THE COMPLETE CAPTAIN BLOOD AND OTHER FAMOUS SABATINI NOVELS

By

Rafael Sabatini

Cover Photograph: greyloch

ISBN: 978-1-78139-251-5

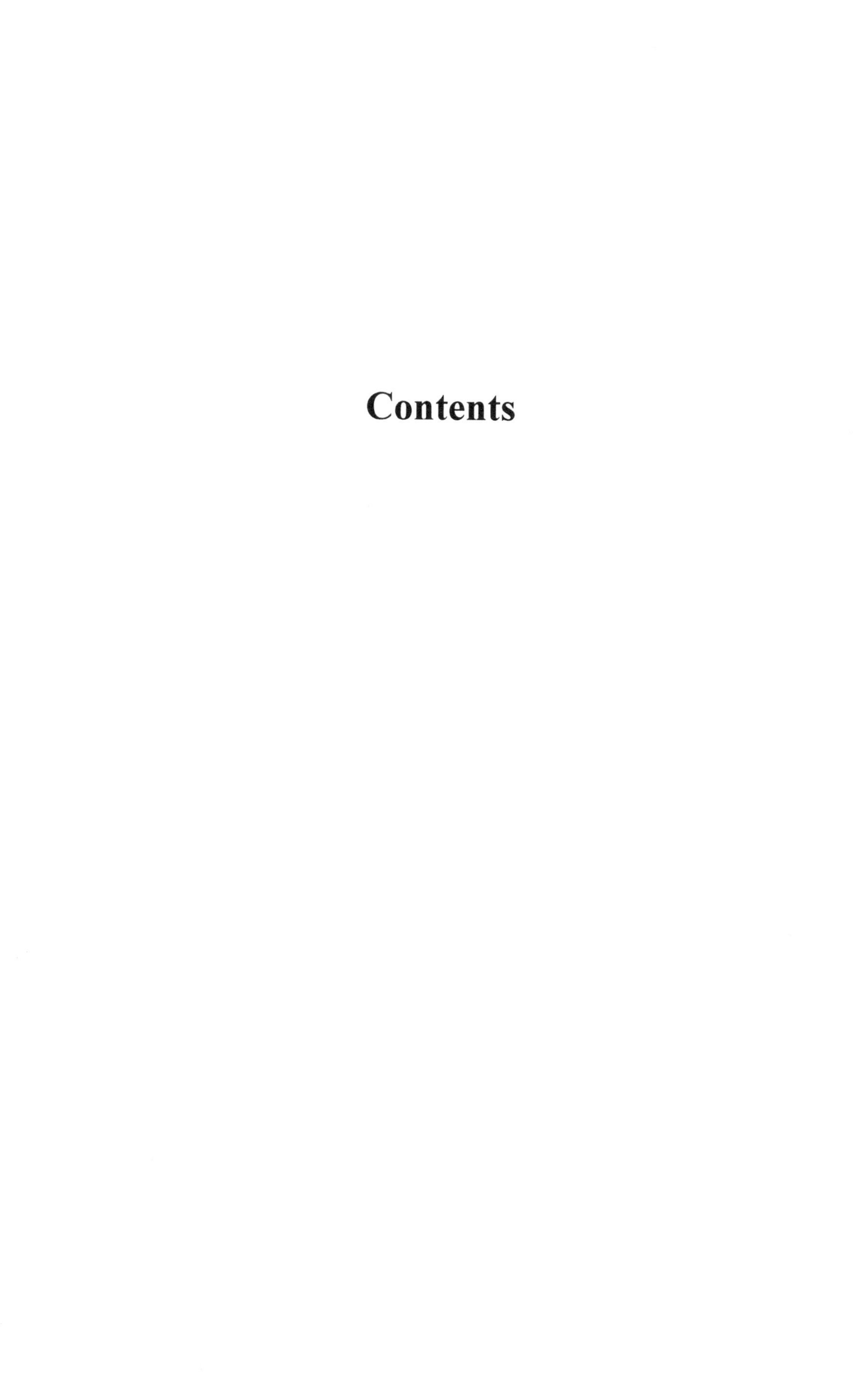

Contents

CAPTAIN BLOOD

CAPTAIN BLOOD RETURNS

THE FORTUNES OF CAPTAIN BLOOD

SCARAMOUCHE

BOOK I: THE ROBE

BOOK II: THE BUSKIN

BOOK III: THE SWORD

THE SEA-HAWK

CAPTAIN BLOOD

By

Rafael Sabatini

CAPTAIN BLOOD HIS ODYSSEY

CHAPTER I. THE MESSENGER

Peter Blood, bachelor of medicine and several other things besides, smoked a pipe and tended the geraniums boxed on the sill of his window above Water Lane in the town of Bridgewater.

Sternly disapproving eyes considered him from a window opposite, but went disregarded. Mr. Blood's attention was divided between his task and the stream of humanity in the narrow street below; a stream which poured for the second time that day towards Castle Field, where earlier in the afternoon Ferguson, the Duke's chaplain, had preached a sermon containing more treason than divinity.

These straggling, excited groups were mainly composed of men with green boughs in their hats and the most ludicrous of weapons in their hands. Some, it is true, shouldered fowling pieces, and here and there a sword was brandished; but more of them were armed with clubs, and most of them trailed the mammoth pikes fashioned out of scythes, as formidable to the eye as they were clumsy to the hand. There were weavers, brewers, carpenters, smiths, masons, bricklayers, cobblers, and representatives of every other of the trades of peace among these improvised men of war. Bridgewater, like Taunton, had yielded so generously of its manhood to the service of the bastard Duke that for any to abstain whose age and strength admitted of his bearing arms was to brand himself a coward or a papist.

Yet Peter Blood, who was not only able.to bear arms, but trained and skilled in their use, who was certainly no coward, and a papist only when it suited him, tended his geraniums and smoked his pipe on that warm July evening as indifferently as if nothing were afoot. One other thing he did. He flung after those war-fevered enthusiasts a line of Horace—a poet for whose work he had early conceived an inordinate affection:

"Quo, quo, scelesti, ruitis?"

And now perhaps you guess why the hot, intrepid blood inherited from the roving sires of his Somersetshire mother remained cool amidst all this frenzied fanatical heat of rebellion; why the turbulent spirit which had forced him once from the sedate academical bonds his father would have imposed upon him, should now remain quiet in the very midst of turbulence. You realize how he regarded these men who were rallying to the banners of liberty—the banners woven by the virgins of Taunton, the girls from the seminaries of Miss Blake and Mrs. Musgrove, who—as the ballad runs—had ripped open their silk petticoats to make colours for King Monmouth's army. That Latin line, contemptuously flung after them as they clattered down the cobbled street, reveals his mind. To him they were fools rushing in wicked frenzy upon their ruin.

You see, he knew too much about this fellow Monmouth and the pretty brown slut who had borne him, to be deceived by the legend of legitimacy, on the strength of which this standard of rebellion had been raised. He had read the absurd proclamation posted at the Cross at Bridgewater—as it had been posted also at Taunton and elsewhere—setting forth that "upon the decease of our Sovereign Lord Charles the Second, the right of succession to the Crown of England, Scotland, France, and Ireland, with the dominions and territories thereunto belonging, did legally descend and devolve upon the most illustrious and high-born Prince James, Duke of Monmouth, son and heir apparent to the said King Charles the Second."

It had moved him to laughter, as had the further announcement that "James Duke of York did first cause the said late King to be poysoned, and immediately thereupon did usurp and invade the Crown."

He knew not which was the greater lie. For Mr. Blood had spent a third of his life in the Netherlands, where this same James Scott—who now proclaimed himself James the Second, by the grace of God, King, et cetera—first saw the light some six-and-thirty years ago, and he was acquainted with the story current there of the fellow's real paternity. Far from being legitimate—by virtue of a pretended secret marriage between Charles Stuart and Lucy Walter—it was possible that this Monmouth who now proclaimed himself King of England was not even the illegitimate child of the late sovereign. What but ruin and disaster could be the end of this grotesque pretension? How could it be hoped that England would ever swallow such a Perkin? And it was on his behalf, to uphold his fantastic claim, that these West Country clods, led by a few armigerous Whigs, had been seduced into rebellion!

"Quo, quo, scelesti, ruitis?"

He laughed and sighed in one; but the laugh dominated the sigh, for Mr. Blood was unsympathetic, as are most self-sufficient men; and he was very self-sufficient; adversity had taught him so to be. A more tender-hearted man, possessing his vision and his knowledge, might have found cause for tears in the contemplation of these ardent, simple, Nonconformist sheep going forth to the shambles—escorted to the rallying ground on Castle Field by wives and daughters, sweethearts and mothers, sustained by the delusion that they were to take the field in defence of Right, of Liberty, and of Religion. For he knew, as all Bridgewater knew and had known now for some hours, that it was Monmouth's intention to deliver battle that same night. The Duke was to lead a surprise attack upon the Royalist army under Feversham that was now encamped on Sedgemoor. Mr. Blood assumed that Lord Feversham would be equally well-informed, and if in this assumption he was wrong, at least he was justified of it. He was not to suppose the Royalist commander so indifferently skilled in the trade he followed.

Mr. Blood knocked the ashes from his pipe, and drew back to close his window. As he did so, his glance travelling straight across the street met at last the glance of those hostile eyes that watched him. There were two pairs, and they belonged to the Misses Pitt, two amiable, sentimental maiden ladies who yielded to none in Bridgewater in their worship of the handsome Monmouth.

Mr. Blood smiled and inclined his head, for he was on friendly terms with these ladies, one of whom, indeed, had been for a little while his patient. But there was no response to his greeting. Instead, the eyes gave him back a stare of cold disdain. The smile on his thin lips grew a little broader, a little less pleasant. He understood the reason of that hostility, which had been daily growing in this past week since Monmouth had come to turn the brains of women of all ages. The Misses Pitt, he apprehended, contemned him that he, a young and vigorous man, of a military training which might now be valuable to the Cause, should stand aloof; that he should placidly smoke his pipe and tend his geraniums on this evening of all evenings, when men of spirit were rallying to the Protestant Champion, offering their blood to place him on the throne where he belonged.

If Mr. Blood had condescended to debate the matter with these ladies, he might have urged that having had his fill of wandering and adventuring, he was now embarked upon the career for which he had been originally intended and for which his studies had equipped him; that he was a man of medicine and not of war; a healer, not a slayer. But they would have answered him, he knew, that in such a cause it behoved every man who deemed himself a man to take up arms. They would have pointed out that their own nephew Jeremiah, who was by trade a sailor, the master of a ship—which by an ill-chance for that young man had come to anchor at this season in Bridgewater Bay—had quitted the helm to snatch up a musket in defence of Right. But Mr. Blood was not of those who argue. As I have said, he was a self-sufficient man.

He closed the window, drew the curtains, and turned to the pleasant, candle-lighted room, and the table on which Mrs. Barlow, his housekeeper, was in the very act of spreading supper. To her, however, he spoke aloud his thought.

"It's out of favour I am with the vinegary virgins over the way."

He had a pleasant, vibrant voice, whose metallic ring was softened and muted by the Irish accent which in all his wanderings he had never lost. It was a voice that could woo seductively and caressingly, or command in such a way as to compel obedience. Indeed, the man's whole nature was in that voice of his. For the rest of him, he was tall and spare, swarthy of tint as a gipsy, with eyes that were startlingly blue in that dark face and under those level black brows. In their glance those eyes, flanking a high-bridged, intrepid nose, were of singular penetration and of a steady haughtiness that went well with his firm lips. Though dressed in black as became his calling, yet it was with an elegance derived from the love of clothes that is peculiar to the adventurer he had been, rather than to the staid medicus he now was. His coat was of fine camlet, and it was laced with silver; there were ruffles of Mechlin at his wrists and a Mechlin cravat encased his throat. His great black periwig was as sedulously curled as any at Whitehall.

Seeing him thus, and perceiving his real nature, which was plain upon him, you might have been tempted to speculate how long such a man would be content to lie by in this little backwater of the world into which chance had swept him some six months ago; how long he would continue to pursue the trade for which he had qualified himself before he had begun to live. Difficult of belief though it may be when you know his history, previous and subsequent, yet it is possible that but for the trick that Fate was about to play him, he might have continued this peaceful existence, settling down completely to the life of a doctor in this Somersetshire haven. It is possible, but not probable.

He was the son of an Irish medicus, by a Somersetshire lady in whose veins ran the rover blood of the Frobishers, which may account for a certain wildness that had early manifested itself in his disposition. This wildness had profoundly alarmed his father, who for an Irishman was of a singularly peace-loving nature. He had early resolved that the boy should follow his own honourable profession, and Peter Blood, being quick to learn and oddly greedy of knowledge, had satisfied his parent by receiving at the age of twenty the degree of baccalaureus medicinae at Trinity College, Dublin. His father survived that satisfaction by three months only. His mother had then been dead some years already. Thus Peter Blood came into an inheritance of some few hundred pounds, with which he had set out to see the world and give for a season a free rein to that restless spirit by which he was imbued. A set of curious chances led him to take service with the Dutch, then at war with France; and a predilection for the sea made him elect that this service should be upon that element. He had the advantage of a commission under the famous de Ruyter, and fought in the Mediterranean engagement in which that great Dutch admiral lost his life.

After the Peace of Nimeguen his movements are obscure. But we know that he spent two years in a Spanish prison, though we do not know how he contrived to get there. It may be due to this that upon his release he took his sword to France, and saw service with the French in their warring upon the Spanish Netherlands. Having reached, at last, the age of thirty-two, his appetite for adventure surfeited, his health having grown indifferent as the result of a neglected wound, he was suddenly overwhelmed by homesickness. He took ship from Nantes with intent to cross to Ireland. But the vessel being driven by stress of weather into Bridgewater Bay, and Blood's health having grown worse during the voyage, he decided to go ashore there, additionally urged to it by the fact that it was his mother's native soil.

Thus in January of that year 1685 he had come to Bridgewater, possessor of a fortune that was approximately the same as that with which he had originally set out from Dublin eleven years ago.

Because he liked the place, in which his health was rapidly restored to him, and because he conceived that he had passed through adventures enough for a man's lifetime, he determined to settle there, and take up at last the profession of medicine from which he had, with so little profit, broken away.

That is all his story, or so much of it as matters up to that night, six months later, when the battle of Sedgemoor was fought.

Deeming the impending action no affair of his, as indeed it was not, and indifferent to the activity with which Bridgewater was that night agog, Mr. Blood closed his ears to the sounds of it, and went early to bed. He was peacefully asleep long before eleven o'clock, at which hour, as you know, Monmouth rode but with his rebel host along the Bristol Road, circuitously to avoid the marshland that lay directly between himself and the Royal Army. You also know that his numerical advantage—possibly counter-balanced by the greater steadiness of the regular troops on the other side—and the advantages he derived from falling by surprise upon an army that was more or less asleep, were all lost to him by blundering and bad leadership before ever he was at grips with Feversham.

The armies came into collision in the neighbourhood of two o'clock in the morning. Mr. Blood slept undisturbed through the distant boom of cannon. Not until four o'clock, when the sun was rising to dispel the last wisps of mist over that stricken field of battle, did he awaken from his tranquil slumbers.

He sat up in bed, rubbed the sleep from his eyes, and collected himself. Blows were thundering upon the door of his house, and a voice was calling incoherently. This was the noise that had aroused him. Conceiving that he had to do with some urgent obstetrical case, he reached for bedgown and slippers, to go below. On the landing he almost collided with Mrs. Barlow, new-risen and unsightly, in a state of panic. He quieted her cluckings with a word of reassurance, and went himself to open.

There in slanting golden light of the new-risen sun stood a breathless, wild-eyed man and a steaming horse. Smothered in dust and grime, his clothes in disarray, the left sleeve of his doublet hanging in rags, this young man opened his lips to speak, yet for a long moment remained speechless.

In that moment Mr. Blood recognized him for the young shipmaster, Jeremiah Pitt, the nephew of the maiden ladies opposite, one who had been drawn by the general enthusiasm into the vortex of that rebellion. The street was rousing, awakened by the sailor's noisy advent; doors were opening, and lattices were being unlatched for the protrusion of anxious, inquisitive heads.

"Take your time, now," said Mr. Blood. "I never knew speed made by overhaste."

But the wild-eyed lad paid no heed to the admonition. He plunged, headlong, into speech, gasping, breathless.

"It is Lord Gildoy," he panted. "He is sore wounded... at Oglethorpe's Farm by the river. I bore him thither... and... and he sent me for you. Come away! Come away!"

He would have clutched the doctor, and haled him forth by force in bedgown and slippers as he was. But the doctor eluded that too eager hand.

"To be sure, I'll come," said he. He was distressed. Gildoy had been a very friendly, generous patron to him since his settling in these parts. And Mr. Blood was eager enough to do what he now could to discharge the debt, grieved that the occasion should have arisen, and in such a manner—for he knew quite well that the rash young nobleman had been an active agent of the Duke's. "To be sure, I'll come. But first give me leave to get some clothes and other things that I may need."

"There's no time to lose."

"Be easy now. I'll lose none. I tell ye again, ye'll go quickest by going leisurely. Come in... take a chair..." He threw open the door of a parlour.

Young Pitt waved aside the invitation.

"I'll wait here. Make haste, in God's name." Mr. Blood went off to dress and to fetch a case of instruments.

Questions concerning the precise nature of Lord Gildoy's hurt could wait until they were on their way. Whilst he pulled on his boots, he gave Mrs. Barlow instructions for the day, which included the matter of a dinner he was not destined to eat.

When at last he went forth again, Mrs. Barlow clucking after him like a disgruntled fowl, he found young Pitt smothered in a crowd of scared, half-dressed townsfolk—mostly women—who had come hastening for news of how the battle had sped. The news he gave them was to be read in the lamentations with which they disturbed the morning air.

At sight of the doctor, dressed and booted, the case of instruments tucked under his arm, the messenger disengaged himself from those who pressed about, shook off his weariness and the two tearful aunts that clung most closely, and seizing the bridle of his horse, he climbed to the saddle.

"Come along, sir," he cried. "Mount behind me."

Mr. Blood, without wasting words, did as he was bidden. Pitt touched the horse with his spur. The little crowd gave way, and thus, upon the crupper of that doubly-laden horse, clinging to the belt of his companion, Peter Blood set out upon his Odyssey. For this Pitt, in whom he beheld no more than the messenger of a wounded rebel gentleman, was indeed the very messenger of Fate.

CHAPTER II. KIRKE'S DRAGOONS

Oglethorpe's farm stood a mile or so to the south of Bridgewater on the right bank of the river. It was a straggling Tudor building showing grey above the ivy that clothed its lower parts. Approaching it now, through the fragrant orchards amid which it seemed to drowse in Arcadian peace beside the waters of the Parrett, sparkling in the morning sunlight, Mr. Blood might have had a difficulty in believing it part of a world tormented by strife and bloodshed.

On the bridge, as they had been riding out of Bridgewater, they had met a vanguard of fugitives from the field of battle, weary, broken men, many of them wounded, all of them terror-stricken, staggering in speedless haste with the last remnants of their strength into the shelter which it was their vain illusion the town would afford them. Eyes glazed with lassitude and fear looked up piteously out of haggard faces at Mr. Blood and his companion as they rode forth; hoarse voices cried a warning that merciless pursuit was not far behind. Undeterred, however, young Pitt rode amain along the dusty road by which these poor fugitives from that swift rout on Sedgemoor came flocking in ever-increasing numbers. Presently he swung aside, and quitting the road took to a pathway that crossed the dewy meadowlands. Even here they met odd groups of these human derelicts, who were scattering in all directions, looking fearfully behind them as they came through the long grass, expecting at every moment to see the red coats of the dragoons.

But as Pitt's direction was a southward one, bringing them ever nearer to Feversham's headquarters, they were presently clear of that human flotsam and jetsam of the battle, and riding through the peaceful orchards heavy with the ripening fruit that was soon to make its annual yield of cider.

At last they alighted on the kidney stones of the courtyard, and Baynes, the master, of the homestead, grave of countenance and flustered of manner, gave them welcome.

In the spacious, stone-flagged hall, the doctor found Lord Gildoy—a very tall and dark young gentleman, prominent of chin and nose—stretched on a cane daybed under one of the tall mullioned windows, in the care of Mrs. Baynes and her comely daughter. His cheeks were leaden-hued, his eyes closed, and from his blue lips came with each laboured breath a faint, moaning noise.

Mr. Blood stood for a moment silently considering his patient. He deplored that a youth with such bright hopes in life as Lord Gildoy's should have risked all, perhaps existence itself, to forward the ambition of a worthless adventurer. Because he had liked and honoured this brave lad he paid his case the tribute of a sigh. Then he knelt to his task, ripped away doublet and underwear to lay bare his lordship's mangled side, and called for water and linen and what else he needed for his work.

He was still intent upon it a half-hour later when the dragoons invaded the homestead. The clatter of hooves and hoarse shouts that heralded their approach disturbed him not at all. For one thing, he was not easily disturbed; for another, his task absorbed him. But his lordship, who had now recovered consciousness, showed considerable alarm, and the battle-stained Jeremy Pitt sped to cover in a clothes-press. Baynes was uneasy, and his wife and daughter trembled. Mr. Blood reassured them.

"Why, what's to fear?" he said. "It's a Christian country, this, and Christian men do not make war upon the wounded, nor upon those who harbour them." He still had, you see, illusions about Christians. He held a glass of cordial, prepared under his directions, to his lordship's lips. "Give your mind peace, my lord. The worst is done."

And then they came rattling and clanking into the stone-flagged hall—a round dozen jack-booted, lobster-coated troopers of the Tangiers Regiment, led by a sturdy, black-browed fellow with a deal of gold lace about the breast of his coat.

Baynes stood his ground, his attitude half-defiant, whilst his wife and daughter shrank away in renewed fear. Mr. Blood, at the head of the day-bed, looked over his shoulder to take stock of the invaders.

The officer barked an order, which brought his men to an attentive halt, then swaggered forward, his gloved hand bearing down the pummel of his sword, his spurs jingling musically as he moved. He announced his authority to the yeoman.

"I am Captain Hobart, of Colonel Kirke's dragoons. What rebels do you harbour?"

The yeoman took alarm at that ferocious truculence. It expressed itself in his trembling voice.

"I... I am no harbourer of rebels, sir. This wounded gentleman...."

"I can see for myself." The Captain stamped forward to the day-bed, and scowled down upon the grey-faced sufferer.

"No need to ask how he came in this state and by his wounds. A damned rebel, and that's enough for me." He flung a command at his dragoons. "Out with him, my lads."

Mr. Blood got between the day-bed and the troopers.

"In the name of humanity, sir!" said he, on a note of anger. "This is England, not Tangiers. The gentleman is in sore case. He may not be moved without peril to his life."

Captain Hobart was amused.

"Oh, I am to be tender of the lives of these rebels! Odds blood! Do you think it's to benefit his health we're taking him? There's gallows being planted along the road from Weston to Bridgewater, and he'll serve for one of them as well as another. Colonel Kirke'll learn these nonconforming oafs something they'll not forforget in generations."

"You're hanging men without trial? Faith, then, it's mistaken I am. We're in Tangiers, after all, it seems, where your regiment belongs."

The Captain considered him with a kindling eye. He looked him over from the soles of his riding-boots to the crown of his periwig. He noted the spare, active frame, the arrogant poise of the head, the air of authority that invested Mr. Blood, and soldier recognized soldier. The Captain's eyes narrowed. Recognition went further.

"Who the hell may you be?" he exploded.

"My name is Blood, sir—Peter Blood, at your service."

"Aye—aye! Codso! That's the name. You were in French service once, were you not?"

If Mr. Blood was surprised, he did not betray it.

"I was."

"Then I remember you—five years ago, or more, you were in Tangiers."

"That is so. I knew your colonel."

"Faith, you may be renewing the acquaintance." The Captain laughed unpleasantly. "What brings you here, sir?"

"This wounded gentleman. I was fetched to attend him. I am a medicus."

"A doctor—you?" Scorn of that lie—as he conceived it—rang in the heavy, hectoring voice.

"Medicinae baccalaureus," said Mr. Blood.

"Don't fling your French at me, man," snapped Hobart. "Speak English!"

Mr. Blood's smile annoyed him.

"I am a physician practising my calling in the town of Bridgewater."

The Captain sneered. "Which you reached by way of Lyme Regis in the following of your bastard Duke."

It was Mr. Blood's turn to sneer. "If your wit were as big as your voice, my dear, it's the great man you'd be by this."

For a moment the dragoon was speechless. The colour deepened in his face.

"You may find me great enough to hang you."

"Faith, yes. Ye've the look and the manners of a hangman. But if you practise your trade on my patient here, you may be putting a rope round your own neck. He's not the kind you may string up and no questions asked. He has the right to trial, and the right to trial by his peers."

"By his peers?"

The Captain was taken aback by these three words, which Mr. Blood had stressed.

"Sure, now, any but a fool or a savage would have asked his name before ordering him to the gallows. The gentleman is my Lord Gildoy."

And then his lordship spoke for himself, in a weak voice.

"I make no concealment of my association with the Duke of Monmouth. I'll take the consequences. But, if you please, I'll take them after trial—by my peers, as the doctor has said."

The feeble voice ceased, and was followed by a moment's silence. As is common in many blustering men, there was a deal of timidity deep down in Hobart. The announcement of his lordship's rank had touched those depths. A servile upstart, he stood in awe of titles. And he stood in awe of his colonel. Percy Kirke was not lenient with blunderers.

By a gesture he checked his men. He must consider. Mr. Blood, observing his pause, added further matter for his consideration.

"Ye'll be remembering, Captain, that Lord Gildoy will have friends and relatives on the Tory side, who'll have something to say to Colonel Kirke if his lordship should be handled like a common felon. You'll go warily, Captain, or, as I've said, it's a halter for your neck ye'll be weaving this morning."

Captain Hobart swept the warning aside with a bluster of contempt, but he acted upon it none the less. "Take up the day-bed," said he, "and convey him on that to Bridgewater. Lodge him in the gaol until I take order about him."

"He may not survive the journey," Blood remonstrated. "He's in no case to be moved."

"So much the worse for him. My affair is to round up rebels." He confirmed his order by a gesture. Two of his men took up the day-bed, and swung to depart with it.

Gildoy made a feeble effort to put forth a hand towards Mr. Blood. "Sir," he said, "you leave me in your debt. If I live I shall study how to discharge it."

Mr. Blood bowed for answer; then to the men: "Bear him steadily," he commanded. "His life depends on it."

As his lordship was carried out, the Captain became brisk. He turned upon the yeoman.

"What other cursed rebels do you harbour?"

"None other, sir. His lordship...."

"We've dealt with his lordship for the present. We'll deal with you in a moment when we've searched your house. And, by God, if you've lied to me...." He broke off, snarling, to give an order. Four of his dragoons went out. In a moment they were heard moving noisily in the adjacent room. Meanwhile, the Captain was questing about the hall, sounding the wainscoting with the butt of a pistol.

Mr. Blood saw no profit to himself in lingering.

"By your leave, it's a very good day I'll be wishing you," said he.

"By my leave, you'll remain awhile," the Captain ordered him.

Mr. Blood shrugged, and sat down. "You're tiresome," he said. "I wonder your colonel hasn't discovered it yet."

But the Captain did not heed him. He was stooping to pick up a soiled and dusty hat in which there was pinned a little bunch of oak leaves. It had been lying near the clothes-press in which the unfortunate Pitt had taken refuge. The Captain smiled malevolently. His eyes raked the room, resting first sardonically on the yeoman, then on the two women in the background, and finally on Mr. Blood, who sat with one leg thrown over the other in an attitude of indifference that was far from reflecting his mind.

Then the Captain stepped to the press, and pulled open one of the wings of its massive oaken door. He took the huddled inmate by the collar of his doublet, and lugged him out into the open.

"And who the devil's this?" quoth he. "Another nobleman?"

Mr. Blood had a vision of those gallows of which Captain Hobart had spoken, and of this unfortunate young shipmaster going to adorn one of them, strung up without trial, in the place of the other victim of whom the Captain had been cheated. On the spot he invented not only a title but a whole family for the young rebel.

"Faith, ye've said it, Captain. This is Viscount Pitt, first cousin to Sir Thomas Vernon, who's married to that slut Moll Kirke, sister to your own colonel, and sometime lady in waiting upon King James's queen."

Both the Captain and his prisoner gasped. But whereas thereafter young Pitt discreetly held his peace, the Captain rapped out a nasty oath. He considered his prisoner again.

"He's lying, is he not?" he demanded, seizing the lad by the shoulder, and glaring into his face. "He's rallying rue, by God!"

"If ye believe that," said Blood, "hang him, and see what happens to you."

The dragoon glared at the doctor and then at his prisoner. "Pah!" He thrust the lad into the hands of his men. "Fetch him along to Bridgewater. And make fast that fellow also," he pointed to Baynes. "We'll show him what it means to harbour and comfort rebels."

There was a moment of confusion. Baynes struggled in the grip of the troopers, protesting vehemently. The terrified women screamed until silenced by a greater terror. The Captain strode across to them. He took the girl by the shoulders. She was a pretty, golden-headed creature, with soft blue eyes that looked up entreatingly, piteously into the face of the dragoon. He leered upon her, his eyes aglow, took her chin in his hand, and set her shuddering by his brutal kiss.

"It's an earnest," he said, smiling grimly. "Let that quiet you, little rebel, till I've done with these rogues."

And he swung away again, leaving her faint and trembling in the arms of her anguished mother. His men stood, grinning, awaiting orders, the two prisoners now fast pinioned.

"Take them away. Let Cornet Drake have charge of them." His smouldering eye again sought the cowering girl. "I'll stay awhile—to search out this place. There may be other rebels hidden here." As an afterthought, he added: "And take this fellow with you." He pointed to Mr. Blood. "Bestir!"

Mr. Blood started out of his musings. He had been considering that in his case of instruments there was a lancet with which he might perform on Captain Hobart a beneficial operation. Beneficial, that is, to humanity. In any case, the dragoon was obviously plethoric and would be the better for a blood-letting. The difficulty lay in making the opportunity. He was beginning to wonder if he could lure the Captain aside with some tale of hidden treasure, when this untimely interruption set a term to that interesting speculation.

He sought to temporize.

"Faith it will suit me very well," said he. "For Bridgewater is my destination, and but that ye detained me I'd have been on my way thither now."

"Your destination there will be the gaol."

"Ah, bah! Ye're surely joking!"

"There's a gallows for you if you prefer it. It's merely a question of now or later."

Rude hands seized Mr. Blood, and that precious lancet was in the case on the table out of reach. He twisted out of the grip of the dragoons, for he was strong and agile, but they closed with him again immediately, and bore him down. Pinning him to the ground, they tied his wrists behind his back, then roughly pulled him to his feet again.

"Take him away," said Hobart shortly, and turned to issue his orders to the other waiting troopers. "Go search the house, from attic to cellar; then report to me here."

The soldiers trailed out by the door leading to the interior. Mr. Blood was thrust by his guards into the courtyard, where Pitt and Baynes already waited. From the threshold of the hall, he looked back at Captain Hobart, and his sapphire eyes were blazing. On his lips trembled a threat of what he would do to Hobart if he should happen to survive this business. Betimes he remembered that to utter it were probably to extinguish his chance of living to execute it. For to-day the King's men were masters in the West, and the West was regarded as enemy country, to be subjected to the worst horror of war by the victorious side. Here a captain of horse was for the moment lord of life and death.

Under the apple-trees in the orchard Mr. Blood and his companions in misfortune were made fast each to a trooper's stirrup leather. Then at the sharp order of the cornet, the little troop started for Bridgewater. As they set out there was the fullest confirmation of Mr. Blood's hideous assumption that to the dragoons this was a conquered enemy country. There were sounds of rending timbers, of furniture smashed and overthrown, the shouts and laughter of brutal men, to announce that this hunt for rebels was no more than a pretext for pillage and destruction. Finally above all other sounds came the piercing screams of a woman in acutest agony.

Baynes checked in his stride, and swung round writhing, his face ashen. As a consequence he was jerked from his feet by the rope that attached him to the stirrup leather, and he was dragged helplessly a yard or two before the trooper reined in, cursing him foully, and striking him with the flat of his sword.

It came to Mr. Blood, as he trudged forward under the laden apple-trees on that fragrant, delicious July morning, that man—as he had long suspected—was the vilest work of God, and that only a fool would set himself up as a healer of a species that was best exterminated.

CHAPTER III. THE LORD CHIEF JUSTICE

It was not until two months later—on the 19th of September, if you must have the actual date—that Peter Blood was brought to trial, upon a charge of high treason. We know that he was not guilty of this; but we need not doubt that he was quite capable of it by the time he was indicted. Those two months of inhuman, unspeakable imprisonment had moved his mind to a cold and deadly hatred of King James and his representatives. It says something for his fortitude that in all the circumstances he should still have had a mind at all. Yet, terrible as was the position of this entirely innocent man, he had cause for thankfulness on two counts. The first of these was that he should have been brought to trial at all; the second, that his trial took place on the date named, and not a day earlier. In the very delay which exacerbated him lay—although he did not realize it—his only chance of avoiding the gallows.

Easily, but for the favour of Fortune, he might have been one of those haled, on the morrow of the battle, more or less haphazard from the overflowing gaol at Bridgewater to be summarily hanged in the market-place by the bloodthirsty Colonel Kirke. There was about the Colonel of the Tangiers Regiment a deadly despatch which might have disposed in like fashion of all those prisoners, numerous as they were, but for the vigorous intervention of Bishop Mews, which put an end to the drumhead courts-martial.

Even so, in that first week after Sedgemoor, Kirke and Feversham contrived between them to put to death over a hundred men after a trial so summary as to be no trial at all. They required human freights for the gibbets with which they were planting the countryside, and they little cared how they procured them or what innocent lives they took. What, after all, was the life of a clod? The executioners were kept busy with rope and chopper and cauldrons of pitch. I spare you the details of that nauseating picture. It is, after all, with the fate of Peter Blood that we are concerned rather than with that of the Monmouth rebels.

He survived to be included in one of those melancholy droves of prisoners who, chained in pairs, were marched from Bridgewater to Taunton. Those who were too sorely wounded to march were conveyed in carts, into which they were brutally crowded, their wounds undressed and festering. Many were fortunate enough to die upon the way. When Blood insisted upon his right to exercise his art so as to relieve some of this suffering, he was accounted importunate and threatened with a flogging. If he had one regret now it was that he had not been out with Monmouth. That, of course, was illogical; but you can hardly expect logic from a man in his position.

His chain companion on that dreadful march was the same Jeremy Pitt who had been the agent of his present misfortunes. The young shipmaster had remained his close companion after their common arrest. Hence, fortuitously, had they been chained together in the crowded prison, where they were almost suffocated by the heat and the stench during those days of July, August, and September.

Scraps of news filtered into the gaol from the outside world. Some may have been deliberately allowed to penetrate. Of these was the tale of Monmouth's execution. It created profoundest dismay amongst those men who were suffering for the Duke and for the religious cause he had professed to champion. Many refused utterly to believe it. A wild story began to circulate that a man resembling Monmouth had offered himself up in the Duke's stead, and that Monmouth survived to come again in glory to deliver Zion and make war upon Babylon.

Mr. Blood heard that tale with the same indifference with which he had received the news of Monmouth's death. But one shameful thing he heard in connection with this which left him not quite so unmoved, and served to nourish the contempt he was forming for King James. His Majesty had consented to see Monmouth. To have done so unless he intended to pardon him was a thing execrable and damnable beyond belief; for the only other object in granting that interview could be the evilly mean satisfaction of spurning the abject penitence of his unfortunate nephew.

Later they heard that Lord Grey, who after the Duke—indeed, perhaps, before him—was the main leader of the rebellion, had purchased his own pardon for forty thousand pounds. Peter Blood found this of a piece with the rest. His contempt for King James blazed out at last.

"Why, here's a filthy mean creature to sit on a throne. If I had known as much of him before as I know to-day, I don't doubt I should have given cause to be where I am now." And then on a sudden thought: "And where will Lord Gildoy be, do you suppose?" he asked.

Young Pitt, whom he addressed, turned towards him a face from which the ruddy tan of the sea had faded almost completely during those months of captivity. His grey eyes were round and questioning. Blood answered him.

"Sure, now, we've never seen his lordship since that day at Oglethorpe's. And where are the other gentry that were taken?—the real leaders of this plaguey rebellion. Grey's case explains their absence, I think. They are wealthy men that can ransom themselves. Here awaiting the gallows are none but the unfortunates who followed; those who had the honour to lead them go free. It's a curious and instructive reversal of the usual way of these things. Faith, it's an uncertain world entirely!"

He laughed, and settled down into that spirit of scorn, wrapped in which he stepped later into the great hall of Taunton Castle to take his trial. With him went Pitt and the yeoman Baynes. The three of them were to be tried together, and their case was to open the proceedings of that ghastly day.

The hall, even to the galleries—thronged with spectators, most of whom were ladies—was hung in scarlet; a pleasant conceit, this, of the Lord Chief Justice's, who naturally enough preferred the colour that should reflect his own bloody mind.

At the upper end, on a raised dais, sat the Lords Commissioners, the five judges in their scarlet robes and heavy dark periwigs, Baron Jeffreys of Wem enthroned in the middle place.

The prisoners filed in under guard. The crier called for silence under pain of imprisonment, and as the hum of voices gradually became hushed, Mr. Blood considered with interest the twelve good men and true that composed the jury. Neither good nor true did they look. They were scared, uneasy, and hangdog as any set of thieves caught with their hands in the pockets of their neighbours. They were twelve shaken men, each of whom stood between the sword of the Lord Chief Justice's recent bloodthirsty charge and the wall of his own conscience.

From them Mr. Blood's calm, deliberate glance passed on to consider the Lords Commissioners, and particularly the presiding Judge, that Lord Jeffreys, whose terrible fame had come ahead of him from Dorchester.

He beheld a tall, slight man on the young side of forty, with an oval face that was delicately beautiful. There were dark stains of suffering or sleeplessness under the low-lidded eyes, heightening their brilliance and their gentle melancholy. The face was very pale, save for the vivid colour of the full lips and the hectic flush on the rather high but inconspicuous cheek-bones. It was something in those lips that marred the perfection of that countenance; a fault, elusive but undeniable, lurked there to belie the fine sensitiveness of those nostrils, the tenderness of those dark, liquid eyes and the noble calm of that pale brow.

The physician in Mr. Blood regarded the man with peculiar interest knowing as he did the agonizing malady from which his lordship suffered, and the amazingly irregular, debauched life that he led in spite of it—perhaps because of it.

"Peter Blood, hold up your hand!"

Abruptly he was recalled to his position by the harsh voice of the clerk of arraigns. His obedience was mechanical, and the clerk droned out the wordy indictment which pronounced Peter Blood a false traitor against the Most Illustrious and Most Excellent Prince, James the Second, by the grace of God, of England, Scotland, France, and Ireland King, his supreme and natural lord. It informed him that, having no fear of God in his heart, but being moved and seduced by the instigation of the Devil, he had failed in the love and true and due natural obedience towards his said lord the King, and had moved to disturb the peace and tranquillity of the kingdom and to stir up war and rebellion to depose his said lord the King from the title, honour, and the regal name of the imperial crown—and much more of the same kind, at the end of all of which he was invited to say whether he was guilty or not guilty. He answered more than was asked.

"It's entirely innocent I am."

A small, sharp-faced man at a table before and to the right of him bounced up. It was Mr. Pollexfen, the Judge-Advocate.

"Are you guilty or not guilty?" snapped this peppery gentleman. "You must take the words."

"Words, is it?" said Peter Blood. "Oh—not guilty." And he went on, addressing himself to the bench. "On this same subject of words, may it please your lordships, I am guilty of nothing to justify any of those words I have heard used to describe me, unless it be of a want of patience at having been closely confined for two months and longer in a foetid gaol with great peril to my health and even life."

Being started, he would have added a deal more; but at this point the Lord Chief Justice interposed in a gentle, rather plaintive voice.

"Look you, sir: because we must observe the common and usual methods of trial, I must interrupt you now. You are no doubt ignorant of the forms of law?"

"Not only ignorant, my lord, but hitherto most happy in that ignorance. I could gladly have forgone this acquaintance with them."

A pale smile momentarily lightened the wistful countenance.

"I believe you. You shall be fully heard when you come to your defence. But anything you say now is altogether irregular and improper."

Enheartened by that apparent sympathy and consideration, Mr. Blood answered thereafter, as was required of him, that he would be tried by God and his country. Whereupon, having prayed to God to send him a good deliverance, the clerk called upon Andrew Baynes to hold up his hand and plead.

From Baynes, who pleaded not guilty, the clerk passed on to Pitt, who boldly owned his guilt. The Lord Chief Justice stirred at that.

"Come; that's better," quoth he, and his four scarlet brethren nodded. "If all were as obstinate as his two fellow-rebels, there would never be an end."

After that ominous interpolation, delivered with an inhuman iciness that sent a shiver through the court, Mr. Pollexfen got to his feet. With great prolixity he stated the general case against the three men, and the particular case against Peter Blood, whose indictment was to be taken first.

The only witness called for the King was Captain Hobart. He testified briskly to the manner in which he had found and taken the three prisoners, together with Lord Gildoy. Upon the orders of his colonel he would have hanged Pitt out of hand, but was restrained by the lies of the prisoner Blood, who led him to believe that Pitt was a peer of the realm and a person of consideration.

As the Captain's evidence concluded, Lord Jeffreys looked across at Peter Blood.

"Will the prisoner Blood ask the witness any questions?"

"None, my lord. He has correctly related what occurred."

"I am glad to have your admission of that without any of the prevarications that are usual in your kind. And I will say this, that here prevarication would avail you little. For we always have the truth in the end. Be sure of that."

Baynes and Pitt similarly admitted the accuracy of the Captain's evidence, whereupon the scarlet figure of the Lord Chief Justice heaved a sigh of relief.

"This being so, let us get on, in God's name; for we have much to do." There was now no trace of gentleness in his voice. It was brisk and rasping, and the lips through which it passed were curved in scorn. "I take it, Mr. Pollexfen, that the wicked treason of these three rogues being established—indeed, admitted by them—there is no more to be said."

Peter Blood's voice rang out crisply, on a note that almost seemed to contain laughter.

"May it please your lordship, but there's a deal more to be said."

His lordship looked at him, first in blank amazement at his audacity, then gradually with an expression of dull anger. The scarlet lips fell into unpleasant, cruel lines that transfigured the whole countenance.

"How now, rogue? Would you waste our time with idle subterfuge?"

"I would have your lordship and the gentlemen of the jury hear me on my defence, as your lordship promised that I should be heard."

"Why, so you shall, villain; so you shall." His lordship's voice was harsh as a file. He writhed as he spoke, and for an instant his features were distorted. A delicate dead-white hand, on which the veins showed blue, brought forth a handkerchief with which he dabbed his lips and then his brow. Observing him with his physician's eye, Peter Blood judged him a prey to the pain of the disease that was destroying him. "So you shall. But after the admission made, what defence remains?"

"You shall judge, my lord."

"That is the purpose for which I sit here."

"And so shall you, gentlemen." Blood looked from judge to jury. The latter shifted uncomfortably under the confident flash of his blue eyes. Lord Jeffreys's bullying charge had whipped the spirit out of them. Had they, themselves, been prisoners accused of treason, he could not have arraigned them more ferociously.

Peter Blood stood boldly forward, erect, self-possessed, and saturnine. He was freshly shaven, and his periwig, if out of curl, was at least carefully combed and dressed.

"Captain Hobart has testified to what he knows—that he found me at Oglethorpe's Farm on the Monday morning after the battle at Weston. But he has not told you what I did there."

Again the Judge broke in. "Why, what should you have been doing there in the company of rebels, two of whom—Lord Gildoy and your fellow there—have already admitted their guilt?"

"That is what I beg leave to tell your lordship."

"I pray you do, and in God's name be brief, man. For if I am to be troubled with the say of all you traitor dogs, I may sit here until the Spring Assizes."

"I was there, my lord, in my quality as a physician, to dress Lord Gildoy's wounds."

"What's this? Do you tell us that you are a physician?"

"A graduate of Trinity College, Dublin."

"Good God!" cried Lord Jeffreys, his voice suddenly swelling, his eyes upon the jury. "What an impudent rogue is this! You heard the witness say that he had known him in Tangiers some years ago, and that he was then an officer in the French service. You heard the prisoner admit that the witness had spoken the truth?"

"Why, so he had. Yet what I am telling you is also true, so it is. For some years I was a soldier; but before that I was a physician, and I have been one again since January last, established in Bridgewater, as I can bring a hundred witnesses to prove."

"There's not the need to waste our time with that. I will convict you out of your own rascally mouth. I will ask you only this: How came you, who represent yourself as a physician peacefully following your calling in the town of Bridgewater, to be with the army of the Duke of Monmouth?"

"I was never with that army. No witness has sworn to that, and I dare swear that no witness will. I never was attracted to the late rebellion. I regarded the adventure as a wicked madness. I take leave to ask your lordship" (his brogue became more marked than ever) "what should I, who was born and bred a papist, be doing in the army of the Protestant Champion?"

"A papist thou?" The judge gloomed on him a moment. "Art more like a snivelling, canting Jack Presbyter. I tell you, man, I can smell a Presbyterian forty miles."

"Then I'll take leave to marvel that with so keen a nose your lordship can't smell a papist at four paces."

There was a ripple of laughter in the galleries, instantly quelled by the fierce glare of the Judge and the voice of the crier.

Lord Jeffreys leaned farther forward upon his desk. He raised that delicate white hand, still clutching its handkerchief, and sprouting from a froth of lace.

"We'll leave your religion out of account for the moment, friend," said he. "But mark what I say to you." With a minatory forefinger he beat the time of his words. "Know, friend, that there is no religion a man can pretend to can give a countenance to lying. Thou hast a precious immortal soul, and there is nothing in the world equal to it in value. Consider that the great God of Heaven and Earth, before Whose tribunal thou and we and all persons are to stand at the last day, will take vengeance on thee for every falsehood, and justly strike thee into eternal flames, make thee drop into the bottomless pit of fire and brimstone, if thou offer to deviate the least from the truth and nothing but the truth. For I tell thee God is not mocked. On that I charge you to answer truthfully. How came you to be taken with these rebels?"

Peter Blood gaped at him a moment in consternation. The man was incredible, unreal, fantastic, a nightmare judge. Then he collected himself to answer.

"I was summoned that morning to succour Lord Gildoy, and I conceived it to be the duty imposed upon me by my calling to answer that summons."

"Did you so?" The Judge, terrible now of aspect—his face white, his twisted lips red as the blood for which they thirsted—glared upon him in evil mockery. Then he controlled himself as if by an effort. He sighed. He resumed his earlier gentle plaintiveness. "Lord! How you waste our time. But I'll have patience with you. Who summoned you?"

"Master Pitt there, as he will testify."

"Oh! Master Pitt will testify—he that is himself a traitor self-confessed. Is that your witness?"

"There is also Master Baynes here, who can answer to it."

"Good Master Baynes will have to answer for himself; and I doubt not he'll be greatly exercised to save his own neck from a halter. Come, come, sir; are these your only witnesses?"

"I could bring others from Bridgewater, who saw me set out that morning upon the crupper of Master Pitt's horse."

His lordship smiled. "It will not be necessary. For, mark me, I do not intend to waste more time on you. Answer me only this: When Master Pitt, as you pretend, came to summon you, did you know that he had been, as you have heard him confess, of Monmouth's following?"

"I did, My lord."

"You did! Ha!" His lordship looked at the cringing jury and uttered a short, stabbing laugh. "Yet in spite of that you went with him?"

"To succour a wounded man, as was my sacred duty."

"Thy sacred duty, sayest thou?" Fury blazed out of him again. "Good God! What a generation of vipers do we live in! Thy sacred duty, rogue, is to thy King and to God. But let it pass. Did he tell you whom it was that you were desired to succour?"

"Lord Gildoy—yes."

"And you knew that Lord Gildoy had been wounded in the battle, and on what side he fought?"

"I knew."

"And yet, being, as you would have us believe, a true and loyal subject of our Lord the King, you went to succour him?"

Peter Blood lost patience for a moment. "My business, my lord, was with his wounds, not with his politics."

A murmur from the galleries and even from the jury approved him. It served only to drive his terrible judge into a deeper fury.

"Jesus God! Was there ever such an impudent villain in the world as thou?" He swung, white-faced, to the jury. "I hope, gentlemen of the jury, you take notice of the horrible carriage of this traitor rogue, and withal you cannot but observe the spirit of this sort of people, what a villainous and devilish one it is. Out of his own mouth he has said enough to hang him a dozen times. Yet is there more. Answer me this, sir: When you cozened Captain Hobart with your lies concerning the station of this other traitor Pitt, what was your business then?"

"To save him from being hanged without trial, as was threatened."

"What concern was it of yours whether or how the wretch was hanged?"

"Justice is the concern of every loyal subject, for an injustice committed by one who holds the King's commission is in some sense a dishonour to the King's majesty."

It was a shrewd, sharp thrust aimed at the jury, and it reveals, I think, the alertness of the man's mind, his self-possession ever steadiest in moments of dire peril. With any other jury it must have made the impression that he hoped to make. It may even have made its impression upon these poor pusillanimous sheep. But the dread judge was there to efface it.

He gasped aloud, then flung himself violently forward.

"Lord of Heaven!" he stormed. "Was there ever such a canting, impudent rascal? But I have done with you. I see thee, villain, I see thee already with a halter round thy neck."

Having spoken so, gloatingly, evilly, he sank back again, and composed himself. It was as if a curtain fell. All emotion passed again from his pale face. Back to invest it again came that gentle melancholy. Speaking after a moment's pause, his voice was soft, almost tender, yet every word of it carried sharply through that hushed court.

"If I know my own heart it is not in my nature to desire the hurt of anybody, much less to delight in his eternal perdition. It is out of compassion for you that I have used all these words—because I would have you have some regard for your immortal soul, and not ensure its damnation by obdurately persisting in falsehood and prevarication. But I see that all the pains in the world, and all compassion and charity are lost upon you, and therefore I will say no more to you." He turned again to the jury that countenance of wistful beauty. "Gentlemen, I must tell you for law, of which we are the judges, and not you, that if any person be in actual rebellion against the King, and another person—who really and actually was not in rebellion—does knowingly receive, harbour, comfort, or succour him, such a person is as much a traitor as he who indeed bore arms. We are bound by our oaths and consciences to declare to you what is law; and you are bound by your oaths and your consciences to deliver and to declare to us by your verdict the truth of the facts."

Upon that he proceeded to his summing-up, showing how Baynes and Blood were both guilty of treason, the first for having harboured a traitor, the second for having succoured that traitor by dressing his wounds. He interlarded his address by sycophantic allusions to his natural lord and lawful sovereign, the King, whom God had set over them, and with vituperations of Nonconformity and of Monmouth, of whom—in his own words—he dared boldly affirm that the meanest subject within the kingdom that was of legitimate birth had a better title to the crown. "Jesus God! That ever we should have such a generation of vipers among us," he burst out in rhetorical frenzy. And then he sank back as if exhausted by the violence he had used. A moment he was still, dabbing his lips again; then he moved uneasily; once more his features were twisted by pain, and in a few snarling, almost incoherent words he dismissed the jury to consider the verdict.

Peter Blood had listened to the intemperate, the blasphemous, and almost obscene invective of that tirade with a detachment that afterwards, in retrospect, surprised him. He was so amazed by the man, by the reactions taking place in him between mind and body, and by his methods of bullying and coercing the jury into bloodshed, that he almost forgot that his own life was at stake.

The absence of that dazed jury was a brief one. The verdict found the three prisoners guilty. Peter Blood looked round the scarlet-hung court. For an instant that foam of white faces seemed to heave before him. Then he was himself again, and a voice was asking him what he had to say for himself, why sentence of death should not be passed upon him, being convicted of high treason.

He laughed, and his laugh jarred uncannily upon the deathly stillness of the court. It was all so grotesque, such a mockery of justice administered by that wistful-eyed jack-pudding in scarlet, who was himself a mockery—the venal instrument of a brutally spiteful and vindictive king. His laughter shocked the austerity of that same jack-pudding.

"Do you laugh, sirrah, with the rope about your neck, upon the very threshold of that eternity you are so suddenly to enter into?"

And then Blood took his revenge.

"Faith, it's in better case I am for mirth than your lordship. For I have this to say before you deliver judgment. Your lordship sees me—an innocent man whose only offence is that I practised charity—with a halter round my neck. Your lordship, being the justiciar, speaks with knowledge of what is to come to me. I, being a physician, may speak with knowledge of what is to come to your lordship. And I tell you that I would not now change places with you—that I would not exchange this halter that you fling about my neck for the stone that you carry in your body. The death to which you may doom me is a light pleasantry by contrast with the death to which your lordship has been doomed by that Great Judge with whose name your lordship makes so free."

The Lord Chief Justice sat stiffly upright, his face ashen, his lips twitching, and whilst you might have counted ten there was no sound in that paralyzed court after Peter Blood had finished speaking. All those who knew Lord Jeffreys regarded this as the lull before the storm, and braced themselves for the explosion. But none came.

Slowly, faintly, the colour crept back into that ashen face. The scarlet figure lost its rigidity, and bent forward. His lordship began to speak. In a muted voice and briefly—much more briefly than his wont on such occasions and in a manner entirely mechanical, the manner of a man whose thoughts are elsewhere while his lips are speaking—he delivered sentence of death in the prescribed form, and without the least allusion to what Peter Blood had said. Having delivered it, he sank back exhausted, his eyes half-closed, his brow agleam with sweat.

The prisoners filed out.

Mr. Pollexfen—a Whig at heart despite the position of Judge-Advocate which he occupied—was overheard by one of the jurors to mutter in the ear of a brother counsel:

"On my soul, that swarthy rascal has given his lordship a scare. It's a pity he must hang. For a man who can frighten Jeffreys should go far."

CHAPTER IV. HUMAN MERCHANDISE

Mr. Pollexfen was at one and the same time right and wrong—a condition much more common than is generally supposed.

He was right in his indifferently expressed thought that a man whose mien and words could daunt such a lord of terror as Jeffreys, should by the dominance of his nature be able to fashion himself a considerable destiny. He was wrong—though justifiably so—in his assumption that Peter Blood must hang.

I have said that the tribulations with which he was visited as a result of his errand of mercy to Oglethorpe's Farm contained—although as yet he did not perceive it, perhaps—two sources of thankfulness: one that he was tried at all; the other that his trial took place on the 19th of September. Until the 18th, the sentences passed by the court of the Lords Commissioners had been carried out literally and expeditiously. But on the morning of the 19th there arrived at Taunton a courier from Lord Sunderland, the Secretary of State, with a letter for Lord Jeffreys wherein he was informed that His Majesty had been graciously pleased to command that eleven hundred rebels should be furnished for transportation to some of His Majesty's southern plantations, Jamaica, Barbados, or any of the Leeward Islands.

You are not to suppose that this command was dictated by any sense of mercy. Lord Churchill was no more than just when he spoke of the King's heart as being as insensible as marble. It had been realized that in these wholesale hangings there was taking place a reckless waste of valuable material. Slaves were urgently required in the plantations, and a healthy, vigorous man could be reckoned worth at least from ten to fifteen pounds. Then, there were at court many gentlemen who had some claim or other upon His Majesty's bounty. Here was a cheap and ready way to discharge these claims. From amongst the convicted rebels a certain number might be set aside to be bestowed upon those gentlemen, so that they might dispose of them to their own profit.

My Lord Sunderland's letter gives precise details of the royal munificence in human flesh. A thousand prisoners were to be distributed among some eight courtiers and others, whilst a postscriptum to his lordship's letter asked for a further hundred to be held at the disposal of the Queen. These prisoners were to be transported at once to His Majesty's southern plantations, and to be kept there for the space of ten years before being restored to liberty, the parties to whom they were assigned entering into security to see that transportation was immediately effected.

We know from Lord Jeffreys's secretary how the Chief Justice inveighed that night in drunken frenzy against this misplaced clemency to which His Majesty had been persuaded. We know how he attempted by letter to induce the King to reconsider his decision. But James adhered to it. It was—apart from the indirect profit he derived from it—a clemency full worthy of him. He knew that to spare lives in this fashion was to convert them into living deaths. Many must succumb in torment to the horrors of West Indian slavery, and so be the envy of their surviving companions.

Thus it happened that Peter Blood, and with him Jeremy Pitt and Andrew Baynes, instead of being hanged, drawn, and quartered as their sentences directed, were conveyed to Bristol and there shipped with some fifty others aboard the Jamaica Merchant. From close confinement under hatches, ill-nourishment and foul water, a sickness broke out amongst them, of which eleven died. Amongst these was the unfortunate yeoman from Oglethorpe's Farm, brutally torn from his quiet homestead amid the fragrant cider orchards for no other sin but that he had practised mercy.

The mortality might have been higher than it was but for Peter Blood. At first the master of the Jamaica Merchant had answered with oaths and threats the doctor's expostulations against permitting men to perish in this fashion, and his insistence that he should be made free of the medicine chest and given leave to minister to the sick. But presently Captain Gardner came to see that he might be brought to task for these too heavy losses of human merchandise and because of this he was belatedly glad to avail himself of the skill of Peter Blood. The doctor went to work zealously and zestfully, and wrought so ably that, by his ministrations and by improving the condition of his fellow-captives, he checked the spread of the disease.

Towards the middle of December the Jamaica Merchant dropped anchor in Carlisle Bay, and put ashore the forty-two surviving rebels-convict.

If these unfortunates had imagined—as many of them appear to have done—that they were coming into some wild, savage country, the prospect, of which they had a glimpse before they were hustled over the ship's side into the waiting boats, was enough to correct the impression. They beheld a town of sufficiently imposing proportions composed of houses built upon European notions of architecture, but without any of the huddle usual in European cities. The spire of a church rose dominantly above the red roofs, a fort guarded the entrance of the wide harbour, with guns thrusting their muzzles between the crenels, and the wide facade of Government House revealed itself dominantly placed on a gentle hill above the town. This hill was vividly green as is an English hill in April, and the day was such a day as April gives to England, the season of heavy rains being newly ended.

On a wide cobbled space on the sea front they found a guard of red-coated militia drawn up to receive them, and a crowd—attracted by their arrival—which in dress and manner differed little from a crowd in a seaport at home save that it contained fewer women and a great number of negroes.

To inspect them, drawn up there on the mole, came Governor Steed, a short, stout, red-faced gentleman, in blue taffetas burdened by a prodigious amount of gold lace, who limped a little and leaned heavily upon a stout ebony cane. After him, in the uniform of a colonel of the Barbados Militia, rolled a tall, corpulent man who towered head and shoulders above the Governor, with malevolence plainly written on his enormous yellowish countenance. At his side, and contrasting oddly with his grossness, moving with an easy stripling grace, came a slight young lady in a modish riding-gown. The broad brim of a grey hat with scarlet sweep of ostrich plume shaded an oval face upon which the climate of the Tropic of Cancer had made no impression, so delicately fair was its complexion. Ringlets of red-brown hair hung to her shoulders. Frankness looked out from her hazel eyes which were set wide; commiseration repressed now the mischievousness that normally inhabited her fresh young mouth.

Peter Blood caught himself staring in a sort of amazement at that piquant face, which seemed here so out of place, and finding his stare returned, he shifted uncomfortably. He grew conscious of the sorry figure that he cut. Unwashed, with rank and matted hair and a disfiguring black beard upon his face, and the erstwhile splendid suit of black camlet in which he had been taken prisoner now reduced to rags that would have disgraced a scarecrow, he was in no case for inspection by such dainty eyes as these. Nevertheless, they continued to inspect him with round-eyed, almost childlike wonder and pity. Their owner put forth a hand to touch the scarlet sleeve of her companion, whereupon with an ill-tempered grunt the man swung his great bulk round so that he directly confronted her.

Looking up into his face, she was speaking to him earnestly, but the Colonel plainly gave her no more than the half of his attention. His little beady eyes, closely flanking a fleshly, pendulous nose, had passed from her and were fixed upon fair-haired, sturdy young Pitt, who was standing beside Blood.

The Governor had also come to a halt, and for a moment now that little group of three stood in conversation. What the lady said, Peter could not hear at all, for she lowered her voice; the Colonel's reached him in a confused rumble, but the Governor was neither considerate nor indistinct; he had a high-pitched voice which carried far, and believing himself witty, he desired to be heard by all.

"But, my dear Colonel Bishop, it is for you to take first choice from this dainty nosegay, and at your own price. After that we'll send the rest to auction."

Colonel Bishop nodded his acknowledgment. He raised his voice in answering. "Your excellency is very good. But, faith, they're a weedy lot, not likely to be of much value in the plantation." His beady eyes scanned them again, and his contempt of them deepened the malevolence of his face. It was as if he were annoyed with them for being in no better condition. Then he beckoned forward Captain

Gardner, the master of the Jamaica Merchant, and for some minutes stood in talk with him over a list which the latter produced at his request.

Presently he waved aside the list and advanced alone towards the rebels-convict, his eyes considering them, his lips pursed. Before the young Somersetshire shipmaster he came to a halt, and stood an instant pondering him. Then he fingered the muscles of the young man's arm, and bade him open his mouth that he might see his teeth. He pursed his coarse lips again and nodded.

He spoke to Gardner over his shoulder.

"Fifteen pounds for this one."

The Captain made a face of dismay. "Fifteen pounds! It isn't half what I meant to ask for him."

"It is double what I had meant to give," grunted the Colonel.

"But he would be cheap at thirty pounds, your honour."

"I can get a negro for that. These white swine don't live. They're not fit for the labour."

Gardner broke into protestations of Pitt's health, youth, and vigour. It was not a man he was discussing; it was a beast of burden. Pitt, a sensitive lad, stood mute and unmoving. Only the ebb and flow of colour in his cheeks showed the inward struggle by which he maintained his self-control.

Peter Blood was nauseated by the loathsome haggle.

In the background, moving slowly away down the line of prisoners, went the lady in conversation with the Governor, who smirked and preened himself as he limped beside her. She was unconscious of the loathly business the Colonel was transacting. Was she, wondered Blood, indifferent to it?

Colonel Bishop swung on his heel to pass on.

"I'll go as far as twenty pounds. Not a penny more, and it's twice as much as you are like to get from Crabston."

Captain Gardner, recognizing the finality of the tone, sighed and yielded. Already Bishop was moving down the line. For Mr. Blood, as for a weedy youth on his left, the Colonel had no more than a glance of contempt. But the next man, a middle-aged Colossus named Wolverstone, who had lost an eye at Sedgemoor, drew his regard, and the haggling was recommenced.

Peter Blood stood there in the brilliant sunshine and inhaled the fragrant air, which was unlike any air that he had ever breathed. It was laden with a strange perfume, blend of logwood flower, pimento, and aromatic cedars. He lost himself in unprofitable speculations born of that singular fragrance. He was in no mood for conversation, nor was Pitt, who stood dumbly at his side, and who was afflicted mainly at the moment by the thought that he was at last about to be separated from this man with whom he had stood shoulder to shoulder throughout all these troublous months, and whom he had come to love and depend upon for guidance and sustenance. A sense of loneliness and misery pervaded him by contrast with which all that he had endured seemed as nothing. To Pitt, this separation was the poignant climax of all his sufferings.

Other buyers came and stared at them, and passed on. Blood did not heed them. And then at the end of the line there was a movement. Gardner was speaking in a loud voice, making an announcement to the general public of buyers that had waited until Colonel Bishop had taken his choice of that human merchandise. As he finished, Blood, looking in his direction, noticed that the girl was speaking to Bishop, and pointing up the line with a silver-hilted riding-whip she carried. Bishop shaded his eyes with his hand to look in the direction in which she was pointing. Then slowly, with his ponderous, rolling gait, he approached again accompanied by Gardner, and followed by the lady and the Governor.

On they came until the Colonel was abreast of Blood. He would have passed on, but that the lady tapped his arm with her whip.

"But this is the man I meant," she said.

"This one?" Contempt rang in the voice. Peter Blood found himself staring into a pair of beady brown eyes sunk into a yellow, fleshly face like currants into a dumpling. He felt the colour creeping into his face under the insult of that contemptuous inspection. "Bah! A bag of bones. What should I do with him?"

He was turning away when Gardner interposed.

"He maybe lean, but he's tough; tough and healthy. When half of them was sick and the other half sickening, this rogue kept his legs and doctored his fellows. But for him there'd ha' been more deaths than there was. Say fifteen pounds for him, Colonel. That's cheap enough. He's tough, I tell your honour—tough and strong, though he be lean. And he's just the man to bear the heat when it comes. The climate'll never kill him."

There came a chuckle from Governor Steed. "You hear, Colonel. Trust your niece. Her sex knows a man when it sees one." And he laughed, well pleased with his wit.

But he laughed alone. A cloud of annoyance swept across the face of the Colonel's niece, whilst the Colonel himself was too absorbed in the consideration of this bargain to heed the Governor's humour. He twisted his lip a little, stroking his chin with his hand the while. Jeremy Pitt had almost ceased to breathe.

"I'll give you ten pounds for him," said the Colonel at last.

Peter Blood prayed that the offer might be rejected. For no reason that he could have given you, he was taken with repugnance at the thought of becoming the property of this gross animal, and in some sort the property of that hazel-eyed young girl. But it would need more than repugnance to save him from his destiny. A slave is a slave, and has no power to shape his fate. Peter Blood was sold to Colonel Bishop—a disdainful buyer—for the ignominious sum of ten pounds.

CHAPTER V. ARABELLA BISHOP

One sunny morning in January, about a month after the arrival of the Jamaica Merchant at Bridgetown, Miss Arabella Bishop rode out from her uncle's fine house on the heights to the northwest of the city. She was attended by two negroes who trotted after her at a respectful distance, and her destination was Government House, whither she went to visit the Governor's lady, who had lately been ailing. Reaching the summit of a gentle, grassy slope, she met a tall, lean man dressed in a sober, gentlemanly fashion, who was walking in the opposite direction. He was a stranger to her, and strangers were rare enough in the island. And yet in some vague way he did not seem quite a stranger.

Miss Arabella drew rein, affecting to pause that she might admire the prospect, which was fair enough to warrant it. Yet out of the corner of those hazel eyes she scanned this fellow very attentively as he came nearer. She corrected her first impression of his dress. It was sober enough, but hardly gentlemanly. Coat and breeches were of plain homespun; and if the former sat so well upon him it was more by virtue of his natural grace than by that of tailoring. His stockings were of cotton, harsh and plain, and the broad castor, which he respectfully doffed as he came up with her, was an old one unadorned by band or feather. What had seemed to be a periwig at a little distance was now revealed for the man's own lustrous coiling black hair.

Out of a brown, shaven, saturnine face two eyes that were startlingly blue considered her gravely. The man would have passed on but that she detained him.

"I think I know you, sir," said she.

Her voice was crisp and boyish, and there was something of boyishness in her manner—if one can apply the term to so dainty a lady. It arose perhaps from an ease, a directness, which disdained the artifices of her sex, and set her on good terms with all the world. To this it may be due that Miss Arabella had reached the age of five and twenty not merely unmarried but unwooed. She used with all men a sisterly frankness which in itself contains a quality of aloofness, rendering it difficult for any man to become her lover.

Her negroes had halted at some distance in the rear, and they squatted now upon the short grass until it should be her pleasure to proceed upon her way.

The stranger came to a standstill upon being addressed.

"A lady should know her own property," said he.

"My property?"

"Your uncle's, leastways. Let me present myself. I am called Peter Blood, and I am worth precisely ten pounds. I know it because that is the sum your uncle paid for me. It is not every man has the same opportunities of ascertaining his real value."

She recognized him then. She had not seen him since that day upon the mole a month ago, and that she should not instantly have known him again despite the interest he had then aroused in her is not surprising, considering the change he had wrought in his appearance, which now was hardly that of a slave.

"My God!" said she. "And you can laugh!"

"It's an achievement," he admitted. "But then, I have not fared as ill as I might."

"I have heard of that," said she.

What she had heard was that this rebel-convict had been discovered to be a physician. The thing had come to the ears of Governor Steed, who suffered damnably from the gout, and Governor Steed had borrowed the fellow from his purchaser. Whether by skill or good fortune, Peter Blood had afforded the Governor that relief which his excellency had failed to obtain from the ministrations of either of the two physicians practising in Bridgetown. Then the Governor's lady had desired him to attend her for the megrims. Mr. Blood had found her suffering from nothing worse than peevishness—the result of a natural petulance aggravated by the dulness of life in Barbados to a lady of her social aspirations. But he had prescribed for her none the less, and she had conceived herself the better for his prescription. After that the fame of him had gone through Bridgetown, and Colonel Bishop had found that there was more profit to be made out of this new slave by leaving him to pursue his profession than by setting him to work on the plantations, for which purpose he had been originally acquired.

"It is yourself, madam, I have to thank for my comparatively easy and clean condition," said Mr. Blood, "and I am glad to take this opportunity of doing so."

The gratitude was in his words rather than in his tone. Was he mocking, she wondered, and looked at him with the searching frankness that another might have found disconcerting. He took the glance for a question, and answered it.

"If some other planter had bought me," he explained, "it is odds that the facts of my shining abilities might never have been brought to light, and I should be hewing and hoeing at this moment like the poor wretches who were landed with me."

"And why do you thank me for that? It was my uncle who bought you."

"But he would not have done so had you not urged him. I perceived your interest. At the time I resented it."

"You resented it?" There was a challenge in her boyish voice.

"I have had no lack of experiences of this mortal life; but to be bought and sold was a new one, and I was hardly in the mood to love my purchaser."

"If I urged you upon my uncle, sir, it was that I commiserated you." There was a slight severity in her tone, as if to reprove the mixture of mockery and flippancy in which he seemed to be speaking.

She proceeded to explain herself. "My uncle may appear to you a hard man. No doubt he is. They are all hard men, these planters. It is the life, I suppose. But there are others here who are worse. There is Mr. Crabston, for instance, up at Speightstown. He was there on the mole, waiting to buy my uncle's leavings, and if you had fallen into his hands... A dreadful man. That is why."

He was a little bewildered.

"This interest in a stranger..." he began. Then changed the direction of his probe. "But there were others as deserving of commiseration."

"You did not seem quite like the others."

"I am not," said he.

"Oh!" She stared at him, bridling a little. "You have a good opinion of yourself."

"On the contrary. The others are all worthy rebels. I am not. That is the difference. I was one who had not the wit to see that England requires purifying. I was content to pursue a doctor's trade in Bridgewater whilst my betters were shedding their blood to drive out an unclean tyrant and his rascally crew."

"Sir!" she checked him. "I think you are talking treason."

"I hope I am not obscure," said he.

"There are those here who would have you flogged if they heard you."

"The Governor would never allow it. He has the gout, and his lady has the megrims."

"Do you depend upon that?" She was frankly scornful.

"You have certainly never had the gout; probably not even the megrims," said he.

She made a little impatient movement with her hand, and looked away from him a moment, out to sea. Quite suddenly she looked at him again; and now her brows were knit.

"But if you are not a rebel, how come you here?"

He saw the thing she apprehended, and he laughed. "Faith, now, it's a long story," said he.

"And one perhaps that you would prefer not to tell?"

Briefly on that he told it her.

"My God! What an infamy!" she cried, when he had done.

"Oh, it's a sweet country England under King James! There's no need to commiserate me further. All things considered I prefer Barbados. Here at least one can believe in God."

He looked first to right, then to left as he spoke, from the distant shadowy bulk of Mount Hillbay to the limitless ocean ruffled by the winds of heaven. Then, as if the fair prospect rendered him conscious of his own littleness and the insignificance of his woes, he fell thoughtful.

"Is that so difficult elsewhere?" she asked him, and she was very grave.

"Men make it so."

"I see." She laughed a little, on a note of sadness, it seemed to him. "I have never deemed Barbados the earthly mirror of heaven," she confessed. "But no doubt you know your world better than I." She touched her horse with her little silver-hilted whip. "I congratulate you on this easing of your misfortunes."

He bowed, and she moved on. Her negroes sprang up, and went trotting after her.

Awhile Peter Blood remained standing there, where she left him, conning the sunlit waters of Carlisle Bay below, and the shipping in that spacious haven about which the gulls were fluttering noisily.

It was a fair enough prospect, he reflected, but it was a prison, and in announcing that he preferred it to England, he had indulged that almost laudable form of boasting which lies in belittling our misadventures.

He turned, and resuming his way, went off in long, swinging strides towards the little huddle of huts built of mud and wattles—a miniature village enclosed in a stockade which the plantation slaves inhabited, and where he, himself, was lodged with them.

Through his mind sang the line of Lovelace:

> "Stone walls do not a prison make,
> Nor iron bars a cage."

But he gave it a fresh meaning, the very converse of that which its author had intended. A prison, he reflected, was a prison, though it had neither walls nor bars, however spacious it might be. And as he realized it that morning so he was to realize it increasingly as time sped on. Daily he came to think more of his clipped wings, of his exclusion from the world, and less of the fortuitous liberty he enjoyed. Nor did the contrasting of his comparatively easy lot with that of his unfortunate fellow-convicts bring him the satisfaction a differently constituted mind might have derived from it. Rather did the contemplation of their misery increase the bitterness that was gathering in his soul.

Of the forty-two who had been landed with him from the Jamaica Merchant, Colonel Bishop had purchased no less than twenty-five. The remainder had gone to lesser planters, some of them to Speightstown, and others still farther north. What may have been the lot of the latter he could not tell, but amongst Bishop's slaves Peter Blood came and went freely, sleeping in their quarters, and their lot he knew to be a brutalizing misery. They toiled in the sugar plantations from sunrise to sunset, and if their labours flagged, there were the whips of the overseer and his men to quicken them. They went in rags, some almost naked; they dwelt in squalor, and they were ill-nourished on salted meat and maize dumplings—food which to many of them was for a season at least so nauseating that two of them sickened and died before Bishop remembered that their lives had a certain value in labour to him and yielded to Blood's intercessions for a better care of such as fell ill. To curb insubordination, one of them who had rebelled against Kent, the brutal overseer, was lashed to death by negroes under his comrades' eyes, and another who had been so misguided as to run away into the woods was tracked, brought back, flogged, and then branded on the forehead with the letters "F. T.," that all might know him for a fugitive traitor as long as he lived. Fortunately for him the poor fellow died as a consequence of the flogging.

After that a dull, spiritless resignation settled down upon the remainder. The most mutinous were quelled, and accepted their unspeakable lot with the tragic fortitude of despair.

Peter Blood alone, escaping these excessive sufferings, remained outwardly unchanged, whilst inwardly the only change in him was a daily deeper hatred of his kind, a daily deeper longing to escape from this place where man defiled so foully the lovely work of his Creator. It was a longing too vague to amount to a hope. Hope here was inadmissible. And yet he did not yield to despair. He set a mask of laughter on his saturnine countenance and went his way, treating the sick to the profit of Colonel Bishop, and encroaching further and further upon the preserves of the two other men of medicine in Bridgetown.

Immune from the degrading punishments and privations of his fellow-convicts, he was enabled to keep his self-respect, and was treated without harshness even by the soulless planter to whom he had been sold. He owed it all to gout and megrims. He had won the esteem of Governor Steed, and—what is even more important—of Governor Steed's lady, whom he shamelessly and cynically flattered and humoured.

Occasionally he saw Miss Bishop, and they seldom met but that she paused to hold him in conversation for some moments, evincing her interest in him. Himself, he was never disposed to linger. He was not, he told himself, to be deceived by her delicate exterior, her sapling grace, her easy, boyish ways and pleasant, boyish voice. In all his life—and it had been very varied—he had never met a man whom he accounted more beastly than her uncle, and he could not dissociate her from the man. She was his niece, of his own blood, and some of the vices of it, some of the remorseless cruelty of the wealthy planter must, he argued, inhabit that pleasant body of hers. He argued this very often to himself, as if answering and convincing some instinct that pleaded otherwise, and arguing it he avoided her when it was possible, and was frigidly civil when it was not.

Justifiable as his reasoning was, plausible as it may seem, yet he would have done better to have trusted the instinct that was in conflict with it. Though the same blood ran in her veins as in those of Colonel Bishop, yet hers was free of the vices that tainted her uncle's, for these vices were not natural to that blood; they were, in his case, acquired. Her father, Tom Bishop—that same Colonel Bishop's brother—had been a kindly, chivalrous, gentle soul, who, broken-hearted by the early death of a young wife, had abandoned the Old World and sought an anodyne for his grief in the New. He had come out to the Antilles, bringing with him his little daughter, then five years of age, and had given himself up to the life of a planter. He had prospered from the first, as men sometimes will who care nothing for prosperity. Prospering, he had bethought him of his younger brother, a soldier at home reputed somewhat wild. He had advised him to come out to Barbados; and the advice, which at another season William Bishop might have scorned, reached him at a moment when his wildness was beginning to bear such fruit that a change of climate was desirable. William came, and was admitted by his generous brother to a partnership in the prosperous plantation. Some six years later, when Arabella was fifteen, her father died, leaving her in her uncle's guardianship. It was perhaps his one mistake. But the goodness of his own nature coloured his views of other men; moreover, himself, he had conducted the education of his daughter, giving her an independence of character upon which perhaps he counted unduly. As things were, there was little love between uncle and niece. But she was dutiful to him, and he was circumspect in his behaviour before her. All his life, and for all his wildness, he had gone in a certain awe of his brother, whose worth he had the wit to recognize; and now it was almost as if some of that awe was transferred to his brother's child, who was also, in a sense, his partner, although she took no active part in the business of the plantations.

Peter Blood judged her—as we are all too prone to judge—upon insufficient knowledge.

He was very soon to have cause to correct that judgment. One day towards the end of May, when the heat was beginning to grow oppressive, there crawled into Carlisle Bay a wounded, battered English ship, the Pride of Devon, her freeboard scarred and broken, her coach a gaping wreck, her mizzen so shot away that only a jagged stump remained to tell the place where it had stood. She had been in action off Martinique with two Spanish treasure ships, and although her captain swore that the Spaniards had beset him without provocation, it is difficult to avoid a suspicion that the encounter had been brought about quite otherwise. One of the Spaniards had fled from the combat, and if the Pride of Devon had not given chase it was probably because she was by then in no case to do so. The other had been sunk, but not before the English ship had transferred to her own hold a good deal of the treasure aboard the Spaniard. It was, in fact, one of those piratical affrays which were a perpetual source of trouble between the courts of St. James's and the Escurial, complaints emanating now from one and now from the other side.

Steed, however, after the fashion of most Colonial governors, was willing enough to dull his wits to the extent of accepting the English seaman's story, disregarding any evidence that might belie it. He shared the hatred so richly deserved by arrogant, overbearing Spain that was common to men of every other nation from the Bahamas to the Main. Therefore he gave the Pride of Devon the shelter she sought in his harbour and every facility to careen and carry out repairs.

But before it came to this, they fetched from her hold over a score of English seamen as battered and broken as the ship herself, and together with these some half-dozen Spaniards in like case, the only survivors of a boarding party from the Spanish galleon that had invaded the English ship and found itself unable to retreat. These wounded men were conveyed to a long shed on the wharf, and the medical skill of Bridgetown was summoned to their aid. Peter Blood was ordered to bear a hand in this work, and partly because he spoke Castilian—and he spoke it as fluently as his own native tongue—partly because of his inferior condition as a slave, he was given the Spaniards for his patients.

Now Blood had no cause to love Spaniards. His two years in a Spanish prison and his subsequent campaigning in the Spanish Netherlands had shown him a side of the Spanish character which he had found anything but admirable. Nevertheless he performed his doctor's duties zealously and painstakingly, if emotionlessly, and even with a certain superficial friendliness towards each of his patients. These were so surprised at having their wounds healed instead of being summarily hanged that they manifested a docility very unusual in their kind. They were shunned, however, by all those charitably disposed inhabitants of Bridgetown who flocked to the improvised hospital with gifts of fruit and flowers and delicacies for the injured English seamen. Indeed, had the wishes of some of these inhabitants been regarded, the Spaniards would have been left to die like vermin, and of this Peter Blood had an example almost at the very outset.

With the assistance of one of the negroes sent to the shed for the purpose, he was in the act of setting a broken leg, when a deep, gruff voice, that he had come to know and dislike as he had never disliked the voice of living man, abruptly challenged him.

"What are you doing there?"

Blood did not look up from his task. There was not the need. He knew the voice, as I have said.

"I am setting a broken leg," he answered, without pausing in his labours.

"I can see that, fool." A bulky body interposed between Peter Blood and the window. The half-naked man on the straw rolled his black eyes to stare up fearfully out of a clay-coloured face at this intruder. A knowledge of English was unnecessary to inform him that here came an enemy. The harsh, minatory note of that voice sufficiently expressed the fact. "I can see that, fool; just as I can see what the rascal is. Who gave you leave to set Spanish legs?"

"I am a doctor, Colonel Bishop. The man is wounded. It is not for me to discriminate. I keep to my trade."

"Do you, by God! If you'd done that, you wouldn't now be here."

"On the contrary, it is because I did it that I am here."

"Aye, I know that's your lying tale." The Colonel sneered; and then, observing Blood to continue his work unmoved, he grew really angry. "Will you cease that, and attend to me when I am speaking?"

Peter Blood paused, but only for an instant. "The man is in pain," he said shortly, and resumed his work.

"In pain, is he? I hope he is, the damned piratical dog. But will you heed me, you insubordinate knave?"

The Colonel delivered himself in a roar, infuriated by what he conceived to be defiance, and defiance expressing itself in the most unruffled disregard of himself. His long bamboo cane was raised to strike. Peter Blood's blue eyes caught the flash of it, and he spoke quickly to arrest the blow.

"Not insubordinate, sir, whatever I may be. I am acting upon the express orders of Governor Steed."

The Colonel checked, his great face empurpling. His mouth fell open.

"Governor Steed!" he echoed. Then he lowered his cane, swung round, and without another word to Blood rolled away towards the other end of the shed where the Governor was standing at the moment.

Peter Blood chuckled. But his triumph was dictated less by humanitarian considerations than by the reflection that he had baulked his brutal owner.

The Spaniard, realizing that in this altercation, whatever its nature, the doctor had stood his friend, ventured in a muted voice to ask him what had happened. But the doctor shook his head in silence, and pursued his work. His ears were straining to catch the words now passing between Steed and Bishop. The Colonel was blustering and storming, the great bulk of him towering above the wizened little overdressed figure of the Governor. But the little fop was not to be browbeaten. His excellency was conscious that he had behind him the force of public opinion to support him. Some there might be, but they were not many, who held such ruthless views as Colonel Bishop. His excellency asserted his authority. It was by his orders that Blood had devoted himself to the wounded Spaniards, and his orders were to be carried out. There was no more to be said.

Colonel Bishop was of another opinion. In his view there was a great deal to be said. He said it, with great circumstance, loudly, vehemently, obscenely—for he could be fluently obscene when moved to anger.

"You talk like a Spaniard, Colonel," said the Governor, and thus dealt the Colonel's pride a wound that was to smart resentfully for many a week. At the moment it struck him silent, and sent him stamping out of the shed in a rage for which he could find no words.

It was two days later when the ladies of Bridgetown, the wives and daughters of her planters and merchants, paid their first visit of charity to the wharf, bringing their gifts to the wounded seamen.

Again Peter Blood was there, ministering to the sufferers in his care, moving among those unfortunate Spaniards whom no one heeded. All the charity, all the gifts were for the members of the crew of the Pride of Devon. And this Peter Blood accounted natural enough. But rising suddenly from the re-dressing of a wound, a task in which he had been absorbed for some moments, he saw to his surprise that one lady, detached from the general throng, was placing some plantains and a bundle of succulent sugar cane on the cloak that served one of his patients for a coverlet. She was elegantly dressed in lavender silk and was followed by a half-naked negro carrying a basket.

Peter Blood, stripped of his coat, the sleeves of his coarse shirt rolled to the elbow, and holding a bloody rag in his hand, stood at gaze a moment. The lady, turning now to confront him, her lips parting in a smile of recognition, was Arabella Bishop.

"The man's a Spaniard," said he, in the tone of one who corrects a misapprehension, and also tinged never so faintly by something of the derision that was in his soul.

The smile with which she had been greeting him withered on her lips. She frowned and stared at him a moment, with increasing haughtiness.

"So I perceive. But he's a human being none the less," said she.

That answer, and its implied rebuke, took him by surprise.

"Your uncle, the Colonel, is of a different opinion," said he, when he had recovered. "He regards them as vermin to be left to languish and die of their festering wounds."

She caught the irony now more plainly in his voice. She continued to stare at him.

"Why do you tell me this?"

"To warn you that you may be incurring the Colonel's displeasure. If he had had his way, I should never have been allowed to dress their wounds."

"And you thought, of course, that I must be of my uncle's mind?" There was a crispness about her voice, an ominous challenging sparkle in her hazel eyes.

"I'd not willingly be rude to a lady even in my thoughts," said he. "But that you should bestow gifts on them, considering that if your uncle came to hear of it...." He paused, leaving the sentence unfinished. "Ah, well—there it is!" he concluded.

But the lady was not satisfied at all.

"First you impute to me inhumanity, and then cowardice. Faith! For a man who would not willingly be rude to a lady even in his thoughts, it's none so bad." Her boyish laugh trilled out, but the note of it jarred his ears this time.

He saw her now, it seemed to him, for the first time, and saw how he had misjudged her.

"Sure, now, how was I to guess that... that Colonel Bishop could have an angel for his niece?" said he recklessly, for he was reckless as men often are in sudden penitence.

"You wouldn't, of course. I shouldn't think you often guess aright." Having withered him with that and her glance, she turned to her negro and the basket that he carried. From this she lifted now the fruits and delicacies with which it was laden, and piled them in such heaps upon the beds of the six Spaniards that by the time she had so served the last of them her basket was empty, and there was nothing left for her own fellow-countrymen. These, indeed, stood in no need of her bounty—as she no doubt observed—since they were being plentifully supplied by others.

Having thus emptied her basket, she called her negro, and without another word or so much as another glance at Peter Blood, swept out of the place with her head high and chin thrust forward.

Peter watched her departure. Then he fetched a sigh.

It startled him to discover that the thought that he had incurred her anger gave him concern. It could not have been so yesterday. It became so only since he had been vouchsafed this revelation of her true nature. "Bad cess to it now, it serves me right. It seems I know nothing at all of human nature. But how the devil was I to guess that a family that can breed a devil like Colonel Bishop should also breed a saint like this?"

CHAPTER VI. PLANS OF ESCAPE

After that Arabella Bishop went daily to the shed on the wharf with gifts of fruit, and later of money and of wearing apparel for the Spanish prisoners. But she contrived so to time her visits that Peter Blood never again met her there. Also his own visits were growing shorter in a measure as his patients healed. That they all throve and returned to health under his care, whilst fully one third of the wounded in the care of Whacker and Bronson—the two other surgeons—died of their wounds, served to increase the reputation in which this rebel-convict stood in Bridgetown. It may have been no more than the fortune of war. But the townsfolk did not choose so to regard it. It led to a further dwindling of the practices of his free colleagues and a further increase of his own labours and his owner's profit. Whacker and Bronson laid their heads together to devise a scheme by which this intolerable state of things should be brought to an end. But that is to anticipate.

One day, whether by accident or design, Peter Blood came striding down the wharf a full half-hour earlier than usual, and so met Miss Bishop just issuing from the shed. He doffed his hat and stood aside to give her passage. She took it, chin in the air, and eyes which disdained to look anywhere where the sight of him was possible.

"Miss Arabella," said he, on a coaxing, pleading note.

She grew conscious of his presence, and looked him over with an air that was faintly, mockingly searching.

"La!" said she. "It's the delicate-minded gentleman!"

Peter groaned. "Am I so hopelessly beyond forgiveness? I ask it very humbly."

"What condescension!"

"It is cruel to mock me," said he, and adopted mock-humility. "After all, I am but a slave. And you might be ill one of these days."

"What, then?"

"It would be humiliating to send for me if you treat me like an enemy."

"You are not the only doctor in Bridgetown."

"But I am the least dangerous."

She grew suddenly suspicious of him, aware that he was permitting himself to rally her, and in a measure she had already yielded to it. She stiffened, and looked him over again.

"You make too free, I think," she rebuked him.

"A doctor's privilege."

"I am not your patient. Please to remember it in future." And on that, unquestionably angry, she departed.

"Now is she a vixen or am I a fool, or is it both?" he asked the blue vault of heaven, and then went into the shed.

It was to be a morning of excitements. As he was leaving an hour or so later, Whacker, the younger of the other two physicians, joined him—an unprecedented condescension this, for hitherto neither of them had addressed him beyond an occasional and surly "good-day!"

"If you are for Colonel Bishop's, I'll walk with you a little way, Doctor Blood," said he. He was a short, broad man of five-and-forty with pendulous cheeks and hard blue eyes.

Peter Blood was startled. But he dissembled it.

"I am for Government House," said he.

"Ah! To be sure! The Governor's lady." And he laughed; or perhaps he sneered. Peter Blood was not quite certain. "She encroaches a deal upon your time, I hear. Youth and good looks, Doctor Blood! Youth and good looks! They are inestimable advantages in our profession as in others—particularly where the ladies are concerned."

Peter stared at him. "If you mean what you seem to mean, you had better say it to Governor Steed. It may amuse him."

"You surely misapprehend me."

"I hope so."

"You're so very hot, now!" The doctor linked his arm through Peter's. "I protest I desire to be your friend—to serve you. Now, listen." Instinctively his voice grew lower. "This slavery in which you find yourself must be singularly irksome to a man of parts such as yourself."

"What intuitions!" cried sardonic Mr. Blood. But the doctor took him literally.

"I am no fool, my dear doctor. I know a man when I see one, and often I can tell his thoughts."

"If you can tell me mine, you'll persuade me of it," said Mr. Blood.

Dr. Whacker drew still closer to him as they stepped along the wharf. He lowered his voice to a still more confidential tone. His hard blue eyes peered up into the swart, sardonic face of his companion, who was a head taller than himself.

"How often have I not seen you staring out over the sea, your soul in your eyes! Don't I know what you are thinking? If you could escape from this hell of slavery, you could exercise the profession of which you are an ornament as a free man with pleasure and profit to yourself. The world is large. There are many nations besides England where a man of your parts would be warmly welcomed. There are many colonies besides these English ones." Lower still came the voice until it was no more than a whisper. Yet there was no one within earshot. "It is none so far now to the Dutch settlement of Curacao. At this time of the year the voyage may safely be undertaken in a light craft. And Curacao need be no more than a stepping-stone to the great world, which would lie open to you once you were delivered from this bondage."

Dr. Whacker ceased. He was pale and a little out of breath. But his hard eyes continued to study his impassive companion.

"Well?" he said after a pause. "What do you say to that?"

Yet Blood did not immediately answer. His mind was heaving in tumult, and he was striving to calm it that he might take a proper survey of this thing flung into it to create so monstrous a disturbance. He began where another might have ended.

"I have no money. And for that a handsome sum would be necessary."

"Did I not say that I desired to be your friend?"

"Why?" asked Peter Blood at point-blank range.

But he never heeded the answer. Whilst Dr. Whacker was professing that his heart bled for a brother doctor languishing in slavery, denied the opportunity which his gifts entitled him to make for himself, Peter Blood pounced like a hawk upon the obvious truth. Whacker and his colleague desired to be rid of one who threatened to ruin them. Sluggishness of decision was never a fault of Blood's. He leapt where another crawled. And so this thought of evasion never entertained until planted there now by Dr. Whacker sprouted into instant growth.

"I see, I see," he said, whilst his companion was still talking, explaining, and to save Dr. Whacker's face he played the hypocrite. "It is very noble in you—very brotherly, as between men of medicine. It is what I myself should wish to do in like case."

The hard eyes flashed, the husky voice grew tremulous as the other asked almost too eagerly:

"You agree, then? You agree?"

"Agree?" Blood laughed. "If I should be caught and brought back, they'd clip my wings and brand me for life."

"Surely the thing is worth a little risk?" More tremulous than ever was the tempter's voice.

"Surely," Blood agreed. "But it asks more than courage. It asks money. A sloop might be bought for twenty pounds, perhaps."

"It shall be forthcoming. It shall be a loan, which you shall repay us—repay me, when you can."

That betraying "us" so hastily retrieved completed Blood's understanding. The other doctor was also in the business.

They were approaching the peopled part of the mole. Quickly, but eloquently, Blood expressed his thanks, where he knew that no thanks were due.

"We will talk of this again, sir—to-morrow," he concluded. "You have opened for me the gates of hope."

In that at least he tittered no more than the bare truth, and expressed it very baldly. It was, indeed, as if a door had been suddenly flung open to the sunlight for escape from a dark prison in which a man had thought to spend his life.

He was in haste now to be alone, to straighten out his agitated mind and plan coherently what was to be done. Also he must consult another. Already he had hit upon that other. For such a voyage a navigator would be necessary, and a navigator was ready to his hand in Jeremy Pitt. The first thing was to take counsel with the young shipmaster, who must be associated with him in this business if it were to be undertaken. All that day his mind was in turmoil with this new hope, and he was sick with impatience for night and a chance to discuss the matter with his chosen partner. As a result Blood was betimes that evening in the spacious stockade that enclosed the huts of the slaves together with the big white house of the overseer, and he found an opportunity of a few words with Pitt, unobserved by the others.

"To-night when all are asleep, come to my cabin. I have something to say to you."

The young man stared at him, roused by Blood's pregnant tone out of the mental lethargy into which he had of late been lapsing as a result of the dehumanizing life he lived. Then he nodded understanding and assent, and they moved apart.

The six months of plantation life in Barbados had made an almost tragic mark upon the young seaman. His erstwhile bright alertness was all departed. His face was growing vacuous, his eyes were dull and lack-lustre, and he moved in a cringing, furtive manner, like an over-beaten dog. He had survived the ill-nourishment, the excessive work on the sugar plantation under a pitiless sun, the lashes of the overseer's whip when his labours flagged, and the deadly, unrelieved animal life to which he was condemned. But the price he was paying for survival was the usual price. He was in danger of becoming no better than an animal, of sinking to the level of the negroes who sometimes toiled beside him. The man, however, was still there, not yet dormant, but merely torpid from a surfeit of despair; and the man in him promptly shook off that torpidity and awoke at the first words Blood spoke to him that night—awoke and wept.

"Escape?" he panted. "O God!" He took his head in his hands, and fell to sobbing like a child.

"Sh! Steady now! Steady!" Blood admonished him in a whisper, alarmed by the lad's blubbering. He crossed to Pitt's side, and set a restraining hand upon his shoulder. "For God's sake, command yourself. If we're overheard we shall both be flogged for this."

Among the privileges enjoyed by Blood was that of a hut to himself, and they were alone in this. But, after all, it was built of wattles thinly plastered with mud, and its door was composed of bamboos, through which sound passed very easily. Though the stockade was locked for the night, and all within it asleep by now—it was after midnight—yet a prowling overseer was not impossible, and a sound of voices must lead to discovery. Pitt realized this, and controlled his outburst of emotion.

Sitting close thereafter they talked in whispers for an hour or more, and all the while those dulled wits of Pitt's were sharpening themselves anew upon this precious whetstone of hope. They would need to recruit others into their enterprise, a half-dozen at least, a half-score if possible, but no more than that. They must pick the best out of that score of survivors of the Monmouth men that Colonel Bishop had acquired. Men who understood the sea were desirable. But of these there were only two in that unfortunate gang, and their knowledge was none too full. They were Hagthorpe, a gentleman who had served in the Royal Navy, and Nicholas Dyke, who had been a petty officer in the late king's time, and there was another who had been a gunner, a man named Ogle.

It was agreed before they parted that Pitt should begin with these three and then proceed to recruit some six or eight others. He was to move with the utmost caution, sounding his men very carefully before making anything in the nature of a disclosure, and even then avoid rendering that disclosure so full that its betrayal might frustrate the plans which as yet had to be worked out in detail. Labouring with them in the plantations, Pitt would not want for opportunities of broaching the matter to his fellow-slaves.

"Caution above everything," was Blood's last recommendation to him at parting. "Who goes slowly, goes safely, as the Italians have it. And remember that if you betray yourself, you ruin all, for you are the only navigator amongst us, and without you there is no escaping."

Pitt reassured him, and slunk off back to his own hut and the straw that served him for a bed.

Coming next morning to the wharf, Blood found Dr. Whacker in a generous mood. Having slept on the matter, he was prepared to advance the convict any sum up to thirty pounds that would enable him to acquire a boat capable of taking him away from the settlement. Blood expressed his thanks becomingly, betraying no sign that he saw clearly into the true reason of the other's munificence.

"It's not money I'll require," said he, "but the boat itself. For who will be selling me a boat and incurring the penalties in Governor Steed's proclamation? Ye'll have read it, no doubt?"

Dr. Whacker's heavy face grew overcast. Thoughtfully he rubbed his chin. "I've read it—yes. And I dare not procure the boat for you. It would be discovered. It must be. And the penalty is a fine of two hundred pounds besides imprisonment. It would ruin me. You'll see that?"

The high hopes in Blood's soul, began to shrink. And the shadow of his despair overcast his face.

"But then..." he faltered. "There is nothing to be done."

"Nay, nay: things are not so desperate." Dr. Whacker smiled a little with tight lips. "I've thought of it. You will see that the man who buys the boat must be one of those who goes with you—so that he is not here to answer questions afterwards."

"But who is to go with me save men in my own case? What I cannot do, they cannot."

"There are others detained on the island besides slaves. There are several who are here for debt, and would be glad enough to spread their wings. There's a fellow Nuttall, now, who follows the trade of a shipwright, whom I happen to know would welcome such a chance as you might afford him."

"But how should a debtor come with money to buy a boat? The question will be asked."

"To' be sure it will. But if you contrive shrewdly, you'll all be gone before that happens."

Blood nodded understanding, and the doctor, setting a hand upon his sleeve, unfolded the scheme he had conceived.

"You shall have the money from me at once. Having received it, you'll forget that it was I who supplied it to you. You have friends in England—relatives, perhaps—who sent it out to you through the agency of one of your Bridgetown patients, whose name as a man of honour you will on no account divulge lest you bring trouble upon him. That is your tale if there are questions."

He paused, looking hard at Blood. Blood nodded understanding and assent. Relieved, the doctor continued:

"But there should be no questions if you go carefully to work. You concert matters With Nuttall. You enlist him as one of your companions and a shipwright should be a very useful member of your crew. You engage him to discover a likely sloop whose owner is disposed to sell. Then let your preparations all be made before the purchase is effected, so that your escape may follow instantly upon it before the inevitable questions come to be asked. You take me?"

So well did Blood take him that within an hour he contrived to see Nuttall, and found the fellow as disposed to the business as Dr. Whacker had predicted. When he left the shipwright, it was agreed that Nuttall should seek the boat required, for which Blood would at once produce the money.

The quest took longer than was expected by Blood, who waited impatiently with the doctor's gold concealed about his person. But at the end of some three weeks, Nuttall—whom he was now meeting daily—informed him that he had found a serviceable wherry, and that its owner was disposed to sell it for twenty-two pounds. That evening, on the beach, remote from all eyes, Peter Blood handed that sum to his new associate, and Nuttall went off with instructions to complete the purchase late on the following day. He was to bring the boat to the wharf, where under cover of night Blood and his fellow-convicts would join him and make off.

Everything was ready. In the shed, from which all the wounded men had now been removed and which had since remained untenanted, Nuttall had concealed the necessary stores: a hundredweight of bread, a quantity of cheese, a cask of water and some few bottles of Canary, a compass, quadrant, chart, half-hour glass, log and line, a tarpaulin, some carpenter's tools, and a lantern and candles. And in the stockade, all was likewise in readiness. Hagthorpe, Dyke, and Ogle had agreed to join the venture, and eight others had been carefully recruited. In Pitt's hut, which he shared with five other rebels-convict, all of whom were to join in this bid for liberty, a ladder had been constructed in secret during those nights of waiting. With this they were to surmount the stockade and gain the open. The risk of detection, so that they made little noise, was negligible. Beyond locking them all into that stockade at night, there was no great precaution taken. Where, after all, could any so foolish as to attempt escape hope to conceal himself in that island? The chief risk lay in discovery by those of their companions who were to be left behind. It was because of these that they must go cautiously and in silence.

The day that was to have been their last in Barbados was a day of hope and anxiety to the twelve associates in that enterprise, no less than to Nuttall in the town below.

Towards sunset, having seen Nuttall depart to purchase and fetch the sloop to the prearranged moorings at the wharf, Peter Blood came sauntering towards the stockade, just as the slaves were being driven in from the fields. He stood aside at the entrance to let them pass, and beyond the message of hope flashed by his eyes, he held no communication with them.

He entered the stockade in their wake, and as they broke their ranks to seek their various respective huts, he beheld Colonel Bishop in talk with Kent, the overseer. The pair were standing by the stocks, planted in the middle of that green space for the punishment of offending slaves.

As he advanced, Bishop turned to regard him, scowling. "Where have you been this while?" he bawled, and although a minatory note was normal to the Colonel's voice, yet Blood felt his heart tightening apprehensively.

"I've been at my work in the town," he answered. "Mrs. Patch has a fever and Mr. Dekker has sprained his ankle."

"I sent for you to Dekker's, and you were not there. You are given to idling, my fine fellow. We shall have to quicken you one of these days unless you cease from abusing the liberty you enjoy. D'ye forget that ye're a rebel convict?"

"I am not given the chance," said Blood, who never could learn to curb his tongue.

"By God! Will you be pert with me?"

Remembering all that was at stake, growing suddenly conscious that from the huts surrounding the enclosure anxious ears were listening, he instantly practised an unusual submission.

"Not pert, sir. I... I am sorry I should have been sought...."

"Aye, and you'll be sorrier yet. There's the Governor with an attack of gout, screaming like a wounded horse, and you nowhere to be found. Be off, man—away with you at speed to Government House! You're awaited, I tell you. Best lend him a horse, Kent, or the lout'll be all night getting there."

They bustled him away, choking almost from a reluctance that he dared not show. The thing was unfortunate; but after all not beyond remedy. The escape was set for midnight, and he should easily be back by then. He mounted the horse that Kent procured him, intending to make all haste.

"How shall I reenter the stockade, sir?" he enquired at parting.

"You'll not reenter it," said Bishop. "When they've done with you at Government House, they may find a kennel for you there until morning."

Peter Blood's heart sank like a stone through water.

"But..." he began.

"Be off, I say. Will you stand there talking until dark? His excellency is waiting for you." And with his cane Colonel Bishop slashed the horse's quarters so brutally that the beast bounded forward all but unseating her rider.

Peter Blood went off in a state of mind bordering on despair. And there was occasion for it. A postponement of the escape at least until to-morrow night was necessary now, and postponement must mean the discovery of Nuttall's transaction and the asking of questions it would be difficult to answer.

It was in his mind to slink back in the night, once his work at Government House were done, and from the outside of the stockade make known to Pitt and the others his presence, and so have them join him that their project might still be carried out. But in this he reckoned without the Governor, whom he found really in the thrall of a severe attack of gout, and almost as severe an attack of temper nourished by Blood's delay.

The doctor was kept in constant attendance upon him until long after midnight, when at last he was able to ease the sufferer a little by a bleeding. Thereupon he would have withdrawn. But Steed would not hear of it. Blood must sleep in his own chamber to be at hand in case of need. It was as if Fate made sport of him. For that night at least the escape must be definitely abandoned.

Not until the early hours of the morning did Peter Blood succeed in making a temporary escape from Government House on the ground that he required certain medicaments which he must, himself, procure from the apothecary.

On that pretext, he made an excursion into the awakening town, and went straight to Nuttall, whom he found in a state of livid panic. The unfortunate debtor, who had sat up waiting through the night, conceived that all was discovered and that his own ruin would be involved. Peter Blood quieted his fears.

"It will be for to-night instead," he said, with more assurance than he felt, "if I have to bleed the Governor to death. Be ready as last night."

"But if there are questions meanwhile?" bleated Nuttall. He was a thin, pale, small-featured, man with weak eyes that now blinked desperately.

"Answer as best you can. Use your wits, man. I can stay no longer." And Peter went off to the apothecary for his pretexted drugs.

Within an hour of his going came an officer of the Secretary's to Nuttall's miserable hovel. The seller of the boat had—as by law required since the coming of the rebels-convict—duly reported the sale at the Secretary's office, so that he might obtain the reimbursement of the ten-pound surety into which every keeper of a small boat was compelled to enter. The Secretary's office postponed this reimbursement until it should have obtained confirmation of the transaction.

"We are informed that you have bought a wherry from Mr. Robert Farrell," said the officer.

"That is so," said Nuttall, who conceived that for him this was the end of the world.

"You are in no haste, it seems, to declare the same at the Secretary's office." The emissary had a proper bureaucratic haughtiness.

Nuttall's weak eyes blinked at a redoubled rate.

"To... to declare it?"

"Ye know it's the law."

"I... I didn't, may it please you."

"But it's in the proclamation published last January."

"I... I can't read, sir. I... I didn't know."

"Faugh!" The messenger withered him with his disdain.

"Well, now you're informed. See to it that you are at the Secretary's office before noon with the ten pounds surety into which you are obliged to enter."

The pompous officer departed, leaving Nuttall in a cold perspiration despite the heat of the morning. He was thankful that the fellow had not asked the question he most dreaded, which was how he, a debtor, should come by the money to buy a wherry. But this he knew was only a respite. The question would presently be asked of a certainty, and then hell would open for him. He cursed the hour in which he had been such a fool as to listen to Peter Blood's chatter of escape. He thought it very likely that the whole plot would be discovered, and that he would probably be hanged, or at least branded and sold into slavery like those other damned rebels-convict, with whom he had been so mad as to associate himself. If only he had the ten pounds for this infernal surety, which until this moment had never entered into their calculations, it was possible that the thing might be done quickly and questions postponed until later. As the Secretary's messenger had overlooked the fact that he was a debtor, so might the others at the Secretary's office, at least for a day or two; and in that time he would, he hoped, be beyond the reach of their questions. But in the meantime what was to be done about this money? And it was to be found before noon!

Nuttall snatched up his hat, and went out in quest of Peter Blood. But where look for him? Wandering aimlessly up the irregular, unpaved street, he ventured to enquire of one or two if they had seen Dr. Blood that morning. He affected to be feeling none so well, and indeed his appearance bore out the deception. None could give him information; and since Blood had never told him of Whacker's share in this business, he walked in his unhappy ignorance past the door of the one man in Barbados who would eagerly have saved him in this extremity.

Finally he determined to go up to Colonel Bishop's plantation. Probably Blood would be there. If he were not, Nuttall would find Pitt, and leave a message with him. He was acquainted with Pitt and knew of Pitt's share in this business. His pretext for seeking Blood must still be that he needed medical assistance.

And at the same time that he set out, insensitive in his anxiety to the broiling heat, to climb the heights to the north of the town, Blood was setting out from Government House at last, having so far eased the Governor's condition as to be permitted to depart. Being mounted, he would, but for an unexpected delay, have reached the stockade ahead of Nuttall, in which case several unhappy events might have been averted. The unexpected delay was occasioned by Miss Arabella Bishop.

They met at the gate of the luxuriant garden of Government House, and Miss Bishop, herself mounted, stared to see Peter Blood on horseback. It happened that he was in good spirits. The fact that the Governor's condition had so far improved as to restore him his freedom of movement had sufficed to remove the depression under which he had been labouring for the past twelve hours and more. In its rebound the mercury of his mood had shot higher far than present circumstances warranted. He was disposed to be optimistic. What had failed last night would certainly not fail again to-night. What was a day, after all? The Secretary's office might be troublesome, but not really troublesome for another twenty-four hours at least; and by then they would be well away.

This joyous confidence of his was his first misfortune. The next was that his good spirits were also shared by Miss Bishop, and that she bore no rancour. The two things conjoined to make the delay that in its consequences was so deplorable.

"Good-morning, sir," she hailed him pleasantly. "It's close upon a month since last I saw you."

"Twenty-one days to the hour," said he. "I've counted them."

"I vow I was beginning to believe you dead."

"I have to thank you for the wreath."

"The wreath?"

"To deck my grave," he explained.

"Must you ever be rallying?" she wondered, and looked at him gravely, remembering that it was his rallying on the last occasion had driven her away in dudgeon.

"A man must sometimes laugh at himself or go mad," said he. "Few realize it. That is why there are so many madmen in the world."

"You may laugh at yourself all you will, sir. But sometimes I think you laugh at me, which is not civil."

"Then, faith, you're wrong. I laugh only at the comic, and you are not comic at all."

"What am I, then?" she asked him, laughing.

A moment he pondered her, so fair and fresh to behold, so entirely maidenly and yet so entirely frank and unabashed.

"You are," he said, "the niece of the man who owns me his slave." But he spoke lightly. So lightly that she was encouraged to insistence.

"Nay, sir, that is an evasion. You shall answer me truthfully this morning."

"Truthfully? To answer you at all is a labour. But to answer truthfully! Oh, well, now, I should say of you that he'll be lucky who counts you his friend." It was in his mind to add more. But he left it there.

"That's mighty civil," said she. "You've a nice taste in compliments, Mr. Blood. Another in your place...."

"Faith, now, don't I know what another would have said? Don't I know my fellow-man at all?"

"Sometimes I think you do, and sometimes I think you don't. Anyway, you don't know your fellow-woman. There was that affair of the Spaniards."

"Will ye never forget it?"

"Never."

"Bad cess to your memory. Is there no good in me at all that you could be dwelling on instead?"

"Oh, several things."

"For instance, now?" He was almost eager.

"You speak excellent Spanish."

"Is that all?" He sank back into dismay.

"Where did you learn it? Have you been in Spain?"

"That I have. I was two years in a Spanish prison."

"In prison?" Her tone suggested apprehensions in which he had no desire to leave her.

"As a prisoner of war," he explained. "I was taken fighting with the French—in French service, that is."

"But you're a doctor!" she cried.

"That's merely a diversion, I think. By trade I am a soldier—at least, it's a trade I followed for ten years. It brought me no great gear, but it served me better than medicine, which, as you may observe, has brought me into slavery. I'm thinking it's more pleasing in the sight of Heaven to kill men than to heal them. Sure it must be."

"But how came you to be a soldier, and to serve the French?"

"I am Irish, you see, and I studied medicine. Therefore—since it's a perverse nation we are—.... Oh, but it's a long story, and the Colonel will be expecting my return." She was not in that way to be defrauded of her entertainment. If he would wait a moment they would ride back together. She had but come to enquire of the Governor's health at her uncle's request.

So he waited, and so they rode back together to Colonel Bishop's house. They rode very slowly, at a walking pace, and some whom they passed marvelled to see the doctor-slave on such apparently intimate terms with his owner's niece. One or two may have promised themselves that they would drop a hint to the Colonel. But the two rode oblivious of all others in the world that morning. He was telling her the story of his early turbulent days, and at the end of it he dwelt more fully than hitherto upon the manner of his arrest and trial.

The tale was barely done when they drew up at the Colonel's door, and dismounted, Peter Blood surrendering his nag to one of the negro grooms, who informed them that the Colonel was from home at the moment.

Even then they lingered a moment, she detaining him.

"I am sorry, Mr. Blood, that I did not know before," she said, and there was a suspicion of moisture in those clear hazel eyes. With a compelling friendliness she held out her hand to him.

"Why, what difference could it have made?" he asked.

"Some, I think. You have been very hardly used by Fate."

"Och, now...." He paused. His keen sapphire eyes considered her steadily a moment from under his level black brows. "It might have been worse," he said, with a significance which brought a tinge of colour to her cheeks and a flutter to her eyelids.

He stooped to kiss her hand before releasing it, and she did not deny him. Then he turned and strode off towards the stockade a half-mile away, and a vision of her face went with him, tinted with a rising blush and a sudden unusual shyness. He forgot in that little moment that he was a rebel-convict with ten years of slavery before him; he forgot that he had planned an escape, which was to be carried into effect that night; forgot even the peril of discovery which as a result of the Governor's gout now overhung him.

CHAPTER VII. PIRATES

Mr. James Nuttall made all speed, regardless of the heat, in his journey from Bridgetown to Colonel Bishop's plantation, and if ever man was built for speed in a hot climate that man was Mr. James Nuttall, with his short, thin body, and his long, fleshless legs. So withered was he that it was hard to believe there were any juices left in him, yet juices there must have been, for he was sweating violently by the time he reached the stockade.

At the entrance he almost ran into the overseer Kent, a squat, bow-legged animal with the arms of a Hercules and the jowl of a bulldog.

"I am seeking Doctor Blood," he announced breathlessly.

"You are in a rare haste," growled Kent. "What the devil is it? Twins?"

"Eh? Oh! Nay, nay. I'm not married, sir. It's a cousin of mine, sir."

"What is?"

"He is taken bad, sir," Nuttall lied promptly upon the cue that Kent himself had afforded him. "Is the doctor here?"

"That's his hut yonder." Kent pointed carelessly. "If he's not there, he'll be somewhere else." And he took himself off. He was a surly, ungracious beast at all times, readier with the lash of his whip than with his tongue.

Nuttall watched him go with satisfaction, and even noted the direction that he took. Then he plunged into the enclosure, to verify in mortification that Dr. Blood was not at home. A man of sense might have sat down and waited, judging that to be the quickest and surest way in the end. But Nuttall had no sense. He flung out of the stockade again, hesitated a moment as to which direction he should take, and finally decided to go any way but the way that Kent had gone. He sped across the parched savannah towards the sugar plantation which stood solid as a rampart and gleaming golden in the dazzling June sunshine. Avenues intersected the great blocks of ripening amber cane. In the distance down one of these he espied some slaves at work. Nuttall entered the avenue and advanced upon them. They eyed him dully, as he passed them. Pitt was not of their number, and he dared not ask for him. He continued his search for best part of an hour, up one of those lanes and then down another. Once an overseer challenged him, demanding to know his business. He was looking, he said, for Dr. Blood. His cousin was taken ill. The overseer bade him go to the devil, and get out of the plantation. Blood was not there. If he was anywhere he would be in his hut in the stockade.

Nuttall passed on, upon the understanding that he would go. But he went in the wrong direction; he went on towards the side of the plantation farthest from the stockade, towards the dense woods that fringed it there. The overseer was too contemptuous and perhaps too languid in the stifling heat of approaching noontide to correct his course.

Nuttall blundered to the end of the avenue, and round the corner of it, and there ran into Pitt, alone, toiling with a wooden spade upon an irrigation channel. A pair of cotton drawers, loose and ragged, clothed him from waist to knee; above and below he was naked, save for a broad hat of plaited straw that sheltered his unkempt golden head from the rays of the tropical sun. At sight of him Nuttall returned thanks aloud to his Maker. Pitt stared at him, and the shipwright poured out his dismal news in a dismal tone. The sum of it was that he must have ten pounds from Blood that very morning or they were all undone. And all he got for his pains and his sweat was the condemnation of Jeremy Pitt.

"Damn you for a fool!" said the slave. "If it's Blood you're seeking, why are you wasting your time here?"

"I can't find him," bleated Nuttall. He was indignant at his reception. He forgot the jangled state of the other's nerves after a night of anxious wakefulness ending in a dawn of despair. "I thought that you...."

"You thought that I could drop my spade and go and seek him for you? Is that what you thought? My God! that our lives should depend upon such a dummer-head. While you waste your time here, the hours are passing! And if an overseer should catch you talking to me? How'll you explain it?"

For a moment Nuttall was bereft of speech by such ingratitude. Then he exploded.

"I would to Heaven I had never had no hand in this affair. I would so! I wish that...."

What else he wished was never known, for at that moment round the block of cane came a big man in biscuit-coloured taffetas followed by two negroes in cotton drawers who were armed with cutlasses. He was not ten yards away, but his approach over the soft, yielding marl had been unheard.

Mr. Nuttall looked wildly this way and that a moment, then bolted like a rabbit for the woods, thus doing the most foolish and betraying thing that in the circumstances it was possible for him to do. Pitt groaned and stood still, leaning upon his spade.

"Hi, there! Stop!" bawled Colonel Bishop after the fugitive, and added horrible threats tricked out with some rhetorical indecencies.

But the fugitive held amain, and never so much as turned his head. It was his only remaining hope that Colonel Bishop might not have seen his face; for the power and influence of Colonel Bishop was quite sufficient to hang any man whom he thought would be better dead.

Not until the runagate had vanished into the scrub did the planter sufficiently recover from his indignant amazement to remember the two negroes who followed at his heels like a brace of hounds. It was a bodyguard without which he never moved in his plantations since a slave had made an attack upon him and all but strangled him a couple of years ago.

"After him, you black swine!" he roared at them. But as they started he checked them. "Wait! Get to heel, damn you!"

It occurred to him that to catch and deal with the fellow there was not the need to go after him, and perhaps spend the day hunting him in that cursed wood. There was Pitt here ready to his hand, and Pitt should tell him the identity of his bashful friend, and also the subject of that close and secret talk he had disturbed. Pitt might, of course, be reluctant. So much the worse for Pitt. The ingenious Colonel Bishop knew a dozen ways—some of them quite diverting—of conquering stubbornness in these convict dogs.

He turned now upon the slave a countenance that was inflamed by heat internal and external, and a pair of heady eyes that were alight with cruel intelligence. He stepped forward swinging his light bamboo cane.

"Who was that runagate?" he asked with terrible suavity. Leaning over on his spade, Jeremy Pitt hung his head a little, and shifted uncomfortably on his bare feet. Vainly he groped for an answer in a mind that could do nothing but curse the idiocy of Mr. James Nuttall.

The planter's bamboo cane fell on the lad's naked shoulders with stinging force.

"Answer me, you dog! What's his name?"

Jeremy looked at the burly planter out of sullen, almost defiant eyes.

"I don't know," he said, and in his voice there was a faint note at least of the defiance aroused in him by a blow which he dared not, for his life's sake, return. His body had remained unyielding under it, but the spirit within writhed now in torment.

"You don't know? Well, here's to quicken your wits." Again the cane descended. "Have you thought of his name yet?"

"I have not."

"Stubborn, eh?" For a moment the Colonel leered. Then his passion mastered him. "'Swounds! You impudent dog! D'you trifle with me? D'you think I'm to be mocked?"

Pitt shrugged, shifted sideways on his feet again, and settled into dogged silence. Few things are more provocative; and Colonel Bishop's temper was never one that required much provocation. Brute fury now awoke in him. Fiercely now he lashed those defenceless shoulders, accompanying each blow by blasphemy and foul abuse, until, stung beyond endurance, the lingering embers of his manhood fanned into momentary flame, Pitt sprang upon his tormentor.

But as he sprang, so also sprang the watchful blacks. Muscular bronze arms coiled crushingly about the frail white body, and in a moment the unfortunate slave stood powerless, his wrists pinioned behind him in a leathern thong.

Breathing hard, his face mottled, Bishop pondered him a moment. Then: "Fetch him along," he said.

Down the long avenue between those golden walls of cane standing some eight feet high, the wretched Pitt was thrust by his black captors in the Colonel's wake, stared at with fearful eyes by his fellow-slaves at work there. Despair went with him. What torments might immediately await him he cared little, horrible though he knew they would be. The real source of his mental anguish lay in the conviction that the elaborately planned escape from this unutterable hell was frustrated now in the very moment of execution.

They came out upon the green plateau and headed for the stockade and the overseer's white house. Pitt's eyes looked out over Carlisle Bay, of which this plateau commanded a clear view from the fort on one side to the long sheds of the wharf on the other. Along this wharf a few shallow boats were moored, and Pitt caught himself wondering which of these was the wherry in which with a little luck they might have been now at sea. Out over that sea his glance ranged miserably.

In the roads, standing in for the shore before a gentle breeze that scarcely ruffled the sapphire surface of the Caribbean, came a stately red-hulled frigate, flying the English ensign.

Colonel Bishop halted to consider her, shading his eyes with his fleshly hand. Light as was the breeze, the vessel spread no canvas to it beyond that of her foresail. Furled was her every other sail, leaving a clear view of the majestic lines of her hull, from towering stern castle to gilded beakhead that was aflash in the dazzling sunshine.

So leisurely an advance argued a master indifferently acquainted with these waters, who preferred to creep forward cautiously, sounding his way. At her present rate of progress it would be an hour, perhaps, before she came to anchorage within the harbour. And whilst the Colonel viewed her, admiring, perhaps, the gracious beauty of her, Pitt was hurried forward into the stockade, and clapped into the stocks that stood there ready for slaves who required correction.

Colonel Bishop followed him presently, with leisurely, rolling gait.

"A mutinous cur that shows his fangs to his master must learn good manners at the cost of a striped hide," was all he said before setting about his executioner's job.

That with his own hands he should do that which most men of his station would, out of self-respect, have relegated to one of the negroes, gives you the measure of the man's beastliness. It was almost as if with relish, as if gratifying some feral instinct of cruelty, that he now lashed his victim about head and shoulders. Soon his cane was reduced, to splinters by his violence. You know, perhaps, the sting of a flexible bamboo cane when it is whole. But do you realize its murderous quality when it has been split into several long lithe blades, each with an edge that is of the keenness of a knife?

When, at last, from very weariness, Colonel Bishop flung away the stump and thongs to which his cane had been reduced, the wretched slave's back was bleeding pulp from neck to waist.

As long as full sensibility remained, Jeremy Pitt had made no sound. But in a measure as from pain his senses were mercifully dulled, he sank forward in the stocks, and hung there now in a huddled heap, faintly moaning.

Colonel Bishop set his foot upon the crossbar, and leaned over his victim, a cruel smile on his full, coarse face.

"Let that teach you a proper submission," said he. "And now touching that shy friend of yours, you shall stay here without meat or drink—without meat or drink, d' ye hear me?—until you please to tell me his name and business." He took his foot from the bar. "When you've had enough of this, send me word, and we'll have the branding-irons to you."

On that he swung on his heel, and strode out of the stockade, his negroes following.

Pitt had heard him, as we hear things in our dreams. At the moment so spent was he by his cruel punishment, and so deep was the despair into which he had fallen, that he no longer cared whether he lived or died.

Soon, however, from the partial stupor which pain had mercifully induced, a new variety of pain aroused him. The stocks stood in the open under the full glare of the tropical sun, and its blistering rays streamed down upon that mangled, bleeding back until he felt as if flames of fire were searing it. And, soon, to this was added a torment still more unspeakable. Flies, the cruel flies of the Antilles, drawn by the scent of blood, descended in a cloud upon him.

Small wonder that the ingenious Colonel Bishop, who so well understood the art of loosening stubborn tongues, had not deemed it necessary to have recourse to other means of torture. Not all his fiendish cruelty could devise a torment more cruel, more unendurable than the torments Nature would here procure a man in Pitt's condition.

The slave writhed in his stocks until he was in danger of breaking his limbs, and writhing, screamed in agony.

Thus was he found by Peter Blood, who seemed to his troubled vision to materialize suddenly before him. Mr. Blood carried a large palmetto leaf. Having whisked away with this the flies that were devouring Jeremy's back, he slung it by a strip of fibre from the lad's neck, so that it protected him from further attacks as well as from the rays of the sun. Next, sitting down beside him, he drew the sufferer's head down on his own shoulder, and bathed his face from a pannikin of cold water. Pitt shuddered and moaned on a long, indrawn breath.

"Drink!" he gasped. "Drink, for the love of Christ!" The pannikin was held to his quivering lips. He drank greedily, noisily, nor ceased until he had drained the vessel. Cooled and revived by the draught, he attempted to sit up.

"My back!" he screamed.

There was an unusual glint in Mr. Blood's eyes; his lips were compressed. But when he parted them to speak, his voice came cool and steady.

"Be easy, now. One thing at a time. Your back's taking no harm at all for the present, since I've covered it up. I'm wanting to know what's happened to you. D' ye think we can do without a navigator that ye go and provoke that beast Bishop until he all but kills you?"

Pitt sat up and groaned again. But this time his anguish was mental rather than physical.

"I don't think a navigator will be needed this time, Peter."

"What's that?" cried Mr. Blood.

Pitt explained the situation as briefly as he could, in a halting, gasping speech. "I'm to rot here until I tell him the identity of my visitor and his business."

Mr. Blood got up, growling in his throat. "Bad cess to the filthy slaver!" said he. "But it must be contrived, nevertheless. To the devil with Nuttall! Whether he gives surety for the boat or not, whether he explains it or not, the boat remains, and we're going, and you're coming with us."

"You're dreaming, Peter," said the prisoner. "We're not going this time. The magistrates will confiscate the boat since the surety's not paid, even if when they press him Nuttall does not confess the whole plan and get us all branded on the forehead."

Mr. Blood turned away, and with agony in his eyes looked out to sea over the blue water by which he had so fondly hoped soon to be travelling back to freedom.

The great red ship had drawn considerably nearer shore by now. Slowly, majestically, she was entering the bay. Already one or two wherries were putting off from the wharf to board her. From where he stood, Mr. Blood could see the glinting of the brass cannons mounted on the prow above the curving beak-head, and he could make out the figure of a seaman in the forechains on her larboard side, leaning out to heave the lead.

An angry voice aroused him from his unhappy thoughts.

"What the devil are you doing here?"

The returning Colonel Bishop came striding into the stockade, his negroes following ever.

Mr. Blood turned to face him, and over that swarthy countenance—which, indeed, by now was tanned to the golden brown of a half-caste Indian—a mask descended.

"Doing?" said he blandly. "Why, the duties of my office."

The Colonel, striding furiously forward, observed two things. The empty pannikin on the seat beside the prisoner, and the palmetto leaf protecting his back. "Have you dared to do this?" The veins on the planter's forehead stood out like cords.

"Of course I have." Mr. Blood's tone was one of faint surprise.

"I said he was to have neither meat nor drink until I ordered it."

"Sure, now, I never heard ye."

"You never heard me? How should you have heard me when you weren't here?"

"Then how did ye expect me to know what orders ye'd given?" Mr. Blood's tone was positively aggrieved. "All that I knew was that one of your slaves was being murthered by the sun and the flies. And I says to myself, this is one of the Colonel's slaves, and I'm the Colonel's doctor, and sure it's my duty to be looking after the Colonel's property. So I just gave the fellow a spoonful of water and covered his back from the sun. And wasn't I right now?"

"Right?" The Colonel was almost speechless.

"Be easy, now, be easy!" Mr. Blood implored him. "It's an apoplexy ye'll be contacting if ye give way to heat like this."

The planter thrust him aside with an imprecation, and stepping forward tore the palmetto leaf from the prisoner's back.

"In the name of humanity, now...." Mr. Blood was beginning.

The Colonel swung upon him furiously. "Out of this!" he commanded. "And don't come near him again until I send for you, unless you want to be served in the same way."

He was terrific in his menace, in his bulk, and in the power of him. But Mr. Blood never flinched. It came to the Colonel, as he found himself steadily regarded by those light-blue eyes that looked so arrestingly odd in that tawny face—like pale sapphires set in copper—that this rogue had for some time now been growing presumptuous. It was a matter that he must presently correct. Meanwhile Mr. Blood was speaking again, his tone quietly insistent.

"In the name of humanity," he repeated, "ye'll allow me to do what I can to ease his sufferings, or I swear to you that I'll forsake at once the duties of a doctor, and that it's devil another patient will I attend in this unhealthy island at all."

For an instant the Colonel was too amazed to speak. Then—

"By God!" he roared. "D'ye dare take that tone with me, you dog? D'ye dare to make terms with me?"

"I do that." The unflinching blue eyes looked squarely into the Colonel's, and there was a devil peeping out of them, the devil of recklessness that is born of despair.

Colonel Bishop considered him for a long moment in silence. "I've been too soft with you," he said at last. "But that's to be mended." And he tightened his lips. "I'll have the rods to you, until there's not an inch of skin left on your dirty back."

"Will ye so? And what would Governor Steed do, then?"

"Ye're not the only doctor on the island."

Mr. Blood actually laughed. "And will ye tell that to his excellency, him with the gout in his foot so bad that he can't stand? Ye know very well it's devil another doctor will he tolerate, being an intelligent man that knows what's good for him."

But the Colonel's brute passion thoroughly aroused was not so easily to be baulked. "If you're alive when my blacks have done with you, perhaps you'll come to your senses."

He swung to his negroes to issue an order. But it was never issued. At that moment a terrific rolling thunderclap drowned his voice and shook the very air. Colonel Bishop jumped, his negroes jumped with him, and so even did the apparently imperturbable Mr. Blood. Then the four of them stared together seawards.

Down in the bay all that could be seen of the great ship, standing now within a cable's-length of the fort, were her topmasts thrusting above a cloud of smoke in which she was enveloped. From the cliffs a flight of startled seabirds had risen to circle in the blue, giving tongue to their alarm, the plaintive curlew noisiest of all.

As those men stared from the eminence on which they stood, not yet understanding what had taken place, they saw the British Jack dip from the main truck and vanish into the rising cloud below. A moment more, and up through that cloud to replace the flag of England soared the gold and crimson banner of Castile. And then they understood.

"Pirates!" roared the Colonel, and again, "Pirates!"

Fear and incredulity were blent in his voice. He had paled under his tan until his face was the colour of clay, and there was a wild fury in his beady eyes. His negroes looked at him, grinning idiotically, all teeth and eyeballs.

CHAPTER VIII. SPANIARDS

The stately ship that had been allowed to sail so leisurely into Carlisle Bay under her false colours was a Spanish privateer, coming to pay off some of the heavy debt piled up by the predaceous Brethren of the Coast, and the recent defeat by the Pride of Devon of two treasure galleons bound for Cadiz. It happened that the galleon which escaped in a more or less crippled condition was commanded by Don Diego de Espinosa y Valdez, who was own brother to the Spanish Admiral Don Miguel de Espinosa, and who was also a very hasty, proud, and hot-tempered gentleman.

Galled by his defeat, and choosing to forget that his own conduct had invited it, he had sworn to teach the English a sharp lesson which they should remember. He would take a leaf out of the book of Morgan and those other robbers of the sea, and make a punitive raid upon an English settlement. Unfortunately for himself and for many others, his brother the Admiral was not at hand to restrain him when for this purpose he fitted out the Cinco Llagas at San Juan de Porto Rico. He chose for his objective the island of Barbados, whose natural strength was apt to render her defenders careless. He chose it also because thither had the Pride of Devon been tracked by his scouts, and he desired a measure of poetic justice to invest his vengeance. And he chose a moment when there were no ships of war at anchor in Carlisle Bay.

He had succeeded so well in his intentions that he had aroused no suspicion until he saluted the fort at short range with a broadside of twenty guns.

And now the four gaping watchers in the stockade on the headland beheld the great ship creep forward under the rising cloud of smoke, her mainsail unfurled to increase her steering way, and go about close-hauled to bring her larboard guns to bear upon the unready fort.

With the crashing roar of that second broadside, Colonel Bishop awoke from stupefaction to a recollection of where his duty lay. In the town below drums were beating frantically, and a trumpet was bleating, as if the peril needed further advertising. As commander of the Barbados Militia, the place of Colonel Bishop was at the head of his scanty troops, in that fort which the Spanish guns were pounding into rubble.

Remembering it, he went off at the double, despite his bulk and the heat, his negroes trotting after him.

Mr. Blood turned to Jeremy Pitt. He laughed grimly. "Now that," said he, "is what I call a timely interruption. Though what'll come of it," he added as an afterthought, "the devil himself knows."

As a third broadside was thundering forth, he picked up the palmetto leaf and carefully replaced it on the back of his fellow-slave.

And then into the stockade, panting and sweating, came Kent followed by best part of a score of plantation workers, some of whom were black and all of whom were in a state of panic. He led them into the low white house, to bring them forth again, within a moment, as it seemed, armed now with muskets and hangers and some of them equipped with bandoleers.

By this time the rebels-convict were coming in, in twos and threes, having abandoned their work upon finding themselves unguarded and upon scenting the general dismay.

Kent paused a moment, as his hastily armed guard dashed forth, to fling an order to those slaves.

"To the woods!" he bade them. "Take to the woods, and lie close there, until this is over, and we've gutted these Spanish swine."

On that he went off in haste after his men, who were to be added to those massing in the town, so as to oppose and overwhelm the Spanish landing parties.

The slaves would have obeyed him on the instant but for Mr. Blood.

"What need for haste, and in this heat?" quoth he. He was surprisingly cool, they thought. "Maybe there'll be no need to take to the woods at all, and, anyway, it will be time enough to do so when the Spaniards are masters of the town."

And so, joined now by the other stragglers, and numbering in all a round score—rebels-convict all—they stayed to watch from their vantage-ground the fortunes of the furious battle that was being waged below.

The landing was contested by the militia and by every islander capable of bearing arms with the fierce resoluteness of men who knew that no quarter was to be expected in defeat. The ruthlessness of Spanish soldiery was a byword, and not at his worst had Morgan or L'Ollonais ever perpetrated such horrors as those of which these Castilian gentlemen were capable.

But this Spanish commander knew his business, which was more than could truthfully be said for the Barbados Militia. Having gained the advantage of a surprise blow, which had put the fort out of action, he soon showed them that he was master of the situation. His guns turned now upon the open space behind the mole, where the incompetent Bishop had marshalled his men, tore the militia into bloody rags, and covered the landing parties which were making the shore in their own boats and in several of those which had rashly gone out to the great ship before her identity was revealed.

All through the scorching afternoon the battle went on, the rattle and crack of musketry penetrating ever deeper into the town to show that the defenders were being driven steadily back. By sunset two hundred and fifty Spaniards were masters of Bridgetown, the islanders were disarmed, and at Government House, Governor Steed—his gout forgotten in his panic—supported by Colonel Bishop and some lesser officers, was being informed by Don Diego, with an urbanity that was itself a mockery, of the sum that would be required in ransom.

For a hundred thousand pieces of eight and fifty head of cattle, Don Diego would forbear from reducing the place to ashes. And what time that suave and courtly commander was settling these details with the apoplectic British Governor, the Spaniards were smashing and looting, feasting, drinking, and ravaging after the hideous manner of their kind.

Mr. Blood, greatly daring, ventured down at dusk into the town. What he saw there is recorded by Jeremy Pitt to whom he subsequently related it—in that voluminous log from which the greater part of my narrative is derived. I have no intention of repeating any of it here. It is all too loathsome and nauseating, incredible, indeed, that men however abandoned could ever descend such an abyss of bestial cruelty and lust.

What he saw was fetching him in haste and white-faced out of that hell again, when in a narrow street a girl hurtled into him, wild-eyed, her unbound hair streaming behind her as she ran. After her, laughing and cursing in a breath, came a heavy-booted Spaniard. Almost he was upon her, when suddenly Mr. Blood got in his way. The doctor had taken a sword from a dead man's side some little time before and armed himself with it against an emergency.

As the Spaniard checked in anger and surprise, he caught in the dusk the livid gleam of that sword which Mr. Blood had quickly unsheathed.

"Ah, perro ingles!" he shouted, and flung forward to his death.

"It's hoping I am ye're in a fit state to meet your Maker," said Mr. Blood, and ran him through the body. He did the thing skilfully: with the combined skill of swordsman and surgeon. The man sank in a hideous heap without so much as a groan.

Mr. Blood swung to the girl, who leaned panting and sobbing against a wall. He caught her by the wrist.

"Come!" he said.

But she hung back, resisting him by her weight. "Who are you?" she demanded wildly.

"Will ye wait to see my credentials?" he snapped. Steps were clattering towards them from beyond the corner round which she had fled from that Spanish ruffian. "Come," he urged again. And this time, reassured perhaps by his clear English speech, she went without further questions.

They sped down an alley and then up another, by great good fortune meeting no one, for already they were on the outskirts of the town. They won out of it, and white-faced, physically sick, Mr. Blood dragged her almost at a run up the hill towards Colonel Bishop's house. He told her briefly who and what he was, and thereafter there was no conversation between them until they reached the big white house. It was all in darkness, which at least was reassuring. If the Spaniards had reached it, there would be lights. He knocked, but had to knock again and yet again before he was answered. Then it was by a voice from a window above.

"Who is there?" The voice was Miss Bishop's, a little tremulous, but unmistakably her own.

Mr. Blood almost fainted in relief. He had been imagining the unimaginable. He had pictured her down in that hell out of which he had just come. He had conceived that she might have followed her uncle into Bridgetown, or committed some other imprudence, and he turned cold from head to foot at the mere thought of what might have happened to her.

"It is I—Peter Blood," he gasped.

"What do you want?"

It is doubtful whether she would have come down to open. For at such a time as this it was no more than likely that the wretched plantation slaves might be in revolt and prove as great a danger as the Spaniards. But at the sound of her voice, the girl Mr. Blood had rescued peered up through the gloom.

"Arabella!" she called. "It is I, Mary Traill."

"Mary!" The voice ceased above on that exclamation, the head was withdrawn. After a brief pause the door gaped wide. Beyond it in the wide hall stood Miss Arabella, a slim, virginal figure in white, mysteriously revealed in the gleam of a single candle which she carried.

Mr. Blood strode in followed by his distraught companion, who, falling upon Arabella's slender bosom, surrendered herself to a passion of tears. But he wasted no time.

"Whom have you here with you? What servants?" he demanded sharply.

The only male was James, an old negro groom.

"The very man," said Blood. "Bid him get out horses. Then away with you to Speightstown, or even farther north, where you will be safe. Here you are in danger—in dreadful danger."

"But I thought the fighting was over..." she was beginning, pale and startled.

"So it is. But the deviltry's only beginning. Miss Traill will tell you as you go. In God's name, madam, take my word for it, and do as I bid you."

"He... he saved me," sobbed Miss Traill.

"Saved you?" Miss Bishop was aghast. "Saved you from what, Mary?"

"Let that wait," snapped Mr. Blood almost angrily. "You've all the night for chattering when you're out of this, and away beyond their reach. Will you please call James, and do as I say—and at once!"

"You are very peremptory...."

"Oh, my God! I am peremptory! Speak, Miss Trail!, tell her whether I've cause to be peremptory."

"Yes, yes," the girl cried, shuddering. "Do as he says—Oh, for pity's sake, Arabella."

Miss Bishop went off, leaving Mr. Blood and Miss Traill alone again.

"I... I shall never forget what you did, sir," said she, through her diminishing tears. She was a slight wisp of a girl, a child, no more.

"I've done better things in my time. That's why I'm here," said Mr. Blood, whose mood seemed to be snappy.

She didn't pretend to understand him, and she didn't make the attempt.

"Did you... did you kill him?" she asked, fearfully.

He stared at her in the flickering candlelight. "I hope so. It is very probable, and it doesn't matter at all," he said. "What matters is that this fellow James should fetch the horses." And he was stamping off to accelerate these preparations for departure, when her voice arrested him.

"Don't leave me! Don't leave me here alone!" she cried in terror.

He paused. He turned and came slowly back. Standing above her he smiled upon her.

"There, there! You've no cause for alarm. It's all over now. You'll be away soon—away to Speightstown, where you'll be quite safe."

The horses came at last—four of them, for in addition to James who was to act as her guide, Miss Bishop had her woman, who was not to be left behind.

Mr. Blood lifted the slight weight of Mary Traill to her horse, then turned to say good-bye to Miss Bishop, who was already mounted. He said it, and seemed to have something to add. But whatever it was, it remained unspoken. The horses started, and receded into the sapphire starlit night, leaving him standing there before Colonel Bishop's door. The last he heard of them was Mary Traill's childlike voice calling back on a quavering note—

"I shall never forget what you did, Mr. Blood. I shall never forget."

But as it was not the voice he desired to hear, the assurance brought him little satisfaction. He stood there in the dark watching the fireflies amid the rhododendrons, till the hoofbeats had faded. Then he sighed and roused himself. He had much to do. His journey into the town had not been one of idle curiosity to see how the Spaniards conducted themselves in victory. It had been inspired by a very different purpose, and he had gained in the course of it all the information he desired. He had an extremely busy night before him, and must be moving.

He went off briskly in the direction of the stockade, where his fellow-slaves awaited him in deep anxiety and some hope.

CHAPTER IX. THE REBELS-CONVICT

There were, when the purple gloom of the tropical night descended upon the Caribbean, not more than ten men on guard aboard the Cinco Llagas, so confident—and with good reason—were the Spaniards of the complete subjection of the islanders. And when I say that there were ten men on guard, I state rather the purpose for which they were left aboard than the duty which they fulfilled. As a matter of fact, whilst the main body of the Spaniards feasted and rioted ashore, the Spanish gunner and his crew—who had so nobly done their duty and ensured the easy victory of the day—were feasting on the gun-deck upon the wine and the fresh meats fetched out to them from shore. Above, two sentinels only kept vigil, at stem and stern. Nor were they as vigilant as they should have been, or else they must have observed the two wherries that under cover of the darkness came gliding from the wharf, with well-greased rowlocks, to bring up in silence under the great ship's quarter.

From the gallery aft still hung the ladder by which Don Diego had descended to the boat that had taken him ashore. The sentry on guard in the stern, coming presently round this gallery, was suddenly confronted by the black shadow of a man standing before him at the head of the ladder.

"Who's there?" he asked, but without alarm, supposing it one of his fellows.

"It is I," softly answered Peter Blood in the fluent Castillan of which he was master.

"Is it you, Pedro?" The Spaniard came a step nearer.

"Peter is my name; but I doubt I'll not be the Peter you're expecting."

"How?" quoth the sentry, checking.

"This way," said Mr. Blood.

The wooden taffrail was a low one, and the Spaniard was taken completely by surprise. Save for the splash he made as he struck the water, narrowly missing one of the crowded boats that waited under the counter, not a sound announced his misadventure. Armed as he was with corselet, cuissarts, and headpiece, he sank to trouble them no more.

"Whist!" hissed Mr. Blood to his waiting rebels-convict. "Come on, now, and without noise."

Within five minutes they had swarmed aboard, the entire twenty of them overflowing from that narrow gallery and crouching on the quarter-deck itself. Lights showed ahead. Under the great lantern in the prow they saw the black figure of the other sentry, pacing on the forecastle. From below sounds reached them of the orgy on the gun-deck: a rich male voice was singing an obscene ballad to which the others chanted in chorus:

"Y estos son los usos de Castilla y de Leon!"

"From what I've seen to-day I can well believe it," said Mr. Blood, and whispered: "Forward—after me."

Crouching low, they glided, noiseless as shadows, to the quarter-deck rail, and thence slipped without sound down into the waist. Two thirds of them were armed with muskets, some of which they had found in the overseer's house, and others supplied from the secret hoard that Mr. Blood had so laboriously assembled against the day of escape. The remainder were equipped with knives and cutlasses.

In the vessel's waist they hung awhile, until Mr. Blood had satisfied himself that no other sentinel showed above decks but that inconvenient fellow in the prow. Their first attention must be for him. Mr. Blood, himself, crept forward with two companions, leaving the others in the charge of that Nathaniel Hagthorpe whose sometime commission in the King's Navy gave him the best title to this office.

Mr. Blood's absence was brief. When he rejoined his comrades there was no watch above the Spaniards' decks.

Meanwhile the revellers below continued to make merry at their ease in the conviction of complete security. The garrison of Barbados was overpowered and disarmed, and their companions were ashore in complete possession of the town, glutting themselves hideously upon the fruits of victory. What, then, was there to fear? Even when their quarters were invaded and they found themselves surrounded by a score of wild, hairy, half-naked men, who—save that they appeared once to have been white—looked like a horde of savages, the Spaniards could not believe their eyes.

Who could have dreamed that a handful of forgotten plantation-slaves would have dared to take so much upon themselves?

The half-drunken Spaniards, their laughter suddenly quenched, the song perishing on their lips, stared, stricken and bewildered at the levelled muskets by which they were checkmated.

And then, from out of this uncouth pack of savages that beset them, stepped a slim, tall fellow with light-blue eyes in a tawny face, eyes in which glinted the light of a wicked humour. He addressed them in the purest Castilian.

"You will save yourselves pain and trouble by regarding yourselves my prisoners, and suffering yourselves to be quietly bestowed out of harm's way."

"Name of God!" swore the gunner, which did no justice at all to an amazement beyond expression.

"If you please," said Mr. Blood, and thereupon those gentlemen of Spain were induced without further trouble beyond a musket prod or two to drop through a scuttle to the deck below.

After that the rebels-convict refreshed themselves with the good things in the consumption of which they had interrupted the Spaniards. To taste palatable Christian food after months of salt fish and maize dumplings was in itself a feast to these unfortunates. But there were no excesses. Mr. Blood saw to that, although it required all the firmness of which he was capable.

Dispositions were to be made without delay against that which must follow before they could abandon themselves fully to the enjoyment of their victory. This, after all, was no more than a preliminary skirmish, although it was one that afforded them the key to the situation. It remained to dispose so that the utmost profit might be drawn from it. Those dispositions occupied some very considerable portion of the night. But, at least, they were complete before the sun peeped over the shoulder of Mount Hilibay to shed his light upon a day of some surprises.

It was soon after sunrise that the rebel-convict who paced the quarter-deck in Spanish corselet and headpiece, a Spanish musket on his shoulder, announced the approach of a boat. It was Don Diego de Espinosa y Valdez coming aboard with four great treasure-chests, containing each twenty-five thousand pieces of eight, the ransom delivered to him at dawn by Governor Steed. He was accompanied by his son, Don Esteban, and by six men who took the oars.

Aboard the frigate all was quiet and orderly as it should be. She rode at anchor, her larboard to the shore, and the main ladder on her starboard side. Round to this came the boat with Don Diego and his treasure. Mr. Blood had disposed effectively. It was not for nothing that he had served under de Ruyter. The swings were waiting, and the windlass manned. Below, a gun-crew held itself in readiness under the command of Ogle, who—as I have said—had been a gunner in the Royal Navy before he went in for politics and followed the fortunes of the Duke of Monmouth. He was a sturdy, resolute fellow who inspired confidence by the very confidence he displayed in himself.

Don Diego mounted the ladder and stepped upon the deck, alone, and entirely unsuspicious. What should the poor man suspect?

Before he could even look round, and survey this guard drawn up to receive him, a tap over the head with a capstan bar efficiently handled by Hagthorpe put him to sleep without the least fuss.

He was carried away to his cabin, whilst the treasure-chests, handled by the men he had left in the boat, were being hauled to the deck. That being satisfactorily accomplished, Don Esteban and the fellows who had manned the boat came up the ladder, one by one, to be handled with the same quiet efficiency. Peter Blood had a genius for these things, and almost, I suspect, an eye for the dramatic. Dramatic, certainly, was the spectacle now offered to the survivors of the raid.

With Colonel Bishop at their head, and gout-ridden Governor Steed sitting on the ruins of a wall beside him, they glumly watched the departure of the eight boats containing the weary Spanish ruffians who had glutted themselves with rapine, murder, and violences unspeakable.

They looked on, between relief at this departure of their remorseless enemies, and despair at the wild ravages which, temporarily at least, had wrecked the prosperity and happiness of that little colony.

The boats pulled away from the shore, with their loads of laughing, jeering Spaniards, who were still flinging taunts across the water at their surviving victims. They had come midway between the wharf and the ship, when suddenly the air was shaken by the boom of a gun.

A round shot struck the water within a fathom of the foremost boat, sending a shower of spray over its occupants. They paused at their oars, astounded into silence for a moment. Then speech burst from them like an explosion. Angrily voluble they anathematized this dangerous carelessness on the part of their gunner, who should know better than to fire a salute from a cannon loaded with shot. They were still cursing him when a second shot, better aimed than the first, came to crumple one of the boats into splinters, flinging its crew, dead and living, into the water.

But if it silenced these, it gave tongue, still more angry, vehement, and bewildered to the crews of the other seven boats. From each the suspended oars stood out poised over the water, whilst on their feet in the excitement the Spaniards screamed oaths at the ship, begging Heaven and Hell to inform them what madman had been let loose among her guns.

Plump into their middle came a third shot, smashing a second boat with fearful execution. Followed again a moment of awful silence, then among those Spanish pirates all was gibbering and jabbering and splashing of oars, as they attempted to pull in every direction at once. Some were for going ashore, others for heading straight to the vessel and there discovering what might be amiss. That something was very gravely amiss there could be no further doubt, particularly as whilst they discussed and fumed and cursed two more shots came over the water to account for yet a third of their boats.

The resolute Ogle was making excellent practice, and fully justifying his claims to know something of gunnery. In their consternation the Spaniards had simplified his task by huddling their boats together.

After the fourth shot, opinion was no longer divided amongst them. As with one accord they went about, or attempted to do so, for before they had accomplished it two more of their boats had been sunk.

The three boats that remained, without concerning themselves with their more unfortunate fellows, who were struggling in the water, headed back for the wharf at speed.

If the Spaniards understood nothing of all this, the forlorn islanders ashore understood still less, until to help their wits they saw the flag of Spain come down from the mainmast of the Cinco Llagas, and the flag of England soar to its empty place. Even then some bewilderment persisted, and it was with fearful eyes that they observed the return of their enemies, who might vent upon them the ferocity aroused by these extraordinary events.

Ogle, however, continued to give proof that his knowledge of gunnery was not of yesterday. After the fleeing Spaniards went his shots. The last of their boats flew into splinters as it touched the wharf, and its remains were buried under a shower of loosened masonry.

That was the end of this pirate crew, which not ten minutes ago had been laughingly counting up the pieces of eight that would fall to the portion of each for his share in that act of villainy. Close upon threescore survivors contrived to reach the shore. Whether they had cause for congratulation, I am unable to say in the absence of any records in which their fate may be traced. That lack of records is in itself eloquent. We know that they were made fast as they landed, and considering the offence they had given I am not disposed to doubt that they had every reason to regret the survival.

The mystery of the succour that had come at the eleventh hour to wreak vengeance upon the Spaniards, and to preserve for the island the extortionate ransom of a hundred thousand pieces of eight, remained yet to be probed. That the Cinco Llagas was now in friendly hands could no longer be doubted after the proofs it had given. But who, the people of Bridgetown asked one another, were the men in possession of her, and whence had they come? The only possible assumption ran the truth very closely. A resolute party of islanders must have got aboard during the night, and seized the ship. It remained to ascertain the precise identity of these mysterious saviours, and do them fitting honour.

Upon this errand—Governor Steed's condition not permitting him to go in person—went Colonel Bishop as the Governor's deputy, attended by two officers.

As he stepped from the ladder into the vessel's waist, the Colonel beheld there, beside the main hatch, the four treasure-chests, the contents of one of which had been contributed almost entirely by himself. It was a gladsome spectacle, and his eyes sparkled in beholding it.

Ranged on either side, athwart the deck, stood a score of men in two well-ordered files, with breasts and backs of steel, polished Spanish morions on their heads, overshadowing their faces, and muskets ordered at their sides.

Colonel Bishop could not be expected to recognize at a glance in these upright, furbished, soldierly figures the ragged, unkempt scarecrows that but yesterday had been toiling in his plantations. Still less could he be expected to recognize at once the courtly gentleman who advanced to greet him—a lean, graceful gentleman, dressed in the Spanish fashion, all in black with silver lace, a gold-hilted sword dangling beside him from a gold embroidered baldrick, a broad castor with a sweeping plume set above carefully curled ringlets of deepest black.

"Be welcome aboard the Cinco Llagas, Colonel, darling," a voice vaguely familiar addressed the planter. "We've made the best of the Spaniards' wardrobe in honour of this visit, though it was scarcely yourself we had dared hope to expect. You find yourself among friends—old friends of yours, all." The Colonel stared in stupefaction. Mr. Blood tricked out in all this splendour—indulging therein his natural taste—his face carefully shaven, his hair as carefully dressed, seemed transformed into a younger man. The fact is he looked no more than the thirty-three years he counted to his age.

"Peter Blood!" It was an ejaculation of amazement. Satisfaction followed swiftly. "Was it you, then...?"

"Myself it was—myself and these, my good friends and yours." Mr. Blood tossed back the fine lace from his wrist, to wave a hand towards the file of men standing to attention there.

The Colonel looked more closely. "Gad's my life!" he crowed on a note of foolish jubilation. "And it was with these fellows that you took the Spaniard and turned the tables on those dogs! Oddswounds! It was heroic!"

"Heroic, is it? Bedad, it's epic! Ye begin to perceive the breadth and depth of my genius."

Colonel Bishop sat himself down on the hatch-coaming, took off his broad hat, and mopped his brow.

"Y'amaze me!" he gasped. "On my soul, y'amaze me! To have recovered the treasure and to have seized this fine ship and all she'll hold! It will be something to set against the other losses we have suffered. As Gad's my life, you deserve well for this."

"I am entirely of your opinion."

"Damme! You all deserve well, and damme, you shall find me grateful."

"That's as it should be," said Mr. Blood. "The question is how well we deserve, and how grateful shall we find you?"

Colonel Bishop considered him. There was a shadow of surprise in his face.

"Why—his excellency shall write home an account of your exploit, and maybe some portion of your sentences shall be remitted."

"The generosity of King James is well known," sneered Nathaniel Hagthorpe, who was standing by, and amongst the ranged rebels-convict some one ventured to laugh.

Colonel Bishop started up. He was pervaded by the first pang of uneasiness. It occurred to him that all here might not be as friendly as appeared.

"And there's another matter," Mr. Blood resumed. "There's a matter of a flogging that's due to me. Ye're a man of your word in such matters, Colonel—if not perhaps in others—and ye said, I think, that ye'd not leave a square inch of skin on my back."

The planter waved the matter aside. Almost it seemed to offend him.

"Tush! Tush! After this splendid deed of yours, do you suppose I can be thinking of such things?"

"I'm glad ye feel like that about it. But I'm thinking it's mighty lucky for me the Spaniards didn't come to-day instead of yesterday, or it's in the same plight as Jeremy Pitt I'd be this minute. And in that case where was the genius that would have turned the tables on these rascally Spaniards?"

"Why speak of it now?"

Mr. Blood resumed: "ye'll please to understand that I must, Colonel, darling. Ye've worked a deal of wickedness and cruelty in your time, and I want this to be a lesson to you, a lesson that ye'll remember—for the sake of others who may come after us. There's Jeremy up there in the round-house with a back that's every colour of the rainbow; and the poor lad'll not be himself again for a month. And if it hadn't been for the Spaniards maybe it's dead he'd be by now, and maybe myself with him."

Hagthorpe lounged forward. He was a fairly tall, vigorous man with a clear-cut, attractive face which in itself announced his breeding.

"Why will you be wasting words on the hog?" wondered that sometime officer in the Royal Navy. "Fling him overboard and have done with him."

The Colonel's eyes bulged in his head. "What the devil do you mean?" he blustered.

"It's the lucky man ye are entirely, Colonel, though ye don't guess the source of your good fortune."

And now another intervened—the brawny, one-eyed Wolverstone, less mercifully disposed than his more gentlemanly fellow-convict.

"String him up from the yardarm," he cried, his deep voice harsh and angry, and more than one of the slaves standing to their arms made echo.

Colonel Bishop trembled. Mr. Blood turned. He was quite calm.

"If you please, Wolverstone," said he, "I conduct affairs in my own way. That is the pact. You'll please to remember it." His eyes looked along the ranks, making it plain that he addressed them all. "I desire that Colonel Bishop should have his life. One reason is that I require him as a hostage. If ye insist on hanging him, ye'll have to hang me with him, or in the alternative I'll go ashore."

He paused. There was no answer. But they stood hang-dog and half-mutinous before him, save Hagthorpe, who shrugged and smiled wearily.

Mr. Blood resumed: "Ye'll please to understand that aboard a ship there is one captain. So." He swung again to the startled Colonel. "Though I promise you your life, I must—as you've heard—keep you aboard as a hostage for the good behaviour of Governor Steed and what's left of the fort until we put to sea."

"Until you..." Horror prevented Colonel Bishop from echoing the remainder of that incredible speech.

"Just so," said Peter Blood, and he turned to the officers who had accompanied the Colonel. "The boat is waiting, gentlemen. You'll have heard what I said. Convey it with my compliments to his excellency."

"But, sir..." one of them began.

"There is no more to be said, gentlemen. My name is Blood—Captain Blood, if you please, of this ship the Cinco Llagas, taken as a prize of war from Don Diego de Espinosa y Valdez, who is my prisoner aboard. You are to understand that I have turned the tables on more than the Spaniards. There's the ladder. You'll find it more convenient than being heaved over the side, which is what'll happen if you linger."

They went, though not without some hustling, regardless of the bellowings of Colonel Bishop, whose monstrous rage was fanned by terror at finding himself at the mercy of these men of whose cause to hate him he was very fully conscious.

A half-dozen of them, apart from Jeremy Pitt, who was utterly incapacitated for the present, possessed a superficial knowledge of seamanship. Hagthorpe, although he had been a fighting officer, untrained in navigation, knew how to handle a ship, and under his directions they set about getting under way.

The anchor catted, and the mainsail unfurled, they stood out for the open before a gentle breeze, without interference from the fort.

As they were running close to the headland east of the bay, Peter Blood returned to the Colonel, who, under guard and panic-stricken, had dejectedly resumed his seat on the coamings of the main batch.

"Can ye swim, Colonel?"

Colonel Bishop looked up. His great face was yellow and seemed in that moment of a preternatural flabbiness; his beady eyes were beadier than ever.

"As your doctor, now, I prescribe a swim to cool the excessive heat of your humours." Blood delivered the explanation pleasantly, and, receiving still no answer from the Colonel, continued: "It's a mercy for you I'm not by nature as bloodthirsty as some of my friends here. And it's the devil's own labour I've had to prevail upon them not to be vindictive. I doubt if ye're worth the pains I've taken for you."

He was lying. He had no doubt at all. Had he followed his own wishes and instincts, he would certainly have strung the Colonel up, and accounted it a meritorious deed. It was the thought of Arabella Bishop that had urged him to mercy, and had led him to oppose the natural vindictiveness of his fellow-slaves until he had been in danger of precipitating a mutiny. It was entirely to the fact that the Colonel was her uncle, although he did not even begin to suspect such a cause, that he owed such mercy as was now being shown him.

"You shall have a chance to swim for it," Peter Blood continued. "It's not above a quarter of a mile to the headland yonder, and with ordinary luck ye should manage it. Faith, you're fat enough to float. Come on! Now, don't be hesitating or it's a long voyage ye'll be going with us, and the devil knows what may happen to you. You're not loved any more than you deserve."

Colonel Bishop mastered himself, and rose. A merciless despot, who had never known the need for restraint in all these years, he was doomed by ironic fate to practise restraint in the very moment when his feelings had reached their most violent intensity.

Peter Blood gave an order. A plank was run out over the gunwale, and lashed down.

"If you please, Colonel," said he, with a graceful flourish of invitation.

The Colonel looked at him, and there was hell in his glance. Then, taking his resolve, and putting the best face upon it, since no other could help him here, he kicked off his shoes, peeled off his fine coat of biscuit-coloured taffetas, and climbed upon the plank.

A moment he paused, steadied by a hand that clutched the ratlines, looking down in terror at the green water rushing past some five-and-twenty feet below.

"Just take a little walk, Colonel, darling," said a smooth, mocking voice behind him.

Still clinging, Colonel Bishop looked round in hesitation, and saw the bulwarks lined with swarthy faces—the faces of men that as lately as yesterday would have turned pale under his frown, faces that were now all wickedly agrin.

For a moment rage stamped out his fear. He cursed them aloud venomously and incoherently, then loosed his hold and stepped out upon the plank. Three steps he took before he lost his balance and went tumbling into the green depths below.

When he came to the surface again, gasping for air, the Cinco Llagas was already some furlongs to leeward. But the roaring cheer of mocking valediction from the rebels-convict reached him across the water, to drive the iron of impotent rage deeper into his soul.

CHAPTER X. DON DIEGO

Don Diego de Espinosa y Valdez awoke, and with languid eyes in aching head, he looked round the cabin, which was flooded with sunlight from the square windows astern. Then he uttered a moan, and closed his eyes again, impelled to this by the monstrous ache in his head. Lying thus, he attempted to think, to locate himself in time and space. But between the pain in his head and the confusion in his mind, he found coherent thought impossible.

An indefinite sense of alarm drove him to open his eyes again, and once more to consider his surroundings.

There could be no doubt that he lay in the great cabin of his own ship, the Cinco Llagas, so that his vague disquiet must be, surely, ill-founded. And yet, stirrings of memory coming now to the assistance of reflection, compelled him uneasily to insist that here something was not as it should be. The low position of the sun, flooding the cabin with golden light from those square ports astern, suggested to him at first that it was early morning, on the assumption that the vessel was headed westward. Then the alternative occurred to him. They might be sailing eastward, in which case the time of day would be late afternoon. That they were sailing he could feel from the gentle forward heave of the vessel under him. But how did they come to be sailing, and he, the master, not to know whether their course lay east or west, not to be able to recollect whither they were bound?

His mind went back over the adventure of yesterday, if of yesterday it was. He was clear on the matter of the easily successful raid upon the Island of Barbados; every detail stood vividly in his memory up to the moment at which, returning aboard, he had stepped on to his own deck again. There memory abruptly and inexplicably ceased.

He was beginning to torture his mind with conjecture, when the door opened, and to Don Diego's increasing mystification he beheld his best suit of clothes step into the cabin. It was a singularly elegant and characteristically Spanish suit of black taffetas with silver lace that had been made for him a year ago in Cadiz, and he knew each detail of it so well that it was impossible he could now be mistaken.

The suit paused to close the door, then advanced towards the couch on which Don Diego was extended, and inside the suit came a tall, slender gentleman of about Don Diego's own height and shape. Seeing the wide, startled eyes of the Spaniard upon him, the gentleman lengthened his stride.

"Awake, eh?" said he in Spanish.

The recumbent man looked up bewildered into a pair of light-blue eyes that regarded him out of a tawny, sardonic face set in a cluster of black ringlets. But he was too bewildered to make any answer.

The stranger's fingers touched the top of Don Diego's head, whereupon Don Diego winced and cried out in pain.

"Tender, eh?" said the stranger. He took Don Diego's wrist between thumb and second finger. And then, at last, the intrigued Spaniard spoke.

"Are you a doctor?"

"Among other things." The swarthy gentleman continued his study of the patient's pulse. "Firm and regular," he announced at last, and dropped the wrist. "You've taken no great harm."

Don Diego struggled up into a sitting position on the red velvet couch.

"Who the devil are you?" he asked. "And what the devil are you doing in my clothes and aboard my ship?"

The level black eyebrows went up, a faint smile curled the lips of the long mouth.

"You are still delirious, I fear. This is not your ship. This is my ship, and these are my clothes."

"Your ship?" quoth the other, aghast, and still more aghast he added: "Your clothes? But... then...." Wildly his eyes looked about him. They scanned the cabin once again, scrutinizing each familiar object. "Am I mad?" he asked at last. "Surely this ship is the Cinco Llagas?"

"The Cinco Llagas it is."

"Then...." The Spaniard broke off. His glance grew still more troubled. "Valga me Dios!" he cried out, like a man in anguish. "Will you tell me also that you are Don Diego de Espinosa?"

"Oh, no, my name is Blood—Captain Peter Blood. This ship, like this handsome suit of clothes, is mine by right of conquest. Just as you, Don Diego, are my prisoner."

Startling as was the explanation, yet it proved soothing to Don Diego, being so much less startling than the things he was beginning to imagine.

"But... Are you not Spanish, then?"

"You flatter my Castilian accent. I have the honour to be Irish. You were thinking that a miracle had happened. So it has—a miracle wrought by my genius, which is considerable."

Succinctly now Captain Blood dispelled the mystery by a relation of the facts. It was a narrative that painted red and white by turns the Spaniard's countenance. He put a hand to the back of his head, and there discovered, in confirmation of the story, a lump as large as a pigeon's egg. Lastly, he stared wild-eyed at the sardonic Captain Blood.

"And my son? What of my son?" he cried out. "He was in the boat that brought me aboard."

"Your son is safe; he and the boat's crew together with your gunner and his men are snugly in irons under hatches."

Don Diego sank back on the couch, his glittering dark eyes fixed upon the tawny face above him. He composed himself. After all, he possessed the stoicism proper to his desperate trade. The dice had fallen against him in this venture. The tables had been turned upon him in the very moment of success. He accepted the situation with the fortitude of a fatalist.

With the utmost calm he enquired:

"And now, Senior Capitan?"

"And now," said Captain Blood—to give him the title he had assumed—"being a humane man, I am sorry to find that ye're not dead from the tap we gave you. For it means that you'll be put to the trouble of dying all over again."

"Ah!" Don Diego drew a deep breath. "But is that necessary?" he asked, without apparent perturbation.

Captain Blood's blue eyes approved his bearing. "Ask yourself," said he. "Tell me, as an experienced and bloody pirate, what in my place would you do, yourself?"

"Ah, but there is a difference." Don Diego sat up to argue the matter. "It lies in the fact that you boast yourself a humane man."

Captain Blood perched himself on the edge of the long oak table. "But I am not a fool," said he, "and I'll not allow a natural Irish sentimentality to stand in the way of my doing what is necessary and proper. You and your ten surviving scoundrels are a menace on this ship. More than that, she is none so well found in water and provisions. True, we are fortunately a small number, but you and your party inconveniently increase it. So that on every hand, you see, prudence suggests to us that we should deny ourselves the pleasure of your company, and, steeling our soft hearts to the inevitable, invite you to be so obliging as to step over the side."

"I see," said the Spaniard pensively. He swung his legs from the couch, and sat now upon the edge of it, his elbows on his knees. He had taken the measure of his man, and met him with a mock-urbanity and a suave detachment that matched his own. "I confess," he admitted, "that there is much force in what you say."

"You take a load from my mind," said Captain Blood. "I would not appear unnecessarily harsh, especially since I and my friends owe you so very much. For, whatever it may have been to others, to us your raid upon Barbados was most opportune. I am glad, therefore, that you agree the I have no choice."

"But, my friend, I did not agree so much."

"If there is any alternative that you can suggest, I shall be most happy to consider it."

Don Diego stroked his pointed black beard.

"Can you give me until morning for reflection? My head aches so damnably that I am incapable of thought. And this, you will admit, is a matter that asks serious thought."

Captain Blood stood up. From a shelf he took a half-hour glass, reversed it so that the bulb containing the red sand was uppermost, and stood it on the table.

"I am sorry to press you in such a matter, Don Diego, but one glass is all that I can give you. If by the time those sands have run out you can propose no acceptable alternative, I shall most reluctantly be driven to ask you to go over the side with your friends."

Captain Blood bowed, went out, and locked the door. Elbows on his knees and face in his hands, Don Diego sat watching the rusty sands as they filtered from the upper to the lower bulb. And what time he watched, the lines in his lean brown face grew deeper. Punctually as the last grains ran out, the door reopened.

The Spaniard sighed, and sat upright to face the returning Captain Blood with the answer for which he came.

"I have thought of an alternative, sir captain; but it depends upon your charity. It is that you put us ashore on one of the islands of this pestilent archipelago, and leave us to shift for ourselves."

Captain Blood pursed his lips. "It has its difficulties," said he slowly.

"I feared it would be so." Don Diego sighed again, and stood up. "Let us say no more."

The light-blue eyes played over him like points of steel.

"You are not afraid to die, Don Diego?"

The Spaniard threw back his head, a frown between his eyes.

"The question is offensive, sir."

"Then let me put it in another way—perhaps more happily: You do not desire to live?"

"Ah, that I can answer. I do desire to live; and even more do I desire that my son may live. But the desire shall not make a coward of me for your amusement, master mocker." It was the first sign he had shown of the least heat or resentment.

Captain Blood did not directly answer. As before he perched himself on the corner of the table.

"Would you be willing, sir, to earn life and liberty—for yourself, your son, and the other Spaniards who are on board?"

"To earn it?" said Don Diego, and the watchful blue eyes did not miss the quiver that ran through him. "To earn it, do you say? Why, if the service you would propose is one that cannot hurt my honour...."

"Could I be guilty of that?" protested the Captain. "I realize that even a pirate has his honour." And forthwith he propounded his offer. "If you will look from those windows, Don Diego, you will see what appears to be a cloud on the horizon. That is the island of Barbados well astern. All day we have been sailing east before the wind with but one intent—to set as great a distance between Barbados and ourselves as possible. But now, almost out of sight of land, we are in a difficulty. The only man among us schooled in the art of navigation is fevered, delirious, in fact, as a result of certain ill-treatment he received ashore before we carried him away with us. I can handle a ship in action, and there are one or two men aboard who can assist me; but of the higher mysteries of seamanship and of the art of finding a way over the trackless wastes of ocean, we know nothing. To hug the land, and go blundering about what you so aptly call this pestilent archipelago, is for us to court disaster, as you can perhaps conceive. And so it comes to this: We desire to make for the Dutch settlement of Curacao as straightly as possible. Will you pledge me your honour, if I release you upon parole, that you will navigate us thither? If so, we will release you and your surviving men upon arrival there."

Don Diego bowed his head upon his breast, and strode away in thought to the stern windows. There he stood looking out upon the sunlit sea and the dead water in the great ship's wake—his ship, which these English dogs had wrested from him; his ship, which he was asked to bring safely into a port where she would be completely lost to him and refitted perhaps to make war upon his kin. That was in one scale; in the other were the lives of sixteen men. Fourteen of them mattered little to him, but the remaining two were his own and his son's.

He turned at length, and his back being to the light, the Captain could not see how pale his face had grown.

"I accept," he said.

CHAPTER XI. FILIAL PIETY

By virtue of the pledge he had given, Don Diego de Espinosa enjoyed the freedom of the ship that had been his, and the navigation which he had undertaken was left entirely in his hands. And because those who manned her were new to the seas of the Spanish Main, and because even the things that had happened in Bridgetown were not enough to teach them to regard every Spaniard as a treacherous, cruel dog to be slain at sight, they used him with the civility which his own suave urbanity invited. He took his meals in the great cabin with Blood and the three officers elected to support him: Hagthorpe, Wolverstone, and Dyke.

They found Don Diego an agreeable, even an amusing companion, and their friendly feeling towards him was fostered by his fortitude and brave equanimity in this adversity.

That Don Diego was not playing fair it was impossible to suspect. Moreover, there was no conceivable reason why he should not. And he had been of the utmost frankness with them. He had denounced their mistake in sailing before the wind upon leaving Barbados. They should have left the island to leeward, heading into the Caribbean and away from the archipelago. As it was, they would now be forced to pass through this archipelago again so as to make Curacao, and this passage was not to be accomplished without some measure of risk to themselves. At any point between the islands they might come upon an equal or superior craft; whether she were Spanish or English would be equally bad for them, and being undermanned they were in no case to fight. To lessen this risk as far as possible, Don Diego directed at first a southerly and then a westerly course; and so, taking a line midway between the islands of Tobago and Grenada, they won safely through the danger-zone and came into the comparative security of the Caribbean Sea.

"If this wind holds," he told them that night at supper, after he had announced to them their position, "we should reach Curacao inside three days."

For three days the wind held, indeed it freshened a little on the second, and yet when the third night descended upon them they had still made no landfall. The Cinco Llagas was ploughing through a sea contained on every side by the blue bowl of heaven. Captain Blood uneasily mentioned it to Don Diego.

"It will be for to-morrow morning," he was answered with calm conviction.

"By all the saints, it is always 'to-morrow morning' with you Spaniards; and to-morrow never comes, my friend."

"But this to-morrow is coming, rest assured. However early you may be astir, you shall see land ahead, Don Pedro."

Captain Blood passed on, content, and went to visit Jerry Pitt, his patient, to whose condition Don Diego owed his chance of life. For twenty-four hours now the fever had left the sufferer, and under Peter Blood's dressings, his lacerated back was beginning to heal satisfactorily. So far, indeed, was he recovered that he complained of his confinement, of the heat in his cabin. To indulge him Captain Blood consented that he should take the air on deck, and so, as the last of the daylight was fading from the sky, Jeremy Pitt came forth upon the Captain's arm.

Seated on the hatch-coamings, the Somersetshire lad gratefully filled his lungs with the cool night air, and professed himself revived thereby. Then with the seaman's instinct his eyes wandered to the darkling vault of heaven, spangled already with a myriad golden points of light. Awhile he scanned it idly, vacantly; then, his attention became sharply fixed. He looked round and up at Captain Blood, who stood beside him.

"D'ye know anything of astronomy, Peter?" quoth he.

"Astronomy, is it? Faith, now, I couldn't tell the Belt of Orion from the Girdle of Venus."

"Ah! And I suppose all the others of this lubberly crew share your ignorance."

"It would be more amiable of you to suppose that they exceed it."

Jeremy pointed ahead to a spot of light in the heavens over the starboard bow. "That is the North Star," said he.

"Is it now? Glory be, I wonder ye can pick it out from the rest."

"And the North Star ahead almost over your starboard bow means that we're steering a course, north, northwest, or maybe north by west, for I doubt if we are standing more than ten degrees westward."

"And why shouldn't we?" wondered Captain Blood.

"You told me—didn't you?—that we came west of the archipelago between Tobago and Grenada, steering for Curacao. If that were our present course, we should have the North Star abeam, out yonder."

On the instant Mr. Blood shed his laziness. He stiffened with apprehension, and was about to speak when a shaft of light clove the gloom above their heads, coming from the door of the poop cabin which had just been opened. It closed again, and presently there was a step on the companion. Don Diego was approaching. Captain Blood's fingers pressed Jerry's shoulder with significance. Then he called the Don, and spoke to him in English as had become his custom when others were present.

"Will ye settle a slight dispute for us, Don Diego?" said he lightly. "We are arguing, Mr. Pitt and I, as to which is the North Star."

"So?" The Spaniard's tone was easy; there was almost a suggestion that laughter lurked behind it, and the reason for this was yielded by his next sentence. "But you tell me Mr. Pitt he is your navigant?"

"For lack of a better," laughed the Captain, good-humouredly contemptuous. "Now I am ready to wager him a hundred pieces of eight that that is the North Star." And he flung out an arm towards a point of light in the heavens straight abeam. He afterwards told Pitt that had Don Diego confirmed him, he would have run him through upon that instant. Far from that, however, the Spaniard freely expressed his scorn.

"You have the assurance that is of ignorance, Don Pedro; and you lose. The North Star is this one." And he indicated it.

"You are sure?"

"But my dear Don Pedro!" The Spaniard's tone was one of amused protest. "But is it possible that I mistake? Besides, is there not the compass? Come to the binnacle and see there what course we make."

His utter frankness, and the easy manner of one who has nothing to conceal resolved at once the doubt that had leapt so suddenly in the mind of Captain Blood. Pitt was satisfied less easily.

"In that case, Don Diego, will you tell me, since Curacao is our destination, why our course is what it is?"

Again there was no faintest hesitation on Don Diego's part. "You have reason to ask," said he, and sighed. "I had hope' it would not be observe'. I have been careless—oh, of a carelessness very culpable. I neglect observation. Always it is my way. I make too sure. I count too much on dead reckoning. And so to-day I find when at last I take out the quadrant that we do come by a half-degree too much south, so that Curacao is now almost due north. That is what cause the delay. But we will be there to-morrow."

The explanation, so completely satisfactory, and so readily and candidly forthcoming, left no room for further doubt that Don Diego should have been false to his parole. And when presently Don Diego had withdrawn again, Captain Blood confessed to Pitt that it was absurd to have suspected him. Whatever his antecedents, he had proved his quality when he announced himself ready to die sooner than enter into any undertaking that could hurt his honour or his country.

New to the seas of the Spanish Main and to the ways of the adventurers who sailed it, Captain Blood still entertained illusions. But the next dawn was to shatter them rudely and for ever.

Coming on deck before the sun was up, he saw land ahead, as the Spaniard had promised them last night. Some ten miles ahead it lay, a long coast-line filling the horizon east and west, with a massive headland jutting forward straight before them. Staring at it, he frowned. He had not conceived that Curacao was of such considerable dimensions. Indeed, this looked less like an island than the main itself.

Beating out aweather, against the gentle landward breeze he beheld a great ship on their starboard bow, that he conceived to be some three or four miles off, and—as well as he could judge her at that distance—of a tonnage equal if not superior to their own. Even as he watched her she altered her course, and going about came heading towards them, close-hauled.

A dozen of his fellows were astir on the forecastle, looking eagerly ahead, and the sound of their voices and laughter reached him across the length of the stately Cinco Llagas.

"There," said a soft voice behind him in liquid Spanish, "is the Promised Land, Don Pedro."

It was something in that voice, a muffled note of exultation, that awoke suspicion in him, and made whole the half-doubt he had been entertaining. He turned sharply to face Don Diego, so sharply that the sly smile was not effaced from the Spaniard's countenance before Captain Blood's eyes had flashed upon it.

"You find an odd satisfaction in the sight of it—all things considered," said Mr. Blood.

"Of course." The Spaniard rubbed his hands, and Mr. Blood observed that they were unsteady. "The satisfaction of a mariner."

"Or of a traitor—which?" Blood asked him quietly. And as the Spaniard fell back before him with suddenly altered countenance that confirmed his every suspicion, he flung an arm out in the direction of the distant shore. "What land is that?" he demanded. "Will you have the effrontery to tell me that is the coast of Curacao?"

He advanced upon Don Diego suddenly, and Don Diego, step by step, fell back. "Shall I tell you what land it is? Shall I?" His fierce assumption of knowledge seemed to dazzle and daze the Spaniard. For still Don Diego made no answer. And then Captain Blood drew a bow at a venture—or not quite at a venture. Such a coast-line as that, if not of the main itself, and the main he knew it could not be, must belong to either Cuba or Hispaniola. Now knowing Cuba to lie farther north and west of the two, it followed, he reasoned swiftly, that if Don Diego meant betrayal he would steer for the nearer of these Spanish territories. "That land, you treacherous, forsworn Spanish dog, is the island of Hispaniola."

Having said it, he closely watched the swarthy face now overspread with pallor, to see the truth or falsehood of his guess reflected there. But now the retreating Spaniard had come to the middle of the quarter-deck, where the mizzen sail made a screen to shut them off from the eyes of the Englishmen below. His lips writhed in a snarling smile.

"Ah, perro ingles! You know too much," he said under his breath, and sprang for the Captain's throat.

Tight-locked in each other's arms, they swayed a moment, then together went down upon the deck, the Spaniard's feet jerked from under him by the right leg of Captain Blood. The Spaniard had depended upon his strength, which was considerable. But it proved no match for the steady muscles of the Irishman, tempered of late by the vicissitudes of slavery. He had depended upon choking the life out of Blood, and so gaining the half-hour that might be necessary to bring up that fine ship that was beating towards them—a Spanish ship, perforce, since none other would be so boldly cruising in these Spanish waters off Hispaniola. But all that Don Diego had accomplished was to betray himself completely, and to no purpose. This he realized when he found himself upon his back, pinned down by

Blood, who was kneeling on his chest, whilst the men summoned by their Captain's shout came clattering up the companion.

"Will I say a prayer for your dirty soul now, whilst I am in this position?" Captain Blood was furiously mocking him.

But the Spaniard, though defeated, now beyond hope for himself, forced his lips to smile, and gave back mockery for mockery.

"Who will pray for your soul, I wonder, when that galleon comes to lie board and board with you?"

"That galleon!" echoed Captain Blood with sudden and awful realization that already it was too late to avoid the consequences of Don Diego's betrayal of them.

"That galleon," Don Diego repeated, and added with a deepening sneer: "Do you know what ship it is? I will tell you. It is the Encarnacion, the flagship of Don Miguel de Espinosa, the Lord Admiral of Castile, and Don Miguel is my brother. It is a very fortunate encounter. The Almighty, you see, watches over the destinies of Catholic Spain."

There was no trace of humour or urbanity now in Captain Blood. His light eyes blazed: his face was set.

He rose, relinquishing the Spaniard to his men. "Make him fast," he bade them. "Truss him, wrist and heel, but don't hurt him—not so much as a hair of his precious head."

The injunction was very necessary. Frenzied by the thought that they were likely to exchange the slavery from which they had so lately escaped for a slavery still worse, they would have torn the Spaniard limb from limb upon the spot. And if they now obeyed their Captain and refrained, it was only because the sudden steely note in his voice promised for Don Diego Valdez something far more exquisite than death.

"You scum! You dirty pirate! You man of honour!" Captain Blood apostrophized his prisoner.

But Don Diego looked up at him and laughed.

"You underrated me." He spoke English, so that all might hear. "I tell you that I was not fear death, and I show you that I was not fear it. You no understand. You just an English dog."

"Irish, if you please," Captain Blood corrected him. "And your parole, you tyke of Spain?"

"You think I give my parole to leave you sons of filth with this beautiful Spanish ship, to go make war upon other Spaniards! Ha!" Don Diego laughed in his throat. "You fool! You can kill me. Pish! It is very well. I die with my work well done. In less than an hour you will be the prisoners of Spain, and the Cinco Llagas will go belong to Spain again."

Captain Blood regarded him steadily out of a face which, if impassive, had paled under its deep tan. About the prisoner, clamant, infuriated, ferocious, the rebels-convict surged, almost literally "athirst for his blood."

"Wait," Captain Blood imperiously commanded, and turning on his heel, he went aside to the rail. As he stood there deep in thought, he was joined by Hagthorpe, Wolverstone, and Ogle the gunner. In silence they stared with him across the water at that other ship. She had veered a point away from the wind, and was running now on a line that must in the end converge with that of the Cinco Llagas.

"In less than half-an-hour," said Blood presently, "we shall have her athwart our hawse, sweeping our decks with her guns."

"We can fight," said the one-eyed giant with an oath.

"Fight!" sneered Blood. "Undermanned as we are, mustering a bare twenty men, in what case are we to fight? No, there would be only one way. To persuade her that all is well aboard, that we are Spaniards, so that she may leave us to continue on our course."

"And how is that possible?" Hagthorpe asked.

"It isn't possible," said Blood. "If it...." And then he broke off, and stood musing, his eyes upon the green water. Ogle, with a bent for sarcasm, interposed a suggestion bitterly.

"We might send Don Diego de Espinosa in a boat manned by his Spaniards to assure his brother the Admiral that we are all loyal subjects of his Catholic Majesty."

The Captain swung round, and for an instant looked as if he would have struck the gunner. Then his expression changed: the light of inspiration Was in his glance.

"Bedad! ye've said it. He doesn't fear death, this damned pirate; but his son may take a different view. Filial piety's mighty strong in Spain." He swung on his heel abruptly, and strode back to the knot of men about his prisoner. "Here!" he shouted to them. "Bring him below." And he led the way down to the waist, and thence by the booby hatch to the gloom of the 'tween-decks, where the air was rank with the smell of tar and spun yarn. Going aft he threw open the door of the spacious wardroom, and went in followed by a dozen of the hands with the pinioned Spaniard. Every man aboard would have followed him but for his sharp command to some of them to remain on deck with Hagthorpe.

In the ward-room the three stern chasers were in position, loaded, their muzzles thrusting through the open ports, precisely as the Spanish gunners had left them.

"Here, Ogle, is work for you," said Blood, and as the burly gunner came thrusting forward through the little throng of gaping men, Blood pointed to the middle chaser; "Have that gun hauled back," he ordered.

When this was done, Blood beckoned those who held Don Diego.

"Lash him across the mouth of it," he bade them, and whilst, assisted by another two, they made haste to obey, he turned to the others. "To the roundhouse, some of you, and fetch the Spanish prisoners. And you, Dyke, go up and bid them set the flag of Spain aloft."

Don Diego, with his body stretched in an arc across the cannon's mouth, legs and arms lashed to the carriage on either side of it, eyeballs rolling in his head, glared maniacally at Captain Blood. A man may not fear to die, and yet be appalled by the form in which death comes to him.

From frothing lips he hurled blasphemies and insults at his tormentor.

"Foul barbarian! Inhuman savage! Accursed heretic! Will it not content you to kill me in some Christian fashion?" Captain Blood vouchsafed him a malignant smile, before he turned to meet the fifteen manacled Spanish prisoners, who were thrust into his presence.

Approaching, they had heard Don Diego's outcries; at close quarters now they beheld with horror-stricken eyes his plight. From amongst them a comely, olive-skinned stripling, distinguished in bearing and apparel from his companions, started forward with an anguished cry of "Father!"

Writhing in the arms that made haste to seize and hold him, he called upon heaven and hell to avert this horror, and lastly, addressed to Captain Blood an appeal for mercy that was at once fierce and piteous. Considering him, Captain Blood thought with satisfaction that he displayed the proper degree of filial piety.

He afterwards confessed that for a moment he was in danger of weakening, that for a moment his mind rebelled against the pitiless thing it had planned. But to correct the sentiment he evoked a memory of what these Spaniards had performed in Bridgetown. Again he saw the white face of that child Mary Traill as she fled in horror before the jeering ruffian whom he had slain, and other things even more unspeakable seen on that dreadful evening rose now before the eyes of his memory to stiffen his faltering purpose. The Spaniards had shown themselves without mercy or sentiment or decency of any kind; stuffed with religion, they were without a spark of that Christianity, the Symbol of which was mounted on the mainmast of the approaching ship. A moment ago this cruel, vicious Don Diego had insulted the Almighty by his assumption that He kept a specially benevolent watch over the destinies of Catholic Spain. Don Diego should be taught his error.

Recovering the cynicism in which he had approached his task, the cynicism essential to its proper performance, he commanded Ogle to kindle a match and remove the leaden apron from the touch-hole of the gun that bore Don Diego. Then, as the younger Espinosa broke into fresh intercessions mingled with imprecations, he wheeled upon him sharply.

"Peace!" he snapped. "Peace, and listen! It is no part of my intention to blow your father to hell as he deserves, or indeed to take his life at all."

Having surprised the lad into silence by that promise—a promise surprising enough in all the circumstances—he proceeded to explain his aims in that faultless and elegant Castilian of which he was fortunately master—as fortunately for Don Diego as for himself.

"It is your father's treachery that has brought us into this plight and deliberately into risk of capture and death aboard that ship of Spain. Just as your father recognized his brother's flagship, so will his brother have recognized the Cinco Llagas. So far, then, all is well. But presently the Encarnacion will be sufficiently close to perceive that here all is not as it should be. Sooner or later, she must guess or discover what is wrong, and then she will open fire or lay us board and board. Now, we are in no case to fight, as your father knew when he ran us into this trap. But fight we will, if we are driven to it. We make no tame surrender to the ferocity of Spain."

He laid his hand on the breech of the gun that bore Don Diego.

"Understand this clearly: to the first shot from the Encarnacion this gun will fire the answer. I make myself clear, I hope?"

White-faced and trembling, young Espinosa stared into the pitiless blue eyes that so steadily regarded him.

"If it is clear?" he faltered, breaking the utter silence in which all were standing. "But, name of God, how should it be clear? How should I understand? Can you avert the fight? If you know a way, and if I, or these, can help you to it—if that is what you mean—in Heaven's name let me hear it."

"A fight would be averted if Don Diego de Espinosa were to go aboard his brother's ship, and by his presence and assurances inform the Admiral that all is well with the Cinco Llagas, that she is indeed still a ship of Spain as her flag now announces. But of course Don Diego cannot go in person, because he is... otherwise engaged. He has a slight touch of fever—shall we say?—that detains him in his cabin. But you, his son, may convey all this and some other matters together with his homage to your uncle. You shall go in a boat manned by six of these Spanish prisoners, and I—a distinguished Spaniard delivered from captivity in Barbados by your recent raid—will accompany you to keep you in countenance. If I return alive, and without accident of any kind to hinder our free sailing hence, Don Diego shall have his life, as shall every one of you. But if there is the least misadventure, be it from treachery or ill-fortune—I care not which—the battle, as I have had the honour to explain, will be opened on our side by this gun, and your father will be the first victim of the conflict."

He paused a moment. There was a hum of approval from his comrades, an anxious stirring among the Spanish prisoners. Young Espinosa stood before him, the colour ebbing and flowing in his cheeks. He waited for some direction from his father. But none came. Don Diego's courage, it seemed, had sadly waned under that rude test. He hung limply in his fearful bonds, and was silent. Evidently he dared not encourage his son to defiance, and presumably was ashamed to urge him to yield. Thus, he left decision entirely with the youth.

"Come," said Blood. "I have been clear enough, I think. What do you say?"

Don Esteban moistened his parched lips, and with the back of his hand mopped the anguish-sweat from his brow. His eyes gazed wildly a moment upon the shoulders of his father, as if beseeching guidance. But his father remained silent. Something like a sob escaped the boy.

"I... I accept," he answered at last, and swung to the Spaniards. "And you—you will accept too," he insisted passionately. "For Don Diego's sake and for your own—for all our sakes. If you do not, this man will butcher us all without mercy."

Since he yielded, and their leader himself counselled no resistance, why should they encompass their own destruction by a gesture of futile heroism? They answered without much hesitation that they would do as was required of them.

Blood turned, and advanced to Don Diego.

"I am sorry to inconvenience you in this fashion, but..." For a second he checked and frowned as his eyes intently observed the prisoner. Then, after that scarcely perceptible pause, he continued, "but I do not think that you have anything beyond this inconvenience to apprehend, and you may depend upon me to shorten it as far as possible." Don Diego made him no answer.

Peter Blood waited a moment, observing him; then he bowed and stepped back.

CHAPTER XII. DON PEDRO SANGRE

The Cinco Llagas and the Encarnacion, after a proper exchange of signals, lay hove to within a quarter of a mile of each other, and across the intervening space of gently heaving, sunlit waters sped a boat from the former, manned by six Spanish seamen and bearing in her stern sheets Don Esteban de Espinosa and Captain Peter Blood.

She also bore two treasure-chests containing fifty thousand pieces of eight. Gold has at all times been considered the best of testimonies of good faith, and Blood was determined that in all respects appearances should be entirely on his side. His followers had accounted this a supererogation of pretence. But Blood's will in the matter had prevailed. He carried further a bulky package addressed to a grande of Spain, heavily sealed with the arms of Espinosa—another piece of evidence hastily manufactured in the cabin of the Cinco Llagas—and he was spending these last moments in completing his instructions to his young companion.

Don Esteban expressed his last lingering uneasiness:

"But if you should betray yourself?" he cried.

"It will be unfortunate for everybody. I advised your father to say a prayer for our success. I depend upon you to help me more materially."

"I will do my best. God knows I will do my best," the boy protested.

Blood nodded thoughtfully, and no more was said until they bumped alongside the towering mass of the Encarnadon. Up the ladder went Don Esteban closely followed by Captain Blood. In the waist stood the Admiral himself to receive them, a handsome, self-sufficient man, very tall and stiff, a little older and greyer than Don Diego, whom he closely resembled. He was supported by four officers and a friar in the black and white habit of St. Dominic.

Don Miguel opened his arms to his nephew, whose lingering panic he mistook for pleasurable excitement, and having enfolded him to his bosom turned to greet Don Esteban's companion.

Peter Blood bowed gracefully, entirely at his ease, so far as might be judged from appearances.

"I am," he announced, making a literal translation of his name, "Don Pedro Sangre, an unfortunate gentleman of Leon, lately delivered from captivity by Don

Esteban's most gallant father." And in a few words he sketched the imagined conditions of his capture by, and deliverance from, those accursed heretics who held the island of Barbados. "Benedicamus Domino," said the friar to his tale.

"Ex hoc nunc et usque in seculum," replied Blood, the occasional papist, with lowered eyes.

The Admiral and his attending officers gave him a sympathetic hearing and a cordial welcome. Then came the dreaded question.

"But where is my brother? Why has he not come, himself, to greet me?"

It was young Espinosa who answered this:

"My father is afflicted at denying himself that honour and pleasure. But unfortunately, sir uncle, he is a little indisposed—oh, nothing grave; merely sufficient to make him keep his cabin. It is a little fever, the result of a slight wound taken in the recent raid upon Barbados, which resulted in this gentleman's happy deliverance."

"Nay, nephew, nay," Don Miguel protested with ironic repudiation. "I can have no knowledge of these things. I have the honour to represent upon the seas His Catholic Majesty, who is at peace with the King of England. Already you have told me more than it is good for me to know. I will endeavour to forget it, and I will ask you, sirs," he added, glancing at his officers, "to forget it also." But he winked into the twinkling eyes of Captain Blood; then added matter that at once extinguished that twinkle. "But since Diego cannot come to me, why, I will go across to him."

For a moment Don Esteban's face was a mask of pallid fear. Then Blood was speaking in a lowered, confidential voice that admirably blended suavity, impressiveness, and sly mockery.

"If you please, Don Miguel, but that is the very thing you must not do—the very thing Don Diego does not wish you to do. You must not see him until his wounds are healed. That is his own wish. That is the real reason why he is not here. For the truth is that his wounds are not so grave as to have prevented his coming. It was his consideration of himself and the false position in which you would be placed if you had direct word from him of what has happened. As your excellency has said, there is peace between His Catholic Majesty and the King of England, and your brother Don Diego...." He paused a moment. "I am sure that I need say no more. What you hear from us is no more than a mere rumour. Your excellency understands."

His excellency frowned thoughtfully. "I understand... in part," said he.

Captain Blood had a moment's uneasiness. Did the Spaniard doubt his bona fides? Yet in dress and speech he knew himself to be impeccably Spanish, and was not Don Esteban there to confirm him? He swept on to afford further confirmation before the Admiral could say another word.

"And we have in the boat below two chests containing fifty thousand pieces of eight, which we are to deliver to your excellency."

His excellency jumped; there was a sudden stir among his officers.

"They are the ransom extracted by Don Diego from the Governor of...."

"Not another word, in the name of Heaven!" cried the Admiral in alarm. "My brother wishes me to assume charge of this money, to carry it to Spain for him? Well, that is a family matter between my brother and myself. So, it can be done. But I must not know...." He broke off. "Hum! A glass of Malaga in my cabin, if you please," he invited them, "whilst the chests are being hauled aboard."

He gave his orders touching the embarkation of these chests, then led the way to his regally appointed cabin, his four officers and the friar following by particular invitation.

Seated at table there, with the tawny wine before them, and the servant who had poured it withdrawn, Don Miguel laughed and stroked his pointed, grizzled beard.

"Virgen santisima! That brother of mine has a mind that thinks of everything. Left to myself, I might have committed a fine indiscretion by venturing aboard his ship at such a moment. I might have seen things which as Admiral of Spain it would be difficult for me to ignore."

Both Esteban and Blood made haste to agree with him, and then Blood raised his glass, and drank to the glory of Spain and the damnation of the besotted James who occupied the throne of England. The latter part of his toast was at least sincere.

The Admiral laughed.

"Sir, sir, you need my brother here to curb your imprudences. You should remember that His Catholic Majesty and the King of England are very good friends. That is not a toast to propose in this cabin. But since it has been proposed, and by one who has such particular personal cause to hate these English hounds, why, we will honour it—but unofficially."

They laughed, and drank the damnation of King James—quite unofficially, but the more fervently on that account. Then Don Esteban, uneasy on the score of his father, and remembering that the agony of Don Diego was being protracted with every moment that they left him in his dreadful position, rose and announced that they must be returning.

"My father," he explained, "is in haste to reach San Domingo. He desired me to stay no longer than necessary to embrace you. If you will give us leave, then, sir uncle."

In the circumstances "sir uncle" did not insist.

As they returned to the ship's side, Blood's eyes anxiously scanned the line of seamen leaning over the bulwarks in idle talk with the Spaniards in the cock-boat that waited at the ladder's foot. But their manner showed him that there was no ground for his anxiety. The boat's crew had been wisely reticent.

The Admiral took leave of them—of Esteban affectionately, of Blood ceremoniously.

"I regret to lose you so soon, Don Pedro. I wish that you could have made a longer visit to the Encarnacion."

"I am indeed unfortunate," said Captain Blood politely.

"But I hope that we may meet again."

"That is to flatter me beyond all that I deserve."

They reached the boat; and she cast off from the great ship. As they were pulling away, the Admiral waving to them from the taffrail, they heard the shrill whistle of the bo'sun piping the hands to their stations, and before they had reached the Cinco Llagas, they beheld the Encarnacion go about under sail. She dipped her flag to them, and from her poop a gun fired a salute.

Aboard the Cinco Llagas some one—it proved afterwards to be Hagthorpe—had the wit to reply in the same fashion. The comedy was ended. Yet there was something else to follow as an epilogue, a thing that added a grim ironic flavour to the whole.

As they stepped into the waist of the Cinco Llagas, Hagthorpe advanced to receive them. Blood observed the set, almost scared expression on his face.

"I see that you've found it," he said quietly.

Hagthorpe's eyes looked a question. But his mind dismissed whatever thought it held.

"Don Diego..." he was beginning, and then stopped, and looked curiously at Blood.

Noting the pause and the look, Esteban bounded forward, his face livid.

"Have you broken faith, you curs? Has he come to harm?" he cried—and the six Spaniards behind him grew clamorous with furious questionings.

"We do not break faith," said Hagthorpe firmly, so firmly that he quieted them. "And in this case there was not the need. Don Diego died in his bonds before ever you reached the Encarnacion."

Peter Blood said nothing.

"Died?" screamed Esteban. "You killed him, you mean. Of what did he die?"

Hagthorpe looked at the boy. "If I am a judge," he said, "Don Diego died of fear."

Don Esteban struck Hagthorpe across the face at that, and Hagthorpe would have struck back, but that Blood got between, whilst his followers seized the lad.

"Let be," said Blood. "You provoked the boy by your insult to his father."

"I was not concerned to insult," said Hagthorpe, nursing his cheek. "It is what has happened. Come and look."

"I have seen," said Blood. "He died before I left the Cinco Llagas. He was hanging dead in his bonds when I spoke to him before leaving."

"What are you saying?" cried Esteban.

Blood looked at him gravely. Yet for all his gravity he seemed almost to smile, though without mirth.

"If you had known that, eh?" he asked at last. For a moment Don Esteban stared at him wide-eyed, incredulous. "I don't believe you," he said at last.

"Yet you may. I am a doctor, and I know death when I see it."

Again there came a pause, whilst conviction sank into the lad's mind.

"If I had known that," he said at last in a thick voice, "you would be hanging from the yardarm of the Encarnacion at this moment."

"I know," said Blood. "I am considering it—the profit that a man may find in the ignorance of others."

"But you'll hang there yet," the boy raved.

Captain Blood shrugged, and turned on his heel. But he did not on that account disregard the words, nor did Hagthorpe, nor yet the others who overheard them, as they showed at a council held that night in the cabin.

This council was met to determine what should be done with the Spanish prisoners. Considering that Curaçao now lay beyond their reach, as they were running short of water and provisions, and also that Pitt was hardly yet in case to undertake the navigation of the vessel, it had been decided that, going east of Hispaniola, and then sailing along its northern coast, they should make for Tortuga, that haven of the buccaneers, in which lawless port they had at least no danger of recapture to apprehend. It was now a question whether they should convey the Spaniards thither with them, or turn them off in a boat to make the best of their way to the coast of Hispaniola, which was but ten miles off. This was the course urged by Blood himself.

"There's nothing else to be done," he insisted. "In Tortuga they would be flayed alive."

"Which is less than the swine deserve," growled Wolverstone.

"And you'll remember, Peter," put in Hagthorpe, "that boy's threat to you this morning. If he escapes, and carries word of all this to his uncle, the Admiral, the execution of that threat will become more than possible."

It says much for Peter Blood that the argument should have left him unmoved. It is a little thing, perhaps, but in a narrative in which there is so much that tells against him, I cannot—since my story is in the nature of a brief for the defence—afford to slur a circumstance that is so strongly in his favour, a circumstance revealing that the cynicism attributed to him proceeded from his reason and from a brooding over wrongs rather than from any natural instincts. "I care nothing for his threats."

"You should," said Wolverstone. "The wise thing'd be to hang him, along o' all the rest."

"It is not human to be wise," said Blood. "It is much more human to err, though perhaps exceptional to err on the side of mercy. We'll be exceptional. Oh, faugh! I've no stomach for cold-blooded killing. At daybreak pack the Spaniards into a boat with a keg of water and a sack of dumplings, and let them go to the devil."

That was his last word on the subject, and it prevailed by virtue of the authority they had vested in him, and of which he had taken so firm a grip. At daybreak Don Esteban and his followers were put off in a boat.

Two days later, the Cinco Llagas sailed into the rock-bound bay of Cayona, which Nature seemed to have designed for the stronghold of those who had appropriated it.

CHAPTER XIII. TORTUGA

It is time fully to disclose the fact that the survival of the story of Captain Blood's exploits is due entirely to the industry of Jeremy Pitt, the Somersetshire shipmaster. In addition to his ability as a navigator, this amiable young man appears to have wielded an indefatigable pen, and to have been inspired to indulge its fluency by the affection he very obviously bore to Peter Blood.

He kept the log of the forty-gun frigate Arabella, on which he served as master, or, as we should say to-day, navigating officer, as no log that I have seen was ever kept. It runs into some twenty-odd volumes of assorted sizes, some of which are missing altogether and others of which are so sadly depleted of leaves as to be of little use. But if at times in the laborious perusal of them—they are preserved in the library of Mr. James Speke of Comerton—I have inveighed against these lacunae, at others I have been equally troubled by the excessive prolixity of what remains and the difficulty of disintegrating from the confused whole the really essential parts.

I have a suspicion that Esquemeling—though how or where I can make no surmise—must have obtained access to these records, and that he plucked from them the brilliant feathers of several exploits to stick them into the tail of his own hero, Captain Morgan. But that is by the way. I mention it chiefly as a warning, for when presently I come to relate the affair of Maracaybo, those of you who have read Esquemeling may be in danger of supposing that Henry Morgan really performed those things which here are veraciously attributed to Peter Blood. I think, however, that when you come to weigh the motives actuating both Blood and the Spanish Admiral, in that affair, and when you consider how integrally the event is a part of Blood's history—whilst merely a detached incident in Morgan's—you will reach my own conclusion as to which is the real plagiarist.

The first of these logs of Pitt's is taken up almost entirely with a retrospective narrative of the events up to the time of Blood's first coming to Tortuga. This and the Tannatt Collection of State Trials are the chief—though not the only—sources of my history so far.

Pitt lays great stress upon the fact that it was the circumstances upon which I have dwelt, and these alone, that drove Peter Blood to seek an anchorage at Tortuga. He insists at considerable length, and with a vehemence which in itself makes it plain that an opposite opinion was held in some quarters, that it was no part of the design of Blood or of any of his companions in misfortune to join hands with the buccaneers who, under a semi-official French protection, made of Tortuga a lair whence they could sally out to drive their merciless piratical trade chiefly at the expense of Spain.

It was, Pitt tells us, Blood's original intention to make his way to France or Holland. But in the long weeks of waiting for a ship to convey him to one or the other of these countries, his resources dwindled and finally vanished. Also, his chronicler thinks that he detected signs of some secret trouble in his friend, and he attributes to this the abuses of the potent West Indian spirit of which Blood became guilty in those days of inaction, thereby sinking to the level of the wild ad-adventurers with whom ashore he associated.

I do not think that Pitt is guilty in this merely of special pleading, that he is putting forward excuses for his hero. I think that in those days there was a good deal to oppress Peter Blood. There was the thought of Arabella Bishop—and that this thought loomed large in his mind we are not permitted to doubt. He was maddened by the tormenting lure of the unattainable. He desired Arabella, yet knew her beyond his reach irrevocably and for all time. Also, whilst he may have desired to go to France or Holland, he had no clear purpose to accomplish when he reached one or the other of these countries. He was, when all is said, an escaped slave, an outlaw in his own land and a homeless outcast in any other. There remained the sea, which is free to all, and particularly alluring to those who feel themselves at war with humanity. And so, considering the adventurous spirit that once already had sent him a-roving for the sheer love of it, considering that this spirit was heightened now by a recklessness begotten of his outlawry, that his training and skill in militant seamanship clamorously supported the temptations that were put before him, can you wonder, or dare you blame him, that in the end he succumbed? And remember that these temptations proceeded not only from adventurous buccaneering acquaintances in the taverns of that evil haven of Tortuga, but even from M. d'Ogeron, the governor of the island, who levied as his harbour dues a percentage of one tenth of all spoils brought into the bay, and who profited further by commissions upon money which he was desired to convert into bills of exchange upon France.

A trade that might have worn a repellent aspect when urged by greasy, half-drunken adventurers, boucan-hunters, lumbermen, beach-combers, English, French, and Dutch, became a dignified, almost official form of privateering when advocated by the courtly, middle-aged gentleman who in representing the French West India Company seemed to represent France herself.

Moreover, to a man—not excluding Jeremy Pitt himself, in whose blood the call of the sea was insistent and imperative—those who had escaped with Peter Blood from the Barbados plantations, and who, consequently, like himself, knew not whither to turn, were all resolved upon joining the great Brotherhood of the Coast, as those rovers called themselves. And they united theirs to the other voices that were persuading Blood, demanding that he should continue now in the leadership which he had enjoyed since they had left Barbados, and swearing to follow him loyally whithersoever he should lead them.

And so, to condense all that Jeremy has recorded in the matter, Blood ended by yielding to external and internal pressure, abandoned himself to the stream of Destiny. "Fata viam invenerunt," is his own expression of it.

If he resisted so long, it was, I think, the thought of Arabella Bishop that restrained him. That they should be destined never to meet again did not weigh at first, or, indeed, ever. He conceived the scorn with which she would come to hear of his having turned pirate, and the scorn, though as yet no more than imagined, hurt him as if it were already a reality. And even when he conquered this, still the thought of her was ever present. He compromised with the conscience that her memory kept so disconcertingly active. He vowed that the thought of her should continue ever before him to help him keep his hands as clean as a man might in this desperate trade upon which he was embarking. And so, although he might entertain no delusive hope of ever winning her for his own, of ever even seeing her again, yet the memory of her was to abide in his soul as a bitter-sweet, purifying influence. The love that is never to be realized will often remain a man's guiding ideal. The resolve being taken, he went actively to work. Ogeron, most accommodating of governors, advanced him money for the proper equipment of his ship the Cinco Llagas, which he renamed the Arabella. This after some little hesitation, fearful of thus setting his heart upon his sleeve. But his Barbados friends accounted it merely an expression of the ever-ready irony in which their leader dealt.

To the score of followers he already possessed, he added threescore more, picking his men with caution and discrimination—and he was an exceptional judge of men—from amongst the adventurers of Tortuga. With them all he entered into the articles usual among the Brethren of the Coast under which each man was to be paid by a share in the prizes captured. In other respects, however, the articles were different. Aboard the Arabella there was to be none of the ruffianly indiscipline that normally prevailed in buccaneering vessels. Those who shipped with him undertook obedience and submission in all things to himself and to the officers appointed by election. Any to whom this clause in the articles was distasteful might follow some other leader.

Towards the end of December, when the hurricane season had blown itself out, he put to sea in his well-found, well-manned ship, and before he returned in the following May from a protracted and adventurous cruise, the fame of Captain Peter Blood had run like ripples before the breeze across the face of the Caribbean Sea. There was a fight in the Windward Passage at the outset with a Spanish galleon, which had resulted in the gutting and finally the sinking of the Spaniard. There was a daring raid effected by means of several appropriated piraguas upon a Spanish pearl fleet in the Rio de la Hacha, from which they had taken a particularly rich haul of pearls. There was an overland expedition to the goldfields of Santa Maria, on the Main, the full tale of which is hardly credible, and there were lesser adventures through all of which the crew of the Arabella came with credit and profit if not entirely unscathed.

And so it happened that before the Arabella came homing to Tortuga in the following May to refit and repair—for she was not without scars, as you conceive—the fame of her and of Peter Blood her captain had swept from the Bahamas to the Windward Isles, from New Providence to Trinidad.

An echo of it had reached Europe, and at the Court of St. James's angry representations were made by the Ambassador of Spain, to whom it was answered that it must not be supposed that this Captain Blood held any commission from the King of England; that he was, in fact, a proscribed rebel, an escaped slave, and that any measures against him by His Catholic Majesty would receive the cordial approbation of King James II.

Don Miguel de Espinosa, the Admiral of Spain in the West Indies, and his nephew Don Esteban who sailed with him, did not lack the will to bring the adventurer to the yardarm. With them this business of capturing Blood, which was now an international affair, was also a family matter.

Spain, through the mouth of Don Miguel, did not spare her threats. The report of them reached Tortuga, and with it the assurance that Don Miguel had behind him not only the authority of his own nation, but that of the English King as well.

It was a brutum fulmen that inspired no terrors in Captain Blood. Nor was he likely, on account of it, to allow himself to run to rust in the security of Tortuga. For what he had suffered at the hands of Man he had chosen to make Spain the scapegoat. Thus he accounted that he served a twofold purpose: he took compensation and at the same time served, not indeed the Stuart King, whom he despised, but England and, for that matter, all the rest of civilized mankind which cruel, treacherous, greedy, bigoted Castile sought to exclude from intercourse with the New World.

One day as he sat with Hagthorpe and Wolverstone over a pipe and a bottle of rum in the stifling reek of tar and stale tobacco of a waterside tavern, he was accosted by a splendid ruffian in a gold-laced coat of dark-blue satin with a crimson sash, a foot wide, about the waist.

"C'est vous qu'on appelle Le Sang?" the fellow hailed him.

Captain Blood looked up to consider the questioner before replying. The man was tall and built on lines of agile strength, with a swarthy, aquiline face that was brutally handsome. A diamond of great price flamed on the indifferently clean hand resting on the pummel of his long rapier, and there were gold rings in his ears, half-concealed by long ringlets of oily chestnut hair.

Captain Blood took the pipe-stem from between his lips.

"My name," he said, "is Peter Blood. The Spaniards know me for Don Pedro Sangre and a Frenchman may call me Le Sang if he pleases."

"Good," said the gaudy adventurer in English, and without further invitation he drew up a stool and sat down at that greasy table. "My name," he informed the three men, two of whom at least were eyeing him askance, "it is Levasseur. You may have heard of me."

They had, indeed. He commanded a privateer of twenty guns that had dropped anchor in the bay a week ago, manned by a crew mainly composed of French boucanhunters from Northern Hispaniola, men who had good cause to hate the Spaniard with an intensity exceeding that of the English. Levasseur had brought them back to Tortuga from an indifferently successful cruise. It would need more, however, than lack of success to abate the fellow's monstrous vanity. A roaring, quarrelsome, hard-drinking, hard-gaming scoundrel, his reputation as a buccaneer stood high among the wild Brethren of the Coast. He enjoyed also a reputation of another sort. There was about his gaudy, swaggering raffishness something that the women found singularly alluring. That he should boast openly of his bonnes fortunes did not seem strange to Captain Blood; what he might have found strange was that there appeared to be some measure of justification for these boasts.

It was current gossip that even Mademoiselle d'Ogeron, the Governor's daughter, had been caught in the snare of his wild attractiveness, and that Levasseur had gone the length of audacity of asking her hand in marriage of her father. M. d'Ogeron had made him the only possible answer. He had shown him the door. Levasseur had departed in a rage, swearing that he would make mademoiselle his wife in the teeth of all the fathers in Christendom, and that M. d'Ogeron should bitterly rue the affront he had put upon him.

This was the man who now thrust himself upon Captain Blood with a proposal of association, offering him not only his sword, but his ship and the men who sailed in her.

A dozen years ago, as a lad of barely twenty, Levasseur had sailed with that monster of cruelty L'Ollonais, and his own subsequent exploits bore witness and did credit to the school in which he had been reared. I doubt if in his day there was a greater scoundrel among the Brethren of the Coast than this Levasseur. And yet, repulsive though he found him, Captain Blood could not deny that the fellow's proposals displayed boldness, imagination, and resource, and he was forced to admit that jointly they could undertake operations of a greater magnitude than was possible singly to either of them. The climax of Levasseur's project was to be a raid upon the wealthy mainland city of Maracaybo; but for this, he admitted, six hundred men at the very least would be required, and six hundred men were not to be conveyed in the two bottoms they now commanded. Preliminary cruises must take place, having for one of their objects the capture of further ships.

Because he disliked the man, Captain Blood would not commit himself at once. But because he liked the proposal he consented to consider it. Being afterwards pressed by both Hagthorpe and Wolverstone, who did not share his own personal dislike of the Frenchman, the end of the matter was that within a week articles were drawn up between Levasseur and Blood, and signed by them and—as was usual—by the chosen representatives of their followers.

These articles contained, inter alia, the common provisions that, should the two vessels separate, a strict account must afterwards be rendered of all prizes severally taken, whilst the vessel taking a prize should retain three fifths of its value, surrendering two fifths to its associate. These shares were subsequently to be subdivided among the crew of each vessel, in accordance with the articles already obtaining between each captain and his own men. For the rest, the articles contained all the clauses that were usual, among which was the clause that any man found guilty of abstracting or concealing any part of a prize, be it of the value of no more than a peso, should be summarily hanged from the yardarm.

All being now settled they made ready for sea, and on the very eve of sailing, Levasseur narrowly escaped being shot in a romantic attempt to scale the wall of the Governor's garden, with the object of taking passionate leave of the infatuated Mademoiselle d'Ogeron. He desisted after having been twice fired upon from a fragrant ambush of pimento trees where the Governor's guards were posted, and he departed vowing to take different and very definite measures on his return.

That night he slept on board his ship, which with characteristic flamboyance he had named La Foudre, and there on the following day he received a visit from Captain Blood, whom he greeted half-mockingly as his admiral. The Irishman came to settle certain final details of which all that need concern us is an understanding that, in the event of the two vessels becoming separated by accident or design, they should rejoin each other as soon as might be at Tortuga.

Thereafter Levasseur entertained his admiral to dinner, and jointly they drank success to the expedition, so copiously on the part of Levasseur that when the time came to separate he was as nearly drunk as it seemed possible for him to be and yet retain his understanding.

Finally, towards evening, Captain Blood went over the side and was rowed back to his great ship with her red bulwarks and gilded ports, touched into a lovely thing of flame by the setting sun.

He was a little heavy-hearted. I have said that he was a judge of men, and his judgment of Levasseur filled him with misgivings which were growing heavier in a measure as the hour of departure approached.

He expressed it to Wolverstone, who met him as he stepped aboard the Arabella:

"You over persuaded me into those articles, you blackguard; and it'll surprise me if any good comes of this association."

The giant rolled his single bloodthirsty eye, and sneered, thrusting out his heavy jaw. "We'll wring the dog's neck if there's any treachery."

"So we will—if we are there to wring it by then." And on that, dismissing the matter: "We sail in the morning, on the first of the ebb," he announced, and went off to his cabin.

CHAPTER XIV. LEVASSEUR'S HEROICS

It would be somewhere about ten o'clock on the following morning, a full hour before the time appointed for sailing, when a canoe brought up alongside La Foudre, and a half-caste Indian stepped out of her and went up the ladder. He was clad in drawers of hairy, untanned hide, and a red blanket served him for a cloak. He was the bearer of a folded scrap of paper for Captain Levasseur.

The Captain unfolded the letter, sadly soiled and crumpled by contact with the half-caste's person. Its contents may be roughly translated thus:

"My well-beloved—I am in the Dutch brig Jongvrow, which is about to sail. Resolved to separate us for ever, my cruel father is sending me to Europe in my brother's charge. I implore you, come to my rescue. Deliver me, my well-beloved hero!—Your desolated Madeleine, who loves you."

The well-beloved hero was moved to the soul of him by that passionate appeal. His scowling glance swept the bay for the Dutch brig, which he knew had been due to sail for Amsterdam with a cargo of hides and tobacco.

She was nowhere to be seen among the shipping in that narrow, rock-bound harbour. He roared out the question in his mind.

In answer the half-caste pointed out beyond the frothing surf that marked the position of the reef constituting one of the stronghold's main defences. Away beyond it, a mile or so distant, a sail was standing out to sea. "There she go," he said.

"There!" The Frenchman gazed and stared, his face growing white. The man's wicked temper awoke, and turned to vent itself upon the messenger. "And where have you been that you come here only now with this? Answer me!"

The half-caste shrank terrified before his fury. His explanation, if he had one, was paralyzed by fear. Levasseur took him by the throat, shook him twice, snarling the while, then hurled him into the scuppers. The man's head struck the gunwale as he fell, and he lay there, quite still, a trickle of blood issuing from his mouth.

Levasseur dashed one hand against the other, as if dusting them.

"Heave that muck overboard," he ordered some of those who stood idling in the waist. "Then up anchor, and let us after the Dutchman."

"Steady, Captain. What's that?" There was a restraining hand upon his shoulder, and the broad face of his lieutenant Cahusac, a burly, callous Breton scoundrel, was stolidly confronting him.

Levasseur made clear his purpose with a deal of unnecessary obscenity.

Cahusac shook his head. "A Dutch brig!" said he. "Impossible! We should never be allowed."

"And who the devil will deny us?" Levasseur was between amazement and fury.

"For one thing, there's your own crew will be none too willing. For another there's Captain Blood."

"I care nothing for Captain Blood...."

"But it is necessary that you should. He has the power, the weight of metal and of men, and if I know him at all he'll sink us before he'll suffer interference with the Dutch. He has his own views of privateering, this Captain Blood, as I warned you."

"Ah!" said Levasseur, showing his teeth. But his eyes, riveted upon that distant sail, were gloomily thoughtful. Not for long. The imagination and resource which Captain Blood had detected in the fellow soon suggested a course.

Cursing in his soul, and even before the anchor was weighed, the association into which he had entered, he was already studying ways of evasion. What Cahusac implied was true: Blood would never suffer violence to be done in his presence to a Dutchman; but it might be done in his absence; and, being done, Blood must perforce condone it, since it would then be too late to protest.

Within the hour the Arabella and La Foudre were beating out to sea together. Without understanding the change of plan involved, Captain Blood, nevertheless, accepted it, and weighed anchor before the appointed time upon perceiving his associate to do so.

All day the Dutch brig was in sight, though by evening she had dwindled to the merest speck on the northern horizon. The course prescribed for Blood and Levasseur lay eastward along the northern shores of Hispaniola. To that course the Arabella continued to hold steadily throughout the night. When day broke again, she was alone. La Foudre under cover of the darkness had struck away to The northeast with every rag of canvas on her yards.

Cahusac had attempted yet again to protest against this.

"The devil take you!" Levasseur had answered him. "A ship's a ship, be she Dutch or Spanish, and ships are our present need. That will suffice for the men."

His lieutenant said no more. But from his glimpse of the letter, knowing that a girl and not a ship was his captain's real objective, he gloomily shook his head as he rolled away on his bowed legs to give the necessary orders.

Dawn found La Foudre close on the Dutchman's heels, not a mile astern, and the sight of her very evidently flustered the Jongvrow. No doubt mademoiselle's brother recognizing Levasseur's ship would be responsible for the Dutch uneasiness. They saw the Jongvrow crowding canvas in a futile endeavour to outsail them, whereupon they stood off to starboard and raced on until they were in a position whence they could send a warning shot across her bow. The Jongvrow veered, showed them her rudder, and opened fire with her stern chasers. The small shot went whistling through La Foudre's shrouds with some slight damage to her canvas. Followed a brief running fight in the course of which the Dutchman let fly a broadside.

Five minutes after that they were board and board, the Jongvrow held tight in the clutches of La Foudre's grapnels, and the buccaneers pouring noisily into her waist.

The Dutchman's master, purple in the face, stood forward to beard the pirate, followed closely by an elegant, pale-faced young gentleman in whom Levasseur recognized his brother-in-law elect.

"Captain Levasseur, this is an outrage for which you shall be made to answer. What do you seek aboard my ship?"

"At first I sought only that which belongs to me, something of which I am being robbed. But since you chose war and opened fire on me with some damage to my ship and loss of life to five of my men, why, war it is, and your ship a prize of war."

From the quarter rail Mademoiselle d'Ogeron looked down with glowing eyes in breathless wonder upon her well-beloved hero. Gloriously heroic he seemed as he stood towering there, masterful, audacious, beautiful. He saw her, and with a glad shout sprang towards her. The Dutch master got in his way with hands upheld to arrest his progress. Levasseur did not stay to argue with him: he was too impatient to reach his mistress. He swung the poleaxe that he carried, and the Dutchman went down in blood with a cloven skull. The eager lover stepped across the body and came on, his countenance joyously alight.

But mademoiselle was shrinking now, in horror. She was a girl upon the threshold of glorious womanhood, of a fine height and nobly moulded, with heavy coils of glossy black hair above and about a face that was of the colour of old ivory. Her countenance was cast in lines of arrogance, stressed by the low lids of her full dark eyes.

In a bound her well-beloved was beside her, flinging away his bloody poleaxe, he opened wide his arms to enfold her. But she still shrank even within his embrace, which would not be denied; a look of dread had come to temper the normal arrogance of her almost perfect face.

"Mine, mine at last, and in spite of all!" he cried exultantly, theatrically, truly heroic.

But she, endeavouring to thrust him back, her hands against his breast, could only falter: "Why, why did you kill him?"

He laughed, as a hero should; and answered her heroically, with the tolerance of a god for the mortal to whom he condescends: "He stood between us. Let his death be a symbol, a warning. Let all who would stand between us mark it and beware."

It was so splendidly terrific, the gesture of it was so broad and fine and his magnetism so compelling, that she cast her silly tremors and yielded herself freely, intoxicated, to his fond embrace. Thereafter he swung her to his shoulder, and stepping with ease beneath that burden, bore her in a sort of triumph, lustily cheered by his men, to the deck of his own ship. Her inconsiderate brother might have ruined that romantic scene but for the watchful Cahusac, who quietly tripped him up, and then trussed him like a fowl.

Thereafter, what time the Captain languished in his lady's smile within the cabin, Cahusac was dealing with the spoils of war. The Dutch crew was ordered into the longboat, and bidden go to the devil. Fortunately, as they numbered fewer than thirty, the longboat, though perilously overcrowded, could yet contain them. Next, Cahusac having inspected the cargo, put a quartermaster and a score of men aboard the Jongvrow, and left her to follow La Foudre, which he now headed south for the Leeward Islands.

Cahusac was disposed to be ill-humoured. The risk they had run in taking the Dutch brig and doing violence to members of the family of the Governor of Tortuga, was out of all proportion to the value of their prize. He said so, sullenly, to Levasseur.

"You'll keep that opinion to yourself," the Captain answered him. "Don't think I am the man to thrust my neck into a noose, without knowing how I am going to take it out again. I shall send an offer of terms to the Governor of Tortuga that he will be forced to accept. Set a course for the Virgen Magra. We'll go ashore, and settle things from there. And tell them to fetch that milksop Ogeron to the cabin."

Levasseur went back to the adoring lady.

Thither, too, the lady's brother was presently conducted. The Captain rose to receive him, bending his stalwart height to avoid striking the cabin roof with his head. Mademoiselle rose too.

"Why this?" she asked Levasseur, pointing to her brother's pinioned wrists—the remains of Cahusac's precautions.

"I deplore it," said he. "I desire it to end. Let M. d'Ogeron give me his parole...."

"I give you nothing," flashed the white-faced youth, who did not lack for spirit.

"You see." Levasseur shrugged his deep regret, and mademoiselle turned protesting to her brother.

"Henri, this is foolish! You are not behaving as my friend. You...."

"Little fool," her brother answered her—and the "little" was out of place; she was the taller of the twain. "Little fool, do you think I should be acting as your friend to make terms with this blackguard pirate?"

"Steady, my young cockerel!" Levasseur laughed. But his laugh was not nice.

"Don't you perceive your wicked folly in the harm it has brought already? Lives have been lost—men have died—that this monster might overtake you. And don't you yet realize where you stand—in the power of this beast, of this cur born in a kennel and bred in thieving and murder?"

He might have said more but that Levasseur struck him across the mouth. Levasseur, you see, cared as little as another to hear the truth about himself.

Mademoiselle suppressed a scream, as the youth staggered back under the blow. He came to rest against a bulkhead, and leaned there with bleeding lips. But his spirit was unquenched, and there was a ghastly smile on his white face as his eyes sought his sister's.

"You see," he said simply. "He strikes a man whose hands are bound."

The simple words, and, more than the words, their tone of ineffable disdain, aroused the passion that never slumbered deeply in Levasseur.

"And what should you do, puppy, if your hands were unbound?" He took his prisoner by the breast of his doublet and shook him. "Answer me! What should you do? Tchah! You empty windbag! You...." And then came a torrent of words unknown to mademoiselle, yet of whose foulness her intuitions made her conscious.

With blanched cheeks she stood by the cabin table, and cried out to Levasseur to stop. To obey her, he opened the door, and flung her brother through it.

"Put that rubbish under hatches until I call for it again," he roared, and shut the door.

Composing himself, he turned to the girl again with a deprecatory smile. But no smile answered him from her set face. She had seen her beloved hero's nature in curl-papers, as it were, and she found the spectacle disgusting and terrifying. It recalled the brutal slaughter of the Dutch captain, and suddenly she realized that what her brother had just said of this man was no more than true. Fear growing to panic was written on her face, as she stood there leaning for support against the table.

"Why, sweetheart, what is this?" Levasseur moved towards her. She recoiled before him. There was a smile on his face, a glitter in his eyes that fetched her heart into her throat.

He caught her, as she reached the uttermost limits of the cabin, seized her in his long arms and pulled her to him.

"No, no!" she panted.

"Yes, yes," he mocked her, and his mockery was the most terrible thing of all. He crushed her to him brutally, deliberately hurtful because she resisted, and kissed her whilst she writhed in his embrace. Then, his passion mounting, he grew angry and stripped off the last rag of hero's mask that still may have hung upon his face. "Little fool, did you not hear your brother say that you are in my power? Remember it, and remember that of your own free will you came. I am not the man with whom a woman can play fast and loose. So get sense, my girl, and accept what you have invited." He kissed her again, almost contemptuously, and flung her off. "No more scowls," he said. "You'll be sorry else."

Some one knocked. Cursing the interruption, Levasseur strode off to open. Cahusac stood before him. The Breton's face was grave. He came to report that they had sprung a leak between wind and water, the consequence of damage sustained from one of the Dutchman's shots. In alarm Levasseur went off with him. The leakage was not serious so long as the weather kept fine; but should a storm overtake them it might speedily become so. A man was slung overboard to make a partial stoppage with a sail-cloth, and the pumps were got to work.

Ahead of them a low cloud showed on the horizon, which Cahusac pronounced one of the northernmost of the Virgin Islands.

"We must run for shelter there, and careen her," said Levasseur. "I do not trust this oppressive heat. A storm may catch us before we make land."

"A storm or something else," said Cahusac grimly. "Have you noticed that?" He pointed away to starboard.

Levasseur looked, and caught his breath. Two ships that at the distance seemed of considerable burden were heading towards them some five miles away.

"If they follow us what is to happen?" demanded Cahusac.

"We'll fight whether we're in case to do so or not," swore Levasseur.

"Counsels of despair." Cahusac was contemptuous. To mark it he spat upon the deck. "This comes of going to sea with a lovesick madman. Now, keep your temper, Captain, for the hands will be at the end of theirs if we have trouble as a result of this Dutchman business."

For the remainder of that day Levasseur's thoughts were of anything but love. He remained on deck, his eyes now upon the land, now upon those two slowly gaining ships. To run for the open could avail him nothing, and in his leaky condition would provide an additional danger. He must stand at bay and fight. And then, towards evening, when within three miles of shore and when he was about to give the order to strip for battle, he almost fainted from relief to hear a voice from the crow's-nest above announce that the larger of the two ships was the Arabella. Her companion was presumably a prize.

But the pessimism of Cahusac abated nothing.

"That is but the lesser evil," he growled. "What will Blood say about this Dutchman?"

"Let him say what he pleases." Levasseur laughed in the immensity of his relief.

"And what about the children of the Governor of Tortuga?"

"He must not know."

"He'll come to know in the end."

"Aye, but by then, morbleu, the matter will be settled. I shall have made my peace with the Governor. I tell you I know the way to compel Ogeron to come to terms."

Presently the four vessels lay to off the northern coast of La Virgen Magra, a narrow little island arid and treeless, some twelve miles by three, uninhabited save by birds and turtles and unproductive of anything but salt, of which there were considerable ponds to the south.

Levasseur put off in a boat accompanied by Cahusac and two other officers, and went to visit Captain Blood aboard the Arabella.

"Our brief separation has been mighty profitable," was Captain Blood's greeting. "It's a busy morning we've both had." He was in high good-humour as he led the way to the great cabin for a rendering of accounts.

The tall ship that accompanied the Arabella was a Spanish vessel of twenty-six guns, the Santiago from Puerto Rico with a hundred and twenty thousand weight of cacao, forty thousand pieces of eight, and the value of ten thousand more in jewels. A rich capture of which two fifths under the articles went to Levasseur and his crew. Of the money and jewels a division was made on the spot. The cacao it was agreed should be taken to Tortuga to be sold.

Then it was the turn of Levasseur, and black grew the brow of Captain Blood as the Frenchman's tale was unfolded. At the end he roundly expressed his disapproval. The Dutch were a friendly people whom it was a folly to alienate, particularly for so paltry a matter as these hides and tobacco, which at most would fetch a bare twenty thousand pieces.

But Levasseur answered him, as he had answered Cahusac, that a ship was a ship, and it was ships they needed against their projected enterprise. Perhaps because things had gone well with him that day, Blood ended by shrugging the matter aside. Thereupon Levasseur proposed that the Arabella and her prize should return to Tortuga there to unload the cacao and enlist the further adventurers that could now be shipped. Levasseur meanwhile would effect certain necessary repairs, and then proceeding south, await his admiral at Saltatudos, an island conveniently situated—in the latitude of 11 deg. 11' N.—for their enterprise against Maracaybo.

To Levasseur's relief, Captain Blood not only agreed, but pronounced himself ready to set sail at once.

No sooner had the Arabella departed than Levasseur brought his ships into the lagoon, and set his crew to work upon the erection of temporary quarters ashore for himself, his men, and his enforced guests during the careening and repairing of La Foudre.

At sunset that evening the wind freshened; it grew to a gale, and from that to such a hurricane that Levasseur was thankful to find himself ashore and his ships in safe shelter. He wondered a little how it might be faring with Captain Blood out there at the mercy of that terrific storm; but he did not permit concern to trouble him unduly.

CHAPTER XV. THE RANSOM

In the glory of the following morning, sparkling and clear after the storm, with an invigorating, briny tang in the air from the salt-ponds on the south of the island, a curious scene was played on the beach of the Virgen Magra, at the foot of a ridge of bleached dunes, beside the spread of sail from which Levasseur had improvised a tent.

Enthroned upon an empty cask sat the French filibuster to transact important business: the business of making himself safe with the Governor of Tortuga.

A guard of honour of a half-dozen officers hung about him; five of them were rude boucan-hunters, in stained jerkins and leather breeches; the sixth was Cahusac. Before him, guarded by two half-naked negroes, stood young d'Ogeron, in frilled shirt and satin small-clothes and fine shoes of Cordovan leather. He was stripped of doublet, and his hands were tied behind him. The young gentleman's comely face was haggard. Near at hand, and also under guard, but unpinioned, mademoiselle his sister sat hunched upon a hillock of sand. She was very pale, and it was in vain that she sought to veil in a mask of arrogance the fears by which she was assailed.

Levasseur addressed himself to M. d'Ogeron. He spoke at long length. In the end—

"I trust, monsieur," said he, with mock suavity, "that I have made myself quite clear. So that there may be no misunderstandings, I will recapitulate. Your ransom is fixed at twenty thousand pieces of eight, and you shall have liberty on parole to go to Tortuga to collect it. In fact, I shall provide the means to convey you thither, and you shall have a month in which to come and go. Meanwhile, your sister remains with me as a hostage. Your father should not consider such a sum excessive as the price of his son's liberty and to provide a dowry for his daughter. Indeed, if anything, I am too modest, pardi! M. d'Ogeron is reputed a wealthy man."

M. d'Ogeron the younger raised his head and looked the Captain boldly in the face.

"I refuse—utterly and absolutely, do you understand? So do your worst, and be damned for a filthy pirate without decency and without honour."

"But what words!" laughed Levasseur. "What heat and what foolishness! You have not considered the alternative. When you do, you will not persist in your refusal. You will not do that in any case. We have spurs for the reluctant. And I warn you against giving me your parole under stress, and afterwards playing me false. I shall know how to find and punish you. Meanwhile, remember your sister's honour is in pawn to me. Should you forget to return with the dowry, you will not consider it unreasonable that I forget to marry her."

Levasseur's smiling eyes, intent upon the young man's face, saw the horror that crept into his glance. M. d'Ogeron cast a wild glance at mademoiselle, and observed the grey despair that had almost stamped the beauty from her face. Disgust and fury swept across his countenance.

Then he braced himself and answered resolutely:

"No, you dog! A thousand times, no!"

"You are foolish to persist." Levasseur spoke without anger, with a coldly mocking regret. His fingers had been busy tying knots in a length of whipcord. He held it up. "You know this? It is a rosary of pain that has wrought the conversion of many a stubborn heretic. It is capable of screwing the eyes out of a man's head by way of helping him to see reason. As you please."

He flung the length of knotted cord to one of the negroes, who in an instant made it fast about the prisoner's brows. Then between cord and cranium the black inserted a short length of metal, round and slender as a pipe-stem. That done he rolled his eyes towards Levasseur, awaiting the Captain's signal.

Levasseur considered his victim, and beheld him tense and braced, his haggard face of a leaden hue, beads of perspiration glinting on his pallid brow just beneath the whipcord.

Mademoiselle cried out, and would have risen: but her guards restrained her, and she sank down again, moaning.

"I beg that you will spare yourself and your sister," said the Captain, "by being reasonable. What, after all, is the sum I have named? To your wealthy father a bagatelle. I repeat, I have been too modest. But since I have said twenty thousand pieces of eight, twenty thousand pieces it shall be."

"And for what, if you please, have you said twenty thousand pieces of eight?"

In execrable French, but in a voice that was crisp and pleasant, seeming to echo some of the mockery that had invested Levasseur's, that question floated over their heads.

Startled, Levasseur and his officers looked up and round. On the crest of the dunes behind them, in sharp silhouette against the deep cobalt of the sky, they beheld a tall, lean figure scrupulously dressed in black with silver lace, a crimson ostrich plume curled about the broad brim of his hat affording the only touch of colour. Under that hat was the tawny face of Captain Blood.

Levasseur gathered himself up with an oath of amazement. He had conceived Captain Blood by now well below the horizon, on his way to Tortuga, assuming him to have been so fortunate as to have weathered last night's storm.

Launching himself upon the yielding sand, into which he sank to the level of the calves of his fine boots of Spanish leather, Captain Blood came sliding erect to the beach. He was followed by Wolverstone, and a dozen others. As he came to a standstill, he doffed his hat, with a flourish, to the lady. Then he turned to Levasseur.

"Good-morning, my Captain," said he, and proceeded to explain his presence. "It was last night's hurricane compelled our return. We had no choice but to ride before it with stripped poles, and it drove us back the way we had gone. Moreover—as the devil would have it!—the Santiago sprang her mainmast; and so I was glad to put into a cove on the west of the island a couple of miles away, and we've walked across to stretch our legs, and to give you good-day. But who are these?" And he designated the man and the woman.

Cahusac shrugged his shoulders, and tossed his long arms to heaven.

"Voila!" said he, pregnantly, to the firmament.

Levasseur gnawed his lip, and changed colour. But he controlled himself to answer civilly:

"As you see, two prisoners."

"Ah! Washed ashore in last night's gale, eh?"

"Not so." Levasseur contained himself with difficulty before that irony. "They were in the Dutch brig."

"I don't remember that you mentioned them before."

"I did not. They are prisoners of my own—a personal matter. They are French."

"French!" Captain Blood's light eyes stabbed at Levasseur, then at the prisoners.

M. d'Ogeron stood tense and braced as before, but the grey horror had left his face. Hope had leapt within him at this interruption, obviously as little expected by his tormentor as by himself. His sister, moved by a similar intuition, was leaning forward with parted lips and gaping eyes.

Captain Blood fingered his lip, and frowned thoughtfully upon Levasseur.

"Yesterday you surprised me by making war upon the friendly Dutch. But now it seems that not even your own countrymen are safe from you."

"Have I not said that these... that this is a matter personal to me?"

"Ah! And their names?"

Captain Blood's crisp, authoritative, faintly disdainful manner stirred Levasseur's quick anger. The blood crept slowly back into his blenched face, and his glance grew in insolence, almost in menace. Meanwhile the prisoner answered for him.

"I am Henri d'Ogeron, and this is my sister."

"D'Ogeron?" Captain Blood stared. "Are you related by chance to my good friend the Governor of Tortuga?"

"He is my father."

Levasseur swung aside with an imprecation. In Captain Blood, amazement for the moment quenched every other emotion.

"The saints preserve us now! Are you quite mad, Levasseur? First you molest the Dutch, who are our friends; next you take prisoners two persons that are French, your own countrymen; and now, faith, they're no less than the children of the Governor of Tortuga, which is the one safe place of shelter that we enjoy in these islands...."

Levasseur broke in angrily:

"Must I tell you again that it is a matter personal to me? I make myself alone responsible to the Governor of Tortuga."

"And the twenty thousand pieces of eight? Is that also a matter personal to you?"

"It is."

"Now I don't agree with you at all." Captain Blood sat down on the cask that Levasseur had lately occupied, and looked up blandly. "I may inform you, to save time, that I heard the entire proposal that you made to this lady and this gentleman, and I'll also remind you that we sail under articles that admit no ambiguities. You have fixed their ransom at twenty thousand pieces of eight. That sum then belongs to your crews and mine in the proportions by the articles established. You'll hardly wish to dispute it. But what is far more grave is that you have concealed from me this part of the prizes taken on your last cruise, and for such an offence as that the articles provide certain penalties that are something severe in character."

"Ho, ho!" laughed Levasseur unpleasantly. Then added: "If you dislike my conduct we can dissolve the association."

"That is my intention. But we'll dissolve it when and in the manner that I choose, and that will be as soon as you have satisfied the articles under which we sailed upon this cruise.

"What do you mean?"

"I'll be as short as I can," said Captain Blood. "I'll waive for the moment the unseemliness of making war upon the Dutch, of taking French prisoners, and of provoking the anger of the Governor of Tortuga. I'll accept the situation as I find it. Yourself you've fixed the ransom of this couple at twenty thousand pieces, and, as I gather, the lady is to be your perquisite. But why should she be your perquisite more than another's, seeing that she belongs by the articles to all of us, as a prize of war?"

Black as thunder grew the brow of Levasseur.

"However," added Captain Blood, "I'll not dispute her to you if you are prepared to buy her."

"Buy her?"

"At the price you have set upon her."

Levasseur contained his rage, that he might reason with the Irishman. "That is the ransom of the man. It is to be paid for him by the Governor of Tortuga."

"No, no. Ye've parcelled the twain together—very oddly, I confess. Ye've set their value at twenty thousand pieces, and for that sum you may have them, since you desire it; but you'll pay for them the twenty thousand pieces that are ultimately to come to you as the ransom of one and the dowry of the other; and that sum shall be divided among our crews. So that you do that, it is conceivable that our followers may take a lenient view of your breach of the articles we jointly signed."

Levasseur laughed savagely. "Ah ca! Credieu! The good jest!"

"I quite agree with you," said Captain Blood.

To Levasseur the jest lay in that Captain Blood, with no more than a dozen followers, should come there attempting to hector him who had a hundred men within easy call. But it seemed that he had left out of his reckoning something which his opponent had counted in. For as, laughing still, Levasseur swung to his officers, he saw that which choked the laughter in his throat. Captain Blood had shrewdly played upon the cupidity that was the paramount inspiration of those adventurers. And Levasseur now read clearly on their faces how completely they adopted Captain Blood's suggestion that all must participate in the ransom which their leader had thought to appropriate to himself.

It gave the gaudy ruffian pause, and whilst in his heart he cursed those followers of his, who could be faithful only to their greed, he perceived—and only just in time—that he had best tread warily.

"You misunderstand," he said, swallowing his rage. "The ransom is for division, when it comes. The girl, meanwhile, is mine on that understanding."

"Good!" grunted Cahusac. "On that understanding all arranges itself."

"You think so?" said Captain Blood. "But if M. d'Ogeron should refuse to pay the ransom? What then?" He laughed, and got lazily to his feet. "No, no. If Captain Levasseur is meanwhile to keep the girl, as he proposes, then let him pay this ransom, and be his the risk if it should afterwards not be forthcoming."

"That's it!" cried one of Levasseur's officers. And Cahusac added: "It's reasonable, that! Captain Blood is right. It is in the articles."

"What is in the articles, you fools?" Levasseur was in danger of losing his head. "Sacre Dieu! Where do you suppose that I have twenty thousand pieces? My whole share of the prizes of this cruise does not come to half that sum. I'll be your debtor until I've earned it. Will that content you?"

All things considered, there is not a doubt that it would have done so had not Captain Blood intended otherwise.

"And if you should die before you have earned it? Ours is a calling fraught with risks, my Captain."

"Damn you!" Levasseur flung upon him livid with fury. "Will nothing satisfy you?"

"Oh, but yes. Twenty thousand pieces of eight for immediate division."

"I haven't got it."

"Then let some one buy the prisoners who has."

"And who do you suppose has it if I have not?"

"I have," said Captain Blood.

"You have!" Levasseur's mouth fell open. "You... you want the girl?"

"Why not? And I exceed you in gallantry in that I will make sacrifices to obtain her, and in honesty in that I am ready to pay for what I want."

Levasseur stared at him foolishly agape. Behind him pressed his officers, gaping also.

Captain Blood sat down again on the cask, and drew from an inner pocket of his doublet a little leather bag. "I am glad to be able to resolve a difficulty that at one moment seemed insoluble." And under the bulging eyes of Levasseur and his officers, he untied the mouth of the bag and rolled into his left palm four or five pearls each of the size of a sparrow's egg. There were twenty such in the bag, the very pick of those taken in that raid upon the pearl fleet. "You boast a knowledge of pearls, Cahusac. At what do you value this?"

The Breton took between coarse finger and thumb the proffered lustrous, delicately iridescent sphere, his shrewd eyes appraising it.

"A thousand pieces," he answered shortly.

"It will fetch rather more in Tortuga or Jamaica," said Captain Blood, "and twice as much in Europe. But I'll accept your valuation. They are almost of a size, as you can see. Here are twelve, representing twelve thousand pieces of eight, which is La Foudre's share of three fifths of the prize, as provided by the articles. For the eight thousand pieces that go to the Arabella, I make myself responsible to my own men. And now, Wolverstone, if you please, will you take my property aboard the Arabella?" He stood up again, indicating the prisoners.

"Ah, no!" Levasseur threw wide the floodgates of his fury. "Ah, that, no, by example! You shall not take her...." He would have sprung upon Captain Blood, who stood aloof, alert, tight-lipped, and watchful.

But it was one of Levasseur's own officers who hindered him.

"Nom de Dieu, my Captain! What will you do? It is settled; honourably settled with satisfaction to all."

"To all?" blazed Levasseur. "Ah ca! To all of you, you animals! But what of me?"

Cahusac, with the pearls clutched in his capacious hand, stepped up to him on the other side. "Don't be a fool, Captain. Do you want to provoke trouble between the crews? His men outnumber us by nearly two to one. What's a girl more or less? In Heaven's name, let her go. He's paid handsomely for her, and dealt fairly with us."

"Dealt fairly?" roared the infuriated Captain. "You...." In all his foul vocabulary he could find no epithet to describe his lieutenant. He caught him a blow that almost sent him sprawling. The pearls were scattered in the sand.

Cahusac dived after them, his fellows with him. Vengeance must wait. For some moments they groped there on hands and knees, oblivious of all else. And yet in those moments vital things were happening.

Levasseur, his hand on his sword, his face a white mask of rage, was confronting Captain Blood to hinder his departure.

"You do not take her while I live!" he cried.

"Then I'll take her when you're dead," said Captain Blood, and his own blade flashed in the sunlight. "The articles provide that any man of whatever rank concealing any part of a prize, be it of the value of no more than a peso, shall be hanged at the yardarm. It's what I intended for you in the end. But since ye prefer it this way, ye muckrake, faith, I'll be humouring you."

He waved away the men who would have interfered, and the blades rang together.

M. d'Ogeron looked on, a man bemused, unable to surmise what the issue either way could mean for him. Meanwhile, two of Blood's men who had taken the place of the Frenchman's negro guards, had removed the crown of whipcord from his brow. As for mademoiselle, she had risen, and was leaning forward, a hand pressed tightly to her heaving breast, her face deathly pale, a wild terror in her eyes.

It was soon over. The brute strength, upon which Levasseur so confidently counted, could avail nothing against the Irishman's practised skill. When, with both lungs transfixed, he lay prone on the white sand, coughing out his rascally life, Captain Blood looked calmly at Cahusac across the body.

"I think that cancels the articles between us," he said. With soulless, cynical eyes Cahusac considered the twitching body of his recent leader. Had Levasseur been a man of different temper, the affair might have ended in a very different manner. But, then, it is certain that Captain Blood would have adopted in dealing with him different tactics. As it was, Levasseur commanded neither love nor loyalty. The men who followed him were the very dregs of that vile trade, and cupidity was their only inspiration. Upon that cupidity Captain Blood had deftly played, until he had brought them to find Levasseur guilty of the one offence they deemed unpardonable, the crime of appropriating to himself something which might be converted into gold and shared amongst them all.

Thus now the threatening mob of buccaneers that came hastening to the theatre of that swift tragi-comedy were appeased by a dozen words of Cahusac's.

Whilst still they hesitated, Blood added something to quicken their decision.

"If you will come to our anchorage, you shall receive at once your share of the booty of the Santiago, that you may dispose of it as you please."

They crossed the island, the two prisoners accompanying them, and later that day, the division made, they would have parted company but that Cahusac, at the instances of the men who had elected him Levasseur's successor, offered Captain Blood anew the services of that French contingent.

"If you will sail with me again," the Captain answered him, "you may do so on the condition that you make your peace with the Dutch, and restore the brig and her cargo."

The condition was accepted, and Captain Blood went off to find his guests, the children of the Governor of Tortuga.

Mademoiselle d'Ogeron and her brother—the latter now relieved of his bonds—sat in the great cabin of the Arabella, whither they had been conducted.

Wine and food had been placed upon the table by Benjamin, Captain Blood's negro steward and cook, who had intimated to them that it was for their entertainment. But it had remained untouched. Brother and sister sat there in agonized bewilderment, conceiving that their escape was but from frying-pan to fire. At length, overwrought by the suspense, mademoiselle flung herself upon her knees before her brother to implore his pardon for all the evil brought upon them by her wicked folly.

M. d'Ogeron was not in a forgiving mood.

"I am glad that at least you realize what you have done. And now this other filibuster has bought you, and you belong to him. You realize that, too, I hope."

He might have said more, but he checked upon perceiving that the door was opening. Captain Blood, coming from settling matters with the followers of Levasseur, stood on the threshold. M. d'Ogeron had not troubled to restrain his high-pitched voice, and the Captain had overheard the Frenchman's last two sentences. Therefore he perfectly understood why mademoiselle should bound up at sight of him, and shrink back in fear.

"Mademoiselle," said he in his vile but fluent French, "I beg you to dismiss your fears. Aboard this ship you shall be treated with all honour. So soon as we are in case to put to sea again, we steer a course for Tortuga to take you home to your father. And pray do not consider that I have bought you, as your brother has just said. All that I have done has been to provide the ransom necessary to bribe a gang of scoundrels to depart from obedience to the arch-scoundrel who commanded them, and so deliver you from all peril. Count it, if you please, a friendly loan to be repaid entirely at your convenience."

Mademoiselle stared at him in unbelief. M. d'Ogeron rose to his feet.

"Monsieur, is it possible that you are serious?"

"I am. It may not happen often nowadays. I may be a pirate. But my ways are not the ways of Levasseur, who should have stayed in Europe, and practised purse-cutting. I have a sort of honour—shall we say, some rags of honour?—remaining me from better days." Then on a brisker note he added: "We dine in an hour, and I trust that you will honour my table with your company. Meanwhile, Benjamin will see, monsieur, that you are more suitably provided in the matter of wardrobe."

He bowed to them, and turned to depart again, but mademoiselle detained him.

"Monsieur!" she cried sharply.

He checked and turned, whilst slowly she approached him, regarding him between dread and wonder.

"Oh, you are noble!"

"I shouldn't put it as high as that myself," said he.

"You are, you are! And it is but right that you should know all."

"Madelon!" her brother cried out, to restrain her.

But she would not be restrained. Her surcharged heart must overflow in confidence.

"Monsieur, for what befell I am greatly at fault. This man—this Levasseur...."

He stared, incredulous in his turn. "My God! Is it possible? That animal!"

Abruptly she fell on her knees, caught his hand and kissed it before he could wrench it from her.

"What do you do?" he cried.

"An amende. In my mind I dishonoured you by deeming you his like, by conceiving your fight with Levasseur a combat between jackals. On my knees, monsieur, I implore you to forgive me."

Captain Blood looked down upon her, and a smile broke on his lips, irradiating the blue eyes that looked so oddly light in that tawny face.

"Why, child," said he, "I might find it hard to forgive you the stupidity of having thought otherwise."

As he handed her to her feet again, he assured himself that he had behaved rather well in the affair. Then he sighed. That dubious fame of his that had spread so quickly across the Caribbean would by now have reached the ears of Arabella Bishop. That she would despise him, he could not doubt, deeming him no better than all the other scoundrels who drove this villainous buccaneering trade. Therefore he hoped that some echo of this deed might reach her also, and be set by her against some of that contempt. For the whole truth, which he withheld from Mademoiselle d'Ogeron, was that in venturing his life to save her, he had been driven by the thought that the deed must be pleasing in the eyes of Miss Bishop could she but witness it.

CHAPTER XVI. THE TRAP

That affair of Mademoiselle d'Ogeron bore as its natural fruit an improvement in the already cordial relations between Captain Blood and the Governor of Tortuga. At the fine stone house, with its green-jalousied windows, which M. d'Ogeron had built himself in a spacious and luxuriant garden to the east of Cayona, the Captain became a very welcome guest. M. d'Ogeron was in the Captain's debt for more than the twenty thousand pieces of eight which he had provided for mademoiselle's ransom; and shrewd, hard bargain-driver though he might be, the Frenchman could be generous and understood the sentiment of gratitude. This he now proved in every possible way, and under his powerful protection the credit of Captain Blood among the buccaneers very rapidly reached its zenith.

So when it came to fitting out his fleet for that enterprise against Maracaybo, which had originally been Levasseur's project, he did not want for either ships or men to follow him. He recruited five hundred adventurers in all, and he might have had as many thousands if he could have offered them accommodation. Similarly without difficulty he might have increased his fleet to twice its strength of ships but that he preferred to keep it what it was. The three vessels to which he confined it were the Arabella, the La Foudre, which Cahusac now commanded with a contingent of some sixscore Frenchmen, and the Santiago, which had been refitted and rechristened the Elizabeth, after that Queen of England whose seamen had humbled Spain as Captain Blood now hoped to humble it again. Hagthorpe, in virtue of his service in the navy, was appointed by Blood to command her, and the appointment was confirmed by the men.

It was some months after the rescue of Mademoiselle d'Ogeron—in August of that year 1687—that this little fleet, after some minor adventures which I pass over in silence, sailed into the great lake of Maracaybo and effected its raid upon that opulent city of the Main.

The affair did not proceed exactly as was hoped, and Blood's force came to find itself in a precarious position. This is best explained in the words employed by Cahusac—which Pitt has carefully recorded—in the course of an altercation that broke out on the steps of the Church of Nuestra Senora del Carmen, which Captain Blood had impiously appropriated for the purpose of a corps-de-garde. I have said already that he was a papist only when it suited him.

The dispute was being conducted by Hagthorpe, Wolverstone, and Pitt on the one side, and Cahusac, out of whose uneasiness it all arose, on the other. Behind them in the sun-scorched, dusty square, sparsely fringed by palms, whose fronds drooped listlessly in the quivering heat, surged a couple of hundred wild fellows belonging to both parties, their own excitement momentarily quelled so that they might listen to what passed among their leaders.

Cahusac appeared to be having it all his own way, and he raised his harsh, querulous voice so that all might hear his truculent denunciation. He spoke, Pitt tells us, a dreadful kind of English, which the shipmaster, however, makes little attempt to reproduce. His dress was as discordant as his speech. It was of a kind to advertise his trade, and ludicrously in contrast with the sober garb of Hagthorpe and the almost foppish daintiness of Jeremy Pitt. His soiled and blood-stained shirt of blue cotton was open in front, to cool his hairy breast, and the girdle about the waist of his leather breeches carried an arsenal of pistols and a knife, whilst a cutlass hung from a leather baldrick loosely slung about his body; above his countenance, broad and flat as a Mongolian's, a red scarf was swathed, turban-wise, about his head.

"Is it that I have not warned you from the beginning that all was too easy?" he demanded between plaintiveness and fury. "I am no fool, my friends. I have eyes, me. And I see. I see an abandoned fort at the entrance of the lake, and nobody there to fire a gun at us when we came in. Then I suspect the trap. Who would not that had eyes and brain? Bah! we come on. What do we find? A city, abandoned like the fort; a city out of which the people have taken all things of value. Again I warn Captain Blood. It is a trap, I say. We are to come on; always to come on, without opposition, until we find that it is too late to go to sea again, that we cannot go back at all. But no one will listen to me. You all know so much more. Name of God! Captain Blood, he will go on, and we go on. We go to Gibraltar. True that at last, after long time, we catch the Deputy-Governor; true, we make him pay big ransom for Gibraltar; true between that ransom and the loot we return here with some two thousand pieces of eight. But what is it, in reality, will you tell me? Or shall I tell you? It is a piece of cheese—a piece of cheese in a mousetrap, and we are the little mice. Goddam! And the cats—oh, the cats they wait for us! The cats are those four Spanish ships of war that have come meantime. And they wait for us outside the bottle-neck of this lagoon. Mort de Dieu! That is what comes of the damned obstinacy of your fine Captain Blood."

Wolverstone laughed. Cahusac exploded in fury.

"Ah, sangdieu! Tu ris, animal? You laugh! Tell me this: How do we get out again unless we accept the terms of Monsieur the Admiral of Spain?"

From the buccaneers at the foot of the steps came an angry rumble of approval. The single eye of the gigantic Wolverstone rolled terribly, and he clenched his great fists as if to strike the Frenchman, who was exposing them to mutiny. But Cahusac was not daunted. The mood of the men enheartened him.

"You think, perhaps, this your Captain Blood is the good God. That he can make miracles, eh? He is ridiculous, you know, this Captain Blood; with his grand air and his...."

He checked. Out of the church at that moment, grand air and all, sauntered Peter Blood. With him came a tough, long-legged French sea-wolf named Yberville, who, though still young, had already won fame as a privateer commander before the loss of his own ship had driven him to take service under Blood. The Captain advanced towards that disputing group, leaning lightly upon his long ebony cane, his face shaded by a broad-plumed hat. There was in his appearance nothing of the buccaneer. He had much more the air of a lounger in the Mall or the Alameda—the latter rather, since his elegant suit of violet taffetas with gold-embroidered button-holes was in the Spanish fashion. But the long, stout, serviceable rapier, thrust up behind by the left hand resting lightly on the pummel, corrected the impression. That and those steely eyes of his announced the adventurer.

"You find me ridiculous, eh, Cahusac?" said he, as he came to a halt before the Breton, whose anger seemed already to have gone out of him. "What, then, must I find you?" He spoke quietly, almost wearily. "You will be telling them that we have delayed, and that it is the delay that has brought about our danger. But whose is the fault of that delay? We have been a month in doing what should have been done, and what but for your blundering would have been done, inside of a week.'"

"Ah ca! Nom de Dieu! Was it my fault that...."

"Was it any one else's fault that you ran your ship La Foudre aground on the shoal in the middle of the lake? You would not be piloted. You knew your way. You took no soundings even. The result was that we lost three precious days in getting canoes to bring off your men and your gear. Those three days gave the folk at Gibraltar not only time to hear of our coming, but time in which to get away. After that, and because of it, we had to follow the Governor to his infernal island fortress, and a fortnight and best part of a hundred lives were lost in reducing it. That's how we come to have delayed until this Spanish fleet is fetched round from La Guayra by a guarda-costa; and if ye hadn't lost La Foudre, and so reduced our fleet from three ships to two, we should even now be able to fight our way through with a reasonable hope of succeeding. Yet you think it is for you to come hectoring here, upbraiding us for a situation that is just the result of your own ineptitude."

He spoke with a restraint which I trust you will agree was admirable when I tell you that the Spanish fleet guarding the bottle-neck exit of the great Lake of Maracaybo, and awaiting there the coming forth of Captain Blood with a calm confidence based upon its overwhelming strength, was commanded by his implacable enemy, Don Miguel de Espinosa y Valdez, the Admiral of Spain. In addition to his duty to his country, the Admiral had, as you know, a further personal incentive arising out of that business aboard the Encarnacion a year ago, and the death of his brother Don Diego; and with him sailed his nephew Esteban, whose vindictive zeal exceeded the Admiral's own.

Yet, knowing all this, Captain Blood could preserve his calm in reproving the cowardly frenzy of one for whom the situation had not half the peril with which it was fraught for himself. He turned from Cahusac to address the mob of buccaneers, who had surged nearer to hear him, for he had not troubled to raise his voice. "I hope that will correct some of the misapprehension that appears to have been disturbing you," said he.

"There's no good can come of talking of what's past and done," cried Cahusac, more sullen now than truculent. Whereupon Wolverstone laughed, a laugh that was like the neighing of a horse. "The question is: what are we to do now?"

"Sure, now, there's no question at all," said Captain Blood.

"Indeed, but there is," Cahusac insisted. "Don Miguel, the Spanish Admiral, have offer us safe passage to sea if we will depart at once, do no damage to the town, release our prisoners, and surrender all that we took at Gibraltar."

Captain Blood smiled quietly, knowing precisely how much Don Miguel's word was worth. It was Yberville who replied, in manifest scorn of his compatriot:

"Which argues that, even at this disadvantage as he has us, the Spanish Admiral is still afraid of us."

"That can be only because he not know our real weakness," was the fierce retort. "And, anyway, we must accept these terms. We have no choice. That is my opinion."

"Well, it's not mine, now," said Captain Blood. "So, I've refused them."

"Refuse'!" Cahusac's broad face grew purple. A muttering from the men behind enheartened him. "You have refuse'? You have refuse' already—and without consulting me?"

"Your disagreement could have altered nothing. You'd have been outvoted, for Hagthorpe here was entirely of my own mind. Still," he went on, "if you and your own French followers wish to avail yourselves of the Spaniard's terms, we shall not hinder you. Send one of your prisoners to announce it to the Admiral. Don Miguel will welcome your decision, you may be sure."

Cahusac glowered at him in silence for a moment. Then, having controlled himself, he asked in a concentrated voice:

"Precisely what answer have you make to the Admiral?"

A smile irradiated the face and eyes of Captain Blood. "I have answered him that unless within four-and-twenty hours we have his parole to stand out to sea, ceasing to dispute our passage or hinder our departure, and a ransom of fifty thousand pieces of eight for Maracaybo, we shall reduce this beautiful city to ashes, and thereafter go out and destroy his fleet."

The impudence of it left Cahusac speechless. But among the English buccaneers in the square there were many who savoured the audacious humour of the trapped dictating terms to the trappers. Laughter broke from them. It spread into a roar of acclamation; for bluff is a weapon dear to every adventurer. Presently, when they understood it, even Cahusac's French followers were carried off their feet by that wave of jocular enthusiasm, until in his truculent obstinacy Cahusac remained the only dissentient. He withdrew in mortification. Nor was he to be mollified until the following day brought him his revenge. This came in the shape of a messenger from Don Miguel with a letter in which the Spanish Admiral solemnly vowed to God that, since the pirates had refused his magnanimous offer to permit them to surrender with the honours of war, he would now await them at the mouth of the lake there to destroy them on their coming forth. He added that should they delay their departure, he would so soon as he was reenforced by a fifth ship, the Santo Nino, on its way to join him from La Guayra, himself come inside to seek them at Maracaybo.

This time Captain Blood was put out of temper.

"Trouble me no more," he snapped at Cahusac, who came growling to him again. "Send word to Don Miguel that you have seceded from me. He'll give you safe conduct, devil a doubt. Then take one of the sloops, order your men aboard and put to sea, and the devil go with you."

Cahusac would certainly have adopted that course if only his men had been unanimous in the matter. They, however, were torn between greed and apprehension. If they went they must abandon their share of the plunder, which was considerable, as well as the slaves and other prisoners they had taken. If they did this, and Captain Blood should afterwards contrive to get away unscathed—and from their knowledge of his resourcefulness, the thing, however unlikely, need not be impossible—he must profit by that which they now relinquished. This was a contingency too bitter for contemplation. And so, in the end, despite all that Cahusac could say, the surrender was not to Don Miguel, but to Peter Blood. They had come into the venture with him, they asserted, and they would go out of it with him or not at all. That was the message he received from them that same evening by the sullen mouth of Cahusac himself.

He welcomed it, and invited the Breton to sit down and join the council which was even then deliberating upon the means to be employed. This council occupied the spacious patio of the Governor's house—which Captain Blood had appropriated to his own uses—a cloistered stone quadrangle in the middle of which a fountain played coolly under a trellis of vine. Orange-trees grew on two sides of it, and the still, evening air was heavy with the scent of them. It was one of those pleasant exterior-interiors which Moorish architects had introduced to Spain and the Spaniards had carried with them to the New World.

Here that council of war, composed of six men in all, deliberated until late that night upon the plan of action which Captain Blood put forward.

The great freshwater lake of Maracaybo, nourished by a score of rivers from the snow-capped ranges that surround it on two sides, is some hundred and twenty miles in length and almost the same distance across at its widest. It is—as has been indicated—in the shape of a great bottle having its neck towards the sea at Maracaybo.

Beyond this neck it widens again, and then the two long, narrow strips of land known as the islands of Vigilias and Palomas block the channel, standing lengthwise across it. The only passage out to sea for vessels of any draught lies in the narrow strait between these islands. Palomas, which is some ten miles in length, is unapproachable for half a mile on either side by any but the shallowest craft save at its eastern end, where, completely commanding the narrow passage out to sea, stands the massive fort which the buccaneers had found deserted upon their coming. In the broader water between this passage and the bar, the four Spanish ships were at anchor in mid-channel. The Admiral's Encarnacion, which we already know, was a mighty galleon of forty-eight great guns and eight small. Next in importance was the Salvador with thirty-six guns; the other two, the Infanta and the San Felipe, though smaller vessels, were still formidable enough with their twenty guns and a hundred and fifty men apiece.

Such was the fleet of which the gauntlet was to be run by Captain Blood with his own Arabella of forty guns, the Elizabeth of twenty-six, and two sloops captured at Gibraltar, which they had indifferently armed with four culverins each. In men they had a bare four hundred survivors of the five hundred-odd that had left Tortuga, to oppose to fully a thousand Spaniards manning the galleons.

The plan of action submitted by Captain Blood to that council was a desperate one, as Cahusac uncompromisingly pronounced it.

"Why, so it is," said the Captain. "But I've done things more desperate." Complacently he pulled at a pipe that was loaded with that fragrant Sacerdotes tobacco for which Gibraltar was famous, and of which they had brought away some hogsheads. "And what is more, they've succeeded. Audaces fortuna juvat. Bedad, they knew their world, the old Romans."

He breathed into his companions and even into Cahusac some of his own spirit of confidence, and in confidence all went busily to work. For three days from sunrise to sunset, the buccaneers laboured and sweated to complete the preparations for the action that was to procure them their deliverance. Time pressed. They must strike before Don Miguel de Espinosa received the reenforcement of that fifth galleon, the Santo Nino, which was coming to join him from La Guayra.

Their principal operations were on the larger of the two sloops captured at Gibraltar; to which vessel was assigned the leading part in Captain Blood's scheme. They began by tearing down all bulkheads, until they had reduced her to the merest shell, and in her sides they broke open so many ports that her gunwale was converted into the semblance of a grating. Next they increased by a half-dozen the scuttles in her deck, whilst into her hull they packed all the tar and pitch and brimstone that they could find in the town, to which they added six barrels of gunpowder, placed on end like guns at the open ports on her larboard side. On the evening of the fourth day, everything being now in readiness, all were got aboard, and the empty, pleasant city of Maracaybo was at last abandoned. But they did not weigh anchor until some two hours after midnight. Then, at last, on the first of the ebb, they drifted silently down towards the bar with all canvas furled save only their spiltsails, which, so as to give them steering way, were spread to the faint breeze that stirred through the purple darkness of the tropical night.

The order of their going was as follows: Ahead went the improvised fire-ship in charge of Wolverstone, with a crew of six volunteers, each of whom was to have a hundred pieces of eight over and above his share of plunder as a special reward. Next came the Arabella. She was followed at a distance by the Elizabeth, commanded by Hagthorpe, with whom was the now shipless Cahusac and the bulk of his French followers. The rear was brought up by the second sloop and some eight canoes, aboard of which had been shipped the prisoners, the slaves, and most of the captured merchandise. The prisoners were all pinioned, and guarded by four buccaneers with musketoons who manned these boats in addition to the two fellows who were to sail them. Their place was to be in the rear and they were to take no part whatever in the coming fight.

As the first glimmerings of opalescent dawn dissolved the darkness, the straining eyes of the buccaneers were able to make out the tall rigging of the Spanish vessels, riding at anchor less than a quarter of a mile ahead. Entirely without suspicion as the Spaniards were, and rendered confident by their own overwhelming strength, it is unlikely that they used a vigilance keener than their careless habit. Certain it is that they did not sight Blood's fleet in that dim light until some time after Blood's fleet had sighted them. By the time that they had actively roused themselves, Wolverstone's sloop was almost upon them, speeding under canvas which had been crowded to her yards the moment the galleons had loomed into view.

Straight for the Admiral's great ship, the Encarnacion, did Wolverstone head the sloop; then, lashing down the helm, he kindled from a match that hung ready lighted beside him a great torch of thickly plaited straw that had been steeped in bitumen. First it glowed, then as he swung it round his head, it burst into flame, just as the slight vessel went crashing and bumping and scraping against the side of the flagship, whilst rigging became tangled with rigging, to the straining of yards and snapping of spars overhead. His six men stood at their posts on the larboard side, stark naked, each armed with a grapnel, four of them on the gunwale, two of them aloft. At the moment of impact these grapnels were slung to bind the Spaniard to them, those aloft being intended to complete and preserve the entanglement of the rigging.

Aboard the rudely awakened galleon all was confused hurrying, scurrying, trumpeting, and shouting. At first there had been a desperately hurried attempt to get up the anchor; but this was abandoned as being already too late; and conceiving themselves on the point of being boarded, the Spaniards stood to arms to ward off the onslaught. Its slowness in coming intrigued them, being so different from the usual tactics of the buccaneers. Further intrigued were they by the sight of the gigantic Wolverstone speeding naked along his deck with a great flaming torch held high. Not until he had completed his work did they begin to suspect the truth—that he was lighting slow-matches—and then one of their officers rendered reckless by panic ordered a boarding-party on to the shop.

The order came too late. Wolverstone had seen his six fellows drop overboard after the grapnels were fixed, and then had sped, himself, to the starboard gunwale. Thence he flung his flaming torch down the nearest gaping scuttle into the hold, and thereupon dived overboard in his turn, to be picked up presently by the longboat from the Arabella. But before that happened the sloop was a thing of fire, from which explosions were hurling blazing combustibles aboard the Encarnacion, and long tongues of flame were licking out to consume the galleon, beating back those daring Spaniards who, too late, strove desperately to cut her adrift.

And whilst the most formidable vessel of the Spanish fleet was thus being put out of action at the outset, Blood had sailed in to open fire upon the Salvador. First athwart her hawse he had loosed a broadside that had swept her decks with terrific effect, then going on and about, he had put a second broadside into her hull at short range. Leaving her thus half-crippled, temporarily, at least, and keeping to his course, he had bewildered the crew of the Infanta by a couple of shots from the chasers on his beak-head, then crashed alongside to grapple and board her, whilst Hagthorpe was doing the like by the San Felipe.

And in all this time not a single shot had the Spaniards contrived to fire, so completely had they been taken by surprise, and so swift and paralyzing had been Blood's stroke.

Boarded now and faced by the cold steel of the buccaneers, neither the San Felipe nor the Infanta offered much resistance. The sight of their admiral in flames, and the Salvador drifting crippled from the action, had so utterly disheartened them that they accounted themselves vanquished, and laid down their arms.

If by a resolute stand the Salvador had encouraged the other two undamaged vessels to resistance, the Spaniards might well have retrieved the fortunes of the day. But it happened that the Salvador was handicapped in true Spanish fashion by being the treasure-ship of the fleet, with plate on board to the value of some fifty thousand pieces. Intent above all upon saving this from falling into the hands of the pirates, Don Miguel, who, with a remnant of his crew, had meanwhile transferred himself aboard her, headed her down towards Palomas and the fort that guarded the passage. This fort the Admiral, in those days of waiting, had taken the precaution secretly to garrison and rearm. For the purpose he had stripped the fort of Cojero, farther out on the gulf, of its entire armament, which included some cannon-royal of more than ordinary range and power.

With no suspicion of this, Captain Blood gave chase, accompanied by the Infanta, which was manned now by a prize-crew under the command of Yberville. The stern chasers of the Salvador desultorily returned the punishing fire of the pursuers; but such was the damage she, herself, sustained, that presently, coming under the guns of the fort, she began to sink, and finally settled down in the shallows with part of her hull above water. Thence, some in boats and some by swimming, the Admiral got his crew ashore on Palomas as best he could.

And then, just as Captain Blood accounted the victory won, and that his way out of that trap to the open sea beyond lay clear, the fort suddenly revealed its formidable and utterly unsuspected strength. With a roar the cannons-royal proclaimed themselves, and the Arabella staggered under a blow that smashed her bulwarks at the waist and scattered death and confusion among the seamen gathered there.

Had not Pitt, her master, himself seized the whipstaff and put the helm hard over to swing her sharply off to starboard, she must have suffered still worse from the second volley that followed fast upon the first.

Meanwhile it had fared even worse with the frailer Infanta. Although hit by one shot only, this had crushed her larboard timbers on the waterline, starting a leak that must presently have filled her, but for the prompt action of the experienced Yberville in ordering her larboard guns to be flung overboard. Thus lightened, and listing now to starboard, he fetched her about, and went staggering after the retreating Arabella, followed by the fire of the fort, which did them, however, little further damage.

Out of range, at last, they lay to, joined by the Elizabeth and the San Felipe, to consider their position.

CHAPTER XVII. THE DUPES

It was a crestfallen Captain Blood who presided over that hastily summoned council held on the poop-deck of the Arabella in the brilliant morning sunshine. It was, he declared afterwards, one of the bitterest moments in his career. He was compelled to digest the fact that having conducted the engagement with a skill of which he might justly be proud, having destroyed a force so superior in ships and guns and men that Don Miguel de Espinosa had justifiably deemed it overwhelming, his victory was rendered barren by three lucky shots from an unsuspected battery by which they had been surprised. And barren must their victory remain until they could reduce the fort that still remained to defend the passage.

At first Captain Blood was for putting his ships in order and making the attempt there and then. But the others dissuaded him from betraying an impetuosity usually foreign to him, and born entirely of chagrin and mortification, emotions which will render unreasonable the most reasonable of men. With returning calm, he surveyed the situation. The Arabella was no longer in case to put to sea; the Infanta was merely kept afloat by artifice, and the San Felipe was almost as sorely damaged by the fire she had sustained from the buccaneers before surrendering.

Clearly, then, he was compelled to admit in the end that nothing remained but to return to Maracaybo, there to refit the ships before attempting to force the passage.

And so, back to Maracaybo came those defeated victors of that short, terrible fight. And if anything had been wanting further to exasperate their leader, he had it in the pessimism of which Cahusac did not economize expressions. Transported at first to heights of dizzy satisfaction by the swift and easy victory of their inferior force that morning, the Frenchman was now plunged back and more deeply than ever into the abyss of hopelessness. And his mood infected at least the main body of his own followers.

"It is the end," he told Captain Blood. "This time we are checkmated."

"I'll take the liberty of reminding you that you said the same before," Captain Blood answered him as patiently as he could. "Yet you've seen what you've seen, and you'll not deny that in ships and guns we are returning stronger than we went. Look at our present fleet, man."

"I am looking at it," said Cahusac.

"Pish! Ye're a white-livered cur when all is said."

"You call me a coward?"

"I'll take that liberty."

The Breton glared at him, breathing hard. But he had no mind to ask satisfaction for the insult. He knew too well the kind of satisfaction that Captain Blood was likely to afford him. He remembered the fate of Levasseur. So he confined himself to words.

"It is too much! You go too far!" he complained bitterly.

"Look you, Cahusac: it's sick and tired I am of your perpetual whining and complaining when things are not as smooth as a convent dining-table. If ye wanted things smooth and easy, ye shouldn't have taken to the sea, and ye should never ha' sailed with me, for with me things are never smooth and easy. And that, I think, is all I have to say to you this morning."

Cahusac flung away cursing, and went to take the feeling of his men.

Captain Blood went off to give his surgeon's skill to the wounded, among whom he remained engaged until late afternoon. Then, at last, he went ashore, his mind made up, and returned to the house of the Governor, to indite a truculent but very scholarly letter in purest Castilian to Don Miguel.

"I have shown your excellency this morning of what I am capable," he wrote. "Although outnumbered by more than two to one in men, in ships, and in guns, I have sunk or captured the vessels of the great fleet with which you were to come to Maracaybo to destroy us. So that you are no longer in case to carry out your boast, even when your reenforcements on the Santo Nino, reach you from La Guayra. From what has occurred, you may judge of what must occur. I should not trouble your excellency with this letter but that I am a humane man, abhorring bloodshed. Therefore before proceeding to deal with your fort, which you may deem invincible, as I have dealt already with your fleet, which you deemed invincible, I make you, purely out of humanitarian considerations, this last offer of terms. I will spare this city of Maracaybo and forthwith evacuate it, leaving behind me the forty prisoners I have taken, in consideration of your paying me the sum of fifty thousand pieces of eight and one hundred head of cattle as a ransom, thereafter granting me unmolested passage of the bar. My prisoners, most of whom are persons of consideration, I will retain as hostages until after my departure, sending them back in the canoes which we shall take with us for that purpose. If your excellency should be so ill-advised as to refuse these terms, and thereby impose upon me the necessity of reducing your fort at the cost of some lives, I warn you that you may expect no quarter from us, and that I shall begin by leaving a heap of ashes where this pleasant city of Maracaybo now stands."

The letter written, he bade them bring him from among the prisoners the Deputy-Governor of Maracaybo, who had been taken at Gibraltar. Disclosing its contents to him, he despatched him with it to Don Miguel.

His choice of a messenger was shrewd. The Deputy-Governor was of all men the most anxious for the deliverance of his city, the one man who on his own account would plead most fervently for its preservation at all costs from the fate with which Captain Blood was threatening it. And as he reckoned so it befell. The Deputy-Governor added his own passionate pleading to the proposals of the letter.

But Don Miguel was of stouter heart. True, his fleet had been partly destroyed and partly captured. But then, he argued, he had been taken utterly by surprise. That should not happen again. There should be no surprising the fort. Let Captain Blood do his worst at Maracaybo, there should be a bitter reckoning for him when eventually he decided—as, sooner or later, decide he must—to come forth. The Deputy-Governor was flung into panic. He lost his temper, and said some hard things to the Admiral. But they were not as hard as the thing the Admiral said to him in answer.

"Had you been as loyal to your King in hindering the entrance of these cursed pirates as I shall be in hindering their going forth again, we should not now find ourselves in our present straits. So weary me no more with your coward counsels. I make no terms with Captain Blood. I know my duty to my King, and I intend to perform it. I also know my duty to myself. I have a private score with this rascal, and I intend to settle it. Take you that message back."

So back to Maracaybo, back to his own handsome house in which Captain Blood had established his quarters, came the Deputy-Governor with the Admiral's answer. And because he had been shamed into a show of spirit by the Admiral's own stout courage in adversity, he delivered it as truculently as the Admiral could have desired. "And is it like that?" said Captain Blood with a quiet smile, though the heart of him sank at this failure of his bluster. "Well, well, it's a pity now that the Admiral's so headstrong. It was that way he lost his fleet, which was his own to lose. This pleasant city of Maracaybo isn't. So no doubt he'll lose it with fewer misgivings. I am sorry. Waste, like bloodshed, is a thing abhorrent to me. But there ye are! I'll have the faggots to the place in the morning, and maybe when he sees the blaze to-morrow night he'll begin to believe that Peter Blood is a man of his word. Ye may go, Don Francisco."

The Deputy-Governor went out with dragging feet, followed by guards, his momentary truculence utterly spent.

But no sooner had he departed than up leapt Cahusac, who had been of the council assembled to receive the Admiral's answer. His face was white and his hands shook as he held them out in protest.

"Death of my life, what have you to say now?" he cried, his voice husky. And without waiting to hear what it might be, he raved on: "I knew you not frighten the Admiral so easy. He hold us entrap', and he knows it; yet you dream that he will yield himself to your impudent message. Your fool letter it have seal' the doom of us all."

"Have ye done?" quoth Blood quietly, as the Frenchman paused for breath.

"No, I have not."

"Then spare me the rest. It'll be of the same quality, devil a doubt, and it doesn't help us to solve the riddle that's before us."

"But what are you going to do? Is it that you will tell me?" It was not a question, it was a demand.

"How the devil do I know? I was hoping you'd have some ideas yourself. But since Ye're so desperately concerned to save your skin, you and those that think like you are welcome to leave us. I've no doubt at all the Spanish Admiral will welcome the abatement of our numbers even at this late date. Ye shall have the sloop as a parting gift from us, and ye can join Don Miguel in the fort for all I care, or for all the good ye're likely to be to us in this present pass."

"It is to my men to decide," Cahusac retorted, swallowing his fury, and on that stalked out to talk to them, leaving the others to deliberate in peace.

Next morning early he sought Captain Blood again. He found him alone in the patio, pacing to and fro, his head sunk on his breast. Cahusac mistook consideration for dejection. Each of us carries in himself a standard by which to measure his neighbour.

"We have take' you at your word, Captain," he announced, between sullenness and defiance. Captain Blood paused, shoulders hunched, hands behind his back, and mildly regarded the buccaneer in silence. Cahusac explained himself. "Last night I send one of my men to the Spanish Admiral with a letter. I make him offer to capitulate if he will accord us passage with the honours of war. This morning I receive his answer. He accord us this on the understanding that we carry nothing away with us. My men they are embarking them on the sloop. We sail at once."

"Bon voyage," said Captain Blood, and with a nod he turned on his heel again to resume his interrupted mediation.

"Is that all that you have to say to me?" cried Cahusac.

"There are other things," said Blood over his shoulder. "But I know ye wouldn't like them."

"Ha! Then it's adieu, my Captain." Venomously he added: "It is my belief that we shall not meet again."

"Your belief is my hope," said Captain Blood.

Cahusac flung away, obscenely vituperative. Before noon he was under way with his followers, some sixty dejected men who had allowed themselves to be persuaded by him into that empty-handed departure—in spite even of all that Yberville could do to prevent it. The Admiral kept faith with him, and allowed him free passage out to sea, which, from his knowledge of Spaniards, was more than Captain Blood had expected.

Meanwhile, no sooner had the deserters weighed anchor than Captain Blood received word that the Deputy-Governor begged to be allowed to see him again. Admitted, Don Francisco at once displayed the fact that a night's reflection had quickened his apprehensions for the city of Maracaybo and his condemnation of the Admiral's intransigence.

Captain Blood received him pleasantly.

"Good-morning to you, Don Francisco. I have postponed the bonfire until nightfall. It will make a better show in the dark."

Don Francisco, a slight, nervous, elderly man of high lineage and low vitality, came straight to business.

"I am here to tell you, Don Pedro, that if you will hold your hand for three days, I will undertake to raise the ransom you demand, which Don Miguel de Espinosa refuses."

Captain Blood confronted him, a frown contracting the dark brows above his light eyes:

"And where will you be raising it?" quoth he, faintly betraying his surprise.

Don Francisco shook his head. "That must remain my affair," he answered. "I know where it is to be found, and my compatriots must contribute. Give me leave for three days on parole, and I will see you fully satisfied. Meanwhile my son remains in your hands as a hostage for my return." And upon that he fell to pleading. But in this he was crisply interrupted.

"By the Saints! Ye're a bold man, Don Francisco, to come to me with such a tale—to tell me that ye know where the ransom's to be raised, and yet to refuse to say. D'ye think now that with a match between your fingers ye'd grow more communicative?"

If Don Francisco grew a shade paler, yet again he shook his head.

"That was the way of Morgan and L'Ollonais and other pirates. But it is not the way of Captain Blood. If I had doubted that I should not have disclosed so much."

The Captain laughed. "You old rogue," said he. "Ye play upon my vanity, do you?"

"Upon your honour, Captain."

"The honour of a pirate? Ye're surely crazed!"

"The honour of Captain Blood," Don Francisco insisted. "You have the repute of making war like a gentleman."

Captain Blood laughed again, on a bitter, sneering note that made Don Francisco fear the worst. He was not to guess that it was himself the Captain mocked.

"That's merely because it's more remunerative in the end. And that is why you are accorded the three days you ask for. So about it, Don Francisco. You shall have what mules you need. I'll see to it."

Away went Don Francisco on his errand, leaving Captain Blood to reflect, between bitterness and satisfaction, that a reputation for as much chivalry as is consistent with piracy is not without its uses.

Punctually on the third day the Deputy-Governor was back in Maracaybo with his mules laden with plate and money to the value demanded and a herd of a hundred head of cattle driven in by negro slaves.

These bullocks were handed over to those of the company who ordinarily were boucan-hunters, and therefore skilled in the curing of meats, and for best part of a week thereafter they were busy at the waterside with the quartering and salting of carcases.

While this was doing on the one hand and the ships were being refitted for sea on the other, Captain Blood was pondering the riddle on the solution of which his own fate depended. Indian spies whom he employed brought him word that the Spaniards, working at low tide, had salved the thirty guns of the Salvador, and thus had added yet another battery to their already overwhelming strength. In the end, and hoping for inspiration on the spot, Captain Blood made a reconnaissance in person. At the risk of his life, accompanied by two friendly Indians, he crossed to the island in a canoe under cover of dark. They concealed themselves and the canoe in the short thick scrub with which that side of the island was densely covered, and lay there until daybreak. Then Blood went forward alone, and with infinite precaution, to make his survey. He went to verify a suspicion that he had formed, and approached the fort as nearly as he dared and a deal nearer than was safe.

On all fours he crawled to the summit of an eminence a mile or so away, whence he found himself commanding a view of the interior dispositions of the stronghold. By the aid of a telescope with which he had equipped himself he was able to verify that, as he had suspected and hoped, the fort's artillery was all mounted on the seaward side.

Satisfied, he returned to Maracaybo, and laid before the six who composed his council—Pitt, Hagthorpe, Yberville, Wolverstone, Dyke, and Ogle—a proposal to storm the fort from the landward side. Crossing to the island under cover of night, they would take the Spaniards by surprise and attempt to overpower them before they could shift their guns to meet the onslaught.

With the exception of Wolverstone, who was by temperament the kind of man who favours desperate chances, those officers received the proposal coldly. Hagthorpe incontinently opposed it.

"It's a harebrained scheme, Peter," he said gravely, shaking his handsome head. "Consider now that we cannot depend upon approaching unperceived to a distance whence we might storm the fort before the cannon could be moved. But even if we could, we can take no cannon ourselves; we must depend entirely upon our small arms, and how shall we, a bare three hundred" (for this was the number to which Cahusac's defection had reduced them), "cross the open to attack more than twice that number under cover?"

The others—Dyke, Ogle, Yberville, and even Pitt, whom loyalty to Blood may have made reluctant—loudly approved him. When they had done, "I have considered all," said Captain Blood. "I have weighed the risks and studied how to lessen them. In these desperate straits...."

He broke off abruptly. A moment he frowned, deep in thought; then his face was suddenly alight with inspiration. Slowly he drooped his head, and sat there considering, weighing, chin on breast. Then he nodded, muttering, "Yes," and again, "Yes." He looked up, to face them. "Listen," he cried. "You may be right. The risks may be too heavy. Whether or not, I have thought of a better way. That which should have been the real attack shall be no more than a feint. Here, then, is the plan I now propose."

He talked swiftly and clearly, and as he talked one by one his officers' faces became alight with eagerness. When he had done, they cried as with one voice that he had saved them.

"That is yet to be proved in action," said he.

Since for the last twenty-four hours all had been in readiness for departure, there was nothing now to delay them, and it was decided to move next morning.

Such was Captain Blood's assurance of success that he immediately freed the prisoners held as hostages, and even the negro slaves, who were regarded by the others as legitimate plunder. His only precaution against those released prisoners was to order them into the church and there lock them up, to await deliverance at the hands of those who should presently be coming into the city.

Then, all being aboard the three ships, with the treasure safely stowed in their holds and the slaves under hatches, the buccaneers weighed anchor and stood out for the bar, each vessel towing three piraguas astern.

The Admiral, beholding their stately advance in the full light of noon, their sails gleaming white in the glare of the sunlight, rubbed his long, lean hands in satisfaction, and laughed through his teeth.

"At last!" he cried. "God delivers him into my hands!" He turned to the group of staring officers behind him. "Sooner or later it had to be," he said. "Say now, gentlemen, whether I am justified of my patience. Here end to-day the troubles caused to the subjects of the Catholic King by this infamous Don Pedro Sangre, as he once called himself to me."

He turned to issue orders, and the fort became lively as a hive. The guns were manned, the gunners already kindling fuses, when the buccaneer fleet, whilst still heading for Palomas, was observed to bear away to the west. The Spaniards watched them, intrigued.

Within a mile and a half to westward of the fort, and within a half-mile of the shore—that is to say, on the very edge of the shoal water that makes Palomas unapproachable on either side by any but vessels of the shallowest draught—the four ships cast anchor well within the Spaniards' view, but just out of range of their heaviest cannon.

Sneeringly the Admiral laughed.

"Aha! They hesitate, these English dogs! Por Dios, and well they may."

"They will be waiting for night," suggested his nephew, who stood at his elbow quivering with excitement.

Don Miguel looked at him, smiling. "And what shall the night avail them in this narrow passage, under the very muzzles of my guns? Be sure, Esteban, that to-night your father will be paid for."

He raised his telescope to continue his observation of the buccaneers. He saw that the piraguas towed by each vessel were being warped alongside, and he wondered a little what this manoeuver might portend. Awhile those piraguas were hidden from view behind the hulls. Then one by one they reappeared, rowing round and away from the ships, and each boat, he observed, was crowded with armed men. Thus laden, they were headed for the shore, at a point where it was densely wooded to the water's edge. The eyes of the wondering Admiral followed them until the foliage screened them from his view.

Then he lowered his telescope and looked at his officers.

"What the devil does it mean?" he asked.

None answered him, all being as puzzled as he was himself.

After a little while, Esteban, who kept his eyes on the water, plucked at his uncle's sleeve. "There they go!" he cried, and pointed.

And there, indeed, went the piraguas on their way back to the ships. But now it was observed that they were empty, save for the men who rowed them. Their armed cargo had been left ashore.

Back to the ships they pulled, to return again presently with a fresh load of armed men, which similarly they conveyed to Palomas. And at last one of the Spanish officers ventured an explanation:

"They are going to attack us by land—to attempt to storm the fort."

"Of course." The Admiral smiled. "I had guessed it. Whom the gods would destroy they first make mad."

"Shall we make a sally?" urged Esteban, in his excitement.

"A sally? Through that scrub? That would be to play into their hands. No, no, we will wait here to receive this attack. Whenever it comes, it is themselves will be destroyed, and utterly. Have no doubt of that."

But by evening the Admiral's equanimity was not quite so perfect. By then the piraguas had made a half-dozen journeys with their loads of men, and they had landed also—as Don Miguel had clearly observed through his telescope—at least a dozen guns.

His countenance no longer smiled; it was a little wrathful and a little troubled now as he turned again to his officers.

"Who was the fool who told me that they number but three hundred men in all? They have put at least twice that number ashore already."

Amazed as he was, his amazement would have been deeper had he been told the truth: that there was not a single buccaneer or a single gun ashore on Palomas. The deception had been complete. Don Miguel could not guess that the men he had beheld in those piraguas were always the same; that on the journeys to the shore they sat and stood upright in full view; and that on the journeys back to the ships, they lay invisible at the bottom of the boats, which were thus made to appear empty.

The growing fears of the Spanish soldiery at the prospect of a night attack from the landward side by the entire buccaneer force—and a force twice as strong as they had suspected the pestilent Blood to command—began to be communicated to the Admiral.

In the last hours of fading daylight, the Spaniards did precisely what Captain Blood so confidently counted that they would do—precisely what they must do to meet the attack, preparations for which had been so thoroughly simulated. They set themselves to labour like the damned at those ponderous guns emplaced to command the narrow passage out to sea.

Groaning and sweating, urged on by the curses and even the whips of their officers, they toiled in a frenzy of panic-stricken haste to shift the greater number and the more powerful of their guns across to the landward side, there to emplace them anew, so that they might be ready to receive the attack which at any moment now might burst upon them from the woods not half a mile away.

Thus, when night fell, although in mortal anxiety of the onslaught of those wild devils whose reckless courage was a byword on the seas of the Main, at least the Spaniards were tolerably prepared for it. Waiting, they stood to their guns.

And whilst they waited thus, under cover of the darkness and as the tide began to ebb, Captain Blood's fleet weighed anchor quietly; and, as once before, with no more canvas spread than that which their sprits could carry, so as to give them steering way—and even these having been painted black—the four vessels, without a light showing, groped their way by soundings to the channel which led to that narrow passage out to sea.

The Elizabeth and the Infanta, leading side by side, were almost abreast of the fort before their shadowy bulks and the soft gurgle of water at their prows were detected by the Spaniards, whose attention until that moment had been all on the other side. And now there arose on the night air such a sound of human baffled fury as may have resounded about Babel at the confusion of tongues. To heighten that confusion, and to scatter disorder among the Spanish soldiery, the Elizabeth emptied her larboard guns into the fort as she was swept past on the swift ebb.

At once realizing—though not yet how—he had been duped, and that his prey was in the very act of escaping after all, the Admiral frantically ordered the guns that had been so laboriously moved to be dragged back to their former emplacements, and commanded his gunners meanwhile to the slender batteries that of all his powerful, but now unavailable, armament still remained trained upon the channel. With these, after the loss of some precious moments, the fort at last made fire.

It was answered by a terrific broadside from the Arabella, which had now drawn abreast, and was crowding canvas to her yards. The enraged and gibbering Spaniards had a brief vision of her as the line of flame spurted from her red flank, and the thunder of her broadside drowned the noise of the creaking halyards. After that they saw her no more. Assimilated by the friendly darkness which the lesser Spanish guns were speculatively stabbing, the escaping ships fired never another shot that might assist their baffled and bewildered enemies to locate them.

Some slight damage was sustained by Blood's fleet. But by the time the Spaniards had resolved their confusion into some order of dangerous offence, that fleet, well served by a southerly breeze, was through the narrows and standing out to sea.

Thus was Don Miguel de Espinosa left to chew the bitter cud of a lost opportunity, and to consider in what terms he would acquaint the Supreme Council of the Catholic King that Peter Blood had got away from Maracaybo, taking with him two twenty-gun frigates that were lately the property of Spain, to say nothing of two hundred and fifty thousand pieces of eight and other plunder. And all this in spite of Don Miguel's four galleons and his heavily armed fort that at one time had held the pirates so securely trapped.

Heavy, indeed, grew the account of Peter Blood, which Don Miguel swore passionately to Heaven should at all costs to himself be paid in full.

Nor were the losses already detailed the full total of those suffered on this occasion by the King of Spain. For on the following evening, off the coast of Oruba, at the mouth of the Gulf of Venezuela, Captain Blood's fleet came upon the belated Santo Nino, speeding under full sail to reenforce Don Miguel at Maracaybo.

At first the Spaniard had conceived that she was meeting the victorious fleet of Don Miguel, returning from the destruction of the pirates. When at comparatively close quarters the pennon of St. George soared to the Arabella's masthead to disillusion her, the Santo Nino chose the better part of valour, and struck her flag.

Captain Blood ordered her crew to take to the boats, and land themselves at Oruba or wherever else they pleased. So considerate was he that to assist them he presented them with several of the piraguas which he still had in tow.

"You will find," said he to her captain, "that Don Miguel is in an extremely bad temper. Commend me to him, and say that I venture to remind him that he must blame himself for all the ills that have befallen him. The evil has recoiled upon him which he loosed when he sent his brother unofficially to make a raid upon the island of Barbados. Bid him think twice before he lets his devils loose upon an English settlement again."

With that he dismissed the Captain, who went over the side of the Santo Nino, and Captain Blood proceeded to investigate the value of this further prize. When her hatches were removed, a human cargo was disclosed in her hold.

"Slaves," said Wolverstone, and persisted in that belief cursing Spanish devilry until Cahusac crawled up out of the dark bowels of the ship, and stood blinking in the sunlight.

There was more than sunlight to make the Breton pirate blink. And those that crawled out after him—the remnants of his crew—cursed him horribly for the pusillanimity which had brought them into the ignominy of owing their deliverance to those whom they had deserted as lost beyond hope.

Their sloop had encountered and had been sunk three days ago by the Santo Nino, and Cahusac had narrowly escaped hanging merely that for some time he might be a mock among the Brethren of the Coast.

For many a month thereafter he was to hear in Tortuga the jeering taunt:

"Where do you spend the gold that you brought back from Maracaybo?"

CHAPTER XVIII. THE MILAGROSA

The affair at Maracaybo is to be considered as Captain Blood's buccaneering masterpiece. Although there is scarcely one of the many actions that he fought—recorded in such particular detail by Jeremy Pitt—which does not afford some instance of his genius for naval tactics, yet in none is this more shiningly displayed than in those two engagements by which he won out of the trap which Don Miguel de Espinosa had sprung upon him.

The fame which he had enjoyed before this, great as it already was, is dwarfed into insignificance by the fame that followed. It was a fame such as no buccaneer—not even Morgan—has ever boasted, before or since.

In Tortuga, during the months he spent there refitting the three ships he had captured from the fleet that had gone out to destroy him, he found himself almost an object of worship in the eyes of the wild Brethren of the Coast, all of whom now clamoured for the honour of serving under him. It placed him in the rare position of being able to pick and choose the crews for his augmented fleet, and he chose fastidiously. When next he sailed away it was with a fleet of five fine ships in which went something over a thousand men. Thus you behold him not merely famous, but really formidable. The three captured Spanish vessels he had renamed with a certain scholarly humour the Clotho, Lachesis, and Atropos, a grimly jocular manner of conveying to the world that he made them the arbiters of the fate of any Spaniards he should henceforth encounter upon the seas.

In Europe the news of this fleet, following upon the news of the Spanish Admiral's defeat at Maracaybo, produced something of a sensation. Spain and England were variously and unpleasantly exercised, and if you care to turn up the diplomatic correspondence exchanged on the subject, you will find that it is considerable and not always amiable.

And meanwhile in the Caribbean, the Spanish Admiral Don Miguel de Espinosa might be said—to use a term not yet invented in his day—to have run amok. The disgrace into which he had fallen as a result of the disasters suffered at the hands of Captain Blood had driven the Admiral all but mad. It is impossible, if we impose our minds impartially, to withhold a certain sympathy from Don Miguel. Hate was now this unfortunate man's daily bread, and the hope of vengeance an obsession to his mind. As a madman he went raging up and down the Caribbean seeking his enemy, and in the meantime, as an hors d'oeuvre to his vindictive appetite, he fell upon any ship of England or of France that loomed above his horizon.

I need say no more to convey the fact that this illustrious sea-captain and great gentleman of Castile had lost his head, and was become a pirate in his turn. The Supreme Council of Castile might anon condemn him for his practices. But how should that matter to one who already was condemned beyond redemption? On the contrary, if he should live to lay the audacious and ineffable Blood by the heels, it was possible that Spain might view his present irregularities and earlier losses with a more lenient eye.

And so, reckless of the fact that Captain Blood was now in vastly superior strength, the Spaniard sought him up and down the trackless seas. But for a whole year he sought him vainly. The circumstances in which eventually they met are very curious.

An intelligent observation of the facts of human existence will reveal to shallow-minded folk who sneer at the use of coincidence in the arts of fiction and drama that life itself is little more than a series of coincidences. Open the history of the past at whatsoever page you will, and there you shall find coincidence at work bringing about events that the merest chance might have averted. Indeed, coincidence may be defined as the very tool used by Fate to shape the destinies of men and nations.

Observe it now at work in the affairs of Captain Blood and of some others.

On the 15th September of the year 1688—a memorable year in the annals of England—three ships were afloat upon the Caribbean, which in their coming conjunctions were to work out the fortunes of several persons.

The first of these was Captain Blood's flagship the Arabella, which had been separated from the buccaneer fleet in a hurricane off the Lesser Antilles. In somewhere about 17 deg. N. Lat., and 74 deg. Long., she was beating up for the Windward Passage, before the intermittent southeasterly breezes of that stifling season, homing for Tortuga, the natural rendezvous of the dispersed vessels.

The second ship was the great Spanish galleon, the Milagrosa, which, accompanied by the smaller frigate Hidalga, lurked off the Caymites, to the north of the long peninsula that thrusts out from the southwest corner of Hispaniola. Aboard the Milagrosa sailed the vindictive Don Miguel.

The third and last of these ships with which we are at present concerned was an English man-of-war, which on the date I have given was at anchor in the French port of St. Nicholas on the northwest coast of Hispaniola. She was on her way from Plymouth to Jamaica, and carried on board a very distinguished passenger in the person of Lord Julian Wade, who came charged by his kinsman, my Lord Sunderland, with a mission of some consequence and delicacy, directly arising out of that vexatious correspondence between England and Spain.

The French Government, like the English, excessively annoyed by the depredations of the buccaneers, and the constant straining of relations with Spain that ensued, had sought in vain to put them down by enjoining the utmost severity against them upon her various overseas governors. But these, either—like the Governor of Tortuga—throve out of a scarcely tacit partnership with the filibusters, or—like the Governor of French Hispaniola—felt that they were to be encouraged as a check upon the power and greed of Spain, which might otherwise be exerted to the disadvantage of the colonies of other nations. They looked, indeed, with apprehension upon recourse to any vigorous measures which must result in driving many of the buccaneers to seek new hunting-grounds in the South Sea.

To satisfy King James's anxiety to conciliate Spain, and in response to the Spanish Ambassador's constant and grievous expostulations, my Lord Sunderland, the Secretary of State, had appointed a strong man to the deputy-governorship of Jamaica. This strong man was that Colonel Bishop who for some years now had been the most influential planter in Barbados.

Colonel Bishop had accepted the post, and departed from the plantations in which his great wealth was being amassed with an eagerness that had its roots in a desire to pay off a score of his own with Peter Blood.

From his first coming to Jamaica, Colonel Bishop had made himself felt by the buccaneers. But do what he might, the one buccaneer whom he made his particular quarry—that Peter Blood who once had been his slave—eluded him ever, and continued undeterred and in great force to harass the Spaniards upon sea and land, and to keep the relations between England and Spain in a state of perpetual ferment, particularly dangerous in those days when the peace of Europe was precariously maintained.

Exasperated not only by his own accumulated chagrin, but also by the reproaches for his failure which reached him from London, Colonel Bishop actually went so far as to consider hunting his quarry in Tortuga itself and making an attempt to clear the island of the buccaneers it sheltered. Fortunately for himself, he abandoned the notion of so insane an enterprise, deterred not only by the enormous natural strength of the place, but also by the reflection that a raid upon what was, nominally at least, a French settlement, must be attended by grave offence to France. Yet short of some such measure, it appeared to Colonel Bishop that he was baffled. He confessed as much in a letter to the Secretary of State.

This letter and the state of things which it disclosed made my Lord Sunderland despair of solving this vexatious problem by ordinary means. He turned to the consideration of extraordinary ones, and bethought him of the plan adopted with Morgan, who had been enlisted into the King's service under Charles II. It occurred to him that a similar course might be similarly effective with Captain Blood. His lordship did not omit the consideration that Blood's present outlawry might well have been undertaken not from inclination, but under stress of sheer necessity; that he had been forced into it by the circumstances of his transportation, and that he would welcome the opportunity of emerging from it.

Acting upon this conclusion, Sunderland sent out his kinsman, Lord Julian Wade, with some commissions made out in blank, and full directions as to the course which the Secretary considered it desirable to pursue and yet full discretion in the matter of pursuing them. The crafty Sunderland, master of all labyrinths of intrigue, advised his kinsman that in the event of his finding Blood intractable, or judging for other reasons that it was not desirable to enlist him in the King's service, he should turn his attention to the officers serving under him, and by seducing them away from him leave him so weakened that he must fall an easy victim to Colonel Bishop's fleet.

The Royal Mary—the vessel bearing that ingenious, tolerably accomplished, mildly dissolute, entirely elegant envoy of my Lord Sunderland's—made a good passage to St. Nicholas, her last port of call before Jamaica. It was understood that as a preliminary Lord Julian should report himself to the Deputy-Governor at Port Royal, whence at need he might have himself conveyed to Tortuga. Now it happened that the Deputy-Governor's niece had come to St. Nicholas some months earlier on a visit to some relatives, and so that she might escape the insufferable heat of Jamaica in that season. The time for her return being now at hand, a passage was sought for her aboard the Royal Mary, and in view of her uncle's rank and position promptly accorded.

Lord Julian hailed her advent with satisfaction. It gave a voyage that had been full of interest for him just the spice that it required to achieve perfection as an experience. His lordship was one of your gallants to whom existence that is not graced by womankind is more or less of a stagnation. Miss Arabella Bishop—this straight up and down slip of a girl with her rather boyish voice and her almost boyish ease of movement—was not perhaps a lady who in England would have commanded much notice in my lord's discerning eyes. His very sophisticated, carefully educated tastes in such matters inclined him towards the plump, the languishing, and the quite helplessly feminine. Miss Bishop's charms were undeniable. But they were such that it would take a delicate-minded man to appreciate them; and my Lord Julian, whilst of a mind that was very far from gross, did not possess the necessary degree of delicacy. I must not by this be understood to imply anything against him.

It remained, however, that Miss Bishop was a young woman and a lady; and in the latitude into which Lord Julian had strayed this was a phenomenon sufficiently rare to command attention. On his side, with his title and position, his personal grace and the charm of a practised courtier, he bore about him the atmosphere of the great world in which normally he had his being—a world that was little more than a name to her, who had spent most of her life in the Antilles. It is not therefore wonderful that they should have been attracted to each other before the Royal Mary was warped out of St. Nicholas. Each could tell the other much upon which the other desired information. He could regale her imagination with stories of St. James's—in many of which he assigned himself a heroic, or at least a distinguished part—and she could enrich his mind with information concerning this new world to which he had come.

Before they were out of sight of St. Nicholas they were good friends, and his lordship was beginning to correct his first impressions of her and to discover the charm of that frank, straightforward attitude of comradeship which made her treat every man as a brother. Considering how his mind was obsessed with the business of his mission, it is not wonderful that he should have come to talk to her of Captain Blood. Indeed, there was a circumstance that directly led to it.

"I wonder now," he said, as they were sauntering on the poop, "if you ever saw this fellow Blood, who was at one time on your uncle's plantations as a slave."

Miss Bishop halted. She leaned upon the taffrail, looking out towards the receding land, and it was a moment before she answered in a steady, level voice:

"I saw him often. I knew him very well."

"Ye don't say!" His lordship was slightly moved out of an imperturbability that he had studiously cultivated. He was a young man of perhaps eight-and-twenty, well above the middle height in stature and appearing taller by virtue of his exceeding leanness. He had a thin, pale, rather pleasing hatchet-face, framed in the curls of a golden periwig, a sensitive mouth and pale blue eyes that lent his countenance a dreamy expression, a rather melancholy pensiveness. But they were alert, observant eyes notwithstanding, although they failed on this occasion to observe the slight change of colour which his question had brought to Miss Bishop's cheeks or the suspiciously excessive composure of her answer.

"Ye don't say!" he repeated, and came to lean beside her. "And what manner of man did you find him?"

"In those days I esteemed him for an unfortunate gentleman."

"You were acquainted with his story?"

"He told it me. That is why I esteemed him—for the calm fortitude with which he bore adversity. Since then, considering what he has done, I have almost come to doubt if what he told me of himself was true."

"If you mean of the wrongs he suffered at the hands of the Royal Commission that tried the Monmouth rebels, there's little doubt that it would be true enough. He was never out with Monmouth; that is certain. He was convicted on a point of law of which he may well have been ignorant when he committed what was construed into treason. But, faith, he's had his revenge, after a fashion."

"That," she said in a small voice, "is the unforgivable thing. It has destroyed him—deservedly."

"Destroyed him?" His lordship laughed a little. "Be none so sure of that. He has grown rich, I hear. He has translated, so it is said, his Spanish spoils into French gold, which is being treasured up for him in France. His future father-in-law, M. d'Ogeron, has seen to that."

"His future father-in-law?" said she, and stared at him round-eyed, with parted lips. Then added: "M. d'Ogeron? The Governor of Tortuga?"

"The same. You see the fellow's well protected. It's a piece of news I gathered in St. Nicholas. I am not sure that I welcome it, for I am not sure that it makes any easier a task upon which my kinsman, Lord Sunderland, has sent me hither. But there it is. You didn't know?"

She shook her head without replying. She had averted her face, and her eyes were staring down at the gently heaving water. After a moment she spoke, her voice steady and perfectly controlled.

"But surely, if this were true, there would have been an end to his piracy by now. If he... if he loved a woman and was betrothed, and was also rich as you say, surely he would have abandoned this desperate life, and..."

"Why, so I thought," his lordship interrupted, "until I had the explanation. D'Ogeron is avaricious for himself and for his child. And as for the girl, I'm told she's a wild piece, fit mate for such a man as Blood. Almost I marvel that he doesn't marry her and take her a-roving with him. It would be no new experience for her. And I marvel, too, at Blood's patience. He killed a man to win her."

"He killed a man for her, do you say?" There was horror now in her voice.

"Yes—a French buccaneer named Levasseur. He was the girl's lover and Blood's associate on a venture. Blood coveted the girl, and killed Levasseur to win her. Pah! It's an unsavoury tale, I own. But men live by different codes out in these parts...."

She had turned to face him. She was pale to the lips, and her hazel eyes were blazing, as she cut into his apologies for Blood.

"They must, indeed, if his other associates allowed him to live after that."

"Oh, the thing was done in fair fight, I am told."

"Who told you?"

"A man who sailed with them, a Frenchman named Cahusac, whom I found in a waterside tavern in St. Nicholas. He was Levasseur's lieutenant, and he was present on the island where the thing happened, and when Levasseur was killed."

"And the girl? Did he say the girl was present, too?"

"Yes. She was a witness of the encounter. Blood carried her off when he had disposed of his brother-buccaneer."

"And the dead man's followers allowed it?" He caught the note of incredulity in her voice, but missed the note of relief with which it was blent. "Oh, I don't believe the tale. I won't believe it!"

"I honour you for that, Miss Bishop. It strained my own belief that men should be so callous, until this Cahusac afforded me the explanation."

"What?" She checked her unbelief, an unbelief that had uplifted her from an inexplicable dismay. Clutching the rail, she swung round to face his lordship with that question. Later he was to remember and perceive in her present behaviour a certain oddness which went disregarded now.

"Blood purchased their consent, and his right to carry the girl off. He paid them in pearls that were worth more than twenty thousand pieces of eight." His lordship laughed again with a touch of contempt. "A handsome price! Faith, they're scoundrels all—just thieving, venal curs. And faith, it's a pretty tale this for a lady's ear."

She looked away from him again, and found that her sight was blurred. After a moment in a voice less steady than before she asked him:

"Why should this Frenchman have told you such a tale? Did he hate this Captain Blood?"

"I did not gather that," said his lordship slowly. "He related it... oh, just as a commonplace, an instance of buccaneering ways.

"A commonplace!" said she. "My God! A commonplace!"

"I dare say that we are all savages under the cloak that civilization fashions for us," said his lordship. "But this Blood, now, was a man of considerable parts, from what else this Cahusac told me. He was a bachelor of medicine."

"That is true, to my own knowledge."

"And he has seen much foreign service on sea and land. Cahusac said—though this I hardly credit—that he had fought under de Ruyter."

"That also is true," said she. She sighed heavily. "Your Cahusac seems to have been accurate enough. Alas!"

"You are sorry, then?"

She looked at him. She was very pale, he noticed.

"As we are sorry to hear of the death of one we have esteemed. Once I held him in regard for an unfortunate but worthy gentleman. Now...."

She checked, and smiled a little crooked smile. "Such a man is best forgotten."

And upon that she passed at once to speak of other things. The friendship, which it was her great gift to command in all she met, grew steadily between those two in the little time remaining, until the event befell that marred what was promising to be the pleasantest stage of his lordship's voyage.

The marplot was the mad-dog Spanish Admiral, whom they encountered on the second day out, when halfway across the Gulf of Gonaves. The Captain of the Royal Mary was not disposed to be intimidated even when Don Miguel opened fire on him. Observing the Spaniard's plentiful seaboard towering high above the water and offering him so splendid a mark, the Englishman was moved to scorn. If this Don who flew the banner of Castile wanted a fight, the Royal Mary was just the ship to oblige him. It may be that he was justified of his gallant confidence, and that he would that day have put an end to the wild career of Don Miguel de Espinosa, but that a lucky shot from the Milagrosa got among some powder stored in his forecastle, and blew up half his ship almost before the fight had started. How the powder came there will never now be known, and the gallant Captain himself did not survive to enquire into it.

Before the men of the Royal Mary had recovered from their consternation, their captain killed and a third of their number destroyed with him, the ship yawing and rocking helplessly in a crippled state, the Spaniards boarded her.

In the Captain's cabin under the poop, to which Miss Bishop had been conducted for safety, Lord Julian was seeking to comfort and encourage her, with assurances that all would yet be well, at the very moment when Don Miguel was stepping aboard. Lord Julian himself was none so steady, and his face was undoubtedly pale. Not that he was by any means a coward. But this cooped-up fighting on an unknown element in a thing of wood that might at any moment founder under his feet into the depths of ocean was disturbing to one who could be brave enough ashore. Fortunately Miss Bishop did not appear to be in desperate need of the poor comfort he was in case to offer. Certainly she, too, was pale, and her hazel eyes may have looked a little larger than usual. But she had herself well in hand. Half sitting, half leaning on the Captain's table, she preserved her courage sufficiently to seek to calm the octoroon waiting-woman who was grovelling at her feet in a state of terror.

And then the cabin-door flew open, and Don Miguel himself, tall, sunburned, and aquiline of face, strode in. Lord Julian span round, to face him, and clapped a hand to his sword.

The Spaniard was brisk and to the point.

"Don't be a fool," he said in his own tongue, "or you'll come by a fool's end. Your ship is sinking."

There were three or four men in morions behind Don Miguel, and Lord Julian realized the position. He released his hilt, and a couple of feet or so of steel slid softly back into the scabbard. But Don Miguel smiled, with a flash of white teeth behind his grizzled beard, and held out his hand.

"If you please," he said.

Lord Julian hesitated. His eyes strayed to Miss Bishop's. "I think you had better," said that composed young lady, whereupon with a shrug his lordship made the required surrender.

"Come you—all of you—aboard my ship," Don Miguel invited them, and strode out.

They went, of course. For one thing the Spaniard had force to compel them; for another a ship which he announced to be sinking offered them little inducement to remain. They stayed no longer than was necessary to enable Miss Bishop to collect some spare articles of dress and my lord to snatch up his valise.

As for the survivors in that ghastly shambles that had been the Royal Mary, they were abandoned by the Spaniards to their own resources. Let them take to the boats, and if those did not suffice them, let them swim or drown. If Lord Julian and Miss Bishop were retained, it was because Don Miguel perceived their obvious value. He received them in his cabin with great urbanity. Urbanely he desired to have the honour of being acquainted with their names.

Lord Julian, sick with horror of the spectacle he had just witnessed, commanded himself with difficulty to supply them. Then haughtily he demanded to know in his turn the name of their aggressor. He was in an exceedingly ill temper. He realized that if he had done nothing positively discreditable in the unusual and difficult position into which Fate had thrust him, at least he had done nothing creditable. This might have mattered less but that the spectator of his indifferent performance was a lady. He was determined if possible to do better now.

"I am Don Miguel de Espinosa," he was answered. "Admiral of the Navies of the Catholic King."

Lord Julian gasped. If Spain made such a hubbub about the depredations of a runagate adventurer like Captain Blood, what could not England answer now?

"Will you tell me, then, why you behave like a damned pirate?" he asked. And added: "I hope you realize what will be the consequences, and the strict account to which you shall be brought for this day's work, for the blood you have murderously shed, and for your violence to this lady and to myself."

"I offer you no violence," said the Admiral, smiling, as only the man who holds the trumps can smile. "On the contrary, I have saved your lives...."

"Saved our lives!" Lord Julian was momentarily speechless before such callous impudence. "And what of the lives you have destroyed in wanton butchery? By God, man, they shall cost you dear."

Don Miguel's smile persisted. "It is possible. All things are possible. Meantime it is your own lives that will cost you dear. Colonel Bishop is a rich man; and you, milord, are no doubt also rich. I will consider and fix your ransom."

"So that you're just the damned murderous pirate I was supposing you," stormed his lordship. "And you have the impudence to call yourself the Admiral of the Navies of the Catholic King? We shall see what your Catholic King will have to say to it."

The Admiral ceased to smile. He revealed something of the rage that had eaten into his brain. "You do not understand," he said. "It is that I treat you English heretic dogs just as you English heretic dogs have treated Spaniards upon the seas—you robbers and thieves out of hell! I have the honesty to do it in my own name—but you, you perfidious beasts, you send your Captain Bloods, your Hagthorpes, and your Morgans against us and disclaim responsibility for what they do. Like Pilate, you wash your hands." He laughed savagely. "Let Spain play the part of Pilate. Let her disclaim responsibility for me, when your ambassador at the Escurial shall go whining to the Supreme Council of this act of piracy by Don Miguel de Espinosa."

"Captain Blood and the rest are not admirals of England!" cried Lord Julian.

"Are they not? How do I know? How does Spain know? Are you not liars all, you English heretics?"

"Sir!" Lord Julian's voice was harsh as a rasp, his eyes flashed. Instinctively he swung a hand to the place where his sword habitually hung. Then he shrugged and sneered: "Of course," said he, "it sorts with all I have heard of Spanish honour and all that I have seen of yours that you should insult a man who is unarmed and your prisoner."

The Admiral's face flamed scarlet. He half raised his hand to strike. And then, restrained, perhaps, by the very words that had cloaked the retorting insult, he turned on his heel abruptly and went out without answering.

CHAPTER XIX. THE MEETING

As the door slammed after the departing Admiral, Lord Julian turned to Arabella, and actually smiled. He felt that he was doing better, and gathered from it an almost childish satisfaction—childish in all the circumstances. "Decidedly I think I had the last word there," he said, with a toss of his golden ringlets.

Miss Bishop, seated at the cabin-table, looked at him steadily, without returning his smile. "Does it matter, then, so much, having the last word? I am thinking of those poor fellows on the Royal Mary. Many of them have had their last word, indeed. And for what? A fine ship sunk, a score of lives lost, thrice that number now in jeopardy, and all for what?"

"You are overwrought, ma'am. I...."

"Overwrought!" She uttered a single sharp note of laughter. "I assure you I am calm. I am asking you a question, Lord Julian. Why has this Spaniard done all this? To what purpose?"

"You heard him." Lord Julian shrugged angrily. "Blood-lust," he explained shortly.

"Blood-lust?" she asked. She was amazed. "Does such a thing exist, then? It is insane, monstrous."

"Fiendish," his lordship agreed. "Devil's work."

"I don't understand. At Bridgetown three years ago there was a Spanish raid, and things were done that should have been impossible to men, horrible, revolting things which strain belief, which seem, when I think of them now, like the illusions of some evil dream. Are men just beasts?"

"Men?" said Lord Julian, staring. "Say Spaniards, and I'll agree." He was an Englishman speaking of hereditary foes. And yet there was a measure of truth in what he said. "This is the Spanish way in the New World. Faith, almost it justifies such men as Blood of what they do."

She shivered, as if cold, and setting her elbows on the table, she took her chin in her hands, and sat staring before her.

Observing her, his lordship noticed how drawn and white her face had grown. There was reason enough for that, and for worse. Not any other woman of his acquaintance would have preserved her self-control in such an ordeal; and of fear, at least, at no time had Miss Bishop shown any sign. It is impossible that he did not find her admirable.

A Spanish steward entered bearing a silver chocolate service and a box of Peruvian candies, which he placed on the table before the lady.

"With the Admiral's homage," he said, then bowed, and withdrew.

Miss Bishop took no heed of him or his offering, but continued to stare before her, lost in thought. Lord Julian took a turn in the long low cabin, which was lighted by a skylight above and great square windows astern. It was luxuriously appointed: there were rich Eastern rugs on the floor, well-filled bookcases stood against the bulkheads, and there was a carved walnut sideboard laden with silverware. On a long, low chest standing under the middle stern port lay a guitar that was gay with ribbons. Lord Julian picked it up, twanged the strings once as if moved by nervous irritation, and put it down.

He turned again to face Miss Bishop.

"I came out here," he said, "to put down piracy. But—blister me!—I begin to think that the French are right in desiring piracy to continue as a curb upon these Spanish scoundrels."

He was to be strongly confirmed in that opinion before many hours were past. Meanwhile their treatment at the hands of Don Miguel was considerate and courteous. It confirmed the opinion, contemptuously expressed to his lordship by Miss Bishop, that since they were to be held to ransom they need not fear any violence or hurt. A cabin was placed at the disposal of the lady and her terrified woman, and another at Lord Julian's. They were given the freedom of the ship, and bidden to dine at the Admiral's table; nor were his further intentions regarding them mentioned, nor yet his immediate destination.

The Milagrosa, with her consort the Hidalga rolling after her, steered a south by westerly course, then veered to the southeast round Cape Tiburon, and thereafter, standing well out to sea, with the land no more than a cloudy outline to larboard, she headed directly east, and so ran straight into the arms of Captain Blood, who was making for the Windward Passage, as we know. That happened early on the following morning. After having systematically hunted his enemy in vain for a year, Don Miguel chanced upon him in this unexpected and entirely fortuitous fashion. But that is the ironic way of Fortune. It was also the way of Fortune that Don Miguel should thus come upon the Arabella at a time when, separated from the rest of the fleet, she was alone and at a disadvantage. It looked to Don Miguel as if the luck which so long had been on Blood's side had at last veered in his own favour.

Miss Bishop, newly risen, had come out to take the air on the quarter-deck with his lordship in attendance—as you would expect of so gallant a gentleman—when she beheld the big red ship that had once been the Cinco Llagas out of Cadiz. The vessel was bearing down upon them, her mountains of snowy canvas bellying forward, the long pennon with the cross of St. George fluttering from her main truck in the morning breeze, the gilded portholes in her red hull and the gilded beak-head aflash in the morning sun.

Miss Bishop was not to recognize this for that same Cinco Llagas which she had seen once before—on a tragic day in Barbados three years ago. To her it was just a great ship that was heading resolutely, majestically, towards them, and an Englishman to judge by the pennon she was flying. The sight thrilled her curiously; it awoke in her an uplifting sense of pride that took no account of the danger to herself in the encounter that must now be inevitable.

Beside her on the poop, whither they had climbed to obtain a better view, and equally arrested and at gaze, stood Lord Julian. But he shared none of her exultation. He had been in his first sea-fight yesterday, and he felt that the experience would suffice him for a very considerable time. This, I insist, is no reflection upon his courage.

"Look," said Miss Bishop, pointing; and to his infinite amazement he observed that her eyes were sparkling. Did she realize, he wondered, what was afoot? Her next sentence resolved his doubt. "She is English, and she comes resolutely on. She means to fight."

"God help her, then," said his lordship gloomily. "Her captain must be mad. What can he hope to do against two such heavy hulks as these? If they could so easily blow the Royal Mary out of the water, what will they do to this vessel? Look at that devil Don Miguel. He's utterly disgusting in his glee."

From the quarter-deck, where he moved amid the frenzy of preparation, the Admiral had turned to flash a backward glance at his prisoners. His eyes were alight, his face transfigured. He flung out an arm to point to the advancing ship, and bawled something in Spanish that was lost to them in the noise of the labouring crew.

They advanced to the poop-rail, and watched the bustle. Telescope in hand on the quarter-deck, Don Miguel was issuing his orders. Already the gunners were kindling their matches; sailors were aloft, taking in sail; others were spreading a stout rope net above the waist, as a protection against falling spars. And meanwhile Don Miguel had been signalling to his consort, in response to which the Hidalga had drawn steadily forward until she was now abeam of the Milagrosa, half cable's length to starboard, and from the height of the tall poop my lord and Miss Bishop could see her own bustle of preparation. And they could discern signs of it now aboard the advancing English ship as well. She was furling tops and mainsail, stripping in fact to mizzen and sprit for the coming action. Thus, almost silently without challenge or exchange of signals, had action been mutually determined.

Of necessity now, under diminished sail, the advance of the Arabella was slower; but it was none the less steady. She was already within saker shot, and they could make out the figures stirring on her forecastle and the brass guns gleaming on her prow. The gunners of the Milagrosa raised their linstocks and blew upon their smouldering matches, looking up impatiently at the Admiral.

But the Admiral solemnly shook his head.

"Patience," he exhorted them. "Save your fire until we have him. He is coming straight to his doom—straight to the yardarm and the rope that have been so long waiting for him."

"Stab me!" said his lordship. "This Englishman may be gallant enough to accept battle against such odds. But there are times when discretion is a better quality than gallantry in a commander."

"Gallantry will often win through, even against overwhelming strength," said Miss Bishop. He looked at her, and noted in her bearing only excitement. Of fear he could still discern no trace. His lordship was past amazement. She was not by any means the kind of woman to which life had accustomed him.

"Presently," he said, "you will suffer me to place you under cover."

"I can see best from here," she answered him. And added quietly: "I am praying for this Englishman. He must be very brave."

Under his breath Lord Julian damned the fellow's bravery.

The Arabella was advancing now along a course which, if continued, must carry her straight between the two Spanish ships. My lord pointed it out. "He's crazy surely!" he cried. "He's driving straight into a death-trap. He'll be crushed to splinters between the two. No wonder that black-faced Don is holding his fire. In his place, I should do the same."

But even at that moment the Admiral raised his hand; in the waist, below him, a trumpet blared, and immediately the gunner on the prow touched off his guns. As the thunder of them rolled out, his lordship saw ahead beyond the English ship and to larboard of her two heavy splashes. Almost at once two successive spurts of flame leapt from the brass cannon on the Arabella's beak-head, and scarcely had the watchers on the poop seen the shower of spray, where one of the shots struck the water near them, then with a rending crash and a shiver that shook the Milagrosa from stem to stern, the other came to lodge in her forecastle. To avenge that blow, the Hidalga blazed at the Englishman with both her forward guns. But even at that short range—between two and three hundred yards—neither shot took effect.

At a hundred yards the Arabella's forward guns, which had meanwhile been reloaded, fired again at the Milagrosa, and this time smashed her bowsprit into splinters; so that for a moment she yawed wildly to port. Don Miguel swore profanely, and then, as the helm was put over to swing her back to her course, his own prow replied. But the aim was too high, and whilst one of the shots tore through the Arabella's shrouds and scarred her mainmast, the other again went wide. And when the smoke of that discharge had lifted, the English ship was found almost between the Spaniards, her bows in line with theirs and coming steadily on into what his lordship deemed a death-trap.

Lord Julian held his breath, and Miss Bishop gasped, clutching the rail before her. She had a glimpse of the wickedly grinning face of Don Miguel, and the grinning faces of the men at the guns in the waist.

At last the Arabella was right between the Spanish ships prow to poop and poop to prow. Don Miguel spoke to the trumpeter, who had mounted the quarter-deck and stood now at the Admiral's elbow. The man raised the silver bugle that was to give the signal for the broadsides of both ships. But even as he placed it to his lips, the Admiral seized his arm, to arrest him. Only then had he perceived what was so obvious—or should have been to an experienced sea-fighter: he had delayed too long and Captain Blood had outmanoeuvred him. In attempting to fire now upon the Englishman, the Milagrosa and her consort would also be firing into each other. Too late he ordered his helmsman to put the tiller hard over and swing the ship to larboard, as a preliminary to manoeuvring for a less impossible position of attack. At that very moment the Arabella seemed to explode as she swept by. Eighteen guns from each of her flanks emptied themselves at that point-blank range into the hulls of the two Spanish vessels.

Half stunned by that reverberating thunder, and thrown off her balance by the sudden lurch of the ship under her feet, Miss Bishop hurtled violently against Lord Julian, who kept his feet only by clutching the rail on which he had been leaning. Billowing clouds of smoke to starboard blotted out everything, and its acrid odour, taking them presently in the throat, set them gasping and coughing.

From the grim confusion and turmoil in the waist below arose a clamour of fierce Spanish blasphemies and the screams of maimed men. The Milagrosa staggered slowly ahead, a gaping rent in her bulwarks; her foremast was shattered, fragments of the yards hanging in the netting spread below. Her beak-head was in splinters, and a shot had smashed through into the great cabin, reducing it to wreckage.

Don Miguel was bawling orders wildly, and peering ever and anon through the curtain of smoke that was drifting slowly astern, in his anxiety to ascertain how it might have fared with the Hidalga.

Suddenly, and ghostly at first through that lifting haze, loomed the outline of a ship; gradually the lines of her red hull became more and more sharply defined as she swept nearer with poles all bare save for the spread of canvas on her sprit.

Instead of holding to her course as Don Miguel had expected she would, the Arabella had gone about under cover of the smoke, and sailing now in the same direction as the Milagrosa, was converging sharply upon her across the wind, so sharply that almost before the frenzied Don Miguel had realized the situation, his vessel staggered under the rending impact with which the other came hurtling alongside. There was a rattle and clank of metal as a dozen grapnels fell, and tore and caught in the timbers of the Milagrosa, and the Spaniard was firmly gripped in the tentacles of the English ship.

Beyond her and now well astern the veil of smoke was rent at last and the Hidalga was revealed in desperate case. She was bilging fast, with an ominous list to larboard, and it could be no more than a question of moments before she settled down. The attention of her hands was being entirely given to a desperate endeavour to launch the boats in time.

Of this Don Miguel's anguished eyes had no more than a fleeting but comprehensive glimpse before his own decks were invaded by a wild, yelling swarm of boarders from the grappling ship. Never was confidence so quickly changed into despair, never was hunter more swiftly converted into helpless prey. For helpless the Spaniards were. The swiftly executed boarding manoeuvre had caught them almost unawares in the moment of confusion following the punishing broadside they had sustained at such short range. For a moment there was a valiant effort by some of Don Miguel's officers to rally the men for a stand against these invaders. But the Spaniards, never at their best in close-quarter fighting, were here demoralized by knowledge of the enemies with whom they had to deal. Their hastily formed ranks were smashed before they could be steadied; driven across the waist to the break of the poop on the one side, and up to the forecastle bulkheads on the other, the fighting resolved itself into a series of skirmishes between groups. And whilst this was doing above, another horde of buccaneers swarmed through the hatch to the main deck below to overpower the gun-crews at their stations there.

On the quarter deck, towards which an overwhelming wave of buccaneers was sweeping, led by a one-eyed giant, who was naked to the waist, stood Don Miguel, numbed by despair and rage. Above and behind him on the poop, Lord Julian and Miss Bishop looked on, his lordship aghast at the fury of this cooped-up fighting, the lady's brave calm conquered at last by horror so that she reeled there sick and faint.

Soon, however, the rage of that brief fight was spent. They saw the banner of Castile come fluttering down from the masthead. A buccaneer had slashed the halyard with his cutlass. The boarders were in possession, and on the upper deck groups of disarmed Spaniards stood huddled now like herded sheep.

Suddenly Miss Bishop recovered from her nausea, to lean forward staring wild-eyed, whilst if possible her cheeks turned yet a deadlier hue than they had been already.

Picking his way daintily through that shambles in the waist came a tall man with a deeply tanned face that was shaded by a Spanish headpiece. He was armed in back-and-breast of black steel beautifully damascened with golden arabesques. Over this, like a stole, he wore a sling of scarlet silk, from each end of which hung a silver-mounted pistol. Up the broad companion to the quarter-deck he came, toying with easy assurance, until he stood before the Spanish Admiral. Then he bowed stiff and formally. A crisp, metallic voice, speaking perfect Spanish, reached those two spectators on the poop, and increased the admiring wonder in which Lord Julian had observed the man's approach.

"We meet again at last, Don Miguel," it said. "I hope you are satisfied. Although the meeting may not be exactly as you pictured it, at least it has been very ardently sought and desired by you."

Speechless, livid of face, his mouth distorted and his breathing laboured, Don Miguel de Espinosa received the irony of that man to whom he attributed his ruin and more beside. Then he uttered an inarticulate cry of rage, and his hand swept to his sword. But even as his fingers closed upon the hilt, the other's closed upon his wrist to arrest the action.

"Calm, Don Miguel!" he was quietly but firmly enjoined. "Do not recklessly invite the ugly extremes such as you would, yourself, have practised had the situation been reversed."

A moment they stood looking into each other's eyes.

"What do you intend by me?" the Spaniard enquired at last, his voice hoarse.

Captain Blood shrugged. The firm lips smiled a little. "All that I intend has been already accomplished. And lest it increase your rancour, I beg you to observe that you have brought it entirely upon yourself. You would have it so." He turned and pointed to the boats, which his men were heaving from the boom amidships. "Your boats are being launched. You are at liberty to embark in them with your men before we scuttle this ship. Yonder are the shores of Hispaniola. You should make them safely. And if you'll take my advice, sir, you'll not hunt me again. I think I am unlucky to you. Get you home to Spain, Don Miguel, and to concerns that you understand better than this trade of the sea."

For a long moment the defeated Admiral continued to stare his hatred in silence, then, still without speaking, he went down the companion, staggering like a drunken man, his useless rapier clattering behind him. His conqueror, who had not even troubled to disarm him, watched him go, then turned and faced those two immediately above him on the poop. Lord Julian might have observed, had he been less taken up with other things, that the fellow seemed suddenly to stiffen, and that he turned pale under his deep tan. A moment he stood at gaze; then suddenly and swiftly he came up the steps. Lord Julian stood forward to meet him.

"Ye don't mean, sir, that you'll let that Spanish scoundrel go free?" he cried.

The gentleman in the black corselet appeared to become aware of his lordship for the first time.

"And who the devil may you be?" he asked, with a marked Irish accent. "And what business may it be of yours, at all?"

His lordship conceived that the fellow's truculence and utter lack of proper deference must be corrected. "I am Lord Julian Wade," he announced, with that object.

Apparently the announcement made no impression.

"Are you, indeed! Then perhaps ye'll explain what the plague you're doing aboard this ship?"

Lord Julian controlled himself to afford the desired explanation. He did so shortly and impatiently.

"He took you prisoner, did he—along with Miss Bishop there?"

"You are acquainted with Miss Bishop?" cried his lordship, passing from surprise to surprise.

But this mannerless fellow had stepped past him, and was making a leg to the lady, who on her side remained unresponsive and forbidding to the point of scorn. Observing this, he turned to answer Lord Julian's question.

"I had that honour once," said he. "But it seems that Miss Bishop has a shorter memory."

His lips were twisted into a wry smile, and there was pain in the blue eyes that gleamed so vividly under his black brows, pain blending with the mockery of his voice. But of all this it was the mockery alone that was perceived by Miss Bishop; she resented it.

"I do not number thieves and pirates among my acquaintance, Captain Blood," said she; whereupon his lordship exploded in excitement.

"Captain Blood!" he cried. "Are you Captain Blood?"

"What else were ye supposing?"

Blood asked the question wearily, his mind on other things. "I do not number thieves and pirates among my acquaintance." The cruel phrase filled his brain, reechoing and reverberating there.

But Lord Julian would not be denied. He caught him by the sleeve with one hand, whilst with the other he pointed after the retreating, dejected figure of Don Miguel.

"Do I understand that ye're not going to hang that Spanish scoundrel?"

"What for should I be hanging him?"

"Because he's just a damned pirate, as I can prove, as I have proved already."

"Ah!" said Blood, and Lord Julian marvelled at the sudden haggardness of a countenance that had been so devil-may-care but a few moments since. "I am a damned pirate, myself; and so I am merciful with my kind. Don Miguel goes free."

Lord Julian gasped. "After what I've told you that he has done? After his sinking of the Royal Mary? After his treatment of me—of us?" Lord Julian protested indignantly.

"I am not in the service of England, or of any nation, sir. And I am not concerned with any wrongs her flag may suffer."

His lordship recoiled before the furious glance that blazed at him out of Blood's haggard face. But the passion faded as swiftly as it had arisen. It was in a level voice that the Captain added:

"If you'll escort Miss Bishop aboard my ship, I shall be obliged to you. I beg that you'll make haste. We are about to scuttle this hulk."

He turned slowly to depart. But again Lord Julian interposed. Containing his indignant amazement, his lordship delivered himself coldly. "Captain Blood, you disappoint me. I had hopes of great things for you."

"Go to the devil," said Captain Blood, turning on his heel, and so departed.

CHAPTER XX. THIEF AND PIRATE

Captain Blood paced the poop of his ship alone in the tepid dusk, and the growing golden radiance of the great poop lantern in which a seaman had just lighted the three lamps. About him all was peace. The signs of the day's battle had been effaced, the decks had been swabbed, and order was restored above and below. A group of men squatting about the main hatch were drowsily chanting, their hardened natures softened, perhaps, by the calm and beauty of the night. They were the men of the larboard watch, waiting for eight bells which was imminent.

Captain Blood did not hear them; he did not hear anything save the echo of those cruel words which had dubbed him thief and pirate.

Thief and pirate!

It is an odd fact of human nature that a man may for years possess the knowledge that a certain thing must be of a certain fashion, and yet be shocked to discover through his own senses that the fact is in perfect harmony with his beliefs. When first, three years ago, at Tortuga he had been urged upon the adventurer's course which he had followed ever since, he had known in what opinion Arabella Bishop must hold him if he succumbed. Only the conviction that already she was for ever lost to him, by introducing a certain desperate recklessness into his soul had supplied the final impulse to drive him upon his rover's course.

That he should ever meet her again had not entered his calculations, had found no place in his dreams. They were, he conceived, irrevocably and for ever parted. Yet, in spite of this, in spite even of the persuasion that to her this reflection that was his torment could bring no regrets, he had kept the thought of her ever before him in all those wild years of filibustering. He had used it as a curb not only upon himself, but also upon those who followed him. Never had buccaneers been so rigidly held in hand, never had they been so firmly restrained, never so debarred from the excesses of rapine and lust that were usual in their kind as those who sailed with Captain Blood. It was, you will remember, stipulated in their articles that in these as in other matters they must submit to the commands of their leader. And because of the singular good fortune which had attended his leadership, he had been able to impose that stern condition of a discipline unknown before among buccaneers. How would not these men laugh at him now if he were to tell them that this he had done out of respect for a slip of a girl of whom he had fallen romantically enamoured? How would not that laughter swell if he added that this girl had that day informed him that she did not number thieves and pirates among her acquaintance.

Thief and pirate!

How the words clung, how they stung and burnt his brain!

It did not occur to him, being no psychologist, nor learned in the tortuous workings of the feminine mind, that the fact that she should bestow upon him those epithets in the very moment and circumstance of their meeting was in itself curious. He did not perceive the problem thus presented; therefore he could not probe it. Else he might have concluded that if in a moment in which by delivering her from captivity he deserved her gratitude, yet she expressed herself in bitterness, it must be because that bitterness was anterior to the gratitude and deep-seated. She had been moved to it by hearing of the course he had taken. Why? It was what he did not ask himself, or some ray of light might have come to brighten his dark, his utterly evil despondency. Surely she would never have been so moved had she not cared—had she not felt that in what he did there was a personal wrong to herself. Surely, he might have reasoned, nothing short of this could have moved her to such a degree of bitterness and scorn as that which she had displayed.

That is how you will reason. Not so, however, reasoned Captain Blood. Indeed, that night he reasoned not at all. His soul was given up to conflict between the almost sacred love he had borne her in all these years and the evil passion which she had now awakened in him. Extremes touch, and in touching may for a space become confused, indistinguishable. And the extremes of love and hate were to-night so confused in the soul of Captain Blood that in their fusion they made up a monstrous passion.

Thief and pirate!

That was what she deemed him, without qualification, oblivious of the deep wrongs he had suffered, the desperate case in which he found himself after his escape from Barbados, and all the rest that had gone to make him what he was. That he should have conducted his filibustering with hands as clean as were possible to a man engaged in such undertakings had also not occurred to her as a charitable thought with which to mitigate her judgment of a man she had once esteemed. She had no charity for him, no mercy. She had summed him up, convicted him and sentenced him in that one phrase. He was thief and pirate in her eyes; nothing more, nothing less. What, then, was she? What are those who have no charity? he asked the stars.

Well, as she had shaped him hitherto, so let her shape him now. Thief and pirate she had branded him. She should be justified. Thief and pirate should he prove henceforth; no more nor less; as bowelless, as remorseless, as all those others who had deserved those names. He would cast out the maudlin ideals by which he had sought to steer a course; put an end to this idiotic struggle to make the best of two worlds. She had shown him clearly to which world he belonged.

Let him now justify her. She was aboard his ship, in his power, and he desired her.

He laughed softly, jeeringly, as he leaned on the taffrail, looking down at the phosphorescent gleam in the ship's wake, and his own laughter startled him by its evil note. He checked suddenly, and shivered. A sob broke from him to end that ribald burst of mirth. He took his face in his hands and found a chill moisture on his brow.

Meanwhile, Lord Julian, who knew the feminine part of humanity rather better than Captain Blood, was engaged in solving the curious problem that had so completely escaped the buccaneer. He was spurred to it, I suspect, by certain vague stirrings of jealousy. Miss Bishop's conduct in the perils through which they had come had brought him at last to perceive that a woman may lack the simpering graces of cultured femininity and yet because of that lack be the more admirable. He wondered what precisely might have been her earlier relations with Captain Blood, and was conscious of a certain uneasiness which urged him now to probe the matter.

His lordship's pale, dreamy eyes had, as I have said, a habit of observing things, and his wits were tolerably acute.

He was blaming himself now for not having observed certain things before, or, at least, for not having studied them more closely, and he was busily connecting them with more recent observations made that very day.

He had observed, for instance, that Blood's ship was named the Arabella, and he knew that Arabella was Miss Bishop's name. And he had observed all the odd particulars of the meeting of Captain Blood and Miss Bishop, and the curious change that meeting had wrought in each.

The lady had been monstrously uncivil to the Captain. It was a very foolish attitude for a lady in her circumstances to adopt towards a man in Blood's; and his lordship could not imagine Miss Bishop as normally foolish. Yet, in spite of her rudeness, in spite of the fact that she was the niece of a man whom Blood must regard as his enemy, Miss Bishop and his lordship had been shown the utmost consideration aboard the Captain's ship. A cabin had been placed at the disposal of each, to which their scanty remaining belongings and Miss Bishop's woman had been duly transferred. They were given the freedom of the great cabin, and they had sat down to table with Pitt, the master, and Wolverstone, who was Blood's lieutenant, both of whom had shown them the utmost courtesy. Also there was the fact that Blood, himself, had kept almost studiously from intruding upon them.

His lordship's mind went swiftly but carefully down these avenues of thought, observing and connecting. Having exhausted them, he decided to seek additional information from Miss Bishop. For this he must wait until Pitt and Wolverstone should have withdrawn. He was hardly made to wait so long, for as Pitt rose from table to follow Wolverstone, who had already departed, Miss Bishop detained him with a question:

"Mr. Pitt," she asked, "were you not one of those who escaped from Barbados with Captain Blood?"

"I was. I, too, was one of your uncle's slaves."

"And you have been with Captain Blood ever since?"

"His shipmaster always, ma'am."

She nodded. She was very calm and self-contained; but his lordship observed that she was unusually pale, though considering what she had that day undergone this afforded no matter for wonder.

"Did you ever sail with a Frenchman named Cahusac?"

"Cahusac?" Pitt laughed. The name evoked a ridiculous memory. "Aye. He was with us at Maracaybo."

"And another Frenchman named Levasseur?"

His lordship marvelled at her memory of these names.

"Aye. Cahusac was Levasseur's lieutenant, until he died."

"Until who died?"

"Levasseur. He was killed on one of the Virgin Islands two years ago."

There was a pause. Then, in an even quieter voice than before, Miss Bishop asked:

"Who killed him?"

Pitt answered readily. There was no reason why he should not, though he began to find the catechism intriguing.

"Captain Blood killed him."

"Why?"

Pitt hesitated. It was not a tale for a maid's ears.

"They quarrelled," he said shortly.

"Was it about a... a lady?" Miss Bishop relentlessly pursued him.

"You might put it that way."

"What was the lady's name?"

Pitt's eyebrows went up; still he answered.

"Miss d'Ogeron. She was the daughter of the Governor of Tortuga. She had gone off with this fellow Levasseur, and... and Peter delivered her out of his dirty clutches. He was a black-hearted scoundrel, and deserved what Peter gave him."

"I see. And... and yet Captain Blood has not married her?"

"Not yet," laughed Pitt, who knew the utter groundlessness of the common gossip in Tortuga which pronounced Mdlle. d'Ogeron the Captain's future wife.

Miss Bishop nodded in silence, and Jeremy Pitt turned to depart, relieved that the catechism was ended. He paused in the doorway to impart a piece of information.

"Maybe it'll comfort you to know that the Captain has altered our course for your benefit. It's his intention to put you both ashore on the coast of Jamaica, as near Port Royal as we dare venture. We've gone about, and if this wind holds ye'll soon be home again, mistress."

"Vastly obliging of him," drawled his lordship, seeing that Miss Bishop made no shift to answer. Sombre-eyed she sat, staring into vacancy.

"Indeed, ye may say so," Pitt agreed. "He's taking risks that few would take in his place. But that's always been his way."

He went out, leaving his lordship pensive, those dreamy blue eyes of his intently studying Miss Bishop's face for all their dreaminess; his mind increasingly uneasy. At length Miss Bishop looked at him, and spoke.

"Your Cahusac told you no more than the truth, it seems."

"I perceived that you were testing it," said his lordship. "I am wondering precisely why."

Receiving no answer, he continued to observe her silently, his long, tapering fingers toying with a ringlet of the golden periwig in which his long face was set.

Miss Bishop sat bemused, her brows knit, her brooding glance seeming to study the fine Spanish point that edged the tablecloth. At last his lordship broke the silence.

"He amazes me, this man," said he, in his slow, languid voice that never seemed to change its level. "That he should alter his course for us is in itself matter for wonder; but that he should take a risk on our behalf—that he should venture into Jamaica waters.... It amazes me, as I have said."

Miss Bishop raised her eyes, and looked at him. She appeared to be very thoughtful. Then her lip flickered curiously, almost scornfully, it seemed to him. Her slender fingers drummed the table.

"What is still more amazing is that he does not hold us to ransom," said she at last.

"It's what you deserve."

"Oh, and why, if you please?"

"For speaking to him as you did."

"I usually call things by their names."

"Do you? Stab me! I shouldn't boast of it. It argues either extreme youth or extreme foolishness." His lordship, you see, belonged to my Lord Sunderland's school of philosophy. He added after a moment: "So does the display of ingratitude."

A faint colour stirred in her cheeks. "Your lordship is evidently aggrieved with me. I am disconsolate. I hope your lordship's grievance is sounder than your views of life. It is news to me that ingratitude is a fault only to be found in the young and the foolish."

"I didn't say so, ma'am." There was a tartness in his tone evoked by the tartness she had used. "If you would do me the honour to listen, you would not misapprehend me. For if unlike you I do not always say precisely what I think, at least I say precisely what I wish to convey. To be ungrateful may be human; but to display it is childish."

"I... I don't think I understand." Her brows were knit. "How have I been ungrateful and to whom?"

"To whom? To Captain Blood. Didn't he come to our rescue?"

"Did he?" Her manner was frigid. "I wasn't aware that he knew of our presence aboard the Milagrosa."

His lordship permitted himself the slightest gesture of impatience.

"You are probably aware that he delivered us," said he. "And living as you have done in these savage places of the world, you can hardly fail to be aware of what is known even in England: that this fellow Blood strictly confines himself to making war upon the Spaniards. So that to call him thief and pirate as you did was to overstate the case against him at a time when it would have been more prudent to have understated it."

"Prudence?" Her voice was scornful. "What have I to do with prudence?"

"Nothing—as I perceive. But, at least, study generosity. I tell you frankly, ma'am, that in Blood's place I should never have been so nice. Sink me! When you consider what he has suffered at the hands of his fellow-countrymen, you may marvel with me that he should trouble to discriminate between Spanish and English. To be sold into slavery! Ugh!" His lordship shuddered. "And to a damned colonial planter!" He checked abruptly. "I beg your pardon, Miss Bishop. For the moment...."

"You were carried away by your heat in defence of this... sea-robber." Miss Bishop's scorn was almost fierce.

His lordship stared at her again. Then he half-closed his large, pale eyes, and tilted his head a little. "I wonder why you hate him so," he said softly.

He saw the sudden scarlet flame upon her cheeks, the heavy frown that descended upon her brow. He had made her very angry, he judged. But there was no explosion. She recovered.

"Hate him? Lord! What a thought! I don't regard the fellow at all."

"Then ye should, ma'am." His lordship spoke his thought frankly. "He's worth regarding. He'd be an acquisition to the King's navy—a man that can do the things he did this morning. His service under de Ruyter wasn't wasted on him. That was a great seaman, and—blister me!—the pupil's worthy the master if I am a judge of anything. I doubt if the Royal Navy can show his equal. To thrust himself deliberately between those two, at point-blank range, and so turn the tables on them! It asks courage, resource, and invention. And we land-lubbers were not the only ones he tricked by his manoeuvre. That Spanish Admiral never guessed the intent until it was too late and Blood held him in check. A great man, Miss Bishop. A man worth regarding."

Miss Bishop was moved to sarcasm.

"You should use your influence with my Lord Sunderland to have the King offer him a commission."

His lordship laughed softly. "Faith, it's done already. I have his commission in my pocket." And he increased her amazement by a brief exposition of the circumstances. In that amazement he left her, and went in quest of Blood. But he was still intrigued. If she were a little less uncompromising in her attitude towards Blood, his lordship would have been happier.

He found the Captain pacing the quarter-deck, a man mentally exhausted from wrestling with the Devil, although of this particular occupation his lordship could have no possible suspicion. With the amiable familiarity he used, Lord Julian slipped an arm through one of the Captain's, and fell into step beside him.

"What's this?" snapped Blood, whose mood was fierce and raw. His lordship was not disturbed.

"I desire, sir, that we be friends," said he suavely.

"That's mighty condescending of you!"

Lord Julian ignored the obvious sarcasm.

"It's an odd coincidence that we should have been brought together in this fashion, considering that I came out to the Indies especially to seek you."

"Ye're not by any means the first to do that," the other scoffed. "But they've mainly been Spaniards, and they hadn't your luck."

"You misapprehend me completely," said Lord Julian. And on that he proceeded to explain himself and his mission.

When he had done, Captain Blood, who until that moment had stood still under the spell of his astonishment, disengaged his arm from his lordship's, and stood squarely before him.

"Ye're my guest aboard this ship," said he, "and I still have some notion of decent behaviour left me from other days, thief and pirate though I may be. So I'll not be telling you what I think of you for daring to bring me this offer, or of my Lord Sunderland—since he's your kinsman for having the impudence to send it. But it does not surprise me at all that one who is a minister of James Stuart's should conceive that every man is to be seduced by bribes into betraying those who trust him." He flung out an arm in the direction of the waist, whence came the half-melancholy chant of the lounging buccaneers.

"Again you misapprehend me," cried Lord Julian, between concern and indignation. "That is not intended. Your followers will be included in your commission."

"And d' ye think they'll go with me to hunt their brethren—the Brethren of the Coast? On my soul, Lord Julian, it is yourself does the misapprehending. Are there not even notions of honour left in England? Oh, and there's more to it than that, even. D'ye think I could take a commission of King James's? I tell you I wouldn't be soiling my hands with it—thief and pirate's hands though they be. Thief and pirate is what you heard Miss Bishop call me to-day—a thing of scorn, an outcast. And who made me that? Who made me thief and pirate?"

"If you were a rebel...?" his lordship was beginning.

"Ye must know that I was no such thing—no rebel at all. It wasn't even pretended. If it were, I could forgive them. But not even that cloak could they cast upon their foulness. Oh, no; there was no mistake. I was convicted for what I did, neither more nor less. That bloody vampire Jeffreys—bad cess to him!—sentenced me to death, and his worthy master James Stuart afterwards sent me into slavery, because I had performed an act of mercy; because compassionately and without thought for creed or politics I had sought to relieve the sufferings of a fellow-creature; because I had dressed the wounds of a man who was convicted of treason. That was all my offence. You'll find it in the records. And for that I was sold into slavery: because by the law of England, as administered by James Stuart in violation of the laws of God, who harbours or comforts a rebel is himself adjudged guilty of rebellion. D'ye dream man, what it is to be a slave?"

He checked suddenly at the very height of his passion. A moment he paused, then cast it from him as if it had been a cloak. His voice sank again. He uttered a little laugh of weariness and contempt.

"But there! I grow hot for nothing at all. I explain myself, I think, and God knows, it is not my custom. I am grateful to you, Lord Julian, for your kindly intentions. I am so. But ye'll understand, perhaps. Ye look as if ye might."

Lord Julian stood still. He was deeply stricken by the other's words, the passionate, eloquent outburst that in a few sharp, clear-cut strokes had so convincingly presented the man's bitter case against humanity, his complete apologia and justification for all that could be laid to his charge. His lordship looked at that keen, intrepid face gleaming lividly in the light of the great poop lantern, and his own eyes were troubled. He was abashed.

He fetched a heavy sigh. "A pity," he said slowly. "Oh, blister me—a cursed pity!" He held out his hand, moved to it on a sudden generous impulse. "But no offence between us, Captain Blood!"

"Oh, no offence. But... I'm a thief and a pirate." He laughed without mirth, and, disregarding the proffered hand, swung on his heel.

Lord Julian stood a moment, watching the tall figure as it moved away towards the taffrail. Then letting his arms fall helplessly to his sides in dejection, he departed.

Just within the doorway of the alley leading to the cabin, he ran into Miss Bishop. Yet she had not been coming out, for her back was towards him, and she was moving in the same direction. He followed her, his mind too full of Captain Blood to be concerned just then with her movements.

In the cabin he flung into a chair, and exploded, with a violence altogether foreign to his nature.

"Damme if ever I met a man I liked better, or even a man I liked as well. Yet there's nothing to be done with him."

"So I heard," she admitted in a small voice. She was very white, and she kept her eyes upon her folded hands.

He looked up in surprise, and then sat conning her with brooding glance. "I wonder, now," he said presently, "if the mischief is of your working. Your words have rankled with him. He threw them at me again and again. He wouldn't take the King's commission; he wouldn't take my hand even. What's to be done with a fellow like that? He'll end on a yardarm for all his luck. And the quixotic fool is running into danger at the present moment on our behalf."

"How?" she asked him with a sudden startled interest.

"How? Have you forgotten that he's sailing to Jamaica, and that Jamaica is the headquarters of the English fleet? True, your uncle commands it...."

She leaned across the table to interrupt him, and he observed that her breathing had grown labored, that her eyes were dilating in alarm.

"But there is no hope for him in that!" she cried. "Oh, don't imagine it! He has no bitterer enemy in the world! My uncle is a hard, unforgiving man. I believe that it was nothing but the hope of taking and hanging Captain Blood that made my uncle leave his Barbados plantations to accept the deputy-governorship of Jamaica. Captain Blood doesn't know that, of course...." She paused with a little gesture of helplessness.

"I can't think that it would make the least difference if he did," said his lordship gravely. "A man who can forgive such an enemy as Don Miguel and take up this uncompromising attitude with me isn't to be judged by ordinary rules. He's chivalrous to the point of idiocy."

"And yet he has been what he has been and done what he has done in these last three years," said she, but she said it sorrowfully now, without any of her earlier scorn.

Lord Julian was sententious, as I gather that he often was. "Life can be infernally complex," he sighed.

CHAPTER XXI. THE SERVICE OF KING JAMES

Miss Arabella Bishop was aroused very early on the following morning by the brazen voice of a bugle and the insistent clanging of a bell in the ship's belfry. As she lay awake, idly watching the rippled green water that appeared to be streaming past the heavily glazed porthole, she became gradually aware of the sounds of swift, laboured bustle—the clatter of many feet, the shouts of hoarse voices, and the persistent trundlings of heavy bodies in the ward-room immediately below the deck of the cabin. Conceiving these sounds to portend a more than normal activity, she sat up, pervaded by a vague alarm, and roused her still slumbering woman.

In his cabin on the starboard side Lord Julian, disturbed by the same sounds, was already astir and hurriedly dressing. When presently he emerged under the break of the poop, he found himself staring up into a mountain of canvas. Every foot of sail that she could carry had been crowded to the Arabella's yards, to catch the morning breeze. Ahead and on either side stretched the limitless expanse of ocean, sparkling golden in the sun, as yet no more than a half-disc of flame upon the horizon straight ahead.

About him in the waist, where all last night had been so peaceful, there was a frenziedly active bustle of some threescore men. By the rail, immediately above and behind Lord Julian, stood Captain Blood in altercation with a one-eyed giant, whose head was swathed in a red cotton kerchief, whose blue shirt hung open at the waist. As his lordship, moving forward, revealed himself, their voices ceased, and Blood turned to greet him.

"Good-morning to you," he said, and added "I've blundered badly, so I have. I should have known better than to come so close to Jamaica by night. But I was in haste to land you. Come up here. I have something to show you."

Wondering, Lord Julian mounted the companion as he was bidden. Standing beside Captain Blood, he looked astern, following the indication of the Captain's hand, and cried out in his amazement. There, not more than three miles away, was land—an uneven wall of vivid green that filled the western horizon. And a couple of miles this side of it, bearing after them, came speeding three great white ships.

"They fly no colours, but they're part of the Jamaica fleet." Blood spoke without excitement, almost with a certain listlessness. "When dawn broke we found ourselves running to meet them. We went about, and it's been a race ever since.

But the Arabella 's been at sea these four months, and her bottom's too foul for the speed we're needing."

Wolverstone hooked his thumbs into his broad leather belt, and from his great height looked down sardonically upon Lord Julian, tall man though his lordship was. "So that you're like to be in yet another sea-fight afore ye've done wi' ships, my lord."

"That's a point we were just arguing," said Blood. "For I hold that we're in no case to fight against such odds."

"The odds be damned!" Wolverstone thrust out his heavy jowl. "We're used to odds. The odds was heavier at Maracaybo; yet we won out, and took three ships. They was heavier yesterday when we engaged Don Miguel."

"Aye—but those were Spaniards."

"And what better are these?—Are ye afeard of a lubberly Barbados planter? Whatever ails you, Peter? I've never known ye scared afore."

A gun boomed out behind them.

"That'll be the signal to lie to," said Blood, in the same listless voice; and he fetched a sigh.

Wolverstone squared himself defiantly before his captain

"I'll see Colonel Bishop in hell or ever I lies to for him." And he spat, presumably for purposes of emphasis.

His lordship intervened.

"Oh, but—by your leave—surely there is nothing to be apprehended from Colonel Bishop. Considering the service you have rendered to his niece and to me...."

Wolverstone's horse-laugh interrupted him. "Hark to the gentleman!" he mocked. "Ye don't know Colonel Bishop, that's clear. Not for his niece, not for his daughter, not for his own mother, would he forgo the blood what he thinks due to him. A drinker of blood, he is. A nasty beast. We knows, the Cap'n and me. We been his slaves."

"But there is myself," said Lord Julian, with great dignity.

Wolverstone laughed again, whereat his lordship flushed. He was moved to raise his voice above its usual languid level.

"I assure you that my word counts for something in England."

"Oh, aye—in England. But this ain't England, damme."

Came the roar of a second gun, and a round shot splashed the water less than half a cable's-length astern. Blood leaned over the rail to speak to the fair young man immediately below him by the helmsman at the whipstaff.

"Bid them take in sail, Jeremy," he said quietly. "We lie to."

But Wolverstone interposed again.

"Hold there a moment, Jeremy!" he roared. "Wait!" He swung back to face the Captain, who had placed a hand on is shoulder and was smiling, a trifle wistfully.

"Steady, Old Wolf! Steady!" Captain Blood admonished him.

"Steady, yourself, Peter. Ye've gone mad! Will ye doom us all to hell out of tenderness for that cold slip of a girl?"

"Stop!" cried Blood in sudden fury.

But Wolverstone would not stop. "It's the truth, you fool. It's that cursed petticoat's making a coward of you. It's for her that ye're afeard—and she, Colonel Bishop's niece! My God, man, ye'll have a mutiny aboard, and I'll lead it myself sooner than surrender to be hanged in Port Royal."

Their glances met, sullen defiance braving dull anger, surprise, and pain.

"There is no question," said Blood, "of surrender for any man aboard save only myself. If Bishop can report to England that I am taken and hanged, he will magnify himself and at the same time gratify his personal rancour against me. That should satisfy him. I'll send him a message offering to surrender aboard his ship, taking Miss Bishop and Lord Julian with me, but only on condition that the Arabella is allowed to proceed unharmed. It's a bargain that he'll accept, if I know him at all."

"It's a bargain he'll never be offered," retorted Wolverstone, and his earlier vehemence was as nothing to his vehemence now. "Ye're surely daft even to think of it, Peter!"

"Not so daft as you when you talk of fighting that." He flung out an arm as he spoke to indicate the pursuing ships, which were slowly but surely creeping nearer. "Before we've run another half-mile we shall be within range."

Wolverstone swore elaborately, then suddenly checked. Out of the tail of his single eye he had espied a trim figure in grey silk that was ascending the companion. So engrossed had they been that they had not seen Miss Bishop come from the door of the passage leading to the cabin. And there was something else that those three men on the poop, and Pitt immediately below them, had failed to observe. Some moments ago Ogle, followed by the main body of his gun-deck crew, had emerged from the booby hatch, to fall into muttered, angrily vehement talk with those who, abandoning the gun-tackles upon which they were labouring, had come to crowd about him.

Even now Blood had no eyes for that. He turned to look at Miss Bishop, marvelling a little, after the manner in which yesterday she had avoided him, that she should now venture upon the quarter-deck. Her presence at this moment, and considering the nature of his altercation with Wolverstone, was embarrassing.

Very sweet and dainty she stood before him in her gown of shimmering grey, a faint excitement tinting her fair cheeks and sparkling in her clear, hazel eyes, that looked so frank and honest. She wore no hat, and the ringlets of her gold-brown hair fluttered distractingly in the morning breeze.

Captain Blood bared his head and bowed silently in a greeting which she returned composedly and formally.

"What is happening, Lord Julian?" she enquired.

As if to answer her a third gun spoke from the ships towards which she was looking intent and wonderingly. A frown rumpled her brow. She looked from one to the other of the men who stood there so glum and obviously ill at ease.

"They are ships of the Jamaica fleet," his lordship answered her.

It should in any case have been a sufficient explanation. But before more could be added, their attention was drawn at last to Ogle, who came bounding up the broad ladder, and to the men lounging aft in his wake, in all of which, instinctively, they apprehended a vague menace.

At the head of the companion, Ogle found his progress barred by Blood, who confronted him, a sudden sternness in his face and in every line of him.

"What's this?" the Captain demanded sharply. "Your station is on the gundeck. Why have you left it?"

Thus challenged, the obvious truculence faded out of Ogle's bearing, quenched by the old habit of obedience and the natural dominance that was the secret of the Captain's rule over his wild followers. But it gave no pause to the gunner's intention. If anything it increased his excitement.

"Captain," he said, and as he spoke he pointed to the pursuing ships, "Colonel Bishop holds us. We're in no case either to run or fight."

Blood's height seemed to increase, as did his sternness.

"Ogle," said he, in a voice cold and sharp as steel, "your station is on the gundeck. You'll return to it at once, and take your crew with you, or else...."

But Ogle, violent of mien and gesture, interrupted him.

"Threats will not serve, Captain."

"Will they not?"

It was the first time in his buccaneering career that an order of his had been disregarded, or that a man had failed in the obedience to which he pledged all those who joined him. That this insubordination should proceed from one of those whom he most trusted, one of his old Barbados associates, was in itself a bitterness, and made him reluctant to that which instinct told him must be done. His hand closed over the butt of one of the pistols slung before him.

"Nor will that serve you," Ogle warned him, still more fiercely. "The men are of my thinking, and they'll have their way."

"And what way may that be?"

"The way to make us safe. We'll neither sink nor hang whiles we can help it."

From the three or four score men massed below in the waist came a rumble of approval. Captain Blood's glance raked the ranks of those resolute, fierce-eyed fellows, then it came to rest again on Ogle. There was here quite plainly a vague threat, a mutinous spirit he could not understand. "You come to give advice, then, do you?" quoth he, relenting nothing of his sternness.

"That's it, Captain; advice. That girl, there." He flung out a bare arm to point to her. "Bishop's girl; the Governor of Jamaica's niece.... We want her as a hostage for our safety."

"Aye!" roared in chorus the buccaneers below, and one or two of them elaborated that affirmation.

In a flash Captain Blood saw what was in their minds. And for all that he lost nothing of his outward stern composure, fear invaded his heart.

"And how," he asked, "do you imagine that Miss Bishop will prove such a hostage?"

"It's a providence having her aboard; a providence. Heave to, Captain, and signal them to send a boat, and assure themselves that Miss is here. Then let them know that if they attempt to hinder our sailing hence, we'll hang the doxy first and fight for it after. That'll cool Colonel Bishop's heat, maybe."

"And maybe it won't." Slow and mocking came Wolverstone's voice to answer the other's confident excitement, and as he spoke he advanced to Blood's side, an unexpected ally. "Some o' them dawcocks may believe that tale." He jerked a contemptuous thumb towards the men in the waist, whose ranks were steadily being increased by the advent of others from the forecastle. "Although even some o' they should know better, for there's still a few was on Barbados with us, and are acquainted like me and you with Colonel Bishop. If ye're counting on pulling Bishop's heartstrings, ye're a bigger fool, Ogle, than I've always thought you was with anything but guns. There's no heaving to for such a matter as that unless you wants to make quite sure of our being sunk. Though we had a cargo of Bishop's nieces it wouldn't make him hold his hand. Why, as I was just telling his lordship here, who thought like you that having Miss Bishop aboard would make us safe, not for his mother would that filthy slaver forgo what's due to him. And if ye' weren't a fool, Ogle, you wouldn't need me to tell you this. We've got to fight, my lads...."

"How can we fight, man?" Ogle stormed at him, furiously battling the conviction which Wolverstone's argument was imposing upon his listeners. "You may be right, and you may be wrong. We've got to chance it. It's our only chance...."

The rest of his words were drowned in the shouts of the hands insisting that the girl be given up to be held as a hostage. And then louder than before roared a gun away to leeward, and away on their starboard beam they saw the spray flung up by the shot, which had gone wide.

"They are within range," cried Ogle. And leaning from the rail, "Put down the helm," he commanded.

Pitt, at his post beside the helmsman, turned intrepidly to face the excited gunner.

"Since when have you commanded on the main deck, Ogle? I take my orders from the Captain."

"You'll take this order from me, or, by God, you'll...."

"Wait!" Blood bade him, interrupting, and he set a restraining hand upon the gunner's arm. "There is, I think, a better way."

He looked over his shoulder, aft, at the advancing ships, the foremost of which was now a bare quarter of a mile away. His glance swept in passing over Miss Bishop and Lord Julian standing side by side some paces behind him. He observed her pale and tense, with parted lips and startled eyes that were fixed upon him, an anxious witness of this deciding of her fate. He was thinking swiftly, reckoning the chances if by pistolling Ogle he were to provoke a mutiny. That some of the men would rally to him, he was sure. But he was no less sure that the main body would oppose him, and prevail in spite of all that he could do, taking the chance that holding Miss Bishop to ransom seemed to afford them. And if they did that, one way or the other, Miss Bishop would be lost. For even if Bishop yielded to their demand, they would retain her as a hostage.

Meanwhile Ogle was growing impatient. His arm still gripped by Blood, he thrust his face into the Captain's.

"What better way?" he demanded. "There is none better. I'll not be bubbled by what Wolverstone has said. He may be right, and he may be wrong. We'll test it. It's our only chance, I've said, and we must take it."

The better way that was in Captain Blood's mind was the way that already he had proposed to Wolverstone. Whether the men in the panic Ogle had aroused among them would take a different view from Wolverstone's he did not know. But he saw quite clearly now that if they consented, they would not on that account depart from their intention in the matter of Miss Bishop; they would make of Blood's own surrender merely an additional card in this game against the Governor of Jamaica.

"It's through her that we're in this trap," Ogle stormed on. "Through her and through you. It was to bring her to Jamaica that you risked all our lives, and we're not going to lose our lives as long as there's a chance to make ourselves safe through her."

He was turning again to the helmsman below, when Blood's grip tightened on his arm. Ogle wrenched it free, with an oath. But Blood's mind was now made up. He had found the only way, and repellent though it might be to him, he must take it.

"That is a desperate chance," he cried. "Mine is the safe and easy way. Wait!" He leaned over the rail. "Put the helm down," he bade Pitt. "Heave her to, and signal to them to send a boat."

A silence of astonishment fell upon the ship—of astonishment and suspicion at this sudden yielding. But Pitt, although he shared it, was prompt to obey. His voice rang out, giving the necessary orders, and after an instant's pause, a score of hands sprang to execute them. Came the creak of blocks and the rattle of slatting sails as they swung aweather, and Captain Blood turned and beckoned Lord Julian forward. His lordship, after a moment's hesitation, advanced in surprise and mistrust—a mistrust shared by Miss Bishop, who, like his lordship and all else aboard, though in a different way, had been taken aback by Blood's sudden submission to the demand to lie to.

Standing now at the rail, with Lord Julian beside him, Captain Blood explained himself.

Briefly and clearly he announced to all the object of Lord Julian's voyage to the Caribbean, and he informed them of the offer which yesterday Lord Julian had made to him.

"That offer I rejected, as his lordship will tell you, deeming myself affronted by it. Those of you who have suffered under the rule of King James will understand me. But now in the desperate case in which we find ourselves—outsailed, and likely to be outfought, as Ogle has said—I am ready to take the way of Morgan: to accept the King's commission and shelter us all behind it."

It was a thunderbolt that for a moment left them all dazed. Then Babel was reenacted. The main body of them welcomed the announcement as only men who have been preparing to die can welcome a new lease of life. But many could not resolve one way or the other until they were satisfied upon several questions, and chiefly upon one which was voiced by Ogle.

"Will Bishop respect the commission when you hold it?"

It was Lord Julian who answered:

"It will go very hard with him if he attempts to flout the King's authority. And though he should dare attempt it, be sure that his own officers will not dare to do other than oppose him."

"Aye," said Ogle, "that is true."

But there were some who were still in open and frank revolt against the course. Of these was Wolverstone, who at once proclaimed his hostility.

"I'll rot in hell or ever I serves the King," he bawled in a great rage.

But Blood quieted him and those who thought as he did.

"No man need follow me into the King's service who is reluctant. That is not in the bargain. What is in the bargain is that I accept this service with such of you as may choose to follow me. Don't think I accept it willingly. For myself, I am entirely of Wolverstone's opinion. I accept it as the only way to save us all from the certain destruction into which my own act may have brought us. And even those of you who do not choose to follow me shall share the immunity of all, and shall afterwards be free to depart. Those are the terms upon which I sell myself to the King. Let Lord Julian, the representative of the Secretary of State, say whether he agrees to them."

Prompt, eager, and clear came his lordship's agreement. And that was practically the end of the matter. Lord Julian, the butt now of good-humouredly ribald jests and half-derisive acclamations, plunged away to his cabin for the commission, secretly rejoicing at a turn of events which enabled him so creditably to discharge the business on which he had been sent.

Meanwhile the bo'sun signalled to the Jamaica ships to send a boat, and the men in the waist broke their ranks and went noisily flocking to line the bulwarks and view the great stately vessels that were racing down towards them.

As Ogle left the quarter-deck, Blood turned, and came face to face with Miss Bishop. She had been observing him with shining eyes, but at sight of his dejected countenance, and the deep frown that scarred his brow, her own expression changed. She approached him with a hesitation entirely unusual to her. She set a hand lightly upon his arm.

"You have chosen wisely, sir," she commended him, "however much against your inclinations."

He looked with gloomy eyes upon her for whom he had made this sacrifice.

"I owed it to you—or thought I did," he said.

She did not understand. "Your resolve delivered me from a horrible danger," she admitted. And she shivered at the memory of it. "But I do not understand why you should have hesitated when first it was proposed to you. It is an honourable service."

"King James's?" he sneered.

"England's," she corrected him in reproof. "The country is all, sir; the sovereign naught. King James will pass; others will come and pass; England remains, to be honourably served by her sons, whatever rancour they may hold against the man who rules her in their time."

He showed some surprise. Then he smiled a little. "Shrewd advocacy," he approved it. "You should have spoken to the crew."

And then, the note of irony deepening in his voice: "Do you suppose now that this honourable service might redeem one who was a pirate and a thief?"

Her glance fell away. Her voice faltered a little in replying. "If he... needs redeeming. Perhaps... perhaps he has been judged too harshly."

The blue eyes flashed, and the firm lips relaxed their grim set.

"Why... if ye think that," he said, considering her, an odd hunger in his glance, "life might have its uses, after all, and even the service of King James might become tolerable."

Looking beyond her, across the water, he observed a boat putting off from one of the great ships, which, hove to now, were rocking gently some three hundred yards away. Abruptly his manner changed. He was like one recovering, taking himself in hand again. "If you will go below, and get your gear and your woman, you shall presently be sent aboard one of the ships of the fleet." He pointed to the boat as he spoke.

She left him, and thereafter with Wolverstone, leaning upon the rail, he watched the approach of that boat, manned by a dozen sailors, and commanded by a scarlet figure seated stiffly in the stern sheets. He levelled his telescope upon that figure.

"It'll not be Bishop himself," said Wolverstone, between question and assertion.

"No." Blood closed his telescope. "I don't know who it is."

"Ha!" Wolverstone vented an ejaculation of sneering mirth. "For all his eagerness, Bishop'd be none so willing to come, hisself. He's been aboard this hulk afore, and we made him swim for it that time. He'll have his memories. So he sends a deputy."

This deputy proved to be an officer named Calverley, a vigorous, self-sufficient fellow, comparatively fresh from England, whose manner made it clear that he came fully instructed by Colonel Bishop upon the matter of how to handle the pirates.

His air, as he stepped into the waist of the Arabella, was haughty, truculent, and disdainful.

Blood, the King's commission now in his pocket, and Lord Julian standing beside him, waited to receive him, and Captain Calverley was a little taken aback at finding himself confronted by two men so very different outwardly from anything that he had expected. But he lost none of his haughty poise, and scarcely deigned a glance at the swarm of fierce, half-naked fellows lounging in a semicircle to form a background.

"Good-day to you, sir," Blood hailed him pleasantly. "I have the honour to give you welcome aboard the Arabella. My name is Blood—Captain Blood, at your service. You may have heard of me."

Captain Calverley stared hard. The airy manner of this redoubtable buccaneer was hardly what he had looked for in a desperate fellow, compelled to ignominious surrender. A thin, sour smile broke on the officer's haughty lips.

"You'll ruffle it to the gallows, no doubt," he said contemptuously. "I suppose that is after the fashion of your kind. Meanwhile it's your surrender I require, my man, not your impudence."

Captain Blood appeared surprised, pained. He turned in appeal to Lord Julian.

"D'ye hear that now? And did ye ever hear the like? But what did I tell ye? Ye see, the young gentleman's under a misapprehension entirely. Perhaps it'll save broken bones if your lordship explains just who and what I am."

Lord Julian advanced a step and bowed perfunctorily and rather disdainfully to that very disdainful but now dumbfounded officer. Pitt, who watched the scene from the quarter-deck rail, tells us that his lordship was as grave as a parson at a hanging. But I suspect this gravity for a mask under which Lord Julian was secretly amused.

"I have the honour to inform you, sir," he said stiffly, "that Captain Blood holds a commission in the King's service under the seal of my Lord Sunderland, His Majesty's Secretary of State."

Captain Calverley's face empurpled; his eyes bulged. The buccaneers in the background chuckled and crowed and swore among themselves in their relish of this comedy. For a long moment Calverley stared in silence at his lordship, observing the costly elegance of his dress, his air of calm assurance, and his cold, fastidious speech, all of which savoured distinctly of the great world to which he belonged.

"And who the devil may you be?" he exploded at last.

Colder still and more distant than ever grew his lordship's voice.

"You're not very civil, sir, as I have already noticed. My name is Wade—Lord Julian Wade. I am His Majesty's envoy to these barbarous parts, and my Lord Sunderland's near kinsman. Colonel Bishop has been notified of my coming."

The sudden change in Calverley's manner at Lord Julian's mention of his name showed that the notification had been received, and that he had knowledge of it.

"I... I believe that he has," said Calverley, between doubt and suspicion. "That is: that he has been notified of the coming of Lord Julian Wade. But... but... aboard this ship...?" The officer made a gesture of helplessness, and, surrendering to his bewilderment, fell abruptly silent.

"I was coming out on the Royal Mary...."

"That is what we were advised."

"But the Royal Mary fell a victim to a Spanish privateer, and I might never have arrived at all but for the gallantry of Captain Blood, who rescued me."

Light broke upon the darkness of Calverley's mind. "I see. I understand."

"I will take leave to doubt it." His lordship's tone abated nothing of its asperity. "But that can wait. If Captain Blood will show you his commission, perhaps that will set all doubts at rest, and we may proceed. I shall be glad to reach Port Royal."

Captain Blood thrust a parchment under Calverley's bulging eyes. The officer scanned it, particularly the seals and signature. He stepped back, a baffled, impotent man. He bowed helplessly.

"I must return to Colonel Bishop for my orders," he informed them.

At that moment a lane was opened in the ranks of the men, and through this came Miss Bishop followed by her octoroon woman. Over his shoulder Captain Blood observed her approach.

"Perhaps, since Colonel Bishop is with you, you will convey his niece to him. Miss Bishop was aboard the Royal Mary also, and I rescued her together with his lordship. She will be able to acquaint her uncle with the details of that and of the present state of affairs."

Swept thus from surprise to surprise, Captain Calverley could do no more than bow again.

"As for me," said Lord Julian, with intent to make Miss Bishop's departure free from all interference on the part of the buccaneers, "I shall remain aboard the Arabella until we reach Port Royal. My compliments to Colonel Bishop. Say that I look forward to making his acquaintance there."

CHAPTER XXII. HOSTILITIES

In the great harbour of Port Royal, spacious enough to have given moorings to all the ships of all the navies of the world, the Arabella rode at anchor. Almost she had the air of a prisoner, for a quarter of a mile ahead, to starboard, rose the lofty, massive single round tower of the fort, whilst a couple of cables'-length astern, and to larboard, rode the six men-of-war that composed the Jamaica squadron.

Abeam with the Arabella, across the harbour, were the flat-fronted white buildings of that imposing city that came down to the very water's edge. Behind these the red roofs rose like terraces, marking the gentle slope upon which the city was built, dominated here by a turret, there by a spire, and behind these again a range of green hills with for ultimate background a sky that was like a dome of polished steel.

On a cane day-bed that had been set for him on the quarter-deck, sheltered from the dazzling, blistering sunshine by an improvised awning of brown sail-cloth, lounged Peter Blood, a calf-bound, well-thumbed copy of Horace's Odes neglected in his hands.

From immediately below him came the swish of mops and the gurgle of water in the scuppers, for it was still early morning, and under the directions of Hayton, the bo'sun, the swabbers were at work in the waist and forecastle. Despite the heat and the stagnant air, one of the toilers found breath to croak a ribald buccaneering ditty:

"For we laid her board and board,
And we put her to the sword,
And we sank her in the deep blue sea.
So It's heigh-ho, and heave-a-ho!
Who'll sail for the Main with me?"

Blood fetched a sigh, and the ghost of a smile played over his lean, sun-tanned face. Then the black brows came together above the vivid blue eyes, and thought swiftly closed the door upon his immediate surroundings.

Things had not sped at all well with him in the past fortnight since his acceptance of the King's commission. There had been trouble with Bishop from the moment of landing. As Blood and Lord Julian had stepped ashore together, they had been met by a man who took no pains to dissemble his chagrin at the turn of events and his determination to change it. He awaited them on the mole, supported by a group of officers.

"You are Lord Julian Wade, I understand," was his truculent greeting. For Blood at the moment he had nothing beyond a malignant glance.

Lord Julian bowed. "I take it I have the honour to address Colonel Bishop, Deputy-Governor of Jamaica." It was almost as if his lordship were giving the Colonel a lesson in deportment. The Colonel accepted it, and belatedly bowed, removing his broad hat. Then he plunged on.

"You have granted, I am told, the King's commission to this man." His very tone betrayed the bitterness of his rancour. "Your motives were no doubt worthy... your gratitude to him for delivering you from the Spaniards. But the thing itself is unthinkable, my lord. The commission must be cancelled."

"I don't think I understand," said Lord Julian distantly.

"To be sure you don't, or you'd never ha' done it. The fellow's bubbled you. Why, he's first a rebel, then an escaped slave, and lastly a bloody pirate. I've been hunting him this year past."

"I assure you, sir, that I was fully informed of all. I do not grant the King's commission lightly."

"Don't you, by God! And what else do you call this? But as His Majesty's Deputy-Governor of Jamaica, I'll take leave to correct your mistake in my own way."

"Ah! And what way may that be?"

"There's a gallows waiting for this rascal in Port Royal."

Blood would have intervened at that, but Lord Julian forestalled him.

"I see, sir, that you do not yet quite apprehend the circumstances. If it is a mistake to grant Captain Blood a commission, the mistake is not mine. I am acting upon the instructions of my Lord Sunderland; and with a full knowledge of all the facts, his lordship expressly designated Captain Blood for this commission if Captain Blood could be persuaded to accept it."

Colonel Bishop's mouth fell open in surprise and dismay.

"Lord Sunderland designated him?" he asked, amazed.

"Expressly."

His lordship waited a moment for a reply. None coming from the speechless Deputy-Governor, he asked a question: "Would you still venture to describe the matter as a mistake, sir? And dare you take the risk of correcting it?"

"I... I had not dreamed...."

"I understand, sir. Let me present Captain Blood."

Perforce Bishop must put on the best face he could command. But that it was no more than a mask for his fury and his venom was plain to all.

From that unpromising beginning matters had not improved; rather had they grown worse.

Blood's thoughts were upon this and other things as he lounged there on the day-bed. He had been a fortnight in Port Royal, his ship virtually a unit now in the

Jamaica squadron. And when the news of it reached Tortuga and the buccaneers who awaited his return, the name of Captain Blood, which had stood so high among the Brethren of the Coast, would become a byword, a thing of execration, and before all was done his life might pay forfeit for what would be accounted a treacherous defection. And for what had he placed himself in this position? For the sake of a girl who avoided him so persistently and intentionally that he must assume that she still regarded him with aversion. He had scarcely been vouchsafed a glimpse of her in all this fortnight, although with that in view for his main object he had daily haunted her uncle's residence, and daily braved the unmasked hostility and baffled rancour in which Colonel Bishop held him. Nor was that the worst of it. He was allowed plainly to perceive that it was the graceful, elegant young trifler from St. James's, Lord Julian Wade, to whom her every moment was devoted. And what chance had he, a desperate adventurer with a record of outlawry, against such a rival as that, a man of parts, moreover, as he was bound to admit?

You conceive the bitterness of his soul. He beheld himself to be as the dog in the fable that had dropped the substance to snatch at a delusive shadow.

He sought comfort in a line on the open page before him:

"levius fit patientia quicquid corrigere est nefas."

Sought it, but hardly found it.

A boat that had approached unnoticed from the shore came scraping and bumping against the great red hull of the Arabella, and a raucous voice sent up a hailing shout. From the ship's belfry two silvery notes rang clear and sharp, and a moment or two later the bo'sun's whistle shrilled a long wail.

The sounds disturbed Captain Blood from his disgruntled musings. He rose, tall, active, and arrestingly elegant in a scarlet, gold-laced coat that advertised his new position, and slipping the slender volume into his pocket, advanced to the carved rail of the quarter-deck, just as Jeremy Pitt was setting foot upon the companion.

"A note for you from the Deputy-Governor," said the master shortly, as he proffered a folded sheet.

Blood broke the seal, and read. Pitt, loosely clad in shirt and breeches, leaned against the rail the while and watched him, unmistakable concern imprinted on his fair, frank countenance.

Blood uttered a short laugh, and curled his lip. "It is a very peremptory summons," he said, and passed the note to his friend.

The young master's grey eyes skimmed it. Thoughtfully he stroked his golden beard.

"You'll not go?" he said, between question and assertion.

"Why not? Haven't I been a daily visitor at the fort...?"

"But it'll be about the Old Wolf that he wants to see you. It gives him a grievance at last. You know, Peter, that it is Lord Julian alone has stood between Bishop and his hate of you. If now he can show that...."

"What if he can?" Blood interrupted carelessly. "Shall I be in greater danger ashore than aboard, now that we've but fifty men left, and they lukewarm rogues who would as soon serve the King as me? Jeremy, dear lad, the Arabella's a prisoner here, bedad, 'twixt the fort there and the fleet yonder. Don't be forgetting that."

Jeremy clenched his hands. "Why did ye let Wolverstone and the others go?" he cried, with a touch of bitterness. "You should have seen the danger."

"How could I in honesty have detained them? It was in the bargain. Besides, how could their staying have helped me?" And as Pitt did not answer him: "Ye see?" he said, and shrugged. "I'll be getting my hat and cane and sword, and go ashore in the cock-boat. See it manned for me."

"Ye're going to deliver yourself into Bishop's hands," Pitt warned him.

"Well, well, maybe he'll not find me quite so easy to grasp as he imagines. There's a thorn or two left on me." And with a laugh Blood departed to his cabin.

Jeremy Pitt answered the laugh with an oath. A moment he stood irresolute where Blood had left him. Then slowly, reluctance dragging at his feet, he went down the companion to give the order for the cock-boat.

"If anything should happen to you, Peter," he said, as Blood was going over the side, "Colonel Bishop had better look to himself. These fifty lads may be lukewarm at present, as you say, but—sink me!—they'll be anything but lukewarm if there's a breach of faith."

"And what should be happening to me, Jeremy? Sure, now, I'll be back for dinner, so I will."

Blood climbed down into the waiting boat. But laugh though he might, he knew as well as Pitt that in going ashore that morning he carried his life in his hands. Because of this, it may have been that when he stepped on to the narrow mole, in the shadow of the shallow outer wall of the fort through whose crenels were thrust the black noses of its heavy guns, he gave order that the boat should stay for him at that spot. He realized that he might have to retreat in a hurry.

Walking leisurely, he skirted the embattled wall, and passed through the great gates into the courtyard. Half-a-dozen soldiers lounged there, and in the shadow cast by the wall, Major Mallard, the Commandant, was slowly pacing. He stopped short at sight of Captain Blood, and saluted him, as was his due, but the smile that lifted the officer's stiff mostachios was grimly sardonic. Peter Blood's attention, however, was elsewhere.

On his right stretched a spacious garden, beyond which rose the white house that was the residence of the Deputy-Governor. In that garden's main avenue, that was fringed with palm and sandalwood, he had caught sight of Miss Bishop alone. He crossed the courtyard with suddenly lengthened stride.

"Good-morning to ye, ma'am," was his greeting as he overtook her; and hat in hand now, he added on a note of protest: "Sure, it's nothing less than uncharitable to make me run in this heat."

"Why do you run, then?" she asked him coolly, standing slim and straight before him, all in white and very maidenly save in her unnatural composure. "I am pressed," she informed him. "So you will forgive me if I do not stay."

"You were none so pressed until I came," he protested, and if his thin lips smiled, his blue eyes were oddly hard.

"Since you perceive it, sir, I wonder that you trouble to be so insistent."

That crossed the swords between them, and it was against Blood's instincts to avoid an engagement.

"Faith, you explain yourself after a fashion," said he. "But since it was more or less in your service that I donned the King's coat, you should suffer it to cover the thief and pirate."

She shrugged and turned aside, in some resentment and some regret. Fearing to betray the latter, she took refuge in the former. "I do my best," said she.

"So that ye can be charitable in some ways!" He laughed softly. "Glory be, now, I should be thankful for so much. Maybe I'm presumptuous. But I can't forget that when I was no better than a slave in your uncle's household in Barbados, ye used me with a certain kindness."

"Why not? In those days you had some claim upon my kindness. You were just an unfortunate gentleman then."

"And what else would you be calling me now?"

"Hardly unfortunate. We have heard of your good fortune on the seas—how your luck has passed into a byword. And we have heard other things: of your good fortune in other directions."

She spoke hastily, the thought of Mademoiselle d'Ogeron in her mind. And instantly would have recalled the words had she been able. But Peter Blood swept them lightly aside, reading into them none of her meaning, as she feared he would.

"Aye—a deal of lies, devil a doubt, as I could prove to you."

"I cannot think why you should trouble to put yourself on your defence," she discouraged him.

"So that ye may think less badly of me than you do."

"What I think of you can be a very little matter to you, sir."

This was a disarming stroke. He abandoned combat for expostulation.

"Can ye say that now? Can ye say that, beholding me in this livery of a service I despise? Didn't ye tell me that I might redeem the past? It's little enough I am concerned to redeem the past save only in your eyes. In my own I've done nothing at all that I am ashamed of, considering the provocation I received."

Her glance faltered, and fell away before his own that was so intent.

"I... I can't think why you should speak to me like this," she said, with less than her earlier assurance.

"Ah, now, can't ye, indeed?" he cried. "Sure, then, I'll be telling ye."

"Oh, please." There was real alarm in her voice. "I realize fully what you did, and I realize that partly, at least, you may have been urged by consideration for myself. Believe me, I am very grateful. I shall always be grateful."

"But if it's also your intention always to think of me as a thief and a pirate, faith, ye may keep your gratitude for all the good it's like to do me."

A livelier colour crept into her cheeks. There was a perceptible heave of the slight breast that faintly swelled the flimsy bodice of white silk. But if she resented his tone and his words, she stifled her resentment. She realized that perhaps she had, herself, provoked his anger. She honestly desired to make amends.

"You are mistaken," she began. "It isn't that."

But they were fated to misunderstand each other.

Jealousy, that troubler of reason, had been over-busy with his wits as it had with hers.

"What is it, then?" quoth he, and added the question: "Lord Julian?"

She started, and stared at him blankly indignant now.

"Och, be frank with me," he urged her, unpardonably. "'Twill be a kindness, so it will."

For a moment she stood before him with quickened breathing, the colour ebbing and flowing in her cheeks. Then she looked past him, and tilted her chin forward.

"You... you are quite insufferable," she said. "I beg that you will let me pass."

He stepped aside, and with the broad feathered hat which he still held in his hand, he waved her on towards the house.

"I'll not be detaining you any longer, ma'am. After all, the cursed thing I did for nothing can be undone. Ye'll remember afterwards that it was your hardness drove me."

She moved to depart, then checked, and faced him again. It was she now who was on her defence, her voice quivering with indignation.

"You take that tone! You dare to take that tone!" she cried, astounding him by her sudden vehemence. "You have the effrontery to upbraid me because I will not take your hands when I know how they are stained; when I know you for a murderer and worse?"

He stared at her open-mouthed.

"A murderer—I?" he said at last.

"Must I name your victims? Did you not murder Levasseur?"

"Levasseur?" He smiled a little. "So they've told you about that!"

"Do you deny it?"

"I killed him, it is true. I can remember killing another man in circumstances that were very similar. That was in Bridgetown on the night of the Spanish raid. Mary Traill would tell you of it. She was present."

He clapped his hat on his head with a certain abrupt fierceness, and strode angrily away, before she could answer or even grasp the full significance of what he had said.

CHAPTER XXIII. HOSTAGES

Peter Blood stood in the pillared portico of Government House, and with unseeing eyes that were laden with pain and anger, stared out across the great harbour of Port Royal to the green hills rising from the farther shore and the ridge of the Blue Mountains beyond, showing hazily through the quivering heat.

He was aroused by the return of the negro who had gone to announce him, and following now this slave, he made his way through the house to the wide piazza behind it, in whose shade Colonel Bishop and my Lord Julian Wade took what little air there was.

"So ye've come," the Deputy-Governor hailed him, and followed the greeting by a series of grunts of vague but apparently ill-humoured import.

He did not trouble to rise, not even when Lord Julian, obeying the instincts of finer breeding, set him the example. From under scowling brows the wealthy Barbados planter considered his sometime slave, who, hat in hand, leaning lightly upon his long beribboned cane, revealed nothing in his countenance of the anger which was being steadily nourished by this cavalier reception.

At last, with scowling brow and in self-sufficient tones, Colonel Bishop delivered himself.

"I have sent for you, Captain Blood, because of certain news that has just reached me. I am informed that yesterday evening a frigate left the harbour having on board your associate Wolverstone and a hundred men of the hundred and fifty that were serving under you. His lordship and I shall be glad to have your explanation of how you came to permit that departure."

"Permit?" quoth Blood. "I ordered it."

The answer left Bishop speechless for a moment. Then:

"You ordered it?" he said in accents of unbelief, whilst Lord Julian raised his eyebrows. "'Swounds! Perhaps you'll explain yourself? Whither has Wolverstone gone?"

"To Tortuga. He's gone with a message to the officers commanding the other four ships of the fleet that is awaiting me there, telling them what's happened and why they are no longer to expect me."

Bishop's great face seemed to swell and its high colour to deepen. He swung to Lord Julian.

"You hear that, my lord? Deliberately he has let Wolverstone loose upon the seas again—Wolverstone, the worst of all that gang of pirates after himself. I hope your lordship begins at last to perceive the folly of granting the King's commission to such a man as this against all my counsels. Why, this thing is... it's just mutiny... treason! By God! It's matter for a court-martial."

"Will you cease your blather of mutiny and treason and courts-martial?" Blood put on his hat, and sat down unbidden. "I have sent Wolverstone to inform Hagthorpe and Christian and Yberville and the rest of my lads that they've one clear month in which to follow my example, quit piracy, and get back to their boucans or their logwood, or else sail out of the Caribbean Sea. That's what I've done."

"But the men?" his lordship interposed in his level, cultured voice. "This hundred men that Wolverstone has taken with him?"

"They are those of my crew who have no taste for King James's service, and have preferred to seek work of other kinds. It was in our compact, my lord, that there should be no constraining of my men."

"I don't remember it," said his lordship, with sincerity.

Blood looked at him in surprise. Then he shrugged. "Faith, I'm not to blame for your lordship's poor memory. I say that it was so; and I don't lie. I've never found it necessary. In any case ye couldn't have supposed that I should consent to anything different."

And then the Deputy-Governor exploded.

"You have given those damned rascals in Tortuga this warning so that they may escape! That is what you have done. That is how you abuse the commission that has saved your own neck!"

Peter Blood considered him steadily, his face impassive. "I will remind you," he said at last, very quietly, "that the object in view was—leaving out of account your own appetites which, as every one knows, are just those of a hangman—to rid the Caribbean of buccaneers. Now, I've taken the most effective way of accomplishing that object. The knowledge that I've entered the King's service should in itself go far towards disbanding the fleet of which I was until lately the admiral."

"I see!" sneered the Deputy-Governor malevolently. "And if it does not?"

"It will be time enough then to consider what else is to be done."

Lord Julian forestalled a fresh outburst on the part of Bishop.

"It is possible," he said, "that my Lord Sunderland will be satisfied, provided that the solution is such as you promise."

It was a courteous, conciliatory speech. Urged by friendliness towards Blood and understanding of the difficult position in which the buccaneer found himself, his lordship was disposed to take his stand upon the letter of his instructions. Therefore he now held out a friendly hand to help him over the latest and most difficult obstacle which Blood himself had enabled Bishop to place in the way of his redemption. Unfortunately the last person from whom Peter Blood desired assistance at that moment was this young nobleman, whom he regarded with the jaundiced eyes of jealousy.

"Anyway," he answered, with a suggestion of defiance and more than a suggestion of a sneer, "it's the most ye should expect from me, and certainly it's the most ye'll get."

His lordship frowned, and dabbed his lips with a handkerchief.

"I don't think that I quite like the way you put it. Indeed, upon reflection, Captain Blood, I am sure that I do not."

"I am sorry for that, so I am," said Blood impudently. "But there it is. I'm not on that account concerned to modify it."

His lordship's pale eyes opened a little wider. Languidly he raised his eyebrows.

"Ah!" he said. "You're a prodigiously uncivil fellow. You disappoint me, sir. I had formed the notion that you might be a gentleman."

"And that's not your lordship's only mistake," Bishop cut in. "You made a worse when you gave him the King's commission, and so sheltered the rascal from the gallows I had prepared for him in Port Royal."

"Aye—but the worst mistake of all in this matter of commissions," said Blood to his lordship, "was the one that trade this greasy slaver Deputy-Governor of Jamaica instead of its hangman, which is the office for which he's by nature fitted."

"Captain Blood!" said his lordship sharply in reproof. "Upon my soul and honour, sir, you go much too far. You are...."

But here Bishop interrupted him. He had heaved himself to his feet, at last, and was venting his fury in unprintable abuse. Captain Blood, who had also risen, stood apparently impassive, for the storm to spend itself. When at last this happened, he addressed himself quietly to Lord Julian, as if Colonel Bishop had not spoken.

"Your lordship was about to say?" he asked, with challenging smoothness.

But his lordship had by now recovered his habitual composure, and was again disposed to be conciliatory. He laughed and shrugged.

"Faith! here's a deal of unnecessary heat," said he. "And God knows this plaguey climate provides enough of that. Perhaps, Colonel Bishop, you are a little uncompromising; and you, sir, are certainly a deal too peppery. I have said, speaking on behalf of my Lord Sunderland, that I am content to await the result of your experiment."

But Bishop's fury had by now reached a stage in which it was not to be restrained.

"Are you, indeed?" he roared. "Well, then, I am not. This is a matter in which your lordship must allow me to be the better judge. And, anyhow, I'll take the risk of acting on my own responsibility."

Lord Julian abandoned the struggle. He smiled wearily, shrugged, and waved a hand in implied resignation. The Deputy-Governor stormed on.

"Since my lord here has given you a commission, I can't regularly deal with you out of hand for piracy as you deserve. But you shall answer before a court-martial for your action in the matter of Wolverstone, and take the consequences."

"I see," said Blood. "Now we come to it. And it's yourself as Deputy-Governor will preside over that same court-martial. So that ye can wipe off old scores by hanging me, it's little ye care how ye do it!" He laughed, and added: "Praemonitus, praemunitus."

"What shall that mean?" quoth Lord Julian sharply.

"I had imagined that your lordship would have had some education."

He was at pains, you see, to be provocative.

"It's not the literal meaning I am asking, sir," said Lord Julian, with frosty dignity. "I want to know what you desire me to understand?"

"I'll leave your lordship guessing," said Blood. "And I'll be wishing ye both a very good day." He swept off his feathered hat, and made them a leg very elegantly.

"Before you go," said Bishop, "and to save you from any idle rashness, I'll tell you that the Harbour-Master and the Commandant have their orders. You don't leave Port Royal, my fine gallows bird. Damme, I mean to provide you with permanent moorings here, in Execution Dock."

Peter Blood stiffened, and his vivid blue eyes stabbed the bloated face of his enemy. He passed his long cane into his left hand, and with his right thrust negligently into the breast of his doublet, he swung to Lord Julian, who was thoughtfully frowning.

"Your lordship, I think, promised me immunity from this."

"What I may have promised," said his lordship, "your own conduct makes it difficult to perform." He rose. "You did me a service, Captain Blood, and I had hoped that we might be friends. But since you prefer to have it otherwise...." He shrugged, and waved a hand towards the Deputy-Governor.

Blood completed the sentence in his own way:

"Ye mean that ye haven't the strength of character to resist the urgings of a bully." He was apparently at his ease, and actually smiling. "Well, well—as I said before—praemonitus, praemunitus. I'm afraid that ye're no scholar, Bishop, or ye'd know that I means forewarned, forearmed."

"Forewarned? Ha!" Bishop almost snarled. "The warning comes a little late. You do not leave this house." He took a step in the direction of the doorway, and raised his voice. "Ho there..." he was beginning to call.

Then with a sudden audible catch in his breath, he stopped short. Captain Blood's right hand had reemerged from the breast of his doublet, bringing with it a long pistol with silver mountings richly chased, which he levelled within a foot of the Deputy-Governor's head.

"And forearmed," said he. "Don't stir from where you are, my lord, or there may be an accident."

And my lord, who had been moving to Bishop's assistance, stood instantly arrested. Chap-fallen, with much of his high colour suddenly departed, the Deputy-Governor was swaying on unsteady legs. Peter Blood considered him with a grimness that increased his panic.

"I marvel that I don't pistol you without more ado, ye fat blackguard. If I don't, it's for the same reason that once before I gave ye your life when it was forfeit. Ye're not aware of the reason, to be sure; but it may comfort ye to know that it exists. At the same time I'll warn ye not to put too heavy a strain on my generosity, which resides at the moment in my trigger-finger. Ye mean to hang me, and since that's the worst that can happen to me anyway, you'll realize that I'll not boggle at increasing the account by spilling your nasty blood." He cast his cane from him, thus disengaging his left hand. "Be good enough to give me your arm, Colonel Bishop. Come, come, man, your arm."

Under the compulsion of that sharp tone, those resolute eyes, and that gleaming pistol, Bishop obeyed without demur. His recent foul volubility was stemmed. He could not trust himself to speak. Captain Blood tucked his left arm through the Deputy-Governor's proffered right. Then he thrust his own right hand with its pistol back into the breast of his doublet.

"Though invisible, it's aiming at ye none the less, and I give you my word of honour that I'll shoot ye dead upon the very least provocation, whether that provocation is yours or another's. Ye'll bear that in mind, Lord Julian. And now, ye greasy hangman, step out as brisk and lively as ye can, and behave as naturally as ye may, or it's the black stream of Cocytus ye'll be contemplating." Arm in arm they passed through the house, and down the garden, where Arabella lingered, awaiting Peter Blood's return.

Consideration of his parting words had brought her first turmoil of mind, then a clear perception of what might be indeed the truth of the death of Levasseur. She perceived that the particular inference drawn from it might similarly have been drawn from Blood's deliverance of Mary Traill. When a man so risks his life for a woman, the rest is easily assumed. For the men who will take such risks without hope of personal gain are few. Blood was of those few, as he had proved in the case of Mary Traill.

It needed no further assurances of his to convince her that she had done him a monstrous injustice. She remembered words he had used—words overheard aboard his ship (which he had named the Arabella) on the night of her deliverance from the Spanish admiral; words he had uttered when she had approved his acceptance of the King's commission; the words he had spoken to her that very morning, which had but served to move her indignation. All these assumed a fresh meaning in her mind, delivered now from its unwarranted preconceptions.

Therefore she lingered there in the garden, awaiting his return that she might make amends; that she might set a term to all misunderstanding. In impatience she awaited him. Yet her patience, it seemed, was to be tested further. For when at last he came, it was in company—unusually close and intimate company—with her uncle. In vexation she realized that explanations must be postponed. Could she have guessed the extent of that postponement, vexation would have been changed into despair.

He passed, with his companion, from that fragrant garden into the courtyard of the fort. Here the Commandant, who had been instructed to hold himself in readiness with the necessary men against the need to effect the arrest of Captain Blood, was amazed by the curious spectacle of the Deputy-Governor of Jamaica strolling forth arm in arm and apparently on the friendliest terms with the intended prisoner. For as they went, Blood was chatting and laughing briskly.

They passed out of the gates unchallenged, and so came to the mole where the cock-boat from the Arabella was waiting. They took their places side by side in the stern sheets, and were pulled away together, always very close and friendly, to the great red ship where Jeremy Pitt so anxiously awaited news.

You conceive the master's amazement to see the Deputy-Governor come toiling up the entrance ladder, with Blood following very close behind him.

"Sure, I walked into a trap, as ye feared, Jeremy," Blood hailed him. "But I walked out again, and fetched the trapper with me. He loves his life, does this fat rascal."

Colonel Bishop stood in the waist, his great face blenched to the colour of clay, his mouth loose, almost afraid to look at the sturdy ruffians who lounged about the shot-rack on the main hatch.

Blood shouted an order to the bo'sun, who was leaning against the forecastle bulkhead.

"Throw me a rope with a running noose over the yardarm there, against the need of it. Now, don't be alarming yourself, Colonel, darling. It's no more than a provision against your being unreasonable, which I am sure ye'll not be. We'll talk the matter over whiles we are dining, for I trust ye'll not refuse to honour my table by your company."

He led away the will-less, cowed bully to the great cabin. Benjamin, the negro steward, in white drawers and cotton shirt, made haste by his command to serve dinner.

Colonel Bishop collapsed on the locker under the stern ports, and spoke now for the first time.

"May I ask wha... what are your intentions?" he quavered.

"Why, nothing sinister, Colonel. Although ye deserve nothing less than that same rope and yardarm, I assure you that it's to be employed only as a last resource. Ye've said his lordship made a mistake when he handed me the commission which the Secretary of State did me the honour to design for me. I'm disposed to agree with you; so I'll take to the sea again. Cras ingens iterabimus aequor. It's the fine Latin scholar ye'll be when I've done with ye. I'll be getting back to Tortuga and my buccaneers, who at least are honest, decent fellows. So I've fetched ye aboard as a hostage."

"My God!" groaned the Deputy-Governor. "Ye... ye never mean that ye'll carry me to Tortuga!"

Blood laughed outright. "Oh, I'd never serve ye such a bad turn as that. No, no. All I want is that ye ensure my safe departure from Port Royal. And, if ye're reasonable, I'll not even trouble you to swim for it this time. Ye've given certain orders to your Harbour-Master, and others to the Commandant of your plaguey fort. Ye'll be so good as to send for them both aboard here, and inform them in my presence that the Arabella is leaving this afternoon on the King's service and is to pass out unmolested. And so as to make quite sure of their obedience, they shall go a little voyage with us, themselves. Here's what you require. Now write—unless you prefer the yardarm."

Colonel Bishop heaved himself up in a pet. "You constrain me with violence..." he was beginning.

Blood smoothly interrupted him.

"Sure, now, I am not constraining you at all. I'm giving you a perfectly free choice between the pen and the rope. It's a matter for yourself entirely."

Bishop glared at him; then shrugging heavily, he took up the pen and sat down at the table. In an unsteady hand he wrote that summons to his officers. Blood despatched it ashore; and then bade his unwilling guest to table.

"I trust, Colonel, your appetite is as stout as usual."

The wretched Bishop took the seat to which he was commanded. As for eating, however, that was not easy to a man in his position; nor did Blood press him. The Captain, himself, fell to with a good appetite. But before he was midway through the meal came Hayton to inform him that Lord Julian Wade had just come aboard, and was asking to see him instantly.

"I was expecting him," said Blood. "Fetch him in."

Lord Julian came. He was very stem and dignified. His eyes took in the situation at a glance, as Captain Blood rose to greet him.

"It's mighty friendly of you to have joined us, my lord."

"Captain Blood," said his lordship with asperity, "I find your humour a little forced. I don't know what may be your intentions; but I wonder do you realize the risks you are running."

"And I wonder does your lordship realize the risk to yourself in following us aboard as I had counted that you would."

"What shall that mean, sir?"

Blood signalled to Benjamin, who was standing behind Bishop.

"Set a chair for his lordship. Hayton, send his lordship's boat ashore. Tell them he'll not be returning yet awhile."

"What's that?" cried his lordship. "Blister me! D'ye mean to detain me? Are ye mad?"

"Better wait, Hayton, in case his lordship should turn violent," said Blood. "You, Benjamin, you heard the message. Deliver it."

"Will you tell me what you intend, sir?" demanded his lordship, quivering with anger.

"Just to make myself and my lads here safe from Colonel Bishop's gallows. I've said that I trusted to your gallantry not to leave him in the lurch, but to follow him hither, and there's a note from his hand gone ashore to summon the Harbour-Master and the Commandant of the fort. Once they are aboard, I shall have all the hostages I need for our safety."

"You scoundrel!" said his lordship through his teeth.

"Sure, now, that's entirely a matter of the point of view," said Blood. "Ordinarily it isn't the kind of name I could suffer any man to apply to me. Still, considering that ye willingly did me a service once, and that ye're likely unwillingly to do me another now, I'll overlook your discourtesy, so I will."

His lordship laughed. "You fool," he said. "Do you dream that I came aboard your pirate ship without taking my measures? I informed the Commandant of exactly how you had compelled Colonel Bishop to accompany you. Judge now whether he or the Harbour-Master will obey the summons, or whether you will be allowed to depart as you imagine."

Blood's face became grave. "I'm sorry for that," said he.

I thought you would be, answered his lordship.

"Oh, but not on my own account. It's the Deputy-Governor there I'm sorry for. D'ye know what Ye've done? Sure, now, ye've very likely hanged him."

"My God!" cried Bishop in a sudden increase of panic.

"If they so much as put a shot across my bows, up goes their Deputy-Governor to the yardarm. Your only hope, Colonel, lies in the fact that I shall send them word of that intention. And so that you may mend as far as you can the harm you have done, it's yourself shall bear them the message, my lord."

"I'll see you damned before I do," fumed his lordship.

"Why, that's unreasonable and unreasoning. But if ye insist, why, another messenger will do as well, and another hostage aboard—as I had originally intended—will make my hand the stronger."

Lord Julian stared at him, realizing exactly what he had refused.

"You'll think better of it now that ye understand?" quoth Blood.

"Aye, in God's name, go, my lord," spluttered Bishop, "and make yourself obeyed. This damned pirate has me by the throat."

His lordship surveyed him with an eye that was not by any means admiring. "Why, if that is your wish..." he began. Then he shrugged, and turned again to Blood.

"I suppose I can trust you that no harm will come to Colonel Bishop if you are allowed to sail?"

"You have my word for it," said Blood. "And also that I shall put him safely ashore again without delay."

Lord Julian bowed stiffly to the cowering Deputy-Governor. "You understand, sir, that I do as you desire," he said coldly.

"Aye, man, aye!" Bishop assented hastily.

"Very well." Lord Julian bowed again and took his departure. Blood escorted him to the entrance ladder at the foot of which still swung the Arabella's own cock-boat.

"It's good-bye, my lord," said Blood. "And there's another thing." He proffered a parchment that he had drawn from his pocket. "It's the commission. Bishop was right when he said it was a mistake."

Lord Julian considered him, and considering him his expression softened.

"I am sorry," he said sincerely.

"In other circumstances..." began Blood. "Oh, but there! Ye'll understand. The boat's waiting."

Yet with his foot on the first rung of the ladder, Lord Julian hesitated.

"I still do not perceive—blister me if I do!—why you should not have found some one else to carry your message to the Commandant, and kept me aboard as an added hostage for his obedience to your wishes."

Blood's vivid eyes looked into the other's that were clear and honest, and he smiled, a little wistfully. A moment he seemed to hesitate. Then he explained himself quite fully.

"Why shouldn't I tell you? It's the same reason that's been urging me to pick a quarrel with you so that I might have the satisfaction of slipping a couple of feet of steel into your vitals. When I accepted your commission, I was moved to think it might redeem me in the eyes of Miss Bishop—for whose sake, as you may have guessed, I took it. But I have discovered that such a thing is beyond accomplishment. I should have known it for a sick man's dream. I have discovered also that if she's choosing you, as I believe she is, she's choosing wisely between us, and that's why I'll not have your life risked by keeping you aboard whilst the message goes by another who might bungle it. And now perhaps ye'll understand."

Lord Julian stared at him bewildered. His long, aristocratic face was very pale.

"My God!" he said. "And you tell me this?"

"I tell you because... Oh, plague on it!—so that ye may tell her; so that she may be made to realize that there's something of the unfortunate gentleman left under the thief and pirate she accounts me, and that her own good is my supreme desire. Knowing that, she may... faith, she may remember me more kindly—if It's only in her prayers. That's all, my lord."

Lord Julian continued to look at the buccaneer in silence. In silence, at last, he held out his hand; and in silence Blood took it.

"I wonder whether you are right," said his lordship, "and whether you are not the better man."

"Where she is concerned see that you make sure that I am right. Good-bye to you."

Lord Julian wrung his hand in silence, went down the ladder, and was pulled ashore. From the distance he waved to Blood, who stood leaning on the bulwarks watching the receding cock-boat.

The Arabella sailed within the hour, moving lazily before a sluggish breeze. The fort remained silent and there was no movement from the fleet to hinder her departure. Lord Julian had carried the message effectively, and had added to it his own personal commands.

CHAPTER XXIV. WAR

Five miles out at sea from Port Royal, whence the details of the coast of Jamaica were losing their sharpness, the Arabella hove to, and the sloop she had been towing was warped alongside.

Captain Blood escorted his compulsory guest to the head of the ladder. Colonel Bishop, who for two hours and more had been in a state of mortal anxiety, breathed freely at last; and as the tide of his fears receded, so that of his deep-rooted hate of this audacious buccaneer resumed its normal flow. But he practised circumspection. If in his heart he vowed that once back in Port Royal there was no effort he would spare, no nerve he would not strain, to bring Peter Blood to final moorings in Execution Dock, at least he kept that vow strictly to himself.

Peter Blood had no illusions. He was not, and never would be, the complete pirate. There was not another buccaneer in all the Caribbean who would have denied himself the pleasure of stringing Colonel Bishop from the yardarm, and by thus finally stifling the vindictive planter's hatred have increased his own security. But Blood was not of these. Moreover, in the case of Colonel Bishop there was a particular reason for restraint. Because he was Arabella Bishop's uncle, his life must remain sacred to Captain Blood.

And so the Captain smiled into the sallow, bloated face and the little eyes that fixed him with a malevolence not to be dissembled.

"A safe voyage home to you, Colonel, darling," said he in valediction, and from his easy, smiling manner you would never have dreamt of the pain he carried in his breast. "It's the second time ye've served me for a hostage. Ye'll be well advised to avoid a third. I'm not lucky to you, Colonel, as you should be perceiving."

Jeremy Pitt, the master, lounging at Blood's elbow, looked darkly upon the departure of the Deputy-Governor. Behind them a little mob of grim, stalwart, suntanned buccaneers were restrained from cracking Bishop like a flea only by their submission to the dominant will of their leader. They had learnt from Pitt while yet in Port Royal of their Captain's danger, and whilst as ready as he to throw over the King's service which had been thrust upon them, yet they resented the manner in which this had been rendered necessary, and they marvelled now at Blood's restraint where Bishop was concerned. The Deputy-Governor looked round and met the lowering hostile glances of those fierce eyes. Instinct warned him that his life at that moment was held precariously, that an injudicious word might precipitate an explosion of hatred from which no human power could save him. Therefore he said nothing. He inclined his head in silence to the Captain, and went blundering and stumbling in his haste down that ladder to the sloop and its waiting negro crew.

They pushed off the craft from the red hull of the Arabella, bent to their sweeps, then, hoisting sail, headed back for Port Royal, intent upon reaching it before darkness should come down upon them. And Bishop, the great bulk of him huddled in the stem sheets, sat silent, his black brows knitted, his coarse lips pursed, malevolence and vindictiveness so whelming now his recent panic that he forgot his near escape of the yardarm and the running noose.

On the mole at Port Royal, under the low, embattled wall of the fort, Major Mallard and Lord Julian waited to receive him, and it was with infinite relief that they assisted him from the sloop.

Major Mallard was disposed to be apologetic.

"Glad to see you safe, sir," said he. "I'd have sunk Blood's ship in spite of your excellency's being aboard but for your own orders by Lord Julian, and his lordship's assurance that he had Blood's word for it that no harm should come to you so that no harm came to him. I'll confess I thought it rash of his lordship to accept the word of a damned pirate...."

"I have found it as good as another's," said his lordship, cropping the Major's too eager eloquence. He spoke with an unusual degree of that frosty dignity he could assume upon occasion. The fact is that his lordship was in an exceedingly bad humour. Having written jubilantly home to the Secretary of State that his mission had succeeded, he was now faced with the necessity of writing again to confess that this success had been ephemeral. And because Major Mallard's crisp mostachios were lifted by a sneer at the notion of a buccaneer's word being acceptable, he added still more sharply: "My justification is here in the person of Colonel Bishop safely returned. As against that, sir, your opinion does not weigh for very much. You should realize it."

"Oh, as your lordship says." Major Mallard's manner was tinged with irony. "To be sure, here is the Colonel safe and sound. And out yonder is Captain Blood, also safe and sound, to begin his piratical ravages all over again."

"I do not propose to discuss the reasons with you, Major Mallard."

"And, anyway, it's not for long," growled the Colonel, finding speech at last. "No, by....." He emphasized the assurance by an unprintable oath. "If I spend the last shilling of my fortune and the last ship of the Jamaica fleet, I'll have that rascal in a hempen necktie before I rest. And I'll not be long about it." He had empurpled in his angry vehemence, and the veins of his forehead stood out like whipcord. Then he checked.

"You did well to follow Lord Julian's instructions," he commended the Major. With that he turned from him, and took his lordship by the arm. "Come, my lord. We must take order about this, you and I."

They went off together, skirting the redoubt, and so through courtyard and garden to the house where Arabella waited anxiously. The sight of her uncle brought her infinite relief, not only on his own account, but on account also of Captain Blood.

"You took a great risk, sir," she gravely told Lord Julian after the ordinary greetings had been exchanged.

But Lord Julian answered her as he had answered Major Mallard. "There was no risk, ma'am."

She looked at him in some astonishment. His long, aristocratic face wore a more melancholy, pensive air than usual. He answered the enquiry in her glance:

"So that Blood's ship were allowed to pass the fort, no harm could come to Colonel Bishop. Blood pledged me his word for that."

A faint smile broke the set of her lips, which hitherto had been wistful, and a little colour tinged her cheeks. She would have pursued the subject, but the Deputy-Governor's mood did not permit it. He sneered and snorted at the notion of Blood's word being good for anything, forgetting that he owed to it his own preservation at that moment.

At supper, and for long thereafter he talked of nothing but Blood—of how he would lay him by the heels, and what hideous things he would perform upon his body. And as he drank heavily the while, his speech became increasingly gross and his threats increasingly horrible; until in the end Arabella withdrew, white-faced and almost on the verge of tears. It was not often that Bishop revealed himself to his niece. Oddly enough, this coarse, overbearing planter went in a certain awe of that slim girl. It was as if she had inherited from her father the respect in which he had always been held by his brother.

Lord Julian, who began to find Bishop disgusting beyond endurance, excused himself soon after, and went in quest of the lady. He had yet to deliver the message from Captain Blood, and this, he thought, would be his opportunity. But Miss Bishop had retired for the night, and Lord Julian must curb his impatience—it amounted by now to nothing less—until the morrow.

Very early next morning, before the heat of the day came to render the open intolerable to his lordship, he espied her from his window moving amid the azaleas in the garden. It was a fitting setting for one who was still as much a delightful novelty to him in womanhood as was the azalea among flowers. He hurried forth to join her, and when, aroused from her pensiveness, she had given him a good-morrow, smiling and frank, he explained himself by the announcement that he bore her a message from Captain Blood.

He observed her little start and the slight quiver of her lips, and observed thereafter not only her pallor and the shadowy rings about her eyes, but also that unusually wistful air which last night had escaped his notice.

They moved out of the open to one of the terraces, where a pergola of orange-trees provided a shaded sauntering space that was at once cool and fragrant. As they went, he considered her admiringly, and marvelled at himself that it should have taken him so long fully to realize her slim, unusual grace, and to find her, as he now did, so entirely desirable, a woman whose charm must irradiate all the life of a man, and touch its commonplaces into magic.

He noted the sheen of her red-brown hair, and how gracefully one of its heavy ringlets coiled upon her slender, milk-white neck. She wore a gown of shimmering grey silk, and a scarlet rose, fresh-gathered, was pinned at her breast like a splash of blood. Always thereafter when he thought of her it was as he saw her at that moment, as never, I think, until that moment had he seen her.

In silence they paced on a little way into the green shade. Then she paused and faced him.

"You said something of a message, sir," she reminded him, thus betraying some of her impatience.

He fingered the ringlets of his periwig, a little embarrassed how to deliver himself, considering how he should begin. "He desired me," he said at last, "to give you a message that should prove to you that there is still something left in him of the unfortunate gentleman that... that.., for which once you knew him."

"That is not now necessary," said she very gravely. He misunderstood her, of course, knowing nothing of the enlightenment that yesterday had come to her.

"I think..., nay, I know that you do him an injustice," said he.

Her hazel eyes continued to regard him.

"If you will deliver the message, it may enable me to judge."

To him, this was confusing. He did not immediately answer. He found that he had not sufficiently considered the terms he should employ, and the matter, after all, was of an exceeding delicacy, demanding delicate handling. It was not so much that he was concerned to deliver a message as to render it a vehicle by which to plead his own cause. Lord Julian, well versed in the lore of womankind and usually at his ease with ladies of the beau-monde, found himself oddly constrained before this frank and unsophisticated niece of a colonial planter.

They moved on in silence and as if by common consent towards the brilliant sunshine where the pergola was intersected by the avenue leading upwards to the house. Across this patch of light fluttered a gorgeous butterfly, that was like black and scarlet velvet and large as a man's hand. His lordship's brooding eyes followed it out of sight before he answered.

"It is not easy. Stab me, it is not. He was a man who deserved well. And amongst us we have marred his chances: your uncle, because he could not forget his rancour; you, because... because having told him that in the King's service he would find his redemption of what was past, you would not afterwards admit to him that he was so redeemed. And this, although concern to rescue you was the chief motive of his embracing that same service."

She had turned her shoulder to him so that he should not see her face.

"I know. I know now," she said softly. Then after a pause she added the question: "And you? What part has your lordship had in this—that you should incriminate yourself with us?"

"My part?" Again he hesitated, then plunged recklessly on, as men do when determined to perform a thing they fear. "If I understood him aright, if he understood aright, himself, my part, though entirely passive, was none the less effective. I implore you to observe that I but report his own words. I say nothing for myself." His lordship's unusual nervousness was steadily increasing. "He thought, then—so he told me—that my presence here had contributed to his inability to redeem himself in your sight; and unless he were so redeemed, then was redemption nothing."

She faced him fully, a frown of perplexity bringing her brows together above her troubled eyes.

"He thought that you had contributed?" she echoed. It was clear she asked for enlightenment. He plunged on to afford it her, his glance a little scared, his cheeks flushing.

"Aye, and he said so in terms which told me something that I hope above all things, and yet dare not believe, for, God knows, I am no coxcomb, Arabella. He said... but first let me tell you how I was placed. I had gone aboard his ship to demand the instant surrender of your uncle whom he held captive. He laughed at me. Colonel Bishop should be a hostage for his safety. By rashly venturing aboard his ship, I afforded him in my own person yet another hostage as valuable at least as Colonel Bishop. Yet he bade me depart; not from the fear of consequences, for he is above fear, nor from any personal esteem for me whom he confessed that he had come to find detestable; and this for the very reason that made him concerned for my safety."

"I do not understand," she said, as he paused. "Is not that a contradiction in itself?"

"It seems so only. The fact is, Arabella, this unfortunate man has the... the temerity to love you."

She cried out at that, and clutched her breast whose calm was suddenly disturbed. Her eyes dilated as she stared at him.

"I... I've startled you," said he, with concern. "I feared I should. But it was necessary so that you may understand."

"Go on," she bade him.

"Well, then: he saw in me one who made it impossible that he should win you—so he said. Therefore he could with satisfaction have killed me. But because my death might cause you pain, because your happiness was the thing that above all things he desired, he surrendered that part of his guarantee of safety which my person afforded him. If his departure should be hindered, and I should lose my life in what might follow, there was the risk that... that you might mourn me. That risk he would not take. Him you deemed a thief and a pirate, he said, and added that—I am giving you his own words always—if in choosing between us two, your choice, as he believed, would fall on me, then were you in his opinion choosing wisely. Because of that he bade me leave his ship, and had me put ashore."

She looked at him with eyes that were aswim with tears. He took a step towards her, a catch in his breath, his hand held out.

"Was he right, Arabella? My life's happiness hangs upon your answer."

But she continued silently to regard him with those tear-laden eyes, without speaking, and until she spoke he dared not advance farther.

A doubt, a tormenting doubt beset him. When presently she spoke, he saw how true had been the instinct of which that doubt was born, for her words revealed the fact that of all that he had said the only thing that had touched her consciousness and absorbed it from all other considerations was Blood's conduct as it regarded herself.

"He said that!" she cried. "He did that! Oh!" She turned away, and through the slender, clustering trunks of the bordering orange-trees she looked out across the glittering waters of the great harbour to the distant hills. Thus for a little while, my lord standing stiffly, fearfully, waiting for fuller revelation of her mind. At last it came, slowly, deliberately, in a voice that at moments was half suffocated. "Last night when my uncle displayed his rancour and his evil rage, it began to be borne in upon me that such vindictiveness can belong only to those who have wronged. It is the frenzy into which men whip themselves to justify an evil passion. I must have known then, if I had not already learnt it, that I had been too credulous of all the unspeakable things attributed to Peter Blood. Yesterday I had his own explanation of that tale of Levasseur that you heard in St. Nicholas. And now this... this but gives me confirmation of his truth and worth. To a scoundrel such as I was too readily brought to believe him, the act of which you have just told me would have been impossible."

"That is my own opinion," said his lordship gently.

"It must be. But even if it were not, that would now weigh for nothing. What weighs—oh, so heavily and bitterly—is the thought that but for the words in which yesterday I repelled him, he might have been saved. If only I could have spoken to him again before he went! I waited for him; but my uncle was with him, and I had no suspicion that he was going away again. And now he is lost—back at his outlawry and piracy, in which ultimately he will be taken and destroyed. And the fault is mine—mine!"

"What are you saying? The only agents were your uncle's hostility and his own obstinacy which would not study compromise. You must not blame yourself for anything."

She swung to him with some impatience, her eyes aswim in tears. "You can say that, and in spite of his message, which in itself tells how much I was to blame! It was my treatment of him, the epithets I cast at him that drove him. So much he has told you. I know it to be true."

"You have no cause for shame," said he. "As for your sorrow—why, if it will afford you solace—you may still count on me to do what man can to rescue him from this position."

She caught her breath.

"You will do that!" she cried with sudden eager hopefulness. "You promise?" She held out her hand to him impulsively. He took it in both his own.

"I promise," he answered her. And then, retaining still the hand she had surrendered to him—"Arabella," he said very gently, "there is still this other matter upon which you have not answered me."

"This other matter?" Was he mad, she wondered.

Could any other matter signify in such a moment.

"This matter that concerns myself; and all my future, oh, so very closely. This thing that Blood believed, that prompted him..., that ... that you are not indifferent to me." He saw the fair face change colour and grow troubled once more.

"Indifferent to you?" said she. "Why, no. We have been good friends; we shall continue so, I hope, my lord."

"Friends! Good friends?" He was between dismay and bitterness. "It is not your friendship only that I ask, Arabella. You heard what I said, what I reported. You will not say that Peter Blood was wrong?"

Gently she sought to disengage her hand, the trouble in her face increasing. A moment he resisted; then, realizing what he did, he set her free.

"Arabella!" he cried on a note of sudden pain.

"I have friendship for you, my lord. But only friendship." His castle of hopes came clattering down about him, leaving him a little stunned. As he had said, he was no coxcomb. Yet there was something that he did not understand. She confessed to friendship, and it was in his power to offer her a great position, one to which she, a colonial planter's niece, however wealthy, could never have aspired even in her dreams. This she rejected, yet spoke of friendship. Peter Blood had been mistaken, then. How far had he been mistaken? Had he been as mistaken in her feelings towards himself as he obviously was in her feelings towards his lordship? In that case ... His reflections broke short. To speculate was to wound himself in vain. He must know. Therefore he asked her with grim frankness:

"Is it Peter Blood?"

"Peter Blood?" she echoed. At first she did not understand the purport of his question. When understanding came, a flush suffused her face.

"I do not know," she said, faltering a little.

This was hardly a truthful answer. For, as if an obscuring veil had suddenly been rent that morning, she was permitted at last to see Peter Blood in his true relations to other men, and that sight, vouchsafed her twenty-four hours too late, filled her with pity and regret and yearning.

Lord Julian knew enough of women to be left in no further doubt. He bowed his head so that she might not see the anger in his eyes, for as a man of honour he took shame in that anger which as a human being he could not repress.

And because Nature in him was stronger—as it is in most of us—than training, Lord Julian from that moment began, almost in spite of himself, to practise something that was akin to villainy. I regret to chronicle it of one for whom—if I have done him any sort of justice—you should have been conceiving some esteem. But the truth is that the lingering remains of the regard in which he had held Peter Blood were choked by the desire to supplant and destroy a rival. He had passed his word to Arabella that he would use his powerful influence on Blood's behalf. I deplore to set it down that not only did he forget his pledge, but secretly set himself to aid and abet Arabella's uncle in the plans he laid for the trapping and undoing of the buccaneer. He might reasonably have urged—had he been taxed with it—that he conducted himself precisely as his duty demanded. But to that he might have been answered that duty with him was but the slave of jealousy in this.

When the Jamaica fleet put to sea some few days later, Lord Julian sailed with Colonel Bishop in Vice-Admiral Craufurd's flagship. Not only was there no need for either of them to go, but the Deputy-Governor's duties actually demanded that he should remain ashore, whilst Lord Julian, as we know, was a useless man aboard a ship. Yet both set out to hunt Captain Blood, each making of his duty a pretext for the satisfaction of personal aims; and that common purpose became a link between them, binding them in a sort of friendship that must otherwise have been impossible between men so dissimilar in breeding and in aspirations.

The hunt was up. They cruised awhile off Hispaniola, watching the Windward Passage, and suffering the discomforts of the rainy season which had now set in. But they cruised in vain, and after a month of it, returned empty-handed to Port Royal, there to find awaiting them the most disquieting news from the Old World.

The megalomania of Louis XIV had set Europe in a blaze of war. The French legionaries were ravaging the Rhine provinces, and Spain had joined the nations leagued to defend themselves from the wild ambitions of the King of France. And there was worse than this: there were rumours of civil war in England, where the people had grown weary of the bigoted tyranny of King James. It was reported that William of Orange had been invited to come over.

Weeks passed, and every ship from home brought additional news. William had crossed to England, and in March of that year 1689 they learnt in Jamaica that he had accepted the crown and that James had thrown himself into the arms of France for rehabilitation.

To a kinsman of Sunderland's this was disquieting news, indeed. It was followed by letters from King William's Secretary of State informing Colonel Bishop that there was war with France, and that in view of its effect upon the Colonies a Governor-General was coming out to the West Indies in the person of Lord Willoughby, and that with him came a squadron under the command of Admiral van der Kuylen to reenforce the Jamaica fleet against eventualities.

Bishop realized that this must mean the end of his supreme authority, even though he should continue in Port Royal as Deputy-Governor. Lord Julian, in the lack of direct news to himself, did not know what it might mean to him. But he had been very close and confidential with Colonel Bishop regarding his hopes of Arabella, and Colonel Bishop more than ever, now that political events put him in danger of being retired, was anxious to enjoy the advantages of having a man of Lord Julian's eminence for his relative.

They came to a complete understanding in the matter, and Lord Julian disclosed all that he knew.

"There is one obstacle in our path," said he. "Captain Blood. The girl is in love with him."

"Ye're surely mad!" cried Bishop, when he had recovered speech.

"You are justified of the assumption," said his lordship dolefully. "But I happen to be sane, and to speak with knowledge."

"With knowledge?"

"Arabella herself has confessed it to me."

"The brazen baggage! By God, I'll bring her to her senses." It was the slave-driver speaking, the man who governed with a whip.

"Don't be a fool, Bishop." His lordship's contempt did more than any argument to calm the Colonel. "That's not the way with a girl of Arabella's spirit. Unless you want to wreck my chances for all time, you'll hold your tongue, and not interfere at all."

"Not interfere? My God, what, then?"

"Listen, man. She has a constant mind. I don't think you know your niece. As long as Blood lives, she will wait for him."

"Then with Blood dead, perhaps she will come to her silly senses."

"Now you begin to show intelligence," Lord Julian commended him. "That is the first essential step."

"And here is our chance to take it." Bishop warmed to a sort of enthusiasm. "This war with France removes all restrictions in the matter of Tortuga. We are free to invest it in the service of the Crown. A victory there and we establish ourselves in the favour of this new government."

"Ah!" said Lord Julian, and he pulled thoughtfully at his lip.

"I see that you understand," Bishop laughed coarsely. "Two birds with one stone, eh? We'll hunt this rascal in his lair, right under the beard of the King of France, and we'll take him this time, if we reduce Tortuga to a heap of ashes."

On that expedition they sailed two days later—which would be some three months after Blood's departure—taking every ship of the fleet, and several lesser vessels as auxiliaries. To Arabella and the world in general it was given out that they were going to raid French Hispaniola, which was really the only expedition that could have afforded Colonel Bishop any sort of justification for leaving Jamaica at all at such a time. His sense of duty, indeed, should have kept him fast in Port Royal; but his sense of duty was smothered in hatred—that most fruitless and corruptive of all the emotions. In the great cabin of Vice-Admiral Craufurd's flagship, the Imperator, the Deputy-Governor got drunk that night to celebrate his conviction that the sands of Captain Blood's career were running out.

CHAPTER XXV. THE SERVICE OF KING LOUIS

Meanwhile, some three months before Colonel Bishop set out to reduce Tortuga, Captain Blood, bearing hell in his soul, had blown into its rockbound harbour ahead of the winter gales, and two days ahead of the frigate in which Wolverstone had sailed from Port Royal a day before him.

In that snug anchorage he found his fleet awaiting him—the four ships which had been separated in that gale off the Lesser Antilles, and some seven hundred men composing their crews. Because they had been beginning to grow anxious on his behalf, they gave him the greater welcome. Guns were fired in his honour and the ships made themselves gay with bunting. The town, aroused by all this noise in the harbour, emptied itself upon the jetty, and a vast crowd of men and women of all creeds and nationalities collected there to be present at the coming ashore of the great buccaneer.

Ashore he went, probably for no other reason than to obey the general expectation. His mood was taciturn; his face grim and sneering. Let Wolverstone arrive, as presently he would, and all this hero-worship would turn to execration.

His captains, Hagthorpe, Christian, and Yberville, were on the jetty to receive him, and with them were some hundreds of his buccaneers. He cut short their greetings, and when they plagued him with questions of where he had tarried, he bade them await the coming of Wolverstone, who would satisfy their curiosity to a surfeit. On that he shook them off, and shouldered his way through that heterogeneous throng that was composed of bustling traders of several nations—English, French, and Dutch—of planters and of seamen of various degrees, of buccaneers who were fruit-selling half-castes, negro slaves, some doll-tearsheets and dunghill-queans from the Old World, and all the other types of the human family that converted the quays of Cayona into a disreputable image of Babel.

Winning clear at last, and after difficulties, Captain Blood took his way alone to the fine house of M. d'Ogeron, there to pay his respects to his friends, the Governor and the Governor's family.

At first the buccaneers jumped to the conclusion that Wolverstone was following with some rare prize of war, but gradually from the reduced crew of the Arabella a very different tale leaked out to stem their satisfaction and convert it into perplexity. Partly out of loyalty to their captain, partly because they perceived that if he was guilty of defection they were guilty with him, and partly because being simple, sturdy men of their hands, they were themselves in the main a little confused as to what really had happened, the crew of the Arabella practised reticence with their brethren in Tortuga during those two days before Wolverstone's arrival. But they were not reticent enough to prevent the circulation of certain uneasy rumours and extravagant stories of discreditable adventures—discreditable, that is, from the buccaneering point of view—of which Captain Blood had been guilty.

But that Wolverstone came when he did, it is possible that there would have been an explosion. When, however, the Old Wolf cast anchor in the bay two days later, it was to him all turned for the explanation they were about to demand of Blood.

Now Wolverstone had only one eye; but he saw a deal more with that one eye than do most men with two; and despite his grizzled head—so picturesquely swathed in a green and scarlet turban—he had the sound heart of a boy, and in that heart much love for Peter Blood.

The sight of the Arabella at anchor in the bay had at first amazed him as he sailed round the rocky headland that bore the fort. He rubbed his single eye clear of any deceiving film and looked again. Still he could not believe what it saw. And then a voice at his elbow—the voice of Dyke, who had elected to sail with him—assured him that he was not singular in his bewilderment.

"In the name of Heaven, is that the Arabella or is it the ghost of her?"

The Old Wolf rolled his single eye over Dyke, and opened his mouth to speak. Then he closed it again without having spoken; closed it tightly. He had a great gift of caution, especially in matters that he did not understand. That this was the Arabella he could no longer doubt. That being so, he must think before he spoke. What the devil should the Arabella be doing here, when he had left her in Jamaica? And was Captain Blood aboard and in command, or had the remainder of her hands made off with her, leaving the Captain in Port Royal?

Dyke repeated his question. This time Wolverstone answered him.

"Ye've two eyes to see with, and ye ask me, who's only got one, what it is ye see!"

"But I see the Arabella."

"Of course, since there she rides. What else was you expecting?"

"Expecting?" Dyke stared at him, open-mouthed. "Was you expecting to find the Arabella here?"

Wolverstone looked him over in contempt, then laughed and spoke loud enough to be heard by all around him. "Of course. What else?" And he laughed again, a laugh that seemed to Dyke to be calling him a fool. On that Wolverstone turned to give his attention to the operation of anchoring.

Anon when ashore he was beset by questioning buccaneers, it was from their very questions that he gathered exactly how matters stood, and perceived that either from lack of courage or other motive Blood, himself, had refused to render any account of his doings since the Arabella had separated from her sister ships. Wolverstone congratulated himself upon the discretion he had used with Dyke.

"The Captain was ever a modest man," he explained to Hagthorpe and those others who came crowding round him. "It's not his way to be sounding his own praises. Why, it was like this. We fell in with old Don Miguel, and when we'd scuttled him we took aboard a London pimp sent out by the Secretary of State to offer the Captain the King's commission if so be him'd quit piracy and be o' good behaviour. The Captain damned his soul to hell for answer. And then we fell in wi' the Jamaica fleet and that grey old devil Bishop in command, and there was a sure end to Captain Blood and to every mother's son of us all. So I goes to him, and 'accept this poxy commission,' says I; 'turn King's man and save your neck and ours.' He took me at my word, and the London pimp gave him the King's commission on the spot, and Bishop all but choked hisself with rage when he was told of it. But happened it had, and he was forced to swallow it. We were King's men all, and so into Port Royal we sailed along o' Bishop. But Bishop didn't trust us. He knew too much. But for his lordship, the fellow from London, he'd ha' hanged the Captain, King's commission and all. Blood would ha' slipped out o' Port Royal again that same night. But that hound Bishop had passed the word, and the fort kept a sharp lookout. In the end, though it took a fortnight, Blood bubbled him. He sent me and most o' the men off in a frigate that I bought for the voyage. His game—as he'd secretly told me—was to follow and give chase. Whether that's the game he played or not I can't tell ye; but here he is afore me as I'd expected he would be."

There was a great historian lost in Wolverstone. He had the right imagination that knows just how far it is safe to stray from the truth and just how far to colour it so as to change its shape for his own purposes.

Having delivered himself of his decoction of fact and falsehood, and thereby added one more to the exploits of Peter Blood, he enquired where the Captain might be found. Being informed that he kept his ship, Wolverstone stepped into a boat and went aboard, to report himself, as he put it.

In the great cabin of the Arabella he found Peter Blood alone and very far gone in drink—a condition in which no man ever before remembered to have seen him. As Wolverstone came in, the Captain raised bloodshot eyes to consider him. A moment they sharpened in their gaze as he brought his visitor into focus. Then he laughed, a loose, idiot laugh, that yet somehow was half a sneer.

"Ah! The Old Wolf!" said he. "Got here at last, eh? And whatcher gonnerdo wi' me, eh?" He hiccoughed resoundingly, and sagged back loosely in his chair.

Old Wolverstone stared at him in sombre silence. He had looked with untroubled eye upon many a hell of devilment in his time, but the sight of Captain Blood in this condition filled him with sudden grief. To express it he loosed an oath. It was his only expression for emotion of all kinds. Then he rolled forward, and dropped into a chair at the table, facing the Captain.

"My God, Peter, what's this?"

"Rum," said Peter. "Rum, from Jamaica." He pushed bottle and glass towards Wolverstone.

Wolverstone disregarded them.

"I'm asking you what ails you?" he bawled.

"Rum," said Captain Blood again, and smiled. "Jus' rum. I answer all your queshons. Why donjerr answer mine? Whatcher gonerdo wi' me?"

"I've done it," said Wolverstone. "Thank God, ye had the sense to hold your tongue till I came. Are ye sober enough to understand me?"

"Drunk or sober, allus 'derstand you."

"Then listen." And out came the tale that Wolverstone had told. The Captain steadied himself to grasp it.

"It'll do as well asertruth," said he when Wolverstone had finished. "And... oh, no marrer! Much obliged to ye, Old Wolf—faithful Old Wolf! But was it worthertrouble? I'm norrer pirate now; never a pirate again. 'S finished'" He banged the table, his eyes suddenly fierce.

"I'll come and talk to you again when there's less rum in your wits," said Wolverstone, rising. "Meanwhile ye'll please to remember the tale I've told, and say nothing that'll make me out a liar. They all believes me, even the men as sailed wi' me from Port Royal. I've made 'em. If they thought as how you'd taken the King's commission in earnest, and for the purpose o' doing as Morgan did, ye guess what would follow."

"Hell would follow," said the Captain. "An' tha's all I'm fit for."

"Ye're maudlin," Wolverstone growled. "We'll talk again to-morrow."

They did; but to little purpose, either that day or on any day thereafter while the rains—which set in that night—endured. Soon the shrewd Wolverstone discovered that rum was not what ailed Blood. Rum was in itself an effect, and not by any means the cause of the Captain's listless apathy. There was a canker eating at his heart, and the Old Wolf knew enough to make a shrewd guess of its nature. He cursed all things that daggled petticoats, and, knowing his world, waited for the sickness to pass.

But it did not pass. When Blood was not dicing or drinking in the taverns of Tortuga, keeping company that in his saner days he had loathed, he was shut up in his cabin aboard the Arabella, alone and uncommunicative. His friends at Government House, bewildered at this change in him, sought to reclaim him. Mademoiselle d'Ogeron, particularly distressed, sent him almost daily invitations, to few of which he responded.

Later, as the rainy season approached its end, he was sought by his captains with proposals of remunerative raids on Spanish settlements. But to all he manifested an indifference which, as the weeks passed and the weather became settled, begot first impatience and then exasperation.

Christian, who commanded the Clotho, came storming to him one day, upbraiding him for his inaction, and demanding that he should take order about what was to do.

"Go to the devil!" Blood said, when he had heard him out. Christian departed fuming, and on the morrow the Clotho weighed anchor and sailed away, setting an example of desertion from which the loyalty of Blood's other captains would soon be unable to restrain their men.

Sometimes Blood asked himself why had he come back to Tortuga at all. Held fast in bondage by the thought of Arabella and her scorn of him for a thief and a pirate, he had sworn that he had done with buccaneering. Why, then, was he here? That question he would answer with another: Where else was he to go? Neither backward nor forward could he move, it seemed.

He was degenerating visibly, under the eyes of all. He had entirely lost the almost foppish concern for his appearance, and was grown careless and slovenly in his dress. He allowed a black beard to grow on cheeks that had ever been so carefully shaven; and the long, thick black hair, once so sedulously curled, hung now in a lank, untidy mane about a face that was changing from its vigorous swarthiness to an unhealthy sallow, whilst the blue eyes, that had been so vivid and compelling, were now dull and lacklustre.

Wolverstone, the only one who held the clue to this degeneration, ventured once—and once only—to beard him frankly about it.

"Lord, Peter! Is there never to be no end to this?" the giant had growled. "Will you spend your days moping and swilling 'cause a white-faced ninny in Port Royal'll have none o' ye? 'Sblood and 'ounds! If ye wants the wench, why the plague doesn't ye go and fetch her?"

The blue eyes glared at him from under the jet-black eyebrows, and something of their old fire began to kindle in them. But Wolverstone went on heedlessly.

"I'll be nice wi' a wench as long as niceness be the key to her favour. But sink me now if I'd rot myself in rum on account of anything that wears a petticoat. That's not the Old Wolf's way. If there's no other expedition'll tempt you, why not Port Royal? What a plague do it matter if it is an English settlement? It's commanded by Colonel Bishop, and there's no lack of rascals in your company'd follow you to hell if it meant getting Colonel Bishop by the throat. It could be done, I tell you. We've but to spy the chance when the Jamaica fleet is away. There's enough plunder in the town to tempt the lads, and there's the wench for you. Shall I sound them on 't?"

Blood was on his feet, his eyes blazing, his livid face distorted. "Ye'll leave my cabin this minute, so ye will, or, by Heaven, it's your corpse'll be carried out of it. Ye mangy hound, d'ye dare come to me with such proposals?"

He fell to cursing his faithful officer with a virulence the like of which he had never yet been known to use. And Wolverstone, in terror before that fury, went out without another word. The subject was not raised again, and Captain Blood was left to his idle abstraction.

But at last, as his buccaneers were growing desperate, something happened, brought about by the Captain's friend M. d'Ogeron. One sunny morning the Governor of Tortuga came aboard the Arabella, accompanied by a chubby little gentleman, amiable of countenance, amiable and self-sufficient of manner.

"My Captain," M. d'Ogeron delivered himself, "I bring you M. de Cussy, the Governor of French Hispaniola, who desires a word with you."

Out of consideration for his friend, Captain Blood pulled the pipe from his mouth, shook some of the rum out of his wits, and rose and made a leg to M. de Cussy.

"Serviteur!" said he.

M. de Cussy returned the bow and accepted a seat on the locker under the stem windows.

"You have a good force here under your command, my Captain," said he.

"Some eight hundred men."

"And I understand they grow restive in idleness."

"They may go to the devil when they please."

M. de Cussy took snuff delicately. "I have something better than that to propose," said he.

"Propose it, then," said Blood, without interest.

M. de Cussy looked at M. d'Ogeron, and raised his eyebrows a little. He did not find Captain Blood encouraging. But M. d'Ogeron nodded vigorously with pursed lips, and the Governor of Hispaniola propounded his business.

"News has reached us from France that there is war with Spain."

"That is news, is it?" growled Blood.

"I am speaking officially, my Captain. I am not alluding to unofficial skirmishes, and unofficial predatory measures which we have condoned out here. There is war—formally war—between France and Spain in Europe. It is the intention of France that this war shall be carried into the New World. A fleet is coming out from Brest under the command of M. le Baron de Rivarol for that purpose. I have letters from him desiring me to equip a supplementary squadron and raise a body of not less than a thousand men to reenforce him on his arrival. What I have come to propose to you, my Captain, at the suggestion of our good friend M. d'Ogeron, is, in brief, that you enroll your ships and your force under M. de Rivarol's flag."

Blood looked at him with a faint kindling of interest. "You are offering to take us into the French service?" he asked. "On what terms, monsieur?"

"With the rank of Capitaine de Vaisseau for yourself, and suitable ranks for the officers serving under you. You will enjoy the pay of that rank, and you will be entitled, together with your men, to one-tenth share in all prizes taken."

"My men will hardly account it generous. They will tell you that they can sail out of here to-morrow, disembowel a Spanish settlement, and keep the whole of the plunder."

"Ah, yes, but with the risks attaching to acts of piracy. With us your position will be regular and official, and considering the powerful fleet by which M. de Rivarol is backed, the enterprises to be undertaken will be on a much vaster scale than anything you could attempt on your own account. So that the one tenth in this case may be equal to more than the whole in the other."

Captain Blood considered. This, after all, was not piracy that was being proposed. It was honourable employment in the service of the King of France.

"I will consult my officers," he said; and he sent for them.

They came and the matter was laid before them by M. de Cussy himself. Hagthorpe announced at once that the proposal was opportune. The men were grumbling at their protracted inaction, and would no doubt be ready to accept the service which M. de Cussy offered on behalf of France. Hagthorpe looked at Blood as he spoke. Blood nodded gloomy agreement. Emboldened by this, they went on to discuss the terms. Yberville, the young French filibuster, had the honour to point out to M. de Cussy that the share offered was too small. For one fifth of the prizes, the officers would answer for their men; not for less.

M. de Cussy was distressed. He had his instructions. It was taking a deal upon himself to exceed them. The buccaneers were firm. Unless M. de Cussy could make it one fifth there was no more to be said. M. de Cussy finally consenting to exceed his instructions, the articles were drawn up and signed that very day. The buccaneers were to be at Petit Goave by the end of January, when M. de Rivarol had announced that he might be expected.

After that followed days of activity in Tortuga, refitting the ships, boucanning meat, laying in stores. In these matters which once would have engaged all Captain Blood's attention, he now took no part. He continued listless and aloof. If he had given his consent to the undertaking, or, rather, allowed himself to be swept into it by the wishes of his officers—it was only because the service offered was of a regular and honourable kind, nowise connected with piracy, with which he swore in his heart that he had done for ever. But his consent remained passive. The service entered awoke no zeal in him. He was perfectly indifferent—as he told Hagthorpe, who ventured once to offer a remonstrance—whether they went to Petit Goave or to Hades, and whether they entered the service of Louis XIV or of Satan.

CHAPTER XXVI. M. de RIVAROL

Captain Blood was still in that disgruntled mood when he sailed from Tortuga, and still in that mood when he came to his moorings in the bay of Petit Goave. In that same mood he greeted M. le Baron de Rivarol when this nobleman with his fleet of five men-of-war at last dropped anchor alongside the buccaneer ships, in the middle of February. The Frenchman had been six weeks on the voyage, he announced, delayed by unfavourable weather.

Summoned to wait on him, Captain Blood repaired to the Castle of Petit Goave, where the interview was to take place. The Baron, a tall, hawk-faced man of forty, very cold and distant of manner, measured Captain Blood with an eye of obvious disapproval. Of Hagthorpe, Yberville, and Wolverstone who stood ranged behind their captain, he took no heed whatever. M. de Cussy offered Captain Blood a chair.

"A moment, M. de Cussy. I do not think M. le Baron has observed that I am not alone. Let me present to you, sir, my companions: Captain Hagthorpe of the Elizabeth, Captain Wolverstone of the Atropos, and Captain Yberville of the Lachesis."

The Baron stared hard and haughtily at Captain Blood, then very distantly and barely perceptibly inclined his head to each of the other three. His manner implied plainly that he despised them and that he desired them at once to understand it. It had a curious effect upon Captain Blood. It awoke the devil in him, and it awoke at the same time his self-respect which of late had been slumbering. A sudden shame of his disordered, ill-kempt appearance made him perhaps the more defiant. There was almost a significance in the way he hitched his sword-belt round, so that the wrought hilt of his very serviceable rapier was brought into fuller view. He waved his captains to the chairs that stood about.

"Draw up to the table, lads. We are keeping the Baron waiting."

They obeyed him, Wolverstone with a grin that was full of understanding. Haughtier grew the stare of M. de Rivarol. To sit at table with these bandits placed him upon what he accounted a dishonouring equality. It had been his notion that—with the possible exception of Captain Blood—they should take his instructions standing, as became men of their quality in the presence of a man of his. He did the only thing remaining to mark a distinction between himself and them. He put on his hat.

"Ye're very wise now," said Blood amiably. "I feel the draught myself." And he covered himself with his plumed castor.

M. de Rivarol changed colour. He quivered visibly with anger, and was a moment controlling himself before venturing to speak. M. de Cussy was obviously very ill at ease.

"Sir," said the Baron frostily, "you compel me to remind you that the rank you hold is that of Capitaine de Vaisseau, and that you are in the presence of the General of the Armies of France by Sea and Land in America. You compel me to remind you further that there is a deference due from your rank to mine."

"I am happy to assure you," said Captain Blood, "that the reminder is unnecessary. I am by way of accounting myself a gentleman, little though I may look like one at present; and I should not account myself that were I capable of anything but deference to those whom nature or fortune may have placed above me, or to those who being placed beneath me in rank may labour under a disability to resent my lack of it." It was a neatly intangible rebuke. M. de Rivarol bit his lip. Captain Blood swept on without giving him time to reply: "Thus much being clear, shall we come to business?"

M. de Rivarol's hard eyes considered him a moment. "Perhaps it will be best," said he. He took up a paper. "I have here a copy of the articles into which you entered with M. de Cussy. Before going further, I have to observe that M. de Cussy has exceeded his instructions in admitting you to one fifth of the prizes taken. His authority did not warrant his going beyond one tenth."

"That is a matter between yourself and M. de Cussy, my General."

"Oh, no. It is a matter between myself and you."

"Your pardon, my General. The articles are signed. So far as we are concerned, the matter is closed. Also out of regard for M. de Cussy, we should not desire to be witnesses of the rebukes you may consider that he deserves."

"What I may have to say to M. de Cussy is no concern of yours."

"That is what I am telling you, my General."

"But—nom de Dieu!—it is your concern, I suppose, that we cannot award you more than one tenth share." M. de Rivarol smote the table in exasperation. This pirate was too infernally skillful a fencer.

"You are quite certain of that, M. le Baron—that you cannot?"

"I am quite certain that I will not."

Captain Blood shrugged, and looked down his nose. "In that case," said he, "it but remains for me to present my little account for our disbursement, and to fix the sum at which we should be compensated for our loss of time and derangement in coming hither. That settled, we can part friends, M. le Baron. No harm has been done."

"What the devil do you mean?" The Baron was on his feet, leaning forward across the table.

"Is it possible that I am obscure? My French, perhaps, is not of the purest, but...."

"Oh, your French is fluent enough; too fluent at moments, if I may permit myself the observation. Now, look you here, M. le filibustier, I am not a man with whom it is safe to play the fool, as you may very soon discover. You have accepted service of the King of France—you and your men; you hold the rank and draw the pay of a Capitaine de Vaisseau, and these your officers hold the rank of lieutenants. These ranks carry obligations which you would do well to study, and penalties for failing to discharge them which you might study at the same time. They are something severe. The first obligation of an officer is obedience. I commend it to your attention. You are not to conceive yourselves, as you appear to be doing, my allies in the enterprises I have in view, but my subordinates. In me you behold a commander to lead you, not a companion or an equal. You understand me, I hope."

"Oh, be sure that I understand," Captain Blood laughed. He was recovering his normal self amazingly under the inspiring stimulus of conflict. The only thing that marred his enjoyment was the reflection that he had not shaved. "I forget nothing, I assure you, my General. I do not forget, for instance, as you appear to be doing, that the articles we signed are the condition of our service; and the articles provide that we receive one-fifth share. Refuse us that, and you cancel the articles; cancel the articles, and you cancel our services with them. From that moment we cease to have the honour to hold rank in the navies of the King of France."

There was more than a murmur of approval from his three captains.

Rivarol glared at them, checkmated.

"In effect..." M. de Cussy was beginning timidly.

"In effect, monsieur, this is your doing," the Baron flashed on him, glad to have some one upon whom he could fasten the sharp fangs of his irritation. "You should be broke for it. You bring the King's service into disrepute; you force me, His Majesty's representative, into an impossible position."

"Is it impossible to award us the one-fifth share?" quoth Captain Blood silkily. "In that case, there is no need for beat or for injuries to M. de Cussy. M. de Cussy knows that we would not have come for less. We depart again upon your assurance that you cannot award us more. And things are as they would have been if M. de Cussy had adhered rigidly to his instructions. I have proved, I hope, to your satisfaction, M. le Baron, that if you repudiate the articles you can neither claim our services nor hinder our departure—not in honour."

"Not in honour, sir? To the devil with your insolence! Do you imply that any course that were not in honour would be possible to me?"

"I do not imply it, because it would not be possible," said Captain Blood. "We should see to that. It is, my General, for you to say whether the articles are repudiated."

The Baron sat down. "I will consider the matter," he said sullenly. "You shall be advised of my resolve."

Captain Blood rose, his officers rose with him. Captain Blood bowed.

"M. le Baron!" said he.

Then he and his buccaneers removed themselves from the August and irate presence of the General of the King's Armies by Land and Sea in America.

You conceive that there followed for M. de Cussy an extremely bad quarter of an hour. M. de Cussy, in fact, deserves your sympathy. His self-sufficiency was blown from him by the haughty M. de Rivarol, as down from a thistle by the winds of autumn. The General of the King's Armies abused him—this man who was Governor of Hispaniola as if he were a lackey. M. de Cussy defended himself by urging the thing that Captain Blood had so admirably urged already on his behalf—that if the terms he had made with the buccaneers were not confirmed there was no harm done. M. de Rivarol bullied and browbeat him into silence.

Having exhausted abuse, the Baron proceeded to indignities. Since he accounted that M. de Cussy had proved himself unworthy of the post he held, M. de Rivarol took over the responsibilities of that post for as long as he might remain in Hispaniola, and to give effect to this he began by bringing soldiers from his ships, and setting his own guard in M. de Cussy's castle.

Out of this, trouble followed quickly. Wolverstone coming ashore next morning in the picturesque garb that he affected, his head swathed in a coloured handkerchief, was jeered at by an officer of the newly landed French troops. Not accustomed to derision, Wolverstone replied in kind and with interest. The officer passed to insult, and Wolverstone struck him a blow that felled him, and left him only the half of his poor senses. Within the hour the matter was reported to M. de Rivarol, and before noon, by M. de Rivarol's orders, Wolverstone was under arrest in the castle.

The Baron had just sat down to dinner with M. de Cussy when the negro who waited on them announced Captain Blood. Peevishly M. de Rivarol bade him be admitted, and there entered now into his presence a spruce and modish gentleman, dressed with care and sombre richness in black and silver, his swarthy, clear-cut face scrupulously shaven, his long black hair in ringlets that fell to a collar of fine point. In his right hand the gentleman carried a broad black hat with a scarlet ostrich-plume, in his left hand an ebony cane. His stockings were of silk, a bunch of ribbons masked his garters, and the black rosettes on his shoes were finely edged with gold.

For a moment M. de Rivarol did not recognize him. For Blood looked younger by ten years than yesterday. But the vivid blue eyes under their level black brows were not to be forgotten, and they proclaimed him for the man announced even before he had spoken. His resurrected pride had demanded that he should put himself on an equality with the baron and advertise that equality by his exterior.

"I come inopportunely," he courteously excused himself. "My apologies. My business could not wait. It concerns, M. de Cussy, Captain Wolverstone of the Lachesis, whom you have placed under arrest."

"It was I who placed him under arrest," said M. de Rivarol.

"Indeed! But I thought that M. de Cussy was Governor of Hispaniola."

"Whilst I am here, monsieur, I am the supreme authority. It is as well that you should understand it."

"Perfectly. But it is not possible that you are aware of the mistake that has been made."

"Mistake, do you say?"

"I say mistake. On the whole, it is polite of me to use that word. Also it is expedient. It will save discussions. Your people have arrested the wrong man, M. de Rivarol. Instead of the French officer, who used the grossest provocation, they have arrested Captain Wolverstone. It is a matter which I beg you to reverse without delay."

M. de Rivarol's hawk-face flamed scarlet. His dark eyes bulged.

"Sir, you... you are insolent! But of an insolence that is intolerable!" Normally a man of the utmost self-possession he was so rudely shaken now that he actually stammered.

"M. le Baron, you waste words. This is the New World. It is not merely new; it is novel to one reared amid the superstitions of the Old. That novelty you have not yet had time, perhaps, to realize; therefore I overlook the offensive epithet you have used. But justice is justice in the New World as in the Old, and injustice as intolerable here as there. Now justice demands the enlargement of my officer and the arrest and punishment of yours. That justice I invite you, with submission, to administer."

"With submission?" snorted the Baron in furious scorn.

"With the utmost submission, monsieur. But at the same time I will remind M. le Baron that my buccaneers number eight hundred; your troops five hundred; and M. de Cussy will inform you of the interesting fact that any one buccaneer is equal in action to at least three soldiers of the line. I am perfectly frank with you, monsieur, to save time and hard words. Either Captain Wolverstone is instantly set at liberty, or we must take measures to set him at liberty ourselves. The consequences may be appalling. But it is as you please, M. le Baron. You are the supreme authority. It is for you to say."

M. de Rivarol was white to the lips. In all his life he had never been so bearded and defied. But he controlled himself.

"You will do me the favour to wait in the ante-room, M. le Capitaine. I desire a word with M. de Cussy. You shall presently be informed of my decision."

When the door had closed, the baron loosed his fury upon the head of M. de Cussy.

"So, these are the men you have enlisted in the King's service, the men who are to serve under me—men who do not serve, but dictate, and this before the enterprise that has brought me from France is even under way! What explanations do you offer me, M. de Cussy? I warn you that I am not pleased with you. I am, in fact, as you may perceive, exceedingly angry."

The Governor seemed to shed his chubbiness. He drew himself stiffly erect.

"Your rank, monsieur, does not give you the right to rebuke me; nor do the facts. I have enlisted for you the men that you desired me to enlist. It is not my fault if you do not know how to handle them better. As Captain Blood has told you, this is the New World."

"So, so!" M. de Rivarol smiled malignantly. "Not only do you offer no explanation, but you venture to put me in the wrong. Almost I admire your temerity. But there!" he waved the matter aside. He was supremely sardonic. "It is, you tell me, the New World, and—new worlds, new manners, I suppose. In time I may conform my ideas to this new world, or I may conform this new world to my ideas." He was menacing on that. "For the moment I must accept what I find. It remains for you, monsieur, who have experience of these savage by-ways, to advise me out of that experience how to act."

"M. le Baron, it was a folly to have arrested the buccaneer captain. It would be madness to persist. We have not the forces to meet force."

"In that case, monsieur, perhaps you will tell me what we are to do with regard to the future. Am I to submit at every turn to the dictates of this man Blood? Is the enterprise upon which we are embarked to be conducted as he decrees? Am I, in short, the King's representative in America, to be at the mercy of these rascals?"

"Oh, by no means. I am enrolling volunteers here in Hispaniola, and I am raising a corps of negroes. I compute that when this is done we shall have a force of a thousand men, the buccaneers apart."

"But in that case why not dispense with them?"

"Because they will always remain the sharp edge of any weapon that we forge. In the class of warfare that lies before us they are so skilled that what Captain Blood has just said is not an overstatement. A buccaneer is equal to three soldiers of the line. At the same time we shall have a sufficient force to keep them in control. For the rest, monsieur, they have certain notions of honour. They will stand by their articles, and so that we deal justly with them, they will deal justly with us, and give no trouble. I have experience of them, and I pledge you my word for that."

M. de Rivarol condescended to be mollified. It was necessary that he should save his face, and in a degree the Governor afforded him the means to do so, as well as a certain guarantee for the future in the further force he was raising.

"Very well," he said. "Be so good as to recall this Captain Blood."

The Captain came in, assured and very dignified. M. de Rivarol found him detestable; but dissembled it.

"M. le Capitaine, I have taken counsel with M. le Gouverneur. From what he tells me, it is possible that a mistake has been committed. Justice, you may be sure, shall be done. To ensure it, I shall myself preside over a council to be composed of two of my senior officers, yourself and an officer of yours. This council shall hold at once an impartial investigation into the affair, and the offender, the man guilty of having given provocation, shall be punished."

Captain Blood bowed. It was not his wish to be extreme. "Perfectly, M. le Baron. And now, sir, you have had the night for reflection in this matter of the articles. Am I to understand that you confirm or that you repudiate them?"

M. de Rivarol's eyes narrowed. His mind was full of what M. de Cussy had said—that these buccaneers must prove the sharp edge of any weapon he might forge. He could not dispense with them. He perceived that he had blundered tactically in attempting to reduce the agreed share. Withdrawal from a position of that kind is ever fraught with loss of dignity. But there were those volunteers that M. de Cussy was enrolling to strengthen the hand of the King's General. Their presence might admit anon of the reopening of this question. Meanwhile he must retire in the best order possible.

"I have considered that, too," he announced. "And whilst my opinion remains unaltered, I must confess that since M. de Cussy has pledged us, it is for us to fulfil the pledges. The articles are confirmed, sir."

Captain Blood bowed again. In vain M. de Rivarol looked searchingly for the least trace of a smile of triumph on those firm lips. The buccaneer's face remained of the utmost gravity.

Wolverstone was set at liberty that afternoon, and his assailant sentenced to two months' detention. Thus harmony was restored. But it had been an unpromising beginning, and there was more to follow shortly of a similar discordant kind.

Blood and his officers were summoned a week later to a council which sat to determine their operations against Spain. M. de Rivarol laid before them a project for a raid upon the wealthy Spanish town of Cartagena. Captain Blood professed astonishment. Sourly invited by M. de Rivarol to state his grounds for it, he did so with the utmost frankness.

"Were I General of the King's Armies in America," said he, "I should have no doubt or hesitation as to the best way in which to serve my Royal master and the French nation. That which I think will be obvious to M. de Cussy, as it is to me, is that we should at once invade Spanish Hispaniola and reduce the whole of this fruitful and splendid island into the possession of the King of France."

"That may follow," said M. de Rivarol. "It is my wish that we begin with Cartagena."

"You mean, sir, that we are to sail across the Caribbean on an adventurous expedition, neglecting that which lies here at our very door. In our absence, a Spanish invasion of French Hispaniola is possible. If we begin by reducing the Spaniards here, that possibility will be removed. We shall have added to the Crown of France the most coveted possession in the West Indies. The enterprise offers no particular difficulty; it may be speedily accomplished, and once accomplished, it would be time to look farther afield. That would seem the logical order in which this campaign should proceed."

He ceased, and there was silence. M. de Rivarol sat back in his chair, the feathered end of a quill between his teeth. Presently he cleared his throat and asked a question.

"Is there anybody else who shares Captain Blood's opinion?"

None answered him. His own officers were overawed by him; Blood's followers naturally preferred Cartagena, because offering the greater chance of loot. Loyalty to their leader kept them silent.

"You seem to be alone in your opinion," said the Baron with his vinegary smile.

Captain Blood laughed outright. He had suddenly read the Baron's mind. His airs and graces and haughtiness had so imposed upon Blood that it was only now that at last he saw through them, into the fellow's peddling spirit. Therefore he laughed; there was really nothing else to do. But his laughter was charged with more anger even than contempt. He had been deluding himself that he had done with piracy. The conviction that this French service was free of any taint of that was the only consideration that had induced him to accept it. Yet here was this haughty, supercilious gentleman, who dubbed himself General of the Armies of France, proposing a plundering, thieving raid which, when stripped of its mean, transparent mask of legitimate warfare, was revealed as piracy of the most flagrant.

M. de Rivarol, intrigued by his mirth, scowled upon him disapprovingly.

"Why do you laugh, monsieur?"

"Because I discover here an irony that is supremely droll. You, M. le Baron, General of the King's Armies by Land and Sea in America, propose an enterprise of a purely buccaneering character; whilst I, the buccaneer, am urging one that is more concerned with upholding the honour of France. You perceive how droll it is."

M. de Rivarol perceived nothing of the kind. M. de Rivarol in fact was extremely angry. He bounded to his feet, and every man in the room rose with him—save only M. de Cussy, who sat on with a grim smile on his lips. He, too, now read the Baron like an open book, and reading him despised him.

"M. le filibustier," cried Rivarol in a thick voice, "it seems that I must again remind you that I am your superior officer."

"My superior officer! You! Lord of the World! Why, you are just a common pirate! But you shall hear the truth for once, and that before all these gentlemen who have the honour to serve the King of France. It is for me, a buccaneer, a sea-robber, to stand here and tell you what is in the interest of French honour and the French Crown. Whilst you, the French King's appointed General, neglecting this, are for spending the King's resources against an outlying settlement of no account, shedding French blood in seizing a place that cannot be held, only because it has been reported to you that there is much gold in Cartagena, and that the plunder of it will enrich you. It is worthy of the huckster who sought to haggle with us about our share, and to beat us down after the articles pledging you were already signed. If I am wrong—let M. de Cussy say so. If I am wrong, let me be proven wrong, and I will beg your pardon. Meanwhile, monsieur, I withdraw from this council. I will have no further part in your deliberations. I accepted the service of the King of France with intent to honour that service. I cannot honour that service by lending countenance to a waste of life and resources in raids upon unimportant settlements, with plunder for their only object. The responsibility for such decisions must rest with you, and with you alone. I desire M. de Cussy to report me to the Ministers of France. For the rest, monsieur, it merely remains for you to give me your orders. I await them aboard my ship—and anything else, of a personal nature, that you may feel I have provoked by the terms I have felt compelled to use in this council. M. le Baron, I have the honour to wish you good-day."

He stalked out, and his three captains—although they thought him mad—rolled after him in loyal silence.

M. de Rivarol was gasping like a landed fish. The stark truth had robbed him of speech. When he recovered, it was to thank Heaven vigorously that the council was relieved by Captain Blood's own act of that gentleman's further participation in its deliberations. Inwardly M. de Rivarol burned with shame and rage. The mask had been plucked from him, and he had been held up to scorn—he, the General of the King's Armies by Sea and Land in America.

Nevertheless, it was to Cartagena that they sailed in the middle of March. Volunteers and negroes had brought up the forces directly under M. de Rivarol to twelve hundred men. With these he thought he could keep the buccaneer contingent in order and submissive.

They made up an imposing fleet, led by M. de Rivarol's flagship, the Victorieuse, a mighty vessel of eighty guns. Each of the four other French ships was at least as powerful as Blood's Arabella, which was of forty guns. Followed the lesser buccaneer vessels, the Elizabeth, Lachesis, and Atropos, and a dozen frigates laden with stores, besides canoes and small craft in tow.

Narrowly they missed the Jamaica fleet with Colonel Bishop, which sailed north for Tortuga two days after the Baron de Rivarol's southward passage.

CHAPTER XXVII. CARTAGENA

Having crossed the Caribbean in the teeth of contrary winds, it was not until the early days of April that the French fleet hove in sight of Cartagena, and M. de Rivarol summoned a council aboard his flagship to determine the method of assault.

"It is of importance, messieurs," he told them, "that we take the city by surprise, not only before it can put itself into a state of defence; but before it can remove its treasures inland. I propose to land a force sufficient to achieve this to the north of the city to-night after dark." And he explained in detail the scheme upon which his wits had laboured.

He was heard respectfully and approvingly by his officers, scornfully by Captain Blood, and indifferently by the other buccaneer captains present. For it must be understood that Blood's refusal to attend councils had related only to those concerned with determining the nature of the enterprise to be undertaken.

Captain Blood was the only one amongst them who knew exactly what lay ahead. Two years ago he had himself considered a raid upon the place, and he had actually made a survey of it in circumstances which he was presently to disclose.

The Baron's proposal was one to be expected from a commander whose knowledge of Cartagena was only such as might be derived from maps.

Geographically and strategically considered, it is a curious place. It stands almost four-square, screened east and north by hills, and it may be said to face south upon the inner of two harbours by which it is normally approached. The entrance to the outer harbour, which is in reality a lagoon some three miles across, lies through a neck known as the Boca Chica—or Little Mouth—and defended by a fort. A long strip of densely wooded land to westward acts here as a natural breakwater, and as the inner harbour is approached, another strip of land thrusts across at right angles from the first, towards the mainland on the east. Just short of this it ceases, leaving a deep but very narrow channel, a veritable gateway, into the secure and sheltered inner harbour. Another fort defends this second passage. East and north of Cartagena lies the mainland, which may be left out of account. But to the west and northwest this city, so well guarded on every other side, lies directly open to the sea. It stands back beyond a half-mile of beach, and besides this and the stout Walls which fortify it, would appear to have no other defences.

But those appearances are deceptive, and they had utterly deceived M. de Rivarol, when he devised his plan.

It remained for Captain Blood to explain the difficulties when M. de Rivarol informed him that the honour of opening the assault in the manner which he prescribed was to be accorded to the buccaneers.

Captain Blood smiled sardonic appreciation of the honour reserved for his men. It was precisely what he would have expected. For the buccaneers the dangers; for M. de Rivarol the honour, glory and profit of the enterprise.

"It is an honour which I must decline," said he quite coldly.

Wolverstone grunted approval and Hagthorpe nodded. Yberville, who as much as any of them resented the superciliousness of his noble compatriot, never wavered in loyalty to Captain Blood. The French officers—there were six of them present—stared their haughty surprise at the buccaneer leader, whilst the Baron challengingly fired a question at him.

"How? You decline it, 'sir? You decline to obey orders, do you say?"

"I understood, M. le Baron, that you summoned us to deliberate upon the means to be adopted."

"Then you understood amiss, M. le Capitaine. You are here to receive my commands. I have already deliberated, and I have decided. I hope you understand."

"Oh, I understand," laughed Blood. "But, I ask myself, do you?" And without giving the Baron time to set the angry question that was bubbling to his lips, he swept on: "You have deliberated, you say, and you have decided. But unless your decision rests upon a wish to destroy my buccaneers, you will alter it when I tell you something of which I have knowledge. This city of Cartagena looks very vulnerable on the northern side, all open to the sea as it apparently stands. Ask yourself, M. le Baron, how came the Spaniards who built it where it is to have been at such trouble to fortify it to the south, if from the north it is so easily assailable."

That gave M. de Rivarol pause.

"The Spaniards," Blood pursued, "are not quite the fools you are supposing them. Let me tell you, messieurs, that two years ago I made a survey of Cartagena as a preliminary to raiding it. I came hither with some friendly trading Indians, myself disguised as an Indian, and in that guise I spent a week in the city and studied carefully all its approaches. On the side of the sea where it looks so temptingly open to assault, there is shoal water for over half a mile out—far enough out, I assure you, to ensure that no ship shall come within bombarding range of it. It is not safe to venture nearer land than three quarters of a mile."

"But our landing will be effected in canoes and piraguas and open boats," cried an officer impatiently.

"In the calmest season of the year, the surf will hinder any such operation. And you will also bear in mind that if landing were possible as you are suggesting, that landing could not be covered by the ships' guns. In fact, it is the landing parties would be in danger from their own artillery."

"If the attack is made by night, as I propose, covering will be unnecessary. You should be ashore in force before the Spaniards are aware of the intent."

"You are assuming that Cartagena is a city of the blind, that at this very moment they are not conning our sails and asking themselves who we are and what we intend."

"But if they feel themselves secure from the north, as you suggest," cried the Baron impatiently, "that very security will lull them."

"Perhaps. But, then, they are secure. Any attempt to land on this side is doomed to failure at the hands of Nature."

"Nevertheless, we make the attempt," said the obstinate Baron, whose haughtiness would not allow him to yield before his officers.

"If you still choose to do so after what I have said, you are, of course, the person to decide. But I do not lead my men into fruitless danger."

"If I command you..." the Baron was beginning. But Blood unceremoniously interrupted him.

"M. le Baron, when M. de Cussy engaged us on your behalf, it was as much on account of our knowledge and experience of this class of warfare as on account of our strength. I have placed my own knowledge and experience in this particular matter at your disposal. I will add that I abandoned my own project of raiding Cartagena, not being in sufficient strength at the time to force the entrance of the harbour, which is the only way into the city. The strength which you now command is ample for that purpose."

"But whilst we are doing that, the Spaniards will have time to remove great part of the wealth this city holds. We must take them by surprise."

Captain Blood shrugged. "If this is a mere pirating raid, that, of course, is a prime consideration. It was with me. But if you are concerned to abate the pride of Spain and plant the Lilies of France on the forts of this settlement, the loss of some treasure should not really weigh for much."

M. de Rivarol bit his lip in chagrin. His gloomy eye smouldered as it considered the self-contained buccaneer.

"But if I command you to go—to make the attempt?" he asked. "Answer me, monsieur, let us know once for all where we stand, and who commands this expedition."

"Positively, I find you tiresome," said Captain Blood, and he swung to M. de Cussy, who sat there gnawing his lip, intensely uncomfortable. "I appeal to you, monsieur, to justify me to the General."

M. de Cussy started out of his gloomy abstraction. He cleared his throat. He was extremely nervous.

"In view of what Captain Blood has submitted...."

"Oh, to the devil with that!" snapped Rivarol. "It seems that I am followed by poltroons. Look you, M. le Capitaine, since you are afraid to undertake this thing, I will myself undertake it. The weather is calm, and I count upon making good my landing. If I do so, I shall have proved you wrong, and I shall have a word to say to you to-morrow which you may not like. I am being very generous with you, sir." He waved his hand regally. "You have leave to go."

It was sheer obstinacy and empty pride that drove him, and he received the lesson he deserved. The fleet stood in during the afternoon to within a mile of the coast, and under cover of darkness three hundred men, of whom two hundred were negroes—the whole of the negro contingent having been pressed into the undertaking—were pulled away for the shore in the canoes, piraguas, and ships' boats. Rivarol's pride compelled him, however much he may have disliked the venture, to lead them in person.

The first six boats were caught in the surf, and pounded into fragments before their occupants could extricate themselves. The thunder of the breakers and the cries of the shipwrecked warned those who followed, and thereby saved them from sharing the same fate. By the Baron's urgent orders they pulled away again out of danger, and stood about to pick up such survivors as contrived to battle towards them. Close upon fifty lives were lost in the adventure, together with half-a-dozen boats stored with ammunition and light guns.

The Baron went back to his flagship an infuriated, but by no means a wiser man. Wisdom—not even the pungent wisdom experience thrusts upon us—is not for such as M. de Rivarol. His anger embraced all things, but focussed chiefly upon Captain Blood. In some warped process of reasoning he held the buccaneer chiefly responsible for this misadventure. He went to bed considering furiously what he should say to Captain Blood upon the morrow.

He was awakened at dawn by the rolling thunder of guns. Emerging upon the poop in nightcap and slippers, he beheld a sight that increased his unreasonable and unreasoning fury. The four buccaneer ships under canvas were going through extraordinary manoeuvre half a mile off the Boca Chica and little more than half a mile away from the remainder of the fleet, and from their flanks flame and smoke were belching each time they swung broadside to the great round fort that guarded that narrow entrance. The fort was returning the fire vigorously and viciously. But the buccaneers timed their broadsides with extraordinary judgment to catch the defending ordnance reloading; then as they drew the Spaniards' fire, they swung away again not only taking care to be ever moving targets, but, further, to present no more than bow or stern to the fort, their masts in line, when the heaviest cannonades were to be expected.

Gibbering and cursing, M. de Rivarol stood there and watched this action, so presumptuously undertaken by Blood on his own responsibility. The officers of the Victorieuse crowded round him, but it was not until M. de Cussy came to join the group that he opened the sluices of his rage. And M. de Cussy himself invited the deluge that now caught him. He had come up rubbing his hands and taking a proper satisfaction in the energy of the men whom he had enlisted.

"Aha, M. de Rivarol!" he laughed. "He understands his business, eh, this Captain Blood. He'll plant the Lilies of France on that fort before breakfast."

The Baron swung upon him snarling. "He understands his business, eh? His business, let me tell you, M. de Cussy, is to obey my orders, and I have not ordered this. Par la Mordieu! When this is over I'll deal with him for his damned insubordination."

"Surely, M. le Baron, he will have justified it if he succeeds."

"Justified it! Ah, parbleu! Can a soldier ever justify acting without orders?" He raved on furiously, his officers supporting him out of their detestation of Captain Blood.

Meanwhile the fight went merrily on. The fort was suffering badly. Yet for all their manoeuvring the buccaneers were not escaping punishment. The starboard gunwale of the Atropos had been hammered into splinters, and a shot had caught her astern in the coach. The Elizabeth was badly battered about the forecastle, and the Arabella's maintop had been shot away, whilst' towards the end of that engagement the Lachesis came reeling out of the fight with a shattered rudder, steering herself by sweeps.

The absurd Baron's fierce eyes positively gleamed with satisfaction.

"I pray Heaven they may sink all his infernal ships!" he cried in his frenzy.

But Heaven didn't hear him. Scarcely had he spoken than there was a terrific explosion, and half the fort went up in fragments. A lucky shot from the buccaneers had found the powder magazine.

It may have been a couple of hours later, when Captain Blood, as spruce and cool as if he had just come from a levee, stepped upon the quarter-deck of the Victoriense, to confront M. de Rivarol, still in bedgown and nightcap.

"I have to report, M. le Baron, that we are in possession of the fort on Boca Chica. The standard of France is flying from what remains of its tower, and the way into the outer harbour is open to your fleet."

M. de Rivarol was compelled to swallow his fury, though it choked him. The jubilation among his officers had been such that he could not continue as he had begun. Yet his eyes were malevolent, his face pale with anger.

"You are fortunate, M. Blood, that you succeeded," he said. "It would have gone very ill with you had you failed. Another time be so good as to await my orders, lest you should afterwards lack the justification which your good fortune has procured you this morning."

Blood smiled with a flash of white teeth, and bowed. "I shall be glad of your orders now, General, for pursuing our advantage. You realize that speed in striking is the first essential."

Rivarol was left gaping a moment. Absorbed in his ridiculous anger, he had considered nothing. But he made a quick recovery. "To my cabin, if you please," he commanded peremptorily, and was turning to lead the way, when Blood arrested him.

"With submission, my General, we shall be better here. You behold there the scene of our coming action. It is spread before you like a map." He waved his hand towards the lagoon, the country flanking it and the considerable city standing back from the beach. "If it is not a presumption in me to offer a suggestion...." He paused. M. de Rivarol looked at him sharply, suspecting irony. But the swarthy face was bland, the keen eyes steady.

"Let us hear your suggestion," he consented.

Blood pointed out the fort at the mouth of the inner harbour, which was just barely visible above the waving palms on the intervening tongue of land. He announced that its armament was less formidable than that of the outer fort, which they had reduced; but on the other hand, the passage was very much narrower than the Boca Chica, and before they could attempt to make it in any case, they must dispose of those defences. He proposed that the French ships should enter the outer harbour, and proceed at once to bombardment. Meanwhile, he would land three hundred buccaneers and some artillery on the eastern side of the lagoon, beyond the fragrant garden islands dense with richly bearing fruit-trees, and proceed simultaneously to storm the fort in the rear. Thus beset on both sides at once, and demoralized by the fate of the much stronger outer fort, he did not think the Spaniards would offer a very long resistance. Then it would be for M. de Rivarol to garrison the fort, whilst Captain Blood would sweep on with his men, and seize the Church of Nuestra Senora de la Poupa, plainly visible on its hill immediately eastward of the town. Not only did that eminence afford them a valuable and obvious strategic advantage, but it commanded the only road that led from Cartagena to the interior, and once it were held there would be no further question of the Spaniards attempting to remove the wealth of the city.

That to M. de Rivarol was—as Captain Blood had judged that it would be—the crowning argument. Supercilious until that moment, and disposed for his own pride's sake to treat the buccaneer's suggestions with cavalier criticism, M. de Rivarol's manner suddenly changed. He became alert and brisk, went so far as tolerantly to commend Captain Blood's plan, and issued orders that action might be taken upon it at once.

It is not necessary to follow that action step by step. Blunders on the part of the French marred its smooth execution, and the indifferent handling of their ships led to the sinking of two of them in the course of the afternoon by the fort's gunfire. But by evening, owing largely to the irresistible fury with which the buccaneers stormed the place from the landward side, the fort had surrendered, and before dusk Blood and his men with some ordnance hauled thither by mules dominated the city from the heights of Nuestra Senora de la Poupa.

At noon on the morrow, shorn of defences and threatened with bombardment, Cartagena sent offers of surrender to M. de Rivarol.

Swollen with pride by a victory for which he took the entire credit to himself, the Baron dictated his terms. He demanded that all public effects and office accounts be delivered up; that the merchants surrender all moneys and goods held by them for their correspondents; the inhabitants could choose whether they would remain in the city or depart; but those who went must first deliver up all their property, and those who elected to remain must surrender half, and become the subjects of France; religious houses and churches should be spared, but they must render accounts of all moneys and valuables in their possession.

Cartagena agreed, having no choice in the matter, and on the next day, which was the 5th of April, M. de Rivarol entered the city and proclaimed it now a

French colony, appointing M. de Cussy its Governor. Thereafter he proceeded to the Cathedral, where very properly a Te Deum was sung in honour of the conquest. This by way of grace, whereafter M. de Rivarol proceeded to devour the city. The only detail in which the French conquest of Cartagena differed from an ordinary buccaneering raid was that under the severest penalties no soldier was to enter the house of any inhabitant. But this apparent respect for the persons and property of the conquered was based in reality upon M. de Rivarol's anxiety lest a doubloon should be abstracted from all the wealth that was pouring into the treasury opened by the Baron in the name of the King of France. Once the golden stream had ceased, he removed all restrictions and left the city in prey to his men, who proceeded further to pillage it of that part of their property which the inhabitants who became French subjects had been assured should remain inviolate. The plunder was enormous. In the course of four days over a hundred mules laden with gold went out of the city and down to the boats waiting at the beach to convey the treasure aboard the ships.

CHAPTER XXVIII. THE HONOUR OF M. DE RIVAROL

During the capitulation and for some time after, Captain Blood and the greater portion of his buccaneers had been at their post on the heights of Nuestra Senora de la Poupa, utterly in ignorance of what was taking place. Blood, although the man chiefly, if not solely, responsible for the swift reduction of the city, which was proving a veritable treasure-house, was not even shown the consideration of being called to the council of officers which with M. de Rivarol determined the terms of the capitulation.

This was a slight that at another time Captain Blood would not have borne for a moment. But at present, in his odd frame of mind, and its divorcement from piracy, he was content to smile his utter contempt of the French General. Not so, however, his captains, and still less his men. Resentment smouldered amongst them for a while, to flame out violently at the end of that week in Cartagena. It was only by undertaking to voice their grievance to the Baron that their captain was able for the moment to pacify them. That done, he went at once in quest of M. de Rivarol.

He found him in the offices which the Baron had set up in the town, with a staff of clerks to register the treasure brought in and to cast up the surrendered account-books, with a view to ascertaining precisely what were the sums yet to be delivered up. The Baron sat there scrutinizing ledgers, like a city merchant, and checking figures to make sure that all was correct to the last peso. A choice occupation this for the General of the King's Armies by Sea and Land. He looked up irritated by the interruption which Captain Blood's advent occasioned.

"M. le Baron," the latter greeted him. "I must speak frankly; and you must suffer it. My men are on the point of mutiny."

M. de Rivarol considered him with a faint lift of the eyebrows.

"Captain Blood, I, too, will speak frankly; and you, too, must suffer it. If there is a mutiny, you and your captains shall be held personally responsible. The mistake you make is in assuming with me the tone of an ally, whereas I have given you clearly to understand from the first that you are simply in the position of having accepted service under me. Your proper apprehension of that fact will save the waste of a deal of words."

Blood contained himself with difficulty. One of these fine days, he felt, that for the sake of humanity he must slit the comb of this supercilious, arrogant cockerel.

"You may define our positions as you please," said he. "But I'll remind you that the nature of a thing is not changed by the name you give it. I am concerned with facts; chiefly with the fact that we entered into definite articles with you. Those articles provide for a certain distribution of the spoil. My men demand it. They are not satisfied."

"Of what are they not satisfied?" demanded the Baron.

"Of your honesty, M. de Rivarol."

A blow in the face could scarcely have taken the Frenchman more aback. He stiffened, and drew himself up, his eyes blazing, his face of a deathly pallor. The clerks at the tables laid down their pens, and awaited the explosion in a sort of terror.

For a long moment there was silence. Then the great gentleman delivered himself in a voice of concentrated anger. "Do you really dare so much, you and the dirty thieves that follow you? God's Blood! You shall answer to me for that word, though it entail a yet worse dishonour to meet you. Faugh!"

"I will remind you," said Blood, "that I am speaking not for myself, but for my men. It is they who are not satisfied, they who threaten that unless satisfaction is afforded them, and promptly, they will take it."

"Take it?" said Rivarol, trembling in his rage. "Let them attempt it, and...."

"Now don't be rash. My men are within their rights, as you are aware. They demand to know when this sharing of the spoil is to take place, and when they are to receive the fifth for which their articles provide."

"God give me patience! How can we share the spoil before it has been completely gathered?"

"My men have reason to believe that it is gathered; and, anyway, they view with mistrust that it should all be housed aboard your ships, and remain in your possession. They say that hereafter there will be no ascertaining what the spoil really amounts to."

"But—name of Heaven!—I have kept books. They are there for all to see."

"They do not wish to see account-books. Few of them can read. They want to view the treasure itself. They know—you compel me to be blunt—that the accounts have been falsified. Your books show the spoil of Cartagena to amount to some ten million livres. The men know—and they are very skilled in these computations—that it exceeds the enormous total of forty millions. They insist that the treasure itself be produced and weighed in their presence, as is the custom among the Brethren of the Coast."

"I know nothing of filibuster customs." The gentleman was disdainful.

"But you are learning quickly."

"What do you mean, you rogue? I am a leader of armies, not of plundering thieves."

"Oh, but of course!" Blood's irony laughed in his eyes. "Yet, whatever you may be, I warn you that unless you yield to a demand that I consider just and therefore uphold, you may look for trouble, and it would not surprise me if you never leave Cartagena at all, nor convey a single gold piece home to France."

"Ah, pardieu! Am I to understand that you are threatening me?"

"Come, come, M. le Baron! I warn you of the trouble that a little prudence may avert. You do not know on what a volcano you are sitting. You do not know the ways of buccaneers. If you persist, Cartagena will be drenched in blood, and whatever the outcome the King of France will not have been well served."

That shifted the basis of the argument to less hostile ground. Awhile yet it continued, to be concluded at last by an ungracious undertaking from M. de Rivarol to submit to the demands of the buccaneers. He gave it with an extreme ill-grace, and only because Blood made him realize at last that to withhold it longer would be dangerous. In an engagement, he might conceivably defeat Blood's followers. But conceivably he might not. And even if he succeeded, the effort would be so costly to him in men that he might not thereafter find himself in sufficient strength to maintain his hold of what he had seized.

The end of it all was that he gave a promise at once to make the necessary preparations, and if Captain Blood and his officers would wait upon him on board the Victorieuse to-morrow morning, the treasure should be produced, weighed in their presence, and their fifth share surrendered there and then into their own keeping.

Among the buccaneers that night there was hilarity over the sudden abatement of M. de Rivarol's monstrous pride. But when the next dawn broke over Cartagena, they had the explanation of it. The only ships to be seen in the harbour were the Arabella and the Elizabeth riding at anchor, and the Atropos and the Lachesis careened on the beach for repair of the damage sustained in the bombardment. The French ships were gone. They had been quietly and secretly warped out of the harbour under cover of night, and three sails, faint and small, on the horizon to westward was all that remained to be seen of them. The absconding M. de Rivarol had gone off with the treasure, taking with him the troops and mariners he had brought from France. He had left behind him at Cartagena not only the empty-handed buccaneers, whom he had swindled, but also M. de Cussy and the volunteers and negroes from Hispaniola, whom he had swindled no less.

The two parties were fused into one by their common fury, and before the exhibition of it the inhabitants of that ill-fated town were stricken with deeper terror than they had yet known since the coming of this expedition.

Captain Blood alone kept his head, setting a curb upon his deep chagrin. He had promised himself that before parting from M. de Rivarol he would present a reckoning for all the petty affronts and insults to which that unspeakable fellow—now proved a scoundrel—had subjected him.

"We must follow," he declared. "Follow and punish."

At first that was the general cry. Then came the consideration that only two of the buccaneer ships were seaworthy—and these could not accommodate the whole force, particularly being at the moment indifferently victualled for a long voyage. The crews of the Lachesis and Atropos and with them their captains, Wolverstone and Yberville, renounced the intention. After all, there would be a deal of treasure still hidden in Cartagena. They would remain behind to extort it whilst fitting their ships for sea. Let Blood and Hagthorpe and those who sailed with them do as they pleased.

Then only did Blood realize the rashness of his proposal, and in attempting to draw back he almost precipitated a battle between the two parties into which that same proposal had now divided the buccaneers. And meanwhile those French sails on the horizon were growing less and less. Blood was reduced to despair. If he went off now, Heaven knew what would happen to the town, the temper of those whom he was leaving being what it was. Yet if he remained, it would simply mean that his own and Hagthorpe's crews would join in the saturnalia and increase the hideousness of events now inevitable. Unable to reach a decision, his own men and Hagthorpe's took the matter off his hands, eager to give chase to Rivarol. Not only was a dastardly cheat to be punished but an enormous treasure to be won by treating as an enemy this French commander who, himself, had so villainously broken the alliance.

When Blood, torn as he was between conflicting considerations, still hesitated, they bore him almost by main force aboard the Arabella.

Within an hour, the water-casks at least replenished and stowed aboard, the Arabella and the Elizabeth put to sea upon that angry chase.

"When we were well at sea, and the Arabella's course was laid," writes Pitt, in his log, "I went to seek the Captain, knowing him to be in great trouble of mind over these events. I found him sitting alone in his cabin, his head in his hands, torment in the eyes that stared straight before him, seeing nothing."

"What now, Peter?" cried the young Somerset mariner. "Lord, man, what is there here to fret you? Surely 't isn't the thought of Rivarol!"

"No," said Blood thickly. And for once he was communicative. It may well be that he must vent the thing that oppressed him or be driven mad by it. And Pitt, after all, was his friend and loved him, and, so, a proper man for confidences. "But if she knew! If she knew! O God! I had thought to have done with piracy; thought to have done with it for ever. Yet here have I been committed by this scoundrel to the worst piracy that ever I was guilty of. Think of Cartagena! Think of the hell those devils will be making of it now! And I must have that on my soul!"

"Nay, Peter—'t isn't on your soul; but on Rivarol's. It is that dirty thief who has brought all this about. What could you have done to prevent it?"

"I would have stayed if it could have availed."

"It could not, and you know it. So why repine?"

"There is more than that to it," groaned Blood. "What now? What remains? Loyal service with the English was made impossible for me. Loyal service with France has led to this; and that is equally impossible hereafter. What to live clean, I believe the only thing is to go and offer my sword to the King of Spain."

But something remained—the last thing that he could have expected—something towards which they were rapidly sailing over the tropical, sunlit sea. All this against which he now inveighed so bitterly was but a necessary stage in the shaping of his odd destiny.

Setting a course for Hispaniola, since they judged that thither must Rivarol go to refit before attempting to cross to France, the Arabella and the Elizabeth ploughed briskly northward with a moderately favourable wind for two days and nights without ever catching a glimpse of their quarry. The third dawn brought with it a haze which circumscribed their range of vision to something between two and three miles, and deepened their growing vexation and their apprehension that M. de Rivarol might escape them altogether.

Their position then—according to Pitt's log—was approximately 75 deg. 30' W. Long. by 17 deg. 45' N. Lat., so that they had Jamaica on their larboard beam some thirty miles to westward, and, indeed, away to the northwest, faintly visible as a bank of clouds, appeared the great ridge of the Blue Mountains whose peaks were thrust into the clear upper air above the low-lying haze. The wind, to which they were sailing very close, was westerly, and it bore to their ears a booming sound which in less experienced ears might have passed for the breaking of surf upon a lee shore.

"Guns!" said Pitt, who stood with Blood upon the quarter-deck. Blood nodded, listening.

"Ten miles away, perhaps fifteen—somewhere off Port Royal, I should judge," Pitt added. Then he looked at his captain. "Does it concern us?" he asked.

"Guns off Port Royal... that should argue Colonel Bishop at work. And against whom should he be in action but against friends of ours I think it may concern us. Anyway, we'll stand in to investigate. Bid them put the helm over."

Close-hauled they tacked aweather, guided by the sound of combat, which grew in volume and definition as they approached it. Thus for an hour, perhaps. Then, as, telescope to his eye, Blood raked the haze, expecting at any moment to behold the battling ships, the guns abruptly ceased.

They held to their course, nevertheless, with all hands on deck, eagerly, anxiously scanning the sea ahead. And presently an object loomed into view, which soon defined itself for a great ship on fire. As the Arabella with the Elizabeth following closely raced nearer on their north-westerly tack, the outlines of the blazing vessel grew clearer. Presently her masts stood out sharp and black above the smoke and flames, and through his telescope Blood made out plainly the pennon of St. George fluttering from her maintop.

"An English ship!" he cried.

He scanned the seas for the conqueror in the battle of which this grim evidence was added to that of the sounds they had heard, and when at last, as they drew closer to the doomed vessel, they made out the shadowy outlines of three tall ships, some three or four miles away, standing in toward Port Royal, the first and natural assumption was that these ships must belong to the Jamaica fleet, and that the burning vessel was a defeated buccaneer, and because of this they sped on to pick up the three boats that were standing away from the blazing hulk. But Pitt, who through the telescope was examining the receding squadron, observed things apparent only to the eye of the trained mariner, and made the incredible announcement that the largest of these three vessels was Rivarol's Victorieuse.

They took in sail and hove to as they came up with the drifting boats, laden to capacity with survivors. And there were others adrift on some of the spars and wreckage with which the sea was strewn, who must be rescued.

CHAPTER XXIX. THE SERVICE OF KING WILLIAM

One of the boats bumped alongside the Arabella, and up the entrance ladder came first a slight, spruce little gentleman in a coat of mulberry satin laced with gold, whose wizened, yellow, rather peevish face was framed in a heavy black periwig. His modish and costly apparel had nowise suffered by the adventure through which he had passed, and he carried himself with the easy assurance of a man of rank. Here, quite clearly, was no buccaneer. He was closely followed by one who in every particular, save that of age, was his physical opposite, corpulent in a brawny, vigorous way, with a full, round, weather-beaten face whose mouth was humourous and whose eyes were blue and twinkling. He was well dressed without fripperies, and bore with him an air of vigorous authority.

As the little man stepped from the ladder into the waist, whither Captain Blood had gone to receive him, his sharp, ferrety dark eyes swept the uncouth ranks of the assembled crew of the Arabella.

"And where the devil may I be now?" he demanded irritably. "Are you English, or what the devil are you?"

"Myself, I have the honour to be Irish, sir. My name is Blood—Captain Peter Blood, and this is my ship the Arabella, all very much at your service.

"Blood!" shrilled the little man. "O 'Sblood! A pirate!" He swung to the Colossus who followed him—"A damned pirate, van der Kuylen. Rend my vitals, but we're come from Scylla to Charybdis."

"So?" said the other gutturally, and again, "So?" Then the humour of it took him, and he yielded to it.

"Damme! What's to laugh at, you porpoise?" spluttered mulberry-coat. "A fine tale this'll make at home! Admiral van der Kuylen first loses his fleet in the night, then has his flagship fired under him by a French squadron, and ends all by being captured by a pirate. I'm glad you find it matter for laughter. Since for my sins I happen to be with you, I'm damned if I do."

"There's a misapprehension, if I may make so bold as to point it out," put in Blood quietly. "You are not captured, gentlemen; you are rescued. When you realize it, perhaps it will occur to you to acknowledge the hospitality I am offering you. It may be poor, but it is the best at my disposal."

The fierce little gentleman stared at him. "Damme! Do you permit yourself to be ironical?" he disapproved him, and possibly with a view to correcting any such tendency, proceeded to introduce himself. "I am Lord Willoughby, King William's Governor-General of the West Indies, and this is Admiral van der Kuylen, commander of His Majesty's West Indian fleet, at present mislaid somewhere in this damned Caribbean Sea."

"King William?" quoth Blood, and he was conscious that Pitt and Dyke, who were behind him, now came edging nearer, sharing his own wonder. "And who may be King William, and of what may he be King?"

"What's that?" In a wonder greater than his own, Lord Willoughby stared back at him. At last: "I am alluding to His Majesty King William III—William of Orange—who, with Queen Mary, has been ruling England for two months and more."

There was a moment's silence, until Blood realized what he was being told.

"D'ye mean, sir, that they've roused themselves at home, and kicked out that scoundrel James and his gang of ruffians?"

Admiral van der Kuylen nudged his lordship, a humourous twinkle in his blue eyes.

"His bolitics are fery sound, I dink," he growled.

His lordship's smile brought lines like gashes into his leathery cheeks. "'Slife! hadn't you heard? Where the devil have you been at all?"

"Out of touch with the world for the last three months," said Blood.

"Stab me! You must have been. And in that three months the world has undergone some changes." Briefly he added an account of them. King James was fled to France, and living under the protection of King Louis, wherefore, and for other reasons, England had joined the league against her, and was now at war with France. That was how it happened that the Dutch Admiral's flagship had been attacked by M. de Rivarol's fleet that morning, from which it clearly followed that in his voyage from Cartagena, the Frenchman must have spoken some ship that gave him the news.

After that, with renewed assurances that aboard his ship they should be honourably entreated, Captain Blood led the Governor-General and the Admiral to his cabin, what time the work of rescue went on. The news he had received had set Blood's mind in a turmoil. If King James was dethroned and banished, there was an end to his own outlawry for his alleged share in an earlier attempt to drive out that tyrant. It became possible for him to return home and take up his life again at the point where it was so unfortunately interrupted four years ago. He was dazzled by the prospect so abruptly opened out to him. The thing so filled his mind, moved him so deeply, that he must afford it expression. In doing so, he revealed of himself more than he knew or intended to the astute little gentleman who watched him so keenly the while.

"Go home, if you will," said his lordship, when Blood paused. "You may be sure that none will harass you on the score of your piracy, considering what it was that drove you to it. But why be in haste? We have heard of you, to be sure, and we know of what you are capable upon the seas. Here is a great chance for you, since you declare yourself sick of piracy. Should you choose to serve King William out here during this war, your knowledge of the West Indies should render you a very valuable servant to His Majesty's Government, which you would not find ungrateful. You should consider it. Damme, sir, I repeat: it is a great chance you are given.

"That your lordship gives me," Blood amended, "I am very grateful. But at the moment, I confess, I can consider nothing but this great news. It alters the shape of the world. I must accustom myself to view it as it now is, before I can determine my own place in it."

Pitt came in to report that the work of rescue was at an end, and the men picked up—some forty-five in all—safe aboard the two buccaneer ships. He asked for orders. Blood rose.

"I am negligent of your lordship's concerns in my consideration of my own. You'll be wishing me to land you at Port Royal."

"At Port Royal?" The little man squirmed wrathfully on his seat. Wrathfully and at length he informed Blood that they had put into Port Royal last evening to find its Deputy-Governor absent. "He had gone on some wild-goose chase to Tortuga after buccaneers, taking the whole of the fleet with him."

Blood stared in surprise a moment; then yielded to laughter.

"He went, I suppose, before news reached him of the change of government at home, and the war with France?"

"He did not," snapped Willoughby. "He was informed of both, and also of my coming before he set out."

"Oh, impossible!"

"So I should have thought. But I have the information from a Major Mallard whom I found in Port Royal, apparently governing in this fool's absence."

"But is he mad, to leave his post at such a time?" Blood was amazed.

"Taking the whole fleet with him, pray remember, and leaving the place open to French attack. That is the sort of Deputy-Governor that the late Government thought fit to appoint: an epitome of its misrule, damme! He leaves Port Royal unguarded save by a ramshackle fort that can be reduced to rubble in an hour. Stab me! It's unbelievable!"

The lingering smile faded from Blood's face. "Is Rivarol aware of this?" he cried sharply.

It was the Dutch Admiral who answered him. "Vould he go dere if he were not? M. de Rivarol he take some of our men prisoners. Berhabs dey dell him. Berhabs he make dem tell. Id is a great obbordunidy."

His lordship snarled like a mountain-cat. "That rascal Bishop shall answer for it with his head if there's any mischief done through this desertion of his post. What if it were deliberate, eh? What if he is more knave than fool? What if this is his way of serving King James, from whom he held his office?"

Captain Blood was generous. "Hardly so much. It was just vindictiveness that urged him. It's myself he's hunting at Tortuga, my lord. But, I'm thinking that while he's about it, I'd best be looking after Jamaica for King William." He laughed, with more mirth than he had used in the last two months.

"Set a course for Port Royal, Jeremy, and make all speed. We'll be level yet with M. de Rivarol, and wipe off some other scores at the same time."

Both Lord Willoughby and the Admiral were on their feet.

"But you are not equal to it, damme!" cried his lordship. "Any one of the Frenchman's three ships is a match for both yours, my man."

"In guns aye," said Blood, and he smiled. "But there's more than guns that matter in these affairs. If your lordship would like to see an action fought at sea as an action should be fought, this is your opportunity."

Both stared at him. "But the odds!" his lordship insisted.

"Id is imbossible," said van der Kuylen, shaking his great head. "Seamanship is imbordand. Bud guns is guns."

"If I can't defeat him, I can sink my own ships in the channel, and block him in until Bishop gets back from his wild-goose chase with his squadron, or until your own fleet turns up."

"And what good will that be, pray?" demanded Willoughby.

"I'll be after telling you. Rivarol is a fool to take this chance, considering what he's got aboard. He carried in his hold the treasure plundered from Cartagena, amounting to forty million livres." They jumped at the mention of that colossal sum. "He has gone into Port Royal with it. Whether he defeats me or not, he doesn't come out of Port Royal with it again, and sooner or later that treasure shall find its way into King William's coffers, after, say, one fifth share shall have been paid to my buccaneers. Is that agreed, Lord Willoughby?"

His lordship stood up, and shaking back the cloud of lace from his wrist, held out a delicate white hand.

"Captain Blood, I discover greatness in you," said he.

"Sure it's your lordship has the fine sight to perceive it," laughed the Captain.

"Yes, yes! Bud how vill you do id?" growled van der Kuylen.

"Come on deck, and it's a demonstration I'll be giving you before the day's much older."

CHAPTER XXX. THE LAST FIGHT OF THE ARABELLA

"VHY do you vait, my friend?" growled van der Kuylen.

"Aye—in God's name!" snapped Willoughby.

It was the afternoon of that same day, and the two buccaneer ships rocked gently with idly flapping sails under the lee of the long spit of land forming the great natural harbour of Port Royal, and less than a mile from the straits leading into it, which the fort commanded. It was two hours and more since they had brought up thereabouts, having crept thither unobserved by the city and by M. de Rivarol's ships, and all the time the air had been aquiver with the roar of guns from sea and land, announcing that battle was joined between the French and the defenders of Port Royal. That long, inactive waiting was straining the nerves of both Lord Willoughby and van der Kuylen.

"You said you vould show us zome vine dings. Vhere are dese vine dings?"

Blood faced them, smiling confidently. He was arrayed for battle, in back-and-breast of black steel. "I'll not be trying your patience much longer. Indeed, I notice already a slackening in the fire. But it's this way, now: there's nothing at all to be gained by precipitancy, and a deal to be gained by delaying, as I shall show you, I hope."

Lord Willoughby eyed him suspiciously. "Ye think that in the meantime Bishop may come back or Admiral van der Kuylen's fleet appear?"

"Sure, now, I'm thinking nothing of the kind. What I'm thinking is that in this engagement with the fort M. de Rivarol, who's a lubberly fellow, as I've reason to know, will be taking some damage that may make the odds a trifle more even. Sure, it'll be time enough to go forward when the fort has shot its bolt."

"Aye, aye!" The sharp approval came like a cough from the little Governor-General. "I perceive your object, and I believe ye're entirely right. Ye have the qualities of a great commander, Captain Blood. I beg your pardon for having misunderstood you."

"And that's very handsome of your lordship. Ye see, I have some experience of this kind of action, and whilst I'll take any risk that I must, I'll take none that I needn't. But...." He broke off to listen. "Aye, I was right. The fire's slackening. It'll mean the end of Mallard's resistance in the fort. Ho there, Jeremy!"

He leaned on the carved rail and issued orders crisply. The bo'sun's pipe shrilled out, and in a moment the ship that had seemed to slumber there, awoke to life. Came the padding of feet along the decks, the creaking of blocks and the hoisting of sail. The helm was put over hard, and in a moment they were moving, the Elizabeth following, ever in obedience to the signals from the Arabella, whilst Ogle the gunner, whom he had summoned, was receiving Blood's final instructions before plunging down to his station on the main deck.

Within a quarter of an hour they had rounded the head, and stood in to the harbour mouth, within saker shot of Rivarol's three ships, to which they now abruptly disclosed themselves.

Where the fort had stood they now beheld a smoking rubbish heap, and the victorious Frenchman with the lily standard trailing from his mastheads was sweeping forward to snatch the rich prize whose defences he had shattered.

Blood scanned the French ships, and chuckled. The Victorieuse and the Medusa appeared to have taken no more than a few scars; but the third ship, the Baleine, listing heavily to larboard so as to keep the great gash in her starboard well above water, was out of account.

"You see!" he cried to van der Kuylen, and without waiting for the Dutchman's approving grunt, he shouted an order: "Helm, hard-a-port!"

The sight of that great red ship with her gilt beak-head and open ports swinging broadside on must have given check to Rivarol's soaring exultation. Yet before he could move to give an order, before he could well resolve what order to give, a volcano of fire and metal burst upon him from the buccaneers, and his decks were swept by the murderous scythe of the broadside. The Arabella held to her course, giving place to the Elizabeth, which, following closely, executed the same manoeuver. And then whilst still the Frenchmen were confused, panic-stricken by an attack that took them so utterly by surprise, the Arabella had gone about, and was returning in her tracks, presenting now her larboard guns, and loosing her second broadside in the wake of the first. Came yet another broadside from the Elizabeth and then the Arabella's trumpeter sent a call across the water, which Hagthorpe perfectly understood.

"On, now, Jeremy!" cried Blood. "Straight into them before they recover their wits. Stand by, there! Prepare to board! Hayton ... the grapnels! And pass the word to the gunner in the prow to fire as fast as he can load."

He discarded his feathered hat, and covered himself with a steel head-piece, which a negro lad brought him. He meant to lead this boarding-party in person. Briskly he explained himself to his two guests. "Boarding is our only chance here. We are too heavily outgunned."

Of this the fullest demonstration followed quickly. The Frenchmen having recovered their wits at last, both ships swung broadside on, and concentrating upon the Arabella as the nearer and heavier and therefore more immediately dangerous of their two opponents, volleyed upon her jointly at almost the same moment.

Unlike the buccaneers, who had fired high to cripple their enemies above decks, the French fifed low to smash the hull of their assailant. The Arabella rocked and staggered under that terrific hammering, although Pitt kept her headed towards the French so that she should offer the narrowest target. For a moment she seemed to hesitate, then she plunged forward again, her beak-head in splinters, her forecastle smashed, and a gaping hole forward, that was only just above the water-line. Indeed, to make her safe from bilging, Blood ordered a prompt jettisoning of the forward guns, anchors, and water-casks and whatever else was moveable.

Meanwhile, the Frenchmen going about, gave the like reception to the Elizabeth. The Arabella, indifferently served by the wind, pressed forward to come to grips. But before she could accomplish her object, the Victorieuse had loaded her starboard guns again, and pounded her advancing enemy with a second broadside at close quarters. Amid the thunder of cannon, the rending of timbers, and the screams of maimed men, the half-necked Arabella plunged and reeled into the cloud of smoke that concealed her prey, and then from Hayton went up the cry that she was going down by the head.

Blood's heart stood still. And then in that very moment of his despair, the blue and gold flank of the Victorieuse loomed through the smoke. But even as he caught that enheartening glimpse he perceived, too, how sluggish now was their advance, and how with every second it grew more sluggish. They must sink before they reached her.

Thus, with an oath, opined the Dutch Admiral, and from Lord Willoughby there was a word of blame for Blood's seamanship in having risked all upon this gambler's throw of boarding.

"There was no other chance!" cried Blood, in broken-hearted frenzy. "If ye say it was desperate and foolhardy, why, so it was; but the occasion and the means demanded nothing less. I fail within an ace of victory."

But they had not yet completely failed. Hayton himself, and a score of sturdy rogues whom his whistle had summoned, were crouching for shelter amid the wreckage of the forecastle with grapnels ready. Within seven or eight yards of the Victorieuse, when their way seemed spent, and their forward deck already awash under the eyes of the jeering, cheering Frenchmen, those men leapt up and forward, and hurled their grapnels across the chasm. Of the four they flung, two reached the Frenchman's decks, and fastened there. Swift as thought itself, was then the action of those sturdy, experienced buccaneers. Unhesitatingly all threw themselves upon the chain of one of those grapnels, neglecting the other, and heaved upon it with all their might to warp the ships together. Blood, watching from his own quarter-deck, sent out his voice in a clarion call:

"Musketeers to the prow!"

The musketeers, at their station at the waist, obeyed him with the speed of men who know that in obedience is the only hope of life. Fifty of them dashed forward instantly, and from the ruins of the forecastle they blazed over the heads of Hayton's men, mowing down the French soldiers who, unable to dislodge the irons, firmly held where they had deeply bitten into the timbers of the Victorieuse, were themselves preparing to fire upon the grapnel crew.

Starboard to starboard the two ships swung against each other with a jarring thud. By then Blood was down in the waist, judging and acting with the hurricane speed the occasion demanded. Sail had been lowered by slashing away the ropes that held the yards. The advance guard of boarders, a hundred strong, was ordered to the poop, and his grapnel-men were posted, and prompt to obey his command at the very moment of impact. As a result, the foundering Arabella was literally kept afloat by the half-dozen grapnels that in an instant moored her firmly to the Victorieuse.

Willoughby and van der Kuylen on the poop had watched in breathless amazement the speed and precision with which Blood and his desperate crew had gone to work. And now he came racing up, his bugler sounding the charge, the main host of the buccaneers following him, whilst the vanguard, led by the gunner Ogle, who had been driven from his guns by water in the gun-deck, leapt shouting to the prow of the Victorieuse, to whose level the high poop of the water-logged Arabella had sunk. Led now by Blood himself, they launched themselves upon the French like hounds upon the stag they have brought to bay. After them went others, until all had gone, and none but Willoughby and the Dutchman were left to watch the fight from the quarter-deck of the abandoned Arabella.

For fully half-an-hour that battle raged aboard the Frenchman. Beginning in the prow, it surged through the forecastle to the waist, where it reached a climax of fury. The French resisted stubbornly, and they had the advantage of numbers to encourage them. But for all their stubborn valour, they ended by being pressed back and back across the decks that were dangerously canted to starboard by the pull of the water-logged Arabella. The buccaneers fought with the desperate fury of men who know that retreat is impossible, for there was no ship to which they could retreat, and here they must prevail and make the Victorieuse their own, or perish.

And their own they made her in the end, and at a cost of nearly half their numbers. Driven to the quarter-deck, the surviving defenders, urged on by the infuriated Rivarol, maintained awhile their desperate resistance. But in the end, Rivarol went down with a bullet in his head, and the French remnant, numbering scarcely a score of whole men, called for quarter.

Even then the labours of Blood's men were not at an end. The Elizabeth and the Medusa were tight-locked, and Hagthorpe's followers were being driven back aboard their own ship for the second time. Prompt measures were demanded. Whilst Pitt and his seamen bore their part with the sails, and Ogle went below with a gun-crew, Blood ordered the grapnels to be loosed at once. Lord Willoughby and the Admiral were already aboard the Victorieuse. As they swung off to the rescue of Hagthorpe, Blood, from the quarter-deck of the conquered vessel, looked his last upon the ship that had served him so well, the ship that had become to him almost as a part of himself. A moment she rocked after her release, then slowly and gradually settled down, the water gurgling and eddying about her topmasts, all that remained visible to mark the spot where she had met her death.

As he stood there, above the ghastly shambles in the waist of the Victorieuse, some one spoke behind him. "I think, Captain Blood, that it is necessary I should beg your pardon for the second time. Never before have I seen the impossible made possible by resource and valour, or victory so gallantly snatched from defeat."

He turned, and presented to Lord Willoughby a formidable front. His headpiece was gone, his breastplate dinted, his right sleeve a rag hanging from his shoulder about a naked arm. He was splashed from head to foot with blood, and there was blood from a scalp-wound that he had taken matting his hair and mixing with the grime of powder on his face to render him unrecognizable.

But from that horrible mask two vivid eyes looked out preternaturally bright, and from those eyes two tears had ploughed each a furrow through the filth of his cheeks.

CHAPTER XXXI. HIS EXCELLENCY THE GOVERNOR

When the cost of that victory came to be counted, it was found that of three hundred and twenty buccaneers who had left Cartagena with Captain Blood, a bare hundred remained sound and whole. The Elizabeth had suffered so seriously that it was doubtful if she could ever again be rendered seaworthy, and Hagthorpe, who had so gallantly commanded her in that last action, was dead. Against this, on the other side of the account, stood the facts that, with a far inferior force and by sheer skill and desperate valour, Blood's buccaneers had saved Jamaica from bombardment and pillage, and they had captured the fleet of M. de Rivarol, and seized for the benefit of King William the splendid treasure which she carried.

It was not until the evening of the following day that van der Kuylen's truant fleet of nine ships came to anchor in the harbour of Port Royal, and its officers, Dutch and English, were made acquainted with their Admiral's true opinion of their worth.

Six ships of that fleet were instantly refitted for sea. There were other West Indian settlements demanding the visit of inspection of the new Governor-General, and Lord Willoughby was in haste to sail for the Antilles.

"And meanwhile," he complained to his Admiral, "I am detained here by the absence of this fool of a Deputy-Governor."

"So?" said van der Kuylen. "But vhy should dad dedam you?"

"That I may break the dog as he deserves, and appoint his successor in some man gifted with a sense of where his duty lies, and with the ability to perform it."

"Aha! But id is not necessary you remain for dat. And he vill require no insdrucshons, dis one. He vill know how to make Port Royal safe, bedder nor you or me."

"You mean Blood?"

"Of gourse. Could any man be bedder? You haf seen vhad he can do."

"You think so, too, eh? Egad! I had thought of it; and, rip me, why not? He's a better man than Morgan, and Morgan was made Governor."

Blood was sent for. He came, spruce and debonair once more, having exploited the resources of Port Royal so to render himself. He was a trifle dazzled by the honour proposed to him, when Lord Willoughby made it known. It was so far beyond anything that he had dreamed, and he was assailed by doubts of his capacity to undertake so onerous a charge.

"Damme!" snapped Willoughby, "Should I offer it unless I were satisfied of your capacity? If that's your only objection...."

"It is not, my lord. I had counted upon going home, so I had. I am hungry for the green lanes of England." He sighed. "There will be apple-blossoms in the orchards of Somerset."

"Apple-blossoms!" His lordship's voice shot up like a rocket, and cracked on the word. "What the devil...? Apple-blossoms!" He looked at van der Kuylen.

The Admiral raised his brows and pursed his heavy lips. His eyes twinkled humourously in his great face.

"So!" he said. "Fery boedical!"

My lord wheeled fiercely upon Captain Blood. "You've a past score to wipe out, my man!" he admonished him. "You've done something towards it, I confess; and you've shown your quality in doing it. That's why I offer you the governorship of Jamaica in His Majesty's name—because I account you the fittest man for the office that I have seen."

Blood bowed low. "Your lordship is very good. But...."

"Tchah! There's no 'but' to it. If you want your past forgotten, and your future assured, this is your chance. And you are not to treat it lightly on account of apple-blossoms or any other damned sentimental nonsense. Your duty lies here, at least for as long as the war lasts. When the war's over, you may get back to Somerset and cider or your native Ireland and its potheen; but until then you'll make the best of Jamaica and rum."

Van der Kuylen exploded into laughter. But from Blood the pleasantry elicited no smile. He remained solemn to the point of glumness. His thoughts were on Miss Bishop, who was somewhere here in this very house in which they stood, but whom he had not seen since his arrival. Had she but shown him some compassion....

And then the rasping voice of Willoughby cut in again, upbraiding him for his hesitation, pointing out to him his incredible stupidity in trifling with such a golden opportunity as this. He stiffened and bowed.

"My lord, you are in the right. I am a fool. But don't be accounting me an ingrate as well. If I have hesitated, it is because there are considerations with which I will not trouble your lordship."

"Apple-blossoms, I suppose?" sniffed his lordship.

This time Blood laughed, but there was still a lingering wistfulness in his eyes.

"It shall be as you wish—and very gratefully, let me assure your lordship. I shall know how to earn His Majesty's approbation. You may depend upon my loyal service.

"If I didn't, I shouldn't offer you this governorship."

Thus it was settled. Blood's commission was made out and sealed in the presence of Mallard, the Commandant, and the other officers of the garrison, who looked on in round-eyed astonishment, but kept their thoughts to themselves.

"Now ve can aboud our business go," said van der Kuylen.

"We sail to-morrow morning," his lordship announced.

Blood was startled.

"And Colonel Bishop?" he asked.

"He becomes your affair. You are now the Governor. You will deal with him as you think proper on his return. Hang him from his own yardarm. He deserves it."

"Isn't the task a trifle invidious?" wondered Blood.

"Very well. I'll leave a letter for him. I hope he'll like it."

Captain Blood took up his duties at once. There was much to be done to place Port Royal in a proper state of defence, after what had happened there. He made an inspection of the ruined fort, and issued instructions for the work upon it, which was to be started immediately. Next he ordered the careening of the three French vessels that they might be rendered seaworthy once more. Finally, with the sanction of Lord Willoughby, he marshalled his buccaneers and surrendered to them one fifth of the captured treasure, leaving it to their choice thereafter either to depart or to enrol themselves in the service of King William.

A score of them elected to remain, and amongst these were Jeremy Pitt, Ogle, and Dyke, whose outlawry, like Blood's, had come to an end with the downfall of King James. They were—saving old Wolverstone, who had been left behind at Cartagena—the only survivors of that band of rebels-convict who had left Barbados over three years ago in the Cinco Llagas.

On the following morning, whilst van der Kuylen's fleet was making finally ready for sea, Blood sat in the spacious whitewashed room that was the Governor's office, when Major Mallard brought him word that Bishop's homing squadron was in sight.

"That is very well," said Blood. "I am glad he comes before Lord Willoughby's departure. The orders, Major, are that you place him under arrest the moment he steps ashore. Then bring him here to me. A moment." He wrote a hurried note. "That to Lord Willoughby aboard Admiral van der Kuylen's flagship."

Major Mallard saluted and departed. Peter Blood sat back in his chair and stared at the ceiling, frowning. Time moved on. Came a tap at the door, and an elderly negro slave presented himself. Would his excellency receive Miss Bishop?

His excellency changed colour. He sat quite still, staring at the negro a moment, conscious that his pulses were drumming in a manner wholly unusual to them. Then quietly he assented.

He rose when she entered, and if he was not as pale as she was, it was because his tan dissembled it. For a moment there was silence between them, as they stood looking each at the other. Then she moved forward, and began at last to speak, haltingly, in an unsteady voice, amazing in one usually so calm and deliberate.

"I... I... Major Mallard has just told me...."

"Major Mallard exceeded his duty," said Blood, and because of the effort he made to steady his voice it sounded harsh and unduly loud.

He saw her start, and stop, and instantly made amends. "You alarm yourself without reason, Miss Bishop. Whatever may lie between me and your uncle, you may be sure that I shall not follow the example he has set me. I shall not abuse my position to prosecute a private vengeance. On the contrary, I shall abuse it to protect him. Lord Willoughby's recommendation to me is that I shall treat him without mercy. My own intention is to send him back to his plantation in Barbados."

She came slowly forward now. "I... I am glad that you will do that. Glad, above all, for your own sake." She held out her hand to him.

He considered it critically. Then he bowed over it. "I'll not presume to take it in the hand of a thief and a pirate," said he bitterly.

"You are no longer that," she said, and strove to smile.

"Yet I owe no thanks to you that I am not," he answered. "I think there's no more to be said, unless it be to add the assurance that Lord Julian Wade has also nothing to apprehend from me. That, no doubt, will be the assurance that your peace of mind requires?"

"For your own sake—yes. But for your own sake only. I would not have you do anything mean or dishonouring."

"Thief and pirate though I be?"

She clenched her hand, and made a little gesture of despair and impatience.

"Will you never forgive me those words?"

"I'm finding it a trifle hard, I confess. But what does it matter, when all is said?"

Her clear hazel eyes considered him a moment wistfully. Then she put out her hand again.

"I am going, Captain Blood. Since you are so generous to my uncle, I shall be returning to Barbados with him. We are not like to meet again—ever. Is it impossible that we should part friends? Once I wronged you, I know. And I have said that I am sorry. Won't you... won't you say 'good-bye'?"

He seemed to rouse himself, to shake off a mantle of deliberate harshness. He took the hand she proffered. Retaining it, he spoke, his eyes sombrely, wistfully considering her.

"You are returning to Barbados?" he said slowly. "Will Lord Julian be going with you?"

"Why do you ask me that?" she confronted him quite fearlessly.

"Sure, now, didn't he give you my message, or did he bungle it?"

"No. He didn't bungle it. He gave it me in your own words. It touched me very deeply. It made me see clearly my error and my injustice. I owe it to you that I should say this by way of amend. I judged too harshly where it was a presumption to judge at all."

He was still holding her hand. "And Lord Julian, then?" he asked, his eyes watching her, bright as sapphires in that copper-coloured face.

"Lord Julian will no doubt be going home to England. There is nothing more for him to do out here."

"But didn't he ask you to go with him?"

"He did. I forgive you the impertinence."

A wild hope leapt to life within him.

"And you? Glory be, ye'll not be telling me ye refused to become my lady, when...."

"Oh! You are insufferable!" She tore her hand free and backed away from him. "I should not have come. Good-bye!" She was speeding to the door.

He sprang after her, and caught her. Her face flamed, and her eyes stabbed him like daggers. "These are pirate's ways, I think! Release me!"

"Arabella!" he cried on a note of pleading. "Are ye meaning it? Must I release ye? Must I let ye go and never set eyes on ye again? Or will ye stay and make this exile endurable until we can go home together? Och, ye're crying now! What have I said to make ye cry, my dear?"

"I... I thought you'd never say it," she mocked him through her tears.

"Well, now, ye see there was Lord Julian, a fine figure of a...."

"There was never, never anybody but you, Peter."

They had, of course, a deal to say thereafter, so much, indeed, that they sat down to say it, whilst time sped on, and Governor Blood forgot the duties of his office. He had reached home at last. His odyssey was ended.

And meanwhile Colonel Bishop's fleet had come to anchor, and the Colonel had landed on the mole, a disgruntled man to be disgruntled further yet. He was accompanied ashore by Lord Julian Wade.

A corporal's guard was drawn up to receive him, and in advance of this stood Major Mallard and two others who were unknown to the Deputy-Governor: one slight and elegant, the other big and brawny.

Major Mallard advanced. "Colonel Bishop, I have orders to arrest you. Your sword, sir!"

"By order of the Governor of Jamaica," said the elegant little man behind Major Mallard. Bishop swung to him.

"The Governor? Ye're mad!" He looked from one to the other. "I am the Governor."

"You were," said the little man dryly. "But we've changed that in your absence. You're broke for abandoning your post without due cause, and thereby imperiling the settlement over which you had charge. It's a serious matter, Colonel Bishop, as you may find. Considering that you held your office from the Government of King James, it is even possible that a charge of treason might lie against you. It rests with your successor entirely whether ye're hanged or not."

Bishop rapped out an oath, and then, shaken by a sudden fear: "Who the devil may you be?" he asked.

"I am Lord Willoughby, Governor General of His Majesty's colonies in the West Indies. You were informed, I think, of my coming."

The remains of Bishop's anger fell from him like a cloak. He broke into a sweat of fear. Behind him Lord Julian looked on, his handsome face suddenly white and drawn.

"But, my lord..." began the Colonel.

"Sir, I am not concerned to hear your reasons," his lordship interrupted him harshly. "I am on the point of sailing and I have not the time. The Governor will hear you, and no doubt deal justly by you." He waved to Major Mallard, and Bishop, a crumpled, broken man, allowed himself to be led away.

To Lord Julian, who went with him, since none deterred him, Bishop expressed himself when presently he had sufficiently recovered.

"This is one more item to the account of that scoundrel Blood," he said, through his teeth. "My God, what a reckoning there will be when we meet!"

Major Mallard turned away his face that he might conceal his smile, and without further words led him a prisoner to the Governor's house, the house that so long had been Colonel Bishop's own residence. He was left to wait under guard in the hall, whilst Major Mallard went ahead to announce him.

Miss Bishop was still with Peter Blood when Major Mallard entered. His announcement startled them back to realities.

"You will be merciful with him. You will spare him all you can for my sake, Peter," she pleaded.

"To be sure I will," said Blood. "But I'm afraid the circumstances won't."

She effaced herself, escaping into the garden, and Major Mallard fetched the Colonel.

"His excellency the Governor will see you now," said he, and threw wide the door.

Colonel Bishop staggered in, and stood waiting.

At the table sat a man of whom nothing was visible but the top of a carefully curled black head. Then this head was raised, and a pair of blue eyes solemnly regarded the prisoner. Colonel Bishop made a noise in his throat, and, paralyzed by amazement, stared into the face of his excellency the Deputy-Governor of Jamaica, which was the face of the man he had been hunting in Tortuga to his present undoing.

The situation was best expressed to Lord Willoughby by van der Kuylen as the pair stepped aboard the Admiral's flagship.

"Id is fery boedigal!" he said, his blue eyes twinkling. "Cabdain Blood is fond of boedry—you remember de abble-blossoms. So? Ha, ha!"

CAPTAIN BLOOD RETURNS

OR

THE CHRONICLES OF CAPTAIN BLOOD

by

Rafael Sabatini

INTRODUCTORY NOTE

The Odyssey of Captain Blood, given to the world some years ago, was derived from various sources, disclosed in the course of its compilation, of which the most important is the log of the *Arabella*, kept by the young Somersetshire shipmaster Jeremy Pitt. This log amounts to just such a chronicle of Blood's activities upon the Caribbean as that which Esquemeling, in similar case, has left of the exploits of that other great buccaneer, Sir Henry Morgan.

The compilation of the Odyssey, whilst it exhausted all other available collateral sources of information, was very far from exhausting the material left by Pitt. From that log of his were taken only those episodes which bore more or less directly upon the main outline of Blood's story, which it was then proposed to relate and elucidate. The selection presented obvious difficulties; and omissions, reluctantly made, were compelled by the necessity of presenting a straightforward and consecutive narrative.

It has since been felt, however, that some of the episodes then omitted might well be assembled in a supplementary volume which may shed additional light upon the methods and habits of the buccaneering fraternity in general and Captain Blood in particular.

It will be remembered by those who have read the volume entitled *Captain Blood: His Odyssey*, and it may briefly be repeated here for the information of those who have not, that Peter Blood was the son of an Irish medicus, who had desired that his son should follow in his own honourable and humane profession. Complying with this parental wish, Peter Blood had received, at the early age of twenty, the degree of baccalaureus medicinae at Trinity College, Dublin. He showed, however, little disposition to practice the peaceful art for which he had brilliantly qualified. Perhaps a roving strain derived from his Somersetshire mother, in whose veins ran the blood of the Frobishers, was responsible for his restiveness. Losing his father some three months after taking his degree, he set out to see the world, preferring to open himself a career with the sword of the adventurer rather than with the scalpel of the surgeon.

After some vague wanderings on the continent of Europe we find him in the service of the Dutch, then at war with France. Again it may have been the Frobisher blood and a consequent predilection for the sea which made him elect to serve upon that element. He enjoyed the advantage of holding a commission under the great De Ruyter, and he fought in the Mediterranean engagement in which that famous Dutch Admiral lost his life. What he learnt under him Pitt's chronicle shows him applying in his later days when he had become the most formidable buccaneer leader on the Caribbean.

After the Peace of Nimeguen and until the beginning of 1685, when he reappears in England, little is known of his fortune, beyond the facts that he spent two years in a Spanish prison--where we must suppose that he acquired the fluent and impeccable Castilian which afterwards served him so often and so well--and that later he was for a while in the service of France, which similarly accounts for his knowledge of the French language.

In January of 1685 we find him at last, at the age of thirty-two, settling down in Bridgewater to practise the profession for which he had been trained. But for the Monmouth Rebellion, in whose vortex he was quite innocently caught up some six months later, this might have been the end of his 'career as an adventurer. And but for the fact that what came to him, utterly uninvited by him, was not in its ultimate manifestation unacceptable, we should have to regard him as one of the victims of the ironical malignity of Fortune aided and abetted, as it ever is, by the stupidity and injustice of man.

In his quality as a surgeon he was summoned on the morning after the battle of Sedgemoor to the bedside of a wounded gentleman who had been out with Monmouth, The dignity of his calling did not permit him to weigh legal quibbles or consider the position in which he might place himself in the eyes of a rigid and relentless law. All that counted with him was that a human being required his medical assistance, and he went to give it.

Surprised in the performance of that humanitarian duty by a party of dragoons who were hunting fugitives from the battle, he was arrested together with his patient. His patient being convicted of high treason for having been in arms against his king, Peter Blood suffered with him the same conviction under the statute which ordains that who succours or comforts a traitor is himself a traitor.

He was tried at Taunton before Judge Jeffreys in the course of the Bloody Assize, and sentenced to death.

Afterwards the sentence was commuted to transportation, not out of any spirit of mercy, but because it was discovered that to put to death the thousands that were implicated in the Monmouth Rebellion was to destroy valuable human merchandise which could be converted into money in the colonies. Slaves were required for work in the plantations, and the wealthy planters overseas who were willing to pay handsomely for the negroes rounded up in Africa by slavers would be no less ready to purchase white men. Accordingly, these unfortunate rebels under sentence of death were awarded in batches to this lady or that gentleman of the Court to be turned by them to profitable account.

Peter Blood was in one of these batches, which included also Jeremy Pitt and some others who were later to be associated with him in an even closer bond than that of their present common misfortune.

This batch was shipped to Barbadoes, and sold there. And then, at last, Fate eased by a little her cruel grip of Peter Blood. When it was discovered that he was a man of medicine, and because in Barbadoes a medical man of ability was urgently required, his purchaser perceived how he could turn this slave to better account than by merely sending him to the sugar plantations. He was allowed to practise as a doctor. And since the pursuit of this demanded a certain liberty of action, this liberty, within definite limits, was accorded him. He employed it to plan an escape in association with a number of his fellow slaves.

The attempt was practically frustrated, when the arrival of a Spanish ship of war at Bridgetown and the circumstances attending it suddenly disclosed to the ready wits and resolute will of Peter Blood a better way of putting it into execution.

The Spaniards, having subjected Bridgetown to bombardment, effected a landing there and took possession of the place, holding it to ransom. To accomplish this, and having nothing to fear from a town which had been completely subdued, they left their fine ship, the *Cinco Llagas* out of Cadiz, at anchor in the bay with not more than a half-score of men aboard to guard her. Nor did these keep careful watch. Persuaded, like their brethren ashore, that there was nothing to be apprehended from the defeated English colonists, they abandoned themselves that night, again like their brethren ashore, to a jovial carousal.

This was Blood's opportunity. With a score of plantation slaves to whom none gave a thought at such a time, he quietly boarded the *Cinco Llagas*, overpowered the watch and took possession of her.

In the morning, when the glutted Spaniards were returning in boats laden with the plunder of Bridgetown, Peter Blood turned their own guns upon them, smashed their boats with round shot, and sailed away with his crew of rebels-convict to turn their reconquered liberty to such account as Fate might indicate.

I - THE BLANK SHOT

Captain Easterling, whose long duel with Peter Blood finds an important place in the chronicles which Jeremy Pitt has left us, must be regarded as the instrument chosen by Fate to shape the destiny of those rebels-convict who fled from Barbadoes in the captured *Cinco Llagas*.

The lives of men are at the mercy of the slenderest chances. A whole destiny may be influenced by no more than the set of the wind at a given moment. And Peter Blood's, at a time when it was still fluid, was certainly fashioned by the October hurricane which blew Captain Easterling's ten-gun sloop into Cayona Bay, where the *Cinco Llagas* had been riding idly at anchor for close upon a month.

Blood and his associates had run to this buccaneer stronghold of Tortuga, assured of finding shelter there whilst they deliberated upon their future courses. They had chosen it because it was the one haven in the Caribbean where they could count upon being unmolested and where no questions would be asked of them. No English settlement would harbour them because of their antecedents. The hand of Spain would naturally be against them not only because they were English, but, further, because they were in possession of a Spanish ship. They could trust themselves to no ordinary French colony because of the recent agreement between the Governments of France and England for the apprehension and interchange of any persons escaping from penal settlements. There remained the Dutch, who were neutral. But Blood regarded neutrality as the most untrustworthy of all conditions, since it implies liberty of action in any direction. Therefore he steered clear of the Dutch as of the others and made for Tortuga, which, belonging to the French West India Company, was nominally French, but nominally only. Actually it was of no nationality, unless the Brethren of the Coast, as the buccaneering fraternity was called, could be deemed to constitute a nation. At least it can be said that no law ran in Tortuga that was at issue with the laws governing that great brotherhood. It suited the French Government to give the protection of its flag to these lawless men, so that in return they might serve French interests by acting as a curb upon Spanish greed and aggressiveness in the West Indies.

At Tortuga, therefore, the escaped rebels-convict dwelt in peace aboard the *Cinco Llagas* until Easterling came to disturb that peace and force them into action and into plans for their future, which, without him, they might have continued to postpone.

This Easterling--as nasty a scoundrel as ever sailed the Caribbean--carried under hatches some tons of cacao of which he had lightened a Dutch merchantman homing from the Antilles. The exploit, he realized, had not covered him with glory; for glory in that pirate's eyes was measurable by profit; and the meagre profit in this instance was not likely to increase him in the poor esteem in which he knew himself to be held by the Brethren of the Coast. Had he suspected the Dutchman of being no more richly laden he would have let her pass unchallenged. But having engaged and boarded her, he had thought it incumbent upon him and his duty to his crew of rascals to relieve her of what she carried. That she should have carried nothing of more value than cacao was a contingency for which he blamed the evil fortune which of late had dogged him--an evil fortune which was making it increasingly difficult for him to find men to sail with him.

Considering these things, and dreaming of great enterprises, he brought his sloop *Bonaventure* into the shelter of the rock-bound harbour of Tortuga, a port designed by very Nature for a stronghold. Walls of rock, rising sheer, and towering like mountains, protect it upon either side and shape it into a miniature gulf. It is only to be approached by two channels demanding skilful pilotage. These were commanded by the Mountain Fort, a massive fortress with which man had supplemented the work of Nature. Within the shelter of this harbour, the French and English buccaneers who made it their lair might deride the might of the King of Spain, whom they regarded as their natural enemy, since it was his persecution of them when they had been peaceful boucan-hunters which had driven them to the grim trade of sea-rovers.

Within that harbour Easterling dismissed his dreams to gaze upon a curious reality. It took the shape of a great red-hulled ship riding proudly at anchor among the lesser craft, like a swan amid a gaggle of geese. When he had come near enough to read the name *Cinco Llagas* boldly painted in letters of gold above her counter, and under this the port of origin, Cadiz, he rubbed his eyes so that he might read again. Thereafter he sought in conjecture an explanation of the presence of that magnificent ship of Spain in this pirates' nest of Tortuga. A thing of beauty she was, from gilded beak-head above which the brass cannons glinted in the morning sun, to towering sterncastle, and a thing of power as announced by the forty guns which Easterling's practised eye computed her to carry behind her closed ports.

The *Bonaventure* cast anchor within a cable's length of the great ship, in ten fathoms, close under the shadow of the Mountain Fort on the harbour's western side, and Easterling went ashore to seek the explanation of this mystery.

In the market-place beyond the mole he mingled with the heterogeneous crowd that converted the quays of Cayona into an image of Babel. There were bustling traders of many nations, chiefly English, French and Dutch; planters and seamen of various degrees; buccaneers who were still genuine boucanhunters and buccaneers who were frankly pirates; lumbermen, beachcombers, Indians, fruit-selling half-castes, negro slaves, and all the other types of the human family that daily loafed or trafficked there. He found presently a couple of well-informed rogues very ready with the singular tale of how that noble vessel out of Cadiz came to ride so peacefully at anchor in Cayona Bay, manned by a parcel of escaped plantation slaves.

To such a man as Easterling, it was an amusing and even an impressive tale. He desired more particular knowledge of the men who had engaged in such an enterprise. He learned that they numbered not above a score and that they were all political offenders--rebels who in England had been out with Monmouth, preserved from the gallows because of the need of slaves in the West Indian plantations. He learned all that was known of their leader, Peter Blood: that he was by trade a man of medicine, and the rest.

It was understood that, because of this, and with a view of resuming his profession, Blood desired to take ship for Europe at the first occasion and that most of his followers would accompany him. But one or two wilder spirits, men who had been trained to the sea, were likely to remain behind and join the Brotherhood of the Coast.

All this Easterling learned in the market-place behind the mole, whence his fine, bold eyes continued to con the great red ship.

With such a vessel as that under his feet there was no limit to the things he might achieve. He began to see visions. The fame of Henry Morgan, with whom once he had sailed and under whom he had served his apprenticeship to piracy, should become a pale thing beside his own. These poor escaped convicts should be ready enough to sell a ship which had served its purpose by them, and they should not be exorbitant in their notions of her value. The cacao aboard the *Bonaventure* should more than suffice to pay for her.

Captain Easterling smiled as he stroked his crisp black beard. It had required his own keen wits to perceive at once an opportunity to which all others had been blind during that long month in which the vessel had been anchored there. It was for him to profit by his perceptions.

He made his way through the rudely-built little town by the road white with coral dust--so white under the blazing sun that a man's eyes ached to behold it and sought instinctively the dark patches made by the shadows of the limp exiguous palms by which it was bordered.

He went so purposefully that he disregarded the hails greeting him from the doorway of the tavern of The King of France, nor paused to crush a cup with the gaudy buccaneers who filled the place with their noisy mirth. The Captain's business that morning was with Monsieur d'Ogeron, the courtly, middle-aged Governor of Tortuga, who in representing the French West India Company seemed to represent France herself, and who, with the airs of a minister of state, conducted affairs of questionable probity but of unquestionable profit to his company.

In the fair, white, green-shuttered house, pleasantly set amid fragrant pimento trees and other aromatic shrubs, Captain Easterling was received with dignified friendliness by the slight, elegant Frenchman who brought to the wilds of Tortuga a faint perfume of the elegancies of Versailles. Coming from the white glare outside into the cool spacious room, to which was admitted only such light as filtered between the slats of the closed shutters, the Captain found himself almost in darkness until his eyes had adjusted themselves.

The Governor offered him a chair and gave him his attention.

In the matter of the cacao there was no difficulty. Monsieur d'Ogeron cared not whence it came. That he had no illusions on the subject was shown by the price per quintal at which he announced himself prepared to purchase. It was a price representing rather less than half the value of the merchandise. Monsieur d'Ogeron was a diligent servant of the French West India Company.

Easterling haggled vainly, grumbled, accepted, and passed to the major matter. He desired to acquire the Spanish ship in the bay. Would Monsieur d'Ogeron undertake the purchase for him from the fugitive convicts who, he understood, were in possession of her.

Monsieur d'Ogeron took time to reply. "It is possible," he said at last, "that they may not wish to sell."

"Not sell? A God's name what use is the ship to those poor ragamuffins?"

"I mention only a possibility," said Monsieur d'Ogeron. "Come to me again this evening, and you shall have your answer."

When Easterling returned as bidden, Monsieur d'Ogeron was not alone. As the Governor rose to receive his visitor, there rose with him a tall, spare man in the early thirties from whose shaven face, swarthy as a gipsy's, a pair of eyes looked out that were startlingly blue, level, and penetrating. If Monsieur d'Ogeron in dress and air suggested Versailles, his companion as markedly suggested the Alameda. He was very richly dressed in black in the Spanish fashion, with an abundance of silver lace and a foam of fine point at throat and wrists, and he wore a heavy black periwig whose curls descended to his shoulders.

Monsieur d'Ogeron presented him: "Here, Captain, is Mr Peter Blood to answer you in person."

Easterling was almost disconcerted, so different was the man's appearance from anything that he could have imagined. And now this singular escaped convict was bowing with the grace of a courtier, and the buccaneer was reflecting that these fine Spanish clothes would have been filched from the locker of the commander of the *Cinco Llagas*. He remembered something else.

"Ah yes. To be sure. The physician," he said, and laughed for no apparent reason.

Mr. Blood began to speak. He had a pleasant voice whose metallic quality was softened by a drawling Irish accent. But what he said made Captain Easterling impatient. It was not his intention to sell the *Cinco Llagas*.

Aggressively before the elegant Mr. Blood stood now the buccaneer, a huge, hairy, dangerous-looking man, in coarse shirt and leather breeches, his cropped head swathed in a red-and-yellow kerchief. Aggressively he demanded Blood's reasons for retaining a ship that could be of no use to him and his fellow convicts.

Blood's voice was softly courteous in reply, which but increased Easterling's contempt of him. Captain Easterling heard himself assured that he was mistaken in his assumptions. It was probable that the fugitives from Barbadoes would employ the vessel to return to Europe, so as to make their way to France or Holland.

"Maybe we're not quite as ye're supposing us, Captain. One of my companions is a shipmaster, and three others have served, in various ways, in the King's Navy."

"Bah!" Easterling's contempt exploded loudly. "The notion's crazy. What of the perils of the sea, man? Perils of capture? How will ye face those with your paltry crew? Have ye considered that?"

Still Captain Blood preserved his pleasant temper. "What we lack in men we make up in weight of metal. Whilst I may not be able to navigate a ship across the ocean, I certainly know how to fight a ship at need. I learnt it under de Ruyter."

The famous name gave pause to Easterling's scorn. "Under de Ruyter?"

"I held a commission with him some years ago." Easterling was plainly dumbfounded. "I thought it's a doctor ye was."

"I am that, too," said the Irishman simply.

The buccaneer expressed his disgusted amazement in a speech liberally festooned with oaths. And then Monsieur d'Ogeron made an end of the interview. "So that you see, Captain Easterling, there is no more to be said in the matter."

Since, apparently, there was not, Captain Easterling sourly took his leave. But on his disgruntled way back to the mole he thought that although there was no more to be said there was a good deal to be done. Having already looked upon the majestic *Cinco Llagas* as his own, he was by no means disposed to forgo the prospect of possession.

Monsieur d'Ogeron also appeared to think that there was still at least a word to be added, and he added it after Easterling's departure. "That," he said quietly, "is a nasty and a dangerous man. You will do well to bear it in mind, Monsieur Blood."

Blood treated the matter lightly. "The warning was hardly necessary. The fellow's person would have announced the blackguard to me even if I had not known him for a pirate."

A shadow that was almost suggestive of annoyance flitted across the delicate features of the Governor of Tortuga.

"Oh, but a filibuster is not of necessity a blackguard, nor is the career of a filibuster one for your contempt, Monsieur Blood. There are those among the buccaneers who do good service to your country and to mine by setting a restraint upon the rapacity of Spain, a rapacity which is responsible for their existence. But for the buccaneers, in these waters, where neither France nor England can maintain a fleet, the Spanish dominion would be as absolute as it is inhuman. You will remember that your country honoured Henry Morgan with a knighthood and the deputy-governorship of Jamaica. And he was an even worse pirate, if it is possible, than your Sir Francis Drake, or Hawkins or Frobisher, or several others I could name, whose memory your country also honours."

Followed upon this from Monsieur d'Ogeron, who derived considerable revenues from the percentages he levied by way of harbour dues on all prizes brought into Tortuga, solemn counsels that Mr. Blood should follow in the footsteps of those heroes. Being outlawed as he was, in possession of a fine ship and the nucleus of an able following, and being, as he had proved, a man of unusual resource, Monsieur d'Ogeron did not doubt that he would prosper finely as a filibuster.

Mr. Blood didn't doubt it himself. He never doubted himself. But he did not on that account incline to the notion. Nor, probably, but for that which ensued, would he ever have so inclined, however much the majority of his followers might have sought to persuade him.

Among these, Hagthorpe, Pitt, and the giant Wolverstone, who had lost an eye at Sedgemoor, were perhaps the most persistent. It was all very well for Blood, they told him, to plan a return to Europe. He was master of a peaceful art in the pursuit of which he might earn a livelihood in France or Flanders. But they were men of the sea, and knew no other trade. Dyke, who had been a petty officer in the Navy before he embarked on politics and rebellion, held similar views, and Ogle, the gunner, demanded to know of Heaven and Hell and Mr. Blood what guns they thought the British Admiralty would entrust to a man who had been out with Monmouth.

Things were reaching a stage in which Peter Blood could see no alternative to that of parting from these men whom a common misfortune had endeared to him. It was in this pass that Fate employed the tool she had forged in Captain Easterling.

One morning, three days after his interview with Mr. Blood at the Governor's house, the Captain came alongside the *Cinco Llagas* in the cockboat from his sloop. As he heaved his massive bulk into the waist of the ship, his bold, dark eyes were everywhere at once. The *Cinco Llagas* was not only well-found, but irreproachably kept. Her decks were scoured, her cordage stowed, and everything in place. The muskets were ranged in the rack about the mainmast, and the brass-work on the scuttle-butts shone like gold in the bright sunshine. Not such lubberly fellows, after all, these escaped rebels-convict who composed Mr. Blood's crew.

And there was Mr. Blood himself in his black and silver, looking like a Grandee of Spain, doffing a black hat with a sweep of claret ostrich plume about it, and bowing until the wings of his periwig met across his face like the pendulous ears of a spaniel. With him stood Nathaniel Hagthorpe, a pleasant gentleman of Mr. Blood's own age, whose steady eye and clear-cut face announced the man of breeding; Jeremy Pitt, the flaxen-haired young Somerset shipmaster; the short, sturdy Nicholas Dyke, who had been a petty officer and had served under King James when he was Duke of York. There was nothing of the' ragamuffin about these, as Easterling had so readily imagined. Even the burly, rough-voiced Wolverstone had crowded his muscular bulk into Spanish fripperies for the occasion.

Having presented them, Mr. Blood invited the captain of the *Bonaventure* to the great cabin in the stern, which for spaciousness and richness of furniture surpassed any cabin Captain Easterling had ever entered.

A negro servant in a white jacket--a lad hired here in Tortuga--brought, besides the usual rum and sugar and fresh limes, a bottle of golden Canary which had been in the ship's original equipment and which Mr. Blood recommended with solicitude to his unbidden guest.

Remembering Monsieur d'Ogeron's warning that Captain Easterling was dangerous, Mr. Blood deemed it wise to use him with all civility, if only so that being at his ease he should disclose in what he might be dangerous now.

They occupied the elegantly cushioned seats about the table of black oak, and Captain Easterling praised the Canary liberally to justify the liberality with which he consumed it. Thereafter he came to business by asking if Mr. Blood, upon reflection, had not perhaps changed his mind about selling the ship.

"If so be that you have," he added, with a glance at Blood's four companions, "considering among how many the purchase money will be divided, you'll find me generous."

If by this he had hoped to make an impression upon those four, their stolid countenances disappointed him.

Mr. Blood shook his head. "It's wasting your time, ye are, Captain. Whatever else we decide, we keep the *Cinco Llagas*."

"Whatever you decide?" The great black brows went up on that shallow brow. "Ye're none so decided than as ye was about this voyage to Europe? Why, then, I'll come at once to the business I'd propose if ye wouldn't sell. It is that with this ship ye join the *Bonaventure* in a venture--a bonaventure," and he laughed noisily at his own jest with a flash of white teeth behind the great black beard.

"You honour us. But we haven't a mind to piracy."

Easterling gave no sign of offence. He waved a great ham of a hand as if to dismiss the notion. "It ain't piracy I'm proposing."

"What then?"

"I can trust you?"--Easterling asked, and his eyes included the four of them.

"Ye're not obliged to. And it's odds ye'll waste your time in any case."

It was not encouraging. Nevertheless, Easterling proceeded. It might be known to them that he had sailed with Morgan. He had been with Morgan in the great march across the Isthmus of Panama. Now it was notorious that when the spoil came to be divided after the sack of that Spanish city it was found to be far below the reasonable expectations of the buccaneers. There were murmurs that Morgan had not dealt fairly with his men; that he had abstracted before the division a substantial portion of the treasure taken. Those murmurs, Easterling could tell them, were well founded. There were pearls and jewels from San Felipe of fabulous value, which Morgan had secretly appropriated for himself. But as the rumours grew and reached his ears, he became afraid of a search that should convict him. And so, midway on the journey across the Isthmus, he one night buried the treasure he had filched.

"Only one man knew this," said Captain Easterling to his attentive listeners--for the tale was of a quality that at all times commands attention. "The man who helped him in a labour he couldn't ha' done alone. I am that man."

He paused a moment to let the impressive fact sink home, and then resumed.

The business he proposed was that the fugitives on the *Cinco Llagas* should join him in an expedition to Darien to recover the treasure, sharing equally in it with his own men and on the scale usual among the Brethren of the Coast.

"If I put the value of what Morgan buried at five hundred thousand pieces of eight, I am being modest."

It was a sum to set his audience staring. Even Blood stared, but not quite with the expression of the others.

"Sure, now, it's very odd," said he thoughtfully. "What is odd, Mr. Blood?"

Mr. Blood's answer took the form of another question. "How many do you number aboard the *Bonaventure*?"

"Something less than two hundred men."

"And the twenty men who are with me make such a difference that you deem it worth while to bring us this proposal?"

Easterling laughed outright, a deep, guttural laugh. "I see that ye don't understand at all." His voice bore a familiar echo of Mr. Blood's Irish intonation. "It's not the men I lack so much as a stout ship in which to guard the treasure when we have it. In a bottom such as this we'd be as snug as in a fort, and I'd snap my fingers at any Spanish galleon that attempted to molest me."

"Faith, now I understand," said Wolverstone, and Pitt and Dyke and Hagthorpe nodded with him. But the glittering blue eye of Peter Blood continued to stare unwinkingly upon the bulky pirate.

"As Wolverstone says, it's understandable. But a tenth of the prize, which, by heads, is all that would come to the *Cinco Llagas*, is far from adequate in the circumstances."

Easterling blew out his cheeks and waved his great hand in a gesture of bonhomie. "What share would you propose?"

"That's to be considered. But it would not be less than one-fifth."

The buccaneer's face remained impassive. He bowed his gaudily swathed head. "Bring these friends of yours to dine to-morrow aboard the *Bonaventure*, and we'll draw up the articles."

For a moment Blood seemed to hesitate. Then in courteous terms he accepted the invitation.

But when the buccaneer had departed he checked the satisfaction of his followers.

"I was warned that Captain Easterling is a dangerous man. That's to flatter him. For to be dangerous a man must be clever, and Captain Easterling is not clever."

"What maggot's burrowing under your periwig, Peter?" wondered Wolverstone.

"I'm thinking of the reason he gave for desiring our association. It was the best he could do when bluntly asked the question."

"It could not have been more reasonable," said Hagthorpe, emphatically. He was finding Blood unnecessarily difficult.

"Reasonable!" Blood laughed. "Specious, if you will. Specious until you come to examine it. Faith now, it glitters, to be sure. But it isn't gold. A ship as strong as a fort in which to stow a half-million pieces of eight, and this fortress ship in the hands of ourselves. A trusting fellow this Easterling for a scoundrel!"

They thought it out, and their eyes grew round. Pitt, however, was not yet persuaded. "In his need he'll trust our honour."

Blood looked at him with scorn. "I never knew a man with eyes like Easterling's to trust to anything but possession. If he means to stow that treasure aboard this ship, and I could well believe that part of it, it is because he means to be in possession of this ship by the time he does so. Honour! Bah! Could such a man believe that honour would prevent us from giving him the slip one night once we had the treasure aboard, or even of bringing our weight of metal to bear upon his sloop and sinking her? It's fatuous you are, Jeremy, with your talk of honour."

Still the thing was not quite clear to Hagthorpe. "What, then, do you suppose to be his reason for inviting us to join him?"

"The reason that he gave. He wants our ship, be it for the conveyance of his treasure, if it exists, be it for other reasons. Didn't he first seek to buy the *Cinco Llagas*? Oh, he wants her, naturally enough; but he wants not us, nor would he keep us long, be sure of that."

And yet, perhaps because the prospect of a share in Morgan's treasure was, as Blood said, a glittering one, his associates were reluctant to abandon it. To gain alluring objects men are always ready to take chances, ready to believe what they hope. So now Hagthorpe, Pitt, and Dyke. They came to the opinion that Blood was leaping to conclusions from a prejudice sown in him by Monsieur d'Ogeron, who may have had reasons of his own to serve. Let them at least dine to-morrow with Easterling, and hear what articles he proposed.

"Can you be sure that we shall not be poisoned?" wondered Blood.

But this was pushing prejudice too far. They mocked him freely. How could they be poisoned by meat and drink that Easterling must share with them? And what end would thus be served? How would that give Easterling possession of the Cinco Llagas?

"By swarming aboard her with a couple of score of his ruffians and taking the men here unawares at a time when there would be none to lead them."

"What?" cried Hagthorpe. "Here in Tortuga? In this haven of the buccaneers? Come, come, Peter! I must suppose there is some honour among thieves."

"You may suppose it. I prefer to suppose nothing of the kind. I hope no man will call me timorous; and yet I'd as soon be called that as rash."

The weight of opinion, however, was against him.

Every man of the rebels-convict crew was as eager for the enterprise when it came to be disclosed as were the three leaders.

And so, despite himself, at eight bells on the morrow, Captain Blood went over with Hagthorpe, Pitt, and Dyke, to dine aboard the *Bonaventure*. Wolverstone was left behind in charge of the *Cinco Llagas*.

Easterling welcomed them boisterously, supported by his entire crew of ruffians. Some eight score of them swarmed in the waist, on the forecastle, and even on the poop, and all were armed. It was not necessary that Mr. Blood should point out to his companions how odd it was that all these fellows should have been summoned for the occasion from the taverns ashore which they usually frequented. Their presence and the leering mockery stamped upon their villainous countenances made Blood's three followers ask themselves at last if Blood had not been justified of his misgivings, and made them suspect with him that they had walked into a trap.

It was too late to retreat. By the break of the poop, at the entrance of the gangway leading to the cabin, stood Captain Easterling waiting to conduct them.

Blood paused there a moment to look up into the pellucid sky above the rigging about which the gulls were circling. He glanced round and up at the grey fort perched on its rocky eminence, all bathed in ardent sunshine. He looked towards the mole, forsaken now in the noontide heat, and then across the crystalline sparkling waters towards the great red *Cinco Llagas* where she rode in majesty and strength. To his uneasy companions it seemed as if he were wondering from what quarter help might come if it were needed. Then, responding to Easterling's inviting gesture, he passed into the gloom of the gangway, followed by the others.

Like the rest of the ship, which the first glance had revealed for dishevelled and unclean, the cabin was in no way comparable with that of the stately *Cinco Llagas*. It was so low that there was barely headroom for tall men like Blood and Hagthorpe. It was ill-furnished, containing little more than the cushioned lockers set about a deal table that was stained and hacked. Also, for all that the horn windows astern were open, the atmosphere of the place was heavy with an acrid blend of vile smells in which spunyarn and bilge predominated.

The dinner proved to be much as the surroundings promised. The fresh pork and fresh vegetables had been befouled in cooking, so that, in forcing himself to eat, the fastidious stomach of Mr. Blood was almost turned.

The company provided by Easterling matched the rest. A half-dozen of his fellows served him as a guard of honour. They had been elected, he announced, by the men, so that they might agree the articles on behalf of all. To these had been added a young Frenchman named Joinville, who was secretary to Monsieur d'Ogeron and stood there to represent the Governor and to lend, as it were, a legal sanction to what was to be done. If the presence of this rather vacuous pale-eyed gentleman served to reassure Mr. Blood a little, it served to intrigue him more.

Amongst them they crowded the narrow confines of the cabin, and Easterling's fellows were so placed along the two sides of the table that no two of the men from the *Cinco Llagas* sat together. Blood and the captain of the *Bonaventure* immediately faced each other across the board.

I - THE BLANK SHOT

Business was left until dinner was over and the negro who waited on them had withdrawn. Until then the men of the *Bonaventure* kept things gay with the heavily salted talk that passed for wit amongst them. At last, the table cleared of all save bottles, and pens and ink being furnished together with a sheet of paper each to Easterling and Blood, the captain of the *Bonaventure* opened the matter of the terms, and Peter Blood heard himself for the first time addressed, as Captain. Easterling's first words were to inform him shortly that the one-fifth share he had demanded was by the men of the *Bonaventure* accounted excessive.

Momentarily Peter Blood's hopes rose.

"Shall we deal in plain terms now, Captain? Do you mean that they'll not be consenting to them?"

"What else should I mean?"

"In that case, Captain, it only remains for us to take our leave, in your debt for this liberal entertainment and the richer for the improvement in our acquaintance."

The elaborate courtesy of those grossly inaccurate terms did not seem to touch the ponderous Easterling. His bold, craftily-set eyes stared blankly from his great red face. He mopped the sweat from his brow before replying.

"You'll take your leave?" There was a sneering undertone to his guttural voice. "I'll trouble you in turn to be plain with me. I likes plain men and lain words. D'ye mean that yell quit from the business?"

Two or three of his followers made a rumbling challenging echo to his question.

Captain Blood--to give him now the title Easterling had bestowed upon him--had the air of being intimidated. He hesitated, looking as if for guidance to his companions, who returned him only uneasy glances.

"If," he said at length, "you find our terms unreasonable, I must assume ye'll not be wishing to go further, and it only remains for us to withdraw."

He spoke with a diffidence which amazed his own followers, who had never known him other than bold in the face of any odds. It provoked a sneer from Easterling, who found no more than he had been expecting from a leech turned adventurer by circumstances.

"Faith, Doctor," said he, "ye were best to get back to your cupping and bleeding, and leave ships to men as can handle them."

There was a lightning flash from those blue eyes, as vivid as it was transient. The swarthy countenance never lost its faint air of diffidence. Meanwhile Easterling had swung to the Governor's representative, who sat on his immediate right.

"What d'ye think of that, Mossoo Joinville?"

The fair, flabby young Frenchman smiled amiably upon Blood's diffidence. "Would it not be wise and proper, sir, to hear what terms Captain Easterling now proposes?"

"I'll hear them. But--"

"Leave the buts till after, Doctor," Easterling cut in. "The terms we'll grant are the terms I told ye. Your men share equally with mine."

"But that means no more than a tenth for the *Cinco Llagas*." And Blood, too, now appealed to M. Joinville. "Do you, sir, account that fair? I have explained to Captain Easterling that for what we lack in men we more than make up in weight of metal, and our guns are handled by a gunner such as I dare swear has no compeer in the Caribbean. A fellow named Ogle--Ned Ogle. A remarkable gunner is Ned Ogle. The very devil of a gunner, as you'd believe if you'd seen him pick those Spanish boats off the water in Bridgetown Harbour."

He would have continued upon the subject of Ned Ogle had not Easterling interrupted him. "Hell, man! What's a gunner more or less?"

"Oh, an ordinary gunner, maybe. But this is no ordinary gunner. An eye he has. Gunners like Ogle are like poets: they are born, so they are. He'll put you a shot between wind and water, will Ogle, as neatly as you might pick your teeth."

Easterling banged the table. "What's all this to the point?"

"It may be something. And meanwhile it shows you the valuable ally ye're acquiring." And he was off again on the subject of his gunner. "He was trained in the King's Navy, was Ned Ogle, and a bad day for the King's Navy it was when Ogle took to politics and followed the Protestant champion to Sedgemoor."

"Leave that," growled one of the officers of the *Bonaventure*, a ruffian who answered to the name of Chard. "Leave it, I say, or we'll waste the day in talk."

Easterling confirmed this with a coarse oath. Captain Blood observed that they did not mean to spare offensiveness, and his speculations on their aims starting from that took a fresh turn.

Joinville intervened. "Could you not compromise with Captain Blood? After all, there is some reason on his side. He might reasonably claim to put a hundred men aboard his ship, and in that case he would naturally take a heavier share."

"In that case he might be worth it," was the truculent answer.

"I am worth it as it is," Blood insisted.

"Ah, bah!" he was answered, with a flick of finger and thumb under his very nose.

He began to suspect that Easterling sought to entice him into an act of rashness, in reply to which he and his followers would probably be butchered where they sat, and M. Joinville would afterwards be constrained to bear witness to the Governor that the provocation had proceeded from the guests. He perceived at last the probable reason for the Frenchman's presence.

But at the moment Joinville was remonstrating. "Come, come, Captain Easterling! Thus you will never reach agreement. Captain Blood's ship is of advantage to you, and we have to pay for what is advantageous. Could you not offer him an eighth or even a seventh share?"

Easterling silenced the growl of disagreement from Chard, and became almost suave. "What would Captain Blood say to that?"

Captain Blood considered for a long moment. Then he shrugged. "I say what you know I must say: that I can say nothing until I have taken the wishes of my followers. We'll resume the discussion when I have done so--another day."

"Oh, s'death!" roared Easterling. "Do you play with us? Haven't you brought your officers with you, and ain't they empowered to speak for your men same as mine? Whatever we settles here, my men abides by. That's the custom of the Brethren of the Coast. And I expect the same from you. And I've the right to expect it, as you can tell him, Mossoo Joinville."

The Frenchman nodded gloomily, and Easterling roared on.

"We are not children, by God! And we're not here to play, but to agree terms. And, by God, we'll agree them before you leave."

"Or not, as the case may be," said Blood quietly. It was to be remarked that he had lost his diffidence by now.

"Or not? What the devil do you mean with your `or not'?" Easterling came to his feet in a vehemence that Peter Blood believed assumed, as the proper note at this stage of the comedy he was playing.

"I mean or not, quite simply." He accounted that the time had come to compel the buccaneers to show their hand. "If we fail to agree terms, why, that's the end of the matter."

"Oho! The end of the matter, eh? Stab me, but it may prove the beginning of it."

Blood smiled up into his face, and cool as ice he commented: "That's what I was supposing. But the beginning of what, if you please, Captain Easterling?"

"Indeed, indeed, Captain!" cried Joinville. "What can you mean?"

"Mean?" Captain Easterling glared at the Frenchman. He appeared to be extremely angry. "Mean?" he repeated. "Look you, Mossoo, this fellow here, this Blood, this doctor, this escaped convict, made believe that he would enter into articles with us so as to get from me the secret of Morgan's treasure. Now that he's got it, he makes difficulties about the articles. He no longer wants to join us, it seems. He proposes to withdraw. It'll be plain to you why he proposes to withdraw, Mossoo Joinville; just as it'll be plain to you why I can't permit it."

"Why, here's paltry invention!" sneered Blood. "What do I know of his secret beyond his tale of a treasure buried somewhere?"

"Not somewhere. You know where. For I've been fool enough to tell you."

Blood actually laughed, and by his laughter scared his companions, to whom the danger of their situation was now clear enough.

"Somewhere on the Isthmus of Darien! There's precision, on my soul! With that information I can go straight to the spot and set my hand on it! As for the rest, M. Joinville, I invite you to observe it's not myself is making difficulties about the articles. On the one-fifth share which I asked from the outset, I might have been prepared to join Captain Easterling. But now that I'm confirmed in all that I suspected of him and more, why, I wouldn't join him for a half share in this treasure, supposing it to exist at all, which I do not."

That brought every man of the *Bonaventure* to his feet as if it had been a signal, and they were clamorous too, until Easterling waved them into silence. Upon that silence cut the tenor voice of M. Joinville.

"You are a singularly rash man, Captain Blood."

"Maybe, maybe," says Blood, light and airily. "Time will show. The last word's not yet been said."

"Then here's to say it," quoth Easterling, quietly sinister on a sudden. "I was about to warn you that ye'll not be allowed to leave this ship with the information ye possess until the articles is signed. But since ye so clearly show your intentions, why, things have gone beyond warnings."

From his seat at the table, which he retained, Captain Blood looked up at the sinister bulk of the captain of the *Bonaventura*, and the three men from the *Cinco Llagas* observed with mingled amaze-men and dismay that he was smiling. At first so unusually diffident and timid; now so deliberately and recklessly provoking. He was beyond understanding. It was Hagthorpe who spoke for them.

"What do you mean, Captain? What do you intend by us?"

"Why, to clap you into irons, and stow you under hatches, where you can do no harm."

"My God, sir--" Hagthorpe was beginning, when Captain Blood's crisp pleasant voice cut across his speech.

"And you, M. Joinville, will permit this without protest?"

Joinville spread his hands, thrust out a nether lip, and shrugged. "You have brought it on yourself, Captain Blood."

"So that is what you are here to report to Monsieur d'Ogeron! Well, well!" He laughed with a touch of bitterness.

And then, abruptly, on the noontide stillness outside came the thunder of a gun to shake them all. Followed the screaming of startled gulls, a pause in which men eyed one another, and then, a shade uneasily, came the question from Easterling, addressed to no one in particular:

"What the devil's that?"

It was Blood who answered him pleasantly. "Now don't let it alarm ye, Captain darling. It's just a salute fired in your honour by Ogle, the gunner--the highly skilful gunner--of the *Cinco Llagas*. Have I told you about him yet?" His eyes embraced the company in the question.

"A salute?" quoth Easterling. "By Hell, what do you mean? A salute?"

"Why, just a courtesy, as a reminder to us and a warning to you. It's reminder to us that we've taken up an hour of your time, and that we must put no further strain upon your hospitality." He got to his feet, and stood, easy and elegant in his Spanish suit of black and silver. "It's a very good day we'll be wishing you, Captain."

Inflamed of countenance, Easterling plucked a pistol from his belt. "You play-acting buffoon! Ye don't leave this ship!"

But Captain Blood continued to smile. "Fith, that will be very bad for the ship, and for all aboard her, including this ingenuous Monsieur Joinville, who really believes you'll pay him the promised share of your phantom treasure for bearing false witness against me, so as to justify you in the eyes of the Governor for seizing the *Cinco Llagas*. Ye see, I am under no delusions concerning you, my dear Captain. For a rogue ye're a thought too transparent."

Easterling loosed a volley of minatory obscenity, waving his pistol. He was restrained from using it only by an indefinable uneasiness aroused by his guest's bantering manner.

"We are wasting time," Blood interrupted him, "and the moments, believe me, are growing singularly precious. You'd best know where you stand. My orders to Ogle were that if within ten minutes of his firing that salute I and my friends here were not over the side of the *Bonaventure*, he was to put a round shot into your forecastle along the water-line, and as many more after that as may be necessary to sink you by the head. I do not think that many will be necessary. Ogle is a singularly skilful marksman. He served with distinction as a gunner in the King's Navy. I think I've told you about him."

It was Joinville who broke the moment's silence that followed. "God of my life!" he bleated, bounding to his feet. "Let me out of this!"

"Oh, stow your squealing, you French rat!" snarled the infuriated Easterling. Then he turned his fury upon Blood, balancing the pistol ominously. "You sneaking leech! You college offal! You'd ha' done better to ha' stuck to your cupping and bleedings, as I told you."

His murderous intention was plain. But Blood was too swift for him. Before any could so much as guess his purpose, he had snatched up by its neck the flagon of Canary that stood before him and crashed it across Captain Easterling's left temple.

As the captain of the *Bonaventure* reeled back against the cabin bulkhead, Peter Blood bowed slightly to him.

"I regret," said he, "that I have no cup; but, as you see, I can practise phlebotomy with a bottle."

Easterling sagged down in a limp unconscious mass at the foot of the bulkhead. The spectacle stirred his officers. There was a movement towards Captain Blood, and a din of raucous voices, and someone laid hands upon him. But above the uproar rang his vibrant voice.

"Be warned! The moments are speeding. The ten minutes have all but fled, and either I and my friends depart, or we all sink together in this bottom."

"In God's name, bethink you of it!" cried Joinville, and started for the door.

A buccaneer who did bethink him of it and who was of a practical turn of mind, seized him about the body and flung him back.

"You there;" he shouted to Captain Blood. "You and your men go first. And bestir yourselves! We've no mind to drown like rats."

They went as they were bidden, curses pursuing them and threats of a reckoning to follow with Captain Easterling.

Either the ruffians aswarm on the deck above were not in the secret of Easterling's intentions, or else a voice of authority forbade them to hinder the departure of Captain Blood and his companions.

In the cock-boat, midway between the two vessels, Hagthorpe found his voice at last.

"On my soul's salvation, Peter, there was a moment when I thought our sands were run."

"Ay, ay," said Pitt with fervour. "And even as it was they might have been." He swung to Peter Blood, where he sat in the sternsheets. "Suppose that for one reason or another we had not got out in those ten minutes, and Ogle had opened fire in earnest? What then?"

"Ah!" said Blood. "Our real danger lay in that he wasn't like to do it."

"But if you so ordered him?"

"Nay, that's just what I forgot to do. All I told him was to loose a blank shot when we had been gone an hour. I thought that however things went it might prove useful. And on my soul, I believe it did. Lord!" He took off his hat, and mopped his brow under the staring eyes of his companions.

"I wonder now if it's the heat that's making me sweat like this."

II - THE TREASURE SHIP

It was a saying of Captain Blood's that the worth of a man manifests itself not so much in the ability to plan great undertakings as in the vision which perceives opportunity and the address which knows how to seize it.

He had certainly displayed these qualities in possessing himself of that fine Spanish ship the *Cinco Llagas*, and he had displayed them again in foiling the designs of that rascally buccaneer Captain Easterling to rob him of that noble vessel.

Meanwhile his own and his vessel's near escape made it clear to all who followed him that there was little safety for them in Tortuga waters, and little trust to be placed in buccaneers. At a general council held that same afternoon in the ship's waist Blood propounded the simple philosophy that when a man is attacked he must either fight or run.

"And since we are in no case to fight when attacked, as no doubt we shall be, it but remains to play the coward's part if only so that we may survive to prove ourselves brave men some other day."

They agreed with him. But whilst the decision to run was taken, it was left to be determined later whither they should run. At the moment all that mattered was to get away from Tortuga and the further probable attentions of Captain Easterling.

Thus it fell out that in the dead of the following night, which if clear was moonless, the great frigate which lately had been the pride of the Cadiz shipyards weighed anchor as quietly as such an operation might be performed. With canvas spread to the faint favouring breeze from the shore, and with the ebb tide to help the manoeuvre, the *Cinco Llagas* stood out to sea. If groan of windlass, rattle of chain, and creak of blocks had betrayed the action to Easterling aboard the *Bonaventure*, a cable's length away, it was not in Easterling's power to thwart Blood's intention.

At least three-quarters of his rascally crew were in the taverns ashore, and Easterling was not disposed to attempt boarding operations with the remnant of his men, even though that remnant outnumbered by two to one the hands of the *Cinco Llagas*. Moreover, even had his full complement of two hundred been aboard, Easterling would still have offered no opposition to that departure. Whilst in Tortuga waters he might have attempted to get possession of the *Cinco Llagas* quietly and by strategy, not even his recklessness could consider seizing her violently by force in such a sanctuary, especially as the French Governor, Monsieur d'Ogeron, appeared to be friendly disposed towards Blood and his fellow fugitives.

Out on the open sea it would be another matter; and the tale he would afterwards tell of the manner in which the *Cinco Llagas* should have come into his possession would be such as no one in Cayona would be in a position to contradict.

So Captain Easterling suffered Peter Blood to depart unhindered, and was well content to let him go. Nor did he display any undue and betraying haste to follow. He made his preparations with leisureliness, and did not weigh anchor until the afternoon of the morrow. He trusted his wits to give him the direction Blood must take and depended upon the greater speed of the *Bonaventure* to overhaul him before he should have gone far enough for safety. His reasoning was shrewd enough. Since he knew that the *Cinco Llagas* was not victualled for a long voyage, there could be no question yet of any direct attempt to sail for Europe.

First she must be equipped, and since to equip her Blood dared approach no English or Spanish settlement, it followed that he must steer for one of the neutral Dutch colonies, and there take his only remaining chance. Nor was Blood likely without experienced pilotage to venture among the dangerous reefs of the Bahamas. It was therefore an easy inference that his destination would be the Leeward Islands with intent to put in at San Martin, Saba, or Santa Eustacia. Confident, then, of overtaking him before he could make the nearest of those Dutch settlements, two hundred leagues away, the pursuing *Bonaventure* steered an easterly course along the northern shores of Hispaniola.

Things, however, were not destined to be so simple as Easterling conjectured. The wind, at first favourable, veered towards evening to the east, and increased throughout the night in vehemence; so that by dawn--an angry dawn with skies ominously flushed--the *Bonaventure* had not merely made no progress, but had actually drifted some miles out of her course. Then the wind shifted to the south towards noon, and it came on to blow harder than ever. It blew up a storm from the Caribbean, and for twenty-four hours the *Bonaventure* rode it out with bare yards and hatches battened against the pounding seas that broke athwart her and tossed her like a cork from trough to crest.

It was fortunate that the burly Easterling was not only a stout fighter but also an able seaman. Under his skilled handling the *Bonaventure* came through the ordeal unscathed, to resume the chase when at last the storm had passed and the wind had settled to a steady breeze from the south-west. With crowded canvas the sloop now went scudding through the heaving seas which the storm had left.

Easterling heartened his followers with the reminder that the hurricane which had delayed them must no less have delayed the *Cinco Llagas*; that, indeed, considering the lubbers who handled the erstwhile Spanish frigate, it was likely that the storm had made things easier for the *Bonaventure*.

II - THE TREASURE SHIP

What exactly the storm had done for them they were to discover on the following morning, when off Cape Engaño they sighted a galleon which at first, in the distance, they supposed to be their quarry, but which very soon they perceived to be some other vessel. That she was Spanish was advertised not only by the towering build, but by the banner of Castile which she flew beneath the Crucifix at the head of her mainmast. On the yards of this mainmast all canvas was close-reefed, and under the spread of only foresail mizzen and spirit she was labouring clumsily towards the Mona Passage with the wind on her larboard quarter.

The sight of her in her partially maimed condition stirred Easterling like a hound at sight of a deer. For the moment the quest of the *Cinco Llagas* was forgotten. Here was more immediate prey, and of a kind to be easily reduced.

At the poop rail he bawled his orders rapidly. In obedience the decks were cleared with feverish speed and the nettings spread from stem to stern to catch any spars that might be shot down in the approaching action. Chard, Easterling's lieutenant, a short, powerful man, who was a dullard in all things save the handling Of a ship and the wielding of a cutlass, took the helm. The gunners at their stations cleared the leaden aprons from the touchholes and swung their glowing matches, ready for the word of command. For however disorderly and unruly Easterling's crew might be at ordinary times, it knew the need for discipline when battle was to be joined.

Watchful on the poop, the buccaneer captain surveyed the Spaniard upon which he was rapidly bearing down, and observed with scorn the scurry of preparation on her decks. His practised eye read her immediate past history at a glance, and his harsh guttural voice announced what he read to Chard, who stood below him at the whipstaff.

"She would be homing for Spain when the hurricane caught her. She's sprung her mainmast and likely suffered other damage besides, and she's beating back for San Domingo for repairs." Easterling laughed in his throat and stroked his dense black beard. The dark, bold eyes in his great red face glinted wickedly. "Give me a homing Spaniard, Chard. There'll be treasure aboard that hulk. By God, we're in luck at last."

He was indeed. It had long been his grievance, and the true reason of his coveting the *Cinco Llagas*, that his sloop the *Bonaventure* was unequal to tackling the real prizes of the Caribbean. And he would never have dared to attack this heavily-armed galleon but that in her crippled condition she was unable to manoeuvre so as to bring her guns to bear upon his flanks.

She, gave him now a broadside from her starboard quarter, and by doing so sealed her own doom. The *Bonaventure*, coming head on, presented little target, and save for a round shot in her forecastle took no damage. Easterling answered the fire with the chasers on his prow, aiming high, and sweeping the Spaniard's decks. Then, nimbly avoiding her clumsy attempt to go about and change their relative positions, the *Bonaventure* was alongside on the quarter of her empty guns. There was a rattling, thudding jar, a creak of entangled rigging, a crack and clatter of broken spars and the thud of grapnels rending into the Spaniard's timbers to bind her fast, mid then, tight-locked, the two vessels went drifting down wind, whilst the buccaneers, led by the colossal Easterling, and after discharging a volley of musketry, swarmed like ants over the Spaniard's bulwarks. Two hundred of them there were, fierce fellows in loose leathern breeches, some with shirts as well, but the majority naked to the waist, and by that brown muscular nakedness the more terrific of aspect.

To receive them stood a bare fifty Spaniards in corselet and morion, drawn up in the galleon's waist as if upon parade, with muskets calmly levelled and a hawk-faced officer in a plumed hat commanding them.

The officer spoke an order, and a volley from the muskets momentarily checked the assault. Then, like an engulfing wave, the buccaneer mob went over the Spanish soldiers, and the ship, the *Santa Barbara*, was taken.

There was not perhaps upon the seas at the time a more cruel, ruthless man than Easterling and those who sailed with him adopted, as men will, their captain's standard of ferocity. Brutally they exterminated the Spanish soldiery, heaving the bodies overboard, and as brutally they dealt with those manning the guns on the main deck below, although these unfortunates readily surrendered in the vain hope of being allowed to keep their lives.

Within ten minutes of the invasion of the *Santa Barbara* there remained alive upon her of her original crew only the captain, Don Ildefonso de Paiva, whom Easterling had stunned with the butt of a pistol, the navigating officer, and four deck-hands, who had been aloft at the moment of boarding. These six Easterling spared for the present because he accounted that they might prove useful.

Whilst his men were busy in the shrouds about the urgent business of disentangling and where necessary repairing, the buccaneer captain began upon the person of Don Ildefonso the investigation of his capture.

The Spaniard, sickly and pallid and with a lump on his brow where the pistol-butt had smitten him, sat on a locker in the handsome roomy cabin, with pinioned wrists, but striving nevertheless to preserve the haughty demeanour proper to a gentleman of Castile in the presence of an impudent sea-robber. Thus until Easterling, towering over him, savagely threatened to loosen his tongue by the artless persuasions of torture. Then Don Ildefonso, realizing the futility of resistance, curtly answered the pirate's questions. From these answers and his subsequent investigations, Easterling discovered his capture to exceed every hope he could have formed.

There had fallen into his hands--which of late had known so little luck--one of those prizes which had been the dream of every sea-rover since the days of Francis Drake. The *Santa Barbara* was a treasure-ship from Porto Bello, laden with gold and silver which had been conveyed across the Isthmus from Panama. She had put forth under the escort of three strong ships of war, with intent to call at San Domingo to revictual before crossing to Spain. But in the recent storm which had swept the Caribbean she had been separated from her consorts, and with damaged mainmast had been driven through the Mona Passage by this gale. She had been beating hack for San Domingo in the hope of rejoining there her escort or else awaiting there another fleet for Spain.

The treasure in her hold was computed by Easterling when his gleaming eyes came to consider those ingots at between two and three hundred thousand pieces of eight. It was a prize such as does not come the way of a pirate twice in his career, and it meant fortune for himself and those who sailed with him.

Now the possession of fortune is inevitably attended by anxiety, and Easterling's besetting anxiety at the moment was to convey his prize with all possible speed to the security of Tortuga.

From his own sloop he took two score men to form a prize crew for the Spaniard, and himself remained aboard her because he could not suffer himself to be parted from the treasure. Then, with damage hurriedly repaired, the two ships went about, and started upon their voyage. Progress was slow, the wind being none too favourable and the *Santa Barbara* none too manageable, and it was past noon before they once more had Cape Raphael abeam. Easterling was uneasy in this near proximity to Hispaniola, and was for taking a wide sweep that would carry them well out to sea, when from the crow's nest of the *Santa Barbara* came a hail, and a moment later the object first espied by the look-out was visible to them all.

There, rounding Cape Raphael, not two miles away, and steering almost to meet them, came a great red ship under full sail. Easterling's telescope confirmed at once what the naked eye had led him incredulously to suspect. This vessel was the *Cinco Llagas*, the original object of his pursuit, which in his haste he must have outsailed.

The truth was that, overtaken by the storm as they approached Samana, Jeremy Pitt, who navigated the *Cinco Llagas*, had run for the shelter of Samana Bay, and under the lee of a headland had remained snug and unperceived, to come forth again when the gale had spent itself.

Easterling, caring little how the thing had happened, perceived in this sudden and unexpected appearance of the *Cinco Llagas* a sign that Fortune, hitherto so niggardly, was disposed now to overwhelm him with her favours. Let him convey himself and the *Santa Barbara's* treasure aboard that stout red ship, and in strength he could make good speed home.

Against a vessel so heavily armed and so undermanned as the *Cinco Llagas* there could be no question of any but boarding tactics, and it did not seem to Captain Easterling that this should offer much difficulty to the swifter and more easily handled *Bonaventure*, commanded by a man experienced in seamanship and opposed by a lubberly follower who was by trade a surgeon.

So Easterling signalled Chard to be about the easy business, and Chard, eager enough to square accounts with the man who once already had done them the injury of slipping like water through their fingers, put the helm over and ordered his men to their stations.

Captain Blood, summoned from the cabin by Pitt, mounted the poop, and telescope in hand, surveyed t he activities aboard his old friend the *Bonaventure*. He remained in no doubt of their significance. He might be a surgeon, but hardly a lubberly one, as Chard so rashly judged him. His service under de Ruyter in those earlier adventurous days when medicine was neglected by him had taught him more of fighting tactics than Easterling had ever known. He was not perturbed. He would show these pirates how he had profited by the lessons learnt under that great admiral.

Just as for the *Bonaventure* it was essential to employ boarding tactics, so for the *Cinco Llagas* it was vital to depend on gunfire. For with no more than twenty men in all, she could not face the odds of almost ten to one, as Blood computed them, of a hand-to-hand engagement. So now he ordered Pitt to put down the helm, and, keeping as close to the wind as possible, to steer a course that would bring them on to the *Bonaventure's* quarter. To the main deck below he ordered Ogle, that sometime gunner of the King's Navy, taking for his gun crew all but six of the hands who would be required for work above.

Chard perceived at once the aim of the manoeuvre, and swore through his teeth, for Blood had the weather gauge of him. He was further handicapped by the fact that since the *Cinco Llagas* was to be captured for their own purposes it must be no part of his work to cripple her by gunfire before attempting to board. Moreover, he perceived the risk to himself of the attempt, resulting from the longer range and heavier calibre of the guns of the *Cinco Llagas*, if she were resolutely handled. And there appeared to be no lack of resolution about her present master.

Meanwhile the distance between the ships was rapidly lessening, and Chard realized that unless he acted quickly he would be within range with his flank exposed. Unable to bring his ship any closer to the wind, he went about on a south-easterly course with intent to circle widely and so get to windward to the *Cinco Llagas*.

Easterling, watching the manoeuvre from the deck of the *Santa Barbara*, and not quite understanding its purpose, cursed Chard for a fool. He cursed him the more virulently when he saw the *Cinco Llagas* veer suddenly to larboard and follow as if giving chase. Chard, however, welcomed this, and taking in sail allowed the other to draw closer. Then with all canvas spread once more, the *Bonaventure* was off with the wind on her quarter to attempt her circling movement.

Blood understood, and took in sail in his turn, standing so that as the *Bonaventure* turned north she must offer him her flank within range of his heavy guns. Hence Chard, to avoid this, must put up his helm and run south once more.

Easterling watched the two ships sailing away from him in a succession of such manoeuvres for position, and, purple with rage, demanded of Heaven and Hell whether he could believe his eyes, which told him only Chard was running away from the lubberly leech. Chard, however, was far from any such intention. With masterly patience and self-control he awaited his chance to run in and grapple. And with equal patience and doggedness Blood saw to it that he should be given no such chance.

In the end it became a question of who should commit the first blunder, and it was Chard who committed it. In his almost excessive anxiety to avoid coming broadside on with the *Cinco Llagas*, he forgot the chasers on her beak-head, and at last in playing for position allowed her to come too near. He realized his blunder when those two guns roared suddenly behind him and the shot went tearing through his shrouds. It angered him, and in his anger he replied with his stern chasers; but their inferior calibre left their fire ineffective. Then, utterly enraged, he swung the *Bonaventure* about, so as to put a broadside athwart the hawse of the other, and by crippling her sailing powers lay her at the mercy of his boarders.

The heavy ground swell, however, combined with the length of the range utterly to defeat his object, and his broadside thundered forth in impotence to leave a cloud of smoke between himself and the *Cinco Llagas*. Instantly Blood swung broadside on, and emptied his twenty larboard guns into that smoke-cloud, hoping to attain the *Bonaventure's* exposed flank beyond. The attempt was equally unsuccessful, but it served to show Chard the mettle of the man he was engaging--a man with whom it was not safe to take such chances. Nevertheless, one more chance he took, and went briskly about, so as to charge through the billowing smoke, and so bear down upon the other ship before she could suspect the design. The manoeuvre, however, was too protracted for success. By the time the *Bonaventure* was upon her fresh course the smoke had dispersed sufficiently to betray her tactics to Blood, and the *Cinco Llagas*, lying well over to larboard, was ripping through the water at twice the speed of the *Bonaventure*, now ill-served by the wind.

Again Chard put the helm over and raced to intercept the other and to get to windward of her. But Blood, now a mile away, and with a safety margin of time, went, about and returned so as to bring his star board guns to bear at the proper moment. To elude this Chard once more headed south and presented no more than his counter as a target.

In this manner the two vessels worked gradually away until the *Santa Barbara*, with the raging, blaspheming Easterling aboard, was no more than a speck on the northern horizon; and still they were as far as ever from joining battle.

Chard cursed the wind which favoured Captain Blood, and cursed Captain Blood who knew so well how to take and maintain the advantage of his position. The lubberly surgeon appeared possessed of perfect understanding of the situation and uncannily ready to meet each move of his opponent. Occasional shots continued to be exchanged by the chasers of each vessel, each aiming high so as to damage the other's sailing powers, yet, at the long range separating them, without success.

Peter Blood at the poop rail, in a fine back-and-breast and steel cap of black damascened steel, which had been the property of the original Spanish commander of the *Cinco Llagas*, was growing weary and anxious. To Hagthorpe similarly armed beside him, to Wolverstone whom no armour aboard would fit, and to Pitt at the whipstaff, immediately below, he confessed it in the tone of his question:

"How long can this ducking and dodging continue? And however long it continues what end can it have but one? Sooner or later the wind will drop or veer, or else it's ourselves will drop from sheer weariness. When that happens we'll be at that scoundrel's mercy."

"There's always the unexpected," said young Pitt.

"Why, so there is, and I thank you for reminding me of it, Jerry. Let's put our hopes in it, for all that I can't see whence it's to come."

It was coming at that moment, and coming quickly, although Blood was the only one of them who recognized it when he saw it. They were standing in towards the land at the end of a long westerly run, when round the point of Espada, less than a mile away, a towering heavily-armed ship came sailing as close to the wind as she dared, her ports open and the mouths of a score of guns gaping along her larboard flank, the banner of Castile flapping aloft in the breeze.

At sight of this fresh enemy of another sort Wolverstone loosed an oath that sounded like a groan. "And that's the end of us!" he cried.

"I'm by no means sure, now, that it may not be the beginning," Blood answered him, with something that sounded like laughter in his voice, which when last heard had been jaded and dispirited. And his orders, flowing fast, showed clearly what was in his mind. "Run me the flag of Spain aloft, and bid Ogle empty his chasers at the *Bonaventure* as we go about."

As Pitt put the helm over, and with straining cordage and creaking blocks the *Cinco Llagas* swung slowly round, the gold and scarlet banner of Castile broke bravely from her maintruck. An instant later the two guns on her forecastle thundered forth, ineffectually in one way, but very effectually in another. Their fire conveyed very plainly to the Spanish newcomer that here he beheld a compatriot ship in pursuit of an English rover.

Explanations no doubt must follow, especially if upon the discovery of the identity of the *Cinco Llagas* the Spaniards should happen to be already acquainted with her recent history. But that could not come until they had disposed of the *Bonaventure*, and Blood was more than content to let the future take care of itself.

Meanwhile the Spanish ship, a guarda-costa from San Domingo, which whilst on patrol had been attracted beyond the Point of Espada by the sound of gunfire out at sea, behaved precisely as was to be expected. Even without the flag now floating at her masthead, the Spanish origin of the *Cinco Llagas* was plain to read in the lines of her; that she was engaged with this equally obvious English sloop was no less plain. The guarda-costa went into the fight without a moment's hesitation, and loosed a broadside at the *Bonaventure* as she was in the act of going about to escape this sudden and unforeseen peril.

Chard raged like a madman as the sloop shuddered under blows at stem and stern and her shattered bowsprit hung in a tangle of cordage athwart her bows. In his frenzy he ordered the fire to be returned, and did some damage to the guarda-costa, but not of a kind to impair her mobility. The Spaniard, warming to the battle, went about so as to pound the sloop with her starboard guns, and Chard, having lost his head by now, swung round also so as to return or even anticipate that fire.

Not until he had done so did it occur to him that with empty guns he was helplessly vulnerable to an onslaught from the *Cinco Llagas*. For Blood, too, espying the opportunity whilst yet it was shaping, had gone about, drawn level, and hurled at him the contents of his heavy artillery. That broadside at comparatively short range swept his deck, shattered the windows of the coach, and one well-placed shot opened a wound in the bows of the *Bonaventure* almost on the waterline, through which the sea rushed into the hold at every roll of the crippled vessel.

Chard realized that he was doomed, and his bitterness was deepened by perception of the misapprehension at the root of his destruction. He saw the Spanish flag at the masthead of the *Cinco Llagas*, and grinned in livid malice.

On a last inspiration, he struck his colours in token of surrender. It was his forlorn hope that the guardacosta, accepting this, and ignorant of his strength in men, would rush in to grapple him, in which case he would turn the tables on the Spaniards and, possessing himself of the guarda-costa, might yet come out of the adventure with safety and credit.

But the vigilant Captain Blood guessed, if not the intention, at least the possibility, as well as the alternative possibility of explanations dangerous to himself from the captured Chard to the Spanish commander. To provide against either danger, he sent for Ogle, and under his instructions that skilful gunner crashed a thirty-two-pound shot into the *Bonaventure's* waterline amidships, so as to supplement the leakage already occurring forward.

The captain of the guarda-costa may have wondered why his compatriot should continue to fire upon a ship that had struck her colours, but the circumstance would hardly seem to him suspicious, although it might be vexatious, for its consequence appeared to be the inevitable destruction of a vessel that might yet have been turned to account.

As for Chard, he had no time for speculations of any kind. The *Bonaventure* was now making water so fast that his only hope of saving the lives of himself and his men lay in attempting to run her aground before she sank. So he headed her for, the shoals at the foot of the Point of Espada, thanking God that she might now run before the wind, although at an ominously diminishing speed, despite the fact that the buccaneers heaved their cannon overboard to lighten her as they went. She grounded at last in the shallows, with the seas breaking over her stern and forecastles, which alone remained above water. These and the shrouds were now black with the men who had climbed to safety. The guardacosta stood off with idly flapping sails, waiting, her captain wondering to behold the *Cinco Llagas* half a mile away already heading northwards.

Aboard her presently Captain Blood was inquiring of Pitt if a knowledge of Spanish signals was included in his lore of the sea, and if so would he read the signals that the guarda-costa was flying. The young ship-master confessed that it was not, and expressed the opinion that as a consequence they had but escaped the frying-pan to fall into the fire.

"Now here's a lack of faith in Madame Fortune," said Blood. "We'll just be dipping our flag in salute to them, to imply that we've business elsewhere, and be off to attend to it. We look like honest Spaniards. Even through a telescope, in this Spanish armour, Hagthorpe and I must look like a pair of dons. Let's go and see how it's faring with the ingenious Easterling. I'm thinking the time has come to improve our acquaintance with him."

The guarda-costa, if surprised at the unceremonious departure of the vessel she had assisted in the destruction of that pirate sloop, cannot have suspected her bona-fides. Either taking it for granted that she had business elsewhere, or else because too intent upon making prisoners of the crew of the *Bonaventure*, she made no attempt to follow.

And so it fell out that some two hours later Captain Easterling, waiting off the coast between Cape Raphael and Cape Engaño, beheld to his stupefaction and horror the swift approach of Peter Blood's red ship. He had listened attentively and in some uneasiness to the distant cannonade, but he had assumed its cessation to that the *Cinco Llagas* was taken. The sight now of that frigate, sailing briskly, jauntily, and undamaged, defied belief. What had happened to Chard? There was no sign of him upon the sea. Could he have blundered so badly as to have allowed. Captain Blood to sink him?

Speculation on this point was presently quenched by speculation of an infinitely graver character. What might be this damned doctor-convict's present intention? If Easterling had been in case to board him he would have known no apprehension, for even his prize crew on the *Santa Barbara* outnumbered Blood's men by more than two to one. But the crippled *Santa Barbara* could never be laid board and board with the *Cinco Llagas* unless Blood desired it, and if Wood meant mischief as a result of what had happened with the *Bonaventure* the *Santa Barbara* must lie at the mercy of his guns.

The reflexion, vexatious enough in itself, was maddening to Easterling when he considered what he carried under hatches. Fortune, it now began to seem, had not favoured him at all. She had merely mocked him by allowing him to grasp something which he could not hold.

But this was by no means the end of his vexation. For now, as if the circumstances in themselves had not been enough to enrage a man, his prize crew turned almost mutinous. Led by a scoundrel named Gunning, a man almost as massive and ruthless as Easterling himself, they furiously blamed their captain and his excessive and improvident greed for the peril in which they found themselves--a peril of death or capture embittered by the thought of the wealth they held. With such a prize in his hands, Easterling should have taken no risks. He should have kept the *Bonaventure* at hand for protection, and paid no heed to the empty hulk of the *Cinco Llagas*. This they told him in terms of fiercest vituperation, whose very justice left him without answer other than insults, which he liberally supplied.

Whilst they wrangled, the *Cinco Llagas* drew nearer, and now Easterling's quartermaster called his attention to the signals she was flying. These demanded the immediate presence aboard her of the commander of the *Santa Barbara*.

Easterling was taken with panic. The high colour receded from his cheeks, his heavy lips grew purple. He vowed that he would see Doctor Blood in Hell before he went.

His men assured him that they would see him in Hell, and shortly, if he did not go.

Gunning reminded him that Blood could not possibly know what the *Santa Barbara* carried, and that therefore it should be possible to cozen him into allowing her to go her ways without further molestation.

A gun thundered from the *Cinco Llagas*, to send a warning shot across the bows of the *Santa Barbara*. That was enough. Gunning thrust the quartermaster aside, and himself seized the helm and put it over, so that the ship lay hove to, as a first intimation of compliance. After that the buccaneers launched the cock-boat and a half-dozen of them swarmed down to man her, whilst, almost at pistol-point, Gunning compelled Captain Easterling to follow them.

When presently he climbed into the waist of the *Cinco Llagas* where she lay hove to, a cable's length away across the sunlit waters, there was hell in his eyes and terror in his soul. Straight and tall, in Spanish corselet and headpiece, the despised doctor stood forward to receive him. Behind him stood Hagthorpe and a half-score of his followers. He seemed to smile.

"At last, Captain, ye stand where ye have so long hoped to stand: on the deck of the *Cinco Llagas*."

Easterling grunted ragefully for only answer to that raillery. His great hands twitched as if he would have them at his Irish mocker's throat. Captain Blood continued to address him.

"It's an ill thing, Captain, to attempt to grasp more than you can comfortably hold. Ye'll not be the first to find himself empty-handed as a consequence. That was a fine fast-sailing sloop of yours, the *Bonaventure*. Ye should have been content. It's a pity that she'll sail no more; for she's sunk, or will be entirely at high water." Abruptly he asked: '"How many hands are with you?" and he had to repeat the question before he was sullenly answered that forty men remained aboard the *Santa Barbara*.

"What boats does she carry?"

"Three with the cock-boat."

"That should be enough to accommodate your following. You'll order them into those boats at once if you value their lives, for in fifteen minutes from now I shall open fire on the ship and sink her. This because I can spare no men for a prize crew, nor can I leave her afloat to be repossessed by you and turned to further mischief."

Easterling began a furious protest that was mixed with remonstrances of the peril to him and his of landing on Hispaniola. Blood cropped it short.

"Ye're receiving such mercy as you probably never showed to any whom ye compelled to surrender. Ye'd best profit by my tenderness. If the Spaniards on Hispaniola spare you when you land there, you can get back to your hunting and boucanning, for which ye're better fitted than the sea. Away with you now."

But Easterling did not at once depart. He stood with feet planted wide, swaying on his powerful legs, clenching and unclenching his hands. At last he took his decision.

"Leave me that ship, and in Tortuga, when I get there, I'll pay you fifty thousand pieces of eight. That's better nor the empty satisfaction of turning us adrift."

"Away with you!" was all that Blood answered him, his tone more peremptory.

"A hundred thousand!" cried Easterling.

"Why not a million?" wondered Blood. "It's as easily promised, and the promise as easily broken. Oh, I'm like to take your word, Captain Easterling, as like as I am to believe that ye command such a sum as a hundred thousand pieces of eight."

Easterling's baleful eyes narrowed. Behind his black beard his thick lips tightened. Almost they smiled. Since there was nothing to be done without disclosures, nothing should be done at all. Let Blood sink a treasure which in any case must now be lost to Easterling. There was in the thought a certain bitter negative satisfaction.

"I pray that we may meet again, Captain Blood," he said, falsely, grimly unctuous. "I'll have something to tell you then that'll make you sorry for what you do now."

"If we meet again I've no doubt the occasion will be one for many regrets. Good-day to you, Captain Easterling. Ye've just fifteen minutes, ye'll remember."

Easterling sneered and shrugged, and then abruptly turned and climbed down to the rocking boat that awaited him below.

When he came to announce Blood's message to his buccaneers they stormed and raged so fiercely at the prospect of thus being cheated of everything that they could be heard across the water aboard the *Cinco Llagas*, to the faintly scornful amusement of Blood, who was far from suspecting the true reason of all this hubbub.

He watched the lowering of the boats, and was thereafter amazed to see the decks of the *Santa Barbara* empty of that angry vociferous mob. The buccaneers had gone below before leaving each man intent upon taking as much of the treasure as he could carry upon his person. Captain Blood became impatient.

"Pass the word down to Ogle to put a shot into her forecastle. Those rogues need quickening."

The roar of the gun, and the impact of the twenty-four-pound shot as it smashed through the timbers of the high forward structure, brought the buccaneers swarming upon deck again, and thence to the waiting boats with the speed of fear. Yet a certain order they preserved for their safety's sake, for in the sea that was running the capsizing of a boat would have been an easy matter.

They pushed off, their wet oars flashed in the brilliant sunlight, and they began to draw away towards the promontory not more than two miles to windward. Once they were clear, Blood gave the word to open fire, when Hagthorpe clutched his arm.

"Wait, man! Wait! Look! There's someone still aboard her!"

Surprised, Blood looked, first with his naked eye, then through his telescope. He beheld a bareheaded gentleman in corselet and thigh-boots, who clearly was no buccaneer of the kind that sailed with Easterling, and who stood on the poop frantically waving a scarf. Blood with quick to guess his identity.

"It'll be one of the Spaniards who were aboard when Easterling took the ship and whose throat he forgot to cut."

He ordered a boat to be launched, and sent six men with Dyke, who had some knowledge of Spanish, to bring the Spaniard off.

Don Ildefonso, who, callously left to drown in the doomed ship, had worked himself free of the thong that bound his wrists, stood in the forechains to await the coming of that boat. He was quivering with excitement at this deliverance of himself and the vessel in his charge with her precious freight--a deliverance which he regarded as little short of miraculous. For like the guarda-costa, Don Ildefonso, even if he had not recognized the Spanish lines of this great ship which had come so unexpectedly to the rescue, must have been relieved of all doubt by the flag of Spain which had been allowed to remain floating at the masthead of the *Cinco Llagas*.

So with speech bubbling eagerly out of him in that joyous excitement of his, the Spanish commander poured into the ears of Dyke, when the boat brought up alongside, the tale of what had happened to them and what they carried. Because of this it was necessary that they should lend him a dozen men so that with the six now under hatches on the *Santa Barbara* he might bring his precious cargo safely into San Domingo.

To Dyke this was an amazing and exciting narrative. But he did not on that account lose grip of his self-possession. Lest too much Spanish should betray him to Don Ildefonso, he took refuge in curtness.

"Bueno," said he. "I'll inform my captain." Under his breath he ordered his men to push off and head back for the *Cinco Llagas*.

When Blood heard the tale and had digested his amazement, he laughed.

"So this is what that rogue would have told me if ever we met again. Faith it's a satisfaction to be denied him."

Ten minutes later the *Cinco Llagas* lay board and board with the *Santa Barbara*.

In the distance Easterling and his men, observing the operation, rested on their oars to stare and mutter. They saw themselves cheated of even the meagre satisfaction for which they had looked in the sinking of an unsuspected treasure. Easterling burst into fresh profanity.

"It'll be that damned Spaniard I forgot in the cabin who'll ha' blabbed of the gold; Oh, 'sdeath! This is what comes o' being soft-hearted; if only I'd cut his throat now..."

Meanwhile to Don Ildefonso, who had been able to make nothing of this boarding manoeuvre, Captain Blood, save for the light eyes in his bronzed face, looking every inch a Spaniard, and delivering himself in the impeccable Castilian of which he was master, was offering explanations.

He was unable to spare a crew to man the *Santa Barbara*, for his own following was insufficient. Nor dared he leave her afloat, since in that case she would he repossessed by the abominable pirates whom he had constrained to abandon her. It remained, therefore, before scuttling her only to tranship the treasure with which Don Ildefonso informed him she was laden. At the same time he would be happy to offer Don Ildefonso and his six surviving hands the hospitality of the *Cinco Llagas* as far as Tortuga, or, if Don Ildefonso preferred it, as seemed probable, Captain Blood would seize a favourable moment for allowing them to take one of his boats and land themselves upon the coast of Hispaniola.

Now this speech was the most amazing thing that had yet happened to Don Ildefonso in that day of amazements.

"Tortuga!" he exclaimed. "Tortuga! You sail to Tortuga, do you say? But what to do there? In God's name who are you, then? What are you?"

"As for who I am, I am called Peter Blood. As for what I am, faith, I scarce know myself."

"You are English!" cried the Spaniard in sudden horror of partial understanding.

"Ah no. That, at least, I am not." Captain Blood drew himself up with great dignity. "I have the honour to be Irish."

"Ah, bah! Irish or English, it is all one."

"Indeed and it is not. There's all the difference in the world between the two."

The Spaniard looked at him with angry eyes. His face was livid, his mouth scornful. "English or Irish, the truth is you are just a cursed pirate."

Blood's eyes looked wistful. He fetched a sigh. "I'm afraid you are right," he admitted. "It's a thing I've sought to avoid. But what am I to do now, when Fate thrusts it upon me in this fashion, and insists that I make so excellent a beginning?"

III - THE KING'S MESSENGER

On a brilliant May morning of the year 1690 a gentleman stepped ashore at Santiago de Porto Rico, followed by a negro servant shouldering a valise. He had been brought to the mole in a cock-boat from the yellow galleon standing in the roadstead, with the flag of Spain floating from her maintruck. Having landed him, the cock-boat went smartly about, and was pulled back to the ship, from which circumstances the gaping idlers on the mole assumed that this gentleman had come to stay.

They stared at him with interest, as they would have stared at any stranger. This, however, was a man whose exterior repaid their attention, a man to take the eye. Even the wretched white slaves toiling half-naked on the fortifications, and the Spanish soldiery guarding them, stood at gaze.

Tall, straight, and vigorously spare, our gentleman was dressed with sombre Spanish elegance in black And silver. The curls of his black periwig fell to his shoulders, and his keen shaven face with its high-bridged nose and disdainful lips was shaded by a broad black hat about the crown of which swept a black ostrich plume. Jewels flashed at his breast, a foam of Mechlin almost concealed his hands, and there were ribbons to the long gold-mounted ebony cane he carried. A fop from the Alameda he must have seemed but for the manifest vigour of him and the air of assurance and consequence with which he bore himself. He carried his dark finery with an indifference to the broiling tropical heat which argued an iron constitution, and his glance was so imperious that the eyes of the inquisitive fell away abashed before it.

He asked the way to the Governor's residence, and the officer commanding the guard over the toiling white prisoners detached a soldier to conduct him.

Beyond the square, which architecturally, and saving for the palm trees throwing patches of black shadow on the dazzling white sun-drenched ground, might have belonged to some little town in Old Spain, past the church with its twin spires and marble steps, they came, by tall, wrought-iron gates, into a garden, and by an avenue of acacias to a big white house with deep external galleries all clad in jessamine. Negro servants in ridiculously rich red-and-yellow liveries admitted our gentleman, and went to announce to the Governor of Porto Rico the arrival of Don Pedro de Queiroz on a mission from King Philip.

Not every day did a messenger from the King of Spain arrive in this almost the least of his Catholic Majesty's overseas dominions. Indeed, the thing had never happened before, and Don Jayme de Villamarga, whilst thrilled to the marrow by the announcement, knew not whether to assign the thrill to pride or to alarm.

A man of middle height, big of head and paunch, and of less than mediocre intelligence, Don Jayme was one of those gentlemen who best served Spain by being absent from her, and this no doubt had been considered in appointing him Governor of Porto Rico. Not even his awe of majesty, represented by Don Pedro, could repress his naturally self-sufficient manner he was pompous in his reception of him, and remained unintimidated by the cold haughty stare of Don Pedro's eyes--eyes of a singularly deep blue, contrasting oddly with his bronzed face. A Dominican monk, elderly, tall and gaunt, kept his excellency company.

"Sir, I give you welcome." Don Jayme spoke as if his mouth were full. "I trust you will announce to me that I have the honour to meet with his majesty's approbation."

Don Pedro made him a deep obeisance, with a sweep of his plumed hat, which, together with his cane, he thereafter handed to one of the negro lackeys. "It is to signify the royal approbation that I am here, happily, after some adventures. I have just landed from the *San Tomas*, after a voyage of some vicissitudes. She has gone on to San Domingo, and it may be three or four days before she returns to take me off again. For that brief while I must make free with your excellency's hospitality." He seemed to claim it as a right rather than ask it as a favour.

"Ah!" was all that Don Jayme permitted himself to answer. And with head on one side, a fatuous smile on the thick lips under his grizzled moustache, he waited for the visitor to enter into details of the royal message.

The visitor, however, displayed no haste. He looked about him at the cool spacious room with its handsome furnishings of carved oak and walnut, its tapestries and pictures, all imported from the Old World, and inquired, in that casual manner of the man who is at home in every environment, if he might be seated. His excellency with some loss of dignity made haste to set a chair.

Composedly, with a thin smile which Don Jayme disliked, the messenger sat down and crossed his legs.

"We are," he announced, "in some sort related, Don Jayme."

Don Jayme stared. "I am not aware of the honour."

"That is why I am at the trouble of informing you. Your marriage, sir, established the bond. I am a distant cousin of Doña Hernanda."

"Oh! My wife!" His excellency's tone in some subtle way implied contempt for that same wife and her relations. "I had remarked your name: Queiroz." This also explained to him the rather hard and open accent of Don Pedro's otherwise impeccable Castilian. "You will, then, be Portuguese, like Doña Hernanda?" and again his tone implied contempt of Portuguese, and particularly perhaps of Portuguese who were in the service of the King of Spain, from whom Portugal had reestablished her independence a half-century ago.

"Half Portuguese, of course. My family--"

"Yes, yes." Thus the testy Don Jayme interrupted him. "But your message from his majesty?"

"Ah yes. Your impatience, Don Jayme, is natural." Don Pedro was faintly ironical. "You will forgive me that I should have intruded family matters. My message, then. It will be no surprise to you, sir, that eulogistic reports should have reached his majesty, whom God preserve--" he bowed his head in reverence, compelling Don Jayme to do the same--"not only of the good government of this important island of Porto Rico, but also of the diligence employed by you to rid these seas of the pestilent rovers, particularly the English buccaneers who trouble our shipping and the peace of our Spanish settlements."

There was nothing in this to surprise Don Jayme. Not even upon reflection. Being a fool, he did not suspect that Porto Rico was the worst governed of any Spanish settlement in the West Indies. As for the rest, he had certainly encouraged the extirpation of the buccaneers from the Caribbean. Quite recently, and quite fortuitously be it added, he had actually contributed materially to this desirable end, as he was not slow to mention.

With chin high and chest puffed out, he moved, strutting, before Don Pedro as he delivered himself. It was gratifying to be appreciated in the proper quarter. It encouraged endeavour. He desired to be modest. Yet in justice to himself he must assert that under his government the island was tranquil and prosperous. Frey Luis here could bear him out in this. The Faith was firmly planted, and there was no heresy in any form in Porto Rico. And as for the matter of the buccaneers, he had done all that a man in his position could do. Not perhaps as much as he could have desired to do. After all, his office kept him ashore. Had Don Pedro remarked the new fortifications he was building? The work was all but complete, and he did not think that even the infamous Captain Blood would have the hardihood to pay him a visit. He had already shown that redoubtable buccaneer that he was not a man with whom it was prudent to trifle. A party of this Captain Blood's men had dared to land on the southern side of the island a few days ago. But Don Jayme's followers were vigilant. He saw to that. A troop of horse was in the neighbourhood at the time. It had descended upon the pirates and had taught them a sharp lesson. He laughed as he spoke of it; laughed at the thought of it; and Don Pedro politely laughed with him, desiring with courteous and appreciative interest to know more of this.

"You killed them all, of course?" he suggested, his contempt of them implicit in his tone.

"Not yet." His excellency spoke with a relish almost fierce. "But I have them under my hand. Six of them, who were captured. We have not yet decided upon their end. Perhaps the rope. Perhaps an auto-da-fé and the fires of the Faith for them. They are heretics all, of course. It is a matter I am still considering with Frey Luis here."

"Well, well," said Don Pedro, as if the subject began to weary him. "Will your excellency hear the remainder of my message?"

The Governor was annoyed by this suggestion that his lengthy exposition had amounted to an interruption. Stiffly he bowed to the representative of majesty. "My apologies," said he in a voice of ice.

But the lofty Don Pedro paid little heed to his manner. He drew from an inner pocket of his rich coat a folded parchment and a small flat leather case.

"I have to explain, your excellency, the condition in which this comes to you. I have said, although I do not think you heeded it, that I arrive here after a voyage of many vicissitudes. Indeed, it is little short of a miracle that I am here at all, considering what I have undergone. I, too, have been a victim of that infernal dog, Captain Blood. The ship on which I originally sailed from Cadiz was sunk by him a week ago. More fortunate than my cousin Don Rodrigo de Queiroz, who accompanied me and who remains a prisoner in that infamous pirate's hands, I made my escape. It is a long tale with which I will not weary you."

"It would not weary me," exclaimed his excellency, forgetting his dignity in his interest.

But Don Pedro waved aside the implied request for details. "Later! Later, perhaps, if you care to hear of it. It is not important. What is important on your excellency's account is that I escaped. I was picked up by the *San Tomas*, which has brought me here, and so I am happily able to discharge my mission." He held up the folded parchment. "I but mention it to explain how this has come to suffer by sea-water, though not to the extent of being illegible. It is a letter from his majesty's Secretary of State informing you that our Sovereign, whom God preserve, has been graciously pleased to create you, in recognition of the services I have mentioned, a knight of the most noble order of St. James of Compostella."

Don Jayme went first white, then red, in his incredulous excitement. With trembling fingers he took the letter and unfolded it. It was certainly damaged by sea-water. Some words were scarcely legible. The ink in which his own surname had been written had run into a smear, as had that of his government of Porto Rico, and some other words here and there. But the amazing substance of the letter was indeed as Don Pedro announced, and the royal signature was unimpaired.

As Don Jayme raised his eyes at last from the document, Don Pedro, proffering the leather case, touched a spring in it. It flew open, and the Governor gazed upon rubies that glowed like live coals against their background of black velvet.

"And here," said Don Pedro, "is the insignia; the cross of the most noble order in which you are invested."

Don Jayme took the case gingerly, as if it had been some holy thing, and gazed upon the smouldering cross. The friar came to stand beside him, murmuring congratulatory words. Any knighthood would have been an honourable, an unexpected, reward for Don Jayme's services to the crown of Spain. But that of all orders this most exalted and coveted order of St. James of Compostella should have been conferred upon him was something that almost defied belief. The Governor of Porto Rico was momentarily awed by the greatness of the thing that had befallen him.

And yet when a few minutes later the room was entered by a little lady, young and delicately lovely, Don Jayme had already recovered his habitual poise of self-sufficiency.

The lady, beholding a stranger, an elegant, courtly stranger, who rose instantly upon her advent, paused in the doorway, hesitating, timid. Then she addressed Don Jayme.

"Pardon. I did not know you occupied."

Don Jayme appealed, sneering, to the friar. "She did not know me occupied! I am the King's representative in Porto Rico, his majesty's Governor of this island, and my wife does not know that I am occupied, conceives that I have leisure. It is unbelievable. But come in, Hernanda. Come in." He grew more playful. "Acquaint yourself with the honours the King bestows upon his poor servant. This may help you to realize what his majesty does me the justice to realize, although you may have failed to do so: that my occupations here are onerous."

Timidly she advanced, obedient to his invitation. "What is it, Jayme?"

"What is it?" He seemed to mimic her. "It is merely this." He displayed the order. "His majesty invests me with the cross of Saint James of Compostella, that is all."

She grew conscious that she was mocked. Her pale, delicate face flushed a little. But there was no accompanying sparkle of her great, dark, wistful eyes to proclaim it a flush of pleasure. Rather, thought Don Pedro, she flushed from shame and resentment at being so contemptuously used before a stranger and at the boorishness of a husband who could so use her.

"I am glad, Jayme," she said, in a gentle, weary voice. "I felicitate you. I am glad."

"Ah! You are glad. Frey Alonso, you will observe that Doña Hernanda is glad." Thus he sneered at her without even the poor, grace of being witty. "This gentleman, by whose hand the order came, is a kinsman of yours, Hernanda."

She turned aside, to look again at that elegant stranger. Her gaze was blank. Yet she hesitated to deny him. Kinship when claimed by gentlemen charged by kings with missions of investiture is not lightly to be denied in the presence of such a husband as Don Jayme. And, after all, hers was a considerable family, and must include many with whom she was not personally acquainted.

The stranger bowed until the curls of his periwig met across his face. "You will not remember me, Doña Hernanda. I am, nevertheless, your cousin, and you will have heard of me from our other cousin, Rodrigo. I am Pedro de Queiroz."

"You are Pedro?" She stared the harder. "Why, then..." She laughed a little. "Oh, but I remember Pedro. We played together as children. Pedro and I."

Something in her tone seemed to deny him. But he confronted her unperturbed.

"That would be at Santarem," said he.

"At Santarem it was." His readiness appeared now to bewilder her. "But you were a fat, sturdy boy then, and your hair was golden."

He laughed. "I have become lean in growing, and I favour a black periwig."

"Which makes your eyes a startling blue. I do not remember that you had blue eyes."

"God help us, ninny!" croaked her husband. "You never could remember anything."

She turned to look at him, and for all that her lip quivered, her eyes steadily met his sneering glance. She seemed about to speak, checked herself, and then spoke at last, very quietly. "Oh yes. There are some things a woman never forgets."

"And on the subject of memory," said Don Pedro, addressing the Governor with cold dignity, "I do not remember that there are any ninnies in our family."

"Faith, then, you needed to come to Porto Rico to discover it," his excellency retorted with his loud, coarse laugh.

"Ah!" Don Pedro sighed. "That may not be the end of my discoveries."

There was something in his tone which Don Jayme did not like. He threw back his big 'head and frowned. "You mean?" he demanded.

Don Pedro was conscious of an appeal in the little lady's dark, liquid eyes. He yielded to it, laughed, and answered:

"I have yet to discover where your excellency proposes to lodge me during the days in which I must inflict myself upon you. If I might now withdraw..."

The Governor swung to Doña Hernanda. "You hear? Your kinsman needs to remind us of our duty to a guest. It will not have occurred to you to make provision for him."

"But I did not know...I was not told of his presence until I found him here."

"Well, well. You know now. And we dine in half an hour."

At dinner Don Jayme was in high spirits, which is to say that he was alternately pompous and boisterous, and occasionally filled the room with his loud jarring laugh.

Don Pedro scarcely troubled to dissemble his dislike of him. His manner became more and more frigidly aloof, and he devoted his attention and addressed his conversation more and more exclusively to the despised wife.

"I have news for you," he told her, when they had come to the dessert, "of our Cousin Rodrigo."

"Ah!" sneered her husband. "She'll welcome news of him. She ever had a particular regard for her Cousin Rodrigo, and he for her."

She flushed, keeping her troubled eyes lowered. Don Pedro came to the rescue, swiftly, easily. "Regard for one another is common among the members of our family. Every Queiroz owes a duty to every other, and is at all times ready to perform it." He looked very straightly at Don Jayme as he spoke, as if inviting him to discover more in the words than they might seem to carry. "And that is at the root of what I am to tell you, cousin Hernanda. As I have already informed his excellency, the ship in which Don Rodrigo and I sailed from Spain together was set upon and sunk by that infamous pirate Captain Blood. We were both captured, but I was so fortunate as to make my escape."

"You have not told us how. You must tell us how," the Governor interrupted him.

Don Pedro waved a hand disdainfully. "It is no great matter, and I soon weary of talking of myself. But...if you insist...some other time. At present I am to tell you of Rodrigo. He remains a prisoner in the hands of Captain Blood. But do not be unduly alarmed."

There was need for his reassuring tone. Doña I Hernanda, who had been hanging on his words, had turned deathly white.

"Do not be alarmed. Rodrigo is in good health, and his life is safe. Also, from my own experience, I know that this Blood, infamous pirate though he be, is not without chivalrous ideals, and, piracy apart, he is a man of honour."

"Piracy apart?" Laughter exploded from Don

Jayme. "On my soul, that's humorous! You deal in paradox, Don Pedro. Eh, Frey Alonso?" The lean friar smiled mechanically. Doña Hernanda, pale and piteous, suffered in silence the interruption. Don Pedro frowned.

"The paradox is not in me, but in Captain Blood. An indemoniated robber, yet he practises no wanton cruelty, and he keeps his word. Therefore, I say you need have no apprehension on the score of Don Rodrigo's fate. His ransom has been agreed between himself and Captain Blood, and I have undertaken to procure it. Meanwhile he is well and courteously treated, and, indeed, a sort of friendship has come to exist between himself and his pirate captor."

"Faith, that I can believe!" cried the Governor, Whilst Doña Hernanda sank back in her chair with a sigh of relief. "Rodrigo was ever ready to consort with rogues. Was he not, Hernanda?"

"I..." She bridled indignantly, then curbed herself, "I never observed it."

"You never observed it! I ask myself have you ever observed anything? Well, well, and so Rodrigo's to be ransomed. At what is his ransom fixed?"

"You desire to contribute?" cried Don Pedro with a certain friendly eagerness.

The Governor started as if he had been stung. His countenance became gravely blank. "Not I, by the Virgin! Not I. That is entirely a matter for the family of Queiroz."

Don Pedro's smile perished. He sighed. "True! True! And yet...I've a notion you'll come to contribute something before all is ended."

"Dismiss it," laughed Don Jayme, "for that way lies disappointment."

They rose from table soon thereafter and withdrew to the noontide rest the heat made necessary.

They did not come together again until supper, which was served in that same room, in the comparative cool of eventide and by the light of a score of candles in heavy silver branches brought from Spain.

The Governor's satisfaction at the signal honour of which he was the recipient appeared to have grown with contemplation of it. He was increasingly jovial and facetious, but not on this account did he spare Doña Hernanda his sneers. Rather did he make her the butt of his coarse humours, inviting the two men to laugh with him at the shortcomings he indicated in her. Don Pedro, however, did not laugh. He remained preternaturally grave, indeed almost compassionate, as he observed the tragic patience on that long-suffering wife's sweet face.

She looked so slight and frail in her stiff black satin gown, which rendered more dazzling by contrast the whiteness of her neck and shoulders, even as her lustrous, smoothly-dressed black hair stressed the warm pallor of her gentle countenance. A little statue in ebony and ivory she seemed to Don Pedro's fancy, and almost as lifeless until after supper he found himself alone with her in the deep jessamine-clad galleries that stood open to the cool night breezes blowing from the sea.

His excellency had gone off to indite a letter of grateful acknowledgment to the King, and had taken the friar to assist him. He had commended his guest to the attention of his wife, whilst commiserating with him upon the necessity. She had led Don Pedro out into the scented purple tropic night, and stepping now beside him came at last to life, and addressed him in a breathless anxiety.

"What you told us to-day of Don Rodrigo de Queiroz, is it true? That he is a prisoner in the hands of Captain Blood, but unhurt and safe, awaiting ransom?"

"Most scrupulously true in all particulars."

"You...you pledge your word for that? Your honour as a gentleman? For I must assume you a gentleman, since you bear commissions from the King."

"And on no other ground?" quoth he, a little taken aback.

"Do you pledge me your word?" she insisted.

"Unhesitatingly. My word of honour. Why should you doubt me?"

"You give me cause. You are not truthful in all things. Why, for instance, do you say you are my cousin?"

"You do not, then, remember me?"

"I remember Pedro de Queiroz. The years might have given you height and slenderness; the sun might have tanned your face, and under your black periwig your hair may still be fair, though I take leave to doubt it. But what, I ask myself, could have changed the colour of your eyes? For your eyes are blue, and Pedro's were dark brown."

He was silent a moment, like a man considering, and she watched his stern, handsome face, made plain by the light beating upon it from the windows of the house. He did not meet her glance. Instead his eyes sought the sea, gleaming under the bright stars and reflecting the twinkling lights of ships in the roadstead, watched the fireflies flitting among the bushes in pursuit of moths, looked anywhere but at the little figure at his side.

At last he spoke, quietly, almost humorously, in admission of the imposture. "We hoped you would have forgotten such a detail."

"We?" she questioned him.

"Rodrigo and I. He is at least my friend. He was hastening to you when this thing befell him. That is how we came to be on the same ship."

"And he desired you to do this?"

"He shall tell you so himself when he arrives. He will be here in a few days, depend on it. As soon as I can ransom him, which will be very soon after my departure. When I was escaping--for, unlike him, I had given no parole--he desired that if I came here I should claim to be your cousin, so as to stand at need in his place until he comes."

She was thoughtful, and her bosom rose and fell in agitation. In silence they moved a little way in step.

"You took a foolish risk," she said, thereby showing her acceptance of his explanation.

"A gentleman," said he sententiously, "will always take a risk to serve a lady."

"Were you serving me?"

"Does it seem to you that I could be serving myself?"

"No. You could not have been doing that."

"Why question further, then? Rodrigo wished it so. He will explain his motives fully when he comes. Meanwhile, as your cousin, I am in his place. If this boorish husband burdens you overmuch..."

"What are you saying?" Her voice rang with alarm.

"That I am Rodrigo's deputy. So that you remember it, that is all I ask."

"I thank you, cousin," she said, and left him.

Three days Don Pedro continued as the guest of the Governor of Porto Rico, and they were much as that first day, saving that daily Don Jayme continued to increase in consciousness of his new dignity as a knight of Saint James of Compostella, and became, consequently, daily more insufferable. Yet Don Pedro suffered him with exemplary fortitude, and at times seemed even disposed to feed the Governor's egregious vanity. Thus, on the third night at supper, Don Pedro cast out the suggestion that his excellency should signalize the honour with which the King had distinguished him by some gesture that should mark the occasion and render it memorable in the annals of the island.

Don Jayme swallowed the suggestion avidly. "Ah yes! That is an admirable thought. What do you counsel that I do?"

Don Pedro smiled with flattering deprecation. "Not for me to counsel Don Jayme de Villamarga. But the gesture should be worthy of the occasion."

"Indeed, yes. That is true." But the dullard's wits are barren of ideas. "The question now is what might be considered worthy?"

Frey' Alonso suggested a ball at Government House, and was applauded in this by Doña Hernanda. Don Pedro, apologetically to the lady, thought a ball would have significance only for those who were bidden to it. Something was required that should impress all social orders in Porto Rico.

"Why not an amnesty?" he inquired at last.

"An amnesty?" The three of them looked at him in questioning wonder.

"Why not? It is a royal gesture, true. But is not a governor in some sort royal, a viceroy, a representative of royalty, the one to whom men look for royal gestures? To mark your accession to this dignity, throw open your gaols, Don Jayme, as do kings upon, their coronation."

Don Jayme conquered his stupefaction at the magnitude of the act suggested, and smote the table with his fist, protesting that here was a notion worth adopting.

To-morrow he would announce it in a proclamation, and set all prisoners free, their sentences remitted.

"That is," he added, "all but six, whose pardon would hardly please the colony."

"I think," said Don Pedro, "that exceptions would stultify the act. There should be no exceptions."

"But these are exceptional prisoners. Can you have forgotten that I told you I had made captive six buccaneers out of a party that had the temerity to land on Porto Rico?"

Don Pedro frowned, reflecting. "Ah, true!" he cried at last. "I remember."

"And did I tell you, sir, that one of these men is that dog Wolverstone?" He pronounced it Volverstohn.

"Wolverstone?" said Don Pedro, who also pronounced it Volverstohn. "You have captured Wolverstone!" It was clear that he was profoundly impressed; as well he might be, for Wolverstone, who was nowadays the foremost of Blood's lieutenants, was almost as well known to Spaniards and as detested by them as Blood himself. "You have captured Wolverstone!" he repeated, and for the first time looked at Don Jayme with eyes of unmistakable respect. "You did not tell me that. Why, in that case, my friend, you have clipped one of Blood's wings. Without Wolverstone he is shorn of half his power. His own destruction may follow now at any moment, and Spain will owe that to you."

Don Jayme spread his hands in an affectation of modesty. "It is something towards deserving the honour his majesty has bestowed upon me."

"Something?" echoed Don Pedro. "If the King had known this, he might have accounted the order of Saint James of Compostella inadequate."

Doña Hernanda looked at him sharply, to see whether he dealt in irony. But he seemed quite sincere, so much so that for once he had shed the hauteur in which he usually arrayed himself. He resumed after a moment's pause.

"Of course, of course, you cannot include these men in the amnesty. They are pot common malefactors. They are enemies of Spain." Abruptly, with a hint of purpose, he asked: "How will you deal with them?"

Don Jayme thrust out a nether lip considering. "I am still undecided whether to hang them out of hand or to let Frey Alonso hold his auto-da-fé upon them and consign them to the fire as heretics. I think I told you so."

"Yes, yes. But I did not then know that Wolverstone is one of them. That makes a difference."

"What difference?"

"Oh, but consider. Give this matter thought. With thought you'll see for yourself what you should do. It's plain enough."

Don Jayme considered awhile as he was bidden. Then shrugged his shoulders.

"Faith, sir, it may be plain enough to you. But I confess that I see no choice beyond that of rope or fire."

"Ultimately, yes. One or the other. But not here in Porto Rico. That is to smother the effulgence of your achievement. Send them to Spain, Don Jayme.

Send them to his majesty, as an earnest of the zeal for which he has been pleased to honour you. Show him thus how richly you deserve that honour and even greater honours. Let that be your acknowledgment."

Don Jayme was staring at him with dilating eyes. His face glowed. "I vow to Heaven I should never have thought of it," he said at last.

"Your modesty made you blind to the opportunity."

"It may be that," Don Jayme admitted.

"But you perceive it now that I indicate it?"

"Oh, I perceive it. Yes, the King of Spain shall be impressed."

Frey Alonso seemed downcast. He had been counting upon his auto-da-fé. Doña Hernanda was chiefly intrigued by the sudden geniality of her hitherto haughty and disdainful pretended cousin. Meanwhile Don Pedro piled Pelion upon Ossa.

"It should prove to his majesty that your excellency is wasted in so small a settlement as Porto Rico. I see you as governor of some more important colony. Perhaps as viceroy...Who shall say? You have displayed a zeal such as has rarely been displayed by any Spanish governor overseas."

"But how and when to send them to Spain?" wondered Don Jayme, who no longer questioned the expediency of doing so.

"Why, that is a matter in which I can serve your excellency. I can convey them for you on the *San Tomas*, which should call for me at any moment now. You will write another letter to his majesty, offering him these evidences of your zeal, and I will bear it together with these captives. Your general amnesty can wait until I've sailed with them. Thus there will be nothing to mar it. It will be complete and properly imposing."

So elated and so grateful to his guest for his suggestion was Don Jayme that he actually went the length of addressing him as cousin in the course of thanking him.

The matter, it seemed, had presented itself for discussion only just in time. For early on the following morning Santiago was startled by the boom of a gun, and turning out to ascertain the reason, beheld again the yellow Spanish ship which had brought Don Pedro coming to anchor in the bay.

Don Pedro himself sought the Governor with the information that this was the signal for his departure, expressing a polite regret that duty did not permit him longer to encroach upon Don Jayme's princely hospitality.

Whilst his negro valet was packing his effects he went to take his leave of Doña Hernanda, and again assured that wistful little lady that she need be under no apprehension on the score of her cousin Rodrigo, who would soon now be with her.

After this Don Jayme, with an officer in attendance, carried Don Pedro off to the town gaol, where the pirates were lodged.

In a dark, unpaved stone chamber, lighted only by a small, heavily-barred, unglazed window set near the ceiling, they were herded with perhaps a score of other malefactors of all kinds and colours. The atmosphere of the place was so indescribably foul and noisome that Don Pedro recoiled as from a blow when it first assailed him. Don Jayme's loud, coarse laugh derided his fastidiousness. Nevertheless, the Governor flicked out a handkerchief that was sprayed with verbena, and thereafter at intervals held it to his nostrils.

Wolverstone and his five associates, heavily loaded with irons, were in a group a little apart from their fellow-prisoners. They squatted against the wall on the foul dank straw that was their bedding. Unshaven, dishevelled and filthy, for no means of grooming themselves had been allowed them, they huddled together there as if seeking strength in union against the common rogues with whom they were confined. Wolverstone, almost a giant in build, might from his dress have been a merchant. Dyke, that sometime petty officer in the King's Navy, had similarly been arrayed like a citizen of some consequence. The other four wore the cotton shirts and leather breeches which had been the dress of the boucan-hunters before they took to the sea, and their heads were swathed in coloured kerchiefs.

They did not stir when the door creaked on its ponderous hinges and a half-dozen corseletted Spaniards with pikes entered to form a guard of honour as well as a protection for the Governor. When that august personage made his appearance attended by his officer and accompanied by his distinguished-looking guest, the other prisoners sprang up and ranged themselves in awe and reverence. The pirates stolidly sat on. But they were not quite indifferent. As Don Pedro sauntered in, languidly leaning on his beribboned cane, dabbing his lips with a handkerchief, which he, too, had deemed it well to produce, Wolverstone stirred on his foul bed, and his single eye (he had lost the other one at Sedgemoor) rolled with almost portentous ferocity.

Don Jayme indicated the group by a wave of his hand. "There are your cursed pirates, Don Pedro, hanging together like a brood of carrion birds."

"These?" quoth Don Pedro haughtily, and pointed with his cane. "Faith, they look their trade, the villains."

Wolverstone glared more fiercely than ever, but was contemptuously silent. A stubborn rogue, it was plain.

Don Pedro advanced towards them, a superb figure in his black and silver, seeming to symbolise the pride and majesty of Spain. The thick-set Governor, in pale green taffetas, kept pace with him, and presently, when they had come to a halt before the buccaneers, he addressed them.

"You begin to know, you English dogs, what it means to defy the might of Spain. And you'll know it better before all is done. I deny myself the pleasure of hanging you as I intended, so that you may go to Spain, to feed a bonfire."

Wolverstone leered at him. "You are noble," he said, in execrable, but comprehensible Spanish. "Noble with the nobility of Spain. You insult the helpless."

The Governor raged at him, calling him the unprintably foul names that come so readily to an angry Spaniard's lips. This until Don Pedro checked him with a hand upon his arm.

"Is this waste of breath worth while?" He spoke disdainfully. "It but serves to detain us in this noisome place."

The buccaneers stared at him in a sort of wonder. Abruptly he turned on his heel.

"Come, Don Jayme." His tone was peremptory. "Have them out of this. The *San Tomas* is waiting, and the tide is on the turn."

The Governor hesitated, flung a last insult at them, then gave an order to the officer, and stalked after his guest, who was already moving away. The officer transferred the order to his men. With the butts of their pikes and many foul words the soldiers stirred the buccaneers. They rose with clank of gyves and manacles, and went stumbling out into the clean air and the sunshine, herded by the pikemen. Hang-dog, foul and weary, they dragged themselves across the square, where the palms waved in the sea breeze, and the islanders stood to watch them pass, and so they came to the mole, where a wherry of eight oars awaited them.

The Governor and his guest stood by whilst they were being packed into the sternsheets, whither the pikemen followed them. Then Don Pedro and Don Jayme took their places in the prow with Don Pedro's negro, who carried his valise. The wherry pushed off and was rowed across the blue water to the stately ship from whose masthead floated the flag of Spain.

They came bumping along her yellow side at the foot of the entrance-ladder, to which a sailor hitched a boathook.

Don Pedro, from the prow of the wherry, called peremptorily for a file of musketeers to stand to order in the waist. A morioned head appeared over the bulwarks to answer him that it was done already. Then, with the pikemen urging them, and moving awkwardly and painfully in their irons, the buccaneer prisoners climbed the ladder and dropped one by one over the ship's side.

Don Pedro waved his black servant after them with the valise, and finally invited Don Jayme to precede him aboard. Himself, Don Pedro followed close, and when at the ladder's head Don Jayme came to a sudden halt, it was Don Pedro's continuing ascent that thrust him forward, and this so sharply that he almost tumbled headlong into the vessel's waist. There were a dozen ready hands to steady him, and a babble of voices to give him laughing welcome. But the voices were English, and the hands belonged to men whose garments and accoutrements proclaimed them buccaneers. They swarmed in the waist, and already some of them were at work to strike the irons from Wolverstone and his mates.

Gasping, livid, bewildered, Don Jayme de Villamarga swung round to Don Pedro who followed. That very Spanish gentleman had paused at the head of the ladder and stood there steadying himself by a ratline, surveying the scene below him. He was calmly smiling.

"You have nothing to apprehend, Don Jayme. I give you my word for that. And my word is good. I am Captain Blood."

He came down to the deck under the stare of the bulging eyes of the Governor, who understood nothing. Before enlightenment finally came his dull, bewildered wits were to understand still less.

A tall, slight gentleman, very elegantly arrayed, stepped forward to meet the Captain. This, to the Governor's increasing amazement, was his wife's cousin, Don Rodrigo. Captain Blood greeted him in a friendly manner.

"I have brought your ransom, as you see, Don Rodrigo," and he waved a hand in the direction of the group of manacled prisoners. "You are free now to depart with Don Jayme. We'll cut short our farewells, for we take up the anchor at once. Hagthorpe, give the order."

Don Jayme thought that he began to understand. Furiously, he turned upon this cousin of his wife's.

"My God, are you in this? Have you plotted with these enemies of Spain to--?"

A hand gripped his shoulder, and a boatswain's whistle piped somewhere forward. "We are weighing the anchor," said Captain Blood. "You were best over the side, believe me. It has been an honour to know you. In future be more respectful to your wife. Go with God, Don Jayme."

The Governor found himself, as in a nightmare, bustled over the side and down the ladder. Don Rodrigo followed him after taking courteous leave of Captain Blood.

Don Jayme collapsed limply in the sternsheets of the wherry as it put off. But soon he roused himself furiously to demand an explanation whilst at the same time overwhelming his companion with threats.

Don Rodrigo strove to preserve his calm. "You had better listen. I was on that ship, the *San Tomas*, on my way to San Domingo, when Blood captured her. He put the crew ashore on one of the Virgin Islands. But me he retained for ransom because of my rank."

"And to save your skin and your purse you made this infamous bargain with him?"

"I have said that you had better listen. It was not NO at all. He treated me honourably, and we became In some sort friends. He is a man of engaging ways, as you may have discovered. In the course of our talks he gleaned from me a good deal of my private life and yours, which in a way, through my Cousin Hernanda, is linked with it. A week ago, after the capture of the men who had gone ashore with Wolverstone, he decided to use the knowledge he had gained; that and my papers, of which he had, of course, possessed himself. He told me what he intended to do, and promised me that if by the use of my name and the rest he succeeded in delivering those followers of his, he would require no further ransom from me."

"And you? You agreed?"

"Agreed? Sometimes, indeed often, you are fatuous. My agreement was not asked. I was merely informed. Your own foolishness and the order of Saint James of Compostella did the rest. I suppose he conferred it upon you, and so dazzled you with it that you were prepared to believe anything he told you?"

"You were bringing it to me? It was among your papers?" quoth Don Jayme, who thought he began to understand.

There was a grim smile on Don Rodrigo's long, sallow face. "I was taking it to the Governor of Hispaniola Don Jayme de Guzman, to whom the letter was addressed."

Don Jayme's mouth fell open. He turned pale. "Not even that, then? The order was not intended for me? It was part of his infernal comedy?"

"You should have examined the letter more attentively."

"It was damaged by sea-water!" roared the Governor furiously.

"You should have examined your conscience, then. It would have told you that you had done nothing to deserve the cross of Saint James."

Don Jayme was too stunned to resent the gibe. Not until he was home again and in the presence of his wife did he recover himself sufficiently to hector her with the tale of how he had been bubbled. Thus he brought upon himself his worst humiliation.

"How does it come, madam," he demanded, "that you recognized him for your cousin?"

"I did not," she answered him, and dared at last to laugh at him, taking payment in that moment for all the browbeating she had suffered at his hands.

"You did not! You mean that you knew he was not your cousin?"

"That is what I mean."

"And you did not tell me?" The world was rocking about him.

"You would not allow me. When I told him that I did not remember that my Cousin Pedro had blue eyes, you told me that I never remembered anything, and you called me ninny. Because I did not wish to be called ninny again before a stranger I said nothing further."

Don Jayme mopped the sweat from his brow, and appealed in livid fury to her cousin Rodrigo, who stood by. "And what do you say to that?" he demanded.

"For myself, nothing. But I might remind you of Captain Blood's advice to you at parting. I think it was that in future you be more respectful to your wife."

IV - THE WAR INDEMNITY

If it was incredibly gallant, it was no less incredibly foolish of the *Atrevida* to have meddled with the *Arabella*, considering the Spaniard's inferior armament and the orders under which she sailed.

The *Arabella* had once been the *Cinco Llagas* out of Cadiz, of which Peter Blood had so gallantly possessed himself. He had so re-named her in honour of a lady in Barbadoes, whose memory was ever to serve him as an inspiration and to set restraint upon his activities as a buccaneer. She was going westward in haste to overtake her consorts, which were a full day ahead, was looking neither to right nor to left, when somewhere about 19°of northern longitude and 66°of western latitude, the *Atrevida* espied her, turned aside to steer across her course, and opened the attack by a shot athwart her hawse.

The Spaniard's commander, Don Vicente de Casanegra was actuated by a belief in himself that was tempered by no consciousness of his limitations.

The result was precisely what might have been expected. The *Arabella* went promptly about on a southern tack which presently brought her on to the *Atrevida's* windward quarter, thus scoring the first tactical advantage. Thence, whilst still out of range of the Spaniard's sakers, the *Arabella* poured in a crippling fire from her demi-cannons, which went far towards deciding the business. At closer quarters she followed this up with cross-bar and langrel, and so cut and slashed the *Atrevida's* rigging that she could no longer have fled, even had Don Vicente been prudently disposed to do so. Finally within pistol-range the *Arabella* hammered her with a broadside that converted the trim Spanish frigate into a staggering impotent hulk. When, after that, they grappled, the Spaniards avoided death by surrender, and it was to Captain Blood himself that the grey-faced, mortified Don Vicente delivered up his sword.

"This will teach you not to bark at me when I am passing peacefully by," said Captain Blood. "I see that you call yourself the *Atrevida*. But I account you more impudent than daring."

His opinion was even lower when, in the course of investigating his capture, he found among the ship's papers, a letter from the Spanish Admiral, Don Miguel de Espinosa y Valdez, containing Don Vicente's sailing orders. In these he was instructed to join the Admiral's squadron with all speed at Spanish Key off

Bieque, for the purpose of a raid upon the English settlement of Antigua. Don Miguel was conveniently expressive in his letter.

Although, he wrote, *his Catholic Majesty is at peace with England, yet England makes no endeavour to repress the damnable activities of the pirate Blood in Spanish waters. Therefore it becomes necessary to make reprisals and obtain compensation for all that Spain has suffered at the hands of this indemoniated filibuster.*

Having stowed the disarmed Spaniards under hatches--all save the rash Don Vicente, who, under parole, was taken aboard the *Arabella*--Blood put a prize crew into the *Atrevida*, patched up her wounds, and set a south-easterly course for the passage between Anegada and the Virgin Islands.

He explained the changed intentions which this implied at a council held that evening in the great cabin and attended by Wolverstone, his lieutenant, Pitt, his shipmaster, Ogle, who commanded on the main-deck, and two representatives of the main body of his followers, one of whom, Albin, was a Frenchman. This because one-third of the buccaneers aboard the *Arabella* at the time were French.

He met with some opposition when he announced the intention of making for Antigua.

This opposition was epitomized by Wolverstone who banged the table with a fist that was like a ham before delivering himself. "To Hell with King James and all who serve him! It's enough that we never make war upon English ships or English settlements. But I'll be damned if I account it our duty to protect folk whose hands are against us."

Captain Blood explained. "The impending Spanish raid is in the nature of reprisals for damage suffered by Spaniards at our hands. This seems to me to impose a duty upon us. We may not be patriots, as ye say, Wolverstone, and we may not be altruists. If we go to warn and remain to assist, we do so as mercenaries, whose services are to be paid for by a garrison which should be very glad to hire them, thus we reconcile duty with profit."

By these arguments he prevailed.

At dawn, having negotiated the passage, they hove to with the southernmost point of the Virgen Gorda on their starboard quarter, some four miles away. The sea being calm, Captain Blood ordered the boats of the *Atrevida* to be launched, and her Spanish crew to depart in them, whereafter the two ships proceeded on their way to the Leeward Islands.

Going south of Saba with gentle breezes, they were off the west coast of Antigua on the morning of the next day, and with the Union Jack flying from the maintruck they came to cast anchor in ten fathoms on the north side of the shoal that divides the entrance to Fort Bay.

A few minutes after noon, just as Colonel Courtney, the Captain-General of the Leeward Islands, whose seat of government was in Antigua, was sitting down to dinner with Mrs. Courtney and Captain Macartney, he was astounded by the announcement that Captain Blood had landed at St. John's and desired to wait upon him.

Colonel Courtney, a tall, dried-up man of forty-five, sandy and freckled, stared with pale, red-rimmed eyes at Mr. Ives, his young secretary, who had brought the message. "Captain Blood, did you say? Captain Blood? What Captain Blood? Surely not the damned pirate of that name, the gallows-bird from Barbadoes?"

Mr. Ives permitted himself to smile upon his excellency's excitement. "The same, sir."

Colonel Courtney flung his napkin amid the dishes on the spread table and rose, still incredulous. "And he's here? Here? Is he mad? Has the sun touched him? Stab me, I'll have him in irons for his impudence before I dine, and on his way to England before..." He broke off. "Egad!" he cried, and swung to his second in command. "We'd better have him in, Macartney."

Macartney's round face, as red as his coat, showed an amazement no less than the Governor's. That a rascal with a price on his head should have the impudence to pay a morning call on the governor of an English settlement was something that left Captain Macartney almost speechless and more incapable of thought than usual.

Mr. Ives admitted into the long, cool, sparsely-furnished room a tall, spare gentleman, very elegant in a suit of biscuit-coloured taffetas. A diamond of price gleamed amid the choice lace at his throat, a diamond buckle flashed from the band of the plumed hat he carried, a long pear-shaped pearl hung from his left ear and glowed against the black curls of his periwig. He leaned upon a gold-mounted ebony cane. So unlike a buccaneer was this modish gentleman that they stared in silence into the long, lean, sardonic countenance with its high-bridged nose, and eyes that looked startlingly blue and cold in a face that was burnt to the colour of a Red Indian's. More and more incredulous, the Colonel brought out a question with a jerk.

"You are Captain Blood?"

The gentleman bowed. Captain Macartney gasped and desired his vitals to be stabbed. The Colonel said "Egad!" again, and his pale eyes bulged. He looked at his pallid wife, at Macartney, and then again at Captain Blood. "You're a daring rogue. A daring rogue, egad!"

"I see you've heard of me."

"But not enough to credit this. Ye'll not have come to surrender?"

The buccaneer sauntered forward to the table. Instinctively Macartney rose.

"If you'll be reading this it will save a world of explanations," and he laid before his excellency the letter from the Spanish Admiral. "The fortune of war brought it into my hands together with the gentleman to whom it is addressed."

Colonel Courtney read, changed colour, and handed the sheet to Macartney. Then he stared again at Blood, who spoke as if answering the stare.

"It's here to warn you I am, and at need to serve you."

"To serve me?"

"Ye seem in need of it. Your ridiculous fort will not stand an hour under Spanish gunfire, and after that you'll have these gentlemen of Castile in the town.

Maybe you know how they conduct themselves on these occasions. If not, I'll be after telling you."

"But--stab me!" spluttered Macartney; "we're not at war with Spain!"

Colonel Courtney turned in cold fury upon Blood. "It is you who are the author of all our woes. It is your rascalities which bring these reprisals upon us."

"That's why I've come. Although I think I am a pretext rather than a reason." Captain Blood sat down. "You've been finding gold in Antigua, as I've heard. Don Miguel will have heard it too. Your militia garrison is not two hundred strong, and your fort, as I've said, is so much rubbish. I bring you a strong ship very heavily armed, and two hundred of the toughest fighting-men to be found in the Caribbean, or anywhere in the world. Of course I'm a damned pirate, and there's a price on my head, and if ye're fastidiously scrupulous yell have nothing to say to me. But if ye've any sense, as I hope ye have, it's thanking God ye'll be that I've come, and ye'll make terms with me."

"Terms?"

Captain Blood explained himself. His men did not risk their lives for the honour and glory of it, and there were in his following a number who were French, and who therefore lacked all patriotic feeling where a British colony was concerned. They would expect a trifle for the valuable services they were about to render.

"Also, Colonel," Blood concluded, "there's a point of honour for you. Whilst it may be difficult for you to enter into alliance with us, there's no difficulty about hiring us, and you may pursue us again without scruple once this job is done."

The Governor looked at him with gloomy eyes. "If I did my duty I would have you in irons and send you home to England to be hanged."

Captain Blood was unperturbed. "Your immediate duty is to preserve the colony of which ye're governor. Ye'll perceive its danger. And the danger is so imminent that even moments may count. Ye'd do well, faith, not to be wasting them."

The Governor looked at Macartney. Macartney's face was as blank as his mind. Then the lady, who had sat a scared and silent witness, suddenly stood up. Like her husband, she was tall and angular, and a tropical climate had prematurely aged her and consumed her beauty. Apparently, thought Blood, it had not consumed her reason.

"James, how can you hesitate? Think of what will happen to the women--the women and the children--if these Spaniards land. Remember what they did at Bridgetown."

The Governor stood with his chin upon his breast, frowning gloomily. "Yet I cannot enter into alliance with...I cannot make terms with outlaws. My duty here is clear. Quite clear." There was finality in his tone.

"Fiat officium, ruat ccelum," said the classical-minded Blood. He sighed, and rose. "If that's your last word, I'll be wishing you a very good day. I've no mind to be caught unawares by the Caribbean Squadron."

"You don't leave," said the Colonel sharply. "There too my duty is clear. The guard, Macartney."

"Och, don't be a fool now, Colonel." Blood's gesture arrested Macartney.

"I'm not a fool, sir, and I know what becomes me. I must do my duty."

"And is your duty demanding so scurvy a return for the valuable service I've already rendered you by my warning? Give it thought now, Colonel."

Again the Colonel's lady acted as Blood's advocate--and acted passionately in her clear apprehension of the only really material issue.

Exasperated, the Colonel flung himself down into his chair again. "But I cannot. I will not make terms with a rebel, an outlaw, a pirate. The dignity of my office...I...I cannot."

In his heart Captain Blood cursed the stupidity of governments that sent such men as this to represent them overseas.

"Will the dignity of your office restrain the Spanish Admiral, d'ye suppose?"

"And the women, James!" his lady again reminded him. "Surely, James, in this extreme need--a whole squadron coming to attack you--his majesty must approve your enlisting any aid."

Thus she began and thus continued, and now Macartney was moved to alliance with her against his excellency's narrow stubbornness, until in the end the Captain-General was brought to sacrifice dignity to expediency. Still reluctant, he demanded ill-humouredly to know the terms of the buccaneers.

"For myself," said Blood, "I ask nothing. I will organize your defences for the sake of the blood in my veins. But when the Spaniards have been driven off I shall require a hundred pieces of eight for each of my men. I have two hundred of them."

His excellency was scandalized. "Twenty thousand pieces!" He choked, and so far forgot his dignity as to haggle. But Blood was coldly firm, and in the end the price was agreed.

That afternoon he set to work upon the defences of St. John's.

Fort Bay is an inlet some two miles in depth and a mile across its widest part. It narrows a little at the mouth, forming a slight bottle-neck. In the middle of this neck ran a long, narrow spit of sand, partly uncovered at extreme low water, with a channel on either side. The southern channel was safe only for vessels of shallow draught; in the narrow, northern channel, however, at the entrance to which the *Arabella* now rode at anchor, there was never less than eight fathoms, at times slightly increased by the small tides of this sea, so that this was the only gateway to the bay.

The fort guarded this channel, occupying a shallow eminence on the northern promontory. It was a square, squat, machicolated structure of grey stone, and its armament consisted of a dozen ancient sakers and a half-dozen faucons with an extreme range of two thousand yards--guns these which provoked Captain Blood's contempt. He supplemented them by twelve sakers of more modern fashion, which he brought ashore from the *Atrevida*.

Twelve more guns he landed from the Spanish ship, including two twelve-pounders. These, however, he reserved for another purpose. Fifty yards west of the fort on the extreme edge of the promontory he set about the construction of earthworks--and set about it at a rate which allowed Colonel Courtney some insight into buccaneer methods and the secret of their success.

He landed a hundred of his men for the purpose and had them toiling almost naked in the broiling sun. To these he added three hundred whites and as many negroes from St. John's--practically the whole of its efficient male population--and he had them digging, banking, and filling the wickerwork gabions into the making of which he impressed the women. Others were sent to cut turf and fell trees, and fetch one and the other to the site of these operations. Throughout the afternoon the promontory seethed and crawled like an ant-heap. By sunset all was done. It seemed a miracle to the Captain-General. In six hours, under Blood's direction and the drive of his will, another fort had been constructed which by ordinary methods could not have been built in less than a week.

And it was not only built and armed with the remaining twelve guns brought from the *Atrevida* and with a half-dozen powerful demi-cannons landed from the *Arabella*; it was so effectively dissembled that from the sea no suspicion of its existence could be formed. Strips of turf faced it so that it merged into the background of shallow cliff; coconut palm stopped it and rose about it; clumps of white acacia and arnotto trees masked the gun emplacements so effectively as to render them invisible at half a mile.

Colonel Courtney conceived that here was a deal of wasted labour. Why trouble to conceal fortifications whose display should have the effect of deterring an assailant?

Blood explained. "If he's intimidated, he'll merely be postponing attack until some time when I'm not here to defend you. I mean either to destroy him or so to maul him that he'll be glad to leave British settlements alone in future."

That night Blood slept aboard the *Arabella* at her anchorage under the bluff. In the morning St. John's was awakened and alarmed by the sound of heavy gunfire. The Captain-General ran from his house in a bedgown, conceiving that the Spaniards were already here. The firing, however, proceeded from the new earthworks, and was directed upon the completely dismasted hull of the *Atrevida*, which had been anchored fore and aft athwart the narrow fairway, right in the middle of the channel.

The Captain-General dressed in haste, took horse, and rode out to the bluff with Macartney. As he reached it the firing ceased. The hulk, riddled with shot, was slowly settling down. She sank with a gurgle, as the now furious Governor flung himself from his horse beside the earthworks. Of Captain Blood, who with a knot of his rude followers was observing the end of the *Atrevida*, he stormily demanded to know in the name of Heaven and of Hell what folly this might be. Did Captain Blood realize that he had completely blocked the entrance to the harbour for all but vessels of the lightest draught?

"That was the aim," said Blood. "I've been at pains to find the shallowest part of the channel. She lies in six fathoms, reducing the depth to a bare two."

The Captain-General conceived that he was being mocked. Livid, he demanded why so insane a measure should have been taken, and this without consulting him. With a note of weariness in his voice Captain Blood explained what should have been obvious. It gave some pause to the Governor's anger. Yet the suspicions natural to a man of such limited vision were not quieted.

"But if to sink the hulk there was your only object, why in the devil's name did you waste shot and powder on her? Why didn't you scuttle her?"

Blood shrugged. "A little gunnery practice. We accomplished two objects in one."

"Gunnery practice?" His excellency was savage. "At that range? What are you telling me, man?"

"You'll understand better when Don Miguel arrives."

"I'll understand now, if you please. I will so. Stab me! Ye'll observe that I command here in Antigua."

Blood was annoyed. He had never learned to suffer fools gladly. "Faith, then your command outstrips your understanding if my object isn't plain. Meanwhile, there are some other matters yet to be settled, and time may be short." With that he swung on his heel, and left the Captain-General spluttering.

Blood had surveyed the coast and found a snug inlet, known as Willoughby's Cove, not two miles away, where the *Arabella* could lie concealed and yet so conveniently at hand that he and all his men might remain aboard. This at least was good news to Colonel Courtney, who was in dread of having pirates quartered on the town. Blood demanded that his men should be victualled, and required fifty head of cattle and twenty hogs. The Captain-General would have haggled with him, but was overborne in terms which did not improve their relations. The beasts were duly delivered, and in the days that followed the buccaneers became buccaneers in earnest; the boucan fires were lighted on the shores of Willoughby's Cove, and there the flesh of the slaughtered animals was boucanned, together with a quantity of turtle which the adventurers captured thereabouts.

In these peaceful arts three days were consumed, until the Captain-General began to ask himself if the whole thing were not some evil game to cover nefarious ends of Captain Blood and his pirates. Blood, however, explained the delay. Not until Don Miguel had abandoned hope of being joined by Don Vicente de Casanegra with the *Atrevida* would he decide to sail without him.

Another four days of inactivity went by, on each of which the Captain-General rode out to Willoughby's Cove to vent his suspicions in searching questions. The interviews increased daily in acrimony. Daily Blood expressed more and more plainly to the Captain-General that he saw little hope for the colonial future of a country which exercised so little discrimination in the election of her overseas governors.

IV - THE WAR INDEMNITY

Don Miguel's squadron appeared off Antigua only just in time to avert an open rupture between the Captain-General and his buccaneer ally.

Word being brought of this to Willoughby's Cove, early one Monday morning, by one of the guards left in charge of the earthworks, Captain Blood landed a hundred of his men and marched them across to the bluff. Wolverstone was left in command aboard. Ogle, that formidable gunner, was already quartered at the fort with a gun-crew.

Six miles out at sea, standing directly for the harbour of St. John's, with a freshening breeze from the north-west to temper the increasing heat of the morning sun, came four stately ships under full spread of sail, the banner of Castile afloat from the head of each mainmast.

From the parapet of the old fort Captain Blood surveyed them through his telescope. At his elbow, with Macartney in attendance, stood the Captain-General, persuaded at last that the Spanish menace was a reality.

Don Miguel commanded at the time the *Virgen del Pilar*, the finest and most powerful vessel in which he had yet sailed since Blood had sunk the *Milagrosa* some months before. She was a great black-hulled galleon of forty guns, including in her armament several heavy demi-cannon with a range of three thousand yards. Of the other three ships, two, if inferior, were still formidable thirty-gun frigates, whilst the last was really little better than a sloop of ten guns.

Blood closed his telescope and prepared for action in the old fort. The new one was for the moment left inactive.

Within a half-hour battle was joined. Don Miguel's advance had all the rashness which Blood knew of old. He made no attempt to shorten sail until within two thousand yards. He conceived, no doubt, that he was taking the place entirely unawares, and that the antiquated guns of the fort would probably be inadequate. Nevertheless, he must dispose of them before attempting to enter the harbour. To be sure of making short work of it, he continued to advance until Blood computed him within a thousand yards.

"On my soul," said Blood, "he'll be meaning to get within pistol-range, or else he thinks the fort of no account at all. Wake him up, Ogle. Let him have a salute."

Ogle's crew had been carefully laying their guns, and they had followed the advance with the twelve sakers from the *Atrevida*. Others stood at hand with linstocks, rammers and water-tubs, to serve the gunners.

Ogle gave the word, and the twelve guns were touched off as one, with a deafening roar. Within that easy range even the five-pound shot of these comparatively small cannon did some little damage to two of the Spanish ships. The moral effect of thus surprising those who came to surprise was even greater. The Admiral instantly signalled them to go about. In doing so they poured broadside after broadside into the fort, and for some minutes the place was a volcano, smoke and dust rising in a dense column above the flying stones and crumbling masonry. Blinded by it, the buccaneers had no vision of what the Spaniards might be doing. But Blood guessed it, and cleared every man from the fort into shelter behind it during the brief respite before the second broadsides came.

When that was over he drove them back again into the battered fortress, which for awhile now had nothing more to fear, and the original antiquated guns of St. John's were brought into action. The faucons were fired at random through the cloud of dust that hid them merely as a display and to let the Spaniards know that the fort was still alive. Then, as the cloud lifted, the five-pounders spoke, in twos and threes, carefully aimed at the ships which were now beating to windward. They did little damage; but this was less important than to keep the Spaniards in play.

Meanwhile the gun-crews were busy with the sakers from the *Atrevida*. Water-tubs had been emptied over them, and now with swabs and wads and rammers at work the reloading was proceeding.

The Captain-General, idle amid this terrific activity, required presently to know why powder was so ineffectively being wasted by these pop-guns, when in the earthworks there were cannon of long range which might be hammering the Spaniards with twenty-four and thirty-pound shot. When he was answered evasively, he passed from suggestion to command, whereupon he was invited not to interfere with carefully laid plans.

An altercation was saved by the return of the Spaniards to the attack and a repetition of all that had gone before. Again the fort was smashed and pounded, and this time two negroes were killed and a half-dozen buccaneers were injured by flying masonry, despite Blood's precaution to get them out of the place before the broadsides came.

When the second attack had been beaten off and the Spaniards were again retiring to reload, Blood resolved to withdraw the guns from the fort in which another half-dozen broadsides might completely bury them. Negroes and buccaneers and men of the Antiguan militia were indiscriminately employed on the business and harnessed to the guns. Even so it took an hour to get them all dear of the rubble and emplaced anew on the landward side of the fort, where Ogle and his men proceeded once more to load and carefully to lay them. The body of the fort meanwhile served to screen the operation from the Spaniards as they sailed in for the third time. Now the English held their fire whilst another storm of metal crashed upon those battered but now empty ramparts. When it was over, the fort was a shapeless heap of rubble, and the little army lying concealed behind the ruins heard the Spanish cheer that announced their conviction that all was done, since no single shot had been fired to answer their bombardment.

Proudly, confidently, Don Miguel came on. No need now to stand off to reload. Already the afternoon was well advanced and he would house his men in St. John's before nightfall. The haze of dust and smoke, whilst serving to screen the defenders and their new emplacements from the sight of the enemy, could yet be penetrated at close quarters by the watchful eyes of the buccaneers. The *Virgen del Pilar* was within five hundred yards of the harbour's mouth, when six sakers, charged now with langrel, chain and cross-bar, swept her decks with murderous effect and some damage to her shrouds. Six faucons, similarly charged, followed after a moment's pause, and if their fire was less effective yet it served to increase the confusion and the alarm of so unexpected an attack.

In the pause they could hear the blare of a trumpet aboard the *Virgen*, screeching the Admiral's orders to the other ships of his squadron. Then, as in the haste of their manoeuvre to go about the Spaniards yawed a moment, broadside on, Blood gave the signal, and two by two the remaining sakers sent their five-pound round shot in search of Spanish timbers. Odd ones took effect, and one very fortunate cannon ball smashed the mainmast of one of the frigates. In her rippled state and the desperate haste resulting from it, she fouled the sloop, and before the two vessels could disentangle themselves and follow the retreat of the others, their decks had been raked again and again by langrel and cross-bar from water-cooled and hurriedly reloaded guns.

Blood, who had been crouching with the rest, stood up at last as the firing ceased, its work temporarily accomplished. He looked into the long, solemn face of Colonel Courtney and laughed.

"Faith! It's another slaughter of the innocents, so it is!"

The Captain-General smiled sourly back at him. "If you had done as I desired you--"

Blood interrupted without ceremony. "On my soul, now! Are ye not content? If I'd done as you desired me, I'd have put all my cards on the table by now. It's saving my trumps I am until the Admiral plays as I want him to."

"And if the Admiral doesn't, Captain Blood?"

"He will, for one thing because it's in the nature of him; for another because there's no other way to play at all. And so ye may go home and sleep in peace, placing your trust in Providence and me."

"I do not care for the association, sir," said the Governor frostily.

"But you will. On my soul, you will. For we do fine things when we work together, Providence and I."

An hour before sunset the Spaniards were hove to a couple of miles out at sea, and becalmed. The Antiguans, white and black, dismissed by Blood, went home to sup--all but some two score whom he retained for emergencies. Then his buccaneers sat down under the sky to a generous supply of meat and a limited amount of rum.

The sun went down into the jade waters of the Caribbean, and darkness followed almost as upon the extinction of a lamp--the soft, purple darkness of a moonless night irradiated by a myriad stars.

Captain Blood stood up and nosed the air. The north-westerly breeze, which had died down towards evening, was springing up again. He ordered all res and lights to be extinguished, so as to encourage that for which he hoped.

Out at sea in the fine cabin of the *Virgen del Pilar*, the proud, noble, brave, incompetent admiral of the Caribbean held a council of war which was no council, for he had summoned his captains merely so that he might impose his will upon them. At dead midnight, by when all in St. John's should be asleep, in the conviction that no further attack would come until morning, they would creep past the fort under cover of darkness and with all lights extinguished. Daylight should find them at anchor a mile or more beyond it, in the bay, with their guns trained upon the town. That must be checkmate to the Antiguans.

Upon this they acted, and with sails trimmed to the favouring breeze, and shortened so as to lessen the gurgle of water at their prows, they nosed gently forward through the velvety gloom. With the *Virgen* leading they reached the entrance of the harbour and the darker waters between the shadowy bluffs on either side. Here all was deathly still. Not a light showed save the distant phosphorescent line where the waters met the shore; not a sound disturbed the stillness save the silken rustle of the sea against their sides.

Already within two hundred yards of the fort, and of the spot where the *Atrevida* had been sunk to block the channel, the *Virgen* crept on, her bulwarks lined with silent, watchful men, Don Miguel, leaning immovable as a statue upon the poop-rail. He was abreast of the fort and counting the victory already won, when suddenly his keel grated, and, grating ever harder, drove shuddering onwards for some yards, to be finally gripped and held as if by some monstrous hand in the depths below, whilst overhead under pressure of a wind to which the vessel no longer yielded, the sails drummed loudly to an accompaniment of groaning cordage and clattering blocks.

And then, before the Admiral could even conjecture what had happened to him, the gloom to larboard was split by flame, the silence smashed by a roar of guns, the rending of timbers, and the crashing of spars, as the demi-cannons landed from the *Arabella*, and held in reserve until now in the dissembled earthworks, hurled their thirty-two-pound shot into the Spanish flagship at merciless short range. The deadly accuracy of these guns might have revealed to Colonel Courtney precisely why Captain Blood had elected to sink the *Atrevida* by gunfire instead of scuttling her. Thus he had obtained the exact range which enabled him to fire so accurately through the darkness.

One frantic, wildly-aimed broadside the *Virgen* discharged in answer before, smashed and riddled and held above water only by the hulk on which she had stuck fast, the Admiral abandoned her. With his survivors he clambered aboard one of the frigates, the *Indiana*, which, unable to check her way in time, had crashed into him astern. Moving very slowly, the *Indiana* had suffered little damage beyond a smashed bowsprit, and her captain, acting promptly, had taken in what little sail he carried.

Mercifully at that moment the guns ashore were reloading. In that brief respite the *Indiana* received the fugitives from the flagship, whilst the sloop which had been next in line, perceiving the situation, took in all sail at once, and getting out her sweeps, warped the *Indiana* astern from her entanglement, and out into the open, where the other frigate lay hove to firing desultorily in the direction of the now silent earthworks on the bluff. The only effect of this was to betray her whereabouts to the buccaneers, and presently the demi-cannons were roaring again, though no longer collectively. A shot from one of them completed the crippling of the *Indiana* by smashing her rudder; so that having been warped out of the harbour she had to be taken in tow by her sister ship.

The firing ceased on both sides, and the peace and silence of the tropical night would again have descended on St. John's but that all in the town were now afoot and hastening out to the bluff for information.

When daylight broke the only ship on the blue expanse of the Caribbean within the vision of Antigua was the red-hulled *Arabella* at anchor in the shadow of the bluff to receive the demi-cannons she had lent the enterprise, and the battered *Virgen del Pilar* listing heavily to starboard where she had stuck on the submerged hull of the *Atrevida.* About the wrecked flagship swarmed a fleet of small boats and canoes in which the buccaneers were salving every object of value to be found aboard her. They brought all ashore: arms and armour, some of great price, a service of gold plate, vessels of gold and silver, two steel-bound coffers being, presumably, the treasury of the squadron and containing some six thousand pieces of eight, besides jewels, clothes, oriental carpets and rich brocades from the great cabin. All were piled up beside the fort for subsequent division as provided by the articles under which the buccaneers sailed.

A string of four pack-mules came along the shallow cliff as the salving was concluded and drew up beside the precious heap.

"What's this?" quoth Blood, who was present at the spot.

"From his excellency the Captain-General," replied the negro muleteer, "fo' dah conveying ob dah treasure."

Blood was taken aback. When he recovered: "Much obliged," said he, and ordered the mules to be laden and conducted to the end of the bluff, to the boats which were to carry the spoils aboard the *Arabella.*

After that he went to wait upon the Captain-General.

He was shown into a long narrow room from one end of which a portrait of his late sardonic majesty King Charles II looked into a mirror on the other. There was a long, narrow table on which stood some books, a guitar, a bowl of heavily-scented white acacia, and there were some tall-backed chairs of black oak without upholstery.

The Captain-General came in followed by Macartney. His face looked longer and narrower than ever.

Captain Blood, telescope under his arm and plumed hat in his hand, bowed low.

"I come to take my leave, your excellency."

"I was about to send for you." The Colonel's pale eyes sought to meet the Captain's steady gaze, but failed. "I hear of considerable treasure taken from the Spanish wreck. I am told your men have carried this aboard your ship. You are aware, sir--or are you not?--that these spoils are the property of the King?"

"I am not aware of it," said Captain Blood. "You are not? Then I inform you of it now." Captain Blood shook his head, smiling tolerantly.

"It is a prize of war."

"Exactly. And the war was being waged on behalf of his majesty and in defence of this his majesty's colony."

"Save that I did not hold the King's commission."

"Tacitly, and temporarily, I granted it you when I consented to enlist you and your men in the defence of the island."

Blood stared at him in amused astonishment.

"What were you, sir, before they made you Captain-General of the Leeward Islands? A lawyer?"

"Captain Blood, I think you mean to be insolent."

"You may be sure I do, and more. You consented to enlist me, did you? Here's condescension! Where should you be now if I hadn't brought you the assistance you consented to receive?"

"We will take one thing at a time, if you please." The Colonel was coldly prim. "When you entered the service of King James, you became subject to the laws that govern his forces. Your appropriation of treasure from the Spanish flagship is an act of brigandage contrary to all those laws and severely punishable under them."

Captain Blood found the situation increasingly humorous. He laughed.

"My clear duty," added Colonel Courtney, "is to place you under arrest."

"But I hope you're not thinking of performing it?"

"Not if you choose to take advantage of my leniency, and depart at once."

"I'll depart as soon as I receive the twenty thousand pieces of eight for which I hired you my services."

"You have chosen, sir, to take payment in another fashion. You have committed a breach of the law. I have nothing more to say to you, Captain Blood."

Blood considered him with narrowing eyes. Was the man so utterly a fool, or was he merely dishonest?

"Oh, sharper than the serpent's tooth!" he laughed. "Sure now I must spend the remainder of my days in succouring British colonies in distress. Meanwhile, here I am and here I stay until I have my twenty thousand pieces." He flung his hat on the table, drew up a chair, sat down, and crossed his legs. "It's a warm day, Colonel, so it is."

The Colonel's eyes flashed. "Captain Macartney, the guard is waiting in the gallery. Be good enough to call it."

"Will ye be intending to arrest me?"

The Colonel's eyes gloomed at him. "Naturally, sir. It is my clear duty. It has been my duty from the moment that you landed here. You show me that I should have considered nothing else whatever my own needs." He waved a hand to the soldier who had paused by the door. "If you please, Captain Macartney."

"Oh, a moment yet, Captain Macartney. A moment yet, Colonel." Blood raised his hand. "This amounts to a declaration of war."

The Colonel shrugged contemptuously. "You may so regard it if you choose. It is not material."

Captain Blood's doubts about the man's honesty were completely dissipated. He was just a fool with a mental vision that could perceive one object only at a time.

"Indeed, and it's most material. Since you declare war on me, war you shall have; and I warn you that you'll find me as ruthless an opponent as the Spaniards found me yesterday when I was your ally."

"By God!" swore Macartney. "Here's fine talk from a man whose person we hold!"

"Others have held me before, Captain Macartney. Don't be attaching too much importance to that." He paused to smile, and then resumed. "It's fortunate now for Antigua that the war you have declared on me may be fought without bloodshed. Indeed, you may perceive at a glance that it has been fought already, that the strategic advantages lie with me, and, therefore, that nothing remains for you but capitulation."

"I perceive nothing of the kind, sir."

"That is because you are slow to perceive the obvious. I am coming to think that at home they regard this as a necessary qualification in a Colonial Governor. A moment's patience, Colonel, while I point out to you that my ship is off the harbour. She carries two hundred of the toughest fighting-men, who would devour your spineless militia at a gulp. She carries forty guns, the half of which could be landed on the bluff within an hour, and within another hour St. John's would be a dust-heap. If you think they would hesitate because this colony is English, I'll remind you that a third of my following is French and the other two-thirds are outlaws like myself. They would sack this town with pleasure, firstly because it is held in the name of King James, a name detestable to all of them, and secondly because the gold you have been finding in Antigua should make it well worth the sacking."

Macartney, purple in the face, was fingering his sword-hilt. But it was the Colonel, livid with passion, who answered, waving one of his bony freckled hands.

"You infamous pirate scoundrel! You damned escaped convict! You've forgot one thing: that until you can get back to your pestilential buccaneers none of this can happen."

"We have to thank him for the warning, sir," Captain Macartney jeered.

"Ah, bah! Ye've no imagination, as I suspected yesterday. Your muleteer gave me a glimpse of what to expect from you. I took my measures accordingly, so I did. I left orders with my lieutenant to assume at twelve o'clock that war had been declared, and to land the guns and haul them to the fort, whence they command the town. I left your mules with him for the purpose." He glanced at the timepiece on the overmantel. "It's nearly half-past twelve already. From your windows here you can see the fort." He stood up and proffered his telescope. "Assure yourself that what I have said is happening."

There was a pause in which the Captain-General considered him with eyes of hate. Then in silence he took the telescope and went to the window. When he turned from it again he was fierce as a rattlesnake. "But you forget one thing still. That we hold you. I'll send word to your pirate scum that at the first shot from them I'll hang you. The guard, Macartney. There's been talk enough."

"Oh, a moment yet," Blood begged. "Ye're so plaguily hasty in your conclusions. Wolverstone has my orders, and no threat to my life will swerve him from them by a hair's breadth. Hang me if you will." He shrugged. "If I set great store by life I should hardly follow the trade of a buccaneer. But when you've hanged me be sure that not one stone of St. John's will be left upon another, not man, woman or child will my buccaneers spare in avenging me. Consider that, and consider at the same time your duty to this colony and to your King--this duty by which you rightly set such store."

The Governor's pale eyes stabbed him as if they would reach his soul. Calm and intrepid he stood before them, so calm in all the circumstances as almost to intimidate.

The Colonel looked at Macartney, as if for help. He found none there. Irritably he broke out at last: "Oh, stab me! I am well served for dealing with a pirate. To be rid of you, I'll pay you your twenty thousand pieces, and so farewell and be damned to you."

"Twenty thousand pieces!" Blood raised his eyebrows in surprise. "But that was whilst I was your ally; that was before ye declared war upon me."

"What the devil do you mean now?"

"That since ye admit defeat, we will pass to the discussion of terms."

"Terms! What terms?" The Captain-General's exasperation was swiftly mounting.

"You shall hear them. First, the twenty thousand pieces of eight that you owe my men for services rendered. Next, thirty thousand for the redemption of the town from the bombardment that is preparing."

"What? By God, sir!..."

"Next," Captain Blood pursued relentlessly, "ten thousand pieces for your own ransom, ten thousand for the ransom of your own family, and five thousand for that of other persons of consequence in St. John's, including Captain Macartney here. That makes seventy-five thousand pieces of eight, and they must be paid within the next hour, since later will be too late."

The Captain-General looked unutterable things. He tried to speak. But speech failed him. He sat down heavily. At last he found his voice. It came thick and quavering.

"You...you abuse my patience. You surely...You think me mad?"

"Best hang him, Colonel, and have done," Macartney exploded.

"And thereby destroy the colony it is your duty at all costs--at all costs, mark you--to preserve."

The Captain-General passed a hand across his wet, pallid brow, and groaned.

They talked, of course, for some time yet; but ever within the circle of what had been said already, until in the end Colonel Courtney broke into a laugh that was almost hysterical.

"Stab me, sir! It only remains to marvel at your moderation. You might have asked seven hundred thousand pieces, or seven millions--"

"True," Blood interrupted him. "But then I am by nature moderate, and also I have a notion of the resources of your treasury."

"But the time!" cried the Governor desperately, to show that he had yielded. "How can I collect the sum within an hour?"

"I'll be reasonable. Send me the money to the bluff by sunset, and I'll withdraw. And now I'll take my leave at once, so as to suspend the operations. It's a very good day I'll be wishing you."

They let him go, perforce. And at sunset Captain Macartney rode out to the gun emplacements of the buccaneers followed by a negro leading a mule on which the gold was laden.

Captain Blood came forward alone to receive him. "It isn't what you'd have got from me," said the choleric captain through his teeth.

"I'll remember that in case you should ever command a settlement. And now, sir, to business. What do these sacks hold?"

"You'll find five thousand pieces in each."

"Then set me down four of them: the twenty thousand pieces for which I agreed to serve Antigua. The rest you can take back to the Captain-General with my compliments. Let the experience teach him, and you too, Captain darling, that a man's first duty is less to his office than to his own honour, and that he cannot perform it unless he fulfils the engagements of his word."

Captain Macartney sucked in his breath. "Gads-life!" he exclaimed huskily. "And you're a pirate!"

Sternly came the vibrant metallic voice of the buccaneer. "I am Captain Blood."

V - BLOOD MONEY

Captain Blood was pleased with the world--which is but another way of saying that he was pleased with himself.

He stood on the mole at Cayona and surveyed the shipping in the rockbound harbour. With pride he considered the five great ships that now made up his fleet, every spar and timber of which had once been the property of Spain. There was his own flagship, the *Arabella*, of forty guns, that once had been the *Cinco Llagas* out of Cadiz, with her red bulwarks and gilded ports aflame in the evening sunlight, with the scarcely less powerful blue and white *Elizabeth* beside her. Beyond them rode the three smaller twenty-gun vessels captured in the great affair at Maracaybo from which Blood was lately returned. These ships, originally named the *Infanta*, the *San Felipe*, and the *Santo Niño*, Blood had renamed after the three Parcae, the *Clotho*, the *Lachesis*, and the *Atropos*, by which it was his intention playfully to convey that they were the arbiters of the fate of any Spaniard henceforth encountered by them upon the seas.

Captain Blood took satisfaction in his own delicate, scholarly humour. He was, as I have said, well pleased with himself. His following numbered close upon a thousand men, and he could double this number whenever he pleased. For his luck was passing into a proverb, and luck is the highest quality that can be sought in a leader of hazardous enterprises. Not the great Henry Morgan himself in his best days had wielded such authority and power. Not even Montbar--surnamed by Spain the Exterminator--had been more dreaded by Spaniards in his day that was Don Pedro Sangre, as they translated Peter Blood's name, accounting it most apt.

Order, he knew, was being taken against him. Not only the King of Spain, of whose power he had made a mock, but also the King of England, whom he accounted, and with some reason, a contemptible fellow, were concerting measures for his destruction; and news had lately come to Tortuga that, nearer at hand, the Spanish Admiral, Don Miguel de Espinosa, who had been the latest and most terrible sufferer at his hands, had proclaimed that he would pay ten thousand pieces of eight to any man who should deliver up to him the person of Captain Blood alive. Don Miguel's was a vindictiveness that was not to be satisfied by mere death.

Peter Blood was not intimidated, nor on that account was he likely to mistrust his luck so much as to let himself run to rust in the security of Tortuga. For that which he had suffered--and he had suffered much--at the hands of man, he had chosen to make Spain the scapegoat. Thus he accounted that he served a twofold purpose. He took compensation, and at the same time served, not indeed the Stuart King, whom he despised--although himself born an Irishman and bred a Papist--but England, and, for that matter, all the rest of civilized mankind, which cruel, treacherous, greedy, bigoted Castile sought to debar from intercourse with the New World.

He was turning from the mole, almost deserted by now of its usual bustling heterogeneous crowd, when the voice of Hayton, the boatswain of the *Arabella*, called after him from the boat that had brought him ashore.

"Back at eight bells, Captain?"

"At eight bells," said Blood over his shoulder, and sauntered on, swinging his long ebony cane, elegant and courtly in a suit of grey and silver.

He took his way up towards the town, saluted as he went by most of those whom he met, and stared at by the rest. He chose to go by way of the wide, unpaved Rue du Roi de France, which the townsfolk had sought to embellish by flanking it with rows of palm-trees. As he approached the tavern of The King of France the little crowd about its portals drew to attention. From within came a steady drone of voices as a muffled accompaniment to foul exclamations, snatches of coarse songs, and the shrill, foolish laughter of women. Through all ran the rattle of dice and the clinking of drinking-cans.

Blood realized that his buccaneers were making merry with the gold they had brought back from Maracaybo. The ruffians overflowing from that house of infamy hailed him with a ringing cheer. Was he not the king of all the ruffians that made up the great Brotherhood of the Coast?

He acknowledged their greeting by a lift of the hand that held the cane, and passed on. He had business with M. d'Ogeron, the Governor, and this business took him now to the handsome white house crowning the eminence to the east of the town.

The Captain was an orderly, provident man, and he was busily providing against the day when the death or downfall of King James II might make it possible for him to return home. For some time now it had been his practice to make over the bulk of his share of prizes to the Governor against bills of exchange on France, which he forwarded to Paris for collection and deposit. Peter Blood was ever a welcome visitor at the Governor's house, not only because these transactions were profitable to M. d'Ogeron, but in a still deeper measure because of a signal service that the Captain had once done him and his in rescuing his daughter Madeleine from the hands of a ruffianly pirate who had attempted to carry her off. By M. d'Ogeron, his son and his two daughters, Captain Blood had ever since been regarded as something more than an ordinary friend.

It was therefore nowise extraordinary that when, his business being transacted, he was departing on this particular evening, Mademoiselle d'Ogeron should choose to escort Captain Blood down the short avenue of her father's fragrant garden.

A pale-faced, black-haired beauty, tall and statuesque of figure, and richly gowned in the latest mode of France, Mademoiselle d'Ogeron was as romantic of appearance as of temperament. And as she stepped gracefully beside the Captain in the gathering dusk she showed her purpose to be not without a certain romantic quality also.

"Monsieur," she said in French, hesitating a little, "I have come to implore you to be ever on your guard. You have too many enemies."

He halted and, half-turning, hat in hand, he bowed until his long black ringlets almost met across his clear-cut, gipsy-tinted face.

"Mademoiselle, your concern is flattering; but so flattering." Erect again, his bold eyes, so startlingly light under their black brows and in a face so burnt and swarthy, laughed into her own. "I do not want for enemies, true. It is the penalty of greatness. Only he who is without anything is without enemies. But at least they are not in Tortuga."

"Are you so very sure of that?"

Her tone gave him pause. He frowned, and considered her solemnly for an instant before replying.

"Mademoiselle, you speak as if from some knowledge."

"Hardly so much. My knowledge is but the knowledge of what a slave told me to-day. He says that the Spanish Admiral has placed a price upon your head."

"That is just the Spanish Admiral's notion of flattery, mademoiselle."

"And that Cahusac has been heard to say he will make you rue the wrong you did him at Maracaybo."

"Cahusac?"

The name revealed to him the rashness of his assertion that he had no enemy in Tortuga. He had forgotten Cahusac; but he realized that Cahusac would not be likely to have forgotten him. Cahusac had been with him at Maracaybo, and had been trapped with him there by the arrival of Don Miguel de Espinosa's fleet. The French rover had taken fright, had charged Blood with rashness in his conduct of the enterprise, had quarrelled with him and had made terms with the Spanish Admiral for himself and his own French contingent. Granted a safe-conduct by Don Miguel, he had departed empty-handed, leaving Captain Blood to his fate. But it proved not at all as the timorous Cahusac conceived it. Captain Blood had not only broken out of the Spanish trap, but he had sorely mauled the Admiral, captured three of his ships, and returned to Tortuga laden with rich spoils of victory.

To Cahusac this was gall and wormwood. With the faculty for confusing cause and effect which is the chief disability of stupid egoists, he came to account himself cheated by Captain Blood. And he was making no secret of his unfounded resentment.

"He is saying that, is he?" said Captain Blood. "Now, that is indiscreet of him. Besides, all the world knows he was not wronged. He was allowed to depart in safety as he wished when he thought the situation grew too dangerous."

"But by doing so he sacrificed his share of the prizes, and for that he and his companions have since been the mock of Tortuga. Can you not conceive what must be that ruffian's feelings?"

They had reached the gate.

"You will take precautions? You will guard yourself?" she begged him.

He smiled upon her friendly anxiety.

"If only so that I may live on to serve you." With formal courtesy he bowed low over her hand and kissed it.

Seriously concerned, however, by her warning he was not. That Cahusac should be vindictive he could well believe. But that Cahusac should utter threats here in Tortuga was an indiscretion too dangerous to be credible in the case of a cur who took no risks.

He stepped out briskly through the night that was closing down, soft and warm, and came soon within sight of the lights of the Rue du Roi de France. As he reached the head of that now deserted thoroughfare a shadow detached itself from the mouth of a lane on his right to intercept him.

Even as he checked: prepared to fall on guard, he made out the figure to be a woman's, and heard his name called softly in a woman's voice.

"Captain Blood!"

As he halted she came closer, and addressed him quickly, breathlessly. "I saw you pass two hours since. But I dursn't be seen speaking to you in daylight here in the street. So I have been on the watch for your return. Don't go on, Captain. You are walking into danger; walking to your death."

At last his puzzled mind recognized her: and before the eyes of his memory flashed a scene enacted a week ago at The King of France. Two drunken ruffians had quarrelled over a woman--a fragment of the human wreckage of Europe washed up on the shores of the New World--an unfortunate creature of a certain comeliness, which, however, like the castoff finery she wore, was tarnished, soiled, and crumpled. The woman, arrogating a voice in a dispute of which she was the object, was brutally struck by one of her companions, and Blood, upon an impulse of chivalrous anger, had felled her assailant and escorted her from the place.

"They're lying in wait for you down yonder," she was saying, "and they mean to kill you."

"Who does?" he asked her, Mademoiselle d'Ogeron's words of warning sharply recalled.

"There's a score of them. And if they was to know--if they was to see me here a-warning you--my own throat would be cut before morning."

She peered fearfully about her through the gloom as she spoke, and fear quivered in her voice. Then she cried out huskily, as if with mounting terror.

"Oh, don't let us stand here! Come with me; I'll make you safe until daylight. Then you can go back to your ship, and if you're wise you'll stay on board after this, or else come ashore in company. Come!" she ended, and caught him by the sleeve.

"Whisht now! Whisht!" said he, resisting the pressure on his arm. "Whither will you be taking me!"

"Oh, what odds, so long as I make you safe?" She was dragging on him with all her weight. "You was kind to me, and I can't leave you to be killed. And we'll both be murdered unless you come."

Yielding at last, as much for her sake as his own, he allowed her to lead him from the wide street into the byway from which she had issued to intercept him. It was a narrow lane with little one-storied houses that were mostly timber standing at wide intervals along one side of it. Along the other ran a palisade enclosing a plantation.

At the second house she stopped. The little door stood open, and the interior was dimly lighted by the naked flame of a brass oil lamp set upon a table.

"Go in," she bade him in a shuddering whisper.

Two steps led down to the floor of the house, which was below the level of the street. Down these went Captain Blood, and on into the room, whose air was rank with the reek of stale tobacco and the sickly odour of the little oil lamp. The woman followed, and closed the door. And then, before Captain Blood could turn to inspect his surroundings in that dim light, he was struck over the head from behind with something heavy and hard-driven, which, if it did not stun him outright, at least stretched him sick and faint upon the grimy naked earth of the unpaved floor.

At the same moment a woman's scream, that ended abruptly in a stifled gurgle, cut sharply upon the silence.

In an instant, before Captain Blood could move to help himself, before he could even recover from his bewildered surprise, swift, sinewy, skilful hands had done their work upon him. Thongs of hide lashed his ankles and his wrists, which' had been dragged behind him. Then he was rolled over on to his back, lifted, forced into a chair, and lashed by the waist to that.

A man of low stature and powerful, apelike build, long in the body and short in the legs, was leaning over him. The sleeves of his blue shirt were rolled to the elbows of his prodigious, long, muscular and hairy arms. Little black eyes twinkled wickedly in a broad face that was almost as flat and sallow as a mulatto's. A red and blue scarf swathed his head, completely concealing his hair; heavy gold rings hung in the lobes of the great ears.

Captain Blood considered him for a long moment, setting a curb upon the violent rage that rose in him in a measure as his senses cleared. Instinctively he realized that violence and passion would help him not at all, and that at all costs they must be suppressed. And he suppressed them.

"Cahusac!" he said slowly. And then added: "This is an unexpected pleasure entirely!"

"Ye've dropped anchor at last, Captain," said Cahusac, and he laughed softly with infinite malice.

Blood looked beyond him towards the door, where the woman was writhing in the grasp of Cahusac's companion.

"Will you be quiet, you slut, or must I quiet you?" the ruffian was threatening.

"What are you going to do with him, Sam?" she whimpered.

"No business of yours, my girl."

"Oh yes, it is! You told me he was in danger, and I believed you, you lying tyke!"

"Well, so he was. But he's safe and snug now. You go in there, Molly." He pointed across the room to the black entrance of an alcove.

"I'll not--" she was beginning angrily.

"Go on," he snarled, "or it'll be the worse for you!"

He seized her roughly again at neck and waist and thrust her, still resisting, across the room and into the alcove. He closed the door and bolted it.

"Stay you there, you slut, and keep quiet, or I'll quiet you once for all."

From behind the door he was answered by a moan. Then there was the creak of a bed as the woman flung herself violently upon it, and thereafter silence.

Captain Blood accounted her part in this business explained, and more or less ended. He looked up into the face of his sometime associate, and his lips smiled to simulate a calm he was far from feeling.

"Would it be an impertinence to inquire what ye're intending, Cahusac?" said he.

Cahusac's companion laughed, and lounged across the table, a tall, loose-limbed fellow, with a long face of an almost Indian cast of features. His dress implied the hunter. He answered for Cahusac, who glowered, morosely silent.

"We intend to hand you over to Don Miguel de Espinosa."

He stooped to give his attention to the lamp, pulling up the wick and trimming it, so that the light in the shabby little room was suddenly increased.

"C'est ça!" said Cahusac. "And Don Miguel, no doubt, he'll intend to hang you from the yardarm."

"So Don Miguel's in this, is he? Glory be! I suppose it's the blood-money that's tempted ye. Sure now, it's the very work that ye're fitted for, devil a doubt. But have ye considered all? There are reefs ahead, my lad. Hayton was to have met me with a boat at the mole at eight bells. I'm late as it is. Eight bells was made an hour ago and more. Presently they'll take alarm. They knew where I was going. They'll follow and track me. To find me, the boys will be turning Tortuga inside out like a sack. And what'll happen to ye then, Cahusac? Have you thought of that? The pity of it is that ye're entirely without foresight. It was lack of foresight that sent ye away empty-handed from Maracaybo. And even then, but for me, ye'd be hauling at the oar of a Spanish galley this very minute. Yet ye're aggrieved, being a poor-spirited, cross-grained cur, and to vent your spite you're running straight upon destruction. If ye've a spark of sense you'll haul in sail, my lad, and heave-to before it's too late."

Cahusac leered at him for only answer, and then in silence went through the Captain's pockets. The other, meanwhile, sat down on a three-legged stool of pine.

"What's o'clock, Cahusac?" he asked.

Cahusac consulted the Captain's watch.

"Near half-past nine, Sam."

"Plague on it!" grumbled Sam. "Three hours to wait!"

"There's dice in the cupboard," said Cahusac, "and here's something to be played for."

He jerked his thumb towards the yield of Captain Blood's pockets, which made a little pile upon the table. There were some twenty gold pieces, a little silver, an onion-shaped gold watch, a gold tobacco-box, a pistol, and, lastly, a jewel which Cahusac had detached from the lace at the Captain's throat, besides a sword and rich balrick of grey leather heavily wrought in gold.

Sam rose, went to a cupboard, and fetched thence the dice. He set them on the table, and drawing up his stool, again resumed his seat. The money he divided into two equal halves. Then he added the sword and the watch to one pile, and the jewel, the pistol, and the tobacco-box to the other.

Blood, very alert and watchful--so concentrated, indeed, upon the problem of winning free from this trap that he was hardly conscious of the pain in' his head from the blow that had felled him--began to speak again. Resolutely he refused to admit the fear and hopelessness that were knocking at his heart.

"There's another thing ye've not considered," said he slowly, almost drawlingly, "and that is that I might be willing to ransom myself at a far more handsome price than the Spanish Admiral has offered for me."

But they weren't impressed. Cahusac merely mocked him.

"Tiens! And your certainty that Hayton will come to your rescue then? What of that?"

He laughed, and Sam laughed with him.

"It's probable," said Blood, "most probable. But not certain; nothing is, in this uncertain world. Not even that the Spaniard will pay you the ten thousand pieces of eight they tell me he has been after offering for me. You could make a better bargain with me, Cahusac."

He paused, and his keen, watchful glance observed the sudden gleam of covetousness in the Frenchman's eye, as well as the frown contracting the brow of the other ruffian. Therefore he continued.

"You might make such a bargain as would compensate you for what you missed at Maracaybo. For every thousand pieces that the Spaniard offers, sure now I'll offer two."

Cahusac's jaw fell, his eyes widened.

"Twenty thousand pieces!" he gasped in blank amazement.

And then Sam's great fist crashed down upon the rickety table, and he swore foully and fiercely.

"None of that!" he roared. "I've made my bargain, and I abides by it. It'll be the worse for me if I doesn't--ay, and for you, Cahusac. Besides, are you such a gull that you think this pretty hawk'll keep faith with you?"

"He knows that I would," said Blood, "he's sailed with me. He knows that my word is accounted good even by Spaniards."

"Maybe. But it's not accounted good by me." Sam stood over him, the long, evil face, with its sloping brows and heavy eyelids, grown dark and menacing. "I'm pledged to deliver you safely at midnight, and when I pledges myself to a job I does it. Understand?"

Captain Blood looked up at him, and actually smiled.

"Faith," said he. "You don't leave much to a man's imagination."

And he meant it literally; for what he had clearly gathered was that it was Sam who had entered into league with the Spanish agents, and dared not for his life's sake break with them.

"Then that's as well," Sam assured him. "If you want to be spared the discomfort of a gag for the next three hours, you'll just hold your plaguey tongue. Understand that?"

He thrust his long face forward into his captive's, sneering and menacing.

Understanding, Captain Blood abandoned his desperate clutch of the only slender straw of hope that he had discovered in the situation. He realized that he was to wait here, helpless in his bonds, until the time appointed for his delivery to someone who should carry him off to Don Miguel de Espinosa. Upon what would happen to him then he scarcely dared to dwell. He knew the revolting cruelties of which a Spaniard was capable, and he could guess what a spur of rage would be the Spanish admiral's. A sweat of horror broke upon his skin. Was he indeed to end his gloriously hazardous career in this mean way? Was he, who had so proudly sailed the seas of the Main as a conqueror, to founder thus in a dirty backwater? He could found no hope upon the search that. Hayton and the others would presently be making. That, as he had said, they would turn the place inside out, he never doubted. But he never doubted, either, that they would come too late. They might hunt down his betrayers, and wreak a terrible vengeance upon them. But how should that avail him?

The fogs of passion thickened in his mind; despair smothered the power of thought. He had close upon a thousand devoted men here in Tortuga, almost within hail, and he bound and helpless, and so to be delivered to the vindictive justice of Castile! That insistent, ever-recurring thought beat backwards and forwards like a pendulum in his brain, distracting it.

And then, in a sense, he came to himself again. His mind grew clear once more, preternaturally clear and active. Cahusac he knew for a venal scoundrel, who would keep faith with none if he saw profit in treachery. And the other was probably no better; indeed, probably worse, since interest alone--that Spanish blood-money--had lured him to his present task. He concluded that he had too soon abandoned the attempt to outbid the Spanish admiral. That way he might yet throw a bone of contention to these mangy curs, over which they would perhaps end by tearing at each other's throats.

A moment he surveyed them now, observing the evil greed in the eyes of each as they watched the fall of the dice over their trifling stakes from the gold and trinkets of which they had rifled him, and over which they were gaming to beguile the time of waiting.

And then he heard his own crisp voice breaking the silence.

"You gamble there for halfpence with a fortune within your reach."

"Are you beginning again?" growled Sam. But the Captain went on undaunted.

"I'll outbid the Spanish admiral's blood-money by forty thousand pieces. I offer you fifty thousand pieces of eight for my life."

Sam, who had risen in anger, stood suddenly arrested by the mention of so vast a sum.

Cahusac had risen too, and now both men stood, one on each side of the table, tense with excitement, which, if unexpressed as yet, was none the less to be read in the sudden pallor of their faces and dilation of their eyes. At last the Frenchman broke the silence.

"God of God! Fifty thousand pieces of eight!" He uttered the words slowly, as if to impress the figure upon his own and his companion's mind. And he repeated. "Fifty thousand pieces of eight! Twenty-five thousand for each! Pardi! but that is worth some risk! Eh, Sam?"

"A mort of money, true," said Sam, thoughtfully. And then he recovered. "Bah! What's a promise, anyhow? Who's to trust him? Once he's free, who's to make him pay, and he's--"

"Oh, I pay," said Blood. "Cahusac will tell you that I always pay." And he continued. "Consider that such a sum, even when divided, will make each of you wealthy, to lead a life of ease and plenty. Muchoviño, muchas mugeres!" he laughed in Spanish. "To be sure now, you'll be wise."

Cahusac licked his lips and looked at his companion. "It could be done," he muttered persuasively. "It's not yet ten, and between this and midnight we could put ourselves beyond the reach of your Spanish friends."

But Sam was not to be persuaded. He had been thinking; yet, tempting as he must find the lure, he dared not yield, discerning a double peril within it. Committed now by Spain to this venture, he dared neither draw back nor shift his course. Between the certain rage of the Spaniards should he play them false, and the probable resentment of Blood once he was restored to liberty, Sam saw himself inevitably crushed. Better an assured five thousand pieces to be enjoyed in comparative safety than a possible twenty-five thousand accompanied by such intolerable risks.

"It could not be done at all!" he cried angrily. "So let us hear no more about it. I've warned you once already."

"Mordieu!" cried Cahusac thickly. "But I say it could! And I say it's worth the risk."

"You say so, do you? And where's the risk for you? The Spaniards do not even know that you're in the business. It's easy for you, my lad, to talk about risks that you won't be called upon to run. But it's not quite the same for me. If I fails the Don, he'll want to know the reason. And, anyhow, I've pledged myself, and I'm a man of my word. So let's hear no more about it."

He towered there, fierce and determined, and Cahusac, after a scowling stare into that long, resolute face, uttered a sigh of exasperation, and sat down again.

Blood perceived quite clearly the inward rage that consumed the Frenchman. Vindictive though he might be towards the Captain, the venal scoundrel preferred his enemy's gold to his blood, and it was easy to guess the bitterness in which he saw himself compelled to forgo the more tangible satisfaction, simply because of the risks with which acceptance would be fraught for his associate.

For a while there was no word spoken between the twain, nor did Blood judge that he could further serve his ends by adding anything to what he had already said. He took heart, meanwhile, from the clear perception of the mischief he had already made.

When at last he broke the brooding silence, his words seemed to have no bearing whatever upon the situation.

"Though you may mean to sell me to Spain, sure there's no reason why ye should let me die of thirst in the meantime. I've a throat that's like the salt ponds on Saltatudos, so I have."

Although he had a definite purpose to serve, to which he made his thirst a pretext, yet that thirst itself was real, and it was suffered by his captors in common with himself. The air of the room, whose door and window were tight-barred, was stifling. Sam passed a hand across his dank brow and swept away the moisture.

"Hell! The heat!" he muttered. "And now I thirst myself."

Cahusac licked his dry lips.

"Is there nothing in the house?" he asked.

"No. But it's only a step to The King of France."

He rose. "I'll go fetch a jack of wine."

Hope soared wildly in the breast of Captain Blood.

It was precisely for this that he had played. Knowing their drinking habit, and how easily suggestion must arouse their desire to indulge it, he had hoped to send one of them upon that errand, and that the one to go would be Sam. With Cahusac he was sure he could make a deal at once.

And then Cahusac, the fool, ruined all by his excessive eagerness. He, too, was on his feet.

"A jack of wine! Yes, yes!" he cried. "Make haste. I, too, am thirsty."

Almost was there a quiver in his voice. Sam's ears detected it. He stood arrested, pondering his associate, and reading in his face the little rascal's treacherous intent.

He smiled a little.

"On second thoughts," said he, slowly, "it will be best if you goes and I stays on guard."

Cahusac's mouth fell open; almost he turned pale. Inwardly Captain Blood cursed him for a triple fool. "D'ye mean that ye don't trust me?" he demanded. "It ain't that--not exactly," he was answered.

"But it's me that stays."

Cahusac became really and vehemently angry. "Ah, ca! Name of God! If you don't trust me with him, I don't trust you neither."

"You don't need to. You know that I dursn't be tempted by his promises. That's why I'm the one to stay."

For a long moment the two ruffianly associates glowered at each other in angry silence. Then Cahusac's glance became sullen. He shrugged and turned aside, as if grudgingly admittingly that Sam's reasoning was unanswerable. He stood pondering with narrowed eyes. Finally he bestirred himself as if with sudden resolve.

"Ah, bah, I go!" he declared, and abruptly went.

As the door closed on the departing Frenchman, Sam resumed his seat at the table. Blood listened to the quickly receding footsteps until they had faded in the distance; then he broke the silence with a laugh that startled his companion.

Sam looked up sharply.

"What's amusing you now, Captain?"

Blood would have preferred, as we know, to deal with Cahusac. Cahusac was a certainty. Sam was hardly a possibility, obsessed as he obviously was by the fear of Spain. Still, that possibility must be exploited, however slender it might appear.

"Your rashness, bedad!" answered Captain Blood. "Yell not trust him to remain on guard, yet ye trust him out of your sight."

"And what harm can he do?"

"He might not return alone," said the Captain darkly.

"Blister me!" cried Sam. "If he tries any such tricks, I'll pistol him at sight. That's how I serves them that gets tricky with me."

"Ye'd be wise to serve him so in any case. He's a treacherous tyke, Sam, as I should know. Ye've baffled him to-night, and he's not the man to forgive. Ye should know that from his betrayal of me. But ye don't know. Ye've eyes, Sam, but no more sight than a blind puppy. And a head, Sam, but no more brains than are contained in a melon, or you'd never hesitate between Spain and me."

"Oh, that's it, is it?"

"Just that. Just fifty thousand pieces of eight that I offer, and that I pledge my honour to pay you, as well as pledging my honour to bear no malice and seek no vengeance. Even Cahusac assures you that my word is good, and was ready enough to accept it."

He paused. The rascally hunter was considering him silently, his face clay-coloured and the perspiration standing in beads upon his brow.

Presently he spoke hoarsely.

"Fifty thousand pieces, you said?" quoth he softly.

"To be sure. For where's the need to share with the French cur? D'ye dream he'd share with you if he could make it all his own by slipping a knife into your back? Come, Sam, make a bold bid for fortune. Damn your fears of Spain! Spain's a phantom! I'll protect you from Spain. You can lie safe aboard my flagship."

Sam's eyes flashed momentarily, then grew troubled again by thought.

"Fifty thousand. Ah, but the risk!"

"Sure, there's no risk at all," said Blood. "Not half the risk you run when it comes out that you sold me to Spain, as come out it will. Man, ye'll never leave Tortuga alive. And if ye did, my buccaneers would hunt ye to the end of the earth."

"But who's to tell?"

"There's always someone. Ye were a fool to undertake this job, a bigger fool to have taken Cahusac for partner. Hasn't he talked openly of vengeance? And won't he, therefore, be the first man suspected? And when they get him, as get him they will, isn't it as sure as judgment that he'll tell on you?"

"By Heaven, I believe you in that!" cried the man, presented with facts which he had never paused to consider.

"Faith, you may believe me in the rest as readily, Sam."

"Wait! Let me think!"

As once before, Captain Blood judged wisely that he had said enough for the moment. So far his success with Sam had been greater than he had dared to hope. The seed he had sown might now be left awhile to germinate.

The minutes sped, and Sam, elbows on the table and head in his hand, sat still and thoughtful. When at last he looked up, and the yellow light beat once more upon his face, Blood saw that it was pallid and gleaming. He tried to conjecture how far the poison he had dropped into Sam's mind might have done its work. Presently Sam plucked a pistol from his belt and examined the priming. This seemed to Blood significant. But it was more significant still that he did not replace the pistol in his belt. He sat nursing it, his yellowish face grimly set, his coarse lips tight with purpose.

"Sam," said Captain Blood softly, "what have you decided?"

"I'll put it out of the power of that French mongrel to bubble me," said the ruffian.

"And nothing else?"

"The rest can wait."

With difficulty Captain Blood bridled his eagerness to force the pace.

Followed an apparently interminable time of waiting, in a silence broken only by the ticking of the Captain's watch where it lay upon the table. Then, faintly at first, but swiftly growing louder as it drew nearer, came a patter of steps in the lane outside. The door was pushed open, and Cahusac appeared carrying a great black jack.

Sam was already on his feet beyond the table, his right hand behind him.

"You've been a long time gone!" he grumbled. "What kept you?"

Cahusac was pale, and breathing rather hard, as if he had been running. Blood, whose mind was preternaturally alert, knowing that he had not run, looked elsewhere for a reason, and guessed it to lie in either fear or excitement.

"I made all haste," was the Frenchman's answer. "But I was athirst myself, and I stayed to quench it. Here's your wine."

He set the leathern jack upon the table.

And on the instant, almost at point-blank range, Sam shot him through the heart.

Through the rising cloud of smoke, whose acrid smell took him sharply in the throat and set him coughing, Blood saw a picture that he was to retain in his mind to the end of his days. Face downwards on the floor lay Cahusac with twitching limbs, whilst Sam leaned forward, across the table to watch him, a grin on his long, animal face.

"I take no risk with French swines like you," he explained himself, as if his victim could still hear him. Then he put down the pistol and reached for the jack. He raised it to his mouth, and poured a full draught down his parched throat. Noisily he smacked his lips as he set down the vessel. Then as a bitter after-taste caught him in the throat he made a grimace, and apprehension charged suddenly through his mind and spread upon his countenance. He snatched up the jack again and thrust his nose into it, sniffing audibly like a questing dog. Then, with eyes dilating in horror, he stared at Blood out of a countenance that was leather-hued, and in an awful voice screamed a single word:

"Manzanilla!"

Then he swung round, and, uttering horrible, blood-curdling blasphemies, he hurled the jack and the remainder of its contents at the dead man on the floor.

A moment later he was doubled up by pain, and his hands were clawing and clutching at his stomach. Then he mastered himself, and without any thought now for Blood, or anything but the torment at work upon his vitals, he reeled across the room and pulled the door wide. The effort seemed to increase his agony. Again he was taken by a cramp that doubled him until his chest was upon his knees, and he howled the while, blaspheming at first, but presently uttering mere inarticulate, animal noises. He collapsed at last upon the floor, a raving, writhing lunatic.

Captain Blood considered him grimly, amazed but no whit intrigued. The riddle did not even require the key supplied by the single word that Sam had ejaculated. It was very plain to read.

Never had poetic retribution more fitly and promptly overtaken a pair of villains. Cahusac had loaded the wine with the poison of the manchineel apple, so readily procurable in Tortuga. With this, and so that he might be free to make a bargain with Captain Blood, and secure to himself the whole of the ransom the Captain offered, he had murdered his associate in the very moment in which, with the same intent, his associate had murdered him.

If Captain Blood had his own wits to thank for much, he had his luck to thank for more.

Gradually and slowly, as it seemed to the captive spectator, though in reality very quickly, the poisoned man's struggles grew fainter. Presently they were merely, and ever decreasingly, sporadic, and finally they ceased altogether, as did his breathing, which at the last had grown stertorous. He lay quite still in a cramped huddle against the open door.

By then Captain Blood was giving his attention to himself, and he had already wasted some moments and some strength in ineffectual straining at his bonds. A drumming on the door of the alcove reminded him of the presence of the woman who had been used unconsciously to decoy him. The shot and Sam's utterances had aroused her into activity. Captain Blood called to her.

"Break down the door! There's no one left here but myself."

Fortunately, that door was but a feeble screen of slender planks, and it yielded quickly to the shoulder that she set against it. Wild-eyed and dishevelled, she broke at 'last into the room, then checked and screamed at what she beheld there.

Captain Blood spoke sharply, to steady her.

"Now, don't be screeching for nothing, my dear. They're both as dead as the planks of the table, and dead men never harmed anyone. There's a knife yonder. Just be slipping it through these plaguey thongs."

In an instant he was free and on his feet, shaking out his ruffled plumage. Then he recovered his sword, his pistol, his watch, and his tobacco-box. The gold and the jewels he pushed together in a little heap upon the table.

"Ye'll have a home somewhere in the world, no doubt. This will help you back to it, my girl."

She began to weep. He took up his hat, picked up his ebony cane from the floor, bade her goodnight, and stepped out into the lane.

Ten minutes later he walked into an excited, torch-lit mob of buccaneers upon the mole, whom Hagthorpe and Wolverstone were organizing into search-parties to scour the town. Wolverstone's single eye fiercely conned the Captain.

"Where the devil have you been?" he asked. "Observing the luck that goes with blood-money," said Captain Blood.

VI - THE GOLD AT SANTA MARIA

The buccaneer fleet of five tall ships rode snugly at anchor in a sequestered creek on the western coast of the Gulf of Darien. A cable's length away, across gently heaving, pellucid waters, shot with opalescence by the morning sun, stretched a broad crescent of silver-grey sand; behind this rose the forest, vividly green from the rains now overpast, abrupt and massive as a cliff. At its foot, among the flaming rhododendrons thrusting forward like outposts of the jungle, stood the tents and rude log huts, palmetto thatched--the buccaneer encampment during that season of careening, of refitting, and of victualling with the fat turtles abounding thereabouts. The buccaneer host, some eight hundred strong, surged there like a swarming hive, a motley mob, English and French in the main, but including odd Dutchmen, and even a few West Indian half-castes. There were boucan-hunters from Hispaniola, lumbermen from Campeachy, vagrant seamen, runagate convicts from the plantations, and proscribed outlaws from the Old World and the New.

Out of the jungle into their midst stepped, on that glowing April morning, three Darien Indians, the foremost of whom was of a tall, commanding presence, broad in the shoulder and long in the arm. He was clad in drawers of hairy, untanned hide, and a red blanket served him for a cloak. His naked breast was streaked in black and reds in his nose he wore a crescent-shaped plate of beaten gold that hung down to his lip, and there were massive gold rings in his ears. A tuft of eagle's feathers sprouted from his sleek black hair, and he was armed with a javelin which he used as a stag.

He advanced calmly and without diffidence into their staring midst, and in primitive Spanish announced himself as the cacique Guanahani, called by the Spaniards Brazo Largo. He begged to be taken before their captain, to whom he referred also by his Hispanicised name of Don Pedro Sangre.

They conducted him aboard the flagship, the *Arabella*, and there, in the captain's cabin, the Indian cacique was courteously made welcome by a spare gentleman of a good height, very elegant in the Spanish fashion, whose resolute face, in cast of features and deep coppery tan, might, but for the eyes of a vivid blue, have been that of a Darien Indian.

Brazo Largo came to the point with a directness and economy of words to which his limited knowledge of Spanish constrained him.

"Usted venir conmigo. Yo llevar usted mucho oro Espanol. Caramba!" said he, in deep, guttural tones. Literally this may be rendered: "You to come with me. I take you much Spanish gold," with the added vague expletive "Caramba!"

The blue eyes flashed with interest. And, in the fluent Spanish acquired in less unregenerate days, Captain Blood answered him with a laugh:

"You are very opportune. Caramba! Where is this Spanish gold?"

"Yonder." The cacique pointed vaguely westward. "March ten days."

Blood's face grew overcast. Remembering Morgan's exploit across the isthmus, he leapt at a conclusion.

"Panama?" quoth he.

But the Indian shook his head, a certain impatience in his sternly wistful features.

"No. Santa Maria."

And he proceeded clumsily to explain that there, on the river of that name, was collected all the gold mined in the mountains of the district for ultimate transmission to Panama. Now was the time when the accumulations were heaviest. Soon the gold would be removed. If Captain Blood desired it--and Brazo Largo knew that there was a prodigious store--he must come at once.

Of the Indian's sincerity and goodwill towards himself Captain Blood entertained no single doubt. The bitter hatred of Spain smouldering in the breast of all Indians under Spanish rule made them the instinctive allies of any enemy of Spain.

Captain Blood sat on the locker under the stern windows and looked out over the sun-kissed waters of the lagoon.

"How many men would be required?" he asked at last.

"Forty ten, fifty ten, perhaps," said Brazo Largo, from which the Captain adduced that he meant four or five hundred.

He questioned him closely as to the nature of the country they would have to cross and the fortifications defending Santa Maria. Brazo Largo put everything in the most favourable light, smoothed away all difficulties, and promised not only himself to guide them, but to provide bearers to convey their gear. And all the time, with gleaming, anxious eyes, he kept repeating to Captain Blood:

"Much gold. Much Spanish gold. Caramba!"

So often did he repeat this parrot-cry, and with such obvious intent to allure, that Blood began to ask himself did not this Indian protest too vehemently for utter honesty.

Pondering him, the Captain voiced his suspicion in a question.

"You are very eager that we should go, my friend?"

"Go. Yes. Go you," the Indian answered. "Spaniards love gold. Guanahani no love Spaniards."

"So that you want to spite them? Indeed, you seem to hate them very bitterly."

"Hate!" said Brazo Largo. His lips writhed, and he made guttural noises of emphatic affirmation. "Huh! Huh!"

"Well, well, I must consider."

He called the boatswain and delivered the cacique into his care for entertainment.

A council, summoned by bugle-call from the quarter-deck of the *Arabella*, was held as soon there after as those concerned were come aboard.

Assembled about the oak table in the admiral's cabin, they formed a motley group, truly representative of the motley host encamped ashore. Blood, at the table's head, looking like a grande of Spain in the sombre richness of his black and silver, the long ringlets of his sable hair reaching to his collar of fine point; young Jerry Pitt, ingenuous of face, and in plain grey homespun, like the West of England Puritan that he had been; Hagthorpe, stiffly built, stern-faced, wearing showy clothes without grace, looked the simple, downright captain of fortune he was become; Wolverstone, herculean of build, bronzed of skin, and picturesquely untidy of person, with a single eye of a fierceness far beyond his nature, was perhaps the only one whose appearance really sorted with his trade; Mackett and James had the general appearance of mariners; lastly, Yberville, who commanded a French contingent, vying in elegance with Blood, had more the air and manner of a Versailles exquisite than of a leader of desperate and bloody pirates.

The admiral--for such was the title by now bestowed by his following upon Captain Blood--laid before them the proposal brought by Brazo Largo. He merely added that it came opportunely, inasmuch as they were without immediate plans.

Opposition sprang naturally enough from those who were, first and foremost, seamen--from Pitt, Mackett, and James. Each in turn dwelt upon the hardships and the dangers attending long overland expeditions. Hagthorpe and Wolverstone, intent upon striking the Spaniard where he most would feel it, favoured the proposal, and reminded the council of Morgan's successful raid upon Panama. Yberville, a French Huguenot proscribed and banished for his faith, and chiefly intent upon slitting the throats of Spanish bigots, wherever and whenever it might be done, proclaimed himself also for the venture in accents as mild and gentle as his words were hot and bloodthirsty.

Thus stood the council equally divided, and it remained for Blood to cast the vote that should determine the matter. But the admiral hesitated, and in the end resolved to leave the decision to the men themselves. He would call for volunteers, and if their numbers reached the necessary, he would lead them across the isthmus, leaving the others with the ships.

The captains approving this, they went ashore at once, taking the Indians with them. There Blood harangued the buccaneers, fairly expounding what was to be said for and what against the venture.

"I myself," he announced, "have resolved to go if so be that I am sufficiently supported." And then, after the manner of Pizarro on a similar occasion, he whipped out his rapier, and with the point of it drew a line in the sand. "Let those who choose to follow me across the isthmus, step now to windward of this line."

A full half of them responded noisily to his invitation. They included to a man the boucan-hunters from Hispaniola--who were by now amphibious fighters, and the hardiest of all that hardy host--and most of the lumbermen from Campeachy, for whom swamp and jungle had no terrors.

Brazo Largo, his coppery face aglow with satisfaction, departed to collect his bearers; and he marched them, fifty stalwart savages, into the camp next morning. The adventurers were ready. They were divided into three companies, each commanded respectively by Wolverstone, Yberville--who had shred his fripperies and dressed himself in the leather garb of the hunter--and Hagthorpe.

In this order they set out, preceded by the Indian bearers, who carried their heavier gear--their tents, six small brass cannons of the kind known as sakers, cans for fireballs, good store of victuals--doughboys and strips of dried turtle--and the medicine-chest. From the decks of the fleet bugles called farewell, and, in pure ostentation, Pitt, who was left in charge, fired a salute from his guns as the jungle swallowed the adventurers.

Ten days later, having covered a distance of some 160 miles, they encamped within striking distance of their destination.

The first part of the journey had been the worst, when their way lay over precipitous mountains, laboriously scaled on the one side and almost as laboriously descended on the other. On the seventh they rested in a great Indian village, where dwelt the king or chief cacique of the Indians of Darien, who, informed by Brazo Largo of their object, received and treated them with all honour and consideration. Gifts were exchanged, knives, scissors, and beads on the one side, against plantains and sugarcane on the other; and, reinforced here by scores of Indians, the buccaneers pushed on.

They came on the morrow to the river of Santa Maria, on which they embarked in a fleet of some seventy canoes of Indian providing. But it was a method of travelling that afforded at first little of the ease it had seemed to promise. All that day and the next they were constrained, at the distance of every stone's cast, to turn out, to haul the boats over shallows or rocks or over trees that had fallen across the channel. At last the navigation grew clearer, and presently, the river becoming broad and deep, the Indians discarded the poles, with which hitherto they had guided the canoes, and took to paddles and oars.

And so they came at length by night within sakershot of Santa Maria. The town stood on the riverbank a half-mile beyond the next bend.

The buccaneers proceeded to unload their arms, which were fast lashed to the insides of the canoes, the locks, as well as their cartridge-boxes and powder-horns, well cased and waxed down. Then, not daring to make a fire lest they should betray their presence, they posted sentries, and lay down to rest until daybreak.

It was Blood's hope to take the Spaniards so completely by surprise as to seize their town before they could put themselves in posture of defence, and so snatch a bloodless victory. This hope, however, was dispelled at dawn, when a distant discharge of musketry, followed by a drum beating frenziedly a travailler within the town, warned the buccaneers that they had not stolen upon the Spaniards as unobserved as they imagined.

To Wolverstone fell the honour of leading the vanguard, and two score of his men were equipped with firepots--shallow cylindrical cans filled with resin and gunpowder--whilst others bore forward the sakers, which were under the special command of Ogle, the gunner from the *Arabella*. Next came Hagthorpe's company, whilst Yberville's brought up the rear.

They marched briskly through the woods to the very edge of the savannah, where, at a distance of perhaps two furlongs, they beheld their Eldorado.

Its appearance was disappointing. Here was no handsome city of New Spain, such as they had been expecting, but a mere huddle of one-storeyed wooden buildings, thatched with wild cane and palmetto royal, clustering about a church, and defended by a fort. The place existed solely as a receiving station for the gold produced by the neighbouring mountains, and it numbered few inhabitants apart from the garrison and the slaves who worked in the goldfields. Fully half the area occupied by the town was taken up by the mud fort, which, whilst built to front the river, presented its flank to the savannah. For further defence against the very hostile Indians of Darien, Santa Maria was encircled by a stout palisade, some twelve feet high, pierced by loopholes for musketry at frequent intervals.

Within the town drums had ceased, but a hum of human movement reached the buccaneers as they reconnoitred from the wood's edge before adventuring upon the open ground. On the parapet of the fort stood a little knot of men in morion and corselet. Above the palisade quivered a thin line of smoke, to announce that Spanish musketeers were at their posts with matches ready lighted.

Blood ordered the sakers forward, having decided to breach the palisade towards the north-east angle, where a storming party would be least attainable by the gunners of the fort. Accordingly, Ogle mounted his battery at a point where a projecting spur of the forest on his left gave him cover. But now a faint easterly breeze beginning to stir carried forward the smoke of their fuses, to betray their whereabouts and invite the speculative fire of the Spanish musketeers. Bullets were already flicking and spattering through the branches about them when Ogle opened with his guns. At that short range it was an easy matter to smash a breach through wooden pales that had never been constructed to resist such weapons. Into that breach, to hold it, rushed the badly-captained Spanish troops. A withering volley from the buccaneers scattered them, whereupon Blood ordered Wolverstone to charge.

"Fireballs to the van! Scatter as you advance, and keep low. God speed you, Ned! Forward!"

Forth they leapt at the double, and they were halfway across the open before the Spaniards brought any considerable body of fire to bear upon them. Then they dropped, and lay supine in the short gamma grass until that frenzied musketry had slackened, when they leapt up again, and on at speed before the Spaniards could reload. And meanwhile Ogle had swung his sakers round to the right, and he was freely hurling his five-pound shot into the town on the flank of the advancing buccaneers.

Seven of Wolverstone's men lay on the ground where they had paused, ten more were picked off, during that second forward rush, and now Wolverstone was at the breach. Over went a score of fireballs to scatter death and terror, and before the Spaniards could recover from the confusion caused by these, the dread enemy was upon them, yelling as they burst through the cloud of smoke and dust.

Nevertheless, the Spanish commander, a courageous if unimaginative officer named Don Domingo Fuentes, rallied his men so effectively that for a quarter of an hour the battle swayed furiously backwards and forwards in the breach.

But in a battle of cold steel there were no troops in the world that, in anything approaching equality of numbers, could have stood long against these hardy, powerful, utterly reckless fellows. Gradually, but relentlessly and inevitably, the cursing, screaming Spaniards were borne back by Wolverstone, supported now by the main host, with Blood himself in command.

Back and back they were thrust, fighting with a wild fury of despair, until the beaten-out line of their resistance suddenly snapped. They broke and scattered, to re-form again, and by a rearguard action gain the shelter of the fort, leaving the buccaneers in possession of the town.

Within the fort, with the two hundred demoralized survivors of his garrison of three hundred men, Don Domingo Fuentes took counsel, and presently sent a flag of truce to Captain Blood, offering to surrender with the honours of war.

But this was more than Blood could prudently concede. He knew that his men would probably be drunk before night, and he could not take the risk of having two hundred armed Spaniards in the neighbourhood at such a time. Being, however, averse to unnecessary bloodshed, and eager to make an end without further fighting, he returned a message to Don Domingo, pledging his word that if he would surrender at discretion, no violence should be done to the life or ultimate liberty of the garrison or the inhabitants of Santa Maria.

The Spaniards piled arms in the great square within the fort, and the buccaneers marched in with banners flying and trumpets blaring. The commander stood forward to make formal surrender of his sword. Behind him were ranged his two hundred disarmed men, and behind these again the scanty inhabitants of the town, who had sought refuge with them. They numbered not more than sixty, amongst whom were perhaps a dozen women, a few negroes, and three friars in the black-and-white habit of Saint Dominic. The black slave population, it was presently ascertained, were at the mines in the mountains, whither they had just returned.

Don Domingo, a tall, personable man of thirty, in corselet and headpiece of black steel, with a little peaked beard that added length to his long, narrow face, addressed Captain Blood almost contemptuously.

"I have accepted your word," he said, "because, although you are a pirate scoundrel and a heretic in every other way dishonourable, you have at least the reputation of observing your pledges."

Captain Blood bowed. He was not looking his best. Half the coat had been torn from his back, and he had taken a scalp wound in the battle. But, however begrimed with blood and sweat, dust and gunpowder, his grace of deportment remained unimpaired.

"You disarm me by your courtesy," said he.

"I have no courtesies for pirate rogues," answered the uncompromising Castilian. Whereupon Yberville, that fierce hater of all Spaniards, thrust himself forward, breathing hard, but was restrained by Captain Blood.

"I am waiting," Don Domingo intrepidly continued, "to learn your detestable purpose here; to learn why you, the subject of a nation at peace with Spain, dare to levy war upon Spaniards."

Blood laughed.

"Faith, now, it's just the lure of gold, which is as potent with pirates as with more respectable scoundrels all the world over--the very lure that has brought you Spaniards to plant this town conveniently near the goldfields. To be plain, Captain, we've come to relieve you of the season's yield, and as soon as ye've handed it over we'll relieve you also of our detestable presence."

The Spaniard laughed, and looked round at his men as if inviting them to laugh with him. "To be sure, you conceive me a fool!" he said.

"Far from it. I'm hoping, for your own sake, that ye're not."

"Do you think that, forewarned as I was of your coming, I kept the gold at Santa Maria?" He was derisive. "You are too late, Captain Blood. It is already on its way to Panama. We embarked it in canoes during the night, and sent a hundred men to guard it. That is how my garrison comes to be depleted, and that is why I have not hesitated to surrender."

He laughed again, observing Blood's rueful countenance.

A gust of rage swept through the ranks of the buccaneers pressing behind their leader. The news had run as swiftly as flame over gunpowder, and with similar effect in the explosion it produced. With yells of execration and sinister baring of weapons, they would have flung themselves upon the Spanish commander, who--in their view--had cheated them, and they would have torn him there and then to pieces, had not Blood swung round and made of his own body a shield for Don Domingo.

"Hold!" he commanded, in a voice that blared like a trumpet. "Don Domingo is my prisoner, and I have pledged my word that he shall suffer no violence!"

Yberville it was who fiercely voiced the common thought.

"Will you keep faith with a Spanish dog who has cheated us? Let him be hanged!"

"It was his duty, and I'll have no man hanged for doing no more than that!"

For a moment Blood's voice was drowned in uproar. But he stood his ground impassively, his light eyes stern, his hand upheld, imposing some measure of restraint upon them.

"Silence, there, and listen! You are wasting time. The harm is far from being beyond repair. The gold has but a few hours' start. You, Yberville, and you, Hagthorpe, re-embark your companies at once, and follow. You should come up with them before they reach the Gulf, but even if you don't, it is still a far cry to Panama, and you'll overtake them long before they're in sight of it. Away with you! Wolverstone's company will await your return here with me."

It was the only thing that could have stayed their fury and prevented a massacre of the unarmed Spaniards. They did not wait to be told a second time, but poured out of the fort and out of the town faster than they had poured into it. The only grumblers were the six score men of Wolverstone's company who were bidden to remain behind. They locked up the Spaniards, all together, in one of the long pent-houses that made up the interior of the fort. Then they scattered about the little town in quest of victuals and such loot as there might be.

Blood turned his attention to the wounded. These, both his own men and the Spaniards, had been carried into another of the pent-houses, where beds of hay and dried leaves had been improvised for them. There were between forty and fifty of them in all, of which number one quarter were buccaneers. In killed and wounded the Spanish loss had been upwards of a hundred men; that of the buccaneers between thirty and forty.

With a half dozen assistants, of whom one was a Spaniard who had some knowledge of medicine, Blood went briskly to work to set limbs and patch up wounds. Absorbed in his task, he paid no heed to the sounds outside, where the Indians, who had gone to earth during the fighting, were now encamped, until suddenly a piercing scream disturbed him.

Before he could move or speak, the door of the hut was wrenched open, and a woman, hugging an infant to her breast, reeled in, calling him wildly by his Hispanicised name.

"Don Pedro! Don Pedro Sangre!" Then, as he stepped forward, frowning, she gasped for breath, clutched her throat, and fell on her knees before him, crying agonisedly in Spanish: "Save him! They are murdering him--murdering him!"

She was a lithe young thing that had scarcely yet crossed the threshold of womanhood, whom at a casual glance you might, from her apparel and general appearance, have supposed a Spaniard of the peasant class. Her blue-black hair and liquid black eyes were such as you might see in many an Andalusian, nor was her skin much swarthier. Only the high cheekbones and peculiar, dusky lips proclaimed, upon a closer inspection, her real race.

"What is it?" said Blood. "Whom are they murdering?"

A shadow darkened the sunlit doorway and Brazo Largo entered, dignified and grimly purposeful.

Overmastering terror of the advancing Indian froze the crouching woman's tongue.

Now he was standing over her. He stooped and set his hand upon her shrinking shoulder. He spoke to her swiftly in the guttural tongue of Darien, and though Blood understood no word of it, yet he could not mistake the note of stern command.

Wildly, a mad thing, she looked up at Captain Blood.

"He bids me go to see them roasting him alive! Mercy, Don Pedro! Save him!"

"Save whom?" barked the Captain, almost in exasperation.

Brazo Largo answered him, explaining:

"She to be my daughter--this. Captain Domingo, he come village, one year now, and carry her away with him. Caramba! Now I roast him, and take her home." He turned to the girl. "Vamos," he commanded, continuing to use his primitive Spanish, "you to come with me. You see him roast, then you come back village."

Captain Blood found the explanation ample. In a flash he recalled Guanahani's excessive eagerness to conduct him to the Spanish gold at Santa Maria, and how that eagerness had momentarily awakened suspicion in him. Now he understood. In urging this raid on Santa Maria, Brazo Largo had used him and his buccaneers to exploit a private vengeance and to recover an abducted daughter from Domingo Fuentes. But however deserving of punishment that abduction might appear, it was also revealed that, whether the girl had gone off willingly or not with the Spanish captain, his subsequent treatment of her had been such that she now desired to stay with him, and was concerned to the point of madness for his life and safety.

"Is it true what he says--that Don Domingo is your lover?" the Captain asked her.

"He is my husband, my married husband, and my love," she answered, a passion of entreaty in her liquid eyes. "This is our little baby. Do not let them kill him, Don Pedro! Oh, if they do," she moaned, "I shall kill myself!"

Captain Blood looked across at the grim-faced Indian.

"You hear? The Spaniard has been good to her. She desires his life. And his offence being as you say, it is her will that decked his fate. What have you done with him?"

Both clamoured at once, the father in angry, almost incoherent, remonstrance, the girl in passionate gratitude. She sprang up and caught Blood's arm to drag him thence.

But Brazo Largo, still protesting, barred the way. He conveyed that in his view Captain Blood was violating the alliance between them.

"Alliance!" snorted Blood. "You have been using me for purposes of your own. You should have been frank with me and told me of your quarrel with Don Domingo before I pledged myself that he should suffer no violence. As it is..."

He shrugged, and went out quickly with the young mother. Brazo Largo stalked after them, glowering and thoughtful.

Outside, Blood ran into Wolverstone and a score of men who were returning from the town. He ordered them to follow him, telling them that the Indians were murdering the Spanish captain.

"Good luck to them!" quoth Wolverstone, who had been drinking.

Nevertheless, he followed, and his men with him, being in reality less bloody in deed than in speech.

Beyond the breach in the palisade they came upon the Indians--some forty of them--kindling a fire. Near at hand lay the helpless Don Domingo, bound with leather thongs. The girl sped to him, crooning soft Spanish endearments. He smiled in answer out of a white face that yet retained something of scornful calm. Captain Blood, more practical, followed with a knife and slashed away the prisoner's bonds.

There was a movement of anger among the Indians, instantly quelled by Brazo Largo. He spoke to them rapidly, and they stood disappointed but impassive. Wolverstone's men were there, musket in hand, blowing on their fuses.

They escorted Don Domingo back to the fort, his little wife tripping between him an the buccaneer captain, whom she enlightened on the score of the Indians' ready obedience to her father.

"He told them that you must have your way since you had pledged your word that Domingo's life should be safe. But that presently you would depart. Then they would return and deal with him and the other few Spaniards left here."

"We must provide against it," said Captain Blood, to reassure her.

When they got back to the fort they found that, in their absence, the remainder of the Indians, numbering rather more than a score, had broken into the shed where the Spaniards were confined. Fortunately the business had only just begun, and the Spaniards, although unarmed, were sufficiently numerous to offer a resistance, which, so far, had been effective. Nevertheless, Captain Blood came no more than in time to prevent a general massacre.

When he had driven off his savage allies, the Spanish commander desired a word with him.

"Don Pedro," he said, "I owe you my life. It is difficult to thank you."

"Pray don't give yourself the trouble," said Captain Blood. "I did what I did, not for your sake, but for the sake of my pledged word, though concern for your little Indian wife may have had some part in it."

The Spaniard smiled almost wistfully as his glance rested on her standing near him, her fond eyes devouring him.

"I was discourteous to you this morning. I beg your pardon."

"That is an ample amend."

The Captain was very dignified.

"You are generous. May I ask, sir, what is your intention regarding us--myself and the others?"

"Nothing against your liberty, as I promised. So soon as my men return, we shall march away and leave you."

The Spaniard sighed.

"It is what I feared. You will leave us, weakened in strength, our defences wrecked, at the mercy of Brazo Largo and his Indians, who will butcher us the moment your backs are turned. For don't imagine that they will leave Santa Maria until that is done."

Captain Blood considered, frowning.

"You have certainly stirred up a personal vengeance, which Brazo Largo will prosecute without pity. But what can I do?"

"You could suffer us to depart for Panama at once, whilst you are here to cover our retreat from your Indian allies."

Captain Blood made a gesture of impatience.

"Ah, wait, Don Pedro! I would not propose it did I not deem you, from what I have seen, to be a man of heart, a gallant gentleman, pirate though you may be. Also you will observe that, since you have disavowed any intention of retaining us as prisoners, I am really not asking for anything at all."

It was quite true, and, upon turning it over in his mind, Captain Blood came to the conclusion that they would be much better off at Santa Maria without these Spaniards, who had to be guarded on the one hand and protected on the other. Therefore he consented. Wolverstone demurred. But when Blood asked him what possible purpose could be served by keeping the Spaniards at Santa Maria, Wolverstone confessed that he did not know. All that he could say was that he trusted no living Spaniard, which did not seem to have any bearing on the question.

So Captain Blood went off to find Brazo Largo, who was sulking on the wooden jetty below the fort.

The Indian rose at his approach, an exaggerated impassivity on his countenance.

"Brazo Largo," said the Captain, "your men have set my word at naught and put my honour in danger."

"I not understand," the Indian answered him. "You make friends with Spanish thieves?"

"Make friends! No. But when they surrendered to me I promised, as the condition of their surrender, that no harm should come to them. Your men would have murdered them in violation of that promise had I not prevented it."

The Indian was contemptuous.

"Huh! Huh! You not my friend. I bring you to Spanish gold, and you turn against me."

"There is no gold," said Blood. "But I am not quarrelling on that. You should have told me, my friend, before we came this journey, that you were using me so that we might deliver up to you your Spanish enemy and your daughter. Then I should not have passed my word to Don Domingo that he would be safe, and you could have drunk the blood of every Spaniard in the place. But you deceived me, Brazo Largo."

"Huh! Huh!" said Brazo Largo. "I not say anything more."

"But I do. There are your men. After what has happened, I cannot trust them. And my pledged word compels me to defend the Spaniards so long as I am here."

The Indian bowed.

"Perfectamente! So long as you here. What then?"

"If there is trouble again, there may be shooting, and some of your braves may be hurt. I should regret that more than the loss of the Spanish gold. It must not happen, Brazo Largo. You must summon your men, and let me consign them to one of the huts in the fort for the present--for their own sakes."

Brazo Largo considered. Then he nodded. He was a very reasonable savage. And so the Indians were assembled, and Brazo Largo, smiling the smile of a man who knew how to wait, submitted to confinement with them in one of the penthouses.

The assembled buccaneers murmured a little among themselves, and Wolverstone ventured to express the general disapproval.

"Ye're pushing matters rather far, Captain, to risk trouble with the Indians for the sake of those Spanish dogs!"

"Oh, not for their sake. For the sake of my pledged word, and that bit of an Indian girl with her baby. The Spanish commander has been good to her, and he's a gallant fellow."

"God help us!" said Wolverstone, and swung away in disgust.

An hour later the Spaniards were embarking from the jetty, under the eyes of the buccaneers, who, from the mud wall of the fort, watched their departure with some misgivings. The only weapons Blood allowed the voyagers were half a dozen fowling-pieces. They took with them, however, a plentiful supply of victuals, and Don Domingo, like a prudent captain, was very particular in the matter of water. Himself he saw the casks stowed aboard the canoes. Then he took his leave of Captain Blood.

"Don Pedro," he said, "I have no words in which to praise your generosity. I am proud to have had you for my enemy."

"Let us say that you are fortunate."

"Fortunate, too. I shall tell it wherever there are Spaniards to hear me that Don Pedro Sangre is a very gallant gentleman."

"I shouldn't," said Captain Blood. "For no one will believe you."

Protesting still, Don Domingo stepped aboard the piragua that carried his Indian wife and their half-caste baby. His men pushed the vessel off into the current, and he started on his journey to Panama, armed with a note in Captain Blood's hand, ordering Yberville and Hagthorpe to pass him unscathed in the event of his coming up with them.

In the cool of the evening the buccaneers sat down to a feast in the open square of the fort. They had found great stores of fowls in the town, and some goats, besides several hogsheads of excellent wine in the house of the Dominican fathers. Blood, with Wolverstone and Ogle, supped in the departed commander's well-equipped quarters, and through the open windows watched with satisfaction the gaiety of his feasting followers. But his satisfaction was not shared by Wolverstone, whose humour was pessimistic.

"Stick to the sea in future, Captain, says I," he grumbled between mouthfuls. "There's no packing off a treasure there when we come within saker-shot. Here we are, after ten days' marching, with another ten days' marching in front of us! And I'll thank God if we get back as light as we came, for as likely as not we shall have differences to set! with old Brazo Largo, and we'll be lucky if we get back at all, ever. Ye've bungled it this time, Captain."

"Ye're just a foolish heap of brawn, Ned," said the Captain. "I've bungled nothing at all. And as for Brazo Largo, he's an understanding savage, so he is, who'll keep friends with us if only because he hates the Spaniards."

"And ye behave as if ye loved 'em," said Wolverstone. "Ye're all smirks and bows for this plaguey commander who cheated us out of the gold, and ye--"

"Sure now, he was a gallant fellow, Spaniard or no Spaniard," said Blood. "In packing off the gold when he heard of our approach he did his duty. Had he been less gallant, he would have gone off with it himself, instead of remaining here at his post. Gallantry calls to gallantry; and that's all I have to say about it."

And then, before Wolverstone could make answer, sharp and clear above the noise the buccaneers were making rang the note of a bugle from the side of the river. Blood leapt to his feet.

"It will be Hagthorpe and Yberville returning!" he cried.

"Pray God they've got the gold at last!" said Wolverstone.

They dashed out into the open and made for the parapet, to which the men were already swarming. As Blood reached it, the first of the returning canoes swung alongside of the jetty, and Hagthorpe sprang out of it.

"Ye're soon returned," cried Blood, leaping down to meet him. "What luck?"

Hagthorpe, tall and square, his head swathed in a yellow kerchief, faced him in the dusk.

"Certainly not the luck that you deserve, Captain." His tone was curious.

"Do you mean that you didn't overtake them?" Yberville, stepping ashore at that moment, answered for his fellow-leader.

"There was nobody to overtake, Captain. He fooled you, that treacherous Spaniard; he lied when he told you that he had sent off the gold; and you--you believed him--you believed a Spaniard!"

"If ye'd come to the point now!" said Captain Blood. "Did I hear ye say he had not sent off the gold? D'ye mean that it is still here?"

"No," said Hagthorpe. "What we mean is that, after he had so fooled you with his lies that ye didn't even trouble to make search, you allowed them to go off scot-free, taking the gold with them."

"What?" the Captain barked at him. "How do you know this?"

"A dozen miles or so from here we came upon an Indian village; and we had the wit to stop and inquire how long it might be since a Spanish fleet of canoes had gone that way. They answered that no such fleet had passed to-day, or yesterday, or any day since the last rains. That's how we knew that your gallant Spaniard had lied. We put about at once to return, and midway back we ran into Don Domingo's party. The meeting took him by surprise. He had not reckoned that we'd seek information so soon. But he was as smooth and specious as ever, and a deal more courteous. He confessed quite frankly that he had lied to you, adding that subsequently, after our departure, he had purchased his liberty, and that of all who accompanied him, by surrendering the gold to you. He was instructed by you, he said, to order us to return at once; and he showed us your note of hand, which made him safe."

And then Yberville took up the tale.

"But we being not quite so trustful of Spaniards, and arguing that he who lies once will lie again, took them ashore and subjected them to a search."

"And d'ye tell me that you found the gold?" cried Blood, aghast.

Yberville paused a moment and smiled.

"You had permitted them to victual themselves generously against that journey. Did you observe at what spring Don Domingo filled his water-casks?"

"His water-casks?" quoth Blood.

"Were casks of gold--there's six or seven hundred-weight of it at the least. We've brought it with us."

By the time the joyous uproar excited by that announcement had settled down, Captain Blood had recovered from his chagrin. He laughed.

"I give you best," he said to Hagthorpe and Yberville. "And the least I can do, by way of amends for having suffered myself to be so utterly fooled, is to forgo my share of the booty." And then, on a graver note: "What did you do with Don Domingo?"

"I would have shot him for his perfidy!" said Hagthorpe fiercely. "But Yberville here--Yberville, of all men--turned mawkish, and besought me to let him go."

Shamefacedly the young Frenchman hung his head, avoiding the Captain's glance of questioning surprise.

"Oh, but after all," he flung out, defiant almost in self-defence, "what would you? There was a lady in the case--his little Indian wife."

"Faith, now, it was of her that I was thinking," said Blood. "And for her sake and his--oh, and also for our own--it will be best to tell Brazo Largo that Don Domingo and his wife were slain in the fight for the gold. The sight of the recovered water-casks will amply confirm the story. Thus there should be peace for all concerned, himself included."

And so, although they brought back that rich booty from Santa Maria, Blood's part in that transaction was rated as one of his few failures. Not so, however, did he himself account it.

VII - THE LOVE STORY OF JEREMY PITT

The love-story of Jeremy Pitt, the young Somerset-shire shipmaster, whose fate had been linked with Peter Blood's since the disastrous night of Sedgemoor, belongs to the later days of Blood's career as a buccaneer, to the great days when he commanded a fleet of five ships and over a thousand men of mixed nationality, held in a discipline to which his skill and good fortune made them willing to submit.

He had lately returned from a very successful raid upon the Spanish pearling fleet in the Rio de la Hache. He had come back to Tortuga to refit, and this not before it was necessary. There were several other buccaneer vessels in the harbour of Cayona at the time, and the little town was boisterous with their revelry. Its taverns and rum-shops throve, whilst the taverners and the women, white and half-castes, as mixed in origin and nationality as the buccaneers themselves, eased the rovers of a good deal of the plunder of which they had eased the Spaniards, who, again, were seldom better than robbers.

Usually these were unquiet times for Monsieur d'Ogeron, the agent of the French West India Company and Governor of Tortuga.

Ogeron himself, as we know, did very well out of the buccaneers in the percentages on their prizes which they very readily paid as harbour dues, and in other ways. But M. d'Ogeron had two daughters, the dark and stately Madeleine and the slight and joyous brunette Lucienne. Now Madeleine, for all her stateliness, had once succumbed to the wooing of a ruffianly buccaneer named Levasseur. To abstract her from this danger her father had shipped her off to France. But Levasseur, getting wind of it in time, had followed, seized the ship that carried her, and the worst might have befallen her but for the timely intervention of Captain Blood, who delivered her, unscathed, from his clutches and restored her, sobered by the experience, to her father.

Since then M. d'Ogeron had sought to practise discretion in the guests he received in the big white house set in its fragrant garden just above the town.

Captain Blood, by the service he had rendered the family on that occasion, had come to be regarded almost as a member of it. And since his officers, all of them driven to their trade as a consequence of transportation suffered for a political offence, were men of a different stamp from the ordinary buccaneer, they, too, were well received.

Now this in itself created a difficulty. If Monsieur d'Ogeron's house was open to the captains who followed Blood, he could not without offence close it to other buccaneer commanders. Therefore he was constrained to tolerate the visits of some whom he neither liked nor trusted, and this despite the protests of a guest from France, the fastidious and delicate Monsieur de Mercoeur, who cared little for the company of any of them.

Monsieur de Mercoeur was the son of one of the governors of the French West India Company, sent by his father on a voyage of instruction to the settlements in which the company was interested. The frigate *Cygne*, which had brought him a week ago, had been at anchor since in Cayona Bay, and would continue there until the young gentleman should see fit to depart again. From this his social consequence may be inferred. Obviously he was a person whose wishes a colonial governor would do his utmost to respect. But how was he to respect them, for instance, where such a truculent, swaggering fellow as Captain Tondeur of the *Reine Margot* was concerned? Monsieur d'Ogeron did not quite see how he could forbid him the house, as Monsieur de Mercoeur would have desired, not even when it became apparent that the rascal was attracted thither by Mademoiselle Lucienne.

Another who was yielding to the same attraction was young Jeremy Pitt. But Pitt was a fellow of a very different stamp, and if his courtship of Lucienne occasioned Monsieur d'Ogeron some distress, at least it caused him no such uneasiness as that begotten by Tondeur.

If ever there was a man designed by nature for a lover, that man was Jeremy Pitt, with his frank, smooth, comely face, his ingenuous blue eyes, his golden locks and his neatly-apparelled, graceful figure. With the vigour of a man he combined the gentleness of a woman. Anything less like a conspirator, which he had been, and a buccaneer, which he was, it would be impossible to conceive. He had, too, ingratiating ways and a gift of almost poetical expression to complete his equipment as the ideal lover.

His instincts--or it may have been his hopes--and perhaps something in the lady's kindly manner, led him to believe that Lucienne was not indifferent to him; and so one evening, under the fragrant pimento trees in her father's garden, he told her that he loved her, and whilst she was still breathless from the effects of that avowal he kissed her lips.

Quivering and troubled she stood before him after that operation. "Monsieur Jeremy...you...you should not...you should not have done that." In the fading light Mr. Pitt saw that there were tears in her eyes. "If my father knew..."

Jeremy interrupted her with emphasis.

"He shall. I mean him to know. He shall know now." And as Monsieur de Mercoeur and Madeleine were at that moment approaching, Jeremy departed at once in quest of the Governor of Tortuga.

Monsieur d'Ogeron, that slight, elegant gentleman who had brought with him to the New World the courtliness of the 01d, could scarcely dissemble his distress. Monsieur d'Ogeron had grown wealthy in his governorship and he had ambitions for his motherless daughters, whom he contemplated removing before, very long to France.

He said so, not crudely or bluntly, but with an infinite delicacy calculated to spare Mr. Pitt's feelings, and he added that she was already promised in marriage.

Jeremy's face was overspread by blank astonishment.

"Promised! But she told me nothing of this!" He forgot that he had never really given her such opportunity.

"It may be that she does not realize. You know how these things are contrived in France."

Mr. Pitt began an argument upon the advantages of natural selection, nipped by Monsieur d'Ogeron before he had properly developed it.

"My dear Mr. Pitt, my friend, consider, I beg, your position in the world. You are a filibuster in--short, an adventurer. I do not use the term offensively. I merely mean that you are a man who lives by adventure. What prospect of security, of domesticity, could you offer a delicately-nurtured girl? If you, yourself, had a daughter, should you gladly give her to such a man?"

"If she loved him," said Mr. Pitt.

"Ah! But what is love, my friend?"

Although perfectly aware of what it was from his late rapture and present misery, Jeremy found a difficulty in giving expression to his knowledge. Monsieur d'Ogeron smiled benignly upon his hesitation.

"To a lover, love is sufficient, I know. To a parent, more is necessary so as to quiet his sense of responsibility. You have done me an honour, Monsieur Pitt. I am desolated that I must decline it. It will be better that we do not trouble our mutual esteem by speaking of this again."

Now when a young man discovers that a certain woman is necessary to his existence, and when he believes with pardonable egotism that he is equally necessary to hers, he does not abandon the quest at the first obstacle.

At the moment, however, the matter could be pursued no further because of the interruption afforded by the entrance of the stately Madeleine accompanied by Monsieur de Mercoeur. The young Frenchman's eyes and voice sought Lucienne. He had charming eyes and a charming voice, and was altogether a charming person, impeccable as to dress and manners. In build he was almost tall, but so slight and frail that he looked as if a strong wind might blow him over; yet he possessed an assurance of address oddly at variance with his almost valetudinarian air.

He seemed surprised not to find Lucienne with her father. He desired, he announced, to persuade her to sing again some of those Provençal songs with which last night she had delighted them. His gesture took in the harpsichord standing in a corner of the well-appointed room. Madeleine departed to seek her sister. Mr. Pitt rose to take his leave. In his present mood he did not think he could bear to sit and hear Lucienne singing Provençal songs for the delight of Monsieur de Mercoeur.

He went off with his woes to Captain Blood, whom he found in the great cabin of the *Arabella*, that splendid red-hulled ship which once had been the *Cinco*

Llagas, but since re-named by Blood after the little lady to whom all his life he remained faithful, as has been elsewhere related.

The Captain laid down his well-thumbed copy of Horace to lend an ear to the plaint of his young friend and shipmaster. Lounging on the cushioned locker under the sternports, Captain Blood thereafter delivered himself, as sympathetic in manner as he was uncompromising in matter. Monsieur d'Ogeron was entirely right, the Captain opined, when he said that Jeremy's occupation in life did not justify him in taking a wife.

"And that's only half the reason for abandoning this notion. The other is that Lucienne charming and seductive child though she may be, is a thought too light to promise any peace and security to a husband not always at hand to guard and check her. That fellow Tondeur goes daily to the Governor's house. It hasn't occurred to you, now, to ask yourself what is attracting him? And why does this frail French dandy, Monsieur de Mercoeur, linger in Tortuga? Oh, and there are others I could name who have had, no doubt, your own delectable experience with a lady who's never reluctant to listen to a tale of love."

"Now devil take your lewdness!" roared out Pitt, with all a lover's unbounded indignation. "By what right do you say such a thing as that?"

"By the right of sanity and an unclouded vision. Ye'll not be the first to have kissed Mademoiselle Lucienne's lips; and ye'll not be the last neither, not even if ye marry her. She has a beckoning eye, so she has, and it's the uneasy husband I should be at sea if she were my wife. Be thankful ye're not the husband of her father's choice. Lovely things like Lucienne d'Ogeron were created just to trouble the world."

Jeremy would listen to no more of this blasphemy. It was like Blood, whom he bitterly denounced as without faith and without ideals, to think so vilely of the sweetest, purest saint in all the world. On that he flung out of the cabin, and left the Captain free to return to his Horace.

Blood, however, had planted a rankling seed in our young lover's heart. The clear perception of grounds for jealousy is a sword that can slay love at a stroke; but the mere suspicion of their existence is a goad to drive a lover on. Feverishly, then, on the morrow, and utterly oblivious of Monsieur d'Ogeron's rejection of his suit, Mr. Pitt made his way betimes to the white house above the town. It was earlier than his wont, and he came upon the lady of his dreams walking in the garden. With her walked Captain Tondeur, that man of sinister reputation. It was said of him that once he had been a fencing-master in Paris, and that he had taken to the sea so as to escape the justice it was desired to mete out to him by the family of a gentleman he had killed in a duel. He was a man of middle height and deceptive slimness, for he was as tough as whipcord. He dressed with a certain raffish elegance and moved with agile grace. His countenance was undistinguished save for the eyes, which, if small and round and black ere singularly penetrating. They were penetrating Mr. Pitt now with an arrogant stare that seemed to invite him to depart again. The Captain's right arm was about the waist of Mademoiselle Lucienne. It remained there notwithstanding Mr. Pitt's appearance, until presently, after a moments surprised pause, the lady disengaged herself in some embarrassment.

"It is Monsieur Jeremy!" she cried, and added, quite needlessly, thought Mr. Pitt: "I was not expecting you."

Jeremy took the hand she proffered and bore it to his lips, more or less mechanically, whilst mumbling a greeting in his indifferent French. Followed an exchange of commonplaces, and then an awkward pause, at the end of which said Tondeur with a scowl.

"When a lady tells me that I am unexpected, I understand her to mean that I am inopportune."

"No doubt a common experience in your life." Captain Tondeur smiled. Your practised, duellist is always self-possessed.

"At least not a subject for pertness. It is not always wise to be pert. The moment's glitter may lead to painful instruction."

Lucienne intervened. She was a little breathless. Her eyes were scared.

"But what is this? What are you saying? You are wrong, Monsieur le Capitaine, to assume Monsieur Jeremy inopportune. Monsieur Jeremy is my friend, and my friends are never inopportune."

"Not perhaps to you, Mademoiselle. But to other friends of yours they can be monstrously so."

"Again you are mistaken." Her manner was frigid. "He is no friend of mine to whom other friends of mine are unwelcome in my presence."

The Captain bit his lip, and Jeremy took a fragment of comfort, for all that he still hotly remembered that arm about the waist of the woman whose lips he had kissed last night and also Captain Blood's condemnation of her.

The elements of a very pretty quarrel were shattered by the sudden appearance of Monsieur d'Ogeron and Monsieur de Mercoeur. Both were out of breath as if they had been hurrying. They checked, however, and seemed relieved when they saw who was present. It was as if Monsieur d'Ogeron found not quite what he had expected, and relief upon the safety for Lucienne which is believed to reside in numbers. Their advent put an end to acrimony, and perhaps because he was in the humour for little else, Captain Tondeur presently took his leave. A smile of disquieting significance accompanied his parting words to Jeremy.

"I shall look forward, monsieur, to an early opportunity of continuing our interesting discussion." Anon, when Jeremy, too, would have departed, Monsieur d'Ogeron detained him. "Remain yet a moment, Monsieur Pitt."

He took the young man by the arm in a friendly manner and drew him away from Monsieur de Mercoeur and Lucienne. They moved up the avenue and entered a tunnel fashioned of over-arching orange trees imported from Europe; a cool place this where the ripe fruit glowed like lamps against the dusky green.

"I did not like the parting words of Captain Tondeur, nor yet his smile. That is a very dangerous man. You would be wise to beware of him."

Jeremy bridled a little. "Do you suppose I fear him?"

"I suppose you would be prudent to do so. A very dangerous man. A canaille. He comes here too much."

"Regarding him as you do, why do you permit it?"

Monsieur d'Ogeron made a grimace. "Regarding him as I do, I cannot do otherwise."

"You are afraid of him?"

"I confess it. Oh, not for myself, Monsieur Pitt. But there is Lucienne. He pays his court to her."

Jeremy quivered with fury. "Could you not forbid him your house?"

"Of course." Monsieur d'Ogeron smiled crookedly. "I did something of the kind once before, in the case of Levasseur. You know the story."

"Oh, but...Oh, but..." Jeremy encountered a difficulty, but finally surmounted it. "Mademoiselle Madeleine was so misguided as to lend herself to the scheme of Levasseur. You do not dream that Mademoiselle Lucienne--"

"Why should I not dream it? This Tondeur canaille though he be, is not without attraction, and he has over Levasseur the advantage that he was once a gentleman and can still display the manners of one when it suits him. An inexperienced child like Lucienne is easily allured by your bold, enterprising wooer."

Mr. Pitt was a little sick at heart and bewildered. "Yet what good can temporising do? Sooner or later you will have to reject him. And then...What then?"

"It is what I ask myself," said Monsieur d'Ogeron almost lugubriously. "Yet an evil that is postponed may ultimately be removed by chance." And then, suddenly, his manner changed. "Oh, but your pardon, my dear Mr. Pitt. Our talk is taking a turn very far from what I intended. A father's anxiety! I meant to do no more than utter a warning, and I beg that you will heed it."

Mr. Pitt thought he understood. What was in Monsieur d'Ogeron's mind was that Tondeur scented a rival in Jeremy and that such a man would take prompt means to eliminate a rival.

"I am obliged to you, Monsieur d'Ogeron. I can take care of myself."

"I trust so. Sincerely I trust so." And on that they parted.

Jeremy went back to dine on board the *Arabella*, and after dinner, pacing the poop with Blood, he told him what had passed.

Captain Blood was thoughtful. "There is cause enough to warn you. Though why the Governor should be troubling to do so is just a trifle odd. I'll pay him a visit, so I will. I may be able to help him, though I don't yet see how. Meanwhile, Jerry, if ye're prudent, yell be keeping the ship. Devil a doubt but Tondeur will be looking for you."

"And I am to avoid him, am I?" snorted Jeremy.

"If ye're wise."

"If I'm a coward."

"Now isn't a live coward better than a dead fool, which is what ye'll be if ye come to grips with Master Tondeur? Ye'll not be forgetting the man's a fencing-master; whilst you...Pshaw! It would be just murder, so it would. And where's the glory of suffering that?"

Pitt knew it in his heart and yet would not admit the humiliating knowledge. Therefore, neglecting Blood's advice, he went ashore on the morrow, and was sitting with Hagthorpe and Wolverstone in the tavern of the King of France when Tondeur found him.

It was in the neighbourhood of noon, and the common-room was thronged with buccaneers, a few ordinary seamen from the *Cygne*, beachcombers and the land-sharks of both sexes who prey upon seafaring men, and particularly upon buccaneers, who are ever prodigal of their broad pieces of eight. The air of the ill-lighted place was heavy with the reek of rum, tobacco, spun-yarn and humanity.

Tondeur came forward leisurely, his left hand resting on his hilt, exchanging nods and bringing up at last before Jeremy's table.

"You permit?" quoth he, and without waiting for an answer, he drew up a stool and sat down. "I am fortunate so soon to be able to resume the little discussion that yesterday was interrupted."

Jeremy, understanding perfectly what was coming, stared at him uneasily. His two companions, understanding nothing, stared with him.

"We discussed inopportuneness, I think, and your sluggishness in perceiving that your presence was not required."

Jeremy leaned forward. "What we discussed is no matter. You are here, I think, to pick a quarrel with me."

"I?" Captain Tondeur stared and frowned. "Why should you suppose that? You do me no harm. It is not in your power to do me harm. Yo are not even in my way. If you were, I should crack you like a flea." He laughed contemptuously, offensively, and by that laugh flung Jeremy, as he intended, into a passion.

"I am no flea for your cracking."

"Are you not?" Tondeur got up. "Then be careful not to pester me again, or you may find yourself under my thumbnail. You have your warning." He spoke loudly, so that all might hear him, and his tone brought a hush upon the crowded room.

He was turning away contemptuously when Jeremy's answer arrested him.

"You insolent dog!"

Captain Tondeur checked. He raised his brows. A snarling smile lifted an end of his little moustache. And meanwhile the burly Wolverstone, still understanding nothing, sought instinctively to restrain Jeremy, who had also risen.

"Dog?" said the Captain slowly. "Dog, eh? It is apt enough. The dog and the flea. All the same, I do not like dog. You will be so good as to retract' dog. You will retract it at once. I am not a patient man, Monsieur Pitt."

"Certainly I will retract it," said Jeremy. "I'll not insult an animal."

"Meaning me?"

"Meaning the dog. I'll substitute instead--"

"Substitute rat," said a sharp voice from the background, which made Tondeur spin round where he stood.

Just within the doorway lounged Captain Blood, tall and elegant in his black and silver, leaning upon his ebony cane. The intensely blue eyes in his clear-cut, sun-tanned face met and held the stare of Captain Tondeur. He sauntered forward, speaking easily and without stress as he came.

"Rat, I think, describes you better, Captain Tondeur." And he stood waiting for the Frenchman's answer.

It came presently in the wake of a sneering laugh. "I see. I see. The little shipmaster here is to be protected. Papa Blood intervenes to save the little coward."

"Certainly he is to be protected. I will not have my shipmaster murdered by a bully-swordsman. That is why I intervene. You might have foreseen it, Captain Tondeur. As for cowardice, you paltry rascal, that is the attribute of the rat to which I liken you. You trade upon a certain skill with the sword; but you are careful to employ it only against those you have reason to believe unskilled. That is the coward's way. Oh, and the murderer's, which is, I believe, what they call you in France."

"That's a lie, anyway," said Tondeur, livid.

Captain Blood was unperturbed. He was deliberately playing Tondeur's own game of baiting an opponent into fury. "You may proceed to prove it upon me, in which case I shall retract, either before or after killing you. Thus you will die in honour, having lived in dishonour. The inner room there is spacious and empty. We can--"

But Tondeur interrupted him, sneering. "I am not so easily distracted. My affair is with Mr. Pitt."

"Let it wait until you have settled mine."

Tondeur contained himself. He was white with passion and breathing hard.

"Look you, Captain Blood: I have been insulted by this shipmaster of yours, who called me dog in the presence here of these. You deliberately seek to thrust yourself into a quarrel that does not concern you. It is not to be tolerated. I appeal me to the company."

It was a shrewd move and the result justified it. The company was on his side. Such of Captain Blood's own men who were present kept silent, whilst the remainder loudly gave the Frenchman reason. Not even Hagthorpe and Wolverstone could do more than shrug, and Jeremy made matters utterly hopeless by declaring himself on the side of the enemy.

"Captain Tondeur is in the right, Peter. You are not concerned in this affair."

"You hear?" cried Tondeur.

"I am concerned, whatever may be said. You mean murder, you scum, and I mean to prevent it." Captain Blood abandoned his cane, and carried his hand to his sword.

But dozens sprang to restrain him, protesting so forcibly and angrily that, finding himself without even the support of his own followers, Captain Blood was forced to give way.

Even the staunch and loyal Wolverstone was muttering in his ear: "Nay, Peter! A God's name! Ye'll provoke a riot for naught. Ye were just too late. The lad had committed himself."

"And what were you doing to let him? Well, well! There he goes, the rash fool."

Pitt was already leading the way to the inner room: a lamb not merely going to the slaughter, but actually conducting the butcher. Hagthorpe was with him. Tondeur followed closely, and others brought up the rear.

Captain Blood, with Wolverstone at his side, went with the crowd, controlling himself now with difficulty.

The inner room was spacious and almost bare. What few chairs and tables it contained were swiftly thrust aside. The place was little more than a shed or penthouse built of wood, and open from the height of some three feet along the whole of one side. Through this opening the afternoon sun was flooding the place with light and heat.

Sword in hand, stripped to the waist, the two men faced each other on the bare earthen floor, Jeremy, the taller of the two, sturdy and vigorous; the other, light, sinewy and agile as a cat. The taverner and the drawers were among the press of onlookers ranged against the inner wall; two or three young viragos were in the crowd, but most of the women had remained in the common-room.

Captain Blood and Wolverstone had come to stand towards the upper end of the room at a table on which there were various objects cleared from the others: some drinking-cans, a couple of flagons, a jack and a pair of brass candlesticks with wide saucer-like stands. In the moments of waiting, whilst preliminaries were being settled, Blood, pale under his tan and with a wicked look in his blue eyes, had glanced at these objects, idly fingering one or two of them as if he would have employed them as missiles.

Hagthorpe was seconding Jeremy. Ventadour, the lieutenant of the *Reine Margot*, stood by Tondeur. The antagonists faced each other along the length of the room, with the sunlight on their flank. As they took up their positions, Jeremy's eyes sought Blood's. The lad smiled to him. Blood, unsmiling, answered by a sign. For a moment there was inquiry in Jeremy's glance, then understanding followed.

Ventadour gave the word: "Allez, messieurs!" and the blades rang together.

Instantly, obeying that signal which he had received from his captain, Jeremy broke ground, and attacked Tondeur on his left. This had the effect of causing Tondeur to veer to that side, with the result that he had the sun in his eyes. Now was Jeremy's chance if he could take it, as Blood had foreseen when he had signalled the manoeuvre. Jeremy did his best, and by the assiduity of his endeavours kept his opponent pinned in that position of disadvantage. But Tondeur was too strong for him. The practised swordsman never lost touch of the opposing blade, and presently, venturing a riposte, availed himself of the ensuing disengage to break ground in his turn, and thus level the position, the antagonists having now completely changed places.

Blood ground his teeth to see Jeremy lose the only advantage he possessed over the sometime fencing-master who was bent on murdering him. Yet the end did not come as swiftly as he expected. Jeremy had certain advantages of reach and vigour. But these did not account for the delay, nor yet did the fact that the fencing-master may have been a little rusty from lack of recent practice. Tondeur played a closely circling blade which found openings everywhere in the other's wide and clumsy guard. Yet he did not go in to finish. Was he deliberately playing with his victim as cat with mouse, or was it perhaps that, standing a little in awe of Blood and of possible consequences should he kill Pitt outright, he aimed merely at disabling him?

The spectators, beholding what they beheld, were puzzled by the delay. They were puzzled still more when Tondeur again broke ground, so as to place his back to the sun and turn his helpless opponent into the position of disadvantage in which Tondeur had erstwhile found himself. To the onlookers this seemed a refinement of cruelty.

Blood, who now directly faced Tondeur, picked up in that moment one of the brass candlesticks from the table beside him. None observed him, every eye being upon the combatants. Blood alone appeared entirely to have lost interest in them. His attention was bestowed entirely upon the candlestick. So as to examine the socket intended for the candle, he raised the object until its broad saucer-like base was vertical. At that moment, for no apparent reason, Tondeur's blade faltered in its guard, and failed to deflect a clumsy thrust with which Jeremy was mechanically in the act of countering. Meeting no opposition, Jeremy's blade drove on until some inches of it came out through Tondeur's back.

Almost before the amazed company had realized this sudden and unexpected conclusion, Captain Blood was on his knees beside the prostrate man. He called for water and clean linen, the surgeon in him now paramount whilst Jeremy--the most amazed in that amazed crowd--stood foolishly looking on beside him.

Whilst Blood was dressing the wound, Tondeur recovered from his momentary swoon he stared with eyes that slowly focussed the man who was bending over him.

"Assassin!" he said through his teeth, and then his head lolled limply on his shoulder once more.

"On the contrary," said Blood, his finger deftly swathing the body which Ventadour was supporting, "I'm your preserver." And to the company he announced: "He will not die of this, for all that it went through him.. With luck he'll be ruffling it again within the month. But he'd best not be moved from here for some days, and he'll need care."

Jeremy never knew how he found himself once more aboard the *Arabella*. The events of the afternoon were dim to him as the transactions of a dream. He had looked, as he conceived, into the grim face of death, and yet he had survived. That evening at supper in the great cabin he made philosophy upon it.

"It serves," he said, "to show the advantages of never losing heart or admitting defeat in an encounter. I might so easily have been slain to-day; and it would have been simply and solely by a preconception: the preconception that Tondeur was the better swordsman."

"It is still possible that he was," said Blood.

"Then how came Ito run him through so easily?"

"How indeed, Peter?" demanded Wolverstone, and the other half-dozen present echoed the question, whilst Hagthorpe enlarged upon the theme.

"The fact is the rascal's reputation for swordsmanship rested solely upon his own boasting. It's the source of many a reputation." And there the discussion was allowed to drop.

In the morning Captain Blood suggested that they should pay a visit to Monsieur d'Ogeron, and render their account to him of what had taken place. As Governor of Tortuga, some formal explanation was due to him, even though his acquaintance with the combatants should render it almost unnecessary. Jeremy, at all times ready to visit the Governor's house on any pretext, was this morning more than willing, the events having set about him a heroic halo.

As they were being rowed ashore Captain Blood observed that the *Cygne* was gone from her moorings in the bay, which would mean, Jeremy opined with faint interest, that Monsieur de Mercoeur had at last departed from Tortuga.

The little Governor gave them a very friendly welcome. He had heard of the affair at The King of France. They need not trouble themselves with any explanations. No official cognizance would be taken of the matter. He knew but too well the causes which had led to it.

"Had things gone otherwise," he said quite frankly, "it would have been different. Knowing who would be the aggressor--as I warned you, Monsieur Pitt--I must have taken some action against Tondeur, and I might have had to call upon you, Captain Blood, to assist me. Order must be preserved even in such a colony as this. But as it is, why, the affair could not have had a more fortunate conclusion. You have made me very happy, Monsieur Pitt."

This augured so well that Mr. Pitt presently asked leave to pay his homage to Mademoiselle Lucienne.

Monsieur d'Ogeron looked at him as if surprised by the request.

"Lucienne? But Lucienne has gone. She sailed for France this morning on the *Cygne* with her husband."

"Her...her husband?" echoed Jeremy, with a sudden feeling of nausea.

"Monsieur de Mercoeur. Did I not tell you she was promised? They were married at cock-crow by Father Benoit. That is why I say you have made me very happy, Monsieur Pitt. Until Captain Tondeur was laid by the heels I dared not permit this thing to take place. Remembering Levasseur, I could not allow Lucienne to depart before. Like Levasseur, it is certain that Tondeur would have followed, and on the high seas would have dared that which he dared not here in Tortuga."

"Therefore," said Captain Blood, in his driest tone, "you set the other two by the ears, so that whilst they were quarrelling over the bone, the third dog might make off with it. That, Monsieur d'Ogeron, was more shrewd than friendly."

"You are angry with me, Captain!" Monsieur d'Ogeron appeared genuinely distressed. "But I had to think of my child, and besides, I had no doubt of the issue. This dear Monsieur Pitt could not fail to prevail against a man like Tondeur."

"This dear Monsieur Pitt," said Captain Blood, "might very easily have lost his life for love of your daughter so as to forward your marriage schemes for her. There's a pretty irony in the thought." He linked his arm through that of his young shipmaster, who stood there white and hang-dog. "You see, Jerry, the pitfalls injudicious loving can dig for a man. Let's be going, my lad. Good day to you, Monsieur d'Ogeron."

He almost dragged the boy away. Then, because he was very angry, he paused when they had reached the door, and there was an unpleasant smile on the face he turned to the Governor.

"Why do you suppose that I should not do on Mr. Pitt's behalf what you feared Tondeur might do? Why shouldn't I go after the *Cygne* and capture your daughter for my shipmaster?"

"My God!" ejaculated Monsieur d'Ogeron, suddenly appalled by the prospect of so merited a vengeance. "You would never do that!"

"No, I would not. But do you know why?"

"Because I've trusted you. Because you are a man of honour."

"Honour! Bah! I'm just a pirate. It's because I don't think she is good enough for Mr. Pitt, as I told him from the outset, and as I hope he now believes."

That was all the revenge he took of Monsieur d'Ogeron for his foxy part in the affair. Having taken it, he departed, and the stricken Jeremy suffered himself to be led away.

But by the time they had reached the mole the lads numbness had given place to rage. He had been duped and tricked, his very life had been put in pawn to serve the schemes of those others, and somebody must pay.

"If ever I meet Monsieur de Mercoeur..." he was raging.

"You'll do fine things," the Captain mocked him. "I'll serve him as I served that dog Tondeur." And now Captain Blood stood still that he might laugh.

"Oh! It's the fine swordsman ye've become all at once, Jerry. The very butcher of a silk button. I'd best be disillusioning you, my young Tybalt, before ye swagger into mischief."

"Disillusioning me?" Jeremy stared at him, a frown darkening that fair, honest face. "Did I, or did I not, lay low that French duellist yesterday?"

And Blood, still laughing, answered him: "You did not!"

"I did not? I did not?" Jeremy set his arms akimbo. "Well ye tell me, then, who did?"

"I did," said the Captain, and on that grew serious. "I did it with the bright bottom of a brass candlestick. I flashed enough reflected sunlight into his eyes to blind him whilst you were doing the business."

He saw Jeremy turn pale, and added the reminder: "He would have murdered you else." Then there was a whimsical twist of his firm lips, a queer flash from his vivid eyes, and he added on a note of conscious pride: "I am Captain Blood."

VIII - THE EXPIATION OF MADAME DE-COULEVAIN

On a day-bed under the wide square sternposts of the luxurious cabin of the *Estremadura* lounged Don Juan de la Fuente, Count of Medians, twanging a beribboned guitar and singing an indelicate song, well known in Malaga at the time, in a languorous baritone voice.

He was a young man of thirty, graceful and elegant, with soft dark eyes and full red lips that were half veiled by small moustaches and a little peaked black beard. Face, figure, dress and posture advertised the voluptuary, and the setting afforded him by the cabin of the great forty-gun galleon he commanded was proper to its tenant. From bulkheads painted an olive green detached gilded carvings of cupids and dolphins, fruit and flowers, whilst each stanchion was in the shape of a fish-tailed caryatid. Against the forward bulkhead a handsome buffet was laden with gold and silver plate; between the doors of two cabins on the larboard side hung a painting of Aphrodite; the floor was spread with a rich Eastern carpet; a finer one covered the quadrangular table, above which was suspended a ponderous lamp of chiselled silver. There were books in a rack: the Ars Amatoria of Ovid, the Satiricon, a Boccaccio and a Poggio, to bear witness to the classico-licentious character of this student. The chairs, like the daybed on which Don Juan was sprawling, were of Cordovan leather, painted and gilded, and although the sternports stood open to the mild airs that barely moved the galleon, the place was heavy with ambergris and other perfumes.

Don Juan's song extolled life's carnal joys and, in particular, bewailed the Pope's celibacy amid opulence:

> "Vida sin niña no es vida, es muerte, Y del Padre
> Santo muy triste es la suerte."

That was its envoy and at the same time its mildest ribaldry. You conceive the rest.

Don Juan was singing this song of his to Captain Blood, who sat with an elbow leaning on the table and a leg thrown across a second chair. On his dark aquiline face there was a set mechanical smile, put on like a mask, to dissemble his weariness and disgust. He wore a suit of grey camlet with silver lace, which had come from Don Juan's wardrobe, for they were much of the same height and shape as they were akin in age, and a black periwig, that was likewise of Don Juan's providing, framed his countenance.

A succession of odd chances had brought about this incredible situation, in which that detested enemy of Spain came to find himself an honoured guest aboard a Spanish galleon, crawling north across the Caribbean, with the Windward Islands some twenty miles abeam. Let it be explained at once that the languorous Don who entertained him was very far from suspecting whom he entertained.

The tale of how he came there, set forth at great and almost tedious length by Pitt in his chronicle, must here be briefly summarized.

A week ago, on Margarita, in a secluded cove of which his own great ship the *Arabella* was careened to clear her keel of accumulated foulness, word had been brought him by some friendly Carib Indians of a Spanish pearling fleet at work in the Gulf of Cariaco, which had already collected a rich harvest.

The temptation to raid it proved irresistible to Captain Blood. In his left ear he wore a great pear-shaped pearl of enormous price that was part of the magnificent haul they had once made from a similar fleet in the Rio de la Hacha. So with three piraguas and forty men carefully picked from his crew of close upon two hundred, Blood slipped one night across the narrow sea between Margarita and the Main, and lay most of the following day under the coast, to creep towards evening into the Gulf of Cariaco. There, however they were surprised by a Spanish guarda-costa whose presence they had been far from suspecting.

They put about in haste, and ran for the open. But the guardship gave chase in the brief dusk, opened fire, and shattered the frail boats that bore the raiders. Of the forty buccaneers, some must have been shot, some drowned, and others picked up to be made prisoners. Blood himself had spent the night clinging to a stout piece of wreckage. A stiffish southerly breeze had sprung up at sunset, and driven by this and borne by the currents, he had miraculously been washed ashore at dawn, exhausted, benumbed, and almost pickled by the long briny immersion, on one of the diminutive islands of the Hermanos group.

It was an island not more than a mile and a half in length and less than a mile across, sparsely grown with coconut palms and aloes, and normally uninhabited save by sea-birds and turtles. But at the time of Blood's arrival there, it happened to be tenanted in addition by a couple of castaway Spaniards. These unfortunates had escaped in a sailing pinnace from the English settlement of Saint Vincent, where they had been imprisoned. Ignorant of navigation, they had entrusted themselves to the sea, and with water and provisions exhausted, and at the point of death from thirst and hunger, they had fortuitously made their landfall a month ago. Not daring after that experience to venture forth again, they had subsisted there on shell-fish taken from the rocks and on coconuts, yams, and berries.

Since Captain Blood could not be sure that Spaniards, even when in these desperate straits, would not slit his throat if they guessed his real identity, he announced himself as shipwrecked from a Dutch brig which had been on its way to Curaco, gave himself the name of Peter Vandermeer, and attributed to himself a mixed parentage of Dutch father and Spanish mother, thus accounting for the fluent Castilian which he spoke.

Finding the pinnace in good order, he provisioned her with a store of yams and of turtle, which he himself boucanned, filled her water-casks, and put to sea with the two castaways. By sun and stars he trusted to steer a course due east for Tobago, whose Dutch settlers were sufficiently neutral to, give them shelter. He deemed it prudent, however to inform his trusting companions that he was making for Trinidad.

But neither Trinidad nor Tobago was to prove their destination. On the third day out they were picked up by the Spanish galleon *Estremadura*, to the jubilation of the two Spaniards and the dismay at first of Captain Blood. However he put a bold face on the matter and trusted to fortune and to the ragged condition in which he went aboard the galleon to escape recognition. When questioned he maintained the fictions of his shipwreck, his Dutch nationality and his mixed parentage, and conceiving that since he was plunging he might as well plunge deeply, and that since he claimed a Spanish mother, he might as well choose one amongst the noblest Spain could afford, he announced her a Trasmiera of the family of the Duke of Arcos, who, therefore, was his kinsman.

The authoritative bearing, which not even his ragged condition could diminish, his intrepid aquiline countenance, dark skin and black hair, and, above all, his fluent, cultured Castilian, made credible the imposture. And, anyway, since he desired no more than to be set ashore on some Dutch or French settlement, whence he could resume his voyage to Curacao, there seemed no reason why he should magnify his identity.

The sybaritic Don Juan de la Fuente who commanded the *Estremadura*, impressed by this shipwrecked gentleman's tale of high connections, treated him generously, placed a choice and extensive wardrobe at his disposal, gave him a stateroom off the main cabin, and used him in every way as one person of distinction should use another. It contributed to this that Don Juan found in Peter Vandermeer a man after his own heart. He insisted upon calling him Don Pedro, as if to stress the Spanish part in him, swearing that his Vandermeer blood had been entirely beneaped by that of the Trasmieras. It was a subject on which the Spanish gentleman made some ribaldries. Indeed, ribaldry flowed from him naturally and copiously on all occasions, and infected his officers, four of whom, young gentlemen of lineage, dined and supped with him daily in the great cabin.

Proclivities which in a raw lad of eighteen Blood might have condoned, trusting to time to correct them, he found frankly disgusting in this man of thirty. Under the courtly elegant exterior he perceived the unclean spirit of the rakehell. But he was far indeed from betraying his contempt. His own safety, resting precariously as it did upon maintaining the good impression he had made at the outset, compelled him to adapt himself to the company, to represent himself as a man of their own licentious kidney.

Thus it came about that during those days when, almost becalmed on the tropical sea, they crawled slowly north under a mountain of canvas that was often limp, something akin to a friendship sprang up between Don Juan and this Don Pedro. Don Juan found much to admire in him: his obvious vigour of body and of spirit, the deep knowledge of men and of the world which he displayed, his ready wit and the faintly cynical philosophy which his talk revealed. Spending long hours together daily, their intimacy grew at the rate peculiar to growths in that tropical region.

And that, briefly, is how you come to find these two closeted together on this the sixth day of Blood's voyage as a guest of honour in a ship in which he would have been travelling in irons had his identity been so much as suspected. Meanwhile her commander wearied him with lascivious songs, whilst Blood pondered the amusing side of the situation, which, nevertheless, it would be well to end at the earliest opportunity.

So presently, when the song had ceased and the Spaniard was munching Peruvian sweetmeats from a silver box beside him, Captain Blood approached the question. The pinnace in which he had travelled with the castaway Spaniards had been taken in tow by the *Estremadura*, and the time, he thought, had come to use it.

"We should now be abeam of Martinique," he said. "It cannot be more than six or seven leagues to land."

"Very true, thanks to this cursed lack of wind. I could blow harder from my own lungs."

"You cannot, of course, put in for me," said Blood. There was war at the time between France and Spain, which Blood understood to be one of the reasons of Don Juan's presence in these waters. "But in this calm sea I could easily pull myself ashore in the boat that brought me. Suppose, Don Juan, I take my leave of you this evening."

Don Juan looked aggrieved. "Here's a sudden haste to leave us! Was it not agreed that I carry you to Saint Martin?"

"True. But, thinking of it, I remember that ships are rare there, and I may be delayed some time in finding a vessel for Curacao; whereas from Martinique..."

"Ah, no," he was peevishly interrupted. "You shall land, if you please, at Mariegalante, where I myself have business, or at Guadeloupe if you prefer it, as I think you may. But I vow I do not let you go just yet."

Captain Blood had checked in the act of filling himself a pipe of finest Sacerdotes tobacco from a jar of broken leaf upon the table. "You have business at Mariegalante?" So surprised was he that he abandoned for that question the matter more personal to himself. "What business is possible at present between you and the French?"

Don Juan smiled darkly. "The business of war, my friend. Am I not a man of war?"

"You are going to raid Mariegalante?"

The Spaniard was some time in answering. Softly he stirred the chords of his guitar into sound. The smile still hovered about his full red lips, but it had assumed a faintly cruel character and his dark eyes glowed.

"The garrison at Basseterre is commanded by a dog named Coulevain with whom I have an account to settle. It is over a year old, but at last we are approaching pay-day. The war gives me my opportunity. I serve Spain and myself at a sin-single stroke."

Blood kindled a light, applied it to his pipe, and fell to smoking. It did not seem to him to be a very commendable service to Spain to risk one of her ships in an attack upon so negligible a settlement as Mariegalante. When presently he spoke, however, it was to utter the half of his thought upon another subject, and he said nothing more of landing on Martinique.

"It will be something to add to my experience, to have been aboard a ship in action. It will be something not easily forgotten--unless we are sunk by the guns of Basseterre."

Don Juan laughed. For all his profligacy, the fellow seemed of a high stomach, not easily disturbed at the imminence of a fight. Rather did the prospect fill him now with glee. This increased when that evening, at last, the breeze freshened and they began to make better speed, and that night in the cabin of the *Estremadura* spirits ran high, boisterously led by Don Juan himself. There was deep drinking of heady Spanish wines and a deal of easily excited laughter.

Captain Blood conjectured that heavy indeed must be the account of the French commander of Mariegalante with Don Juan if the prospect of a settlement could so exalt the Spaniard. His own sympathies went out freely to the French settlers who were about to suffer one of those revolting raids by which the Spaniards had rendered themselves so deservedly detested in the New World. But he was powerless to raise a finger or utter a word in their defence, compelled to join in this brutal mirth at the prospect of French slaughter, and to drink damnation to the French in general and to Colonel de Coulevain in particular.

In the morning, when he went on deck, Captain Blood beheld the long coastline of Dominica, ten or twelve miles away on the larboard quarter, and in the distance ahead a vague grey mass which he knew to be the mountain that rises in the middle of the round Island of Mariegalante. They had come south of Dominica in the night, and so had passed out of the Caribbean Sea into the open Atlantic.

Don Juan, in high spirits and apparently none the worse for last night's carouse, came to join him on the poop and to inform him of that which he already knew, but of which he was careful to betray no knowledge.

For a couple of hours they held to their course, driving straight before the wind with shortened sail. When within ten miles of the island, which now seemed to rise from the turquoise sea like a wall of green, the crew became active under sharp words of command and shrill notes from the boatswain's pipe. Nettings were spread above the *Estremadura's* decks to catch any spars that might be brought down in action; the shot-racks were filled; the leaden aprons were cleared from the guns, and buckets for seawater were distributed beside them.

From the carved poop-rail, at Don Juan's side, Captain Blood looked on with interest and approval as the musketeers in corselet and peaked headpiece were marshalled in the waist. And all the while Don Juan was explaining to him the significance of things with which no man afloat was better acquainted than Captain Blood.

At eight bells they went below to dine, Don Juan less boisterous now that action was imminent. His face had lost some of its colour, and there was a restlessness about his long slender hands, a feverish glitter in his velvet eyes. He ate little, and this little quickly; but he drank copiously; and he was still at table when one of his officers, a squat youngster named Veraguas, who had remained on duty, came to announce that it was time for him to take command.

He rose, and, with the aid of his negro steward Absolom, armed himself quickly in back and breast and steel cap; then went on deck. Captain Blood accompanied him, despite the Spaniard's warning that he should not expose himself without body-armour.

The *Estremadura* had come within three miles of the port of Basseterre. She flew no flag, from a natural reluctance to advertise her nationality more than it was advertised already by her lines and rig. Within a mile Don Juan could, through his telescope, survey the whole of the wide-mouthed harbour, and he announced that at least no ships of war were present. The fort would be the only antagonist in the preliminary duel.

A shot just then across the *Estremadura's* bows proclaimed that at least the commandant of the fort was a man who understood his business. Despite that definite signal to heave to, the *Estremadura* raced on and met the roar of a dozen guns. Unscathed by the volley, she held to her course, reserving her fire. Thus Don Juan earned the unspoken approval of Captain Blood. He ran the gauntlet of a second volley, and still held his fire until almost at point-blank range. Then he loosed a broadside, went smartly about, loosed another, and then ran off, close-hauled, to reload, offering only the narrow target of his stern to the French gunners.

When he returned to the attack he trailed astern the three boats that hitherto had been on the booms amidship, in addition to the useful pinnace in which Captain Blood had travelled.

He suffered now some damage to the mizzen yards, and the tall deck structures of his ornate forecastle were heavily battered. But there was nothing in this to distress him, and, handling his ship with great judgment, he smashed at the fort with two more heavy broadsides of twenty guns each, so well-delivered that he effectively silenced it for the moment.

He was off again, and when next he returned the boats in tow were filled with his musketeers. He brought them to within a hundred yards of the cliff, to seaward of the fort and at an angle at which the guns could hardly reach him, and sending the boats ashore, he stood there to cover their landing. A party of French that issued from the half-ruined fortress to oppose them were mown down by a discharge of gangrel and case-shot. Then the Spaniards were ashore and swarming up the gentle slope to the attack whilst the empty boats were being rowed back for reinforcements.

Whilst this was happening, Don Juan moved forward again and crashed yet another broadside at the fort to create a diversion and further to increase the distress and confusion there. Four or five guns answered him, and a twelve-pound shot came to splinter his bulwarks amidships; but he was away again without further harm, and going about to meet his boats. He was, still loading them with a further contingent when the musketry ashore fell silent. Then a lusty Spanish cheer came over the water, and soon thereafter the ring of hammers upon metal to announce the spiking of the fort's now undefended guns...

Hitherto Captain Blood's attitude had been one of dispassionate criticism of proceedings in which he was something of an authority. Now, however, his mind turned to what must follow, and from his knowledge of the ways of Spanish soldiery on a raid, and his acquaintance with the rakehell who was to lead them, he shuddered, hardened buccaneer though he might be, at the prospective sequel. To him war was war, and he could engage in it ruthlessly against men as ruthless. But the sacking of towns with the remorselessness of a brutal inflamed soldiery towards peaceful colonists and their women was something he had never tolerated.

That Don Juan de la Fuente, delicately bred gentleman of Spain though he might be, shared no particle of Blood's scruples was evident. For Don Juan, his dark eyes aglow with expectancy, went ashore with his reinforcements, personally to lead that raid. At the last, with a laugh, he invited his guest to accompany him, promising him rare sport and a highly diverting addition to his experiences of life. Blood commanded himself and remained outwardly cold.

"My nationality forbids it, Don Juan. The Dutch are not at war with France."

"Why, who's to know you're Dutch? Be entirely a Spaniard for once, Don Pedro, and enjoy yourself. Who is to know?"

"I am," said Blood. "It is a question of honour." Don Juan stared at him as if he were ludicrous. "You must be the victim of your scruples, then;" and still laughing he went down the accommodation ladder to the waiting boat.

Captain Blood remained upon the poop, whence he could watch the town above the shore, less than a mile away; for the *Estremadura* now rode at anchor in the roadstead. Of the officers, only Veraguas remained aboard, and of the men not more than fourteen or fifteen. But they kept a sharp watch, and there was a master gunner amongst them for emergencies.

Don Sebastian Veraguas bewailed his fate that he should have been left out of the landing party, and spoke wistfully of the foul joys that might have been his ashore. He was a sturdy, bovine fellow of five and-twenty, prominent of nose and chin, and he chattered self-sufficiently whilst Blood kept his glance upon the little town. Even at that distance they could hear the sounds of the horrid Spanish handiwork, and already more than one house was in flames. Too well Blood knew what was taking place at the instigation of a gentleman of Spain, and as grim-faced he watched, he would have given much to have had a hundred of his buccaneers at hand with whom to sweep this Spanish rubbish from the earth. Once before he had witnessed at close quarters such a raid, and he had sworn then that never thereafter would he show mercy to a Spaniard. To that oath he had been false in the past; but he vowed now that he would not fail to keep it in future.

And meanwhile the young man at his elbow, whom he could gladly have strangled with his hands, was calling down the whole heavenly hierarchy to witness his disappointment at being absent from that Hell.

It was evening when the raiders returned, coming, as they had gone, by the road which led to the now silent fort, and there taking boat to cross a hundred yards of jade-green water to the anchored ship. They sang as they came, boisterous and hilarious, a few of them with bandaged wounds, many of them flushed with wine and rum, and all of them laden with spoils. They made vile jests of the desolation they had left behind and viler boasts of the abominations they had practised. No buccaneers in the world, thought Blood, could ever have excelled them in brutality. The raid had been entirely successful and they had lost not more than a half-dozen men whose deaths had been terribly avenged.

And then in the last boat came Don Juan. Ahead of him up the accommodation ladder went two of his men bearing a heaving bundle, which Blood presently made out to be a woman whose head and shoulders were muffled in a cloak. Below the black folds of this he beheld a petticoat of flowered silk and caught a glimpse of agitated legs in silken hose and dainty high-heeled shoes. In mounting horror he judged from this that the woman was a person of quality.

Don Juan, with face and hands begrimed with sweat and powder, followed closely. From the head of the ladder he uttered a command: "To my cabin."

Blood saw her borne across the deck, through the ranks of men who jeered their ribaldries, and then she vanished in the arms of her captors down the gangway.

Now whatever he may have been towards men, towards women Blood had never been other than chivalrous. This, perhaps, for the sake of that sweet lady in Barbadoes to whom he accounted himself nothing, but who was to him an inspiration to more honour than would be thought possible in a buccaneer. That chivalry arose in him now full-armed. Had he yielded to it completely and blindly he would there and then have fallen upon Don Juan, and thus wrecked at once all possibility of being of service to his unfortunate captive. Her presence here could be no mystery to any. She was the particular prize that the profligate Spanish commander reserved to himself, and Blood felt his flesh go crisp and cold at the thought.

Yet when presently he came down the companion and crossed the deck to the gangway he was calm and smiling. In that narrow passage he joined Don Juan's officers, the three who had been ashore with him as well as Veraguas. They were all talking at once and laughing boisterously, and the subject of their approving mirth was their captain's vileness.

Together they burst into the cabin, Blood coming last. The negro servant had laid the table for supper with the usual six places, and had just lighted the great silver lamp, for with sunset the daylight faded almost instantly.

Don Juan was emerging at that moment from one of the larboard cabins. He closed the door, and stood for a dozen heart-beats with his back to it, surveying that invasion almost mistrustfully. It determined him to turn the key in the lock, draw it out and put it in his pocket. From that lesser cabin, in which clearly the lady had been bestowed, there came no sound.

"She's quiet at last, God be praised," laughed one of the officers.

"Worn out with screeching," explained another. "Lord! Was there ever such a wild-cat? A woman of spirit that, from the way she fought; a little devil worth the taming. It's a task I envy you, Juan."

Veraguas hailed the prize as well-deserved by such brilliant leadership, and then whilst questionable quips and jests were still being bandied, Don Juan, smiling grimly, introspectively, ordered them to table.

"We'll sup briefly, if you please," he announced, as he unbuckled his harness, and by the remark produced a fresh storm of hilarity on the subject of his haste and at the expense of the poor victim beyond that door.

When at last they sat down Captain Blood thrust himself upon Don Juan's notice with a question: "And Colonel de Coulevain?"

The handsome face darkened. "A malediction on him! He was away from Basseterre, organizing defences at Les Carmes."

Blood raised his brows, adopted a tone of faint concern. "Then the account remains unsettled in spite of all your brave efforts."

"Not quite. Not quite."

"By Heaven, no!" said another with a laugh. "Madame de Coulevain should give an ample quittance."

"Madame de Coulevain?" said Blood, although the question was unnecessary as were the glances that travelled towards the locked cabin door to answer him. He laughed. "Now that..." He paused. "That is an artistic vengeance, Don Juan, whatever the offence." And, with Hell in his soul, he laughed again, softly, in admiring approval.

Don Juan shrugged and sighed. "Yet I would I had found him and made him pay in full."

But Captain Blood would not leave it there. "If you really hate the man, think of the torment to which you have doomed him, always assuming that he loves his wife. Surely by comparison with that the peace of death would be no punishment at all."

"Maybe, maybe." Don Juan was short. Disappointment seemed to have spoiled his temper, or perhaps impatience fretted him. "Give me wine, Absolom. God of my life! How I thirst!"

The negro poured for them. Don Juan drained his bumper at a draught. Blood did the same, and the goblets were replenished.

Blood toasted the Spanish commander in voluble terms. He was no great judge, he declared, of an action afloat; but he could not conceive that the one he had witnessed that day could have been better fought by any commander living.

Don Juan smiled his gratification; the toast was drunk with relish, and the cups were filled again. Then others talked, and Blood lapsed into thought.

He reflected that soon now, supper being done, Don Juan would drive them all to their quarters. Captain Blood's own were on the starboard side of the great cabin. But would he be suffered to remain there now, so near at hand? If so, he might yet avail that unhappy lady, and already he knew precisely how. The danger lay in that he might be sent elsewhere to-night.

He roused himself and broke in upon the talk, called noisily for more wine, and after that for yet more, in which the others who had sweated profusely in that day's action kept him company gladly enough. He broke into renewed eulogies of Don Juan's skill and valour, and it was presently observed that his speech was slurred and indistinct, and that he hiccoughed and repeated himself foolishly.

Thus he provoked ridicule, and when it was forthcoming he displayed annoyance, and appealed to Don Juan to inform these merry and befuddled gentlemen that he at least was sober; but his speech grew thicker even whilst he was protesting.

When Veraguas taxed him with being drunk he grew almost violent, spoke of his Dutch origin to remind them that he came of a nation of great drinkers, and offered to drink any man in the Caribbean under the table. Boastfully, to prove his words, he called for more wine, and having drunk it lapsed gradually into silence. His eyelids dropped heavily, his body sagged, and presently, to the hilarity of all who beheld here a boaster confounded, he slid from his chair and came to rest upon the cabin floor, nor attempted to rise again.

Veraguas stirred him contemptuously and ungently with his foot. He gave no sign of life. He lay inert as a log, breathing stertorously.

Don Juan got up abruptly. "Put the fool to bed. And get you gone too; all of you."

Don Pedro was borne, insensible, amid laughter and some rude handling, to his cabin. His neckcloth was loosed, and so they left him, closing the door upon him.

Then, in compliance with Don Juan's renewed command, they all departed noisily, and the commander locked the door of the now empty great cabin.

Alone, he came slowly back to the table, and stood a moment listening to the uncertain steps and the merry voices retreating down the gangway. His goblet stood half-full. He picked it up and drank. Then, setting it down, and proceeding without haste, he drew from his pocket the key of the cabin in which Madame de Coulevain had been bestowed. He crossed the floor, thrust the key into the lock and turned it. But before he could throw open the door a sound behind him made him turn again.

His drunken guest was leaning against the bulkhead beside the open door of his stateroom. His clothes were in disorder, his face vacuous, and he stood so precariously that it was a wonder the gentle heave of the ship did not pitch him off his balance. He moved his lips like a man nauseated, and parted them with a dry click.

"Wha's o'clock?" was his foolish question.

Don Juan relaxed his stare to smile, although a thought impatiently.

The drunkard babbled on: "I...I don't...remember..." He broke off. He lurched forward. "Thousand devils! I...I thirst!"

"To bed with you! To bed!" cried Don Juan. "To bed? Of...of course to bed. Whither...else? Eh? But first...a cup."

He reached the table. He lurched round it, a man carried forward by his own impetus, and came to rest opposite the Spaniard, whose velvet eyes watched him with angry contempt. He found a goblet and a jug, a heavy, encrusted silver jug, shaped like an amphora with a handle on either side of its long neck. He poured himself wine, drank, and set down the cup; then he stood swaying slightly, and put forth his right hand as if to steady himself. It came to rest on the neck of the silver jug.

Don Juan, watching him ever with impatient scorn, may have seen for the fraction of a second the vacuity leave that countenance, and the vivid blue eyes under their black brows grow cold and hard as sapphires. But before the second was spent, before the brain could register what the eyes beheld, the body of that silver jug had crashed into his brow, and the commander of the *Estremadura* knew nothing more.

Captain Blood, without a trace now of drunkenness in face or gait, stepped quickly round the table, and went down on one knee beside the man he had felled. Don Juan lay quite still on the gay Eastern carpet, his handsome face clay-coloured with a trickle of blood across it from the wound between the half-closed eyes. Captain Blood contemplated his work without pity or compunction. If there was cowardice in the blow which had taken the Spaniard unawares from a hand which he supposed friendly, that cowardice was born of no fear for himself, but for the helpless lady in that larboard cabin. On her account he could take no risk of Don Juan's being able to give the alarm; and, anyway, this cruel, soulless profligate deserved no honourable consideration.

He stood up briskly, then stooped and placed his hand under the inert Spaniard's armpits. Raising the limp body, he dragged it with trailing heels to the stern window, which stood open to the soft, purple, tropical night. He took Don Juan in his arms, and, laden with him, mounted the day-bed. A moment he steadied his heavy burden upon the sill; then he thrust it forth, and, supporting himself by his grip of a stanchion, leaned far out to observe the Spaniard's fall.

The splash he made in the phosphorescent wake of the gently moving ship was merged into the gurgle of water about the vessel. For an instant as it took the sea the body glowed, sharply defined in an incandescence that was as suddenly extinguished. Phosphorescent bubbles arose and broke in the luminous line astern; then all was as it had been.

Captain Blood was still leaning far out, still peering down, when a voice in the cabin behind him came to startle him. It brought him instantly erect, alert; but he did not yet turn round. Indeed, he checked himself in the very act, and remained stiffly poised, his left hand supporting him still upon the stanchion, his back turned squarely upon the speaker.

For the voice was the voice of a woman. Its tone was tender, gentle, inviting. The words it had uttered in French were:

"Juan! Juan! Why do you stay? What do you there? I have been waiting. Juan!"

Speculation treading close upon amazement, he continued to stand there, waiting for more that should help him to understand. The voice came again, more insistently now.

"Juan! Don't you hear me? Juan!"

He swung round at last, and beheld her near the open door of her cabin, from which she had emerged: a tall, handsome woman, in the middle twenties, partly dressed, with a mantle of unbound golden tresses about her white shoulders. He had imagined this lady cowering, terror-stricken, helpless, probably pinioned, in the cabin to which the Spanish ravisher had consigned her. Because of that mental picture, intolerable to his chivalrous nature, he had done what he had done. Yet there she stood, not merely free, nor merely having come forth of her own free will, but summoning Don Juan in accents that are used to a lover.

Horror stunned him: horror of himself and of the dreadful murderous blunder he had committed in his haste to play at knight-errantry: to usurp the place of Providence.

And then another deeper horror welled up to submerge the first: horror of this woman as she stood suddenly revealed to him. That dreadful raid on Basseterre had been no more than a pretext to cloak her elopement, and must have been undertaken at her invitation. The rest, her forcible conveyance aboard, her bestowal in the cabin, had all been part of a loathly comedy she had played--a comedy set against a background of fire and rape and murder, by all of which she remained so soullessly unperturbed that she could come forth to coo her lover's name on that seductive note.

It was for this harpy, who waded complacently through blood and the wreckage of a hundred lives to the fulfilment of her desires, that he had soiled his hands. The situation seemed to transmute his chivalrously-inspired deed into a foulness.

He shivered as he regarded her, and she, confronted by that stern aquiline face and those ice-cold blue eyes, that were certainly not Don Juan's, gasped, recoiled, and clutched her flimsy silken body-garment chosen to her generous breast.

"Who are you?" she demanded. "Where is Don Juan de la Fuente?"

He stepped down from the day-bed, and something bodeful in his countenance changed her surprise to incipient alarm.

"You are Madame de Coulevain?" he asked, using her own language. He must make no mistake.

She nodded. "Yes, yes." Her tone was impatient, but the fear abode in her eyes. "Who are you? Why do you question me?" She stamped her foot. "Where is Don Juan?"

He knew that truth is commonly the shortest road, and he took it. He jerked a thumb backwards over his shoulder. "I've just thrown him through the window."

She stared and stared at this cold, calm man about whom she perceived something so remorseless and terrifying that she could not doubt his incredible words.

Suddenly she loosed a scream. It did not disconcert or even move him. He began to speak again, and, dominated by those brilliant intolerable eyes which were like points of steel, she controlled herself to listen.

"You are supposing me one of Don Juan's companions; perhaps even that, covetous of the noble prize he took to-day at Basseterre I have murdered him to possess it. That far indeed from the truth. Deceived like the rest by the comedy of your being brought forcibly aboard, imagining you the unhappy victim of a man I knew for a profligate voluptuary, I was moved to unutterable compassion on your behalf, and to save you from the horror I foresaw for you I killed him. And now," he added with a bitter smile, "it seems that you were in no need of saving, that I have thwarted you no less than I have thwarted him. This comes of playing Providence."

"You killed him!" she said. She staggered where she stood, and, ashen-faced, looked as if she would swoon. "You killed him! Killed him! Oh, my God! My God! You've killed my Juan." Thus far she had spoken dully, as if she were repeating something so that she might force it upon her own understanding. But now she wrought herself to frenzy. "You beast! You assassin!" she screamed. "You shall pay! I'll rouse the ship! You shall answer, as God's in Heaven!"

She was already across the cabin hammering on the door; already her hand was upon the key when he came up with her. She struggled like a wild-cat in his grip, screaming the while for help. At last he wrenched her away, swung her round and hurled her from him. Then he withdrew, and pocketed the key.

She lay on the floor, by the table, where he had flung her, and sent scream after scream to alarm the ship.

Captain Blood surveyed her coldly. "Aye, aye, breathe your lungs, my child," he bade her. "It will do you good and me no harm."

He sat down to await the exhaustion of her paroxysm. But his words had already quieted her. Her round eyes asked a question. He smiled sourly as he answered it.

"No man aboard this ship will stir a foot for all your cries, or even heed them, unless it be as a matter for amusement. That is the kind of men they are who follow Don Juan de la Fuente."

He saw by her stricken expression how well she understood. He nodded with that faint sardonic smile which she found hateful. "Aye, madame. That's the situation. You were best bring yourself to a calm contemplation of it."

She got to her feet, and stood leaning heavily against the table, surveying him with rage and loathing. "If they do not come to-night, they will come to-morrow. Some time they must come. And when they come it will be very ill for you, whoever you may be."

"Will it not also be very ill for you?" quoth Blood.

"For me? I did not murder him."

"You'll not be accused of it. But in him you've lost your only protector aboard this ship. What will betide you, do you suppose, when you are alone and helpless in their power, a prisoner of war, the captive of a raid, in the hands of these merry gentlemen of Spain?"

"God of Heaven!" She clutched her breast in terror.

"Quiet you," he bade her, almost contemptuously. "I did not rescue you, as I supposed, from one wolf, merely to fling you to the pack. That will not happen--unless you yourself prefer it to returning to your husband."

She grew hysterical.

"To my husband? Ah, that, no! Never that! Never that!"

"It is that or..."--he pointed to the door--"...The pack. I perceive no choice for you save between those alternatives."

"Who are you?" she asked abruptly. "What are you, you devil, who have destroyed me and yet torment me?"

"I am your saviour, not your destroyer. Your husband, for his own sake, shall be left to suppose, as all have been led to suppose, that you were violently carried off. He will receive you back with relief of his own anguish and with tenderness, and make amends to you for all that the poor fool will fancy you have suffered."

She laughed on a note of hysteria.

"Tenderness! Tenderness in my husband! If he had ever been tender I should not be where I now am." And suddenly, to his surprise, she was moved to explain, to exculpate herself. "I was married to a cold, gross, stupid, cruel animal. That is Monsieur de Coulevain, a fool who has squandered his possessions and is forced to accept a command in these raw barbarous colonies to which he has dragged me.

"Oh, you think the worst of me, of course. You account me just a light woman. But you shall know the truth.

"At the height of my disillusion some few months after my marriage, Don Juan de la Fuente came to us at Pau, where we lived, for my husband is a Gascon. My Don Juan was travelling in France. We loved each other from our first meeting. He saw my unhappiness, which was plain to all. He urged me to fly to Spain with him, and I would to Heaven I had yielded then, and so put an end to misery. Foolishly I resisted. A sense of duty kept me faithful to my vows. I dismissed him. Since then my cup of misery and shame has overflowed, and when a letter from him was brought to me here at Basseterre on the outbreak of war with Spain, to show me that his fond, loyal, noble heart had not forgotten, I answered him, and in my despair I bade him come for me whenever he would."

She paused a moment, looking at Captain Blood with tragic eyes from which the tears were flowing.

"Now, sir, you know precisely what you have done, what havoc you have made."

Blood's expression had lost some of its sternness. His voice, as he answered her, assumed a gentler note.

"The havoc exists only in your mind, madame. The change which you conceived to be from hell to heaven would have been from hell to deeper hell. You did not know this man, this loyal, noble heart, this Don Juan de la Fuente. You were taken by the external glitter of him. But it was the glitter, I tell you of decay, for at the core the man was rotten, and in his hands your fate would have been infamy."

"Do you mend your case or mine by maligning the man you've murdered?"

"Malign him? Nay, madame. Proof of what I say is under my hand. You were in Basseterre to-day. You know something of the bloodshed, the slaughter of almost defenceless men, the dreadful violence to women..."

Faintly she interrupted him. "These things...in the way of war..."

"The way of war?" he roared. "Madame, undeceive yourself. Look truth boldly in the face though it condemn you both. Of what consequence Mariegalante to Spain? And, having been taken, is it held? War served your lover as a pretext. He let loose his dreadful soldiery upon the ill-defended place, solely so that he might answer your invitation. Men who to-day have been wantonly butchered, and unfortunate women who have suffered brutal violence, would now be sleeping tranquilly in their beds but for you and your evil lover. But for you--"

She interrupted him. She had covered her face with her hands while he was speaking, and sat rocking herself and moaning feebly. Now suddenly she uncovered her face again, and he saw that her eyes were fierce.

"No more!" she commanded, and stood up. "I'll hear no more. It's false! False what you say! You distort things to justify your own wicked deed."

He considered her grimly with those cold, penetrating eyes of his.

"Your kind," he said slowly, "will always believe what it chooses to believe. I do not think that I need pity you too much. But since I know that I have distorted nothing, I am content that expiation now awaits you. You shall choose the form of it, madame. Shall I leave you to these Spanish gentlemen, or will you come with me to your husband?"

She looked at him, her eyes distraught, her bosom in tumult. She began to plead with him. Awhile he listened; then he cut her short.

"Madame, I am not the arbiter of your fate. You have shaped it for yourself. I but point out the only two roads it leaves you free to tread."

"How...how can you take me back to Basseterre?" she asked him presently.

He told her, and without waiting for her consent, which he knew could not be withheld, he made swift preparation. He flung some provisions into a napkin, took a skin of wine, and a little cask of water, and by a rope which he fetched from his state-room lowered these things to the pinnace, which was again in tow, and which he drew under the counter of the galleon.

Next he lashed the shortened tow-rope to a cleat on one of the stanchions, then summoned her to make with him the airy passage down that rope.

It appalled her. But he conquered her fears, and when she had come to stand beside him, he seized the rope and swung out on it and slid down a little way to make room for her above him. At his command, although almost sick with terror, she grasped the rope and placed her feet on his shoulders. Then she slid down between the rope and him, until his hold embraced her knees and held her firmly.

Gently now, foot by foot, they began to descend. From the decks above came the sound of voices raised in song. The men were singing some Spanish scrannel in chorus.

At last his toe was on the gunwale of the pinnace. He worked her nose forward with that foot, sufficiently to enable him to plant the other firmly in the foresheets. After that it was an easy matter to step backwards, drawing her after him whilst still she clung to the rope. Thus he hauled the boat a little farther under the counter until he could take his companion about the waist and gently lower her.

After that he attacked the tow-rope with a knife and sawed it swiftly through. The galleon with its glowing sternport and the three great golden poop lamps sped serenely on close-hauled to the breeze, leaving them gently oscillating in her wake.

When he had recovered breath he bestowed Madame de Coulevain in the sternsheets, then hoisting the sail and trimming it, he broached to, and with his eyes on the brilliant stars in the tropical sky he steered a course which, with the wind astern, should bring them to Basseterre before sunrise.

In the sternsheets the woman was now gently weeping. With her, expiation had begun, as it does when it is possible to sin no more.

IX - THE GRATITUDE OF MONSIEUR DE COULEVAIN

All through the tepid night the pinnace, gently driven by the southerly breeze, ploughed steadily through a calm sea, which after moonrise became of liquid silver.

At the tiller sat Captain Blood. Beside him in the stern-sheets crouched the woman, who between silences was now whimpering, now vituperative, now apologetic. Of the gratitude which he accounted due to him he perceived no sign. But he was a tolerant, understanding man, and he did not, therefore, account himself aggrieved. Madame de Coulevain's case, however regarded, was a hard one; and she had little, after all, for which to be thankful to Fate or to Man.

Her mixed and alternating emotions did not surprise him.

He perceived quite clearly the sources of the hatred that rang in her voice whenever in the darkness she upbraided him and that glared in her pallid face when the dawn at last began to render it visible.

They were then within a couple of miles of land: a green flat coast with a single great mountain towering in the background. To larboard a tall ship was sweeping past them, steering for the bay ahead, and in her lines and rig Captain Blood read her English nationality. From her furled topsails he assumed that her master, evidently strange to these waters, was cautiously groping his way in. And this was confirmed by the seaman visible on the starboard forechains, leaning far out to take soundings. His chanting voice reached them across the sunlit waters as he told the fathoms.

Madame de Coulevain, who latterly had fallen into a drowsy stupor, roused herself to stare across at the frigate, aglow in the golden glory of the risen sun.

"No need for fear, madame. She is not Spanish."

"Fear?" She glared at him, blear-eyed from sleeplessness and weeping. She was a handsome woman, golden-headed and built on the generous lines of Hebe. Her full lips writhed into bitterness. "What have I to fear more than the fate you thrust upon me?"

"I, madame? I thrust no fate upon you. You are overtaken by the fate your own actions have invited."

Fiercely she interrupted him. "Have I invited this? That I should return to my husband?"

Captain Blood sighed in weariness. "Are we to have the argument all over again? Must I remind you that yourself you refused the only alternative, which was to remain at the mercy of those Spanish gallants on that Spanish ship? For the rest, your husband shall be left to suppose that you were carried off against your will."

"It if had not been for you, you assassin..."

"If it had not been for me, madame, your fate would have been even worse than you tell me that it is going to be."

"Nothing could be worse! Nothing! This man who has brought me out to these savage lands because, discredited and debt-ridden as he is, there was no longer a place for him at home, is...Oh, but why do I talk to you? Why do I try to explain to one who obstinately refuses to understand, to one who desires only to blame?"

"Madame, I do not desire to blame. I desire that you should blame yourself, for the horror you brought upon Basseterre. If you will accept whatever comes as an expiation, you may find some peace of mind."

"Peace of mind! Peace of mind!" Her scorn was fulminating.

He became sententious. "Expiation cleanses conscience. And when that has happened calm will return to your spirit."

"You preach to me! You! A filibuster, a sea-robber! And you preach of things you do not understand. I owe no expiation. I have done no wrong. I was a desperate woman, hard-driven by a man who is a beast, a cruel drunken beast, a broken gamester without honour; not even honest. I took my only chance to save my soul. Was I to know that Don Juan was what you say he is? Do I know it even now?"

"Do you not?" he asked her. "Did you see the ruin and desolation wantonly wrought in Basseterre, the horrors that he loosed his men to perpetrate, and do you still doubt his nature? And can you contemplate that havoc wrought so as to give you to your lover's arms, and still protest that you did no wrong? That, madame, is the offence that calls for expiation; not anything that may lie between yourself and your husband, or yourself and Don Juan."

Her mind refused admission to a conviction which it dared not harbour. Therefore she ranted on. Blood ceased to listen. He gave his attention to the sail; hauled it a little closer, so that the craft heeled over and headed straight for the bay.

It was an hour later when they brought up at the mole. A longboat was alongside, manned by English sailors from the frigate which in the meantime had come to anchor in the roadstead.

Odd groups of men and women, white and black, idling, cowed, at the waterside, with the horror of yesterday's events still heavy upon them, stared round-eyed at Madame de Coulevain as she was handed from the boat by her stalwart, grim-faced escort, in his crumpled coat of silver-laced grey camlet and black periwig that was rather out of curl.

The little mob moved forward in wonder, slowly at first, then with quickening steps, to crowd about the unsuspected author of their woes with questions of welcome and thanksgiving for this miracle of her return, of her deliverance, as they accounted it.

Blood waited, grim and silent, his eyes upon the sparse town which showed yesterday's ugly wounds as yet unscarred. Houses displayed shattered doors and broken windows, whilst here and there a heap of ashes smouldered where a house had stood. Pieces of broken furniture lay about in the open. From the belfry of the little church standing amid the acacias in the open square came the mournful note of a passing-bell. Within the walled enclosure about it there was an ominous activity, and negroes could be seen at work there with pick and shovel.

Captain Blood's cold blue eyes played swiftly over all this and more. Then, almost roughly, he extricated the lady from that little mob of stricken questioning sympathisers who little guessed to what extent she was the author of their woes. At once conducted and conducting, he made his way up the gently rising ground. They passed a party of British sailors filling water-casks at a fountain which had been contrived by the damming of a brook. They passed the church with its busy graveyard. They passed a company of militia at drill; men in blue coats with red facings who had been hurriedly brought over by Colonel de Coulevain from Les Carmes after the harm was done.

Delayed on the way by others whom they met and who must stop to cry out in wonder at sight of Madame de Coulevain, accompanied by this tall, stern stranger, they came at last by a wide gateway into a luxuriant garden, and by an avenue of palms to a long, low house of stone and timber.

There were no signs of damage here. The Spaniards who had yesterday invaded the place, if, indeed, they had invaded it, had wrought no other mischief than to carry off the Governor's lady. The elderly negro who admitted them broke into shrill cries upon beholding his dishevelled mistress in her crumpled gown of flowered silk. He laughed and wept at once. He uttered scraps of prayer. He capered like a dog. He caught her hand and slobbered kisses on it.

"You appear to be loved, madame," said Captain Blood when at last they stood alone in the long dining-room.

"Of course that must surprise you," she sneered, with that twist of her full lips which he had come to know.

The door of a connecting-room was abruptly flung open, and a tall, heavily-built man with prominent features and sallow, deeply-lined cheeks stood at gaze. His militia coat, of blue with red facings, was stiff with tarnished gold lace. His dark bloodshot eyes opened wide at sight of her. He turned pale under his tan.

"Antoinette!" he ejaculated. He came forward unsteadily and took her by the shoulders. "Is it really you? They told me...But where have you been since yesterday?"

"Where they told you I was, no doubt." There was little in her tone besides weariness. "Fortunately, or unfortunately, this gentleman delivered me, and he has brought me safely back."

"Fortunately or unfortunately?" he echoed, and scowled. His lip curled. The dislike of her in his eyes was not to be mistaken. He took his hands from her shoulders, and half turned to consider her companion. "This gentleman?" Then his glance darkened further. "A Spaniard?"

Captain Blood met the frown with a smile. "A Dutchman, sir," he lied. But the rest of his tale was true. "By great good fortune I was aboard that Spanish ship, the *Estremadura*. I had been picked up by her at sea a few days before. I had access to the great cabin in which the Spanish commander had locked himself with Madame your wife. I interrupted his amorous intentions. In fact, I killed him with my hands." And he added a brief account of how, thereafter, he had conveyed her from the galleon.

Monsieur de Coulevain swore profoundly to express his wonder; stood silently pondering the thing he had been told; then swore again. Blood accounted him a dull, brutish fellow whom any woman would be justified in leaving. If the Colonel felt any tenderness towards his wife, or thankfulness for her delivery from the dreadful fate to which he must suppose her to have been exposed, he kept the emotions to himself. He showed presently, however, that he could be emotional enough over the memory of yesterday's catastrophe. This Blood accounted reasonable until he came to perceive that the man's real concern was less with the sufferings of the people of Basseterre than with the possible consequences to himself when an account of his stewardship should come to be asked of him by the French Government.

Madame, her beauty sadly impaired by her pallor, her weariness and dishevelled condition, interrupted his lament, to recall him to the demands of common courtesy.

"You have not yet thanked this gentleman for the heroic service he has rendered us."

Blood caught the sneer and perceived its double edge. At last he found it in his heart to pity her a little, to understand the despair which had driven her, reckless of what might betide others, so that she should escape from this boorish egotist.

Belatedly and clumsily M. de Coulevain expressed his thanks. When that was done, Madame took her leave of them. She confessed herself exhausted, and it was the old negro, who had remained in attendance in the background, who came forward to proffer his arm and to assist her. On the threshold a negro woman waited, all tenderness and solicitude, to put her weary mistress to bed.

Coulevain, heavy-eyed, watched her depart, and remained staring until Captain Blood's brisk voice aroused him.

"If you were to offer me some breakfast, sir, that would be a practical measure of repayment."

Coulevain swore. "Death of my life! How negligent I am! These troubles, sir...the ruin of the town...the abduction of my wife...It is too much, sir. You'll understand. It discomposes a man. You forgive me, Monsieur...I have not the honour to know your name."

"Vandermeer. Peter Vandermeer, at your service."

And then another voice cut in, a voice that spoke French with a rasping English accent. "Are you quite sure that that is your name?"

Blood span round. On the threshold of the adjacent room from which Colonel de Coulevain had earlier issued stood now the stocky figure of a youngish man in a red coat that was laced with silver. In the plump, florid countenance Captain Blood recognized at a glance his old acquaintance Captain Macartney, who had been second in command at Antigua when some months before Captain Blood had slipped through the fingers of the British there. His momentary surprise at finding Macartney here was dispelled by remembrance of the English frigate which had passed him as they were approaching Basseterre.

The officer was smiling hatefully. "Good morning, Captain Blood. This time you have no buccaneers at your heels, no ships, no demi-cannons with which to intimidate us."

So ominous was the tone, so clear its hint of the speaker's intention, that Blood's hand flew instinctively to his left side. The Englishman's smile became a laugh.

"Not even a sword, Captain Blood."

"Its absence will no doubt encourage your impertinences."

But now the Colonel was intervening. "Captain Blood, did you say? Captain Blood? Not the filibuster? Not...?"

"The filibuster indeed; the buccaneer, the transported rebel, the escaped convict on whose head the British Government has placed the price of a thousand pounds."

"A thousand pounds!" Coulevain sucked his breath. His dark, blood-injected eyes returned to the contemplation of his wife's preserver. "Sir, sir! Is this true, sir?"

Blood shrugged. "Of course it's true. Who else do you suppose could have done what I have told you that I did last night?"

Coulevain continued to stare at him with increasing wonder. "And you contrived to pass yourself off as a Dutchman on a Spanish ship?"

"Who else but Captain Blood could have done that?"

"My God!" said Coulevain.

"I hope, none the less, you'll give me some breakfast, my Colonel?"

"Aboard the *Royal Duchess*," said Macartney, evilly facetious, "you shall have all the breakfast you require."

"Much obliged. But I have a prior claim on the hospitality of Colonel de Coulevain, for services rendered to his wife."

Major Macartney--he had been promoted since Blood's last meeting with him--smiled. "My claim can wait, then, until your fast is broken."

"What claim is that?" quoth Coulevain.

"To do my duty by arresting this damned pirate, and delivering him to the hangman."

M. de Coulevain seemed shocked. "Arrest him? You want to laugh, I think. This, sir, is France. Your warrant does not run on French soil."

"Perhaps not. But there is an agreement between France and England for the prompt exchange of any prisoners who may have escaped from a penal settlement. Under that agreement, sir, you dare not refuse to surrender Captain Blood to me."

"Surrender him to you? My guest? The man who has served me so nobly? Who is here as a direct consequence of that service? Sir, it...it is unthinkable." Thus he displayed to Captain Blood certain remains of decent feeling.

Macartney was gravely calm. "I perceive your scruples. I respect them. But duty is duty."

"I care nothing for your duty, sir."

The Major's manner became more stern. "Colonel de Coulevain, you will forgive me for pointing out to you that I have the means at hand to enforce my demand, and my duty will compel me to employ it."

"What?" Colonel de Coulevain was aghast. "You would land your men under arms on French soil?"

"If you are obstinate in your misplaced chivalry you will leave me no choice."

"But...God of my life! That would be an act of war. War between the nations would be the probable result."

Macartney shook his round head. "The certain result would be the cashiering of Colonel de Coulevain for having made the act necessary in defiance of the existing agreement." He smiled maliciously. "I think you will be sufficiently under a cloud already, my Colonel, for yesterday's events here."

Coulevain sat down heavily, dragged forth a handkerchief and mopped his brow. He was perspiring freely. He appealed in his distress to Captain Blood. "Death of my life! What am I to do?"

"I am afraid," said Captain Blood, "that his reasoning is faultless." He stifled a yawn. "You'll forgive me. I was out in the open all night." And he, too, sat down. "Do not permit yourself to be distressed, my Colonel. This business of playing Providence is seldom properly requited by Fortune."

"But what am I to do, sir? What am I to do?"

Under his sleepy exterior, Captain Blood's wits were wide-awake and busy. It was within his experience of these officers sent overseas that they belonged almost without exception to one of two classes: they were either men who, like Coulevain, had dissipated their fortunes, or else younger sons with no fortunes to dissipate. Now, as he afterwards expressed it, he heaved the lead so as to sound the depth of Macartney's disinterestedness and honesty of purpose.

"You will give me up, of course, my Colonel. And the British Government will pay you the reward of a thousand pounds--five thousands pieces of eight."

Each officer made a sharp movement at that, and from each came an almost inarticulate ejaculation of inquiry.

Captain Blood explained himself. "It is so provided by the agreement under which Major Macartney claims my surrender. Any reward for the apprehension of an escaped prisoner is payable to the person surrendering him to the authorities. Here, on French soil, it will be you, my Colonel, who will surrender me. Major Macartney is merely the representative of the authorities--the British Government--to whom I am surrendered."

The Englishman's face lost some of its high colour; it lengthened; his mouth drooped; his very breathing quickened. Blood had heaved the lead to some purpose. It had given him the exact depth of Macartney, who stood now tongue-tied and crestfallen, forbidden by decency from making the least protest against the suddenly vanished prospect of a thousand pounds which he had been reckoning as good as in his pocket.

But this was not the only phenomenon produced by Blood's disclosure of the exact situation. Colonel de Coulevain, too, was oddly stricken. The sudden prospect of so easily acquiring this magnificent sum seemed to have affected him as oddly as the contrary had affected Macartney. This was an unexpected complication to the observant Captain Blood. But it led him at once to remember that Madame de Coulevain had described her husband as a broken gamester harassed by creditors. He wondered what would be the ultimate clash of the evil forces he was releasing, and almost ventured to hope that in that, when it came, as once before in a similar situation, would lie his opportunity.

"There is no more to be said, my Colonel," he drawled. "Circumstances have been too much for me. I know when I've lost, and I must pay." He yawned again. "Meanwhile, if I might have a little food and rest, I should be grateful. Perhaps Major Macartney will give me leave until this evening, when he can come to fetch me with an escort."

Macartney swung aside, and paced towards the open windows. The elation, the masterfulness, had completely left him. He dragged his feet. His shoulders drooped. "Very well," he said sourly, and checked his aimless wandering to turn towards the door. "I'll return for you at six o'clock."

But on the threshold he paused..."You'll play me no tricks, Captain Blood?"

"Tricks? What tricks can I play?" The Captain smiled wistfully. "I have no buccaneers, no ship, no demi-cannon. Not even a sword, as you remarked, Major. For the only trick I might yet play you..." He broke off, and changed his tone to add more briskly: "Major Macartney, since there's no thousand pounds to be earned by you for taking me, should you not be a fool to refuse a thousand pounds for leaving me? For forgetting that you have seen me?"

Macartney flushed. "What the devil do you mean?"

"Now don't be getting hot, Major. Think it over until this evening. A thousand pounds is a deal of money. You don't earn it every day, or every year, in the service of King James; and you perceive quite clearly by now that you won't earn it by arresting me."

Macartney bit his lip, looking searchingly meanwhile at the Colonel. "It...it's unthinkable!" he exploded. "I am not to be bribed. Unthinkable! If it were known..."

Captain Blood chuckled. "Is that what's troubling you? But who's to tell? Colonel de Coulevain owes me silence at least."

The brooding Colonel roused himself. "Oh, at least, at least. Have no doubt of that, sir."

Macartney looked from one to the other of them, a man plainly in the grip of temptation. He swore in his throat. "I'll return at six," he announced shortly.

"With an escort, Major, or alone?" was Blood's sly question.

"That's...that's as may be."

He strode out, and they heard his angrily-planted feet go clattering across the hall. Captain Blood winked at the Colonel, and rose. "I'll wager you a thousand pounds that there will be no escort."

"I cannot take the wager since I am of the same opinion."

"Now that's a pity, for I shall require the money, and I don't know how else to obtain it. It is possible he may consent to accept my note of hand."

"No need to distress yourself on that score."

Captain Blood searched the Colonel's heavy, blood-hound countenance. It wore a smile, a smile intended to be friendly. But somehow Captain Blood did not like the face any better on that account.

The smile broadened to an increasing friendliness. "You may break your fast and take your rest with an easy mind, sir. I will deal with Maj or Macartney when he returns."

"You will deal with him? Do you mean that you will advance the money?"

"I owe you no less, my dear Captain."

Again Captain Blood gave him a long searching stare before he bowed and spoke his eloquent thanks. The proposal was amazing. So amazing coming from a broken gamester harassed by creditors, that it was not to be believed--at least not by a man of Captain Blood's experience.

When, having broken his fast, he repaired to the curtained bed which Abraham had prepared for him in a fair room above stairs, he lay despite his weariness for some time considering it all. He recalled the subtle sudden betraying change in Coulevain's manner when it was disclosed that the reward would go to him; he saw again the oily smile on the Colonel's face when he had announced that he would deal with Major Macartney. If he knew men at all, Coulevain was the last whom he would trust. Of himself he was aware that he was an extremely negotiable security. The British Government had set a definite price upon his head. But it was widely known that the Spaniards whom he had harassed and pillaged without mercy would pay three or four times that price for him alive, so that they might have the pleasure of roasting him in the fires of the Faith. Had this scoundrel Coulevain suddenly perceived that the advent in Mariegalante of this saviour of his wife's honour was something in the nature of a windfall with which to repair his battered fortunes? If the half of what Madame de Coulevain had said of her husband in the course of that night's sailing was true there was no reason to suppose that any nice scruples would restrain him.

The more he considered, the more the Captain's uneasiness increased. He began to perceive that he was in an extremely tight corner. He even' went so far as to ask himself if the most prudent course might not be to rise, weary as he was, slip down to the mole, get aboard the pinnace which already had served him so well, and trust himself in her to the mercies of the ocean. But whither steer a course in that frail cockleshell? Only the neighbouring islands were possible, and they were all either French or British. On British soil he was certain of arrest with the gallows to follow, whilst on French soil he could hardly expect to fare better, considering his experience here where the commander was so deeply in his debt. If only he had money with which to purchase a passage on some ship that might pick him up at sea, money enough to induce a shipmaster to ask no questions whilst landing him off Tortuga. But he had none. The only thing of value in his possession was the great pearl in his left ear, worth perhaps five hundred pieces.

He was disposed to curse that raid in canoes upon the pearl fisheries of Cariaco which had resulted in disaster, had separated him from his ship, and had left him since adrift. But since cursing past events was the least profitable method of averting future ones, he decided to take the sleep of which he stood in need, hoping for the counsel which sleep is said to bring.

He timed himself to awaken at six o'clock, the hour at which Major Macartney was to return, and, his well-trained senses responding to that command, he awakened punctually. The angle of the sun was his sufficient dock. He slipped from the bed, found his shoes, which Abraham had cleaned, his coat, which had been brushed, and his periwig, which had been combed by the good negro. He had scarcely donned them when through the open window floated up to him the sound of a voice. It was the voice of Macartney, and it was answered instantly by the Colonel's with a hearty: "Come you in, sir. Come in."

In the nick of time, thought Blood; and he accepted the circumstances as a good omen. Cautiously he made his way below, meeting no one on the stairs or in the hall. Outside the door of the dining-room he stood listening. A hum of voices reached him. But they were distant. They came from the room beyond. Noiselessly he opened the door and slid across the threshold. The place was empty, as he had expected. The door of the adjacent room stood ajar. Through this came now the Major's laugh, and upon the heels of it the Colonel's voice.

"Depend upon it. He is under my hand. Spain, as you've said, will pay three times this sum, or even more, for him. Therefore he should be glad to ransom himself for, say, five times the amount of this advance." He chuckled, adding: "I have the advantage of you, Major, in that I can hold him to ransom, which your position as a British officer makes impossible to you. All things considered, you are fortunate, yes, and wise, to earn a thousand pounds for yourself."

"My God!" said Macartney, rendered suddenly virtuous by envy. "And that's how you pay your debts and reward the man for preserving your wife's life and honour! Faith, I'm glad I'm not your creditor."

"Shall we abstain from comments?" the Colonel suggested sourly.

"Oh, by all means. Give me the money, and I'll go my ways."

There was a chinking squelch twice repeated, as of moneybags that are raised and set down again. "It is in rolls of twenty double moidores. Will you count them?"

There followed a mumbling pause, and at the end of it came the Colonel's voice again. "If you will sign this quittance, the matter is at an end."

"Quittance?"

"I'll read it to you." And the Colonel read: "I acknowledge, and give Colonel Jerome de Coulevain this quittance for the sum of five thousand pieces of eight, received from him in consideration of my forbearing from any action against Captain Blood, and of my undertaking no action whatever hereafter for as long as he may remain the guest of Colonel de Coulevain on the Island of Mariegalante or elsewhere. Given under my hand and seal this tenth day of July of 1688."

As the Colonel's voice trailed off there came an explosion from Macartney.

"God's death, Colonel! Are you mad, or do you think that I am?"

"What do you find amiss? Is it not a correct statement?"

Macartney banged the table in his vehemence. "It puts a rope round my neck."

"Only if you play me false. What other guarantee have I that when you've taken these five thousand pieces you will keep faith with me?"

"You have my word," said Macartney in a passion. "And my word must content you."

"Your word! Your word!" The Frenchman's sneer was unmistakable. "Ah, that, no. Your word is not enough."

"You want to insult me!"

"Pish! Let us be practical, Major. Ask yourself: Would you accept the word of a man in a transaction in which his own part is dishonest?"

"Dishonest, sir? What the devil do you mean?"

"Are you not accepting a bribe to be false to your duty? Is not that dishonesty?"

"By god! This comes well from you, considering your intentions."

"You make it necessary. Besides, have I played the hypocrite as to my part? I have been unnecessarily frank, even to appearing a rogue. But, as in your own case, Major, necessity knows no law with me."

A pause followed upon those conciliatory words. Then: "Nevertheless," said Macartney, "I do not sign that paper."

"You'll sign and seal it, or I do not pay the money. What do you fear, Major? I give you my word--"

"Your word! Hell and the devil! In what is your word better than mine?"

"The circumstances make it better. On my side there can be no temptation to break faith, as on yours. It cannot profit me."

It was clear by now to Blood that since Macartney had not struck the Frenchman for his insults, he would end by signing. Only a desperate need of money could so have curbed the Englishman. He therefore heard with surprise Macartney's angry outburst.

"Give me the pen. Let us have done."

Another pause followed, then the Colonel's voice: "And now seal it here, where I have set the wax. The signet on your finger will serve."

Captain Blood waited for no more. The long windows stood open to the garden over which the dusk was rapidly descending. He stepped noiselessly out and vanished amid the shrubs. About the stem of a tall silk-cotton tree he found a tough slender liana swarming like a snake. He brought out his knife, slashed it near the root, and drew it down.

As Captain Macartney, softly humming to himself, a heavy leathern bag in the crook of each arm, came presently down the avenue between the palms where the evening shadows were deepest, he tripped over what he conceived to be a rope stretched taut across the path, and spread-eagled forward with a crash.

Lying momentarily half-stunned by the heavy fall, a weight descended on his back, and in his ear a pleasant voice was murmuring in English, with a strong Irish accent: "I have no buccaneers, Major, no ship, no demi-cannon, and, as you remarked, not even a sword. But I still have my hands and my wits, and they should more than suffice to deal with a paltry rogue like you."

"By God!" swore Macartney, though half-choked. "You shall hang for this, Captain Blood! By God, you shall!" Frenziedly he struggled to elude the grip of his assailant. His sword being useless in his present position, he sought to reach the pocket in which he carried a pistol, but, by the movement, merely betrayed its presence. Captain Blood possessed himself of it.

"Will you be quiet now?" he asked. "Or must I be blowing out your brains?"

"You dirty Judas! You thieving pirate! Is this how you keep faith?"

"I pledged you no faith, you nasty rogue. Your bargain was with the French colonel, not with me. It was he who bribed you to be false to your duty. I had no part in it."

"Had you not? You lying dog! You're a pretty pair of scoundrels, on my soul! Working in con-conjunction."

"Now that," said Blood, "is needlessly and foolishly offensive."

Macartney broke into fresh expletives.

"You talk too much," said Captain Blood, and tapped him twice over the head with the butt of the pistol, using great science. The Major sank forward gently, like a man asleep.

Captain Blood rose, and peered about him through the dusk. All was still. He went to pick up the leather bags which Macartney had dropped as he fell. He made a sling for them with his scarf, and so hung them from his neck. Then he raised the unconscious Major, swung him skilfully to his shoulder, and, thus burdened, went staggering down the avenue and out into the open.

The night was hot and Macartney was heavy. The sweat ran from Blood's pores. But he went steadily ahead until he reached the low wall of the churchyard, just as the moon was beginning to rise. On to the summit of this wall he eased himself of his burden, toppled it over into the churchyard, and then climbed after it. What he had to do there was quickly done by the light of the moon under the shelter of that wall. With the man's own sash he trussed him up at wrists and ankles. Then he stuffed some of the Major's periwig into his mouth, using the fellow's neckcloth to hold this unpleasant gag in position and taking care to leave his nostrils free.

As he was concluding the operation, Macartney opened his eyes and glared at him.

"Sure now it's only me: your old friend, Captain Blood. I'm just after making you comfortable for the night. When they find you in the morning, ye can tell them any convenient lie that will save you the trouble of explaining what can't be explained at all. It's a very good night I'll be wishing you, Maj or darling."

He went over the wall and briskly down the road that led to the sea.

On the mole lounged the British sailors who manned the longboat from the *Royal Duchess*, awaiting the Major's return. Further on, some men of Mariegalante were landing their haul from a fishing-boat that had just come in. None gave heed to Blood as he stepped along to the mole's end where that morning he had moored the pinnace. In the locker, where he stowed the heavy bags of gold, there was still some of the food that he had brought away last night from the *Estremadura*. He could not take the risk of adding to it. But he filled the two small water-casks at the fountain.

Then he stepped aboard, cast off and got out the sweeps. Another night on the open sea lay ahead of him. The wind, however, was still in the same quarter as last night and would favour the run to Guadeloupe upon which he had determined.

Once out of the bay he hoisted sail, and ran northward along the coast and the shallow cliffs which cast an inky shadow against the moon's white radiance. On he crawled through a sea of rippling quicksilver until he reached the island's end; then he headed straight across the ten miles of intervening water.

Off Grand Terre, the eastern of the two main islands of Guadeloupe, he lay awaiting sunrise. When it came, bringing a freshening of the wind, he ran close past Saint Anne, which was empty of shipping, and, hugging the coast, sailed on in a north-easterly direction until he came, some two hours later, to Port du Moule.

There were half a dozen ships in the harbour, and Blood scanned them with anxiety until his glance alighted on a black brigantine that was bellied like a Flemish alderman. Those lines were a sufficient advertisement of her Dutch origin, and Captain Blood, sweeping alongside, hailed her with confidence and climbed to her deck.

"I am in haste," he informed her sturdy captain, "to reach the northern coast of French Hispaniola, and I will pay you well for a passage thither."

The Dutchman eyed him without favour. "If you're in haste you had better seek what you need elsewhere. I am for Curacao."

"I've said I'll pay you well. Five thousand pieces of eight should compensate you for delays."

"Five thousand pieces!" The Dutchman stared. The sum was as much as he could hope to earn by his present voyage. "Who are you, sir?"

"What's that to the matter? I am one who will pay five thousand pieces."

The skipper of the brigantine screwed up his little blue eyes. "Will you pay in advance?"

"The half of it. The other half I shall obtain when my destination is reached. But you may hold me aboard until you have the money." Thus he ensured that the

Dutchman, ignorant of the fact that the entire sum was already under his hand, should keep faith.

"I could sail to-night," said the other slowly.

Blood at once produced one of the two bags. The other he had stowed in one of the water-casks in the locker of the pinnace, and there it remained unsuspected until four days later, when they were in the narrow seas between Hispaniola and Tortuga.

Then Captain Blood, announcing that he would put himself ashore, paid over the balance of the money, and climbed down the side of the brig to re-enter the pinnace. When, presently, the Dutchman observed him to be steering not, indeed, towards Hispaniola, but a northerly course in the direction of Tortuga, that stronghold of the buccaneers, his growing suspicions may have been fully confirmed. He remained, however, untroubled, the only man who, in addition to Blood himself, had really profited by that transaction on the Island of Mariegalante.

Thus Captain Blood came back at last to Tortuga and to the fleet that was by now mourning him as dead. With that fleet of five tall ships he sailed into the harbour of Basseterre a month later with intent to settle a debt which he conceived to lie between Colonel de Coulevain and himself.

His appearance there in such force fluttered both the garrison and the inhabitants. But he came too late for his purposes. Colonel de Coulevain was no longer there to be fluttered. He had been sent back to France under arrest.

Captain Blood was informed of this by Colonel Sancerre, who had succeeded to the military command of Mariegalante, and who received him with the courtesy due to a filibuster who comes backed by the powerful fleet that Blood had anchored in the roadstead.

Captain Blood fetched a sigh when he heard the news. "A pity! I had a little word to say to him; a little debt to settle."

"A little debt of five thousand pieces of eight, I think," said the Frenchman.

"On my faith, you are well informed."

The Colonel explained. "When the General of the Armies of France in America came here to inquire into the matter of the Spanish raid on Mariegalante, he discovered that Colonel de Coulevain had robbed the French Colonial Treasury of that sum. There was proof of it in a quittance that was found among M. de Coulevain's papers."

"So that's where he got the money!"

"I see that you understand." The Commandant looked grave. "Robbery is a serious, shameful matter, Captain Blood."

"I know it is. I've practised a good deal of it myself."

"And I've little doubt that they will hang M. de Coulevain, poor devil."

Captain Blood nodded. "No doubt of that. But we'll save our tears to water some nobler grave, my Colonel."

Colonel Sancerre eyed him with cold disapproval. "This hardly comes well from you, Captain Blood. It was to save you from the English that Colonel de Coulevain paid over the money, was it not?"

"Hardly to save me from them. To buy me from them so that he might sell me again to Spain at a handsome profit. He had an eye to a profit, your Colonel de Coulevain."

"But what do you tell me?" cried Sancerre.

"That it's entirely a poetic thing that the quittance he took on my behalf should be the means of hanging him."

X - GALLOWS KEY

It is impossible now to determine whether Gallows Key took its name from the events I am about to relate or bore it already previously among seafaring men. Jeremy Pitt in his log gives no hint, and the miniature island is not now to be identified with precision. All that we know positively, and this from Pitt's log of the *Arabella*, is that it forms part of the group known as the Albuquerque Keys, lying in 12°northern latitude and 85°western longitude, some sixty miles north-west of Porto Bello.

It is little more than a barren rock, frequented only by sea-birds and the turtles that come to deposit their eggs in the golden sand of the reef-enclosed lagoon on its eastern side. This strip of beach shelves rapidly to a depth of some sixty fathoms, and the entrance to the lagoon is by a gap of not more than twenty yards in the rocky amphitheatre which goes to form it.

Into this secure if desolate haven sailed Captain Easterling one April day of the year 1688 in his thirty-gun frigate the *Avenger*, followed by the two ships that made up his fleet: the *Hermes*, a frigate of twenty-six guns, commanded by Roger Galloway, and the *Valiant*, a brigantine carrying twenty, in charge of Crosby Pike, who once had sailed with Captain Blood and was realizing his mistake in making a change of admiral.

You will remember this scoundrel Easterling, how once he had tried a fall with Peter Blood, when Blood was on the very threshold of his career as a buccaneer, and how, as a consequence, Easterling's ship had been blown from under him and himself swept from the seas.

But laboriously, with the patience and tenacity found in bad men as in good, Easterling had won back to his old position, and was afloat once more and in greater strength than ever before upon the Caribbean.

He was, in Peter Blood's own words, just a filthy pirate, a ruthless, bloodthirsty robber, without a spark even of that honour which is said to prevail among thieves. His followers made up a lawless mob, of mixed nationalities, subject to no discipline and obeying no rules save those which concerned the division of their spoils. They practised no discrimination in their piracy. They would attack an English or Dutch merchantman as readily as a Spanish galleon, and deal out the same ruthless brutality to the one as to the other.

Now, despite his ill-repute even among buccaneers, he had succeeded in luring away from Blood's following the resolute Crosby Pike, with his twenty-gun ship and well-disciplined crew of a hundred and thirty men. The lure had been that old story of Morgan's treasure with which Easterling once had unsuccessfully attempted to beguile Blood.

Again he told that hoary tale of how he had sailed with Henry Morgan and had been with him at the sack of Panama; how--as was well known--on the return march across the Isthmus there had been all but mutiny among Morgan's followers on a suspicion that the booty divided among them was very far from being all the booty taken; how it was murmured that Morgan had secretly abstracted a great portion for himself; how Morgan, becoming alarmed lest a mutinous search of his personal baggage should reveal the truth of the rumour, had taken Easterling into his confidence and sought his aid in what he was to do. Between them they had buried that treasure--a treasure of pearls and precious stones of the fabulous value of at least half a million pieces of eight--at a spot on the banks of the Chagres River. They were to return to unearth it later when opportunity should serve. Morgan, however, swept by destiny along other profitable pursuits, was still postponing his return when death overtook him. Easterling had never returned because never before had he commanded the necessary force for the penetration of Spanish territory, or the necessary strength of ships for the safe conveyance of the treasure once it was reclaimed.

Such had been the tale to which Blood had scorned to lend an ear but to which Pike succumbed, in spite of Blood's warning against joining forces with so unscrupulous a rogue and his freely expressed conviction that no such treasure existed.

Pitying Pike for his credulity, Blood bore him no resentment for his defection, and feared rather than hoped that the sequel would punish him sufficiently.

Blood himself at this time had been planning an expedition to Darien. But since Easterling's activities on the isthmus might put the Spaniards on the alert, he found it prudent to postpone the business. His fleet, consisting in those days of five stout ships, scattered and went a-roving without definite objective. This was at the beginning of April, and it was concerted that they should reassemble at Mosquito Keys, at the end of May, when the expedition to Darien could be considered anew.

The *Arabella*, going south by the Windward Passage, and then east along the southern coast of Hispaniola, came, some twenty miles beyond Cape Tiburon, upon an English merchantman in a foundering condition. She was kept precariously afloat so long as the sea was calm by the shifting of her guns and all other heavy gear to larboard, so as to keep above water the gaping wounds in her starboard quarter. Her broken spars and fractured mainmast told an eloquent tale, and Blood imagined that Spaniards had been at work. He discovered instead, when he went to her assistance, that she had yesterday been attacked and plundered by Easterling, who had put half her crew to the sword and brutally killed her captain for not having struck his colours when summoned to do so.

The *Arabella* towed her within ten miles of Port Royal, and daring to go no nearer, lest she should draw down upon herself the Jamaica Squadron, left her there to complete alone what little remained of the voyage to safety.

That done, however, the *Arabella* did not sail east again, but headed south for the Main. To Pitt, his shipmaster, Blood explained his motives.

"We'll be keeping an eye on this blackguard Easterling, so we will, Jerry, and maybe more than an eye."

And south they sailed, since that was the way Easterling had gone. To the tale of his treasure, Blood, as we know, attached no faith. He regarded it as an invention to gull such credulous fellows as Pike into association. In this, however, he was presently to be proven wrong.

Creeping down the Mosquito Coast, he found a snug anchorage in a cove of one of the numerous islands in the Lagoon of Chiriqui. There for the moment he elected to lie concealed, and thence he watched the operations of Easterling, twenty miles away, through the eyes of friendly Mosquito Indians whom he employed as scouts. From these he learned that Easterling had cast anchor a little to westward of the mouth of the Chagres, that he had landed a force of three hundred and fifty men, and that he was penetrating with them into the isthmus. From his knowledge of Easterling's total strength, Blood computed that hardly more than a hundred men had been left behind to guard the waiting ships.

Whilst waiting in his turn, Blood took his ease. On a cane day-bed set under an improvised awning on the poop (for the weather was growing hot) the buccaneer found sufficient adventure for his spirit in the verse of Horace and the prose of Suetonius. When physical activity was desired, he would swim in the clear, jade-green waters of the lagoon, or, landing on the palm-fringed shore of that uninhabited island, he would take a hand with his men in the capture of turtle, or in the hewing of wood to provide the fuel for the boucan fires in which their succulent flesh was being cured.

Meanwhile his Indians brought him news, first of a skirmish between Easterling's men and a party of Spaniards who evidently had got wind of the presence on Darien of the buccaneers. Then came word that Easterling was marching back to the coast; a couple of days later he was informed of another encounter between Easterling and a Spanish force, in which the buccaneers had suffered severely, although in the end they had beaten off the attack. Lastly came news of yet a third engagement, and this was brought, together with other precious details, by one who had taken part in it.

He was one of Pike's men, a hard-bitten old adventurer, who had given up logwood-cutting to take to the sea. His name was Cunley, and he had been rendered helpless by a gunshot wound in the thigh and left by Easterling's retreating force to die where he had fallen. Overlooked by the Spaniards, he had dragged himself into the scrub for shelter and thus into the hands of the watchful Indians. They had handled him tenderly, so that he should survive to tell his tale to Captain Blood, and they had quieted his alarms with assertions in their broken Spanish that it was to Don Pedro Sangre that he was being conveyed.

Tenderly they hoisted the crippled fellow aboard the *Arabella*, where Blood's first care was to employ his surgeon's skill to dress the hideous festering wound. Thereafter, in the ward-room, converted for the moment into a sick bay, Cunley told in bitterness the tale of the adventure.

Morgan's treasure was real enough. The buccaneers were bearing it back to the waiting ships, and in value it exceeded all that Easterling had represented. But it was being dearly bought--most dearly by Pike's contingent, whence the bitterness investing Cunley's tale. Going and coming they had been harassed by Spaniards and once by a party of hostile Indians. Further, they had been reduced by fever and sickness on that difficult march through a miasmic country where mosquitoes had almost eaten them alive. Of the three hundred and fifty men who had left the ships, Cunley computed that after the last engagement, in which he had been wounded, not more than two hundred remained alive. But the ugly fact was that not more than twenty of these men were Pike's. Yet Pike had brought ashore by Easterling's orders the heaviest of the three contingents, landing a hundred and thirty men, and leaving a bare score to guard the *Valiant*, whilst fifty men at least had been left on each of the other ships.

Easterling had so contrived that Pike's contingent was ever in the van, so that it had borne the brunt of every attack the buccaneers had suffered. It was not to be supposed that Pike had submitted to this without remonstrances. Protests had grown increasingly bitter as the ill continued. But Easterling, backed by his earlier associate, Roger Galloway, who commanded the *Hermes*, had browbeaten Pike into submission, whilst the ruffianly followers of those two captains, by preponderance of numbers remaining at comparatively full strength, had easily imposed their will upon the dwindling force of the *Valiant*. If all her present survivors got back to the ship, the *Valiant* could now muster a crew of barely forty hands, whilst the other two combined a strength of nearly three hundred men.

"Ye see, Captain," Cunley concluded grimly, "how this Easterling has used us. As the monkey used the cat. And now him and Galloway--them two black-hearted bastards--is in such strength that Crosby Pike dursn't say a word o' protest. It was a black day for all of us, Captain, when the *Valiant* left your fleet to join that blackguard Easterling's, treasure or no treasure."

"Treasure or no treasure," Captain Blood repeated. "And I'm thinking that for Captain Pike no treasure it will prove."

He rose from his chair by the sick man's bed, tall, graceful and vigorous in his black small clothes, silver-broidered waistcoat and full white cambric sleeves. His coat of black and silver he had discarded before commencing his surgical ministrations. He waved away the white-clad negro who attended with bowl and lint and forceps, and, alone with Cunley, he paced to the wardroom ports and back. His long supple fingers toyed thoughtfully with the curls of his black periwig; his eyes, blue as sapphires, were now as hard.

"I thought that Pike would prove a minnow in the jaws of Easterling. It but remains for Easterling to swallow him, and faith, it's what he'll be doing."

"Ye've said it, Captain. It's plaguey little o' that treasure me and my mates o' the *Valiant* or Captain Pike himself'll ever see. The thirty that's left of us 'll be lucky if they gets away alive. That's my faith, Captain."

"And mine, bedad," said Captain Blood. But his mouth was grim.

"Can ye do nothing for the honour of the Brethren of the Coast and for the sake o' justice, Captain?"

"It's thinking of it, I am. If the fleet were with me I'd sail in this minute and take a hand. But with just this one ship..." He broke off and shrugged. "The odds are a trifle heavy. But I'll watch, and I'll consider."

Cunley's opinion that it was a black day for the *Valiant* when she joined Easterling's fleet was now being shared by every survivor of her crew, and by none more fully than by Captain Pike himself. He had become. apprehensive of the final issue of the adventure, and his apprehensions received the fullest confirmation on the morrow of their sailing from the Chagres, when they came to anchorage in that lagoon of Gallows Key to which I have alluded.

Easterling's *Avenger* led the way into that diminutive circular harbour, and anchored nearest to the shore. Next came the *Hermes*. The *Valiant*, now bringing up the rear, was compelled, for lack of room within, to anchor in the narrow roadstead. Thus again Pike was given the most vulnerable station in the event of attack--a station in which his ship must act as a shield for the others.

Trenam, Pike's sturdy young Cornish lieutenant, who from the outset had been against association with Easterling, perceiving the object of this disposition, was not ashamed to urge Pike to take up anchor and be off in the night, abandoning Easterling and the treasure before worse befell them. But Pike, as obstinate as he was courageous, repudiated this for a coward counsel.

"By God!" he swore. "It's what Easterling desires! We've earned our share of that treasure, and we're not sailing without it."

But the practical Trenam, shook his fair head. "That will be as Easterling chooses. He's got the strength to enforce his will, and the will to play the rogue, or I'm a fool else."

Pike silenced him by making oath that he was not afraid of twenty Easterlings.

And his air was as truculent when next morning, in response to a signal from the flagship, he went aboard the *Avenger*.

He was awaited in the cabin not only by Easterling, arrayed in tawdry splendour, but by Galloway, who favoured the loose leather breeches and cotton shirt that made up the habitual garb of a boucan-hunter. Easterling was massively built and swarthy--a man still young, with fine eyes and a full black beard, behind which, when he laughed, there was a flash of strong white teeth. Galloway, squat and broad, was not apelike in build, with his long arms and short powerful legs, but oddly apelike in countenance, out of which two bright little wicked eyes sparkled under a shallow wrinkled brow.

They received Captain Pike with every show of friendliness, sate him down at the greasy table, poured rum for him and pledged him, whereafter Easterling came promptly to business.

"We've sent for ye, Captain Pike, because at present we're carrying, as it were, all our eggs in one basket. This treasure," and he waved a hand in the direction of the chests containing it, "is best divided without more ado, so that each of us can go about his business."

Pike took heart at this promising beginning. "Ye mean to break up the fleet, then?" said he indifferently.

"Why not, since the job's done? Roger here and me has decided to quit piracy. We're for home with the fortune we've made. I'll belike turn farmer somewhere in Devon." He laughed.

Pike smiled, but offered no comment. He was not at any time a man of many words, as his long, dour, weatherbeaten face announced.

Easterling cleared his throat and resumed. "Me and Roger's been considering that some change in the provisions o' the articles would be only fair. They do run that one-third of what's left over after I've taken my fifth goes to each of the three ships."

"Ay, that's how they run, and that's fair enough for me," said Pike.

"That's not our opinion, Roger's and mine, now that we comes to think it over."

Pike opened his mouth to answer, but Easterling, giving him no time, ran on:

"Roger and me don't see as you should take a third to share among thirty men, while we share each of us the same among a hundred and fifty."

Captain Pike was swept by sudden passion. "Was, that why ye saw to it that my men were always put where the Spaniards could kill them until we're reduced to less than a quarter of our strength at the outset?"

Easterling's black brows met above eyes that were suddenly malevolent.

"Now what the devil do you mean by that, Captain Pike, if you please?"

"It's an imputation," said Galloway dryly. "A nasty imputation."

"No imputation at all," said Pike. "It's a fact."

"A fact, eh?" Easterling was smiling, and the lean, tough, resolute Pike grew uneasy under that smile. Galloway's bright little ape's eyes were considering him oddly. The very air of that untidy, evil-smelling cabin became charged with menace. Pike had a vision of brutalities witnessed in the course of his association with Easterling, wanton, unnecessary brutalities springing from the sheer lust of cruelty. He recalled words in which Captain Blood had warned him against association with a man whom he described as treacherous and foul by nature. If he had hugged a doubt of the deliberate calculation by which is own men had been sacrificed on Darien, that doubt was now dispelled.

He was as a sleepwalker who awakens suddenly to find himself on the edge of a precipice into which another step must have projected him. The instinct of self-preservation made him recoil from an attitude of truculence which might lead to his being pistolled on the spot. He pushed back the hair from his moist brow and commanded himself to answer in level tones.

"What I mean is that if my men have been reduced, they've suffered this in the common cause. They will consider it unfair to break the articles on any such grounds."

He argued on. He reminded Easterling of the practice of matelotage among buccaneers, whereby every man enters into a partnership with another in which the two make common cause and under which each is the other's heir. In this alone lay reason why many of his men who were to inherit should feel defrauded by any change in the articles.

Easterling's evil grin gave way again to a scowl. "What's it to me what any of your mangy followers may feel? I'm admiral of this fleet, and my word is law."

"So it is," said Pike. "And your word is in the articles under which we sailed with you."

"To hell with the articles!" roared Captain Easterling.

He rose and stood over Pike, towering and menacing, his head almost touching the ceiling of the cabin. He spoke deliberately. "I'm telling you things is changed since we signed them articles. What I says is more nor any articles, and what I says is that the *Valiant* can have a tenth share of the plunder. Ye'd be wise to take it, remembering the saying that who tries to grasp too much ends by holding nothing."

Pike stared up at him with fallen jaw. He had turned pale from the stress of the conflict within him between rage and prudence.

"By God, Easterling..." He broke off abruptly.

Easterling scowled down upon him. "Continue," he commanded. "Finish what ye has to say."

Pike shrugged despondently. "Ye know I dursn't accept your offer. Ye know my men would tear me in pieces if I did so without consulting them."

"Then away with you to consult them. I've a mind to slit your pimpish ears so that they may see what happens to them as gets pert with Captain Easterling. You may tell your scum that if they has the impudence to refuse my offer they needn't trouble to send you here again. They can up anchor and be off to Hell. Remind 'em of what I says: that who tries to grasp too much ends by holding nothing. Away with you, Captain Pike, with that message."

Not until he was back aboard his own ship did Captain Pike release the rage from which he all but bursted. And the sound of it, the tale he told in the ship's waist with the survivors of his crew about him, aroused in his violent followers a rage to match his own. Trenam added fuel to the flames by the views he expressed.

"If the swine means to break faith is it likely he'll stop half-way? Depend on it, if we accept this tenth, he'll find a pretext to cheat us of all. Captain Blood was in the right. We should never ha' put our trust in that son of a dog."

One of the hands spoke up, voicing the feelings of all. "But since we've put it, we've got to see he keeps it."

Pike, who was leaning by now to Trenam's despondent view of their case, waited for the chorus of angry approval to subside.

"Will you tell me how we are to do it? We are some forty men against three hundred. A twenty-gun brig against two frigates with fifty guns of heavier weight between them."

This gave them pause until another bold one spoke. "He says a tenth or naught. Our answer is a third or naught. There's honour among buccaneers, and we hold him to his pledge, to the articles upon which the dirty thief enlisted us."

As one man the crew supported him. "Go you back with that answer, Captain."

"And if he refuses?"

It was Trenam who now thought he held the answer.

"There's ways of compelling him. Tell him we'll raise the whole Brotherhood of the Coast against him. Captain Blood will see that we have justice. Captain Blood's none so fond of him, as he well knows. Remind him of that, Captain. Go you back and tell him."

It was a powerful card to play. Pike realized this: yet he confessed that he did not relish the task of playing it. But his men turned upon him with up-braidings. It was he who had persuaded them to follow Easterling. It was he who had not known how to make a stand against Easterling's encroachments from the outset. They had done their part. It was for him to see to it that they were not cheated of their pay.

So back from the *Valiant* at her anchorage in the very neck of the harbour went Captain Pike in the cockboat to convey his men's answer to Captain Easterling, and to hoist the bogey of Captain Blood and the Brethren of the Coast, upon which he depended now for his own safety.

The interview took place in the waist of the *Avenger* before an audience of her crew and in the presence of Captain Galloway, who was still aboard her. It was short and violent.

When Captain Pike had stated that his men insisted upon the fulfilment of the terms of the articles, Easterling laughed. His crew laughed with him; some there were who cheered Pike ironically.

"If that's their last word, my man," said Easterling, "they can up anchor and away to the devil. I've no more to say to them."

"It'll be the worse for you, Captain, if they go," said Pike steadily.

"D'ye threaten, by God!" The man's great bulk seemed to swell with rage.

"I warn you, Captain."

"You warn me? Warn me of what?"

"That the Brethren of the Coast, the whole buccaneering fraternity, will be raised against you for this breach of faith."

"Breach of faith!" Easterling's voice soared in pitch. "Breach of faith, ye bastard scum! D'ye dare stand before my face and say that to me?" He plucked a pistol from his belt. "Be off this ship at once, and tell your blackguards that if the *Valiant* is still there by noon I'll blow her out of the water. Away with you."

Pike, choking with indignation, and made bold by it, played his master card.

"Very well," said he. "You'll have Captain Blood to deal with for this."

Pike had reckoned upon intimidating, but neither upon the extent to which his words would achieve it, nor the blind fury that follows panic in such natures as that of the man with whom he dealt.

"Captain Blood?" Easterling spoke through his teeth, his great face purple. "You'll go whining to Captain Blood, will you? Go whine in Hell, then."

And on the word, at point-blank range, he shot Pike through the head.

The buccaneers standing about them recoiled in momentary horror as the man's body went backwards across the hatch coaming. Easterling jeered coarsely at their squeamishness. Galloway looked on, his little eyes glittering, his face inscrutable.

"Take up that carrion." Easterling pointed with his still smoking pistol. "Hang it from the yard-arm. Let it serve as a warning to those swine on the *Valiant* of what happens to them as gets pert with Captain Easterling."

A long-drawn cry, in which anger, fear and pity were all blended, went up from the deck of Pike's ship when her crew, crowding the larboard bulwarks, perceived through the rigging of the *Hermes*, the limp body of their captain swinging from the yardarm of the *Avenger*. So intent were these men that they paid no heed to the two long Indian canoes that came alongside to starboard, or even to the tall gentleman in black and silver who stepped from the accommodation ladder to the deck behind them. Not until his crisp dry voice rang out were they aware of him.

"I arrive a trifle late, it seems."

They turned and beheld him on the hatch-coaming, his left hand on the pummel of his rapier, his face in the shadow of his broad plumed hat, his eyes hard and cold with anger. Asking themselves how he came there, they stared at him as if he were an apparition, mystified, incredulous, doubting their vision.

At last young Trenam sprang towards him, his eyes blazing with excitement in his grey face. "Captain Blood! Is it indeed you? But how--?"

Captain Blood quieted him by a wave of the long supple hand emerging from the foam of lace at his wrist. "I've never been far from you ever since you landed on Darien. I know your case, and this is no more than I foresaw. But I had hoped to avert it."

"You'll call a reckoning from that treacherous dog?"

"To be sure I will, and at once. That hideous gesture demands an instant answer." His voice was as grim as his countenance. "You have men here to lay the guns. Get them below at once."

The *Valiant* had been swinging with the first of the gentle ebb when Blood stepped aboard; she stood now. In the line of the channel, so that the operation of opening the gun-ports could not be discerned from the other ships.

"The guns?" gasped Trenam. "But, Captain, we're in no case to fight. We've neither the men nor the metal."

"Enough for what's to do. Men and guns are not all that count in these affairs. Easterling gave you this station so that you should cover the other ships." Blood uttered a short stern laugh. "He shall learn the strategic disadvantages of it, so he shall. Get your gun crew below." Then he gave other orders briskly. "Eight of you to man the longboat. There are two canoes astern well-manned to assist you warp your ship broadside when the time comes. The ebbing tide will help you. Send aloft every man you can spare, to loose sail once we're out of the channel. Bestir, Trenam! Bestir!"

He dived below to the main deck, where the gun crew was already at work clearing the guns for action. He stimulated the men by his words and manner, and received unquestioning obedience from them; for, without understanding what might be afoot, they were stirred almost to enthusiasm by their confidence in him and their assurance that he would avenge upon Easterling their captain's murder and their own wrongs.

When all was ready and the matches glowing he went on deck again.

The two canoes manned by Mosquito Indians and the *Valiant's* longboat were astern under her counter and invisible to those aboard the other two ships. Towing-ropes had been attached, and the men waited for the word of command.

At Blood's suggestion Trenam, did not wait to take up anchor, but slipped his cable, and the oarsmen bent to their task of warping the ship round. Labours which would not in themselves have sufficed were made easy by the ebb, and slowly the brigantine began to swing broadside across the channel. Already Blood was below again, directing the hands that manned the starboard guns. Five of these were to be concentrated on the rudder of the *Hermes*, the other five were to sweep her shrouds.

As the *Valiant* swung about and the warping operations became apparent to the men on the other ships it was assumed by them that, panic-stricken by the fate of their captain, the crew of the brigantine had resolved on flight. From the decks of the *Hermes* a derisive valedictory cheer rang out. But scarcely had it died away, and just as it was being taken up by the *Avenger*, it was answered by the roar of ten guns at point-blank range.

The *Hermes* rocked and shuddered under the impact of that unexpected broadside, and the fierce outcries of her men were mingled with the hoarse voices of the startled sea-birds that rose to circle in alarm.

Blood was on deck again almost before the reverberations had rolled away. He peered through the rising cloud of smoke and smiled. The rudder of the *Hermes* had been shattered, her mainmast was broken and hung precariously suspended in her shrouds, whilst a rent showed in the bulwarks of her forecastle.

"And now?" quoth Trenam in uneasy excitement.

Blood looked round. They were moving steadily if slowly down the short channel, and were already almost in the open sea. A steady breeze was blowing from the north. "Crowd on sail, and let her run before the wind."

"They'll follow," said the young mariner. "Why, so I trust. But not yet awhile. Take a look at their plight."

It was only the that Trenam understood precisely what Blood had done. With her broken rudder and shattered mainmast, the *Hermes*, whilst being herself unmanageable, was blocking the way and making it impossible for the raging Easterling to get past her and attack the *Valiant*.

Trenam perceived and admired, but was still far from easy. "If you've invited pursuit, it's true that you've certainly delayed it. But it will surely come, and we shall be as surely sunk when it does. It's just what that devil Easterling desires."

"Indeed, and I hope so; and, anyway, I've quickened those same desires of his."

They had picked up the crew of the longboat, whilst the Indian canoes could be seen making off to the north along the reef. The *Valiant* was now running before the wind and Gallows Key was dropping swiftly astern. All hands were on deck. From the pooprail, where he leaned beside Trenam, Blood spoke to the man at the whipstaff below.

"Put up the helm. We go about." Perceiving Trenam's alarm, he smiled. "Quiet you. Have faith in me, and man the larboard guns. They'll not yet have disentangled themselves, and we'll give them a salute in passing. Faith now, ye may trust me. It's by no means the first action I've fought, and I know the fool I'm engaging. It won't have occurred to him that we might have the impudence to return, and I'll wager your share of Morgan's treasure that he won't have so much as opened his ports as yet."

It fell out as he foretold. When they ran in, close-hauled, they saw that the *Hermes* had only just been warped aside to give passage to the *Avenger*, which with sprit-sail, sweeps, and the ebb to assist her, was crawling towards the channel.

Easterling must have rubbed his eyes at this reappearance of the *Valiant*, which he was imagining in full flight; he must have ground his strong white teeth when she hung there an instant with slatting sails and poured a broadside athwart his decks before going off again on a north-easterly tack. He replied in haste and ineffectively with his chasers, and whilst the mess made by the *Valiant's* guns was being cleared up, he settled down vindictively to a pursuit which must end in the sinking of the audacious brigantine with every hand aboard.

The *Valiant* was perhaps a mile away to the northeast when Trenam beheld the *Avenger* emerge from the narrow roadstead and take the open sea to come ploughing after them with crowded yards. It was a dismaying vision. He turned to Captain Blood.

"And now, Captain? What remains?"

"To go about again," was the surprising answer. "Bid the helmsman steer for the northernmost point of the Key yonder."

"That will bring us within range."

"No matter. We'll run the gauntlet of his fire. At need we can round the point. But I've a notion the need will not present itself."

They went about, and ran in once more, Blood scanning the rocky coast of the island the while through the telescope. Trenam stood fretful at his elbow.

"What do you look for, Captain?" he wondered with faint hope.

"My Indian friends. They've made good speed. They've gone. All should be well."

To Trenam it seemed that things would be anything but well. The *Avenger* had veered a point nearer to the wind, so as to shorten the work of intercepting them. From her forward ports a gun boomed, and a round shot flung up the spray half a cable's length astern of the *Valiant*.

"He's getting the range," said Blood indifferently.

"Aye," agreed Trenam with bitter dryness. "We've let you have your way unquestioned, Captain. But what's to be the end?"

"I fancy it's coming yonder under full sail," said Captain Blood, and he pointed with the telescope.

Round the northern point of Gallows Key came a great red-hulled ship under a mountain of canvas that gleamed like snow in the noontide sunshine. Veering south as she appeared, she swept majestically on before the wind, a thing of beauty and of power, from gilded beak-head to lofty poop-lantern. She was abeam of the *Valiant* between the brigantine and island, before the dumbfounded Trenam found his voice, and before the voices of the crew were raised to cheer and cheer again.

Pale with excitement, his eyes sparkling, Trenam swung to Captain Blood. "The *Arabella*!"

Blood smiled upon him quizzically. "To be sure ye supposed I swam here, or crossed the ocean in a canoe; or may be ye thought I wanted to be chased by Easterling just for the fun of running away and the joy of being drowned at the end of it. Ye hadn't thought about these things maybe. Neither, had Easterling. But he's thinking about them now, so he is. Thinking hard, I dare swear."

But Easterling was doing nothing of the kind. His wits were paralysed. In the madness of despair, seeing himself beset by that formidable ship, which, moreover, had the weather gauge of him, he attempted to run for shelter back to the harbour from which he had been lured. Once there, with the guns of the *Hermes* to support his own, he might have held the narrow roadstead against all comers. But he should have known that he would never be allowed to reach it. When he ignored the shot athwart his bows, summoning him to strike his colours, a broadside of twenty heavy guns crashed into his exposed flank, and wrought such damage in it that he was bereft of even the satisfaction of replying. The *Arabella*, well handled by old Wolverstone, who was in command of her, went promptly about, and at still closer range poured in a second broadside to complete the business. Hard hit between wind and water, the *Avenger* was seen to be settling down by the head.

A sound like a wail arose from the deck of the *Valiant*. It startled Blood.

"What is it? What do they cry?"

"The treasure!" Trenam answered him. "Morgan's treasure!"

Blood frowned. "Faith, Wolverstone must ha' forgotten it in his fury." Then the frown cleared. He sighed and shrugged. "Ah well! It's gone now, so it has. Bad cess to it."

The *Arabella* hove to and lowered her boats to pick up the survivors struggling in the water. Easterling, lacking the courage to drown, was amongst them, and by

Blood's direction he was brought aboard the *Valiant*. Thus was the iron driven deep into his soul. But deeper still was it to be driven when he stepped on to the deck of Pike's ship to find himself confronting Captain Blood. It had been no bogey, then, with which Pike's last words had threatened him. He recoiled as if at last, and for once in his life, afraid. The dark eyes smouldered in his grey face with the mingled fury and terror to be seen in those of a trapped animal.

"So it was you!" he ejaculated.

"If ye mean it was I who took Pike's place when ye murdered him, ye're right. Ye'd had done better to have been honest with him. There's a maxim ye should have learnt at school, that honesty is the best policy. Though perhaps ye never were at school. But there's another maxim of which I made you a present years ago and which they tell me that ye're fond of quoting: Who seeks to grasp too much ends by holding nothing."

He waited for a reply, but none came. Easterling, his great bulk sagging, glowered at him silently with those dark feral eyes.

Blood sighed, and moved towards the head of the accommodation ladder.

"Ye're no affair of mine. I leave ye to these men you have wronged, and whose leader you have murdered. It is for them to judge you."

He went down to the boat that had brought Easterling aboard, and so back to the *Arabella*, his task accomplished, and his long duel with Easterling at last concluded.

An hour later the *Arabella* and the *Valiant* were running south together. Gallows Key was falling rapidly astern, and Galloway and his crew aboard the crippled *Hermes* imprisoned in the lagoon were left to conjecture what had happened outside and to extricate themselves as best they could from their own difficulties.

THE FORTUNES OF CAPTAIN BLOOD

By

Rafael Sabatini

This is a fictional work and all characters are drawn from the author's imagination.
Any resemblance or similarities are entirely coincidental.

Episode 1

THE DRAGON'S JAW

I

She was a beautiful ship, in the frigate class, fashioned, not merely in her lines, but in her details, with an extreme of that loving care that Spanish builders not infrequently bestowed. She had been named, as if to blend piety with loyalty, the *San Felipe,* and she had been equipped with a fastidiousness to match the beauty of her lines.

The great cabin, flooded with sunlight from the tall stern windows of horn, which now stood open above the creaming wake, had been made luxurious by richly carved furnishings, by hangings of green damask and by the gilded scroll-work of the bulkheads. Here Peter Blood, her present owner, bending over the Spaniard who reclined on a day bed by the stern locker, was reverting for the moment to his original trade of surgery. His hands, as strong as they were shapely, and by deftness rendered as delicate of touch as a woman's, had renewed the dressing of the Spaniard's thigh, where the fractured bone had pierced the flesh. He made now a final adjustment of the strappings that held the splint in place, stood up, and by a nod dismissed the negro steward who had been his acolyte.

'It is very well, Don Ilario.' He spoke quietly in a Spanish that was fluent and even graceful. 'I can now give you my word that you will walk on your two legs again.'

A wan smile dispelled some of the shadows from the hollows which suffering had dug in the patient's patrician countenance. 'For that,' he said, 'the thanks to God and you. A miracle.'

'No miracle at all. Just surgery.'

'Ah! But the surgeon, then? That is the miracle. Will men believe me when I say I was made whole again by Captain Blood?'

The Captain, tall and lithe, was in the act of rolling down the sleeves of his fine cambric shirt. Eyes startlingly blue under black eyebrows, in a hawk-face tanned to the colour of mahogany, gravely considered the Spaniard.

'Once a surgeon, always a surgeon,' he said, as if by way of explanation. 'And I was a surgeon once, as you may have heard.'

'As I have discovered for myself, to my profit. But by what queer alchemy of Fate does a surgeon become a buccaneer?'

Captain Blood smiled reflectively. 'My troubles came upon me from considering only--as in your case--a surgeon's duty; from beholding in a wounded man a patient, without concern for how he came by his wounds. He was a poor rebel who had been out with the Duke of Monmouth. Who comforts a rebel is himself a rebel. So runs the law among Christian men. I was taken red-handed in the abominable act of dressing his wounds, and for that I was sentenced to death. The penalty was commuted, not from mercy. Slaves were needed in the plantations. With a shipload of other wretches, I was carried overseas to be sold in Barbados. I escaped, and I think I must have died at somewhere about the time that Captain Blood came to life. But the ghost of the surgeon still walks in the body of the buccaneer, as you have found, Don Ilario.'

'To my great profit and deep gratitude. And the ghost still practises the dangerous charity that slew the surgeon?'

'Ah!' The vivid eyes flashed him a searching look, observed the flush on the Spaniard's pallid cheekbones, the queer expression of his glance.

'You are not afraid that history may repeat itself?'

'I do not care to be afraid of anything,' said Captain Blood, and he reached for his coat. He settled to his shoulders the black satin garment rich with silver lace, adjusted before a mirror the costly Mechlin at his throat, shook out the curls of his black periwig, and stood forth, an elegant incarnation of virility, more proper to the ante-chambers of the Escurial than to the quarter-deck of a buccaneer ship.

'You must rest now and endeavour to sleep until eight bells is made. You show no sign of fever. But tranquillity is still my prescription for you. At eight bells I will return.'

The patient, however, showed no disposition to be tranquil.

'Don Pedro. . . Before you go. . . Wait. This situation puts me to shame. I cannot lie so under this great obligation to you. I sail under false colours.'

Blood's shaven lips had an ironic twist. 'I have, myself, found it convenient at times.'

'Ah, but how different! My honour revolts.' Abruptly, his dark eyes steadily meeting the Captain's, he continued: 'You know me only as one of four shipwrecked Spaniards you rescued from that rock of the St Vincent Keys and have generously undertaken to land at San Domingo. Honour insists that you should know more.'

Blood seemed mildly amused. 'I doubt if you could add much to my knowledge. You are Don Ilario de Saavedra, the King of Spain's new Governor of Hispaniola. Before the gale that wrecked you, your ship formed part of the squadron of the Marquis of Riconete, who is to co-operate with you in the Caribbean in the extermination of that endemonized pirate and buccaneer, that enemy of God and Spain, whose name is Peter Blood.'

Don Ilario's blank face betrayed the depth of his astonishment. 'Virgen Santissima--Virgin Most Holy! You know that?'

'With commendable prudence you put your commission in your pocket when your ship was about to founder. With a prudence no less commendable, I took a look at it soon after you came aboard. We are not fastidious in my trade.'

If the simple explanation removed one astonishment, it replaced it by another. 'And in spite of that, you not only use me tenderly, you actually convey me to San Domingo!' Then his expression changed. 'Ah, I see. You trust my gratitude, and. . .'

But there Captain Blood interrupted him. 'Gratitude?' He laughed. 'It is the last emotion in which I should put my trust. I trust to nothing but myself, sir. I have told you that I do not care to be afraid of anything. Your obligation is not to the buccaneer, it is to the surgeon; and that is an obligation to a ghost. So dismiss it. Do not trouble your mind with problems of where your duty lies: whether to me or to your king. I am forewarned. That is enough for me. Give yourself peace, Don Ilario.'

He departed, leaving the Spaniard bewildered and bemused.

Coming out into the waist, where some two score of his buccaneers, the half of the ship's full company, were idling, he detected a sullenness in the air, which earlier had been fresh and clear. There had, however, been no steadiness in the weather since the hurricane some ten days ago, on the morrow of which he had rescued the injured Don Ilario and his three companions from the rocky islet on which the storm had cast them up. It was due to these country winds of some violence, with intermittent breathless calms, that the *San Felipe* was still no nearer to her destination than a point some twenty miles south of Saona. She was barely crawling over a gently heaving oily sea of deepest violet, her sails alternately swelling and sagging. The distant highlands of Hispaniola on the starboard quarter, which earlier had been clearly visible, had vanished now behind an ashen haze.

Chaffinch, the sailing master, standing by the whip staff at the break of the poop, spoke to him as he passed. 'There's more mischief coming, Captain. I begin to doubt if we'll ever make San Domingo. We've a Jonah aboard.'

So far as the mischief went, Chaffinch was not mistaken. It came on to blow from the west at noon, and brought up such a storm that his lightly expressed doubt of ever making San Domingo came before midnight to be seriously entertained by every man aboard. Under a deluge of rain, to the crash of thunder, and with great seas pounding over her, the *San Felipe* rode out a gale that bore her steadily northwestwards. Not until daybreak did the last of the hurricane sweep past her, leaving her, dipping and heaving on a black sea of long smooth rollers, to cast up her damage and lick her wounds. Her poop-rail had been shorn away, and her swivel-guns had gone with it overboard. From the boom amidships one of her boats had been carried off, and some parts of the wreckage of another lay tangled in the forechains.

But of all that she had suffered above deck the most serious damage was to her mainmast. It had been sprung, and was not merely useless but a source of danger. Against all this, however, they could set it that the storm had all but swept them to their destination. Less than five miles ahead, to the north, stood El Rosarto, beyond which lay San Domingo. Into the Spanish waters of that harbour and under the guns of King Philip's fortresses, Don Ilario, for his own sake, must supply them with safe conduct.

It was still early morning, brilliant now and sparkling after the tempest, when the battered ship, with mizzen and foresails ballooning to the light airs, but not a rag on her mainmast save the banner of Castile at its summit, staggered past the natural breakwater, which the floods of the Ozama have long since eroded, and came by the narrow eastern passage that was known as the Dragon's Jaw into the harbour of San Domingo.

She found eight fathoms close alongside of a shore that was reared like a mole on a foundation of coral, forming an island less than a quarter of a mile in width by nearly a mile in length, with a shallow ridge along the middle of it crowned by some clusters of cabbage-palms. Here the *San Felipe* dropped anchor and fired a gun to salute the noblest city of New Spain across the spacious harbour.

White and fair that city stood in its emerald setting of wide savannahs, a place of squares and palaces and churches that might have been transported from Castile, dominated by the spire of the cathedral that held the ashes of Columbus.

There was a stir along the white mole, and soon a string of boats came speeding towards the *San Felipe,* led by a gilded barge of twenty oars, trailing the red-and-yellow flag of Spain. Under a red awning fringed with gold sat a portly, swarthy, blue-jowled gentleman in pale-brown taffetas and a broad plumed hat, who wheezed and sweated when presently he climbed the accommodation-ladder to the waist of the *San Felipe.*

There Captain Blood, in black-and-silver splendour, stood to receive him beside the day-bed on which the helpless Don Ilario had been carried from the cabin. In attendance upon him stood his three shipwrecked companions, and for background there was a file of buccaneers, tricked out in headpieces and corselets to look like Spanish infantry, standing with ordered muskets.

But Don Clemente Pedroso, the retiring Governor, whom Don Ilario came to replace, was not deceived. A year ago, off Puerto Rico, on the deck of a galleon that Captain Blood had boarded and sacked, Pedroso had stood face to face with the buccaneer, and Blood's was not a countenance that was easily forgotten. Don Clemente checked abruptly in his advance. Into his swarthy, pear-shaped face came a blend of fear and fury.

Urbanely, plumed hat in hand, the Captain bowed to him.

'Your Excellency's memory honours me, I think. But do not suppose that I fly false colours.' He pointed aloft to the flag which had earned the *San Felipe* the civility of this visit. 'That is due to the presence aboard of Don Ilario de Saavedra, King Philip's new Governor of Hispaniola.'

Don Clemente lowered his eyes to the pallid, proud face of the man on the day-bed, and stood speechless, breathing noisily, whilst Don Ilario in a few words explained the situation and proffered a commission still legible if sadly blurred by seawater. The three Spaniards who had been rescued with him were also presented, and there was assurance that all further confirmation would be supplied by the Marquis of Riconete, the Admiral of the Ocean-Sea, whose squadron should very soon be at San Domingo.

In a scowling silence Don Clemente listened; in scowling silence he scanned the new Governor's commission. Thereafter he strove, from prudence, to wrap in a cold dignity the rage which the situation and the sight of Captain Blood aroused in him.

But he was in obvious haste to depart. 'My barge, Don Ilario, is at your Excellency's orders. There is, I think, nothing to detain us.'

And he half turned away scorning in his tremendous dignity further to notice Captain Blood.

'Nothing,' said Don Ilario, 'beyond expressions of gratitude to my preserver and provision for his requital.'

Don Clemente, without turning, answered sourly. 'Naturally, I suppose, it becomes necessary to permit him a free withdrawal.'

'I should be shamed by so poor and stingy an acknowledgment,' said Don Ilario, 'especially in the present condition of his ship. It is a poor enough return for the great service he has rendered me to permit him to supply himself here with wood and water and fresh victuals and with boats to replace those which he has lost. He must also be accorded sanctuary at San Domingo to carry out repairs.'

Captain Blood interposed. 'For those repairs I need not be troubling San Domingo. The island here will excellently serve, and, by your leave, Don Clemente, I shall temporarily take possession of it.'

Don Clemente, who had stood fuming during Don Ilario's announcement, swung about now and exploded. 'By my leave?' His face was yellow. 'I render thanks to God and His Saints that I am relieved of that shame since Don Ilario is now the Governor.'

Saavedra frowned. He spoke with languid sternness.

'You will bear that in your memory, if you please, Don Clemente, and trim your tone to it.'

'Oh, your Excellency's servant.' The deposed Governor bowed in raging irony. 'It is, of course, yours to command how long this enemy of God and of Spain shall enjoy the hospitality and protection of His Catholic Majesty.'

'For as long as he may need so as to carry out his repairs.'

'I see. And once these are effected, he is, of course, to be free to depart, so that he may continue to harass and plunder the ships of Spain?'

Frostily Saavedra answered: 'He has my word that he shall be free to go, and that for forty-eight hours thereafter there shall be no pursuit or other measure against him.'

'And he has your word for that? By all the Hells! He has your word. . .'

Blandly Captain Blood cut in. 'And it occurs to me that it would be prudent to have your word as well, my friend.'

He was moved by no fear for himself, but only by generosity to Don Ilario: to link the old Governor and the new in responsibility, so that Don Clemente might not hereafter make for his successor the mischief of which Blood perceived him capable.

Don Clemente was aghast. Furiously he waved his fat hands. 'My word? My word!' He choked with rage. His countenance swelled as if it would burst. 'You think I'll pass my word to a pirate rogue? You think. . .'

'Oh, as you please. If you prefer it I can put you under hatches and in irons, and keep both you and Don Ilario aboard until I am ready to sail again.'

'It's an outrage.'

Captain Blood shrugged. 'You may call it that. I call it holding hostages.'

Don Clemente glared at him with increasing malice. 'I must protest. Under constraint. . .'

'There's no constraint at all. You'll give me your word, or I'll put you in irons. Ye've a free choice. Where's the constraint?'

Then Don Ilario cut in. 'Come, sir, come! This wrangling is monstrously ungracious. You'll pledge your word, sir, or take the consequences.'

And so, for all his bitterness, Don Clemente suffered the reluctant pledge to be wrung from him.

After that, in contrast with his furious departure was Don Ilario's gracious leave-taking when they were about to lower his day-bed in slings to the waiting barge. He and Captain Blood parted with mutual compliments and expressions of goodwill, which it was perfectly understood should nowise hinder the active hostility imposed by duty upon Don Ilario once the armistice were at an end.

Blood smiled as he watched the red barge with its trailing flag ploughing with flash of oars across the harbour towards the mole. Some of the lesser boats went with it. Others, laden with fruit and vegetables, fresh meat and fish, remained on the flank of the *San Felipe,* little caring, in their anxiety to trade their wares, that she might be a pirate.

Wolverstone, the one-eyed giant who had shared Blood's escape from Barbados and had since been one of his closest associates, leaned beside him on the bulwarks. 'Ye'll not be trusting overmuch, I hope, to the word of that flabby, blue-faced Governor?'

'It's hateful, so it is, to be by nature suspicious, Ned. Hasn't he pledged himself, and would ye do him the wrong to suspect his bona fides? I cry shame on you, Ned; but all the same we'll be removing temptation from him, so we will, by fortifying ourselves on the island here.'

II

They set about it at once, with the swift, expert activity of their kind. Gangways were constructed, connecting the ship with the island, and on that strip of sand and coral they landed the twenty-four guns of the *San Felipe,* and so emplaced them that they commanded the harbour. They erected a tent of sail-cloth, felling palms to supply the poles, set up a forge, and, having unstepped the damaged mast, hauled it ashore so that they might repair it there. Meanwhile the carpenters aboard went about making good the damage to the upper works, whilst parties of buccaneers in the three boats supplied to them by the orders of Don Ilario went to procure wood and water and the necessary stores, for all of which Captain Blood scrupulously paid.

For two days they laboured without disturbance or distraction. When on the morning of the third day the alarm came, it was not from the harbour or the town before them, but from the open sea at their backs.

Captain Blood was fetched ashore at sunrise, so that from the summit of the ridge he might survey the approaching peril. With him went Wolverstone and Chaffinch, Hagthorpe, the West Country gentleman who shared their fortunes, and Ogle, who once had been a gunner in the King's Navy.

Less than a mile away they beheld a squadron of five tall ships approaching in a bravery of ensigns and pennants, all canvas spread to the light but quickening morning airs. Even as they gazed, a white cloud of smoke blossomed like a cauliflower on the flank of the leading galleon, and the boom of a saluting gun came to arouse a city that as yet was barely stirring.

'A lovely sight,' said Chaffinch.

'For a poet or a shipmaster,' said Blood. 'But I'm neither of those this morning. I'm thinking this will be King Philip's Admiral of the Ocean-Sea, the Marquis of Riconete.'

'And he's pledged no word not to molest us,' was Wolverstone's grim and unnecessary reminder.

'But I'll see to it that he does before ever we let him through the Dragon's Jaw.' Blood turned on his heel, and, making a trumpet of his hands, sounded his orders sharp and clearly to some two or three score buccaneers who stood also at gaze, some way behind them, by the guns.

Instantly those hands were seething to obey, and for the next five minutes all was a bustle of heaving and hauling to drag the *San Felipe's* two stern chasers to the summit of the ridge. They were demi-cannon, with a range of fully a mile and a half, and they were no sooner in position than Ogle was laying one of them. At a word from Blood he touched off the gun, and sent a thirty-pound shot athwart the bows of the advancing Admiral, three-quarters of a mile away.

There is no signal to lie hove to that will command a more prompt compliance. Whatever the Marquis of Riconete's astonishment at this thunderbolt from a clear sky, it brought him up with a round turn. The helm was put over hard, and the Admiral swung to larboard with idly flapping sails. Faintly over the sunlit waters came the sound of a trumpet, and the four ships that followed executed the same manoeuvre. Then from the Admiral a boat was lowered, and came speeding towards the reef to investigate this portent.

Peter Blood, with Chaffinch and a half-score men, was at the water's edge when the boat grounded. Wolverstone and Hagthorpe had taken station on the other side of the island, so as to watch the harbour and the mole, which was now all agog.

An elegant young officer stepped ashore to request on the Admiral's behalf an explanation of the sinister greeting he had received. It was supplied.

'I am here refitting my ship by permission of Don Ilario de Saavedra, in return for some small service I had the honour to do him when he was lately ship-wrecked. Before I can suffer the Admiral of the Ocean-Sea to enter this harbour I must possess his confirmation of Don Ilario's sanction and his pledge that he will leave me in peace to complete my repairs.'

The young officer stiffened with indignation. 'These are extraordinary words, sir. Who are you?'

'My name is Blood. Captain Blood, at your service.'

'Captain . . . Captain Blood!' The young man's eyes were round. 'You are Captain Blood?' Suddenly he laughed. 'You have the effrontery to suppose. . .'

He was interrupted. 'I do not like "effrontery". And as for what I suppose, be good enough to come with me. It will save argument.' He led the way to the summit of the ridge, the Spaniard sullenly following. There he paused. 'You were about to tell me, of course, that I had better be making my soul, because the guns of your squadron will blow me off this island. Be pleased to observe.'

He pointed with his long ebony cane to the activity below, where a motley buccaneer host was swarming about the landed cannon. Six of the guns were being hauled into a new position so as completely to command at point-blank range the narrow channel of the Dragon's Jaw. On the seaward side, whence it might be assailed, this battery was fully protected by the ridge.

'You will understand the purpose of these measures,' said Captain Blood. 'And you may have heard that my gunnery is of exceptional excellence. Even if it were not, I might without boasting assert--and you, I am sure, are of intelligence to perceive--that the first ship to thrust her bowsprit across that line will be sunk before she can bring a gun to bear.' He leaned upon his tall cane, the embodiment of suavity. 'Inform your Admiral, with my service, of what you have seen, and assure him from me that he may enter the harbour of San Domingo the moment he has given me the pledge I ask; but not a moment sooner.' He waved a hand in dismissal. 'God be with you, sir. Chaffinch, escort the gentleman to his boat.'

In his anger the Spaniard failed to do justice to so courteous an occasion. He muttered some Spanish mixture of theology and bawdiness, and flung away in a pet, without farewells. Back to the Admiral he was rowed. But either he did not report accurately or else the Admiral was of those who will not be convinced. For an hour later the ridge was being ploughed by round-shot, and the morning air shaken by the thunder of the squadron's guns. It distressed the gulls and set them circling and screaming overhead. But it distressed the buccaneers not at all, sheltered behind the natural bastion of the ridge from that storm of iron.

During a slackening of the fire, Ogle wriggled snakewise up to the demi-cannons which had been so emplaced that they thrust their muzzles and no more above the ridge. He laid one of them with slow care. The Spaniards, formed in line ahead for the purposes of their bombardment, three-quarters of a mile away, offered a target that could hardly be missed. Ogle touched off the unsuspected gun, and a thirty-pound shot crashed amidships into the bulwarks of the middle galleon. It went to warn the Marquis that he was not to be allowed to practise his gunnery with impunity.

There was a blare of trumpets and a hasty going about of the entire squadron to beat up against the freshening wind. To speed them, Ogle fired the second gun, and although lethally the shot was harmless, morally it could scarcely fail of its alarming purpose. Then he whistled up his gun-crew to re-load at leisure in that moment of the enemy's fleeing panic.

All day the Spaniards remained hove to a mile and a half away, where they accounted themselves out of range. Blood took advantage of this to order six more guns to be hauled to the ridge, and so as to form a breastwork half the palms on the island were felled. Whilst the main body of the buccaneers, clothed only in loose leather breeches, made short work of this, the remainder under the orders of the carpenter calmly pursued the labours of refitting. The fire glowed in the forge, and the anvils pealed bell-like under the hammers.

Across the harbour and into this scene of heroic activity came towards evening Don Clemente Pedroso, greatly daring and more yellow-faced than ever. Conducted to the ridge, where Captain Blood with the help of Ogle was still directing the construction of the breastwork, his Excellency demanded furiously to know what the buccaneers supposed must be the end of this farce.

'If you think you're propounding a problem,' said Captain Blood, 'ye're mistook. It'll end when the Admiral gives me the pledge I've asked that he'll not molest me.'

Don Clemente's black eyes were malevolent, and malevolent was the crease at the base of his beaky nose. 'You do not know the Marquis of Riconete.'

'What's more to the matter is that the Marquis does not know me. But I think we shall soon be better acquainted.'

'You deceive yourself. The Admiral is bound by no promise made you by Don Ilario. He will never make terms with you.'

Captain Blood laughed in his face. 'In that case, faith, he can stay where he is until he reaches the bottom of his water-casks. Then he can either die of thirst or sail away to find water. Indeed, we may not have to wait so long. You've not observed perhaps that the wind is freshening from the south. If it should come to blow in earnest, your Marquis may be in some discomfort off this coast.'

Don Clemente wasted some energy in vague blasphemies. Captain Blood was amused. 'I know how you suffer. You were already counting upon seeing me hanged.'

'Few things in this life would bring me greater satisfaction.'

'Alas! I must hope to disappoint your Excellency. You'll stay to sup aboard with me?'

'Sir, I do not sup with pirates.'

'Then you may go sup with the devil,' said Captain Blood. And on his short fat legs Don Clemente stalked in dudgeon back to his barge.

Wolverstone watched his departure with a brooding eye.

'Odslife, Peter, you'ld be wise to hold that Spanish gentleman. His pledge binds him no more than would a cobweb. The treacherous dog will spare nothing to do us a mischief, pledge or no pledge.'

'You're forgetting Don Ilario.'

'I'm thinking Don Clemente may forget him, too.'

'We'll be vigilant,' Blood promised confidently

That night the buccaneers slept as usual in their quarters aboard, but they left a gun-crew ashore and set a watch in a boat anchored in the Dragon's Jaw, lest the Admiral of Ocean-Sea should attempt to creep in. But although the night was clear, other risks apart, the Spaniards would not attempt the hazardous channel in the dark.

Throughout the next day, which was Sunday, the condition of stalemate continued. But on Monday morning the exasperated Admiral once more plastered the island with shot, and then stood boldly in to force a passage.

Ogle's battery had suffered no damage because the Admiral knew neither its position nor extent. Nor did Ogle now disclose it until the enemy was within a half-mile. Then four of his guns blazed at the leading ship. Two shots went wide, a third smashed into her tall forecastle, and the fourth caught her between wind and water and opened a breach through which the sea poured into her. The other three Spaniards veered in haste to starboard, and went off on an easterly tack. The crippled listed galleon went staggering after them, jettisoning in desperate haste her guns, and what other heavy gear she could spare, so as to bring the wound in her flank above the water-level.

Thus ended that attempt to force a way in, and by noon the Spaniards had gone about again and were back in their old position a mile and a half away. They were still there twenty-four hours later when a boat went out from San Domingo with a letter from Don Ilario in which the new Governor required the Marquis of Riconete to accord Captain Blood the terms he demanded. The boat had to struggle against a rising sea, for it was coming on to blow again, and from the south dark, ominous banks of cloud were rolling up. Apprehensions on the score of the weather may well have combined with Don Ilario's letter in persuading the Marquis to yield where obstinacy seemed to promise only humiliation.

So the officer by whom Captain Blood had already been visited came again to the island at the harbour's mouth, bringing him the required letter of undertaking from the Admiral, as a result of which the Spanish ships were that evening allowed to come into shelter from the rising storm. Unmolested they sailed through the Dragon's Jaw, and went to drop anchor across the harbour, by the town.

III

The wounds in the pride of the Marquis of Riconete were raw, and at the Governor's Palace that night there was a discussion of some heat. It beat to and fro between the dangerous doctrine expounded by the Admiral and supported by Don Clemente that an undertaking obtained by threats was not in honour binding, and the firm insistence of the chivalrous Don Ilario that the terms must be kept.

Wolverstone's mistrust of the operation of the Spanish conscience continued unabated, and nourished his contempt of Blood's faith in the word that had been pledged. Nor would he account sufficient the measures taken in emplacing the guns anew, so that all but six still left to command the Dragon's Jaw were now trained upon the harbour. His single eye remained apprehensively watchful in the three or four peaceful days that followed, but it was not until the morning of Friday, by when, the mast repaired, they were almost ready to put to sea, that he observed anything that he could account significant. What he observed then led him to call Captain Blood to the poop of the *San Felipe.*

'There's a queer coming and going of boats over yonder, between the Spanish squadron and the mole. Ye can see it for yourself. And it's been going on this half-hour and more. The boats go fully laden to the mole, and come back empty to the ships. Maybe ye'll guess the meaning of it.'

'The meaning's plain enough,' said Blood. 'The crews are being put ashore.'

'It's what I was supposing,' said Wolverstone. 'But will you tell me what sense or purpose there can be in that? Where there's no sense there's usually mischief. There'ld be no harm in having the men stand to their arms on the island tonight.'

The cloud on Blood's brow showed that his lieutenant had succeeded in stirring his suspicions. 'It's plaguily odd, so it is. And yet. . . Faith, I'll not believe Don Ilario would play me false.'

'I'm not thinking of Don Ilario, but of that bile-laden curmudgeon Don Clemente. That's not the man to let a pledged word thwart his spite. And if this Riconete is such another, as well he may be. . .'

'Don Ilario is the man in authority now.'

'Maybe. But he's crippled by a broken leg, and those other two might easily overbear him, knowing that King Philip himself would condone it.'

'But if they mean mischief, why should they be putting the crews ashore?'

'That's what I hoped you might guess, Peter.'

'Since I can't, I'd better go and find out.' A fruit-barge had just come alongside. Captain Blood leaned over the rail. 'Hey, you!' he hailed the owner. 'Bring me your yams aboard.'

He turned to beckon some of the hands in the waist and issued orders briefly whilst the fruit-seller was climbing the accommodation-ladder with a basket of yams balanced on his head. He was invited aft to the Captain's cabin, and, unsuspecting, went, after which he was seen no more that day. His half-caste mate, who had remained in the barge, was similarly lured aboard, and went to join his master under hatches. Then an unclean, bare-legged, sunburned fellow in the greasy shirt, loose calico breeches and swathed head of a waterside hawker went over the side of the *San Felipe,* climbed down into the barge, and pulled away across the harbour towards the Spanish ships, followed by anxious eyes from the bulwarks of the buccaneer vessel.

Bumping alongside of the Admiral, the hawker bawled his wares for some time in vain. The utter silence within those wooden walls was significant. After a while steps rang out on the deck. A sentry in a headpiece looked over the rail to bid him take his fruit to the devil, adding the indiscreet but already superfluous information that if he were not a fool he would know that there was no one aboard.

Bawling ribaldries in return, the hawker pulled away for the mole, climbed out of the barge, and went to refresh himself at a wayside tavern that was thronged with Spaniards from the ships. Over a pot of wine he insinuated himself into a group of these seamen, with an odd tale of wrongs suffered at the hands of pirates and a fiercely rancorous criticism of the Admiral for suffering the buccaneers to remain on the island at the harbour's mouth instead of blowing them to perdition.

His fluent Spanish admitted of no suspicion. His truculence and obvious hatred of pirates won him sympathy.

'It's not the Admiral,' a petty officer assured him. 'He'ld never have parleyed with these dogs. It's this weak-kneed new Governor of Hispaniola who's to blame. It's he who has given them leave to repair their ship.'

'If I were an Admiral of Castile,' said the hawker, 'I vow to the Virgin I'd take matters into my own hands.'

There was a general laugh, and a corpulent Spaniard clapped him on the back. 'The Admiral's of the same mind, my lad.'

'In spite of his flabbiness the Governor,' said a second.

'That's why we're all ashore,' nodded a third.

And now in scraps which the hawker was left to piece together forth came the tale of mischief that was preparing for the buccaneers.

So much to his liking did the hawker find the Spaniards, and so much to their liking did they find him, that the afternoon was well advanced before he rolled out of the tavern to find his barge and resume his trade. The pursuit of it took him back across the harbour, and when at last he came alongside the *San Felipe* he was seen to have a second and very roomy barge in tow. Making fast at the foot of the accommodation-ladder, he climbed to the ship's waist, where Wolverstone received him with relief and not without wrath.

'Ye said naught of going ashore, Peter. Where the plague was the need o' that? You'll be thrusting your head into a noose once too often.'

Captain Blood laughed. 'I've thrust my head into no noose at all. And if I had the result would have been worth the risk. I'm justified of my faith in Don Ilario. It's only because he's a man of his word that we may all avoid having our throats cut this night. For if he had given his consent to employ the men of the garrison, as Don Clemente wished, we should never have known anything about it until too late. Because he refused, Don Clemente has made alliance with that other forswarn scoundrel, the Admiral. Between them they've concocted a sweet plan behind Don Ilario's back. And that's why the Marquis has taken his crews ashore, so as to hold them in readiness for the job.

'They're to slip out to sea in boatloads at midnight by the shallow western passage, land on the unguarded southwest side of the island, and then, having entered by the back door as it were, creep across to surprise us on board the *San Felipe* and cut our throats whilst we sleep. There'll be some four hundred of them at the least. Practically every mother's son from the squadron. The Marquis of Riconete means to make sure that the odds are in his favour.'

'And we with eighty men in all!' Wolverstone rolled his single eye. 'But we're forewarned. We can shift the guns so as to smash them as they land.'

Blood shook his head. 'It can't be done without being noticed. If they saw us move the guns they must suppose we've got wind of what's coming. They'd change their plans, and that wouldn't suit me at all.'

'Wouldn't suit you! Does this camisado suit you?'

'Let me see the trap that's set for me, and it's odd if I can't turn it against the trapper. Did ye notice that I brought a second barge back with me? Forty men can pack into those two bottoms, the remainder can go in the four boats we have.'

'Go? Go where? D'ye mean to run, Peter?'

'To be sure I do. But no farther than will suit my purpose.'

He cut things fine. It wanted only an hour to midnight when he embarked his men. And even then he was in no haste to set out. He waited until the silence of the night was disturbed by a distant creak of rowlocks, which warned him that the Spaniards were well upon their way to the shallow passage on the western side of the island. Then, at last, he gave the word to push off, and the *San Felipe* was abandoned to the enemy stealing upon her through the night.

It would be fully an hour later, when the Spaniards, having landed, came like shadows over the ridge, some to take possession of the guns, others to charge across the gangways. They preserved a ghostly silence until they were aboard the *San Felipe.* Then they gave tongue loudly as stormers will, to encourage themselves. To their surprise, however, not all the din they made sufficed to arouse these pirate dogs, who, apparently, were all asleep so trustfully that they had set no watch.

A sense of something outside their calculations began to pervade them as they stood at fault, unable to understand this lack of life aboard the ship they had invaded. Then, suddenly, the darkness of the night was split by tongues of flame from across the harbour, and with a roar as of thunder a broadside of twenty guns crashed its metal into the flank of the *San Felipe.*

The surprise-party thus, itself, surprised, filled the night with a screaming babel of imprecations, and turned in frenzy to escape from a vessel that was beginning to founder. In the mad panic of men assailed by forces of destruction which they cannot understand, the Spaniards fought one another to reach the gangways and regain the comparative safety of the shore without thought or care for those who had been wounded by that murderous volley.

The Marquis of Riconete, a tall, gaunt man, strove furiously to rally them.

'Stand firm! In the name of God, stand firm, you dogs!'

His officers plunged this way and that into the fleeing mob, and with blows and oaths succeeded in restoring some measure of order. Whilst the *San Felipe* was settling down in eight fathoms, the men, ashore and re-formed at last, stood to their arms, waiting. But they no more knew for what they waited than did the Marquis, who was furiously demanding of Heaven and Hell the explanation of happenings so unaccountable.

It was soon afforded. Against the blackness of the night loomed ahead, in deeper blackness, the shape of a great ship that was slowly advancing towards the Dragon's Jaw. The splash of oars and the grating of rowlocks told that she was being warped out of the harbour, and to the straining ears of the Spaniards the creak of blocks and the rattle of spars presently bore the message that she was hoisting sail.

To the Marquis, peering with Don Clemente through the gloom, the riddle was solved. Whilst he had been leading the men of his squadron to seize a ship that he supposed to be full of buccaneers, the buccaneers had stolen across the harbour to take possession of a ship that they knew to be untenanted, and to turn her guns upon the Spaniards in the *San Felipe.* It was in that same vessel, the Admiral's flagship, the magnificent *Maria Gloriosa* of forty guns, with a fortune in her hold, that those accursed pirates were now putting to sea under the Admiral's impotent nose.

He said so in bitterness, and in bitterness raged awhile with Don Clemente, until the latter suddenly remembered the guns that Blood had trained upon the passage, guns that would still be emplaced and of a certainty loaded, since they had not been used. Frantically he informed the Admiral of how he might yet turn the tables on the buccaneers, and at the information the Admiral instantly took fire.

'I vow to Heaven,' he cried, 'that those dogs shall not leave San Domingo, though I have to sink my own ship. Ho there! The guns! To the guns!'

He led the way at a run, half a hundred men stumbling after him in the dark towards the channel battery. They reached it just as the *Maria Gloriosa* was entering the Dragon's Jaw. In less than five minutes she would be within point-blank range. A miss would be impossible at such close quarters, and six guns stood ready trained.

'A gunner!' bawled the Marquis. 'At once a gunner, to sink me that infernal pirate into Hell.'

A man stood briskly forward. From the rear came a gleam of light, and a lantern was passed forward from hand to hand until it reached the gunner. He snatched it, ignited from its flames a length of fuse, then stepped to the nearest gun.

'Wait,' the Marquis ordered. 'Wait until she is abreast.'

But by the light of the lantern the gunner perceived at once that waiting could avail them nothing. With an imprecation he sprang to the nearest gun, shed light upon the touch-hole, and again passed on. Thus from gun to gun he sped until he had reached the last. Then he came back, swinging the lantern in one hand and the spluttering fuse in the other, so slowly that the Marquis was moved to frenzy.

Not a hundred yards away the *Maria Gloriosa* was slowly passing, her hull a dark shadow, her sails faintly grey above.

'Make haste, fool! Make haste! Touch them off!' roared the Admiral of the Ocean-Sea.

'Look for yourself, Excellency.' The gunner set down the lantern on the gun so that its light fell directly upon the touch-hole. 'Spiked. A soft nail has been rammed home. It is the same with all of them.'

The Admiral of the Ocean-Sea swore with the picturesque and horrible fervour that only a Spaniard can achieve. 'He forgets nothing, that endemonized pirate dog.'

A musket-shot, carefully aimed by a buccaneer from the bulwarks of the passing ship, came to shatter the lantern. It was followed by an ironic cheer and a burst of still more ironic laughter from the deck of the *Maria Gloriosa* as she passed on her stately way through the Dragon's Jaw to the open sea.

Episode 2

THE PRETENDER

I

Mobility, as everyone knows, is a quality that has been in all times a conspicuous factor of success with most great commanders by land and sea. So, too, with Captain Blood. There were occasions when his onslaught was sudden as the stoop of a hawk. And there was a time, coinciding with his attainment of the summit of his fame, when this mobility assumed proportions conveying such an impression of ubiquity that it led the Spaniards to believe and assert that only a compact with Satan could enable a man so miraculously to annihilate space.

Not content to be mildly amused by the echoes that reached him from time to time of the supernatural powers with which Spanish superstition endowed him, Captain Blood was diligent to profit where possible by the additional terror in which his name came thus to be held. But when shortly after his capture at San Domingo of the *Maria Gloriosa,* the powerful, richly laden flagship of the Spanish Admiral of the Ocean-Sea, the Marquis of Riconete, he heard it positively and circumstantially reported that on the very morrow of his sailing from San Domingo he had been raiding Cartagena, two hundred miles away, it occurred to him that one or two other fantastic tales of his doings that had lately reached his ears might possess a foundation less vague than was supplied by mere superstitious imaginings.

It was in a water-side tavern at Christianstadt on the island of Sainte Croix, where the *Maria Gloriosa* (impudently re-named the *Andalusian Lass,* and as impudently flying the flag of the Union) had put in for wood and water, that he overheard an account of horrors practised by himself and his buccaneers at Cartagena in the course of that same raid.

He had sought the tavern in accordance with his usual custom when roving at a venture, without definite object. These resorts of seafaring men were of all places the likeliest in which to pick up scraps of information that might be turned to account. Nor was this the first time that the information he picked up concerned himself, though never yet had it been of quite so surprising a nature.

The narrator was a big Dutchman, red of hair and face, named Claus, master of a merchant ship from the Scheldt, and he was entertaining with his lurid tale of pillage, rape and murder two traders of the town, members of the French West India Company.

Uninvited, Blood thrust himself into this group with the object of learning more, and the intrusion was not merely accepted with the tolerance that prevailed in such resorts, but welcomed by virtue of the elegance of this stranger's appointments and the quiet authority of his manner.

'My greetings, messieurs.' If his French had not the native fluency of his Spanish, acquired during two years at Seville in a prison of the Holy Office, yet it was serviceably smooth. He drew up a stool, sat down without ceremony, and rapped with his knuckles on the stained deal table to summon the taverner. 'When do you say that this occurred?'

'Ten days ago it was,' the Dutchman answered him.

'Impossible.' Blood shook his periwigged head. 'To my certain knowledge, Captain Blood ten days ago was at San Domingo. Besides, his ways are hardly as villainous as those you describe.'

Claus, that rough man, of a temper to match his fiery complexion, displayed impatience of the contradiction. 'Pirates are pirates, and all are foul.' He spat ostentatiously upon the sanded floor, as if to mark his nausea.

'Faith, I'll not argue with you on that. But since I know that ten days ago Captain Blood was at San Domingo, it follows that he could not at the same time have been at Cartagena.'

'Cock-sure, are you not?' the Dutchman sneered. 'Then let me tell you, sir, that I had the tale two days since at San Juan de Puerto Rico from the captain of one of two battered Spanish plate-ships that had been beset in Cartagena by the raiders. You'll not pretend to know better than he. Those two galleons ran into San Juan for shelter. They had been hunted across the Caribbean by that damned buccaneer, and they would never have escaped him but that a lucky shot of theirs damaged his foremast and compelled him to shorten sail.'

But Blood was not impressed by this citation of an eyewitness. 'Bah!' said he. 'The Spaniards were in a mistake. That's all.'

The traders looked uneasily at the dark face of this newcomer, whose eyes, so vividly blue under their black eyebrows, were coldly contemptuous. The timely arrival of the taverner brought a pause to the discussion, and Blood softened the mounting irritation of the Dutchman by inviting these habitual rum-drinkers to share with him a bottle of more elegant Canary Sack.

'My good sir,' Claus insisted, 'there could be no mistake. Blood's big red ship, the *Arabella,* is not to be mistaken.'

'If they say that the *Arabella* chased them, they make it the more certain that they lied. For, again to my certain knowledge, the *Arabella* is at Tortuga, careened for graving and refitting.'

'You know a deal,' said the Dutchman, with his heavy sarcasm.

'I keep myself informed,' was the plausible answer, civilly delivered. 'It's prudent.'

'Ay, provided that you inform yourself correctly. This time you're sorely at fault. Believe me, sir, at present Captain Blood is somewhere hereabouts.'

Captain Blood smiled. 'That I can well believe. What I don't perceive is why you should suppose it.'

The Dutchman thumped the table with his great fist. 'Didn't I tell you that somewhere off Puerto Rico his foremast was strained, in action with these Spaniards? What better reason than that? He'll have run to one of these islands for repairs. That's certain.'

'What's much more certain is that your Spaniards, in panic of Captain Blood, see an *Arabella* in every ship they sight.'

Only the coming of the Sack made the Dutchman tolerant of such obstinacy in error. When they had drunk, he confined his talk to the plate-ships. Not only were they at Puerto Rico for repairs, but after their late experience, and because they were very richly laden, they would not again put to sea until they could be convoyed.

Now here, at last, was matter of such interest to Captain Blood that he was not concerned to dispute further about the horrors imputed to him at Cartagena and the other falsehood of his engagement with those same plate-ships.

That evening in the cabin of the *Andalusian Lass,* in whose splendid equipment of damasks and velvets, of carved and gilded bulkheads, of crystal and silver, was reflected the opulence of the Spanish Admiral to whom she had so lately belonged, Captain Blood summoned a council of war. It was composed of the one-eyed giant Wolverstone, of Nathaniel Hagthorpe, that pleasant mannered West Country gentleman, and of Chaffinch, the little sailing master, all of them men who had been transported with Blood for their share in the Monmouth rising. As a result of their deliberations, the *Andalusian Lass* weighed anchor that same night, and slipped away from Sainte Croix, to appear two days later off San Juan de Puerto Rico.

Flying now the red and gold of Spain at her maintruck, she hove to in the roads, fired a gun in salute, and lowered a boat.

Through his telescope, Blood scanned the harbour for confirmation of the Dutchman's tale. There he made out quite clearly among the lesser shipping two tall yellow galleons, vessels of thirty guns, whose upper works bore signs of extensive damage, now in course of repair. So far, then, it seemed, Mynheer Claus had told the truth. And this was all that mattered.

It was necessary to proceed with caution. Not only was the harbour protected by a considerable fort, with a garrison which no doubt would be kept more than usually alert in view of the presence of the treasure-ships, but Blood disposed of no more than eighty hands aboard the *Andalusian Lass,* so that he was not in sufficient strength to effect a landing, even if his gunnery should have the good fortune to subdue the fortress. He must trust to guile rather than to strength, and in the lowered cock-boat Captain Blood went audaciously ashore upon a reconnaissance.

II

It was so improbable as to be accounted impossible that news of Captain Blood's capture of the Spanish flagship at San Domingo could already have reached Puerto Rico; therefore the white-and-gold splendours, and the pronouncedly Spanish lines, of the *Maria Gloriosa* should be his sufficient credentials at the outset. He had made free with the Marquis of Riconete's extensive wardrobe, and he came arrayed in a suit of violet taffetas, with stockings of lilac silk and a baldrick of finest Cordovan of the same colour that was stiff with silver bullion. A broad black hat with a trailing claret feather covered his black periwig and shaded his weathered, high-bred face.

Tall, straight, and vigorously spare, his head high, and authority in every line of him, he came to stand, leaning upon his tall gold-headed cane, before the Captain-General of Puerto Rico, Don Sebastian Mendes, and to explain himself in that fluent Castilian so painfully acquired.

Some Spaniards, making a literal translation of his name, spoke of him as Don Pedro Sangre, others alluded to him as El Diablo Encarnado. Humorously blending now the two, he impudently announced himself as Don Pedro Encarnado, deputy of the Admiral of the Ocean-Sea, the Marquis of Riconete, who could not come ashore in person because chained to his bed aboard by an attack of gout. From a Dutch vessel, spoken off Sainte Croix, his Excellency the Admiral had heard of an attack by scoundrelly buccaneers upon two ships of Spain from Cartagena, which had sought shelter here at San Juan. These ships he had seen in the harbour, but the Marquis desired more precise information in the matter.

Don Sebastian supplied it tempestuously. He was a big, choleric man, flabby and sallow, with little black moustachios surmounting lips as thick almost as an African's, and he possessed a number of chins, all of them blue from the razor.

His reception of the false Don Pedro had been marked, first by all the ceremony due to the deputy of a representative of the Catholic King, and then by the cordiality proper from one Castilian gentleman to another; he presented him to his dainty, timid, still youthful little wife, and kept him to dinner, which was spread in a cool white patio under the green shade of a trellis of vines, and served by liveried negro slaves at the orders of a severely formal Spanish majordomo.

At table the tempestuousness aroused in Don Sebastian by his visitor's questions was maintained. It was true enough--por Dios!--that the plate-ships had been set upon by buccaneers, the same vile hijos de puta who had lately transformed Cartagena into the likeness of Hell. There were nauseating details, which the Captain-General supplied without regard for the feelings of Doña Leocadia, who shuddered and crossed herself more than once while his horrible tale was telling.

If it shocked Captain Blood to learn that such things were being imputed to him and his followers, he forgot this in the interest aroused in him by the information that there was bullion aboard those plate-ships to the value of two hundred thousand pieces of eight, to say nothing of pepper and spices worth almost the like amount.

'What a prize would not that have been for that incarnate devil Blood, and what a mercy of the Lord it was that the ships were able not only to get away from Cartagena, but to escape his subsequent pursuit of them!'

'Captain Blood?' said the visitor. 'Is it certain, then, that this was his work?'

'Not a doubt of it. Who else is afloat today who would dare so much? Let me lay hands on him, and as Heaven hears me I'll have the skin off his bones to make myself a pair of breeches.'

'Sebastian, my love!' Doña Leocadia shudderingly remonstrated. 'What horror!'

'Let me lay hands on him,' Don Sebastian fiercely repeated.

Captain Blood smiled amiably. 'It may come to pass. He may be nearer to you than you suppose.'

'I pray God he may be.' And the Captain-General twirled his absurd moustache.

After dinner the visitor took a ceremonious leave, regretfully, but of necessity since he must report to his Admiral. But on the morrow he was back again, and when the boat that brought him ashore had returned to the white-and-gold flagship, the great galleon was observed by the idlers on the mole to take up her anchor and to be hoisting sail. Before the freshening breeze that set a sparkling ruffle on the sunlit violet waters, she moved majestically eastwards along the peninsula on which San Juan is built.

Penmanship had occupied some of Captain Blood's time aboard since yesterday, and the Admiral's writing-coffer had supplied his needs: the Admiral's seal and a sheet of parchment surmounted by the arms of Spain. Hence an imposing document, which he now placed before Don Sebastian. Explanations plausibly accompanied it.

'Your assurance that Captain Blood is in these waters has persuaded the Admiral to hunt him out. In his Excellency's absence, he commands me, as you observe, to remain here.'

The Captain-General was poring over the parchment with its great slab of red wax bearing the arms of the Marquis of Riconete. It ordered Don Sebastian to make over to Don Pedro Encarnado the command of the military establishment of San Juan de Puerto Rico, the Fort of Santo Antonio, and its garrison.

It was not an order that Don Sebastian could be expected to receive with equanimity. He frowned and blew out his fat lips. 'I do not understand this at all. Colonel Vargas who commands the fort under my orders is a competent, experienced officer. Besides,' he bristled, 'I have been under the impression that it is I who am Captain-General of Puerto Rico, and that it is for me to appoint my officers.'

No speech or manner could have been more conciliatory than Captain Blood's. 'In your place, Don Sebastian, I must confess--oh, but entirely between ourselves--that I should feel precisely as you do. But. . . What would you? It is necessary to have patience. The Admiral is moved to excessive anxiety for the safety of the plate-ships.'

'Is not their safety in San Juan my affair? Am I not the King's representative in Puerto Rico? Let the Admiral command as he pleases on the ocean; but here on land. . .'

Suavely Captain Blood interrupted him, a hand familiarly upon his shoulder. 'My dear Don Sebastian!' He lowered his voice to a confidential tone. 'You know how it is with these royal favourites.'

'Royal. . .' Don Sebastian choked down his annoyance in sudden apprehension. 'I never heard that the Marquis of Riconete is a royal favourite.'

'A lap-dog to his Majesty. That, of course, between ourselves. Hence his audacity. I should not blame you for holding the opinion that he abuses the King's affection for him. You know how the royal favour goes to a man's head.' He paused and sighed. 'It distresses me to be the instrument of this encroachment upon your province but I am as helpless as yourself, my friend.'

Thus brought to imagine that he trod dangerous ground, Don Sebastian suppressed the heat begotten of this indignity to his office, and philosophically consented, as Captain Blood urged him, to take comfort in the thought that the Admiral's interference possessed at least the advantage for him of relieving him of all responsibility for what might follow.

After this, and in the two succeeding days, Peter Blood displayed a tact that made things easy, not only for the Captain-General, but also for Colonel Vargas, who at first had been disposed to verbal violence on the subject of his supersession. It reconciled the Colonel, at least in part, to discover that the new commandant showed no inclination to interfere with any of his military measures. Far from it, having made a close inspection of the fort, its armament, garrison, and munitions, he warmly commended all that he beheld, and generously confessed that he should not know how to improve upon the Colonel's dispositions.

It was on the first Friday in June that the false Don Pedro had come ashore to take command. On the following Sunday morning in the courtyard of the Captain-General's quarters, a breathless young officer reeled from the saddle of a lathered, spent, and quivering horse. To Don Sebastian, who was at breakfast with his lady and his temporary Commandant, this messenger brought the alarming news that a powerfully armed ship that flew no flag and was manifestly a pirate was threatening San Patrico, fifty miles away. It had opened a bombardment of the settlement, so far without damage because it dared not come within range of the fire maintained by the guns of the harbour fort. Lamentably, however, the fort was very short of ammunition, and once this were exhausted there was no adequate force in men to resist a landing.

Such was Don Sebastian's amazement that it transcended his alarm. 'In the devil's name, what should pirates seek at San Patrico? There's nothing there but sugarcane and maize.'

'I think I understand,' said Captain Blood. 'San Patrico is the back door to San Juan and the plate-ships.'

'The back door?'

'Don't you see? Because these pirates dare not venture a frontal attack against your heavily armed fort of Santo Antonio here, they hoped to march overland from San Patrico and take you in the rear.'

The Captain-General was profoundly impressed by this prompt display of military acumen.

'By all the Saints, I believe you explain it.' He heaved himself up, announcing that he would take order at once, dismissed the officer to rest and refreshment, and despatched a messenger to fetch Colonel Vargas from the fort.

Stamping up and down the long room, which was kept in cool shadow by the slatted blinds, he gave thanks to his patron saint, the martyred centurion, that Santo Antonio was abundantly munitioned, thanks to his foresight, and could spare all the powder and shot that San Patrico might require so as to hold these infernal pirates at bay.

The timid glance of Doña Leocadia followed him about the room, then was turned upon the new commandant when his voice, cool and calm, invaded the Captain-General's pause for breath.

'With submission, sir, it would be an error to take munitions from Santo Antonio. We may require all that we have. Several things are possible. These buccaneers may change their plans, when they find the landing at San Patrico less easy than they suppose. Or'--and now he stated what he knew to be the case, since it was precisely what he had commanded--'the attack on San Patrico may be no more than a feint, to draw thither your strength.'

Don Sebastian stared blankly, passing a jewelled hand over his ponderous blue jowl. 'That is possible. Yes, God help me!' And thankful now for the presence of this calm, discerning commandant, whose coming at first had so offended him, he cast himself entirely upon the man's resourcefulness.

Don Pedro was prompt to take command. 'I have a note of the munitions aboard the plate-ships. They are considerable. Abundant for the needs of San Patrico, and useless at present to the vessels. We will take not only their powder and shot, but their guns as well, and haul them at once to San Patrico.'

'You'll disarm the plate-ships?' Don Sebastian stared alarm.

'What need to keep them armed whilst in harbour here? It is the fort that will defend the entrance if it should come to need defending. The emergency is at San Patrico.' He became more definite. 'You will be good enough to order the necessary mules and oxen for the transport. As for men, there are two hundred and thirty at Santo Antonio and a hundred and twenty aboard the plate-ships. What is the force at San Patrico?'

'Between forty and fifty.'

'God help us! If these buccaneers intend a landing, it follows that they must be four or five hundred strong. To oppose them San Patrico will need every man we can spare. I shall have to send Colonel Vargas thither with a hundred and fifty men from Santo Antonio and a hundred men from the ships.'

'And leave San Juan defenceless?' In his horror Don Sebastian could not help adding: 'Are you mad?'

Captain Blood's air was that of a man whose knowledge of his business places him beyond all wavering. 'I think not. We have the fort with a hundred guns, half of them of powerful calibre. A hundred men should abundantly suffice to serve them. And lest you suppose that I subject you to risks I am not prepared to share, I shall, myself, remain here to command them.'

When Vargas came, he was as horrified as Don Sebastian at this depletion of the defence of San Juan. In the heat of his arguments against it he became almost discourteous. He looked down his nose at the Admiral's deputy, and spoke of the Art of War as if from an eminence where it had no secrets. From that eminence, the new commandant coolly dislodged him. 'If you tell me that we can attempt to resist a landing at San Patrico with fewer than three hundred men, I shall understand that you have still to learn the elements of your profession. And, anyway,' he added, rising, so as to mark the end of the discussion, 'I have the honour to command here, and the responsibility is mine. I shall be glad if you will give my orders your promptest obedience.'

Colonel Vargas bowed stiffly, biting his lip, and the Captain-General returned explosive thanks to Heaven that he held a parchment from the Admiral of the Ocean-Sea which must relieve him of all blame for whatever consequences might attend this rashness.

As the Cathedral bells were summoning the faithful to High Mass, and notwithstanding the approaching sweltering heat of noontide, the matter admitting of no delay, Colonel Vargas marched his men out of San Juan. At the head of the column, and followed by a long train of mules, laden with ammunition, and of oxen-teams hauling the guns, the Colonel took the road across the gently undulating plains to San Patrico, fifty miles away.

III

You will have conceived that the pirate threatening San Patrico was the erstwhile flagship of the Spanish Admiral of the Ocean-Sea, now the *Andalusian Lass,* despatched thither on that business by Captain Blood. Wolverstone had been placed in command of her, and his orders were to maintain his demonstration and keep the miserable little fort of San Patrico in play for forty-eight hours. At the end of that time, and under cover of night, he was to slip quietly away before the arrival of the reinforcements from San Juan, which by then would be well upon their way, and, abandoning the feint, come round at speed to deliver the real blow at the now comparatively defenceless San Juan.

Messengers from San Patrico arriving at regular intervals throughout Monday brought reports that showed how faithfully Wolverstone was fulfilling his instructions. The messages gave assurance that the constant fire of the fort was compelling the pirates to keep their distance.

It was heartening news to the Captain-General, persuaded that every hour that passed increased the chances that the raiders would be caught red-handed by the

Admiral of the Ocean-Sea, who must be somewhere in the neighbourhood, and incontinently destroyed. 'By tomorrow,' he said, 'Vargas will be at San Patrico with the reinforcements and the pirates' chance of landing will be at an end.'

But what the morrow brought was something very different from the expectations of all concerned. Soon after daybreak, San Juan was awakened by the roar of guns. Don Sebastian's first uplifting thought, as he thrust a leg out of bed, was that here was the Marquis of Riconete announcing his return by a fully royal salute. The continuous bombardment, however, stirred his misgivings even before he reached the terrace of his fine house. Once there, and having seen what his telescope could show him in detail, his misgivings were changed to stark consternation.

Captain Blood's first awakening emotions had been the very opposite to Don Sebastian's. But his annoyed assumptions were at once dismissed. Even if Wolverstone should have left San Patrico before midnight, which was unlikely, it was impossible, in the teeth of the keen westerly wind now blowing, that he could reach San Juan for another twelve hours. Moreover, Wolverstone was not the man to act in such careless disregard of his instructions.

Half dressed, Captain Blood made haste to seek at Don Sebastian's side the explanation of this artillery, and there experienced a consternation no whit inferior to the Captain-General's, though vastly different of source. For the great red ship whose guns were pounding the fort from the roads, a half-mile away, had all the appearance of his own *Arabella,* which he had left careened in Tortuga less than a month ago.

He remembered the false current tale of a raid by Captain Blood on Cartagena, and he asked himself was it possible that Pitt and Dyke and other associates whom he had left behind had gone roving in his absence, conducting their raids with inhuman cruelties such as those which had disgraced Morgan and Montbars. He could not believe it of them; and yet here stood his ship under a billowing cloud of smoke from her own gunfire, delivering broadsides that were bringing down the walls of a fort that had the appearance of being massive and substantial, but the mortar of which, as he had been glad to ascertain when inspecting it, was mere adobe.

At his side the Captain-General of Puerto Rico was invoking alternately all the saints in the calendar and all the fiends in Hell to bear witness that here was that incarnate devil Captain Blood.

Tight-lipped, that incarnate devil at his very elbow gave no heed to his imprecations. With a hand to his brow, so as to shade his eyes from the morning sun, he scanned the lines of that red ship from gilded beak-head to towering poop. It was the *Arabella,* and yet it was not the *Arabella.* The difference eluded him, yet a difference he perceived.

As he looked, the great vessel came broadside on in the act of going about. Then, even without counting her gunports, he obtained a clear assurance. She carried four guns less than his own flagship.

'That is not Captain Blood,' he said.

'Not Captain Blood? You'll tell me that I am not Sebastian Mendes. Is not his ship named the *Arabella?'*

'That is not the *Arabella.'*

Don Sebastian looked him over with a contemptuous, blood-injected eye. Then he proffered his telescope.

'Read the name on the counter for yourself.'

Captain Blood took the glass. The ship was swinging, so as to bring her starboard guns to bear, and her counter came fully into view. In letters of gold, he read there the name *Arabella,* and his bewilderment was renewed.

'I do not understand,' he said. But the roar of her broadside drowned his words and loosened some further tons of the fort's masonry. And then, at last, the guns of the fort thundered in their turn for the first time. The fire was wild and wide of the mark, but at least it had the effect of compelling the attacking ship to stand off, so as to get out of range.

'By God, they're awake at last!' cried Don Sebastian, with bitter irony.

Blood departed in search of his boots, ordering the scared servants who stood about to find and saddle him a horse.

When, five minutes later, booted, but still not more than half dressed, he was setting his foot to the stirrup, the Captain-General surged beside him. 'It's your responsibility,' he raged. 'Yours and your precious Admiral's. Your fatuous measures have left us defenceless. I hope you'll be able to answer for it. I hope so.'

'I hope so too; and to that brigand, whoever he may be.' Captain Blood spoke through his teeth in an anger more bitter if less boisterous than the Captain-General's. For he was experiencing the condition of being hoist with his own petard and all the emotions that accompany it. He had been at such elaborate and crafty pains to disarm San Juan, merely, it seemed, so as to make it easy for a pestilential interloper to come and snatch from under his very nose the prize for which he played. He could not conjecture the identity of the interloper, but he had more than a suspicion that it was not by mere coincidence that this red ship was named the *Arabella,* and not a doubt but that her master was the author of those horrors in Cartagena which were being assigned to Captain Blood.

However that might be, what mattered now was to do what might be done so as to frustrate this most inopportune of interlopers. And so, by a singular irony, Captain Blood rode forth upon the hope, rendered forlorn by his own contriving, of organizing the defences of a Spanish place against an attack by buccaneers.

He found the fortress in a state of desolation and confusion. Half the guns were already out of action under the heaped rubble. Of the hundred men that had been left to garrison it, ten had been killed and thirty disabled. The sixty that remained whole were resolute and steady men--there were no better troops in the world than those of the Spanish infantry--but reduced to helplessness by the bewildered incompetence of the young officer in command.

Captain Blood came amongst them just as another broadside shore away twenty yards of ramparts. In the well-like courtyard, half choked with the dust of crumbling masonry and the acrid fumes of gunpowder, he stormed at the officer who ran to meet him.

'Will you keep your company cowering here until men and guns are all buried together in these ruins?'

Captain Araña bridled. He threw a chest. 'We can die at our posts, sir, to pay for your errors.'

'So can any fool. But if you had as much intelligence as impertinence you would be saving some of the guns. They'll be needed presently. Haul a score of them out of this, and have them posted in that cover.' He pointed to a pimento grove less than a half-mile away in the direction of the city. 'Leave me a dozen hands to serve the guns that remain, and take every other man with you. And get your wounded out of this death-trap. When you're in the grove send out for teams of mules, horses, oxen, what you will, against the need for further haulage. Load with canister. Use your wits, man, and waste no time. About it!'

If Captain Araña lacked imagination to conceive, at least he possessed energy to execute the conceptions of another. Dominated by the commandant's brisk authority fired by admiration for measures whose simple soundness he at once perceived, he went diligently to work, whilst Blood took charge of a battery of ten guns emplaced on the southern rampart which best commanded the bay. A dozen men, aroused from their inertia by his vigour, and stimulated by his own indifference to danger, carried out his orders calmly and swiftly.

The buccaneer, having emptied her starboard guns, was going about so as to bring her larboard broadside to bear. Taking advantage of the manoeuvre, and gauging as best he could the station from which her next fire would be delivered, Blood passed from gun to gun, laying each with his own hands, deliberately and carefully. He had just laid the last of them when the red ship, having put the helm over, presented her larboard flank. He snatched the spluttering match from the hand of a musketeer, and instantly touched off the gun at that broad target. If the shot was not as lucky as he hoped, yet it was lucky enough. It shore away the pirate's bowsprit. She yawed under the shock and listed slightly, and this at the very moment that her broadside was delivered. As a consequence of that fortuitously altered elevation, the discharge soared harmlessly over the fort and went to plough the ground away in its rear. At once she swung downwind so as to run out of range.

'Fire!' roared Blood, and the other nine guns blazed as one.

The buccaneer's stern presenting but a narrow mark, Blood could hope for little more than a moral effect. But again luck favoured him, and if eight of the twenty-four-pound missiles merely flung up the spray about the ship, the ninth crashed into her stern-coach, to speed her on her way.

The Spaniards sent up a cheer. 'Viva Don Pedro!' And it was actually with laughter that they set about reloading, their courage resurrected by that first if slight success.

There was no need now for haste. It took the buccaneer some time to clear the wreckage of her bowsprit, and it was quite an hour before she was beating back, close-hauled against the breeze, to take her revenge.

In that most valuable respite, Araña had got the guns into the cover of the grove a quarter of a mile away. Thither Blood might have retreated to join him. But, greatly daring, he stayed, first to repeat his earlier tactics. This time, however, his fire went wide, and the full force of the red ship's broadside came smashing into the fort to open another wound in its crumbling flank. Then, infuriated perhaps by the mishap suffered, and judging, no doubt, from the fort's previous volley that only a few of its guns remained effective and that these would now be empty the buccaneer ran in close, and, going about, delivered her second broadside at point-blank range.

The result was an explosion that shook the buildings in San Juan, a mile away.

Blood felt as if giant hands had seized him, lifted him and cast him violently from them upon the subsiding ground. He lay winded and half stunned, while rubble came spattering down in a titanic hailstorm; and to the roar as of a continuous cataract, the walls of the fort slid down as if suddenly turned liquid, and came to rest in a shapeless heap of ruin.

An unlucky shot had found the powder-magazine. It was the end of the fort.

The cheer that came over the water from the buccaneer ship was like an echo of the explosion.

Blood roused himself, shook himself free of the mortar and rubble in which he was half buried, coughed the dust from his throat, and made a mental examination of his condition. His hip was hurt, but the gradually subsiding pain assured him that there was no permanent damage. He got slowly to his knees, still half dazed, then, at last, to his feet. Badly shaken, his hands cut and bleeding, smothered in dust and grime, he was, at least, whole. He had broken nothing. But of the twelve who had been with him he found only five as sound as they had been before the explosion; a sixth lay groaning with a broken thigh, a seventh sat nursing a dislocated shoulder. The other five were gone, buried in that heaped-up mound.

He collected wits that had been badly scattered, straightened his dusty periwig, and decided that there could be no purpose in lingering on this rubbish-heap that lately had been a fort. To the five survivors he ordered the care of their two crippled fellows, saw these borne away towards the pimento grove, and went staggering after them.

By the time he reached the shelter of that belt of perfumed trees, the buccaneers were disposing for the tactics that logically followed upon the destruction of the fort. Their preparations for landing were clearly discernible to Blood as he paused on the edge of the grove to observe them, shading his eyes from the glare of the sun. He saw that five boats had been lowered, and that, manned to overcrowding, these were pulling away for the beach, whilst the red ship rode now at anchor to cover the landing.

There was no time to lose. Blood entered the cool green shade of the plantation, where Araña and his men awaited him. He approved the emplacement there of the guns unsuspected by the buccaneers, and charged with canister as he had directed. Carefully judging the spot, less than a mile away, where the enemy should come ashore, he ordered and himself supervised the training of the guns upon it. He took for mark a fishing-boat that stood upside down upon the beach, half a cable's length from the water's creamy edge.

'We'll wait,' he explained to Araña, 'until those sons of dogs are in line with it, and then we'll give them a passport into Hell.' From that, so as to beguile the waiting moments, he went on to lecture the Spanish captain upon the finer details of the art of war.

'You begin to perceive the advantages that may lie in departing from schoolroom rules and preconceptions, and in abandoning a fort that can't be held, so as to improvise another one that can be. By these tactics we hold those ruffians at our mercy. In a moment you'll see them swept to perdition, and victory plucked from the appearance of defeat.'

No doubt it is what would have happened but for the supervention of the unexpected. As a matter of fact, Captain Araña was having an even more instructive morning than Captain Blood intended. He was now to receive a demonstration of the futility of divided command.

IV

The trouble came from Don Sebastian, who, meanwhile, had unfortunately not been idle. As Captain-General of Puerto Rico he conceived it to be his duty to arm every man of the town who was able to lift a weapon. Without taking the precaution of consulting Don Pedro, or even of informing him of what he proposed, he had brought the improvised army, some five or six score strong, under cover of the white buildings, to within a hundred yards of the water. There he held them in ambush, to launch them in a charge against the landing buccaneers at the very last moment. In this way he calculated to make it impossible for the ship's artillery to play upon his force, and he was exultantly proud of his tactical conception.

In themselves these tactics were as sound as they were obvious; but they suffered from the unsuspected disadvantage that in serving to baulk the buccaneer gunners on the ship, they no less baulked the Spanish battery in the grove. Before Blood could deliver the fire he was holding, he beheld to his dismay the yelling improvised army of Puerto Rican townsfolk go charging down the beach upon the invader, so that in a moment all was a heaving, writhing, battling, screaming press, in which friend and foe were inextricably mixed.

In this confusion that fighting mob surged up the beach slowly at first, but steadily gathering impetus in a measure as Don Sebastian's forces gave way before the fury of little more than half their number of buccaneers. Firing, and shouting, they all vanished together into the town, leaving some bodies behind them on the sands.

Whilst Captain Blood was cursing Don Sebastian's untimely interference, Captain Araña was urging a rescue. He received yet another lesson.

'Battles are not won by heroics, my friend, but by calculation. The ruffians aboard will number at least twice those that have been landed; and these are by now masters of the situation, thanks to the heroics of Don Sebastian. If we march in now, we shall be taken in the rear by the next landing-party and thus find ourselves caught between two fires. So we'll wait, if you please, for the second landing-party, and when we've destroyed that, we'll deal with the blackguards who are by now in possession of the town. Thus we make sure.'

The time of waiting, however, was considerable. In each of the boats only two men had been left to pull back to the ship, and their progress was slow. Slow, too, was the second loading and return. So that close upon two hours had passed since the first landing before the second party leapt ashore.

It may have appeared to this second party that there was no need for haste, since all the signs went clearly to show that the feeble opposition offered by San Juan had already been fully overcome.

Therefore no haste they made even when their keels grated on the beach. In leisurely fashion they climbed out of the boats, a motley crowd, like that which had composed the first landing-party: some in hats, some few in morions, others with heads swathed in dirty, gaudy scarves, and offering the same variety in the remainder of their dress. It was representative of every class, from the frank buccaneer in cotton shirt and raw-hide breeches to the hidalgo in a laced coat, whilst here and there a back-and-breast supplied a more military equipment. They were uniform at least in that everybody was scarved by a bandoleer, every shoulder bore a musket, and from every belt hung a sword of some description.

They numbered perhaps fifty, and one who seemed set in authority, and wore a gaudy scarlet coat with tarnished lace, marshalled them at the water's edge into a parody of military formation, then, placing himself at their head, waved his sword and gave the word to march.

They marched, breaking into song, so as to supply a rhythm. Raucously bawling their lewd ditty, they advanced in close order, whilst in the pimento grove the gunners blew on their matches, their eyes on Captain Blood, who watched and waited, his right arm raised. At last the raiders were in line with the boat which had served the Spaniards for a mark. Blood's arm fell, and five guns were touched off as one.

That hail of canister swept away the head of the column together with the sword-waving leader in his fine red coat. The unexpectedness of the blow struck the remainder with a sudden palsy, from which few recovered in time. For twice more did Blood's arm rise and fall, and twice more did the charge of five guns mow through those too serried ranks, until almost all that remained of them were heaped about the beach below, some writhing and some still. A few, a half-dozen perhaps, escaped miraculously whole and unscathed, and these, not daring to return to the boats which stood unmanned and empty where they had been drawn up, were making for the shelter of the town, and wriggling on their stomachs lest yet another murderous blast should sweep death across that beach. Captain Blood smiled terribly into the startled eyes of Captain Araña. He resumed the military education of that worthy Spanish officer.

'We may advance now with confidence, Captain, since we have made our rear secure from attack. You may have observed that with deplorable rashness the pirates have employed all their boats in their landings. What men remain aboard that ship are safely marooned in her.'

'But they have guns,' objected Araña. 'What if in vindictiveness they open fire upon the town?'

'Whilst their captain and his first landing-party are in it? Not likely. Still, so as to make sure, we'll leave a dozen men here to serve these guns. If those on board should turn desperate and lose their heads, a volley or two will drive them out of range.'

Dispositions made, an orderly company of fifty Spanish musketeers, unsuspected by the buccaneers to have survived the demolition of the fort, were advancing from the pimento grove at the double upon the town.

V

The pirate captain--whose name has not survived--was set down by Blood as a lubberly idiot, who, like all idiots, took too much for granted, otherwise he would have been at pains to make sure that the force which had opposed his landing comprised the full strength of San Juan.

Ludicrous, too, was the grasping covetousness which had inspired that landing. In this Captain Blood accounted him just a cheap thief, who stayed to rake up crumbs where a feast was spread. With the great prize for which the scoundrel played, the two treasure-ships which he had chased across the Caribbean from Cartagena now lying all but at his mercy, it was a stupid rashness not to have devoted all his energy to making himself master of them at once. From the circumstance that those ships had never fired a gun, he must have inferred--if he was capable of inferences--that the crews were ashore; and if he was not capable of inferences, his telescope--and Captain Blood supposed that the fellow would at least possess a telescope--should have enabled him to ascertain the fact by observation.

But here Blood's reasoning is possibly at fault. For it may well have been the actual perception that the ships were unmanned, and easily to be reduced into possession, which induced the captain to let them wait until his excessive greed should have been satisfied by the plunder of the town. After all, he will have remembered, there was often great store of wealth in these cities of New Spain, and there would be a royal treasury in the keeping of the governor. It would be just such a temptation as this which had led him to plunder the city of Cartagena whilst those treasure-ships were putting to sea. Evidently not even this had sufficed to teach him that who seeks to grasp too much ends by holding nothing; and here he was in San Juan pursuing the same inexpert methods, and pursuing them in the same disgusting manner as that in which at Cartagena he had dishonoured--

as Captain Blood was now fully persuaded--the name of the great buccaneer leader which he had assumed.

I will not say that in what he had done Captain Blood was not actuated by the determination that no interloper should come and snatch from him the prize for which he had laboured and the capture of which his dispositions had rendered easy, but I account it beyond doubt that his manner of doing it gathered an unusual ferocity because of his deep resentment of that foul impersonation at Cartagena and the horrors perpetrated there in his name. The sins of a career which harsh fortune had imposed upon him were heavy enough already. He could not patiently suffer that still worse offences should be attributed to him as a result of the unrestrained methods of this low pretender and his crew of ruthless blackguards.

So it was a grimly resolute, not to say a vindictive, Captain Blood who marched that little column of Spanish musketeers to clean up a place which his impersonator would now be defiling. As they approached the town gate the sounds that met them abundantly justified his assumptions of the nature of the raider's activities.

The buccaneer captain had swept invincibly through a place whose resistance had been crushed at the outset. Finding it at his mercy, he had delivered it to his men for pillage. Let them make holiday here awhile in their brutal fashion before settling down to the main business of the raid and possessing themselves of the plate-ships in the harbour. And so that evil crew, composed of the scourings of the gaols of every land, had broken up into groups which had scattered through the town on a voluptuous course of outrage, smashing, burning, pillaging and murdering in sheer lust of destruction.

For himself the leader marked down what should prove the richest prize in San Juan. With a half-dozen followers he broke into the house of the Captain-General, where Don Sebastian had shut himself up after the rout of his inopportunely improvised force.

Having laid violent hands upon Don Sebastian and his comely, panic-stricken little lady, the captain delivered over the main plunder of the house to the men who were with him. Two of these, however, he retained, to assist him in the particular kind of robbery upon which he was intent, whilst the other four were left remorselessly to pillage the Spaniard's property and guzzle the fine wines that he had brought from Spain.

A tall, swarthy raffish fellow of not more than thirty, who had announced himself as Captain Blood, and who flaunted the black and silver that was notoriously Blood's common wear, the pirate sprawled at his ease in Don Sebastian's dining-room. He sat at the head of the long table of dark oak, one leg hooked over the arm of his chair, his plumed hat cocked over one eye, and a leer on his thick, shaven lips.

Opposite to him, at the table's foot, between two of the captain's ruffians, stood Don Sebastian in shirt and breeches, without his wig, his hands pinioned behind him, his face the colour of lead, yet with defiance in his dark eyes.

Midway between them, but away from the table, in a tall chair, with her back to one of the open windows, sat Doña Leocadia in a state of terror that brought her to the verge of physical sickness but otherwise robbed her of movement.

The captain's fingers were busy with a length of whipcord, making knots in it. In slow, mocking tones and in clumsy, scarcely intelligible Spanish, he addressed his victim.

'So you won't talk, eh? You'ld put me to the trouble of pulling down this damned hovel of yours stone by stone so as to find what I want. Your error, my hidalgo. You'll not only talk, you'll be singing presently. Here's to provide the music.'

He flung the knotted whipcord up the table, signing to one of his men to take and use it. In a moment it was tightly encircling the Captain-General's brow, and the grinning ape whose dirty fingers had bound it there took up a silver spoon from the Spaniard's sideboard, and passed the handle of it between the cord and the flesh.

'Hold there,' his captain bade him. 'Now Don Gubernador, you know what's coming if you don't loose your obstinate tongue and tell me where you hide your pieces of eight.' He paused, watching the Spaniard from under lowered eyelids, a curl of contemptuous amusement on his lip. 'If you prefer it, we can give you a lighted match between the fingers, or a hot iron to the soles of your feet. We've all manner of ingenious miracles for restoring speech to the dumb. It's as you please, my friend. But you'll gain nothing by being mute. Come now. These doubloons. Where do you hide them?'

But the Spaniard, his head high, his lips tight, glared at him in silent detestation.

The pirate's smile broadened in deepening, contemptuous menace. He sighed. 'Well, well! I'm a patient man. You shall have a minute to think it over. One minute.' He held up a dirty forefinger. 'Time for me to drink this.' He poured himself a bumper of dark, syrupy Malaga from a silver jug, and quaffed it at a draught. He set down the lovely glass so violently that the stem snapped. He used it as an illustration. 'And that's how I'll serve your ugly neck in the end, you Spanish pimp, if you play the mule with me. Now then: these doubloons. Vamos, maldito! Soy Don Pedro Sangre, yo! Haven't you heard that you can't trifle with Captain Blood.'

Hate continued to glare at him from Don Sebastian's eyes. 'I've heard nothing of you that's as obscene as the reality, you foul pirate dog. I tell you nothing.'

The lady stirred, and made a whimpering, incoherent sound, that presently resolved itself into speech. 'For pity's sake, Sebastian! In God's name, tell him. Tell him. Let him take all we have. What does it matter?'

'What, indeed, if ye've no life with which to enjoy it?' the captain mocked him. 'Give heed to your pullet's better sense. No?' He banged the table in anger. 'So be it! Squeeze it out of his cuckoldy head, my lads.' And he settled himself more comfortably in his chair, in expectation of entertainment.

One of the brigands laid hands upon the spoon he had thrust between cord and brow. But before he had begun to twist it the captain checked him again.

'Wait. There's perhaps a surer way.' The cruel coarse mouth broadened in a smile. He unhooked his leg from the chair-arm, and sat up. 'These dons be mighty proud o' their women.' He turned, and beckoned Doña Leocadia. 'Aqui, muger! Aqui!' he commanded.

'Don't heed him, Leocadia,' cried her husband. 'Don't move.'

'He . . . he can always fetch me,' she answered, pathetically practical in her disobedience.

'You hear, fool? It's a pity you've none of her good sense. Come along, madam.'

The frail, pallid little woman, quaking with fear, dragged herself to the side of his chair. He looked up at her with his odious smile, and in his close-set eyes there was insulting appraisal of this dainty, timid wisp of womanhood. He flung an arm about her waist and pulled her to him.

'Come closer, woman. What the devil!'

Don Sebastian closed his eyes, and groaned between pain and fury. For a moment he strove desperately in the powerful hands that held him.

The captain, handling the little lady as if she were invertebrate, as indeed horror had all but rendered her, hauled her to sit upon his knee.

'Never heed his jealous bellowing, little one. He shan't harm you, on the word of Captain Blood.' He tilted up her chin, and smiled into dark eyes that panic was dilating. This and his lingering kiss she bore as a corpse might have borne them. 'There'll be more o' that to follow, my pullet, unless your loutish husband comes to his senses. I've got her, you see, Don Gubernador, and I dare swear she'd enjoy a voyage with me. But you can ransom her with the doubloons you hide. You'll allow that's generous, now. For I can help myself to both if I've a mind to it.'

The threatened woolding could not have put Don Sebastian in a greater anguish.

'You dog! Even if I yield, what assurance have I that you will keep faith?'

'The word of Captain Blood.'

A sudden burst of gunfire shook the house. It was closely followed by a second and yet a third.

Momentarily it startled them.

'What the devil. . .' the captain was beginning, when he checked, prompt to find the explanation. 'Bah! My children amuse themselves. That's all.'

But he would hardly have laughed as heartily as he did could he have guessed that those bursts of gunfire had mown down some fifty of those children of his, in the very act of landing to reinforce him, or that some fifty Spanish musketeers were advancing at the double from the pimento grove, led by the authentic Captain Blood, who came to deal with the pirates scattered through the town. And deal with them he did with sharp efficiency as fast as he came upon them, in groups of four, or six, or ten at most. Some were shot at sight, and the remainder rounded up and taken prisoners, so that no chance was ever theirs to assemble and offer an organized resistance.

In the Captain-General's dining-room, the buccaneer captain, unhurried because deriving more and more evil relish from the situation in a measure as he grew more fuddled by the heady Malaga wine, gave little heed to the increasing sounds outside, the shots, the screams and the bursts of musketry. In his complete persuasion that all power of resistance had been crushed, he supposed these to be the ordinary indications that his children continued to amuse themselves. Idle gunfire was a common practice among jubilant filibusters, and who but his own men should now have muskets to fire in San Juan?

So he continued at his leisure to savour the voluptuous humour of tormenting the Captain-General with a choice between losing his wife or his doubloons until at last Don Sebastian's spirit broke, and he told them where the King's treasure-chest was stored.

But the evil in the buccaneer was not allayed. 'Too late,' he declared. 'You've been trifling with me overlong. And in the meantime I've grown fond of this dainty piece of yours. So fond that I couldn't bear now to be parted from her. Your life you may have, you Spanish dog. And after your cursed obstinacy that's more than you deserve. But your money and your women go with me, like the plate-ships of the King of Spain.'

'You pledged me your word!' cried the demented Spaniard.

'Ay ay! But that was long since. You didn't accept when the chance was yours. You chose to trifle with me.' Thus the filibuster mocked him, and in the room none heeded the quick approach of steps. 'And I warned you that it is not safe to trifle with Captain Blood.'

The last word was not out of him when the door was flung open, and a crisp, metallic voice was answering him on a grimly humorous note.

'Faith, I'm glad to hear you say it, whoever you may be.' A tall man in a dishevelled black periwig without a hat, his violet coat in rags, his lean face smeared with sweat and grime, came in, sword in hand. At his heels followed three musketeers in Spanish corselets and steel caps. The sweep of his glance took in the situation.

'So. So. No more than in time, I think.'

Startled, the ruffian flung Doña Leocadia from him and bounded to his feet, a hand on one of the pistols he carried slung before him at the ends of an embroidered stole.

'What's this? In Hell's name, who are you?'

The newcomer stepped close to him, and out of that begrimed countenance eyes blue as sapphires and as hard sent a chill through him. 'You poor pretender! You dung-souled impostor!'

Whatever the ruffian may or may not have understood, he was in no doubt that here was need for instant action. He plucked forth the pistol on which his hand was resting. But before he could level it, Captain Blood had stepped back. His rapier licked forth, sudden as a viper's tongue, to transfix the pirate's arm, and the pistol clattered from a nerveless hand.

'You should have had it in the heart, you dog, but for a vow I've made that, God helping me, Captain Blood shall never be hanged by any hand but mine.'

One of the musketeers closed with the disabled man, and bore him down, snarling and cursing, whilst Blood and the others dealt swiftly and efficiently with his men.

Above the din of that brutal struggle rang the scream of Doña Leocadia, who reeled to a chair, fell into it, and fainted.

Don Sebastian, scarcely in better case when his bonds were cut, babbled weakly an incoherent mixture of thanksgivings for this timely miracle and questions upon how it had been wrought.

'Look to your lady,' Blood advised him, 'and give yourself no other thought. San Juan is cleared of this blight. Some thirty of these scoundrels are safe in the town gaol, the others, safer still, in Hell. If any have got away at all, they'll find a party waiting for them at the boats. We've the dead to bury, the wounded to attend, the fugitives from the town to recall. Look to your lady and your household, and leave the rest to me.'

He was away again, as abruptly as he had come, and gone too were his musketeers, bearing the raging captive with them.

VI

He came back at suppertime to find order restored to the Captain-General's house, the servants at their posts once more, and the table spread. Doña Leocadia burst into tears at sight of him, still all begrimed from battle. Don Sebastian hugged him to his ample bosom, the grime notwithstanding, proclaiming him the saviour of San Juan, a hero of the true Castilian pattern, a worthy representative of the great Admiral of the Ocean-Sea. And this, too, was the opinion of the town, which resounded that night with cries of 'Viva Don Pedro! Long live the hero of San Juan de Puerto Rico!'

It was all very pleasant and touching, and induced in Captain Blood, as he afterwards confessed to Jeremy Pitt, a mood of reflection upon the virtue of service to the cause of law and order. Cleansed and re-clothed, in garments at once too loose and too short, borrowed from Don Sebastian's wardrobe, he sat down to supper at the Captain-General's table, ate heartily and did justice to some excellent Spanish wine that had survived the raid upon the Captain-General's cellar.

He slept peacefully, in the consciousness of a good action performed and the assurance that, being without boats and very short of men, the pretended *Arabella* was powerless to accomplish upon the treasure-ships the real object of her descent upon San Juan. So as to make doubly sure, however, a Spanish company kept watch at the guns in the pimento grove. But there was no alarm, and when day broke it showed them the pirate ship hull down on the horizon, and, in a majesty of full sail, the sometime *Maria Gloriosa* entering the roads.

At breakfast, when he came to it, Don Pedro Encarnado was greeted by Don Sebastian with news that his Admiral's ship had just dropped anchor in the bay.

'He is very punctual,' said Don Pedro, thinking of Wolverstone.

'Punctual? He's behind the fair. He arrives just too late to complete your glorious work by sinking that pirate craft. I shall hope to tell him so.'

Don Pedro frowned. 'That would be imprudent, considering his favour with the King. It is not well to ruffle the Marquis. Fortunately he is not likely to come ashore. The gout, you see.'

'But I shall pay him a visit aboard his ship.'

There was no make-believe in Captain Blood's frown. Unless he could turn Don Sebastian from that reasonable intention the smooth plan he had evolved would be disastrously wrecked.

'No, no. I shouldn't do that,' he said.

'Not do it? Of course I shall. It is my duty.'

'Oh no, no. You would derogate. Think of the great position you occupy Captain-General of Puerto Rico; which is to say, Governor, Viceroy almost. It is not for you to wait upon admirals, but for admirals to wait upon you. And the Marquis of Riconete is well aware of it. That is why, being unable, from his plaguey gout, to come in person, he sent me to be his deputy. What you have to say to the Marquis, you can say here, at your ease, to me.'

Impressed, Don Sebastian passed a reflective hand over his several chins. 'There is, of course, a certain truth in what you say. Yes, yes. Nevertheless, in this case I have a special duty to perform, which must be performed in person. I must acquaint the Admiral very fully with the heroic part you have played in saving Puerto Rico and the King's treasury here, not to mention the plate-ships. Honour where honour is due. I must see, Don Pedro, that you have your deserts.'

And Doña Leocadia, remembering with a shudder the horrors of yesterday which the gallantry of Don Pedro had cut short, and further possible horrors which his timely coming had averted, was warm and eager in reinforcement of her husband's generous intentions.

But before that display of so much goodwill Don Pedro's face grew more and more forbidding. Sternly he shook his head.

'It is as I feared,' he said--'something which I cannot permit. If you insist, Don Sebastian, you will affront me. What I did yesterday was no more than was imposed upon me by my office. Neither thanks nor praise are due for a performance of bare duty. They are heroes only who without thought of risk to themselves or concern for their own interests, perform deeds which are not within their duties. That, at least, is my conception. And, as I have said, to insist upon making a ballad of my conduct yesterday would be to affront me. You would not, I am sure, wish to do that, Don Sebastian.'

'Oh, but what modesty!' exclaimed the lady, joining her hands and casting up her eyes. 'How true it is that the great are always humble.'

Don Sebastian looked crestfallen. He sighed. 'It is an attitude worthy of a hero. True. But it disappoints me, my friend. It is a little return that I could make. . .'

'No return is due, Don Sebastian.' Don Pedro was forbiddingly peremptory. 'Let us speak of it no more, I beg of you.' He rose. 'I had better go aboard at once, to receive the Admiral's orders. I will inform him, in my own terms, of what has taken place here. And I can point to the gallows you are erecting on the beach for this pestilent Captain Blood. That will be most reassuring to his Excellency.'

Of how reassuring it was Don Pedro brought news when towards noon he came ashore again, no longer in the borrowed ill-fitting clothes, but arrayed once more in all the glories of a grandee of Spain.

'The Marquis of Riconete asks me to inform you that since the Caribbean is happily delivered of the infamous Captain Blood, his Excellency's mission in these waters is at an end, and nothing now prevents him from yielding to the urgency of returning to Spain at once. He has decided to convoy the plate-ships across the ocean, and he begs you to instruct their captains to be ready to weigh anchor on the first of the ebb: this afternoon at three.'

Don Sebastian was aghast. 'But did you not tell him, sir, that it is impossible?'

Don Pedro shrugged. 'One does not argue with the Admiral of the Ocean-Sea.'

'But, my dear Don Pedro, more than half the crews are absent and the ships are without guns.'

'Be sure that I did not fail to inform his Excellency of that. It merely annoyed him. He takes the view that since each ship carries hands enough to sail her, no more is necessary. The *Maria Gloriosa* is sufficiently armed to protect them.'

'He does not pause, then, to reflect what may happen should they become separated?'

'That also I pointed out. It made no impression. His Excellency is of a high confidence.'

Don Sebastian blew out his cheeks. 'So! So! To be sure, it is his affair. And I thank God for it. The plate-ships have brought trouble enough upon San Juan de Puerto Rico, and I'll be glad to see the last of them. But permit me to observe that your Admiral of the Ocean-Sea is a singularly rash man. It comes, I suppose, of being a royal favourite.'

Don Pedro's sly little smile suggested subtly complete agreement. 'It is understood, then, that you will give orders for the promptest victualling of the ships. His Excellency must not be kept waiting, and, anyway, the ebb will not wait even for him.'

'Oh, perfectly,' said Don Sebastian. Irony exaggerated his submission. 'I will give the orders at once.'

'I will inform his Excellency. He will be gratified. I take my leave, then, Don Sebastian.' They embraced. 'Believe me, I shall long treasure the memory of our happy and profitable association. My homage to Doña Leocadia.'

'But will you not stay to see the hanging of Captain Blood? It is to take place at noon.'

'The Admiral expects me aboard at eight bells. I dare not keep him waiting.'

But on his way to the harbour, Captain Blood paused at the town gaol. By the officer in charge he was received with the honour due to the saviour of San Juan, and doors were unlocked at his bidding.

Beyond a yard in which the heavily ironed, dejected prisoners of yesterday's affray were herded, he came to a stone chamber lighted by a small window set high and heavily barred. In this dark, noisome hole sat the great buccaneer, hunched on a stool, his head in his manacled hands. He looked up as the door groaned on its hinges, and out of a livid face he glared at his visitor. He did not recognize his grimy opponent of yesterday in this elegant gentleman in black and silver, whose sedulously curled black periwig fell to his shoulders and who swung a gold-headed ebony cane as he advanced.

'Is it time?' he growled in his bad Spanish.

The apparent Castilian nobleman answered him in the English that is spoken in Ireland. 'Och now, don't be impatient. Ye've still time to be making your soul; that is, if ye've a soul to make at all; still time to repent the nasty notion that led you into this imposture. I could forgive you the pretence that you are Captain Blood. There's a sort of compliment in that. But I can't be forgiving you the things you did in Cartagena: the wantonly murdered men, the violated women, the loathsome cruelties for cruelty's sake by which you slaked your evil lusts and dishonoured the name you assumed.'

The ruffian sneered. 'You talk like a canting parson sent to shrive me.'

'I talk like the man I am, the man whose name ye've befouled with the filth of your nature. I'll be leaving you to ponder, in the little time that's left you, the poetic justice by which mine is the hand that hangs you. For I am Captain Blood.'

A moment still he remained inscrutably surveying the doomed impostor whom amazement had rendered speechless; then, turning on his heel, he went to rejoin the waiting Spanish officer.

Thence, past the gallows erected on the beach, he repaired to the waiting boat, and was pulled back to the white-and-gold flagship in the roads.

And so it befell that on that same day the false Captain Blood was hanged on the beach of San Juan de Puerto Rico, and the real Captain Blood sailed away for Tortuga in the *Maria Gloriosa,* or *Andalusian Lass,* convoying the richly laden plate-ships, which had neither guns nor crews with which to offer resistance when the truth of their situation was later discovered to their captains.

Episode 3

THE DEMONSTRATION

I

'Fortune,' Captain Blood was wont to say, 'detests a niggard. Her favours are reserved for the man who knows how to spend nobly and to stake boldly.'

Whether you hold him right or wrong in this opinion, it is at least beyond question that he never shrank from acting upon it. Instances of his prodigality are abundant in that record of his fortunes and hazards which Jeremy Pitt has left us, but none is more recklessly splendid than that supplied by his measures to defeat the West Indian policy of Monsieur de Louvois when it was threatening the great buccaneering brotherhood with extinction.

The Marquis de Louvois, who succeeded the great Colbert in the service of Louis XIV, was universally hated whilst he lived, and as universally lamented when he died. Than this conjunction of estimates there can be, I take it, no higher testimonial to the worth of a minister of State. Nothing was either too great or too small for Monsieur de Louvois' attention. Once he had set the machinery of State moving smoothly at home, he turned in his reorganizing lust to survey the French possessions in the Caribbean, where the activities of the buccaneers distressed his sense of orderliness.

Thither, in the King's twenty-four-gun ship the *Béarnais,* he dispatched the Chevalier de Saintonges, an able, personable gentleman in the early thirties, who had earned a confidence which Monsieur de Louvois did not lightly bestow, and who bore now clear instructions upon how to proceed so as to put an end to the evil, as Monsieur de Louvois accounted it.

To Monsieur de Saintonges, whose circumstances in life were by no means opulent, this was to prove an unsuspected and Heaven-sent chance of fortune; for in the course of serving his King to the best of his ability he found occasion, with an ability even greater, very abundantly to serve himself. During his sojourn in Martinique, which the events induced him to protract far beyond what was strictly necessary, he met, wooed at tropical speed, and married, Madame de Veynac. This young and magnificently handsome widow of Hommaire de Veynac had inherited from her late husband those vast West Indian possessions which comprised nearly a third of the island of Martinique, with plantations of sugar, spices, and tobacco producing annual revenues that were nothing short of royal. Thus richly endowed, she came to the arms of the stately but rather impecunious Chevalier de Saintonges.

The Chevalier was too conscientious a man and too profoundly imbued with the sense of the importance of his mission to permit this marriage to be more than a splendid interlude in the diligent performance of the duties which had brought him to the New World. The nuptials having been celebrated in Saint Pierre with all the pomp and luxury proper to the lady's importance, Monsieur de Saintonges resumed his task with the increased consequence which he derived from the happy change in his circumstances. He took his bride aboard the *Béarnais,* and sailed away from Saint Pierre to complete his tour of inspection before setting a course for France and the full enjoyment of the fabulous wealth that was now his.

Dominica, Guadeloupe, and the Grenadines he had already visited, as well as Sainte Croix, which properly speaking was the property not of the French Crown but of the French West India Company. The most important part of his mission, however, remained yet to be accomplished at Tortuga, that other property of the French West India Company, which had become the stronghold of those buccaneers, English, French and Dutch, for whose extermination it was the Chevalier's duty to take order.

His confidence in his ability to succeed in this difficult matter had been materially augmented by the report that Peter Blood, the most dangerous and enterprising of all these filibusters, had lately been caught by the Spaniards and hanged at San Juan de Puerto Rico.

In calm but torrid August weather the *Béarnais* made a good passage and came to drop anchor in the Bay of Cayona, that rockbound harbour which Nature might have designed expressly to be a pirates' lair.

The Chevalier took his bride ashore with him, bestowing her in a chair expressly procured, for which his seamen opened a way through the heterogeneous crowd of Europeans, Negroes, Maroons, and Mulattos of both sexes who swarmed to view this great lady from the French ship. Two half-caste porters, all but naked, bore the chair with its precious cargo, whilst the rather pompous Monsieur de Saintonges, clad in the lightest of blue taffetas, cane in one hand and the hat with which he fanned himself in the other, stalked beside it, damning the heat, the flies, and the smells. A tall, florid man, already inclining slightly at this early age to embonpoint, he perspired profusely, and his head ran wet under his elaborate golden periwig.

Up the gentle acclivity of the main unpaved street of Cayona with its fierce white glare of coral dust and its fringe of languid palms, he toiled to the blessed fragrant shade of the Governor's garden and eventually to the cool twilight of chambers from which the sun's ardour was excluded by green, slatted blinds. Here cool drinks, in which rum and limes and sugar-cane were skilfully compounded, accompanied the cordial welcome extended by the Governor and his two handsome daughters to these distinguished visitors.

But the heat in which Monsieur de Saintonges arrived was destined to be only temporarily allayed. Soon after Madame de Saintonges had been carried off by the Governor's daughters, a discussion ensued which reopened all the Chevalier's pores.

Monsieur d'Ogeron, who governed Tortuga on behalf of the French West India Company, had listened with a gravity increasing to gloom to the forcible expositions made by his visitor in the name of Monsieur de Louvois.

A slight, short, elegant man was this Monsieur d'Ogeron, who retained in this outlandish island of his rule something of the courtly airs of the great world from which he came, just as he surrounded himself in his house and its equipment with the elegancies proper to a French gentleman of birth. Only breeding and good manners enabled him now to dissemble his impatience. At the end of the Chevalier's blunt and pompous peroration, he fetched a sigh in which there was some weariness.

'I suspect,' he ventured, 'that Monsieur de Louvois is indifferently informed upon West Indian conditions.'

Monsieur de Saintonges was aghast at this hint of opposition. His sense of the importance and omniscience of Monsieur de Louvois was almost as high as his sense of his own possession of these qualities.

'I doubt, sir, if there are any conditions in the world upon which Monsieur le Marquis is not fully informed.'

Monsieur d'Ogeron's smile was gentle and courteous. 'All the world is of course aware of Monsieur de Louvois' high worth. But his Excellency does not possess my own experience of these remotenesses, and this, I venture to think, lends some value to my opinion.'

By an impatient gesture the Chevalier waved aside the matter of Monsieur d'Ogeron's opinions. 'We lose sight of the point, I think. Suffer me to be quite blunt, sir. Tortuga is under the flag of France. Monsieur de Louvois takes the view, in which I venture to concur, that it is in the last degree improper. . . In short, that it is not to the honour of the flag of France that it should protect a horde of brigands.'

Monsieur d'Ogeron's gentle smile was still all deprecation. 'Sir, sir, it is not the flag of France that protects the filibusters, but the filibusters that protect the flag of France.'

The tall, blond, rather imposing representative of the Crown came to his feet, as if to mark his indignation. 'Monsieur, that is an outrageous statement.'

The Governor's urbanity remained unimpaired. 'It is the fact that is outrageous, not the statement. Permit me to observe to you, monsieur, that a hundred and fifty years ago, His Holiness the Pope bestowed upon Spain the New World of Columbus' discovery. Since then other nations, the French, the English, the Dutch, have paid less heed to that papal bull than Spain considers proper. They have attempted, themselves, to settle some of these lands--lands of which the Spaniards have never taken actual possession. Because Spain insists upon regarding this as a violation of her rights, the Caribbean for years has been a cockpit.

'These buccaneers themselves, whom you regard with such contempt, were originally peaceful hunters, cultivators, and traders. The Spaniards chased them out of Hispaniola, drove them, English and French, from St Christopher and the Dutch from Sainte Croix, by ruthless massacres which did not spare even their women and children. In self-defence these men forsook their peaceful boucans, took arms, banded themselves together into a brotherhood, and hunted the Spaniard in their turn. That the Virgin Islands today belong to the English Crown is due to these Brethren of the Coast, as they call themselves, these buccaneers who took possession of those lands in the name of England. This very island of Tortuga, like the island of Sainte Croix, came to belong to the French West India Company, and so to France, in the same way.

'You spoke, sir, of the protection of the French flag enjoyed by these buccaneers. There is here a confusion of ideas. If there were no buccaneers to hold the rapacity of Spain in check, I ask myself, Monsieur de Saintonges, if this voyage of yours would ever have been undertaken, for I doubt if there would have been any French possessions in the Caribbean to be visited.' He paused to smile upon the blank amazement of his guest. 'I hope, monsieur, that I have said enough to justify the opinion, which I take the liberty of holding in opposition to that of Monsieur de Louvois, that the suppression of the buccaneers might easily result in disaster to the French West Indian colonies.'

At this point Monsieur de Saintonges exploded. As so commonly happens, it was actually a sense of the truth underlying the Governor's argument that produced his exasperation. The reckless terms of his rejoinder lead us to doubt the wisdom of Monsieur de Louvois in choosing him for an ambassador.

'You have said enough, monsieur . . . more than enough to persuade me that a reluctance to forgo the profits accruing to your Company and to yourself personally from the plunder marketed in Tortuga, is rendering you negligent of the honour of France, upon which this traffic is a stain.'

Monsieur d'Ogeron smiled no longer. Stricken in his turn by the amount of truth in the Chevalier's accusation; he came to his feet suddenly, white with anger. But, a masterful, self-contained little man, he was without any of the bluster of his tall visitor. His voice was as cold as ice and very level.

'Such an assertion, monsieur, can be made to me only sword in hand.'

Saintonges strode about the long room, and waved his arms.

'That is of a piece with the rest! Preposterous! If that's your humour, you had better send your cartel to Monsieur de Louvois. I am but his mouthpiece. I have said what I was charged to say, and what I would not have said if I had found you reasonable. You are to understand, monsieur, that I have not come all the way from France to fight duels on behalf of the Crown, but to explain the Crown's views and issue the Crown's orders. If they appear distasteful to you, that is not my affair. The orders I have for you are that Tortuga must cease to be a haven for buccaneers. And that is all that needs to be said.'

'God give me patience, sir,' cried Monsieur d'Ogeron in his distress. 'Will you be good enough to tell me at the same time how I am to enforce these orders?'

'Where is the difficulty? Close the market in which you receive the plunder. If you make an end of the traffic, the buccaneers will make an end of themselves.'

'How simple! But how very simple! And what if the buccaneers make an end of me and of this possession of the West India Company? What if they seize the island of Tortuga for themselves, which is no doubt what would happen? What then, if you please, Monsieur de Saintonges?'

'The might of France will know how to enforce her rights.'

'Much obliged. Does the might of France realize how mighty it will have to be? Has Monsieur de Louvois any conception of the strength and organization of these buccaneers? Have you never, for instance, heard in France of Morgan's march on Panama? Is it realized that there are in all some five or six thousand of these men afloat, the most formidable sea-fighters the world has ever seen? If they were banded together by such a menace of extinction, they could assemble a navy of forty or fifty ships that would sweep the Caribbean from end to end.'

At last the Governor had succeeded in putting Monsieur de Saintonges out of countenance by these realities. For a moment the Chevalier stared chapfallen at his host. Then he rallied obstinately. 'Surely, sir, surely you exaggerate.'

'I exaggerate nothing. I desire you to understand that I am actuated by something more than the self-interest you so offensively attribute to me.'

'Monsieur de Louvois will regret, I am sure, the injustice of that assumption when I report to him fully, making clear what you have told me. For the rest, sir, however, you have your orders.'

'But surely, sir, you have been granted some discretion in the fulfilment of your mission. Finding things as you do, as I have explained them, it seems to me that you would do no disservice to the Crown in recommending to Monsieur de Louvois that until France is in a position to place a navy in the Caribbean so as to protect her possessions, she would be well-advised not to disturb the existing state of things.'

The Chevalier merely stiffened further. 'That, monsieur, is not a recommendation that would become me. You have the orders of Monsieur de Louvois, which are that this mart for the plunder of the seas must at once be closed. I trust that you will enable me to assure Monsieur de Louvois of your immediate compliance.'

Monsieur d'Ogeron was in despair before the stupidity of this official intransigence. 'I must still protest, monsieur, that your description is not a just one. No plunder comes here but the plunder of Spain to compensate us for all the plunder we have suffered and shall continue to suffer at the hands of the gentlemen of Castile.'

'That, sir, is fantastic. There is peace between Spain and France.'

'In the Caribbean, Monsieur de Saintonges, there is never peace. If we abolish the buccaneers, we lay down our arms and offer our throats to the knife. That is all.'

There were, however, no arguments that could move Monsieur de Saintonges from the position he had taken up. 'I must regard that as a personal opinion, more or less coloured--suffer me to say it without offence--by the interests of your Company and yourself. Anyway, the orders are clear. You realize that you will neglect them at your peril.'

'And also that I shall fulfil them at my peril,' said the Governor, with a twist of the lips. He shrugged and sighed. 'You place me, sir, between the sword and the wall.'

'Do me the justice to understand that I discharge my duty,' said the lofty Chevalier de Saintonges, and the concession of those words was the only concession Monsieur d'Ogeron could wring from his obstinate self-sufficiency.

II

Monsieur de Saintonges sailed away with his wife that same evening from Tortuga, setting a course for Port au Prince, where he desired to pay a call before finally steering for France and the opulent ease which he could now command there. Admiring himself for the firmness with which he had resisted all the Governor of Tortuga's special pleading, he took Madame de Saintonges into his confidence in the matter, so that she too might admire him.

'That little trafficker in brigandage might have persuaded me from my duty if I had been less alert,' he laughed. 'But I am not easily deceived. That is why Monsieur de Louvois chose me for a mission of this importance. He knew the difficulties I should meet, and knew that I should not be duped by misrepresentations however specious.'

She was a tall, handsome, languorous lady, sloe-eyed, black-haired, with a skin like ivory and a bosom of Hebe. Her languishing eyes considered in awe and reverence this husband from the great world, who was to open for her social gates in France that would have been closed against the wife of a mere planter, however rich. Yet for all her admiring confidence in his acumen, she ventured to wonder was he correct in regarding as purely self-interested the arguments which Monsieur d'Ogeron had presented. She had not spent her life in the West Indies without learning something of the predatoriness of Spain, although perhaps she had never until now suspected the extent to which the activities of the buccaneers might be keeping that predatoriness in check. Spain maintained a considerable fleet in the Caribbean, mainly for the purpose of guarding her settlements from filibustering raids. The suppression of the filibusters would render that fleet comparatively idle, and in idleness there is no knowing to what devilry men may turn, especially if they be Spaniards.

Thus, meekly, Madame de Saintonges to her adored husband. But the adored husband, with the high spirit that rendered him so adorable, refused to be shaken.

'In such an event, be sure that the King of France, my master, will take order.'

Nevertheless, his mind was no longer quite at rest. His wife's very submissive and tentative support of Monsieur d'Ogeron's argument had unsettled him. It was easy to gird at the self-interest of the Governor of Tortuga, and to assign to it his dread of Spain. Monsieur de Saintonges, because, himself, he had acquired a sudden and enormous interest in French West Indian possessions, began to ask himself whether, after all, he might not have been too ready to believe that Monsieur d'Ogeron had exaggerated.

And the Governor of Tortuga had not exaggerated. However much his interests may have jumped with his arguments, there can be no doubt whatever that these were well founded. Because of this he could perceive ahead of him no other course but to resign his office and return at once to France, leaving Monsieur de Louvois to work out the destinies of the French West Indies and of Tortuga in his own fashion. It would be a desertion of the interests of the West India Company. But if the new minister's will prevailed, very soon the West India Company would have no interests to protect.

The little Governor spent a disturbed night, and slept late on the following morning, to be eventually aroused by gunfire.

The boom of cannon and the rattle of musketry were so continuous that it took him some time to realize that the din did not betoken an attack upon the harbour, but a feu-de-joie such as the rocks of Cayona had never yet echoed. The reason for it, when he discovered it, served to dispel some part of his dejection. The report that Peter Blood had been taken and hanged at San Juan de Puerto Rico was being proven false by the arrival in Cayona of Peter Blood himself. He had sailed into the harbour aboard a captured Spanish vessel, the sometime *Maria Gloriosa,* lately the flagship of the Marquis of Riconete, the Admiral of the Ocean-Sea, trailing in her wake the two richly laden Spanish galleons, the plate-ships taken at Puerto Rico.

The guns that thundered their salutes were the guns of Blood's own fleet of three ships, which had been refitting at Tortuga in his absence and aboard which during the past week all had been mourning and disorientation.

Rejoicing as fully as any of those jubilant buccaneers in this return from the dead of a man whom he too had mourned--for a real friendship existed between the Governor of Tortuga and the great Captain--Monsieur d'Ogeron and his daughters prepared for Peter Blood a feast of welcome, to which the Governor brought some of those bottles 'from behind the faggots', as he described the choice wines that he received from France.

The Captain came in great good humour to the feast, and entertained them at table with an account of the queer adventure in Puerto Rico, which had ended in the hanging of a poor scoundrelly pretender to the name and fame of Captain Blood, and had enabled him to sail away unchallenged with the two plate-ships that were now anchored in the harbour of Tortuga.

'I never made a richer haul, and I doubt if many richer have ever been made. Of the gold alone my own share must be a matter of twenty-five thousand pieces of eight, which I'll be depositing with you against bills of exchange on France. Then the peppers and spices in one of the galleons should be worth over a hundred thousand pieces to the West India Company. It awaits your valuation, my friend.'

But an announcement which should have increased the Governor's good humour merely served to precipitate him visibly into the depths of gloom by reminding him of how the circumstances had altered. Sorrowfully he looked across the table at his guest, and sorrowfully he shook his head.

'All that is finished, my friend. I am under a cursed interdict.' And forth in fullest detail came the tale of the visit of the Chevalier de Saintonges with its curtailment of Monsieur d'Ogeron's activities. 'So you see, my dear Captain, the markets of the West India Company are now closed to you.'

The keen, shaven, suntanned face in its frame of black curls showed an angry consternation.

'Name of God! But didn't you tell this lackey from Court that--'

'There was nothing I did not tell him to which a man of sense should have listened, no argument that I did not present. To all that I had to say he wearied me with insistence that he doubted if there were any conditions in the world upon which Monsieur de Louvois is not informed. To the Chevalier de Saintonges there is no god but Louvois, and Saintonges is his prophet. So much was plain. A consequential gentleman this Monsieur de Saintonge, like all these Court minions. Lately in Martinique he married the widow of Hommaire de Veynac. That will make him one of the richest men in France. You know the effect of great possessions on a self-sufficient man.' Monsieur d'Ogeron spread his hands. 'It is finished, my friend.'

But with this Captain Blood could not agree. 'That is to bend your head to the axe. Oh no, no. Defeat is not to be accepted so easily by men of our strength.'

'For you, who dwell outside the law, all things are possible. But for me. . . Here in Tortuga I represent the law of France. I must serve and uphold it. And the law has pronounced.'

'Had I arrived a day sooner the law might have been made to pronounce differently.'

D'Ogeron was wistfully sardonic. 'You imagine, in spite of all that I have said, that you could have persuaded this coxcomb of his folly?'

'There is nothing of which a man cannot be persuaded if the proper arguments are put before him in the proper manner.'

'I tell you that I put before him all the arguments that exist.'

'No, no. You presented only those that occurred to you.'

'If you mean that I should have put a pistol to the head of this insufferable puppy. . .'

'Oh, my friend! That is not an argument. It is a constraint. We are all of us self-interested, and none are more so than those who, like this Chevalier de Saintonges, are ready to accuse others of that fault. An appeal to his interests might have been persuasive.'

'Perhaps. But what do I know of his interests?'

'What do you know of them? Oh, but think. Have you not, yourself, just told me that he lately married the widow of Hommaire de Veynac? That gives him great West Indian interests. You spoke vaguely and generally of Spanish raids upon the settlements of other nations. You should have been more particular. You should have dwelt upon the possibility of a raid upon wealthy Martinique. That would have given him to think. And now he's gone, and the chance is lost.'

But d'Ogeron would see no reason for sharing any regrets of that lost opportunity.

'His obstinacy would have prevented him from taking fright. He would not have listened. The last thing he said to me before he sailed for Port au Prince. . .'

'For Port au Prince!' ejaculated Captain Blood, to interrupt him, 'He's gone to Port au Prince?'

'That was his destination when he departed yesterday. It's his last port of call before he sails for France.'

'So, so!' The Captain was thoughtful. 'That means, then, that he will be returning by way of the Tortuga Channel?'

'Of course, since in the alternative he would have to sail round Hispaniola.'

'Now, glory be, I may not be too late, after all. Couldn't I intercept him as he returns, and try my persuasive arts on him?'

'You'd waste your time, Captain.'

'You make too sure. It's the great gift of persuasion I have. Sustain your hopes awhile, my friend, until I put Monsieur de Saintonges to the test.'

But to raise from their nadir the hopes of Monsieur d'Ogeron something more was necessary than mere light-hearted assurances. It was with the sigh of an abiding despondency that he bade farewell that day to Captain Blood, and without confidence that he wished him luck in whatever he might adventure.

What form the adventure might take, Captain Blood, himself, did not yet know when he quitted the Governor's house and went aboard his own splendid forty-gun ship the *Arabella,* which, ready for sea, fitted, armed and victualled, had been standing idle during his late absence. But the thought he gave the matter was to such good purpose that late that same afternoon, with a definite plan conceived, he held a council of war in the great cabin, and assigned particular duties to his leading associates.

Hagthorpe and Dyke were to remain in Tortuga in charge of the treasure-ships. Wolverstone was given command of the Spanish Admiral's captured flagship, the *Maria Gloriosa,* and was required to sail at once, with very special and detailed instructions. To Yberville, the French buccaneer who was associated with him, Blood entrusted the *Elizabeth,* with orders to make ready to put to sea.

That same evening, at sunset, the *Arabella* was warped out of the swarm of lesser shipping that had collected about her anchorage. With Blood, himself, in command, with Pitt for sailing master and Ogle for master gunner, she set sail from Cayona, followed closely by the *Elizabeth.* The *Maria Gloriosa* was already hull down on the horizon.

Beating up against gentle easterly breezes, the two buccaneer ships, the *Arabella* and her consort, were off Point Palmish on the northern coast of Hispaniola by the following evening. Hereabouts, where the Tortuga Channel narrows to a mere five miles between Palmish and Portugal Point, Captain Blood decided to take up his station for what was to be done.

III

At about the time that the *Arabella* and the *Elizabeth* were casting anchor in that lonely cove on the northern coast of Hispaniola, the *Béarnais* was weighing at Port au Prince. The smells of the place offended the delicate nostrils of Madame dè Saintonges, and on this account--since wives so well endowed are to be pampered--the Chevalier cut short his visit even at the cost of scamping the King's business. Glad to have set a term to this at last, with the serene conviction of having discharged his mission in a manner that must deserve the praise of Monsieur de Louvois, the Chevalier now turned his face towards France and his thoughts to lighter and more personal matters.

With a light wind abeam, the progress of the *Béarnais* was so slow that it took her twenty-four hours to round Cape St Nicholas at the Western end of the Tortuga Channel; so that it was somewhere about sunset on the day following that of her departure from Port au Prince when she entered that narrow passage.

Monsieur de Saintonges at the time was lounging elegantly on the poop, beside a day-bed set under an awning of brown sailcloth. On this day-bed reclined his handsome Creole wife. There was about this superbly proportioned lady, from the deep mellowness of her voice to the great pearls entwined in her glossy black hair, nothing that did not announce her opulence. It was enhanced at present by profound contentment in this marriage in which each party so perfectly complemented the other. She seemed to glow and swell with it as she lay there luxuriously, faintly waving her jewelled fan, her rich laugh so ready to pay homage to the wit with which her bridegroom sought to dazzle her.

Into this idyll stepped, more or less abruptly, and certainly intrusively, Monsieur Luzan, the Captain of the *Béarnais,* a lean, brown, hook-nosed man something above the middle height, whose air and carriage were those of a soldier rather than a seaman. As he approached, he took the telescope from under his arm and pointed aft with it.

'Yonder is something that is odd,' he said. And he held out the glass. 'Take a look, Chevalier.'

Monsieur de Saintonges rose slowly, and his eyes followed the indication. Some three miles to westward a sail was visible.

'A ship,' he said, and languidly accepted the proffered telescope. He stepped aside, to the rail, whence the view was clearer and where he could find a support on which to steady his elbow.

Through the glass he beheld a big white vessel very high in the poop. She was veering northward, on a starboard tack against the easterly breeze, and so displayed a noble flank pierced for twenty-four guns, the ports gleaming gold against the white. From her maintopmast, above a mountain of snowy canvas, floated the red-and-gold banner of Castile, and above this a crucifix was mounted.

The Chevalier lowered the glass. 'A Spaniard,' was his casual comment. 'What oddness do you discover in her, Captain?'

'Oh, a Spaniard manifestly. But she was steering south when first we sighted her. A little later she veered into our wake and crowded sail. That is what is odd. For the inference is that she decided to follow us.'

'What then?'

'Just so. What then?' He paused as if for a reply, then resumed. 'From the position of her flag she is an admiral's ship. You will have observed that she is of a heavy armament. She carries forty-eight guns besides stern and forechasers.' Again he paused, finally to add with some force: 'When I am followed by a ship like that I like to know the reason.'

Madame stirred languidly on her day-bed to an accompaniment of deep, rich laughter. 'Are you a man to start at shadows, Captain?'

'Invariably, when cast by a Spaniard, Madame.' Luzan's tone was sharp. He was of a peppery temper, and this was stirred by the reflection upon his courage which he found implied in Madame's question.

The Chevalier, disliking the tone, permitted himself some sarcasms where he would have been better employed in inquiring into the reasons for the Captain's misgivings. Luzan departed in annoyance.

That night the wind dropped to the merest breath, and so slow was their progress that by the following dawn they were still some five or six miles to the west of Portugal Point and the exit of the straits. And daylight showed them the big Spanish ship ever at about the same distance astern. Uneasily and at length Captain Luzan scanned her once more, then passed his glass to his lieutenant.

'See what she can tell you.'

The lieutenant looked long, and whilst he looked he saw her making the addition of stunsails to the mountain of canvas that she already carried. This he announced to the Captain at his elbow, and then, having scanned the pennant on her foretopmast, he was able to add the information that she was the flagship of the Spanish Admiral of the Ocean-Sea, the Marquis of Riconete.

That she should put out stunsails so as to catch the last possible ounce of the light airs increased the Captain's suspicion that her aim was to overhaul him, and being imbued, as became an experienced seaman, whilst in these waters with a healthy mistrust of the intentions of all Spaniards, he took his decision. Crowding all possible sail, and as close-hauled as he dared run, he headed south for the shelter of one of the harbours of the northern coast of French Hispaniola. Thither this Spaniard, if she was indeed in pursuit, would hardly dare to follow him. If she did, she would scarcely venture to display hostility. The manoeuvre would also serve to apply a final test to her intentions.

The result supplied Luzan with almost immediate certainty. At once the great galleon was seen to veer in the same direction, actually thrusting her nose yet a point nearer to such wind as there was. It became as clear that she was in pursuit of the *Béarnais* as that the *Béarnais* would be cut off before ever she could reach the green coast that was now almost ahead of her, but still some four miles distant.

Madame de Saintonges, greatly incommoded in her cabin by the apparently quite unnecessary list to starboard, demanded impatiently to be informed by Heaven or Hell what might be amiss that morning with the fool who commanded the *Béarnais.* The uxorious Chevalier, in bed-gown and slippers, and with a hurriedly donned periwig, the curls of which hung like a row of tallow candles about his flushed countenance, made haste to go and ascertain.

He reeled along the almost perpendicular deck of the gangway to the ship's waist, and stood there bawling angrily for Luzan.

The Captain appeared at the poop-rail to answer him with a curt account of his apprehensions.

'Are you still under that absurd persuasion?' quoth Monsieur de Saintonges. 'Absurd! Why should a Spaniard be in pursuit of us?'

'It will be better to continue to ask ourselves that question than to wait to discover the answer,' snapped Luzan, thus, by his lack of deference, increasing the Chevalier's annoyance.

'But it is imbecile, this!' raved Saintonges. 'To run away from nothing. And it is infamous to discompose Madame de Saintonges by fears so infantile.'

Luzan's patience completely left him. 'She'll be infinitely more discomposed,' he sneered, 'if these infantile fears are realized.' And he added bluntly: 'Madame de Saintonges is a handsome woman, and Spaniards are Spaniards.'

A shrill exclamation was his answer, to announce that Madame herself had now emerged from the companionway. She was in a state of undress that barely preserved the decencies; for without waiting to cast more than a wrap over her night-rail, and with a mane of lustrous black hair like a cloak about her splendid shoulders, she had come to ascertain for herself what might be happening.

Luzan's remark, overheard as she was stepping into the ship's waist, brought upon him now a torrent of shrill abuse, in the course of which he heard himself described as a paltry coward and a low, coarse wretch. And before she had done, the Chevalier was adding his voice to hers.

'You are mad, sir. Mad! What can we possibly have to fear from a Spanish ship, a King's ship, you tell me, an Admiral? We fly the flag of France, and Spain is not at war with France.'

Luzan controlled himself to answer as quietly as he might. 'In these waters, sir, it is impossible to say with whom Spain may be at war. Spain is persuaded that God created the Americas especially for her delight. I have been telling you this ever since we entered the Caribbean.'

The Chevalier remembered not only this, but also that from someone else he had lately heard expressions very similar. Madame, however, was distracting his attention. 'The fellow's wits are turned by panic,' she railed in furious contempt. 'It is terrible that such a man should be entrusted with a ship. He would be better fitted to command a kitchen battery.'

Heaven alone knows what might have been the answer to that insult and what the consequences of it if at that very moment the boom of a gun had not come to save Luzan the trouble of a reply, and abruptly to change the scene and the tempers of the actors.

'Righteous Heaven!' screamed Madame, and 'Ventredieu!' swore her husband.

The lady clutched her bosom. The Chevalier, with a face of chalk, put an arm protectingly about her. From the poop the Captain whom they had so freely accused of cowardice laughed outright with a well-savoured malice.

'You are answered, Madame. And you, sir. Another time perhaps you will reflect before you call my fears infantile and my conduct imbecile.'

With that he turned his back upon them, so that he might speak to the lieutenant who had hastened to his elbow. He bawled an order. It was instantly followed by the whistle of the boatswain's pipe, and in the waist about Saintonges and his bride there was a sudden jostling stir as the hands came pouring from their quarters to be marshalled for whatever the Captain might require of them. Aloft there was another kind of activity. Men were swarming the ratlines and spreading nets whose purpose was to catch any spars that might be brought down in the course of action.

A second gun boomed from the Spaniard and then a third; after that there was a pause, and then they were saluted by what sounded like the thunder of a whole broadside.

The Chevalier lowered his white and shaking wife, whose knees had suddenly turned to water, to a seat on the hatch-coaming. He was futilely profane in his distress.

From the rail Luzan, taking pity on them, and entirely unruffled, uttered what he believed to be reassurance.

'At present she is burning powder to no purpose. Mere Spanish bombast. She'll come within range before I fire a shot. My gunners have their orders.'

But, far from reassuring them, this was merely to increase the Chevalier's fury and distress.

'God of my life! Return her fire? You mustn't think of it. You can't deliver battle.'

'Can't I? You shall see.'

'But you cannot go into action with Madame de Saintonges on board.'

'You want to laugh,' said Luzan. 'If I had the Queen of France on board I must still fight my ship. And I have no choice, pray observe. We are being overhauled too fast to make harbour in time. And how do I know that we should be safe even then?'

The Chevalier stamped in rage.

'But they are brigands, then, these Spaniards?'

There was another roar of artillery at closer quarters now which if still not close enough for damage was close enough to increase the panic of Monsieur and Madame de Saintonges.

The Captain was no longer heeding them. His lieutenant had clutched his arm, and was pointing westward. Luzan with the telescope to his eye was following that indication.

A mile or so off on their starboard beam, midway between the *Béarnais* and the Spanish Admiral, a big red forty-gun ship under full sail was creeping into view round a headland of the Hispaniola coast. Close in her wake came a second ship of an armament only a little less powerful. They flew no flag, and it was in increasing apprehension that Luzan watched their movements, wondering were they fresh assailants. To his almost incredulous relief, he saw them veer to larboard, heading in the direction of the Spaniard half hidden still in the smoke of her last cannonade, which that morning's gentle airs were slow to disperse.

Light though the wind might be, the newcomers had the advantage of it, and with the weather-gauge of the Spaniard they advanced upon him, like hawks stooping to a heron, opening fire with their forechasers as they went.

Through a veil of rising smoke the Spaniard could be discerned easing up to receive them; then a half-dozen guns volleyed from her flank, and she was again lost to view in the billowing white clouds they had belched. But she seemed to have fired wildly in her excessive haste, for the red ship and her consort held steadily for some moments on their course, evidently unimpaired, then swung to starboard, and delivered each an answering broadside at the Spaniard.

By now, under Luzan's directions, and despite the protests of Monsieur de Saintonges, the *Béarnais* too had eased up, until she stood with idly flapping sails, suddenly changed from actor to spectator in this drama of the seas.

'Why do you pause, sir?' cried Saintonges. 'Keep to your course. Take advantage of this check to make that harbour.'

'Whilst others fight my battles for me?'

'You have a lady on board,' Saintonges raged at him. 'Madame de Saintonges must be placed in safety.'

'She is in no danger at present. And we may be needed. A while ago you accused me of cowardice. Now you would persuade me to become a coward. For the sake of Madame de Saintonges I will not go into battle save in the last extremity. But for that last extremity I must stand prepared.'

He was so grimly firm that Saintonges dared insist no further. Instead, setting his hopes upon those Heaven-sent rescuers, he stood on the hatch-coaming, and from that elevation sought to follow the fortunes of the battle which was roaring away to westward. But there was nothing to be seen now save a great curtain of smoke, like a vast spreading, deepening cloud that hung low over the sea and extended for perhaps two miles in the sluggish air. From somewhere within the heart of it they continued for awhile to hear the thunder of the guns. Then came a spell of silence, and after a while on the southern edge of the cloud two ships appeared that were at first as the wraiths of ships. Gradually rigging and hulls assumed definition as the smoke rolled away from them, and at about the same time the heart of the cloud began to assume a rosy tint, deepening swiftly to orange, until through the thinning smoke it was seen to proceed from the flames of a ship on fire.

From the poop-rail, Luzan's announcement brought relief at last to the Chevalier. 'The Spanish Admiral is burning. It is the end of her.'

IV

One of the two ships responsible for the destruction of the Spanish galleon remained hove to on the scene of action, her boats lowered and ranging the waters in her neighbourhood. This Luzan made out through his telescope. The other and larger vessel, emerging from that brief decisive engagement without visible scars, headed eastward, and came beating up against the wind towards the *Béarnais,* her red hull and gilded beakhead aglow in the morning sunshine. Still she displayed no flag, and this circumstance renewed in Monsieur de Saintonges the apprehensions which the issue of the battle had allayed.

With his lady still in half-clad condition, he was now on the poop at Luzan's side, and to the Captain he put the question was it prudent to remain hove to whilst this ship of undeclared nationality advanced upon them.

'But hasn't she proved a friend? A friend in need?' said the Captain.

Madame de Saintonges had not yet forgiven Luzan his plain speaking. Out of her hostility she answered him. 'You assume too much. All that we really know is that she proved an enemy to that Spanish ship. How do you know that these are not pirates to whom every ship is a prey? How do we know that since fire has robbed them of their Spanish prize they may not be intent now upon compensating themselves at our expense?'

Luzan looked at her without affection. 'There is one thing I know,' said he tartly. 'Her sailing powers are as much in excess of our own as her armament. It would avail us little to turn a craven tail if she means to overtake us. And there is another thing. If they meant us mischief one of those ships would not have remained behind. The two of them would be heading for us. So we need not fear to do what courtesy dictates.'

This argument was reassuring, and so the *Béarnais* waited whilst in the breeze that was freshening now the stranger came rippling forward over the sunlit water. At a distance of less than a quarter of a mile she hove to. A boat was lowered to the calm sea and came speeding with flash of yellow oars towards the *Béarnais.* Out of her a tall man climbed the Jacob's ladder of the French vessel, and stood at last upon the poop in an elegance of black and silver, from which you might suppose him to come straight from Versailles or the Alameda rather than from the deck of a ship in action.

To the group that received him there--Monsieur de Saintonges and his wife in their disarray, with Luzan and his lieutenant--this stately gentleman bowed until the curls of his periwig met across his square chin, whilst the claret feather in his doffed hat swept the deck.

'I come,' he announced in fairly fluent French, 'to bear and receive felicitations, and to assure myself before sailing away that you are in no need of further assistance and that you suffered no damage before we had the honour to intervene and dispose of that Spanish brigand who was troubling you.'

Such gallant courtesy completely won them, especially the lady. They reassured him on their own score and were solicitous as to what hurts he might have taken in the fight, for all that none were manifest.

Of these he made light. He had suffered some damage on the larboard quarter, which they could not see, but so slight as not to be worth remarking, whilst his men had taken scarcely a scratch. The fight, he explained, had been as brief as, in one sense, it was regrettable. He had hoped to make a prize of that fine galleon. But before he could close with her, a shot had found and fired her powder-magazine, and so the little affair ended almost before it was well begun. He had picked up most of her crew, and his consort was still at that work of rescue.

'As for the flagship of the Admiral of the Ocean-Sea, you see what's left of her, and very soon you will not see even that.'

They carried off this airy, elegant preserver to the great cabin, and in the wine of France they pledged his opportuneness and the victory which had rescued them from ills unnamable. Yet throughout there was from black-and-silver no hint of his identity or nationality, although this they guessed from his accent to be English. Saintonges, at last, approached the matter obliquely.

'You fly no flag, sir,' he said, when they had drunk.

The swarthy gentleman laughed. He conveyed the impression that laughter came to him readily. 'Sir, to be frank with you, I am of those who fly any flag that the occasion may demand. It might have been reassuring if I had approached you under French colours. But in the stress of the hour I gave no thought to it. You could hardly mistake me for a foe.'

'Of those that fly no flag?' the Chevalier echoed, staring bewilderment.

'Just so.' And airily he continued: 'At present I am on my way to Tortuga, and in haste. I am to assemble men and ships for an expedition to Martinique.'

It was the lady's turn to grow round-eyed. 'To Martinique?' She seemed suddenly a little out of breath. 'An expedition to Martinique? An expedition? But to what end?'

Her intervention had the apparent effect of taking him by surprise. He looked up, raising his brows. He smiled a little, and his answer had the tone of humouring her.

'There is a possibility--I will put it no higher--that Spain may be fitting out a squadron for a raid upon Saint Pierre. The loss of the Admiral which I have left in flames out yonder may delay their preparations, and so give us more time. It is what I hope.'

Rounder still grew her dark eyes, paler her cheeks. Her deep bosom was heaving now in tumult.

'Do you say that Spaniards propose a raid upon Martinique? Upon Martinique?'

And the Chevalier in an excitement scarcely less marked than his wife's added at once: 'Impossible, sir. Your information must be at fault. God of my life! That would be an act of war. And France and Spain are at peace.'

The dark brows of their preserver were raised again as if in amusement at their simplicity. 'An act of war. Perhaps. But was it not an act of war for that Spanish ship to fire upon the French flag this morning? Would the peace that prevails in Europe have availed you in the West Indies if you had been sunk?'

'An account--a strict account--would have been asked of Spain.'

'And it would have been rendered, not a doubt. With apologies of the fullest and some lying tales of a misunderstanding. But would that have set your ship afloat again if she had been sunk this morning, or restored you to life so that you might expose the lies by which Spanish men of State would cover the misdeed? Has this not happened, too, and often, when Spain has raided the settlements of other nations?'

'But not of late, sir,' Saintonges retorted.

Black-and-silver shrugged. 'Perhaps that is just the reason why the Spaniards in the Caribbean grow restive.'

And by that answer Monsieur de Saintonges was silenced, bewildered.

'But Martinique!' wailed the lady.

Black-and-silver shrugged expressively. 'The Spaniards call it Martinico, Madame. You are to remember that Spain believes that God created the New World especially for her profit, and that the Divine Will approves her resentment of all interlopers.'

'Isn't that just what I told you, Chevalier?' said Luzan. 'Almost my own words to you this morning when you would not believe there could be danger from a Spanish ship.'

There was an approving gleam from the bright blue eyes of the swarthy stranger as they rested on the French captain.

'So, so. Yes. It is hard to believe. But you have now the proof of it, I think, that in these waters, as in the islands of the Caribbean Sea, Spain respects no flag but her own unless force is present to compel respect. The settlers of every other nation have experienced in turn the Spaniards' resentment of their presence here. It expresses itself in devastating raids, in rapine, and in massacre. I need not enumerate instances. They will be present in your mind. If today it should happen, indeed, to be the turn of Martinico, we can but wonder that it should not have come before. For that is an island worth plundering and possessing, and France maintains no force in the West Indies that is adequate to restrain these conquistadores. Fortunately we still exist. If it were not for us. . .'

'For you?' Saintonges interrupted him, his voice suddenly sharp. 'You exist, you say. Of whom do you speak, sir? Who are you?'

The question seemed to take the stranger by surprise.

He stared, expressionless, for a moment; then his answer, for all that it confirmed the suspicions of the Chevalier and the convictions of Luzan, was nevertheless as a thunderbolt to Saintonges.

'I speak of the Brethren of the Coast, of course. The buccaneers, sir.' And he added, almost it seemed with a sort of pride: 'I am Captain Blood.'

Blankly, his jaw fallen, Saintonges looked across the table into that dark, smiling face of the redoubtable filibuster who had been reported dead.

To be faithful to his mission he should place this man in irons and carry him a prisoner to France. But not only would that in the circumstances of the moment be an act of blackest ingratitude, it would be rendered impossible by the presence at hand of two heavily armed buccaneer ships. Moreover, in the light so suddenly vouchsafed to him, Monsieur de Saintonges perceived that it would be an act of grossest folly. He considered what had happened that morning: the direct and very disturbing evidence of Spain's indiscriminate predatoriness; the evidence of a buccaneer activity which he could not now regard as other than salutary, supplied by that burning ship a couple of miles away; the further evidence of one and the other contained in this news of an impending Spanish raid on Martinique and the intended buccaneer intervention to save it where France had not the means at hand.

Considering all this--and the Martinique business touched him so closely and personally that from being perhaps the richest man in France he might find himself as a result of it no better than he had been before this voyage--it leapt to the eye that for once, at least, the omniscient Monsieur de Louvois had been at fault. So clear was it, and so demonstrable, that Saintonges began to conceive it his duty to shoulder the burden of that demonstration.

Something of all these considerations and emotions quivered in the hoarse voice in which, still staring blankly at Captain Blood, he ejaculated: 'You are that brigand of the sea!'

Blood displayed no resentment. He smiled. 'Oh, but a benevolent brigand, as you perceive. Benevolent, that is, to all but Spain.'

Madame de Saintonges swung in a breathless excitement to her husband, clutching his arm. In the movement the wrap slipped from her shoulders, so that still more of her opulent charms became revealed. But this went unheeded by her. In such an hour of crisis modesty became a negligible matter.

'Charles, what will you do?'

'Do?' said he dully.

'The orders you left in Tortuga may mean ruin to me, and. . .'

He raised a hand to stem this betrayal of self-interest. In whatever might have to be done, of course, no interest but the interest of his master the King of France must be permitted to sway him.

'I see, my dear. I see. Duty becomes plain. We have received a valuable lesson this morning. Fortunately before it is too late.'

She drew a deep breath of relief, and swung excitedly, anxiously to Captain Blood, 'You have no doubt in your mind, sir, that your buccaneers can ensure the safety of Martinique?'

'None, Madame.' His voice was of a hard confidence. 'The Bay of Saint Pierre will prove a mousetrap for the Spaniards if they are so rash as to sail into it. I shall know what is to do. And the plunder of their ships alone will richly defray the costs of the expedition.'

And then Saintonges laughed.

'Ah, yes,' said he. 'The plunder, to be sure. I understand. The ships of Spain are a rich prey, when all is said. Oh, I do not sneer, sir. I hope I am not so ungenerous.'

'I could not suppose it, sir,' said Captain Blood. He pushed back his chair, and rose. 'I will be taking my leave. The breeze is freshening and I should seize the advantage. If it holds I shall be in Tortuga this evening.'

He stood, inclined a little, before Madame de Saintonges, awaiting the proffer of her hand, when the Chevalier took him by the shoulder.

'A moment yet, sir. Keep Madame company whilst I write a letter which you shall carry for me to the Governor of Tortuga.'

'A letter!' Captain Blood assumed astonishment. 'To commend this poor exploit of ours? Sir, sir, never be at so much trouble.'

Monsieur de Saintonges was for a moment ill at ease. 'It . . . it has a further purpose,' he said at last.

'Ah! If it is to serve some purpose of your own, that is another matter. Pray command me.'

V

In the faithful discharge of that courier's office Captain Blood laid the letter from the Chevalier de Saintonges on the evening of that same day before the Governor of Tortuga, without any word of explanation.

'From the Chevalier de Saintonges, you say?' Monsieur d'Ogeron was frowning thoughtfully. 'To what purpose?'

'I could guess,' said Captain Blood. 'But why should I, when the letter is in your hands? Read it, and we shall know.'

'In what circumstances did you obtain this letter?'

'Read it. It may tell you, and so save my breath.'

D'Ogeron broke the seal and spread the sheet. With knitted brows he read the formal retraction by the representative of the Crown of France of the orders left with the Governor of Tortuga for the cessation of all traffic with the buccaneers. Monsieur d'Ogeron was required to continue relations with them as heretofore pending fresh instructions from France. And the Chevalier added the conviction that these instructions when and if they came would nowise change the existing order of things. He was confident that when he had fully laid before the Marquis de Louvois the demonstration he had received of the conditions prevailing in the West Indies, his Excellency would be persuaded of the inexpediency at present of enforcing his decrees against the buccaneers.

Monsieur d'Ogeron blew out his cheeks. 'But will you tell me, then, how you worked this miracle with that obstinate numskull?'

'Every argument depends, as I said to you, upon the manner of its presentation. You and I both said the same thing to the Chevalier de Saintonges. But you said it in words. I said it chiefly in action. Knowing that fools learn only by experience, I supplied experience for him. It was thus.' And he rendered a full account of that early morning sea-fight off the northern coast of Hispaniola.

The Governor listened, stroking his chin. 'Yes,' he said slowly, when the tale was done. 'Yes. That would be persuasive. And to scare him with this bogey of a raid on Martinque and the probable loss of his new-found wealth was well conceived. But don't you flatter yourself a little, my friend, on the score of your shrewdness? Are you not forgetting how amazingly fortunate it was for you that in such a place and at such a time a Spanish galleon should have had the temerity to attack the *Béarnais?* Amazingly fortunate! It fits your astounding luck most oddly!'

'Most oddly, as you say,' Blood solemnly agreed.

'What ship was this you burnt and sank? And what fool commanded her? Do you know?'

'Oh yes. The *Maria Gloriosa,* the flagship of the Marquis of Riconete, the Spanish Admiral of the Ocean-Sea.'

D'Ogeron looked up sharply. 'The *Maria Gloriosa?* What are you telling me? Why, you captured her yourself at San Domingo, and came back here in her when you brought the treasure-ships.'

'Just so. And therefore I had her in hand for this little demonstration of Spanish turpitude and buccaneer prowess. She sailed with Wolverstone in command and just enough hands to work her and to man the half-dozen guns I spared her for the sacrifice.'

'God save us! Do you tell me, then, that it was all a comedy?'

'Mostly played behind a curtain of the smoke of battle. It was a very dense curtain. We supplied an abundance of smoke from guns loaded with powder only, and the light airs assisted us. Wolverstone set fire to the ship at the height of the supposed battle, and under cover of that friendly smoke came aboard the *Arabella* with his crew.'

The Governor continued to glare amazement. 'And you tell me that this was convincing?'

'That it was convincing, no. That it convinced.'

'And you deliberately--deliberately burnt that splendid Spanish ship.'

'That is what convinced. Merely to have driven her off might not have done it.'

'But the waste! Oh my heavens, the waste!'

'Do you complain? Will you be cheese-paring? Do you think that it is by economies that great enterprises are carried through? Look at the letter in your hand again. It amounts to a Government charter for a traffic against which there was a Government decree. Do you think such things can be obtained by fine phrases? You tried them, and you know what came of it.' He slapped the little Governor on the shoulder. 'Let's come to business. For now I shall be able to sell you my spices, and I warn you that I shall expect a good price for them: the price of three Spanish ships at least.'

Episode 4

THE DELIVERANCE

I

For a year and more after his escape from Barbados with Peter Blood, it was the abiding sorrow of Nathaniel Hagthorpe, that West Country gentleman whom the force of adversity had made a buccaneer, that his younger brother Tom should still continue in the enslaved captivity from which, himself, he had won free.

Both these brothers had been out with Monmouth, and being taken after Sedgemoor, both had been sentenced to be hanged for their share in that rebellion. Then came the harsh commutation of the sentence which doomed them to slavery in the plantations, and with a shipload of other rebels-convict they had been sent out to Barbados, and there had passed into the possession of the brutal Colonel Bishop. But by the time that Blood had come to organize the escape of himself and his fellows from that island, Tom Hagthorpe was no longer there.

Colonel Sir James Court, who was deputy in Nevis for the Governor of the Leeward Islands, had come on a visit to Bishop in Barbados and had brought with him his young wife. She was a dainty, wilful piece of mischief, too young by far to have mated with so elderly a man, and having been raised by her marriage to a station above that into which she had been born, she was the more insistent upon her ladyhood and of exactions and pretensions at which a duchess might have paused.

Newly arrived in the West Indies, she was resentfully slow to adapt herself to some of the necessities of her environment, and among her pretensions arising out of this was the lack of a white groom to attend her when she rode abroad. It did not seem fitting to her that a person of her rank should be accompanied on those occasions by what she contemptuously termed a greasy blackamoor.

Nevis, however, could offer her no other, fume as she might. Although by far the most important slave-mart in the West Indies, it imported this human merchandise only from Africa. Because of this it had been omitted by the Secretary of State at home from the list of islands to which contingents of the West Country rebels had been shipped. Lady Court had a notion that this might be repaired in the course of that visit to Barbados, and it was Tom Hagthorpe's misfortune that her questing eyes should have alighted admiringly upon his clean-limbed almost stripling grace when she beheld him at work, half naked, among Colonel Bishop's golden sugar-cane. She marked him for her own, and thereafter gave Sir James no peace until he had bought the slave from the planter who owned him. Bishop made no difficulty about the sale. To him one slave was much as another, and there was a delicacy about this particular lad which made him of indifferent value in a plantation and easily replaced.

Whilst the separation from his brother was a grief to Tom, yet at first the brothers were so little conscious of his misfortune that they welcomed this deliverance from the lash of the overseer; and although a gentleman born, yet so abjectly was he fallen that they regarded it as a sort of promotion that he should go to Nevis to be a groom to the Colonel's lady. Therefore Nat Hagthorpe, taking comfort in the assurance of the lad's improved condition, did not grievously bewail his departure from Barbados until after his own escape, when the thought of his brother's continuing slavery was an abiding source of bitterness.

Tom Hagthorpe's confidence that at least he would gain by the change of owners and find himself in less uneasy circumstances seems soon to have proved an illusion. We are without absolute knowledge of how this came about. But what we know of the lady, as will presently be disclosed, justifies a suspicion that she may have exercised in vain the witchery of her long narrow eyes on that comely lad; in short that he played Joseph to her Madam Potiphar, and thereby so enraged her that she refused to have him continue in attendance. He was clumsy she complained, ill-mannered and disposed to insolence.

'I warned you,' said Sir James a little wearily, for her exactions constantly multiplying were growing burdensome, 'that he was born a gentleman, and must naturally resent his degradation. Better to have left him in the plantations.'

'You can send him back to them,' she answered. 'For I've done with the rascal.'

And so, deposed from the office for which he had been acquired, he went to toil again at sugar-cane under overseers no whit less brutal than Bishop's, and was given for associates a gang of gaolbirds, thieves, and sharpers lately shipped from England.

Of this, of course, his brother had no knowledge, or he must have been visited by a deeper dejection on Tom's behalf and a fiercer impatience to see him delivered from captivity. For that was an object constantly before Nat Hagthorpe, and one that he constantly urged upon Peter Blood.

'Will you be patient now?' the Captain would answer him, himself driven to the verge of impatience by this reiteration of an almost impossible demand. 'If Nevis were a Spanish settlement, we could set about it without ceremony. But we haven't come yet to the point of making war on English ships and English lands. That would entirely ruin our prospects.'

'Prospects? What prospects have we?' growled Hagthorpe. 'We're outlawed, or aren't we?'

'Maybe, maybe. But we discriminate by being the enemy of Spain alone. We're not hostis humani generis yet, and until we become that, we need not abandon hope, like others of our kind, that one day this outlawry will be lifted. I'll not be putting that in jeopardy by a landing in force on Nevis, not even to save your brother Nat.'

'Is he to languish there until he dies, then?'

'No, no. I'll find the way. Be sure I'll find it. But we'ld be wise to wait awhile.'

'For what?'

'For Chance. It's a great faith I have in the lady. She's obliged me more than once, so she has; and she'll maybe oblige me again. But she's not a lady you can drive. Just put your faith in her, Nat, as I do.'

And in the end he was shown to be justified of that faith. The Chance upon which he depended came with unexpected suddenness to his assistance, soon after the affair of San Juan de Puerto Rico. The news that Captain Blood had been caught by the Spaniards and had expiated his misdeeds on a gallows on the beach of San Juan had swept like a hurricane across the Caribbean, from Hispaniola to the Main. In every Spanish settlement there was exultation over the hanging of the most formidable agent of restraint upon Spain's fierce predatoriness that had ever sailed the seas. For the same reason there was much secret unavowed regret among the English and French colonists, by whom the buccaneers were, at least tacitly, encouraged.

Before very long it must come to be discovered that the treasure-ships which had sailed from San Juan under the convoy of the flagship of the Admiral of the Ocean-Sea had cast anchor not in Cadiz Bay, but in the harbour of Tortuga, and that it was not the Admiral of the Ocean-Sea, but Captain Blood, himself, who had commanded the flagship at the very time when his body could be seen dangling from that gallows on the beach. But until the discovery came, Captain Blood was concerned, like a wise opportunist, to profit by the authoritative report of his demise. He realized that there was no time to be lost if he would take full advantage of the present relaxation of vigilance throughout New Spain, and so he set out from the buccaneer stronghold of Tortuga on a projected descent upon the Main.

He took the seas in the *Arabella,* but she bore a broad white stripe painted along her water-line so as to dissemble her red hull, and on her counter the name displayed was now *Mary of Modena,* so as to supply an ultra-Stuart English antidote to her powerful, shapely Spanish lines. With the white, blue, and red of the Union flag at her maintruck, she put in at St Thomas, ostensibly for wood and water, actually to see what might be picked up. What she picked up was Mr Geoffrey Court, who came to supply the chance for which Nathaniel Hagthorpe had prayed and Captain Blood had confidently waited.

II

Over the emerald water that sparkled in the morning sunlight, in a boat rowed by four moistly gleaming negroes, came Mr Geoffrey Court, a consequential gentleman in a golden periwig and a brave suit of mauve taffetas with silver button-holes.

Whilst the negroes steadied the boat against the great hull, he climbed the accommodation ladder in the prow, and stepped aboard, fanning himself with his plumed hat, inviting Heaven to rot him if he could support this abominable heat, and peremptorily demanding the master of this pestilential vessel.

The adjective was merely a part of his habitual and limited rhetoric. For the deck on which he stood was scrubbed clean as a trencher; the brass of the scuttle-butts and the swivel-guns on the poop-tail gleamed like polished gold; the muskets in the rack about the mainmast could not have been more orderly or better furbished had this been a King's ship; and all the gear was stowed as daintily as in a lady's chamber.

The men lounging on the forecastle and in the waist, few of them wearing more than a cotton shirt and pair of loose calico drawers, observed the gentleman's arrogance with a mild but undisguised amusement to which he was happily blind.

A negro steward led him by a dark gangway to the main cabin astern, which surprised him by its space and the luxury of its appointments. Here, at a table spread with snowy napery on which crystal and silver sparkled, sat three men, and one of these, spare and commanding of height, very elegant in black and silver, his sunburned hawk face framed in the flowing curls of a black periwig, rose to receive the visitor. The other two, who remained seated, if less imposing were yet of engaging aspect. They were Jeremy Pitt, the ship-master, young and fair and slight of build, and Nathaniel Hagthorpe, older and broader and of a graver countenance.

Our gentleman in mauve lost none of his assurance under the calm survey to which those three pairs of eyes subjected him. His self-sufficiency proclaimed itself in the tone in which he desired to be informed whither the *Mary of Modena* might be bound. That he supplied a reason for the question seemed on his part a mere condescension.

'My name is Court. Geoffrey Court, to serve you, sir. I am in haste to reach Nevis, where my cousin commands.'

The announcement made something of a sensation upon his audience. It took the breaths of the three men before him, and from Hagthorpe came a gasping 'God save us!' whilst his sudden pallor must have been apparent even with his face in shadow, for he sat with the tall stern windows at his back. Mr Court, however, was too much engrossed in himself to pay heed to changes in the aspect of another. He desired to impress them with his consequence.

'I am cousin to Sir James Court, who is Deputy in Nevis for the Governor of the Leeward Islands. You will have heard of him, of course.'

'Of course,' said Blood.

Hagthorpe's impatience was not content to wait. 'And you want us to carry you to Nevis?' he cried, out of breath, in an eagerness that would have been noticed by any man less obtuse.

'If your course lies anywhere in that direction. It's this way with me: I came out from home, may I perish, on a plaguey half-rotten ship that met foul weather and all but went to pieces under it. Her seams opened under the strain, and she was leaking like a colander when we ran in here for safety. You can see her at anchor yonder. May I rot if she'll ever be fit to take the seas again. The most cursed luck it was to have sailed in such a worm-eaten wash-tub.'

'And you're in haste to get to Nevis?' quoth Blood.

'In desperate haste, may I burn. I've been expected there this month past.'

It was Hagthorpe who answered him in a voice hoarse with emotion. 'Odslife, but you're singularly in luck, sir. For Nevis is our next port of call.'

'Stab me! And is that so?'

There was a grim smile on Blood's dark face. 'It's a strange chance, so it is,' he said. 'We weigh at eight bells, and if this wind holds it's tomorrow morning we'll be dropping anchor at Charlestown.'

'Nothing, then, could be more fortunate. Nothing, may I perish.' The florid countenance was all delight. 'Fate owes me something for the discomforts I have borne. By your leave, I'll fetch my portmantles at once.' Magnificently he added: 'The price of the passage shall be what you will.'

As magnificently Blood waved a graceful hand that was half smothered in a foam of lace. 'That's a matter of no moment at all. Ye'll take a morning whet with us?'

'With all my heart, Captain. . .'

He paused there, waiting for the name to be supplied to him; but Captain Blood did not appear to heed. He was giving orders to the steward.

Rum and limes and sugar were brought, and over their punch they were reasonably merry, saving Hagthorpe, who was fathoms deep in preoccupation. But no sooner had Mr Court departed than he roused himself to thank Blood for what he supposed had been in his mind when he so readily consented to carry this passenger.

'Didn't I say, now, that if you'ld put your faith in Chance, she'ld be serving us sooner or later? It's not myself ye should be thanking, Nat. It's Fortune. She's just tumbled Mr Court out of her cornucopia into your lap.' He laughed as he mimicked Mr Court: "The price of the passage shall be what you will." What *you* will, Nat; and I'm thinking it's Sir James Court we'll be asking to pay it.'

III

At the very moment that Mr Geoffrey Court was drinking that morning whet in the cabin of the *Arabella,* his cousin Sir James, a tall, spare man of fifty, as vigorous still of body as he was irresolute of mind, sat at his breakfast-table with a satchel of letters that had just arrived from England. They were letters long overdue, for the ship that had brought them, delayed and driven out of her course by gales, had exceeded by fully two months the normal time of the voyage.

Sir James had emptied the satchel on to the table, and had spread the contents for a general preliminary glance. A package bulkier than the rest drew his attention, and he took it up. He scanned the superscription with a frown that gradually drew together his heavy, grizzled brows. He hesitated, passing a brown, bony hand along his chin; then, as if abruptly taking a decision, he broke the seals and tore away the wrapper. From this husk he extracted a dainty volume bound in vellum, with some gold tooling on the spine and the legend, also in gold, *The Poems of Sir John Suckling.*

He sniffed contemptuously, and contemptuously tossed the thing aside. But as it fell, the volume partly opened, and at what he saw his narrow face grew attentive. He took it up again. The fold of vellum on the inner side of the cover had become detached and had slightly curled away from the board. The paste securing that fold had perished, and as he fingered the curled edge the entire flap forming the side of the cover came loose. Between this and the board a folded sheet was now disclosed.

That sheet was still in James' hand ten minutes later, when the room was abruptly invaded by the dainty lady who might have been, in years, his daughter, but was, in fact, his wife. She was scarcely of the middle height and virginally slight of figure, clear-eyed and of a delicate tint unblemished by the climate of the tropics. She was dressed for riding, her face in the shadow of a wide hat, a whip in her hand.

'I have to speak to you,' she announced, her voice musical, but its tone shrewish.

Sir James, sitting with his back to the door, had not turned to see who entered. At the sound of her voice he dropped a napkin over the volume of poems. Then, still without turning, he spoke. 'In that case the King's business may go to the devil.'

'Must you always sneer, sir?' The shrewish note grew sharper. 'Do you transact the King's business at the breakfast-table?'

Always calm, even lethargic, of spirit, Sir James replied: 'Not always. No. But just as often as you must be peremptory.'

'I don't want for cause.' She swept forward and round the table so that she might directly face him. She stood there, very straight, her riding-whip in her gloved hands, held across her slim, vigorous young body. There was a petulance on the sensual lips, an aggressive forward thrust of the little pointed chin.

'I have been insulted,' she announced.

Grey-faced, Sir James considered her. 'To be sure,' he said at last.

'What do you mean--"To be sure"?'

'Doesn't it happen every time that you ride out?'

'And if it does, who shall wonder when yourself you set the example?'

He avoided the offered argument. Argument, at least, was something that he had learnt to refuse this winsome termagant of half his age whom he had married five years ago and who had since poisoned his life with the bad manners and ill-temper brought from her tradesman-father's home.

'Who was it today?' asked his weary voice.

'That dog Hagthorpe. I would to God I had left him rotting in Barbados.'

'Instead of bringing him to rot here. Yes? What did he say to you?'

'Say? You don't conceive he had the effrontery to speak to me?'

He smiled a little sourly. In these days of disillusion he was able to perceive that most of the trouble came from her being too consciously a lady without proper preparation for the role.

'But if he insulted you?'

'It was in the cursed impudent way he looked at me, with a half-smile on his insolent face.'

'A half-smile?' The bushy brows went up. 'It may have been no more than a greeting.'

'You would say that. You would take sides even with your slaves against your wife. Happen what may, I am never in the right. Oh no. Never. A greeting?' she sniffed. 'This was no greeting. And if it was, is a low slave to greet me with smiles?'

'A half-smile, I think you said. And as for low, he may be a slave--poor devil!--but he was born a gentleman.'

'Fine gentleman to be sure! A damned rebel who should have been hanged.'

His deep-set eyes gravely considered her daintiness. 'Are you quite without pity?' he asked her. 'I wonder sometimes. And is there no constancy in you either? You were so taken with the lad when first we saw him in Barbados that nothing would content you until I had bought him so that you might make of him your groom and lavish favours on him only to--'

Her whip crashed down on the table to interrupt him. 'I'll listen to no more of this. It's cowardly always to browbeat and bully me, and put me in the wrong. But I shall know what to do another time. I'll lay my whip across that rogue's smug face. That will teach him to leer at me.'

'It will be worthy,' was the bitter comment. 'It will be brave, towards an unfortunate who must bear whatever comes lest worse should follow.'

But she was no longer listening. The stroke of her whip had scattered some of the letters heaped upon the table. Her attention was sharply diverted.

'Has a packet come from England?' Her breathing seemed to quicken as he watched her.

'I spoke, I think, of the King's business. Here you see it. At the breakfast-table.'

She was already rummaging through the heap, scanning each package in turn. 'Are there letters for me?'

It was a second or two before his suddenly compressed lips parted again to reply evasively: 'I haven't seen all of them yet.'

She continued her search, whilst he watched her from under his brows. At the end she looked at him again.

'Nothing?' she asked, on a note of surprised, aggrieved inquiry. Her brows were knit, her delicate chin seemed to grow more pointed. 'Nothing?'

'You have looked for yourself,' he said.

She turned slowly away, her lip between finger and thumb. He was grimly amused to observe that the furious grievance with which she had sought him was forgotten; that her wrath on the matter of the slave had been quenched in another preoccupation. Slowly she moved to the door, passing out of his range of sight. Her hand upon the knob, she paused. She spoke in a voice that was soft and amiable. 'You have no word from Geoffrey?' He answered without turning. 'I have told you that I have not yet looked through all the letters.'

Still she lingered. 'I did not see his hand on any of them.'

'In that case he has not written to me.'

'Odd!' she said slowly, 'It is very odd. We should have had word by now of when to expect him.'

'I'll not pretend to anxiety for that news.'

'You'll not?' A flush slowly inflamed her face in the pause she made. Then her anger lashed him again. 'And I? You've no thought, of course, for me, chained in this hateful island, with no society but the parson and the commandant and their silly wives. Haven't I sacrificed enough for you that you should grudge me even the rare company of someone from the world, who can give me news of something besides sugar and pepper and the price of blackamoors?' She waited through a silent moment. 'Why don't you answer me?' she shrilled.

He had turned pale under his tan. He swung slowly round in his chair.

'You want an answer, do you?' There was an undertone of thunder in his voice.

Evidently she didn't. For at the mere threat of it she went abruptly out, and slammed the door. He half rose, and she little knew in what peril she stood at that moment from the anger that flamed up in him. Emotion of any kind, however, was short-lived in this lethargic-minded man. An imprecation fluttered from him on a sigh as he sagged back again into his chair. Again unfolding the sheet which his hand had retained during her presence in the room, he resumed his scowling study of it. Then, having sat gloomily in thought for a long while, he rose and went to lock both the letter and the vellum-bound volume in a secretaire that stood between the open windows. After that, at last, he gave his attention to the other packages that awaited him.

IV

Lady Court's yearnings for society from the great world, which were at the root of a good deal of the wretchedness of that household, received some satisfaction on the morrow, when the *Mary of Modena* reached the island of Nevis--that vast green mountain rising from the sea--and came to cast anchor in Charlestown Bay.

Mr Court, all a quivering eagerness to go ashore, was in the very act of ordering Jacob, the steward, to take up his portmantles, when Captain Blood sauntered into the cabin.

'That will be for tomorrow perhaps,' said he.

'Tomorrow?' Mr Court stared at him. 'But this is Nevis, isn't it?'

'To be sure. This is Nevis. But before we set you ashore there's the trifling matter of the price of your passage.'

'Oh! That!' Mr Court was contemptuous. 'Didn't I say you might make it what you please?'

'You did. And, faith, I may be taking you at your word.'

Mr Court did not like the Captain's smile. He interpreted it in his own fashion.

'If you mean to be--ah--extortionate. . .'

'Och, not extortionate at all. Most reasonable, to be sure. Sit down, sir, whilst I explain.'

'Explain? Explain what?'

'Sit down, sir.' Blood's tone and manner were compelling. Bewildered, Mr Court sat down.

'It's this way,' said Captain Blood, and sat down also, on the stern locker, with his back to the open window, the sunshine, the glittering sea and the hawkers' boats that with fruit and vegetables and fowls came crowding about the ship. 'It's this way: For the moment I'll trouble you to be considering yourself, in a manner of speaking, a hostage, Mr Court. A hostage for a very good friend of mine, who at this moment is a slave in the hands of your cousin, Sir James. You've told us how highly Sir James esteems and loves you; so there's no cause for uneasiness at all. In short, sir: my friend's freedom is the price I'll be asking Sir James for your passage. That's all.'

'All?' There was fury in Mr Court's tone, in his prominent eyes. 'This is an outrage!'

'I'll not be depriving you of the comfort of calling it that.'

Mr Court set an obvious restraint upon his feelings. 'And supposing that Sir James should refuse?'

'Och, why will you be vexing your soul by supposing anything so unpleasant? The one certain thing at present is that if Sir James consents you'll be landed at once on Nevis.'

'I am asking you, sir, what will happen if he doesn't.'

Captain Blood smiled amiably. 'I'm an orderly man, and so I like to take one thing at a time. Speculation's mostly a waste of thought. We'll leave that until it happens, for the excellent reason that it may never happen at all.'

Mr Court came to his feet in exasperation.

'But this . . . this is monstrous. Od rot me, sir, you'll do me this violence at your peril.'

'I am Captain Blood,' he was answered, 'so you'll not be supposing that a little peril more or less will daunt me.'

The announcement released some fresh emotions in Mr Court. His eyes threatened to drop from his flushed, angry face.

'You are Captain Blood! Captain Blood! That damned pirate! You may be but, may I perish, I care nothing who you are. . .'

'Why should you now? All I'm asking of you is that you'll step into your cabin. Of course I shall have to place a guard at the door, but there'll be no other restraints, and your comforts shall not suffer.'

'Do you suppose I'll submit to this?'

'I can put you in irons if you prefer it,' said Captain Blood suavely.

Mr Court, having furiously considered him, decided that he would not prefer it.

Captain Blood was rowed ashore, and took his way to the Deputy-Governor's house on the water-front: a fine white house with green slatted sun-blinds set back in a fair garden where azaleas flamed and all was fragrance of orange and pimento.

He found access to Sir James an easy matter. To a person of his obvious distinction, in his becoming coat of dark-blue camlett, his plumed hat and his long sword slung from a gold-embroidered baldrick, colonial doors were readily opened. He announced himself as Captain Peter, which was scarcely false, and he left it to be supposed that his rank was naval and to be understood that the ship in which he now sailed was his own property. His business in Nevis, the most important slave-market of the West Indies, he declared to be the acquisition of a lad of whom he might make a cabin boy. He had been informed that Sir James, himself, did a little slave-dealing, but even if this information were not correct, he had the presumption to hope that he might deserve Sir James' assistance in his quest.

His person was so elegantly engaging, his manner, perfectly blending deference with dignity, so winning, that Sir James professed himself entirely at Captain Peter's service. Just now there were no slaves available, but at any moment a cargo of blacks from the Coast of Guinea should be arriving, and if Captain Peter were not pressed for a day or two there was no doubt that his need would be supplied. Meanwhile, of course, Captain Peter would stay to dine.

And to dine Captain Peter stayed, meeting Lady Court, whom he impressed so favourably that before dinner was over the invitation extended by her husband had been materially enlarged by her.

Meanwhile, considering the ostensible object of Captain Peter's visit to Nevis, it was natural that the conversation should turn to slaves, and to a comparison of the service to be obtained from them with that afforded by European servants. Sir James, by opining that the white man was so superior as to render any comparison ridiculous, opened the way for the Captain's searching probe.

'And yet all the white men out here as a result of the Monmouth rebellion are being wasted in the plantations. It is odd that no one should ever have thought of employing any of them in some other capacity.'

'They are fit for nothing else,' said her ladyship. 'You can't make ordinary servants of such mutinous material. I know because I tried.'

'Ah! Your ladyship tried. Now that is interesting. But you'll not be telling me that the wretches you so rescued from the plantations were so indifferent to this good fortune as not to give good service?'

Sir James interposed. 'My wife's experience is more limited than her assertion might lead you to suppose. She judges from a single trial.'

She acknowledged the hostile criticism by a disdainful glance, and the Captain came gallantly to her support.

'Ab uno omnes, you know, Sir James. That is often true.' He turned to the lady, who met him smiling. 'What was this single trial? What manner of man was it who proved so lacking in grace?'

'One of those rebels-convict shipped to the plantations. We found him in Barbados, and I bought him to make a groom of him. But he was so little grateful, so little sensible of that betterment of his fortunes that in the end I sent him back to work at sugar-cane.'

The Captain's grave nod approved her. 'Faith, he was rightly served. And what became of him?'

'Just that. He's repenting his bad manners on Sir James' plantation here. A surly, mutinous dog.'

Again Sir James spoke, sadly: 'The poor wretch was a gentleman once, like so many of his misguided fellow-rebels. It was a poor mercy not to have hanged them.'

On that he changed the subject, and Captain Blood having obtained the information that he sought was content to allow him to do so.

But whatever the matter of which they talked, the lady's rare young beauty, combined with a sweet, ingenuous charm of manner, which seemed to bring a twist to the lip of Sir James as he watched her, commanded from their visitor the attentive regard which no man of any gallantry could have withheld. She rewarded him by insisting that whilst he waited in Charlestown he should take up his quarters in their house. She would admit of no refusal. She vowed that all the favour would be of the Captain's bestowing. Too rarely did a distinguished visitor from across the ocean come to relieve the monotony of their life on Nevis.

As a further inducement, she enlarged upon the beauties of this island. She must be the Captain's guide to its scented groves, its luxuriant plantations, its crystal streams, so that he should realize what an earthly Paradise was this which her husband had so often heard her denounce a desolate Hell.

Sir James, without illusions, covering his contempt of her light arts with a mask of grave urbanity, confirmed her invitation, whereupon she announced that she would give orders at once to have a room prepared and the Captain must send aboard for what he needed.

Captain Blood accepted this hospitality in graceful terms and without reluctance. Whilst so much may not have been absolutely necessary for the accomplishment of his purpose in Nevis, yet there could be no doubt that residence in the household of Sir James Court might very materially assist him.

V

We have heard Captain Blood expressing his faith in Fortune, or Chance, as he named it to Hagthorpe. Nevertheless, he did not carry his faith to the lengths of sitting still for Fortune to come seeking him. Chances, he knew, were to be created, or at least attracted, by intelligence and diligence, and betimes on the following morning he was afoot and booted, so as to lose no time in his quest. He knew, from the information gathered yesterday, in what direction it should be pursued, and soon after sunrise he was making his way to Sir James' stables to procure the necessary means.

There could be nothing odd in that a guest of early-rising habits should choose to go for a gallop before breakfast, or that for the purpose he should borrow a mount from his host. The fact that he should elect in his ride to go by way of Sir James' plantation could hardly suggest an interest in one of the slaves at work in it.

So far, then, he could depend upon himself. Beyond that--for sight and perhaps speech of the slave he sought--he put his faith again in Fortune.

At the outset it looked as if Fortune that morning were in no kindly mood. For early though the hour, Lady Court, be it because of matutinal habits, because meticulous in her duty as a hostess, or because of an unconquerable and troublesome susceptibility to such attractiveness in the male as her guest displayed, came fresh and sprightly to take him by surprise in the stables, and to call for a horse so that she might ride with him. It was vexatious, but it did not put him out of countenance. When she joyously announced that she would show him the cascades, he secretly cursed her sprightliness. Very politely he demurred on the ground that his first interest was in the plantations.

She puckered her perfect nose in mock disdain of him. 'I vow, sir, you disappoint me. I conceived you more poetical, more romantical, a man to take joy in beauty, in the wild glories of nature.'

'Why, so I am, I hope. But I'm practical as well; and also something of a student. I can admire the orderliness of man's contriving, and inform myself upon it.'

This led to argument; a very pretty and equally silly battle of words, which Captain Blood, with a definite purpose in view, found monstrous tedious. It ended in a compromise. They rode out first to the cascades, in which she could not spur the Captain into more than languid interest, and then home to breakfast by way of the sugar-plantations, in which no interest could have been more disappointingly keen to her than his. For he wasted time there, and her ladyship was growing sharp-set.

So that he might view at leisure every detail, he proceeded at no more than a walking pace through the broad lanes between the walls of cane that were turning golden, past gangs of slaves, of whom a few were white, who were toiling at the irrigation trenches. From time to time the Captain would try the lady's patience by drawing rein, so that he might look about him more searchingly, and once he paused by an overseer, to question him, first on the subject of the cultivation itself, then on that of the slaves employed, their numbers and quality. He was informed that the white ones were transported convicts.

'Rebel knaves, I suppose,' said the Captain. 'Some of those psalm-singers who were out with the Duke of Monmouth.'

'Nay, sir. We've only one o' they; one as came from Barbados wi' a parcel o' thieves and cozeners. That gang's down yonder, at the end of this brake.'

They rode on and came to the group, a dozen or so half-naked unkempt men, some of them burnt so black by the sun that they looked like pale-coloured negroes, and more than one back a criss-cross of scars from the overseer's lash. It was amongst these that Captain Blood's questing eyes alighted on the man he sought in Nevis.

My lady, who could never long sustain a role of amiable docility, was beginning to manifest her loss of patience at these futilities. That loss was complete when her companion now drew rein yet again, and gave a courteous good morning to the burly overseer of these wretched toilers. Almost at once her annoyance found an outlet. A young man, conspicuous for his athletic frame and sun-bleached golden hair, stood leaning upon his hoe, staring up wide-eyed and open-mouthed at the Captain.

She urged her mare forward.

'Why do you stand idle, oaf? Will you never learn not to stare at your betters? Then here's to improve your manners.'

Viciously her riding-switch cut across his naked shoulders. It was raised again, to repeat the stroke; but the slave, who had half swung round so as fully to face her, parried the blow on his left forearm as it descended, whilst his hand, simultaneously closing upon the switch, wrenched it from her with a jerk that almost pulled her from the saddle.

If the other toilers fell idle, to stare in awe, there was instant action from the watchful overseer. With an oath he sprang for the young slave, uncoiling the thong of his whip.

'Cut the flesh from his bones, Walter!' shrilled the lady.

Before this menace the goaded youth flung away the silver-mounted switch and swung his hoe aloft. His light eyes were blazing. 'Touch me with that whip and I'll beat your brains out.'

The big overseer checked. He knew reckless resolve when he saw it, and here it glared at him plainly. The slave, maddened by pain and injustice, was no more in case to count the cost of doing as he threatened than of having dared to employ the threat. The overseer attempted to dominate him by words and tone, so as to gain time until the frenzy should have passed.

'Put down that hoe, Hagthorpe. Put it down at once.'

But Hagthorpe laughed at him; and then my lady laughed too, on a note that was horrible in its evil, spiteful glee.

'Don't argue with the dog. Pistol him. You've my warrant for it, Walter. I'm witness to his mutiny. Pistol him, man.'

Thus insistently and imperatively ordered, the man carried a hand to the holster of his belt. But even as he drew the weapon, the Captain leaned over from the saddle, and the butt of his heavy riding-crop crashed upon the overseer's hand, sending the pistol flying. The fellow cried out in pain and amazement.

'Be easy now,' said Blood. 'I've saved your life, so I have. For it would have cost you no less if you had fired that pistol.'

'Captain Peter!' It was a cry of indignant, incredulous protest from Lady Court.

He turned to her, and the scorn in his eyes, so vividly blue under their black brows, struck her like a blow.

'What are you? A woman? Od's blood, ma'am, in London Town I've seen poor street-walkers carted that were more womanly.'

She gasped. Then fury rallied her courage to answer him. 'I have a husband, sir, I thank God. You shall answer to him for that.' She drove a vicious spur into her horse, and departed at the gallop, leaving him to follow as he listed.

'Sure and I'll answer to all the husbands in the world,' he called after her, and laughed.

Then he beckoned Hagthorpe forward. 'Here, my lad. You'll come and answer with me. I am going to see justice done, and I know better than to leave you at the mercy of an overseer while I'm about it. Take hold of my stirrup-leather. You're coming with me to Sir James. Stand back there, my man, or I'll ride you down. It's to your master I'll be accounting for my actions, not to you.'

Still nursing his hand, the overseer, his face sullen, fell aside before that threat, and Captain Blood moved on at an easy pace down the golden lane with Tom Hagthorpe striding beside him clinging to his stirrup-leather. Out of earshot the young man hoarsely asked a question.

'Peter, by what miracle do you happen here?'

'Miracle, is it? Now didn't ye suppose that sooner or later one or another of us would be coming to look for you?' He laughed. 'I've not only had the luck to find you. That sweet, womanly creature has supplied a pretext for my interest in you. It makes things easy. And, anyway, easy or difficult, by my soul, I'm not leaving Nevis without you.'

VI

In the hall of the Deputy-Governor's house, when they came to it, Captain Blood left the lad to wait for him, whilst, guided by my lady's strident scolding voice, he strode to the dining-room. There he found Sir James seated, cold and sneering, before a neglected breakfast and her ladyship pacing the room as she railed. The opening of the door momentarily checked her. Then with heaving breast and eyes that flamed in a white face she exploded at the intruder.

'You have the effrontery to present yourself?'

'I thought that I might be expected.'

'Expected? Ha!'

He bowed a little. 'I'm far from wishing to intrude. But I supposed that some explanation might be desired of me.'

'Some explanation indeed!'

'And it's not in my sensitive heart to disappoint a lady.'

'A while ago you had another name for me.'

'A while ago you deserved another.'

Sir James rapped the table. His dignity both as Deputy-Governor and as husband demanded, he conceived, this intervention. 'Sir!' His tone was a reproof. Peremptorily he added: 'A plain tale, if you please.'

'Faith, I'll make it plainer than may please you, Sir James. I'll not be mincing words at all.' And forth came a scrupulous account of the events, in the course of rendering which he was more than once compelled to overbear her ladyship's interruptions.

At the end her husband looked at her where she stood fuming, and there was no sympathy in his glance. It was cold and hard and laden with dislike. 'Captain Peter supplies what the tale lacked to make it hang together.'

'It should suffice at least to show you that satisfaction is required, unless you're a poltroon.'

Whilst the Deputy-Governor was wincing at the insult, Captain Blood was making haste to interpose.

'Sir James, I am at your service for satisfaction of whatever sort you choose. But first, for my own satisfaction, let me say that if under the spur of emotions which I trust you will account humane, I have done aught that is offensive, my apologies are freely offered.'

Sir James remained singularly cold and stern. 'You have done little good, and perhaps a deal of harm, by your intervention. This wretched slave, encouraged to mutiny by your action, cannot be suffered to escape the consequences. There would be an end to order and discipline in the plantation if his conduct were overlooked. You perceive that?'

'Does it matter what he perceives?' railed the lady

'What I perceive is that if I had not intervened this man would have been shot on the spot by her ladyship's orders, and this because innocent of all offence he resisted the threat--again by her ladyship's orders--of having the flesh cut from his bones. Those were her gentle words.'

'It is certainly what will happen to him now,' she spitefully announced. 'That is, unless Sir James prefers to hang him.'

'As a scapegoat for me, because I intervened?' demanded the Captain of Sir James, and Sir James, stung by the sneer, made haste to answer: 'No, no. For threatening the overseer.'

This brought down upon him a fresh attack from her ladyship.

'His insolence to me, of course, is of no account. Nor, it seems, is this gentleman's.'

Between the two of them, Sir James was in danger of losing his stern habitual calm. He slapped the table so that the dishes rattled.

'One thing at a time, madam, if you please. The situation is nasty enough, God knows. I've warned you more than once against venting your spleen upon this fellow Hagthorpe. Now you force me to choose between flogging him for an insubordination that I cannot regard as other than fully provoked, and imperilling all discipline among the slaves. Since I cannot afford that, I have to thank your tantrums, madam, for compelling me to be inhuman.'

'Whilst I have none but myself to thank for having mated with a fool.'

'That, madam, is a matter we may presently have occasion to argue,' said he, and there was something so mysteriously minatory in his tone that her astonishment deprived her pertness of an answer.

Softly Blood's voice cut into the pause. 'I might be able, Sir James, to lift you from the horns of this dilemma.' And he went on to explain himself. 'You'll remember that it was to buy a cabin-boy I landed here. I had thought of a negro; but this Hagthorpe seems a likely lad. Sell him to me, and I'll take him off your hands.'

The elderly man considered a moment, and his gloom was seen to lighten a little. 'Egad! It's a solution.'

'You have but to name your price, then, Sir James.'

But her ladyship was there with her spite to close that easy exit.

'What next? The man's a rebel-convict, doomed for life to service in the plantations. You have a clear duty. You dare not be a party to his leaving the West Indies.'

In the troubled hesitation of that irresolute man, Blood saw that all was not yet done, as he had hoped. Cursing the spite of the lovely termagant, he advanced to the foot of the table, and, folding his arms on the tall back of the chair that stood there, he looked grimly from one to other of them.

'Well, well!' said he. 'And so this unfortunate lad is to be flogged.'

'He's to be hanged,' her ladyship corrected.

'No, no,' Sir James protested. 'A flogging will suffice.'

'I see that I can do no more,' said Blood, and his manner became ironically smooth. 'So I'll take my leave. But before I go, Sir James, there's something I'd almost forgot. I found a cousin of yours at St Thomas who was in haste to get to Nevis.'

He intended to surprise them; and he succeeded; but their surprise was no greater than his own at the abrupt and utter change of manner his announcement produced in her ladyship.

'Geoffrey!' she cried, a catch in her voice. 'Do you mean Geoffrey Court?'

'That is his name. Geoffrey Court.'

'And he's at St Thomas, you say?' Again it was her ladyship who questioned him, the change in her manner growing more ludicrously marked. There was a change too in the aspect of Sir James. He was observing his wife from under his bushy eyebrows, the ghost of a sneer on his thin lips.

'No, no,' Blood corrected. 'Mr Court is here. Aboard my ship. I gave him passage from St Thomas.'

'Then. . .' She paused. She was out of breath, and her brows were knit in a puzzled frown. 'Then why has he not landed?'

'I'm disposed to think it's by a dispensation of Providence. Just as it was by a dispensation of Providence that he requested a passage of me. All that need matter to you, Sir James, is that he's still aboard.'

'But is he ill, then?' cried my lady

'As healthy as a fish, ma'am. But he may not so continue. Aboard that ship, Sir James, I am as absolute as you are here ashore.'

It was impossible to misunderstand him. Taken aback, they stared at him a moment, then her ladyship, panting and quavering, exploded.

'There are laws to restrain you, I suppose.'

'No laws at all, ma'am. You have only half my name. I am Captain Peter, yes. Captain Peter Blood.' It had become necessary to disclose himself if his threat was to carry weight. He smiled upon their silent stupefaction. 'Perhaps you'll be seeing the need, for the sake of Cousin Geoffrey, of being more humane in the matter of this unfortunate slave. For I give you my word that whatever you do to young Hagthorpe that same will I do to Mr Geoffrey Court.'

Sir James actually and incomprehensibly laughed, whilst her ladyship gaped in terror for a moment before bracing herself to deal practically with the situation.

'Before you can do anything you'll have to reach your ship again, and you'll never leave Charlestown until Mr Court is safely ashore. You'd forgot to. . .'

'Och, I've forgotten nothing,' he interrupted, with a wave of the hand. 'You're not to suppose that I'm the man to walk into a gin without taking precautions to see that it can't be sprung on me. The *Mary of Modena* carries forty guns in her flanks, all of them demi-cannons. Two of her broadsides will make of Charlestown just a heap of rubble. And it's what'll happen if they have no word of me aboard before eight bells is made. You'll come away from that bell-pull, my lady, if you're prudent.'

She came away white and trembling, whilst Sir James, grey-faced, but still with that suggestion of a sneering smile about his lips, looked up at Captain Blood.

'You play the highwayman, sir. You put a pistol to our heads.'

'No pistol at all. Just forty demi-cannons, and every one of them loaded.'

But for all his bravado Captain Blood fully realized that in the pass to which things were come he might yet have to pistol Sir James so as to win free. He would deplore the necessity; but he was prepared for it. What he was not prepared for was the Deputy-Governor's abrupt and easy acquiescence.

'That simplifies the issue, which is, I think, that whatever I do to Hagthorpe you will do to my cousin.'

'That is the issue exactly.'

'Then if I were to hang Hagthorpe. . .'

'There would be a yard-arm for your cousin.'

'Only one decision, of course, is possible.'

Her ladyship's gasp of relief from her mounting fears was clearly audible. 'You prevail, sir,' she cried. 'We must let Hagthorpe go.'

'On the contrary,' said Sir James. 'I must hang him.'

'You must. . .' She choked as she stared at him, open-mouthed, the horror back again in her wide blue eyes.

'I have a clear duty, madam, as you reminded me. As you said, I dare not be a party to Hagthorpe's leaving the plantations. He must hang. Fiat justitia, ruat coelum. I think that's how it runs. What happens afterwards will not be on my conscience.'

'Not on your conscience!' She was distraught. 'But Geoffrey!' She wrung her hands. 'Geoffrey!' Her tone had become a wail. Then, rallying, she turned in fury on her husband. 'You're mad. Mad! You can't do this. You can't. Hagthorpe must go. What does he matter, after all? What's a slave more or less? In God's name, let him go.'

'And my duty, then? My clear duty?'

His sternness broke her spirit. 'Oh God!' She flung herself on her knees beside his chair, clawing his arm in her anguish.

He cast her off and answered her with a laugh that in its contemptuous mockery was horrible to hear.

Afterwards Captain Blood boasted, perhaps unduly that it was this cruel amusement at the woman's panic that brought light to a situation full of mystery, explained the ready acceptance of it by Sir James, and made plain much else that had been puzzling.

Having laughed his wicked fill, the Deputy-Governor rose, and waved a hand in dismissal of the Captain. 'The matter's settled, then. You'll desire to return to your ship, and I'll not detain you. Yet, stay. You might take a message to my cousin.' He went to unlock the secretaire that stood between the windows. Thence he took a copy of *The Poems of Sir John Suckling* on one of the sides of which the vellum curled away from the board. 'Condole with him on my behalf, and restore him this. I was waiting for him, to hand it to him myself. But it will be much better this way. Assure him from me that the letter it contained, almost as poetical as the volume itself, has now been faithfully delivered.' And to her ladyship he held out a folded sheet. 'It is for you, ma'am. Take it.' She shrank in fear. 'Take it,' he insisted, and flung it at her. 'We will discuss its contents presently. Meanwhile, it will help you to understand my strict regard for that clear duty of which you reminded me.'

Crouching where he had left her beside his empty chair, her shaking fingers unfolded the sheet. She lowered her eyes to the writing; then, after a moment, with a whimpering sound, let the sheet fall.

Captain Blood was taking in his hands the volume that Sir James had proffered. It was now, I think, that full understanding came to him, and for a moment he was in a dilemma. If the unexpected had helped him at the commencement, the unexpected had certainly come to thwart him now, when in sight of the end.

'I'll wish you a very good day, sir,' said Sir James. 'There is nothing to detain you longer.'

'You're in a mistake, Sir James. There's just one thing. I've changed my mind. I may have done many things in my time for which I should take shame. But I've never yet been anyone's hangman, and I'll be damned if I fill that office in your service. I was quite ready to hang this cousin of yours as an act of reprisal. But I'm damned if I'll hang him to oblige you. I'll send him ashore, Sir James, so that you may hang him yourself.'

The sudden dismay in Sir James' face was no more than Captain Blood expected. Having thus wrecked that sweet plan of vengeance, the Captain went on to show where consolation lay.

'If now that I've changed my mind you were to change yours, and sell me this lad to be my cabin-boy, I'ld not only carry your cousin away with me, but I think I could induce him not to trouble you again.'

Sir James' deep-set eyes questioningly searched the face of the buccaneer.

Captain Blood smiled. 'It's entirely a friendly proposal, Sir James,' he said, and the assurance bore conviction to the troubled mind of the Deputy-Governor.

'Very well,' he said at last. 'You may take the lad. On those terms I make you a gift of him.'

VII

Realizing that husband and wife would be having a good deal to say to each other, and that to linger at such a time would be intrusive, Captain Blood took an immediate tactful leave, and departed.

In the hall he summoned the waiting Tom Hagthorpe to accompany him, and the lad, understanding nothing of this amazing deliverance, went with him.

None hindering them, they hired a boat at the mole, and so came to the *Mary of Modena,* in the waist of which the two brothers, reunited, fell into each other's arms, whilst Captain Blood looked on with all the sense of being a beneficent deity.

On the verge of tears, Nat demanded to know by what arts Peter Blood had accomplished this deliverance so speedily and without violence.

'I'll not be saying there was no violence,' said Blood. 'There was, in fact, a deal of it. But it was violence of the emotions. And there's some more of the same kind to be borne yet. But that's for Mr Court.' He turned to the bo'sun who was standing by. 'Pipe the hands to quarters, Jake. We weigh at once.'

He went off to the cabin to which Mr Court was confined. He dismissed the guard posted at the door, and unlocked it. A very furious gentleman greeted him.

'How much longer do you keep me here, you damned scoundrel?'

'And where would you be going now?' wondered Captain Blood.

'Where would I be going? D'ye mock me, you cursed pirate? I'm going ashore, as you well know.'

'Do I, now? I wonder.'

'D'ye mean still to prevent me?'

'Faith, there may not be the need. I have a message for you from Sir James: a message and a book of poetry.'

Faithfully he delivered both. Mr Court changed colour, went limp, and sat down suddenly on a locker.

'Perhaps you'll be less eager now to land on Nevis. It may begin to occur to you that the West Indies are not the healthiest region for dalliance. Jealousy in the tropics can be like the climate--mighty hot and fierce. You'll wisely prefer, I should think, to find a ship somewhere that will carry you safely home to England.'

Mr Court wiped the perspiration from his brow

'Then you're not putting me ashore?'

The thudding of the capstan and the rattle of the anchor chain reached them through the open port of the cabin. Captain Blood's gesture drew attention to the sound.

'We are weighing now. We shall be at sea in half-an-hour.'

'Perhaps it's as well,' Mr Court resignedly admitted.

Episode 5

SACRILEGE

I

Never in the whole course of his outlawry did Captain Blood cease to regard it as distressingly ironical that he who was born and bred in the Romish Faith should owe his exile from England to a charge of having supported the Protestant Champion and should be regarded by Spain as a heretic who would be the better for a burning.

He expatiated at length and aggrievedly upon this to Yberville, his French associate, on a day when he was constrained by inherent scruples to turn his back upon a prospect of great and easy plunder to be made at the cost of a little sacrilege.

Yet Yberville, whose parents had hoped to make a churchman of him, and who had actually been in minor orders before circumstances sent him overseas and turned him into a filibuster instead, was left between indignation and amusement at scruples which he accounted vain. Amusement, however, won the day with him; for this tall and vigorous fellow, already inclining a little to portliness, was of as jovial and easy-going a nature as his humorous mouth and merry brown eye announced. Undoubtedly--although in the end he was to provoke derision by protesting it--a great churchman had been lost in him.

They had put into Bieque, and, ostensibly for the purpose of buying stores, Yberville had gone ashore to see what news might be gleaned that could be turned to account. For this was at a time when the *Arabella* was sailing at a venture, without definite object. A Basque who had spent some years across the border in Spain, Yberville spoke a fluent Castilian which enabled him to pass for a Spaniard when he chose, and so equipped him perfectly for this scouting task in a Spanish settlement.

He had come back to the big red-hulled ship at anchor in the roadstead, with the flag of Spain impudently flaunted from her maintruck, with news that seemed to him to indicate a likely enterprise. He had learnt that Don Ignacio de la Fuente, sometime Grand Inquisitor of Castile, and now appointed Cardinal-Archbishop of

New Spain, was on his way to Mexico on the eighty-gun galleon the *Santa Veronica,* and in passing was visiting the bishoprics of his province. His Eminence had been at San Salvador, and he was now reported on his way to San Juan de Puerto Rico, after which he was expected at San Domingo, perhaps at Santiago de Cuba, and certainly at Havana, before finally crossing to the Main.

Unblushingly Yberville disclosed the profit which his rascally mind conceived might be extracted from these circumstances.

'Next to King Philip himself,' he opined, 'or, at least, next to the Grand inquisitor, the Cardinal-Archbishop of Seville, there is no Spaniard living who would command a higher ransom than this Primate of New Spain.'

Blood checked in his stride. The two were pacing the high poop of the *Arabella* in the bright November sunshine of that region of perpetual summer. Yberville's tall vigour was still set off by the finery of lilac satin in which he had gone ashore, a purple love-knot in his long brown curls. Forward at the capstan and at the braces was the bustle of preparation to get the great ship under way; and in the forechains, Snell, the bo'sun, his bald pate gleaming in a circlet of untidy grey curls, was ordering in obscene and fragmentary Castilian some bumboats to stand off.

Blood's vivid eyes flashed disapproval upon the jovial countenance of his companion. 'What then?' he asked.

'Why, just that. The *Santa Veronica* carries a sacerdotal cargo as rich as the plate in any ship that ever came out of Mexico.' And he laughed.

But Blood did not laugh with him. 'I see. And it's your blackguardly notion that we should lay her board and board, and seize the Archbishop?'

'Just that, my faith! The place to lie in wait for the *Santa Veronica* would be the straits north of Saona. There we should catch his Eminence on his way to San Domingo. It should offer little difficulty.'

Under the shade of his broad hat Blood's countenance had become forbidding. He shook his head. 'That is not for us.'

'Not for us? Why not? Are you deterred by her eighty guns?'

'I am deterred by nothing but the trifle of sacrilege concerned. To lay violent hands on an archbishop, and hold him to ransom! I may be a sinner, God knows; but underneath it all I hope I'm a true son of the Church.'

'You mean a son of the true Church,' Yberville amended. 'I hope I'm no less myself, but not on that account would I make a scruple of holding a Grand Inquisitor to ransom.'

'Maybe not. But then you had the advantage of being bred in a seminary. That makes you free, I suppose, with holy things.'

Yberville laughed at the sarcasm. 'It makes me discriminate between the Faith of Rome and the Faith of Spain. Your Spaniard with his Holy House, his autos de fé and his faggots is very nearly a heretic in my eyes.'

'A sophistry, to justify the abduction of a Cardinal. But I'm not a sophist, Yberville, whatever else I may be. We'll keep out of sacrilege, so we will.'

Before the determination in his tone and face, Yberville fetched a sigh of resignation. 'Well, well! If that's your feeling. . . But it's a great chance neglected.'

And it was now that Captain Blood dilated upon the irony of his fate, until from the capstan to interrupt him came the bo'sun's cry: 'Belay there!' Then his whistle shrilled, and men swarmed aloft to let go the clewlines. The *Arabella* shook out her sails as a bird spreads its wings, and stood out for the open sea, to continue at a venture, without definite aim.

In leisurely fashion, with the light airs prevailing, they skimmed about the Virgin Islands, keeping a sharp look-out for what might blow into their range; but not until some three or four days later, when perhaps a score of miles to the south of Puerto Rico, did they sight a likely quarry. This was a small two-masted carack, very high in the poop, carrying not more than a dozen guns, and obviously a Spaniard, from the picture of Our Lady of Sorrows on the ballooning mainsail.

The *Arabella* shifted a point or two nearer to the wind, hoisted the Union Flag, and coming within range put a shot across the Spaniard's bows, as a signal to heave to.

Considering the presumed Englishman's heavy armament and superior sailing power, it is not surprising that the carack should have been prompt to obey that summons. But it was certainly a surprising contradiction to the decoration of her mainsail that simultaneously with her coming up into the wind the Cross of St George should break from her maintruck. After that she lowered a boat, and sent it speeding across the quarter-mile of gently ruffled sapphire water to the *Arabella.*

Out of his boat, a short, stockily built man, red of hair and of face, decently dressed in bottle green, climbed the Jacob's ladder of Blood's ship. With purposefulness in every line of him, he rolled forward on short, powerful legs towards Captain Blood, who, in a stateliness of black and silver, waited to receive him in the ship's waist. Blood was supported there by the scarcely less splendid Yberville, the giant Wolverstone, who had left an eye at Sedgemoor and boasted that with the one remaining he could see twice as much as any ordinary man, and Jeremy Pitt, the sailing-master of the *Arabella,* from whose entertaining chronicles we derive this account of the affair.

Pitt sums up this newcomer in a sentence. 'Not in all my life did I ever see a hotter man.' There was a scorching penetration in the glance of his small eyes under their beetling sandy brows as they raked his surroundings: the deck that was clean-scoured as a trencher, the gleaming brass of the scuttle butts and of the swivel-gun on the poop-rail, the orderly array of muskets in the rack about the mainmast. All may well have led him to suppose that he was aboard a King's ship.

Finally his questing hazel eyes returned to a second and closer inspection of the waiting group.

'My name is Walker,' he announced with a truculent air and in an accent that proclaimed a northern origin. 'Captain Walker. And I'll be glad to know who the devil you may be that ye're so poxy ready with your gunfire. If ye've put a shot athwart my bows 'cause o' they emblems o' Popery on my mains'l, supposing me a Spaniard, faith, then ye're just the men I be looking for.'

Blood was austere. 'If you are the captain of that ship, it's glad I'd be to learn how that comes to be the case.'

'Ay, ay. So ye may, ecod! It's a long tale, Cap'n, and an ugly.'

Blood took the hint. 'Come below,' he said, 'and let us have it.'

It was in the great cabin of the *Arabella* with its carved and gilded bulkheads, its hangings of green damask, its costly plate and books and pictures and other sybaritic equipment such as the rough little North Country seaman had never dreamed could be found under a ship's deck, that the tale was told. It was told to the four who had received this odd visitor, and after Blood had presented himself and his associates, thereby momentarily abating some of the little shipmaster's truculence. But he recovered all his heat and fury when they came to sit about the table, on which the negro steward had set Canary Sack and Nantes brandy and a jug of meg, and it roared in him as he related what he had endured.

He had sailed, he told them, from Plymouth, six months earlier, bound in the first instance for the Coast of Guinea, where he had taken aboard three hundred able-bodied young negroes, bought with beads and knives and axes from an African chieftain with whom he had already previously done several similar tradings. With this valuable cargo under hatches he was making his way to Jamaica, where a ready market awaited him, when, at the end of September, somewhere off the Bahamas, he was caught by an early storm, forerunner of the approaching hurricane season.

'By the mercy o' God we came through it afloat. But we was so battered and feckless that I had to jettison all my guns. Under the strain we had sprung a leak that kept us pumping for our lives; most o' my upper works was gone, and my mizzen was in such a state that I couldna' wi' safety ha' spread a night-shift on it. I must run to the nearest port for graving, and the nearest port happened to be Havana.

'When the port Alcalde had come aboard, seen for hisself my draggle-tailed condition, and that, anyway, wi'out guns I were toothless, as ye might say, he let me come into the shelter o' the lagoon, and there, without careening, we set about repairs.

'To pay for what we lacked I offered to trade the Alcalde some o' they blacks I carried. Now happen, as I was to learn, that the mines had been swept by a plague o' some kind--smallpox or yellow fever or summut--and they was mighty short o' slaves to work them. The Alcalde would buy the lot, he says, if I would sell. Seeing how it was with me, I were glad enough to lighten the ship by being rid o' the whole cargo, and I looked on the Alcalde's need as a crowning mercy to get me out of all my difficulties. But that weren't the end o' the windfall, as I supposed it. Instead o' gold, the Alcalde proposed to me that I takes payment in green hides, which, as ye may know, is the chief product of the island of Cuba. Naught could ha' suited me better, for I knew as I could sell the hides in England for three times the purchase price, and maybe a trifle over. So he gives me a bill o' lading for the hides, which it were agreed we should take aboard so soon as we was fit to sail.

'I pushed on wi' repairs, counting my fortune made, and looking on a voyage that at one time had seemed as if it must end in shipwreck, like to prove the most profitable as I had ever made.

'But I were reckoning without Spanish villainy. For when we was at last in case to put to sea again, and I sends word to the Alcalde that we was ready to load the hides of his bill of lading, the mate, which I had sent ashore, comes me back wi' a poxy message that the Captain-General--as they call the Governor in Cuba--would not allow the shipment, seeing as how it was against the law for any foreigner to trade in a Spanish settlement, and the Alcalde advised us to put to sea at once, whilst the Captain-General was in a mind to permit it.

'Ye'll maybe guess my feelings. Tom Walker, I may tell ye, bain't the man to let hisself be impudently robbed by anyone, whether pick-pocket or Captain-General. So I goes ashore myself. Not to the Alcalde. Oh no. I goes straight to the Captain-General hisself, a high-and-mighty Castilian grande, wi' a name as long as my arm. For short, they calls him Don Ruiz Perera de Valdoro y Peñascon, no less, and he's Count of Marcos too. A grande of the grandest.

'I slaps down my bill o' lading afore him, and tells him straightly how the thieving Alcalde had dealt by me, certain sure in my fecklessness that justice would be done at once.

'But from the way he shrugged and smiled I knew him for a villain afore ever he spoke. "Ye've been told the law, I believe," says he, wi' a leering curl to his mangy lip. "And ye've been rightly told. It is forbidden us by decree of His Catholic Majesty to buy from or sell to any foreign trader. The hides may not be shipped."

'It were a sour disappointment to me, seeing the profit on which I'd reckoned. But I keeps my temper to myself. "So be it," says I, "although it comes mighty hard on me and the law might ha' been thought of afore I were given this poxy bill o' lading. Howsomever, here it be; and ye can have it back in return for my three hundred negros."

'At that he scowls and tries to stare me down, twirling his moustachios the while. "God gi' me patience wi' you!" says he. "That transaction too were illegal. Ye had no right to trade your slaves here."

'"I traded them at the Alcalde's request, Excellency," I reminds him.

'"My friend," says he, "if you was to commit murder at someone else's request, would that excuse the crime?"

'"It's not me what's broke the law," says I, "but him which bought the slaves from me."

'"Ye're both guilty. Therefore, neither must profit. The slaves is confiscate to the State."

'Now, I've told ye, sirs, as how I was making no ado about suffering the loss of my lawful profit on the hides. But to be stripped naked, as it were, by that heuck-fingered Spanish gentleman, robbed o' a cargo o' blacks, the worth o' which I had agreed at ten thousand pieces of eight--Od rot my soul!--that was more nor I could stomach. My temper got the better o' me, and I ups and storms in a mighty rage at that fine Castilian nobleman--Don Ruiz Perera de Valdoro y Peñascon--crying shame on him for such iniquity, and demanding that at least he pay me in gold the price o' my slaves.

'The cool villain lets me rant myself out, then shows me his teeth again in another o' his wicked, fleering smiles.

'"My friend," says he, "ye've no cause to make this pother, no cause to complain at all. Why, you heretic fool, let me tell you as I am doing far less than my strict duty, which would be to seize your ship, your crew and your person, and send you to Cadiz or Seville there to purge the heresies wi' which your kind be troubling the world."'

Captain Walker paused there, to compose himself a little from the passion into which his memories had whipped him. He mopped his brow, and took a pull at the bumbo before resuming.

'Od rot me for a coward, but my courage went out o' me like sweat at they words. "Better be robbed," says I to myself, "than be cast into the Fires o' the Faith in a fool's coat." So I takes my leave of his Excellency afore his sense o' duty might get the better o' what he calls his compassion--damn his dirty soul!'

Again he paused, and then went on. 'Ye may be supposing that the end o' my trouble. But bide a while; for it weren't, nor yet the worst.

'I gets back aboard in haste, as ye'll understand. We weighs at once, and slips out to sea without no interference from the forts. But we've not gone above four or five miles, when on our heels comes a carack of a guarda-costa and opens fire on us as soon as ever she's within range. It's my belief she had orders from the muckety Captain-General to sink us. And for why? Because the talk of the Holy Office and the Fires of the Faith was so much bluster. The last thing as that thief would wish would be as they should find out in Spain the ways by which he is becoming rich in the New World.

'Howsomever, there was the guarda-costa, pumping round-shot into us as fast and hard as bad Spanish gunnery could contrive it. Without guns as we was it were easy as shooting woodcock. Or so they thought. But, having the weather-gauge o' them, I took the only chance left us. I put the helm hard over, and ran straight for her. Not a doubt but those muck-scutcheons counted on shooting us to pieces afore ever we could reach her, and, on my soul, they all but did. We was sinking fast, leaking like a colander, wi' our decks awash when at last we bumps alongside o' her. But by the mercy o' God to heretics, what were left o', my poor ship got a hold on that guarda-costa's timbers wi' her grapnels, what time we climbs aboard her. After that it were red hell on they decks, for we was all mad wi' rage at those cold-blooded murderers. From stem to stern we swept her wi' cold steel. I had five men killed and a half-score wounded; but the only Spaniards left alive was them as went overboard to drown.'

The slaver paused again, and his fiery eye flung a glance of challenge at his audience. 'That's about all, I think. We kept the carack, of course, my own ship being sunk, and that'll explain they emblems o' Popery on our mainsail. I knew as they'ld bring us trouble afore long. And yet, when, as I supposed, it was on account o' they that ye put a shot athwart my hawse, it came to me that maybe I had found a friend.'

II

The tale was told, and the audience, thrilled and moved by it, sat in silence a while, still under the spell of it after Walker had ceased to speak.

It was Wolverstone, at last, who stirred and growled. 'As ugly a story as I've heard of Castilian subtlety. That Captain-General would be the better for a keel-hauling.'

'Better still for a roasting over a slow fire,' said Yberville. 'It's the only way to give savour to this New Christian pig.'

Blood looked at him across the table. 'New Christian?' he echoed. 'You know him, then?'

'No more than you.' And the sometime seminarist explained. 'In Spain when a Jew is received into the Church he must take a new name. But his choice is not entirely free. The name he takes must be the name of a tree or plant, or the like, so that the source of his house may still be known. This Captain-General bears the name of Perera: Pear tree. The Valdaro and Peñascon have been subsequently added. They are always the readiest, these renegadoes, with threats of the Fires of the Faith.'

Blood gave his attention once more to Captain Walker.

'You'll have a purpose, sir, in giving yourself the trouble of telling us this nasty tale. What service do you seek of us?'

'Why, just a spare set o' sails, if so be ye have them, as I'm supposing ye will. I'll pay you what they're worth; for, burn me, it's inviting trouble to try to cross the ocean with those I carry.'

'And is that all, now! Faith, it was in my mind ye might be asking us to recover the value of your slaves from this Captain-General of Havana, with perhaps just a trifle over for our trouble in the interests of poetic justice. Havana is a wealthy city.'

Walker stared at him. 'Ye're laughing at me, Captain. I know better than to ask the impossible.'

'The impossible!' said Blood, with a lift of his black brows. Then he laughed. 'On my soul, it's almost like a challenge.'

'No challenge at all. Ye'll be bonny fighters, like enough; but the devil himself wouldn't venture to sail a buccaneer ship into Havana.'

'Ah!' Blood rubbed his chin. 'Yet this fellow needs a lesson, bad cess to him. And to rob a thief is a beckoning adventure.' He looked at his associates. 'Will we be paying him a visit, now?'

Pitt's opposition was immediate. 'Not unless we've taken leave of our senses. You don't know Havana, Peter. If there's a Spanish harbour in the New World that may be called impregnable, that harbour is Havana. In all the Caribbean there are no defences more formidable, as Drake discovered already in his day.'

'And that's the fact,' said Walker, whose red eye had momentarily gleamed at Blood's words. 'The place is an arsenal. The entrance is by a channel not more than half a mile across, with three forts, no less, to defend it: the Moro, the Puntal, and El Fuerte. Ye wouldn't stay afloat an hour there.'

Blood's eyes were dreamy. 'Yet you stayed afloat some days.'

'Ay, man. But the circumstances.'

'Glory be, now. Couldn't we be contriving circumstances? It wouldn't be the first time. The thing needs thought, and it's worth thinking about with no other enterprise to engage us.'

'That,' said Yberville, who had never been able to reconcile himself to the neglect of the opportunity presented by the voyage of the Archbishop, 'is only because you're mawkish. The Primate of the New World is still at sea. Let him pay for the sins of his countrymen. His ransom need be no less than the plunder of Havana would yield us, and we could include in it compensation for Captain Walker for the slaves of which they've robbed him.'

'Faith, ye have it,' said Wolverstone, who, being a heretic, was undaunted by any thought of sacrilege. 'It's like burning candles to Satan to be delicate with a Spaniard just because he's an archbishop.'

'And it need not end there,' said Pitt, that other heretic, in a glow of sudden inspiration. 'If we had the Archbishop in the hold, we could sail into Havana without fear of their forts. They'ld never dare to fire on a ship that housed his holiness.'

Blood was pensively toying with a curl of his black periwig. He smiled introspectively. 'I was thinking that same.'

'So!' crowed Yberville. 'Religious scruples begin to yield to reason. Heaven be praised.'

'Faith, now, I'll not say that it might not be worth a trifle of sacrilege--just a trifle, mark you--to squeeze his plunder out of this rogue of a Captain-General. Yes, I think it might be done.' He got up suddenly. 'Captain Walker, if ye've a mind to come with us on this venture and seek to recover what ye've lost, ye'd best be scuttling that guarda-costa and fetching your hands aboard the *Arabella.* Ye can trust us to provide you with a ship to take you home when this is over.'

'Man!' cried the tough little slaver, all the natural fierceness of him sunk fathoms deep in his amazement. 'Ye're not serious?'

'Not very,' said Captain Blood. 'It's just a whim of mine. But a whim that is like to cost this Don What's-his-name Perera dear. So you can come with us to Havana, and take your chance of sailing home again in a tall ship with a full cargo of hides, your fortunes restored, or you can have the set of sails ye're asking for, and go home empty-handed. The choice is yours.'

Looking up at him almost in awe, Captain Walker yielded at once to the vigorous vitality and full-blooded confidence of the buccaneer. The adventurous spirit in him answered to the call. No risk, he swore, was too great that offered a chance to wipe off the score against that forsworn Captain-General.

Yberville, however, was frowning. 'But the Archbishop, then?'

Blood smiled with tight lips. 'The Archbishop certainly. We can do nothing without the Archbishop.' He turned to Pitt with an order that showed how fully he had already resolved not only upon what was to do, but upon how it should be done. 'Jerry you'll lay me a course for Sainte Croix.'

'Why that?' quoth Yberville. 'It's much farther east than we need to go for his Eminence.'

'To be sure it is. But one thing at a time. There's some gear we'll be needing, and Sainte Croix is the place to provide it.'

III

They did not, after all, scuttle the Spanish carack, as Captain Blood proposed. The thrifty nature of the little North Country seaman revolted at the thought of such waste, whilst his caution desired to know how he and his hands were ever to get back to England if Blood's scheme should, after all, miscarry even in part and no such tall ship as he promised should be forthcoming.

For the rest, however, the events followed the course that Captain Blood laid down. Steering in a north-easterly direction, the *Arabella,* with the guarda-costa following, came a couple of days later to the French settlement of Sainte Croix, of which the buccaneers were free. Forty-eight hours they remained there, and Captain Blood, with Yberville and the bald-headed little bo'sun, Snell, who knew his way about every port of the Caribbean, spent most of the time ashore.

Then, leaving the carack to await their return, Walker and his hands transferred themselves to the *Arabella.* She set sail, and laid a westward course once more, in the direction of Puerto Rico. After that she was seen no more until a fortnight later, when her great red hull was sighted off the undulating green hills of the northern coast of Cuba.

In the genial, comparatively temperate airs of that region she sailed along those fertile shores, and so came at last to the entrance of the lagoon on which Havana stood in a majesty of limestone palaces, of churches, monasteries, squares, and market-places that might have been transported bodily from Old Castile to the New World.

Scanning the defences as they approached, Blood realized for himself how little either Walker or Jeremy Pitt had exaggerated their massive strength. The mighty Moro Fort, with its sullen bastions and massive towers, occupied a rocky eminence at the very mouth of the channel; opposite to it stood the Puntal, with its demi-lunar batteries; and facing the entrance loomed El Fuerte, no less menacing. Whatever might have been the strength of the place in the time of Drake, he would be rash, indeed, who would run the gauntlet of those three formidable guardians now.

The *Arabella* hove to in the roadstead, announced herself by firing a gun as a salute, hoisted the Union flag, and awaited events.

They followed soon in the shape of a ten-oared barge, from under the awning of which stepped the Alcalde of the port, Walker's old friend, Don Hieronimo. He puffed his way up the Jacob's ladder, and came aboard to inquire into the purpose of this ship in these waters.

Captain Blood, in a splendour of purple and silver, received him in the waist, attended by Pitt and Wolverstone. A dozen half-naked seamen hovered above the trim decks, and a half dozen more were aloft clewing up the royals.

Nothing could have exceeded the courtliness with which the Alcalde was made welcome. Blood, who announced himself casually as on his way to Jamaica with a valuable cargo of slaves, had been, he said, constrained by lack of wood and water to put in at Havana. He would depend upon the kindliness and courtesy of the Alcalde for these and also for some fresh victuals for which they would be the better, and he would gladly pay in gold for what they took.

The black-coated Don Hieronimo, pasty-faced and flabby, some five and a half feet high and scarcely less round the belly, with the dewlap of an ox, was not to be seduced by the elegant exterior or courteous phrases of any damned heretical foreigner. He responded coldly, his expression one of consequential malevolence, whilst his shrewd black eyes scoured every corner of those decks suspiciously. Thus until the slaves were mentioned. Then a curious change took place; a measure of affability overspread his forbidding surliness. He went so far as to display his yellow teeth in a smile.

To be sure the Señor Captain could purchase whatever he required in Havana. To be sure he was at liberty to enter the port when he pleased, and then not a doubt but that the bumboats would be alongside and able to supply all that he lacked. If not, the Alcalde would be happy to afford him every facility ashore.

Upon these assurances the seaman at the whipstaff was ordered to put down the helm, and Pitt's clear voice rang out in command to the men at the braces to let go and haul. Catching the breeze again, the *Arabella* crept forward past those formidable forts, with the Alcalde's barge in tow, what time the Alcalde with ever-increasing affability was slyly seeking to draw from Captain Blood some information touching this cargo of slaves in his hold. But so vague and lethargic was Captain Blood upon the subject, that in the end, Don Hieronimo was forced to come out into the open and deal frankly.

'I may seem persistent in questioning you about these slaves,' he said. 'But that is because it occurs to me that if you choose, you need not be at the cost of carrying them to Jamaica. You would find a ready market for them here in Havana.'

'In Havana?' Blood raised his eyebrows. 'But is it not against the laws of His Catholic Majesty?'

The Alcalde pursed his thick, dusky lips. 'The law was made when there was no thought for our present difficulties. There has been a scourge of smallpox in the mines, and we are short of hands. Of necessity we must waive the law. If, then, you would care to trade, sir captain, there is no obstacle.'

'I see,' said Blood, without enthusiasm.

'And the prices will be good,' added Don Hieronimo, so as to stir him from his lethargy. 'In fact, they will be unusual.'

'So are my slaves. Very unusual.'

'And that's the fact,' Wolverstone confirmed him in his halting Spanish. 'They'll cost you dear, Señor Alcalde. Though I don't suppose ye'll grudge the price when you've had a look at them.'

'If I might see them,' begged the Spaniard.

'Oh, but why not?' was Blood's ready agreement.

The *Arabella* had come by now through the bottle-neck into the great blue lagoon that is the Bay of Havana, a full three miles across. The leadsman in the forechains was calling the fathoms, and it occurred to Blood that it might be prudent to go no farther. He turned aside for a moment, to order Pitt to anchor where they stood, well away from the forest of masts and spars reared by the shipping over against the town. Then he came back to the Alcalde.

'If you will follow me, Don Hieronimo,' said he, and led the way to a scuttle.

By a short narrow ladder they dropped to the main-deck below, where the gloom was shot by shafts of sunlight from the open gunports, crossed by others from the gratings overhead. The Alcalde looked along that formidable array of cannon, and at the lines of hammocks slung behind them on either side, in some of which men were even now reposing.

Stooping to avoid the stanchions in that shallow place, he followed his tall leader aft, and was followed in turn by the massive Wolverstone. Presently Blood paused, and turned, to ask a curious question.

'Does it happen, sir, that you are acquainted with the Cardinal-Archbishop Don Ignacio de la Fuente, the new Primate of New Spain?'

'Not yet, sir. He has not yet reached Havana. But we look daily now for the honour of receiving him.'

'It may be yours even sooner than you think.'

'But not sooner than we hope. What, sir, do you know of the Cardinal-Archbishop's voyage?'

Blood, however, had already resumed his progress aft, and did not answer him.

They came at last to the door of the wardroom, which was guarded by two musketeers. A muffled sound of chanting, Gregorian of character, which had mystified the Alcalde as they approached, was now so distinct that as they halted he could even distinguish the words of that droned supplication:

'Hostem repellas longius
Pacemque dones protinus;
Ductore sic te praevio
Vitemus omne noxium.'

He frowned, and stared up at Blood. 'Por Dios! Are they your slaves who sing?'

'They appear to find consolation in it.'

Don Hieronimo was suspicious without knowing what to suspect. Something here was not as it should be. 'Oddly devout, are they not?' said he.

'Certainly devout. Not oddly.'

At a sign from him, one of the musketeers had unbarred the door, and as he now flung it wide, the chanting abruptly broke off on the word 'Saeculorum'. The Amen to that hymn was never uttered.

Ceremoniously Blood waved the Alcalde forward. In haste to resolve this riddle, Don Hieronimo stepped boldly and quickly across the threshold, and there abruptly checked, at gaze with horror-stricken, bulging eyes.

In the spacious but sparsely furnished ward-room, invaded by the smell of bilge-water and spunyam, and lighted by a window astern, he beheld a dozen men in the white woollen habit and black cloak of the order of St Dominic. In two rows they sat, silent and immovable as lay-figures, their hands folded within their wide sleeves, their heads bowed and cowled, all save one who stood uncovered and as if in immediate attendance upon a stately figure that sat apart, enthroned on a tall chair. A tall, handsome man of perhaps forty, he was from head to foot a flame of scarlet. A scarlet skullcap covered the tonsure to be presumed in his flowing locks of a rich brown that was almost auburn; a collar of finest point adorned the neck of his silken cassock; a gold cross gleamed on his scarlet breast. His very hands were gloved in red, and on the annular finger of his right flashed the episcopal sapphire, worn over his glove. His calm and the austerity in which he was enveloped lent him a dignity of aspect almost superhuman.

His handsome eyes surveyed the gross fellow who had so abruptly and unceremoniously stumbled into that place. But their lofty calm remained unperturbed. It was as if he left human passions to lesser mortals, such as a bare-headed, red-faced, rather bibulous-looking friar behind him, a man, relieved by nature from recourse to the tonsuring razor, whose hairless pate rose brown and gleaming from a crown of grey, greasy curls. A very human brother, this, to judge by the fierce scowl with which he surveyed the intruder.

Forcibly Captain Blood thrust forward the palsied Alcalde, so as to gain room to enter. Hat in hand, he stepped past him some little way, then turned to beckon him forward.

But before he could speak, the Alcalde, apoplectic and out of breath, was demanding to know what this might mean.

Blood was smilingly bland before that indignation. 'Is it not plain? I understand your surprise. But you'll remember that I warned you that my slaves are unusual.'

'Slaves? These?' The Alcalde seemed to choke. 'For sale? In God's name, who are you that you dare so impious, so infernal a jest?'

'I am called Blood, sir. Captain Blood.' And he added, with a bow, 'To serve you.'

'Blood!' The black eyes grew almost invisible in that congested countenance. 'You are Captain Blood? You are that endemonized pirate out of hell?'

'That is how Spain describes me. But Spain is prejudiced. Leave that, sir, and come.' Again he beckoned him, and what he said confirmed the Alcalde's worst fearful suspicions. 'Let me have the honour of presenting you to His Eminence the

Cardinal-Archbishop Don Ignacio de la Fuente, the Primate of New Spain. I told you that it might be yours to welcome him sooner than you thought.'

'God of mercy!' gurgled the Alcalde.

Stately as a Court usher, Blood advanced a pace, and bowed low to the Cardinal. 'Eminence, condescend to receive a poor sinner who is, nevertheless, a person of some consequence in these parts: the Alcalde of the port of Havana.'

At the same moment Don Hieronimo was thrust violently forward by the herculean arm of Wolverstone, who bawled after him: 'On your knees, sir, to ask a blessing of his Eminence.'

The prelate's calm, inscrutable, deep-set eyes were considering the horrified officer who was now on his knees before him.

'Eminence!' gasped Don Hieronimo, almost in tears. 'Eminence!'

As steady as the glance was the deep, rich voice that murmured: 'Pax tibi, filius meus,' whilst in slow majesty the hand that bore the cardinalitial ring was extended to be kissed.

Faltering 'Eminence!' yet again, the Alcalde fell upon it and bore it to his mouth as if he would eat it. 'What horror!' he wailed. 'My God, what horror! What sacrilege!'

A smile infinitely wistful, infinitely compassionate and saintly broke upon the prelate's handsome face. 'We offer up these ills for our sins, my son, thankful, since that is so, that they are given us to endure. We are for sale, it seems, I and these poor brethren of St Dominic who accompany me and share my duress at the hands of our heretical captors. We must pray for grace to bear it with becoming fortitude, remembering that those great Apostles St Peter and St Paul also suffered incarceration in the fulfilment of their sacred missions.'

Don Hieronimo was scrambling to his feet, moving sluggishly not only from his obesity but also from overpowering emotion. 'But how could such a horror come to pass?' he groaned.

'Let it not distress you, my son, that I should be a prisoner in the hands of this poor, blind heretic.'

'Three errors in three words, Eminence,' was Blood's comment. 'Behold how easy is error, and let it serve as a warning against hasty judgements when you are called upon to judge, as presently you shall be. I am not poor. I am not blind. I am not a heretic. I am a true son of Mother Church. And if I have reluctantly laid violent hands upon your Eminence, it was not only so that you might be a hostage for the righting of a monstrous wrong that has been done in the name of the Catholic King and the Holy Faith, but so that in your wisdom and piety you might, yourself, deliver judgement upon the deed and the doer.'

Through his teeth the bareheaded, red-faced little friar, leaning forward and snarling like a terrier, uttered three words of condemnation. 'Perro hereje maldito!'

Instantly the Cardinal's gloved hand was raised imperiously to rebuke and restrain him. 'Peace, Frey Domingo!

'I spoke, sir, of poverty and blindness of the spirit, not of the flesh,' he quietly answered Blood, and continued, addressing him in the second person singular, as if more signally to mark the gulf between them: 'For in that sense poor and blind thou art.' He sighed. More sternly still he added: 'That thou shouldst confess thyself a son of the True Church is but to confess this outrage more scandalous than I had supposed it.'

'Suspend your judgement, Eminence, until all my motive is disclosed,' said Blood, and taking a step or two in the direction of the open door he raised his voice to call. 'Captain Walker!'

In answer, a bow-legged, red-haired little man, all fire and truculence, advanced with a rolling gait to nod curtly to the scarlet presence, and then, arms akimbo, to confront the Alcalde.

'Good day to you, Don Ladrin, which is what I calls you. You'ld not be expecting to see me again so soon, ye murdering villain. Ye didna know maybe that an English sailor has as many lives as a cat. I've come back for my hides, ye thief. My hides, and my tall ship as your rascals sank under me.'

If anything at that moment could have added to the Alcalde's distress and rage and to the confusion of his wits this reappearance of Captain Walker certainly supplied it. Yellow-faced and shaking from head to foot, he stood gasping and mouthing, desperately seeking words in which to answer. But Captain Blood gave him little time to strain his wits.

'So now, Don Hieronimo, perhaps you begin to understand,' he said. 'We are here in quest of restitution of what was stolen, of reparation for a crime. And for this his Eminence there is no more than a hostage in our hands.

'I will not trouble you to restore the hides out of which you and your Captain-General between you swindled this poor seaman. But you'll pay in gold the price they would have fetched in England; that is twenty thousand pieces of eight. And you'll provide a ship of a burthen at least equal to that which your guarda-costa sank by orders of your Captain-General, this ship to be of not less than twenty guns, all found, armed and victualled for a voyage. Time enough, when that is done, to discuss putting his Eminence ashore.'

There was a streak of blood on the Alcalde's chin, from the wound his teeth had made in his lip. Yet frenzied though he might be by impotent rage, yet he was not so blinded but that he perceived that the guns of the mighty forts of Havana, and of the Admiral's squadron within range of which this pirate vessel impudently rode at anchor, were powerless against her whilst the sacred person of the Primate of New Spain was in her hold. Similarly to attempt to take her by assault must be fraught by a like deadly peril for the Cardinal at the hands of men so desperate and bloody as these. At whatever cost, his Eminence must be delivered, and this with the least delay. In all the circumstances it was perhaps a matter for thankfulness that the pirate's demands should be as modest as they were.

He strove for dignity, drew himself up and thrust out his paunch, and spoke to Blood in the tone of a man addressing his lackey. 'I do not parley with you. I will inform his Excellency the Captain-General.' He turned to the Cardinal, with a change to utmost humility. 'Give me leave, Eminence, accepting my assurance that you will not be allowed to remain in this scandalous duress one moment longer than may be avoidable. Give me leave.' He bowed very low, and would have withdrawn. But the Cardinal gave him no such leave just yet. He had been listening with obvious attention to what passed.

'Wait, sir. Wait. There is something here that I do not understand.' A puzzled frown stood between his brows. 'This man speaks of restitution, of reparation. Has he the right to use such words?'

It was Blood who answered him. 'I desire your Eminence to be the judge of that. That is the judgement to which I alluded. It is so that you may deliver it that I have ventured to lay hands upon your sacred person, for which I shall hope for your absolution in the end.' Thereupon, in a dozen crisp, incisive sentences, he sketched the tale of the robbery of Captain Walker under the cloak of legal justification.

When he had done the Cardinal looked at him with scorn, and from him turned to the fuming Alcalde. His gentle voice was warm with indignation.

'That tale of course is false. Impossible. It does not deceive me. No Castilian man of honour placed by His Catholic Majesty in authority could be guilty of such turpitude. You hear, sir Alcalde, how this misguided pirate imperils his immortal soul by bearing false witness.'

The perspiring Alcalde's answer did not come as promptly as his Eminence expected it. 'But is it possible that you hesitate?' he asked, as if startled, leaning forward.

Desperately Don Hieronimo broke into stumbling speech. 'It is that. . . Dios mio! The tale is grossly exaggerated. It--'

'Exaggerated!' The gentle voice was suddenly and sharply raised. 'Exaggerated? Not wholly false, then?'

The only answer he received was a cringing hunch of the Alcalde's shoulders and a glance that fell in fear under the prelate's stern eyes.

The Cardinal-Archbishop sank back into his chair, his face inscrutable, his voice of an ominous quiet.

'You have leave to go. You will request the Captain-General of Havana to wait upon me here in person. I require to know more of this.'

'He . . . he may require safe-conduct,' stuttered the unfortunate Alcalde.

'It is granted him,' said Captain Blood.

'You hear? I shall expect him at the earliest.' And the scarlet hand with its sapphire ring majestically waved Don Hieronimo away.

Daring no more, the Alcalde bowed himself double and went out backwards as if from a royal presence.

IV

If the tale borne by Don Hieronimo to the Captain-General, of Captain Blood's outrageous and sacrilegious violence to the Cardinal-Archbishop of New Spain filled Don Ruiz with amazement, dismay, and horrified indignation, the summons on which it concluded, and the reasons for it, supplied a stimulus that presently moved his Excellency to almost superhuman activity. If he delayed four hours in answering in person that summons, at least the answer that he then delivered was of such a fullness that it would have taken an ordinary Spaniard in ordinary circumstances as many days to have prepared it.

His conscience shaken into uneasiness by what his subordinate told him, Don Ruiz Perera de Valdoro y Peñascon, who was also Count of Marcos, deemed it well to omit in the Cardinal-Archbishop's service no effort that might be calculated to conciliate his Eminence. It occurred to him, naturally enough, that nothing could be more conciliatory, nothing would be more likely to put the Cardinal in a good humour with him, than if he were to present himself in the role of his Eminence's immediate deliverer from the hands of that abominable pirate who held him captive.

Therefore by exertions unprecedented in all his experience Don Ruiz so contrived that in seeking the Cardinal-Archbishop aboard the *Arabella* he was actually able to fulfil all the conditions upon which he understood that Captain Blood had consented to restore his prisoner to liberty. So great an achievement must fill the Primate with a wonder and gratitude that would leave no room for petty matters.

Thus, then, it fell out almost incredibly that when some four hours after the Alcalde's departure from the *Arabella* the Captain-General came alongside in his barge, a broad-beamed, two-masted, square-rigged brigantine was warped to a station a cable's length from the buccaneer's larboard quarter. In addition to this, Don Ruiz, who climbed the ladder with the Alcalde in close attendance, was followed by two alguaziles, each of whom shouldered a wooden coffer of some weight.

Captain Blood had taken his precautions against treachery. His gun-ports had been opened on the larboard side, and twenty threatening muzzles had been run out. As his Excellency stepped down into the waist, his contemptuous eyes saw the bulwarks lined by men, some half naked, some fully clothed, and some actually in armour, but all with muskets poised and matches glowing.

A tall, narrow-faced gentleman with a bold nose, Don Ruiz came dressed as was demanded by an occasion of such ceremony. He was magnificent in gold-laced black. He wore the cross of St James on his breast, and a gold-hilted sword swung at his side. He carried a long cane in one hand and a gold-edged handkerchief in the other.

Under his little black moustachios his thin lips curled in disdain as he acknowledged the bow with which Captain Blood received him. The deepening sallowness of his face bore witness to the wicked humour upon which he strove to set that mask of lofty contempt.

He delivered himself without preamble. 'Your impudent conditions are fulfilled, Sir Pirate. There is the ship you have demanded, and here in these coffers is the gold--the twenty thousand pieces. It is now for you to keep your part of the bargain struck, and so make an end of the sacrilegious infamy of which you have been guilty.'

Without answering him, Captain Blood turned and beckoned forward the little North-Country shipmaster from the background, where he stood glowering at Don Ruiz.

'You hear, Captain Walker.' He pointed to the coffers, which the alguaziles had set down upon the hatch-coaming. 'There, says his Excellency, is your gold. Verify it, then take it, put your men aboard that brigantine, spread your sails, and be off whilst I am still here to make your departure safe.'

For a moment amazement and emotion before such munificence rendered the little slaver dumb. Then speech bubbled out of him in a maudlin gush of wonder and gratitude which Blood made haste to stem.

'It's wasting good time ye are, my friend. Sure, don't I know all that: that I'm great and noble and that it was the lucky day for you when I put a shot athwart your hawse? Away with you now, and say a good word for Peter Blood in England when ye get there.'

'But this gold,' Walker still protested. 'Ye'll take the half of it at least?'

'Och, now! What's a trifle of gold? I'll know how to repay myself for my trouble, ye may be sure. Gather your hands and be off, and God be with you, my friend.'

When at last he had wrenched his fingers from the crushing grip into which the slaver packed all the emotion that he could not properly utter, Blood gave his attention to Don Ruiz, who had stood aloof with the Alcalde, disdainful of eye and lip.

'If you will follow me, I will conduct you to his Eminence.'

He led the way below, and Pitt and Wolverstone went with them.

In the ward-room, at sight of that majestic figure, glittering in scarlet splendour against the humble monkish background, Don Ruiz, with an inarticulate cry, ran forward to cast himself upon his knees.

'Benedictus sis,' murmured the Primate, and gave him his ring to kiss.

'My lord! Eminence! That these incarnate devils should have subjected your saintliness to such indignity!'

'That is not important, my son,' said the gentle, musical voice. 'By me and these my brethren in Christ suffering is accepted thankfully, as something of which to make an offering to the Throne of Grace. What is important, what gives me deep concern, is the reason pretexted for it, which I learned only this morning here. I have been told, Lord Count, that in the King's name delivery was refused of merchandise that had been sold to an English seaman, that the moneys he had already paid, as the price of that merchandise, were confiscated, that he was driven empty away with threats of prosecution by the Holy Office, and that even when, thus robbed, he had departed, his ship was pursued and sunk by one of your guarda-costas.

'These things I have heard, my son; but although your Alcalde did not contradict them, I must refuse to believe that a gentleman of Spain and a representative of His Catholic Majesty in these parts could be guilty of such conduct.'

Don Ruiz got to his feet. Sallower than ever was his narrow face. But he contrived that his tone should be easy and his manner imposing. By a certain loftiness he hoped to wave the matter away.

'That is all overpast, Eminence. If error there was, it has now been corrected, and with generous interest, as this buccaneer captain will bear me witness. I am here to give myself the honour of escorting your Eminence ashore to the joyous welcome that awaits you and the great reception which expectant Havana has been preparing for some weeks.'

But his ingratiatory smile found no reflection in the Primate's lofty countenance. It remained overcast, sadly grave. 'Ah! You admit the error, then. But you do not explain it.'

Choleric by nature and imperious from long habit of command, the Captain-General was momentarily in danger of forgetting that he stood in the presence of one who was virtually the Pope of the New World, a man whose powers there were inferior only to the King's, and before whom in certain matters even the King, himself, must bow. Although he remembered it in time, a hint of tartness still invested his reply.

'Explanation must prove tedious to your Lordship, and perhaps obscure, since these are matters concerned with my legal office. Your Eminence's great and renowned enlightenment will scarcely cover what is a matter of jurisprudence.'

The most wistful of smiles broke upon that handsome face. 'You are indifferently informed, I fear, Don Ruiz. You can never have heard that I have held the exalted office of Grand Inquisitor of Castile, or you would know--since it must follow--that I am a doctor not only of canon, but also of civil law. Be under no apprehension, then, that I shall fail to follow your legal exposition of the event, and even less on the score of tedium. Many of my duties are tedious, my son; but they are not on that account avoided.'

To that cold, relentless insistence the Captain-General saw himself under the necessity of submitting. He swallowed his annoyance, steadied himself, and provided himself with a scapegoat who would not dare, on his life, to deny him.

'In brief, Eminence, these transactions were permitted without my knowledge by my Alcalde.' The audible gasp from Don Hieronimo, who stood behind him, did not deter his Excellency. He went steadily on. 'When I learned of them, I had no choice but to cancel them, since it is my duty to insist upon the law which forbids all foreigners to trade in His Catholic Majesty's dominions.'

'With that there could be no quarrel. But I understand that this English seaman had already paid for the merchandise.'

'He had traded slaves for them, Eminence.'

'No matter what he had traded. Were his slaves restored to him when the transaction was cancelled by you?'

'The laws which he defied when he traded them decreed their confiscation likewise.'

'Ordinarily that might be so. But this, if I am rightly informed, is no ordinary case. I am told that he was urged to trade his slaves by your Alcalde.'

'Just as I,' Blood interposed, 'was urged by him this morning to trade mine.' And the sweep of his hand indicated the Cardinal-Archbishop and his attendant monks.

'He does not learn by his errors, then, this Alcalde of yours. Perhaps you do not desire that he shall.'

Ostentatiously Don Ruiz turned his shoulder upon Blood, ignoring him. 'Your Eminence cannot account me bound by the illegality of a subordinate.' Then permitting himself a little smile, he added the sophism which he had already used with Captain Walker. 'If a man commit murder it cannot exculpate him to say that he had the sanction of another.'

'That is to be subtle, is it not? I must take thought upon this, Don Ruiz. We will talk of it again.'

Don Ruiz bowed low, his lip in his teeth. 'At your Eminence's disposal,' he said. 'Meanwhile, my barge is waiting to carry your Eminence ashore.'

The Cardinal rose, imposingly tall in his robes, and drew his scarlet cloak about him. The cowled Dominicans, who had stood like statues, stirred responsively into life. His Eminence turned to them.

'Be mindful, my children, to return thanks for this safe deliverance. Let us go.'

And he stepped forward, to be checked at once by Captain Blood. 'Patience yet awhile, Eminence. All is not done.'

The Cardinal threw up his head, a frown darkening his brow. 'How? What, then, remains?'

Blood's answer was delivered rather to the scowling Captain-General than to the prelate. 'So far we have had no more than restitution. Come we now to the question of compensations.'

'Compensations!' cried the Primate, and for once the splendid calm of him was ruffled. Sternly he added the questions:

'What is this? Do you break faith sir?'

'That, at least, has never yet been said of me. I break no faith. On the contrary, I am punctilious. What I told the Alcalde was that when restitution was made we would discuss the matter of your Eminence's landing. That we would discuss it. No more than that.'

Don Ruiz smiled in rage and malice, a smile that displayed his white teeth. 'Ingenious. Yes. And then, you brigand?'

'I could not without disrespect to his Eminence, the Primate of New Spain, set his ransom at less than a hundred thousand ducats.'

Don Ruiz sucked in his breath. He went livid. His jaw fell loose. 'A hundred thousand ducats!'

'That is today. Tomorrow I may not be so modest.'

The Captain-General in his fury swung to the Cardinal, his gestures wild. 'Your Eminence hears what this thief now demands?'

But the Cardinal, having now resumed his unworldly calm, was not again to be shaken from it. 'Patience, my son. Patience! Let us beware the mortal sin of anger, which will scarcely hasten my release for the apostolic labours that await me in Havana.'

It would have needed a great deal more than this to bring Don Ruiz to yield had not the very fury that now possessed him, craving an orgy of vengeance, shown him the way. Trembling a little in his suppressed wrath, yet he was sufficiently master of himself to bow as if to an order, and to promise in comparatively civil terms that the money should at once be forthcoming, in order that his Eminence's deliverance should be procured at the earliest moment.

V

But in his barge as he was returning to shore with the Alcalde, the Captain-General betrayed the fact that it was not the deliverance of the Cardinal-Archbishop that spurred him so much as his eagerness to crush this impudent pirate who defeated him at his own game.

'The fool shall have the gold, so that destruction may overtake him.'

Gloomily the Alcalde shook his head. 'It's a terrible price to pay God of my life! A hundred thousand pieces!'

'There's no help for that.' Almost Don Ruiz implied by his manner that he accounted cheap at the price the destruction of a man who had brought him to such humiliation that he, the Captain-General of Havana, lord of life and death in those parts, had been made to look no better than a schoolboy standing to be birched. 'Nor is it so exorbitant. The Admiral of the Ocean-Sea is willing to pay fifty thousand pieces for the head of Captain Blood. I but double it--out of the royal Treasury.'

'But what the Marquis of Riconete pays would not be lost. Whilst this will be sunk with that scoundrel.'

'But perhaps not beyond recovery. It depends upon where we sink him. Where he's anchored now there's not above four fathoms, and it's all shallow on that side as far as the bar. But that's no matter. What matters is to get the Cardinal-Archbishop out of that ship, so as to put an end to this cursed dog's immunity.'

'Are you so sure that it will end then? That sly devil will demand pledges, oaths.'

Don Ruiz laughed savagely from livid lips. 'He shall have them. All the pledges, all the oaths that he requires. An oath sworn under constraint has never been accounted binding on any man.'

But the Alcalde's gloom was not relieved. 'That will not be his Eminence's view.'

'His Eminence?'

'Can you doubt that this damned pirate will ask a pledge from him--a pledge of safe-conduct for himself? You've seen the man this Cardinal is: a narrow, bigoted zealot, a slave to the letter of a contract. It's an ill thing to set up priests as judges. They're so unfitted for the office. There's no humanity in them, no breadth of understanding. What this prelate swears, that he will do; no matter where or how the oath may have been exacted.'

For a moment dismay darkened still further the Captain-General's soul. A little thought, however, and his tortuous mind had found a way. He laughed again.

'I thank you, Don Hieronimo, for that forewarning. I am not pledged yet, nor will those be upon whom I shall depend, and who shall have my instant orders.'

Back in his palace before coming to the matter of the Cardinal's ransom, he summoned one of his officers.

'The Cardinal-Archbishop of New Spain will land this evening at Havana,' he announced. 'To do him honour, and so that the city may be apprised of this happy event, I shall require a salute to be fired from the gun on the mole. You will take a gunner, and station yourself there. The moment his Eminence sets foot on land you will order the gun to be touched off.'

On that he dismissed the officer, and summoned another one.

'You will take horse at once, and ride to El Fuerte, to the Moro, and the Puntal. In my name you will order the commandant of each of those forts to train his guns on that red ship at anchor yonder, flying the English flag. After that they are to wait for the signal, which will be the firing of the gun on the mole, when the Cardinal-Archbishop of New Spain comes ashore. As soon as they hear it, but not before, they are to open fire upon that pirate ship and sink her. Let there be no mistake.'

Upon the officer's assurance that all was perfectly clear, Don Ruiz dismissed him to carry those orders, and then turned his attention to raiding the royal treasury for the gold which was to deliver the Cardinal from his duress.

So expeditiously did he go about this matter that he was alongside the *Arabella* again by the first dog-watch, and out of his barge four massive chests were hoisted to the deck of the buccaneer.

It had enheartened both him and the Alcalde, who again faithfully accompanied him, to behold, as they approached, the Cardinal-Archbishop on the poop-deck. Mantled and red-hatted, his crozier borne before him by the bareheaded Frey Domingo, and the other Dominicans modestly cowled and ranged behind him, it was clear that already his Eminence was ready and waiting to go ashore. This, and the measure of liberty which his presence on deck announced had already been accorded to him, finally assured Don Ruiz that once the ransom were paid there would be an end of the sacrilege of His Eminence's detention and no further obstacle would delay his departure from that accursed ship. With the removal of that protecting consecrated presence the immunity of the *Arabella* would be at an end and the guns of the Havana forts would make short work of her timbers.

Exulting in this thought, Don Ruiz could not refrain from taking with Blood, who received him at the head of the entrance ladder, the tone proper from a royal representative to a pirate.

'Maldito ladron--accursed thief--there is your gold, the price of a sacrilege for which you'll burn in Hell through all eternity. Verify it, and let us begone.'

Captain Blood gave no hint that he was so much as touched by that insulting speech. He stooped to the massive chests, unlocked each in turn, and cast a casual yet appraising glance over the gleaming contents. Then he beckoned his shipmaster forward. 'Jerry, here is the gold. See it stowed.' Almost disdainfully he added: 'We assume the count to be correct.'

Thereupon he turned to the poop and to the scarlet figure at the rail, and raised his voice. 'My Lord Cardinal, the ransom has been received and the Captain-General's barge waits to take you ashore. You have but to pledge me your word that I shall be allowed to depart without let, hindrance, or pursuit.'

Under his little black moustachios the Captain-General's lip curled in a little smile. The slyness of the man displayed itself in the terms, so calculated to avert suspicion, in which he chose to give expression to his venom.

'You may now depart without let or hindrance, you rogue. But if ever we meet again upon the seas, as meet we shall. . .'

He left his sentence there. But Captain Blood completed it for him. 'It is probable that I shall have the satisfaction of hanging you from that yard-arm, like the forsworn, dishonoured thief that you are, you gentleman of Spain.'

At the head of the companion the advancing Cardinal paused to reprove him for those words.

'Captain Blood, that threat is as ungenerous as I hope the terms of it are untrue.'

Don Ruiz caught his breath, aghast, more enraged even by the reproof than by the offensive terms of the threat that had provoked it.

'You hope!' he cried. 'Your Eminence hopes!'

'Wait!' Slowly the Cardinal descended the steps of the companion, his monks, following him, and came to stand in the waist, a very incarnation of the illimitable power and majesty of the Church.

'I said I hoped that the accusation is untrue, and that implies a doubt, which has offended you. For that doubt, Don Ruiz, I shall hope presently to seek your pardon. But first, since last you were here something has been troubling me which I must ask you to resolve.'

'Ashore, your Eminence will find me ready fully to answer your every question.' And Don Ruiz strode away to place himself at the head of the ladder by which the Cardinal was to descend. Captain Blood at the same moment, hat in hand, passed to its other side and took up his station there, as the courteous speeding of a departing guest demanded.

But the Primate did not move from where he stood. 'Don Ruiz, there is one question that must be answered before I consent to land in a province that you govern.' And so stern and commanding was his mien that Don Ruiz, at whose nod a population trembled, stood in dismay before him, waiting.

The Cardinal's glance passed from him to the attendant Don Hieronimo, and it was to him that the crucial question was set.

'Señor Alcalde, weigh well your answer to me, for your office and perhaps even more will depend upon your accuracy. What was done with the merchandise--the property of that English seaman--which the Captain-General ordered you to confiscate?'

Don Hieronimo's uneasy eyes looked anywhere but at his questioner. Intimidated, he dared not be other than prompt and truthful in his reply. 'It was sold again, Eminence.'

'And the gold it fetched? What became of that?'

'I delivered it to his Excellency, the Captain-General. Some twelve thousand ducats.'

In the hushed pause that followed, Don Ruiz bore the searching scrutiny of those stern, sad eyes, with his head high and a scornful, defiant curl to his lip. But the Primate's next question wiped the last vestige of that arrogance from his countenance.

'And is, then, the Captain-General of Havana also the King's Treasurer?'

'Not so, of course, Eminence,' said Don Ruiz, perforce.

'Then, sir, did you in your turn surrender to the Treasury this gold received for goods you confiscated in the name of the King, your master?'

He dared not prevaricate where verification of his word must so shortly follow. His tone, nevertheless, was surly with resentment of such a question.

'Not yet, Eminence. But. . .'

'Not yet!' The Cardinal allowed him to go no further, and there was an undertone of thunder in that gentle, interrupting voice. 'Not yet? And it is a full month since those events. I am answered, sir. Unhappily I did you no wrong by my doubt, which was that an officer of the Crown who interprets the laws with such sophistries as that which you uttered to me this morning cannot possibly be honest.'

'Eminence!' It was a roar of anger. In his excitement, his face livid, he advanced a step. Such words wherever uttered to him must have moved his wrath. But to be admonished and insulted by this priest in public, to be held up to the scorn and derision of these ruffianly buccaneers, was something beyond the endurance of any Castilian gentleman. In his fury he was seeking words in which to answer the indignity as it deserved, when, as if divining his mind, the Primate launched a scornful fulmination that withered his anger and turned it into fear.

'Silence, man! Will you raise your voice to us? By such means as these you no doubt grow rich in gold, but still richer in dishonour. And there is more. So that this unfortunate English seaman should quietly suffer himself to be robbed, you threatened him with prosecution by the Holy Office and the Fires of the Faith. Even a New Christian, and a New Christian more than any other, should know that to invoke the Holy Office for such base ends is to bring himself within the scope of its just resentment.'

That terrible threat on the lips of a sometime Grand Inquisitor, and the terms in which it was delivered, with its hint of old Christian scorn of New Christian blood, was the lightning-stroke that reduced the Captain-General's heart to ashes. He stood appalled, in fancy already seeing himself dishonoured, ruined, sent home to be arraigned in an auto de fé, stripped of every dignity before being flung to the secular arm for execution. 'My lord!' It was the piteous wail of a broken man. He held out hands in supplication. 'I did not see. . .'

'That I can well believe. Oculos habent et non videbunt. No man who saw would incur that peril.' Then his normal calm descended upon him again. Awhile he stood thoughtful, and about him all was respectful silence. Then he sighed, and advanced to take the stricken Count of Marcos by the arm. He led him away towards the forecastle, out of earshot of the others. He spoke very gently. 'Believe me, my heart bleeds for you, my son. Humanum est errare. Sinners are we all. I practise mercy where I can, against my own need of mercy. Therefore, the little that I can do to help you, I will do. Once I am ashore in Cuba, whilst you are its Captain-General, I must discover it to be my clear duty as Inquisitor of the Faith to take action in this matter. And that action of necessity must break you. To avoid this, my son, I will not land whilst you hold office here. But this is the utmost that I can do. Perhaps even in doing so much I am guilty of a sophistry myself. But I have to think not only of you, but also of the proud Castilian name and the honour of Spain herself, which must suffer in the dishonour of one of her administrators. At the same time, you will see that I cannot suffer that one who has so grossly abused the King's trust should continue in authority, or that his offence should go entirely unpunished.'

He paused a moment, whilst Don Ruiz stood in abjection with lowered head to bear the sentence that he knew must follow.

'You will resign your governorship this very day, on any pretext that you choose, and you will take the first ship to Spain. Then, so long as you do not return to the New World or assume any public office at home, so long shall I avoid official knowledge of your offence. More I cannot do. And may God forgive me if already I do too much.'

If the sentence was harsh, yet the broken man who listened heard it almost in relief, for he had not dared to expect to be so lightly quit. 'So be it, Eminence,' he faltered, his head still bowed. Then he raised eyes of despair and bewilderment to meet the Cardinal's compassionate eyes. 'But if your Eminence does not land. . . ?'

'Do not be concerned for me. I have already sounded this Captain Blood against my possible need. Now that I have taken my resolve, he shall carry me to San Domingo. When my work there is done I can take ship to return here to Havana and by that time you will have departed.'

Thus Don Ruiz saw himself cheated even of his vengeance upon that accursed sea-robber who had brought this ruin upon him. He began a last, weak, despairing attempt to avert at least that.

'But will you trust these pirates, who already have. . . ?'

He was interrupted. 'In this world, my son, I have learnt to place my trust in Heaven rather than in man. And this buccaneer, for all the evil in him, is a son of the true Church, and he has shown me that he is a scrupulous observer of his word. If there are risks I must accept them. See to it by your future conduct that I accept them in a good cause. Now go with God, Don Ruiz. There is no reason why I should detain you longer.'

The Captain-General went down on his knees to kiss the Cardinal's ring and ask a blessing. Over his bowed head the Primate of New Spain extended his right hand, two fingers and the thumb extended, and made the Sign of the Cross.

'Benedictus sis. Pax Domini sit sempre tecum. May the light of grace show you better ways in future. Depart with God.'

But for all the penitence displayed in his attitude at the Cardinal's feet, it is to be doubted if he departed as admonished. Stumbling like a blind man to the entrance-ladder, with a curt summons to the Alcalde to attend him and not so much as a glance or word to anybody else, he went over the side and down to his waiting barge.

And whilst he and the Alcalde raged in mutual sympathy, and damned the Cardinal-Archbishop for a vain, muddling priest, the *Arabella* was weighing anchor. Under full sail she swaggered past the massive forts and out of the bay of Havana, safe from molestation since, because of the imposing scarlet figure that paced the poop, the signal gun could not be fired.

And that is how it came to pass that when a fortnight later that great galleon the *Santa Veronica,* in a bravery of flags and pennants and with guns thundering in salute, sailed into the bay of Havana there was no Captain-General to welcome the arriving Primate of New Spain. To deepen the annoyance of that short, corpulent, choleric little prelate, not only was there no proper preparation for his welcome, but the Alcalde who came aboard in an anguish of bewilderment was within an ace of treating his Eminence as an impostor.

Aboard the *Arabella* in those days, Yberville, divested of his scarlet splendours, which, like the monkish gowns, had been hurriedly procured in Sainte Croix, was giving himself airs and vowing that a great churchman had been lost to the world when he became a buccaneer. Captain Blood, however, would concede no more than that the kiss was that of a great comedian. And in this the bo'sun Snell, whom Nature had so suitably tonsured for the part of Frey Domingo, being a heretic, entirely concurred with Captain Blood.

Episode 6

THE ELOPING HIDALGA

I

Word was brought to Tortuga by a half-caste Indian, who had shipped as one of the hands on a French brig, of the affair in which the unfortunate James Sherarton lost his life. It was a nasty story with which we are only indirectly concerned here, so that it need be no more than briefly stated. Sherarton and the party of English pearl-fishers he directed were at work off one of the Espada Keys near the Gulf of Maracaybo. They had already garnered a considerable harvest, when a Spanish frigate came upon them, and, not content with seizing their sloop and their pearls, ruthlessly put them to the sword. And there were twelve of them, honest, decent men who were breaking no laws from any but the Spanish point of view, which would admit no right of any other nation in the waters of the New World.

Captain Blood was present in the Tavern of the King of France at Cayona when the half-caste told in nauseous detail the story of that massacre.

'Spain shall pay,' he said. And his sense of justice being poetic, he added: 'And she shall pay in pearls.'

Beyond that he gave no hint of the intention which had leapt instantly to his mind. The inspiration was as natural as it was sudden. The very mention of pearl-fisheries had been enough to call to his mind the Rio de la Hacha, that most productive of all the pearl-fisheries in the Caribbean from which such treasures were brought to the surface, to the profit of King Philip.

It was not the first time that the notion of raiding that source of Spanish wealth had occurred to him; but the difficulties and dangers with which the enterprise was fraught had led him hitherto to postpone it in favour of some easier immediate task. Never, however, had those difficulties and dangers been heavier than at this moment, when it almost seemed that the task was imposed upon him by a righteously indignant Nemesis. He was not blind to this. He knew how fiercely vigilant was the Spanish Admiral of the Ocean-Sea, the Marquis of Riconete, who was cruising with a powerful squadron off the Main. So rudely had Captain Blood handled him in that affair at San Domingo that the Admiral dared not show himself again in Spain until he had wiped out the disgrace of it. The depths of his vindictiveness might be gauged from the announcement, which he had published far and wide, that he would pay the enormous sum of fifty thousand pieces of eight for the person of Captain Blood, dead or alive, or for information that should result in his capture.

If, then, a raid on Rio de la Hacha were to succeed, it was of the first importance that it should be carried out smoothly and swiftly. The buccaneers must be away with their plunder before the Admiral could even suspect their presence off the coast. With a view to making sure of this, Captain Blood took the resolve of first reconnoitring the ground in person, and rendering himself familiar with its every detail, so that there should be no fumbling when the raid took place.

Moulting his normal courtly plumage, discarding gold lace and Mechlin, he dissembled his long person in brown homespun, woollen stockings, plain linen bands, and a hat without adornment. He discarded his periwig, and replaced it by a kerchief of black silk that swathed his cropped head like a skullcap.

In this guise, leaving at Tortuga his fleet, which consisted in those days of four ships manned by close upon a thousand buccaneers, he sailed alone for Curaçao in a trading-vessel and there transferred himself to a broad-beamed Dutchman, the *Loewen,* that made regular voyages to and fro between that island and Carthagena. He represented himself as a trader in hides and the like, and assumed the name of Tormillo and a mixed Dutch and Spanish origin.

It was on a Monday that he landed from the Dutchman at Rio de la Hacha. The *Loewen* would be back from Carthagena on the following Friday, and even if no other business should bring her to Rio de la Hacha, she would call there again so as to pick up Señor Tormillo, who would be returning in her to Curaçao. He had contrived, largely at the cost of drinking too much bumbo, to establish the friendliest relations with the Dutch skipper, so as to ensure the faithful observance of this arrangement.

Having been put ashore by the Dutchman's cockboat, he took lodgings at the Escudo de Leon, a decent inn in the upper part of the town, and gave out that he was in Rio de la Hacha to purchase hides. Soon the traders flocked to him, and he won their esteem by the quantity of hides he agreed to purchase, and their amused contempt by the liberal prices he agreed to pay. In the pursuit of his business he went freely and widely about the place, and in the intervals between purchases he contrived to observe what was to be observed and to collect the information that he required.

So well did he employ his time that by the evening of Thursday he had fully accomplished all that he came to do. He was acquainted with the exact armament and condition of the fort that guarded the harbour, with the extent and quality of the military establishment, with the situation and defences of the royal treasury, where the harvest of pearls was stored; he had even contrived to inspect the fishery where the pearling-boats were at work under the protection of a ten-gun guarda-costa; and he had ascertained that the Marquis of Riconete, having flung out swift scouting-vessels, had taken up his headquarters at Carthagena, a hundred and fifty miles away to the south-west. Not only this, but he had fully evolved in his mind the plan by which the Spanish scouts were to be eluded and the place surprised, so that it might quickly be cleaned up before the Admiral's squadron could supervene to hinder.

Content, he came back to the Escudo de Leon on that Thursday evening for his last night in his lodgings there. In the morning the Dutchman should be back to take him off again, his mission smoothly accomplished. And then that happened which altered everything and was destined to change the lives and fortunes of persons of whose existence at that hour he was not even aware.

The landlord met him with the news that a Spanish gentleman, Don Francisco de Villamarga, had just been seeking him at the inn, and would return again in an hour's time. The mention of that name seemed suddenly to diminish the stifling heat of the evening for him. But, at least, he kept his breath and his countenance.

'Don Francisco de Villamarga?' he slowly repeated, giving himself time to think. Was it possible that there were in the New World two Spaniards of that same distinguished name? 'I seem to remember that a Don Francisco de Villamarga was deputy-governor of Maracaybo.'

'It is the same, sir,' the landlord answered him. 'Don Francisco was governor there, or, at least Alcalde, until about a year ago.'

'And he asked for me?'

'For you, Señor Tormillo. He came back from the interior today, he says, with a parcel of green hides which he desires to offer you.'

'Oh!' It was almost a gasp of relief. The Captain breathed more freely, but not yet freely enough. 'Don Francisco with hides to sell? Don Francisco de Villamarga a trader?'

The fat little vintner spread his hands. 'What would you, sir? This is the New World. Here such things can happen to a hidalgo when he is not fortunate. And Don Francisco, poor gentleman, has had sad misfortune, through no fault of his own. The province of his governorship was raided by Captain Blood, that accursed pirate, and Don Francisco fell into disgrace. What would you? It is the way of these things. There is no mercy for a governor who cannot protect a place entrusted to him.'

'I see.' Captain Blood took off his broad hat, and mopped his brow that was beaded with sweat below the line of the black scarf.

So far all was well, thanks to the fortunate chance of his absence when Don Francisco had called. But the danger of recognition which so far had been safely run was now only just round the corner. And there were few men in New Spain by whom Captain Blood would be more reluctant to be recognized than by this sometime deputy-governor of Maracaybo, this proud Spanish gentleman who had been constrained, for the reasons given by the inn-keeper, to soil his hands in trade. The impending encounter was likely to be as sweet for Don Francisco as it would certainly be bitter for Captain Blood. Even in prosperity Don Francisco would not have been likely to spare him. In adversity the prospect of earning fifty thousand pieces of eight would serve to sharpen the vindictiveness of this official who had fallen upon evil days.

Shuddering at the narrowness of the escape, thankful for that timeliest of warnings, Captain Blood perceived that there was only one thing to be done. Impossible now to await the coming of the Dutchman in the morning. In some sort of vessel, alone if need be in an open boat, he must get out of Rio de la Hacha at once. But he must not appear either startled or in flight.

He frowned annoyance. 'What misfortune that I should have been absent when Don Francisco called! It is intolerable to put a gentleman born to the trouble of seeking me again. I will wait upon him at once, if you will tell me where he is lodged.'

'Oh, certainly. You will find his house in the Calle San Bias; that is the first turning on your right; anyone there will show you where Don Francisco lives.'

The Captain waited for no more. 'I go at once,' he said, and stepped out.

But either he forgot or he mistook the landlord's directions, for instead of turning to his right, he turned to his left and took his way briskly down a street, at this hour of supper almost deserted, that led towards the harbour.

He was passing an alley, within fifty yards of the mole, when from the depths of it came ominous sounds of strife; the clash of steel on steel, a woman's cry, a man's harsh, vituperative interjections.

The concern supplied him by his own situation might well have reminded him that these murderous sounds were no affair of his, and that he had enough already on his hands to get out of Rio de la Hacha with his life. But the actual message of the vituperative exclamation overheard arrested his flight.

'Perro inglés! Dog of an Englishman!'

Thus Blood learnt that in that dark alley it was a compatriot who was being murdered. It was enough. In foreign lands, to any man who is not dead to feeling, a compatriot is a brother. He plunged at once into the gloom of that narrow way, his hand groping for the pistol inside the breast of his coat.

As he ran, however, it occurred to him that here was noise enough already. The last thing he desired was to attract spectators by increasing it. So he left the pistol in his pocket and whipped out his rapier instead.

By the little light that lingered, he could make out the group as he advanced upon it. Three men were assailing a fourth, who, with his back to a closed door, and his left arm swathed in his coat so as to make a buckler, offered a defence that was as desperate as it must ultimately prove futile. That he could have stood so long even against such odds was evidence of an unusual toughness.

At a little distance beyond that brawling quartet, the slight figure of a woman, cloaked and hooded by a light mantle of black silk, leaned in helplessness against the wall.

Blood's intervention was stealthy, swift, and practical. He announced his arrival by sending his sword through the back of the nearest of the three assailants.

'That will adjust the odds,' he explained, and cleared his blade just in time to engage a gentleman who whirled to face him, spitting blasphemies with that fluency in which the Castilian's only rival is the Catalan.

Blood broke ground nimbly, enveloped the vicious thrust in a counter-parry, and, in the movement, drove his steel through the blasphemer's sword-arm.

Out of action, the man reeled back, gripping the arm from which the blood was spurting, and cursing more fluently than ever, whilst the only remaining Spaniard, perceiving the sudden change in the odds, from three to one on his side to two to one against it, and not relishing this at all, gave way before Blood's charge. In the next moment he and his wounded comrade were in flight, leaving their friend to lie where he had fallen.

At Blood's side the man he had rescued, breathing in gasps, almost collapsed against him.

'Damned assassins!' he panted. 'Another minute would ha' seen the end of me.'

Then the woman who had darted forward surged at his other side.

'Vamos, Jorgito! Vamos!' she cried in fearful urgency. Then shifted from Spanish to fairly fluent English. 'Quick, my love! Let us get to the boat. We are almost there. Oh, come!'

This mention of a boat was an intimation to Blood that his good action was not likely to go unrewarded. It gave him every ground for hoping that in helping a stranger he had helped himself; for a boat was, of all things, what he most needed at the moment.

His hands played briskly over the man he was supporting, and came away wet from his left shoulder. He made no more ado. He hitched the fellow's right arm round his neck, gripped him about the waist to support him, and bade the girl lead on.

Whatever her panic on the score of her man's hurt, the promptitude of her obedience to the immediate need of getting him away was in itself an evidence of her courage and practical wit. One or two windows in the alley had been thrust open, and from odd doorways white faces dimly seen in the gloom were peering out to discover the cause of the hubbub. These witnesses, though silent, and perhaps timid, stressed the need for haste.

'Come,' she said. 'This way. Follow me.'

Half supporting, half carrying the wounded man, Blood kept pace with her speed, and so came out of the alley and gained the mole. Across this, disregarding the stare of odd wayfarers who paused and turned as they went by, she led him to a spot where a long-boat waited.

Two men rose out of it: Indians, or half-castes, their bodies naked from shoulder to waist. One of them sprang instantly ashore, then checked, peering in the dusk at the man Captain Blood was supporting.

'Que tal el patron?' he asked gruffly

'He has been hurt. Help him down carefully. Oh, make haste! Make haste!'

She remained on the quay, casting fearful glances over her shoulder whilst Blood and the Indians were bestowing the wounded man in the sternsheets. Then Blood, standing in the boat, proffered her his hand.

'Aboard, ma'am.' He was peremptory, and so as to save time and argument he added: 'I am coming with you.'

'But you can't. We sail at once. The boat will not return. We dare not linger, sir.'

'Faith, no more dare I. It is very well. I've said I am coming with you. Aboard, ma'am!' and without more ado, he almost pulled her into the boat, ordering the men to give way.

II

If she found the matter bewildering, she did not pursue it. Concern enough for her at the moment lay in the condition of her Englishman and the evidently urgent need of getting him away before his assailants returned, reinforced, to finish him. She could not waste moments so precious in arguing with an eccentric: possibly she had not even any thoughts to spare him.

As the boat shot away from the mole, she sank down in the sternsheets at the side of her companion, who had swooned. On his other side, Blood was kneeling, and the deft fingers of the buccaneer, who once had been a surgeon, located and gropingly examined that wound, high in the shoulder.

'Give yourself peace,' he comforted the girl. 'This is no great matter. A little bloodletting has made him faint. That is all. You'll soon have him well again.'

She breathed a little prayer of thanks, 'Gracias a Dios,' then, with a backward glance in the direction of the mole, urged the men to greater effort.

As the boat sped over the dark water towards a ship's lantern a half-mile away, the Englishman stirred and looked about him.

'What the plague. . .' he began, and struggled to rise.

Blood's hand restrained him. 'Quiet,' he said. 'There's no need for alarm. We're taking you aboard.'

'Taking me aboard? Who the devil are you?'

'Jorgito,' the girl cried, 'it is the gentleman who saved your life.'

'Odso! You're there, Isabelita?' His next question showed that he took in the situation. 'Are they following?'

When she had reassured him and pointed ahead to the ship's lantern towards which they were heading, he laughed softly, then cursed the Indians.

'Faster, you lazy dogs! Bend your backs to it, you louts.'

The rowers increased their effort, breathing stertorously. The man laughed again, softly, as before, a fleering, mocking sound.

'So, so. We've had the luck to win clear of that gin with no more than a scratch. Yet, God's my life, it's more than a scratch. I'm bleeding like a Christian martyr.'

'It's nothing,' Blood reassured him. 'You've lost some blood. But once aboard we'll staunch the wound and make you comfortable.'

'Faith, you talk like a sawbones.'

'It's what I am.'

'Gadso! Was there ever greater luck. Eh, Isabelita? A swordsman to rescue me and a doctor to heal me, all in one. There's a providence watching over me this night. An omen, sweetheart.'

'A mercy,' she corrected on a crooning note, and drew closer to him.

And now from their scraps of talk, Blood pieced together the tale of their exact relationship. They were an eloping pair, these two--this Englishman, whose name was George Fairfax, and this little hidalga of the great family of Sotomayor. His late assailants were her brother and two friends, bent upon frustrating the elopement. Her brother was the Spaniard who had escaped uninjured from the encounter, and it was his pursuit in force which she dreaded and for which she continually looked back towards the receding mole. By the time, however, that agitated lights came dancing at last along the water's edge, the long-boat was in the black shadow of a two-masted brig, bumping against her side, whilst from her deck a gruff English voice was hailing them.

The lady was the first to swarm the accommodation ladder. Then followed Fairfax, with Blood immediately and so closely behind as to support him and, indeed, partly carry him aboard.

At the head of the ladder they were received by a large man with a face that showed hot in the light of a lantern slung from the mainmast, who overwhelmed them with alarmed questions.

Fairfax, steadying himself against the bulkhead, gasped for breath, and broke into that interrogatory flow sharply to rap out his orders.

'Get under way at once, Tim. No time to get the boat aboard. Take her in tow. And don't stay to take up anchor. Cut the cable. Hoist sail and let's away. Thank God the wind serves. We shall have the Alcalde and all the alguaziles of la Hacha aboard if we delay. So stir your damned bones.'

Tim's roaring voice was passing on the orders and men were leaping to obey, when the lady set a hand on her lover's arm.

'But this gentleman, George. You forget him. He does not know where we go.'

Fairfax supported himself with a hand on Blood's shoulder. He turned his head to peer into the countenance of his preserver, and there was a scowl on the lean, dark face.

'Ye'll have gathered I can't be delayed,' he said.

'Faith, it's very glad to gather it I've been,' was the easy answer. 'And it's little I'm caring where you go, so long as it's away from Rio de la Hacha.'

The dark face lightened. The man laughed softly. 'Running away too, are you? Damn my blood! You're most accommodating. It seems all of a piece. Look alive, Tim. Can't these lubbers of yours move no faster?'

There was a blast from the master's whistle, and naked feet pattered at speed across the deck. Tim spoke briskly and savagely, to stimulate their efforts, then sprang to the side to shout his orders to the Indians still in the boat alongside.

'Get you below, sir,' he begged his employer. 'I'll come to you as soon as we are under way and the course is set.'

It was Blood who assisted Fairfax to the cabin--a place of fair proportions if rudely equipped, lighted by a slush-lamp that swung above the bare table. The lady, breathing tenderest solicitude, followed closely.

To receive them a negro lad emerged from a stateroom on the larboard side. He cried out at sight of the blood with which his master's shirt was drenched, and stood arrested, teeth and eyeballs flashing in that startled dusky face.

Assuming authority, Blood ordered him to lend a hand, and between them they carried Fairfax, whose senses were beginning to swim again, through the doorway which the steward had left open, and there removed his shoes and got him to bed.

Then Blood despatched the boy, who answered to the name of Alcatrace, to the galley for hot water and to the Captain of the ship's medicine-chest.

On the narrow bed, Fairfax, a man as tall and well-knit as Blood himself, reclined in a sitting posture, propped by all the pillows available. He wore his own hair, and the reddish-brown cloud of it half veiled his pallid, bony countenance as with eyes half closed his head lolled weakly forward.

Having disposed of him comfortably, Blood cut away his sodden shirt and laid bare his vigorous torso.

When the steward returned with a can of water, some linen and a cedar box containing the ship's poor store of medicines, the lady followed him into the stateroom, begging to be allowed to help. Through the ports that stood open to the purple tropical night, she heard the creak of blocks and the thud of the sails as they took the wind, and it was with immense relief that she felt at last under her feet the forward heave of the unleashed brig. One anxiety at least was now allayed, and the danger of recapture overpast.

Courteously Blood welcomed her assistance. Observing her now in the light, he found her to agree with the impressions he had already formed. A slight wisp of womanhood, little more than a child, and probably not long out of the hands of the nuns, she showed him a winsome, eager face, and two shining eyes intensely black against the waxen pallor in which they were set. Her gold-laced gown of black, with beautiful point of Spain at throat and wrists, and, some pearls of obvious price entwined in her glossy tresses, were, like the proud air investing her, those of a person of rank.

She proved quick to understand Blood's requirements and deft to execute them, and thus, with her assistance, he worked upon the man for love of whom this little hidalga of the great house of Sotomayor was apparently burning her boats. Carefully, tenderly, he washed the purple lips of the wound in the shoulder, which was still oozing. In the medicine-chest held for him by Alcatrace he discovered at least some arnica, and of this he made a liberal application. It produced a fiercely reviving effect. Fairfax threw up his head.

'Hell-fire!' he cried. 'Do you burn me, damn you?'

'Patience, sir. Patience. It's a healing cautery.'

The lady's arm encircled the patient's head, supporting and soothing him. Her lips lightly touched his dank brow. 'My poor Jorgito,' she murmured.

He grunted for answer, and closed his eyes.

Blood was tearing linen into strips. Out of these, he made a pad for the wound, applied a bandage to hold it in position, and then a second bandage, like a sling, to keep the left arm immovable against the patient's breast. Then Alcatrace found him a fresh shirt, and they passed it over the Englishman's head, leaving the left sleeve empty. The surgical task was finished.

Blood made a readjustment of the pillows. 'Ye'll sleep in that position if you please. And you'll avoid movement as much as possible. If we can keep you quiet, you should be whole again in a week or so. Ye've had a near escape. Had the blade taken you two inches lower, it's another kind of bed we'ld be making for you this minute. Ye've been lucky, so you have.'

'Lucky? May I burn!'

'There's even, perhaps, something for which to render thanks.'

If the quiet reminder brought from Fairfax no more than a grumbled oath, it stirred the lady to a sort of violence. She leaned across the narrow bed to seize both of Blood's hands. Her pale, dark face was solemnly intense. Her lips trembled, as did her voice.

'You have been so good, so brave, so noble.'

Before he could guess her intent, she had carried his hands to her lips and kissed them. Protesting, he wrenched them away. She smiled up at him wistfully.

'But shall I not kiss them, then, those hands? Have they not save' my Jorgito's life? Have they not heal' his wounds? All my life I shall love those hands. All my life I shall be grateful to them.'

Captain Blood had his doubts about this. He was not finding Jorgito prepossessing. The fellow's shallow, sloping animal brow and wide, loose-lipped mouth inspired no confidence, for all that in its total sum, and in a coarse raffish way, the face might be described as handsome. It was a face of strongly marked bone structures, the nose boldly carved, the cheek-bones prominent, the jaw long and powerful. In age, he could not have passed the middle thirties.

His eyes, rather close-set and pale, shifted under Blood's scrutiny, and he began to mutter belated acknowledgments, reminded by the lady's outburst of what was due from him.

'I vow, sir, I am deeply in your debt. Damn my blood! That's nothing new for me, God knows. I've been in somebody's debt ever since I can remember. But this--may I perish--is a debt of another kind. If only you had skewered for me the guts of that pimp who got away, I'ld be still more grateful to you. The world could very well do without Don Serafino de Sotomayor. Damn his blood!'

'Señor Jesus! No digas eso, querido!' Quick and shrill came the remonstrance from the little hidalga. 'Don't say such things, my love.' To soften her protest, she stroked his cheek as she ran on, 'No, no, Jorgito. If that have happen never more will my conscience be quiet. If my brother's blood have been shed, it will kill me.'

'And what of my blood, then? Hasn't there been enough of that shed by him and his plaguey bullies. And didn't he hope to shed it all, the damned cut-throat?'

'Querido,' she soothed him. 'That was for protect me. He think it his duty. I could not have forgive him ever if he kill you. It would have broke my heart,

Jorgito, you know. Yet I can understand Serafino. Oh, let us thank God--God and this so brave gentleman--that no worse have happen.'

And then Tim, the big red ship-master, rolled in to inquire how Mr Fairfax fared, and to report that the course was set, that the *Heron* was moving briskly before a steady southerly breeze, and that already La Hacha was half a dozen miles astern. 'So all's well that ends well, sir. And we've to find quarters for this gentleman who came aboard with you. I'll have a hammock slung for him in the cuddy. See to it, Alcatrace.' He drove the negro out upon that task. 'Pronto Vamos!'

Fairfax reclined with half-closed eyes. 'All's well that ends well,' he echoed. He laughed softly, and Blood observed that always when he laughed his loose mouth seemed to writhe in a sneer. He was recovering vigour of body and of mind with every moment now, since he had been made comfortable and the bleeding had been checked. His hand closed over the lady's where it lay upon the counterpane. 'Ay. All's well that ends well,' he repeated. 'Ye'll have the jewels safe, sweetheart?'

'The jewels?' She started, caught her breath, and for a moment her brows were knit in thought. Then, with consternation overspreading her countenance and a hand on her heart, she came to her feet. 'The jewels!'

Fairfax slewed his head round to look at her fully, his pale eyes suddenly wide, the brows raised. 'What now?' His voice was a croak. 'Ye have them safe?'

Her lip quivered. 'Valga me Dios! I must have drop' the casket when Serafino overtake us.'

There was a long hushed pause, which Blood felt to be of the kind that is the prelude of a storm. 'Ye dropped the casket!' said Fairfax. His tone was ominously quiet. He was staring at her in stupefaction, his jaw loose. 'Ye dropped the casket?' Gradually a blaze kindled in his light eyes. 'D'ye say ye dropped the casket?' This time his voice rose and cracked. 'Damn my blood! It passes belief. Hell! Ye can't have dropped it.'

The sudden fury of him shocked her. She looked at him with frightened eyes. 'You are angry, Jorgito,' she faltered. 'But you must not be angry. That is not right. Think of what happen'. I was distracted. Your life was in danger. What were the jewels then? How can I think of jewels? I let the casket fall. I did not notice. Then when you are wounded, and I think perhaps you will die, can I think of jewels then? You see, Jorgito? It is lastima, yes. But they do not matter. We have each other. They do not matter. Let them go.'

Her fond hand was stealing about his neck again. But in a rage he flung it off.

'Don't matter!' he roared, his loose mouth working. 'Rot my bones! You lose a fortune; you spill thirty thousand ducats in the kennel, and you say it don't matter! Hell and the devil, girl! If that don't matter, tell me what does.'

Blood thought it time to intervene. Gently, but very firmly, he pressed the wounded man back upon his pillows. 'Will you be quiet now, ye bellowing calf? Haven't you spilt enough of your blood this night?'

But Fairfax raged and struggled. 'Quiet? Damn my soul! You don't understand. How can I be quiet? Quiet, when this little fool has. . .'

She interrupted him there. She had drawn herself stiffly erect. Her lips were steady now her eyes more intensely black than ever.

'Is it so much to you that I lose my jewels, George? They were my jewels. You'll please to remember that. If I lose them, I lose them, and it is my affair, my loss. And I should not count it loss in a night when I have gain' so much. Or have I not, George? Were the jewels such great matter to you? More than I, perhaps?'

That challenge brought him to his senses. He beat a retreat before it, in the best order he could contrive, paused, and then broke into a laugh that to Blood was pure play-acting. 'What the devil! Are you angry with me, Isabelita? Plague on it! I am like that. Hot and quick. That's my nature. And thirty thousand ducats is a loss to make a man forget his manners for the moment. But the jewels? Bah! Rot the jewels. If they've gone, they've gone.' He held out a coaxing hand. 'Come, Isabelita. Kiss and forgive, sweetheart. I'll soon be buying you all the jewels you could want.'

'I want no jewels, George.' She was not more than half-mollified. Something of the ugly suspicion he had aroused in her still lingered. But she went to him, and suffered him to put an arm about her. 'You must not be angry with me again, ever, Jorgito. If I had love' you less, I would have think more of the casket.'

'To be sure you would, chick. To be sure.'

Tim shuffled uncomfortably. 'I'd best get back on deck, sir.' He made shift to go, but in the doorway paused to turn to Captain Blood. 'That blackamoor will ha' slung your hammock for you.'

'You may be showing me the way, then. There's no more I can do here for to-night.'

Whilst the ship-master waited, holding the door, he spoke again. 'If this wind holds, we should make Port Royal by Sunday night or Monday morning.'

Blood was brought to a standstill. 'Port Royal?' said he slowly. 'I'ld not care to land there.'

Fairfax looked at him. 'Why not? It's an English settlement. You should have nothing to fear in Jamaica.'

'Still I'ld not care to land there. What port will you be making after that?'

The question seemed to amuse Fairfax. Again he uttered his unpleasant, fleering laugh. 'Faith, that'll depend upon a mort o things.'

Blood's steadily rising dislike of the man sharpened his rejoinder.

'I'ld thank you to make it depend a little upon my convenience, seeing that I'm here for yours.'

'For mine?' Fairfax raised his light brows. 'Od rot me, now! Didn't I understand you was running away too? But we'll see what we can do. Where was you wishing to be put ashore?'

By an effort Blood stifled his indignation and kept to the point. 'From Port Royal, it would be no great matter for you to carry me through the Windward

Passage, and land me either on the northwest coast of Hispaniola or even on Tortuga.'

'Tortuga!' There was such a quickening of the light, shifty eyes, that Blood instantly regretted that he should have mentioned the place. Fairfax was pondering him intently, and behind that searching glance it was obvious that his mind was busy. 'Tortuga, eh? So ye've friends among the buccaneers?' He laughed. 'Well, well! That's your affair, to be sure. Let the *Heron* make Port Royal first, and then we'll be obliging you.'

'I'll be in your debt,' said Blood, with more than a hint of sarcasm. 'Give you good night, sir. And you, ma'am.'

III

For a considerable time after the door had closed upon the departing men, Fairfax lay very still and very thoughtful, his eyes narrowed, a mysterious smile on his lips.

At long last Doña Isabela spoke softly. 'You should sleep, Jorgito. Of what do you think?'

He made her an answer that seemed to hold no sense.

'Of the difference the lack of a periwig makes to a man who's an Irishman and a surgeon and wants to be landed on Tortuga.'

For a moment she wondered whether he had a touch of fever, and it increased her concern that he should sleep. She proposed to leave him. But he would not hear of it. He cursed the burning thirst he discovered in himself, and begged her to give him to drink. That same thirst continued thereafter to torment him and to keep him wakeful, so that she stayed at his side and gave him frequent draughts of water, mixed with the juice of limes, and once, on his insistent demand, with brandy.

The night wore on, with little said between them, and after some three hours of it he turned so quiet that she thought he slept at last and was preparing to creep away, when suddenly he announced his complete wakefulness by an oath and a laugh and ordered her to summon Tim. She obeyed only because to demur would be to excite him.

When Tim returned with her, Fairfax required to know what o'clock it might be and how far the master reckoned they had travelled. Eight bells, said Tim, had just been made, and they had put already a good forty miles between the *Heron* and La Hacha.

Then came a question that was entirely odd: 'How far to Carthagena?'

'A hundred miles maybe. Maybe a trifle more.'

'How long to make it?'

The ship-master's eyes became round with surprise. 'With the wind as it blows, maybe twenty-four hours.'

'Make it, then,' was the astounding order. 'Go about at once.'

The surprise in Tim's hot face was changed to concern.

'Ye've the fever, Captain, surely. What should we be doing back on the Main?'

'I've no fever, man. Ye've heard my order. Go about and lay a course for Carthagena.'

'But Carthagena. . .' The mate and Doña Isabel exchanged glances.

Surprising this, and perceiving what was in their minds, Fairfax's mouth twisted ill-humouredly. 'Od rot you! Wait!' he growled, and fell to thinking.

Had he been in full possession of his vigour he would have admitted no partner to the evil enterprise he had in mind. He would have carried it through single-handed, keeping his own counsel. But his condition making him dependent upon the ship-master left him no choice, as he saw it, but to lay his cards upon the table.

'Riconete is at Carthagena, and Riconete will pay fifty thousand pieces of eight for Captain Blood, dead or alive. Fifty thousand pieces of eight.' He paused a moment, and then added: 'That's a mort o' money, and there'll be five thousand pieces for you, Tim, when it's paid.'

Tim's suspicions were now a certainty. 'To be sure. To be sure.'

Exasperated, Fairfax snarled at him. 'God rot your bones, Tim! Are you humouring me! Ye think I have the fever. Ye'ld be the better yourself for a touch of the fever that's burning me. It might sharpen your paltry wits and quicken your sight.'

'Ay ay,' said Tim. 'But where do we find Captain Blood?'

'In the cuddy where you've bestowed him.'

'Ye're light-headed, sir.'

'Will you harp on that? Damn you for a fool. That is Captain Blood, I tell you. I recognized him the moment he asked to be landed at Tortuga. I'ld ha' known him sooner if I'ld ha' been more than half awake. He wouldn't care to land at Port Royal, he said. Of course he wouldn't. Not while Colonel Bishop is Governor of Jamaica. That'll maybe help you to understand.'

Tim was foolishly blinking his amazement and loosed an oath or two of surprised conviction. 'Ye recognize him, d'ye say?'

'That's what I say, and ye may believe I'm not mistook. Be off now, and put about. That first. Then you'd better see to making this fellow fast. If you take him in his sleep, it'll save trouble. Away with you.'

'Ay, ay,' said Tim, and bustled off in a state of excitement that was tempered by no scruples.

Doña Isabela, in a horror that had been growing steadily with understanding of what she heard, came suddenly to her feet.

'Wait, wait! What is it you will do?'

'No matter for you, sweetheart,' said Fairfax, and a peremptory wave of his sound hand dismissed Tim from the doorway where her voice had arrested him.

'But it is matter for me. I understand. You cannot do this, George.'

'Can't I? Why, the rogue'll be asleep by now. It should be easy. There'll be a surprised awakening for him; there will so.' And his fleering laugh went to increase her horror.

'But--Dios mio!--you cannot, you cannot. You cannot sell the man who save' your life.'

He turned his head to consider her with sneering amusement. Too much of a scoundrel to know how much of a scoundrel he was, he imagined himself opposed by a foolish, sentimental qualm that would be easily allayed. He was confident, too, of his complete ascendancy over a mind whose innocence he mistook for simplicity.

'Rot me, child, it's a duty, no less. You don't understand. This Blood is a pirate rogue, buccaneer, thief, and assassin. The sea'll be cleaner without him.'

She became only more vehement. 'He may be what you say--pirate, buccaneer, and the rest. Of that I know nothing. I care nothing. But I know he save' your life, and I care for that. He is here in your ship because he save' your life.'

'That's a lie, anyway,' growled Fairfax. 'He's here because he's took advantage of my condition. He's come aboard the *Heron* so as to escape from the Main and the justice that is after him. Well, well. He'll find out his mistake tomorrow.'

She wrung her hands, a fierce distress in her white face. Then, growing steadier, she pondered him very solemnly with an expression he had never yet seen on that eager face, an expression that annoyed him.

The faith in this man, of whom, after all, she knew but little, the illusions formed about him in the course of being swept off her maiden feet by a whirlwind wooing, which had made her cast everything away so that at his bidding she might link her fortunes with his own, had been sorely disturbed by the spectacle of his coarse anger at the loss of the jewels. That faith was now in danger of being finally and tragically shattered by this revelation of a nature which must fill her with dread and loathing once she admitted to herself the truth of what she beheld. Against this admission she was still piteously struggling. For if George Fairfax should prove, indeed, the thing she was being compelled to suspect, what could there be for her who was now so completely and irrevocably in his power?

'George,' she said quietly, in a forced calm to which the tumult of her bosom gave the lie, 'it matters not what this man is. You owe him your life. Without him you would lie dead now in that alley in La Hacha. You cannot do what you say. It would be infamy.'

'Infamy? Infamy be damned!' He laughed his ugly, contemptuous laugh. 'Ye just don't understand. It's a duty, I tell you--the duty of every honest gentleman to lay this pirate rogue by the heels.'

Scorn deepened in the dark eyes that continued so disconcertingly to regard him. 'Honest? You say that! Honest to sell the man who save' your life? For fifty thousand pieces of eight, was it not? That is honest? Honest as Judas, who sell the Saviour for thirty pieces.'

He glowered at her in resentment. Then found, as rogues will, an argument to justify himself. 'If you don't like it, you may blame yourself. If in your stupidity you hadn't lost the jewels I shouldn't need to do this. As it is, it's just a providence. For how else am I to find money for Tim and the hands, buy stores at Jamaica, and pay for the graving of the *Heron* against the ocean voyage? How else?'

'How else!' There was a bitter edge to her voice now 'How else since I lost my jewels, eh? It is so. It was for that? My jewels were for that? Que verguenza?' A sob shook her. 'Dios mio, que viltad! Ay de mi! Ay de mi!'

Then, hoping against hope in her despair, she caught his arm in her two hands and changed her tone to one of pleading.

'Jorgito. . .'

But Mr Fairfax, you'll have gathered, was not a patient man. He would be plagued no further. He flung her off with a violence that sent her hurtling against the bulkhead at her back. His evil temper was now thoroughly aroused, and it may have been rendered the more savage because his impetuous movement brought a twinge of pain to his wounded shoulder.

'Enough of that whining, my girl. Devil take you if you haven't set me bleeding again. Ye'll meddle in things you understand and not in my affairs. D'ye think a man's to be pestered so? Ye'll have to learn different afore we're acquainted much longer. Ye will so, by God?' Peremptorily he ended: 'Get you to bed.'

As she still lingered, winded where he had flung her, white-faced, aghast, incredulous, annoying him by the reproach of her stare, he raised his voice in fury. 'D'ye hear me? Get you to bed, rot you! Go!'

She went without another word, so swiftly and quietly that she left him with a sense of something ominous. Uneasy, a sudden suspicion of treachery crossing his mind, he got gingerly down from his bed, despite his condition, and staggered to the door, to spy upon her thence. He was just in time to see her vanish through the doorway of the stateroom opposite, and a moment later, from beyond her closed door, a sound of desolate sobbing reached him across the cabin.

His upper lip curled as he listened. At least, it had not occurred to her to betray his intentions to Captain Blood. Not that it would matter much if she did. Tim and the six hands aboard would easily account for the buccaneer if he should make trouble. Still, the notion might come to her, and it would be safer to provide.

He bawled the name of Alcatrace, who lay stretched, asleep, on the stern locker. The steward, awakened by the call, leapt up to answer it, and received from Fairfax stern, clear orders to remain awake and on guard so as to see that Doña Isabela did not leave the couch. At need, he was to employ violence to prevent it.

Then, with the help of Alcatrace, Fairfax crawled back to his bed, re-settled himself, and soon a heavy list to starboard informing him that they had gone about, this man who accounted his fortune made allowed himself to sink at last into an exhausted sleep.

IV

It should have occurred to them that the list to starboard so reassuring to Mr George Fairfax must present a riddle to Captain Blood if he should happen still to be awake. And awake it happened that he was.

He had doffed no more than his coat and his shoes, and he lay in shirt and breeches in the hammock they had slung for him in the stuffy narrow spaces of the cuddy, vainly wooing a slumber that held aloof. He was preoccupied, and not at all on his own behalf. Not all the rude ways that he had followed and the disillusions that he had suffered had yet sufficed to extinguish the man's sentimental nature. In the case of the little lady of the house of Sotomayor, he found abundant if disturbing entertainment for it this night. He was perplexed and perturbed by the situation in which he discovered her, so utterly in the power of a man who was not merely and unmistakably a scoundrel, but a crude egotist of little mind and less heart. Captain Blood reflected upon the misery and heart-break that so often will follow upon an innocent girl's infatuation for just such a man, who has obtained empire over her by his obvious but flashy vigour and the deceptive ardour of his wooing. In the buccaneer's sentimental eyes she was as a dove in the talons of a hawk, and he would give a deal to deliver her from them before she was torn to pieces. But it was odds that in her infatuation she would not welcome that deliverance, and even if, proving an exception to the rule, she should lend an ear to the sense that Blood could talk to her, he realized that he was in no case to offer her assistance, however ardently he might desire to do so.

With a sigh, he sought to dismiss a problem to which he could supply no happy solution; but it persisted until that list to starboard of a ship that hitherto had ridden on an even keel came to divert his attention into other channels. Was it possible, he wondered, that the wind could have veered with such suddenness? It must be so, because nothing else would explain the fact observed; at least, nothing else that seemed reasonable.

Nevertheless, he was moved to ascertain. He eased himself out of the hammock, groped for his coat and his shoes, put them on, and made his way by the gangway to the ship's waist.

Here one of the hands squatted on the hatch-coaming, softly singing, and at the break of the low poop the helmsman stood at the whipstaff. But Blood asked no questions of either of them. He preferred instead to obtain from the heavens the information that he sought, and the clear, starry sky told him all that he required to know. The North Star was abeam on the starboard quarter. Thus he obtained the surprising knowledge that they had gone about.

Always prudently mistrustful of anything that appeared to be against reason, he climbed the poop in quest of Tim. He beheld him pacing there, a burly silhouette against the light from the two tall stern lanterns, and he stepped briskly towards him.

To the ship-master, Captain Blood's advent was momentarily disconcerting. At that very instant he had been asking himself whether sufficient time had been given their passenger to be fast asleep, so that they might tie him up in his hammock without unnecessary ado. Recovering from his surprise, Tim jovially hailed the Captain as he advanced across the canting deck.

'A fine night, sir.'

Blood took a devious way to his ends, by an answer that applied a test. 'I see the wind has changed.'

'Ay,' the ship-master answered with alacrity. 'It was uncommon sudden. It's come to blow hard from the south.'

'That'll be delaying us in making Port Royal.'

'If it holds. But maybe it'll change again.'

'Maybe it will,' said Blood. 'We'll pray for it.'

Pacing together; they had come to the rail. They leaned upon it, and looked down at the dark water and the white, luminous edge of the wave that curled away from the ship's flank.

Blood made philosophy. 'A queer, uncertain life, this seafaring life, Tim, at the mercy of every wind that blows, driving us now in one direction, now in another, sometimes helping, sometimes hindering, and sometimes defeating and destroying us. I suppose you love your life, Tim?'

'What a question! To be sure I love my life.'

'And ye'll have the fear of death that's common to us all?'

'Od rot me! Ye're talking like a parson.'

'Maybe. Ye see it's opportune to remind you that ye're mortal, Tim. We're all apt to forget it at times and place our self in dangers that are entirely unnecessary. Mortal dangers. Just such a danger as you stand in this very minute, Tim.'

'What's that?' Tim took his elbows from the rail.

'Now don't be moving,' said Blood gently. His hand was inside the breast of his coat, and from the region of it, under cover of the cloth, something hard and tubular was pressed closely into the mate's side just below the ribs. 'My finger's on the trigger, Tim, and if ye were to move suddenly ye might startle me into pulling it. Put your elbows back on the rail, Tim darling while we talk. Ye've nothing to fear. I've no notion of hurting you; that is, provided ye're reasonable, as I think ye will be. Tell me now: Why are we going back to the Main?'

Tim was gasping in mingled surprise and fear, and his fear was greater perhaps than it need have been because he knew now beyond doubt with whom he had to deal. The sweat stood in cold beads on his brow.

'Going back to the Main?' he faltered stupidly

'Just so. Why have ye gone about? And why did ye lie to me about a south wind? D'ye think I'm such a lubber that I can't tell north from south on a clear night like this? Ye're no better than a fool, it seems. But unless ye get sense enough not to lie to me again, ye'll never tell another lie to anyone after this night. Now I'll be asking you again: Why are we going back to the Main? And don't tell me it's Fairfax you're selling.'

There was on Tim's part a thoughtful, hard-breathing pause. Blood might have made him afraid to lie, but he was still more afraid to speak the truth since it was what it was. 'Who else should it be?' he growled.

'Tim, Tim! Ye're lying to me again despite my warning. And your lies have the queer quality of telling me the truth. For if ye were meaning to sell Fairfax, it's La Hacha ye'ld be making for; and if ye were making for La Hacha ye'ld never be reaching so far on this westerly tack unless ye're a lubberly idiot, which I perceive ye're not. I'm saving you the trouble of lying again, Tim, for that--I vow to God--would certainly be the death of you. D'ye know who I am? Let me have the truth of that too. Do you?'

It was just because he did know who his questioner was that, having twice been so easily caught out in falsehood by this man's acuteness, the master stood chilled and palsied, never doubting that if he moved his inside would be blown out by that pistol in his flank. Fear at last tore the truth from him.

'I do, Captain. But. . .'

'Whisht now! Don't be committing suicide by telling me another falsehood; and there's no need. There's no need to tell me more. I know the rest. Ye're heading for Carthagena, of course. That's the market for the goods you carry, and the Marquis of Riconete is your buyer. If the notion is yours, Tim, I can forgive it. For you owe me nothing, and there's no reason in the world why ye shouldn't be earning fifty thousand pieces of eight by sellin' me to Spain. Is the notion yours, now?'

Vehemently Tim invoked the heavenly hierarchy to bear witness that he had done no more than obey the orders of Fairfax, who alone had conceived this infamous notion of making for Carthagena. He was still protesting when Blood cut into that flow of blasphemy-reinforced assertion.

'Yes, yes. I believe you. I had a notion that he recognized me when I spoke of landing on Tortuga. It was incautious of me. But, bad cess to him!--I'd saved his mangy life, and I thought that even the worst blackguard in the Caribbean would hesitate before. . . No matter. Tell me this: What share were you to have of the blood money, Tim?'

'Five thousand pieces, he promised,' said Tim, hang-dog.

'Glory be! Is that all! Ye can't be much of a hand at a bargain; and that's not the only kind of fool you are. How long did you think you'ld live to enjoy the money? Or perhaps you didn't think. Well, think now, Tim, and maybe it'll occur to you that when it was known, as known it would be, how he'd earned it, my buccaneers would hunt you to the ends of the seas. Ye should reflect on these things, Tim, when ye go partners with a scoundrel. Ye'll be wiser to throw in your lot with me, my lad. And if it's five thousand pieces you want, faith, you may still earn them by taking my orders whilst I'm aboard this brig. Do that, and you may call for the money at Tortuga when you please, and be sure of safe-conduct. You have my word for that. And I am Captain Blood.'

Tim required no time for reflection. From the black shadow of imminent death that had been upon him, he saw himself suddenly not only offered safety but a reward as great as that which villainy would have brought him, and free from those overlooked risks to which Blood had just drawn his attention.

'I take the Almighty to be my witness. . .' he was beginning with fervour, when again Blood cut him short.

'Now don't be wasting breath on oaths, for I put no trust in them. My trust is in the gold I offer on the one hand and the lead on the other. I'm not leaving your side from this moment, Tim. I've conceived a kindness for you, my lad. And if I take my pistol from your ribs, don't be presuming upon that. It stays primed and cocked. Ye've no pistols of your own about you, I hope.' He ran his left hand over the master's body, as he spoke, so as to assure himself. 'Very well. We'll not go about again as you might be supposing, because we are still going back to the Main. But not to Carthagena. It's for La Hacha that we'll be steering a course. So you'll just be stepping to the poop-rail with me, and bidding them put the helm over. Ye've run far enough westward. It's more than time we were on the other tack if we are to make La Hacha by morning. Come along now.'

Obediently the master went with him, and from the rail, piped the hands to quarters. When all was ready, his deep voice rang out.

'Let go, and haul!' and a moment later, in response, the foreyards ran round noisily, the deck came level and then canted to larboard, and the brig was heading southwest.

V

All through that clear June night Captain Blood and the master of the *Heron* remained side by side on the poop of the brig, whether sitting or standing or going ever and anon to the rail to issue orders to the crew. And though the voice was always Tim's the orders were always Captain Blood's.

Tim gave him no trouble, it never being in his mind to change a state of things which suited his rascality so well. The reckoning there might have to be with Fairfax gave him no concern. In the main there was silence between them. But when the first grey light of dawn was creeping over the sea, Tim ventured a question that had been perplexing him.

'Sink me if I understand why ye should be wanting to go back to La Hacha. I thought as you was running away from it. Why else did ye ever consent to stop aboard when we weighed anchor?'

Blood laughed softly. 'Maybe it's as well ye should know. Ye'll be the better able to explain things to Mr Fairfax in case they should not be altogether clear to him.

'Ye may find it hard to believe from what you know of me, but there's a streak of chivalry in my nature, a remnant from better days; for indeed, it was that same chivalry that made me what I am. And ye're not to suppose that it's Fairfax I'm taking back to La Hacha and the vengeance of the house of Sotomayor. For I don't care a louse what may happen to the blackguard, and I'm not by nature a vindictive man.

'It's the little hidalga I'm concerned for. It's entirely on her account that we're going back, now that I've sounded the nasty depths of this fellow to whom in a blind evil hour she entrusted herself. We're going to restore her to her family, Tim, safe and undamaged, God be praised. It's little thanks I'm likely to get for it from her. But that may come later, when with a riper knowledge of the world she may have some glimpse of the hell from which I am delivering her.'

Here was something beyond Tim's understanding. He swore in his amazement. Also it placed in jeopardy, it seemed to him, the five thousand pieces he was promised.

'But if ye was running away from La Hacha, there must be danger for ye there. Are ye forgetting that?'

'Faith, I never yet knew a danger that could prevent me from doing what I'm set on. And I'm set on this.'

It persuaded Tim of that streak of chivalry of which Blood had boasted, a quality which the burly master of the *Heron* could not help regarding as a deplorable flaw in a character of so much rascally perfection.

Ahead the growing daylight showed the loom of the coastline. But seven bells had been made before they were rippling through the greenish water at the mouth of the harbour of Rio de la Hacha, with the sun already high abeam on the larboard side.

They ran in to find an anchorage, and from the pooprail the now weary and blear-eyed Tim continued to be the mouthpiece of the tall man who clung to him like his shadow.

'Bid them let go.'

The order was issued, a rattle followed from the capstan, and the *Heron* came to anchor within a quarter of a mile of the mole.

'Summon all hands to the waist.'

When the six men who composed the crew of the brig stood assembled there, Blood's next instructions followed. 'Bid them take the cover from the main hatch.'

It was done at once.

'Now order them all down into the hold. Tell them they are to stow it for cargo to be taken aboard.'

It may have puzzled them, but there was no hesitation to obey, and as the last man disappeared into the darkness, Blood drew the master to the companion. 'You'll go and join them, Tim, if you please.'

There was a momentary rebellion. 'Sink me, Captain, can't you--'

'You'll go and join them,' Blood insisted. 'At once.'

Under the compulsion of that tone and of the eyes so blue and cold that looked with deadly menace into his own, Tim's resistance crumbled, and obediently he climbed down into the hold.

Captain Blood, following close upon his heels, dragged the heavy wooden cover over the hatchway again, and dumped it down, insensible to the storm of howling from those he thus imprisoned in the bowels of the brig.

The noise they made aroused Mr Fairfax from an exhausted slumber, on one side of the cabin, and Doña Isabela from a despondent listlessness on the other.

Mr Fairfax, realizing at once that they were at anchor, and puzzled to the point of uneasiness by the fact, wondering, indeed, whether he could have slept the round of the clock, got stiffly from his couch and staggered to the port. It happened to look out towards the open sea, so that all that he beheld was the green, ruffled water, and some boats at a little distance. Clearly, then, they were in harbour. But in what harbour? It was impossible that they could be in Carthagena. But if in Carthagena, where the devil were they?

He was still asking himself this question when his attention was caught by sounds in the main cabin. He could hear the liquid voice of Alcatrace raised in alarmed, insistent protest.

'De orders, ma'am, are dat you not leabe de cabin. Cap'n's orders, ma'am.'

Doña Isabela, who from her port on the brig's other side had seen and recognized the mole of Rio de la Hacha, without understanding how they came there and without thought even to inquire, had flung in breathless excitement from her stateroom. The resolute negro confronting her and arresting her intended flight almost turned her limp with the sickness of frustration.

'Please, Alcatrace. Please!' On an inspiration she snatched at the pearls in her hair and tore them free. She held them out to him.

'I give you these, Alcatrace. Let me pass.'

What she would do when she had passed and even if she gained the deck she did not stay to think. She was offering all that remained her to bribe a passage of the first obstacle.

The negro's eyes gleamed covetously. But the fear of Fairfax, who might be awake and overhearing, was stronger than his greed. He closed his eyes and shook his head.

'Cap'n's orders, ma'am,' he repeated.

She looked to right and left as a hunted thing will, seeking a way of escape, and her desperate eyes alighted on a brace of pistols on the buffet against the forward bulkhead of the cabin. It was enough. Moving so suddenly as to take him by surprise, she sprang for them, caught them up, and wheeled again to face him with one in each hand, whilst the pearls that had failed her rolled neglected across the cabin floor.

'Out of my way, Alcatrace!'

Before that formidable menace the negro fell back in squealing alarm, and the lady swept out unhindered and made for the deck.

Out there Blood was concluding his preparations for what was yet to do. Most of his anxiety about the immediate future was allayed by the sight of the broad-beamed Dutch ship that was to carry him back to Curaçao beating up into the roads, faithful to the engagement made with him.

But before he could think of boarding the Dutchman, he would take the eloping hidalga ashore, whether she liked it or not, and even if he had to employ force with her. So he went about his preparations. He disengaged the tow-rope of the long-boat from its bollard, and warped the boat forward to the foot of the Jacob's ladder. This done, he made for the gangway leading aft in quest of the lady in whose service the boat was to be employed. He was within a yard of the door when it was suddenly and violently flung open, and he found himself to his amazement confronted by Doña Isabela and her two pistols.

Waving these weapons at him, her voice strident, she addressed him much as she had addressed Alcatrace.

'Out of my way! Out of my way!'

Captain Blood in his time had faced weapons of every kind with imperturbable intrepidity. But he was to confess afterwards that a panic seized him before the threat of those pistols brandished by a woman's trembling hands. Spurred by it to nimbleness, he leapt aside, and flattened himself against a bulkhead in promptest obedience.

He had been prepared for the utmost resistance to his kindly intentions for her, but not for a resistance expressed in so uncompromising and lethal a manner. It was the surprise of it that for a moment put him so utterly out of countenance. When he had recovered from it, he contrived to stand grimly calm before the quivering panic he now perceived in the lady with the pistols.

'Where is Tim?' she demanded. 'I want him. I must be taken ashore at once. At once!'

Blood loosed a breath of relief. 'Glory be! Have ye come to your senses, then, of your own accord? But maybe ye don't know where we are.'

'Oh, I know where I am. I know--' And there, abruptly, she broke off, staring round-eyed at this man whose place and part aboard this ship were suddenly borne in upon her excited senses. His presence, confronting her now, served only to bewilder her. 'But you. . . You. . .' she faltered, breathless, 'You don't know. You are in great danger, sir.'

'I am that, ma'am, for ye will be wagging those pistols at me. Put them down. Put them down, ma'am, a God's name, before we have an accident.' As she obeyed him and lowered her hands, he caught her by the arm. 'Come on ashore with you, then, since that's where ye want to be going. Glory be! Ye're saving me a deal of trouble, for it was ashore I meant to take you whether ye wanted to go or not. Come on.'

But in her amazement she resisted, turning heavy to the suasion of his hand, demanding explanation. 'You meant to take me ashore, you say?'

'Why else do you suppose I brought you back to La Hacha? For it's by my contriving, that we're back here this morning. They say the night brings counsel, but I hardly hoped that a night aboard the brig would bring you such excellent counsel as ye seem to have had.' And again impatiently he sought to hustle her forward.

'You brought me back? You? Captain Blood!'

That gave him pause. His grip of her arm relaxed. His eyes narrowed. 'Ye know that, do you? To be sure he would tell you. Did the blackguard tell you at the same time that he meant to sell me?'

'That,' she said, 'is why I want to go ashore. That is why I thank God to be back in La Hacha.'

'I see. I see.' But his eyes were still grave. 'And when I've put you ashore, can I trust you to hold your tongue until I'm away again?'

There was angry reproach in her glance. She thrust forward her little pointed chin. 'You insult me, sir. Should I betray you? Can you think that?'

'I can't. But I'd like to be sure.'

'I told you last night what I thought of you.'

'So ye did. And heaven knows ye've cause to think better of me still this morning. Come away, then.'

He swept her across the deck, past the hatchway from which the angry sounds of the imprisoned men were still arising, to the Jacob's ladder, and so down into the waiting long-boat.

It was as well they had delayed no longer, for he had no sooner cast off than two faces looked down at them from the head of the ladder in the waist, one black, the other ghastly white in its pallor and terrible in the fury that convulsed it. Mr Fairfax with the help of Alcatrace had staggered to the deck just as Blood and the lady reached the boat.

'Good morning to you, Jorgito!' Blood hailed him. 'Doña Isabela is going ashore with me. But her brother and all the Sotomayors will be alongside presently and devil a doubt but they'll bring the Alcalde with them. They'll be correcting the mistake I made last night when I saved your nasty life.'

'Oh, not that! I do not want that,' Dona Isabela appealed to him.

Blood laughed as he bent his oars. 'D'ye suppose he'll wait? It'll quicken him in getting the cover off the hatch, so as to get under way again. Though the devil knows where he'll go now. Certainly not to Carthagena. It was the notion he took to go there persuaded me he was not the right kind of husband for your ladyship, and decided me to bring you back to your family.'

'That is what made me wish to return,' she said, her dark eyes very wistful. 'All night I prayed for a miracle, and behold my prayer is answered. By you.' She looked at him, a growing wonder in her vivid little face. 'I do not yet know how you did it.'

'Ah!' he said, and rested for a moment on his oars. He drew himself up and sat very erect in the thwart, his lean, intrepid face lighted by a smile half humorous, half complacent. 'I am Captain Blood.'

But before they reached the mole her persistency had drawn a fuller explanation from him, and it brought a great tenderness to eyes that were aswim in tears.

He brought his boat through the swarm of craft with their noisy tenants to the sea-washed steps of the mole, and sprang out under the stare of curious questioning eyes, to hand her from the sternsheets.

Still holding her hand, he said: 'Ye'll forgive me if I don't tarry.'

'Yes, yes. Go. And God go with you.' But she did not yet release her clasp. She leaned nearer. 'Last night I thought you were sent by Heaven to save . . . that man. Today I know that you were sent to save me. Always I shall remember.'

The phrase must have lingered pleasantly in his memory, as we judge from the answer he presently returned to the greeting of the master of the Dutch brig. For with commendable prudence, remembering that Don Francisco de Villamarga was in La Hacha, he denied himself the satisfaction of such thanks as the family of Sotomayor might have been disposed to shower upon him, and pulled steadily away until he brought up against the bulging hull of that most opportunely punctual Dutchman.

Classens, the master, was in the waist to greet him when he climbed aboard.

'Ye're early astir, sir,' the smiling, rubicund Dutchman commended him.

'As becomes a messenger of Heaven,' was the cryptic answer, in which for long thereafter Mynheer Classens vainly sought the jest he supposed to be wrapped in it.

They were in the act of weighing anchor when the *Heron,* crowding canvas, went rippling past them out to sea, a disgruntled, raging, fearful *Heron* in full flight from the neighbourhood of the hawks. And in all this adventure that was Captain Blood's only regret.

SCARAMOUCHE

A ROMANCE OF THE FRENCH REVOLUTION

By

Rafael Sabatini

BOOK I: THE ROBE

CHAPTER I. THE REPUBLICAN

He was born with a gift of laughter and a sense that the world was mad. And that was all his patrimony. His very paternity was obscure, although the village of Gavrillac had long since dispelled the cloud of mystery that hung about it. Those simple Brittany folk were not so simple as to be deceived by a pretended relationship which did not even possess the virtue of originality. When a nobleman, for no apparent reason, announces himself the godfather of an infant fetched no man knew whence, and thereafter cares for the lad's rearing and education, the most unsophisticated of country folk perfectly understand the situation. And so the good people of Gavrillac permitted themselves no illusions on the score of the real relationship between Andre-Louis Moreau—as the lad had been named—and Quintin de Kercadiou, Lord of Gavrillac, who dwelt in the big grey house that dominated from its eminence the village clustering below.

Andre-Louis had learnt his letters at the village school, lodged the while with old Rabouillet, the attorney, who in the capacity of fiscal intendant, looked after the affairs of M. de Kercadiou. Thereafter, at the age of fifteen, he had been packed off to Paris, to the Lycee of Louis Le Grand, to study the law which he was now returned to practise in conjunction with Rabouillet. All this at the charges of his godfather, M. de Kercadiou, who by placing him once more under the tutelage of Rabouillet would seem thereby quite clearly to be making provision for his future.

Andre-Louis, on his side, had made the most of his opportunities. You behold him at the age of four-and-twenty stuffed with learning enough to produce an intellectual indigestion in an ordinary mind. Out of his zestful study of Man, from Thucydides to the Encyclopaedists, from Seneca to Rousseau, he had confirmed into an unassailable conviction his earliest conscious impressions of the general insanity of his own species. Nor can I discover that anything in his eventful life ever afterwards caused him to waver in that opinion.

In body he was a slight wisp of a fellow, scarcely above middle height, with a lean, astute countenance, prominent of nose and cheek-bones, and with lank, black hair that reached almost to his shoulders. His mouth was long, thin-lipped, and humorous. He was only just redeemed from ugliness by the splendour of a pair of ever-questing, luminous eyes, so dark as to be almost black. Of the whimsical quality of his mind and his rare gift of graceful expression, his writings—

unfortunately but too scanty—and particularly his Confessions, afford us very ample evidence. Of his gift of oratory he was hardly conscious yet, although he had already achieved a certain fame for it in the Literary Chamber of Rennes—one of those clubs by now ubiquitous in the land, in which the intellectual youth of France foregathered to study and discuss the new philosophies that were permeating social life. But the fame he had acquired there was hardly enviable. He was too impish, too caustic, too much disposed—so thought his colleagues—to ridicule their sublime theories for the regeneration of mankind. Himself he protested that he merely held them up to the mirror of truth, and that it was not his fault if when reflected there they looked ridiculous.

All that he achieved by this was to exasperate; and his expulsion from a society grown mistrustful of him must already have followed but for his friend, Philippe de Vilmorin, a divinity student of Rennes, who, himself, was one of the most popular members of the Literary Chamber.

Coming to Gavrillac on a November morning, laden with news of the political storms which were then gathering over France, Philippe found in that sleepy Breton village matter to quicken his already lively indignation. A peasant of Gavrillac, named Mabey, had been shot dead that morning in the woods of Meupont, across the river, by a gamekeeper of the Marquis de La Tour d'Azyr. The unfortunate fellow had been caught in the act of taking a pheasant from a snare, and the gamekeeper had acted under explicit orders from his master.

Infuriated by an act of tyranny so absolute and merciless, M. de Vilmorin proposed to lay the matter before M. de Kercadiou. Mabey was a vassal of Gavrillac, and Vilmorin hoped to move the Lord of Gavrillac to demand at least some measure of reparation for the widow and the three orphans which that brutal deed had made.

But because Andre-Louis was Philippe's dearest friend—indeed, his almost brother—the young seminarist sought him out in the first instance. He found him at breakfast alone in the long, low-ceilinged, white-panelled dining-room at Rabouillet's—the only home that Andre-Louis had ever known—and after embracing him, deafened him with his denunciation of M. de La Tour d'Azyr.

"I have heard of it already," said Andre-Louis.

"You speak as if the thing had not surprised you," his friend reproached him.

"Nothing beastly can surprise me when done by a beast. And La Tour d'Azyr is a beast, as all the world knows. The more fool Mabey for stealing his pheasants. He should have stolen somebody else's."

"Is that all you have to say about it?"

"What more is there to say? I've a practical mind, I hope."

"What more there is to say I propose to say to your godfather, M. de Kercadiou. I shall appeal to him for justice."

"Against M. de La Tour d'Azyr?" Andre-Louis raised his eyebrows.

"Why not?"

"My dear ingenuous Philippe, dog doesn't eat dog."

"You are unjust to your godfather. He is a humane man."

"Oh, as humane as you please. But this isn't a question of humanity. It's a question of game-laws."

M. de Vilmorin tossed his long arms to Heaven in disgust. He was a tall, slender young gentleman, a year or two younger than Andre-Louis. He was very soberly dressed in black, as became a seminarist, with white bands at wrists and throat and silver buckles to his shoes. His neatly clubbed brown hair was innocent of powder.

"You talk like a lawyer," he exploded.

"Naturally. But don't waste anger on me on that account. Tell me what you want me to do."

"I want you to come to M. de Kercadiou with me, and to use your influence to obtain justice. I suppose I am asking too much."

"My dear Philippe, I exist to serve you. I warn you that it is a futile quest; but give me leave to finish my breakfast, and I am at your orders."

M. de Vilmorin dropped into a winged armchair by the well-swept hearth, on which a piled-up fire of pine logs was burning cheerily. And whilst he waited now he gave his friend the latest news of the events in Rennes. Young, ardent, enthusiastic, and inspired by Utopian ideals, he passionately denounced the rebellious attitude of the privileged.

Andre-Louis, already fully aware of the trend of feeling in the ranks of an order in whose deliberations he took part as the representative of a nobleman, was not at all surprised by what he heard. M. de Vilmorin found it exasperating that his friend should apparently decline to share his own indignation.

"Don't you see what it means?" he cried. "The nobles, by disobeying the King, are striking at the very foundations of the throne. Don't they perceive that their very existence depends upon it; that if the throne falls over, it is they who stand nearest to it who will be crushed? Don't they see that?"

"Evidently not. They are just governing classes, and I never heard of governing classes that had eyes for anything but their own profit."

"That is our grievance. That is what we are going to change."

"You are going to abolish governing classes? An interesting experiment. I believe it was the original plan of creation, and it might have succeeded but for Cain."

"What we are going to do," said M. de Vilmorin, curbing his exasperation, "is to transfer the government to other hands."

"And you think that will make a difference?"

"I know it will."

"Ah! I take it that being now in minor orders, you already possess the confidence of the Almighty. He will have confided to you His intention of changing the pattern of mankind."

M. de Vilmorin's fine ascetic face grew overcast. "You are profane, Andre," he reproved his friend.

"I assure you that I am quite serious. To do what you imply would require nothing short of divine intervention. You must change man, not systems. Can you and our vapouring friends of the Literary Chamber of Rennes, or any other learned society of France, devise a system of government that has never yet been tried? Surely not. And can they say of any system tried that it proved other than a failure in the end? My dear Philippe, the future is to be read with certainty only in the past. Ab actu ad posse valet consecutio. Man never changes. He is always greedy, always acquisitive, always vile. I am speaking of Man in the bulk."

"Do you pretend that it is impossible to ameliorate the lot of the people?" M. de Vilmorin challenged him.

"When you say the people you mean, of course, the populace. Will you abolish it? That is the only way to ameliorate its lot, for as long as it remains populace its lot will be damnation."

"You argue, of course, for the side that employs you. That is natural, I suppose." M. de Vilmorin spoke between sorrow and indignation.

"On the contrary, I seek to argue with absolute detachment. Let us test these ideas of yours. To what form of government do you aspire? A republic, it is to be inferred from what you have said. Well, you have it already. France in reality is a republic to-day."

Philippe stared at him. "You are being paradoxical, I think. What of the King?"

"The King? All the world knows there has been no king in France since Louis XIV. There is an obese gentleman at Versailles who wears the crown, but the very news you bring shows for how little he really counts. It is the nobles and clergy who sit in the high places, with the people of France harnessed under their feet, who are the real rulers. That is why I say that France is a republic; she is a republic built on the best pattern—the Roman pattern. Then, as now, there were great patrician families in luxury, preserving for themselves power and wealth, and what else is accounted worth possessing; and there was the populace crushed and groaning, sweating, bleeding, starving, and perishing in the Roman kennels. That was a republic; the mightiest we have seen."

Philippe strove with his impatience. "At least you will admit—you have, in fact, admitted it—that we could not be worse governed than we are?"

"That is not the point. The point is should we be better governed if we replaced the present ruling class by another? Without some guarantee of that I should be the last to lift a finger to effect a change. And what guarantees can you give? What is the class that aims at government? I will tell you. The bourgeoisie."

"What?"

"That startles you, eh? Truth is so often disconcerting. You hadn't thought of it? Well, think of it now. Look well into this Nantes manifesto. Who are the authors of it?"

"I can tell you who it was constrained the municipality of Nantes to send it to the King. Some ten thousand workmen—shipwrights, weavers, labourers, and artisans of every kind."

"Stimulated to it, driven to it, by their employers, the wealthy traders and shipowners of that city," Andre-Louis replied. "I have a habit of observing things at close quarters, which is why our colleagues of the Literary Chamber dislike me so cordially in debate. Where I delve they but skim. Behind those labourers and artisans of Nantes, counselling them, urging on these poor, stupid, ignorant toilers to shed their blood in pursuit of the will o' the wisp of freedom, are the sail-makers, the spinners, the ship-owners and the slave-traders. The slave-traders! The men who live and grow rich by a traffic in human flesh and blood in the colonies, are conducting at home a campaign in the sacred name of liberty! Don't you see that the whole movement is a movement of hucksters and traders and peddling vassals swollen by wealth into envy of the power that lies in birth alone? The money-changers in Paris who hold the bonds in the national debt, seeing the parlous financial condition of the State, tremble at the thought that it may lie in the power of a single man to cancel the debt by bankruptcy. To secure themselves they are burrowing underground to overthrow a state and build upon its ruins a new one in which they shall be the masters. And to accomplish this they inflame the people. Already in Dauphiny we have seen blood run like water—the blood of the populace, always the blood of the populace. Now in Brittany we may see the like. And if in the end the new ideas prevail? if the seigneurial rule is overthrown, what then? You will have exchanged an aristocracy for a plutocracy. Is that worth while? Do you 'think that under money-changers and slave-traders and men who have waxed rich in other ways by the ignoble arts of buying and selling, the lot of the people will be any better than under their priests and nobles? Has it ever occurred to you, Philippe, what it is that makes the rule of the nobles so intolerable? Acquisitiveness. Acquisitiveness is the curse of mankind. And shall you expect less acquisitiveness in men who have built themselves up by acquisitiveness? Oh, I am ready to admit that the present government is execrable, unjust, tyrannical—what you will; but I beg you to look ahead, and to see that the government for which it is aimed at exchanging it may be infinitely worse."

Philippe sat thoughtful a moment. Then he returned to the attack.

"You do not speak of the abuses, the horrible, intolerable abuses of power under which we labour at present."

"Where there is power there will always be the abuse of it."

"Not if the tenure of power is dependent upon its equitable administration."

"The tenure of power is power. We cannot dictate to those who hold it."

"The people can—the people in its might."

"Again I ask you, when you say the people do you mean the populace? You do. What power can the populace wield? It can run wild. It can burn and slay for a time. But enduring power it cannot wield, because power demands qualities which the populace does not possess, or it would not be populace. The inevitable, tragic corollary of civilization is populace. For the rest, abuses can be corrected by equity; and equity, if it is not found in the enlightened, is not to be found at all. M. Necker is to set about correcting abuses, and limiting privileges. That is decided. To that end the States General are to assemble."

"And a promising beginning we have made in Brittany, as Heaven hears me!" cried Philippe.

"Pooh! That is nothing. Naturally the nobles will not yield without a struggle. It is a futile and ridiculous struggle—but then... it is human nature, I suppose, to be futile and ridiculous."

M. de Vilmorin became witheringly sarcastic. "Probably you will also qualify the shooting of Mabey as futile and ridiculous. I should even be prepared to hear you argue in defence of the Marquis de La Tour d'Azyr that his gamekeeper was merciful in shooting Mabey, since the alternative would have been a life-sentence to the galleys."

Andre-Louis drank the remainder of his chocolate; set down his cup, and pushed back his chair, his breakfast done.

"I confess that I have not your big charity, my dear Philippe. I am touched by Mabey's fate. But, having conquered the shock of this news to my emotions, I do not forget that, after all, Mabey was thieving when he met his death."

M. de Vilmorin heaved himself up in his indignation.

"That is the point of view to be expected in one who is the assistant fiscal intendant of a nobleman, and the delegate of a nobleman to the States of Brittany."

"Philippe, is that just? You are angry with me!" he cried, in real solicitude.

"I am hurt," Vilmorin admitted. "I am deeply hurt by your attitude. And I am not alone in resenting your reactionary tendencies. Do you know that the Literary Chamber is seriously considering your expulsion?"

Andre-Louis shrugged. "That neither surprises nor troubles me."

M. de Vilmorin swept on, passionately: "Sometimes I think that you have no heart. With you it is always the law, never equity. It occurs to me, Andre, that I was mistaken in coming to you. You are not likely to be of assistance to me in my interview with M. de Kercadiou." He took up his hat, clearly with the intention of departing.

Andre-Louis sprang up and caught him by the arm.

"I vow," said he, "that this is the last time ever I shall consent to talk law or politics with you, Philippe. I love you too well to quarrel with you over other men's affairs."

"But I make them my own," Philippe insisted vehemently.

"Of course you do, and I love you for it. It is right that you should. You are to be a priest; and everybody's business is a priest's business. Whereas I am a lawyer—the fiscal intendant of a nobleman, as you say—and a lawyer's business is the business of his client. That is the difference between us. Nevertheless, you are not going to shake me off."

"But I tell you frankly, now that I come to think of it, that I should prefer you did not see M. de Kercadiou with me. Your duty to your client cannot be a help to me."

His wrath had passed; but his determination remained firm, based upon the reason he gave.

"Very well," said Andre-Louis. "It shall be as you please. But nothing shall prevent me at least from walking with you as far as the chateau, and waiting for you while you make your appeal to M. de Kercadiou."

And so they left the house good friends, for the sweetness of M. de Vilmorin's nature did not admit of rancour, and together they took their way up the steep main street of Gavrillac.

CHAPTER II. THE ARISTOCRAT

The sleepy village of Gavrillac, a half-league removed from the main road to Rennes, and therefore undisturbed by the world's traffic, lay in a curve of the River Meu, at the foot, and straggling halfway up the slope, of the shallow hill that was crowned by the squat manor. By the time Gavrillac had paid tribute to its seigneur—partly in money and partly in service—tithes to the Church, and imposts to the King, it was hard put to it to keep body and soul together with what remained. Yet, hard as conditions were in Gavrillac, they were not so hard as in many other parts of France, not half so hard, for instance, as with the wretched feudatories of the great Lord of La Tour d'Azyr, whose vast possessions were at one point separated from this little village by the waters of the Meu.

The Chateau de Gavrillac owed such seigneurial airs as might be claimed for it to its dominant position above the village rather than to any feature of its own. Built of granite, like all the rest of Gavrillac, though mellowed by some three centuries of existence, it was a squat, flat-fronted edifice of two stories, each lighted by four windows with external wooden shutters, and flanked at either end by two square towers or pavilions under extinguisher roofs. Standing well back in a garden, denuded now, but very pleasant in summer, and immediately fronted by a fine sweep of balustraded terrace, it looked, what indeed it was, and always had been, the residence of unpretentious folk who found more interest in husbandry than in adventure.

Quintin de Kercadiou, Lord of Gavrillac—Seigneur de Gavrillac was all the vague title that he bore, as his forefathers had borne before him, derived no man knew whence or how—confirmed the impression that his house conveyed. Rude as the granite itself, he had never sought the experience of courts, had not even taken service in the armies of his King. He left it to his younger brother, Etienne, to represent the family in those exalted spheres. His own interests from earliest years had been centred in his woods and pastures. He hunted, and he cultivated his acres, and superficially he appeared to be little better than any of his rustic metayers. He kept no state, or at least no state commensurate with his position or with the tastes of his niece Aline de Kercadiou. Aline, having spent some two years in the court atmosphere of Versailles under the aegis of her uncle Etienne, had ideas very different from those of her uncle Quintin of what was befitting seigneurial dignity. But though this only child of a third Kercadiou had exercised, ever since she was left an orphan at the early age of four, a tyrannical rule over the Lord of Gavrillac, who had been father and mother to her, she had never yet succeeded in beating down his stubbornness on that score. She did not yet despair—persistence being a dominant note in her character—although she had been assiduously and fruitlessly at work since her return from the great world of Versailles some three months ago.

She was walking on the terrace when Andre-Louis and M. de Vilmorin arrived. Her slight body was wrapped against the chill air in a white pelisse; her head was encased in a close-fitting bonnet, edged with white fur. It was caught tight in a knot of pale-blue ribbon on the right of her chin; on the left a long ringlet of corn-coloured hair had been permitted to escape. The keen air had whipped so much of her cheeks as was presented to it, and seemed to have added sparkle to eyes that were of darkest blue.

Andre-Louis and M. de Vilmorin had been known to her from childhood. The three had been playmates once, and Andre-Louis—in view of his spiritual relationship with her uncle—she called her cousin. The cousinly relations had persisted between these two long after Philippe de Vilmorin had outgrown the earlier intimacy, and had become to her Monsieur de Vilmorin.

She waved her hand to them in greeting as they advanced, and stood—an entrancing picture, and fully conscious of it—to await them at the end of the terrace nearest the short avenue by which they approached.

"If you come to see monsieur my uncle, you come inopportunely, messieurs," she told them, a certain feverishness in her air. "He is closely—oh, so very closely—engaged."

"We will wait, mademoiselle," said M. de Vilmorin, bowing gallantly over the hand she extended to him. "Indeed, who would haste to the uncle that may tarry a moment with the niece?"

"M. l'abbe," she teased him, "when you are in orders I shall take you for my confessor. You have so ready and sympathetic an understanding."

"But no curiosity," said Andre-Louis. "You haven't thought of that."

"I wonder what you mean, Cousin Andre."

"Well you may," laughed Philippe. "For no one ever knows." And then, his glance straying across the terrace settled upon a carriage that was drawn up before the door of the chateau. It was a vehicle such as was often to be seen in the streets of a great city, but rarely in the country. It was a beautifully sprung two-horse cabriolet of walnut, with a varnish upon it like a sheet of glass and little pastoral scenes exquisitely painted on the panels of the door. It was built to carry two persons, with a box in front for the coachman, and a stand behind for the footman. This stand was empty, but the footman paced before the door, and as he emerged now from behind the vehicle into the range of M. de Vilmorin's vision, he displayed the resplendent blue-and-gold livery of the Marquis de La Tour d'Azyr.

"Why!" he exclaimed. "Is it M. de La Tour d'Azyr who is with your uncle?"

"It is, monsieur," said she, a world of mystery in voice and eyes, of which M. de Vilmorin observed nothing.

"Ah, pardon!" he bowed low, hat in hand. "Serviteur, mademoiselle," and he turned to depart towards the house.

"Shall I come with you, Philippe?" Andre-Louis called after him.

"It would be ungallant to assume that you would prefer it," said M. de Vilmorin, with a glance at mademoiselle. "Nor do I think it would serve. If you will wait..."

M. de Vilmorin strode off. Mademoiselle, after a moment's blank pause, laughed ripplingly. "Now where is he going in such a hurry?"

"To see M. de La Tour d'Azyr as well as your uncle, I should say."

"But he cannot. They cannot see him. Did I not say that they are very closely engaged? You don't ask me why, Andre." There was an arch mysteriousness about her, a latent something that may have been elation or amusement, or perhaps both. Andre-Louis could not determine it.

"Since obviously you are all eagerness to tell, why should I ask?" quoth he.

"If you are caustic I shall not tell you even if you ask. Oh, yes, I will. It will teach you to treat me with the respect that is my due."

"I hope I shall never fail in that."

"Less than ever when you learn that I am very closely concerned in the visit of M. de La Tour d'Azyr. I am the object of this visit." And she looked at him with sparkling eyes and lips parted in laughter.

"The rest, you would seem to imply, is obvious. But I am a dolt, if you please; for it is not obvious to me."

"Why, stupid, he comes to ask my hand in marriage."

"Good God!" said Andre-Louis, and stared at her, chapfallen.

She drew back from him a little with a frown and an upward tilt of her chin. "It surprises you?"

"It disgusts me," said he, bluntly. "In fact, I don't believe it. You are amusing yourself with me."

For a moment she put aside her visible annoyance to remove his doubts. "I am quite serious, monsieur. There came a formal letter to my uncle this morning from M. de La Tour d'Azyr, announcing the visit and its object. I will not say that it did not surprise us a little..."

"Oh, I see," cried Andre-Louis, in relief. "I understand. For a moment I had almost feared..." He broke off, looked at her, and shrugged.

"Why do you stop? You had almost feared that Versailles had been wasted upon me. That I should permit the court-ship of me to be conducted like that of any village wench. It was stupid of you. I am being sought in proper form, at my uncle's hands."

"Is his consent, then, all that matters, according to Versailles?"

"What else?"

"There is your own."

She laughed. "I am a dutiful niece... when it suits me."

"And will it suit you to be dutiful if your uncle accepts this monstrous proposal?"

"Monstrous!" She bridled. "And why monstrous, if you please?"

"For a score of reasons," he answered irritably.

"Give me one," she challenged him.

"He is twice your age."

"Hardly so much," said she.

"He is forty-five, at least."

"But he looks no more than thirty. He is very handsome—so much you will admit; nor will you deny that he is very wealthy and very powerful; the greatest nobleman in Brittany. He will make me a great lady."

"God made you that, Aline."

"Come, that's better. Sometimes you can almost be polite." And she moved along the terrace, Andre-Louis pacing beside her.

"I can be more than that to show reason why you should not let this beast befoul the beautiful thing that God has made."

She frowned, and her lips tightened. "You are speaking of my future husband," she reproved him.

His lips tightened too; his pale face grew paler.

"And is it so? It is settled, then? Your uncle is to agree? You are to be sold thus, lovelessly, into bondage to a man you do not know. I had dreamed of better things for you, Aline."

"Better than to be Marquise de La Tour d'Azyr?"

He made a gesture of exasperation. "Are men and women nothing more than names? Do the souls of them count for nothing? Is there no joy in life, no happiness, that wealth and pleasure and empty, high-sounding titles are to be its only aims? I had set you high—so high, Aline—a thing scarce earthly. There is joy in your heart, intelligence in your mind; and, as I thought, the vision that pierces husks and shams to claim the core of reality for its own. Yet you will surrender all for a parcel of make-believe. You will sell your soul and your body to be Marquise de La Tour d'Azyr."

"You are indelicate," said she, and though she frowned her eyes laughed. "And you go headlong to conclusions. My uncle will not consent to more than to allow my consent to be sought. We understand each other, my uncle and I. I am not to be bartered like a turnip."

He stood still to face her, his eyes glowing, a flush creeping into his pale cheeks.

"You have been torturing me to amuse yourself!" he cried. "Ah, well, I forgive you out of my relief."

"Again you go too fast, Cousin Andre I have permitted my uncle to consent that M. le Marquis shall make his court to me. I like the look of the gentleman. I am flattered by his preference when I consider his eminence. It is an eminence that I may find it desirable to share. M. le Marquis does not look as if he were a dullard. It should be interesting to be wooed by him. It may be more interesting still to marry him, and I think, when all is considered, that I shall probably—very probably—decide to do so."

He looked at her, looked at the sweet, challenging loveliness of that childlike face so tightly framed in the oval of white fur, and all the life seemed to go out of his own countenance.

"God help you, Aline!" he groaned.

She stamped her foot. He was really very exasperating, and something presumptuous too, she thought.

"You are insolent, monsieur."

"It is never insolent to pray, Aline. And I did no more than pray, as I shall continue to do. You'll need my prayers, I think."

"You are insufferable!" She was growing angry, as he saw by the deepening frown, the heightened colour.

"That is because I suffer. Oh, Aline, little cousin, think well of what you do; think well of the realities you will be bartering for these shams—the realities that you will never know, because these cursed shams will block your way to them. When M. de La Tour d'Azyr comes to make his court, study him well; consult your fine instincts; leave your own noble nature free to judge this animal by its intuitions. Consider that..."

"I consider, monsieur, that you presume upon the kindness I have always shown you. You abuse the position of toleration in which you stand. Who are you? What are you, that you should have the insolence to take this tone with me?"

He bowed, instantly his cold, detached self again, and resumed the mockery that was his natural habit.

"My congratulations, mademoiselle, upon the readiness with which you begin to adapt yourself to the great role you are to play."

"Do you adapt yourself also, monsieur," she retorted angrily, and turned her shoulder to him.

"To be as the dust beneath the haughty feet of Madame la Marquise. I hope I shall know my place in future."

The phrase arrested her. She turned to him again, and he perceived that her eyes were shining now suspiciously. In an instant the mockery in him was quenched in contrition.

"Lord, what a beast I am, Aline!" he cried, as he advanced. "Forgive me if you can."

Almost had she turned to sue forgiveness from him. But his contrition removed the need.

"I'll try," said she, "provided that you undertake not to offend again."

"But I shall," said he. "I am like that. I will fight to save you, from yourself if need be, whether you forgive me or not."

They were standing so, confronting each other a little breathlessly, a little defiantly, when the others issued from the porch.

First came the Marquis of La Tour d'Azyr, Count of Solz, Knight of the Orders of the Holy Ghost and Saint Louis, and Brigadier in the armies of the King. He was a tall, graceful man, upright and soldierly of carriage, with his head disdainfully set upon his shoulders. He was magnificently dressed in a full-skirted coat of mulberry velvet that was laced with gold. His waistcoat, of velvet too, was of a golden apricot colour; his breeches and stockings were of black silk, and his lacquered, red-heeled shoes were buckled in diamonds. His powdered hair was tied behind in a broad ribbon of watered silk; he carried a little three-cornered hat under his arm, and a gold-hilted slender dress-sword hung at his side.

Considering him now in complete detachment, observing the magnificence of him, the elegance of his movements, the great air, blending in so extraordinary a manner disdain and graciousness, Andre Louis trembled for Aline. Here was a practised, irresistible wooer, whose bonnes fortunes were become a by-word, a man who had hitherto been the despair of dowagers with marriageable daughters, and the desolation of husbands with attractive wives.

He was immediately followed by M. de Kercadiou, in completest contrast. On legs of the shortest, the Lord of Gavrillac carried a body that at forty-five was beginning to incline to corpulence and an enormous head containing an indifferent allotment of intelligence. His countenance was pink and blotchy, liberally branded by the smallpox which had almost extinguished him in youth. In dress he was careless to the point of untidiness, and to this and to the fact that he had never married—disregarding the first duty of a gentleman to provide himself with an heir—he owed the character of misogynist attributed to him by the countryside.

After M. de Kercadiou came M. de Vilmorin, very pale and self-contained, with tight lips and an overcast brow.

To meet them, there stepped from the carriage a very elegant young gentleman, the Chevalier de Chabrillane, M. de La Tour d'Azyr's cousin, who whilst awaiting his return had watched with considerable interest—his own presence unsuspected—the perambulations of Andre-Louis and mademoiselle.

Perceiving Aline, M. de La Tour d'Azyr detached himself from the others, and lengthening his stride came straight across the terrace to her.

To Andre-Louis the Marquis inclined his head with that mixture of courtliness and condescension which he used. Socially, the young lawyer stood in a curious position. By virtue of the theory of his birth, he ranked neither as noble nor as simple, but stood somewhere between the two classes, and whilst claimed by neither he was used familiarly by both. Coldly now he returned M. de La Tour d'Azyr's greeting, and discreetly removed himself to go and join his friend.

The Marquis took the hand that mademoiselle extended to him, and bowing over it, bore it to his lips.

"Mademoiselle," he said, looking into the blue depths of her eyes, that met his gaze smiling and untroubled, "monsieur your uncle does me the honour to permit that I pay my homage to you. Will you, mademoiselle, do me the honour to receive me when I come to-morrow? I shall have something of great importance for your ear."

"Of importance, M. le Marquis? You almost frighten me." But there was no fear on the serene little face in its furred hood. It was not for nothing that she had graduated in the Versailles school of artificialities.

"That," said he, "is very far from my design."

"But of importance to yourself, monsieur, or to me?"

"To us both, I hope," he answered her, a world of meaning in his fine, ardent eyes.

"You whet my curiosity, monsieur; and, of course, I am a dutiful niece. It follows that I shall be honoured to receive you."

"Not honoured, mademoiselle; you will confer the honour. To-morrow at this hour, then, I shall have the felicity to wait upon you."

He bowed again; and again he bore her fingers to his lips, what time she curtsied. Thereupon, with no more than this formal breaking of the ice, they parted.

She was a little breathless now, a little dazzled by the beauty of the man, his princely air, and the confidence of power he seemed to radiate. Involuntarily almost, she contrasted him with his critic—the lean and impudent Andre-Louis in his plain brown coat and steel-buckled shoes—and she felt guilty of an unpardonable offence in having permitted even one word of that presumptuous criticism. To-morrow M. le Marquis would come to offer her a great position, a great rank. And already she had derogated from the increase of dignity accruing to her from his very intention to translate her to so great an eminence. Not again would she suffer it; not again would she be so weak and childish as to permit Andre-Louis to utter his ribald comments upon a man by comparison with whom he was no better than a lackey.

Thus argued vanity and ambition with her better self and to her vast annoyance her better self would not admit entire conviction.

Meanwhile, M. de La Tour d'Azyr was climbing into his carriage. He had spoken a word of farewell to M. de Kercadiou, and he had also had a word for M. de Vilmorin in reply to which M. de Vilmorin had bowed in assenting silence. The carriage rolled away, the powdered footman in blue-and-gold very stiff behind it, M. de La Tour d'Azyr bowing to mademoiselle, who waved to him in answer.

Then M. de Vilmorin put his arm through that of Andre Louis, and said to him, "Come, Andre."

"But you'll stay to dine, both of you!" cried the hospitable Lord of Gavrillac. "We'll drink a certain toast," he added, winking an eye that strayed towards mademoiselle, who was approaching. He had no subtleties, good soul that he was.

M. de Vilmorin deplored an appointment that prevented him doing himself the honour. He was very stiff and formal.

"And you, Andre?"

"I? Oh, I share the appointment, godfather," he lied, "and I have a superstition against toasts." He had no wish to remain. He was angry with Aline for her smiling reception of M. de La Tour d'Azyr and the sordid bargain he saw her set on making. He was suffering from the loss of an illusion.

CHAPTER III. THE ELOQUENCE OF M. DE VILMORIN

As they walked down the hill together, it was now M. de Vilmorin who was silent and preoccupied, Andre-Louis who was talkative. He had chosen Woman as a subject for his present discourse. He claimed—quite unjustifiably—to have discovered Woman that morning; and the things he had to say of the sex were unflattering, and occasionally almost gross. M. de Vilmorin, having ascertained the subject, did not listen. Singular though it may seem in a young French abbe of his day, M. de Vilmorin was not interested in Woman. Poor Philippe was in several ways exceptional. Opposite the Breton arme—the inn and posting-house at the entrance of the village of Gavrillac—M. de Vilmorin interrupted his companion just as he was soaring to the dizziest heights of caustic invective, and Andre-Louis, restored thereby to actualities, observed the carriage of M. de La Tour d'Azyr standing before the door of the hostelry.

"I don't believe you've been listening to me," said he.

"Had you been less interested in what you were saying, you might have observed it sooner and spared your breath. The fact is, you disappoint me, Andre. You seem to have forgotten what we went for. I have an appointment here with M. le Marquis. He desires to hear me further in the matter. Up there at Gavrillac I could accomplish nothing. The time was ill-chosen as it happened. But I have hopes of M. le Marquis."

"Hopes of what?"

"That he will make what reparation lies in his power. Provide for the widow and the orphans. Why else should he desire to hear me further?"

"Unusual condescension," said Andre-Louis, and quoted "Timeo Danaos et dona ferentes."

"Why?" asked Philippe.

"Let us go and discover—unless you consider that I shall be in the way."

Into a room on the right, rendered private to M. le Marquis for so long as he should elect to honour it, the young men were ushered by the host. A fire of logs was burning brightly at the room's far end, and by this sat now M. de La Tour d'Azyr and his cousin, the Chevalier de Chabrillane. Both rose as M. de Vilmorin came in. Andre-Louis following, paused to close the door.

"You oblige me by your prompt courtesy, M. de Vilmorin," said the Marquis, but in a tone so cold as to belie the politeness of his words. "A chair, I beg. Ah,

Moreau?" The note was frigidly interrogative. "He accompanies you, monsieur?" he asked.

"If you please, M. le Marquis."

"Why not? Find yourself a seat, Moreau." He spoke over his shoulder as to a lackey.

"It is good of you, monsieur," said Philippe, "to have offered me this opportunity of continuing the subject that took me so fruitlessly, as it happens, to Gavrillac."

The Marquis crossed his legs, and held one of his fine hands to the blaze. He replied, without troubling to turn to the young man, who was slightly behind him.

"The goodness of my request we will leave out of question for the moment," said he, darkly, and M. de Chabrillane laughed. Andre-Louis thought him easily moved to mirth, and almost envied him the faculty.

"But I am grateful," Philippe insisted, "that you should condescend to hear me plead their cause."

The Marquis stared at him over his shoulder. "Whose cause?" quoth he.

"Why, the cause of the widow and orphans of this unfortunate Mabey."

The Marquis looked from Vilmorin to the Chevalier, and again the Chevalier laughed, slapping his leg this time.

"I think," said M. de La Tour d'Azyr, slowly, "that we are at cross-purposes. I asked you to come here because the Chateau de Gavrillac was hardly a suitable place in which to carry our discussion further, and because I hesitated to incommode you by suggesting that you should come all the way to Azyr. But my object is connected with certain expressions that you let fall up there. It is on the subject of those expressions, monsieur, that I would hear you further—if you will honour me."

Andre-Louis began to apprehend that there was something sinister in the air. He was a man of quick intuitions, quicker far than those of M. de Vilmorin, who evinced no more than a mild surprise.

"I am at a loss, monsieur," said he. "To what expressions does monsieur allude?"

"It seems, monsieur, that I must refresh your memory." The Marquis crossed his legs, and swung sideways on his chair, so that at last he directly faced M. de Vilmorin. "You spoke, monsieur—and however mistaken you may have been, you spoke very eloquently, too eloquently almost, it seemed to me—of the infamy of such a deed as the act of summary justice upon this thieving fellow Mabey, or whatever his name may be. Infamy was the precise word you used. You did not retract that word when I had the honour to inform you that it was by my orders that my gamekeeper Benet proceeded as he did."

"If," said M. de Vilmorin, "the deed was infamous, its infamy is not modified by the rank, however exalted, of the person responsible. Rather is it aggravated."

"Ah!" said M. le Marquis, and drew a gold snuffbox from his pocket. "You say, 'if the deed was infamous,' monsieur. Am I to understand that you are no longer as convinced as you appeared to be of its infamy?"

M. de Vilmorin's fine face wore a look of perplexity. He did not understand the drift of this.

"It occurs to me, M. le Marquis, in view of your readiness to assume responsibility, that you must believe justification for the deed which is not apparent to myself."

"That is better. That is distinctly better." The Marquis took snuff delicately, dusting the fragments from the fine lace at his throat. "You realize that with an imperfect understanding of these matters, not being yourself a landowner, you may have rushed to unjustifiable conclusions. That is indeed the case. May it be a warning to you, monsieur. When I tell you that for months past I have been annoyed by similar depredations, you will perhaps understand that it had become necessary to employ a deterrent sufficiently strong to put an end to them. Now that the risk is known, I do not think there will be any more prowling in my coverts. And there is more in it than that, M. de Vilmorin. It is not the poaching that annoys me so much as the contempt for my absolute and inviolable rights. There is, monsieur, as you cannot fail to have observed, an evil spirit of insubordination in the air, and there is one only way in which to meet it. To tolerate it, in however slight a degree, to show leniency, however leniently disposed, would entail having recourse to still harsher measures to-morrow. You understand me, I am sure, and you will also, I am sure, appreciate the condescension of what amounts to an explanation from me where I cannot admit that any explanations were due. If anything in what I have said is still obscure to you, I refer you to the game laws, which your lawyer friend there will expound for you at need."

With that the gentleman swung round again to face the fire. It appeared to convey the intimation that the interview was at an end. And yet this was not by any means the intimation that it conveyed to the watchful, puzzled, vaguely uneasy Andre-Louis. It was, thought he, a very curious, a very suspicious oration. It affected to explain, with a politeness of terms and a calculated insolence of tone; whilst in fact it could only serve to stimulate and goad a man of M. de Vilmorin's opinions. And that is precisely what it did. He rose.

"Are there in the world no laws but game laws?" he demanded, angrily. "Have you never by any chance heard of the laws of humanity?"

The Marquis sighed wearily. "What have I to do with the laws of humanity?" he wondered.

M. de Vilmorin looked at him a moment in speechless amazement.

"Nothing, M. le Marquis. That is—alas!—too obvious. I hope you will remember it in the hour when you may wish to appeal to those laws which you now deride."

M. de La Tour d'Azyr threw back his head sharply, his high-bred face imperious.

"Now what precisely shall that mean? It is not the first time to-day that you have made use of dark sayings that I could almost believe to veil the presumption of a threat."

"Not a threat, M. le Marquis—a warning. A warning that such deeds as these against God's creatures... Oh, you may sneer, monsieur, but they are God's creatures, even as you or I—neither more nor less, deeply though the reflection may wound your pride, In His eyes..."

"Of your charity, spare me a sermon, M. l'abbe!"

"You mock, monsieur. You laugh. Will you laugh, I wonder, when God presents His reckoning to you for the blood and plunder with which your hands are full?"

"Monsieur!" The word, sharp as the crack of a whip, was from M. de Chabrillane, who bounded to his feet. But instantly the Marquis repressed him.

"Sit down, Chevalier. You are interrupting M. l'abbe, and I should like to hear him further. He interests me profoundly."

In the background Andre-Louis, too, had risen, brought to his feet by alarm, by the evil that he saw written on the handsome face of M. de La Tour d'Azyr. He approached, and touched his friend upon the arm.

"Better be going, Philippe," said he.

But M. de Vilmorin, caught in the relentless grip of passions long repressed, was being hurried by them recklessly along.

"Oh, monsieur," said he, "consider what you are and what you will be. Consider how you and your kind live by abuses, and consider the harvest that abuses must ultimately bring."

"Revolutionist!" said M. le Marquis, contemptuously. "You have the effrontery to stand before my face and offer me this stinking cant of your modern so-called intellectuals!"

"Is it cant, monsieur? Do you think—do you believe in your soul—that it is cant? Is it cant that the feudal grip is on all things that live, crushing them like grapes in the press, to its own profit? Does it not exercise its rights upon the waters of the river, the fire that bakes the poor man's bread of grass and barley, on the wind that turns the mill? The peasant cannot take a step upon the road, cross a crazy bridge over a river, buy an ell of cloth in the village market, without meeting feudal rapacity, without being taxed in feudal dues. Is not that enough, M. le Marquis? Must you also demand his wretched life in payment for the least infringement of your sacred privileges, careless of what widows or orphans you dedicate to woe? Will naught content you but that your shadow must lie like a curse upon the land? And do you think in your pride that France, this Job among the nations, will suffer it forever?"

He paused as if for a reply. But none came. The Marquis considered him, strangely silent, a half smile of disdain at the corners of his lips, an ominous hardness in his eyes.

Again Andre-Louis tugged at his friend's sleeve.

"Philippe."

Philippe shook him off, and plunged on, fanatically.

"Do you see nothing of the gathering clouds that herald the coming of the storm? You imagine, perhaps, that these States General summoned by M. Necker, and promised for next year, are to do nothing but devise fresh means of extortion to liquidate the bankruptcy of the State? You delude yourselves, as you shall find. The Third Estate, which you despise, will prove itself the preponderating force, and it will find a way to make an end of this canker of privilege that is devouring the vitals of this unfortunate country."

M. le Marquis shifted in his chair, and spoke at last.

"You have, monsieur," said he, "a very dangerous gift of eloquence. And it is of yourself rather than of your subject. For after all, what do you offer me? A rechauffe of the dishes served to out-at-elbow enthusiasts in the provincial literary chambers, compounded of the effusions of your Voltaires and Jean-Jacques and such dirty-fingered scribblers. You have not among all your philosophers one with the wit to understand that we are an order consecrated by antiquity, that for our rights and privileges we have behind us the authority of centuries."

"Humanity, monsieur," Philippe replied, "is more ancient than nobility. Human rights are contemporary with man."

The Marquis laughed and shrugged.

"That is the answer I might have expected. It has the right note of cant that distinguishes the philosophers."

And then M. de Chabrillane spoke.

"You go a long way round," he criticized his cousin, on a note of impatience.

"But I am getting there," he was answered. "I desired to make quite certain first."

"Faith, you should have no doubt by now."

"I have none." The Marquis rose, and turned again to M. de Vilmorin, who had understood nothing of that brief exchange. "M. l'abbe," said he once more, "you have a very dangerous gift of eloquence. I can conceive of men being swayed by it. Had you been born a gentleman, you would not so easily have acquired these false views that you express."

M. de Vilmorin stared blankly, uncomprehending.

"Had I been born a gentleman, do you say?" quoth he, in a slow, bewildered voice. "But I was born a gentleman. My race is as old, my blood as good as yours, monsieur."

From M. le Marquis there was a slight play of eyebrows, a vague, indulgent smile. His dark, liquid eyes looked squarely into the face of M. de Vilmorin.

"You have been deceived in that, I fear."

"Deceived?"

"Your sentiments betray the indiscretion of which madame your mother must have been guilty."

The brutally affronting words were sped beyond recall, and the lips that had uttered them, coldly, as if they had been the merest commonplace, remained calm and faintly sneering.

A dead silence followed. Andre-Louis' wits were numbed. He stood aghast, all thought suspended in him, what time M. de Vilmorin's eyes continued fixed upon M. de La Tour d'Azyr's, as if searching there for a meaning that eluded him. Quite suddenly he understood the vile affront. The blood leapt to his face, fire blazed in his gentle eyes. A convulsive quiver shook him. Then, with an inarticulate cry, he leaned forward, and with his open hand struck M. le Marquis full and hard upon his sneering face.

In a flash M. de Chabrillane was on his feet, between the two men.

Too late Andre-Louis had seen the trap. La Tour d'Azyr's words were but as a move in a game of chess, calculated to exasperate his opponent into some such counter-move as this—a counter-move that left him entirely at the other's mercy.

M. le Marquis looked on, very white save where M. de Vilmorin's finger-prints began slowly to colour his face; but he said nothing more. Instead, it was M. de Chabrillane who now did the talking, taking up his preconcerted part in this vile game.

"You realize, monsieur, what you have done," said he, coldly, to Philippe. "And you realize, of course, what must inevitably follow."

M. de Vilmorin had realized nothing. The poor young man had acted upon impulse, upon the instinct of decency and honour, never counting the consequences. But he realized them now at the sinister invitation of M. de Chabrillane, and if he desired to avoid these consequences, it was out of respect for his priestly vocation, which strictly forbade such adjustments of disputes as M. de Chabrillane was clearly thrusting upon him.

He drew back. "Let one affront wipe out the other," said he, in a dull voice. "The balance is still in M. le Marquis's favour. Let that content him."

"Impossible." The Chevalier's lips came together tightly. Thereafter he was suavity itself, but very firm. "A blow has been struck, monsieur. I think I am correct in saying that such a thing has never happened before to M. le Marquis in all his life. If you felt yourself affronted, you had but to ask the satisfaction due from one gentleman to another. Your action would seem to confirm the assumption that you found so offensive. But it does not on that account render you immune from the consequences."

It was, you see, M. de Chabrillane's part to heap coals upon this fire, to make quite sure that their victim should not escape them.

"I desire no immunity," flashed back the young seminarist, stung by this fresh goad. After all, he was nobly born, and the traditions of his class were strong upon him—stronger far than the seminarist schooling in humility. He owed it to himself, to his honour, to be killed rather than avoid the consequences of the thing he had done.

"But he does not wear a sword, messieurs!" cried Andre Louis, aghast.

"That is easily amended. He may have the loan of mine."

"I mean, messieurs," Andre-Louis insisted, between fear for his friend and indignation, "that it is not his habit to wear a sword, that he has never worn one, that he is untutored in its uses. He is a seminarist—a postulant for holy orders, already half a priest, and so forbidden from such an engagement as you propose."

"All that he should have remembered before he struck a blow," said M. de Chabrillane, politely.

"The blow was deliberately provoked," raged Andre-Louis. Then he recovered himself, though the other's haughty stare had no part in that recovery. "O my God, I talk in vain! How is one to argue against a purpose formed! Come away, Philippe. Don't you see the trap..."

M. de Vilmorin cut him short, and flung him off. "Be quiet, Andre. M. le Marquis is entirely in the right."

"M. le Marquis is in the right?" Andre-Louis let his arms fall helplessly. This man he loved above all other living men was caught in the snare of the world's insanity. He was baring his breast to the knife for the sake of a vague, distorted sense of the honour due to himself. It was not that he did not see the trap. It was that his honour compelled him to disdain consideration of it. To Andre-Louis in that moment he seemed a singularly tragic figure. Noble, perhaps, but very pitiful.

CHAPTER IV. THE HERITAGE

It was M. de Vilmorin's desire that the matter should be settled out of hand. In this he was at once objective and subjective. A prey to emotions sadly at conflict with his priestly vocation, he was above all in haste to have done, so that he might resume a frame of mind more proper to it. Also he feared himself a little; by which I mean that his honour feared his nature. The circumstances of his education, and the goal that for some years now he had kept in view, had robbed him of much of that spirited brutality that is the birthright of the male. He had grown timid and gentle as a woman. Aware of it, he feared that once the heat of his passion was spent he might betray a dishonouring weakness, in the ordeal.

M. le Marquis, on his side, was no less eager for an immediate settlement; and since they had M. de Chabrillane to act for his cousin, and Andre-Louis to serve as witness for M. de Vilmorin, there was nothing to delay them.

And so, within a few minutes, all arrangements were concluded, and you behold that sinisterly intentioned little group of four assembled in the afternoon sunshine on the bowling-green behind the inn. They were entirely private, screened more or less from the windows of the house by a ramage of trees, which, if leafless now, was at least dense enough to provide an effective lattice.

There were no formalities over measurements of blades or selection of ground. M. le Marquis removed his sword-belt and scabbard, but declined—not considering it worth while for the sake of so negligible an opponent—to divest himself either of his shoes or his coat. Tall, lithe, and athletic, he stood to face the no less tall, but very delicate and frail, M. de Vilmorin. The latter also disdained to make any of the usual preparations. Since he recognized that it could avail him nothing to strip, he came on guard fully dressed, two hectic spots above the cheek-bones burning on his otherwise grey face.

M. de Chabrillane, leaning upon a cane—for he had relinquished his sword to M. de Vilmorin—looked on with quiet interest. Facing him on the other side of the combatants stood Andre-Louis, the palest of the four, staring from fevered eyes, twisting and untwisting clammy hands.

His every instinct was to fling himself between the antagonists, to protest against and frustrate this meeting. That sane impulse was curbed, however, by the consciousness of its futility. To calm him, he clung to the conviction that the issue could not really be very serious. If the obligations of Philippe's honour compelled him to cross swords with the man he had struck, M. de La Tour d'Azyr's birth compelled him no less to do no serious hurt to the unfledged lad he had so grievously provoked. M. le Marquis, after all, was a man of honour. He could intend no more than to administer a lesson; sharp, perhaps, but one by which his opponent must live to profit. Andre-Louis clung obstinately to that for comfort.

Steel beat on steel, and the men engaged. The Marquis presented to his opponent the narrow edge of his upright body, his knees slightly flexed and converted into living springs, whilst M. de Vilmorin stood squarely, a full target, his knees wooden. Honour and the spirit of fair play alike cried out against such a match.

The encounter was very short, of course. In youth, Philippe had received the tutoring in sword-play that was given to every boy born into his station of life. And so he knew at least the rudiments of what was now expected of him. But what could rudiments avail him here? Three disengages completed the exchanges, and then without any haste the Marquis slid his right foot along the moist turf, his long, graceful body extending itself in a lunge that went under M. de Vilmorin's clumsy guard, and with the utmost deliberation he drove his blade through the young man's vitals.

Andre-Louis sprang forward just in time to catch his friend's body under the armpits as it sank. Then, his own legs bending beneath the weight of it, he went down with his burden until he was kneeling on the damp turf. Philippe's limp head lay against Andre-Louis' left shoulder; Philippe's relaxed arms trailed at his sides; the blood welled and bubbled from the ghastly wound to saturate the poor lad's garments.

With white face and twitching lips, Andre-Louis looked up at M. de La Tour d'Azyr, who stood surveying his work with a countenance of grave but remorseless interest.

"You have killed him!" cried Andre-Louis.

"Of course."

The Marquis ran a lace handkerchief along his blade to wipe it. As he let the dainty fabric fall, he explained himself. "He had, as I told him, a too dangerous gift of eloquence."

And he turned away, leaving completest understanding with Andre-Louis. Still supporting the limp, draining body, the young man called to him.

"Come back, you cowardly murderer, and make yourself quite safe by killing me too!"

The Marquis half turned, his face dark with anger. Then M. de Chabrillane set a restraining hand upon his arm. Although a party throughout to the deed, the Chevalier was a little appalled now that it was done. He had not the high stomach of M. de La Tour d'Azyr, and he was a good deal younger.

"Come away," he said. "The lad is raving. They were friends."

"You heard what he said?" quoth the Marquis.

"Nor can he, or you, or any man deny it," flung back Andre-Louis. "Yourself, monsieur, you made confession when you gave me now the reason why you killed him. You did it because you feared him."

"If that were true—what, then?" asked the great gentleman.

"Do you ask? Do you understand of life and humanity nothing but how to wear a coat and dress your hair—oh, yes, and to handle weapons against boys and priests? Have you no mind to think, no soul into which you can turn its vision? Must you be told that it is a coward's part to kill the thing he fears, and doubly a coward's part to kill in this way? Had you stabbed him in the back with a knife, you would have shown the courage of your vileness. It would have been a vileness undisguised. But you feared the consequences of that, powerful as you are; and so you shelter your cowardice under the pretext of a duel."

The Marquis shook off his cousin's hand, and took a step forward, holding now his sword like a whip. But again the Chevalier caught and held him.

"No, no, Gervais! Let be, in God's name!"

"Let him come, monsieur," raved Andre-Louis, his voice thick and concentrated. "Let him complete his coward's work on me, and thus make himself safe from a coward's wages."

M. de Chabrillane let his cousin go. He came white to the lips, his eyes glaring at the lad who so recklessly insulted him. And then he checked. It may be that he remembered suddenly the relationship in which this young man was popularly believed to stand to the Seigneur de Gavrillac, and the well-known affection in which the Seigneur held him. And so he may have realized that if he pushed this matter further, he might find himself upon the horns of a dilemma. He would be confronted with the alternatives of shedding more blood, and so embroiling himself with the Lord of Gavrillac at a time when that gentleman's friendship was of the first importance to him, or else of withdrawing with such hurt to his dignity as must impair his authority in the countryside hereafter.

Be it so or otherwise, the fact remains that he stopped short; then, with an incoherent ejaculation, between anger and contempt, he tossed his arms, turned on his heel and strode off quickly with his cousin.

When the landlord and his people came, they found Andre-Louis, his arms about the body of his dead friend, murmuring passionately into the deaf ear that rested almost against his lips:

"Philippe! Speak to me, Philippe! Philippe... Don't you hear me? O God of Heaven! Philippe!"

At a glance they saw that here neither priest nor doctor could avail. The cheek that lay against Andre-Louis's was leaden-hued, the half-open eyes were glazed, and there was a little froth of blood upon the vacuously parted lips.

Half blinded by tears Andre-Louis stumbled after them when they bore the body into the inn. Upstairs in the little room to which they conveyed it, he knelt by the bed, and holding the dead man's hand in both his own, he swore to him out of his impotent rage that M. de La Tour d'Azyr should pay a bitter price for this.

"It was your eloquence he feared, Philippe," he said. "Then if I can get no justice for this deed, at least it shall be fruitless to him. The thing he feared in you, he shall fear in me. He feared that men might be swayed by your eloquence to the undoing of such things as himself. Men shall be swayed by it still. For your eloquence and your arguments shall be my heritage from you. I will make them my own. It matters nothing that I do not believe in your gospel of freedom. I know it—every word of it; that is all that matters to our purpose, yours and mine. If all else fails, your thoughts shall find expression in my living tongue. Thus at least we shall have frustrated his vile aim to still the voice he feared. It shall profit him nothing to have your blood upon his soul. That voice in you would never half so relentlessly have hounded him and his as it shall in me—if all else fails."

It was an exulting thought. It calmed him; it soothed his grief, and he began very softly to pray. And then his heart trembled as he considered that Philippe, a man of peace, almost a priest, an apostle of Christianity, had gone to his Maker with the sin of anger on his soul. It was horrible. Yet God would see the righteousness of that anger. And in no case—be man's interpretation of Divinity what it might—could that one sin outweigh the loving good that Philippe had ever practised, the noble purity of his great heart. God after all, reflected Andre-Louis, was not a grand-seigneur.

CHAPTER V. THE LORD OF GAVRILLAC

For the second time that day Andre-Louis set out for the chateau, walking briskly, and heeding not at all the curious eyes that followed him through the village, and the whisperings that marked his passage through the people, all agog by now with that day's event in which he had been an actor.

He was ushered by Benoit, the elderly body-servant, rather grandiloquently called the seneschal, into the ground-floor room known traditionally as the library. It still contained several shelves of neglected volumes, from which it derived its title, but implements of the chase—fowling-pieces, powder-horns, hunting-bags, sheath-knives—obtruded far more prominently than those of study. The furniture was massive, of oak richly carved, and belonging to another age. Great massive oak beams crossed the rather lofty whitewashed ceiling.

Here the squat Seigneur de Gavrillac was restlessly pacing when Andre-Louis was introduced. He was already informed, as he announced at once, of what had taken place at the Breton arme. M. de Chabrillane had just left him, and he confessed himself deeply grieved and deeply perplexed.

"The pity of it!" he said. "The pity of it!" He bowed his enormous head. "So estimable a young man, and so full of promise. Ah, this La Tour d'Azyr is a hard man, and he feels very strongly in these matters. He may be right. I don't know. I have never killed a man for holding different views from mine. In fact, I have never killed a man at all. It isn't in my nature. I shouldn't sleep of nights if I did. But men are differently made."

"The question, monsieur my godfather," said Andre-Louis, "is what is to be done." He was quite calm and self-possessed, but very white.

M. de Kercadiou stared at him blankly out of his pale eyes.

"Why, what the devil is there to do? From what I am told, Vilmorin went so far as to strike M. le Marquis."

"Under the very grossest provocation."

"Which he himself provoked by his revolutionary language. The poor lad's head was full of this encyclopaedist trash. It comes of too much reading. I have never set much store by books, Andre; and I have never known anything but trouble to come out of learning. It unsettles a man. It complicates his views of life, destroys the simplicity which makes for peace of mind and happiness. Let this miserable affair be a warning to you, Andre. You are, yourself, too prone to these new-fashioned speculations upon a different constitution of the social order. You see what comes of it. A fine, estimable young man, the only prop of his widowed mother too, forgets himself, his position, his duty to that mother—everything; and goes and gets himself killed like this. It is infernally sad. On my soul it is sad." He produced a handkerchief, and blew his nose with vehemence.

Andre-Louis felt a tightening of his heart, a lessening of the hopes, never too sanguine, which he had founded upon his godfather.

"Your criticisms," he said, "are all for the conduct of the dead, and none for that of the murderer. It does not seem possible that you should be in sympathy with such a crime."

"Crime?" shrilled M. de Kercadiou. "My God, boy, you are speaking of M. de La Tour d'Azyr."

"I am, and of the abominable murder he has committed..."

"Stop!" M. de Kercadiou was very emphatic. "I cannot permit that you apply such terms to him. I cannot permit it. M. le Marquis is my friend, and is likely very soon to stand in a still closer relationship."

"Notwithstanding this?" asked Andre-Louis.

M. de Kercadiou was frankly impatient.

"Why, what has this to do with it? I may deplore it. But I have no right to condemn it. It is a common way of adjusting differences between gentlemen."

"You really believe that?"

"What the devil do you imply, Andre? Should I say a thing that I don't believe? You begin to make me angry."

"'Thou shalt not kill,' is the King's law as well as God's."

"You are determined to quarrel with me, I think. It was a duel..."

Andre-Louis interrupted him. "It is no more a duel than if it had been fought with pistols of which only M. le Marquis's was loaded. He invited Philippe to discuss the matter further, with the deliberate intent of forcing a quarrel upon him and killing him. Be patient with me, monsieur my god-father. I am not telling you of what I imagine but what M. le Marquis himself admitted to me."

Dominated a little by the young man's earnestness, M. de Kercadiou's pale eyes fell away. He turned with a shrug, and sauntered over to the window.

"It would need a court of honour to decide such an issue. And we have no courts of honour," he said.

"But we have courts of justice."

With returning testiness the seigneur swung round to face him again. "And what court of justice, do you think, would listen to such a plea as you appear to have in mind?"

"There is the court of the King's Lieutenant at Rennes."

"And do you think the King's Lieutenant would listen to you?"

"Not to me, perhaps, Monsieur. But if you were to bring the plaint..."

"I bring the plaint?" M. de Kercadiou's pale eyes were wide with horror of the suggestion.

"The thing happened here on your domain."

"I bring a plaint against M. de La Tour d'Azyr! You are out of your senses, I think. Oh, you are mad; as mad as that poor friend of yours who has come to this end through meddling in what did not concern him. The language he used here to M. le Marquis on the score of Mabey was of the most offensive. Perhaps you didn't know that. It does not at all surprise me that the Marquis should have desired satisfaction."

"I see," said Andre-Louis, on a note of hopelessness.

"You see? What the devil do you see?"

"That I shall have to depend upon myself alone."

"And what the devil do you propose to do, if you please?"

"I shall go to Rennes, and lay the facts before the King's Lieutenant."

"He'll be too busy to see you." And M. de Kercadiou's mind swung a trifle inconsequently, as weak minds will. "There is trouble enough in Rennes already on the score of these crazy States General, with which the wonderful M. Necker is to repair the finances of the kingdom. As if a peddling Swiss bank-clerk, who is also a damned Protestant, could succeed where such men as Calonne and Brienne have failed."

"Good-afternoon, monsieur my godfather," said Andre-Louis.

"Where are you going?" was the querulous demand.

"Home at present. To Rennes in the morning."

"Wait, boy, wait!" The squat little man rolled forward, affectionate concern on his great ugly face, and he set one of his podgy hands on his godson's shoulder. "Now, listen to me, Andre," he reasoned. "This is sheer knight-errantry—moonshine, lunacy. You'll come to no good by it if you persist. You've read 'Don Quixote,' and what happened to him when he went tilting against windmills. It's what will happen to you, neither more nor less. Leave things as they are, my boy. I wouldn't have a mischief happen to you."

Andre-Louis looked at him, smiling wanly.

"I swore an oath to-day which it would damn my soul to break."

"You mean that you'll go in spite of anything that I may say?" Impetuous as he was inconsequent, M. de Kercadiou was bristling again. "Very well, then, go... Go to the devil!"

"I will begin with the King's Lieutenant."

"And if you get into the trouble you are seeking, don't come whimpering to me for assistance," the seigneur stormed. He was very angry now. "Since you choose to disobey me, you can break your empty head against the windmill, and be damned to you."

Andre-Louis bowed with a touch of irony, and reached the door.

"If the windmill should prove too formidable," said he, from the threshold, "I may see what can be done with the wind. Good-bye, monsieur my godfather."

He was gone, and M. de Kercadiou was alone, purple in the face, puzzling out that last cryptic utterance, and not at all happy in his mind, either on the score of his godson or of M. de La Tour d'Azyr. He was disposed to be angry with them both. He found these headstrong, wilful men who relentlessly followed their own impulses very disturbing and irritating. Himself he loved his ease, and to be at peace with his neighbours; and that seemed to him so obviously the supreme good of life that he was disposed to brand them as fools who troubled to seek other things.

CHAPTER VI. THE WINDMILL

There was between Nantes and Rennes an established service of three stage-coaches weekly in each direction, which for a sum of twenty-four livres—roughly, the equivalent of an English guinea—would carry you the seventy and odd miles of the journey in some fourteen hours. Once a week one of the diligences going in each direction would swerve aside from the highroad to call at Gavrillac, to bring and take letters, newspapers, and sometimes passengers. It was usually by this coach that Andre-Louis came and went when the occasion offered. At present, however, he was too much in haste to lose a day awaiting the passing of that diligence. So it was on a horse hired from the Breton arme that he set out next morning; and an hour's brisk ride under a grey wintry sky, by a half-ruined road through ten miles of flat, uninteresting country, brought him to the city of Rennes.

He rode across the main bridge over the Vilaine, and so into the upper and principal part of that important city of some thirty thousand souls, most of whom, he opined from the seething, clamant crowds that everywhere blocked his way, must on this day have taken to the streets. Clearly Philippe had not overstated the excitement prevailing there.

He pushed on as best he could, and so came at last to the Place Royale, where he found the crowd to be most dense. From the plinth of the equestrian statue of Louis XV, a white-faced young man was excitedly addressing the multitude. His youth and dress proclaimed the student, and a group of his fellows, acting as a guard of honour to him, kept the immediate precincts of the statue.

Over the heads of the crowd Andre-Louis caught a few of the phrases flung forth by that eager voice.

"It was the promise of the King... It is the King's authority they flout... They arrogate to themselves the whole sovereignty in Brittany. The King has dissolved them... These insolent nobles defying their sovereign and the people..."

Had he not known already, from what Philippe had told him, of the events which had brought the Third Estate to the point of active revolt, those few phrases would fully have informed him. This popular display of temper was most opportune to his need, he thought. And in the hope that it might serve his turn by disposing to reasonableness the mind of the King's Lieutenant, he pushed on up the wide and well-paved Rue Royale, where the concourse of people began to diminish. He put up his hired horse at the Come de Cerf, and set out again, on foot, to the Palais de Justice.

There was a brawling mob by the framework of poles and scaffoldings about the building cathedral, upon which work had been commenced a year ago. But he did not pause to ascertain the particular cause of that gathering. He strode on, and thus came presently to the handsome Italianate palace that was one of the few public edifices that had survived the devastating fire of sixty years ago.

He won through with difficulty to the great hall, known as the Salle des Pas Perdus, where he was left to cool his heels for a full half-hour after he had found an usher so condescending as to inform the god who presided over that shrine of Justice that a lawyer from Gavrillac humbly begged an audience on an affair of gravity.

That the god condescended to see him at all was probably due to the grave complexion of the hour. At long length he was escorted up the broad stone staircase, and ushered into a spacious, meagrely furnished anteroom, to make one of a waiting crowd of clients, mostly men.

There he spent another half-hour, and employed the time in considering exactly what he should say. This consideration made him realize the weakness of the case he proposed to set before a man whose views of law and morality were coloured by his social rank.

At last he was ushered through a narrow but very massive and richly decorated door into a fine, well-lighted room furnished with enough gilt and satin to have supplied the boudoir of a lady of fashion.

It was a trivial setting for a King's Lieutenant, but about the King's Lieutenant there was—at least to ordinary eyes—nothing trivial. At the far end of the chamber, to the right of one of the tall windows that looked out over the inner court, before a goat-legged writing-table with Watteau panels, heavily encrusted with ormolu, sat that exalted being. Above a scarlet coat with an order flaming on its breast, and a billow of lace in which diamonds sparkled like drops of water, sprouted the massive powdered head of M. de Lesdiguieres. It was thrown back to scowl upon this visitor with an expectant arrogance that made Andre-Louis wonder almost was a genuflexion awaited from him.

Perceiving a lean, lantern-jawed young man, with straight, lank black hair, in a caped riding-coat of brown cloth, and yellow buckskin breeches, his knee-boots splashed with mud, the scowl upon that august visage deepened until it brought together the thick black eyebrows above the great hooked nose.

"You announce yourself as a lawyer of Gavrillac with an important communication," he growled. It was a peremptory command to make this communication without wasting the valuable time of a King's Lieutenant, of whose immense importance it conveyed something more than a hint. M. de Lesdiguieres accounted himself an imposing personality, and he had every reason to do so, for in his time he had seen many a poor devil scared out of all his senses by the thunder of his voice.

He waited now to see the same thing happen to this youthful lawyer from Gavrillac. But he waited in vain.

Andre-Louis found him ridiculous. He knew pretentiousness for the mask of worthlessness and weakness. And here he beheld pretentiousness incarnate. It was to be read in that arrogant poise of the head, that scowling brow, the inflexion of that reverberating voice. Even more difficult than it is for a man to be a hero to his valet—who has witnessed the dispersal of the parts that make up the imposing whole—is it for a man to be a hero to the student of Man who has witnessed the same in a different sense.

Andre-Louis stood forward boldly—impudently, thought M. de Lesdiguieres.

"You are His Majesty's Lieutenant here in Brittany," he said—and it almost seemed to the august lord of life and death that this fellow had the incredible effrontery to address him as one man speaking to another. "You are the dispenser of the King's high justice in this province."

Surprise spread on that handsome, sallow face under the heavily powdered wig.

"Is your business concerned with this infernal insubordination of the canaille?" he asked.

"It is not, monsieur."

The black eyebrows rose. "Then what the devil do you mean by intruding upon me at a time when all my attention is being claimed by the obvious urgency of this disgraceful affair?"

"The affair that brings me is no less disgraceful and no less urgent."

"It will have to wait!" thundered the great man in a passion, and tossing back a cloud of lace from his hand, he reached for the little silver bell upon his table.

"A moment, monsieur!" Andre-Louis' tone was peremptory. M. de Lesdiguieres checked in sheer amazement at its impudence. "I can state it very briefly..."

"Haven't I said already..."

"And when you have heard it," Andre-Louis went on, relentlessly, interrupting the interruption, "you will agree with me as to its character."

M. de Lesdiguieres considered him very sternly.

"What is your name?" he asked.

"Andre-Louis Moreau."

"Well, Andre-Louis Moreau, if you can state your plea briefly, I will hear you. But I warn you that I shall be very angry if you fail to justify the impertinence of this insistence at so inopportune a moment."

"You shall be the judge of that, monsieur," said Andre-Louis, and he proceeded at once to state his case, beginning with the shooting of Mabey, and passing thence to the killing of M. de Vilmorin. But he withheld until the end the name of the great gentleman against whom he demanded justice, persuaded that did he introduce it earlier he would not be allowed to proceed.

He had a gift of oratory of whose full powers he was himself hardly conscious yet, though destined very soon to become so. He told his story well, without exaggeration, yet with a force of simple appeal that was irresistible. Gradually the great man's face relaxed from its forbidding severity. Interest, warming almost to sympathy, came to be reflected on it.

"And who, sir, is the man you charge with this?"

"The Marquis de La Tour d'Azyr."

The effect of that formidable name was immediate. Dismayed anger, and an arrogance more utter than before, took the place of the sympathy he had been betrayed into displaying.

"Who?" he shouted, and without waiting for an answer, "Why, here's impudence," he stormed on, "to come before me with such a charge against a gentleman of M. de La Tour d'Azyr's eminence! How dare you speak of him as a coward...."

"I speak of him as a murderer," the young man corrected. "And I demand justice against him."

"You demand it, do you? My God, what next?"

"That is for you to say, monsieur."

It surprised the great gentleman into a more or less successful effort of self-control.

"Let me warn you," said he, acidly, "that it is not wise to make wild accusations against a nobleman. That, in itself, is a punishable offence, as you may learn. Now listen to me. In this matter of Mabey—assuming your statement of it to be exact—the gamekeeper may have exceeded his duty; but by so little that it is hardly worth comment. Consider, however, that in any case it is not a matter for the King's Lieutenant, or for any court but the seigneurial court of M. de La Tour d'Azyr himself. It is before the magistrates of his own appointing that such a matter must be laid, since it is matter strictly concerning his own seigneurial jurisdiction. As a lawyer you should not need to be told so much."

"As a lawyer, I am prepared to argue the point. But, as a lawyer I also realize that if that case were prosecuted, it could only end in the unjust punishment of a wretched gamekeeper, who did no more than carry out his orders, but who none the less would now be made a scapegoat, if scapegoat were necessary. I am not concerned to hang Benet on the gallows earned by M. de La Tour d'Azyr."

M. de Lesdiguieres smote the table violently. "My God!" he cried out, to add more quietly, on a note of menace, "You are singularly insolent, my man."

"That is not my intention, sir, I assure you. I am a lawyer, pleading a case—the case of M. de Vilmorin. It is for his assassination that I have come to beg the King's justice."

"But you yourself have said that it was a duel!" cried the Lieutenant, between anger and bewilderment.

"I have said that it was made to appear a duel. There is a distinction, as I shall show, if you will condescend to hear me out."

"Take your own time, sir!" said the ironical M. de Lesdiguieres, whose tenure of office had never yet held anything that remotely resembled this experience.

Andre-Louis took him literally. "I thank you, sir," he answered, solemnly, and submitted his argument. "It can be shown that M. de Vilmorin never practised fencing in all his life, and it is notorious that M. de La Tour d'Azyr is an exceptional swordsman. Is it a duel, monsieur, where one of the combatants alone is armed? For it amounts to that on a comparison of their measures of respective skill."

"There has scarcely been a duel fought on which the same trumpery argument might not be advanced."

"But not always with equal justice. And in one case, at least, it was advanced successfully."

"Successfully? When was that?"

"Ten years ago, in Dauphiny. I refer to the case of M. de Gesvres, a gentleman of that province, who forced a duel upon M. de la Roche Jeannine, and killed him. M. de Jeannine was a member of a powerful family, which exerted itself to obtain justice. It put forward just such arguments as now obtain against M. de La Tour d'Azyr. As you will remember, the judges held that the provocation had proceeded of intent from M. de Gesvres; they found him guilty of premeditated murder, and he was hanged."

M. de Lesdiguieres exploded yet again. "Death of my life!" he cried. "Have you the effrontery to suggest that M. de La Tour d'Azyr should be hanged? Have you?"

"But why not, monsieur, if it is the law, and there is precedent for it, as I have shown you, and if it can be established that what I state is the truth—as established it can be without difficulty?"

"Do you ask me, why not? Have you temerity to ask me that?"

"I have, monsieur. Can you answer me? If you cannot, monsieur, I shall understand that whilst it is possible for a powerful family like that of La Roche Jeannine to set the law in motion, the law must remain inert for the obscure and uninfluential, however brutally wronged by a great nobleman."

M. de Lesdiguieres perceived that in argument he would accomplish nothing against this impassive, resolute young man. The menace of him grew more fierce.

"I should advise you to take yourself off at once, and to be thankful for the opportunity to depart unscathed."

"I am, then, to understand, monsieur, that there will be no inquiry into this case? That nothing that I can say will move you?"

"You are to understand that if you are still there in two minutes it will be very much the worse for you." And M. de Lesdiguieres tinkled the silver hand-bell upon his table.

"I have informed you, monsieur, that a duel—so-called—has been fought, and a man killed. It seems that I must remind you, the administrator of the King's justice, that duels are against the law, and that it is your duty to hold an inquiry. I come as the legal representative of the bereaved mother of M. de Vilmorin to demand of you the inquiry that is due."

The door behind Andre-Louis opened softly. M. de Lesdiguieres, pale with anger, contained himself with difficulty.

"You seek to compel us, do you, you impudent rascal?" he growled. "You think the King's justice is to be driven headlong by the voice of any impudent roturier? I marvel at my own patience with you. But I give you a last warning, master lawyer; keep a closer guard over that insolent tongue of yours, or you will have cause very bitterly to regret its glibness." He waved a jewelled, contemptuous hand, and spoke to the usher standing behind Andre. "To the door!" he said, shortly.

Andre-Louis hesitated a second. Then with a shrug he turned. This was the windmill, indeed, and he a poor knight of rueful countenance. To attack it at closer quarters would mean being dashed to pieces. Yet on the threshold he turned again.

"M. de Lesdiguieres," said he, "may I recite to you an interesting fact in natural history? The tiger is a great lord in the jungle, and was for centuries the terror of lesser beasts, including the wolf. The wolf, himself a hunter, wearied of being hunted. He took to associating with other wolves, and then the wolves, driven to form packs for self-protection, discovered the power of the pack, and took to hunting the tiger, with disastrous results to him. You should study Buffon, M. de Lesdiguieres."

"I have studied a buffoon this morning, I think," was the punning sneer with which M. de Lesdiguieres replied. But that he conceived himself witty, it is probable he would not have condescended to reply at all. "I don't understand you," he added.

"But you will, M. de Lesdiguieres. You will," said Andre-Louis, and so departed.

CHAPTER VII. THE WIND

He had broken his futile lance with the windmill—the image suggested by M. de Kercadiou persisted in his mind—and it was, he perceived, by sheer good fortune that he had escaped without hurt. There remained the wind itself—the whirlwind. And the events in Rennes, reflex of the graver events in Nantes, had set that wind blowing in his favour.

He set out briskly to retrace his steps towards the Place Royale, where the gathering of the populace was greatest, where, as he judged, lay the heart and brain of this commotion that was exciting the city.

But the commotion that he had left there was as nothing to the commotion which he found on his return. Then there had been a comparative hush to listen to the voice of a speaker who denounced the First and Second Estates from the pedestal of the statue of Louis XV. Now the air was vibrant with the voice of the multitude itself, raised in anger. Here and there men were fighting with canes and fists; everywhere a fierce excitement raged, and the gendarmes sent thither by the King's Lieutenant to restore and maintain order were so much helpless flotsam in that tempestuous human ocean.

There were cries of "To the Palais! To the Palais! Down with the assassins! Down with the nobles! To the Palais!"

An artisan who stood shoulder to shoulder with him in the press enlightened Andre-Louis on the score of the increased excitement.

"They've shot him dead. His body is lying there where it fell at the foot of the statue. And there was another student killed not an hour ago over there by the cathedral works. Pardi! If they can't prevail in one way they'll prevail in another." The man was fiercely emphatic. "They'll stop at nothing. If they can't overawe us, by God, they'll assassinate us. They are determined to conduct these States of Brittany in their own way. No interests but their own shall be considered."

Andre-Louis left him still talking, and clove himself a way through that human press.

At the statue's base he came upon a little cluster of students about the body of the murdered lad, all stricken with fear and helplessness.

"You here, Moreau!" said a voice.

He looked round to find himself confronted by a slight, swarthy man of little more than thirty, firm of mouth and impertinent of nose, who considered him with disapproval. It was Le Chapelier, a lawyer of Rennes, a prominent member of the Literary Chamber of that city, a forceful man, fertile in revolutionary ideas and of an exceptional gift of eloquence.

"Ah, it is you, Chapelier! Why don't you speak to them? Why don't you tell them what to do? Up with you, man!" And he pointed to the plinth.

Le Chapelier's dark, restless eyes searched the other's impassive face for some trace of the irony he suspected. They were as wide asunder as the poles, these two, in their political views; and mistrusted as Andre Louis was by all his colleagues of the Literary Chamber of Rennes, he was by none mistrusted so thoroughly as by this vigorous republican. Indeed, had Le Chapelier been able to prevail against the influence of the seminarist Vilmorin, Andre-Louis would long since have found himself excluded from that assembly of the intellectual youth of Rennes, which he exasperated by his eternal mockery of their ideals.

So now Le Chapelier suspected mockery in that invitation, suspected it even when he failed to find traces of it on Andre-Louis' face, for he had learnt by experience that it was a face not often to be trusted for an indication of the real thoughts that moved behind it.

"Your notions and mine on that score can hardly coincide," said he.

"Can there be two opinions?" quoth Andre-Louis.

"There are usually two opinions whenever you and I are together, Moreau—more than ever now that you are the appointed delegate of a nobleman. You see what your friends have done. No doubt you approve their methods." He was coldly hostile.

Andre-Louis looked at him without surprise. So invariably opposed to each other in academic debates, how should Le Chapelier suspect his present intentions?

"If you won't tell them what is to be done, I will," said he.

"Nom de Dieu! If you want to invite a bullet from the other side, I shall not hinder you. It may help to square the account."

Scarcely were the words out than he repented them; for as if in answer to that challenge Andre-Louis sprang up on to the plinth. Alarmed now, for he could only suppose it to be Andre-Louis' intention to speak on behalf of Privilege, of which he was a publicly appointed representative, Le Chapelier clutched him by the leg to pull him down again.

"Ah, that, no!" he was shouting. "Come down, you fool. Do you think we will let you ruin everything by your clowning? Come down!"

Andre-Louis, maintaining his position by clutching one of the legs of the bronze horse, flung his voice like a bugle-note over the heads of that seething mob.

"Citizens of Rennes, the motherland is in danger!"

The effect was electric. A stir ran, like a ripple over water, across that froth of upturned human faces, and completest silence followed. In that great silence they looked at this slim young man, hatless, long wisps of his black hair fluttering in the breeze, his neckcloth in disorder, his face white, his eyes on fire.

Andre-Louis felt a sudden surge of exaltation as he realized by instinct that at one grip he had seized that crowd, and that he held it fast in the spell of his cry and his audacity.

Even Le Chapelier, though still clinging to his ankle, had ceased to tug. The reformer, though unshaken in his assumption of Andre-Louis' intentions, was for a moment bewildered by the first note of his appeal.

And then, slowly, impressively, in a voice that travelled clear to the ends of the square, the young lawyer of Gavrillac began to speak.

"Shuddering in horror of the vile deed here perpetrated, my voice demands to be heard by you. You have seen murder done under your eyes—the murder of one who nobly, without any thought of self, gave voice to the wrongs by which we are all oppressed. Fearing that voice, shunning the truth as foul things shun the light, our oppressors sent their agents to silence him in death."

Le Chapelier released at last his hold of Andre-Louis' ankle, staring up at him the while in sheer amazement. It seemed that the fellow was in earnest; serious for once; and for once on the right side. What had come to him?

"Of assassins what shall you look for but assassination? I have a tale to tell which will show that this is no new thing that you have witnessed here to-day; it will reveal to you the forces with which you have to deal. Yesterday..."

There was an interruption. A voice in the crowd, some twenty paces, perhaps, was raised to shout:

"Yet another of them!"

Immediately after the voice came a pistol-shot, and a bullet flattened itself against the bronze figure just behind Andre-Louis.

Instantly there was turmoil in the crowd, most intense about the spot whence the shot had been fired. The assailant was one of a considerable group of the opposition, a group that found itself at once beset on every side, and hard put to it to defend him.

From the foot of the plinth rang the voice of the students making chorus to Le Chapelier, who was bidding Andre-Louis to seek shelter.

"Come down! Come down at once! They'll murder you as they murdered La Riviere."

"Let them!" He flung wide his arms in a gesture supremely theatrical, and laughed. "I stand here at their mercy. Let them, if they will, add mine to the blood that will presently rise up to choke them. Let them assassinate me. It is a trade they understand. But until they do so, they shall not prevent me from speaking to you, from telling you what is to be looked for in them." And again he laughed, not merely in exaltation as they supposed who watched him from below, but also in amusement. And his amusement had two sources. One was to discover how glibly he uttered the phrases proper to whip up the emotions of a crowd: the other was in the remembrance of how the crafty Cardinal de Retz, for the purpose of inflaming popular sympathy on his behalf, had been in the habit of hiring fellows to fire upon his carriage. He was in just such case as that arch-politician. True, he had not hired the fellow to fire that pistol-shot; but he was none the less obliged to him, and ready to derive the fullest, advantage from the act.

The group that sought to protect that man was battling on, seeking to hew a way out of that angry, heaving press.

"Let them go!" Andre-Louis called down..."What matters one assassin more or less? Let them go, and listen to me, my countrymen!"

And presently, when some measure of order was restored, he began his tale. In simple language now, yet with a vehemence and directness that drove home every point, he tore their hearts with the story of yesterday's happenings at Gavrillac. He drew tears from them with the pathos of his picture of the bereaved widow Mabey and her three starving, destitute children—"orphaned to avenge the death of a pheasant"—and the bereaved mother of that M. de Vilmorin, a student of Rennes, known here to many of them, who had met his death in a noble endeavour to champion the cause of an esurient member of their afflicted order.

"The Marquis de La Tour d'Azyr said of him that he had too dangerous a gift of eloquence. It was to silence his brave voice that he killed him. But he has failed of his object. For I, poor Philippe de Vilmorin's friend, have assumed the mantle of his apostleship, and I speak to you with his voice to-day."

It was a statement that helped Le Chapelier at last to understand, at least in part, this bewildering change in Andre-Louis, which rendered him faithless to the side that employed him.

"I am not here," continued Andre-Louis, "merely to demand at your hands vengeance upon Philippe de Vilmorin's murderers. I am here to tell you the things he would to-day have told you had he lived."

So far at least he was frank. But he did not add that they were things he did not himself believe, things that he accounted the cant by which an ambitious bourgeoisie—speaking through the mouths of the lawyers, who were its articulate part—sought to overthrow to its own advantage the present state of things. He left his audience in the natural belief that the views he expressed were the views he held.

And now in a terrible voice, with an eloquence that amazed himself, he denounced the inertia of the royal justice where the great are the offenders. It was with bitter sarcasm that he spoke of their King's Lieutenant, M. de Lesdiguieres.

"Do you wonder," he asked them, "that M. de Lesdiguieres should administer the law so that it shall ever be favourable to our great nobles? Would it be just, would it be reasonable that he should otherwise administer it?" He paused dramatically to let his sarcasm sink in. It had the effect of reawakening Le Chapelier's doubts, and checking his dawning conviction in Andre-Louis' sincerity. Whither was he going now?

He was not left long in doubt. Proceeding, Andre-Louis spoke as he conceived that Philippe de Vilmorin would have spoken. He had so often argued with him, so often attended the discussions of the Literary Chamber, that he had all the rant of the reformers—that was yet true in substance—at his fingers' ends.

"Consider, after all, the composition of this France of ours. A million of its inhabitants are members of the privileged classes. They compose France. They are France. For surely you cannot suppose the remainder to be anything that matters. It cannot be pretended that twenty-four million souls are of any account, that they can be representative of this great nation, or that they can exist for any purpose but that of servitude to the million elect."

Bitter laughter shook them now, as he desired it should. "Seeing their privileges in danger of invasion by these twenty-four millions—mostly canailles; possibly created by God, it is true, but clearly so created to be the slaves of Privilege—does it surprise you that the dispensing of royal justice should be placed in the stout hands of these Lesdiguieres, men without brains to think or hearts to be touched? Consider what it is that must be defended against the assault of us others—canaille. Consider a few of these feudal rights that are in danger of being swept away should the Privileged yield even to the commands of their sovereign; and admit the Third Estate to an equal vote with themselves.

"What would become of the right of terrage on the land, of parciere on the fruit-trees, of carpot on the vines? What of the corvees by which they command forced labour, of the ban de vendage, which gives them the first vintage, the banvin which enables them to control to their own advantage the sale of wine? What of their right of grinding the last liard of taxation out of the people to maintain their own opulent estate; the cens, the lods-et-ventes, which absorb a fifth of the value of the land, the blairee, which must be paid before herds can feed on communal lands, the pulverage to indemnify them for the dust raised on their roads by the herds that go to market, the sextelage on everything offered for sale in the public markets, the etalonnage, and all the rest? What of their rights over men and animals for field labour, of ferries over rivers, and of bridges over streams, of sinking wells, of warren, of dovecot, and of fire, which last yields them a tax on every peasant hearth? What of their exclusive rights of fishing and of hunting, the violation of which is ranked as almost a capital offence?

"And what of other rights, unspeakable, abominable, over the lives and bodies of their people, rights which, if rarely exercised, have never been rescinded. To this day if a noble returning from the hunt were to slay two of his serfs to bathe and refresh his feet in their blood, he could still claim in his sufficient defence that it was his absolute feudal right to do so.

"Rough-shod, these million Privileged ride over the souls and bodies of twenty-four million contemptible canaille existing but for their own pleasure. Woe betide him who so much as raises his voice in protest in the name of humanity against an excess of these already excessive abuses. I have told you of one remorselessly slain in cold blood for doing no more than that. Your own eyes have witnessed the assassination of another here upon this plinth, of yet another over there by the cathedral works, and the attempt upon my own life.

"Between them and the justice due to them in such cases stand these Lesdiguieres, these King's Lieutenants; not instruments of justice, but walls erected for the shelter of Privilege and Abuse whenever it exceeds its grotesquely excessive rights.

"Do you wonder that they will not yield an inch; that they will resist the election of a Third Estate with the voting power to sweep all these privileges away, to compel the Privileged to submit themselves to a just equality in the eyes of the law with the meanest of the canaille they trample underfoot, to provide that the moneys necessary to save this state from the bankruptcy into which they have all but plunged it shall be raised by taxation to be borne by themselves in the same proportion as by others?

"Sooner than yield to so much they prefer to resist even the royal command."

A phrase occurred to him used yesterday by Vilmorin, a phrase to which he had refused to attach importance when uttered then. He used it now. "In doing this they are striking at the very foundations of the throne. These fools do not perceive that if that throne falls over, it is they who stand nearest to it who will be crushed."

A terrific roar acclaimed that statement. Tense and quivering with the excitement that was flowing through him, and from him out into that great audience, he stood a moment smiling ironically. Then he waved them into silence, and saw by their ready obedience how completely he possessed them. For in the voice with which he spoke each now recognized the voice of himself, giving at last expression to the thoughts that for months and years had been inarticulately stirring in each simple mind.

Presently he resumed, speaking more quietly, that ironic smile about the corner of his mouth growing more marked:

"In taking my leave of M. de Lesdiguieres I gave him warning out of a page of natural history. I told him that when the wolves, roaming singly through the jungle, were weary of being hunted by the tiger, they banded themselves into packs, and went a-hunting the tiger in their turn. M. de Lesdiguieres contemptuously answered that he did not understand me. But your wits are better than his. You understand me, I think? Don't you?"

Again a great roar, mingled now with some approving laughter, was his answer. He had wrought them up to a pitch of dangerous passion, and they were ripe for any violence to which he urged them. If he had failed with the windmill, at least he was now master of the wind.

"To the Palais!" they shouted, waving their hands, brandishing canes, and—here and there—even a sword. "To the Palais! Down with M. de Lesdiguieres! Death to the King's Lieutenant!"

He was master of the wind, indeed. His dangerous gift of oratory—a gift nowhere more powerful than in France, since nowhere else are men's emotions so quick to respond to the appeal of eloquence—had given him this mastery. At his bidding now the gale would sweep away the windmill against which he had flung himself in vain. But that, as he straightforwardly revealed it, was no part of his intent.

"Ah, wait!" he bade them. "Is this miserable instrument of a corrupt system worth the attention of your noble indignation?"

He hoped his words would be reported to M. de Lesdiguieres. He thought it would be good for the soul of M. de Lesdiguieres to hear the undiluted truth about himself for once.

"It is the system itself you must attack and overthrow; not a mere instrument—a miserable painted lath such as this. And precipitancy will spoil everything. Above all, my children, no violence!"

My children! Could his godfather have heard him!

"You have seen often already the result of premature violence elsewhere in Brittany, and you have heard of it elsewhere in France. Violence on your part will call for violence on theirs. They will welcome the chance to assert their mastery by a firmer grip than heretofore. The military will be sent for. You will be faced by the bayonets of mercenaries. Do not provoke that, I implore you. Do not put it into their power, do not afford them the pretext they would welcome to crush you down into the mud of your own blood."

Out of the silence into which they had fallen anew broke now the cry of

"What else, then? What else?"

"I will tell you," he answered them. "The wealth and strength of Brittany lies in Nantes—a bourgeois city, one of the most prosperous in this realm, rendered so by the energy of the bourgeoisie and the toil of the people. It was in Nantes that this movement had its beginning, and as a result of it the King issued his order dissolving the States as now constituted—an order which those who base their power on Privilege and Abuse do not hesitate to thwart. Let Nantes be informed of the precise situation, and let nothing be done here until Nantes shall have given us the lead. She has the power—which we in Rennes have not—to make her will prevail, as we have seen already. Let her exert that power once more, and until she does so do you keep the peace in Rennes. Thus shall you triumph. Thus shall the outrages that are being perpetrated under your eyes be fully and finally avenged."

As abruptly as he had leapt upon the plinth did he now leap down from it. He had finished. He had said all—perhaps more than all—that could have been said by the dead friend with whose voice he spoke. But it was not their will that he should thus extinguish himself. The thunder of their acclamations rose deafeningly upon the air. He had played upon their emotions—each in turn—as a skilful harpist plays upon the strings of his instrument. And they were vibrant with the passions he had aroused, and the high note of hope on which he had brought his symphony to a close.

A dozen students caught him as he leapt down, and swung him to their shoulders, where again he came within view of all the acclaiming crowd.

The delicate Le Chapelier pressed alongside of him with flushed face and shining eyes.

"My lad," he said to him, "you have kindled a fire to-day that will sweep the face of France in a blaze of liberty." And then to the students he issued a sharp command. "To the Literary Chamber—at once. We must concert measures upon the instant, a delegate must be dispatched to Nantes forthwith, to convey to our friends there the message of the people of Rennes."

The crowd fell back, opening a lane through which the students bore the hero of the hour. Waving his hands to them, he called upon them to disperse to their homes, and await there in patience what must follow very soon.

"You have endured for centuries with a fortitude that is a pattern to the world," he flattered them. "Endure a little longer yet. The end, my friends, is well in sight at last."

They carried him out of the square and up the Rue Royale to an old house, one of the few old houses surviving in that city that had risen from its ashes, where in an upper chamber lighted by diamond-shaped panes of yellow glass the Literary Chamber usually held its meetings. Thither in his wake the members of that chamber came hurrying, summoned by the messages that Le Chapelier had issued during their progress.

Behind closed doors a flushed and excited group of some fifty men, the majority of whom were young, ardent, and afire with the illusion of liberty, hailed Andre-Louis as the strayed sheep who had returned to the fold, and smothered him in congratulations and thanks.

Then they settled down to deliberate upon immediate measures, whilst the doors below were kept by a guard of honour that had improvised itself from the masses. And very necessary was this. For no sooner had the Chamber assembled than the house was assailed by the gendarmerie of M. de Lesdiguieres, dispatched in haste to arrest the firebrand who was inciting the people of Rennes to sedition. The force consisted of fifty men. Five hundred would have been too few. The mob broke their carbines, broke some of their heads, and would indeed have torn them into pieces had they not beaten a timely and well-advised retreat before a form of horseplay to which they were not at all accustomed.

And whilst that was taking place in the street below, in the room abovestairs the eloquent Le Chapelier was addressing his colleagues of the Literary Chamber. Here, with no bullets to fear, and no one to report his words to the authorities, Le Chapelier could permit his oratory a full, unintimidated flow. And that considerable oratory was as direct and brutal as the man himself was delicate and elegant.

He praised the vigour and the greatness of the speech they had heard from their colleague Moreau. Above all he praised its wisdom. Moreau's words had come as a surprise to them. Hitherto they had never known him as other than a bitter critic of their projects of reform and regeneration; and quite lately they had heard, not without misgivings, of his appointment as delegate for a nobleman in the States of Brittany. But they held the explanation of his conversion. The murder of their dear colleague Vilmorin had produced this change. In that brutal deed Moreau had beheld at last in true proportions the workings of that evil spirit which they were vowed to exorcise from France. And to-day he had proven himself the stoutest apostle among them of the new faith. He had pointed out to them the only sane and useful course. The illustration he had borrowed from natural history was most apt. Above all, let them pack like the wolves, and to ensure this uniformity of action in the people of all Brittany, let a delegate at once be sent to Nantes, which had already proved itself the real seat of Brittany's power. It but remained to appoint that delegate, and Le Chapelier invited them to elect him.

Andre-Louis, on a bench near the window, a prey now to some measure of reaction, listened in bewilderment to that flood of eloquence.

As the applause died down, he heard a voice exclaiming:

"I propose to you that we appoint our leader here, Le Chapelier, to be that delegate."

Le Chapelier reared his elegantly dressed head, which had been bowed in thought, and it was seen that his countenance was pale. Nervously he fingered a gold spy-glass.

"My friends," he said, slowly, "I am deeply sensible of the honour that you do me. But in accepting it I should be usurping an honour that rightly belongs elsewhere. Who could represent us better, who more deserving to be our representative, to speak to our friends of Nantes with the voice of Rennes, than the champion who once already to-day has so incomparably given utterance to the voice of this great city? Confer this honour of being your spokesman where it belongs—upon Andre-Louis Moreau."

Rising in response to the storm of applause that greeted the proposal, Andre-Louis bowed and forthwith yielded. "Be it so," he said, simply. "It is perhaps fitting that I should carry out what I have begun, though I too am of the opinion that Le Chapelier would have been a worthier representative. I will set out to-night."

"You will set out at once, my lad," Le Chapelier informed him, and now revealed what an uncharitable mind might account the true source of his generosity. "It is not safe after what has happened for you to linger an hour in Rennes. And you must go secretly. Let none of you allow it to be known that he has gone. I would not have you come to harm over this, Andre-Louis. But you must see the risks you run, and if you are to be spared to help in this work of salvation of our afflicted motherland, you must use caution, move secretly, veil your identity even. Or else M. de Lesdiguieres will have you laid by the heels, and it will be goodnight for you."

CHAPTER VIII. OMNES OMNIBUS

Andre-Louis rode forth from Rennes committed to a deeper adventure than he had dreamed of when he left the sleepy village of Gavrillac. Lying the night at a roadside inn, and setting out again early in the morning, he reached Nantes soon after noon of the following day.

Through that long and lonely ride through the dull plains of Brittany, now at their dreariest in their winter garb, he had ample leisure in which to review his actions and his position. From one who had taken hitherto a purely academic and by no means friendly interest in the new philosophies of social life, exercising his wits upon these new ideas merely as a fencer exercises his eye and wrist with the foils, without ever suffering himself to be deluded into supposing the issue a real one, he found himself suddenly converted into a revolutionary firebrand, committed to revolutionary action of the most desperate kind. The representative and delegate of a nobleman in the States of Brittany, he found himself simultaneously and incongruously the representative and delegate of the whole Third Estate of Rennes.

It is difficult to determine to what extent, in the heat of passion and swept along by the torrent of his own oratory, he might yesterday have succeeded in deceiving himself. But it is at least certain that, looking back in cold blood now, he had no single delusion on the score of what he had done. Cynically he had presented to his audience one side only of the great question that he propounded.

But since the established order of things in France was such as to make a rampart for M. de La Tour d'Azyr, affording him complete immunity for this and any other crimes that it pleased him to commit, why, then the established order must take the consequences of its wrong-doing. Therein he perceived his clear justification.

And so it was without misgivings that he came on his errand of sedition into that beautiful city of Nantes, rendered by its spacious streets and splendid port the rival in prosperity of Bordeaux and Marseilles.

He found an inn on the Quai La Fosse, where he put up his horse, and where he dined in the embrasure of a window that looked out over the tree-bordered quay and the broad bosom of the Loire, on which argosies of all nations rode at anchor. The sun had again broken through the clouds, and shed its pale wintry light over the yellow waters and the tall-masted shipping.

Along the quays there was a stir of life as great as that to be seen on the quays of Paris. Foreign sailors in outlandish garments and of harsh-sounding, outlandish speech, stalwart fishwives with baskets of herrings on their heads, voluminous of petticoat above bare legs and bare feet, calling their wares shrilly and almost inarticulately, watermen in woollen caps and loose trousers rolled to the knees, peasants in goatskin coats, their wooden shoes clattering on the round kidney-stones, shipwrights and labourers from the dockyards, bellows-menders, rat-catchers, water-carriers, ink-sellers, and other itinerant pedlars. And, sprinkled through this proletariat mass that came and went in constant movement, Andre-Louis beheld tradesmen in sober garments, merchants in long, fur-lined coats; occasionally a merchant-prince rolling along in his two-horse cabriolet to the whip-crackings and shouts of "Gare!" from his coachman; occasionally a dainty lady carried past in her sedan-chair, with perhaps a mincing abbe from the episcopal court tripping along in attendance; occasionally an officer in scarlet riding disdainfully; and once the great carriage of a nobleman, with escutcheoned panels and a pair of white-stockinged, powdered footmen in gorgeous liveries hanging on behind. And there were Capuchins in brown and Benedictines in black, and secular priests in plenty—for God was well served in the sixteen parishes of Nantes—and by way of contrast there were lean-jawed, out-at-elbow adventurers, and gendarmes in blue coats and gaitered legs, sauntering guardians of the peace.

Representatives of every class that went to make up the seventy thousand inhabitants of that wealthy, industrious city were to be seen in the human stream that ebbed and flowed beneath the window from which Andre-Louis observed it.

Of the waiter who ministered to his humble wants with soup and bouilli, and a measure of vin gris, Andre-Louis enquired into the state of public feeling in the city. The waiter, a staunch supporter of the privileged orders, admitted regretfully that an uneasiness prevailed. Much would depend upon what happened at Rennes. If it was true that the King had dissolved the States of Brittany, then all should be well, and the malcontents would have no pretext for further disturbances. There had been trouble and to spare in Nantes already. They wanted no repetition of it. All manner of rumours were abroad, and since early morning there had been crowds besieging the portals of the Chamber of Commerce for definite news. But definite news was yet to come. It was not even known for a fact that His Majesty actually had dissolved the States.

It was striking two, the busiest hour of the day upon the Bourse, when Andre-Louis reached the Place du Commerce. The square, dominated by the imposing classical building of the Exchange, was so crowded that he was compelled almost to fight his way through to the steps of the magnificent Ionic porch. A word would have sufficed to have opened a way for him at once. But guile moved him to keep silent. He would come upon that waiting multitude as a thunderclap, precisely as yesterday he had come upon the mob at Rennes. He would lose nothing of the surprise effect of his entrance.

The precincts of that house of commerce were jealously kept by a line of ushers armed with staves, a guard as hurriedly assembled by the merchants as it was evidently necessary. One of these now effectively barred the young lawyer's passage as he attempted to mount the steps.

Andre-Louis announced himself in a whisper.

The stave was instantly raised from the horizontal, and he passed and went up the steps in the wake of the usher. At the top, on the threshold of the chamber, he paused, and stayed his guide.

"I will wait here," he announced. "Bring the president to me."

"Your name, monsieur?"

Almost had Andre-Louis answered him when he remembered Le Chapelier's warning of the danger with which his mission was fraught, and Le Chapelier's parting admonition to conceal his identity.

"My name is unknown to him; it matters nothing; I am the mouthpiece of a people, no more. Go."

The usher went, and in the shadow of that lofty, pillared portico Andre-Louis waited, his eyes straying out ever and anon to survey that spread of upturned faces immediately below him.

Soon the president came, others following, crowding out into the portico, jostling one another in their eagerness to hear the news.

"You are a messenger from Rennes?"

"I am the delegate sent by the Literary Chamber of that city to inform you here in Nantes of what is taking place."

"Your name?"

Andre-Louis paused. "The less we mention names perhaps the better."

The president's eyes grew big with gravity. He was a corpulent, florid man, purse-proud, and self-sufficient.

He hesitated a moment. Then—"Come into the Chamber," said he.

"By your leave, monsieur, I will deliver my message from here—from these steps."

"From here?" The great merchant frowned.

"My message is for the people of Nantes, and from here I can speak at once to the greatest number of Nantais of all ranks, and it is my desire—and the desire of those whom I represent—that as great a number as possible should hear my message at first hand."

"Tell me, sir, is it true that the King has dissolved the States?"

Andre-Louis looked at him. He smiled apologetically, and waved a hand towards the crowd, which by now was straining for a glimpse of this slim young man who had brought forth the president and more than half the numbers of the Chamber, guessing already, with that curious instinct of crowds, that he was the awaited bearer of tidings.

"Summon the gentlemen of your Chamber, monsieur," said he, "and you shall hear all."

"So be it."

A word, and forth they came to crowd upon the steps, but leaving clear the topmost step and a half-moon space in the middle.

To the spot so indicated, Andre-Louis now advanced very deliberately. He took his stand there, dominating the entire assembly. He removed his hat, and launched the opening bombshell of that address which is historic, marking as it does one of the great stages of France's progress towards revolution.

"People of this great city of Nantes, I have come to summon you to arms!"

In the amazed and rather scared silence that followed he surveyed them for a moment before resuming.

"I am a delegate of the people of Rennes, charged to announce to you what is taking place, and to invite you in this dreadful hour of our country's peril to rise and march to her defence."

"Name! Your name!" a voice shouted, and instantly the cry was taken up by others, until the multitude rang with the question.

He could not answer that excited mob as he had answered the president. It was necessary to compromise, and he did so, happily. "My name," said he, "is Omnes Omnibus—all for all. Let that suffice you now. I am a herald, a mouthpiece, a voice; no more. I come to announce to you that since the privileged orders, assembled for the States of Brittany in Rennes, resisted your will—our will—despite the King's plain hint to them, His Majesty has dissolved the States."

There was a burst of delirious applause. Men laughed and shouted, and cries of "Vive le Roi!" rolled forth like thunder. Andre-Louis waited, and gradually the preternatural gravity of his countenance came to be observed, and to beget the suspicion that there might be more to follow. Gradually silence was restored, and at last Andre Louis was able to proceed.

"You rejoice too soon. Unfortunately, the nobles, in their insolent arrogance, have elected to ignore the royal dissolution, and in despite of it persist in sitting and in conducting matters as seems good to them."

A silence of utter dismay greeted that disconcerting epilogue to the announcement that had been so rapturously received. Andre-Louis continued after a moment's pause:

"So that these men who were already rebels against the people, rebels, against justice and equity, rebels against humanity itself, are now also rebels against their King. Sooner than yield an inch of the unconscionable privileges by which too long already they have flourished, to the misery of a whole nation, they will make a mock of royal authority, hold up the King himself to contempt. They are determined to prove that there is no real sovereignty in France but the sovereignty of their own parasitic faineantise."

There was a faint splutter of applause, but the majority of the audience remained silent, waiting.

"This is no new thing. Always has it been the same. No minister in the last ten years, who, seeing the needs and perils of the State, counselled the measures that we now demand as the only means of arresting our motherland in its ever-quickening progress to the abyss, but found himself as a consequence cast out of office by the influence which Privilege brought to bear against him. Twice already has M. Necker been called to the ministry, to be twice dismissed when his insistent counsels of reform threatened the privileges of clergy and nobility. For the third time now has he been called to office, and at last it seems we are to have States General in spite of Privilege. But what the privileged orders can no longer prevent, they are determined to stultify. Since it is now a settled thing that these States General are to meet, at least the nobles and the clergy will see to it—unless we take measures to prevent them—by packing the Third Estate with their own creatures, and denying it all effective representation, that they convert the States General into an instrument of their own will for the perpetuation of the abuses by which they live. To achieve this end they will stop at nothing. They have flouted the authority of the King, and they are silencing by assassination those who raise their voices to condemn them. Yesterday in Rennes two young men who addressed the people as I am addressing you were done to death in the streets by assassins at the instigation of the nobility. Their blood cries out for vengeance."

Beginning in a sullen mutter, the indignation that moved his hearers swelled up to express itself in a roar of anger.

"Citizens of Nantes, the motherland is in peril. Let us march to her defence. Let us proclaim it to the world that we recognize that the measures to liberate the Third Estate from the slavery in which for centuries it has groaned find only obstacles in those orders whose phrenetic egotism sees in the tears and suffering of the unfortunate an odious tribute which they would pass on to their generations still unborn. Realizing from the barbarity of the means employed by our enemies to perpetuate our oppression that we have everything to fear from the aristocracy they would set up as a constitutional principle for the governing of France, let us declare ourselves at once enfranchised from it.

"The establishment of liberty and equality should be the aim of every citizen member of the Third Estate; and to this end we should stand indivisibly united, especially the young and vigorous, especially those who have had the good fortune to be born late enough to be able to gather for themselves the precious fruits of the philosophy of this eighteenth century."

Acclamations broke out unstintedly now. He had caught them in the snare of his oratory. And he pressed his advantage instantly.

"Let us all swear," he cried in a great voice, "to raise up in the name of humanity and of liberty a rampart against our enemies, to oppose to their bloodthirsty covetousness the calm perseverance of men whose cause is just. And let us protest here and in advance against any tyrannical decrees that should declare us seditious when we have none but pure and just intentions. Let us make oath upon the honour of our motherland that should any of us be seized by an unjust tribunal, intending against us one of those acts termed of political expediency—which are, in effect, but acts of despotism—let us swear, I say, to give a full expression to the strength that is in us and do that in self-defence which nature, courage, and despair dictate to us."

Loud and long rolled the applause that greeted his conclusion, and he observed with satisfaction and even some inward grim amusement that the wealthy merchants who had been congregated upon the steps, and who now came crowding about him to shake him by the hand and to acclaim him, were not merely participants in, but the actual leaders of, this delirium of enthusiasm.

It confirmed him, had he needed confirmation, in his conviction that just as the philosophies upon which this new movement was based had their source in thinkers extracted from the bourgeoisie, so the need to adopt those philosophies to the practical purposes of life was most acutely felt at present by those bourgeois who found themselves debarred by Privilege from the expansion their wealth permitted them. If it might be said of Andre-Louis that he had that day lighted the torch of the Revolution in Nantes, it might with even greater truth be said that the torch itself was supplied by the opulent bourgeoisie.

I need not dwell at any length upon the sequel. It is a matter of history how that oath which Omnes Omnibus administered to the citizens of Nantes formed the backbone of the formal protest which they drew up and signed in their thousands. Nor were the results of that powerful protest—which, after all, might already be said to harmonize with the expressed will of the sovereign himself—long delayed. Who shall say how far it may have strengthened the hand of Necker, when on the 27th of that same month of November he compelled the Council to adopt the most significant and comprehensive of all those measures to which clergy and nobility had refused their consent? On that date was published the royal decree ordaining that the deputies to be elected to the States General should number at least one thousand, and that the deputies of the Third Estate should be fully representative by numbering as many as the deputies of clergy and nobility together.

CHAPTER IX. THE AFTERMATH

Dusk of the following day was falling when the homing Andre-Louis approached Gavrillac. Realizing fully what a hue and cry there would presently be for the apostle of revolution who had summoned the people of Nantes to arms, he desired as far as possible to conceal the fact that he had been in that maritime city. Therefore he made a wide detour, crossing the river at Bruz, and recrossing it a little above Chavagne, so as to approach Gavrillac from the north, and create the impression that he was returning from Rennes, whither he was known to have gone two days ago.

Within a mile or so of the village he caught in the fading light his first glimpse of a figure on horseback pacing slowly towards him. But it was not until they had come within a few yards of each other, and he observed that this cloaked figure was leaning forward to peer at him, that he took much notice of it. And then he found himself challenged almost at once by a woman's voice.

"It is you, Andre—at last!"

He drew rein, mildly surprised, to be assailed by another question, impatiently, anxiously asked.

"Where have you been?"

"Where have I been, Cousin Aline? Oh... seeing the world."

"I have been patrolling this road since noon to-day waiting for you." She spoke breathlessly, in haste to explain. "A troop of the marechaussee from Rennes descended upon Gavrillac this morning in quest of you. They turned the chateau and the village inside out, and at last discovered that you were due to return with a horse hired from the Breton arme. So they have taken up their quarters at the inn to wait for you. I have been here all the afternoon on the lookout to warn you against walking into that trap."

"My dear Aline! That I should have been the cause of so much concern and trouble!"

"Never mind that. It is not important."

"On the contrary; it is the most important part of what you tell me. It is the rest that is unimportant."

"Do you realize that they have come to arrest you?" she asked him, with increasing impatience. "You are wanted for sedition, and upon a warrant from M. de Lesdiguieres."

"Sedition?" quoth he, and his thoughts flew to that business at Nantes. It was impossible they could have had news of it in Rennes and acted upon it in so short a time.

"Yes, sedition. The sedition of that wicked speech of yours at Rennes on Wednesday."

"Oh, that!" said he. "Pooh!" His note of relief might have told her, had she been more attentive, that he had to fear the consequences of a greater wickedness committed since. "Why, that was nothing."

"Nothing?"

"I almost suspect that the real intentions of these gentlemen of the marechaussee have been misunderstood. Most probably they have come to thank me on M. de Lesdiguieres' behalf. I restrained the people when they would have burnt the Palais and himself inside it."

"After you had first incited them to do it. I suppose you were afraid of your work. You drew back at the last moment. But you said things of M. de Lesdiguieres, if you are correctly reported, which he will never forgive."

"I see," said Andre-Louis, and he fell into thought.

But Mlle. de Kercadiou had already done what thinking was necessary, and her alert young mind had settled all that was to be done.

"You must not go into Gavrillac," she told him, "and you must get down from your horse, and let me take it. I will stable it at the chateau to-night. And sometime to-morrow afternoon, by when you should be well away, I will return it to the Breton arme."

"Oh, but that is impossible."

"Impossible? Why?"

"For several reasons. One of them is that you haven't considered what will happen to you if you do such a thing."

"To me? Do you suppose I am afraid of that pack of oafs sent by M. Lesdiguieres? I have committed no sedition."

"But it is almost as bad to give aid to one who is wanted for the crime. That is the law."

"What do I care for the law? Do you imagine that the law will presume to touch me?"

"Of course there is that. You are sheltered by one of the abuses I complained of at Rennes. I was forgetting."

"Complain of it as much as you please, but meanwhile profit by it. Come, Andre, do as I tell you. Get down from your horse." And then, as he still hesitated, she stretched out and caught him by the arm. Her voice was vibrant with earnestness. "Andre, you don't realize how serious is your position. If these people take you, it is almost certain that you will be hanged. Don't you realize it? You must not go to Gavrillac. You must go away at once, and lie completely lost for a time until this blows over. Indeed, until my uncle can bring influence to bear to obtain your pardon, you must keep in hiding."

"That will be a long time, then," said Andre-Louis. "M. de Kercadiou has never cultivated friends at court."

"There is M. de La Tour d'Azyr," she reminded him, to his astonishment.

"That man!" he cried, and then he laughed. "But it was chiefly against him that I aroused the resentment of the people of Rennes. I should have known that all my speech was not reported to you."

"It was, and that part of it among the rest."

"Ah! And yet you are concerned to save me, the man who seeks the life of your future husband at the hands either of the law or of the people? Or is it, perhaps, that since you have seen his true nature revealed in the murder of poor Philippe, you have changed your views on the subject of becoming Marquise de La Tour d'Azyr?"

"You often show yourself without any faculty of deductive reasoning."

"Perhaps. But hardly to the extent of imagining that M. de La Tour d'Azyr will ever lift a finger to do as you suggest."

"In which, as usual, you are wrong. He will certainly do so if I ask him."

"If you ask him?" Sheer horror rang in his voice.

"Why, yes. You see, I have not yet said that I will be Marquise de La Tour d'Azyr. I am still considering. It is a position that has its advantages. One of them is that it ensures a suitor's complete obedience."

"So, so. I see the crooked logic of your mind. You might go so far as to say to him: 'Refuse me this, and I shall refuse to be your marquise.' You would go so far as that?"

"At need, I might."

"And do you not see the converse implication? Do you not see that your hands would then be tied, that you would be wanting in honour if afterwards you refused him? And do you think that I would consent to anything that could so tie your hands? Do you think I want to see you damned, Aline?"

Her hand fell away from his arm.

"Oh, you are mad!" she exclaimed, quite out of patience.

"Possibly. But I like my madness. There is a thrill in it unknown to such sanity as yours. By your leave, Aline, I think I will ride on to Gavrillac."

"Andre, you must not! It is death to you!" In her alarm she backed her horse, and pulled it across the road to bar his way.

It was almost completely night by now; but from behind the wrack of clouds overhead a crescent moon sailed out to alleviate the darkness.

"Come, now," she enjoined him. "Be reasonable. Do as I bid you. See, there is a carriage coming up behind you. Do not let us be found here together thus."

He made up his mind quickly. He was not the man to be actuated by false heroics about dying, and he had no fancy whatever for the gallows of M. de Lesdiguieres' providing. The immediate task that he had set himself might be accomplished. He had made heard—and ringingly—the voice that M. de La Tour d'Azyr imagined he had silenced. But he was very far from having done with life.

"Aline, on one condition only."

"And that?"

"That you swear to me you will never seek the aid of M. de La Tour d'Azyr on my behalf."

"Since you insist, and as time presses, I consent. And now ride on with me as far as the lane. There is that carriage coming up."

The lane to which she referred was one that branched off the road some three hundred yards nearer the village and led straight up the hill to the chateau itself. In silence they rode together towards it, and together they turned into that thickly hedged and narrow bypath. At a depth of fifty yards she halted him.

"Now!" she bade him.

Obediently he swung down from his horse, and surrendered the reins to her.

"Aline," he said, "I haven't words in which to thank you."

"It isn't necessary," said she.

"But I shall hope to repay you some day."

"Nor is that necessary. Could I do less than I am doing? I do not want to hear of you hanged, Andre; nor does my uncle, though he is very angry with you."

"I suppose he is."

"And you can hardly be surprised. You were his delegate, his representative. He depended upon you, and you have turned your coat. He is rightly indignant, calls you a traitor, and swears that he will never speak to you again. But he doesn't want you hanged, Andre."

"Then we are agreed on that at least, for I don't want it myself."

"I'll make your peace with him. And now—good-bye, Andre. Send me a word when you are safe."

She held out a hand that looked ghostly in the faint light. He took it and bore it to his lips.

"God bless you, Aline."

She was gone, and he stood listening to the receding clopper-clop of hooves until it grew faint in the distance. Then slowly, with shoulders hunched and head sunk on his breast, he retraced his steps to the main road, cogitating whither he should go. Quite suddenly he checked, remembering with dismay that he was almost entirely without money. In Brittany itself he knew of no dependable hiding-place, and as long as he was in Brittany his peril must remain imminent. Yet to leave the province, and to leave it as quickly as prudence dictated, horses would be necessary. And how was he to procure horses, having no money beyond a single louis d'or and a few pieces of silver?

There was also the fact that he was very weary. He had had little sleep since Tuesday night, and not very much then; and much of the time had been spent in the saddle, a wearing thing to one so little accustomed to long rides. Worn as he was, it was unthinkable that he should go far to-night. He might get as far as Chavagne, perhaps. But there he must sup and sleep; and what, then, of to-morrow?

Had he but thought of it before, perhaps Aline might have been able to assist him with the loan of a few louis. His first impulse now was to follow her to the chateau. But prudence dismissed the notion. Before he could reach her, he must be seen by servants, and word of his presence would go forth.

There was no choice for him; he must tramp as far as Chavagne, find a bed there, and leave to-morrow until it dawned. On the resolve he set his face in the direction whence he had come. But again he paused. Chavagne lay on the road to Rennes. To go that way was to plunge further into danger. He would strike south again. At the foot of some meadows on this side of the village there was a ferry that would put him across the river. Thus he would avoid the village; and by placing the river between himself and the immediate danger, he would obtain an added sense of security.

A lane, turning out of the highroad, a quarter of a mile this side of Gavrillac, led down to that ferry. By this lane some twenty minutes later came Andre-Louis with dragging feet. He avoided the little cottage of the ferryman, whose window was alight, and in the dark crept down to the boat, intending if possible to put himself across. He felt for the chain by which the boat was moored, and ran his fingers along this to the point where it was fastened. Here to his dismay he found a padlock.

He stood up in the gloom and laughed silently. Of course he might have known it. The ferry was the property of M. de La Tour d'Azyr, and not likely to be left unfastened so that poor devils might cheat him of seigneurial dues.

There being no possible alternative, he walked back to the cottage, and rapped on the door. When it opened, he stood well back, and aside, out of the shaft of light that issued thence.

"Ferry!" he rapped out, laconically.

The ferryman, a burly scoundrel well known to him, turned aside to pick up a lantern, and came forth as he was bidden. As he stepped from the little porch, he levelled the lantern so that its light fell on the face of this traveller.

"My God!" he ejaculated.

"You realize, I see, that I am pressed," said Andre-Louis, his eyes on the fellow's startled countenance.

"And well you may be with the gallows waiting for you at Rennes," growled the ferryman. "Since you've been so foolish as to come back to Gavrillac, you had better go again as quickly as you can. I will say nothing of having seen you."

"I thank you, Fresnel. Your advice accords with my intention. That is why I need the boat."

"Ah, that, no," said Fresnel, with determination. "I'll hold my peace, but it's as much as my skin is worth to help you.

"You need not have seen my face. Forget that you have seen it."

"I'll do that, monsieur. But that is all I will do. I cannot put you across the river."

"Then give me the key of the boat, and I will put myself across."

"That is the same thing. I cannot. I'll hold my tongue, but I will not—I dare not—help you."

Andre-Louis looked a moment into that sullen, resolute face, and understood. This man, living under the shadow of La Tour d'Azyr, dared exercise no will that might be in conflict with the will of his dread lord.

"Fresnel," he said, quietly, "if, as you say, the gallows claim me, the thing that has brought me to this extremity arises out of the shooting of Mabey. Had not Mabey been murdered there would have been no need for me to have raised my voice as I have done. Mabey was your friend, I think. Will you for his sake lend me the little help I need to save my neck?"

The man kept his glance averted, and the cloud of sullenness deepened on his face.

"I would if I dared, but I dare not." Then, quite suddenly he became angry. It was as if in anger he sought support. "Don't you understand that I dare not? Would you have a poor man risk his life for you? What have you or yours ever done for me that you should ask that? You do not cross to-night in my ferry. Understand that, monsieur, and go at once—go before I remember that it may be dangerous even to have talked to you and not give information. Go!"

He turned on his heel to reenter his cottage, and a wave of hopelessness swept over Andre-Louis.

But in a second it was gone. The man must be compelled, and he had the means. He bethought him of a pistol pressed upon him by Le Chapelier at the moment of his leaving Rennes, a gift which at the time he had almost disdained. True, it was not loaded, and he had no ammunition. But how was Fresnel to know that?

He acted quickly. As with his right hand he pulled it from his pocket, with his left he caught the ferryman by the shoulder, and swung him round.

"What do you want now?" Fresnel demanded angrily. "Haven't I told you that I..."

He broke off short. The muzzle of the pistol was within a foot of his eyes.

"I want the key of the boat. That is all, Fresnel. And you can either give it me at once, or I'll take it after I have burnt your brains. I should regret to kill you, but I shall not hesitate. It is your life against mine, Fresnel; and you'll not find it strange that if one of us must die I prefer that it shall be you."

Fresnel dipped a hand into his pocket, and fetched thence a key. He held it out to Andre-Louis in fingers that shook—more in anger than in fear.

"I yield to violence," he said, showing his teeth like a snarling dog. "But don't imagine that it will greatly profit you."

Andre-Louis took the key. His pistol remained levelled.

"You threaten me, I think," he said. "It is not difficult to read your threat. The moment I am gone, you will run to inform against me. You will set the marechaussee on my heels to overtake me."

"No, no!" cried the other. He perceived his peril. He read his doom in the cold, sinister note on which Andre-Louis addressed him, and grew afraid. "I swear to you, monsieur, that I have no such intention."

"I think I had better make quite sure of you."

"O my God! Have mercy, monsieur!" The knave was in a palsy of terror. "I mean you no harm—I swear to Heaven I mean you no harm. I will not say a word. I will not..."

"I would rather depend upon your silence than your assurances. Still, you shall have your chance. I am a fool, perhaps, but I have a reluctance to shed blood. Go into the house, Fresnel. Go, man. I follow you."

In the shabby main room of that dwelling, Andre-Louis halted him again. "Get me a length of rope," he commanded, and was readily obeyed.

Five minutes later Fresnel was securely bound to a chair, and effectively silenced by a very uncomfortable gag improvised out of a block of wood and a muffler.

On the threshold the departing Andre-Louis turned.

"Good-night, Fresnel," he said. Fierce eyes glared mute hatred at him. "It is unlikely that your ferry will be required again to-night. But some one is sure to come to your relief quite early in the morning. Until then bear your discomfort with what fortitude you can, remembering that you have brought it entirely upon yourself by your uncharitableness. If you spend the night considering that, the lesson should not be lost upon you. By morning you may even have grown so charitable as not to know who it was that tied you up. Good-night."

He stepped out and closed the door.

To unlock the ferry, and pull himself across the swift-running waters, on which the faint moonlight was making a silver ripple, were matters that engaged not more than six or seven minutes. He drove the nose of the boat through the decaying sedges that fringed the southern bank of the stream, sprang ashore, and made the little craft secure. Then, missing the footpath in the dark, he struck out across a sodden meadow in quest of the road.

BOOK II: THE BUSKIN

CHAPTER I. THE TRESPASSERS

Coming presently upon the Redon road, Andre-Louis, obeying instinct rather than reason, turned his face to the south, and plodded wearily and mechanically forward. He had no clear idea of whither he was going, or of whither he should go. All that imported at the moment was to put as great a distance as possible between Gavrillac and himself.

He had a vague, half-formed notion of returning to Nantes; and there, by employing the newly found weapon of his oratory, excite the people into sheltering him as the first victim of the persecution he had foreseen, and against which he had sworn them to take up arms. But the idea was one which he entertained merely as an indefinite possibility upon which he felt no real impulse to act.

Meanwhile he chuckled at the thought of Fresnel as he had last seen him, with his muffled face and glaring eyeballs. "For one who was anything but a man of action," he writes, "I felt that I had acquitted myself none so badly." It is a phrase that recurs at intervals in his sketchy "Confessions." Constantly is he reminding you that he is a man of mental and not physical activities, and apologizing when dire necessity drives him into acts of violence. I suspect this insistence upon his philosophic detachment—for which I confess he had justification enough—to betray his besetting vanity.

With increasing fatigue came depression and self-criticism. He had stupidly overshot his mark in insultingly denouncing M. de Lesdiguieres. "It is much better," he says somewhere, "to be wicked than to be stupid. Most of this world's misery is the fruit not as priests tell us of wickedness, but of stupidity." And we know that of all stupidities he considered anger the most deplorable. Yet he had permitted himself to be angry with a creature like M. de Lesdiguieres—a lackey, a fribble, a nothing, despite his potentialities for evil. He could perfectly have discharged his self-imposed mission without arousing the vindictive resentment of the King's Lieutenant.

He beheld himself vaguely launched upon life with the riding-suit in which he stood, a single louis d'or and a few pieces of silver for all capital, and a knowledge of law which had been inadequate to preserve him from the consequences of infringing it.

He had, in addition—but these things that were to be the real salvation of him he did not reckon—his gift of laughter, sadly repressed of late, and the philosophic outlook and mercurial temperament which are the stock-in-trade of your adventurer in all ages.

Meanwhile he tramped mechanically on through the night, until he felt that he could tramp no more. He had skirted the little township of Guichen, and now within a half-mile of Guignen, and with Gavrillac a good seven miles behind him, his legs refused to carry him any farther.

He was midway across the vast common to the north of Guignen when he came to a halt. He had left the road, and taken heedlessly to the footpath that struck across the waste of indifferent pasture interspersed with clumps of gorse. A stone's throw away on his right the common was bordered by a thorn hedge. Beyond this loomed a tall building which he knew to be an open barn, standing on the edge of a long stretch of meadowland. That dark, silent shadow it may have been that had brought him to a standstill, suggesting shelter to his subconsciousness. A moment he hesitated; then he struck across towards a spot where a gap in the hedge was closed by a five-barred gate. He pushed the gate open, went through the gap, and stood now before the barn. It was as big as a house, yet consisted of no more than a roof carried upon half a dozen tall, brick pillars. But densely packed under that roof was a great stack of hay that promised a warm couch on so cold a night. Stout timbers had been built into the brick pillars, with projecting ends to serve as ladders by which the labourer might climb to pack or withdraw hay. With what little strength remained him, Andre-Louis climbed by one of these and landed safely at the top, where he was forced to kneel, for lack of room to stand upright. Arrived there, he removed his coat and neckcloth, his sodden boots and stockings. Next he cleared a trough for his body, and lying down in it, covered himself to the neck with the hay he had removed. Within five minutes he was lost to all worldly cares and soundly asleep.

When next he awakened, the sun was already high in the heavens, from which he concluded that the morning was well advanced; and this before he realized quite where he was or how he came there. Then to his awakening senses came a drone of voices close at hand, to which at first he paid little heed. He was deliciously refreshed, luxuriously drowsy and luxuriously warm.

But as consciousness and memory grew more full, he raised his head clear of the hay that he might free both ears to listen, his pulses faintly quickened by the nascent fear that those voices might bode him no good. Then he caught the reassuring accents of a woman, musical and silvery, though laden with alarm.

"Ah, mon Dieu, Leandre, let us separate at once. If it should be my father..."

And upon this a man's voice broke in, calm and reassuring:

"No, no, Climene; you are mistaken. There is no one coming. We are quite safe. Why do you start at shadows?"

"Ah, Leandre, if he should find us here together! I tremble at the very thought."

More was not needed to reassure Andre-Louis. He had overheard enough to know that this was but the case of a pair of lovers who, with less to fear of life, were yet—after the manner of their kind—more timid of heart than he. Curiosity drew him from his warm trough to the edge of the hay. Lying prone, he advanced his head and peered down.

In the space of cropped meadow between the barn and the hedge stood a man and a woman, both young. The man was a well-set-up, comely fellow, with a fine head of chestnut hair tied in a queue by a broad bow of black satin. He was dressed with certain tawdry attempts at ostentatious embellishments, which did not prepossess one at first glance in his favour. His coat of a fashionable cut was of faded plum-coloured velvet edged with silver lace, whose glory had long since departed. He affected ruffles, but for want of starch they hung like weeping willows over hands that were fine and delicate. His breeches were of plain black cloth, and his black stockings were of cotton—matters entirely out of harmony with his magnificent coat. His shoes, stout and serviceable, were decked with buckles of cheap, lack-lustre paste. But for his engaging and ingenuous countenance, Andre-Louis must have set him down as a knight of that order which lives dishonestly by its wits. As it was, he suspended judgment whilst pushing investigation further by a study of the girl. At the outset, be it confessed that it was a study that attracted him prodigiously. And this notwithstanding the fact that, bookish and studious as were his ways, and in despite of his years, it was far from his habit to waste consideration on femininity.

The child—she was no more than that, perhaps twenty at the most—possessed, in addition to the allurements of face and shape that went very near perfection, a sparkling vivacity and a grace of movement the like of which Andre-Louis did not remember ever before to have beheld assembled in one person. And her voice too—that musical, silvery voice that had awakened him—possessed in its exquisite modulations an allurement of its own that must have been irresistible, he thought, in the ugliest of her sex. She wore a hooded mantle of green cloth, and the hood being thrown back, her dainty head was all revealed to him. There were glints of gold struck by the morning sun from her light nut-brown hair that hung in a cluster of curls about her oval face. Her complexion was of a delicacy that he could compare only with a rose petal. He could not at that distance discern the colour of her eyes, but he guessed them blue, as he admired the sparkle of them under the fine, dark line of eyebrows.

He could not have told you why, but he was conscious that it aggrieved him to find her so intimate with this pretty young fellow, who was partly clad, as it appeared, in the cast-offs of a nobleman. He could not guess her station, but the speech that reached him was cultured in tone and word. He strained to listen.

"I shall know no peace, Leandre, until we are safely wedded," she was saying. "Not until then shall I count myself beyond his reach. And yet if we marry without his consent, we but make trouble for ourselves, and of gaining his consent I almost despair."

Evidently, thought Andre-Louis, her father was a man of sense, who saw through the shabby finery of M. Leandre, and was not to be dazzled by cheap paste buckles.

"My dear Climene," the young man was answering her, standing squarely before her, and holding both her hands, "you are wrong to despond. If I do not reveal to you all the stratagem that I have prepared to win the consent of your unnatural parent, it is because I am loath to rob you of the pleasure of the surprise that is in store. But place your faith in me, and in that ingenious friend of whom I have spoken, and who should be here at any moment."

The stilted ass! Had he learnt that speech by heart in advance, or was he by nature a pedantic idiot who expressed himself in this set and formal manner? How came so sweet a blossom to waste her perfumes on such a prig? And what a ridiculous name the creature owned!

Thus Andre-Louis to himself from his observatory. Meanwhile, she was speaking.

"That is what my heart desires, Leandre, but I am beset by fears lest your stratagem should be too late. I am to marry this horrible Marquis of Sbrufadelli this very day. He arrives by noon. He comes to sign the contract—to make me the Marchioness of Sbrufadelli. Oh!" It was a cry of pain from that tender young heart. "The very name burns my lips. If it were mine I could never utter it—never! The man is so detestable. Save me, Leandre. Save me! You are my only hope."

Andre-Louis was conscious of a pang of disappointment. She failed to soar to the heights he had expected of her. She was evidently infected by the stilted manner of her ridiculous lover. There was an atrocious lack of sincerity about her words. They touched his mind, but left his heart unmoved. Perhaps this was because of his antipathy to M. Leandre and to the issue involved.

So her father was marrying her to a marquis! That implied birth on her side. And yet she was content to pair off with this dull young adventurer in the tarnished lace! It was, he supposed, the sort of thing to be expected of a sex that all philosophy had taught him to regard as the maddest part of a mad species.

"It shall never be!" M. Leandre was storming passionately. "Never! I swear it!" And he shook his puny fist at the blue vault of heaven—Ajax defying Jupiter. "Ah, but here comes our subtle friend..." (Andre-Louis did not catch the name, M. Leandre having at that moment turned to face the gap in the hedge.) "He will bring us news, I know."

Andre-Louis looked also in the direction of the gap. Through it emerged a lean, slight man in a rusty cloak and a three-cornered hat worn well down over his nose so as to shade his face. And when presently he doffed this hat and made a sweeping bow to the young lovers, Andre-Louis confessed to himself that had he been cursed with such a hangdog countenance he would have worn his hat in precisely such a manner, so as to conceal as much of it as possible. If M. Leandre appeared to be wearing, in part at least, the cast-offs of nobleman, the newcomer appeared to be wearing the cast-offs of M. Leandre. Yet despite his vile clothes and viler face, with its three days' growth of beard, the fellow carried himself with a certain air; he positively strutted as he advanced, and he made a leg in a manner that was courtly and practised.

"Monsieur," said he, with the air of a conspirator, "the time for action has arrived, and so has the Marquis... That is why."

The young lovers sprang apart in consternation; Climene with clasped hands, parted lips, and a bosom that raced distractingly under its white fichu-menteur; M. Leandre agape, the very picture of foolishness and dismay.

Meanwhile the newcomer rattled on. "I was at the inn an hour ago when he descended there, and I studied him attentively whilst he was at breakfast. Having done so, not a single doubt remains me of our success. As for what he looks like, I could entertain you at length upon the fashion in which nature has designed his gross fatuity. But that is no matter. We are concerned with what he is, with the wit of him. And I tell you confidently that I find him so dull and stupid that you may be confident he will tumble headlong into each and all of the traps I have so cunningly prepared for him."

"Tell me, tell me! Speak!" Climene implored him, holding out her hands in a supplication no man of sensibility could have resisted. And then on the instant she caught her breath on a faint scream. "My father!" she exclaimed, turning distractedly from one to the other of those two. "He is coming! We are lost!"

"You must fly, Climene!" said M. Leandre.

"Too late!" she sobbed. "Too late! He is here."

"Calm, mademoiselle, calm!" the subtle friend was urging her. "Keep calm and trust to me. I promise you that all shall be well."

"Oh!" cried M. Leandre, limply. "Say what you will, my friend, this is ruin—the end of all our hopes. Your wits will never extricate us from this. Never!"

Through the gap strode now an enormous man with an inflamed moon face and a great nose, decently dressed after the fashion of a solid bourgeois. There was no mistaking his anger, but the expression that it found was an amazement to Andre-Louis.

"Leandre, you're an imbecile! Too much phlegm, too much phlegm! Your words wouldn't convince a ploughboy! Have you considered what they mean at all? Thus," he cried, and casting his round hat from him in a broad gesture, he took his stand at M. Leandre's side, and repeated the very words that Leandre had lately uttered, what time the three observed him coolly and attentively.

"Oh, say what you will, my friend, this is ruin—the end of all our hopes. Your wits will never extricate us from this. Never!"

A frenzy of despair vibrated in his accents. He swung again to face M. Leandre. "Thus," he bade him contemptuously. "Let the passion of your hopelessness express itself in your voice. Consider that you are not asking Scaramouche here whether he has put a patch in your breeches. You are a despairing lover expressing..."

He checked abruptly, startled. Andre-Louis, suddenly realizing what was afoot, and how duped he had been, had loosed his laughter. The sound of it pealing and booming uncannily under the great roof that so immediately confined him was startling to those below.

The fat man was the first to recover, and he announced it after his own fashion in one of the ready sarcasms in which he habitually dealt.

"Hark!" he cried, "the very gods laugh at you, Leandre." Then he addressed the roof of the barn and its invisible tenant. "Hi! You there!"

Andre-Louis revealed himself by a further protrusion of his tousled head.

"Good-morning," said he, pleasantly. Rising now on his knees, his horizon was suddenly extended to include the broad common beyond the hedge. He beheld there an enormous and very battered travelling chaise, a cart piled up with timbers partly visible under the sheet of oiled canvas that covered them, and a sort of house on wheels equipped with a tin chimney, from which the smoke was slowly curling. Three heavy Flemish horses and a couple of donkeys—all of them hobbled—were contentedly cropping the grass in the neighbourhood of these vehicles. These, had he perceived them sooner, must have given him the clue to the queer scene that had been played under his eyes. Beyond the hedge other figures were moving. Three at that moment came crowding into the gap—a saucy-faced girl with a tip-tilted nose, whom he supposed to be Columbine, the soubrette; a lean, active youngster, who must be the lackey Harlequin; and another rather loutish youth who might be a zany or an apothecary.

All this he took in at a comprehensive glance that consumed no more time than it had taken him to say good-morning. To that good-morning Pantaloon replied in a bellow:

"What the devil are you doing up there?"

"Precisely the same thing that you are doing down there," was the answer. "I am trespassing."

"Eh?" said Pantaloon, and looked at his companions, some of the assurance beaten out of his big red face. Although the thing was one that they did habitually, to hear it called by its proper name was disconcerting.

"Whose land is this?" he asked, with diminishing assurance.

Andre-Louis answered, whilst drawing on his stockings. "I believe it to be the property of the Marquis de La Tour d'Azyr."

"That's a high-sounding name. Is the gentleman severe?"

"The gentleman," said Andre-Louis, "is the devil; or rather, I should prefer to say upon reflection, that the devil is a gentleman by comparison."

"And yet," interposed the villainous-looking fellow who played Scaramouche, "by your own confessing you don't hesitate, yourself, to trespass upon his property."

"Ah, but then, you see, I am a lawyer. And lawyers are notoriously unable to observe the law, just as actors are notoriously unable to act. Moreover, sir, Nature imposes her limits upon us, and Nature conquers respect for law as she conquers all else. Nature conquered me last night when I had got as far as this. And so I slept here without regard for the very high and puissant Marquis de La Tour d'Azyr. At the same time, M. Scaramouche, you'll observe that I did not flaunt my trespass quite as openly as you and your companions."

Having donned his boots, Andre-Louis came nimbly to the ground in his shirt-sleeves, his riding-coat over his arm. As he stood there to don it, the little cunning eyes of the heavy father conned him in detail. Observing that his clothes, if plain, were of a good fashion, that his shirt was of fine cambric, and that he expressed himself like a man of culture, such as he claimed to be, M. Pantaloon was disposed to be civil.

"I am very grateful to you for the warning, sir..." he was beginning.

"Act upon it, my friend. The gardes-champetres of M. d'Azyr have orders to fire on trespassers. Imitate me, and decamp."

They followed him upon the instant through that gap in the hedge to the encampment on the common. There Andre-Louis took his leave of them. But as he was turning away he perceived a young man of the company performing his morning toilet at a bucket placed upon one of the wooden steps at the tail of the house on wheels. A moment he hesitated, then he turned frankly to M. Pantaloon, who was still at his elbow.

"If it were not unconscionable to encroach so far upon your hospitality, monsieur," said he, "I would beg leave to imitate that very excellent young gentleman before I leave you."

"But, my dear sir!" Good-nature oozed out of every pore of the fat body of the master player. "It is nothing at all. But, by all means. Rhodomont will provide what you require. He is the dandy of the company in real life, though a fire-eater on the stage. Hi, Rhodomont!"

The young ablutionist straightened his long body from the right angle in which it had been bent over the bucket, and looked out through a foam of soapsuds. Pantaloon issued an order, and Rhodomont, who was indeed as gentle and amiable off the stage as he was formidable and terrible upon it, made the stranger free of the bucket in the friendliest manner.

So Andre-Louis once more removed his neckcloth and his coat, and rolled up the sleeves of his fine shirt, whilst Rhodomont procured him soap, a towel, and presently a broken comb, and even a greasy hair-ribbon, in case the gentleman should have lost his own. This last Andre-Louis declined, but the comb he gratefully accepted, and having presently washed himself clean, stood, with the towel flung over his left shoulder, restoring order to his dishevelled locks before a broken piece of mirror affixed to the door of the travelling house.

He was standing thus, the gentle Rhodomont babbled aimlessly at his side, when his ears caught the sound of hooves. He looked over his shoulder carelessly, and then stood frozen, with uplifted comb and loosened mouth. Away across the common, on the road that bordered it, he beheld a party of seven horsemen in the blue coats with red facings of the marechaussee.

Not for a moment did he doubt what was the quarry of this prowling gendarmerie. It was as if the chill shadow of the gallows had fallen suddenly upon him.

And then the troop halted, abreast with them, and the sergeant leading it sent his bawling voice across the common.

"Hi, there! Hi!" His tone rang with menace.

Every member of the company—and there were some twelve in all—stood at gaze. Pantaloon advanced a step or two, stalking, his head thrown back, his manner that of a King's Lieutenant.

"Now, what the devil's this?" quoth he, but whether of Fate or Heaven or the sergeant, was not clear.

There was a brief colloquy among the horsemen, then they came trotting across the common straight towards the players' encampment.

Andre-Louis had remained standing at the tail of the travelling house. He was still passing the comb through his straggling hair, but mechanically and unconsciously. His mind was all intent upon the advancing troop, his wits alert and gathered together for a leap in whatever direction should be indicated.

Still in the distance, but evidently impatient, the sergeant bawled a question.

"Who gave you leave to encamp here?"

It was a question that reassured Andre-Louis not at all. He was not deceived by it into supposing or even hoping that the business of these men was merely to round up vagrants and trespassers. That was no part of their real duty; it was something done in passing—done, perhaps, in the hope of levying a tax of their own. It was very long odds that they were from Rennes, and that their real business was the hunting down of a young lawyer charged with sedition. Meanwhile Pantaloon was shouting back.

"Who gave us leave, do you say? What leave? This is communal land, free to all."

The sergeant laughed unpleasantly, and came on, his troop following.

"There is," said a voice at Pantaloon's elbow, "no such thing as communal land in the proper sense in all M. de La Tour d'Azyr's vast domain. This is a terre censive, and his bailiffs collect his dues from all who send their beasts to graze here."

Pantaloon turned to behold at his side Andre-Louis in his shirt-sleeves, and without a neckcloth, the towel still trailing over his left shoulder, a comb in his hand, his hair half dressed.

"God of God!" swore Pantaloon. "But it is an ogre, this Marquis de La Tour d'Azyr!"

"I have told you already what I think of him," said Andre-Louis. "As for these fellows you had better let me deal with them. I have experience of their kind." And without waiting for Pantaloon's consent, Andre-Louis stepped forward to meet the advancing men of the marechaussee. He had realized that here boldness alone could save him.

When a moment later the sergeant pulled up his horse alongside of this half-dressed young man, Andre-Louis combed his hair what time he looked up with a half smile, intended to be friendly, ingenuous, and disarming.

In spite of it the sergeant hailed him gruffly: "Are you the leader of this troop of vagabonds?"

"Yes... that is to say, my father, there, is really the leader." And he jerked a thumb in the direction of M. Pantaloon, who stood at gaze out of earshot in the background. "What is your pleasure, captain?"

"My pleasure is to tell you that you are very likely to be gaoled for this, all the pack of you." His voice was loud and bullying. It carried across the common to the ears of every member of the company, and brought them all to stricken attention where they stood. The lot of strolling players was hard enough without the addition of gaolings.

"But how so, my captain? This is communal land free to all."

"It is nothing of the kind."

"Where are the fences?" quoth Andre-Louis, waving the hand that held the comb, as if to indicate the openness of the place.

"Fences!" snorted the sergeant. "What have fences to do with the matter? This is terre censive. There is no grazing here save by payment of dues to the Marquis de La Tour d'Azyr."

"But we are not grazing," quoth the innocent Andre-Louis.

"To the devil with you, zany! You are not grazing! But your beasts are grazing!"

"They eat so little," Andre-Louis apologized, and again essayed his ingratiating smile.

The sergeant grew more terrible than ever. "That is not the point. The point is that you are committing what amounts to a theft, and there's the gaol for thieves."

"Technically, I suppose you are right," sighed Andre-Louis, and fell to combing his hair again, still looking up into the sergeant's face. "But we have sinned in ignorance. We are grateful to you for the warning." He passed the comb into his left hand, and with his right fumbled in his breeches' pocket, whence there came a faint jingle of coins. "We are desolated to have brought you out of your way. Perhaps for their trouble your men would honour us by stopping at the next inn to drink the health of... of this M. de La Tour d' Azyr, or any other health that they think proper."

Some of the clouds lifted from the sergeant's brow. But not yet all.

"Well, well," said he, gruffly. "But you must decamp, you understand." He leaned from the saddle to bring his recipient hand to a convenient distance. Andre-Louis placed in it a three-livre piece.

"In half an hour," said Andre-Louis.

"Why in half an hour? Why not at once?"

"Oh, but time to break our fast."

They looked at each other. The sergeant next considered the broad piece of silver in his palm. Then at last his features relaxed from their sternness.

"After all," said he, "it is none of our business to play the tipstaves for M. de La Tour d'Azyr. We are of the marechaussee from Rennes." Andre-Louis' eyelids played him false by flickering. "But if you linger, look out for the gardes-champetres of the Marquis. You'll find them not at all accommodating. Well, well—a good appetite to you, monsieur," said he, in valediction.

"A pleasant ride, my captain," answered Andre-Louis.

The sergeant wheeled his horse about, his troop wheeled with him. They were starting off, when he reined up again.

"You, monsieur!" he called over his shoulder. In a bound Andre-Louis was beside his stirrup. "We are in quest of a scoundrel named Andre-Louis Moreau, from Gavrillac, a fugitive from justice wanted for the gallows on a matter of sedition. You've seen nothing, I suppose, of a man whose movements seemed to you suspicious?"

"Indeed, we have," said Andre-Louis, very boldly, his face eager with consciousness of the ability to oblige.

"You have?" cried the sergeant, in a ringing voice. "Where? When?"

"Yesterday evening in the neighbourhood of Guignen..."

"Yes, yes," the sergeant felt himself hot upon the trail.

"There was a fellow who seemed very fearful of being recognized ... a man of fifty or thereabouts..."

"Fifty!" cried the sergeant, and his face fell. "Bah! This man of ours is no older than yourself, a thin wisp of a fellow of about your own height and of black hair, just like your own, by the description. Keep a lookout on your travels, master player. The King's Lieutenant in Rennes has sent us word this morning that he will pay ten louis to any one giving information that will lead to this scoundrel's arrest. So there's ten louis to be earned by keeping your eyes open, and sending word to the nearest justices. It would be a fine windfall for you, that."

"A fine windfall, indeed, captain," answered Andre-Louis, laughing.

But the sergeant had touched his horse with the spur, and was already trotting off in the wake of his men. Andre-Louis continued to laugh, quite silently, as he sometimes did when the humour of a jest was peculiarly keen.

Then he turned slowly about, and came back towards Pantaloon and the rest of the company, who were now all grouped together, at gaze.

Pantaloon advanced to meet him with both hands out-held. For a moment Andre-Louis thought he was about to be embraced.

"We hail you our saviour!" the big man declaimed. "Already the shadow of the gaol was creeping over us, chilling us to the very marrow. For though we be poor, yet are we all honest folk and not one of us has ever suffered the indignity of prison. Nor is there one of us would survive it. But for you, my friend, it might have happened. What magic did you work?"

"The magic that is to be worked in France with a King's portrait. The French are a very loyal nation, as you will have observed. They love their King—and his portrait even better than himself, especially when it is wrought in gold. But even in silver it is respected. The sergeant was so overcome by the sight of that noble visage—on a three-livre piece—that his anger vanished, and he has gone his ways leaving us to depart in peace."

"Ah, true! He said we must decamp. About it, my lads! Come, come..."

"But not until after breakfast," said Andre-Louis. "A half-hour for breakfast was conceded us by that loyal fellow, so deeply was he touched. True, he spoke of possible gardes-champetres. But he knows as well as I do that they are not seriously to be feared, and that if they came, again the King's portrait—wrought in copper this time—would produce the same melting effect upon them. So, my dear

M. Pantaloon, break your fast at your ease. I can smell your cooking from here, and from the smell I argue that there is no need to wish you a good appetite."

"My friend, my saviour!" Pantaloon flung a great arm about the young man's shoulders. "You shall stay to breakfast with us."

"I confess to a hope that you would ask me," said Andre-Louis.

CHAPTER II. THE SERVICE OF THESPIS

They were, thought Andre-Louis, as he sat down to breakfast with them behind the itinerant house, in the bright sunshine that tempered the cold breath of that November morning, an odd and yet an attractive crew. An air of gaiety pervaded them. They affected to have no cares, and made merry over the trials and tribulations of their nomadic life. They were curiously, yet amiably, artificial; histrionic in their manner of discharging the most commonplace of functions; exaggerated in their gestures; stilted and affected in their speech. They seemed, indeed, to belong to a world apart, a world of unreality which became real only on the planks of their stage, in the glare of their footlights. Good-fellowship bound them one to another; and Andre-Louis reflected cynically that this harmony amongst them might be the cause of their apparent unreality. In the real world, greedy striving and the emulation of acquisitiveness preclude such amity as was present here.

They numbered exactly eleven, three women and eight men; and they addressed each other by their stage names: names which denoted their several types, and never—or only very slightly—varied, no matter what might be the play that they performed.

"We are," Pantaloon informed him, "one of those few remaining staunch bands of real players, who uphold the traditions of the old Italian Commedia dell' Arte. Not for us to vex our memories and stultify our wit with the stilted phrases that are the fruit of a wretched author's lucubrations. Each of us is in detail his own author in a measure as he develops the part assigned to him. We are improvisers—improvisers of the old and noble Italian school."

"I had guessed as much," said Andre-Louis, "when I discovered you rehearsing your improvisations."

Pantaloon frowned.

"I have observed, young sir, that your humour inclines to the pungent, not to say the acrid. It is very well. It is I suppose, the humour that should go with such a countenance. But it may lead you astray, as in this instance. That rehearsal—a most unusual thing with us—was necessitated by the histrionic rawness of our Leandre. We are seeking to inculcate into him by training an art with which Nature neglected to endow him against his present needs. Should he continue to fail in doing justice to our schooling... But we will not disturb our present harmony with the unpleasant anticipation of misfortunes which we still hope to avert. We love our Leandre, for all his faults. Let me make you acquainted with our company."

And he proceeded to introduction in detail. He pointed out the long and amiable Rhodomont, whom Andre-Louis already knew.

"His length of limb and hooked nose were his superficial qualifications to play roaring captains," Pantaloon explained. "His lungs have justified our choice. You should hear him roar. At first we called him Spavento or Epouvapto. But that was unworthy of so great an artist. Not since the superb Mondor amazed the world has so thrasonical a bully been seen upon the stage. So we conferred upon him the name of Rhodomont that Mondor made famous; and I give you my word, as an actor and a gentleman—for I am a gentleman, monsieur, or was—that he has justified us."

His little eyes beamed in his great swollen face as he turned their gaze upon the object of his encomium. The terrible Rhodomont, confused by so much praise, blushed like a schoolgirl as he met the solemn scrutiny of Andre-Louis.

"Then here we have Scaramouche, whom also you already know. Sometimes he is Scapin and sometimes Coviello, but in the main Scaramouche, to which let me tell you he is best suited—sometimes too well suited, I think. For he is Scaramouche not only on the stage, but also in the world. He has a gift of sly intrigue, an art of setting folk by the ears, combined with an impudent aggressiveness upon occasion when he considers himself safe from reprisals. He is Scaramouche, the little skirmisher, to the very life. I could say more. But I am by disposition charitable and loving to all mankind."

"As the priest said when he kissed the serving-wench," snarled Scaramouche, and went on eating.

"His humour, like your own, you will observe, is acrid," said Pantaloon. He passed on. "Then that rascal with the lumpy nose and the grinning bucolic countenance is, of course, Pierrot. Could he be aught else?"

"I could play lovers a deal better," said the rustic cherub.

"That is the delusion proper to Pierrot," said Pantaloon, contemptuously. "This heavy, beetle-browed ruffian, who has grown old in sin, and whose appetite increases with his years, is Polichinelle. Each one, as you perceive, is designed by Nature for the part he plays. This nimble, freckled jackanapes is Harlequin; not your spangled Harlequin into which modern degeneracy has debased that first-born of Momus, but the genuine original zany of the Commedia, ragged and patched, an impudent, cowardly, blackguardly clown."

"Each one of us, as you perceive," said Harlequin, mimicking the leader of the troupe, "is designed by Nature for the part he plays."

"Physically, my friend, physically only, else we should not have so much trouble in teaching this beautiful Leandre to become a lover. Then we have Pasquariel here, who is sometimes an apothecary, sometimes a notary, sometimes a lackey—an amiable, accommodating fellow. He is also an excellent cook, being a child of Italy, that land of gluttons. And finally, you have myself, who as the father of the company very properly play as Pantaloon the roles of father. Sometimes, it is true, I am a deluded husband, and sometimes an ignorant, self-sufficient doctor. But it is rarely that I find it necessary to call myself other than Pantaloon. For the rest, I am the only one who has a name—a real name. It is Binet, monsieur.

"And now for the ladies... First in order of seniority we have Madame there." He waved one of his great hands towards a buxom, smiling blonde of five-and-forty, who was seated on the lowest of the steps of the travelling house. "She is our Duegne, or Mother, or Nurse, as the case requires. She is known quite simply and royally as Madame. If she ever had a name in the world, she has long since forgotten it, which is perhaps as well. Then we have this pert jade with the tip-tilted nose and the wide mouth, who is of course our soubrette Columbine, and lastly, my daughter Climene, an amoureuse of talents not to be matched outside the Comedie Francaise, of which she has the bad taste to aspire to become a member."

The lovely Climene—and lovely indeed she was—tossed her nut-brown curls and laughed as she looked across at Andre-Louis. Her eyes, he had perceived by now, were not blue, but hazel.

"Do not believe him, monsieur. Here I am queen, and I prefer to be queen here rather than a slave in Paris."

"Mademoiselle," said Andre-Louis, quite solemnly, "will be queen wherever she condescends to reign."

Her only answer was a timid—timid and yet alluring—glance from under fluttering lids. Meanwhile her father was bawling at the comely young man who played lovers—"You hear, Leandre! That is the sort of speech you should practise."

Leandre raised languid eyebrows. "That?" quoth he, and shrugged. "The merest commonplace."

Andre-Louis laughed approval. "M. Leandre is of a readier wit than you concede. There is subtlety in pronouncing it a commonplace to call Mlle. Climene a queen."

Some laughed, M. Binet amongst them, with good-humoured mockery.

"You think he has the wit to mean it thus? Bah! His subtleties are all unconscious."

The conversation becoming general, Andre-Louis soon learnt what yet there was to learn of this strolling band. They were on their way to Guichen, where they hoped to prosper at the fair that was to open on Monday next. They would make their triumphal entry into the town at noon, and setting up their stage in the old market, they would give their first performance that same Saturday night, in a new canevas—or scenario—of M. Binet's own, which should set the rustics gaping. And then M. Binet fetched a sigh, and addressed himself to the elderly, swarthy, beetle-browed Polichinelle, who sat on his left.

"But we shall miss Felicien," said he. "Indeed, I do not know what we shall do without him."

"Oh, we shall contrive," said Polichinelle, with his mouth full.

"So you always say, whatever happens, knowing that in any case the contriving will not fall upon yourself."

"He should not be difficult to replace," said Harlequin.

"True, if we were in a civilized land. But where among the rustics of Brittany are we to find a fellow of even his poor parts?" M. Binet turned to Andre-Louis. "He was our property-man, our machinist, our stage-carpenter, our man of affairs, and occasionally he acted."

"The part of Figaro, I presume," said Andre-Louis, which elicited a laugh.

"So you are acquainted with Beaumarchais!" Binet eyed the young man with fresh interest.

"He is tolerably well known, I think."

"In Paris, to be sure. But I had not dreamt his fame had reached the wilds of Brittany."

"But then I was some years in Paris—at the Lycee of Louis le Grand. It was there I made acquaintance with his work."

"A dangerous man," said Polichinelle, sententiously.

"Indeed, and you are right," Pantaloon agreed. "Clever—I do not deny him that, although myself I find little use for authors. But of a sinister cleverness responsible for the dissemination of many of these subversive new ideas. I think such writers should be suppressed."

"M. de La Tour d'Azyr would probably agree with you—the gentleman who by the simple exertion of his will turns this communal land into his own property." And Andre-Louis drained his cup, which had been filled with the poor vin gris that was the players' drink.

It was a remark that might have precipitated an argument had it not also reminded M. Binet of the terms on which they were encamped there, and of the fact that the half-hour was more than past. In a moment he was on his feet, leaping up with an agility surprising in so corpulent a man, issuing his commands like a marshal on a field of battle.

"Come, come, my lads! Are we to sit guzzling here all day? Time flees, and there's a deal to be done if we are to make our entry into Guichen at noon. Go, get you dressed. We strike camp in twenty minutes. Bestir, ladies! To your chaise, and see that you contrive to look your best. Soon the eyes of Guichen will be upon you, and the condition of your interior to-morrow will depend upon the impression made by your exterior to-day. Away! Away!"

The implicit obedience this autocrat commanded set them in a whirl. Baskets and boxes were dragged forth to receive the platters and remains of their meagre feast. In an instant the ground was cleared, and the three ladies had taken their departure to the chaise, which was set apart for their use. The men were already climbing into the house on wheels, when Binet turned to Andre-Louis.

"We part here, sir," said he, dramatically, "the richer by your acquaintance; your debtors and your friends." He put forth his podgy hand.

Slowly Andre-Louis took it in his own. He had been thinking swiftly in the last few moments. And remembering the safety he had found from his pursuers in the bosom of this company, it occurred to him that nowhere could he be better hidden for the present, until the quest for him should have died down.

"Sir," he said, "the indebtedness is on my side. It is not every day one has the felicity to sit down with so illustrious and engaging a company."

Binet's little eyes peered suspiciously at the young man, in quest of irony. He found nothing but candour and simple good faith.

"I part from you reluctantly," Andre-Louis continued. "The more reluctantly since I do not perceive the absolute necessity for parting."

"How?" quoth Binet, frowning, and slowly withdrawing the hand which the other had already retained rather longer than was necessary.

"Thus," Andre-Louis explained himself. "You may set me down as a sort of knight of rueful countenance in quest of adventure, with no fixed purpose in life at present. You will not marvel that what I have seen of yourself and your distinguished troupe should inspire me to desire your better acquaintance. On your side you tell me that you are in need of some one to replace your Figaro—your Felicien, I think you called him. Whilst it may be presumptuous of me to hope that I could discharge an office so varied and so onerous..."

"You are indulging that acrid humour of yours again, my friend," Binet interrupted him. "Excepting for that," he added, slowly, meditatively, his little eyes screwed up, "we might discuss this proposal that you seem to be making."

"Alas! we can except nothing. If you take me, you take me as I am. What else is possible? As for this humour—such as it is—which you decry, you might turn it to profitable account."

"How so?"

"In several ways. I might, for instance, teach Leandre to make love."

Pantaloon burst into laughter. "You do not lack confidence in your powers. Modesty does not afflict you."

"Therefore I evince the first quality necessary in an actor."

"Can you act?"

"Upon occasion, I think," said Andre-Louis, his thoughts upon his performance at Rennes and Nantes, and wondering when in all his histrionic career Pantaloon's improvisations had so rent the heart of mobs.

M. Binet was musing. "Do you know much of the theatre?" quoth he.

"Everything," said Andre-Louis.

"I said that modesty will prove no obstacle in your career."

"But consider. I know the work of Beaumarchais, Eglantine, Mercier, Chenier, and many others of our contemporaries. Then I have read, of course, Moliere, Racine, Corneille, besides many other lesser French writers. Of foreign authors, I am intimate with the works of Gozzi, Goldoni, Guarini, Bibbiena, Machiavelli, Secchi, Tasso, Ariosto, and Fedini. Whilst of those of antiquity I know most of the work of Euripides, Aristophanes, Terence, Plautus..."

"Enough!" roared Pantaloon.

"I am not nearly through with my list," said Andre-Louis.

"You may keep the rest for another day. In Heaven's name, what can have induced you to read so many dramatic authors?"

"In my humble way I am a student of man, and some years ago I made the discovery that he is most intimately to be studied in the reflections of him provided for the theatre."

"That is a very original and profound discovery," said Pantaloon, quite seriously. "It had never occurred to me. Yet is it true. Sir, it is a truth that dignifies our art. You are a man of parts, that is clear to me. It has been clear since first I met you. I can read a man. I knew you from the moment that you said 'good-morning.' Tell me, now: Do you think you could assist me upon occasion in the preparation of a scenario? My mind, fully engaged as it is with a thousand details of organization, is not always as clear as I would have it for such work. Could you assist me there, do you think?"

"I am quite sure I could."

"Hum, yes. I was sure you would be. The other duties that were Felicien's you would soon learn. Well, well, if you are willing, you may come along with us. You'd want some salary, I suppose?"

"If it is usual," said Andre-Louis.

"What should you say to ten livres a month?"

"I should say that it isn't exactly the riches of Peru."

"I might go as far as fifteen," said Binet, reluctantly. "But times are bad."

"I'll make them better for you."

"I've no doubt you believe it. Then we understand each other?"

"Perfectly," said Andre-Louis, dryly, and was thus committed to the service of Thespis.

CHAPTER II. THE COMIC MUSE

The company's entrance into the township of Guichen, if not exactly triumphal, as Binet had expressed the desire that it should be, was at least sufficiently startling and cacophonous to set the rustics gaping. To them these fantastic creatures appeared—as indeed they were—beings from another world.

First went the great travelling chaise, creaking and groaning on its way, drawn by two of the Flemish horses. It was Pantaloon who drove it, an obese and massive Pantaloon in a tight-fitting suit of scarlet under a long brown bed-gown, his countenance adorned by a colossal cardboard nose. Beside him on the box sat Pierrot in a white smock, with sleeves that completely covered his hands, loose white trousers, and a black skull-cap. He had whitened his face with flour, and he made hideous noises with a trumpet.

On the roof of the coach were assembled Polichinelle, Scaramouche, Harlequin, and Pasquariel. Polichinelle in black and white, his doublet cut in the fashion of a century ago, with humps before and behind, a white frill round his neck and a black mask upon the upper half of his face, stood in the middle, his feet planted wide to steady him, solemnly and viciously banging a big drum. The other three were seated each at one of the corners of the roof, their legs dangling over. Scaramouche, all in black in the Spanish fashion of the seventeenth century, his face adorned with a pair of mostachios, jangled a guitar discordantly. Harlequin, ragged and patched in every colour of the rainbow, with his leather girdle and sword of lath, the upper half of his face smeared in soot, clashed a pair of cymbals intermittently. Pasquariel, as an apothecary in skull-cap and white apron, excited the hilarity of the onlookers by his enormous tin clyster, which emitted when pumped a dolorous squeak.

Within the chaise itself, but showing themselves freely at the windows, and exchanging quips with the townsfolk, sat the three ladies of the company. Climene, the amoureuse, beautifully gowned in flowered satin, her own clustering ringlets concealed under a pumpkin-shaped wig, looked so much the lady of fashion that you might have wondered what she was doing in that fantastic rabble. Madame, as the mother, was also dressed with splendour, but exaggerated to achieve the ridiculous. Her headdress was a monstrous structure adorned with flowers, and superimposed by little ostrich plumes. Columbine sat facing them, her back to the horses, falsely demure, in milkmaid bonnet of white muslin, and a striped gown of green and blue.

The marvel was that the old chaise, which in its halcyon days may have served to carry some dignitary of the Church, did not founder instead of merely groaning under that excessive and ribald load.

Next came the house on wheels, led by the long, lean Rhodomont, who had daubed his face red, and increased the terror of it by a pair of formidable mostachios. He was in long thigh-boots and leather jerkin, trailing an enormous sword from a crimson baldrick. He wore a broad felt hat with a draggled feather, and as he advanced he raised his great voice and roared out defiance, and threats of blood-curdling butchery to be performed upon all and sundry. On the roof of this vehicle sat Leandre alone. He was in blue satin, with ruffles, small sword, powdered hair, patches and spy-glass, and red-heeled shoes: the complete courtier, looking very handsome. The women of Guichen ogled him coquettishly. He took the ogling as a proper tribute to his personal endowments, and returned it with interest. Like Climene, he looked out of place amid the bandits who composed the remainder of the company.

Bringing up the rear came Andre-Louis leading the two donkeys that dragged the property-cart. He had insisted upon assuming a false nose, representing as for embellishment that which he intended for disguise. For the rest, he had retained his own garments. No one paid any attention to him as he trudged along beside his donkeys, an insignificant rear guard, which he was well content to be.

They made the tour of the town, in which the activity was already above the normal in preparation for next week's fair. At intervals they halted, the cacophony would cease abruptly, and Polichinelle would announce in a stentorian voice that at five o'clock that evening in the old market, M. Binet's famous company of improvisers would perform a new comedy in four acts entitled, "The Heartless Father."

Thus at last they came to the old market, which was the groundfloor of the town hall, and open to the four winds by two archways on each side of its length, and one archway on each side of its breadth. These archways, with two exceptions, had been boarded up. Through those two, which gave admission to what presently would be the theatre, the ragamuffins of the town, and the niggards who were reluctant to spend the necessary sous to obtain proper admission, might catch furtive glimpses of the performance.

That afternoon was the most strenuous of Andre-Louis' life, unaccustomed as he was to any sort of manual labour. It was spent in erecting and preparing the stage at one end of the market-hall; and he began to realize how hard-earned were to be his monthly fifteen livres. At first there were four of them to the task—or really three, for Pantaloon did no more than bawl directions. Stripped of their finery, Rhodomont and Leandre assisted Andre-Louis in that carpentering. Meanwhile the other four were at dinner with the ladies. When a half-hour or so later they came to carry on the work, Andre-Louis and his companions went to dine in their turn, leaving Polichinelle to direct the operations as well as assist in them.

They crossed the square to the cheap little inn where they had taken up their quarters. In the narrow passage Andre-Louis came face to face with Climene, her fine feathers cast, and restored by now to her normal appearance.

"And how do you like it?" she asked him, pertly.

He looked her in the eyes. "It has its compensations," quoth he, in that curious cold tone of his that left one wondering whether he meant or not what he seemed to mean.

She knit her brows. "You... you feel the need of compensations already?"

"Faith, I felt it from the beginning," said he. "It was the perception of them allured me."

They were quite alone, the others having gone on into the room set apart for them, where food was spread. Andre-Louis, who was as unlearned in Woman as he was learned in Man, was not to know, upon feeling himself suddenly extraordinarily aware of her femininity, that it was she who in some subtle, imperceptible manner so rendered him.

"What," she asked him, with demurest innocence, "are these compensations?"

He caught himself upon the brink of the abyss.

"Fifteen livres a month," said he, abruptly.

A moment she stared at him bewildered. He was very disconcerting. Then she recovered.

"Oh, and bed and board," said she. "Don't be leaving that from the reckoning, as you seem to be doing; for your dinner will be going cold. Aren't you coming?"

"Haven't you dined?" he cried, and she wondered had she caught a note of eagerness.

"No," she answered, over her shoulder. "I waited."

"What for?" quoth his innocence, hopefully.

"I had to change, of course, zany," she answered, rudely. Having dragged him, as she imagined, to the chopping-block, she could not refrain from chopping. But then he was of those who must be chopping back.

"And you left your manners upstairs with your grand-lady clothes, mademoiselle. I understand."

A scarlet flame suffused her face. "You are very insolent," she said, lamely.

"I've often been told so. But I don't believe it." He thrust open the door for her, and bowing with an air which imposed upon her, although it was merely copied from Fleury of the Comedie Francaise, so often visited in the Louis le Grand days, he waved her in. "After you, ma demoiselle." For greater emphasis he deliberately broke the word into its two component parts.

"I thank you, monsieur," she answered, frostily, as near sneering as was possible to so charming a person, and went in, nor addressed him again throughout the meal. Instead, she devoted herself with an unusual and devastating assiduity to the suspiring Leandre, that poor devil who could not successfully play the lover with her on the stage because of his longing to play it in reality.

Andre-Louis ate his herrings and black bread with a good appetite nevertheless. It was poor fare, but then poor fare was the common lot of poor people in that winter of starvation, and since he had cast in his fortunes with a company whose affairs were not flourishing, he must accept the evils of the situation philosophically.

"Have you a name?" Binet asked him once in the course of that repast and during a pause in the conversation.

"It happens that I have," said he. "I think it is Parvissimus."

"Parvissimus?" quoth Binet. "Is that a family name?"

"In such a company, where only the leader enjoys the privilege of a family name, the like would be unbecoming its least member. So I take the name that best becomes in me. And I think it is Parvissimus—the very least."

Binet was amused. It was droll; it showed a ready fancy. Oh, to be sure, they must get to work together on those scenarios.

"I shall prefer it to carpentering," said Andre-Louis. Nevertheless he had to go back to it that afternoon, and to labour strenuously until four o'clock, when at last the autocratic Binet announced himself satisfied with the preparations, and proceeded, again with the help of Andre-Louis, to prepare the lights, which were supplied partly by tallow candles and partly by lamps burning fish-oil.

At five o'clock that evening the three knocks were sounded, and the curtain rose on "The Heartless Father."

Among the duties inherited by Andre-Louis from the departed Felicien whom he replaced, was that of doorkeeper. This duty he discharged dressed in a Polichinelle costume, and wearing a pasteboard nose. It was an arrangement mutually agreeable to M. Binet and himself. M. Binet—who had taken the further precaution of retaining Andre-Louis' own garments—was thereby protected against the risk of his latest recruit absconding with the takings. Andre-Louis, without illusions on the score of Pantaloon's real object, agreed to it willingly enough, since it protected him from the chance of recognition by any acquaintance who might possibly be in Guichen.

The performance was in every sense unexciting; the audience meagre and unenthusiastic. The benches provided in the front half of the market contained some twenty-seven persons: eleven at twenty sous a head and sixteen at twelve. Behind these stood a rabble of some thirty others at six sous apiece. Thus the gross takings were two louis, ten livres, and two sous. By the time M. Binet had paid for the use of the market, his lights, and the expenses of his company at the inn over Sunday, there was not likely to be very much left towards the wages of his players. It is not surprising, therefore, that M. Binet's bonhomie should have been a trifle overcast that evening.

"And what do you think of it?" he asked Andre-Louis, as they were walking back to the inn after the performance.

"Possibly it could have been worse; probably it could not," said he.

In sheer amazement M. Binet checked in his stride, and turned to look at his companion.

"Huh!" said he. "Dieu de Dien! But you are frank."

"An unpopular form of service among fools, I know."

"Well, I am not a fool," said Binet.

"That is why I am frank. I pay you the compliment of assuming intelligence in you, M. Binet."

"Oh, you do?" quoth M. Binet. "And who the devil are you to assume anything? Your assumptions are presumptuous, sir." And with that he lapsed into silence and the gloomy business of mentally casting up his accounts.

But at table over supper a half-hour later he revived the topic.

"Our latest recruit, this excellent M. Parvissimus," he announced, "has the impudence to tell me that possibly our comedy could have been worse, but that probably it could not." And he blew out his great round cheeks to invite a laugh at the expense of that foolish critic.

"That's bad," said the swarthy and sardonic Polichinelle. He was grave as Rhadamanthus pronouncing judgment. "That's bad. But what is infinitely worse is that the audience had the impudence to be of the same mind."

"An ignorant pack of clods," sneered Leandre, with a toss of his handsome head.

"You are wrong," quoth Harlequin. "You were born for love, my dear, not criticism."

Leandre—a dull dog, as you will have conceived—looked contemptuously down upon the little man. "And you, what were you born for?" he wondered.

"Nobody knows," was the candid admission. "Nor yet why. It is the case of many of us, my dear, believe me."

"But why"—M. Binet took him up, and thus spoilt the beginnings of a very pretty quarrel—"why do you say that Leandre is wrong?"

"To be general, because he is always wrong. To be particular, because I judge the audience of Guichen to be too sophisticated for 'The Heartless Father.'"

"You would put it more happily," interposed Andre-Louis—who was the cause of this discussion—"if you said that 'The Heartless Father' is too unsophisticated for the audience of Guichen."

"Why, what's the difference?" asked Leandre.

"I didn't imply a difference. I merely suggested that it is a happier way to express the fact."

"The gentleman is being subtle," sneered Binet.

"Why happier?" Harlequin demanded.

"Because it is easier to bring 'The Heartless Father' to the sophistication of the Guichen audience, than the Guichen audience to the unsophistication of 'The Heartless Father.'"

"Let me think it out," groaned Polichinelle, and he took his head in his hands.

But from the tail of the table Andre-Louis was challenged by Climene who sat there between Columbine and Madame.

"You would alter the comedy, would you, M. Parvissimus?" she cried.

He turned to parry her malice.

"I would suggest that it be altered," he corrected, inclining his head.

"And how would you alter it, monsieur?"

"I? Oh, for the better."

"But of course!" She was sleekest sarcasm. "And how would you do it?"

"Aye, tell us that," roared M. Binet, and added: "Silence, I pray you, gentlemen and ladies. Silence for M. Parvissimus."

Andre-Louis looked from father to daughter, and smiled. "Pardi!" said he. "I am between bludgeon and dagger. If I escape with my life, I shall be fortunate. Why, then, since you pin me to the very wall, I'll tell you what I should do. I should go back to the original and help myself more freely from it."

"The original?" questioned M. Binet—the author.

"It is called, I believe, 'Monsieur de Pourceaugnac,' and was written by Moliere."

Somebody tittered, but that somebody was not M. Binet. He had been touched on the raw, and the look in his little eyes betrayed the fact that his bonhomme exterior covered anything but a bonhomme.

"You charge me with plagiarism," he said at last; "with filching the ideas of Moliere."

"There is always, of course," said Andre-Louis, unruffled, "the alternative possibility of two great minds working upon parallel lines."

M. Binet studied the young man attentively a moment. He found him bland and inscrutable, and decided to pin him down.

"Then you do not imply that I have been stealing from Moliere?"

"I advise you to do so, monsieur," was the disconcerting reply.

M. Binet was shocked.

"You advise me to do so! You advise me, me, Antoine Binet, to turn thief at my age!"

"He is outrageous," said mademoiselle, indignantly.

"Outrageous is the word. I thank you for it, my dear. I take you on trust, sir. You sit at my table, you have the honour to be included in my company, and to my face you have the audacity to advise me to become a thief—the worst kind of thief that is conceivable, a thief of spiritual things, a thief of ideas! It is insufferable, intolerable! I have been, I fear, deeply mistaken in you, monsieur; just as you appear to have been mistaken in me. I am not the scoundrel you suppose me, sir, and I will not number in my company a man who dares to suggest that I should become one. Outrageous!"

He was very angry. His voice boomed through the little room, and the company sat hushed and something scared, their eyes upon Andre-Louis, who was the only one entirely unmoved by this outburst of virtuous indignation.

"You realize, monsieur," he said, very quietly, "that you are insulting the memory of the illustrious dead?"

"Eh?" said Binet.

Andre-Louis developed his sophistries.

"You insult the memory of Moliere, the greatest ornament of our stage, one of the greatest ornaments of our nation, when you suggest that there is vileness in doing that which he never hesitated to do, which no great author yet has hesitated to do. You cannot suppose that Moliere ever troubled himself to be original in the matter of ideas. You cannot suppose that the stories he tells in his plays have never been told before. They were culled, as you very well know—though you seem momentarily to have forgotten it, and it is therefore necessary that I should remind you—they were culled, many of them, from the Italian authors, who themselves had culled them Heaven alone knows where. Moliere took those old stories and retold them in his own language. That is precisely what I am suggesting that you should do. Your company is a company of improvisers. You supply the dialogue as you proceed, which is rather more than Moliere ever attempted. You may, if you prefer it—though it would seem to me to be yielding to an excess of scruple—go straight to Boccaccio or Sacchetti. But even then you cannot be sure that you have reached the sources."

Andre-Louis came off with flying colours after that. You see what a debater was lost in him; how nimble he was in the art of making white look black. The company was impressed, and no one more that M. Binet, who found himself supplied with a crushing argument against those who in future might tax him with the impudent plagiarisms which he undoubtedly perpetrated. He retired in the best order he could from the position he had taken up at the outset.

"So that you think," he said, at the end of a long outburst of agreement, "you think that our story of 'The Heartless Father' could be enriched by dipping into 'Monsieur de Pourceaugnac,' to which I confess upon reflection that it may present certain superficial resemblances?"

"I do; most certainly I do—always provided that you do so judiciously. Times have changed since Moliere." It was as a consequence of this that Binet retired soon after, taking Andre-Louis with him. The pair sat together late that night, and were again in close communion throughout the whole of Sunday morning.

After dinner M. Binet read to the assembled company the amended and amplified canevas of "The Heartless Father," which, acting upon the advice of M. Parvissimus, he had been at great pains to prepare. The company had few doubts as to the real authorship before he began to read; none at all when he had read. There was a verve, a grip about this story; and, what was more, those of them who knew their Moliere realized that far from approaching the original more closely, this canevas had drawn farther away from it. Moliere's original part—the title role—had dwindled into insignificance, to the great disgust of Polichinelle, to whom it fell. But the other parts had all been built up into importance, with the exception of Leandre, who remained as before. The two great roles were now Scaramouche, in the character of the intriguing Sbrigandini, and Pantaloon the father. There was, too, a comical part for Rhodomont, as the roaring bully hired by Polichinelle to cut Leandre into ribbons. And in view of the importance now of Scaramouche, the play had been rechristened "Figaro-Scaramouche."

This last had not been without a deal of opposition from M. Binet. But his relentless collaborator, who was in reality the real author—drawing shamelessly, but practically at last upon his great store of reading—had overborne him.

"You must move with the times, monsieur. In Paris Beaumarchais is the rage. 'Figaro' is known to-day throughout the world. Let us borrow a little of his glory. It will draw the people in. They will come to see half a 'Figaro' when they will not come to see a dozen 'Heartless Fathers.' Therefore let us cast the mantle of Figaro upon some one, and proclaim it in our title."

"But as I am the head of the company..." began M. Binet, weakly.

"If you will be blind to your interests, you will presently be a head without a body. And what use is that? Can the shoulders of Pantaloon carry the mantle of Figaro? You laugh. Of course you laugh. The notion is absurd. The proper person for the mantle of Figaro is Scaramouche, who is naturally Figaro's twin-brother."

Thus tyrannized, the tyrant Binet gave way, comforted by the reflection that if he understood anything at all about the theatre, he had for fifteen livres a month acquired something that would presently be earning him as many louis.

The company's reception of the canevas now confirmed him, if we except Polichinelle, who, annoyed at having lost half his part in the alterations, declared the new scenario fatuous.

"Ah! You call my work fatuous, do you?" M. Binet hectored him.

"Your work?" said Polichinelle, to add with his tongue in his cheek: "Ah, pardon. I had not realized that you were the author."

"Then realize it now."

"You were very close with M. Parvissimus over this authorship," said Polichinelle, with impudent suggestiveness.

"And what if I was? What do you imply?"

"That you took him to cut quills for you, of course."

"I'll cut your ears for you if you're not civil," stormed the infuriated Binet.

Polichinelle got up slowly, and stretched himself.

"Dieu de Dieu!" said he. "If Pantaloon is to play Rhodomont, I think I'll leave you. He is not amusing in the part." And he swaggered out before M. Binet had recovered from his speechlessness.

CHAPTER IV. EXIT MONSIEUR PARVISSIMUS

Ar four o'clock on Monday afternoon the curtain rose on "Figaro-Scaramouche" to an audience that filled three quarters of the market-hall. M. Binet attributed this good attendance to the influx of people to Guichen for the fair, and to the magnificent parade of his company through the streets of the township at the busiest time of the day. Andre-Louis attributed it entirely to the title. It was the "Figaro" touch that had fetched in the better-class bourgeoisie, which filled more than half of the twenty-sous places and three quarters of the twelve-sous seats. The lure had drawn them. Whether it was to continue to do so would depend upon the manner in which the canevas over which he had laboured to the glory of Binet was interpreted by the company. Of the merits of the canevas itself he had no doubt. The authors upon whom he had drawn for the elements of it were sound, and he had taken of their best, which he claimed to be no more than the justice due to them.

The company excelled itself. The audience followed with relish the sly intriguings of Scaramouche, delighted in the beauty and freshness of Climene, was moved almost to tears by the hard fate which through four long acts kept her from the hungering arms of the so beautiful Leandre, howled its delight over the ignominy of Pantaloon, the buffooneries of his sprightly lackey Harlequin, and the thrasonical strut and bellowing fierceness of the cowardly Rhodomont.

The success of the Binet troupe in Guichen was assured. That night the company drank Burgundy at M. Binet's expense. The takings reached the sum of eight louis, which was as good business as M. Binet had ever done in all his career. He was very pleased. Gratification rose like steam from his fat body. He even condescended so far as to attribute a share of the credit for the success to M. Parvissimus.

"His suggestion," he was careful to say, by way of properly delimiting that share, "was most valuable, as I perceived at the time."

"And his cutting of quills," growled Polichinelle. "Don't forget that. It is most important to have by you a man who understands how to cut a quill, as I shall remember when I turn author."

But not even that gibe could stir M. Binet out of his lethargy of content.

On Tuesday the success was repeated artistically and augmented financially. Ten louis and seven livres was the enormous sum that Andre-Louis, the doorkeeper, counted over to M. Binet after the performance. Never yet had M. Binet made so much money in one evening—and a miserable little village like Guichen was certainly the last place in which he would have expected this windfall.

"Ah, but Guichen in time of fair," Andre-Louis reminded him. "There are people here from as far as Nantes and Rennes to buy and sell. To-morrow, being the last day of the fair, the crowds will be greater than ever. We should better this evening's receipts."

"Better them? I shall be quite satisfied if we do as well, my friend."

"You can depend upon that," Andre-Louis assured him. "Are we to have Burgundy?"

And then the tragedy occurred. It announced itself in a succession of bumps and thuds, culminating in a crash outside the door that brought them all to their feet in alarm.

Pierrot sprang to open, and beheld the tumbled body of a man lying at the foot of the stairs. It emitted groans, therefore it was alive. Pierrot went forward to turn it over, and disclosed the fact that the body wore the wizened face of Scaramouche, a grimacing, groaning, twitching Scaramouche.

The whole company, pressing after Pierrot, abandoned itself to laughter.

"I always said you should change parts with me," cried Harlequin. "You're such an excellent tumbler. Have you been practising?"

"Fool!" Scaramouche snapped. "Must you be laughing when I've all but broken my neck?"

"You are right. We ought to be weeping because you didn't break it. Come, man, get up," and he held out a hand to the prostrate rogue.

Scaramouche took the hand, clutched it, heaved himself from the ground, then with a scream dropped back again.

"My foot!" he complained.

Binet rolled through the group of players, scattering them to right and left. Apprehension had been quick to seize him. Fate had played him such tricks before.

"What ails your foot?" quoth he, sourly.

"It's broken, I think," Scaramouche complained.

"Broken? Bah! Get up, man." He caught him under the armpits and hauled him up.

Scaramouche came howling to one foot; the other doubled under him when he attempted to set it down, and he must have collapsed again but that Binet supported him. He filled the place with his plaint, whilst Binet swore amazingly and variedly.

"Must you bellow like a calf, you fool? Be quiet. A chair here, some one."

A chair was thrust forward. He crushed Scaramouche down into it.

"Let us look at this foot of yours."

Heedless of Scaramouche's howls of pain, he swept away shoe and stocking.

"What ails it?" he asked, staring. "Nothing that I can see." He seized it, heel in one hand, instep in the other, and gyrated it. Scaramouche screamed in agony, until Climene caught Binet's arm and made him stop.

"My God, have you no feelings?" she reproved her father. "The lad has hurt his foot. Must you torture him? Will that cure it?"

"Hurt his foot!" said Binet. "I can see nothing the matter with his foot—nothing to justify all this uproar. He has bruised it, maybe..."

"A man with a bruised foot doesn't scream like that," said Madame over Climene's shoulder. "Perhaps he has dislocated it."

"That is what I fear," whimpered Scaramouche.

Binet heaved himself up in disgust.

"Take him to bed," he bade them, "and fetch a doctor to see him."

It was done, and the doctor came. Having seen the patient, he reported that nothing very serious had happened, but that in falling he had evidently sprained his foot a little. A few days' rest and all would be well.

"A few days!" cried Binet. "God of God! Do you mean that he can't walk?"

"It would be unwise, indeed impossible for more than a few steps."

M. Binet paid the doctor's fee, and sat down to think. He filled himself a glass of Burgundy, tossed it off without a word, and sat thereafter staring into the empty glass.

"It is of course the sort of thing that must always be happening to me," he grumbled to no one in particular. The members of the company were all standing in silence before him, sharing his dismay. "I might have known that this—or something like it—would occur to spoil the first vein of luck that I have found in years. Ah, well, it is finished. To-morrow we pack and depart. The best day of the fair, on the crest of the wave of our success—a good fifteen louis to be taken, and this happens! God of God!"

"Do you mean to abandon to-morrow's performance?"

All turned to stare with Binet at Andre-Louis.

"Are we to play 'Figaro-Scaramouche' without Scaramouche?" asked Binet, sneering.

"Of course not." Andre-Louis came forward. "But surely some rearrangement of the parts is possible. For instance, there is a fine actor in Polichinelle."

Polichinelle swept him a bow. "Overwhelmed," said he, ever sardonic.

"But he has a part of his own," objected Binet.

"A small part, which Pasquariel could play."

"And who will play Pasquariel?"

"Nobody. We delete it. The play need not suffer."

"He thinks of everything," sneered Polichinelle. "What a man!"

But Binet was far from agreement. "Are you suggesting that Polichinelle should play Scaramouche?" he asked, incredulously.

"Why not? He is able enough!"

"Overwhelmed again," interjected Polichinelle.

"Play Scaramouche with that figure?" Binet heaved himself up to point a denunciatory finger at Polichinelle's sturdy, thick-set shortness.

"For lack of a better," said Andre-Louis.

"Overwhelmed more than ever." Polichinelle's bow was superb this time. "Faith, I think I'll take the air to cool me after so much blushing."

"Go to the devil," Binet flung at him.

"Better and better." Polichinelle made for the door. On the threshold he halted and struck an attitude. "Understand me, Binet. I do not now play Scaramouche in any circumstances whatever." And he went out. On the whole, it was a very dignified exit.

Andre Louis shrugged, threw out his arms, and let them fall to his sides again. "You have ruined everything," he told M. Binet. "The matter could easily have been arranged. Well, well, it is you are master here; and since you want us to pack and be off, that is what we will do, I suppose."

He went out, too. M. Binet stood in thought a moment, then followed him, his little eyes very cunning. He caught him up in the doorway. "Let us take a walk together, M. Parvissimus," said he, very affably.

He thrust his arm through Andre-Louis', and led him out into the street, where there was still considerable movement. Past the booths that ranged about the market they went, and down the hill towards the bridge. "I don't think we shall pack to-morrow," said M. Binet, presently. "In fact, we shall play to-morrow night."

"Not if I know Polichinelle. You have..."

"I am not thinking of Polichinelle."

"Of whom, then?"

"Of yourself."

"I am flattered, sir. And in what capacity are you thinking of me?" There was something too sleek and oily in Binet's voice for Andre-Louis' taste.

"I am thinking of you in the part of Scaramouche."

"Day-dreams," said Andre-Louis. "You are amusing yourself, of course."

"Not in the least. I am quite serious."

"But I am not an actor."

"You told me that you could be."

"Oh, upon occasion... a small part, perhaps..."

"Well, here is a big part—the chance to arrive at a single stride. How many men have had such a chance?"

"It is a chance I do not covet, M. Binet. Shall we change the subject?" He was very frosty, as much perhaps because he scented in M. Binet's manner something that was vaguely menacing as for any other reason.

"We'll change the subject when I please," said M. Binet, allowing a glimpse of steel to glimmer through the silk of him. "To-morrow night you play Scaramouche. You are ready enough in your wits, your figure is ideal, and you have just the kind of mordant humour for the part. You should be a great success."

"It is much more likely that I should be an egregious failure."

"That won't matter," said Binet, cynically, and explained himself. "The failure will be personal to yourself. The receipts will be safe by then."

"Much obliged," said Andre-Louis.

"We should take fifteen louis to-morrow night."

"It is unfortunate that you are without a Scaramouche," said Andre-Louis.

"It is fortunate that I have one, M. Parvissimus."

Andre-Louis disengaged his arm. "I begin to find you tiresome," said he. "I think I will return."

"A moment, M. Parvissimus. If I am to lose that fifteen louis... you'll not take it amiss that I compensate myself in other ways?"

"That is your own concern, M. Binet."

"Pardon, M. Parvissimus. It may possibly be also yours." Binet took his arm again. "Do me the kindness to step across the street with me. Just as far as the post-office there. I have something to show you."

Andre-Louis went. Before they reached that sheet of paper nailed upon the door, he knew exactly what it would say. And in effect it was, as he had supposed, that twenty louis would be paid for information leading to the apprehension of one Andre-Louis Moreau, lawyer of Gavrillac, who was wanted by the King's Lieutenant in Rennes upon a charge of sedition.

M. Binet watched him whilst he read. Their arms were linked, and Binet's grip was firm and powerful.

"Now, my friend," said he, "will you be M. Parvissimus and play Scaramouche to-morrow, or will you be Andre-Louis Moreau of Gavrillac and go to Rennes to satisfy the King's Lieutenant?"

"And if it should happen that you are mistaken?" quoth Andre-Louis, his face a mask.

"I'll take the risk of that," leered M. Binet. "You mentioned, I think, that you were a lawyer. An indiscretion, my dear. It is unlikely that two lawyers will be in hiding at the same time in the same district. You see it is not really clever of me. Well, M. Andre-Louis Moreau, lawyer of Gavrillac, what is it to be?"

"We will talk it over as we walk back," said Andre-Louis.

"What is there to talk over?"

"One or two things, I think. I must know where I stand. Come, sir, if you please."

"Very well," said M. Binet, and they turned up the street again, but M. Binet maintained a firm hold of his young friend's arm, and kept himself on the alert for any tricks that the young gentleman might be disposed to play. It was an unnecessary precaution. Andre-Louis was not the man to waste his energy futilely. He knew that in bodily strength he was no match at all for the heavy and powerful Pantaloon.

"If I yield to your most eloquent and seductive persuasions, M. Binet," said he, sweetly, "what guarantee do you give me that you will not sell me for twenty louis after I shall have served your turn?"

"You have my word of honour for that." M. Binet was emphatic.

Andre-Louis laughed. "Oh, we are to talk of honour, are we? Really, M. Binet? It is clear you think me a fool."

In the dark he did not see the flush that leapt to M. Binet's round face. It was some moments before he replied.

"Perhaps you are right," he growled. "What guarantee do you want?"

"I do not know what guarantee you can possibly give."

"I have said that I will keep faith with you."

"Until you find it more profitable to sell me."

"You have it in your power to make it more profitable always for me to keep faith with you. It is due to you that we have done so well in Guichen. Oh, I admit it frankly."

"In private," said Andre-Louis.

M. Binet left the sarcasm unheeded.

"What you have done for us here with 'Figaro-Scaramouche,' you can do elsewhere with other things. Naturally, I shall not want to lose you. That is your guarantee."

"Yet to-night you would sell me for twenty louis."

"Because—name of God!—you enrage me by refusing me a service well within your powers. Don't you think, had I been entirely the rogue you think me, I could have sold you on Saturday last? I want you to understand me, my dear Parvissimus."

"I beg that you'll not apologize. You would be more tiresome than ever."

"Of course you will be gibing. You never miss a chance to gibe. It'll bring you trouble before you're done with life. Come; here we are back at the inn, and you have not yet given me your decision."

Andre-Louis looked at him. "I must yield, of course. I can't help myself."

M. Binet released his arm at last, and slapped him heartily upon the back. "Well declared, my lad. You'll never regret it. If I know anything of the theatre, I know that you have made the great decision of your life. To-morrow night you'll thank me."

Andre-Louis shrugged, and stepped out ahead towards the inn. But M. Binet called him back.

"M. Parvissimus!"

He turned. There stood the man's great bulk, the moonlight beating down upon that round fat face of his, and he was holding out his hand.

"M. Parvissimus, no rancour. It is a thing I do not admit into my life. You will shake hands with me, and we will forget all this."

Andre-Louis considered him a moment with disgust. He was growing angry. Then, realizing this, he conceived himself ridiculous, almost as ridiculous as that sly, scoundrelly Pantaloon. He laughed and took the outstretched hand. "No rancour?" M. Binet insisted.

"Oh, no rancour," said Andre-Louis.

CHAPTER V. ENTER SCARAMOUCHE

Dressed in the close-fitting suit of a bygone age, all black, from flat velvet cap to rosetted shoes, his face whitened and a slight up-curled moustache glued to his upper lip, a small-sword at his side and a guitar slung behind him, Scaramouche surveyed himself in a mirror, and was disposed to be sardonic—which was the proper mood for the part.

He reflected that his life, which until lately had been of a stagnant, contemplative quality, had suddenly become excessively active. In the course of one week he had been lawyer, mob-orator, outlaw, property-man, and finally buffoon. Last Wednesday he had been engaged in moving an audience of Rennes to anger; on this Wednesday he was to move an audience of Guichen to mirth. Then he had been concerned to draw tears; to-day it was his business to provoke laughter. There was a difference, and yet there was a parallel. Then as now he had been a comedian; and the part that he had played then was, when you came to think of it, akin to the part he was to play this evening. For what had he been at Rennes but a sort of Scaramouche—the little skirmisher, the astute intriguer, spattering the seed of trouble with a sly hand? The only difference lay in the fact that to-day he went forth under the name that properly described his type, whereas last week he had been disguised as a respectable young provincial attorney.

He bowed to his reflection in the mirror.

"Buffoon!" he apostrophized it. "At last you have found yourself. At last you have come into your heritage. You should be a great success."

Hearing his new name called out by M. Binet, he went below to find the company assembled, and waiting in the entrance corridor of the inn.

He was, of course, an object of great interest to all the company. Most critically was he conned by M. Binet and mademoiselle; by the former with gravely searching eyes, by the latter with a curl of scornful lip.

"You'll do," M. Binet commended his make-up. "At least you look the part."

"Unfortunately men are not always what they look," said Climene, acidly.

"That is a truth that does not at present apply to me," said Andre-Louis. "For it is the first time in my life that I look what I am."

Mademoiselle curled her lip a little further, and turned her shoulder to him. But the others thought him very witty—probably because he was obscure. Columbine encouraged him with a friendly smile that displayed her large white teeth, and M. Binet swore yet once again that he would be a great success, since he threw himself with such spirit into the undertaking. Then in a voice that for the moment he appeared to have borrowed from the roaring captain, M. Binet marshalled them for the short parade across to the market-hall.

The new Scaramouche fell into place beside Rhodomont. The old one, hobbling on a crutch, had departed an hour ago to take the place of doorkeeper, vacated of necessity by Andre-Louis. So that the exchange between those two was a complete one.

Headed by Polichinelle banging his great drum and Pierrot blowing his trumpet, they set out, and were duly passed in review by the ragamuffins drawn up in files to enjoy so much of the spectacle as was to be obtained for nothing.

Ten minutes later the three knocks sounded, and the curtains were drawn aside to reveal a battered set that was partly garden, partly forest, in which Climene feverishly looked for the coming of Leandre. In the wings stood the beautiful, melancholy lover, awaiting his cue, and immediately behind him the unfledged Scaramouche, who was anon to follow him.

Andre-Louis was assailed with nausea in that dread moment. He attempted to take a lightning mental review of the first act of this scenario of which he was himself the author-in-chief; but found his mind a complete blank. With the perspiration starting from his skin, he stepped back to the wall, where above a dim lantern was pasted a sheet bearing the brief outline of the piece. He was still studying it, when his arm was clutched, and he was pulled violently towards the wings. He had a glimpse of Pantaloon's grotesque face, its eyes blazing, and he caught a raucous growl:

"Climene has spoken your cue three times already."

Before he realized it, he had been bundled on to the stage, and stood there foolishly, blinking in the glare of the footlights, with their tin reflectors. So utterly foolish and bewildered did he look that volley upon volley of laughter welcomed him from the audience, which this evening packed the hall from end to end. Trembling a little, his bewilderment at first increasing, he stood there to receive that rolling tribute to his absurdity. Climene was eyeing him with expectant mockery, savouring in advance his humiliation; Leandre regarded him in consternation, whilst behind the scenes, M. Binet was dancing in fury.

"Name of a name," he groaned to the rather scared members of the company assembled there, "what will happen when they discover that he isn't acting?"

But they never did discover it. Scaramouche's bewildered paralysis lasted but a few seconds. He realized that he was being laughed at, and remembered that his Scaramouche was a creature to be laughed with, and not at. He must save the situation; twist it to his own advantage as best he could. And now his real bewilderment and terror was succeeded by acted bewilderment and terror far more marked, but not quite so funny. He contrived to make it clearly appear that his terror was of some one off the stage. He took cover behind a painted shrub, and thence, the laughter at last beginning to subside, he addressed himself to Climene and Leandre.

"Forgive me, beautiful lady, if the abrupt manner of my entrance startled you. The truth is that I have never been the same since that last affair of mine with Almaviva. My heart is not what it used to be. Down there at the end of the lane I came face to face with an elderly gentleman carrying a heavy cudgel, and the horrible thought entered my mind that it might be your father, and that our little stratagem to get you safely married might already have been betrayed to him. I think it was the cudgel put such notion in my head. Not that I am afraid. I am not really afraid of anything. But I could not help reflecting that, if it should really have been your father, and he had broken my head with his cudgel, your hopes would have perished with me. For without me, what should you have done, my poor children?"

A ripple of laughter from the audience had been steadily enheartening him, and helping him to recover his natural impudence. It was clear they found him comical. They were to find him far more comical than ever he had intended, and this was largely due to a fortuitous circumstance upon which he had insufficiently reckoned. The fear of recognition by some one from Gavrillac or Rennes had been strong upon him. His face was sufficiently made up to baffle recognition; but there remained his voice. To dissemble this he had availed himself of the fact that Figaro was a Spaniard. He had known a Spaniard at Louis le Grand who spoke a fluent but most extraordinary French, with a grotesque excess of sibilant sounds. It was an accent that he had often imitated, as youths will imitate characteristics that excite their mirth. Opportunely he had bethought him of that Spanish student, and it was upon his speech that to-night he modelled his own. The audience of Guichen found it as laughable on his lips as he and his fellows had found it formerly on the lips of that derided Spaniard.

Meanwhile, behind the scenes, Binet—listening to that glib impromptu of which the scenario gave no indication—had recovered from his fears.

"Dieu de Dieu!" he whispered, grinning. "Did he do it, then, on purpose?"

It seemed to him impossible that a man who had been so terror-stricken as he had fancied Andre-Louis, could have recovered his wits so quickly and completely. Yet the doubt remained.

To resolve it after the curtain had fallen upon a first act that had gone with a verve unrivalled until this hour in the annals of the company, borne almost entirely upon the slim shoulders of the new Scaramouche, M. Binet bluntly questioned him.

They were standing in the space that did duty as green-room, the company all assembled there, showering congratulations upon their new recruit. Scaramouche, a little exalted at the moment by his success, however trivial he might consider it to-morrow, took then a full revenge upon Climene for the malicious satisfaction with which she had regarded his momentary blank terror.

"I do not wonder that you ask," said he. "Faith, I should have warned you that I intended to do my best from the start to put the audience in a good humour with me. Mademoiselle very nearly ruined everything by refusing to reflect any of my terror. She was not even startled. Another time, mademoiselle, I shall give you full warning of my every intention."

She crimsoned under her grease-paint. But before she could find an answer of sufficient venom, her father was rating her soundly for her stupidity—the more soundly because himself he had been deceived by Scaramouche's supreme acting.

Scaramouche's success in the first act was more than confirmed as the performance proceeded. Completely master of himself by now, and stimulated as only success can stimulate, he warmed to his work. Impudent, alert, sly, graceful, he incarnated the very ideal of Scaramouche, and he helped out his own native wit by many a remembered line from Beaumarchais, thereby persuading the better informed among the audience that here indeed was something of the real Figaro, and bringing them, as it were, into touch with the great world of the capital.

When at last the curtain fell for the last time, it was Scaramouche who shared with Climene the honours of the evening, his name that was coupled with hers in the calls that summoned them before the curtains.

As they stepped back, and the curtains screened them again from the departing audience, M. Binet approached them, rubbing his fat hands softly together. This runagate young lawyer, whom chance had blown into his company, had evidently been sent by Fate to make his fortune for him. The sudden success at Guichen, hitherto unrivalled, should be repeated and augmented elsewhere. There would be no more sleeping under hedges and tightening of belts. Adversity was behind him. He placed a hand upon Scaramouche's shoulder, and surveyed him with a smile whose oiliness not even his red paint and colossal false nose could dissemble.

"And what have you to say to me now?" he asked him. "Was I wrong when I assured you that you would succeed? Do you think I have followed my fortunes in the theatre for a lifetime without knowing a born actor when I see one? You are my discovery, Scaramouche. I have discovered you to yourself. I have set your feet upon the road to fame and fortune. I await your thanks."

Scaramouche laughed at him, and his laugh was not altogether pleasant.

"Always Pantaloon!" said he.

The great countenance became overcast. "I see that you do not yet forgive me the little stratagem by which I forced you to do justice to yourself. Ungrateful dog! As if I could have had any purpose but to make you; and I have done so. Continue as you have begun, and you will end in Paris. You may yet tread the stage of the Comedie Francaise, the rival of Talma, Fleury, and Dugazon. When that happens to you perhaps you will feel the gratitude that is due to old Binet, for you will owe it all to this soft-hearted old fool."

"If you were as good an actor on the stage as you are in private," said Scaramouche, "you would yourself have won to the Comedie Francaise long since. But I bear no rancour, M. Binet." He laughed, and put out his hand.

Binet fell upon it and wrung it heartily.

"That, at least, is something," he declared. "My boy, I have great plans for you—for us. To-morrow we go to Maure; there is a fair there to the end of this week. Then on Monday we take our chances at Pipriac, and after that we must consider. It may be that I am about to realize the dream of my life. There must have been upwards of fifteen louis taken to-night. Where the devil is that rascal Cordemais?"

Cordemais was the name of the original Scaramouche, who had so unfortunately twisted his ankle. That Binet should refer to him by his secular designation was a sign that in the Binet company at least he had fallen for ever from the lofty eminence of Scaramouche.

"Let us go and find him, and then we'll away to the inn and crack a bottle of the best Burgundy, perhaps two bottles."

But Cordemais was not readily to be found. None of the company had seen him since the close of the performance. M. Binet went round to the entrance. Cordemais was not there. At first he was annoyed; then as he continued in vain to bawl the fellow's name, he began to grow uneasy; lastly, when Polichinelle, who was with them, discovered Cordemais' crutch standing discarded behind the door, M. Binet became alarmed. A dreadful suspicion entered his mind. He grew visibly pale under his paint.

"But this evening he couldn't walk without the crutch!" he exclaimed. "How then does he come to leave it there and take himself off?"

"Perhaps he has gone on to the inn," suggested some one.

"But he couldn't walk without his crutch," M. Binet insisted.

Nevertheless, since clearly he was not anywhere about the market-hall, to the inn they all trooped, and deafened the landlady with their inquiries.

"Oh, yes, M. Cordemais came in some time ago."

"Where is he now?"

"He went away again at once. He just came for his bag."

"For his bag!" Binet was on the point of an apoplexy. "How long ago was that?"

She glanced at the timepiece on the overmantel. "It would be about half an hour ago. It was a few minutes before the Rennes diligence passed through."

"The Rennes diligence!" M. Binet was almost inarticulate. "Could he... could he walk?" he asked, on a note of terrible anxiety.

"Walk? He ran like a hare when he left the inn. I thought, myself, that his agility was suspicious, seeing how lame he had been since he fell downstairs yesterday. Is anything wrong?"

M. Binet had collapsed into a chair. He took his head in his hands, and groaned.

"The scoundrel was shamming all the time!" exclaimed Climene. "His fall downstairs was a trick. He was playing for this. He has swindled us."

"Fifteen louis at least—perhaps sixteen!" said M. Binet. "Oh, the heartless blackguard! To swindle me who have been as a father to him—and to swindle me in such a moment."

From the ranks of the silent, awe-stricken company, each member of which was wondering by how much of the loss his own meagre pay would be mulcted, there came a splutter of laughter.

M. Binet glared with blood-injected eyes.

"Who laughs?" he roared. "What heartless wretch has the audacity to laugh at my misfortune?"

Andre-Louis, still in the sable glories of Scaramouche, stood forward. He was laughing still.

"It is you, is it? You may laugh on another note, my friend, if I choose a way to recoup myself that I know of."

"Dullard!" Scaramouche scorned him. "Rabbit brained elephant! What if Cordemais has gone with fifteen louis? Hasn't he left you something worth twenty times as much?"

M. Binet gaped uncomprehending.

"You are between two wines, I think. You've been drinking," he concluded.

"So I have—at the fountain of Thalia. Oh, don't you see? Don't you see the treasure that Cordemais has left behind him?"

"What has he left?"

"A unique idea for the groundwork of a scenario. It unfolds itself all before me. I'll borrow part of the title from Moliere. We'll call it 'Les Fourberies de Scaramouche,' and if we don't leave the audiences of Maure and Pipriac with sides aching from laughter I'll play the dullard Pantaloon in future."

Polichinelle smacked fist into palm. "Superb!" he said, fiercely. "To cull fortune from misfortune, to turn loss into profit, that is to have genius."

Scaramouche made a leg. "Polichinelle, you are a fellow after my own heart. I love a man who can discern my merit. If Pantaloon had half your wit, we should have Burgundy to-night in spite of the flight of Cordemais."

"Burgundy?" roared M. Binet, and before he could get farther Harlequin had clapped his hands together.

"That is the spirit, M. Binet. You heard him, landlady. He called for Burgundy."

"I called for nothing of the kind."

"But you heard him, dear madame. We all heard him."

The others made chorus, whilst Scaramouche smiled at him, and patted his shoulder.

"Up, man, a little courage. Did you not say that fortune awaits us? And have we not now the wherewithal to constrain fortune? Burgundy, then, to... to toast 'Les Fourberies de Scaramouche.'"

And M. Binet, who was not blind to the force of the idea, yielded, took courage, and got drunk with the rest.

CHAPTER VI. CLIMENE

Diligent search among the many scenarios of the improvisers which have survived their day, has failed to bring to light the scenario of "Les Fourberies de Scaramouche," upon which we are told the fortunes of the Binet troupe came to be soundly established. They played it for the first time at Maure in the following week, with Andre-Louis—who was known by now as Scaramouche to all the company, and to the public alike—in the title-role. If he had acquitted himself well as Figaro-Scaramouche, he excelled himself in the new piece, the scenario of which would appear to be very much the better of the two.

After Maure came Pipriac, where four performances were given, two of each of the scenarios that now formed the backbone of the Binet repertoire. In both Scaramouche, who was beginning to find himself, materially improved his performances. So smoothly now did the two pieces run that Scaramouche actually suggested to Binet that after Fougeray, which they were to visit in the following week, they should tempt fortune in a real theatre in the important town of Redon. The notion terrified Binet at first, but coming to think of it, and his ambition being fanned by Andre-Louis, he ended by allowing himself to succumb to the temptation.

It seemed to Andre-Louis in those days that he had found his real metier, and not only was he beginning to like it, but actually to look forward to a career as actor-author that might indeed lead him in the end to that Mecca of all comedians, the Comedie Francaise. And there were other possibilities. From the writing of skeleton scenarios for improvisers, he might presently pass to writing plays of dialogue, plays in the proper sense of the word, after the manner of Chenier, Eglantine, and Beaumarchais.

The fact that he dreamed such dreams shows us how very kindly he had taken to the profession into which Chance and M. Binet between them had conspired to thrust him. That he had real talent both as author and as actor I do not doubt, and I am persuaded that had things fallen out differently he would have won for himself a lasting place among French dramatists, and thus fully have realized that dream of his.

Now, dream though it was, he did not neglect the practical side of it.

"You realize," he told M. Binet, "that I have it in my power to make your fortune for you."

He and Binet were sitting alone together in the parlour of the inn at Pipriac, drinking a very excellent bottle of Volnay. It was on the night after the fourth and last performance there of "Les Feurberies." The business in Pipriac had been as excellent as in Maure and Guichen. You will have gathered this from the fact that they drank Volnay.

"I will concede it, my dear Scaramouche, so that I may hear the sequel."

"I am disposed to exercise this power if the inducement is sufficient. You will realize that for fifteen livres a month a man does not sell such exceptional gifts as mine.

"There is an alternative," said M. Binet, darkly.

"There is no alternative. Don't be a fool, Binet."

Binet sat up as if he had been prodded. Members of his company did not take this tone of direct rebuke with him.

"Anyway, I make you a present of it," Scaramouche pursued, airily. "Exercise it if you please. Step outside and inform the police that they can lay hands upon one Andre-Louis Moreau. But that will be the end of your fine dreams of going to Redon, and for the first time in your life playing in a real theatre. Without me, you can't do it, and you know it; and I am not going to Redon or anywhere else, in fact I am not even going to Fougeray, until we have an equitable arrangement."

"But what heat!" complained Binet, "and all for what? Why must you assume that I have the soul of a usurer? When our little arrangement was made, I had no idea how could I?—that you would prove as valuable to me as you are? You had but to remind me, my dear Scaramouche. I am a just man. As from to-day you shall have thirty livres a month. See, I double it at once. I am a generous man."

"But you are not ambitious. Now listen to me, a moment."

And he proceeded to unfold a scheme that filled Binet with a paralyzing terror.

"After Redon, Nantes," he said. "Nantes and the Theatre Feydau."

M. Binet choked in the act of drinking. The Theatre Feydau was a sort of provincial Comedie Francaise. The great Fleury had played there to an audience as critical as any in France. The very thought of Redon, cherished as it had come to be by M. Binet, gave him at moments a cramp in the stomach, so dangerously ambitious did it seem to him. And Redon was a puppet-show by comparison with Nantes. Yet this raw lad whom he had picked up by chance three weeks ago, and who in that time had blossomed from a country attorney into author and actor, could talk of Nantes and the Theatre Feydau without changing colour.

"But why not Paris and the Comedie Francaise?" wondered M. Binet, with sarcasm, when at last he had got his breath.

"That may come later," says impudence.

"Eh? You've been drinking, my friend."

But Andre-Louis detailed the plan that had been forming in his mind. Fougeray should be a training-ground for Redon, and Redon should be a training-ground for Nantes. They would stay in Redon as long as Redon would pay adequately to come and see them, working hard to perfect themselves the while. They would add three or four new players of talent to the company; he would write three or four fresh scenarios, and these should be tested and perfected until the troupe was in possession of at least half a dozen plays upon which they could depend; they would lay out a portion of their profits on better dresses and better scenery, and finally in a couple of months' time, if all went well, they should be ready to make their real bid for fortune at Nantes. It was quite true that distinction was usually demanded of the companies appearing at the Feydau, but on the other hand Nantes had not seen a troupe of improvisers for a generation and longer. They would be supplying a novelty to which all Nantes should flock provided that the work were really well done, and Scaramouche undertook—pledged himself—that if matters were left in his own hands, his projected revival of the Commedia dell' Arte in all its glories would exceed whatever expectations the public of Nantes might bring to the theatre.

"We'll talk of Paris after Nantes," he finished, supremely matter-of-fact, "just as we will definitely decide on Nantes after Redon."

The persuasiveness that could sway a mob ended by sweeping M. Binet off his feet. The prospect which Scaramouche unfolded, if terrifying, was also intoxicating, and as Scaramouche delivered a crushing answer to each weakening objection in a measure as it was advanced, Binet ended by promising to think the matter over.

"Redon will point the way," said Andre-Louis, "and I don't doubt which way Redon will point."

Thus the great adventure of Redon dwindled to insignificance. Instead of a terrifying undertaking in itself, it became merely a rehearsal for something greater. In his momentary exaltation Binet proposed another bottle of Volnay. Scaramouche waited until the cork was drawn before he continued.

"The thing remains possible," said he then, holding his glass to the light, and speaking casually, "as long as I am with you."

"Agreed, my dear Scaramouche, agreed. Our chance meeting was a fortunate thing for both of us."

"For both of us," said Scaramouche, with stress. "That is as I would have it. So that I do not think you will surrender me just yet to the police."

"As if I could think of such a thing! My dear Scaramouche, you amuse yourself. I beg that you will never, never allude to that little joke of mine again."

"It is forgotten," said Andre-Louis. "And now for the remainder of my proposal. If I am to become the architect of your fortunes, if I am to build them as I have planned them, I must also and in the same degree become the architect of my own."

"In the same degree?" M. Binet frowned.

"In the same degree. From to-day, if you please, we will conduct the affairs of this company in a proper manner, and we will keep account-books."

"I am an artist," said M. Binet, with pride. "I am not a merchant."

"There is a business side to your art, and that shall be conducted in the business manner. I have thought it all out for you. You shall not be troubled with details that might hinder the due exercise of your art. All that you have to do is to say yes or no to my proposal."

"Ah? And the proposal?"

"Is that you constitute me your partner, with an equal share in the profits of your company."

Pantaloon's great countenance grew pale, his little eyes widened to their fullest extent as he conned the face of his companion. Then he exploded.

"You are mad, of course, to make me a proposal so monstrous."

"It has its injustices, I admit. But I have provided for them. It would not, for instance, be fair that in addition to all that I am proposing to do for you, I should also play Scaramouche and write your scenarios without any reward outside of the half-profit which would come to me as a partner. Thus before the profits come to be divided, there is a salary to be paid me as actor, and a small sum for each scenario with which I provide the company; that is a matter for mutual agreement. Similarly, you shall be paid a salary as Pantaloon. After those expenses are cleared up, as well as all the other salaries and disbursements, the residue is the profit to be divided equally between us."

It was not, as you can imagine, a proposal that M. Binet would swallow at a draught. He began with a point-blank refusal to consider it.

"In that case, my friend," said Scaramouche, "we part company at once. To-morrow I shall bid you a reluctant farewell."

Binet fell to raging. He spoke of ingratitude in feeling terms; he even permitted himself another sly allusion to that little jest of his concerning the police, which he had promised never again to mention.

"As to that, you may do as you please. Play the informer, by all means. But consider that you will just as definitely be deprived of my services, and that without me you are nothing—as you were before I joined your company."

M. Binet did not care what the consequences might be. A fig for the consequences! He would teach this impudent young country attorney that M. Binet was not the man to be imposed upon.

Scaramouche rose. "Very well," said he, between indifference and resignation. "As you wish. But before you act, sleep on the matter. In the cold light of morning you may see our two proposals in their proper proportions. Mine spells fortune for both of us. Yours spells ruin for both of us. Good-night, M. Binet. Heaven help you to a wise decision."

The decision to which M. Binet finally came was, naturally, the only one possible in the face of so firm a resolve as that of Andre-Louis, who held the trumps. Of course there were further discussions, before all was settled, and M. Binet was brought to an agreement only after an infinity of haggling surprising in one who was an artist and not a man of business. One or two concessions were made by Andre-Louis; he consented, for instance, to waive his claim to be paid for scenarios, and he also consented that M. Binet should appoint himself a salary that was out of all proportion to his deserts.

Thus in the end the matter was settled, and the announcement duly made to the assembled company. There were, of course, jealousies and resentments. But these were not deep-seated, and they were readily swallowed when it was discovered that under the new arrangement the lot of the entire company was to be materially improved from the point of view of salaries. This was a matter that had met with considerable opposition from M. Binet. But the irresistible Scaramouche swept away all objections.

"If we are to play at the Feydau, you want a company of self-respecting comedians, and not a pack of cringing starvelings. The better we pay them in reason, the more they will earn for us."

Thus was conquered the company's resentment of this too swift promotion of its latest recruit. Cheerfully now—with one exception—they accepted the dominance of Scaramouche, a dominance soon to be so firmly established that M. Binet himself came under it.

The one exception was Climene. Her failure to bring to heel this interesting young stranger, who had almost literally dropped into their midst that morning outside Guichen, had begotten in her a malice which his persistent ignoring of her had been steadily inflaming. She had remonstrated with her father when the new partnership was first formed. She had lost her temper with him, and called him a fool, whereupon M. Binet—in Pantaloon's best manner—had lost his temper in his turn and boxed her ears. She piled it up to the account of Scaramouche, and spied her opportunity to pay off some of that ever-increasing score. But opportunities were few. Scaramouche was too occupied just then. During the week of preparation at Fougeray, he was hardly seen save at the performances, whilst when once they were at Redon, he came and went like the wind between the theatre and the inn.

The Redon experiment had justified itself from the first. Stimulated and encouraged by this, Andre-Louis worked day and night during the month that they spent in that busy little town. The moment had been well chosen, for the trade in chestnuts of which Redon is the centre was just then at its height. And every afternoon the little theatre was packed with spectators. The fame of the troupe had gone forth, borne by the chestnut-growers of the district, who were bringing their wares to Redon market, and the audiences were made up of people from the surrounding country, and from neighbouring villages as far out as Allaire, Saint-Perrieux and Saint-Nicholas. To keep the business from slackening, Andre-Louis prepared a new scenario every week. He wrote three in addition to those two with which he had already supplied the company; these were "The Marriage of Pantaloon," "The Shy Lover," and "The Terrible Captain." Of these the last was the greatest success. It was based upon the "Miles Gloriosus" of Plautus, with great opportunities for Rhodomont, and a good part for Scaramouche as the roaring captain's sly lieutenant. Its success was largely due to the fact that Andre-Louis amplified the scenario to the extent of indicating very fully in places the lines which the dialogue should follow, whilst here and there he had gone so far as to supply some of the actual dialogue to be spoken, without, however, making it obligatory upon the actors to keep to the letter of it.

And meanwhile as the business prospered, he became busy with tailors, improving the wardrobe of the company, which was sorely in need of improvement. He ran to earth a couple of needy artists, lured them into the company to play small parts—apothecaries and notaries—and set them to beguile their leisure in painting new scenery, so as to be ready for what he called the conquest of Nantes, which was to come in the new year. Never in his life had he worked so hard; never in his life had he worked at all by comparison with his activities now. His fund of energy and enthusiasm was inexhaustible, like that of his good humour. He came and went, acted, wrote, conceived, directed, planned, and executed, what time M. Binet took his ease at last in comparative affluence, drank Burgundy every night, ate white bread and other delicacies, and began to congratulate himself upon his astuteness in having made this industrious, tireless fellow his partner. Having discovered how idle had been his fears of performing at Redon, he now began to dismiss the terrors with which the notion of Nantes had haunted him.

And his happiness was reflected throughout the ranks of his company, with the single exception always of Climene. She had ceased to sneer at Scaramouche, having realized at last that her sneers left him untouched and recoiled upon herself. Thus her almost indefinable resentment of him was increased by being stifled, until, at all costs, an outlet for it must be found.

One day she threw herself in his way as he was leaving the theatre after the performance. The others had already gone, and she had returned upon pretence of having forgotten something.

"Will you tell me what I have done to you?" she asked him, point-blank.

"Done to me, mademoiselle?" He did not understand.

She made a gesture of impatience. "Why do you hate me?"

"Hate you, mademoiselle? I do not hate anybody. It is the most stupid of all the emotions. I have never hated—not even my enemies."

"What Christian resignation!"

"As for hating you, of all people! Why... I consider you adorable. I envy Leandre every day of my life. I have seriously thought of setting him to play Scaramouche, and playing lovers myself."

"I don't think you would be a success," said she.

"That is the only consideration that restrains me. And yet, given the inspiration that is given Leandre, it is possible that I might be convincing."

"Why, what inspiration do you mean?"

"The inspiration of playing to so adorable a Climene."

Her lazy eyes were now alert to search that lean face of his.

"You are laughing at me," said she, and swept past him into the theatre on her pretended quest. There was nothing to be done with such a fellow. He was utterly without feeling. He was not a man at all.

Yet when she came forth again at the end of some five minutes, she found him still lingering at the door.

"Not gone yet?" she asked him, superciliously.

"I was waiting for you, mademoiselle. You will be walking to the inn. If I might escort you..."

"But what gallantry! What condescension!"

"Perhaps you would prefer that I did not?"

"How could I prefer that, M. Scaramouche? Besides, we are both going the same way, and the streets are common to all. It is that I am overwhelmed by the unusual honour."

He looked into her piquant little face, and noted how obscured it was by its cloud of dignity. He laughed.

"Perhaps I feared that the honour was not sought."

"Ah, now I understand," she cried. "It is for me to seek these honours. I am to woo a man before he will pay me the homage of civility. It must be so, since you, who clearly know everything, have said so. It remains for me to beg your pardon for my ignorance."

"It amuses you to be cruel," said Scaramouche. "No matter. Shall we walk?"

They set out together, stepping briskly to warm their blood against the wintry evening air. Awhile they went in silence, yet each furtively observing the other.

"And so, you find me cruel?" she challenged him at length, thereby betraying the fact that the accusation had struck home.

He looked at her with a half smile. "Will you deny it?"

"You are the first man that ever accused me of that."

"I dare not suppose myself the first man to whom you have been cruel. That were an assumption too flattering to myself. I must prefer to think that the others suffered in silence."

"Mon Dieu! Have you suffered?" She was between seriousness and raillery.

"I place the confession as an offering on the altar of your vanity."

"I should never have suspected it."

"How could you? Am I not what your father calls a natural actor? I was an actor long before I became Scaramouche. Therefore I have laughed. I often do when I am hurt. When you were pleased to be disdainful, I acted disdain in my turn."

"You acted very well," said she, without reflecting.

"Of course. I am an excellent actor."

"And why this sudden change?"

"In response to the change in you. You have grown weary of your part of cruel madam—a dull part, believe me, and unworthy of your talents. Were I a woman and had I your loveliness and your grace, Climene, I should disdain to use them as weapons of offence."

"Loveliness and grace!" she echoed, feigning amused surprise. But the vain baggage was mollified. "When was it that you discovered this beauty and this grace, M. Scaramouche?"

He looked at her a moment, considering the sprightly beauty of her, the adorable femininity that from the first had so irresistibly attracted him.

"One morning when I beheld you rehearsing a love-scene with Leandre."

He caught the surprise that leapt to her eyes, before she veiled them under drooping lids from his too questing gaze.

"Why, that was the first time you saw me."

"I had no earlier occasion to remark your charms."

"You ask me to believe too much," said she, but her tone was softer than he had ever known it yet.

"Then you'll refuse to believe me if I confess that it was this grace and beauty that determined my destiny that day by urging me to join your father's troupe."

At that she became a little out of breath. There was no longer any question of finding an outlet for resentment. Resentment was all forgotten.

"But why? With what object?"

"With the object of asking you one day to be my wife."

She halted under the shock of that, and swung round to face him. Her glance met his own without, shyness now; there was a hardening glitter in her eyes, a faint stir of colour in her cheeks. She suspected him of an unpardonable mockery.

"You go very fast, don't you?" she asked him, with heat.

"I do. Haven't you observed it? I am a man of sudden impulses. See what I have made of the Binet troupe in less than a couple of months. Another might have laboured for a year and not achieved the half of it. Shall I be slower in love than in work? Would it be reasonable to expect it? I have curbed and repressed myself not to scare you by precipitancy. In that I have done violence to my feelings, and more than all in using the same cold aloofness with which you chose to treat me. I have waited—oh! so patiently—until you should tire of that mood of cruelty."

"You are an amazing man," said she, quite colourlessly.

"I am," he agreed with her. "It is only the conviction that I am not commonplace that has permitted me to hope as I have hoped."

Mechanically, and as if by tacit consent, they resumed their walk.

"And I ask you to observe," he said, "when you complain that I go very fast, that, after all, I have so far asked you for nothing."

"How?" quoth she, frowning.

"I have merely told you of my hopes. I am not so rash as to ask at once whether I may realize them."

"My faith, but that is prudent," said she, tartly.

"Of course."

It was his self-possession that exasperated her; for after that she walked the short remainder of the way in silence, and so, for the moment, the matter was left just there.

But that night, after they had supped, it chanced that when Climene was about to retire, he and she were alone together in the room abovestairs that her father kept exclusively for his company. The Binet Troupe, you see, was rising in the world.

As Climene now rose to withdraw for the night, Scaramouche rose with her to light her candle. Holding it in her left hand, she offered him her right, a long, tapering, white hand at the end of a softly rounded arm that was bare to the elbow.

"Good-night, Scaramouche," she said, but so softly, so tenderly, that he caught his breath, and stood conning her, his dark eyes aglow.

Thus a moment, then he took the tips of her fingers in his grasp, and bowing over the hand, pressed his lips upon it. Then he looked at her again. The intense femininity of her lured him on, invited him, surrendered to him. Her face was pale, there was a glitter in her eyes, a curious smile upon her parted lips, and under its fichu-menteur her bosom rose and fell to complete the betrayal of her.

By the hand he continued to hold, he drew her towards him. She came unresisting. He took the candle from her, and set it down on the sideboard by which she stood. The next moment her slight, lithe body was in his arms, and he was kissing her, murmuring her name as if it were a prayer.

"Am I cruel now?" she asked him, panting. He kissed her again for only answer. "You made me cruel because you would not see," she told him next in a whisper.

And then the door opened, and M. Binet came in to have his paternal eyes regaled by this highly indecorous behaviour of his daughter.

He stood at gaze, whilst they quite leisurely, and in a self-possession too complete to be natural, detached each from the other.

"And what may be the meaning of this?" demanded M. Binet, bewildered and profoundly shocked.

"Does it require explaining?" asked Scaramouche. "Doesn't it speak for itself—eloquently? It means that Climene and I have taken it into our heads to be married."

"And doesn't it matter what I may take into my head?"

"Of course. But you could have neither the bad taste nor the bad heart to offer any obstacle."

"You take that for granted? Aye, that is your way, to be sure—to take things for granted. But my daughter is not to be taken for granted. I have very definite views for my daughter. You have done an unworthy thing, Scaramouche. You have betrayed my trust in you. I am very angry with you."

He rolled forward with his ponderous yet curiously noiseless gait. Scaramouche turned to her, smiling, and handed her the candle.

"If you will leave us, Climene, I will ask your hand of your father in proper form."

She vanished, a little fluttered, lovelier than ever in her mixture of confusion and timidity. Scaramouche closed the door and faced the enraged M. Binet, who had flung himself into an armchair at the head of the short table, faced him with the avowed purpose of asking for Climene's hand in proper form. And this was how he did it:

"Father-in-law," said he, "I congratulate you. This will certainly mean the Comedie Francaise for Climene, and that before long, and you shall shine in the glory she will reflect. As the father of Madame Scaramouche you may yet be famous."

Binet, his face slowly empurpling, glared at him in speechless stupefaction. His rage was the more utter from his humiliating conviction that whatever he might say or do, this irresistible fellow would bend him to his will. At last speech came to him.

"You're a damned corsair," he cried, thickly, banging his ham-like fist upon the table. "A corsair! First you sail in and plunder me of half my legitimate gains; and now you want to carry off my daughter. But I'll be damned if I'll give her to a graceless, nameless scoundrel like you, for whom the gallows are waiting already."

Scaramouche pulled the bell-rope, not at all discomposed. He smiled. There was a flush on his cheeks and a gleam in his eyes. He was very pleased with the world that night. He really owed a great debt to M. de Lesdiguieres.

"Binet," said he, "forget for once that you are Pantaloon, and behave as a nice, amiable father-in-law should behave when he has secured a son-in-law of exceptionable merits. We are going to have a bottle of Burgundy at my expense, and it shall be the best bottle of Burgundy to be found in Redon. Compose yourself to do fitting honour to it. Excitations of the bile invariably impair the fine sensitiveness of the palate."

CHAPTER VII. THE CONQUEST OF NANTES

The Binet Troupe opened in Nantes—as you may discover in surviving copies of the "Courrier Nantais"—on the Feast of the Purification with "Les Fourberies de Scaramouche." But they did not come to Nantes as hitherto they had gone to little country villages and townships, unheralded and depending entirely upon the parade of their entrance to attract attention to themselves. Andre-Louis had borrowed from the business methods of the Comedie Francaise. Carrying matters with a high hand entirely in his own fashion, he had ordered at Redon the printing of playbills, and four days before the company's descent upon Nantes, these bills were pasted outside the Theatre Feydau and elsewhere about the town, and had attracted—being still sufficiently unusual announcements at the time—considerable attention. He had entrusted the matter to one of the company's latest recruits, an intelligent young man named Basque, sending him on ahead of the company for the purpose.

You may see for yourself one of these playbills in the Carnavalet Museum. It details the players by their stage names only, with the exception of M. Binet and his daughter, and leaving out of account that he who plays Trivelin in one piece appears as Tabarin in another, it makes the company appear to be at least half as numerous again as it really was. It announces that they will open with "Les Fourberies de Scaramouche," to be followed by five other plays of which it gives the titles, and by others not named, which shall also be added should the patronage to be received in the distinguished and enlightened city of Nantes encourage the Binet Troupe to prolong its sojourn at the Theatre Feydau. It lays great stress upon the fact that this is a company of improvisers in the old Italian manner, the like of which has not been seen in France for half a century, and it exhorts the public of Nantes not to miss this opportunity of witnessing these distinguished mimes who are reviving for them the glories of the Comedie de l'Art. Their visit to Nantes—the announcement proceeds—is preliminary to their visit to Paris, where they intend to throw down the glove to the actors of the Comedie Francaise, and to show the world how superior is the art of the improviser to that of the actor who depends upon an author for what he shall say, and who consequently says always the same thing every time that he plays in the same piece.

It is an audacious bill, and its audacity had scared M. Binet out of the little sense left him by the Burgundy which in these days he could afford to abuse. He had offered the most vehement opposition. Part of this Andre-Louis had swept aside; part he had disregarded.

"I admit that it is audacious," said Scaramouche. "But at your time of life you should have learnt that in this world nothing succeeds like audacity."

"I forbid it; I absolutely forbid it," M. Binet insisted.

"I knew you would. Just as I know that you'll be very grateful to me presently for not obeying you."

"You are inviting a catastrophe."

"I am inviting fortune. The worst catastrophe that can overtake you is to be back in the market-halls of the country villages from which I rescued you. I'll have you in Paris yet in spite of yourself. Leave this to me."

And he went out to attend to the printing. Nor did his preparations end there. He wrote a piquant article on the glories of the Comedie de l'Art, and its resurrection by the improvising troupe of the great mime Florimond Binet. Binet's name was not Florimond; it was just Pierre. But Andre-Louis had a great sense of the theatre. That article was an amplification of the stimulating matter contained in the playbills; and he persuaded Basque, who had relations in Nantes, to use all the influence he could command, and all the bribery they could afford, to get that article printed in the "Courrier Nantais" a couple of days before the arrival of the Binet Troupe.

Basque had succeeded, and, considering the undoubted literary merits and intrinsic interest of the article, this is not at all surprising.

And so it was upon an already expectant city that Binet and his company descended in that first week of February. M. Binet would have made his entrance in the usual manner—a full-dress parade with banging drums and crashing cymbals. But to this Andre-Louis offered the most relentless opposition.

"We should but discover our poverty," said he. "Instead, we will creep into the city unobserved, and leave ourselves to the imagination of the public."

He had his way, of course. M. Binet, worn already with battling against the strong waters of this young man's will, was altogether unequal to the contest now that he found Climene in alliance with Scaramouche, adding her insistence to his, and joining with him in reprobation of her father's sluggish and reactionary wits. Metaphorically, M. Binet threw up his arms, and cursing the day on which he had taken this young man into his troupe, he allowed the current to carry him whither it would. He was persuaded that he would be drowned in the end. Meanwhile he would drown his vexation in Burgundy. At least there was abundance of Burgundy. Never in his life had he found Burgundy so plentiful. Perhaps things were not as bad as he imagined, after all. He reflected that, when all was said, he had to thank Scaramouche for the Burgundy. Whilst fearing the worst, he would hope for the best.

And it was very much the worst that he feared as he waited in the wings when the curtain rose on that first performance of theirs at the Theatre Feydau to a house that was tolerably filled by a public whose curiosity the preliminary announcements had thoroughly stimulated.

Although the scenario of "Lee Fourberies de Scaramouche" has not apparently survived, yet we know from Andre-Louis' "Confessions" that it is opened by Polichinelle in the character of an arrogant and fiercely jealous lover shown in the act of beguiling the waiting-maid, Columbine, to play the spy upon her mistress, Climene. Beginning with cajolery, but failing in this with the saucy Columbine, who likes cajolers to be at least attractive and to pay a due deference to her own very piquant charms, the fierce humpbacked scoundrel passes on to threats of the terrible vengeance he will wreak upon her if she betrays him or neglects to obey him implicitly; failing here, likewise, he finally has recourse to bribery, and after he has bled himself freely to the very expectant Columbine, he succeeds by these means in obtaining her consent to spy upon Climene, and to report to him upon her lady's conduct.

The pair played the scene well together, stimulated, perhaps, by their very nervousness at finding themselves before so imposing an audience. Polichinelle was everything that is fierce, contemptuous, and insistent. Columbine was the essence of pert indifference under his cajolery, saucily mocking under his threats, and finely sly in extorting the very maximum when it came to accepting a bribe. Laughter rippled through the audience and promised well. But M. Binet, standing trembling in the wings, missed the great guffaws of the rustic spectators to whom they had played hitherto, and his fears steadily mounted.

Then, scarcely has Polichinelle departed by the door than Scaramouche bounds in through the window. It was an effective entrance, usually performed with a broad comic effect that set the people in a roar. Not so on this occasion. Meditating in bed that morning, Scaramouche had decided to present himself in a totally different aspect. He would cut out all the broad play, all the usual clowning which had delighted their past rude audiences, and he would obtain his effects by subtlety instead. He would present a slyly humorous rogue, restrained, and of a certain dignity, wearing a countenance of complete solemnity, speaking his lines drily, as if unconscious of the humour with which he intended to invest them. Thus, though it might take the audience longer to understand and discover him, they would like him all the better in the end.

True to that resolve, he now played his part as the friend and hired ally of the lovesick Leandre, on whose behalf he came for news of Climene, seizing the opportunity to further his own amour with Columbine and his designs upon the money-bags of Pantaloon. Also he had taken certain liberties with the traditional costume of Scaramouche; he had caused the black doublet and breeches to be slashed with red, and the doublet to be cut more to a peak, a la Henri III. The conventional black velvet cap he had replaced by a conical hat with a turned-up brim, and a tuft of feathers on the left, and he had discarded the guitar.

M. Binet listened desperately for the roar of laughter that usually greeted the entrance of Scaramouche, and his dismay increased when it did not come. And then he became conscious of something alarmingly unusual in Scaramouche's manner. The sibilant foreign accent was there, but none of the broad boisterousness their audiences had loved.

He wrung his hands in despair. "It is all over!" he said. "The fellow has ruined us! It serves me right for being a fool, and allowing him to take control of everything!"

But he was profoundly mistaken. He began to have an inkling of this when presently himself he took the stage, and found the public attentive, remarked a grin of quiet appreciation on every upturned face. It was not, however, until the thunders of applause greeted the fall of the curtain on the first act that he felt quite sure they would be allowed to escape with their lives.

Had the part of Pantaloon in "Les Fourberies" been other than that of a blundering, timid old idiot, Binet would have ruined it by his apprehensions. As it was, those very apprehensions, magnifying as they did the hesitancy and bewilderment that were the essence of his part, contributed to the success. And a success it proved that more than justified all the heralding of which Scaramouche had been guilty.

For Scaramouche himself this success was not confined to the public. At the end of the play a great reception awaited him from his companions assembled in the green-room of the theatre. His talent, resource, and energy had raised them in a few weeks from a pack of vagrant mountebanks to a self-respecting company of first-rate players. They acknowledged it generously in a speech entrusted to Polichinelle, adding the tribute to his genius that, as they had conquered Nantes, so would they conquer the world under his guidance.

In their enthusiasm they were a little neglectful of the feelings of M. Binet. Irritated enough had he been already by the overriding of his every wish, by the consciousness of his weakness when opposed to Scaramouche. And, although he had suffered the gradual process of usurpation of authority because its every step had been attended by his own greater profit, deep down in him the resentment abode to stifle every spark of that gratitude due from him to his partner. To-night his nerves had been on the rack, and he had suffered agonies of apprehension, for all of which he blamed Scaramouche so bitterly that not even the ultimate success—almost miraculous when all the elements are considered—could justify his partner in his eyes.

And now, to find himself, in addition, ignored by this company—his own company, which he had so laboriously and slowly assembled and selected among the men of ability whom he had found here and there in the dregs of cities—was something that stirred his bile, and aroused the malevolence that never did more than slumber in him. But deeply though his rage was moved, it did not blind him to the folly of betraying it. Yet that he should assert himself in this hour was imperative unless he were for ever to become a thing of no account in this troupe over which he had lorded it for long months before this interloper came amongst them to fill his purse and destroy his authority.

So he stepped forward now when Polichinelle had done. His make-up assisting him to mask his bitter feelings, he professed to add his own to Polichinelle's acclamations of his dear partner. But he did it in such a manner as to make it clear that what Scaramouche had done, he had done by M. Binet's favour, and that in all M. Binet's had been the guiding hand. In associating himself with Polichinelle, he desired to thank Scaramouche, much in the manner of a lord rendering thanks to his steward for services diligently rendered and orders scrupulously carried out.

It neither deceived the troupe nor mollified himself. Indeed, his consciousness of the mockery of it but increased his bitterness. But at least it saved his face and rescued him from nullity—he who was their chief.

To say, as I have said, that it did not deceive them, is perhaps to say too much, for it deceived them at least on the score of his feelings. They believed, after discounting the insinuations in which he took all credit to himself, that at heart he was filled with gratitude, as they were. That belief was shared by Andre-Louis himself, who in his brief, grateful answer was very generous to M. Binet, more than endorsing the claims that M. Binet had made.

And then followed from him the announcement that their success in Nantes was the sweeter to him because it rendered almost immediately attainable the dearest wish of his heart, which was to make Climene his wife. It was a felicity of which he was the first to acknowledge his utter unworthiness. It was to bring him into still closer relations with his good friend M. Binet, to whom he owed all that he had achieved for himself and for them. The announcement was joyously received, for the world of the theatre loves a lover as dearly as does the greater world. So they acclaimed the happy pair, with the exception of poor Leandre, whose eyes were more melancholy than ever.

They were a happy family that night in the upstairs room of their inn on the Quai La Fosse—the same inn from which Andre-Louis had set out some weeks ago to play a vastly different role before an audience of Nantes. Yet was it so different, he wondered? Had he not then been a sort of Scaramouche—an intriguer, glib and specious, deceiving folk, cynically misleading them with opinions that were not really his own? Was it at all surprising that he should have made so rapid and signal a success as a mime? Was not this really all that he had ever been, the thing for which Nature had designed him?

On the following night they played "The Shy Lover" to a full house, the fame of their debut having gone abroad, and the success of Monday was confirmed. On Wednesday they gave "Figaro-Scaramouche," and on Thursday morning the "Courrier Nantais" came out with an article of more than a column of praise of these brilliant improvisers, for whom it claimed that they utterly put to shame the mere reciters of memorized parts.

Andre-Louis, reading the sheet at breakfast, and having no delusions on the score of the falseness of that statement, laughed inwardly. The novelty of the thing, and the pretentiousness in which he had swaddled it, had deceived them finely. He turned to greet Binet and Climene, who entered at that moment. He waved the sheet above his head.

"It is settled," he announced, "we stay in Nantes until Easter."

"Do we?" said Binet, sourly. "You settle everything, my friend."

"Read for yourself." And he handed him the paper.

Moodily M. Binet read. He set the sheet down in silence, and turned his attention to his breakfast.

"Was I justified or not?" quoth Andre-Louis, who found M. Binet's behaviour a thought intriguing.

"In what?"

"In coming to Nantes?"

"If I had not thought so, we should not have come," said Binet, and he began to eat.

Andre-Louis dropped the subject, wondering.

After breakfast he and Climene sallied forth to take the air upon the quays. It was a day of brilliant sunshine and less cold than it had lately been. Columbine tactlessly joined them as they were setting out, though in this respect matters were improved a little when Harlequin came running after them, and attached himself to Columbine.

Andre-Louis, stepping out ahead with Climene, spoke of the thing that was uppermost in his mind at the moment.

"Your father is behaving very oddly towards me," said he. "It is almost as if he had suddenly become hostile."

"You imagine it," said she. "My father is very grateful to you, as we all are."

"He is anything but grateful. He is infuriated against me; and I think I know the reason. Don't you? Can't you guess?"

"I can't, indeed."

"If you were my daughter, Climene, which God be thanked you are not, I should feel aggrieved against the man who carried you away from me. Poor old Pantaloon! He called me a corsair when I told him that I intend to marry you."

"He was right. You are a bold robber, Scaramouche."

"It is in the character," said he. "Your father believes in having his mimes play upon the stage the parts that suit their natural temperaments."

"Yes, you take everything you want, don't you?" She looked up at him, half adoringly, half shyly.

"If it is possible," said he. "I took his consent to our marriage by main force from him. I never waited for him to give it. When, in fact, he refused it, I just snatched it from him, and I'll defy him now to win it back from me. I think that is what he most resents."

She laughed, and launched upon an animated answer. But he did not hear a word of it. Through the bustle of traffic on the quay a cabriolet, the upper half of which was almost entirely made of glass, had approached them. It was drawn by two magnificent bay horses and driven by a superbly livened coachman.

In the cabriolet alone sat a slight young girl wrapped in a lynx-fur pelisse, her face of a delicate loveliness. She was leaning forward, her lips parted, her eyes devouring Scaramouche until they drew his gaze. When that happened, the shock of it brought him abruptly to a dumfounded halt.

Climene, checking in the middle of a sentence, arrested by his own sudden stopping, plucked at his sleeve.

"What is it, Scaramouche?"

But he made no attempt to answer her, and at that moment the coachman, to whom the little lady had already signalled, brought the carriage to a standstill beside them. Seen in the gorgeous setting of that coach with its escutcheoned panels, its portly coachman and its white-stockinged footman—who swung instantly to earth as the vehicle stopped—its dainty occupant seemed to Climene a princess out of a fairy-tale. And this princess leaned forward, with eyes aglow and cheeks aflush, stretching out a choicely gloved hand to Scaramouche.

"Andre-Louis!" she called him.

And Scaramouche took the hand of that exalted being, just as he might have taken the hand of Climene herself, and with eyes that reflected the gladness of her own, in a voice that echoed the joyous surprise of hers, he addressed her familiarly by name, just as she had addressed him.

"Aline!"

CHAPTER VIII. THE DREAM

"The door," Aline commanded her footman, and "Mount here beside me," she commanded Andre-Louis, in the same breath.

"A moment, Aline."

He turned to his companion, who was all amazement, and to Harlequin and Columbine, who had that moment come up to share it. "You permit me, Climene?" said he, breathlessly. But it was more a statement than a question. "Fortunately you are not alone. Harlequin will take care of you. Au revoir, at dinner."

With that he sprang into the cabriolet without waiting for a reply. The footman closed the door, the coachman cracked his whip, and the regal equipage rolled away along the quay, leaving the three comedians staring after it, open-mouthed... Then Harlequin laughed.

"A prince in disguise, our Scaramouche!" said he.

Columbine clapped her hands and flashed her strong teeth. "But what a romance for you, Climene! How wonderful!"

The frown melted from Climene's brow. Resentment changed to bewilderment.

"But who is she?"

"His sister, of course," said Harlequin, quite definitely.

"His sister? How do you know?"

"I know what he will tell you on his return."

"But why?"

"Because you wouldn't believe him if he said she was his mother."

Following the carriage with their glance, they wandered on in the direction it had taken. And in the carriage Aline was considering Andre-Louis with grave eyes, lips slightly compressed, and a tiny frown between her finely drawn eyebrows.

"You have taken to queer company, Andre," was the first thing she said to him. "Or else I am mistaken in thinking that your companion was Mlle. Binet of the Theatre Feydau."

"You are not mistaken. But I had not imagined Mlle. Binet so famous already."

"Oh, as to that..." mademoiselle shrugged, her tone quietly scornful. And she explained. "It is simply that I was at the play last night. I thought I recognized her."

"You were at the Feydau last night? And I never saw you!"

"Were you there, too?"

"Was I there!" he cried. Then he checked, and abruptly changed his tone. "Oh, yes, I was there," he said, as commonplace as he could, beset by a sudden reluctance to avow that he had so willingly descended to depths that she must account unworthy, and grateful that his disguise of face and voice should have proved impenetrable even to one who knew him so very well.

"I understand," said she, and compressed her lips a little more tightly.

"But what do you understand?"

"The rare attractions of Mlle. Binet. Naturally you would be at the theatre. Your tone conveyed it very clearly. Do you know that you disappoint me, Andre? It is stupid of me, perhaps; it betrays, I suppose, my imperfect knowledge of your sex. I am aware that most young men of fashion find an irresistible attraction for creatures who parade themselves upon the stage. But I did not expect you to ape the ways of a man of fashion. I was foolish enough to imagine you to be different; rather above such trivial pursuits. I conceived you something of an idealist."

"Sheer flattery."

"So I perceive. But you misled me. You talked so much morality of a kind, you made philosophy so readily, that I came to be deceived. In fact, your hypocrisy was so consummate that I never suspected it. With your gift of acting I wonder that you haven't joined Mlle. Binet's troupe."

"I have," said he.

It had really become necessary to tell her, making choice of the lesser of the two evils with which she confronted him.

He saw first incredulity, then consternation, and lastly disgust overspread her face.

"Of course," said she, after a long pause, "that would have the advantage of bringing you closer to your charmer."

"That was only one of the inducements. There was another. Finding myself forced to choose between the stage and the gallows, I had the incredible weakness to prefer the former. It was utterly unworthy of a man of my lofty ideals, but—what would you? Like other ideologists, I find it easier to preach than to practise. Shall I stop the carriage and remove the contamination of my disgusting person? Or shall I tell you how it happened?"

"Tell me how it happened first. Then we will decide."

He told her how he met the Binet Troupe, and how the men of the marechaussee forced upon him the discovery that in its bosom he could lie safely lost until the hue and cry had died down. The explanation dissolved her iciness.

"My poor Andre, why didn't you tell me this at first?"

"For one thing, you didn't give me time; for another, I feared to shock you with the spectacle of my degradation."

She took him seriously. "But where was the need of it? And why did you not send us word as I required you of your whereabouts?"

"I was thinking of it only yesterday. I have hesitated for several reasons."

"You thought it would offend us to know what you were doing?"

"I think that I preferred to surprise you by the magnitude of my ultimate achievements."

"Oh, you are to become a great actor?" She was frankly scornful.

"That is not impossible. But I am more concerned to become a great author. There is no reason why you should sniff. The calling is an honourable one. All the world is proud to know such men as Beaumarchais and Chenier."

"And you hope to equal them?"

"I hope to surpass them, whilst acknowledging that it was they who taught me how to walk. What did you think of the play last night?"

"It was amusing and well conceived."

"Let me present you to the author."

"You? But the company is one of the improvisers."

"Even improvisers require an author to write their scenarios. That is all I write at present. Soon I shall be writing plays in the modern manner."

"You deceive yourself, my poor Andre. The piece last night would have been nothing without the players. You are fortunate in your Scaramouche."

"In confidence—I present you to him."

"You—Scaramouche? You?" She turned to regard him fully. He smiled his close-lipped smile that made wrinkles like gashes in his cheeks. He nodded. "And I didn't recognize you!"

"I thank you for the tribute. You imagined, of course, that I was a scene-shifter. And now that you know all about me, what of Gavrillac? What of my god-father?"

He was well, she told him, and still profoundly indignant with Andre-Louis for his defection, whilst secretly concerned on his behalf.

"I shall write to him to-day that I have seen you."

"Do so. Tell him that I am well and prospering. But say no more. Do not tell him what I am doing. He has his prejudices too. Besides, it might not be prudent. And now the question I have been burning to ask ever since I entered your carriage. Why are you in Nantes, Aline?"

"I am on a visit to my aunt, Mme. de Sautron. It was with her that I came to the play yesterday. We have been dull at the chateau; but it will be different now. Madame my aunt is receiving several guests to-day. M. de La Tour d'Azyr is to be one of them."

Andre-Louis frowned and sighed. "Did you ever hear, Aline, how poor Philippe de Vilmorin came by his end?"

"Yes; I was told, first by my uncle; then by M. de La Tour d'Azyr, himself."

"Did not that help you to decide this marriage question?"

"How could it? You forget that I am but a woman. You don't expect me to judge between men in matters such as these?"

"Why not? You are well able to do so. The more since you have heard two sides. For my godfather would tell you the truth. If you cannot judge, it is that you do not wish to judge." His tone became harsh. "Wilfully you close your eyes to justice that might check the course of your unhealthy, unnatural ambition."

"Excellent!" she exclaimed, and considered him with amusement and something else. "Do you know that you are almost droll? You rise unblushing from the dregs of life in which I find you, and shake off the arm of that theatre girl, to come and preach to me."

"If these were the dregs of life I might still speak from them to counsel you out of my respect and devotion, Aline." He was very, stiff and stern. "But they are not the dregs of life. Honour and virtue are possible to a theatre girl; they are impossible to a lady who sells herself to gratify ambition; who for position, riches, and a great title barters herself in marriage."

She looked at him breathlessly. Anger turned her pale. She reached for the cord.

"I think I had better let you alight so that you may go back to practise virtue and honour with your theatre wench."

"You shall not speak so of her, Aline."

"Faith, now we are to have heat on her behalf. You think I am too delicate? You think I should speak of her as a..."

"If you must speak of her at all," he interrupted, hotly, "you'll speak of her as my wife."

Amazement smothered her anger. Her pallor deepened. "My God!" she said, and looked at him in horror. And in horror she asked him presently: "You are married—married to that—?"

"Not yet. But I shall be, soon. And let me tell you that this girl whom you visit with your ignorant contempt is as good and pure as you are, Aline. She has wit and talent which have placed her where she is and shall carry her a deal farther. And she has the womanliness to be guided by natural instincts in the selection of her mate."

She was trembling with passion. She tugged the cord.

"You will descend this instant!" she told him fiercely. "That you should dare to make a comparison between me and that..."

"And my wife-to-be," he interrupted, before she could speak the infamous word. He opened the door for himself without waiting for the footman, and leapt down. "My compliments," said he, furiously, "to the assassin you are to marry." He slammed the door. "Drive on," he bade the coachman.

The carriage rolled away up the Faubourg Gigan, leaving him standing where he had alighted, quivering with rage. Gradually, as he walked back to the inn, his anger cooled. Gradually, as he cooled, he perceived her point of view, and in the end forgave her. It was not her fault that she thought as she thought. Her rearing had been such as to make her look upon every actress as a trull, just as it had qualified her calmly to consider the monstrous marriage of convenience into which she was invited.

He got back to the inn to find the company at table. Silence fell when he entered, so suddenly that of necessity it must be supposed he was himself the subject of the conversation. Harlequin and Columbine had spread the tale of this prince in disguise caught up into the chariot of a princess and carried off by her; and it was a tale that had lost nothing in the telling.

Climene had been silent and thoughtful, pondering what Columbine had called this romance of hers. Clearly her Scaramouche must be vastly other than he had hitherto appeared, or else that great lady and he would never have used such familiarity with each other. Imagining him no better than he was, Climene had made him her own. And now she was to receive the reward of disinterested affection.

Even old Binet's secret hostility towards Andre-Louis melted before this astounding revelation. He had pinched his daughter's ear quite playfully. "Ah, ah, trust you to have penetrated his disguise, my child!"

She shrank resentfully from that implication.

"But I did not. I took him for what he seemed."

Her father winked at her very solemnly and laughed. "To be sure, you did. But like your father, who was once a gentleman, and knows the ways of gentlemen, you detected in him a subtle something different from those with whom misfortune has compelled you hitherto to herd. You knew as well as I did that he never caught that trick of haughtiness, that grand air of command, in a lawyer's musty office, and that his speech had hardly the ring or his thoughts the complexion of the bourgeois that he pretended to be. And it was shrewd of you to have made him yours. Do you know that I shall be very proud of you yet, Climene?"

She moved away without answering. Her father's oiliness offended her. Scaramouche was clearly a great gentleman, an eccentric if you please, but a man born. And she was to be his lady. Her father must learn to treat her differently.

She looked shyly—with a new shyness—at her lover when he came into the room where they were dining. She observed for the first time that proud carriage of the head, with the chin thrust forward, that was a trick of his, and she noticed with what a grace he moved—the grace of one who in youth has had his dancing-masters and fencing-masters.

It almost hurt her when he flung himself into a chair and exchanged a quip with Harlequin in the usual manner as with an equal, and it offended her still more that Harlequin, knowing what he now knew, should use him with the same unbecoming familiarity.

CHAPTER IX. THE AWAKENING

"Do you know," said Climene, "that I am waiting for the explanation which I think you owe me?"

They were alone together, lingering still at the table to which Andre-Louis had come belatedly, and Andre-Louis was loading himself a pipe. Of late—since joining the Binet Troupe—he had acquired the habit of smoking. The others had gone, some to take the air and others, like Binet and Madame, because they felt that it were discreet to leave those two to the explanations that must pass. It was a feeling that Andre-Louis did not share. He kindled a light and leisurely applied it to his pipe. A frown came to settle on his brow.

"Explanation?" he questioned presently, and looked at her. "But on what score?"

"On the score of the deception you have practised on us—on me."

"I have practised none," he assured her.

"You mean that you have simply kept your own counsel, and that in silence there is no deception. But it is deceitful to withhold facts concerning yourself and your true station from your future wife. You should not have pretended to be a simple country lawyer, which, of course, any one could see that you are not. It may have been very romantic, but... Enfin, will you explain?"

"I see," he said, and pulled at his pipe. "But you are wrong, Climene. I have practised no deception. If there are things about me that I have not told you, it is that I did not account them of much importance. But I have never deceived you by pretending to be other than I am. I am neither more nor less than I have represented myself."

This persistence began to annoy her, and the annoyance showed on her winsome face, coloured her voice.

"Ha! And that fine lady of the nobility with whom you are so intimate, who carried you off in her cabriolet with so little ceremony towards myself? What is she to you?"

"A sort of sister," said he.

"A sort of sister!" She was indignant. "Harlequin foretold that you would say so; but he was amusing himself. It was not very funny. It is less funny still from you. She has a name, I suppose, this sort of sister?"

"Certainly she has a name. She is Mlle. Aline de Kercadiou, the niece of Quintin de Kercadiou, Lord of Gavrillac."

"Oho! That's a sufficiently fine name for your sort of sister. What sort of sister, my friend?"

For the first time in their relationship he observed and deplored the taint of vulgarity, of shrewishness, in her manner.

"It would have been more accurate in me to have said a sort of reputed left-handed cousin."

"A reputed left-handed cousin! And what sort of relationship may that be? Faith, you dazzle me with your lucidity."

"It requires to be explained."

"That is what I have been telling you. But you seem very reluctant with your explanations."

"Oh, no. It is only that they are so unimportant. But be you the judge. Her uncle, M. de Kercadiou, is my godfather, and she and I have been playmates from infancy as a consequence. It is popularly believed in Gavrillac that M. de Kercadiou is my father. He has certainly cared for my rearing from my tenderest years, and it is entirely owing to him that I was educated at Louis le Grand. I owe to him everything that I have—or, rather, everything that I had; for of my own free will I have cut myself adrift, and to-day I possess nothing save what I can earn for myself in the theatre or elsewhere."

She sat stunned and pale under that cruel blow to her swelling pride. Had he told her this but yesterday, it would have made no impression upon her, it would have mattered not at all; the event of to-day coming as a sequel would but have enhanced him in her eyes. But coming now, after her imagination had woven for him so magnificent a background, after the rashly assumed discovery of his splendid identity had made her the envied of all the company, after having been in her own eyes and theirs enshrined by marriage with him as a great lady, this disclosure crushed and humiliated her. Her prince in disguise was merely the outcast bastard of a country gentleman! She would be the laughing-stock of every member of her father's troupe, of all those who had so lately envied her this romantic good fortune.

"You should have told me this before," she said, in a dull voice that she strove to render steady.

"Perhaps I should. But does it really matter?"

"Matter?" She suppressed her fury to ask another question. "You say that this M. de Kercadiou is popularly believed to be your father. What precisely do you mean?"

"Just that. It is a belief that I do not share. It is a matter of instinct, perhaps, with me. Moreover, once I asked M. de Kercadiou point-blank, and I received from him a denial. It is not, perhaps, a denial to which one would attach too much importance in all the circumstances. Yet I have never known M de Kercadiou for other than a man of strictest honour, and I should hesitate to disbelieve him—

particularly when his statement leaps with my own instincts. He assured me that he did not know who my father was."

"And your mother, was she equally ignorant?" She was sneering, but he did not remark it. Her back was to the light.

"He would not disclose her name to me. He confessed her to be a dear friend of his."

She startled him by laughing, and her laugh was not pleasant.

"A very dear friend, you may be sure, you simpleton. What name do you bear?"

He restrained his own rising indignation to answer her question calmly: "Moreau. It was given me, so I am told, from the Brittany village in which I was born. But I have no claim to it. In fact I have no name, unless it be Scaramouche, to which I have earned a title. So that you see, my dear," he ended with a smile, "I have practised no deception whatever."

"No, no. I see that now." She laughed without mirth, then drew a deep breath and rose. "I am very tired," she said.

He was on his feet in an instant, all solicitude. But she waved him wearily back.

"I think I will rest until it is time to go to the theatre." She moved towards the door, dragging her feet a little. He sprang to open it, and she passed out without looking at him.

Her so brief romantic dream was ended. The glorious world of fancy which in the last hour she had built with such elaborate detail, over which it should be her exalted destiny to rule, lay shattered about her feet, its debris so many stumbling-blocks that prevented her from winning back to her erstwhile content in Scaramouche as he really was.

Andre-Louis sat in the window embrasure, smoking and looking idly out across the river. He was intrigued and meditative. He had shocked her. The fact was clear; not so the reason. That he should confess himself nameless should not particularly injure him in the eyes of a girl reared amid the surroundings that had been Climene's. And yet that his confession had so injured him was fully apparent.

There, still at his brooding, the returning Columbine discovered him a half-hour later.

"All alone, my prince!" was her laughing greeting, which suddenly threw light upon his mental darkness. Climene had been disappointed of hopes that the wild imagination of these players had suddenly erected upon the incident of his meeting with Aline. Poor child! He smiled whimsically at Columbine.

"I am likely to be so for some little time," said he, "until it becomes a commonplace that I am not, after all, a prince.

"Not a prince? Oh, but a duke, then—at least a marquis."

"Not even a chevalier, unless it be of the order of fortune. I am just Scaramouche. My castles are all in Spain."

Disappointment clouded the lively, good-natured face.

"And I had imagined you..."

"I know," he interrupted. "That is the mischief." He might have gauged the extent of that mischief by Climene's conduct that evening towards the gentlemen of fashion who clustered now in the green-room between the acts to pay their homage to the incomparable amoureuse. Hitherto she had received them with a circumspection compelling respect. To-night she was recklessly gay, impudent, almost wanton.

He spoke of it gently to her as they walked home together, counselling more prudence in the future.

"We are not married yet," she told him, tartly. "Wait until then before you criticize my conduct."

"I trust that there will be no occasion then," said he.

"You trust? Ah, yes. You are very trusting."

"Climene, I have offended you. I am sorry."

"It is nothing," said she. "You are what you are." Still was he not concerned. He perceived the source of her ill-humour; understood, whilst deploring it; and, because he understood, forgave. He perceived also that her ill-humour was shared by her father, and by this he was frankly amused. Towards M. Binet a tolerant contempt was the only feeling that complete acquaintance could beget. As for the rest of the company, they were disposed to be very kindly towards Scaramouche. It was almost as if in reality he had fallen from the high estate to which their own imaginations had raised him; or possibly it was because they saw the effect which that fall from his temporary and fictitious elevation had produced upon Climene.

Leandre alone made himself an exception. His habitual melancholy seemed to be dispelled at last, and his eyes gleamed now with malicious satisfaction when they rested upon Scaramouche, whom occasionally he continued to address with sly mockery as "mon prince."

On the morrow Andre-Louis saw but little of Climene. This was not in itself extraordinary, for he was very hard at work again, with preparations now for "Figaro-Scaramouche" which was to be played on Saturday. Also, in addition to his manifold theatrical occupations, he now devoted an hour every morning to the study of fencing in an academy of arms. This was done not only to repair an omission in his education, but also, and chiefly, to give him added grace and poise upon the stage. He found his mind that morning distracted by thoughts of both Climene and Aline. And oddly enough it was Aline who provided the deeper perturbation. Climene's attitude he regarded as a passing phase which need not seriously engage him. But the thought of Aline's conduct towards him kept rankling, and still more deeply rankled the thought of her possible betrothal to M. de La Tour d'Azyr.

This it was that brought forcibly to his mind the self-imposed but by now half-forgotten mission that he had made his own. He had boasted that he would make the voice which M. de La Tour d'Azyr had sought to silence ring through the length and breadth of the land. And what had he done of all this that he had boasted? He had incited the mob of Rennes and the mob of Nantes in such terms as poor Philippe might have employed, and then because of a hue and cry he had fled like a cur and taken shelter in the first kennel that offered, there to lie quiet and devote himself to other things—self-seeking things. What a fine contrast between the promise and the fulfilment!

Thus Andre-Louis to himself in his self-contempt. And whilst he trifled away his time and played Scaramouche, and centred all his hopes in presently becoming the rival of such men as Chenier and Mercier, M. de La Tour d'Azyr went his proud ways unchallenged and wrought his will. It was idle to tell himself that the seed he had sown was bearing fruit. That the demands he had voiced in Nantes for the Third Estate had been granted by M. Necker, thanks largely to the commotion which his anonymous speech had made. That was not his concern or his mission. It was no part of his concern to set about the regeneration of mankind, or even the regeneration of the social structure of France. His concern was to see that M. de La Tour d'Azyr paid to the uttermost liard for the brutal wrong he had done Philippe de Vilmorin. And it did not increase his self-respect to find that the danger in which Aline stood of being married to the Marquis was the real spur to his rancour and to remembrance of his vow. He was—too unjustly, perhaps—disposed to dismiss as mere sophistries his own arguments that there was nothing he could do; that, in fact, he had but to show his head to find himself going to Rennes under arrest and making his final exit from the world's stage by way of the gallows.

It is impossible to read that part of his "Confessions" without feeling a certain pity for him. You realize what must have been his state of mind. You realize what a prey he was to emotions so conflicting, and if you have the imagination that will enable you to put yourself in his place, you will also realize how impossible was any decision save the one to which he says he came, that he would move, at the first moment that he perceived in what direction it would serve his real aims to move.

It happened that the first person he saw when he took the stage on that Thursday evening was Aline; the second was the Marquis de La Tour d'Azyr. They occupied a box on the right of, and immediately above, the stage. There were others with them—notably a thin, elderly, resplendent lady whom Andre-Louis supposed to be Madame la Comtesse de Sautron. But at the time he had no eyes for any but those two, who of late had so haunted his thoughts. The sight of either of them would have been sufficiently disconcerting. The sight of both together very nearly made him forget the purpose for which he had come upon the stage. Then he pulled himself together, and played. He played, he says, with an unusual nerve, and never in all that brief but eventful career of his was he more applauded.

That was the evening's first shock. The next came after the second act. Entering the green-room he found it more thronged than usual, and at the far end with Climene, over whom he was bending from his fine height, his eyes intent upon her face, what time his smiling lips moved in talk, M. de La Tour d'Azyr. He had her entirely to himself, a privilege none of the men of fashion who were in the habit of visiting the coulisse had yet enjoyed. Those lesser gentlemen had all withdrawn before the Marquis, as jackals withdraw before the lion.

Andre-Louis stared a moment, stricken. Then recovering from his surprise he became critical in his study of the Marquis. He considered the beauty and grace and splendour of him, his courtly air, his complete and unshakable self-possession. But more than all he considered the expression of the dark eyes that were devouring Climene's lovely face, and his own lips tightened.

M. de La Tour d'Azyr never heeded him or his stare; nor, had he done so, would he have known who it was that looked at him from behind the make-up of Scaramouche; nor, again, had he known, would he have been in the least troubled or concerned.

Andre-Louis sat down apart, his mind in turmoil. Presently he found a mincing young gentleman addressing him, and made shift to answer as was expected. Climene having been thus sequestered, and Columbine being already thickly besieged by gallants, the lesser visitors had to content themselves with Madame and the male members of the troupe. M. Binet, indeed, was the centre of a gay cluster that shook with laughter at his sallies. He seemed of a sudden to have emerged from the gloom of the last two days into high good-humour, and Scaramouche observed how persistently his eyes kept flickering upon his daughter and her splendid courtier.

That night there, were high words between Andre-Louis and Climene, the high words proceeding from Climene. When Andre-Louis again, and more insistently, enjoined prudence upon his betrothed, and begged her to beware how far she encouraged the advances of such a man as M. de La Tour d'Azyr, she became roundly abusive. She shocked and stunned him by her virulently shrewish tone, and her still more unexpected force of invective.

He sought to reason with her, and finally she came to certain terms with him.

"If you have become betrothed to me simply to stand as an obstacle in my path, the sooner we make an end the better."

"You do not love me then, Climene?"

"Love has nothing to do with it. I'll not tolerate your insensate jealousy. A girl in the theatre must make it her business to accept homage from all."

"Agreed; and there is no harm, provided she gives nothing in exchange."

White-faced, with flaming eyes she turned on him at that.

"Now, what exactly do you mean?"

"My meaning is clear. A girl in your position may receive all the homage that is offered, provided she receives it with a dignified aloofness implying clearly that she has no favours to bestow in return beyond the favour of her smile. If she is wise she will see to it that the homage is always offered collectively by her admirers, and that no single one amongst them shall ever have the privilege of approaching her alone. If she is wise she will give no encouragement, nourish no hopes that it may afterwards be beyond her power to deny realization."

"How? You dare?"

"I know my world. And I know M. de La Tour d'Azyr," he answered her. "He is a man without charity, without humanity almost; a man who takes what he wants wherever he finds it and whether it is given willingly or not; a man who reckons nothing of the misery he scatters on his self-indulgent way; a man whose only law is force. Ponder it, Climene, and ask yourself if I do you less than honour in warning you."

He went out on that, feeling a degradation in continuing the subject.

The days that followed were unhappy days for him, and for at least one other. That other was Leandre, who was cast into the profoundest dejection by M. de La Tour d'Azyr's assiduous attendance upon Climene. The Marquis was to be seen at every performance; a box was perpetually reserved for him, and invariably he came either alone or else with his cousin M. de Chabrillane.

On Tuesday of the following week, Andre-Louis went out alone early in the morning. He was out of temper, fretted by an overwhelming sense of humiliation, and he hoped to clear his mind by walking. In turning the corner of the Place du Bouffay he ran into a slightly built, sallow-complexioned gentleman very neatly dressed in black, wearing a tie-wig under a round hat. The man fell back at sight of him, levelling a spy-glass, then hailed him in a voice that rang with amazement.

"Moreau! Where the devil have you been hiding your-self these months?"

It was Le Chapelier, the lawyer, the leader of the Literary Chamber of Rennes.

"Behind the skirts of Thespis," said Scaramouche.

"I don't understand."

"I didn't intend that you should. What of yourself, Isaac? And what of the world which seems to have been standing still of late?"

"Standing still!" Le Chapelier laughed. "But where have you been, then? Standing still!" He pointed across the square to a café under the shadow of the gloomy prison. "Let us go and drink a bavaroise. You are of all men the man we want, the man we have been seeking everywhere, and—behold!—you drop from the skies into my path."

They crossed the square and entered the café.

"So you think the world has been standing still! Dieu de Dieu! I suppose you haven't heard of the royal order for the convocation of the States General, or the terms of them—that we are to have what we demanded, what you demanded for us here in Nantes! You haven't heard that the order has gone forth for the primary elections—the elections of the electors. You haven't heard of the fresh uproar in Rennes, last month. The order was that the three estates should sit together at the States General of the bailliages, but in the bailliage of Rennes the nobles must ever be recalcitrant. They took up arms actually—six hundred of them with their valetaille, headed by your old friend M. de La Tour d'Azyr, and they were for slashing us—the members of the Third Estate—into ribbons so as to put an end to our insolence." He laughed delicately. "But, by God, we showed them that we, too, could take up arms. It was what you yourself advocated here in Nantes, last November. We fought them a pitched battle in the streets, under the leadership of your namesake Moreau, the provost, and we so peppered them that they were glad to take shelter in the Cordelier Convent. That is the end of their resistance to the royal authority and the people's will."

He ran on at great speed detailing the events that had taken place, and finally came to the matter which had, he announced, been causing him to hunt for Andre-Louis until he had all but despaired of finding him.

Nantes was sending fifty delegates to the assembly of Rennes which was to select the deputies to the Third Estate and edit their cahier of grievances. Rennes itself was being as fully represented, whilst such villages as Gavrillac were sending two delegates for every two hundred hearths or less. Each of these three had clamoured that Andre-Louis Moreau should be one of its delegates. Gavrillac wanted him because he belonged to the village, and it was known there what sacrifices he had made in the popular cause; Rennes wanted him because it had heard his spirited address on the day of the shooting of the students; and Nantes—to whom his identity was unknown—asked for him as the speaker who had addressed them under the name of Omnes Omnibus and who had framed for them the memorial that was believed so largely to have influenced M. Necker in formulating the terms of the convocation.

Since he could not be found, the delegations had been made up without him. But now it happened that one or two vacancies had occurred in the Nantes representation; and it was the business of filling these vacancies that had brought Le Chapelier to Nantes.

Andre-Louis firmly shook his head in answer to Le Chapelier's proposal.

"You refuse?" the other cried. "Are you mad? Refuse, when you are demanded from so many sides? Do you realize that it is more than probable you will be elected one of the deputies, that you will be sent to the States General at Versailles to represent us in this work of saving France?"

But Andre-Louis, we know, was not concerned to save France. At the moment he was concerned to save two women, both of whom he loved, though in vastly different ways, from a man he had vowed to ruin. He stood firm in his refusal until Le Chapelier dejectedly abandoned the attempt to persuade him.

"It is odd," said Andre-Louis, "that I should have been so deeply immersed in trifles as never to have perceived that Nantes is being politically active."

"Active! My friend, it is a seething cauldron of political emotions. It is kept quiet on the surface only by the persuasion that all goes well. At a hint to the contrary it would boil over."

"Would it so?" said Scaramouche, thoughtfully. "The knowledge may be useful." And then he changed the subject. "You know that La Tour d'Azyr is here?"

"In Nantes? He has courage if he shows himself. They are not a docile people, these Nantais, and they know his record and the part he played in the rising at Rennes. I marvel they haven't stoned him. But they will, sooner or later. It only needs that some one should suggest it."

"That is very likely," said Andre-Louis, and smiled. "He doesn't show himself much; not in the streets, at least. So that he has not the courage you suppose; nor any kind of courage, as I told him once. He has only insolence."

At parting Le Chapelier again exhorted him to give thought to what he proposed. "Send me word if you change your mind. I am lodged at the Cerf, and I shall be here until the day after to-morrow. If you have ambition, this is your moment."

"I have no ambition, I suppose," said Andre-Louis, and went his way.

That night at the theatre he had a mischievous impulse to test what Le Chapelier had told him of the state of public feeling in the city. They were playing "The Terrible Captain," in the last act of which the empty cowardice of the bullying braggart Rhodomont is revealed by Scaramouche.

After the laughter which the exposure of the roaring captain invariably produced, it remained for Scaramouche contemptuously to dismiss him in a phrase that varied nightly, according to the inspiration of the moment. This time he chose to give his phrase a political complexion:

"Thus, O thrasonical coward, is your emptiness exposed. Because of your long length and the great sword you carry and the angle at which you cock your hat, people have gone in fear of you, have believed in you, have imagined you to be as terrible and as formidable as you insolently make yourself appear. But at the first touch of true spirit you crumple up, you tremble, you whine pitifully, and the great sword remains in your scabbard. You remind me of the Privileged Orders when confronted by the Third Estate."

It was audacious of him, and he was prepared for anything—a laugh, applause, indignation, or all together. But he was not prepared for what came. And it came so suddenly and spontaneously from the groundlings and the body of those in the amphitheatre that he was almost scared by it—as a boy may be scared who has held a match to a sun-scorched hayrick. It was a hurricane of furious applause. Men leapt to their feet, sprang up on to the benches, waving their hats in the air, deafening him with the terrific uproar of their acclamations. And it rolled on and on, nor ceased until the curtain fell.

Scaramouche stood meditatively smiling with tight lips. At the last moment he had caught a glimpse of M. de La Tour d'Azyr's face thrust farther forward than usual from the shadows of his box, and it was a face set in anger, with eyes on fire.

"Mon Dieu!" laughed Rhodomont, recovering from the real scare that had succeeded his histrionic terror, "but you have a great trick of tickling them in the right place, Scaramouche."

Scaramouche looked up at him and smiled. "It can be useful upon occasion," said he, and went off to his dressing-room to change.

But a reprimand awaited him. He was delayed at the theatre by matters concerned with the scenery of the new piece they were to mount upon the morrow. By the time he was rid of the business the rest of the company had long since left. He called a chair and had himself carried back to the inn in solitary state. It was one of many minor luxuries his comparatively affluent present circumstances permitted.

Coming into that upstairs room that was common to all the troupe, he found M. Binet talking loudly and vehemently. He had caught sounds of his voice whilst yet upon the stairs. As he entered Binet broke off short, and wheeled to face him.

"You are here at last!" It was so odd a greeting that Andre-Louis did no more than look his mild surprise. "I await your explanations of the disgraceful scene you provoked to night."

"Disgraceful? Is it disgraceful that the public should applaud me?"

"The public? The rabble, you mean. Do you want to deprive us of the patronage of all gentlefolk by vulgar appeals to the low passions of the mob?"

Andre-Louis stepped past M. Binet and forward to the table. He shrugged contemptuously. The man offended him, after all.

"You exaggerate grossly—as usual."

"I do not exaggerate. And I am the master in my own theatre. This is the Binet Troupe, and it shall be conducted in the Binet way."

"Who are the gentlefolk the loss of whose patronage to the Feydau will be so poignantly felt?" asked Andre-Louis.

"You imply that there are none? See how wrong you are. After the play tonight M. le Marquis de La Tour d'Azyr came to me, and spoke to me in the severest terms about your scandalous outburst. I was forced to apologize, and..."

"The more fool you," said Andre-Louis. "A man who respected himself would have shown that gentleman the door." M. Binet's face began to empurple. "You call yourself the head of the Binet Troupe, you boast that you will be master in your own theatre, and you stand like a lackey to take the orders of the first insolent fellow who comes to your green-room to tell you that he does not like a line spoken by one of your company! I say again that had you really respected yourself you would have turned him out."

There was a murmur of approval from several members of the company, who, having heard the arrogant tone assumed by the Marquis, were filled with resentment against the slur cast upon them all.

"And I say further," Andre-Louis went on, "that a man who respects himself, on quite other grounds, would have been only too glad to have seized this pretext to show M. de La Tour d'Azyr the door."

"What do you mean by that?" There was a rumble of thunder in the question.

Andre-Louis' eyes swept round the company assembled at the supper-table. "Where is Climene?" he asked, sharply.

Leandre leapt up to answer him, white in the face, tense and quivering with excitement.

"She left the theatre in the Marquis de La Tour d'Azyr's carriage immediately after the performance. We heard him offer to drive her to this inn."

Andre-Louis glanced at the timepiece on the overmantel. He seemed unnaturally calm.

"That would be an hour ago—rather more. And she has not yet arrived?"

His eyes sought M. Binet's. M. Binet's eyes eluded his glance. Again it was Leandre who answered him.

"Not yet."

"Ah!" Andre-Louis sat down, and poured himself wine. There was an oppressive silence in the room. Leandre watched him expectantly, Columbine commiseratingly. Even M. Binet appeared to be waiting for a cue from Scaramouche. But Scaramouche disappointed him. "Have you left me anything to eat?" he asked.

Platters were pushed towards him. He helped himself calmly to food, and ate in silence, apparently with a good appetite. M. Binet sat down, poured himself wine, and drank. Presently he attempted to make conversation with one and another. He was answered curtly, in monosyllables. M. Binet did not appear to be in favour with his troupe that night.

At long length came a rumble of wheels below and a rattle of halting hooves. Then voices, the high, trilling laugh of Climene floating upwards. Andre-Louis went on eating unconcernedly.

"What an actor!" said Harlequin under his breath to Polichinelle, and Polichinelle nodded gloomily.

She came in, a leading lady taking the stage, head high, chin thrust forward, eyes dancing with laughter; she expressed triumph and arrogance. Her cheeks were flushed, and there was some disorder in the mass of nut-brown hair that crowned her head. In her left hand she carried an enormous bouquet of white camellias. On its middle finger a diamond of great price drew almost at once by its effulgence the eyes of all.

Her father sprang to meet her with an unusual display of paternal tenderness. "At last, my child!"

He conducted her to the table. She sank into a chair, a little wearily, a little nervelessly, but the smile did not leave her face, not even when she glanced across at Scaramouche. It was only Leandre, observing her closely, with hungry, scowling stare, who detected something as of fear in the hazel eyes momentarily seen between the fluttering of her lids.

Andre-Louis, however, still went on eating stolidly, without so much as a look in her direction. Gradually the company came to realize that just as surely as a scene was brooding, just so surely would there be no scene as long as they remained. It was Polichinelle, at last, who gave the signal by rising and withdrawing, and within two minutes none remained in the room but M. Binet, his daughter, and Andre-Louis. And then, at last, Andre-Louis set down knife and fork, washed his throat with a draught of Burgundy, and sat back in his chair to consider Climene.

"I trust," said he, "that you had a pleasant ride, mademoiselle."

"Most pleasant, monsieur." Impudently she strove to emulate his coolness, but did not completely succeed.

"And not unprofitable, if I may judge that jewel at this distance. It should be worth at least a couple of hundred louis, and that is a formidable sum even to so wealthy a nobleman as M. de La Tour d'Azyr. Would it be impertinent in one who has had some notion of becoming your husband, to ask you, mademoiselle, what you have given him in return?"

M. Binet uttered a gross laugh, a queer mixture of cynicism and contempt.

"I have given nothing," said Climene, indignantly.

"Ah! Then the jewel is in the nature of a payment in advance."

"My God, man, you're not decent!" M. Binet protested.

"Decent?" Andre Louis' smouldering eyes turned to discharge upon M. Binet such a fulmination of contempt that the old scoundrel shifted uncomfortably in his chair. "Did you mention decency, Binet? Almost you make me lose my temper, which is a thing that I detest above all others!" Slowly his glance returned to Climene, who sat with elbows on the table, her chin cupped in her palms, regarding him with something between scorn and defiance. "Mademoiselle," he said, slowly, "I desire you purely in your own interests to consider whither you are going."

"I am well able to consider it for myself, and to decide without advice from you, monsieur."

"And now you've got your answer," chuckled Binet. "I hope you like it."

Andre-Louis had paled a little; there was incredulity in his great sombre eyes as they continued steadily to regard her. Of M. Binet he took no notice.

"Surely, mademoiselle, you cannot mean that willingly, with open eyes and a full understanding of what you do, you would exchange an honourable wifehood for... for the thing that such men as M. de La Tour d'Azyr may have in store for you?"

M. Binet made a wide gesture, and swung to his daughter. "You hear him, the mealy-mouthed prude! Perhaps you'll believe at last that marriage with him would be the ruin of you. He would always be there the inconvenient husband—to mar your every chance, my girl."

She tossed her lovely head in agreement with her father. "I begin to find him tiresome with his silly jealousies," she confessed. "As a husband I am afraid he would be impossible."

Andre-Louis felt a constriction of the heart. But—always the actor—he showed nothing of it. He laughed a little, not very pleasantly, and rose.

"I bow to your choice, mademoiselle. I pray that you may not regret it."

"Regret it?" cried M. Binet. He was laughing, relieved to see his daughter at last rid of this suitor of whom he had never approved, if we except those few hours when he really believed him to be an eccentric of distinction. "And what shall she regret? That she accepted the protection of a nobleman so powerful and wealthy that as a mere trinket he gives her a jewel worth as much as an actress earns in a year at the Comedie Francaise?" He got up, and advanced towards Andre-Louis. His mood became conciliatory. "Come, come, my friend, no rancour now. What the devil! You wouldn't stand in the girl's way? You can't really blame her for making this choice? Have you thought what it means to her? Have you thought that under the protection of such a gentleman there are no heights which she may not reach? Don't you see the wonderful luck of it? Surely, if you're fond of her, particularly being of a jealous temperament, you wouldn't wish it otherwise?"

Andre-Louis looked at him in silence for a long moment. Then he laughed again. "Oh, you are fantastic," he said. "You are not real." He turned on his heel and strode to the door.

The action, and more the contempt of his look, laugh, and words stung M. Binet to passion, drove out the conciliatoriness of his mood.

"Fantastic, are we?" he cried, turning to follow the departing Scaramouche with his little eyes that now were inexpressibly evil. "Fantastic that we should prefer the powerful protection of this great nobleman to marriage with a beggarly, nameless bastard. Oh, we are fantastic!"

Andre-Louis turned, his hand upon the door-handle. "No," he said, "I was mistaken. You are not fantastic. You are just vile—both of you." And he went out.

CHAPTER X. CONTRITION

Mlle. de Kercadiou walked with her aunt in the bright morning sunshine of a Sunday in March on the broad terrace of the Chateau de Sautron.

For one of her natural sweetness of disposition she had been oddly irritable of late, manifesting signs of a cynical worldliness, which convinced Mme. de Sautron more than ever that her brother Quintin had scandalously conducted the child's education. She appeared to be instructed in all the things of which a girl is better ignorant, and ignorant of all the things that a girl should know. That at least was the point of view of Mme. de Sautron.

"Tell me, madame," quoth Aline, "are all men beasts?" Unlike her brother, Madame la Comtesse was tall and majestically built. In the days before her marriage with M. de Sautron, ill-natured folk described her as the only man in the family. She looked down now from her noble height upon her little niece with startled eyes.

"Really, Aline, you have a trick of asking the most disconcerting and improper questions."

"Perhaps it is because I find life disconcerting and improper."

"Life? A young girl should not discuss life."

"Why not, since I am alive? You do not suggest that it is an impropriety to be alive?"

"It is an impropriety for a young unmarried girl to seek to know too much about life. As for your absurd question about men, when I remind you that man is the noblest work of God, perhaps you will consider yourself answered."

Mme. de Sautron did not invite a pursuance of the subject. But Mlle. de Kercadiou's outrageous rearing had made her headstrong.

"That being so," said she, "will you tell me why they find such an overwhelming attraction in the immodest of our sex?"

Madame stood still and raised shocked hands. Then she looked down her handsome, high-bridged nose.

"Sometimes—often, in fact, my dear Aline—you pass all understanding. I shall write to Quintin that the sooner you are married the better it will be for all."

"Uncle Quintin has left that matter to my own deciding," Aline reminded her.

"That," said madame with complete conviction, "is the last and most outrageous of his errors. Who ever heard of a girl being left to decide the matter of her own marriage? It is... indelicate almost to expose her to thoughts of such things." Mme. de Sautron shuddered. "Quintin is a boor. His conduct is unheard of. That M. de La Tour d'Azyr should parade himself before you so that you may make up your mind whether he is the proper man for you!" Again she shuddered. "It is of a grossness, of... of a prurience almost... Mon Dieu! When I married your uncle, all this was arranged between our parents. I first saw him when he came to sign the contract. I should have died of shame had it been otherwise. And that is how these affairs should be conducted."

"You are no doubt right, madame. But since that is not how my own case is being conducted, you will forgive me if I deal with it apart from others. M. de La Tour d'Azyr desires to marry me. He has been permitted to pay his court. I should be glad to have him informed that he may cease to do so."

Mme. de Sautron stood still, petrified by amazement. Her long face turned white; she seemed to breathe with difficulty.

"But... but... what are you saying?" she gasped.

Quietly Aline repeated her statement.

"But this is outrageous! You cannot be permitted to play fast-and-loose with a gentleman of M. le Marquis' quality! Why, it is little more than a week since you permitted him to be informed that you would become his wife!"

"I did so in a moment of... rashness. Since then M. le Marquis' own conduct has convinced me of my error."

"But—mon Dieu!" cried the Countess. "Are you blind to the great honour that is being paid you? M. le Marquis will make you the first lady in Brittany. Yet, little fool that you are, and greater fool that Quintin is, you trifle with this extraordinary good fortune! Let me warn you." She raised an admonitory forefinger. "If you continue in this stupid humour M. de La Tour d'Azyr may definitely withdraw his offer and depart in justified mortification."

"That, madame, as I am endeavouring to convey to you, is what I most desire."

"Oh, you are mad."

"It may be, madame, that I am sane in preferring to be guided by my instincts. It may be even that I am justified in resenting that the man who aspires to become my husband should at the same time be paying such assiduous homage to a wretched theatre girl at the Feydau."

"Aline!"

"Is it not true? Or perhaps you do not find it strange that M. de La Tour d'Azyr should so conduct himself at such a time?"

"Aline, you are so extraordinary a mixture. At moments you shock me by the indecency of your expressions; at others you amaze me by the excess of your prudery. You have been brought up like a little bourgeoise, I think. Yes, that is it—a little bourgeoise. Quintin was always something of a shopkeeper at heart."

"I was asking your opinion on the conduct of M. de La Tour d'Azyr, madame. Not on my own."

"But it is an indelicacy in you to observe such things. You should be ignorant of them, and I can't think who is so... so unfeeling as to inform you. But since you are informed, at least you should be modestly blind to things that take place outside the... orbit of a properly conducted demoiselle."

"Will they still be outside my orbit when I am married?"

"If you are wise. You should remain without knowledge of them. It... it deflowers your innocence. I would not for the world that M. de La Tour d'Azyr should know you so extraordinarily instructed. Had you been properly reared in a convent this would never have happened to you."

"But you do not answer me, madame!" cried Aline in despair. "It is not my chastity that is in question; but that of M. de La Tour d'Azyr."

"Chastity!" Madame's lips trembled with horror. Horror overspread her face. "Wherever did you learn that dreadful, that so improper word?"

And then Mme. de Sautron did violence to her feelings. She realized that here great calm and prudence were required. "My child, since you know so much that you ought not to know, there can be no harm in my adding that a gentleman must have these little distractions."

"But why, madame? Why is it so?"

"Ah, mon Dieu, you are asking me riddles of nature. It is so because it is so. Because men are like that."

"Because men are beasts, you mean—which is what I began by asking you."

"You are incorrigibly stupid, Aline."

"You mean that I do not see things as you do, madame. I am not over-expectant as you appear to think; yet surely I have the right to expect that whilst M. de La Tour d'Azyr is wooing me, he shall not be wooing at the same time a drab of the theatre. I feel that in this there is a subtle association of myself with that unspeakable creature which soils and insults me. The Marquis is a dullard whose wooing takes the form at best of stilted compliments, stupid and unoriginal. They gain nothing when they fall from lips still warm from the contamination of that woman's kisses."

So utterly scandalized was madame that for a moment she remained speechless. Then—

"Mon Dieu!" she exclaimed. "I should never have suspected you of so indelicate an imagination."

"I cannot help it, madame. Each time his lips touch my fingers I find myself thinking of the last object that they touched. I at once retire to wash my hands. Next time, madame, unless you are good enough to convey my message to him, I shall call for water and wash them in his presence."

"But what am I to tell him? How... in what words can I convey such a message?" Madame was aghast.

"Be frank with him, madame. It is easiest in the end. Tell him that however impure may have been his life in the past, however impure he intend that it shall be in the future, he must at least study purity whilst approaching with a view to marriage a virgin who is herself pure and without stain."

Madame recoiled, and put her hands to her ears, horror stamped on her handsome face. Her massive bosom heaved.

"Oh, how can you?" she panted. "How can you make use of such terrible expressions? Wherever have you learnt them?"

"In church," said Aline.

"Ah, but in church many things are said that... that one would not dream of saying in the world. My dear child, how could I possibly say such a thing to M. le Marquis? How could I possibly?"

"Shall I say it?"

"Aline!"

"Well, there it is," said Aline. "Something must be done to shelter me from insult. I am utterly disgusted with M. le Marquis—a disgusting man. And however fine a thing it may be to become Marquise de La Tour d'Azyr, why, frankly, I'd sooner marry a cobbler who practised decency."

Such was her vehemence and obvious determination that Mme. de Sautron fetched herself out of her despair to attempt persuasion. Aline was her niece, and such a marriage in the family would be to the credit of the whole of it. At all costs nothing must frustrate it.

"Listen, my dear," she said. "Let us reason. M. le Marquis is away and will not be back until to-morrow."

"True. And I know where he has gone—or at least whom he has gone with. Mon Dieu, and the drab has a father and a lout of a fellow who intends to make her his wife, and neither of them chooses to do anything. I suppose they agree with you, madame, that a great gentleman must have his little distractions." Her contempt was as scorching as a thing of fire. "However, madame, you were about to say?"

"That on the day after to-morrow you are returning to Gavrillac. M. de La Tour d'Azyr will most likely follow at his leisure."

"You mean when this dirty candle is burnt out?"

"Call it what you will." Madame, you see, despaired by now of controlling the impropriety of her niece's expressions. "At Gavrillac there will be no Mlle. Binet. This thing will be in the past. It is unfortunate that he should have met her at such a moment. The chit is very attractive, after all. You cannot deny that. And you must make allowances."

"M. le Marquis formally proposed to me a week ago. Partly to satisfy the wishes of the family, and partly..." She broke off, hesitating a moment, to resume on a note of dull pain, "Partly because it does not seem greatly to matter whom I marry, I gave him my consent. That consent, for the reasons I have given you, madame, I desire now definitely to withdraw."

Madame fell into agitation of the wildest. "Aline, I should never forgive you! Your uncle Quintin would be in despair. You do not know what you are saying, what a wonderful thing you are refusing. Have you no sense of your position, of the station into which you were born?"

"If I had not, madame, I should have made an end long since. If I have tolerated this suit for a single moment, it is because I realize the importance of a suitable marriage in the worldly sense. But I ask of marriage something more; and Uncle Quintin has placed the decision in my hands."

"God forgive him!" said madame. And then she hurried on: "Leave this to me now, Aline. Be guided by me—oh, be guided by me!" Her tone was beseeching. "I will take counsel with your uncle Charles. But do not definitely decide until this unfortunate affair has blown over. Charles will know how to arrange it. M. le Marquis shall do penance, child, since your tyranny demands it; but not in sack-cloth and ashes. You'll not ask so much?"

Aline shrugged. "I ask nothing at all," she said, which was neither assent nor dissent.

So Mme. de Sautron interviewed her husband, a slight, middle-aged man, very aristocratic in appearance and gifted with a certain shrewd sense. She took with him precisely the tone that Aline had taken with herself and which in Aline she had found so disconcertingly indelicate. She even borrowed several of Aline's phrases.

The result was that on the Monday afternoon when at last M. de La Tour d'Azyr's returning berline drove up to the chateau, he was met by M. le Comte de Sautron who desired a word with him even before he changed.

"Gervais, you're a fool," was the excellent opening made by M. le Comte.

"Charles, you give me no news," answered M. le Marquis. "Of what particular folly do you take the trouble to complain?"

He flung himself wearily upon a sofa, and his long graceful body sprawling there he looked up at his friend with a tired smile on that nobly handsome pale face that seemed to defy the onslaught of age.

"Of your last. This Binet girl."

"That! Pooh! An incident; hardly a folly."

"A folly—at such a time," Sautron insisted. The Marquis looked a question. The Count answered it. "Aline," said he, pregnantly. "She knows. How she knows I can't tell you, but she knows, and she is deeply offended."

The smile perished on the Marquis' face. He gathered himself up.

"Offended?" said he, and his voice was anxious.

"But yes. You know what she is. You know the ideals she has formed. It wounds her that at such a time—whilst you are here for the purpose of wooing her—you should at the same time be pursuing this affair with that chit of a Binet girl."

"How do you know?" asked La Tour d'Azyr.

"She has confided in her aunt. And the poor child seems to have some reason. She says she will not tolerate that you should come to kiss her hand with lips that are still contaminated from... Oh, you understand. You appreciate the impression of such a thing upon a pure, sensitive girl such as Aline. She said—I had better tell you—that the next time you kiss her hand, she will call for water and wash it in your presence."

The Marquis' face flamed scarlet. He rose. Knowing his violent, intolerant spirit, M. de Sautron was prepared for an outburst. But no outburst came. The

Marquis turned away from him, and paced slowly to the window, his head bowed, his hands behind his back. Halted there he spoke, without turning, his voice was at once scornful and wistful.

"You are right, Charles, I am a fool—a wicked fool! I have just enough sense left to perceive it. It is the way I have lived, I suppose. I have never known the need to deny myself anything I wanted." Then suddenly he swung round, and the outburst came. "But, my God, I want Aline as I have never wanted anything yet! I think I should kill myself in rage if through my folly I should have lost her." He struck his brow with his hand. "I am a beast!" he said. "I should have known that if that sweet saint got word of these petty devilries of mine she would despise me; and I tell you, Charles, I'd go through fire to regain her respect."

"I hope it is to be regained on easier terms," said Charles; and then to ease the situation which began to irk him by its solemnity, he made a feeble joke. "It is merely asked of you that you refrain from going through certain fires that are not accounted by mademoiselle of too purifying a nature."

"As to that Binet girl, it is finished—finished," said the Marquis.

"I congratulate you. When did you make that decision?"

"This moment. I would to God I had made it twenty-four hours ago. As it is—" he shrugged—"why, twenty-four hours of her have been enough for me as they would have been for any man—a mercenary, self-seeking little baggage with the soul of a trull. Bah!" He shuddered in disgust of himself and her.

"Ah! That makes it easier for you," said M. de Sautron, cynically.

"Don't say it, Charles. It is not so. Had you been less of a fool, you would have warned me sooner."

"I may prove to have warned you soon enough if you'll profit by the warning."

"There is no penance I will not do. I will prostrate myself at her feet. I will abase myself before her. I will make confession in the proper spirit of contrition, and Heaven helping me, I'll keep to my purpose of amendment for her sweet sake." He was tragically in earnest.

To M. de Sautron, who had never seen him other than self-contained, supercilious, and mocking, this was an amazing revelation. He shrank from it almost; it gave him the feeling of prying, of peeping through a keyhole. He slapped his friend's shoulder.

"My dear Gervais, here is a magnificently romantic mood. Enough said. Keep to it, and I promise you that all will presently be well. I will be your ambassador, and you shall have no cause to complain."

"But may I not go to her myself?"

"If you are wise you will at once efface yourself. Write to her if you will—make your act of contrition by letter. I will explain why you have gone without seeing her. I will tell her that you did so upon my advice, and I will do it tactfully. I am a good diplomat, Gervais. Trust me."

M. le Marquis raised his head, and showed a face that pain was searing. He held out his hand. "Very well, Charles. Serve me in this, and count me your friend in all things."

CHAPTER XI. THE FRACAS AT THE THEATRE FEYDAU

Leaving his host to act as his plenipotentiary with Mademoiselle de Kercadiou, and to explain to her that it was his profound contrition that compelled him to depart without taking formal leave of her, the Marquis rolled away from Sautron in a cloud of gloom. Twenty-four hours with La Binet had been more than enough for a man of his fastidious and discerning taste. He looked back upon the episode with nausea—the inevitable psychological reaction—marvelling at himself that until yesterday he should have found her so desirable, and cursing himself that for the sake of that ephemeral and worthless gratification he should seriously have imperilled his chances of winning Mademoiselle de Kercadiou to wife. There is, after all, nothing very extraordinary in his frame of mind, so that I need not elaborate it further. It resulted from the conflict between the beast and the angel that go to make up the composition of every man.

The Chevalier de Chabrillane—who in reality occupied towards the Marquis a position akin to that of gentleman-in-waiting—sat opposite to him in the enormous travelling berline. A small folding table had been erected between them, and the Chevalier suggested piquet. But M. le Marquis was in no humour for cards. His thoughts absorbed him. As they were rattling over the cobbles of Nantes' streets, he remembered a promise to La Binet to witness her performance that night in "The Faithless Lover." And now he was running away from her. The thought was repugnant to him on two scores. He was breaking his pledged word, and he was acting like a coward. And there was more than that. He had led the mercenary little strumpet—it was thus he thought of her at present, and with some justice—to expect favours from him in addition to the lavish awards which already he had made her. The baggage had almost sought to drive a bargain with him as to her future. He was to take her to Paris, put her into her own furniture—as the expression ran, and still runs—and under the shadow of his powerful protection see that the doors of the great theatres of the capital should be opened to her talents. He had not—he was thankful to reflect—exactly committed himself. But neither had he definitely refused her. It became necessary now to come to an understanding, since he was compelled to choose between his trivial passion for her—a passion quenched already—and his deep, almost spiritual devotion to Mademoiselle de Kercadiou.

His honour, he considered, demanded of him that he should at once deliver himself from a false position. La Binet would make a scene, of course; but he knew the proper specific to apply to hysteria of that nature. Money, after all, has its uses.

He pulled the cord. The carriage rolled to a standstill; a footman appeared at the door.

"To the Theatre Feydau," said he.

The footman vanished and the berline rolled on. M. de Chabrillane laughed cynically.

"I'll trouble you not to be amused," snapped the Marquis. "You don't understand." Thereafter he explained himself. It was a rare condescension in him. But, then, he could not bear to be misunderstood in such a matter. Chabrillane grew serious in reflection of the Marquis' extreme seriousness.

"Why not write?" he suggested. "Myself, I confess that I should find it easier."

Nothing could better have revealed M. le Marquis' state of mind than his answer.

"Letters are liable both to miscarriage and to misconstruction. Two risks I will not run. If she did not answer, I should never know which had been incurred. And I shall have no peace of mind until I know that I have set a term to this affair. The berline can wait while we are at the theatre. We will go on afterwards. We will travel all night if necessary."

"Peste!" said M. de Chabrillane with a grimace. But that was all.

The great travelling carriage drew up at the lighted portals of the Feydau, and M. le Marquis stepped out. He entered the theatre with Chabrillane, all unconsciously to deliver himself into the hands of Andre-Louis.

Andre-Louis was in a state of exasperation produced by Climene's long absence from Nantes in the company of M. le Marquis, and fed by the unspeakable complacency with which M. Binet regarded that event of quite unmistakable import.

However much he might affect the frame of mind of the stoics, and seek to judge with a complete detachment, in the heart and soul of him Andre-Louis was tormented and revolted. It was not Climene he blamed. He had been mistaken in her. She was just a poor weak vessel driven helplessly by the first breath, however foul, that promised her advancement. She suffered from the plague of greed; and he congratulated himself upon having discovered it before making her his wife. He felt for her now nothing but a deal of pity and some contempt. The pity was begotten of the love she had lately inspired in him. It might be likened to the dregs of love, all that remained after the potent wine of it had been drained off. His anger he reserved for her father and her seducer.

The thoughts that were stirring in him on that Monday morning, when it was discovered that Climene had not yet returned from her excursion of the previous day in the coach of M. le Marquis, were already wicked enough without the spurring they received from the distraught Leandre.

Hitherto the attitude of each of these men towards the other had been one of mutual contempt. The phenomenon has frequently been observed in like cases. Now, what appeared to be a common misfortune brought them into a sort of alliance. So, at least, it seemed to Leandre when he went in quest of Andre-Louis, who with apparent unconcern was smoking a pipe upon the quay immediately facing the inn.

"Name of a pig!" said Leandre. "How can you take your ease and smoke at such a time?"

Scaramouche surveyed the sky. "I do not find it too cold," said he. "The sun is shining. I am very well here."

"Do I talk of the weather?" Leandre was very excited.

"Of what, then?"

"Of Climene, of course."

"Oh! The lady has ceased to interest me," he lied.

Leandre stood squarely in front of him, a handsome figure handsomely dressed in these days, his hair well powdered, his stockings of silk. His face was pale, his large eyes looked larger than usual.

"Ceased to interest you? Are you not to marry her?"

Andre-Louis expelled a cloud of smoke. "You cannot wish to be offensive. Yet you almost suggest that I live on other men's leavings."

"My God!" said Leandre, overcome, and he stared awhile. Then he burst out afresh. "Are you quite heartless? Are you always Scaramouche?"

"What do you expect me to do?" asked Andre-Louis, evincing surprise in his own turn, but faintly.

"I do not expect you to let her go without a struggle."

"But she has gone already." Andre-Louis pulled at his pipe a moment, what time Leandre clenched and unclenched his hands in impotent rage. "And to what purpose struggle against the inevitable? Did you struggle when I took her from you?"

"She was not mine to be taken from me. I but aspired, and you won the race. But even had it been otherwise where is the comparison? That was a thing in honour; this—this is hell."

His emotion moved Andre-Louis. He took Leandre's arm. "You're a good fellow, Leandre. I am glad I intervened to save you from your fate."

"Oh, you don't love her!" cried the other, passionately. "You never did. You don't know what it means to love, or you'd not talk like this. My God! if she had been my affianced wife and this had happened, I should have killed the man—killed him! Do you hear me? But you... Oh, you, you come out here and smoke, and take the air, and talk of her as another man's leavings. I wonder I didn't strike you for the word."

He tore his arm from the other's grip, and looked almost as if he would strike him now.

"You should have done it," said Andre-Louis. "It's in your part."

With an imprecation Leandre turned on his heel to go. Andre-Louis arrested his departure.

"A moment, my friend. Test me by yourself. Would you marry her now?"

"Would I?" The young man's eyes blazed with passion. "Would I? Let her say that she will marry me, and I am her slave."

"Slave is the right word—a slave in hell."

"It would never be hell to me where she was, whatever she had done. I love her, man, I am not like you. I love her, do you hear me?"

"I have known it for some time," said Andre-Louis. "Though I didn't suspect your attack of the disease to be quite so violent. Well, God knows I loved her, too, quite enough to share your thirst for killing. For myself, the blue blood of La Tour d'Azyr would hardly quench this thirst. I should like to add to it the dirty fluid that flows in the veins of the unspeakable Binet."

For a second his emotion had been out of hand, and he revealed to Leandre in the mordant tone of those last words something of the fires that burned under his icy exterior. The young man caught him by the hand.

"I knew you were acting," said he. "You feel—you feel as I do."

"Behold us, fellows in viciousness. I have betrayed myself, it seems. Well, and what now? Do you want to see this pretty Marquis torn limb from limb? I might afford you the spectacle."

"What?" Leandre stared, wondering was this another of Scaramouche's cynicisms.

"It isn't really difficult provided I have aid. I require only a little. Will you lend it me?"

"Anything you ask," Leandre exploded. "My life if you require it."

Andre-Louis took his arm again. "Let us walk," he said. "I will instruct you."

When they came back the company was already at dinner. Mademoiselle had not yet returned. Sullenness presided at the table. Columbine and Madame wore anxious expressions. The fact was that relations between Binet and his troupe were daily growing more strained.

Andre-Louis and Leandre went each to his accustomed place. Binet's little eyes followed them with a malicious gleam, his thick lips pouted into a crooked smile.

"You two are grown very friendly of a sudden," he mocked.

"You are a man of discernment, Binet," said Scaramouche, the cold loathing of his voice itself an insult. "Perhaps you discern the reason?"

"It is readily discerned."

"Regale the company with it!" he begged; and waited. "What? You hesitate? Is it possible that there are limits to your shamelessness?"

Binet reared his great head. "Do you want to quarrel with me, Scaramouche?" Thunder was rumbling in his deep voice.

"Quarrel? You want to laugh. A man doesn't quarrel with creatures like you. We all know the place held in the public esteem by complacent husbands. But, in God's name, what place is there at all for complacent fathers?"

Binet heaved himself up, a great towering mass of manhood. Violently he shook off the restraining hand of Pierrot who sat on his left.

"A thousand devils!" he roared; "if you take that tone with me, I'll break every bone in your filthy body."

"If you were to lay a finger on me, Binet, you would give me the only provocation I still need to kill you." Andre-Louis was as calm as ever, and therefore the more menacing. Alarm stirred the company. He protruded from his pocket the butt of a pistol—newly purchased. "I go armed, Binet. It is only fair to give you warning. Provoke me as you have suggested, and I'll kill you with no more compunction than I should kill a slug, which after all is the thing you most resemble—a slug, Binet; a fat, slimy body; foulness without soul and without intelligence. When I come to think of it I can't suffer to sit at table with you. It turns my stomach."

He pushed away his platter and got up. "I'll go and eat at the ordinary below stairs."

Thereupon up jumped Columbine.

"And I'll come with you, Scaramouche!" cried she.

It acted like a signal. Had the thing been concerted it couldn't have fallen out more uniformly. Binet, in fact, was persuaded of a conspiracy. For in the wake of Columbine went Leandre, in the wake of Leandre, Polichinelle and then all the rest together, until Binet found himself sitting alone at the head of an empty table in an empty room—a badly shaken man whose rage could afford him no support against the dread by which he was suddenly invaded.

He sat down to think things out, and he was still at that melancholy occupation when perhaps a half-hour later his daughter entered the room, returned at last from her excursion.

She looked pale, even a little scared—in reality excessively self-conscious now that the ordeal of facing all the company awaited her.

Seeing no one but her father in the room, she checked on the threshold.

"Where is everybody?" she asked, in a voice rendered natural by effort.

M. Binet reared his great head and turned upon her eyes that were blood-injected. He scowled, blew out his thick lips and made harsh noises in his throat. Yet he took stock of her, so graceful and comely and looking so completely the lady of fashion in her long fur-trimmed travelling coat of bottle green, her muff and her broad hat adorned by a sparkling Rhinestone buckle above her adorably coiffed brown hair. No need to fear the future whilst he owned such a daughter, let Scaramouche play what tricks he would.

He expressed, however, none of these comforting reflections.

"So you're back at last, little fool," he growled in greeting. "I was beginning to ask myself if we should perform this evening. It wouldn't greatly have surprised me if you had not returned in time. Indeed, since you have chosen to play the fine hand you held in your own way and scorning my advice, nothing can surprise me."

She crossed the room to the table, and leaning against it, looked down upon him almost disdainfully.

"I have nothing to regret," she said.

"So every fool says at first. Nor would you admit it if you had. You are like that. You go your own way in spite of advice from older heads. Death of my life, girl, what do you know of men?"

"I am not complaining," she reminded him.

"No, but you may be presently, when you discover that you would have done better to have been guided by your old father. So long as your Marquis languished for you, there was nothing you could not have done with the fool. So long as you let him have no more than your fingertips to kiss... ah, name of a name! that was the time to build your future. If you live to be a thousand you'll never have such a chance again, and you've squandered it, for what?"

Mademoiselle sat down.—"You're sordid," she said, with disgust.

"Sordid, am I?" His thick lips curled again. "I have had enough of the dregs of life, and so I should have thought have you. You held a hand on which to have won a fortune if you had played it as I bade you. Well, you've played it, and where's the fortune? We can whistle for that as a sailor whistles for wind. And, by Heaven, we'll need to whistle presently if the weather in the troupe continues as it's set in. That scoundrel Scaramouche has been at his ape's tricks with them. They've suddenly turned moral. They won't sit at table with me any more." He was spluttering between anger and sardonic mirth. "It was your friend Scaramouche set them the example of that. He threatened my life actually. Threatened my life! Called me... Oh, but what does that matter? What matters is that the next thing to happen to us will be that the Binet Troupe will discover it can manage without M. Binet and his daughter. This scoundrelly bastard I've befriended has little by little robbed me of everything. It's in his power to-day to rob me of my troupe, and the knave's ungrateful enough and vile enough to make use of his power.

"Let him," said mademoiselle contemptuously.

"Let him?" He was aghast. "And what's to become of us?"

"In no case will the Binet Troupe interest me much longer," said she. "I shall be going to Paris soon. There are better theatres there than the Feydau. There's Mlle. Montansier's theatre in the Palais Royal; there's the Ambigu Comique; there's the Comedie Francaise; there's even a possibility I may have a theatre of my own."

His eyes grew big for once. He stretched out a fat hand, and placed it on one of hers. She noticed that it trembled.

"Has he promised that? Has he promised?"

She looked at him with her head on one side, eyes sly and a queer little smile on her perfect lips.

"He did not refuse me when I asked it," she answered, with conviction that all was as she desired it.

"Bah!" He withdrew his hand, and heaved himself up. There was disgust on his face. "He did not refuse!" he mocked her; and then with passion: "Had you acted as I advised you, he would have consented to anything that you asked, and what is more he would have provided anything that you asked—anything that lay within his means, and they are inexhaustible. You have changed a certainty into a possibility, and I hate possibilities God of God! I have lived on possibilities, and infernally near starved on them."

Had she known of the interview taking place at that moment at the Chateau de Sautron she would have laughed less confidently at her father's gloomy forebodings. But she was destined never to know, which indeed was the cruellest punishment of all. She was to attribute all the evil that of a sudden overwhelmed her, the shattering of all the future hopes she had founded upon the Marquis and the sudden disintegration of the Binet Troupe, to the wicked interference of that villain Scaramouche.

She had this much justification that possibly, without the warning from M. de Sautron, the Marquis would have found in the events of that evening at the Theatre Feydau a sufficient reason for ending an entanglement that was fraught with too much unpleasant excitement, whilst the breaking-up of the Binet Troupe was most certainly the result of Andre-Louis' work. But it was not a result that he intended or even foresaw.

So much was this the case that in the interval after the second act, he sought the dressing-room shared by Polichinelle and Rhodomont. Polichinelle was in the act of changing.

"I shouldn't trouble to change," he said. "The piece isn't likely to go beyond my opening scene of the next act with Leandre."

"What do you mean?"

"You'll see." He put a paper on Polichinelle's table amid the grease-paints. "Cast your eye over that. It's a sort of last will and testament in favour of the troupe. I was a lawyer once; the document is in order. I relinquish to all of you the share produced by my partnership in the company."

"But you don't mean that you are leaving us?" cried Polichinelle in alarm, whilst Rhodomont's sudden stare asked the same question.

Scaramouche's shrug was eloquent. Polichinelle ran on gloomily: "Of course it was to have been foreseen. But why should you be the one to go? It is you who have made us; and it is you who are the real head and brains of the troupe; it is you who have raised it into a real theatrical company. If any one must go, let it be Binet—Binet and his infernal daughter. Or if you go, name of a name! we all go with you!"

"Aye," added Rhodomont, "we've had enough of that fat scoundrel."

"I had thought of it, of course," said Andre-Louis. "It was not vanity, for once; it was trust in your friendship. After to-night we may consider it again, if I survive."

"If you survive?" both cried.

Polichinelle got up. "Now, what madness have you in mind?" he asked.

"For one thing I think I am indulging Leandre; for another I am pursuing an old quarrel."

The three knocks sounded as he spoke.

"There, I must go. Keep that paper, Polichinelle. After all, it may not be necessary."

He was gone. Rhodomont stared at Polichinelle. Polichinelle stared at Rhodomont.

"What the devil is he thinking of?" quoth the latter.

"That is most readily ascertained by going to see," replied Polichinelle. He completed changing in haste, and despite what Scaramouche had said; and then followed with Rhodomont.

As they approached the wings a roar of applause met them coming from the audience. It was applause and something else; applause on an unusual note. As it faded away they heard the voice of Scaramouche ringing clear as a bell:

"And so you see, my dear M. Leandre, that when you speak of the Third Estate, it is necessary to be more explicit. What precisely is the Third Estate?"

"Nothing," said Leandre.

There was a gasp from the audience, audible in the wings, and then swiftly followed Scaramouche's next question:

"True. Alas! But what should it be?"

"Everything," said Leandre.

The audience roared its acclamations, the more violent because of the unexpectedness of that reply.

"True again," said Scaramouche. "And what is more, that is what it will be; that is what it already is. Do you doubt it?"

"I hope it," said the schooled Leandre.

"You may believe it," said Scaramouche, and again the acclamations rolled into thunder.

Polichinelle and Rhodomont exchanged glances: indeed, the former winked, not without mirth.

"Sacred name!" growled a voice behind them. "Is the scoundrel at his political tricks again?"

They turned to confront M. Binet. Moving with that noiseless tread of his, he had come up unheard behind them, and there he stood now in his scarlet suit of Pantaloon under a trailing bedgown, his little eyes glaring from either side of his false nose. But their attention was held by the voice of Scaramouche. He had stepped to the front of the stage.

"He doubts it," he was telling the audience. "But then this M. Leandre is himself akin to those who worship the worm-eaten idol of Privilege, and so he is a little afraid to believe a truth that is becoming apparent to all the world. Shall I convince him? Shall I tell him how a company of noblemen backed by their servants under arms—six hundred men in all—sought to dictate to the Third Estate of

Rennes a few short weeks ago? Must I remind him of the martial front shown on that occasion by the Third Estate, and how they swept the streets clean of that rabble of nobles—cette canaille noble..."

Applause interrupted him. The phrase had struck home and caught. Those who had writhed under that infamous designation from their betters leapt at this turning of it against the nobles themselves.

"But let me tell you of their leader—le pins noble de cette canaille, ou bien le plus canaille de ces nobles! You know him that one. He fears many things, but the voice of truth he fears most. With such as him the eloquent truth eloquently spoken is a thing instantly to be silenced. So he marshalled his peers and their valetailles, and led them out to slaughter these miserable bourgeois who dared to raise a voice. But these same miserable bourgeois did not choose to be slaughtered in the streets of Rennes. It occurred to them that since the nobles decreed that blood should flow, it might as well be the blood of the nobles. They marshalled themselves too—this noble rabble against the rabble of nobles—and they marshalled themselves so well that they drove M. de La Tour d'Azyr and his warlike following from the field with broken heads and shattered delusions. They sought shelter at the hands of the Cordeliers; and the shavelings gave them sanctuary in their convent—those who survived, among whom was their proud leader, M. de La Tour d'Azyr. You have heard of this valiant Marquis, this great lord of life and death?"

The pit was in an uproar a moment. It quieted again as Scaramouche continued:

"Oh, it was a fine spectacle to see this mighty hunter scuttling to cover like a hare, going to earth in the Cordelier Convent. Rennes has not seen him since. Rennes would like to see him again. But if he is valorous, he is also discreet. And where do you think he has taken refuge, this great nobleman who wanted to see the streets of Rennes washed in the blood of its citizens, this man who would have butchered old and young of the contemptible canaille to silence the voice of reason and of liberty that presumes to ring through France to-day? Where do you think he hides himself? Why, here in Nantes."

Again there was uproar.

"What do you say? Impossible? Why, my friends, at this moment he is here in this theatre—skulking up there in that box. He is too shy to show himself—oh, a very modest gentleman. But there he is behind the curtains. Will you not show yourself to your friends, M. de La Tour d'Azyr, Monsieur le Marquis who considers eloquence so very dangerous a gift? See, they would like a word with you; they do not believe me when I tell them that you are here."

Now, whatever he may have been, and whatever the views held on the subject by Andre-Louis, M. de La Tour d'Azyr was certainly not a coward. To say that he was hiding in Nantes was not true. He came and went there openly and unabashed. It happened, however, that the Nantais were ignorant until this moment of his presence among them. But then he would have disdained to have informed them of it just as he would have disdained to have concealed it from them.

Challenged thus, however, and despite the ominous manner in which the bourgeois element in the audience had responded to Scaramouche's appeal to its passions, despite the attempts made by Chabrillane to restrain him, the Marquis swept aside the curtain at the side of the box, and suddenly showed himself, pale but self-contained and scornful as he surveyed first the daring Scaramouche and then those others who at sight of him had given tongue to their hostility.

Hoots and yells assailed him, fists were shaken at him, canes were brandished menacingly.

"Assassin! Scoundrel! Coward! Traitor!"

But he braved the storm, smiling upon them his ineffable contempt. He was waiting for the noise to cease; waiting to address them in his turn. But he waited in vain, as he very soon perceived.

The contempt he did not trouble to dissemble served but to goad them on.

In the pit pandemonium was already raging. Blows were being freely exchanged; there were scuffling groups, and here and there swords were being drawn, but fortunately the press was too dense to permit of their being used effectively. Those who had women with them and the timid by nature were making haste to leave a house that looked like becoming a cockpit, where chairs were being smashed to provide weapons, and parts of chandeliers were already being used as missiles.

One of these hurled by the hand of a gentleman in one of the boxes narrowly missed Scaramouche where he stood, looking down in a sort of grim triumph upon the havoc which his words had wrought. Knowing of what inflammable material the audience was composed, he had deliberately flung down amongst them the lighted torch of discord, to produce this conflagration.

He saw men falling quickly into groups representative of one side or the other of this great quarrel that already was beginning to agitate the whole of France. Their rallying cries were ringing through the theatre.

"Down with the canaille!" from some.

"Down with the privileged!" from others.

And then above the general din one cry rang out sharply and insistently:

"To the box! Death to the butcher of Rennes! Death to La Tour d'Azyr who makes war upon the people!"

There was a rush for one of the doors of the pit that opened upon the staircase leading to the boxes.

And now, whilst battle and confusion spread with the speed of fire, overflowing from the theatre into the street itself, La Tour d'Azyr's box, which had become the main object of the attack of the bourgeoisie, had also become the rallying ground for such gentlemen as were present in the theatre and for those who, without being men of birth themselves, were nevertheless attached to the party of the nobles.

La Tour d'Azyr had quitted the front of the box to meet those who came to join him. And now in the pit one group of infuriated gentlemen, in attempting to reach the stage across the empty orchestra, so that they might deal with the audacious comedian who was responsible for this explosion, found themselves opposed and held back by another group composed of men to whose feelings Andre-Louis had given expression.

Perceiving this, and remembering the chandelier, he turned to Leandre, who had remained beside him.

"I think it is time to be going," said he.

Leandre, looking ghastly under his paint, appalled by the storm which exceeded by far anything that his unimaginative brain could have conjectured, gurgled an inarticulate agreement. But it looked as if already they were too late, for in that moment they were assailed from behind.

M. Binet had succeeded at last in breaking past Polichinelle and Rhodomont, who in view of his murderous rage had been endeavouring to restrain him. Half a dozen gentlemen, habitues of the green-room, had come round to the stage to disembowel the knave who had created this riot, and it was they who had flung aside those two comedians who hung upon Binet. After him they came now, their swords out; but after them again came Polichinelle, Rhodomont, Harlequin, Pierrot, Pasquariel, and Basque the artist, armed with such implements as they could hastily snatch up, and intent upon saving the man with whom they sympathized in spite of all, and in whom now all their hopes were centred.

Well ahead rolled Binet, moving faster than any had ever seen him move, and swinging the long cane from which Pantaloon is inseparable.

"Infamous scoundrel!" he roared. "You have ruined me! But, name of a name, you shall pay!"

Andre-Louis turned to face him. "You confuse cause with effect," said he. But he got no farther... Binet's cane, viciously driven, descended and broke upon his shoulder. Had he not moved swiftly aside as the blow fell it must have taken him across the head, and possibly stunned him. As he moved, he dropped his hand to his pocket, and swift upon the cracking of Binet's breaking cane came the crack of the pistol with which Andre-Louis replied.

"You had your warning, you filthy pander!" he cried. And on the word he shot him through the body.

Binet went down screaming, whilst the fierce Polichinelle, fiercer than ever in that moment of fierce reality, spoke quickly into Andre-Louis' ear:

"Fool! So much was not necessary! Away with you now, or you'll leave your skin here! Away with you!"

Andre-Louis thought it good advice, and took it. The gentlemen who had followed Binet in that punitive rush upon the stage, partly held in check by the improvised weapons of the players, partly intimidated by the second pistol that Scaramouche presented, let him go. He gained the wings, and here found himself faced by a couple of sergeants of the watch, part of the police that was already invading the theatre with a view to restoring order. The sight of them reminded him unpleasantly of how he must stand towards the law for this night's work, and more particularly for that bullet lodged somewhere in Binet's obese body. He flourished his pistol.

"Make way, or I'll burn your brains!" he threatened them, and intimidated, themselves without firearms, they fell back and let him pass. He slipped by the door of the green-room, where the ladies of the company had shut themselves in until the storm should be over, and so gained the street behind the theatre. It was deserted. Down this he went at a run, intent on reaching the inn for clothes and money, since it was impossible that he should take the road in the garb of Scaramouche.

BOOK III: THE SWORD

CHAPTER I. TRANSITION

"You may agree," wrote Andre-Louis from Paris to Le Chapelier, in a letter which survives, "that it is to be regretted I should definitely have discarded the livery of Scaramouche, since clearly there could be no livery fitter for my wear. It seems to be my part always to stir up strife and then to slip away before I am caught in the crash of the warring elements I have aroused. It is a humiliating reflection. I seek consolation in the reminder of Epictetus (do you ever read Epictetus?) that we are but actors in a play of such a part as it may please the Director to assign us. It does not, however, console me to have been cast for a part so contemptible, to find myself excelling ever in the art of running away. But if I am not brave, at least I am prudent; so that where I lack one virtue I may lay claim to possessing another almost to excess. On a previous occasion they wanted to hang me for sedition. Should I have stayed to be hanged? This time they may want to hang me for several things, including murder; for I do not know whether that scoundrel Binet be alive or dead from the dose of lead I pumped into his fat paunch. Nor can I say that I very greatly care. If I have a hope at all in the matter it is that he is dead—and damned. But I am really indifferent. My own concerns are troubling me enough. I have all but spent the little money that I contrived to conceal about me before I fled from Nantes on that dreadful night; and both of the only two professions of which I can claim to know anything—the law and the stage—are closed to me, since I cannot find employment in either without revealing myself as a fellow who is urgently wanted by the hangman. As things are it is very possible that I may die of hunger, especially considering the present price of victuals in this ravenous city. Again I have recourse to Epictetus for comfort. 'It is better,' he says, 'to die of hunger having lived without grief and fear, than to live with a troubled spirit amid abundance.' I seem likely to perish in the estate that he accounts so enviable. That it does not seem exactly enviable to me merely proves that as a Stoic I am not a success."

There is also another letter of his written at about the same time to the Marquis de La Tour d'Azyr—a letter since published by M. Emile Quersac in his "Undercurrents of the Revolution in Brittany," unearthed by him from the archives of Rennes, to which it had been consigned by M. de Lesdiguieres, who had received it for justiciary purposes from the Marquis.

"The Paris newspapers," he writes in this, "which have reported in considerable detail the fracas at the Theatre Feydau and disclosed the true identity of the Scaramouche who provoked it, inform me also that you have escaped the fate I had intended for you when I raised that storm of public opinion and public indignation. I would not have you take satisfaction in the thought that I regret your escape. I do not. I rejoice in it. To deal justice by death has this disadvantage that the victim has no knowledge that justice has overtaken him. Had you died, had you been torn limb from limb that night, I should now repine in the thought of your eternal and untroubled slumber. Not in euthanasia, but in torment of mind should the guilty atone. You see, I am not sure that hell hereafter is a certainty, whilst I am quite sure that it can be a certainty in this life; and I desire you to continue to live yet awhile that you may taste something of its bitterness.

"You murdered Philippe de Vilmorin because you feared what you described as his very dangerous gift of eloquence, I took an oath that day that your evil deed should be fruitless; that I would render it so; that the voice you had done murder to stifle should in spite of that ring like a trumpet through the land. That was my conception of revenge. Do you realize how I have been fulfilling it, how I shall continue to fulfil it as occasion offers? In the speech with which I fired the people of Rennes on the very morrow of that deed, did you not hear the voice of Philippe de Vilmorin uttering the ideas that were his with a fire and a passion greater than he could have commanded because Nemesis lent me her inflaming aid? In the voice of Omnes Omnibus at Nantes my voice again—demanding the petition that sounded the knell of your hopes of coercing the Third Estate, did you not hear again the voice of Philippe de Vilmorin? Did you not reflect that it was the mind of the man you had murdered, resurrected in me his surviving friend, which made necessary your futile attempt under arms last January, wherein your order, finally beaten, was driven to seek sanctuary in the Cordelier Convent? And that night when from the stage of the Feydau you were denounced to the people, did you not hear yet again, in the voice of Scaramouche, the voice of Philippe de Vilmorin, using that dangerous gift of eloquence which you so foolishly imagined you could silence with a sword-thrust? It is becoming a persecution—is it not?—this voice from the grave that insists upon making itself heard, that will not rest until you have been cast into the pit. You will be regretting by now that you did not kill me too, as I invited you on that occasion. I can picture to myself the bitterness of this regret, and I contemplate it with satisfaction. Regret of neglected opportunity is the worst hell that a living soul can inhabit, particularly such a soul as yours. It is because of this that I am glad to know that you survived the riot at the Feydau, although at the time it was no part of my intention that you should. Because of this I am content that you should live to enrage and suffer in the shadow of your evil deed, knowing at last—since you had not hitherto the wit to discern it for yourself—that the voice of Philippe de Vilmorin will follow you to denounce you ever more loudly, ever more insistently, until having lived in dread you shall go down in blood under the just rage which your victim's dangerous gift of eloquence is kindling against you."

I find it odd that he should have omitted from this letter all mention of Mlle. Binet, and I am disposed to account it at least a partial insincerity that he should have assigned entirely to his self-imposed mission, and not at all to his lacerated feelings in the matter of Climene, the action which he had taken at the Feydau.

Those two letters, both written in April of that year 1789, had for only immediate effect to increase the activity with which Andre-Louis Moreau was being sought.

Le Chapelier would have found him so as to lend him assistance, to urge upon him once again that he should take up a political career. The electors of Nantes would have found him—at least, they would have found Omnes Omnibus, of whose identity with himself they were still in ignorance—on each of the several occasions when a vacancy occurred in their body. And the Marquis de La Tour d'Azyr and M. de Lesdiguieres would have found him that they might send him to the gallows.

With a purpose no less vindictive was he being sought by M. Binet, now unhappily recovered from his wound to face completest ruin. His troupe had deserted him during his illness, and reconstituted under the direction of Polichinelle it was now striving with tolerable success to continue upon the lines which Andre-Louis had laid down. M. le Marquis, prevented by the riot from expressing in person to Mlle. Binet his purpose of making an end of their relations, had been constrained to write to her to that effect from Azyr a few days later. He tempered the blow by enclosing in discharge of all liabilities a bill on the Caisse d'Escompte for a hundred louis. Nevertheless it almost crushed the unfortunate and it enabled her father when he recovered to enrage her by pointing out that she owed this turn of events to the premature surrender she had made in defiance of his sound worldly advice. Father and daughter alike were left to assign the Marquis' desertion, naturally enough, to the riot at the Feydau. They laid that with the rest to the account of Scaramouche, and were forced in bitterness to admit that the scoundrel had taken a superlative revenge. Climene may even have come to consider that it would have paid her better to have run a straight course with Scaramouche and by marrying him to have trusted to his undoubted talents to place her on the summit to which her ambition urged her, and to which it was now futile for her to aspire. If so, that reflection must have been her sufficient punishment. For, as Andre-Louis so truly says, there is no worse hell than that provided by the regrets for wasted opportunities.

Meanwhile the fiercely sought Andre-Louis Moreau had gone to earth completely for the present. And the brisk police of Paris, urged on by the King's Lieutenant from Rennes, hunted for him in vain. Yet he might have been found in a house in the Rue du Hasard within a stone's throw of the Palais Royal, whither purest chance had conducted him.

That which in his letter to Le Chapelier he represents as a contingency of the near future was, in fact, the case in which already he found himself. He was destitute. His money was exhausted, including that procured by the sale of such articles of adornment as were not of absolute necessity.

So desperate was his case that strolling one gusty April morning down the Rue du Hasard with his nose in the wind looking for what might be picked up, he stopped to read a notice outside the door of a house on the left side of the street as you approach the Rue de Richelieu. There was no reason why he should have gone down the Rue du Hasard. Perhaps its name attracted him, as appropriate to his case.

The notice written in a big round hand announced that a young man of good address with some knowledge of swordsmanship was required by M. Bertrand des Amis on the second floor. Above this notice was a black oblong board, and on this a shield, which in vulgar terms may be described as red charged with two swords crossed and four fleurs de lys, one in each angle of the saltire. Under the shield, in letters of gold, ran the legend:

BERTRAND DES AMIS
Maitre en fait d'Armes des Academies du Roi

Andre-Louis stood considering. He could claim, he thought, to possess the qualifications demanded. He was certainly young and he believed of tolerable address, whilst the fencing-lessons he had received in Nantes had given him at least an elementary knowledge of swordsmanship. The notice looked as if it had been pinned there some days ago, suggesting that applicants for the post were not very numerous. In that case perhaps M. Bertrand des Amis would not be too exigent. And anyway, Andre-Louis had not eaten for four-and-twenty hours, and whilst the employment here offered—the precise nature of which he was yet to ascertain—did not appear to be such as Andre-Louis would deliberately have chosen, he was in no case now to be fastidious.

Then, too, he liked the name of Bertrand des Amis. It felicitously combined suggestions of chivalry and friendliness. Also the man's profession being of a kind that is flavoured with romance it was possible that M. Bertrand des Amis would not ask too many questions.

In the end he climbed to the second floor. On the landing he paused outside a door, on which was written "Academy of M. Bertrand des Amis." He pushed this open, and found himself in a sparsely furnished, untenanted antechamber. From a room beyond, the door of which was closed, came the stamping of feet, the click and slither of steel upon steel, and dominating these sounds a vibrant sonorous voice speaking a language that was certainly French; but such French as is never heard outside a fencing-school.

"Coulez! Mais, coulez donc!.... So! Now the flanconnade—en carte.... And here is the riposte.... Let us begin again. Come! The ward of fierce.... Make the coupe, and then the quinte par dessus les armes.... O, mais allongez! Allongez! Allez au fond!" the voice cried in expostulation. "Come, that was better." The blades ceased.

"Remember: the hand in pronation, the elbow not too far out. That will do for to-day. On Wednesday we shall see you tirer au mur. It is more deliberate. Speed will follow when the mechanism of the movements is more assured."

Another voice murmured in answer. The steps moved aside. The lesson was at an end. Andre-Louis tapped on the door.

It was opened by a tall, slender, gracefully proportioned man of perhaps forty. Black silk breeches and stockings ending in light shoes clothed him from the waist down. Above he was encased to the chin in a closely fitting plastron of leather, His face was aquiline and swarthy, his eyes full and dark, his mouth firm and his clubbed hair was of a lustrous black with here and there a thread of silver showing.

In the crook of his left arm he carried a fencing-mask, a thing of leather with a wire grating to protect the eyes. His keen glance played over Andre-Louis from head to foot.

"Monsieur?" he inquired, politely.

It was clear that he mistook Andre-Louis' quality, which is not surprising, for despite his sadly reduced fortunes, his exterior was irreproachable, and M. des Amis was not to guess that he carried upon his back the whole of his possessions.

"You have a notice below, monsieur," he said, and from the swift lighting of the fencing-master's eyes he saw that he had been correct in his assumption that applicants for the position had not been jostling one another on his threshold. And then that flash of satisfaction was followed by a look of surprise.

"You are come in regard to that?"

Andre-Louis shrugged and half smiled. "One must live," said he.

"But come in. Sit down there. I shall be at your.... I shall be free to attend to you in a moment."

Andre-Louis took a seat on the bench ranged against one of the whitewashed walls. The room was long and low, its floor entirely bare. Plain wooden forms such as that which he occupied were placed here and there against the wall. These last were plastered with fencing trophies, masks, crossed foils, stuffed plastrons, and a variety of swords, daggers, and targets, belonging to a variety of ages and countries. There was also a portrait of an obese, big-nosed gentleman in an elaborately curled wig, wearing the blue ribbon of the Saint Esprit, in whom Andre-Louis recognized the King. And there was a framed parchment—M. des Amis' certificate from the King's Academy. A bookcase occupied one corner, and near this, facing the last of the four windows that abundantly lighted the long room, there was a small writing-table and an armchair. A plump and beautifully dressed young gentleman stood by this table in the act of resuming coat and wig. M. des Amis sauntered over to him—moving, thought Andre-Louis, with extraordinary grace and elasticity—and stood in talk with him whilst also assisting him to complete his toilet.

At last the young gentleman took his departure, mopping himself with a fine kerchief that left a trail of perfume on the air. M. des Amis closed the door, and turned to the applicant, who rose at once.

"Where have you studied?" quoth the fencing-master abruptly.

"Studied?" Andre-Louis was taken aback by the question. "Oh, at Louis Le Grand."

M. des Amis frowned, looking up sharply as if to see whether his applicant was taking the liberty of amusing himself.

"In Heaven's name! I am not asking you where you did your humanities, but in what academy you studied fencing."

"Oh—fencing!" It had hardly ever occurred to Andre-Louis that the sword ranked seriously as a study. "I never studied it very much. I had some lessons in... in the country once."

The master's eyebrows went up. "But then?" he cried. "Why trouble to come up two flights of stairs?" He was impatient.

"The notice does not demand a high degree of proficiency. If I am not proficient enough, yet knowing the rudiments I can easily improve. I learn most things readily," Andre-Louis commended himself. "For the rest: I possess the other qualifications. I am young, as you observe: and I leave you to judge whether I am wrong in assuming that my address is good. I am by profession a man of the robe, though I realize that the motto here is cedat toga armis."

M. des Amis smiled approvingly. Undoubtedly the young man had a good address, and a certain readiness of wit, it would appear. He ran a critical eye over his physical points. "What is your name?" he asked.

Andre-Louis hesitated a moment. "Andre-Louis," he said.

The dark, keen eyes conned him more searchingly.

"Well? Andre-Louis what?"

"Just Andre-Louis. Louis is my surname."

"Oh! An odd surname. You come from Brittany by your accent. Why did you leave it?"

"To save my skin," he answered, without reflecting. And then made haste to cover the blunder. "I have an enemy," he explained.

M. des Amis frowned, stroking his square chin. "You ran away?"

"You may say so.

"A coward, eh?"

"I don't think so." And then he lied romantically. Surely a man who lived by the sword should have a weakness for the romantic. "You see, my enemy is a swordsman of great strength—the best blade in the province, if not the best blade in France. That is his repute. I thought I would come to Paris to learn something of the art, and then go back and kill him. That, to be frank, is why your notice attracted me. You see, I have not the means to take lessons otherwise. I thought to find work here in the law. But I have failed. There are too many lawyers in Paris as it is, and whilst waiting I have consumed the little money that I had, so that... so that, enfin, your notice seemed to me something to which a special providence had directed me."

M. des Amis gripped him by the shoulders, and looked into his face.

"Is this true, my friend?" he asked.

"Not a word of it," said Andre-Louis, wrecking his chances on an irresistible impulse to say the unexpected. But he didn't wreck them. M. des Amis burst into laughter; and having laughed his fill, confessed himself charmed by his applicant's fundamental honesty.

"Take off your coat," he said, "and let us see what you can do. Nature, at least, designed you for a swordsman. You are light, active, and supple, with a good length of arm, and you seem intelligent. I may make something of you, teach you enough for my purpose, which is that you should give the elements of the art to new pupils before I take them in hand to finish them. Let us try. Take that mask and foil, and come over here."

He led him to the end of the room, where the bare floor was scored with lines of chalk to guide the beginner in the management of his feet.

At the end of a ten minutes' bout, M. des Amis offered him the situation, and explained it. In addition to imparting the rudiments of the art to beginners, he was to brush out the fencing-room every morning, keep the foils furbished, assist the gentlemen who came for lessons to dress and undress, and make himself generally useful. His wages for the present were to be forty livres a month, and he might sleep in an alcove behind the fencing-room if he had no other lodging.

The position, you see, had its humiliations. But, if Andre-Louis would hope to dine, he must begin by eating his pride as an hors d'oeuvre.

"And so," he said, controlling a grimace, "the robe yields not only to the sword, but to the broom as well. Be it so. I stay."

It is characteristic of him that, having made that choice, he should have thrown himself into the work with enthusiasm. It was ever his way to do whatever he did with all the resources of his mind and energies of his body. When he was not instructing very young gentlemen in the elements of the art, showing them the elaborate and intricate salute—which with a few days' hard practice he had mastered to perfection—and the eight guards, he was himself hard at work on those same guards, exercising eye, wrist, and knees.

Perceiving his enthusiasm, and seeing the obvious possibilities it opened out of turning him into a really effective assistant, M. des Amis presently took him more seriously in hand.

"Your application and zeal, my friend, are deserving of more than forty livres a month," the master informed him at the end of a week. "For the present, however, I will make up what else I consider due to you by imparting to you secrets of this noble art. Your future depends upon how you profit by your exceptional good fortune in receiving instruction from me."

Thereafter every morning before the opening of the academy, the master would fence for half an hour with his new assistant. Under this really excellent tuition Andre-Louis improved at a rate that both astounded and flattered M. des Amis. He would have been less flattered and more astounded had he known that at least half the secret of Andre-Louis' amazing progress lay in the fact that he was devouring the contents of the master's library, which was made up of a dozen or so treatises on fencing by such great masters as La Bessiere, Danet, and the syndic of the King's Academy, Augustin Rousseau. To M. des Amis, whose swordsmanship was all based on practice and not at all on theory, who was indeed no theorist or student in any sense, that little library was merely a suitable adjunct to a fencing-academy, a proper piece of decorative furniture. The books themselves meant nothing to him in any other sense. He had not the type of mind that could have read them with profit nor could he understand that another should do so. Andre-Louis, on the contrary, a man with the habit of study, with the acquired faculty of learning from books, read those works with enormous profit, kept their precepts in mind, critically set off those of one master against those of another, and made for himself a choice which he proceeded to put into practice.

At the end of a month it suddenly dawned upon M. des Amis that his assistant had developed into a fencer of very considerable force, a man in a bout with whom it became necessary to exert himself if he were to escape defeat.

"I said from the first," he told him one day, "that Nature designed you for a swordsman. See how justified I was, and see also how well I have known how to mould the material with which Nature has equipped you."

"To the master be the glory," said Andre-Louis.

His relations with M. des Amis had meanwhile become of the friendliest, and he was now beginning to receive from him other pupils than mere beginners. In fact Andre-Louis was becoming an assistant in a much fuller sense of the word. M. des Amis, a chivalrous, open-handed fellow, far from taking advantage of what he had guessed to be the young man's difficulties, rewarded his zeal by increasing his wages to four louis a month.

From the earnest and thoughtful study of the theories of others, it followed now—as not uncommonly happens—that Andre-Louis came to develop theories of his own. He lay one June morning on his little truckle bed in the alcove behind the academy, considering a passage that he had read last night in Danet on double and triple feints. It had seemed to him when reading it that Danet had stopped short on the threshold of a great discovery in the art of fencing. Essentially a theorist, Andre-Louis perceived the theory suggested, which Danet himself in suggesting it had not perceived. He lay now on his back, surveying the cracks in the ceiling and considering this matter further with the lucidity that early morning often brings to an acute intelligence. You are to remember that for close upon two months now the sword had been Andre-Louis' daily exercise and almost hourly thought. Protracted concentration upon the subject was giving him an extraordinary penetration of vision. Swordsmanship as he learnt and taught and saw it daily practised consisted of a series of attacks and parries, a series of disengages from one line into another. But always a limited series. A half-dozen disengages on either side was, strictly speaking, usually as far as any engagement went. Then one recommenced. But even so, these disengages were fortuitous. What if from first to last they should be calculated?

That was part of the thought—one of the two legs on which his theory was to stand; the other was: what would happen if one so elaborated Danet's ideas on the triple feint as to merge them into a series of actual calculated disengages to culminate at the fourth or fifth or even sixth disengage? That is to say, if one were to make a series of attacks inviting ripostes again to be countered, each of which was not intended to go home, but simply to play the opponent's blade into a line that must open him ultimately, and as predetermined, for an irresistible lunge. Each counter of the opponent's would have to be preconsidered in this widening of his guard, a widening so gradual that he should himself be unconscious of it, and throughout intent upon getting home his own point on one of those counters.

Andre-Louis had been in his time a chess-player of some force, and at chess he had excelled by virtue of his capacity for thinking ahead. That virtue applied to fencing should all but revolutionize the art. It was so applied already, of course, but only in an elementary and very limited fashion, in mere feints, single, double, or triple. But even the triple feint should be a clumsy device compared with this method upon which he theorized.

He considered further, and the conviction grew that he held the key of a discovery. He was impatient to put his theory to the test.

That morning he was given a pupil of some force, against whom usually he was hard put to it to defend himself. Coming on guard, he made up his mind to hit him on the fourth disengage, predetermining the four passes that should lead up to it. They engaged in tierce, and Andre-Louis led the attack by a beat and a straightening of the arm. Came the demi-contre he expected, which he promptly countered by a thrust in quinte; this being countered again, he reentered still lower, and being again correctly parried, as he had calculated, he lunged swirling his point into carte, and got home full upon his opponent's breast. The ease of it surprised him.

They began again. This time he resolved to go in on the fifth disengage, and in on that he went with the same ease. Then, complicating the matter further, he decided to try the sixth, and worked out in his mind the combination of the five preliminary engages. Yet again he succeeded as easily as before.

The young gentleman opposed to him laughed with just a tinge of mortification in his voice.

"I am all to pieces this morning," he said.

"You are not of your usual force," Andre-Louis politely agreed. And then greatly daring, always to test that theory of his to the uttermost: "So much so," he added, "that I could almost be sure of hitting you as and when I declare."

The capable pupil looked at him with a half-sneer. "Ah, that, no," said he.

"Let us try. On the fourth disengage I shall touch you. Allons! En garde!"

And as he promised, so it happened.

The young gentleman who, hitherto, had held no great opinion of Andre-Louis' swordsmanship, accounting him well enough for purposes of practice when the master was otherwise engaged, opened wide his eyes. In a burst of mingled generosity and intoxication, Andre-Louis was almost for disclosing his method—a method which a little later was to become a commonplace of the fencing-rooms. Betimes he checked himself. To reveal his secret would be to destroy the prestige that must accrue to him from exercising it.

At noon, the academy being empty, M. des Amis called Andre-Louis to one of the occasional lessons which he still received. And for the first time in all his experience with Andre-Louis, M. des Amis received from him a full hit in the course of the first bout. He laughed, well pleased, like the generous fellow he was.

"Aha! You are improving very fast, my friend." He still laughed, though not so well pleased, when he was hit in the second bout. After that he settled down to fight in earnest with the result that Andre-Louis was hit three times in succession. The speed and accuracy of the fencing-master when fully exerting himself disconcerted Andre-Louis' theory, which for want of being exercised in practice still demanded too much consideration.

But that his theory was sound he accounted fully established, and with that, for the moment, he was content. It remained only to perfect by practice the application of it. To this he now devoted himself with the passionate enthusiasm of the discoverer. He confined himself to a half-dozen combinations, which he practised assiduously until each had become almost automatic. And he proved their infallibility upon the best among M. des Amis' pupils.

Finally, a week or so after that last bout of his with des Amis, the master called him once more to practice.

Hit again in the first bout, the master set himself to exert all his skill against his assistant. But to-day it availed him nothing before Andre-Louis' impetuous attacks.

After the third hit, M. des Amis stepped back and pulled off his mask.

"What's this?" he asked. He was pale, and his dark brows were contracted in a frown. Not in years had he been so wounded in his self-love. "Have you been taught a secret botte?"

He had always boasted that he knew too much about the sword to believe any nonsense about secret bottes; but this performance of Andre-Louis' had shaken his convictions on that score.

"No," said Andre-Louis. "I have been working hard; and it happens that I fence with my brains."

"So I perceive. Well, well, I think I have taught you enough, my friend. I have no intention of having an assistant who is superior to myself."

"Little danger of that," said Andre-Louis, smiling pleasantly. "You have been fencing hard all morning, and you are tired, whilst I, having done little, am entirely fresh. That is the only secret of my momentary success."

His tact and the fundamental good-nature of M. des Amis prevented the matter from going farther along the road it was almost threatening to take. And thereafter, when they fenced together, Andre-Louis, who continued daily to perfect his theory into an almost infallible system, saw to it that M. des Amis always scored against him at least two hits for every one of his own. So much he would grant to discretion, but no more. He desired that M. des Amis should be conscious of his strength, without, however, discovering so much of its real extent as would have excited in him an unnecessary degree of jealousy.

And so well did he contrive that whilst he became ever of greater assistance to the master—for his style and general fencing, too, had materially improved—he was also a source of pride to him as the most brilliant of all the pupils that had ever passed through his academy. Never did Andre-Louis disillusion him by revealing the fact that his skill was due far more to M. des Amis' library and his own mother wit than to any lessons received.

CHAPTER II. QUOS DEUS VULT PERDERE

Once again, precisely as he had done when he joined the Binet troupe, did Andre-Louis now settle down whole-heartedly to the new profession into which necessity had driven him, and in which he found effective concealment from those who might seek him to his hurt. This profession might—although in fact it did not—have brought him to consider himself at last as a man of action. He had not, however, on that account ceased to be a man of thought, and the events of the spring and summer months of that year 1789 in Paris provided him with abundant matter for reflection. He read there in the raw what is perhaps the most amazing page in the history of human development, and in the end he was forced to the conclusion that all his early preconceptions had been at fault, and that it was such exalted, passionate enthusiasts as Vilmorin who had been right.

I suspect him of actually taking pride in the fact that he had been mistaken, complacently attributing his error to the circumstance that he had been, himself, of too sane and logical a mind to gauge the depths of human insanity now revealed.

He watched the growth of hunger, the increasing poverty and distress of Paris during that spring, and assigned it to its proper cause, together with the patience with which the people bore it. The world of France was in a state of hushed, of paralyzed expectancy, waiting for the States General to assemble and for centuries of tyranny to end. And because of this expectancy, industry had come to a standstill, the stream of trade had dwindled to a trickle. Men would not buy or sell until they clearly saw the means by which the genius of the Swiss banker, M. Necker, was to deliver them from this morass. And because of this paralysis of affairs the men of the people were thrown out of work and left to starve with their wives and children.

Looking on, Andre-Louis smiled grimly. So far he was right. The sufferers were ever the proletariat. The men who sought to make this revolution, the electors—here in Paris as elsewhere—were men of substance, notable bourgeois, wealthy traders. And whilst these, despising the canaille, and envying the privileged, talked largely of equality—by which they meant an ascending equality that should confuse themselves with the gentry—the proletariat perished of want in its kennels.

CHAPTER II. QUOS DEUS VULT PERDERE

At last with the month of May the deputies arrived, Andre-Louis' friend Le Chapelier prominent amongst them, and the States General were inaugurated at Versailles. It was then that affairs began to become interesting, then that Andre-Louis began seriously to doubt the soundness of the views he had held hitherto.

When the royal proclamation had gone forth decreeing that the deputies of the Third Estate should number twice as many as those of the other two orders together, Andre-Louis had believed that the preponderance of votes thus assured to the Third Estate rendered inevitable the reforms to which they had pledged them selves.

But he had reckoned without the power of the privileged orders over the proud Austrian queen, and her power over the obese, phlegmatic, irresolute monarch. That the privileged orders should deliver battle in defence of their privileges, Andre-Louis could understand. Man being what he is, and labouring under his curse of acquisitiveness, will never willingly surrender possessions, whether they be justly or unjustly held. But what surprised Andre-Louis was the unutterable crassness of the methods by which the Privileged ranged themselves for battle. They opposed brute force to reason and philosophy, and battalions of foreign mercenaries to ideas. As if ideas were to be impaled on bayonets!

The war between the Privileged and the Court on one side, and the Assembly and the People on the other had begun.

The Third Estate contained itself, and waited; waited with the patience of nature; waited a month whilst, with the paralysis of business now complete, the skeleton hand of famine took a firmer grip of Paris; waited a month whilst Privilege gradually assembled an army in Versailles to intimidate it—an army of fifteen regiments, nine of which were Swiss and German—and mounted a park of artillery before the building in which the deputies sat. But the deputies refused to be intimidated; they refused to see the guns and foreign uniforms; they refused to see anything but the purpose for which they had been brought together by royal proclamation.

Thus until the 10th of June, when that great thinker and metaphysician, the Abbe Sieyes, gave the signal: "It is time," said he, "to cut the cable."

And the opportunity came soon, at the very beginning of July. M. du Chatelet, a harsh, haughty disciplinarian, proposed to transfer the eleven French Guards placed under arrest from the military gaol of the Abbaye to the filthy prison of Bicetre reserved for thieves and felons of the lowest order. Word of that intention going forth, the people at last met violence with violence. A mob four thousand strong broke into the Abbaye, and delivered thence not only the eleven guardsmen, but all the other prisoners, with the exception of one whom they discovered to be a thief, and whom they put back again.

That was open revolt at last, and with revolt Privilege knew how to deal. It would strangle this mutinous Paris in the iron grip of the foreign regiments. Measures were quickly concerted. Old Marechal de Broglie, a veteran of the Seven Years' War, imbued with a soldier's contempt for civilians, conceiving that the sight of a uniform would be enough to restore peace and order, took control with

Besenval as his second-in-command. The foreign regiments were stationed in the environs of Paris, regiments whose very names were an irritation to the Parisians, regiments of Reisbach, of Diesbach, of Nassau, Esterhazy, and Roehmer. Reenforcements of Swiss were sent to the Bastille between whose crenels already since the 30th of June were to be seen the menacing mouths of loaded cannon.

On the 10th of July the electors once more addressed the King to request the withdrawal of the troops. They were answered next day that the troops served the purpose of defending the liberties of the Assembly! And on the next day to that, which was a Sunday, the philanthropist Dr. Guillotin—whose philanthropic engine of painless death was before very long to find a deal of work—came from the Assembly, of which he was a member, to assure the electors of Paris that all was well, appearances notwithstanding, since Necker was more firmly in the saddle than ever. He did not know that at the very moment in which he was speaking so confidently, the oft-dismissed and oft-recalled M. Necker had just been dismissed yet again by the hostile cabal about the Queen. Privilege wanted conclusive measures, and conclusive measures it would have—conclusive to itself.

And at the same time yet another philanthropist, also a doctor, one Jean-Paul Mara, of Italian extraction—better known as Marat, the gallicized form of name he adopted—a man of letters, too, who had spent some years in England, and there published several works on sociology, was writing:

"Have a care! Consider what would be the fatal effect of a seditious movement. If you should have the misfortune to give way to that, you will be treated as people in revolt, and blood will flow."

Andre-Louis was in the gardens of the Palais Royal, that place of shops and puppet-shows, of circus and cafes, of gaming houses and brothels, that universal rendezvous, on that Sunday morning when the news of Necker's dismissal spread, carrying with it dismay and fury. Into Necker's dismissal the people read the triumph of the party hostile to themselves. It sounded the knell of all hope of redress of their wrongs.

He beheld a slight young man with a pock-marked face, redeemed from utter ugliness by a pair of magnificent eyes, leap to a table outside the Café de Foy, a drawn sword in his hand, crying, "To arms!" And then upon the silence of astonishment that cry imposed, this young man poured a flood of inflammatory eloquence, delivered in a voice marred at moments by a stutter. He told the people that the Germans on the Champ de Mars would enter Paris that night to butcher the inhabitants. "Let us mount a cockade!" he cried, and tore a leaf from a tree to serve his purpose—the green cockade of hope.

Enthusiasm swept the crowd, a motley crowd made up of men and women of every class, from vagabond to nobleman, from harlot to lady of fashion. Trees were despoiled of their leaves, and the green cockade was flaunted from almost every head.

"You are caught between two fires," the incendiary's stuttering voice raved on. "Between the Germans on the Champ de Mars and the Swiss in the Bastille. To arms, then! To arms!"

Excitement boiled up and over. From a neighbouring waxworks show came the bust of Necker, and presently a bust of that comedian the Duke of Orleans, who had a party and who was as ready as any other of the budding opportunists of those days to take advantage of the moment for his own aggrandizement. The bust of Necker was draped with crepe.

Andre-Louis looked on, and grew afraid. Marat's pamphlet had impressed him. It had expressed what himself he had expressed more than half a year ago to the mob at Rennes. This crowd, he felt must be restrained. That hot-headed, irresponsible stutterer would have the town in a blaze by night unless something were done. The young man, a causeless advocate of the Palais named Camille Desmoulins, later to become famous, leapt down from his table still waving his sword, still shouting, "To arms! Follow me!" Andre-Louis advanced to occupy the improvised rostrum, which the stutterer had just vacated, to make an effort at counteracting that inflammatory performance. He thrust through the crowd, and came suddenly face to face with a tall man beautifully dressed, whose handsome countenance was sternly set, whose great sombre eyes mouldered as if with suppressed anger.

Thus face to face, each looking into the eyes of the other, they stood for a long moment, the jostling crowd streaming past them, unheeded. Then Andre-Louis laughed.

"That fellow, too, has a very dangerous gift of eloquence, M. le Marquis," he said. "In fact there are a number of such in France to-day. They grow from the soil, which you and yours have irrigated with the blood of the martyrs of liberty. Soon it may be your blood instead. The soil is parched, and thirsty for it."

"Gallows-bird!" he was answered. "The police will do your affair for you. I shall tell the Lieutenant-General that you are to be found in Paris."

"My God, man!" cried Andre-Louis, "will you never get sense? Will you talk like that of Lieutenant-Generals when Paris itself is likely to tumble about your ears or take fire under your feet? Raise your voice, M. le Marquis. Denounce me here, to these. You will make a hero of me in such an hour as this. Or shall I denounce you? I think I will. I think it is high time you received your wages. Hi! You others, listen to me! Let me present you to..."

A rush of men hurtled against him, swept him along with them, do what he would, separating him from M. de La Tour d'Azyr, so oddly met. He sought to breast that human torrent; the Marquis, caught in an eddy of it, remained where he had been, and Andre-Louis' last glimpse of him was of a man smiling with tight lips, an ugly smile.

Meanwhile the gardens were emptying in the wake of that stuttering firebrand who had mounted the green cockade. The human torrent poured out into the Rue de Richelieu, and Andre-Louis perforce must suffer himself to be borne along by it, at least as far as the Rue du Hasard. There he sidled out of it, and having no wish to be crushed to death or to take further part in the madness that was afoot, he slipped down the street, and so got home to the deserted academy. For there were no pupils to-day, and even M. des Amis, like Andre-Louis, had gone out to seek for news of what was happening at Versailles.

This was no normal state of things at the Academy of Bertrand des Amis. Whatever else in Paris might have been at a standstill lately, the fencing academy had flourished as never hitherto. Usually both the master and his assistant were busy from morning until dusk, and already Andre-Louis was being paid now by the lessons that he gave, the master allowing him one half of the fee in each case for himself, an arrangement which the assistant found profitable. On Sundays the academy made half-holiday; but on this Sunday such had been the state of suspense and ferment in the city that no one having appeared by eleven o'clock both des Amis and Andre-Louis had gone out. Little they thought as they lightly took leave of each other—they were very good friends by now—that they were never to meet again in this world.

Bloodshed there was that day in Paris. On the Place Vendome a detachment of dragoons awaited the crowd out of which Andre-Louis had slipped. The horsemen swept down upon the mob, dispersed it, smashed the waxen effigy of M. Necker, and killed one man on the spot—an unfortunate French Guard who stood his ground. That was a beginning. As a consequence Besenval brought up his Swiss from the Champ de Mars and marshalled them in battle order on the Champs Elysees with four pieces of artillery. His dragoons he stationed in the Place Louis XV. That evening an enormous crowd, streaming along the Champs Elysees and the Tuileries Gardens, considered with eyes of alarm that warlike preparation. Some insults were cast upon those foreign mercenaries and some stones were flung. Besenval, losing his head, or acting under orders, sent for his dragoons and ordered them to disperse the crowd, But that crowd was too dense to be dispersed in this fashion; so dense that it was impossible for the horsemen to move without crushing some one. There were several crushed, and as a consequence when the dragoons, led by the Prince de Lambesc, advanced into the Tuileries Gardens, the outraged crowd met them with a fusillade of stones and bottles. Lambesc gave the order to fire. There was a stampede. Pouring forth from the Tuileries through the city went those indignant people with their story of German cavalry trampling upon women and children, and uttering now in grimmest earnest the call to arms, raised at noon by Desmoulins in the Palais Royal.

The victims were taken up and borne thence, and amongst them was Bertrand des Amis, himself—like all who lived by the sword—an ardent upholder of the noblesse, trampled to death under hooves of foreign horsemen launched by the noblesse and led by a nobleman.

To Andre-Louis, waiting that evening on the second floor of No. 13 Rue du Hasard for the return of his friend and master, four men of the people brought that broken body of one of the earliest victims of the Revolution that was now launched in earnest.

CHAPTER III. PRESIDENT LE CHAPELIER

The ferment of Paris which, during the two following days, resembled an armed camp rather than a city, delayed the burial of Bertrand des Amis until the Wednesday of that eventful week. Amid events that were shaking a nation to its foundations the death of a fencing-master passed almost unnoticed even among his pupils, most of whom did not come to the academy during the two days that his body lay there. Some few, however, did come, and these conveyed the news to others, with the result that the master was followed to Pere Lachaise by a score of young men at the head of whom as chief mourner walked Andre-Louis.

There were no relatives to be advised so far as Andre-Louis was aware, although within a week of M. des Amis' death a sister turned up from Passy to claim his heritage. This was considerable, for the master had prospered and saved money, most of which was invested in the Compagnie des Eaux and the National Debt. Andre-Louis consigned her to the lawyers, and saw her no more.

The death of des Amis left him with so profound a sense of loneliness and desolation that he had no thought or care for the sudden access of fortune which it automatically procured him. To the master's sister might fall such wealth as he had amassed, but Andre-Louis succeeded to the mine itself from which that wealth had been extracted, the fencing-school in which by now he was himself so well established as an instructor that its numerous pupils looked to him to carry it forward successfully as its chief. And never was there a season in which fencing-academies knew such prosperity as in these troubled days, when every man was sharpening his sword and schooling himself in the uses of it.

It was not until a couple of weeks later that Andre-Louis realized what had really happened to him, and he found himself at the same time an exhausted man, for during that fortnight he had been doing the work of two. If he had not hit upon the happy expedient of pairing-off his more advanced pupils to fence with each other, himself standing by to criticize, correct and otherwise instruct, he must have found the task utterly beyond his strength. Even so, it was necessary for him to fence some six hours daily, and every day he brought arrears of lassitude from yesterday until he was in danger of succumbing under the increasing burden of fatigue. In the end he took an assistant to deal with beginners, who gave the hardest work. He found him readily enough by good fortune in one of his own pupils named Le Duc. As the summer advanced, and the concourse of pupils steadily increased, it became necessary for him to take yet another assistant—an able young instructor named Galoche—and another room on the floor above.

They were strenuous days for Andre-Louis, more strenuous than he had ever known, even when he had been at work to build up the Binet Company; but it follows that they were days of extraordinary prosperity. He comments regretfully upon the fact that Bertrand des Amis should have died by ill-chance on the very eve of so profitable a vogue of sword-play.

The arms of the Academie du Roi, to which Andre-Louis had no title, still continued to be displayed outside his door. He had overcome the difficulty in a manner worthy of Scaramouche. He left the escutcheon and the legend "Academie de Bertrand des Amis, Maitre en fait d'Armes des Academies du Roi," appending to it the further legend: "Conducted by Andre-Louis."

With little time now in which to go abroad it was from his pupils and the newspapers—of which a flood had risen in Paris with the establishment of the freedom of the Press—that he learnt of the revolutionary processes around him, following upon, as a measure of anticlimax, the fall of the Bastille. That had happened whilst M. des Amis lay dead, on the day before they buried him, and was indeed the chief reason of the delay in his burial. It was an event that had its inspiration in that ill-considered charge of Prince Lambesc in which the fencing-master had been killed.

The outraged people had besieged the electors in the Hotel de Ville, demanding arms with which to defend their lives from these foreign murderers hired by despotism. And in the end the electors had consented to give them arms, or, rather—for arms it had none to give—to permit them to arm themselves. Also it had given them a cockade, of red and blue, the colours of Paris. Because these colours were also those of the liveries of the Duke of Orleans, white was added to them—the white of the ancient standard of France—and thus was the tricolour born. Further, a permanent committee of electors was appointed to watch over public order.

Thus empowered the people went to work with such good effect that within thirty-six hours sixty thousand pikes had been forged. At nine o'clock on Tuesday morning thirty thousand men were before the Invalides. By eleven o'clock they had ravished it of its store of arms amounting to some thirty thousand muskets, whilst others had seized the Arsenal and possessed themselves of powder.

Thus they prepared to resist the attack that from seven points was to be launched that evening upon the city. But Paris did not wait for the attack. It took the initiative. Mad with enthusiasm it conceived the insane project of taking that terrible menacing fortress, the Bastille, and, what is more, it succeeded, as you know, before five o'clock that night, aided in the enterprise by the French Guards with cannon.

The news of it, borne to Versailles by Lambesc in flight with his dragoons before the vast armed force that had sprouted from the paving-stones of Paris, gave the Court pause. The people were in possession of the guns captured from the Bastille. They were erecting barricades in the streets, and mounting these guns upon them. The attack had been too long delayed. It must be abandoned since now it could lead only to fruitless slaughter that must further shake the already sorely shaken prestige of Royalty.

And so the Court, growing momentarily wise again under the spur of fear, preferred to temporize. Necker should be brought back yet once again, the three orders should sit united as the National Assembly demanded. It was the completest surrender of force to force, the only argument. The King went alone to inform the National Assembly of that eleventh-hour resolve, to the great comfort of its members, who viewed with pain and alarm the dreadful state of things in Paris. "No force but the force of reason and argument" was their watchword, and it was so to continue for two years yet, with a patience and fortitude in the face of ceaseless provocation to which insufficient justice has been done.

As the King was leaving the Assembly, a woman, embracing his knees, gave tongue to what might well be the question of all France:

"Ah, sire, are you really sincere? Are you sure they will not make you change your mind?"

Yet no such question was asked when a couple of days later the King, alone and unguarded save by the representatives of the Nation, came to Paris to complete the peacemaking, the surrender of Privilege. The Court was filled with terror by the adventure. Were they not the "enemy," these mutinous Parisians? And should a King go thus among his enemies? If he shared some of that fear, as the gloom of him might lead us to suppose, he must have found it idle. What if two hundred thousand men under arms—men without uniforms and with the most extraordinary motley of weapons ever seen—awaited him? They awaited him as a guard of honour.

Mayor Bailly at the barrier presented him with the keys of the city. "These are the same keys that were presented to Henri IV. He had reconquered his people. Now the people have reconquered their King."

At the Hotel de Ville Mayor Bailly offered him the new cockade, the tricoloured symbol of constitutional France, and when he had given his royal confirmation to the formation of the Garde Bourgeoise and to the appointments of Bailly and Lafayette, he departed again for Versailles amid the shouts of "Vive le Roi!" from his loyal people.

And now you see Privilege—before the cannon's mouth, as it were—submitting at last, where had they submitted sooner they might have saved oceans of blood—chiefly their own. They come, nobles and clergy, to join the National Assembly, to labour with it upon this constitution that is to regenerate France. But the reunion is a mockery—as much a mockery as that of the Archbishop of Paris singing the Te Deum for the fall of the Bastille—most grotesque and incredible of all these grotesque and incredible events. All that has happened to the National Assembly is that it has introduced five or six hundred enemies to hamper and hinder its deliberations.

But all this is an oft-told tale, to be read in detail elsewhere. I give you here just so much of it as I have found in Andre-Louis' own writings, almost in his own words, reflecting the changes that were operated in his mind. Silent now, he came fully to believe in those things in which he had not believed when earlier he had preached them.

Meanwhile together with the change in his fortune had come a change in his position towards the law, a change brought about by the other changes wrought around him. No longer need he hide himself. Who in these days would prefer against him the grotesque charge of sedition for what he had done in Brittany? What court would dare to send him to the gallows for having said in advance what all France was saying now? As for that other possible charge of murder, who should concern himself with the death of the miserable Binet killed by him—if, indeed, he had killed him, as he hoped—in self-defence.

And so one fine day in early August, Andre-Louis gave himself a holiday from the academy, which was now working smoothly under his assistants, hired a chaise and drove out to Versailles to the Café d'Amaury, which he knew for the meeting-place of the Club Breton, the seed from which was to spring that Society of the Friends of the Constitution better known as the Jacobins. He went to seek Le Chapelier, who had been one of the founders of the club, a man of great prominence now, president of the Assembly in this important season when it was deliberating upon the Declaration of the Rights of Man.

Le Chapelier's importance was reflected in the sudden servility of the shirt-sleeved, white-aproned waiter of whom Andre-Louis inquired for the representative.

M. Le Chapelier was above-stairs with friends. The waiter desired to serve the gentleman, but hesitated to break in upon the assembly in which M. le Depute found himself.

Andre-Louis gave him a piece of silver to encourage him to make the attempt. Then he sat down at a marble-topped table by the window looking out over the wide tree-encircled square. There, in that common-room of the café, deserted at this hour of mid-afternoon, the great man came to him. Less than a year ago he had yielded precedence to Andre-Louis in a matter of delicate leadership; to-day he stood on the heights, one of the great leaders of the Nation in travail, and Andre-Louis was deep down in the shadows of the general mass.

The thought was in the minds of both as they scanned each other, each noting in the other the marked change that a few months had wrought. In Le Chapelier, Andre-Louis observed certain heightened refinements of dress that went with certain subtler refinements of countenance. He was thinner than of old, his face was pale and there was a weariness in the eyes that considered his visitor through a gold-rimmed spy-glass. In Andre-Louis those jaded but quick-moving eyes of the Breton deputy noted changes even more marked. The almost constant swordmanship of these last months had given Andre-Louis a grace of movement, a poise, and a curious, indefinable air of dignity, of command. He seemed taller by virtue of this, and he was dressed with an elegance which if quiet was none the less rich. He wore a small silver-hilted sword, and wore it as if used to it, and his black hair that Le Chapelier had never seen other than fluttering lank about his bony cheeks was glossy now and gathered into a club. Almost he had the air of a petit-maitre.

In both, however, the changes were purely superficial, as each was soon to reveal to the other. Le Chapelier was ever the same direct and downright Breton, abrupt of manner and of speech. He stood smiling a moment in mingled surprise and pleasure; then opened wide his arms. They embraced under the awe-stricken gaze of the waiter, who at once effaced himself.

"Andre-Louis, my friend! Whence do you drop?"

"We drop from above. I come from below to survey at close quarters one who is on the heights."

"On the heights! But that you willed it so, it is yourself might now be standing in my place."

"I have a poor head for heights, and I find the atmosphere too rarefied. Indeed, you look none too well on it yourself, Isaac. You are pale."

"The Assembly was in session all last night. That is all. These damned Privileged multiply our difficulties. They will do so until we decree their abolition."

They sat down. "Abolition! You contemplate so much? Not that you surprise me. You have always been an extremist."

"I contemplate it that I may save them. I seek to abolish them officially, so as to save them from abolition of another kind at the hands of a people they exasperate."

"I see. And the King?"

"The King is the incarnation of the Nation. We shall deliver him together with the Nation from the bondage of Privilege. Our constitution will accomplish it. You agree?"

Andre-Louis shrugged. "Does it matter? I am a dreamer in politics, not a man of action. Until lately I have been very moderate; more moderate than you think. But now almost I am a republican. I have been watching, and I have perceived that this King is—just nothing, a puppet who dances according to the hand that pulls the string."

"This King, you say? What other king is possible? You are surely not of those who weave dreams about Orleans? He has a sort of party, a following largely recruited by the popular hatred of the Queen and the known fact that she hates him. There are some who have thought of making him regent, some even more; Robespierre is of the number."

"Who?" asked Andre-Louis, to whom the name was unknown.

"Robespierre—a preposterous little lawyer who represents Arras, a shabby, clumsy, timid dullard, who will make speeches through his nose to which nobody listens—an ultra-royalist whom the royalists and the Orleanists are using for their own ends. He has pertinacity, and he insists upon being heard. He may be listened to some day. But that he, or the others, will ever make anything of Orleans... pish! Orleans himself may desire it, but the man is a eunuch in crime; he would, but he can't. The phrase is Mirabeau's."

He broke off to demand Andre-Louis' news of himself.

"You did not treat me as a friend when you wrote to me," he complained. "You gave me no clue to your whereabouts; you represented yourself as on the verge of destitution and withheld from me the means to come to your assistance. I have been troubled in mind about you, Andre. Yet to judge by your appearance I might have spared myself that. You seem prosperous, assured. Tell me of it."

Andre-Louis told him frankly all that there was to tell. "Do you know that you are an amazement to me?" said the deputy. "From the robe to the buskin, and now from the buskin to the sword! What will be the end of you, I wonder?"

"The gallows, probably."

"Pish! Be serious. Why not the toga of the senator in senatorial France? It might be yours now if you had willed it so."

"The surest way to the gallows of all," laughed Andre-Louis.

At the moment Le Chapelier manifested impatience. I wonder did the phrase cross his mind that day four years later when himself he rode in the death-cart to the Greve.

"We are sixty-six Breton deputies in the Assembly. Should a vacancy occur, will you act as suppleant? A word from me together with the influence of your name in Rennes and Nantes, and the thing is done."

Andre-Louis laughed outright. "Do you know, Isaac, that I never meet you but you seek to thrust me into politics?"

"Because you have a gift for politics. You were born for politics."

"Ah, yes—Scaramouche in real life. I've played it on the stage. Let that suffice. Tell me, Isaac, what news of my old friend, La Tour d'Azyr?"

"He is here in Versailles, damn him—a thorn in the flesh of the Assembly. They've burnt his chateau at La Tour d'Azyr. Unfortunately he wasn't in it at the time. The flames haven't even singed his insolence. He dreams that when this philosophic aberration is at an end, there will be serfs to rebuild it for him."

"So there has been trouble in Brittany?" Andre-Louis had become suddenly grave, his thoughts swinging to Gavrillac.

"An abundance of it, and elsewhere too. Can you wonder? These delays at such a time, with famine in the land? Chateaux have been going up in smoke during the last fortnight. The peasants took their cue from the Parisians, and treated every castle as a Bastille. Order is being restored, there as here, and they are quieter now."

"What of Gavrillac? Do you know?"

"I believe all to be well. M. de Kercadiou was not a Marquis de La Tour d'Azyr. He was in sympathy with his people. It is not likely that they would injure Gavrillac. But don't you correspond with your godfather?"

"In the circumstances—no. What you tell me would make it now more difficult than ever, for he must account me one of those who helped to light the torch that has set fire to so much belonging to his class. Ascertain for me that all is well, and let me know."

"I will, at once."

At parting, when Andre-Louis was on the point of stepping into his cabriolet to return to Paris, he sought information on another matter.

"Do you happen to know if M. de La Tour d'Azyr has married?" he asked.

"I don't; which really means that he hasn't. One would have heard of it in the case of that exalted Privileged."

"To be sure." Andre-Louis spoke indifferently. "Au revoir, Isaac! You'll come and see me—13 Rue du Hasard. Come soon."

"As soon and as often as my duties will allow. They keep me chained here at present."

"Poor slave of duty with your gospel of liberty!"

"True! And because of that I will come. I have a duty to Brittany: to make Omnes Omnibus one of her representatives in the National Assembly."

"That is a duty you will oblige me by neglecting," laughed Andre-Louis, and drove away.

CHAPTER IV. AT MEUDON

Later in the week he received a visit from Le Chapelier just before noon.

"I have news for you, Andre. Your godfather is at Meudon. He arrived there two days ago. Had you heard?"

"But no. How should I hear? Why is he at Meudon?" He was conscious of a faint excitement, which he could hardly have explained.

"I don't know. There have been fresh disturbances in Brittany. It may be due to that."

"And so he has come for shelter to his brother?" asked Andre-Louis.

"To his brother's house, yes; but not to his brother. Where do you live at all, Andre? Do you never hear any of the news? Etienne de Gavrillac emigrated years ago. He was of the household of M. d'Artois, and he crossed the frontier with him. By now, no doubt, he is in Germany with him, conspiring against France. For that is what the emigres are doing. That Austrian woman at the Tuileries will end by destroying the monarchy."

"Yes, yes," said Andre-Louis impatiently. Politics interested him not at all this morning. "But about Gavrillac?"

"Why, haven't I told you that Gavrillac is at Meudon, installed in the house his brother has left? Dieu de Dieu! Don't I speak French or don't you understand the language? I believe that Rabouillet, his intendant, is in charge of Gavrillac. I have brought you the news the moment I received it. I thought you would probably wish to go out to Meudon."

"Of course. I will go at once—that is, as soon as I can. I can't to-day, nor yet to-morrow. I am too busy here." He waved a hand towards the inner room, whence proceeded the click-click of blades, the quick moving of feet, and the voice of the instructor, Le Duc.

"Well, well, that is your own affair. You are busy. I leave you now. Let us dine this evening at the Café de Foy. Kersain will be of the party."

"A moment!" Andre-Louis' voice arrested him on the threshold. "Is Mlle. de Kercadiou with her uncle?"

"How the devil should I know? Go and find out."

He was gone, and Andre-Louis stood there a moment deep in thought. Then he turned and went back to resume with his pupil, the Vicomte de Villeniort, the interrupted exposition of the demi-contre of Danet, illustrating with a small-sword the advantages to be derived from its adoption.

Thereafter he fenced with the Vicomte, who was perhaps the ablest of his pupils at the time, and all the while his thoughts were on the heights of Meudon, his mind casting up the lessons he had to give that afternoon and on the morrow, and wondering which of these he might postpone without deranging the academy. When having touched the Vicomte three times in succession, he paused and wrenched himself back to the present, it was to marvel at the precision to be gained by purely mechanical action. Without bestowing a thought upon what he was doing, his wrist and arm and knees had automatically performed their work, like the accurate fighting engine into which constant practice for a year and more had combined them.

Not until Sunday was Andre-Louis able to satisfy a wish which the impatience of the intervening days had converted into a yearning. Dressed with more than ordinary care, his head elegantly coiffed—by one of those hairdressers to the nobility of whom so many were being thrown out of employment by the stream of emigration which was now flowing freely—Andre-Louis mounted his hired carriage, and drove out to Meudon.

The house of the younger Kercadiou no more resembled that of the head of the family than did his person. A man of the Court, where his brother was essentially a man of the soil, an officer of the household of M. le Comte d'Artois, he had built for himself and his family an imposing villa on the heights of Meudon in a miniature park, conveniently situated for him midway between Versailles and Paris, and easily accessible from either. M. d'Artois—the royal tennis-player—had been amongst the very first to emigrate. Together with the Condes, the Contis, the Polignacs, and others of the Queen's intimate council, old Marshal de Broglie and the Prince de Lambesc, who realized that their very names had become odious to the people, he had quitted France immediately after the fall of the Bastille. He had gone to play tennis beyond the frontier—and there consummate the work of ruining the French monarchy upon which he and those others had been engaged in France. With him, amongst several members of his household went Etienne de Kercadiou, and with Etienne de Kercadiou went his family, a wife and four children. Thus it was that the Seigneur de Gavrillac, glad to escape from a province so peculiarly disturbed as that of Brittany—where the nobles had shown themselves the most intransigent of all France—had come to occupy in his brother's absence the courtier's handsome villa at Meudon.

That he was quite happy there is not to be supposed. A man of his almost Spartan habits, accustomed to plain fare and self-help, was a little uneasy in this sybaritic abode, with its soft carpets, profusion of gilding, and battalion of sleek, silent-footed servants—for Kercadiou the younger had left his entire household behind. Time, which at Gavrillac he had kept so fully employed in agrarian concerns, here hung heavily upon his hands. In self-defence he slept a great deal, and but for Aline, who made no attempt to conceal her delight at this proximity to Paris and the heart of things, it is possible that he would have beat a retreat almost at once from surroundings that sorted so ill with his habits. Later on, perhaps, he would accustom himself and grow resigned to this luxurious inactivity. In the meantime the novelty of it fretted him, and it was into the presence of a peevish and rather somnolent M. de Kercadiou that Andre-Louis was ushered in the early hours of the afternoon of that Sunday in June. He was unannounced, as had ever been the custom at Gavrillac. This because Benoit, M. de Kercadiou's old seneschal, had accompanied his seigneur upon this soft adventure, and was installed—to the ceaseless and but half-concealed hilarity of the impertinent valetaille that M. Etienne had left—as his maitre d'hotel here at Meudon.

Benoit had welcomed M. Andre with incoherencies of delight; almost had he gambolled about him like some faithful dog, whilst conducting him to the salon and the presence of the Lord of Gavrillac, who would—in the words of Benoit—be ravished to see M. Andre again.

"Monseigneur! Monseigneur!" he cried in a quavering voice, entering a pace or two in advance of the visitor. "It is M. Andre... M. Andre, your godson, who comes to kiss your hand. He is here... and so fine that you would hardly know him. Here he is, monseigneur! Is he not beautiful?"

And the old servant rubbed his hands in conviction of the delight that he believed he was conveying to his master.

Andre-Louis crossed the threshold of that great room, soft-carpeted to the foot, dazzling to the eye. It was immensely lofty, and its festooned ceiling was carried on fluted pillars with gilded capitals. The door by which he entered, and the windows that opened upon the garden, were of an enormous height—almost, indeed, the full height of the room itself. It was a room overwhelmingly gilded, with an abundance of ormolu encrustations on the furniture, in which it nowise differed from what was customary in the dwellings of people of birth and wealth. Never, indeed, was there a time in which so much gold was employed decoratively as in this age when coined gold was almost unprocurable, and paper money had been put into circulation to supply the lack. It was a saying of Andre-Louis' that if these people could only have been induced to put the paper on their walls and the gold into their pockets, the finances of the kingdom might soon have been in better case.

The Seigneur—furbished and beruffled to harmonize with his surroundings—had risen, startled by this exuberant invasion on the part of Benoit, who had been almost as forlorn as himself since their coming to Meudon.

"What is it? Eh?" His pale, short-sighted eyes peered at the visitor. "Andre!" said he, between surprise and sternness; and the colour deepened in his great pink face.

Benoit, with his back to his master, deliberately winked and grinned at Andre-Louis to encourage him not to be put off by any apparent hostility on the part of his godfather. That done, the intelligent old fellow discreetly effaced himself.

"What do you want here?" growled M. de Kercadiou.

"No more than to kiss your hand, as Benoit has told you, monsieur my godfather," said Andre-Louis submissively, bowing his sleek black head.

"You have contrived without kissing it for two years."

"Do not, monsieur, reproach me with my misfortune."

The little man stood very stiffly erect, his disproportionately large head thrown back, his pale prominent eyes very stern.

"Did you think to make your outrageous offence any better by vanishing in that heartless manner, by leaving us without knowledge of whether you were alive or dead?"

"At first it was dangerous dangerous to my life—to disclose my whereabouts. Then for a time I was in need, almost destitute, and my pride forbade me, after what I had done and the view you must take of it, to appeal to you for help. Later..."

"Destitute?" The Seigneur interrupted. For a moment his lip trembled. Then he steadied himself, and the frown deepened as he surveyed this very changed and elegant godson of his, noted the quiet richness of his apparel, the paste buckles and red heels to his shoes, the sword hilted in mother-o'-pearl and silver, and the carefully dressed hair that he had always seen hanging in wisps about his face. "At least you do not look destitute now," he sneered.

"I am not. I have prospered since. In that, monsieur, I differ from the ordinary prodigal, who returns only when he needs assistance. I return solely because I love you, monsieur—to tell you so. I have come at the very first moment after hearing of your presence here." He advanced. "Monsieur my godfather!" he said, and held out his hand.

But M. de Kercadiou remained unbending, wrapped in his cold dignity and resentment.

"Whatever tribulations you may have suffered or consider that you may have suffered, they are far less than your disgraceful conduct deserved, and I observe that they have nothing abated your impudence. You think that you have but to come here and say, 'Monsieur my godfather!' and everything is to be forgiven and forgotten. That is your error. You have committed too great a wrong; you have offended against everything by which I hold, and against myself personally, by your betrayal of my trust in you. You are one of those unspeakable scoundrels who are responsible for this revolution."

"Alas, monsieur, I see that you share the common delusion. These unspeakable scoundrels but demanded a constitution, as was promised them from the throne. They were not to know that the promise was insincere, or that its fulfilment would be baulked by the privileged orders. The men who have precipitated this revolution, monsieur, are the nobles and the prelates."

"You dare—and at such a time as this—stand there and tell me such abominable lies! You dare to say that the nobles have made the revolution, when scores of them, following the example of M. le Duc d'Aiguillon, have flung their privileges, even their title-deeds, into the lap of the people! Or perhaps you deny it?"

"Oh, no. Having wantonly set fire to their house, they now try to put it out by throwing water on it; and where they fail they put the entire blame on the flames."

"I see that you have come here to talk politics."

"Far from it. I have come, if possible, to explain myself. To understand is always to forgive. That is a great saying of Montaigne's. If I could make you understand..."

"You can't. You'll never make me understand how you came to render yourself so odiously notorious in Brittany."

"Ah, not odiously, monsieur!"

"Certainly, odiously—among those that matter. It is said even that you were Omnes Omnibus, though that I cannot, will not believe."

"Yet it is true."

M. de Kercadiou choked. "And you confess it? You dare to confess it?"

"What a man dares to do, he should dare to confess—unless he is a coward."

"Oh, and to be sure you were very brave, running away each time after you had done the mischief, turning comedian to hide yourself, doing more mischief as a comedian, provoking a riot in Nantes, and then running away again, to become God knows what—something dishonest by the affluent look of you. My God, man, I tell you that in these past two years I have hoped that you were dead, and you profoundly disappoint me that you are not!" He beat his hands together, and raised his shrill voice to call—"Benoit!" He strode away towards the fireplace, scarlet in the face, shaking with the passion into which he had worked himself. "Dead, I might have forgiven you, as one who had paid for his evil, and his folly. Living, I never can forgive you. You have gone too far. God alone knows where it will end.

"Benoit, the door. M. Andre-Louis Moreau to the door!" The tone argued an irrevocable determination. Pale and self-contained, but with a queer pain at his heart, Andre-Louis heard that dismissal, saw Benoit's white, scared face and shaking hands half-raised as if he were about to expostulate with his master. And then another voice, a crisp, boyish voice, cut in.

"Uncle!" it cried, a world of indignation and surprise in its pitch, and then: "Andre!" And this time a note almost of gladness, certainly of welcome, was blended with the surprise that still remained.

Both turned, half the room between them at the moment, and beheld Aline in one of the long, open windows, arrested there in the act of entering from the garden, Aline in a milk-maid bonnet of the latest mode, though without any of the tricolour embellishments that were so commonly to be seen upon them.

The thin lips of Andre's long mouth twisted into a queer smile. Into his mind had flashed the memory of their last parting. He saw himself again, standing burning with indignation upon the pavement of Nantes, looking after her carriage as it receded down the Avenue de Gigan.

She was coming towards him now with outstretched hands, a heightened colour in her cheeks, a smile of welcome on her lips. He bowed low and kissed her hand in silence.

Then with a glance and a gesture she dismissed Benoit, and in her imperious fashion constituted herself Andre's advocate against that harsh dismissal which she had overheard.

"Uncle," she said, leaving Andre and crossing to M. de Kercadiou, "you make me ashamed of you! To allow a feeling of peevishness to overwhelm all your affection for Andre!"

"I have no affection for him. I had once. He chose to extinguish it. He can go to the devil; and please observe that I don't permit you to interfere."

"But if he confesses that he has done wrong..."

"He confesses nothing of the kind. He comes here to argue with me about these infernal Rights of Man. He proclaims himself unrepentant. He announces himself with pride to have been, as all Brittany says, the scoundrel who hid himself under the sobriquet of Omnes Omnibus. Is that to be condoned?"

She turned to look at Andre across the wide space that now separated them.

"But is this really so? Don't you repent, Andre—now that you see all the harm that has come?"

It was a clear invitation to him, a pleading to him to say that he repented, to make his peace with his godfather. For a moment it almost moved him. Then, considering the subterfuge unworthy, he answered truthfully, though the pain he was suffering rang in his voice.

"To confess repentance," he said slowly, "would be to confess to a monstrous crime. Don't you see that? Oh, monsieur, have patience with me; let me explain myself a little. You say that I am in part responsible for something of all this that has happened. My exhortations of the people at Rennes and twice afterwards at Nantes are said to have had their share in what followed there. It may be so. It would be beyond my power positively to deny it. Revolution followed and bloodshed. More may yet come. To repent implies a recognition that I have done wrong. How shall I say that I have done wrong, and thus take a share of the responsibility for all that blood upon my soul? I will be quite frank with you to show you how far, indeed, I am from repentance. What I did, I actually did against all my convictions at the time. Because there was no justice in France to move against the murderer of Philippe de Vilmorin, I moved in the only way that I imagined could make the evil done recoil upon the hand that did it, and those other hands that had the power but not the spirit to punish. Since then I have come to see that I was wrong, and that Philippe de Vilmorin and those who thought with him were in the right.

"You must realize, monsieur, that it is with sincerest thankfulness that I find I have done nothing calling for repentance; that, on the contrary, when France is given the inestimable boon of a constitution, as will shortly happen, I may take pride in having played my part in bringing about the conditions that have made this possible."

There was a pause. M. de Kercadiou's face turned from pink to purple.

"You have quite finished?" he said harshly.

"If you have understood me, monsieur."

"Oh, I have understood you, and... and I beg that you will go."

Andre-Louis shrugged his shoulders and hung his head. He had come there so joyously, in such yearning, merely to receive a final dismissal. He looked at

Aline. Her face was pale and troubled; but her wit failed to show her how she could come to his assistance. His excessive honesty had burnt all his boats.

"Very well, monsieur. Yet this I would ask you to remember after I am gone. I have not come to you as one seeking assistance, as one driven to you by need. I am no returning prodigal, as I have said. I am one who, needing nothing, asking nothing, master of his own destinies, has come to you driven by affection only, urged by the love and gratitude he bears you and will continue to bear you."

"Ah, yes!" cried Aline, turning now to her uncle. Here at least was an argument in Andre's favour, thought she. "That is true. Surely that..."

Inarticulately he hissed her into silence, exasperated.

"Hereafter perhaps that will help you to think of me more kindly, monsieur."

"I see no occasion, sir, to think of you at all. Again, I beg that you will go."

Andre-Louis looked at Aline an instant, as if still hesitating.

She answered him by a glance at her furious uncle, a faint shrug, and a lift of the eyebrows, dejection the while in her countenance.

It was as if she said: "You see his mood. There is nothing to be done."

He bowed with that singular grace the fencing-room had given him and went out by the door.

"Oh, it is cruel!" cried Aline, in a stifled voice, her hands clenched, and she sprang to the window.

"Aline!" her uncle's voice arrested her. "Where are you going?"

"But we do not know where he is to be found."

"Who wants to find the scoundrel?"

"We may never see him again."

"That is most fervently to be desired."

Aline said "Ouf!" and went out by the window.

He called after her, imperiously commanding her return. But Aline—dutiful child—closed her ears lest she must disobey him, and sped light-footed across the lawn to the avenue there to intercept the departing Andre-Louis.

As he came forth wrapped in gloom, she stepped from the bordering trees into his path.

"Aline!" he cried, joyously almost.

"I did not want you to go like this. I couldn't let you," she explained herself. "I know him better than you do, and I know that his great soft heart will presently melt. He will be filled with regret. He will want to send for you, and he will not know where to send."

"You think that?"

"Oh, I know it! You arrive in a bad moment. He is peevish and cross-grained, poor man, since he came here. These soft surroundings are all so strange to him. He wearies himself away from his beloved Gavrillac, his hunting and tillage, and the truth is that in his mind he very largely blames you for what has happened—for the necessity, or at least, the wisdom, of this change. Brittany, you must know, was becoming too unsafe. The chateau of La Tour d'Azyr, amongst others, was burnt to the ground some months ago. At any moment, given a fresh excitement, it may be the turn of Gavrillac. And for this and his present discomfort he blames you and your friends. But he will come round presently. He will be sorry that he sent you away like this—for I know that he loves you, Andre, in spite of all. I shall reason with him when the time comes. And then we shall want to know where to find you."

"At number 13, Rue du Hasard. The number is unlucky, the name of the street appropriate. Therefore both are easy to remember."

She nodded. "I will walk with you to the gates." And side by side now they proceeded at a leisurely pace down the long avenue in the June sunshine dappled by the shadows of the bordering trees. "You are looking well, Andre; and do you know that you have changed a deal? I am glad that you have prospered." And then, abruptly changing the subject before he had time to answer her, she came to the matter uppermost in her mind.

"I have so wanted to see you in all these months, Andre. You were the only one who could help me; the only one who could tell me the truth, and I was angry with you for never having written to say where you were to be found."

"Of course you encouraged me to do so when last we met in Nantes."

"What? Still resentful?"

"I am never resentful. You should know that." He expressed one of his vanities. He loved to think himself a Stoic. "But I still bear the scar of a wound that would be the better for the balm of your retraction."

"Why, then, I retract, Andre. And now tell me."

"Yes, a self-seeking retraction," said he. "You give me something that you may obtain something." He laughed quite pleasantly. "Well, well; command me."

"Tell me, Andre." She paused, as if in some difficulty, and then went on, her eyes upon the ground: "Tell me—the truth of that event at the Feydau."

The request fetched a frown to his brow. He suspected at once the thought that prompted it. Quite simply and briefly he gave her his version of the affair.

She listened very attentively. When he had done she sighed; her face was very thoughtful.

"That is much what I was told," she said. "But it was added that M. de La Tour d'Azyr had gone to the theatre expressly for the purpose of breaking finally with La Binet. Do you know if that was so?"

"I don't; nor of any reason why it should be so. La Binet provided him the sort of amusement that he and his kind are forever craving..."

"Oh, there was a reason," she interrupted him. "I was the reason. I spoke to Mme. de Sautron. I told her that I would not continue to receive one who came to me contaminated in that fashion." She spoke of it with obvious difficulty, her colour rising as he watched her half-averted face.

"Had you listened to me..." he was beginning, when again she interrupted him.

"M. de Sautron conveyed my decision to him, and afterwards represented him to me as a man in despair, repentant, ready to give proofs—any proofs—of his sincerity and devotion to me. He told me that M. de La Tour d'Azyr had sworn to him that he would cut short that affair, that he would see La Binet no more. And then, on the very next day I heard of his having all but lost his life in that riot at the theatre. He had gone straight from that interview with M. de Sautron, straight from those protestations of future wisdom, to La Binet. I was indignant. I pronounced myself finally. I stated definitely that I would not in any circumstances receive M. de La Tour d'Azyr again! And then they pressed this explanation upon me. For a long time I would not believe it."

"So that you believe it now," said Andre quickly. "Why?"

"I have not said that I believe it now. But... but... neither can I disbelieve. Since we came to Meudon M. de La Tour d'Azyr has been here, and himself he has sworn to me that it was so."

"Oh, if M. de La Tour d'Azyr has sworn..." Andre-Louis was laughing on a bitter note of sarcasm.

"Have you ever known him lie?" she cut in sharply. That checked him. "M. de La Tour d'Azyr is, after all, a man of honour, and men of honour never deal in falsehood. Have you ever known him do so, that you should sneer as you have done?"

"No," he confessed. Common justice demanded that he should admit that virtue at least in his enemy. "I have not known him lie, it is true. His kind is too arrogant, too self-confident to have recourse to untruth. But I have known him do things as vile..."

"Nothing is as vile," she interrupted, speaking from the code by which she had been reared. "It is for liars only—who are first cousin to thieves—that there is no hope. It is in falsehood only that there is real loss of honour."

"You are defending that satyr, I think," he said frostily.

"I desire to be just."

"Justice may seem to you a different matter when at last you shall have resolved yourself to become Marquise de La Tour d'Azyr." He spoke bitterly.

"I don't think that I shall ever take that resolve."

"But you are still not sure—in spite of everything."

"Can one ever be sure of anything in this world?"

"Yes. One can be sure of being foolish."

Either she did not hear or did not heed him.

"You do not of your own knowledge know that it was not as M. de La Tour d'Azyr asserts—that he went to the Feydau that night?"

"I don't," he admitted. "It is of course possible. But does it matter?"

"It might matter. Tell me; what became of La Binet after all?"

"I don't know."

"You don't know?" She turned to consider him. "And you can say it with that indifference! I thought... I thought you loved her, Andre."

"So did I, for a little while. I was mistaken. It required a La Tour d'Azyr to disclose the truth to me. They have their uses, these gentlemen. They help stupid fellows like myself to perceive important truths. I was fortunate that revelation in my case preceded marriage. I can now look back upon the episode with equanimity and thankfulness for my near escape from the consequences of what was no more than an aberration of the senses. It is a thing commonly confused with love. The experience, as you see, was very instructive."

She looked at him in frank surprise.

"Do you know, Andre, I sometimes think that you have no heart."

"Presumably because I sometimes betray intelligence. And what of yourself, Aline? What of your own attitude from the outset where M. de La Tour d'Azyr is concerned? Does that show heart? If I were to tell you what it really shows, we should end by quarrelling again, and God knows I can't afford to quarrel with you now. I... I shall take another way."

"What do you mean?"

"Why, nothing at the moment, for you are not in any danger of marrying that animal."

"And if I were?"

"Ah! In that case affection for you would discover to me some means of preventing it—unless..." He paused.

"Unless?" she demanded, challengingly, drawn to the full of her short height, her eyes imperious.

"Unless you could also tell me that you loved him," said he simply, whereat she was as suddenly and most oddly softened. And then he added, shaking his head: "But that of course is impossible."

"Why?" she asked him, quite gently now.

"Because you are what you are, Aline—utterly good and pure and adorable. Angels do not mate with devils. His wife you might become, but never his mate, Aline—never."

They had reached the wrought-iron gates at the end of the avenue. Through these they beheld the waiting yellow chaise which had brought Andre-Louis. From near at hand came the creak of other wheels, the beat of other hooves, and now another vehicle came in sight, and drew to a stand-still beside the yellow chaise—a handsome equipage with polished mahogany panels on which the gold and azure of armorial bearings flashed brilliantly in the sunlight. A footman swung to earth to throw wide the gates; but in that moment the lady who occupied the carriage, perceiving Aline, waved to her and issued a command.

CHAPTER V. MADAME DE PLOUGASTEL

The postilion drew rein, and the footman opened the door, letting down the steps and proffering his arm to his mistress to assist her to alight, since that was the wish she had expressed. Then he opened one wing of the iron gates, and held it for her. She was a woman of something more than forty, who once must have been very lovely, who was very lovely still with the refining quality that age brings to some women. Her dress and carriage alike advertised great rank.

"I take my leave here, since you have a visitor," said Andre-Louis.

"But it is an old acquaintance of your own, Andre. You remember Mme. la Comtesse de Plougastel?"

He looked at the approaching lady, whom Aline was now hastening forward to meet, and because she was named to him he recognized her. He must, he thought, had he but looked, have recognized her without prompting anywhere at any time, and this although it was some sixteen years since last he had seen her. The sight of her now brought it all back to him—a treasured memory that had never permitted itself to be entirely overlaid by subsequent events.

When he was a boy of ten, on the eve of being sent to school at Rennes, she had come on a visit to his godfather, who was her cousin. It happened that at the time he was taken by Rabouillet to the Manor of Gavrillac, and there he had been presented to Mme. de Plougastel. The great lady, in all the glory then of her youthful beauty, with her gentle, cultured voice—so cultured that she had seemed to speak a language almost unknown to the little Breton lad—and her majestic air of the great world, had scared him a little at first. Very gently had she allayed those fears of his, and by some mysterious enchantment she had completely enslaved his regard. He recalled now the terror in which he had gone to the embrace to which he was bidden, and the subsequent reluctance with which he had left those soft round arms. He remembered, too, how sweetly she had smelled and the very perfume she had used, a perfume as of lilac—for memory is singularly tenacious in these matters.

For three days whilst she had been at Gavrillac, he had gone daily to the manor, and so had spent hours in her company. A childless woman with the maternal instinct strong within her, she had taken this precociously intelligent, wide-eyed lad to her heart.

"Give him to me, Cousin Quintin," he remembered her saying on the last of those days to his godfather. "Let me take him back with me to Versailles as my adopted child."

But the Seigneur had gravely shaken his head in silent refusal, and there had been no further question of such a thing. And then, when she said good-bye to him—the thing came flooding back to him now—there had been tears in her eyes.

"Think of me sometimes, Andre-Louis," had been her last words.

He remembered how flattered he had been to have won within so short a time the affection of this great lady. The thing had given him a sense of importance that had endured for months thereafter, finally to fade into oblivion.

But all was vividly remembered now upon beholding her again, after sixteen years, profoundly changed and matured, the girl—for she had been no more in those old days—sunk in this worldly woman with the air of calm dignity and complete self-possession. Yet, he insisted, he must have known her anywhere again.

Aline embraced her affectionately, and then answering the questioning glance with faintly raised eyebrows that madame was directing towards Aline's companion—

"This is Andre-Louis," she said. "You remember Andre-Louis, madame?"

Madame checked. Andre-Louis saw the surprise ripple over her face, taking with it some of her colour, leaving her for a moment breathless.

And then the voice—the well-remembered rich, musical voice—richer and deeper now than of yore, repeated his name:

"Andre-Louis!"

Her manner of uttering it suggested that it awakened memories, memories perhaps of the departed youth with which it was associated. And she paused a long moment, considering him, a little wide-eyed, what time he bowed before her.

"But of course I remember him," she said at last, and came towards him, putting out her hand. He kissed it dutifully, submissively, instinctively. "And this is what you have grown into?" She appraised him, and he flushed with pride at the satisfaction in her tone. He seemed to have gone back sixteen years, and to be again the little Breton lad at Gavrillac. She turned to Aline. "How mistaken Quintin was in his assumptions. He was pleased to see him again, was he not?"

"So pleased, madame, that he has shown me the door," said Andre-Louis.

"Ah!" She frowned, conning him still with those dark, wistful eyes of hers. "We must change that, Aline. He is of course very angry with you. But it is not the way to make converts. I will plead for you, Andre-Louis. I am a good advocate."

He thanked her and took his leave.

"I leave my case in your hands with gratitude. My homage, madame."

And so it happened that in spite of his godfather's forbidding reception of him, the fragment of a song was on his lips as his yellow chaise whirled him back to Paris and the Rue du Hasard. That meeting with Mme. de Plougastel had enheartened him; her promise to plead his case in alliance with Aline gave him assurance that all would be well.

That he was justified of this was proved when on the following Thursday towards noon his academy was invaded by M. de Kercadiou. Gilles, the boy, brought him word of it, and breaking off at once the lesson upon which he was engaged, he pulled off his mask, and went as he was—in a chamois waistcoat buttoned to the chin and with his foil under his arm to the modest salon below, where his godfather awaited him.

The florid little Lord of Gavrillac stood almost defiantly to receive him.

"I have been over-persuaded to forgive you," he announced aggressively, seeming thereby to imply that he consented to this merely so as to put an end to tiresome importunities.

Andre-Louis was not misled. He detected a pretence adopted by the Seigneur so as to enable him to retreat in good order.

"My blessings on the persuaders, whoever they may have been. You restore me my happiness, monsieur my godfather."

He took the hand that was proffered and kissed it, yielding to the impulse of the unfailing habit of his boyish days. It was an act symbolical of his complete submission, reestablishing between himself and his godfather the bond of protected and protector, with all the mutual claims and duties that it carries. No mere words could more completely have made his peace with this man who loved him.

M. de Kercadiou's face flushed a deeper pink, his lip trembled, and there was a huskiness in the voice that murmured "My dear boy!" Then he recollected himself, threw back his great head and frowned. His voice resumed its habitual shrillness. "You realize, I hope, that you have behaved damnably... damnably, and with the utmost ingratitude?"

"Does not that depend upon the point of view?" quoth Andre-Louis, but his tone was studiously conciliatory.

"It depends upon a fact, and not upon any point of view. Since I have been persuaded to overlook it, I trust that at least you have some intention of reforming."

"I... I will abstain from politics," said Andre-Louis, that being the utmost he could say with truth.

"That is something, at least." His godfather permitted himself to be mollified, now that a concession—or a seeming concession—had been made to his just resentment.

"A chair, monsieur."

"No, no. I have come to carry you off to pay a visit with me. You owe it entirely to Mme. de Plougastel that I consent to receive you again. I desire that you come with me to thank her."

"I have my engagements here..." began Andre-Louis, and then broke off. "No matter! I will arrange it. A moment." And he was turning away to reenter the academy.

"What are your engagements? You are not by chance a fencing-instructor?" M. de Kercadiou had observed the leather waistcoat and the foil tucked under Andre-Louis' arm.

"I am the master of this academy—the academy of the late Bertrand des Amis, the most flourishing school of arms in Paris to-day."

M. de Kercadiou's brows went up.

"And you are master of it?"

"Maitre en fait d'Armes. I succeeded to the academy upon the death of des Amis."

He left M. Kercadiou to think it over, and went to make his arrangements and effect the necessary changes in his toilet.

"So that is why you have taken to wearing a sword," said M. de Kercadiou, as they climbed into his waiting carriage.

"That and the need to guard one's self in these times."

"And do you mean to tell me that a man who lives by what is after all an honourable profession, a profession mainly supported by the nobility, can at the same time associate himself with these peddling attorneys and low pamphleteers who are spreading dissension and insubordination?"

"You forget that I am a peddling attorney myself, made so by your own wishes, monsieur."

M. de Kercadiou grunted, and took snuff. "You say the academy flourishes?" he asked presently.

"It does. I have two assistant instructors. I could employ a third. It is hard work."

"That should mean that your circumstances are affluent."

"I have reason to be satisfied. I have far more than I need."

"Then you'll be able to do your share in paying off this national debt," growled the nobleman, well content that—as he conceived it—some of the evil Andre-Louis had helped to sow should recoil upon him.

Then the talk veered to Mme. de Plougastel. M. de Kercadiou, Andre-Louis gathered, but not the reason for it, disapproved most strongly of this visit. But then Madame la Comtesse was a headstrong woman whom there was no denying, whom all the world obeyed. M. de Plougastel was at present absent in Germany, but would shortly be returning. It was an indiscreet admission from which it was easy to infer that M. de Plougastel was one of those intriguing emissaries who came and went between the Queen of France and her brother, the Emperor of Austria.

The carriage drew up before a handsome hotel in the Faubourg Saint-Denis, at the corner of the Rue Paradis, and they were ushered by a sleek servant into a little boudoir, all gilt and brocade, that opened upon a terrace above a garden that was a park in miniature. Here madame awaited them. She rose, dismissing the young person who had been reading to her, and came forward with both hands outheld to greet her cousin Kercadiou.

"I almost feared you would not keep your word," she said. "It was unjust. But then I hardly hoped that you would succeed in bringing him." And her glance, gentle, and smiling welcome upon him, indicated Andre-Louis.

The young man made answer with formal gallantry.

"The memory of you, madame, is too deeply imprinted on my heart for any persuasions to have been necessary."

"Ah, the courtier!" said madame, and abandoned him her hand. "We are to have a little talk, Andre-Louis," she informed him, with a gravity that left him vaguely ill at ease.

They sat down, and for a while the conversation was of general matters, chiefly concerned, however, with Andre-Louis, his occupations and his views. And all the while madame was studying him attentively with those gentle, wistful eyes, until again that sense of uneasiness began to pervade him. He realized instinctively that he had been brought here for some purpose deeper than that which had been avowed.

At last, as if the thing were concerted—and the clumsy Lord of Gavrillac was the last man in the world to cover his tracks—his godfather rose and, upon a pretext of desiring to survey the garden, sauntered through the windows on to the terrace, over whose white stone balustrade the geraniums trailed in a scarlet riot. Thence he vanished among the foliage below.

"Now we can talk more intimately," said madame. "Come here, and sit beside me." She indicated the empty half of the settee she occupied.

Andre-Louis went obediently, but a little uncomfortably. "You know," she said gently, placing a hand upon his arm, "that you have behaved very ill, that your godfather's resentment is very justly founded?"

"Madame, if I knew that, I should be the most unhappy, the most despairing of men." And he explained himself, as he had explained himself on Sunday to his godfather. "What I did, I did because it was the only means to my hand in a country in which justice was paralyzed by Privilege to make war upon an infamous scoundrel who had killed my best friend—a wanton, brutal act of murder, which there was no law to punish. And as if that were not enough—forgive me if I speak with the utmost frankness, madame—he afterwards debauched the woman I was to have married."

"Ah, mon Dieu!" she cried out.

"Forgive me. I know that it is horrible. You perceive, perhaps, what I suffered, how I came to be driven. That last affair of which I am guilty—the riot that began in the Feydau Theatre and afterwards enveloped the whole city of Nantes—was provoked by this."

"Who was she, this girl?"

It was like a woman, he thought, to fasten upon the unessential.

"Oh, a theatre girl, a poor fool of whom I have no regrets. La Binet was her name. I was a player at the time in her father's troupe. That was after the Rennes business, when it was necessary to hide from such justice as exists in France—the gallows' justice for unfortunates who are not 'born.' This added wrong led me to provoke a riot in the theatre."

"Poor boy," she said tenderly. "Only a woman's heart can realize what you must have suffered; and because of that I can so readily forgive you. But now..."

"Ah, but you don't understand, madame. If to-day I thought that I had none but personal grounds for having lent a hand in the holy work of abolishing Privilege, I think I should cut my throat. My true justification lies in the insincerity of those who intended that the convocation of the States General should be a sham, mere dust in the eyes of the nation."

"Was it not, perhaps, wise to have been insincere in such a matter?"

He looked at her blankly.

"Can it ever be wise, madame, to be insincere?"

"Oh, indeed it can; believe me, who am twice your age, and know my world."

"I should say, madame, that nothing is wise that complicates existence; and I know of nothing that so complicates it as insincerity. Consider a moment the complications that have arisen out of this."

"But surely, Andre-Louis, your views have not been so perverted that you do not see that a governing class is a necessity in any country?"

"Why, of course. But not necessarily a hereditary one."

"What else?"

He answered her with an epigram. "Man, madame, is the child of his own work. Let there be no inheriting of rights but from such a parent. Thus a nation's best will always predominate, and such a nation will achieve greatly."

"But do you account birth of no importance?"

"Of none, madame—or else my own might trouble me." From the deep flush that stained her face, he feared that he had offended by what was almost an indelicacy. But the reproof that he was expecting did not come. Instead—

"And does it not?" she asked. "Never, Andre?"

"Never, madame. I am content."

"You have never... never regretted your lack of parents' care?"

He laughed, sweeping aside her sweet charitable concern that was so superfluous. "On the contrary, madame, I tremble to think what they might have made of me, and I am grateful to have had the fashioning of myself."

She looked at him for a moment very sadly, and then, smiling, gently shook her head.

"You do not want self-satisfaction... Yet I could wish that you saw things differently, Andre. It is a moment of great opportunities for a young man of talent and spirit. I could help you; I could help you, perhaps, to go very far if you would permit yourself to be helped after my fashion."

"Yes," he thought, "help me to a halter by sending me on treasonable missions to Austria on the Queen's behalf, like M. de Plougastel. That would certainly end in a high position for me."

Aloud he answered more as politeness prompted. "I am grateful, madame. But you will see that, holding the ideals I have expressed, I could not serve any cause that is opposed to their realization."

"You are misled by prejudice, Andre-Louis, by personal grievances. Will you allow them to stand in the way of your advancement?"

"If what I call ideals were really prejudices, would it be honest of me to run counter to them whilst holding them?"

"If I could convince you that you are mistaken! I could help you so much to find a worthy employment for the talents you possess. In the service of the King you would prosper quickly. Will you think of it, Andre-Louis, and let us talk of this again?"

He answered her with formal, chill politeness.

"I fear that it would be idle, madame. Yet your interest in me is very flattering, and I thank you. It is unfortunate for me that I am so headstrong."

"And now who deals in insincerity?" she asked him.

"Ah, but you see, madame, it is an insincerity that does not mislead."

And then M. de Kercadiou came in through the window again, and announced fussily that he must be getting back to Meudon, and that he would take his godson with him and set him down at the Rue du Hasard.

"You must bring him again, Quintin," the Countess said, as they took their leave of her.

"Some day, perhaps," said M. de Kercadiou vaguely, and swept his godson out.

In the carriage he asked him bluntly of what madame had talked.

"She was very kind—a sweet woman," said Andre-Louis pensively.

"Devil take you, I didn't ask you the opinion that you presume to have formed of her. I asked you what she said to you."

"She strove to point out to me the error of my ways. She spoke of great things that I might do—to which she would very kindly help me—if I were to come to my senses. But as miracles do not happen, I gave her little encouragement to hope."

"I see. I see. Did she say anything else?"

He was so peremptory that Andre-Louis turned to look at him.

"What else did you expect her to say, monsieur my godfather?"

"Oh, nothing."

"Then she fulfilled your expectations."

"Eh? Oh, a thousand devils, why can't you express yourself in a sensible manner that a plain man can understand without having to think about it?"

He sulked after that most of the way to the Rue du Hasard, or so it seemed to Andre-Louis. At least he sat silent, gloomily thoughtful to judge by his expression.

"You may come and see us soon again at Meudon," he told Andre-Louis at parting. "But please remember—no revolutionary politics in future, if we are to remain friends."

CHAPTER VI. POLITICIANS

One morning in August the academy in the Rue du Hasard was invaded by Le Chapelier accompanied by a man of remarkable appearance, whose herculean stature and disfigured countenance seemed vaguely familiar to Andre-Louis. He was a man of little, if anything, over thirty, with small bright eyes buried in an enormous face. His cheek-bones were prominent, his nose awry, as if it had been broken by a blow, and his mouth was rendered almost shapeless by the scars of another injury. (A bull had horned him in the face when he was but a lad.) As if that were not enough to render his appearance terrible, his cheeks were deeply pock-marked. He was dressed untidily in a long scarlet coat that descended almost to his ankles, soiled buckskin breeches and boots with reversed tops. His shirt, none too clean, was open at the throat, the collar hanging limply over an unknotted cravat, displaying fully the muscular neck that rose like a pillar from his massive shoulders. He swung a cane that was almost a club in his left hand, and there was a cockade in his biscuit-coloured, conical hat. He carried himself with an aggressive, masterful air, that great head of his thrown back as if he were eternally at defiance.

Le Chapelier, whose manner was very grave, named him to Andre-Louis.

"This is M. Danton, a brother-lawyer, President of the Cordeliers, of whom you will have heard."

Of course Andre-Louis had heard of him. Who had not, by then?

Looking at him now with interest, Andre-Louis wondered how it came that all, or nearly all the leading innovators, were pock-marked. Mirabeau, the journalist Desmoulins, the philanthropist Marat, Robespierre the little lawyer from Arras, this formidable fellow Danton, and several others he could call to mind all bore upon them the scars of smallpox. Almost he began to wonder was there any connection between the two. Did an attack of smallpox produce certain moral results which found expression in this way?

He dismissed the idle speculation, or rather it was shattered by the startling thunder of Danton's voice.

"This ——— Chapelier has told me of you. He says that you are a patriotic ———."

More than by the tone was Andre-Louis startled by the obscenities with which the Colossus did not hesitate to interlard his first speech to a total stranger. He laughed outright. There was nothing else to do.

"If he has told you that, he has told you more than the truth! I am a patriot. The rest my modesty compels me to disavow."

"You're a joker too, it seems," roared the other, but he laughed nevertheless, and the volume of it shook the windows. "There's no offence in me. I am like that."

"What a pity," said Andre-Louis.

It disconcerted the king of the markets. "Eh? what's this, Chapelier? Does he give himself airs, your friend here?"

The spruce Breton, a very petit-maitre in appearance by contrast with his companion, but nevertheless of a down-right manner quite equal to Danton's in brutality, though dispensing with the emphasis of foulness, shrugged as he answered him:

"It is merely that he doesn't like your manners, which is not at all surprising. They are execrable."

"Ah, bah! You are all like that, you ——— Bretons. Let's come to business. You'll have heard what took place in the Assembly yesterday? You haven't? My God, where do you live? Have you heard that this scoundrel who calls himself King of France gave passage across French soil the other day to Austrian troops going to crush those who fight for liberty in Belgium? Have you heard that, by any chance?"

"Yes," said Andre-Louis coldly, masking his irritation before the other's hectoring manner. "I have heard that."

"Oh! And what do you think of it?" Arms akimbo, the Colossus towered above him.

Andre-Louis turned aside to Le Chapelier.

"I don't think I understand. Have you brought this gentleman here to examine my conscience?"

"Name of a name! He's prickly as a ——— porcupine!" Danton protested.

"No, no." Le Chapelier was conciliatory, seeking to provide an antidote to the irritant administered by his companion. "We require your help, Andre. Danton here thinks that you are the very man for us. Listen now..."

"That's it. You tell him," Danton agreed. "You both talk the same mincing— sort of French. He'll probably understand you."

Le Chapelier went on without heeding the interruption. "This violation by the King of the obvious rights of a country engaged in framing a constitution that shall make it free has shattered every philanthropic illusion we still cherished. There are those who go so far as to proclaim the King the vowed enemy of France. But that, of course, is excessive."

"Who says so?" blazed Danton, and swore horribly by way of conveying his total disagreement.

Le Chapelier waved him into silence, and proceeded.

"Anyhow, the matter has been more than enough, added to all the rest, to set us by the ears again in the Assembly. It is open war between the Third Estate and the Privileged."

"Was it ever anything else?"

"Perhaps not; but it has assumed a new character. You'll have heard of the duel between Lameth and the Duc de Castries?"

"A trifling affair."

"In its results. But it might have been far other. Mirabeau is challenged and insulted now at every sitting. But he goes his way, cold-bloodedly wise. Others are not so circumspect; they meet insult with insult, blow with blow, and blood is being shed in private duels. The thing is reduced by these swordsmen of the nobility to a system."

Andre-Louis nodded. He was thinking of Philippe de Vilmorin. "Yes," he said, "it is an old trick of theirs. It is so simple and direct—like themselves. I wonder only that they didn't hit upon this system sooner. In the early days of the States General, at Versailles, it might have had a better effect. Now, it comes a little late."

"But they mean to make up for lost time—sacred name!" cried Danton. "Challenges are flying right and left between these bully-swordsmen, these spadassinicides, and poor devils of the robe who have never learnt to fence with anything but a quill. It's just ——— murder. Yet if I were to go amongst messieurs les nobles and crunch an addled head or two with this stick of mine, snap a few aristocratic necks between these fingers which the good God has given me for the purpose, the law would send me to atone upon the gallows. This in a land that is striving after liberty. Why, Dieu me damne! I am not even allowed to keep my hat on in the theatre. But they ——— these ———s!"

"He is right," said Le Chapelier. "The thing has become unendurable, insufferable. Two days ago M. d'Ambly threatened Mirabeau with his cane before the whole Assembly. Yesterday M. de Faussigny leapt up and harangued his order by inviting murder. 'Why don't we fall on these scoundrels, sword in hand?' he asked. Those were his very words: 'Why don't we fall on these scoundrels, sword in hand.'"

"It is so much simpler than lawmaking," said Andre-Louis.

"Lagron, the deputy from Ancenis in the Loire, said something that we did not hear in answer. As he was leaving the Manege one of these bullies grossly insulted him. Lagron no more than used his elbow to push past when the fellow cried out that he had been struck, and issued his challenge. They fought this morning early in the Champs Elysees, and Lagron was killed, run through the stomach deliberately by a man who fought like a fencing-master, and poor Lagron did not even own a sword. He had to borrow one to go to the assignation."

Andre-Louis—his mind ever on Vilmorin, whose case was here repeated, even to the details—was swept by a gust of passion. He clenched his hands, and his jaws set. Danton's little eyes observed him keenly.

"Well? And what do you think of that? Noblesse oblige, eh? The thing is we must oblige them too, these ———-s. We must pay them back in the same coin; meet them with the same weapons. Abolish them; tumble these assassinateurs into the abyss of nothingness by the same means."

"But how?"

"How? Name of God! Haven't I said it?"

"That is where we require your help," Le Chapelier put in. "There must be men of patriotic feeling among the more advanced of your pupils. M. Danton's idca is that a little band of these—say a half-dozen, with yourself at their head—might read these bullies a sharp lesson."

Andre-Louis frowned.

"And how, precisely, had M. Danton thought that this might be done?"

M. Danton spoke for himself, vehemently.

"Why, thus: We post you in the Manege, at the hour when the Assembly is rising. We point out the six leading phlebotomists, and let you loose to insult them before they have time to insult any of the representatives. Then to-morrow morning, six ——— phlebotomists themselves phlebotomized secundum artem. That will give the others something to think about. It will give them a great deal to think about, by ——! If necessary the dose may be repeated to ensure a cure. If you kill the ———-s, so much the better."

He paused, his sallow face flushed with the enthusiasm of his idea. Andre-Louis stared at him inscrutably.

"Well, what do you say to that?"

"That it is most ingenious." And Andre-Louis turned aside to look out of the window.

"And is that all you think of it?"

"I will not tell you what else I think of it because you probably would not understand. For you, M. Danton, there is at least this excuse that you did not know me. But you, Isaac—to bring this gentleman here with such a proposal!"

Le Chapelier was overwhelmed in confusion. "I confess I hesitated," he apologized. "But M. Danton would not take my word for it that the proposal might not be to your taste."

"I would not!" Danton broke in, bellowing. He swung upon Le Chapelier, brandishing his great arms. "You told me monsieur was a patriot. Patriotism knows no scruples. You call this mincing dancing-master a patriot?"

"Would you, monsieur, out of patriotism consent to become an assassin?"

"Of course I would. Haven't I told you so? Haven't I told you that I would gladly go among them with my club, and crack them like so many—fleas?"

"Why not, then?"

"Why not? Because I should get myself hanged. Haven't I said so?"

"But what of that ——— being a patriot? Why not, like another Curtius, jump into the gulf, since you believe that your country would benefit by your death?"

M. Danton showed signs of exasperation. "Because my country will benefit more by my life."

"Permit me, monsieur, to suffer from a similar vanity."

"You? But where would be the danger to you? You would do your work under the cloak of duelling—as they do."

"Have you reflected, monsieur, that the law will hardly regard a fencing-master who kills his opponent as an ordinary combatant, particularly if it can be shown that the fencing-master himself provoked the attack?"

"So! Name of a name!" M. Danton blew out his cheeks and delivered himself with withering scorn. "It comes to this, then: you are afraid!"

"You may think so if you choose—that I am afraid to do slyly and treacherously that which a thrasonical patriot like yourself is afraid of doing frankly and openly. I have other reasons. But that one should suffice you."

Danton gasped. Then he swore more amazingly and variedly than ever.

"By ——! you are right," he admitted, to Andre-Louis' amazement. "You are right, and I am wrong. I am as bad a patriot as you are, and I am a coward as well." And he invoked the whole Pantheon to witness his self-denunciation. "Only, you see, I count for something: and if they take me and hang me, why, there it is! Monsieur, we must find some other way. Forgive the intrusion. Adieu!" He held out his enormous hand..

Le Chapelier stood hesitating, crestfallen.

"You understand, Andre? I am sorry that..."

"Say no more, please. Come and see me soon again. I would press you to remain, but it is striking nine, and the first of my pupils is about to arrive."

"Nor would I permit it," said Danton. "Between us we must resolve the riddle of how to extinguish M. de La Tour d'Azyr and his friends."

"Who?"

Sharp as a pistol-shot came that question, as Danton was turning away. The tone of it brought him up short. He turned again, Le Chapelier with him.

"I said M. de La Tour d'Azyr."

"What has he to do with the proposal you were making me?"

"He? Why, he is the phlebotomist in chief."

And Le Chapelier added. "It is he who killed Lagron."

"Not a friend of yours, is he?" wondered Danton.

"And it is La Tour d'Azyr you desire me to kill?" asked Andre-Louis very slowly, after the manner of one whose thoughts are meanwhile pondering the subject.

"That's it," said Danton. "And not a job for a prentice hand, I can assure you."

"Ah, but this alters things," said Andre-Louis, thinking aloud. "It offers a great temptation."

"Why, then...?" The Colossus took a step towards him again.

"Wait!" He put up his hand. Then with chin sunk on his breast, he paced away to the window, musing.

Le Chapelier and Danton exchanged glances, then watched him, waiting, what time he considered.

At first he almost wondered why he should not of his own accord have decided upon some such course as this to settle that long-standing account of M. de La Tour d'Azyr. What was the use of this great skill in fence that he had come to acquire, unless he could turn it to account to avenge Vilmorin, and to make Aline safe from the lure of her own ambition? It would be an easy thing to seek out La Tour d'Azyr, put a mortal affront upon him, and thus bring him to the point. To-day this would be murder, murder as treacherous as that which La Tour d'Azyr had done upon Philippe de Vilmorin; for to-day the old positions were reversed, and it was Andre-Louis who might go to such an assignation without a doubt of the issue. It was a moral obstacle of which he made short work. But there remained the legal obstacle he had expounded to Danton. There was still a law in France; the same law which he had found it impossible to move against La Tour d'Azyr, but which would move briskly enough against himself in like case. And then, suddenly, as if by inspiration, he saw the way—a way which if adopted would probably bring La Tour d'Azyr to a poetic justice, bring him, insolent, confident, to thrust himself upon Andre-Louis' sword, with all the odium of provocation on his own side.

He turned to them again, and they saw that he was very pale, that his great dark eyes glowed oddly.

"There will probably be some difficulty in finding a suppleant for this poor Lagron," he said. "Our fellow-countrymen will be none so eager to offer themselves to the swords of Privilege."

"True enough," said Le Chapelier gloomily; and then, as if suddenly leaping to the thing in Andre-Louis' mind: "Andre!" he cried. "Would you..."

"It is what I was considering. It would give me a legitimate place in the Assembly. If your Tour d'Azyrs choose to seek me out then, why, their blood be upon their own heads. I shall certainly do nothing to discourage them." He smiled curiously. "I am just a rascal who tries to be honest—Scaramouche always, in fact; a creature of sophistries. Do you think that Ancenis would have me for its representative?"

"Will it have Omnes Omnibus for its representative?" Le Chapelier was laughing, his countenance eager. "Ancenis will be convulsed with pride. It is not Rennes or Nantes, as it might have been had you wished it. But it gives you a voice for Brittany."

"I should have to go to Ancenis..."

"No need at all. A letter from me to the Municipality, and the Municipality will confirm you at once. No need to move from here. In a fortnight at most the thing can be accomplished. It is settled, then?"

Andre-Louis considered yet a moment. There was his academy. But he could make arrangements with Le Duc and Galoche to carry it on for him whilst himself directing and advising. Le Duc, after all, was become a thoroughly efficient master, and he was a trustworthy fellow. At need a third assistant could be engaged.

"Be it so," he said at last.

Le Chapelier clasped hands with him and became congratulatorily voluble, until interrupted by the red-coated giant at the door.

"What exactly does it mean to our business, anyway?" he asked. "Does it mean that when you are a representative you will not scruple to skewer M. le Marquis?"

"If M. le Marquis should offer himself to be skewered, as he no doubt will."

"I perceive the distinction," said M. Danton, and sneered. "You've an ingenious mind." He turned to Le Chapelier. "What did you say he was to begin with—a lawyer, wasn't it?"

"Yes, I was a lawyer, and afterwards a mountebank."

"And this is the result!"

"As you say. And do you know that we are after all not so dissimilar, you and I?"

"What?"

"Once like you I went about inciting other people to go and kill the man I wanted dead. You'll say I was a coward, of course."

Le Chapelier prepared to slip between them as the clouds gathered on the giant's brow. Then these were dispelled again, and the great laugh vibrated through the long room.

"You've touched me for the second time, and in the same place. Oh, you can fence, my lad. We should be friends. Rue des Cordeliers is my address. Any—scoundrel will tell you where Danton lodges. Desmoulins lives underneath. Come and visit us one evening. There's always a bottle for a friend."

CHAPTER VII. THE SPADASSINICIDES

After an absence of rather more than a week, M. le Marquis de La Tour d'Azyr was back in his place on the Cote Droit of the National Assembly. Properly speaking, we should already at this date allude to him as the ci-devant Marquis de La Tour d'Azyr, for the time was September of 1790, two months after the passing—on the motion of that downright Breton leveller, Le Chapelier—of the decree that nobility should no more be hereditary than infamy; that just as the brand of the gallows must not defile the possibly worthy descendants of one who had been convicted of evil, neither should the blazon advertising achievement glorify the possibly unworthy descendants of one who had proved himself good. And so the decree had been passed abolishing hereditary nobility and consigning family escutcheons to the rubbish-heap of things no longer to be tolerated by an enlightened generation of philosophers. M. le Comte de Lafayette, who had supported the motion, left the Assembly as plain M. Motier, the great tribune Count Mirabeau became plain M. Riquetti, and M. le Marquis de La Tour d'Azyr just simple M. Lesarques. The thing was done in one of those exaltations produced by the approach of the great National Festival of the Champ de Mars, and no doubt it was thoroughly repented on the morrow by those who had lent themselves to it. Thus, although law by now, it was a law that no one troubled just yet to enforce.

That, however, is by the way. The time, as I have said, was September, the day dull and showery, and some of the damp and gloom of it seemed to have penetrated the long Hall of the Manege, where on their eight rows of green benches elliptically arranged in ascending tiers about the space known as La Piste, sat some eight or nine hundred of the representatives of the three orders that composed the nation.

The matter under debate by the constitution-builders was whether the deliberating body to succeed the Constituent Assembly should work in conjunction with the King, whether it should be periodic or permanent, whether it should govern by two chambers or by one.

The Abbe Maury, son of a cobbler, and therefore in these days of antitheses orator-in-chief of the party of the Right—the Blacks, as those who fought Privilege's losing battles were known—was in the tribune. He appeared to be urging the adoption of a two-chambers system framed on the English model. He was, if anything, more long-winded and prosy even than his habit; his arguments assumed more and more the form of a sermon; the tribune of the National Assembly became more and more like a pulpit; but the members, conversely, less and less like a congregation. They grew restive under that steady flow of pompous verbiage, and it was in vain that the four ushers in black satin breeches and carefully powdered heads, chain of office on their breasts, gilded sword at their sides, circulated in the Piste, clapping their hands, and hissing,

"Silence! En place!"

Equally vain was the intermittent ringing of the bell by the president at his green-covered table facing the tribune. The Abbe Maury had talked too long, and for some time had failed to interest the members. Realizing it at last, he ceased, whereupon the hum of conversation became general. And then it fell abruptly. There was a silence of expectancy, and a turning of heads, a craning of necks. Even the group of secretaries at the round table below the president's dais roused themselves from their usual apathy to consider this young man who was mounting the tribune of the Assembly for the first time.

"M. Andre-Louis Moreau, deputy suppleant, vice Emmanuel Lagron, deceased, for Ancenis in the Department of the Loire."

M. de La Tour d'Azyr shook himself out of the gloomy abstraction in which he had sat. The successor of the deputy he had slain must, in any event, be an object of grim interest to him. You conceive how that interest was heightened when he heard him named, when, looking across, he recognized indeed in this Andre-Louis Moreau the young scoundrel who was continually crossing his path, continually exerting against him a deep-moving, sinister influence to make him regret that he should have spared his life that day at Gavrillac two years ago. That he should thus have stepped into the shoes of Lagron seemed to M. de La Tour d'Azyr too apt for mere coincidence, a direct challenge in itself.

He looked at the young man in wonder rather than in anger, and looking at him he was filled by a vague, almost a premonitory, uneasiness.

At the very outset, the presence which in itself he conceived to be a challenge was to demonstrate itself for this in no equivocal terms.

"I come before you," Andre-Louis began, "as a deputy-suppleant to fill the place of one who was murdered some three weeks ago."

It was a challenging opening that instantly provoked an indignant outcry from the Blacks. Andre-Louis paused, and looked at them, smiling a little, a singularly self-confident young man.

"The gentlemen of the Right, M. le President, do not appear to like my words. But that is not surprising. The gentlemen of the Right notoriously do not like the truth."

This time there was uproar. The members of the Left roared with laughter, those of the Right thundered menacingly. The ushers circulated at a pace beyond their usual, agitated themselves, clapped their hands, and called in vain for silence.

The President rang his bell.

Above the general din came the voice of La Tour d'Azyr, who had half-risen from his seat: "Mountebank! This is not the theatre!"

"No, monsieur, it is becoming a hunting-ground for bully-swordsmen," was the answer, and the uproar grew.

The deputy-suppleant looked round and waited. Near at hand he met the encouraging grin of Le Chapelier, and the quiet, approving smile of Kersain, another Breton deputy of his acquaintance. A little farther off he saw the great head of Mirabeau thrown back, the great eyes regarding him from under a frown in a sort of wonder, and yonder, among all that moving sea of faces, the sallow countenance of the Arras' lawyer Robespierre—or de Robespierre, as the little snob now called himself, having assumed the aristocratic particle as the prerogative of a man of his distinction in the councils of his country. With his tip-tilted nose in the air, his carefully curled head on one side, the deputy for Arras was observing Andre-Louis attentively. The horn-rimmed spectacles he used for reading were thrust up on to his pale forehead, and it was through a levelled spy-glass that he considered the speaker, his thin-lipped mouth stretched a little in that tiger-cat smile that was afterwards to become so famous and so feared.

Gradually the uproar wore itself out, and diminished so that at last the President could make himself heard. Leaning forward, he gravely addressed the young man in the tribune:

"Monsieur, if you wish to be heard, let me beg of you not to be provocative in your language." And then to the others: "Messieurs, if we are to proceed, I beg that you will restrain your feelings until the deputy-suppleant has concluded his discourse."

"I shall endeavour to obey, M. le President, leaving provocation to the gentlemen of the Right. If the few words I have used so far have been provocative, I regret it. But it was necessary that I should refer to the distinguished deputy whose place I come so unworthily to fill, and it was unavoidable that I should refer to the event which has procured us this sad necessity. The deputy Lagron was a man of singular nobility of mind, a selfless, dutiful, zealous man, inflamed by the high purpose of doing his duty by his electors and by this Assembly. He possessed what his opponents would call a dangerous gift of eloquence."

La Tour d'Azyr writhed at the well-known phrase—his own phrase—the phrase that he had used to explain his action in the matter of Philippe de Vilmorin, the phrase that from time to time had been cast in his teeth with such vindictive menace.

And then the crisp voice of the witty Canales, that very rapier of the Privileged party, cut sharply into the speaker's momentary pause.

"M. le President," he asked with great solemnity, "has the deputy-suppleant mounted the tribune for the purpose of taking part in the debate on the constitution of the legislative assemblies, or for the purpose of pronouncing a funeral oration upon the departed deputy Lagron?"

This time it was the Blacks who gave way to mirth, until checked by the deputy-suppleant.

"That laughter is obscene!" In this truly Gallic fashion he flung his glove into the face of Privilege, determined, you see, upon no half measures; and the rippling laughter perished on the instant quenched in speechless fury.

Solemnly he proceeded.

"You all know how Lagron died. To refer to his death at all requires courage, to laugh in referring to it requires something that I will not attempt to qualify. If I have alluded to his decease, it is because my own appearance among you seemed to render some such allusion necessary. It is mine to take up the burden which he set down. I do not pretend that I have the strength, the courage, or the wisdom of Lagron; but with every ounce of such strength and courage and wisdom as I possess that burden will I bear. And I trust, for the sake of those who might attempt it, that the means taken to impose silence upon that eloquent voice will not be taken to impose silence upon mine."

There was a faint murmur of applause from the Left, splutter of contemptuous laughter from the Right.

"Rhodomont!" a voice called to him.

He looked in the direction of that voice, proceeding from the group of spadassins amid the Blacks across the Piste, and he smiled. Inaudibly his lips answered:

"No, my friend—Scaramouche; Scaramouche, the subtle, dangerous fellow who goes tortuously to his ends." Aloud, he resumed: "M. le President, there are those who will not understand that the purpose for which we are assembled here is the making of laws by which France may be equitably governed, by which France may be lifted out of the morass of bankruptcy into which she is in danger of sinking. For there are some who want, it seems, not laws, but blood; I solemnly warn them that this blood will end by choking them, if they do not learn in time to discard force and allow reason to prevail."

Again in that phrase there was something that stirred a memory in La Tour d'Azyr. He turned in the fresh uproar to speak to his cousin Chabrillane who sat beside him.

"A daring rogue, this bastard of Gavrillac's," said he.

Chabrillane looked at him with gleaming eyes, his face white with anger.

"Let him talk himself out. I don't think he will be heard again after to-day. Leave this to me."

Hardly could La Tour have told you why, but he sank back in his seat with a sense of relief. He had been telling himself that here was matter demanding action, a challenge that he must take up. But despite his rage he felt a singular unwillingness. This fellow had a trick of reminding him, he supposed, too unpleasantly of that young abbe done to death in the garden behind the Breton arme at Gavrillac. Not that the death of Philippe de Vilmorin lay heavily upon M. de La Tour d'Azyr's conscience. He had accounted himself fully justified of his action. It was that the whole thing as his memory revived it for him made an unpleasant picture: that distraught boy kneeling over the bleeding body of the friend he had loved, and almost begging to be slain with him, dubbing the Marquis murderer and coward to incite him.

Meanwhile, leaving now the subject of the death of Lagron, the deputy-suppleant had at last brought himself into order, and was speaking upon the question under debate. He contributed nothing of value to it; he urged nothing definite. His speech on the subject was very brief—that being the pretext and not the purpose for which he had ascended the tribune.

When later he was leaving the hall at the end of the sitting, with Le Chapelier at his side, he found himself densely surrounded by deputies as by a body-guard. Most of them were Bretons, who aimed at screening him from the provocations which his own provocative words in the Assembly could not fail to bring down upon his head. For a moment the massive form of Mirabeau brought up alongside of him.

"Felicitations, M. Moreau," said the great man. "You acquitted yourself very well. They will want your blood, no doubt. But be discreet, monsieur, if I may presume to advise you, and do not allow yourself to be misled by any false sense of quixotry. Ignore their challenges. I do so myself. I place each challenger upon my list. There are some fifty there already, and there they will remain. Refuse them what they are pleased to call satisfaction, and all will be well." Andre-Louis smiled and sighed.

"It requires courage," said the hypocrite.

"Of course it does. But you would appear to have plenty."

"Hardly enough, perhaps. But I shall do my best."

They had come through the vestibule, and although this was lined with eager Blacks waiting for the young man who had insulted them so flagrantly from the rostrum, Andre-Louis' body-guard had prevented any of them from reaching him.

Emerging now into the open, under the great awning at the head of the Carriere, erected to enable carriages to reach the door under cover, those in front of him dispersed a little, and there was a moment as he reached the limit of the awning when his front was entirely uncovered. Outside the rain was falling heavily, churning the ground into thick mud, and for a moment Andre-Louis, with Le Chapelier ever at his side, stood hesitating to step out into the deluge.

The watchful Chabrillane had seen his chance, and by a detour that took him momentarily out into the rain, he came face to face with the too-daring young Breton. Rudely, violently, he thrust Andre-Louis back, as if to make room for himself under the shelter.

Not for a second was Andre-Louis under any delusion as to the man's deliberate purpose, nor were those who stood near him, who made a belated and ineffectual attempt to close about him. He was grievously disappointed. It was not Chabrillane he had been expecting. His disappointment was reflected on his countenance, to be mistaken for something very different by the arrogant Chevalier.

But if Chabrillane was the man appointed to deal with him, he would make the best of it.

"I think you are pushing against me, monsieur," he said, very civilly, and with elbow and shoulder he thrust M. de Chabrillane back into the rain.

"I desire to take shelter, monsieur," the Chevalier hectored.

"You may do so without standing on my feet. I have a prejudice against any one standing on my feet. My feet are very tender. Perhaps you did not know it, monsieur. Please say no more."

"Why, I wasn't speaking, you lout!" exclaimed the Chevalier, slightly discomposed.

"Were you not? I thought perhaps you were about to apologize."

"Apologize?" Chabrillane laughed. "To you! Do you know that you are amusing?" He stepped under the awning for the second time, and again in view of all thrust Andre-Louis rudely back.

"Ah!" cried Andre-Louis, with a grimace. "You hurt me, monsieur. I have told you not to push against me." He raised his voice that all might hear him, and once more impelled M. de Chabrillane back into the rain.

Now, for all his slenderness, his assiduous daily sword-practice had given Andre-Louis an arm of iron. Also he threw his weight into the thrust. His assailant reeled backwards a few steps, and then his heel struck a baulk of timber left on the ground by some workmen that morning, and he sat down suddenly in the mud.

A roar of laughter rose from all who witnessed the fine gentleman's downfall. He rose, mud-bespattered, in a fury, and in that fury sprang at Andre-Louis.

Andre-Louis had made him ridiculous, which was altogether unforgivable.

"You shall meet me for this!" he spluttered. "I shall kill you for it."

His inflamed face was within a foot of Andre-Louis'. Andre-Louis laughed. In the silence everybody heard the laugh and the words that followed.

"Oh, is that what you wanted? But why didn't you say so before? You would have spared me the trouble of knocking you down. I thought gentlemen of your profession invariably conducted these affairs with decency, decorum, and a certain grace. Had you done so, you might have saved your breeches."

"How soon shall we settle this?" snapped Chabrillane, livid with very real fury.

"Whenever you please, monsieur. It is for you to say when it will suit your convenience to kill me. I think that was the intention you announced, was it not?" Andre-Louis was suavity itself.

"To-morrow morning, in the Bois. Perhaps you will bring a friend."

"Certainly, monsieur. To-morrow morning, then. I hope we shall have fine weather. I detest the rain."

Chabrillane looked at him almost with amazement. Andre-Louis smiled pleasantly.

"Don't let me detain you now, monsieur. We quite understand each other. I shall be in the Bois at nine o'clock to-morrow morning."

"That is too late for me, monsieur."

"Any other hour would be too early for me. I do not like to have my habits disturbed. Nine o'clock or not at all, as you please."

"But I must be at the Assembly at nine, for the morning session."

"I am afraid, monsieur, you will have to kill me first, and I have a prejudice against being killed before nine o'clock."

Now this was too complete a subversion of the usual procedure for M. de Chabrillane's stomach. Here was a rustic deputy assuming with him precisely the tone of sinister mockery which his class usually dealt out to their victims of the Third Estate. And to heighten the irritation, Andre-Louis—the actor, Scaramouche always—produced his snuffbox, and proffered it with a steady hand to Le Chapelier before helping himself.

Chabrillane, it seemed, after all that he had suffered, was not even to be allowed to make a good exit.

"Very well, monsieur," he said. "Nine o'clock, then; and we'll see if you'll talk as pertly afterwards."

On that he flung away, before the jeers of the provincial deputies. Nor did it soothe his rage to be laughed at by urchins all the way down the Rue Dauphine because of the mud and filth that dripped from his satin breeches and the tails of his elegant, striped coat.

But though the members of the Third had jeered on the surface, they trembled underneath with fear and indignation. It was too much. Lagron killed by one of these bullies, and now his successor challenged, and about to be killed by another of them on the very first day of his appearance to take the dead man's place. Several came now to implore Andre-Louis not to go to the Bois, to ignore the challenge and the whole affair, which was but a deliberate attempt to put him out of the way. He listened seriously, shook his head gloomily, and promised at last to think it over.

He was in his seat again for the afternoon session as if nothing disturbed him.

But in the morning, when the Assembly met, his place was vacant, and so was M. de Chabrillane's. Gloom and resentment sat upon the members of the Third, and brought a more than usually acrid note into their debates. They disapproved of the rashness of the new recruit to their body. Some openly condemned his lack of circumspection. Very few—and those only the little group in Le Chapelier's confidence—ever expected to see him again.

It was, therefore, as much in amazement as in relief that at a few minutes after ten they saw him enter, calm, composed, and bland, and thread his way to his seat. The speaker occupying the rostrum at that moment—a member of the Privileged—stopped short to stare in incredulous dismay. Here was something that he could not understand at all. Then from somewhere, to satisfy the amazement on both sides of the assembly, a voice explained the phenomenon contemptuously.

"They haven't met. He has shirked it at the last moment."

It must be so, thought all; the mystification ceased, and men were settling back into their seats. But now, having reached his place, having heard the voice that explained the matter to the universal satisfaction, Andre-Louis paused before taking his seat. He felt it incumbent upon him to reveal the true fact.

"M. le President, my excuses for my late arrival." There was no necessity for this. It was a mere piece of theatricality, such as it was not in Scaramouche's nature to forgo. "I have been detained by an engagement of a pressing nature. I bring you also the excuses of M. de Chabrillane. He, unfortunately, will be permanently absent from this Assembly in future."

The silence was complete. Andre-Louis sat down.

CHAPTER VIII. THE PALADIN OF THE THIRD

M. Le Chevalier de Chabrillane had been closely connected, you will remember, with the iniquitous affair in which Philippe de Vilmorin had lost his life. We know enough to justify a surmise that he had not merely been La Tour d'Azyr's second in the encounter, but actually an instigator of the business. Andre-Louis may therefore have felt a justifiable satisfaction in offering up the Chevalier's life to the Manes of his murdered friend. He may have viewed it as an act of common justice not to be procured by any other means. Also it is to be remembered that Chabrillane had gone confidently to the meeting, conceiving that he, a practised ferailleur, had to deal with a bourgeois utterly unskilled in swordsmanship. Morally, then, he was little better than a murderer, and that he should have tumbled into the pit he conceived that he dug for Andre-Louis was a poetic retribution. Yet, notwithstanding all this, I should find the cynical note on which Andre-Louis announced the issue to the Assembly utterly detestable did I believe it sincere. It would justify Aline of the expressed opinion, which she held in common with so many others who had come into close contact with him, that Andre-Louis was quite heartless.

You have seen something of the same heartlessness in his conduct when he discovered the faithlessness of La Binet although that is belied by the measures he took to avenge himself. His subsequent contempt of the woman I account to be born of the affection in which for a time he held her. That this affection was as deep as he first imagined, I do not believe; but that it was as shallow as he would almost be at pains to make it appear by the completeness with which he affects to have put her from his mind when he discovered her worthlessness, I do not believe; nor, as I have said, do his actions encourage that belief. Then, again, his callous cynicism in hoping that he had killed Binet is also an affectation. Knowing that such things as Binet are better out of the world, he can have suffered no compunction; he had, you must remember, that rarely level vision which sees things in their just proportions, and never either magnifies or reduces them by sentimental considerations. At the same time, that he should contemplate the taking of life with such complete and cynical equanimity, whatever the justification, is quite incredible.

Similarly now, it is not to be believed that in coming straight from the Bois de Boulogne, straight from the killing of a man, he should be sincerely expressing his nature in alluding to the fact in terms of such outrageous flippancy. Not quite to such an extent was he the incarnation of Scaramouche. But sufficiently was he so ever to mask his true feelings by an arresting gesture, his true thoughts by an effective phrase. He was the actor always, a man ever calculating the effect he would produce, ever avoiding self-revelation, ever concerned to overlay his real character by an assumed and quite fictitious one. There was in this something of impishness, and something of other things.

Nobody laughed now at his flippancy. He did not intend that anybody should. He intended to be terrible; and he knew that the more flippant and casual his tone, the more terrible would be its effect. He produced exactly the effect he desired.

What followed in a place where feelings and practices had become what they had become is not difficult to surmise. When the session rose, there were a dozen spadassins awaiting him in the vestibule, and this time the men of his own party were less concerned to guard him. He seemed so entirely capable of guarding himself; he appeared, for all his circumspection, to have so completely carried the war into the enemy's camp, so completely to have adopted their own methods, that his fellows scarcely felt the need to protect him as yesterday.

As he emerged, he scanned that hostile file, whose air and garments marked them so clearly for what they were. He paused, seeking the man he expected, the man he was most anxious to oblige. But M. de La Tour d'Azyr was absent from those eager ranks. This seemed to him odd. La Tour d'Azyr was Chabrillane's cousin and closest friend. Surely he should have been among the first to-day. The fact was that La Tour d'Azyr was too deeply overcome by amazement and grief at the utterly unexpected event. Also his vindictiveness was held curiously in leash. Perhaps he, too, remembered the part played by Chabrillane in the affair at Gavrillac, and saw in this obscure Andre-Louis Moreau, who had so persistently persecuted him ever since, an ordained avenger. The repugnance he felt to come to the point, with him, particularly after this culminating provocation, was puzzling even to himself. But it existed, and it curbed him now.

To Andre-Louis, since La Tour was not one of that waiting pack, it mattered little on that Tuesday morning who should be the next. The next, as it happened, was the young Vicomte de La Motte-Royau, one of the deadliest blades in the group.

On the Wednesday morning, coming again an hour or so late to the Assembly, Andre-Louis announced—in much the same terms as he had announced the death of Chabrillane—that M. de La Motte-Royau would probably not disturb the harmony of the Assembly for some weeks to come, assuming that he were so fortunate as to recover ultimately from the effects of an unpleasant accident with which he had quite unexpectedly had the misfortune to meet that morning.

On Thursday he made an identical announcement with regard to the Vidame de Blavon. On Friday he told them that he had been delayed by M. de Troiscantins, and then turning to the members of the Cote Droit, and lengthening his face to a sympathetic gravity:

"I am glad to inform you, messieurs, that M. des Troiscantins is in the hands of a very competent surgeon who hopes with care to restore him to your councils in a few weeks' time."

It was paralyzing, fantastic, unreal; and friend and foe in that assembly sat alike stupefied under those bland daily announcements. Four of the most redoubtable spadassinicides put away for a time, one of them dead—and all this performed with such an air of indifference and announced in such casual terms by a wretched little provincial lawyer!

He began to assume in their eyes a romantic aspect. Even that group of philosophers of the Cote Gauche, who refused to worship any force but the force of reason, began to look upon him with a respect and consideration which no oratorical triumphs could ever have procured him.

And from the Assembly the fame of him oozed out gradually over Paris. Desmoulins wrote a panegyric upon him in his paper "Les Revolutions," wherein he dubbed him the "Paladin of the Third Estate," a name that caught the fancy of the people, and clung to him for some time. Disdainfully was he mentioned in the "Actes des Apotres," the mocking organ of the Privileged party, so light-heartedly and provocatively edited by a group of gentlemen afflicted by a singular mental myopy.

The Friday of that very busy week in the life of this young man who even thereafter is to persist in reminding us that he is not in any sense a man of action, found the vestibule of the Manege empty of swordsmen when he made his leisurely and expectant egress between Le Chapelier and Kersain.

So surprised was he that he checked in his stride.

"Have they had enough?" he wondered, addressing the question to Le Chapelier.

"They have had enough of you, I should think," was the answer. "They will prefer to turn their attention to some one less able to take care of himself."

Now this was disappointing. Andre-Louis had lent himself to this business with a very definite object in view. The slaying of Chabrillane had, as far as it went, been satisfactory. He had regarded that as a sort of acceptable hors d'oeuvre. But the three who had followed were no affair of his at all. He had met them with a certain amount of repugnance, and dealt with each as lightly as consideration of his own safety permitted. Was the baiting of him now to cease whilst the man at whom he aimed had not presented himself? In that case it would be necessary to force the pace!

Out there under the awning a group of gentlemen stood in earnest talk. Scanning the group in a rapid glance, Andre-Louis perceived M. de La Tour d'Azyr amongst them. He tightened his lips. He must afford no provocation. It must be for them to fasten their quarrels upon him. Already the "Actes des Apotres" that morning had torn the mask from his face, and proclaimed him the fencing-master of the Rue du Hasard, successor to Bertrand des Amis. Hazardous as it had been hitherto for a man of his condition to engage in single combat it was rendered doubly so by this exposure, offered to the public as an aristocratic apologia.

Still, matters could not be left where they were, or he should have had all his pains for nothing. Carefully looking away from that group of gentlemen, he raised his voice so that his words must carry to their ears.

"It begins to look as if my fears of having to spend the remainder of my days in the Bois were idle."

Out of the corner of his eye he caught the stir his words created in that group. Its members had turned to look at him; but for the moment that was all. A little more was necessary. Pacing slowly along between his friends he resumed:

"But is it not remarkable that the assassin of Lagron should make no move against Lagron's successor? Or perhaps it is not remarkable. Perhaps there are good reasons. Perhaps the gentleman is prudent."

He had passed the group by now, and he left that last sentence of his to trail behind him, and after it sent laughter, insolent and provoking.

He had not long to wait. Came a quick step behind him, and a hand falling upon his shoulder, spun him violently round. He was brought face to face with M. de La Tour d'Azyr, whose handsome countenance was calm and composed, but whose eyes reflected something of the sudden blaze of passion stirring in him. Behind him several members of the group were approaching more slowly. The others—like Andre-Louis' two companions—remained at gaze.

"You spoke of me, I think," said the Marquis quietly.

"I spoke of an assassin—yes. But to these my friends." Andre-Louis' manner was no less quiet, indeed the quieter of the two, for he was the more experienced actor.

"You spoke loudly enough to be overheard," said the Marquis, answering the insinuation that he had been eavesdropping.

"Those who wish to overhear frequently contrive to do so."

"I perceive that it is your aim to be offensive."

"Oh, but you are mistaken, M. le Marquis. I have no wish to be offensive. But I resent having hands violently laid upon me, especially when they are hands that I cannot consider clean, In the circumstances I can hardly be expected to be polite."

The elder man's eyelids flickered. Almost he caught himself admiring Andre-Louis' bearing. Rather, he feared that his own must suffer by comparison. Because of this, he enraged altogether, and lost control of himself.

"You spoke of me as the assassin of Lagron. I do not affect to misunderstand you. You expounded your views to me once before, and I remember."

"But what flattery, monsieur!"

"You called me an assassin then, because I used my skill to dispose of a turbulent hot-head who made the world unsafe for me. But how much better are you, M. the fencing-master, when you oppose yourself to men whose skill is as naturally inferior to your own!"

M. de La Tour d'Azyr's friends looked grave, perturbed. It was really incredible to find this great gentleman so far forgetting himself as to descend to argument with a canaille of a lawyer-swordsman. And what was worse, it was an argument in which he was being made ridiculous.

"I oppose myself to them!" said Andre-Louis on a tone of amused protest. "Ah, pardon, M. le Marquis; it is they who chose to oppose themselves to me—and so stupidly. They push me, they slap my face, they tread on my toes, they call me by unpleasant names. What if I am a fencing-master? Must I on that account submit to every manner of ill-treatment from your bad-mannered friends? Perhaps had they found out sooner that I am a fencing-master their manners would have been better. But to blame me for that! What injustice!"

"Comedian!" the Marquis contemptuously apostrophized him. "Does it alter the case? Are these men who have opposed you men who live by the sword like yourself?"

"On the contrary, M. le Marquis, I have found them men who died by the sword with astonishing ease. I cannot suppose that you desire to add yourself to their number."

"And why, if you please?" La Tour d'Azyr's face had flamed scarlet before that sneer.

"Oh," Andre-Louis raised his eyebrows and pursed his lips, a man considering. He delivered himself slowly. "Because, monsieur, you prefer the easy victim—the Lagrons and Vilmorins of this world, mere sheep for your butchering. That is why."

And then the Marquis struck him.

Andre-Louis stepped back. His eyes gleamed a moment; the next they were smiling up into the face of his tall enemy.

"No better than the others, after all! Well, well! Remark, I beg you, how history repeats itself—with certain differences. Because poor Vilmorin could not bear a vile lie with which you goaded him, he struck you. Because you cannot bear an equally vile truth which I have uttered, you strike me. But always is the vileness yours. And now as then for the striker there is..." He broke off. "But why name it? You will remember what there is. Yourself you wrote it that day with the point of your too-ready sword. But there. I will meet you if you desire it, monsieur."

"What else do you suppose that I desire? To talk?"

Andre-Louis turned to his friends and sighed. "So that I am to go another jaunt to the Bois. Isaac, perhaps you will kindly have a word with one of these friends of M. le Marquis', and arrange for nine o'clock to-morrow, as usual."

"Not to-morrow," said the Marquis shortly to Le Chapeher. "I have an engagement in the country, which I cannot postpone."

Le Chapelier looked at Andre-Louis.

"Then for M. le Marquis' convenience, we will say Sunday at the same hour."

"I do not fight on Sunday. I am not a pagan to break the holy day."

"But surely the good God would not have the presumption to damn a gentleman of M. le Marquis' quality on that account? Ah, well, Isaac, please arrange for Monday, if it is not a feast-day or monsieur has not some other pressing engagement. I leave it in your hands."

He bowed with the air of a man wearied by these details, and threading his arm through Kersain's withdrew.

"Ah, Dieu de Dieu! But what a trick of it you have," said the Breton deputy, entirely unsophisticated in these matters.

"To be sure I have. I have taken lessons at their hands." He laughed. He was in excellent good-humour. And Kersain was enrolled in the ranks of those who accounted Andre-Louis a man without heart or conscience.

But in his "Confessions" he tells us—and this is one of the glimpses that reveal the true man under all that make-believe—that on that night he went down on his knees to commune with his dead friend Philippe, and to call his spirit to witness that he was about to take the last step in the fulfilment of the oath sworn upon his body at Gavrillac two years ago.

CHAPTER IX. TORN PRIDE

M. de La Tour d'Azyr's engagement in the country on that Sunday was with M. de Kercadiou. To fulfil it he drove out early in the day to Meudon, taking with him in his pocket a copy of the last issue of "Les Actes des Apotres," a journal whose merry sallies at the expense of the innovators greatly diverted the Seigneur de Gavrillac. The venomous scorn it poured upon those worthless rapscallions afforded him a certain solatium against the discomforts of expatriation by which he was afflicted as a result of their detestable energies.

Twice in the last month, had M. de La Tour d'Azyr gone to visit the Lord of Gavrillac at Meudon, and the sight of Aline, so sweet and fresh, so bright and of so lively a mind, had caused those embers smouldering under the ashes of the past, embers which until now he had believed utterly extinct, to kindle into flame once more. He desired her as we desire Heaven. I believe that it was the purest passion of his life; that had it come to him earlier he might have been a vastly different man. The cruelest wound that in all his selfish life he had taken was when she sent him word, quite definitely after the affair at the Feydau, that she could not again in any circumstances receive him. At one blow—through that disgraceful riot—he had been robbed of a mistress he prized and of a wife who had become a necessity to the very soul of him. The sordid love of La Binet might have consoled him for the compulsory renunciation of his exalted love of Aline, just as to his exalted love of Aline he had been ready to sacrifice his attachment to La Binet. But that ill-timed riot had robbed him at once of both. Faithful to his word to Sautron he had definitely broken with La Binet, only to find that Aline had definitely broken with him. And by the time that he had sufficiently recovered from his grief to think again of La Binet, the comedienne had vanished beyond discovery.

For all this he blamed, and most bitterly blamed, Andre-Louis. That low-born provincial lout pursued him like a Nemesis, was become indeed the evil genius of his life. That was it—the evil genius of his life! And it was odds that on Monday... He did not like to think of Monday. He was not particularly afraid of death. He was as brave as his kind in that respect, too brave in the ordinary way, and too confident of his skill, to have considered even remotely such a possibility as that of dying in a duel. It was only that it would seem like a proper consummation of all the evil that he had suffered directly or indirectly through this Andre-Louis

Moreau that he should perish ignobly by his hand. Almost he could hear that insolent, pleasant voice making the flippant announcement to the Assembly on Monday morning.

He shook off the mood, angry with himself for entertaining it. It was maudlin. After all Chabrillane and La Motte-Royau were quite exceptional swordsmen, but neither of them really approached his own formidable calibre. Reaction began to flow, as he drove out through country lanes flooded with pleasant September sunshine. His spirits rose. A premonition of victory stirred within him. Far from fearing Monday's meeting, as he had so unreasonably been doing, he began to look forward to it. It should afford him the means of setting a definite term to this persecution of which he had been the victim. He would crush this insolent and persistent flea that had been stinging him at every opportunity. Borne upward on that wave of optimism, he took presently a more hopeful view of his case with Aline.

At their first meeting a month ago he had used the utmost frankness with her. He had told her the whole truth of his motives in going that night to the Feydau; he had made her realize that she had acted unjustly towards him. True he had gone no farther.

But that was very far to have gone as a beginning. And in their last meeting, now a fortnight old, she had received him with frank friendliness. True, she had been a little aloof. But that was to be expected until he quite explicitly avowed that he had revived the hope of winning her. He had been a fool not to have returned before to-day.

Thus in that mood of new-born confidence—a confidence risen from the very ashes of despondency—came he on that Sunday morning to Meudon. He was gay and jovial with M. de Kercadiou what time he waited in the salon for mademoiselle to show herself. He pronounced with confidence on the country's future. There were signs already—he wore the rosiest spectacles that morning—of a change of opinion, of a more moderate note. The Nation began to perceive whither this lawyer rabble was leading it. He pulled out "The Acts of the Apostles" and read a stinging paragraph. Then, when mademoiselle at last made her appearance, he resigned the journal into the hands of M. de Kercadiou.

M. de Kercadiou, with his niece's future to consider, went to read the paper in the garden, taking up there a position whence he could keep the couple within sight—as his obligations seemed to demand of him—whilst being discreetly out of earshot.

The Marquis made the most of an opportunity that might be brief. He quite frankly declared himself, and begged, implored to be taken back into Aline's good graces, to be admitted at least to the hope that one day before very long she would bring herself to consider him in a nearer relationship.

"Mademoiselle," he told her, his voice vibrating with a feeling that admitted of no doubt, "you cannot lack conviction of my utter sincerity. The very constancy of my devotion should afford you this. It is just that I should have been banished from you, since I showed myself so utterly unworthy of the great honour to which

I aspired. But this banishment has nowise diminished my devotion. If you could conceive what I have suffered, you would agree that I have fully expiated my abject fault."

She looked at him with a curious, gentle wistfulness on her lovely face.

"Monsieur, it is not you whom I doubt. It is myself."

"You mean your feelings towards me?"

"Yes."

"But that I can understand. After what has happened..."

"It was always so, monsieur," she interrupted quietly. "You speak of me as if lost to you by your own action. That is to say too much. Let me be frank with you. Monsieur, I was never yours to lose. I am conscious of the honour that you do me. I esteem you very deeply..."

"But, then," he cried, on a high note of confidence, "from such a beginning..."

"Who shall assure me that it is a beginning? May it not be the whole? Had I held you in affection, monsieur, I should have sent for you after the affair of which you have spoken. I should at least not have condemned you without hearing your explanation. As it was..." She shrugged, smiling gently, sadly. "You see..."

But his optimism far from being crushed was stimulated. "But it is to give me hope, mademoiselle. If already I possess so much, I may look with confidence to win more. I shall prove myself worthy. I swear to do that. Who that is permitted the privilege of being near you could do other than seek to render himself worthy?"

And then before she could add a word, M. de Kercadiou came blustering through the window, his spectacles on his forehead, his face inflamed, waving in his hand "The Acts of the Apostles," and apparently reduced to speechlessness.

Had the Marquis expressed himself aloud he would have been profane. As it was he bit his lip in vexation at this most inopportune interruption.

Aline sprang up, alarmed by her uncle's agitation.

"What has happened?"

"Happened?" He found speech at last. "The scoundrel! The faithless dog! I consented to overlook the past on the clear condition that he should avoid revolutionary politics in future. That condition he accepted, and now"—he smacked the news-sheet furiously—"he has played me false again. Not only has he gone into politics, once more, but he is actually a member of the Assembly, and what is worse he has been using his assassin's skill as a fencing-master, turning himself into a bully-swordsman. My God! Is there any law at all left in France?"

One doubt M. de La Tour d'Azyr had entertained, though only faintly, to mar the perfect serenity of his growing optimism. That doubt concerned this man Moreau and his relations with M. de Kercadiou. He knew what once they had been, and how changed they subsequently were by the ingratitude of Moreau's own behavior in turning against the class to which his benefactor belonged. What he did not know was that a reconciliation had been effected. For in the past month—ever since circumstances had driven Andre-Louis to depart from his undertaking to steer clear of politics—the young man had not ventured to approach Meudon, and as it happened his name had not been mentioned in La Tour d'Azyr's hearing on the occasion of either of his own previous visits. He learnt of that reconciliation now; but he learnt at the same time that the breach was now renewed, and rendered wider and more impassable than ever. Therefore he did not hesitate to avow his own position.

"There is a law," he answered. "The law that this rash young man himself evokes. The law of the sword." He spoke very gravely, almost sadly. For he realized that after all the ground was tender. "You are not to suppose that he is to continue indefinitely his career of evil and of murder. Sooner or later he will meet a sword that will avenge the others. You have observed that my cousin Chabrillane is among the number of this assassin's victims; that he was killed on Tuesday last."

"If I have not expressed my condolence, Azyr, it is because my indignation stifles at the moment every other feeling. The scoundrel! You say that sooner or later he will meet a sword that will avenge the others. I pray that it may be soon."

The Marquis answered him quietly, without anything but sorrow in his voice. "I think your prayer is likely to be heard. This wretched young man has an engagement for to-morrow, when his account may be definitely settled."

He spoke with such calm conviction that his words had all the sound of a sentence of death. They suddenly stemmed the flow of M. de Kercadiou's anger. The colour receded from his inflamed face; dread looked out of his pale eyes, to inform M. de La Tour d'Azyr, more clearly than any words, that M. de Kercadiou's hot speech had been the expression of unreflecting anger, that his prayer that retribution might soon overtake his godson had been unconsciously insincere. Confronted now by the fact that this retribution was about to be visited upon that scoundrel, the fundamental gentleness and kindliness of his nature asserted itself; his anger was suddenly whelmed in apprehension; his affection for the lad beat up to the surface, making Andre-Louis' sin, however hideous, a thing of no account by comparison with the threatened punishment.

M. de Kercadiou moistened his lips.

"With whom is this engagement?" he asked in a voice that by an effort he contrived to render steady.

M. de La Tour d'Azyr bowed his handsome head, his eyes upon the gleaming parquetry of the floor. "With myself," he answered quietly, conscious already with a tightening of the heart that his answer must sow dismay. He caught the sound of a faint outcry from Aline; he saw the sudden recoil of M. de Kercadiou. And then he plunged headlong into the explanation that he deemed necessary.

"In view of his relations with you, M. de Kercadiou, and because of my deep regard for you, I did my best to avoid this, even though as you will understand the death of my dear friend and cousin Chabrillane seemed to summon me to action, even though I knew that my circumspection was becoming matter for criticism among my friends. But yesterday this unbridled young man made further restraint impossible to me. He provoked me deliberately and publicly. He put upon me the very grossest affront, and... to-morrow morning in the Bois... we meet."

He faltered a little at the end, fully conscious of the hostile atmosphere in which he suddenly found himself. Hostility from M. de Kercadiou, the latter's earlier change of manner had already led him to expect; the hostility of mademoiselle came more in the nature of a surprise.

He began to understand what difficulties the course to which he was committed must raise up for him. A fresh obstacle was to be flung across the path which he had just cleared, as he imagined. Yet his pride and his sense of the justice due to be done admitted of no weakening.

In bitterness he realized now, as he looked from uncle to niece—his glance, usually so direct and bold, now oddly furtive—that though to-morrow he might kill Andre-Louis, yet even by his death Andre-Louis would take vengeance upon him. He had exaggerated nothing in reaching the conclusion that this Andre-Louis Moreau was the evil genius of his life. He saw now that do what he would, kill him even though he might, he could never conquer him. The last word would always be with Andre-Louis Moreau. In bitterness, in rage, and in humiliation—a thing almost unknown to him—did he realize it, and the realization steeled his purpose for all that he perceived its futility.

Outwardly he showed himself calm and self-contained, properly suggesting a man regretfully accepting the inevitable. It would have been as impossible to find fault with his bearing as to attempt to turn him from the matter to which he was committed. And so M. de Kercadiou perceived.

"My God!" was all that he said, scarcely above his breath, yet almost in a groan.

M. de La Tour d'Azyr did, as always, the thing that sensibility demanded of him. He took his leave. He understood that to linger where his news had produced such an effect would be impossible, indecent. So he departed, in a bitterness comparable only with his erstwhile optimism, the sweet fruit of hope turned to a thing of gall even as it touched his lips. Oh, yes; the last word, indeed, was with Andre-Louis Moreau—always!

Uncle and niece looked at each other as he passed out, and there was horror in the eyes of both. Aline's pallor was deathly almost, and standing there now she wrung her hands as if in pain.

"Why did you not ask him—beg him..." She broke off.

"To what end? He was in the right, and... and there are things one cannot ask; things it would be a useless humiliation to ask." He sat down, groaning. "Oh, the poor boy—the poor, misguided boy."

In the mind of neither, you see, was there any doubt of what must be the issue. The calm confidence in which La Tour d'Azyr had spoken compelled itself to be shared. He was no vainglorious boaster, and they knew of what a force as a swordsman he was generally accounted.

"What does humiliation matter? A life is at issue—Andre's life."

"I know. My God, don't I know? And I would humiliate myself if by humiliating myself I could hope to prevail. But Azyr is a hard, relentless man, and..."

Abruptly she left him.

She overtook the Marquis as he was in the act of stepping his carriage. He turned as she called, and bowed.

"Mademoiselle?"

At once he guessed her errand, tasted in anticipation the unparalleled bitterness of being compelled to refuse her. Yet at her invitation he stepped back into the cool of the hall.

In the middle of the floor of chequered marbles, black and white, stood a carved table of black oak. By this he halted, leaning lightly against it whilst she sat enthroned in the great crimson chair beside it.

"Monsieur, I cannot allow you so to depart," she said. "You cannot realize, monsieur, what a blow would be dealt my uncle if... if evil, irrevocable evil were to overtake his godson to-morrow. The expressions that he used at first..."

"Mademoiselle, I perceived their true value. Spare yourself. Believe me I am profoundly desolated by circumstances which I had not expected to find. You must believe me when I say that. It is all that I can say."

"Must it really be all? Andre is very dear to his godfather."

The pleading tone cut him like a knife; and then suddenly it aroused another emotion—an emotion which he realized to be utterly unworthy, an emotion which, in his overwhelming pride of race, seemed almost sullying, yet not to be repressed. He hesitated to give it utterance; hesitated even remotely to suggest so horrible a thing as that in a man of such lowly origin he might conceivably discover a rival. Yet that sudden pang of jealousy was stronger than his monstrous pride.

"And to you, mademoiselle? What is this Andre-Louis Moreau to you? You will pardon the question. But I desire clearly to understand."

Watching her he beheld the scarlet stain that overspread her face. He read in it at first confusion, until the gleam of her blue eyes announced its source to lie in anger. That comforted him; since he had affronted her, he was reassured. It did not occur to him that the anger might have another source.

"Andre and I have been playmates from infancy. He is very dear to me, too; almost I regard him as a brother. Were I in need of help, and were my uncle not available, Andre would be the first man to whom I should turn. Are you sufficiently answered, monsieur? Or is there more of me you would desire revealed?"

He bit his lip. He was unnerved, he thought, this morning; otherwise the silly suspicion with which he had offended could never have occurred to him.

He bowed very low. "Mademoiselle, forgive that I should have troubled you with such a question. You have answered more fully than I could have hoped or wished."

He said no more than that. He waited for her to resume. At a loss, she sat in silence awhile, a pucker on her white brow, her fingers nervously drumming on the table. At last she flung herself headlong against the impassive, polished front that he presented.

"I have come, monsieur, to beg you to put off this meeting."

She saw the faint raising of his dark eyebrows, the faintly regretful smile that scarcely did more than tinge his fine lips, and she hurried on. "What honour can await you in such an engagement, monsieur?"

It was a shrewd thrust at the pride of race that she accounted his paramount sentiment, that had as often lured him into error as it had urged him into good.

"I do not seek honour in it, mademoiselle, but—I must say it—justice. The engagement, as I have explained, is not of my seeking. It has been thrust upon me, and in honour I cannot draw back."

"Why, what dishonour would there be in sparing him? Surely, monsieur, none would call your courage in question? None could misapprehend your motives."

"You are mistaken, mademoiselle. My motives would most certainly be misapprehended. You forget that this young man has acquired in the past week a certain reputation that might well make a man hesitate to meet him."

She brushed that aside almost contemptuously, conceiving it the merest quibble.

"Some men, yes. But not you, M. le Marquis."

Her confidence in him on every count was most sweetly flattering. But there was a bitterness behind the sweet.

"Even I, mademoiselle, let me assure you. And there is more than that. This quarrel which M. Moreau has forced upon me is no new thing. It is merely the culmination of a long-drawn persecution..."

"Which you invited," she cut in. "Be just, monsieur."

"I hope that it is not in my nature to be otherwise, mademoiselle."

"Consider, then, that you killed his friend."

"I find in that nothing with which to reproach myself. My justification lay in the circumstances—the subsequent events in this distracted country surely confirm it."

"And..." She faltered a little, and looked away from him for the first time. "And that you... that you... And what of Mademoiselle Binet, whom he was to have married?"

He stared at her for a moment in sheer surprise. "Was to have married?" he repeated incredulously, dismayed almost.

"You did not know that?"

"But how do you?"

"Did I not tell you that we are as brother and sister almost? I have his confidence. He told me, before... before you made it impossible."

He looked away, chin in hand, his glance thoughtful, disturbed, almost wistful.

"There is," he said slowly, musingly, "a singular fatality at work between that man and me, bringing us ever each by turns athwart the other's path..."

He sighed; then swung to face her again, speaking more briskly: "Mademoiselle, until this moment I had no knowledge—no suspicion of this thing. But..."

He broke off, considered, and then shrugged. "If I wronged him, I did so unconsciously. It would be unjust to blame me, surely. In all our actions it must be the intention alone that counts."

"But does it make no difference?"

"None that I can discern, mademoiselle. It gives me no justification to withdraw from that to which I am irrevocably committed. No justification, indeed, could ever be greater than my concern for the pain it must occasion my good friend, your uncle, and perhaps yourself, mademoiselle."

She rose suddenly, squarely confronting him, desperate now, driven to play the only card upon which she thought she might count.

"Monsieur," she said, "you did me the honour to-day to speak in certain terms; to... to allude to certain hopes with which you honour me."

He looked at her almost in fear. In silence, not daring to speak, he waited for her to continue.

"I... I... Will you please to understand, monsieur, that if you persist in this matter, if... unless you can break this engagement of yours to-morrow morning in the Bois, you are not to presume to mention this subject to me again, or, indeed, ever again to approach me."

To put the matter in this negative way was as far as she could possibly go. It was for him to make the positive proposal to which she had thus thrown wide the door.

"Mademoiselle, you cannot mean..."

"I do, monsieur... irrevocably, please to understand." He looked at her with eyes of misery, his handsome, manly face as pale as she had ever seen it. The hand he had been holding out in protest began to shake. He lowered it to his side again, lest she should perceive its tremor. Thus a brief second, while the battle was fought within him, the bitter engagement between his desires and what he conceived to be the demands of his honour, never perceiving how far his honour was buttressed by implacable vindictiveness. Retreat, he conceived, was impossible without shame; and shame was to him an agony unthinkable. She asked too much. She could not understand what she was asking, else she would never be so unreasonable, so unjust. But also he saw that it would be futile to attempt to make her understand.

It was the end. Though he kill Andre-Louis Moreau in the morning as he fiercely hoped he would, yet the victory even in death must lie with Andre-Louis Moreau.

He bowed profoundly, grave and sorrowful of face as he was grave and sorrowful of heart.

"Mademoiselle, my homage," he murmured, and turned to go.

"But you have not answered me!" she called after him in terror.

He checked on the threshold, and turned; and there from the cool gloom of the hall she saw him a black, graceful silhouette against the brilliant sunshine beyond—a memory of him that was to cling as something sinister and menacing in the dread hours that were to follow.

"What would you, mademoiselle? I but spared myself and you the pain of a refusal."

He was gone leaving her crushed and raging. She sank down again into the great red chair, and sat there crumpled, her elbows on the table, her face in her hands—a face that was on fire with shame and passion. She had offered herself, and she had been refused! The inconceivable had befallen her. The humiliation of it seemed to her something that could never be effaced.

Startled, appalled, she stepped back, her hand pressed to her tortured breast.

CHAPTER X. THE RETURNING CARRIAGE

M. de Kercadiou wrote a letter.

"Godson," he began, without any softening adjective, "I have learnt with pain and indignation that you have dishonoured yourself again by breaking the pledge you gave me to abstain from politics. With still greater pain and indignation do I learn that your name has become in a few short days a byword, that you have discarded the weapon of false, insidious arguments against my class—the class to which you owe everything—for the sword of the assassin. It has come to my knowledge that you have an assignation to-morrow with my good friend M. de La Tour d'Azyr. A gentleman of his station is under certain obligations imposed upon him by his birth, which do not permit him to draw back from an engagement. But you labour under no such disadvantages. For a man of your class to refuse an engagement of honour, or to neglect it when made, entails no sacrifice. Your peers will probably be of the opinion that you display a commendable prudence. Therefore I beg you, indeed, did I think that I still exercise over you any such authority as the favours you have received from me should entitle me to exercise, I would command you, to allow this matter to go no farther, and to refrain from rendering yourself to your assignation to-morrow morning. Having no such authority, as your past conduct now makes clear, having no reason to hope that a proper sentiment of gratitude to me will induce to give heed to this my most earnest request, I am compelled to add that should you survive to-morrow's encounter, I can in no circumstances ever again permit myself to be conscious of your existence. If any spark survives of the affection that once you expressed for me, or if you set any value upon the affection, which, in spite of all that you have done to forfeit it, is the chief prompter of this letter, you will not refuse to do as I am asking."

It was not a tactful letter. M. de Kercadiou was not a tactful man. Read it as he would, Andre-Louis—when it was delivered to him on that Sunday afternoon by the groom dispatched with it into Paris—could read into it only concern for M. La Tour d'Azyr, M. de Kercadiou's good friend, as he called him, and prospective nephew-in-law.

He kept the groom waiting a full hour while composing his answer. Brief though it was, it cost him very considerable effort and several unsuccessful attempts. In the end this is what he wrote:

Monsieur my godfather—You make refusal singularly hard for me when you appeal to me upon the ground of affection. It is a thing of which all my life I shall hail the opportunity to give you proofs, and I am therefore desolated beyond anything I could hope to express that I cannot give you the proof you ask to-day. There is too much between M. de La Tour d'Azyr and me. Also you do me and my class—whatever it may be—less than justice when you say that obligations of honour are not binding upon us. So binding do I count them, that, if I would, I could not now draw back.

If hereafter you should persist in the harsh intention you express, I must suffer it. That I shall suffer be assured.

Your affectionate and grateful godson

Andre-Louis

He dispatched that letter by M. de Kercadiou's groom, and conceived this to be the end of the matter. It cut him keenly; but he bore the wound with that outward stoicism he affected.

Next morning, at a quarter past eight, as with Le Chapelier—who had come to break his fast with him—he was rising from table to set out for the Bois, his housekeeper startled him by announcing Mademoiselle de Kercadiou.

He looked at his watch. Although his cabriolet was already at the door, he had a few minutes to spare. He excused himself from Le Chapelier, and went briskly out to the anteroom.

She advanced to meet him, her manner eager, almost feverish.

"I will not affect ignorance of why you have come," he said quickly, to make short work. "But time presses, and I warn you that only the most solid of reasons can be worth stating."

It surprised her. It amounted to a rebuff at the very outset, before she had uttered a word; and that was the last thing she had expected from Andre-Louis. Moreover, there was about him an air of aloofness that was unusual where she was concerned, and his voice had been singularly cold and formal.

It wounded her. She was not to guess the conclusion to which he had leapt. He made with regard to her—as was but natural, after all—the same mistake that he had made with regard to yesterday's letter from his godfather. He conceived that the mainspring of action here was solely concern for M. de La Tour d'Azyr. That it might be concern for himself never entered his mind. So absolute was his own conviction of what must be the inevitable issue of that meeting that he could not conceive of any one entertaining a fear on his behalf.

What he assumed to be anxiety on the score of the predestined victim had irritated him in M. de Kercadiou; in Aline it filled him with a cold anger; he argued from it that she had hardly been frank with him; that ambition was urging her to consider with favour the suit of M. de La Tour d'Azyr. And than this there was no spur that could have driven more relentlessly in his purpose, since to save her was in his eyes almost as momentous as to avenge the past.

She conned him searchingly, and the complete calm of him at such a time amazed her. She could not repress the mention of it.

"How calm you are, Andre!"

"I am not easily disturbed. It is a vanity of mine."

"But... Oh, Andre, this meeting must not take place!" She came close up to him, to set her hands upon his shoulders, and stood so, her face within a foot of his own.

"You know, of course, of some good reason why it should not?" said he.

"You may be killed," she answered him, and her eyes dilated as she spoke.

It was so far from anything that he had expected that for a moment he could only stare at her. Then he thought he had understood. He laughed as he removed her hands from his shoulders, and stepped back. This was a shallow device, childish and unworthy in her.

"Can you really think to prevail by attempting to frighten me?" he asked, and almost sneered.

"Oh, you are surely mad! M. de La Tour d'Azyr is reputed the most dangerous sword in France."

"Have you never noticed that most reputations are undeserved? Chabrillane was a dangerous swordsman, and Chabrillane is underground. La Motte-Royau was an even more dangerous swordsman, and he is in a surgeon's hands. So are the other spadassinicides who dreamt of skewering a poor sheep of a provincial lawyer. And here to-day comes the chief, the fine flower of these bully-swordsmen. He comes, for wages long overdue. Be sure of that. So if you have no other reason to urge..."

It was the sarcasm of him that mystified her. Could he possibly be sincere in his assurance that he must prevail against M. de La Tour d'Azyr? To her in her limited knowledge, her mind filled with her uncle's contrary conviction, it seemed that Andre-Louis was only acting; he would act a part to the very end.

Be that as it might, she shifted her ground to answer him.

"You had my uncle's letter?"

"And I answered it."

"I know. But what he said, he will fulfil. Do not dream that he will relent if you carry out this horrible purpose."

"Come, now, that is a better reason than the other," said he. "If there is a reason in the world that could move me it would be that. But there is too much between La Tour d'Azyr and me. There is an oath I swore on the dead hand of Philippe de Vilmorin. I could never have hoped that God would afford me so great an opportunity of keeping it."

"You have not kept it yet," she warned him.

He smiled at her. "True!" he said. "But nine o'clock will soon be here. Tell me," he asked her suddenly, "why did you not carry this request of yours to M. de La Tour d'Azyr?"

"I did," she answered him, and flushed as she remembered her yesterday's rejection. He interpreted the flush quite otherwise.

"And he?" he asked.

"M. de La Tour d'Azyr's obligations..." she was beginning: then she broke off to answer shortly: "Oh, he refused."

"So, so. He must, of course, whatever it may have cost him. Yet in his place I should have counted the cost as nothing. But men are different, you see." He sighed. "Also in your place, had that been so, I think I should have left the matter there. But then..."

"I don't understand you, Andre."

"I am not so very obscure. Not nearly so obscure as I can be. Turn it over in your mind. It may help to comfort you presently." He consulted his watch again. "Pray use this house as your own. I must be going."

Le Chapelier put his head in at the door.

"Forgive the intrusion. But we shall be late, Andre, unless you..."

"Coming," Andre answered him. "If you will await my return, Aline, you will oblige me deeply. Particularly in view of your uncle's resolve."

She did not answer him. She was numbed. He took her silence for assent, and, bowing, left her. Standing there she heard his steps going down the stairs together with Le Chapelier's. He was speaking to his friend, and his voice was calm and normal.

Oh, he was mad—blinded by self-confidence and vanity. As his carriage rattled away, she sat down limply, with a sense of exhaustion and nausea. She was sick and faint with horror. Andre-Louis was going to his death. Conviction of it—an unreasoning conviction, the result, perhaps, of all M. de Kercadiou's rantings—entered her soul. Awhile she sat thus, paralyzed by hopelessness. Then she sprang up again, wringing her hands. She must do something to avert this horror. But what could she do? To follow him to the Bois and intervene there would be to make a scandal for no purpose. The conventions of conduct were all against her, offering a barrier that was not to be overstepped. Was there no one could help her?

Standing there, half-frenzied by her helplessness, she caught again a sound of vehicles and hooves on the cobbles of the street below. A carriage was approaching. It drew up with a clatter before the fencing-academy. Could it be Andre-Louis returning? Passionately she snatched at that straw of hope. Knocking, loud and urgent, fell upon the door. She heard Andre-Louis' housekeeper, her wooden shoes clanking upon the stairs, hurrying down to open.

She sped to the door of the anteroom, and pulling it wide stood breathlessly to listen. But the voice that floated up to her was not the voice she so desperately hoped to hear. It was a woman's voice asking in urgent tones for M. Andre-Louis—a voice at first vaguely familiar, then clearly recognized, the voice of Mme. de Plougastel.

Excited, she ran to the head of the narrow staircase in time to hear Mme. de Plougastel exclaim in agitation:

"He has gone already! Oh, but how long since? Which way did he take?"

It was enough to inform Aline that Mme. de Plougastel's errand must be akin to her own. At the moment, in the general distress and confusion of her mind, her mental vision focussed entirely on the one vital point, she found in this no matter for astonishment. The singular regard conceived by Mme. de Plougastel for Andre-Louis seemed to her then a sufficient explanation.

Without pausing to consider, she ran down that steep staircase, calling:

"Madame! Madame!"

The portly, comely housekeeper drew aside, and the two ladies faced each other on that threshold. Mme. de Plougastel looked white and haggard, a nameless dread staring from her eyes.

"Aline! You here!" she exclaimed. And then in the urgency sweeping aside all minor considerations, "Were you also too late?" she asked.

"No, madame. I saw him. I implored him. But he would not listen."

"Oh, this is horrible!" Mme. de Plougastel shuddered as she spoke. "I heard of it only half an hour ago, and I came at once, to prevent it at all costs."

The two women looked blankly, despairingly, at each other. In the sunshine-flooded street one or two shabby idlers were pausing to eye the handsome equipage with its magnificent bay horses, and the two great ladies on the doorstep of the fencing-academy. From across the way came the raucous voice of an itinerant bellows-mender raised in the cry of his trade:

"A raccommoder les vieux soufflets!"

Madame swung to the housekeeper.

"How long is it since monsieur left?"

"Ten minutes, maybe; hardly more." Conceiving these great ladies to be friends of her invincible master's latest victim, the good woman preserved a decently stolid exterior.

Madame wrung her hands. "Ten minutes! Oh!" It was almost a moan. "Which way did he go?"

"The assignation is for nine o'clock in the Bois de Boulogne," Aline informed her. "Could we follow? Could we prevail if we did?"

"Ah, my God! The question is should we come in time? At nine o'clock! And it wants but little more than a quarter of an hour. Mon Dieu! Mon Dieu!" Madame clasped and unclasped her hands in anguish. "Do you know, at least, where in the Bois they are to meet?"

"No—only that it is in the Bois."

"In the Bois!" Madame was flung into a frenzy. "The Bois is nearly half as large as Paris." But she swept breathlessly on, "Come, Aline: get in, get in!"

Then to her coachman. "To the Bois de Boulogne by way of the Cours la Reine," she commanded, "as fast as you can drive. There are ten pistoles for you if we are in time. Whip up, man!"

She thrust Aline into the carriage, and sprang after her with the energy of a girl. The heavy vehicle—too heavy by far for this race with time—was moving before she had taken her seat. Rocking and lurching it went, earning the maledictions of more than one pedestrian whom it narrowly avoided crushing against a wall or trampling underfoot.

Madame sat back with closed eyes and trembling lips. Her face showed very white and drawn. Aline watched her in silence. Almost it seemed to her that Mme. de Plougastel was suffering as deeply as herself, enduring an anguish of apprehension as great as her own.

Later Aline was to wonder at this. But at the moment all the thought of which her half-numbed mind was capable was bestowed upon their desperate errand.

The carriage rolled across the Place Louis XV and out on to the Cours la Reine at last. Along that beautiful, tree-bordered avenue between the Champs Elysees and the Seine, almost empty at this hour of the day, they made better speed, leaving now a cloud of dust behind them.

But fast to danger-point as was the speed, to the women in that carriage it was too slow. As they reached the barrier at the end of the Cours, nine o'clock was striking in the city behind them, and every stroke of it seemed to sound a note of doom.

Yet here at the barrier the regulations compelled a momentary halt. Aline enquired of the sergeant-in-charge how long it was since a cabriolet such as she described had gone that way. She was answered that some twenty minutes ago a vehicle had passed the barrier containing the deputy M. le Chapelier and the Paladin of the Third Estate, M. Moreau. The sergeant was very well informed. He could make a shrewd guess, he said, with a grin, of the business that took M. Moreau that way so early in the day.

They left him, to speed on now through the open country, following the road that continued to hug the river. They sat back mutely despairing, staring hopelessly ahead, Aline's hand clasped tight in madame's. In the distance, across the meadows on their right, they could see already the long, dusky line of trees of the Bois, and presently the carriage swung aside following a branch of the road that turned to the right, away from the river and heading straight for the forest.

Mademoiselle broke at last the silence of hopelessness that had reigned between them since they had passed the barrier.

"Oh, it is impossible that we should come in time! Impossible!"

"Don't say it! Don't say it!" madame cried out.

"But it is long past nine, madame! Andre would be punctual, and these... affairs do not take long. It... it will be all over by now."

Madame shivered, and closed her eyes. Presently, however, she opened them again, and stirred. Then she put her head from the window. "A carriage is approaching," she announced, and her tone conveyed the thing she feared.

"Not already! Oh, not already!" Thus Aline expressed the silently communicated thought. She experienced a difficulty in breathing, felt the sudden need of air. Something in her throat was throbbing as if it would suffocate her; a mist came and went before her eyes.

In a cloud of dust an open caleche was speeding towards them, coming from the Bois. They watched it, both pale, neither venturing to speak, Aline, indeed, without breath to do so.

As it approached, it slowed down, perforce, as they did, to effect a safe passage in that narrow road. Aline was at the window with Mme. de Plougastel, and with fearful eyes both looked into this open carriage that was drawing abreast of them.

"Which of them is it, madame? Oh, which of them?" gasped Aline, scarce daring to look, her senses swimming.

On the near side sat a swarthy young gentleman unknown to either of the ladies. He was smiling as he spoke to his companion. A moment later and the man sitting beyond came into view. He was not smiling. His face was white and set, and it was the face of the Marquis de La Tour d'Azyr.

For a long moment, in speechless horror, both women stared at him, until, perceiving them, blankest surprise invaded his stern face.

In that moment, with a long shuddering sigh Aline sank swooning to the carriage floor behind Mme. de Plougastel.

CHAPTER XI. INFERENCES

By fast driving Andre-Louis had reached the ground some minutes ahead of time, notwithstanding the slight delay in setting out. There he had found M. de La Tour d'Azyr already awaiting him, supported by a M. d'Ormesson, a swarthy young gentleman in the blue uniform of a captain in the Gardes du Corps.

Andre-Louis had been silent and preoccupied throughout that drive. He was perturbed by his last interview with Mademoiselle de Kercadiou and the rash inferences which he had drawn as to her motives.

"Decidedly," he had said, "this man must be killed."

Le Chapelier had not answered him. Almost, indeed, had the Breton shuddered at his compatriot's cold-bloodedness. He had often of late thought that this fellow Moreau was hardly human. Also he had found him incomprehensibly inconsistent. When first this spadassinicide business had been proposed to him, he had been so very lofty and disdainful. Yet, having embraced it, he went about it at times with a ghoulish flippancy that was revolting, at times with a detachment that was more revolting still.

Their preparations were made quickly and in silence, yet without undue haste or other sign of nervousness on either side. In both men the same grim determination prevailed. The opponent must be killed; there could be no half-measures here. Stripped each of coat and waistcoat, shoeless and with shirt-sleeves rolled to the elbow, they faced each other at last, with the common resolve of paying in full the long score that stood between them. I doubt if either of them entertained a misgiving as to what must be the issue.

Beside them, and opposite each other, stood Le Chapelier and the young captain, alert and watchful.

"Allez, messieurs!"

The slender, wickedly delicate blades clashed together, and after a momentary glizade were whirling, swift and bright as lightnings, and almost as impossible to follow with the eye. The Marquis led the attack, impetuously and vigorously, and almost at once Andre-Louis realized that he had to deal with an opponent of a very different mettle from those successive duellists of last week, not excluding La Motte-Royau, of terrible reputation.

Here was a man whom much and constant practice had given extraordinary speed and a technique that was almost perfect. In addition, he enjoyed over Andre-Louis physical advantages of strength and length of reach, which rendered him altogether formidable. And he was cool, too; cool and self-contained; fearless and purposeful. Would anything shake that calm, wondered Andre-Louis?

He desired the punishment to be as full as he could make it. Not content to kill the Marquis as the Marquis had killed Philippe, he desired that he should first know himself as powerless to avert that death as Philippe had been. Nothing less would content Andre-Louis. M. le Marquis must begin by tasting of that cup of despair. It was in the account; part of the quittance due.

As with a breaking sweep Andre-Louis parried the heavy lunge in which that first series of passes culminated, he actually laughed—gleefully, after the fashion of a boy at a sport he loves.

That extraordinary, ill-timed laugh made M. de La Tour d'Azyr's recovery hastier and less correctly dignified than it would otherwise have been. It startled and discomposed him, who had already been discomposed by the failure to get home with a lunge so beautifully timed and so truly delivered.

He, too, had realized that his opponent's force was above anything that he could have expected, fencing-master though he might be, and on that account he had put forth his utmost energy to make an end at once.

More than the actual parry, the laugh by which it was accompanied seemed to make of that end no more than a beginning. And yet it was the end of something. It was the end of that absolute confidence that had hitherto inspired M. de La Tour d'Azyr. He no longer looked upon the issue as a thing forgone. He realized that if he was to prevail in this encounter, he must go warily and fence as he had never fenced yet in all his life.

They settled down again; and again—on the principle this time that the soundest defence is in attack—it was the Marquis who made the game. Andre-Louis allowed him to do so, desired him to do so; desired him to spend himself and that magnificent speed of his against the greater speed that whole days of fencing in succession for nearly two years had given the master. With a beautiful, easy pressure of forte on foible Andre-Louis kept himself completely covered in that second bout, which once more culminated in a lunge.

Expecting it now, Andre-Louis parried it by no more than a deflecting touch. At the same moment he stepped suddenly forward, right within the other's guard, thus placing his man so completely at his mercy that, as if fascinated, the Marquis did not even attempt to recover himself.

This time Andre-Louis did not laugh: He just smiled into the dilating eyes of M. de La Tour d'Azyr, and made no shift to use his advantage.

"Come, come, monsieur!" he bade him sharply. "Am I to run my blade through an uncovered man?" Deliberately he fell back, whilst his shaken opponent recovered himself at last.

M. d'Ormesson released the breath which horror had for a moment caught. Le Chapelier swore softly, muttering:

"Name of a name! It is tempting Providence to play the fool in this fashion!"

Andre-Louis observed the ashen pallor that now over spread the face of his opponent.

"I think you begin to realize, monsieur, what Philippe de Vilmorin must have felt that day at Gavrillac. I desired that you should first do so. Since that is accomplished, why, here's to make an end."

He went in with lightning rapidity. For a moment his point seemed to La Tour d'Azyr to be everywhere at once, and then from a low engagement in sixte, Andre-Louis stretched forward with swift and vigorous ease to lunge in tierce. He drove his point to transfix his opponent whom a series of calculated disengages uncovered in that line. But to his amazement and chagrin, La Tour d'Azyr parried the stroke; infinitely more to his chagrin La Tour d'Azyr parried it just too late. Had he completely parried it, all would yet have been well. But striking the blade in the last fraction of a second, the Marquis deflected the point from the line of his body, yet not so completely but that a couple of feet of that hard-driven steel tore through the muscles of his sword-arm.

To the seconds none of these details had been visible. All that they had seen had been a swift whirl of flashing blades, and then Andre-Louis stretched almost to the ground in an upward lunge that had pierced the Marquis' right arm just below the shoulder.

The sword fell from the suddenly relaxed grip of La Tour d'Azyr's fingers, which had been rendered powerless, and he stood now disarmed, his lip in his teeth, his face white, his chest heaving, before his opponent, who had at once recovered. With the blood-tinged tip of his sword resting on the ground, Andre-Louis surveyed him grimly, as we survey the prey that through our own clumsiness has escaped us at the last moment.

In the Assembly and in the newspapers this might be hailed as another victory for the Paladin of the Third Estate; only himself could know the extent and the bitternest of the failure.

M. d'Ormesson had sprung to the side of his principal.

"You are hurt!" he had cried stupidly.

"It is nothing," said La Tour d'Azyr. "A scratch." But his lip writhed, and the torn sleeve of his fine cambric shirt was full of blood.

D'Ormesson, a practical man in such matters, produced a linen kerchief, which he tore quickly into strips to improvise a bandage.

Still Andre-Louis continued to stand there, looking on as if bemused. He continued so until Le Chapelier touched him on the arm. Then at last he roused himself, sighed, and turned away to resume his garments, nor did he address or look again at his late opponent, but left the ground at once.

As, with Le Chapelier, he was walking slowly and in silent dejection towards the entrance of the Bois, where they had left their carriage, they were passed by the caleche conveying La Tour d'Azyr and his second—which had originally driven almost right up to the spot of the encounter. The Marquis' wounded arm was carried in a sling improvised from his companion's sword-belt. His sky-blue coat with three collars had been buttoned over this, so that the right sleeve hung empty. Otherwise, saving a certain pallor, he looked much his usual self.

And now you understand how it was that he was the first to return, and that seeing him thus returning, apparently safe and sound, the two ladies, intent upon preventing the encounter, should have assumed that their worst fears were realized.

Mme. de Plougastel attempted to call out, but her voice refused its office. She attempted to throw open the door of her own carriage; but her fingers fumbled clumsily and ineffectively with the handle. And meanwhile the caleche was slowly passing, La Tour d'Azyr's fine eyes sombrely yet intently meeting her own anguished gaze. And then she saw something else. M. d'Ormesson, leaning back again from the forward inclination of his body to join his own to his companion's salutation of the Countess, disclosed the empty right sleeve of M. de La Tour d'Azyr's blue coat. More, the near side of the coat itself turned back from the point near the throat where it was caught together by a single button, revealed the slung arm beneath in its blood-sodden cambric sleeve.

Even now she feared to jump to the obvious conclusion—feared lest perhaps the Marquis, though himself wounded, might have dealt his adversary a deadlier wound.

She found her voice at last, and at the same moment signalled to the driver of the caleche to stop.

As it was pulled to a standstill, M. d'Ormesson alighted, and so met madame in the little space between the two carriages.

"Where is M. Moreau?" was the question with which she surprised him.

"Following at his leisure, no doubt, madame," he answered, recovering.

"He is not hurt?"

"Unfortunately it is we who..." M. d'Ormesson was beginning, when from behind him M. de La Tour d'Azyr's voice cut in crisply:

"This interest on your part in M. Moreau, dear Countess..."

He broke off, observing a vague challenge in the air with which she confronted him. But indeed his sentence did not need completing.

There was a vaguely awkward pause. And then she looked at M. d'Ormesson. Her manner changed. She offered what appeared to be an explanation of her concern for M. Moreau.

"Mademoiselle de Kercadiou is with me. The poor child has fainted."

There was more, a deal more, she would have said just then, but for M. d'Ormesson's presence.

Moved by a deep solicitude for Mademoiselle de Kertadiou, de La Tour d'Azyr sprang up despite his wound.

"I am in poor case to render assistance, madame," he said, an apologetic smile on his pale face. "But..."

With the aid of d'Ormesson, and in spite of the latter's protestations, he got down from the caleche, which then moved on a little way, so as to leave the road clear—for another carriage that was approaching from the direction of the Bois.

And thus it happened that when a few moments later that approaching cabriolet overtook and passed the halted vehicles, Andre-Louis beheld a very touching scene. Standing up to obtain a better view, he saw Aline in a half-swooning condition—she was beginning to revive by now—seated in the doorway of the carriage, supported by Mme. de Plougastel. In an attitude of deepest concern, M. de La Tour d'Azyr, his wound notwithstanding, was bending over the girl, whilst behind him stood M. d'Ormesson and madame's footman.

The Countess looked up and saw him as he was driven past. Her face lighted; almost it seemed to him she was about to greet him or to call him, wherefore, to avoid a difficulty, arising out of the presence there of his late antagonist, he anticipated her by bowing frigidly—for his mood was frigid, the more frigid by virtue of what he saw—and then resumed his seat with eyes that looked deliberately ahead.

Could anything more completely have confirmed him in his conviction that it was on M. de La Tour d'Azyr's account that Aline had come to plead with him that morning? For what his eyes had seen, of course, was a lady overcome with emotion at the sight of blood of her dear friend, and that same dear friend restoring her with assurances that his hurt was very far from mortal. Later, much later, he was to blame his own perverse stupidity. Almost is he too severe in his self-condemnation. For how else could he have interpreted the scene he beheld, his preconceptions being what they were?

That which he had already been suspecting, he now accounted proven to him. Aline had been wanting in candour on the subject of her feelings towards M. de La Tour d'Azyr. It was, he supposed, a woman's way to be secretive in such matters, and he must not blame her. Nor could he blame her in his heart for having succumbed to the singular charm of such a man as the Marquis—for not even his hostility could blind him to M. de La Tour d'Azyr's attractions. That she had succumbed was betrayed, he thought, by the weakness that had overtaken her upon seeing him wounded.

"My God!" he cried aloud. "What must she have suffered, then, if I had killed him as I intended!"

If only she had used candour with him, she could so easily have won his consent to the thing she asked. If only she had told him what now he saw, that she loved M. de La Tour d'Azyr, instead of leaving him to assume her only regard for the Marquis to be based on unworthy worldly ambition, he would at once have yielded.

He fetched a sigh, and breathed a prayer for forgiveness to the shade of Vilmorin.

"It is perhaps as well that my lunge went wide," he said.

"What do you mean?" wondered Le Chapelier.

"That in this business I must relinquish all hope of recommencing."

CHAPTER XII. THE OVERWHELMING REASON

M. de La Tour d'Azyr was seen no more in the Manege—or indeed in Paris at all—throughout all the months that the National Assembly remained in session to complete its work of providing France with a constitution. After all, though the wound to his body had been comparatively slight, the wound to such a pride as his had been all but mortal.

The rumour ran that he had emigrated. But that was only half the truth. The whole of it was that he had joined that group of noble travellers who came and went between the Tuileries and the headquarters of the emigres at Coblenz. He became, in short, a member of the royalist secret service that in the end was to bring down the monarchy in ruins.

As for Andre-Louis, his godfather's house saw him no more, as a result of his conviction that M. de Kercadiou would not relent from his written resolve never to receive him again if the duel were fought.

He threw himself into his duties at the Assembly with such zeal and effect that when—its purpose accomplished—the Constituent was dissolved in September of the following year, membership of the Legislative, whose election followed immediately, was thrust upon him.

He considered then, like many others, that the Revolution was a thing accomplished, that France had only to govern herself by the Constitution which had been given her, and that all would now be well. And so it might have been but that the Court could not bring itself to accept the altered state of things. As a result of its intrigues half Europe was arming to hurl herself upon France, and her quarrel was the quarrel of the French King with his people. That was the horror at the root of all the horrors that were to come.

Of the counter-revolutionary troubles that were everywhere being stirred up by the clergy, none were more acute than those of Brittany, and, in view of the influence it was hoped he would wield in his native province, it was proposed to Andre-Louis by the Commission of Twelve, in the early days of the Girondin ministry, that he should go thither to combat the unrest. He was desired to proceed peacefully, but his powers were almost absolute, as is shown by the orders he carried—orders enjoining all to render him assistance and warning those who might hinder him that they would do so at their peril.

He accepted the task, and he was one of the five plenipotentiaries despatched on the same errand in that spring of 1792. It kept him absent from Paris for four months and might have kept him longer but that at the beginning of August he was recalled. More imminent than any trouble in Brittany was the trouble brewing in Paris itself; when the political sky was blacker than it had been since '89. Paris realized that the hour was rapidly approaching which would see the climax of the long struggle between Equality and Privilege. And it was towards a city so disposed that Andre-Louis came speeding from the West, to find there also the climax of his own disturbed career.

Mlle. de Kercadiou, too, was in Paris in those days of early August, on a visit to her uncle's cousin and dearest friend, Mme. de Plougastel. And although nothing could now be plainer than the seething unrest that heralded the explosion to come, yet the air of gaiety, indeed of jocularity, prevailing at Court—whither madame and mademoiselle went almost daily—reassured them. M. de Plougastel had come and gone again, back to Coblenz on that secret business that kept him now almost constantly absent from his wife. But whilst with her he had positively assured her that all measures were taken, and that an insurrection was a thing to be welcomed, because it could have one only conclusion, the final crushing of the Revolution in the courtyard of the Tuileries. That, he added, was why the King remained in Paris. But for his confidence in that he would put himself in the centre of his Swiss and his knights of the dagger, and quit the capital. They would hack a way out for him easily if his departure were opposed. But not even that would be necessary.

Yet in those early days of August, after her husband's departure the effect of his inspiring words was gradually dissipated by the march of events under madame's own eyes. And finally on the afternoon of the ninth, there arrived at the Hotel Plougastel a messenger from Meudon bearing a note from M. de Kercadiou in which he urgently bade mademoiselle join him there at once, and advised her hostess to accompany her.

You may have realized that M. de Kercadiou was of those who make friends with men of all classes. His ancient lineage placed him on terms of equality with members of the noblesse; his simple manners—something between the rustic and the bourgeois—and his natural affability placed him on equally good terms with those who by birth were his inferiors. In Meudon he was known and esteemed of all the simple folk, and it was Rougane, the friendly mayor, who, informed on the 9th of August of the storm that was brewing for the morrow, and knowing of mademoiselle's absence in Paris, had warningly advised him to withdraw her from what in the next four-and-twenty hours might be a zone of danger for all persons of quality, particularly those suspected of connections with the Court party.

Now there was no doubt whatever of Mme. de Plougastel's connection with the Court. It was not even to be doubted—indeed, measure of proof of it was to be forthcoming—that those vigilant and ubiquitous secret societies that watched over the cradle of the young revolution were fully informed of the frequent journeyings of M. de Plougastel to Coblenz, and entertained no illusions on the score of the reason for them. Given, then, a defeat of the Court party in the struggle that was preparing, the position in Paris of Mme. de Plougastel could not be other than fraught with danger, and that danger would be shared by any guest of birth at her hotel.

M. de Kercadiou's affection for both those women quickened the fears aroused in him by Rougane's warning. Hence that hastily dispatched note, desiring his niece and imploring his friend to come at once to Meudon.

The friendly mayor carried his complaisance a step farther, and dispatched the letter to Paris by the hands of his own son, an intelligent lad of nineteen. It was late in the afternoon of that perfect August day when young Rougane presented himself at the Hotel Plougastel.

He was graciously received by Mme. de Plougastel in the salon, whose splendours, when combined with the great air of the lady herself, overwhelmed the lad's simple, unsophisticated soul. Madame made up her mind at once.

M. de Kercadiou's urgent message no more than confirmed her own fears and inclinations. She decided upon instant departure.

"Bien, madame," said the youth. "Then I have the honour to take my leave."

But she would not let him go. First to the kitchen to refresh himself, whilst she and mademoiselle made ready, and then a seat for him in her carriage as far as Meudon. She could not suffer him to return on foot as he had come.

Though in all the circumstances it was no more than his due, yet the kindliness that in such a moment of agitation could take thought for another was presently to be rewarded. Had she done less than this, she would have known—if nothing worse—at least some hours of anguish even greater than those that were already in store for her.

It wanted, perhaps, a half-hour to sunset when they set out in her carriage with intent to leave Paris by the Porte Saint-Martin. They travelled with a single footman behind. Rougane—terrifying condescension—was given a seat inside the carriage with the ladies, and proceeded to fall in love with Mlle. de Kercadiou, whom he accounted the most beautiful being he had ever seen, yet who talked to him simply and unaffectedly as with an equal. The thing went to his head a little, and disturbed certain republican notions which he had hitherto conceived himself to have thoroughly digested.

The carriage drew up at the barrier, checked there by a picket of the National Guard posted before the iron gates.

The sergeant in command strode to the door of the vehicle. The Countess put her head from the window.

"The barrier is closed, madame," she was curtly informed.

"Closed!" she echoed. The thing was incredible. "But... but do you mean that we cannot pass?"

"Not unless you have a permit, madame." The sergeant leaned nonchalantly on his pike. "The orders are that no one is to leave or enter without proper papers."

"Whose orders?"

"Orders of the Commune of Paris."

"But I must go into the country this evening." Madame's voice was almost petulant. "I am expected."

"In that case let madame procure a permit."

"Where is it to be procured?"

"At the Hotel de Ville or at the headquarters of madame's section."

She considered a moment. "To the section, then. Be so good as to tell my coachman to drive to the Bondy Section."

He saluted her and stepped back. "Section Bondy, Rue des Morts," he bade the driver.

Madame sank into her seat again, in a state of agitation fully shared by mademoiselle. Rougane set himself to pacify and reassure them. The section would put the matter in order. They would most certainly be accorded a permit. What possible reason could there be for refusing them? A mere formality, after all!

His assurance uplifted them merely to prepare them for a still more profound dejection when presently they met with a flat refusal from the president of the section who received the Countess.

"Your name, madame?" he had asked brusquely. A rude fellow of the most advanced republican type, he had not even risen out of deference to the ladies when they entered. He was there, he would have told you, to perform the duties of his office, not to give dancing-lessons.

"Plougastel," he repeated after her, without title, as if it had been the name of a butcher or baker. He took down a heavy volume from a shelf on his right, opened it and turned the pages. It was a sort of directory of his section. Presently he found what he sought. "Comte de Plougastel, Hotel Plougastel, Rue du Paradis. Is that it?"

"That is correct, monsieur," she answered, with what civility she could muster before the fellow's affronting rudeness.

There was a long moment of silence, during which he studied certain pencilled entries against the name. The sections had been working in the last few weeks much more systematically than was generally suspected.

"Your husband is with you, madame?" he asked curtly, his eyes still conning that page.

"M. le Comte is not with me," she answered, stressing the title.

"Not with you?" He looked up suddenly, and directed upon her a glance in which suspicion seemed to blend with derision. "Where is he?"

"He is not in Paris, monsieur.

"Ah! Is he at Coblenz, do you think?"

Madame felt herself turning cold. There was something ominous in all this. To what end had the sections informed themselves so thoroughly of the comings and goings of their inhabitants? What was preparing? She had a sense of being trapped, of being taken in a net that had been cast unseen.

"I do not know, monsieur," she said, her voice unsteady.

"Of course not." He seemed to sneer. "No matter. And you wish to leave Paris also? Where do you desire to go?"

"To Meudon."

"Your business there?"

The blood leapt to her face. His insolence was unbearable to a woman who in all her life had never known anything but the utmost deference from inferiors and equals alike. Nevertheless, realizing that she was face to face with forces entirely new, she controlled herself, stifled her resentment, and answered steadily.

"I wish to conduct this lady, Mlle. de Kercadiou, back to her uncle who resides there."

"Is that all? Another day will do for that, madame. The matter is not pressing."

"Pardon, monsieur, to us the matter is very pressing."

"You have not convinced me of it, and the barriers are closed to all who cannot prove the most urgent and satisfactory reasons for wishing to pass. You will wait, madame, until the restriction is removed. Good-evening."

"But, monsieur..."

"Good-evening, madame," he repeated significantly, a dismissal more contemptuous and despotic than any royal "You have leave to go."

Madame went out with Aline. Both were quivering with the anger that prudence had urged them to suppress. They climbed into the coach again, desiring to be driven home.

Rougane's astonishment turned into dismay when they told him what had taken place. "Why not try the Hotel de Ville, madame?" he suggested.

"After that? It would be useless. We must resign ourselves to remaining in Paris until the barriers are opened again."

"Perhaps it will not matter to us either way by then, madame," said Aline.

"Aline!" she exclaimed in horror.

"Mademoiselle!" cried Rougane on the same note. And then, because he perceived that people detained in this fashion must be in some danger not yet discernible, but on that account more dreadful, he set his wits to work. As they were approaching the Hotel Plougastel once more, he announced that he had solved the problem.

"A passport from without would do equally well," he announced. "Listen, now, and trust to me. I will go back to Meudon at once. My father shall give me two permits—one for myself alone, and another for three persons—from Meudon to Paris and back to Meudon. I reenter Paris with my own permit, which I then proceed to destroy, and we leave together, we three, on the strength of the other one, representing ourselves as having come from Meudon in the course of the day. It is quite simple, after all. If I go at once, I shall be back to-night."

"But how will you leave?" asked Aline.

"I? Pooh! As to that, have no anxiety. My father is Mayor of Meudon. There are plenty who know him. I will go to the Hotel de Ville, and tell them what is, after all, true—that I am caught in Paris by the closing of the barriers, and that my father is expecting me home this evening. They will pass me through. It is quite simple."

His confidence uplifted them again. The thing seemed as easy as he represented it.

"Then let your passport be for four, my friend," madame begged him. "There is Jacques," she explained, indicating the footman who had just assisted them to alight.

Rougane departed confident of soon returning, leaving them to await him with the same confidence. But the hours succeeded one another, the night closed in, bedtime came, and still there was no sign of his return.

They waited until midnight, each pretending for the other's sake to a confidence fully sustained, each invaded by vague premonitions of evil, yet beguiling the time by playing tric-trac in the great salon, as if they had not a single anxious thought between them.

At last on the stroke of midnight, madame sighed and rose.

"It will be for to-morrow morning," she said, not believing it.

"Of course," Aline agreed. "It would really have been impossible for him to have returned to-night. And it will be much better to travel to-morrow. The journey at so late an hour would tire you so much, dear madame."

Thus they made pretence.

Early in the morning they were awakened by a din of bells—the tocsins of the sections ringing the alarm. To their startled ears came later the rolling of drums, and at one time they heard the sounds of a multitude on the march. Paris was rising. Later still came the rattle of small-arms in the distance and the deeper boom of cannon. Battle was joined between the men of the sections and the men of the Court. The people in arms had attacked the Tuileries. Wildest rumours flew in all directions, and some of them found their way through the servants to the Hotel Plougastel, of that terrible fight for the palace which was to end in the purposeless massacre of all those whom the invertebrate monarch abandoned there, whilst placing himself and his family under the protection of the Assembly. Purposeless to the end, ever adopting the course pointed out to him by evil counsellors, he prepared for resistance only until the need for resistance really arose, whereupon he ordered a surrender which left those who had stood by him to the last at the mercy of a frenzied mob.

And while this was happening in the Tuileries, the two women at the Hotel Plougastel still waited for the return of Rougane, though now with ever-lessening hope. And Rougane did not return. The affair did not appear so simple to the father as to the son. Rougane the elder was rightly afraid to lend himself to such a piece of deception.

He went with his son to inform M. de Kercadiou of what had happened, and told him frankly of the thing his son suggested, but which he dared not do.

M. de Kercadiou sought to move him by intercessions and even by the offer of bribes. But Rougane remained firm.

"Monsieur," he said, "if it were discovered against me, as it inevitably would be, I should hang for it. Apart from that, and in spite of my anxiety to do all in my power to serve you, it would be a breach of trust such as I could not contemplate. You must not ask me, monsieur."

"But what do you conceive is going to happen?" asked the half-demented gentleman.

"It is war," said Rougane, who was well informed, as we have seen. "War between the people and the Court. I am desolated that my warning should have come too late. But, when all is said, I do not think that you need really alarm yourself. War will not be made on women." M. de Kercadiou clung for comfort to that assurance after the mayor and his son had departed. But at the back of his mind there remained the knowledge of the traffic in which M. de Plougastel was engaged. What if the revolutionaries were equally well informed? And most probably they were. The women-folk political offenders had been known aforetime to suffer for the sins of their men. Anything was possible in a popular upheaval, and Aline would be exposed jointly with Mme. de Plougastel.

Late that night, as he sat gloomily in his brother's library, the pipe in which he had sought solace extinguished between his fingers, there came a sharp knocking at the door.

To the old seneschal of Gavrillac who went to open there stood revealed upon the threshold a slim young man in a dark olive surcoat, the skirts of which reached down to his calves. He wore boots, buckskins, and a small-sword, and round his waist there was a tricolour sash, in his hat a tricolour cockade, which gave him an official look extremely sinister to the eyes of that old retainer of feudalism, who shared to the full his master's present fears.

"Monsieur desires?" he asked, between respect and mistrust.

And then a crisp voice startled him.

"Why, Benoit! Name of a name! Have you completely forgotten me?"

With a shaking hand the old man raised the lantern he carried so as to throw its light more fully upon that lean, wide-mouthed countenance.

"M. Andre!" he cried. "M. Andre!" And then he looked at the sash and the cockade, and hesitated, apparently at a loss.

But Andre-Louis stepped past him into the wide vestibule, with its tessellated floor of black-and-white marble.

"If my godfather has not yet retired, take me to him. If he has retired, take me to him all the same."

"Oh, but certainly, M. Andre—and I am sure he will be ravished to see you. No, he has not yet retired. This way, M. Andre; this way, if you please."

The returning Andre-Louis, reaching Meudon a half-hour ago, had gone straight to the mayor for some definite news of what might be happening in Paris that should either confirm or dispel the ominous rumours that he had met in ever-increasing volume as he approached the capital. Rougane informed him that insurrection was imminent, that already the sections had possessed themselves of the barriers, and that it was impossible for any person not fully accredited to enter or leave the city.

Andre-Louis bowed his head, his thoughts of the gravest. He had for some time perceived the danger of this second revolution from within the first, which might destroy everything that had been done, and give the reins of power to a villainous faction that would plunge the country into anarchy. The thing he had feared was more than ever on the point of taking place. He would go on at once, that very night, and see for himself what was happening.

And then, as he was leaving, he turned again to Rougane to ask if M. de Kercadiou was still at Meudon.

"You know him, monsieur?"

"He is my godfather."

"Your godfather! And you a representative! Why, then, you may be the very man he needs." And Rougane told him of his son's errand into Paris that afternoon and its result.

No more was required. That two years ago his godfather should upon certain terms have refused him his house weighed for nothing at the moment. He left his travelling carriage at the little inn and went straight to M. de Kercadiou.

And M. de Kercadiou, startled in such an hour by this sudden apparition, of one against whom he nursed a bitter grievance, greeted him in terms almost identical with those in which in that same room he had greeted him on a similar occasion once before.

"What do you want here, sir?"

"To serve you if possible, my godfather," was the disarming answer.

But it did not disarm M. de Kercadiou. "You have stayed away so long that I hoped you would not again disturb me."

"I should not have ventured to disobey you now were it not for the hope that I can be of service. I have seen Rougane, the mayor..."

"What's that you say about not venturing to disobey?"

"You forbade me your house, monsieur."

M. de Kercadiou stared at him helplessly.

"And is that why you have not come near me in all this time?"

"Of course. Why else?"

M. de Kercadiou continued to stare. Then he swore under his breath. It disconcerted him to have to deal with a man who insisted upon taking him so literally. He had expected that Andre-Louis would have come contritely to admit his fault and beg to be taken back into favour. He said so.

"But how could I hope that you meant less than you said, monsieur? You were so very definite in your declaration. What expressions of contrition could have served me without a purpose of amendment? And I had no notion of amending. We may yet be thankful for that."

"Thankful?"

"I am a representative. I have certain powers. I am very opportunely returning to Paris. Can I serve you where Rougane cannot? The need, monsieur, would appear to be very urgent if the half of what I suspect is true. Aline should be placed in safety at once."

M. de Kercadiou surrendered unconditionally. He came over and took Andre-Louis' hand.

"My boy," he said, and he was visibly moved, "there is in you a certain nobility that is not to be denied. If I seemed harsh with you, then, it was because I was fighting against your evil proclivities. I desired to keep you out of the evil path of politics that have brought this unfortunate country into so terrible a pass. The enemy on the frontier; civil war about to flame out at home. That is what you revolutionaries have done."

Andre-Louis did not argue. He passed on.

"About Aline?" he asked. And himself answered his own question: "She is in Paris, and she must be brought out of it at once, before the place becomes a shambles, as well it may once the passions that have been brewing all these months are let loose. Young Rougane's plan is good. At least, I cannot think of a better one."

"But Rougane the elder will not hear of it."

"You mean he will not do it on his own responsibility. But he has consented to do it on mine. I have left him a note over my signature to the effect that a safe-conduct for Mlle. de Kercadiou to go to Paris and return is issued by him in compliance with orders from me. The powers I carry and of which I have satisfied him are his sufficient justification for obeying me in this. I have left him that note on the understanding that he is to use it only in an extreme case, for his own protection. In exchange he has given me this safe-conduct."

"You already have it!"

M. de Kercadiou took the sheet of paper that Andre-Louis held out. His hand shook. He approached it to the cluster of candles burning on the console and screwed up his short-sighted eyes to read.

"If you send that to Paris by young Rougane in the morning," said Andre-Louis, "Aline should be here by noon. Nothing, of course, could be done to-night without provoking suspicion. The hour is too late. And now, monsieur my godfather, you know exactly why I intrude in violation of your commands. If there is any other way in which I can serve you, you have but to name it whilst I am here."

"But there is, Andre. Did not Rougane tell you that there were others..."

"He mentioned Mme. de Plougastel and her servant."

"Then why...?" M. de Kercadiou broke off, looking his question.

Very solemnly Andre-Louis shook his head.

"That is impossible," he said.

M. de Kercadiou's mouth fell open in astonishment. "Impossible!" he repeated. "But why?"

"Monsieur, I can do what I am doing for Aline without offending my conscience. Besides, for Aline I would offend my conscience and do it. But Mme. de Plougastel is in very different case. Neither Aline nor any of hers have been concerned in counter-revolutionary work, which is the true source of the calamity that now threatens to overtake us. I can procure her removal from Paris without self-reproach, convinced that I am doing nothing that any one could censure, or that might become the subject of enquiries. But Mme. de Plougastel is the wife of M. le Comte de Plougastel, whom all the world knows to be an agent between the Court and the emigres."

"That is no fault of hers," cried M. de Kercadiou through his consternation.

"Agreed. But she may be called upon at any moment to establish the fact that she is not a party to these manoeuvres. It is known that she was in Paris to-day. Should she be sought to-morrow and should it be found that she has gone, enquiries will certainly be made, from which it must result that I have betrayed my trust, and abused my powers to serve personal ends. I hope, monsieur, that you will understand that the risk is too great to be run for the sake of a stranger."

"A stranger?" said the Seigneur reproachfully.

"Practically a stranger to me," said Andre-Louis.

"But she is not a stranger to me, Andre. She is my cousin and very dear and valued friend. And, mon Dieu, what you say but increases the urgency of getting her out of Paris. She must be rescued, Andre, at all costs—she must be rescued! Why, her case is infinitely more urgent than Aline's!"

He stood a suppliant before his godson, very different now from the stern man who had greeted him on his arrival. His face was pale, his hands shook, and there were beads of perspiration on his brow.

"Monsieur my godfather, I would do anything in reason. But I cannot do this. To rescue her might mean ruin for Aline and yourself as well as for me."

"We must take the risk."

"You have a right to speak for yourself, of course."

"Oh, and for you, believe me, Andre, for you!" He came close to the young man. "Andre, I implore you to take my word for that, and to obtain this permit for Mme. de Plougastel."

Andre looked at him mystified. "This is fantastic," he said. "I have grateful memories of the lady's interest in me for a few days once when I was a child, and again more recently in Paris when she sought to convert me to what she accounts the true political religion. But I do not risk my neck for her—no, nor yours, nor Aline's."

"Ah! But, Andre..."

"That is my last word, monsieur. It is growing late, and I desire to sleep in Paris."

"No, no! Wait!" The Lord of Gavrillac was displaying signs of unspeakable distress. "Andre, you must!"

There was in this insistence and, still more, in the frenzied manner of it, something so unreasonable that Andre could not fail to assume that some dark and mysterious motive lay behind it.

"I must?" he echoed. "Why must I? Your reasons, monsieur?"

"Andre, my reasons are overwhelming."

"Pray allow me to be the judge of that." Andre-Louis' manner was almost peremptory.

The demand seemed to reduce M. de Kercadiou to despair. He paced the room, his hands tight-clasped behind him, his brow wrinkled. At last he came to stand before his godson.

"Can't you take my word for it that these reasons exist?" he cried in anguish.

"In such a matter as this—a matter that may involve my neck? Oh, monsieur, is that reasonable?"

"I violate my word of honour, my oath, if I tell you." M. de Kercadiou turned away, wringing his hands, his condition visibly pitcous: then turned again to Andre. "But in this extremity, in this desperate extremity, and since you so ungenerously insist, I shall have to tell you. God help me, I have no choice. She will realize that when she knows. Andre, my boy..." He paused again, a man afraid. He set a hand on his godson's shoulder, and to his increasing amazement Andre-Louis perceived that over those pale, short-sighted eyes there was a film of tears. "Mme. de Plougastel is your mother."

Followed, for a long moment, utter silence. This thing that he was told was not immediately understood. When understanding came at last Andre-Louis' first impulse was to cry out. But he possessed himself, and played the Stoic. He must ever be playing something. That was in his nature. And he was true to his nature even in this supreme moment. He continued silent until, obeying that queer histrionic instinct, he could trust himself to speak without emotion. "I see," he said, at last, quite coolly.

His mind was sweeping back over the past. Swiftly he reviewed his memories of Mme. de Plougastel, her singular if sporadic interest in him, the curious blend of affection and wistfulness which her manner towards him had always presented, and at last he understood so much that hitherto had intrigued him.

"I see," he said again; and added now, "Of course, any but a fool would have guessed it long ago."

It was M. de Kercadiou who cried out, M. de Kercadiou who recoiled as from a blow.

"My God, Andre, of what are you made? You can take such an announcement in this fashion?"

"And how would you have me take it? Should it surprise me to discover that I had a mother? After all, a mother is an indispensable necessity to getting one's self born."

He sat down abruptly, to conceal the too-revealing fact that his limbs were shaking. He pulled a handkerchief from his pocket to mop his brow, which had grown damp. And then, quite suddenly, he found himself weeping.

At the sight of those tears streaming silently down that face that had turned so pale, M. de Kercadiou came quickly across to him. He sat down beside him and threw an arm affectionately over his shoulder.

"Andre, my poor lad," he murmured. "I... I was fool enough to think you had no heart. You deceived me with your infernal pretence, and now I see... I see..." He was not sure what it was that he saw, or else he hesitated to express it.

"It is nothing, monsieur. I am tired out, and... and I have a cold in the head." And then, finding the part beyond his power, he abruptly threw it up, utterly abandoned all pretence. "Why... why has there been all this mystery?" he asked. "Was it intended that I should never know?"

"It was, Andre. It... it had to be, for prudence' sake."

"But why? Complete your confidence, sir. Surely you cannot leave it there. Having told me so much, you must tell me all."

"The reason, my boy, is that you were born some three years after your mother's marriage with M. de Plougastel, some eighteen months after M. de Plougastel had been away with the army, and some four months before his return to his wife. It is a matter that M. de Plougastel has never suspected, and for gravest family reasons must never suspect. That is why the utmost secrecy has been preserved. That is why none was ever allowed to know. Your mother came betimes into Brittany, and under an assumed name spent some months in the village of Moreau. It was while she was there that you were born."

Andre-Louis turned it over in his mind. He had dried his tears. And sat now rigid and collected.

"When you say that none was ever allowed to know, you are telling me, of course, that you, monsieur..."

"Oh, mon Dieu, no!" The denial came in a violent outburst. M. de Kercadiou sprang to his feet propelled from Andre's side by the violence of his emotions. It was as if the very suggestion filled him with horror. "I was the only other one who knew. But it is not as you think, Andre. You cannot imagine that I should lie to you, that I should deny you if you were my son?"

"If you say that I am not, monsieur, that is sufficient."

"You are not. I was Therese's cousin and also, as she well knew, her truest friend. She knew that she could trust me; and it was to me she came for help in her extremity. Once, years before, I would have married her. But, of course, I am not the sort of man a woman could love. She trusted, however, to my love for her, and I have kept her trust."

"Then, who was my father?"

"I don't know. She never told me. It was her secret, and I did not pry. It is not in my nature, Andre."

Andre-Louis got up, and stood silently facing M. de Kercadiou.

"You believe me, Andre."

"Naturally, monsieur; and I am sorry, I am sorry that I am not your son."

M. de Kercadiou gripped his godson's hand convulsively, and held it a moment with no word spoken. Then as they fell away from each other again:

"And now, what will you do, Andre?" he asked. "Now that you know?"

Andre-Louis stood awhile, considering, then broke into laughter. The situation had its humours. He explained them.

"What difference should the knowledge make? Is filial piety to be called into existence by the mere announcement of relationship? Am I to risk my neck through lack of circumspection on behalf of a mother so very circumspect that she had no intention of ever revealing herself? The discovery rests upon the merest chance, upon a fall of the dice of Fate. Is that to weigh with me?"

"The decision is with you, Andre."

"Nay, it is beyond me. Decide it who can, I cannot."

"You mean that you refuse even now?"

"I mean that I consent. Since I cannot decide what it is that I should do, it only remains for me to do what a son should. It is grotesque; but all life is grotesque."

"You will never, never regret it."

"I hope not," said Andre. "Yet I think it very likely that I shall. And now I had better see Rougane again at once, and obtain from him the other two permits required. Then perhaps it will be best that I take them to Paris myself, in the morning. If you will give me a bed, monsieur, I shall be grateful. I... I confess that I am hardly in case to do more to-night."

CHAPTER XIII. SANCTUARY

Into the late afternoon of that endless day of horror with its perpetual alarms, its volleying musketry, rolling drums, and distant muttering of angry multitudes, Mme. de Plougastel and Aline sat waiting in that handsome house in the Rue du Paradis. It was no longer for Rougane they waited. They realized that, be the reason what it might—and by now many reasons must no doubt exist—this friendly messenger would not return. They waited without knowing for what. They waited for whatever might betide.

At one time early in the afternoon the roar of battle approached them, racing swiftly in their direction, swelling each moment in volume and in horror. It was the frenzied clamour of a multitude drunk with blood and bent on destruction. Near at hand that fierce wave of humanity checked in its turbulent progress. Followed blows of pikes upon a door and imperious calls to open, and thereafter came the rending of timbers, the shivering of glass, screams of terror blending with screams of rage, and, running through these shrill sounds, the deeper diapason of bestial laughter.

It was a hunt of two wretched Swiss guardsmen seeking blindly to escape. And they were run to earth in a house in the neighbourhood, and there cruelly done to death by that demoniac mob. The thing accomplished, the hunters, male and female, forming into a battalion, came swinging down the Rue du Paradis, chanting the song of Marseilles—a song new to Paris in those days:

> Allons, enfants de la patrie!
> Le jour de gloire est arrive
> Contre nous de la tyrannie
> L'etendard sanglant est leve.

Nearer it came, raucously bawled by some hundreds of voices, a dread sound that had come so suddenly to displace at least temporarily the merry, trivial air of the "Ca ira!" which hitherto had been the revolutionary carillon. Instinctively Mme. de Plougastel and Aline clung to each other. They had heard the sound of the ravishing of that other house in the neighbourhood, without knowledge of the reason. What if now it should be the turn of the Hotel Plougastel! There was no real cause to fear it, save that amid a turmoil imperfectly understood and therefore the more awe-inspiring, the worst must be feared always.

The dreadful song so dreadfully sung, and the thunder of heavily shod feet upon the roughly paved street, passed on and receded. They breathed again, almost as if a miracle had saved them, to yield to fresh alarm an instant later, when madame's young footman, Jacques, the most trusted of her servants, burst into their presence unceremoniously with a scared face, bringing the announcement that a man who had just climbed over the garden wall professed himself a friend of madame's, and desired to be brought immediately to her presence.

"But he looks like a sansculotte, madame," the staunch fellow warned her.

Her thoughts and hopes leapt at once to Rougane.

"Bring him in," she commanded breathlessly.

Jacques went out, to return presently accompanied by a tall man in a long, shabby, and very ample overcoat and a wide-brimmed hat that was turned down all round, and adorned by an enormous tricolour cockade. This hat he removed as he entered.

Jacques, standing behind him, perceived that his hair, although now in some disorder, bore signs of having been carefully dressed. It was clubbed, and it carried some lingering vestiges of powder. The young footman wondered what it was in the man's face, which was turned from him, that should cause his mistress to out and recoil. Then he found himself dismissed abruptly by a gesture.

The newcomer advanced to the middle of the salon, moving like a man exhausted and breathing hard. There he leaned against a table, across which he confronted Mme. de Plougastel. And she stood regarding him, a strange horror in her eyes.

In the background, on a settle at the salon's far end, sat Aline staring in bewilderment and some fear at a face which, if unrecognizable through the mask of blood and dust that smeared it, was yet familiar. And then the man spoke, and instantly she knew the voice for that of the Marquis de La Tour d'Azyr.

"My dear friend," he was saying, "forgive me if I startled you. Forgive me if I thrust myself in here without leave, at such a time, in such a manner. But... you see how it is with me. I am a fugitive. In the course of my distracted flight, not knowing which way to turn for safety, I thought of you. I told myself that if I could but safely reach your house, I might find sanctuary."

"You are in danger?"

"In danger?" Almost he seemed silently to laugh at the unnecessary question. "If I were to show myself openly in the streets just now, I might with luck contrive to live for five minutes! My friend, it has been a massacre. Some few of us escaped from the Tuileries at the end, to be hunted to death in the streets. I doubt if by this time a single Swiss survives. They had the worst of it, poor devils. And as for us—my God! They hate us more than they hate the Swiss. Hence this filthy disguise."

He peeled off the shaggy greatcoat, and casting it from him stepped forth in the black satin that had been the general livery of the hundred knights of the dagger who had rallied in the Tuileries that morning to the defence of their king.

His coat was rent across the back, his neckcloth and the ruffles at his wrists were torn and bloodstained; with his smeared face and disordered headdress he was terrible to behold. Yet he contrived to carry himself with his habitual easy assurance, remembered to kiss the trembling hand which Mme. de Plougastel extended to him in welcome.

"You did well to come to me, Gervais," she said. "Yes, here is sanctuary for the present. You will be quite safe, at least for as long as we are safe. My servants are entirely trustworthy. Sit down and tell me all."

He obeyed her, collapsing almost into the armchair which she thrust forward, a man exhausted, whether by physical exertion or by nerve-strain, or both. He drew a handkerchief from his pocket and wiped some of the blood and dirt from his face.

"It is soon told." His tone was bitter with the bitterness of despair. "This, my dear, is the end of us. Plougastel is lucky in being across the frontier at such a time. Had I not been fool enough to trust those who to-day have proved themselves utterly unworthy of trust, that is where I should be myself. My remaining in Paris is the crowning folly of a life full of follies and mistakes. That I should come to you in my hour of most urgent need adds point to it." He laughed in his bitterness.

Madame moistened her dry lips. "And... and now?" she asked him.

"It only remains to get away as soon as may be, if it is still possible. Here in France there is no longer any room for us—at least, not above ground. To-day has proved it." And then he looked up at her, standing there beside him so pale and timid, and he smiled. He patted the fine hand that rested upon the arm of his chair. "My dear Therese, unless you carry charitableness to the length of giving me to drink, you will see me perish of thirst under your eyes before ever the canaille has a chance to finish me."

She started. "I should have thought of it!" she cried in self-reproach, and she turned quickly. "Aline," she begged, "tell Jacques to bring..."

"Aline!" he echoed, interrupting, and swinging round in his turn. Then, as Aline rose into view, detaching from her background, and he at last perceived her, he heaved himself abruptly to his weary legs again, and stood there stiffly bowing to her across the space of gleaming floor. "Mademoiselle, I had not suspected your presence," he said, and he seemed extraordinarily ill-at-ease, a man startled, as if caught in an illicit act.

"I perceived it, monsieur," she answered, as she advanced to do madame's commission. She paused before him. "From my heart, monsieur, I grieve that we should meet again in circumstances so very painful."

Not since the day of his duel with Andre-Louis—the day which had seen the death and burial of his last hope of winning her—had they stood face to face.

He checked as if on the point of answering her. His glance strayed to Mme. de Plougastel, and, oddly reticent for one who could be very glib, he bowed in silence.

"But sit, monsieur, I beg. You are fatigued."

"You are gracious to observe it. With your permission, then." And he resumed his seat. She continued on her way to the door and passed out upon her errand.

When presently she returned they had almost unaccountably changed places. It was Mme. de Plougastel who was seated in that armchair of brocade and gilt, and M. de La Tour d'Azyr who, despite his lassitude, was leaning over the back of it talking earnestly, seeming by his attitude to plead with her. On Aline's entrance he broke off instantly and moved away, so that she was left with a sense of having intruded. Further she observed that the Countess was in tears.

Following her came presently the diligent Jacques, bearing a tray laden with food and wine. Madame poured for her guest, and he drank a long draught of the Burgundy, then begged, holding forth his grimy hands, that he might mend his appearance before sitting down to eat.

He was led away and valeted by Jacques, and when he returned he had removed from his person the last vestige of the rough handling he had received. He looked almost his normal self, the disorder in his attire repaired, calm and dignified and courtly in his bearing, but very pale and haggard of face, seeming suddenly to have increased in years, to have reached in appearance the age that was in fact his own.

As he ate and drank—and this with appetite, for as he told them he had not tasted food since early morning—he entered into the details of the dreadful events of the day, and gave them the particulars of his own escape from the Tuileries when all was seen to be lost and when the Swiss, having burnt their last cartridge, were submitting to wholesale massacre at the hands of the indescribably furious mob.

"Oh, it was all most ill done," he ended critically. "We were timid when we should have been resolute, and resolute at last when it was too late. That is the history of our side from the beginning of this accursed struggle. We have lacked proper leadership throughout, and now—as I have said already—there is an end to us. It but remains to escape, as soon as we can discover how the thing is to be accomplished."

Madame told him of the hopes that she had centred upon Rougane.

It lifted him out of his gloom. He was disposed to be optimistic.

"You are wrong to have abandoned that hope," he assured her. "If this mayor is so well disposed, he certainly can do as his son promised. But last night it would have been too late for him to have reached you, and to-day, assuming that he had come to Paris, almost impossible for him to win across the streets from the other side. It is most likely that he will yet come. I pray that he may; for the knowledge that you and Mlle. de Kercadiou are out of this would comfort me above all."

"We should take you with us," said madame.

"Ah! But how?"

"Young Rougane was to bring me permits for three persons—Aline, myself, and my footman, Jacques. You would take the place of Jacques."

"Faith, to get out of Paris, madame, there is no man whose place I would not take." And he laughed.

Their spirits rose with his and their flagging hopes revived. But as dusk descended again upon the city, without any sign of the deliverer they awaited, those hopes began to ebb once more.

M. de La Tour d'Azyr at last pleaded weariness, and begged to be permitted to withdraw that he might endeavour to take some rest against whatever might have to be faced in the immediate future. When he had gone, madame persuaded Aline to go and lie down.

"I will call you, my dear, the moment he arrives," she said, bravely maintaining that pretence of a confidence that had by now entirely evaporated.

Aline kissed her affectionately, and departed, outwardly so calm and unperturbed as to leave the Countess wondering whether she realized the peril by which they were surrounded, a peril infinitely increased by the presence in that house of a man so widely known and detested as M. de La Tour d'Azyr, a man who was probably being sought for by his enemies at this moment.

Left alone, madame lay down on a couch in the salon itself, to be ready for any emergency. It was a hot summer night, and the glass doors opening upon the luxuriant garden stood wide to admit the air. On that air came intermittently from the distance sounds of the continuing horrible activities of the populace, the aftermath of that bloody day.

Mme. de Plougastel lay there, listening to those sounds for upwards of an hour, thanking Heaven that for the present at least the disturbances were distant, dreading lest at any moment they should occur nearer at hand, lest this Bondy section in which her hotel was situated should become the scene of horrors similar to those whose echoes reached her ears from other sections away to the south and west.

The couch occupied by the Countess lay in shadow; for all the lights in that long salon had been extinguished with the exception of a cluster of candles in a massive silver candle branch placed on a round marquetry table in the middle of the room—an island of light in the surrounding gloom.

The timepiece on the overmantel chimed melodiously the hour of ten, and then, startling in the suddenness with which it broke the immediate silence, another sound vibrated through the house, and brought madame to her feet, in a breathless mingling of hope and dread. Some one was knocking sharply on the door below. Followed moments of agonized suspense, culminating in the abrupt invasion of the room by the footman Jacques. He looked round, not seeing his mistress at first.

"Madame! Madame!" he panted, out of breath.

"What is it, Jacques!" Her voice was steady now that the need for self-control seemed thrust upon her. She advanced from the shadows into that island of light about the table. "There is a man below. He is asking... he is demanding to see you at once."

"A man?" she questioned.

"He... he seems to be an official; at least he wears the sash of office. And he refuses to give any name; he says that his name would convey nothing to you. He insists that he must see you in person and at once."

"An official?" said madame.

"An official," Jacques repeated. "I would not have admitted him, but that he demanded it in the name of the Nation. Madame, it is for you to say what shall be done. Robert is with me. If you wish it... whatever it may be..."

"My good Jacques, no, no." She was perfectly composed. "If this man intended evil, surely he would not come alone. Conduct him to me, and then beg Mlle. de Kercadiou to join me if she is awake."

Jacques departed, himself partly reassured. Madame seated herself in the armchair by the table well within the light. She smoothed her dress with a mechanical hand. If, as it would seem, her hopes had been futile, so had her momentary fears. A man on any but an errand of peace would have brought some following with him, as she had said.

The door opened again, and Jacques reappeared; after him, stepping briskly past him, came a slight man in a wide-brimmed hat, adorned by a tricolour cockade. About the waist of an olive-green riding-coat he wore a broad tricolour sash; a sword hung at his side.

He swept off his hat, and the candlelight glinted on the steel buckle in front of it. Madame found herself silently regarded by a pair of large, dark eyes set in a lean, brown face, eyes that were most singularly intent and searching.

She leaned forward, incredulity swept across her countenance. Then her eyes kindled, and the colour came creeping back into her pale cheeks. She rose suddenly. She was trembling.

"Andre-Louis!" she exclaimed.

CHAPTER XIV. THE BARRIER

That gift of laughter of his seemed utterly extinguished. For once there was no gleam of humour in those dark eyes, as they continued to consider her with that queer stare of scrutiny. And yet, though his gaze was sombre, his thoughts were not. With his cruelly true mental vision which pierced through shams, and his capacity for detached observation—which properly applied might have carried him very far, indeed—he perceived the grotesqueness, the artificiality of the emotion which in that moment he experienced, but by which he refused to be possessed. It sprang entirely from the consciousness that she was his mother; as if, all things considered, the more or less accidental fact that she had brought him into the world could establish between them any real bond at this time of day! The motherhood that bears and forsakes is less than animal. He had considered this; he had been given ample leisure in which to consider it during those long, turbulent hours in which he had been forced to wait, because it would have been almost impossible to have won across that seething city, and certainly unwise to have attempted so to do.

He had reached the conclusion that by consenting to go to her rescue at such a time he stood committed to a piece of purely sentimental quixotry. The quittances which the Mayor of Meudon had exacted from him before he would issue the necessary safe-conducts placed the whole of his future, perhaps his very life, in jeopardy. And he had consented to do this not for the sake of a reality, but out of regard for an idea—he who all his life had avoided the false lure of worthless and hollow sentimentality.

Thus thought Andre-Louis as he considered her now so searchingly, finding it, naturally enough, a matter of extraordinary interest to look consciously upon his mother for the first time at the age of eight-and-twenty.

From her he looked at last at Jacques, who remained at attention, waiting by the open door.

"Could we be alone, madame?" he asked her.

She waved the footman away, and the door closed. In agitated silence, unquestioning, she waited for him to account for his presence there at so extraordinary a time.

"Rougane could not return," he informed her shortly. "At M. de Kercadiou's request, I come instead."

"You! You are sent to rescue us!" The note of amazement in her voice was stronger than that of her relief.

"That, and to make your acquaintance, madame."

"To make my acquaintance? But what do you mean, Andre-Louis?"

"This letter from M. de Kercadiou will tell you." Intrigued by his odd words and odder manner, she took the folded sheet. She broke the seal with shaking hands, and with shaking hands approached the written page to the light. Her eyes grew troubled as she read; the shaking of her hands increased, and midway through that reading a moan escaped her. One glance that was almost terror she darted at the slim, straight man standing so incredibly impassive upon the edge of the light, and then she endeavoured to read on. But the crabbed characters of M. de Kercadiou swam distortedly under her eyes. She could not read. Besides, what could it matter what else he said. She had read enough. The sheet fluttered from her hands to the table, and out of a face that was like a face of wax, she looked now with a wistfulness, a sadness indescribable, at Andre-Louis.

"And so you know, my child?" Her voice was stifled to a whisper.

"I know, madame my mother."

The grimness, the subtle blend of merciless derision and reproach in which it was uttered completely escaped her. She cried out at the new name. For her in that moment time and the world stood still. Her peril there in Paris as the wife of an intriguer at Coblenz was blotted out, together with every other consideration—thrust out of a consciousness that could find room for nothing else beside the fact that she stood acknowledged by her only son, this child begotten in adultery, borne furtively and in shame in a remote Brittany village eight-and-twenty years ago. Not even a thought for the betrayal of that inviolable secret, or the consequences that might follow, could she spare in this supreme moment.

She took one or two faltering steps towards him, hesitating. Then she opened her arms. Sobs suffocated her voice.

"Won't you come to me, Andre-Louis?"

A moment yet he stood hesitating, startled by that appeal, angered almost by his heart's response to it, reason and sentiment at grips in his soul. This was not real, his reason postulated; this poignant emotion that she displayed and that he experienced was fantastic. Yet he went. Her arms enfolded him; her wet cheek was pressed hard against his own; her frame, which the years had not yet succeeded in robbing of its grace, was shaken by the passionate storm within her.

"Oh, Andre-Louis, my child, if you knew how I have hungered to hold you so! If you knew how in denying myself this I have atoned and suffered! Kercadiou should not have told you—not even now. It was wrong—most wrong, perhaps, to you. It would have been better that he should have left me here to my fate, whatever that may be. And yet—come what may of this—to be able to hold you so, to be able to acknowledge you, to hear you call me mother—oh! Andre-Louis, I cannot now regret it. I cannot... I cannot wish it otherwise."

"Is there any need, madame?" he asked her, his stoicism deeply shaken. "There is no occasion to take others into our confidence. This is for to-night alone. To-night we are mother and son. To-morrow we resume our former places, and, outwardly at least, forget."

"Forget? Have you no heart, Andre-Louis?"

The question recalled him curiously to his attitude towards life—that histrionic attitude of his that he accounted true philosophy. Also he remembered what lay before them; and he realized that he must master not only himself but her; that to yield too far to sentiment at such a time might be the ruin of them all.

"It is a question propounded to me so often that it must contain the truth," said he. "My rearing is to blame for that."

She tightened her clutch about his neck even as he would have attempted to disengage himself from her embrace.

"You do not blame me for your rearing? Knowing all, as you do, Andre-Louis, you cannot altogether blame. You must be merciful to me. You must forgive me. You must! I had no choice."

"When we know all of whatever it may be, we can never do anything but forgive, madame. That is the profoundest religious truth that was ever written. It contains, in fact, a whole religion—the noblest religion any man could have to guide him. I say this for your comfort, madame my mother."

She sprang away from him with a startled cry. Beyond him in the shadows by the door a pale figure shimmered ghostly. It advanced into the light, and resolved itself into Aline. She had come in answer to that forgotten summons madame had sent her by Jacques. Entering unperceived she had seen Andre-Louis in the embrace of the woman whom he addressed as "mother." She had recognized him instantly by his voice, and she could not have said what bewildered her more: his presence there or the thing she overheard.

"You heard, Aline?" madame exclaimed.

"I could not help it, madame. You sent for me. I am sorry if..." She broke off, and looked at Andre-Louis long and curiously. She was pale, but quite composed. She held out her hand to him. "And so you have come at last, Andre," said she. "You might have come before."

"I come when I am wanted," was his answer. "Which is the only time in which one can be sure of being received." He said it without bitterness, and having said it stooped to kiss her hand.

"You can forgive me what is past, I hope, since I failed of my purpose," he said gently, half-pleading. "I could not have come to you pretending that the failure was intentional—a compromise between the necessities of the case and your own wishes. For it was not that. And yet, you do not seem to have profited by my failure. You are still a maid."

She turned her shoulder to him.

"There are things," she said, "that you will never understand."

"Life, for one," he acknowledged. "I confess that I am finding it bewildering. The very explanations calculated to simplify it seem but to complicate it further." And he looked at Mme. de Plougastel.

"You mean something, I suppose," said mademoiselle.

"Aline!" It was the Countess who spoke. She knew the danger of half-discoveries. "I can trust you, child, I know, and Andre-Louis, I am sure, will offer no objection." She had taken up the letter to show it to Aline. Yet first her eyes questioned him.

"Oh, none, madame," he assured her. "It is entirely a matter for yourself."

Aline looked from one to the other with troubled eyes, hesitating to take the letter that was now proffered. When she had read it through, she very thoughtfully replaced it on the table. A moment she stood there with bowed head, the other two watching her. Then impulsively she ran to madame and put her arms about her.

"Aline!" It was a cry of wonder, almost of joy. "You do not utterly abhor me!"

"My dear," said Aline, and kissed the tear-stained face that seemed to have grown years older in these last few hours.

In the background Andre-Louis, steeling himself against emotionalism, spoke with the voice of Scaramouche.

"It would be well, mesdames, to postpone all transports until they can be indulged at greater leisure and in more security. It is growing late. If we are to get out of this shambles we should be wise to take the road without more delay."

It was a tonic as effective as it was necessary. It startled them into remembrance of their circumstances, and under the spur of it they went at once to make their preparations.

They left him for perhaps a quarter of an hour, to pace that long room alone, saved only from impatience by the turmoil of his mind. When at length they returned, they were accompanied by a tall man in a full-skirted shaggy greatcoat and a broad hat the brim of which was turned down all around. He remained respectfully by the door in the shadows.

Between them the two women had concerted it thus, or rather the Countess had so concerted it when Aline had warned her that Andre-Louis' bitter hostility towards the Marquis made it unthinkable that he should move a finger consciously to save him.

Now despite the close friendship uniting M. de Kercadiou and his niece with Mme. de Plougastel, there were several matters concerning them of which the Countess was in ignorance. One of these was the project at one time existing of a marriage between Aline and M. de La Tour d'Azyr. It was a matter that Aline—naturally enough in the state of her feelings—had never mentioned, nor had M. de Kercadiou ever alluded to it since his coming to Meudon, by when he had perceived how unlikely it was ever to be realized.

M. de La Tour d'Azyr's concern for Aline on that morning of the duel when he had found her half-swooning in Mme. de Plougastel's carriage had been of a circumspection that betrayed nothing of his real interest in her, and therefore had appeared no more than natural in one who must account himself the cause of her distress. Similarly Mme. de Plougastel had never realized nor did she realize now—for Aline did not trouble fully to enlighten her—that the hostility between the two men was other than political, the quarrel other than that which already had taken Andre-Louis to the Bois on every day of the preceding week. But, at least, she realized that even if Andre-Louis' rancour should have no other source, yet that inconclusive duel was cause enough for Aline's fears.

And so she had proposed this obvious deception; and Aline had consented to be a passive party to it. They had made the mistake of not fully forewarning and persuading M. de La Tour d'Azyr. They had trusted entirely to his anxiety to escape from Paris to keep him rigidly within the part imposed upon him. They had reckoned without the queer sense of honour that moved such men as M. le Marquis, nurtured upon a code of shams.

Andre-Louis, turning to scan that muffled figure, advanced from the dark depths of the salon. As the light beat on his white, lean face the pseudo-footman started. The next moment he too stepped forward into the light, and swept his broad-brimmed hat from his brow. As he did so Andre-Louis observed that his hand was fine and white and that a jewel flashed from one of the fingers. Then he caught his breath, and stiffened in every line as he recognized the face revealed to him.

"Monsieur," that stern, proud man was saying, "I cannot take advantage of your ignorance. If these ladies can persuade you to save me, at least it is due to you that you shall know whom you are saving."

He stood there by the table very erect and dignified, ready to perish as he had lived—if perish he must—without fear and without deception.

Andre-Louis came slowly forward until he reached the table on the other side, and then at last the muscles of his set face relaxed, and he laughed.

"You laugh?" said M. de La Tour d'Azyr, frowning, offended.

"It is so damnably amusing," said Andre-Louis.

"You've an odd sense of humour, M. Moreau."

"Oh, admitted. The unexpected always moves me so. I have found you many things in the course of our acquaintance. To-night you are the one thing I never expected to find you: an honest man."

M. de La Tour d'Azyr quivered. But he attempted no reply.

"Because of that, monsieur, I am disposed to be clement. It is probably a foolishness. But you have surprised me into it. I give you three minutes, monsieur, in which to leave this house, and to take your own measures for your safety. What afterwards happens to you shall be no concern of mine."

"Ah, no, Andre! Listen..." Madame began in anguish.

"Pardon, madame. It is the utmost that I will do, and already I am violating what I conceive to be my duty. If M. de La Tour d'Azyr remains he not only ruins himself, but he imperils you. For unless he departs at once, he goes with me to the headquarters of the section, and the section will have his head on a pike inside the hour. He is a notorious counter-revolutionary, a knight of the dagger, one of those whom an exasperated populace is determined to exterminate. Now, monsieur, you know what awaits you. Resolve yourself and at once, for these ladies' sake."

"But you don't know, Andre-Louis!" Mme. de Plougastel's condition was one of anguish indescribable. She came to him and clutched his arm. "For the love of Heaven, Andre-Louis, be merciful with him! You must!"

"But that is what I am being, madame—merciful; more merciful than he deserves. And he knows it. Fate has meddled most oddly in our concerns to bring us together to-night. Almost it is as if Fate were forcing retribution at last upon him. Yet, for your sakes, I take no advantage of it, provided that he does at once as I have desired him."

And now from beyond the table the Marquis spoke icily, and as he spoke his right hand stirred under the ample folds of his greatcoat.

"I am glad, M. Moreau, that you take that tone with me. You relieve me of the last scruple. You spoke of Fate just now, and I must agree with you that Fate has meddled oddly, though perhaps not to the end that you discern. For years now you have chosen to stand in my path and thwart me at every turn, holding over me a perpetual menace. Persistently you have sought my life in various ways, first indirectly and at last directly. Your intervention in my affairs has ruined my highest hopes—more effectively, perhaps, than you suppose. Throughout you have been my evil genius. And you are even one of the agents of this climax of despair that has been reached by me to-night."

"Wait! Listen!" Madame was panting. She flung away from Andre-Louis, as if moved by some premonition of what was coming. "Gervais! This is horrible!"

"Horrible, perhaps, but inevitable. Himself he has invited it. I am a man in despair, the fugitive of a lost cause. That man holds the keys of escape. And, besides, between him and me there is a reckoning to be paid."

His hand came from beneath the coat at last, and it came armed with a pistol.

Mme. de Plougastel screamed, and flung herself upon him. On her knees now, she clung to his arm with all her strength and might.

Vainly he sought to shake himself free of that desperate clutch.

"Therese!" he cried. "Are you mad? Will you destroy me and yourself? This creature has the safe-conducts that mean our salvation. Himself, he is nothing."

From the background Aline, a breathless, horror-stricken spectator of that scene, spoke sharply, her quick mind pointing out the line of checkmate.

"Burn the safe-conducts, Andre-Louis. Burn them at once—in the candles there."

But Andre-Louis had taken advantage of that moment of M. de La Tour d'Azyr's impotence to draw a pistol in his turn. "I think it will be better to burn his brains instead," he said. "Stand away from him, madame."

Far from obeying that imperious command, Mme. de Plougastel rose to her feet to cover the Marquis with her body. But she still clung to his arm, clung to it with unsuspected strength that continued to prevent him from attempting to use the pistol.

"Andre! For God's sake, Andre!" she panted hoarsely over her shoulder.

"Stand away, madame," he commanded her again, more sternly, "and let this murderer take his due. He is jeopardizing all our lives, and his own has been forfeit these years. Stand away!" He sprang forward with intent now to fire at his enemy over her shoulder, and Aline moved too late to hinder him.

"Andre! Andre!"

Panting, gasping, haggard of face, on the verge almost of hysteria, the distracted Countess flung at last an effective, a terrible barrier between the hatred of those men, each intent upon taking the other's life.

"He is your father, Andre! Gervais, he is your son—our son! The letter there... on the table... O my God!" And she slipped nervelessly to the ground, and crouched there sobbing at the feet of M. de La Tour d'Azyr.

CHAPTER XV. SAFE-CONDUCT

Across the body of that convulsively sobbing woman, the mother of one and the mistress of the other, the eyes of those mortal enemies met, invested with a startled, appalled interest that admitted of no words.

Beyond the table, as if turned to stone by this culminating horror of revelation, stood Aline.

M. de La Tour d'Azyr was the first to stir. Into his bewildered mind came the memory of something that Mme. de Plougastel had said of a letter that was on the table. He came forward, unhindered. The announcement made, Mme. de Plougastel no longer feared the sequel, and so she let him go. He walked unsteadily past this new-found son of his, and took up the sheet that lay beside the candle-branch. A long moment he stood reading it, none heeding him. Aline's eyes were all on Andre-Louis, full of wonder and commiseration, whilst Andre-Louis was staring down, in stupefied fascination, at his mother.

M. de La Tour d'Azyr read the letter slowly through. Then very quietly he replaced it. His next concern, being the product of an artificial age sternly schooled in the suppression of emotion, was to compose himself. Then he stepped back to Mme. de Plougastel's side and stooped to raise her.

"Therese," he said.

Obeying, by instinct, the implied command, she made an effort to rise and to control herself in her turn. The Marquis half conducted, half carried her to the armchair by the table.

Andre-Louis looked on. Still numbed and bewildered, he made no attempt to assist. He saw as in a dream the Marquis bending over Mme. de Plougastel. As in a dream he heard him ask:

"How long have you known this, Therese?"

"I... I have always known it... always. I confided him to Kercadiou. I saw him once as a child... Oh, but what of that?"

"Why was I never told? Why did you deceive me? Why did you tell me that this child had died a few days after birth? Why, Therese? Why?"

"I was afraid. I... I thought it better so—that nobody, nobody, not even you, should know. And nobody has known save Quintin until last night, when to induce him to come here and save me he was forced to tell him."

"But I, Therese?" the Marquis insisted. "It was my right to know."

"Your right? What could you have done? Acknowledge him? And then? Ha!" It was a queer, desperate note of laughter. "There was Plougastel; there was my family. And there was you... you, yourself, who had ceased to care, in whom the fear of discovery had stifled love. Why should I have told you, then? Why? I should not have told you now had there been any other way to... to save you both. Once before I suffered just such dreadful apprehensions when you and he fought in the Bois. I was on my way to prevent it when you met me. I would have divulged the truth, as a last resource, to avert that horror. But mercifully God spared me the necessity then."

It had not occurred to any of them to doubt her statement, incredible though it might seem. Had any done so her present words must have resolved all doubt, explaining as they did much that to each of her listeners had been obscure until this moment.

M. de La Tour d'Azyr, overcome, reeled away to a chair and sat down heavily. Losing command of himself for a moment, he took his haggard face in his hands.

Through the windows open to the garden came from the distance the faint throbbing of a drum to remind them of what was happening around them. But the sound went unheeded. To each it must have seemed that here they were face to face with a horror greater than any that might be tormenting Paris. At last Andre-Louis began to speak, his voice level and unutterably cold.

"M. de La Tour d'Azyr," he said, "I trust that you'll agree that this disclosure, which can hardly be more distasteful and horrible to you than it is to me, alters nothing, since it effaces nothing of all that lies between us. Or, if it alters anything, it is merely to add something to that score. And yet... Oh, but what can it avail to talk! Here, monsieur, take this safe-conduct which is made out for Mme. de Plougastel's footman, and with it make your escape as best you can. In return I will beg of you the favour never to allow me to see you or hear of you again."

"Andre!" His mother swung upon him with that cry. And yet again that question. "Have you no heart? What has he ever done to you that you should nurse so bitter a hatred of him?"

"You shall hear, madame. Once, two years ago in this very room I told you of a man who had brutally killed my dearest friend and debauched the girl I was to have married. M. de La Tour d'Azyr is that man."

A moan was her only answer. She covered her face with her hands.

The Marquis rose slowly to his feet again. He came slowly forward, his smouldering eyes scanning his son's face.

"You are hard," he said grimly. "But I recognize the hardness. It derives from the blood you bear."

"Spare me that," said Andre-Louis.

The Marquis inclined his head. "I will not mention it again. But I desire that you should at least understand me, and you too, Therese. You accuse me, sir, of murdering your dearest friend. I will admit that the means employed were perhaps unworthy. But what other means were at my command to meet an urgency that every day since then proves to have existed? M. de Vilmorin was a revolutionary, a man of new ideas that should overthrow society and rebuild it more akin to the desires of such as himself. I belonged to the order that quite as justifiably desired society to remain as it was. Not only was it better so for me and mine, but I also contend, and you have yet to prove me wrong, that it is better so for all the world; that, indeed, no other conceivable society is possible. Every human society must of necessity be composed of several strata. You may disturb it temporarily into an amorphous whole by a revolution such as this; but only temporarily. Soon out of the chaos which is all that you and your kind can ever produce, order must be restored or life will perish; and with the restoration of order comes the restoration of the various strata necessary to organized society. Those that were yesterday at the top may in the new order of things find themselves dispossessed without any benefit to the whole. That change I resisted. The spirit of it I fought with whatever weapons were available, whenever and wherever I encountered it. M. de Vilmorin was an incendiary of the worst type, a man of eloquence full of false ideals that misled poor ignorant men into believing that the change proposed could make the world a better place for them. You are an intelligent man, and I defy you to answer me from your heart and conscience that such a thing was true or possible. You know that it is untrue; you know that it is a pernicious doctrine; and what made it worse on the lips of M. de Vilmorin was that he was sincere and eloquent. His voice was a danger that must be removed—silenced. So much was necessary in self-defence. In self-defence I did it. I had no grudge against M. de Vilmorin. He was a man of my own class; a gentleman of pleasant ways, amiable, estimable, and able.

"You conceive me slaying him for the very lust of slaying, like some beast of the jungle flinging itself upon its natural prey. That has been your error from the first. I did what I did with the very heaviest heart—oh, spare me your sneer!—I do not lie, I have never lied. And I swear to you here and now, by my every hope of Heaven, that what I say is true. I loathed the thing I did. Yet for my own sake and the sake of my order I must do it. Ask yourself whether M. de Vilmorin would have hesitated for a moment if by procuring my death he could have brought the Utopia of his dreams a moment nearer realization.

"After that. You determined that the sweetest vengeance would be to frustrate my ends by reviving in yourself the voice that I had silenced, by yourself carrying forward the fantastic apostleship of equality that was M. de Vilmorin's. You lacked the vision that would have shown you that God did not create men equals. Well, you are in case to-night to judge which of us was right, which wrong. You see what is happening here in Paris. You see the foul spectre of Anarchy stalking through a land fallen into confusion. Probably you have enough imagination to conceive something of what must follow. And do you deceive yourself that out of this filth and ruin there will rise up an ideal form of society? Don't you understand that society must re-order itself presently out of all this?

"But why say more? I must have said enough to make you understand the only thing that really matters—that I killed M. de Vilmorin as a matter of duty to my order. And the truth—which though it may offend you should also convince you—is that to-night I can look back on the deed with equanimity, without a single regret, apart from what lies between you and me.

"When, kneeling beside the body of your friend that day at Gavrillac, you insulted and provoked me, had I been the tiger you conceived me I must have killed you too. I am, as you may know, a man of quick passions. Yet I curbed the natural anger you aroused in me, because I could forgive an affront to myself where I could not overlook a calculated attack upon my order."

He paused a moment. Andre-Louis stood rigid listening and wondering. So, too, the others. Then M. le Marquis resumed, on a note of less assurance. "In the matter of Mlle. Binet I was unfortunate. I wronged you through inadvertence. I had no knowledge of the relations between you."

Andre-Louis interrupted him sharply at last with a question: "Would it have made a difference if you had?"

"No," he was answered frankly. "I have the faults of my kind. I cannot pretend that any such scruple as you suggest would have weighed with me. But can you—if you are capable of any detached judgment—blame me very much for that?"

"All things considered, monsieur, I am rapidly being forced to the conclusion that it is impossible to blame any man for anything in this world; that we are all of us the sport of destiny. Consider, monsieur, this gathering—this family gathering—here to-night, whilst out there... O my God, let us make an end! Let us go our ways and write 'finis' to this horrible chapter of our lives."

M. le La Tour considered him gravely, sadly, in silence for a moment.

"Perhaps it is best," he said, at length, in a small voice. He turned to Mme. de Plougastel. "If a wrong I have to admit in my life, a wrong that I must bitterly regret, it is the wrong that I have done to you, my dear..."

"Not now, Gervais! Not now!" she faltered, interrupting him.

"Now—for the first and the last time. I am going. It is not likely that we shall ever meet again—that I shall ever see any of you again—you who should have been the nearest and dearest to me. We are all, he says, the sport of destiny. Ah, but not quite. Destiny is an intelligent force, moving with purpose. In life we pay for the evil that in life we do. That is the lesson that I have learnt to-night. By an act of betrayal I begot unknown to me a son who, whilst as ignorant as myself of our relationship, has come to be the evil genius of my life, to cross and thwart me, and finally to help to pull me down in ruin. It is just—poetically just. My full and resigned acceptance of that fact is the only atonement I can offer you."

He stooped and took one of madame's hands that lay limply in her lap.

"Good-bye, Therese!" His voice broke. He had reached the end of his iron self-control.

She rose and clung to him a moment, unashamed before them. The ashes of that dead romance had been deeply stirred this night, and deep down some lingering embers had been found that glowed brightly now before their final extinction. Yet she made no attempt to detain him. She understood that their son had pointed out the only wise, the only possible course, and was thankful that M. de La Tour d'Azyr accepted it.

"God keep you, Gervais," she murmured. "You will take the safe-conduct, and... and you will let me know when you are safe?"

He held her face between his hands an instant; then very gently kissed her and put her from him. Standing erect, and outwardly calm again, he looked across at Andre-Louis who was proffering him a sheet of paper.

"It is the safe-conduct. Take it, monsieur. It is my first and last gift to you, and certainly the last gift I should ever have thought of making you—the gift of life. In a sense it makes us quits. The irony, sir, is not mine, but Fate's. Take it, monsieur, and go in peace."

M. de La Tour d'Azyr took it. His eyes looked hungrily into the lean face confronting him, so sternly set. He thrust the paper into his bosom, and then abruptly, convulsively, held out his hand. His son's eyes asked a question.

"Let there be peace between us, in God's name," said the Marquis thickly.

Pity stirred at last in Andre-Louis. Some of the sternness left his face. He sighed. "Good-bye, monsieur," he said.

"You are hard," his father told him, speaking wistfully. "But perhaps you are in the right so to be. In other circumstances I should have been proud to have owned you as my son. As it is..." He broke off abruptly, and as abruptly added, "Good-bye."

He loosed his son's hand and stepped back. They bowed formally to each other. And then M. de La Tour d'Azyr bowed to Mlle. de Kercadiou in utter silence, a bow that contained something of utter renunciation, of finality.

That done he turned and walked stiffly out of the room, and so out of all their lives. Months later they were to hear of him in the service of the Emperor of Austria.

CHAPTER XVI. SUNRISE

Andre-Louis took the air next morning on the terrace at Meudon. The hour was very early, and the newly risen sun was transmuting into diamonds the dewdrops that still lingered on the lawn. Down in the valley, five miles away, the morning mists were rising over Paris. Yet early as it was that house on the hill was astir already, in a bustle of preparation for the departure that was imminent.

Andre-Louis had won safely out of Paris last night with his mother and Aline, and to-day they were to set out all of them for Coblenz.

To Andre-Louis, sauntering there with hands clasped behind him and head hunched between his shoulders—for life had never been richer in material for reflection—came presently Aline through one of the glass doors from the library.

"You're early astir," she greeted him.

"Faith, yes. I haven't been to bed. No," he assured her, in answer to her exclamation. "I spent the night, or what was left of it, sitting at the window thinking."

"My poor Andre!"

"You describe me perfectly. I am very poor—for I know nothing, understand nothing. It is not a calamitous condition until it is realized. Then..." He threw out his arms, and let them fall again. His face she observed was very drawn and haggard.

She paced with him along the old granite balustrade over which the geraniums flung their mantle of green and scarlet.

"Have you decided what you are going to do?" she asked him.

"I have decided that I have no choice. I, too, must emigrate. I am lucky to be able to do so, lucky to have found no one amid yesterday's chaos in Paris to whom I could report myself as I foolishly desired, else I might no longer be armed with these." He drew from his pocket the powerful passport of the Commission of Twelve, enjoining upon all Frenchmen to lend him such assistance as he might require, and warning those who might think of hindering him that they did so at their own peril. He spread it before her. "With this I conduct you all safely to the frontier. Over the frontier M. de Kercadiou and Mme. de Plougastel will have to conduct me; and then we shall be quits."

"Quits?" quoth she. "But you will be unable to return!"

"You conceive, of course, my eagerness to do so. My child, in a day or two there will be enquiries. It will be asked what has become of me. Things will transpire. Then the hunt will start. But by then we shall be well upon our way, well ahead of any possible pursuit. You don't imagine that I could ever give the government any satisfactory explanation of my absence—assuming that any government remains to which to explain it?"

"You mean... that you will sacrifice your future, this career upon which you have embarked?" It took her breath away.

"In the pass to which things have come there is no career for me down there—at least no honest one. And I hope you do not think that I could be dishonest. It is the day of the Dantons, and the Marats, the day of the rabble. The reins of government will be tossed to the populace, or else the populace, drunk with the conconceit with which the Dantons and the Marats have filled it, will seize the reins by force. Chaos must follow, and a despotism of brutes and apes, a government of the whole by its lowest parts. It cannot endure, because unless a nation is ruled by its best elements it must wither and decay."

"I thought you were a republican," said she.

"Why, so I am. I am talking like one. I desire a society which selects its rulers from the best elements of every class and denies the right of any class or corporation to usurp the government to itself—whether it be the nobles, the clergy, the bourgeoisie, or the proletariat. For government by any one class is fatal to the welfare of the whole. Two years ago our ideal seemed to have been realized. The monopoly of power had been taken from the class that had held it too long and too unjustly by the hollow right of heredity. It had been distributed as evenly as might be throughout the State, and if men had only paused there, all would have been well. But our impetus carried us too far, the privileged orders goaded us on by their very opposition, and the result is the horror of which yesterday you saw no more than the beginnings. No, no," he ended. "Careers there may be for venal place-seekers, for opportunists; but none for a man who desires to respect himself. It is time to go. I make no sacrifice in going."

"But where will you go? What will you do?"

"Oh, something. Consider that in four years I have been lawyer, politician, swordsman, and buffoon—especially the latter. There is always a place in the world for Scaramouche. Besides, do you know that unlike Scaramouche I have been oddly provident? I am the owner of a little farm in Saxony. I think that agriculture might suit me. It is a meditative occupation; and when all is said, I am not a man of action. I haven't the qualities for the part."

She looked up into his face, and there was a wistful smile in her deep blue eyes.

"Is there any part for which you have not the qualities, I wonder?"

"Do you really? Yet you cannot say that I have made a success of any of those which I have played. I have always ended by running away. I am running away now from a thriving fencing-academy, which is likely to become the property of Le Duc. That comes of having gone into politics, from which I am also running away. It is the one thing in which I really excel. That, too, is an attribute of Scaramouche."

"Why will you always be deriding yourself?" she wondered.

"Because I recognize myself for part of this mad world, I suppose. You wouldn't have me take it seriously? I should lose my reason utterly if I did; especially since discovering my parents."

"Don't, Andre!" she begged him. "You are insincere, you know."

"Of course I am. Do you expect sincerity in man when hypocrisy is the very keynote of human nature? We are nurtured on it; we are schooled in it, we live by it; and we rarely realize it. You have seen it rampant and out of hand in France during the past four years—cant and hypocrisy on the lips of the revolutionaries, cant and hypocrisy on the lips of the upholders of the old regime; a riot of hypocrisy out of which in the end is begotten chaos. And I who criticize it all on this beautiful God-given morning am the rankest and most contemptible hypocrite of all. It was this—the realization of this truth kept me awake all night. For two years I have persecuted by every means in my power... M. de La Tour d'Azyr."

He paused before uttering the name, paused as if hesitating how to speak of him.

"And in those two years I have deceived myself as to the motive that was spurring me. He spoke of me last night as the evil genius of his life, and himself he recognized the justice of this. It may be that he was right, and because of that it is probable that even had he not killed Philippe de Vilmorin, things would still have been the same. Indeed, to-day I know that they must have been. That is why I call myself a hypocrite, a poor, self-duping hypocrite."

"But why, Andre?"

He stood still and looked at her. "Because he sought you, Aline. Because in that alone he must have found me ranged against him, utterly intransigeant. Because of that I must have strained every nerve to bring him down—so as to save you from becoming the prey of your own ambition.

"I wish to speak of him no more than I must. After this, I trust never to speak of him again. Before the lines of our lives crossed, I knew him for what he was, I knew the report of him that ran the countryside. Even then I found him detestable. You heard him allude last night to the unfortunate La Binet. You heard him plead, in extenuation of his fault, his mode of life, his rearing. To that there is no answer, I suppose. He conforms to type. Enough! But to me, he was the embodiment of evil, just as you have always been the embodiment of good; he was the embodiment of sin, just as you are the embodiment of purity. I had enthroned you so high, Aline, so high, and yet no higher than your place. Could I, then, suffer that you should be dragged down by ambition, could I suffer the evil I detested to mate with the good I loved? What could have come of it but your own damnation, as I told you that day at Gavrillac? Because of that my detestation of him became a personal, active thing. I resolved to save you at all costs from a fate so horrible. Had you been able to tell me that you loved him it would have been different. I should have hoped that in a union sanctified by love you would have raised him to your own pure heights. But that out of considerations of worldly advancement you should lovelessly consent to mate with him... Oh, it was vile and hopeless.

And so I fought him—a rat fighting a lion—fought him relentlessly until I saw that love had come to take in your heart the place of ambition. Then I desisted."

"Until you saw that love had taken the place of ambition!" Tears had been gathering in her eyes whilst he was speaking. Now amazement eliminated her emotion. "But when did you see that? When?"

"I—I was mistaken. I know it now. Yet, at the time... surely, Aline, that morning when you came to beg me not to keep my engagement with him in the Bois, you were moved by concern for him?"

"For him! It was concern for you," she cried, without thinking what she said.

But it did not convince him. "For me? When you knew—when all the world knew what I had been doing daily for a week!"

"Ah, but he, he was different from the others you had met. His reputation stood high. My uncle accounted him invincible; he persuaded me that if you met nothing could save you."

He looked at her frowning.

"Why this, Aline?" he asked her with some sternness. "I can understand that, having changed since then, you should now wish to disown those sentiments. It is a woman's way, I suppose."

"Oh, what are you saying, Andre? How wrong you are! It is the truth I have told you!"

"And was it concern for me," he asked her, "that laid you swooning when you saw him return wounded from the meeting? That was what opened my eyes."

"Wounded? I had not seen his wound. I saw him sitting alive and apparently unhurt in his caleche, and I concluded that he had killed you as he had said he would. What else could I conclude?"

He saw light, dazzling, blinding, and it scared him. He fell back, a hand to his brow. "And that was why you fainted?" he asked incredulously.

She looked at him without answering. As she began to realize how much she had been swept into saying by her eagerness to make him realize his error, a sudden fear came creeping into her eyes.

He held out both hands to her.

"Aline! Aline!" His voice broke on the name. "It was I..."

"O blind Andre, it was always you—always! Never, never did I think of him, not even for loveless marriage, save once for a little while, when... when that theatre girl came into your life, and then..." She broke off, shrugged, and turned her head away. "I thought of following ambition, since there was nothing left to follow."

He shook himself. "I am dreaming, of course, or else I am mad," he said.

"Blind, Andre; just blind," she assured him.

"Blind only where it would have been presumption to have seen."

"And yet," she answered him with a flash of the Aline he had known of old, "I have never found you lack presumption."

M. de Kercadiou, emerging a moment later from the library window, beheld them holding hands and staring each at the other, beatifically, as if each saw Paradise in the other's face.

THE SEA-HAWK

By

Rafael Sabatini

NOTE

Lord Henry Goade, who had, as we shall see, some personal acquaintance with Sir Oliver Tressilian, tells us quite bluntly that he was ill-favoured. But then his lordship is addicted to harsh judgments and his perceptions are not always normal. He says, for instance, of Anne of Cleves, that she was the "ugliest woman that ever I saw." As far as we can glean from his own voluminous writings it would seem to be extremely doubtful whether he ever saw Anne of Cleves at all, and we suspect him here of being no more than a slavish echo of the common voice, which attributed Cromwell's downfall to the ugliness of this bride he procured for his Bluebeard master. To the common voice from the brush of Holbein, which permits us to form our own opinions and shows us a lady who is certainly very far from deserving his lordship's harsh stricture. Similarly, I like to believe that Lord Henry was wrong in his pronouncement upon Sir Oliver, and I am encouraged in this belief by the pen-portrait which he himself appends to it. "He was," he says, "a tall, powerful fellow of a good shape, if we except that his arms were too long and that his feet and hands were of an uncomely bigness. In face he was swarthy, with black hair and a black forked beard; his nose was big and very high in the bridge, and his eyes sunk deep under beetling eyebrows were very pale-coloured and very cruel and sinister. He had—and this I have ever remarked to be the sign of great virility in a man—a big, deep, rough voice, better suited to, and no doubt oftener employed in, quarter-deck oaths and foulnesses than the worship of his Maker."

Thus my Lord Henry Goade, and you observe how he permits his lingering disapproval of the man to intrude upon his description of him. The truth is that—as there is ample testimony in his prolific writings—is lordship was something of a misanthropist. It was, in fact, his misanthropy which drove him, as it has driven many another, to authorship. He takes up the pen, not so much that he may carry out his professed object of writing a chronicle of his own time, but to the end that he may vent the bitterness engendered in him by his fall from favour. As a consequence he has little that is good to say of anyone, and rarely mentions one of his contemporaries but to tap the sources of a picturesque invective. After all, it is possible to make excuses for him. He was at once a man of thought and a man of action—a combination as rare as it is usually deplorable. The man of action in him might have gone far had he not been ruined at the outset by the man of thought. A magnificent seaman, he might have become Lord High Admiral of England but for a certain proneness to intrigue. Fortunately for him—since head where nature had placed it—he came betimes under a cloud of suspicion. His career suffered a check; but it was necessary to afford him some compensation since, after all, the suspicions could not be substantiated.

Consequently he was removed from his command and appointed by the Queen's Grace her Lieutenant of Cornwall, a position in which it was judged that he could do little mischief. There, soured by this blighting of his ambitions, and living a life of comparative seclusion, he turned, as so many other men similarly placed have turned, to seek consolation in his pen. He wrote his singularly crabbed, narrow and superficial History of Lord Henry Goade: his own Times—which is a miracle of injuvenations, distortions, misrepresentations, and eccentric spelling. In the eighteen enormous folio volumes, which he filled with his minute and gothic characters, he gives his own version of the story of what he terms his downfall, and, having, notwithstanding his prolixity, exhausted this subject in the first five of the eighteen tomes, he proceeds to deal with so much of the history of his own day as came immediately under his notice in his Cornish retirement.

For the purposes of English history his chronicles are entirely negligible, which is the reason why they have been allowed to remain unpublished and in oblivion. But to the student who attempts to follow the history of that extraordinary man, Sir Oliver Tressilian, they are entirely invaluable. And, since I have made this history my present task, it is fitting that I should here at the outset acknowledge my extreme indebtedness to those chronicles. Without them, indeed, it were impossible to reconstruct the life of that Cornish gentleman who became a renegade and a Barbary Corsair and might have become Basha of Algiers—or Argire, as his lordship terms it—but for certain matters which are to be set forth.

Lord Henry wrote with knowledge and authority, and the tale he has to tell is very complete and full of precious detail. He was, himself, an eyewitness of much that happened; he pursued a personal acquaintance with many of those who were connected with Sir Oliver's affairs that he might amplify his chronicles, and he considered no scrap of gossip that was to be gleaned along the countryside too trivial to be recorded. I suspect him also of having received no little assistance from Jasper Leigh in the matter of those events that happened out of England, which seem to me to constitute by far the most interesting portion of his narrative.

R. S.

PART I. SIR OLIVER TRESSILIAN

CHAPTER I. THE HUCKSTER

Sir Oliver Tressilian sat at his ease in the lofty dining-room of the handsome house of Penarrow, which he owed to the enterprise of his father of lamented and lamentable memory and to the skill and invention of an Italian engineer named Bagnolo who had come to England half a century ago as one of the assistants of the famous Torrigiani.

This house of such a startlingly singular and Italianate grace for so remote a corner of Cornwall deserves, together with the story of its construction, a word in passing.

The Italian Bagnolo who combined with his salient artistic talents a quarrelsome, volcanic humour had the mischance to kill a man in a brawl in a Southwark tavern. As a result he fled the town, nor paused in his headlong flight from the consequences of that murderous deed until he had all but reached the very ends of England. Under what circumstances he became acquainted with Tressilian the elder I do not know. But certain it is that the meeting was a very timely one for both of them. To the fugitive, Ralph Tressilian—who appears to have been inveterately partial to the company of rascals of all denominations—afforded shelter; and Bagnolo repaid the service by offering to rebuild the decaying half-timbered house of Penarrow. Having taken the task in hand he went about it with all the enthusiasm of your true artist, and achieved for his protector a residence that was a marvel of grace in that crude age and outlandish district. There arose under the supervision of the gifted engineer, worthy associate of Messer Torrigiani, a noble two-storied mansion of mellow red brick, flooded with light and sunshine by the enormously tall mullioned windows that rose almost from base to summit of each pilastered facade. The main doorway was set in a projecting wing and was overhung by a massive balcony, the whole surmounted by a pillared pediment of extraordinary grace, now partly clad in a green mantle of creepers. Above the burnt red tiles of the roof soared massive twisted chimneys in lofty majesty.

But the glory of Penarrow—that is, of the new Penarrow begotten of the fertile brain of Bagnolo—was the garden fashioned out of the tangled wilderness about the old house that had crowned the heights above Penarrow point. To the labours of Bagnolo, Time and Nature had added their own. Bagnolo had cut those handsome esplanades, had built those noble balustrades bordering the three terraces with their fine connecting flights of steps; himself he had planned the fountain, and with his own hands had carved the granite faun presiding over it and the dozen other statues of nymphs and sylvan gods in a marble that gleamed in white brilliance amid the dusky green. But Time and Nature had smoothed the lawns to a velvet surface, had thickened the handsome boxwood hedges, and thrust up those black spear-like poplars that completed the very Italianate appearance of that Cornish demesne.

Sir Oliver took his ease in his dining-room considering all this as it was displayed before him in the mellowing September sunshine, and found it all very good to see, and life very good to live. Now no man has ever been known so to find life without some immediate cause, other than that of his environment, for his optimism. Sir Oliver had several causes. The first of these—although it was one which he may have been far from suspecting—was his equipment of youth, wealth, and good digestion; the second was that he had achieved honour and renown both upon the Spanish Main and in the late harrying of the Invincible Armada—or, more aptly perhaps might it be said, in the harrying of the late Invincible Armada—and that he had received in that the twenty-fifth year of his life the honour of knighthood from the Virgin Queen; the third and last contributor to his pleasant mood—and I have reserved it for the end as I account this to be the proper place for the most important factor—was Dan Cupid who for once seemed compounded entirely of benignity and who had so contrived matters that Sir Oliver's wooing Of Mistress Rosamund Godolphin ran an entirely smooth and happy course.

So, then, Sir Oliver sat at his ease in his tall, carved chair, his doublet untrussed, his long legs stretched before him, a pensive smile about the firm lips that as yet were darkened by no more than a small black line of moustachios. (Lord Henry's portrait of him was drawn at a much later period.) It was noon, and our gentleman had just dined, as the platters, the broken meats and the half-empty flagon on the board beside him testified. He pulled thoughtfully at a long pipe—for he had acquired this newly imported habit of tobacco-drinking—and dreamed of his mistress, and was properly and gallantly grateful that fortune had used him so handsomely as to enable him to toss a title and some measure of renown into his Rosamund's lap.

By nature Sir Oliver was a shrewd fellow ("cunning as twenty devils," is my Lord Henry's phrase) and he was also a man of some not inconsiderable learning. Yet neither his natural wit nor his acquired endowments appear to have taught him that of all the gods that rule the destinies of mankind there is none more ironic and malicious than that same Dan Cupid in whose honour, as it were, he was now burning the incense of that pipe of his. The ancients knew that innocent-seeming boy for a cruel, impish knave, and they mistrusted him. Sir Oliver either did not know or did not heed that sound piece of ancient wisdom. It was to be borne in upon him by grim experience, and even as his light pensive eyes smiled upon the sunshine that flooded the terrace beyond the long mullioned window, a shadow fell athwart it which he little dreamed to be symbolic of the shadow that was even falling across the sunshine of his life.

After that shadow came the substance—tall and gay of raiment under a broad black Spanish hat decked with blood-red plumes. Swinging a long beribboned cane the figure passed the windows, stalking deliberately as Fate.

The smile perished on Sir Oliver's lips. His swarthy face grew thoughtful, his black brows contracted until no more than a single deep furrow stood between them. Then slowly the smile came forth again, but no longer that erstwhile gentle pensive smile. It was transformed into a smile of resolve and determination, a smile that tightened his lips even as his brows relaxed, and invested his brooding eyes with a gleam that was mocking, crafty and almost wicked.

Came Nicholas his servant to announce Master Peter Godolphin, and close upon the lackey's heels came Master Godolphin himself, leaning upon his beribboned cane and carrying his broad Spanish hat. He was a tall, slender gentleman, with a shaven, handsome countenance, stamped with an air of haughtiness; like Sir Oliver, he had a high-bridged, intrepid nose, and in age he was the younger by some two or three years. He wore his auburn hair rather longer than was the mode just then, but in his apparel there was no more foppishness than is tolerable in a gentleman of his years.

Sir Oliver rose and bowed from his great height in welcome. But a wave of tobacco-smoke took his graceful visitor in the throat and set him coughing and grimacing.

"I see," he choked, "that ye have acquired that filthy habit."

"I have known filthier," said Sir Oliver composedly.

"I nothing doubt it," rejoined Master Godolphin, thus early giving indications of his humour and the object of his visit.

Sir Oliver checked an answer that must have helped his visitor to his ends, which was no part of the knight's intent.

"Therefore," said he ironically, "I hope you will be patient with my shortcomings. Nick, a chair for Master Godolphin and another cup. I bid you welcome to Penarrow."

A sneer flickered over the younger man's white face. "You pay me a compliment, sir, which I fear me 'tis not mine to return to you."

"Time enough for that when I come to seek it," said Sir Oliver, with easy, if assumed, good humour.

"When you come to seek it?"

"The hospitality of your house," Sir Oliver explained.

"It is on that very matter I am come to talk with you."

"Will you sit?" Sir Oliver invited him, and spread a hand towards the chair which Nicholas had set. In the same gesture he waved the servant away.

Master Godolphin ignored the invitation. "You were," he said, "at Godolphin Court but yesterday, I hear." He paused, and as Sir Oliver offered no denial, he added stiffly: "I am come, sir, to inform you that the honour of your visits is one we shall be happy to forgo."

In the effort he made to preserve his self-control before so direct an affront Sir Oliver paled a little under his tan.

"You will understand, Peter," he replied slowly, "that you have said too much unless you add something more." He paused, considering his visitor a moment. "I do not know whether Rosamund has told you that yesterday she did me the honour to consent to become my wife...."

"She is a child that does not know her mind," broke in the other.

"Do you know of any good reason why she should come to change it?" asked Sir Oliver, with a slight air of challenge.

Master Godolphin sat down, crossed his legs and placed his hat on his knee.

"I know a dozen," he answered. "But I need not urge them. Sufficient should it be to remind you that Rosamund is but seventeen and that she is under my guardianship and that of Sir John Killigrew. Neither Sir John nor I can sanction this betrothal."

"Good lack!" broke out Sir Oliver. "Who asks your sanction or Sir John's? By God's grace your sister will grow to be a woman soon and mistress of herself. I am in no desperate haste to get me wed, and by nature—as you may be observing—I am a wondrous patient man. I'll even wait," And he pulled at his pipe.

"Waiting cannot avail you in this, Sir Oliver. 'Tis best you should understand. We are resolved, Sir John and I."

"Are you so? God's light. Send Sir John to me to tell me of his resolves and I'll tell him something of mine. Tell him from me, Master Godolphin, that if he will trouble to come as far as Penarrow I'll do by him what the hangman should have done long since. I'll crop his pimpish ears for him, by this hand!"

"Meanwhile," said Master Godolphin whettingly, "will you not essay your rover's prowess upon me?"

"You?" quoth Sir Oliver, and looked him over with good-humoured contempt. "I'm no butcher of fledgelings, my lad. Besides, you are your sister's brother, and 'tis no aim of mine to increase the obstacles already in my path." Then his tone changed. He leaned across the table. "Come, now, Peter. What is at the root of all this matter? Can we not compose such differences as you conceive exist? Out with them. 'Tis no matter for Sir John. He's a curmudgeon who signifies not a finger's snap. But you, 'tis different. You are her brother. Out with your plaints, then. Let us be frank and friendly."

"Friendly?" The other sneered again. "Our fathers set us an example in that."

"Does it matter what our fathers did? More shame to them if, being neighbours, they could not be friends. Shall we follow so deplorable an example?"

"You'll not impute that the fault lay with my father," cried the other, with a show of ready anger.

"I impute nothing, lad. I cry shame upon them both."

"'Swounds!" swore Master Peter. "Do you malign the dead?"

"If I do, I malign them both. But I do not. I no more than condemn a fault that both must acknowledge could they return to life."

"Then, Sir, confine your condemnings to your own father with whom no man of honour could have lived at peace...."

"Softly, softly, good Sir...."

"There's no call to go softly. Ralph Tressilian was a dishonour, a scandal to the countryside. Not a hamlet between here and Truro, or between here and Helston, but swarms with big Tressilian noses like your own, in memory of your debauched parent."

Sir Oliver's eyes grew narrower: he smiled. "I wonder how you came by your own nose?" he wondered.

Master Godolphin got to his feet in a passion, and his chair crashed over behind him. "Sir," he blazed, "you insult my mother's memory!"

Sir Oliver laughed. "I make a little free with it, perhaps, in return for your pleasantries on the score of my father."

Master Godolphin pondered him in speechless anger, then swayed by his passion he leaned across the board, raised his long cane and struck Sir Oliver sharply on the shoulder.

That done, he strode off magnificently towards the door. Half-way thither he paused.

"I shall expect your friends and the length of your sword," said he.

Sir Oliver laughed again. "I don't think I shall trouble to send them," said he.

Master Godolphin wheeled, fully to face him again. "How? You will take a blow?"

Sir Oliver shrugged. "None saw it given," said he.

"But I shall publish it abroad that I have caned you."

"You'll publish yourself a liar if you do; for none will believe you." Then he changed his tone yet again. "Come, Peter, we are behaving unworthily. As for the blow, I confess that I deserved it. A man's mother is more sacred than his father. So we may cry quits on that score. Can we not cry quits on all else? What can it profit us to perpetuate a foolish quarrel that sprang up between our fathers?"

"There is more than that between us," answered Master Godolphin. "I'll not have my sister wed a pirate."

"A pirate? God's light! I am glad there's none to hear you for since her grace has knighted me for my doings upon the seas, your words go very near to treason. Surely, lad, what the Queen approves, Master Peter Godolphin may approve and even your mentor Sir John Killigrew. You've been listening to him. 'Twas he sent you hither."

"I am no man's lackey," answered the other hotly, resenting the imputation—and resenting it the more because of the truth in it.

"To call me a pirate is to say a foolish thing. Hawkins with whom I sailed has also received the accolade, and who dubs us pirates insults the Queen herself. Apart from that, which, as you see, is a very empty charge, what else have you against me? I am, I hope, as good as any other here in Cornwall; Rosamund honours me with her affection and I am rich and shall be richer still ere the wedding bells are heard."

"Rich with the fruit of thieving upon the seas, rich with the treasures of scuttled ships and the price of slaves captured in Africa and sold to the plantations, rich as the vampire is glutted—with the blood of dead men."

"Does Sir John say that?" asked Sir Oliver, in a soft deadly voice.

"I say it."

"I heard you; but I am asking where you learnt that pretty lesson. Is Sir John your preceptor? He is, he is. No need to tell me. I'll deal with him. Meanwhile let me disclose to you the pure and disinterested source of Sir John's rancour. You shall see what an upright and honest gentleman is Sir John, who was your father's friend and has been your guardian."

"I'll not listen to what you say of him."

"Nay, but you shall, in return for having made me listen to what he says of me. Sir John desires to obtain a licence to build at the mouth of the Fal. He hopes to see a town spring up above the haven there under the shadow of his own Manor of Arwenack. He represents himself as nobly disinterested and all concerned for the prosperity of the country, and he neglects to mention that the land is his own and that it is his own prosperity and that of his family which he is concerned to foster. We met in London by a fortunate chance whilst Sir John was about this business at the Court. Now it happens that I, too, have interests in Truro and Penryn; but, unlike Sir John, I am honest in the matter, and proclaim it. If any growth should take place about Smithick it follows from its more advantageous situation that Truro and Penryn must suffer, and that suits me as little as the other matter would suit Sir John. I told him so, for I can be blunt, and I told the Queen in the form of a counter-petition to Sir John's." He shrugged. "The moment was propitious to me. I was one of the seamen who had helped to conquer the unconquerable Armada of King Philip. I was therefore not to be denied, and Sir John was sent home as empty-handed as he went to Court. D'ye marvel that he hates me? Knowing him for what he is, d'ye marvel that he dubs me pirate and worse? 'Tis natural enough so to misrepresent my doings upon the sea, since it is those doings have afforded me the power to hurt his profit. He has chosen the weapons of calumny for this combat, but those weapons are not mine, as I shall show him this very day. If you do not credit what I say, come with me and be present at the little talk I hope to have with that curmudgeon."

"You forget," said Master Godolphin, "that I, too, have interests in the neighbourhood of Smithick, and that you are hurting those."

"Soho!" crowed Sir Oliver. "Now at last the sun of truth peeps forth from all this cloud of righteous indignation at my bad Tressilian blood and pirate's ways! You, too, are but a trafficker. Now see what a fool I am to have believed you sincere, and to have stood here in talk with you as with an honest man." His voice swelled and his lip curled in a contempt that struck the other like a blow. "I swear I had not wasted breath with you had I known you for so mean and pitiful a fellow."

"These words...." began Master Godolphin, drawing himself up very stiffly.

"Are a deal less than your deserts," cut in the other, and he raised his voice to call—"Nick."

"You shall answer to them," snapped his visitor.

"I am answering now," was the stern answer. "To come here and prate to me of my dead father's dissoluteness and of an ancient quarrel between him and yours, to bleat of my trumped-up course of piracy and my own ways of life as a just cause why I may not wed your sister whilst the real consideration in your mind, the real spur to your hostility is not more than the matter of some few paltry pounds a year that I hinder you from pocketing. A God's name get you gone."

Nick entered at that moment.

"You shall hear from me again, Sir Oliver," said the other, white with anger. "You shall account to me for these words."

"I do not fight with... with hucksters," flashed Sir Oliver.

"D'ye dare call me that?"

"Indeed, 'tis to discredit an honourable class, I confess it. Nick, the door for Master Godolphin."

CHAPTER II. ROSAMUND

Anon, after his visitor had departed, Sir Oliver grew calm again. Then being able in his calm to consider his position, he became angry anew at the very thought of the rage in which he had been, a rage which had so mastered him that he had erected additional obstacles to the already considerable ones that stood between Rosamund and himself. In full blast, his anger swung round and took Sir John Killigrew for its objective. He would settle with him at once. He would so, by Heaven's light!

He bellowed for Nick and his boots.

"Where is Master Lionel? he asked when the boots had been fetched.

"He be just ridden in, Sir Oliver."

"Bid him hither."

Promptly, in answer to that summons, came Sir Oliver's half-brother—a slender lad favouring his mother the dissolute Ralph Tressilian's second wife. He was as unlike Sir Oliver in body as in soul. He was comely in a very gentle, almost womanish way; his complexion was fair and delicate, his hair golden, and his eyes of a deep blue. He had a very charming stripling grace—for he was but in his twenty-first year—and he dressed with all the care of a Court-gallant.

"Has that whelp Godolphin been to visit you?" he asked as he entered.

"Aye," growled Sir Oliver. "He came to tell me some things and to hear some others in return."

"Ha. I passed him just beyond the gates, and he was deaf to my greeting. 'Tis a most cursed insufferable pup."

"Art a judge of men, Lal." Sir Oliver stood up booted. "I am for Arwenack to exchange a compliment or two with Sir John."

His tight-pressed lips and resolute air supplemented his words so well that Lionel clutched his arm.

"You're not... you're not...?"

"I am." And affectionately, as if to soothe the lad's obvious alarm, he patted his brother's shoulder. "Sir John," he explained, "talks too much. 'Tis a fault that wants correcting. I go to teach him the virtue of silence."

"There will be trouble, Oliver."

"So there will—for him. If a man must be saying of me that I am a pirate, a slave-dealer, a murderer, and Heaven knows what else, he must be ready for the consequences. But you are late, Lal. Where have you been?"

"I rode as far as Malpas."

"As far as Malpas?" Sir Oliver's eyes narrowed, as was the trick with him. "I hear it whispered what magnet draws you thither," he said. "Be wary, boy. You go too much to Malpas."

"How?" quoth Lionel a trifle coldly.

"I mean that you are your father's son. Remember it, and strive not to follow in his ways lest they bring you to his own end. I have just been reminded of these predilections of his by good Master Peter. Go not over often to Malpas, I say. No more." But the arm which he flung about his younger brother's shoulders and the warmth of his embrace made resentment of his warning quite impossible.

When he was gone, Lionel sat him down to dine, with Nick to wait on him. He ate but little, and never addressed the old servant in the course of that brief repast. He was very pensive. In thought he followed his brother on that avenging visit of his to Arwenack. Killigrew was no babe, but man of his hands, a soldier and a seaman. If any harm should come to Oliver...He trembled at the thought; and then almost despite him his mind ran on to calculate the consequences to himself. His fortune would be in a very different case, he refected. In a sort of horror, he sought to put so detestable a reflection from his mind; but it returned insistently. It would not be denied. It forced him to a consideration of his own circumstances.

All that he had he owed to his brother's bounty. That dissolute father of theirs had died as such men commonly die, leaving behind him heavily encumbered estates and many debts; the very house of Penarrow was mortgaged, and the moneys raised on it had been drunk, or gambled, or spent on one or another of Ralph Tressilian's many lights o' love. Then Oliver had sold some little property near Helston, inherited from his mother; he had sunk the money into a venture upon the Spanish Main. He had fitted out and manned a ship, and had sailed with Hawkins upon one of those ventures, which Sir John Killigrew was perfectly entitled to account pirate raids. He had returned with enough plunder in specie and gems to disencumber the Tressilian patrimony. He had sailed again and returned still wealthier. And meanwhile, Lionel had remained at home taking his ease. He loved his ease. His nature was inherently indolent, and he had the wasteful extravagant tastes that usually go with indolence. He was not born to toil and struggle, and none had sought to correct the shortcomings of his character in that respect. Sometimes he wondered what the future might hold for him should Oliver come to marry. He feared his life might not be as easy as it was at present. But he did not seriously fear. It was not in his nature—it never is in the natures of such men—to give any excess of consideration to the future. When his thoughts did turn to it in momentary uneasiness, he would abruptly dismiss them with the reflection that when all was said Oliver loved him, and Oliver would never fail to provide adequately for all his wants.

In this undoubtedly he was fully justified. Oliver was more parent than brother to him. When their father had been brought home to die from the wound dealt him by an outraged husband—and a shocking spectacle that sinner's death had been with its hasty terrified repentance—he had entrusted Lionel to his elder brother's care. At the time Oliver was seventeen and Lionel twelve. But Oliver had seemed by so many years older than his age, that the twice-widowed Ralph Tressilian had come to depend upon this steady, resolute, and masterful child of his first marriage. It was into his ear that the dying man had poured the wretched tale of his repentance for the life he had lived and the state in which he was leaving his affairs with such scant provision for his sons. For Oliver he had no fear. It was as if with the prescience that comes to men in his pass he had perceived that Oliver was of those who must prevail, a man born to make the world his oyster. His anxieties were all for Lionel, whom he also judged with that same penetrating insight vouchsafed a man in his last hours. Hence his piteous recommendation of him to Oliver, and Oliver's ready promise to be father, mother, and brother to the youngster.

All this was in Lionel's mind as he sat musing there, and again he struggled with that hideous insistent thought that if things should go ill with his brother at Arwenack, there would be great profit to himself; that these things he now enjoyed upon another's bounty he would then enjoy in his own right. A devil seemed to mock him with the whispered sneer that were Oliver to die his own grief would not be long-lived. Then in revolt against that voice of an egoism so loathsome that in his better moments it inspired even himself with horror, he bethought him of Oliver's unvarying, unwavering affection; he pondered all the loving care and kindness that through these years past Oliver had ever showered upon him; and he cursed the rottenness of a mind that could even admit such thoughts as those which he had been entertaining. So wrought upon was he by the welter of his emotions, by that fierce strife between his conscience and his egotism, that he came abruptly to his feet, a cry upon his lips.

"Vade retro, Sathanas!"

Old Nicholas, looking up abruptly, saw the lad's face, waxen, his brow bedewed with sweat.

"Master Lionel! Master Lionel!" he cried, his small bright eyes concernedly scanning his young master's face. "What be amiss?"

Lionel mopped his brow. "Sir Oliver has gone to Arwenack upon a punitive business," said he.

"An' what be that, zur?" quoth Nicholas.

"He has gone to punish Sir John for having maligned him."

A grin spread upon the weather-beaten countenance of Nicholas.

"Be that so? Marry, 'twere time. Sir John he be over long i' th' tongue."

Lionel stood amazed at the man's easy confidence and supreme assurance of how his master must acquit himself.

"You... you have no fear, Nicholas...." He did not add of what. But the servant understood, and his grin grew broader still.

"Fear? Lackaday! I bain't afeeard for Sir Oliver, and doan't ee be afeeard. Sir Oliver'll be home to sup with a sharp-set appetite—'tis the only difference fighting ever made to he."

The servant was justified of his confidence by the events, though through a slight error of judgment Sir Oliver did not quite accomplish all that promised and intended. In anger, and when he deemed that he had been affronted, he was—as his chronicler never wearies of insisting, and as you shall judge before the end of this tale is reached of a tigerish ruthlessness. He rode to Arwenack fully resolved to kill his calumniator. Nothing less would satisfy him. Arrived at that fine embattled castle of the Killigrews which commanded the entrance to the estuary of the Fal, and from whose crenels the country might be surveyed as far as the Lizard, fifteen miles away, he found Peter Godolphin there before him; and because of Peter's presence Sir Oliver was more deliberate and formal in his accusation of Sir John than he had intended. He desired, in accusing Sir John, also to clear himself in the eyes of Rosamund's brother, to make the latter realize how entirely odious were the calumnies which Sir John had permitted himself, and how basely prompted.

Sir John, however, came halfway to meet the quarrel. His rancour against the Pirate of Penarrow—as he had come to dub Sir Oliver—endered him almost as eager to engage as was his visitor.

They found a secluded corner of the deer-park for their business, and there Sir John—a slim, sallow gentleman of some thirty years of age—made an onslaught with sword and dagger upon Sir Oliver, full worthy of the onslaught he had made earlier with his tongue. But his impetuosity availed him less than nothing. Sir Oliver was come there with a certain purpose, and it was his way that he never failed to carry through a thing to which he set his hand.

In three minutes it was all over and Sir Oliver was carefully wiping his blade, whilst Sir John lay coughing upon the turf tended by white-faced Peter Godolphin and a scared groom who had been bidden thither to make up the necessary tale of witnesses.

Sir Oliver sheathed his weapons and resumed his coat, then came to stand over his fallen foe, considering him critically.

"I think I have silenced him for a little time only," he said. "And I confess that I intended to do better. I hope, however, that the lesson will suffice and that he will lie no more—at least concerning me."

"Do you mock a fallen man?" was Master Godolphin's angry protest.

"God forbid!" said Sir Oliver soberly. "There is no mockery in my heart. There is, believe me, nothing but regret—regret that I should not have done the thing more thoroughly. I will send assistance from the house as I go. Give you good day, Master Peter."

From Arwenack he rode round by Penryn on his homeward way. But he did not go straight home. He paused at the Gates of Godolphin Court, which stood above Trefusis Point commanding the view of Carrick Roads. He turned in under the old gateway and drew up in the courtyard. Leaping to the kidney-stones that paved it, he announced himself a visitor to Mistress Rosamund.

He found her in her bower—a light, turreted chamber on the mansion's eastern side, with windows that looked out upon that lovely sheet of water and the wooded slopes beyond. She was sitting with a book in her lap in the deep of that tall window when he entered, preceded and announced by Sally Pentreath, who, now her tire-woman, had once been her nurse.

She rose with a little exclamation of gladness when he appeared under the lintel—scarce high enough to admit him without stooping—and stood regarding him across the room with brightened eyes and flushing cheeks.

What need is there to describe her? In the blaze of notoriety into which she was anon to be thrust by Sir Oliver Tressilian there was scarce a poet in England who did not sing the grace and loveliness of Rosamund Godolphin, and in all conscience enough of those fragments have survived. Like her brother she was tawny headed and she was divinely tall, though as yet her figure in its girlishness was almost too slender for her height.

"I had not looked for you so early...." she was beginning, when she observed that his countenance was oddly stern. "Why... what has happened?" she cried, her intuitions clamouring loudly of some mischance.

"Naught to alarm you, sweet; yet something that may vex you." He set an arm about that lissom waist of hers above the swelling farthingale, and gently led her back to her chair, then flung himself upon the window-seat beside her. "You hold Sir John Killigrew in some affection?" he said between statement and inquiry.

"Why, yes. He was our guardian until my brother came of full age."

Sir Oliver made a wry face. "Aye, there's the rub. Well, I've all but killed him."

She drew back into her chair, recoiling before him, and he saw horror leap to her eyes and blench her face. He made haste to explain the causes that had led to this, he told her briefly of the calumnies concerning him that Sir John had put about to vent his spite at having been thwarted in a matter of his coveted licence to build at Smithick.

"That mattered little," he concluded. "I knew these tales concerning me were abroad, and I held them in the same contempt as I hold their utterer. But he went further, Rose: he poisoned your brother's mind against me, and he stirred up in him the slumbering rancour that in my father's time was want to lie between our houses. To-day Peter came to me with the clear intent to make a quarrel. He affronted me as no man has ever dared."

She cried out at that, her already great alarm redoubled. He smiled.

"Do not suppose that I could harm him. He is your brother, and, so, sacred to me. He came to tell me that no betrothal was possible between us, forbade me ever again to visit Godolphin Court, dubbed me pirate and vampire to my face and reviled my father's memory. I tracked the evil of all this to its source in Killigrew, and rode straight to Arwenack to dam that source of falsehood for all time. I did not accomplish quite so much as I intended. You see, I am frank, my Rose. It may be that Sir John will live; if so I hope that he may profit by this lesson. I have come straight to you," he concluded, "that you may hear the tale from me before another comes to malign me with false stories of this happening."

"You... you mean Peter?" she cried.

"Alas!" he sighed.

She sat very still and white, looking straight before her and not at all at Sir Oliver. At length she spoke.

"I am not skilled in reading men," she said in a sad, small voice. "How should I be, that am but a maid who has led a cloistered life. I was told of you that you were violent and passionate, a man of bitter enmities, easily stirred to hatreds, cruel and ruthless in the persecution of them."

"You, too, have been listening to Sir John," he muttered, and laughed shortly.

"All this was I told," she pursued as if he had not spoken, "and all did I refuse to believe because my heart was given to you. Yet... yet of what have you made proof to-day?"

"Of forbearance," said he shortly.

"Forbearance?" she echoed, and her lips writhed in a smile of weary irony. "Surely you mock me!"

He set himself to explain.

"I have told you what Sir John had done. I have told you that the greater part of it—and matter all that touched my honour—I know Sir John to have done long since. Yet I suffered it in silence and contempt. Was that to show myself easily stirred to ruthlessness? What was it but forbearance? When, however, he carries his petty huckster's rancour so far as to seek to choke for me my source of happiness in life and sends your brother to affront me, I am still so forbearing that I recognize your brother to be no more than a tool and go straight to the hand that wielded him. Because I know of your affection for Sir John I gave him such latitude as no man of honour in England would have given him."

Then seeing that she still avoided his regard, still sat in that frozen attitude of horror at learning that the man she loved had imbrued his hands with the blood of another whom she also loved, his pleading quickened to a warmer note. He flung himself upon his knees beside her chair, and took in his great sinewy hands the slender fingers which she listlessly surrendered. "Rose," he cried, and his deep voice quivered with intercession, "dismiss all that you have heard from out your mind. Consider only this thing that has befallen. Suppose that Lionel my brother came to you, and that, having some measure of power and authority to support him, he swore to you that you should never wed me, swore to prevent this marriage because he deemed you such a woman as could not bear my name with honour to myself; and suppose that to all this he added insult to the memory of your dead father, what answer would you return him? Speak, Rose! Be honest with thyself and me. Deem yourself in my place, and say in honesty if you can still condemn me for what I have done. Say if it differs much from what you would wish to do in such a case as I have named."

Her eyes scanned now his upturned face, every line of which was pleading to her and calling for impartial judgment. Her face grew troubled, and then almost fierce. She set her hands upon his shoulders, and looked deep into his eyes.

"You swear to me, Noll, that all is as you have told it me—you have added naught, you have altered naught to make the tale more favourable to yourself?"

"You need such oaths from me?" he asked, and she saw sorrow spread upon his countenance.

"If I did I should not love thee, Noll. But in such an hour I need your own assurance. Will you not be generous and bear with me, strengthen me to withstand anything that may be said hereafter?"

"As God's my witness, I have told you true in all," he answered solemnly.

She sank her head to his shoulder. She was weeping softly, overwrought by this climax to all that in silence and in secret she had suffered since he had come a-wooing her.

"Then," she said, "I believe you acted rightly. I believe with you that no man of honour could have acted otherwise. I must believe you, Noll, for did I not, then I could believe in naught and hope for naught. You are as a fire that has seized upon the better part of me and consumed it all to ashes that you may hold it in your heart. I am content so you be true."

"True I shall ever be, sweetheart," he whispered fervently. "Could I be less since you are sent to make me so?"

She looked at him again, and now she was smiling wistfully through her tears.

"And you will bear with Peter?" she implored him.

"He shall have no power to anger me," he answered. "I swear that too. Do you know that but to-day he struck me?"

"Struck you? You did not tell me that!"

"My quarrel was not with him but with the rogue that sent him. I laughed at the blow. Was he not sacred to me?"

"He is good at heart, Noll," she pursued. "In time he will come to love you as you deserve, and you will come to know that he, too, deserves your love."

"He deserves it now for the love he bears to you."

"And you will think ever thus during the little while of waiting that perforce must lie before us?"

"I shall never think otherwise, sweet. Meanwhile I shall avoid him, and that no harm may come should he forbid me Godolphin Court I'll even stay away. In less than a year you will be of full age, and none may hinder you to come and go. What is a year, with such hope as mine to still impatience?"

She stroked his face. "Art very gentle with me ever, Noll," she murmured fondly. "I cannot credit you are ever harsh to any, as they say."

"Heed them not," he answered her. "I may have been something of all that, but you have purified me, Rose. What man that loved you could be aught but gentle." He kissed her, and stood up. "I had best be going now," he said. "I shall walk along the shore towards Trefusis Point to-morrow morning. If you should chance to be similarly disposed...."

She laughed, and rose in her turn. "I shall be there, dear Noll."

"'Twere best so hereafter," he assured her, smiling, and so took his leave.

She followed him to the stair-head, and watched him as he descended with eyes that took pride in the fine upright carriage of that stalwart, masterful lover.

CHAPTER III. THE FORGE

Sir Oliver's wisdom in being the first to bear Rosamund the story of that day's happenings was established anon when Master Godolphin returned home. He went straight in quest of his sister; and in a frame of mind oppressed by fear and sorrow, for Sir John, by his general sense of discomfiture at the hands of Sir Oliver and by the anger begotten of all this he was harsh in manner and disposed to hector.

"Madam," he announced abruptly, "Sir John is like to die."

The astounding answer she returned him—that is, astounding to him—did not tend to soothe his sorely ruffled spirit.

"I know," she said. "And I believe him to deserve no less. Who deals in calumny should be prepared for the wages of it."

He stared at her in a long, furious silence, then exploded into oaths, and finally inveighed against her unnaturalness and pronounced her bewitched by that foul dog Tressilian.

"It is fortunate for me," she answered him composedly, "that he was here before you to give me the truth of this affair." Then her assumed calm and the anger with which she had met his own all fell away from her. "Oh, Peter, Peter," she cried in anguish, "I hope that Sir John will recover. I am distraught by this event. But be just, I implore you. Sir Oliver has told me how hard-driven he had been."

"He shall be driven harder yet, as God's my life! If you think this deed shall go unpunished...."

She flung herself upon his breast and implored him to carry this quarrel no further. She spoke of her love for Sir Oliver and announced her firm resolve to marry him in despite of all opposition that could be made, all of which did not tend to soften her brother's humour. Yet because of the love that ever had held these two in closest bonds he went so far in the end as to say that should Sir John recover he would not himself pursue the matter further. But if Sir John should die—as was very likely—honour compelled him to seek vengeance of a deed to which he had himself so very largely contributed.

"I read that man as if he were an open book," the boy announced, with callow boastfulness. "He has the subtlety of Satan, yet he does not delude me. It was at me he struck through Killigrew. Because he desires you, Rosamund, he could not—as he bluntly told me—deal with me however I provoked him, not even though I went the length of striking him. He might have killed me for't; but he knew that to do so would place a barrier 'twixt him and you. Oh! he is calculating as all the fiends of Hell. So, to wipe out the dishonour which I did him, he shifts the blame of it upon Killigrew and goes out to kill him, which he further thinks may act as a warning to me. But if Killigrew dies...." And thus he rambled on, filling her gentle heart with anguish to see this feud increasing between the two men she loved best in all the world. If the outcome of it should be that either were to kill the other, she knew that she could never again look upon the survivor.

She took heart at last in the memory of Sir Oliver's sworn promise that her brother's life should be inviolate to him, betide what might. She trusted him; she depended upon his word and that rare strength of his which rendered possible to him a course that no weaker man would dare pursue. And in this reflection her pride in him increased, and she thanked God for a lover who in all things was a giant among men.

But Sir John Killigrew did not die. He hovered between this world and a better one for some seven days, at the end of which he began to recover. By October he was abroad again, gaunt and pale, reduced to half the bulk that had been his before, a mere shadow of a man.

One of his first visits was to Godolphin Court. He went to remonstrate with Rosamund upon her betrothal, and he did so at the request of her brother. But his remonstrances were strangely lacking in the force that she had looked for.

The odd fact is that in his near approach to death, and with his earthly interest dwindling, Sir John had looked matters frankly in the face, and had been driven to the conclusion—a conclusion impossible to him in normal health—that he had got no more than he deserved. He realized that he had acted unworthily, if unconscious at the time of the unworthiness of what he did; that the weapons with which he had fought Sir Oliver were not the weapons that become a Gentleman or in which there is credit to be won. He perceived that he had permitted his old enmity for the house of Tressilian, swollen by a sense of injury lately suffered in the matter of the licence to build at Smithick, to warp his judgment and to persuade him that Sir Oliver was all he had dubbed him. He realized that jealousy, too, had taken a hand in the matter. Sir Oliver's exploits upon the seas had brought him wealth, and with this wealth he was building up once more the Tressilian sway in those parts, which Ralph Tressilian had so outrageously diminished, so that he threatened to eclipse the importance of the Killigrews of Arwenack.

Nevertheless, in the hour of reaction he did not go so far as to admit that Sir Oliver Tressilian was a fit mate for Rosamund Godolphin. She and her brother had been placed in his care by their late father, and he had nobly discharged his tutelage until such time as Peter had come to full age. His affection for Rosamund was tender as that of a lover, but tempered by a feeling entirely paternal. He went very near to worshipping her, and when all was said, when he had cleared his mind of all dishonest bias, he still found overmuch to dislike in Oliver Tressilian, and the notion of his becoming Rosamund's husband was repellent.

First of all there was that bad Tressilian blood—notoriously bad, and never more flagrantly displayed than in the case of the late Ralph Tressilian. It was impossible that Oliver should have escaped the taint of it; nor could Sir John perceive any signs that he had done so. He displayed the traditional Tressilian turbulence. He was passionate and brutal, and the pirate's trade to which he had now set his hand was of all trades the one for which he was by nature best equipped. He was harsh and overbearing, impatient of correction and prone to trample other men's feelings underfoot. Was this, he asked himself in all honesty, a mate for Rosamund? Could he entrust her happiness to the care of such a man? Assuredly he could not.

Therefore, being whole again, he went to remonstrate with her as he accounted it his duty and as Master Peter had besought him. Yet knowing the bias that had been his he was careful to understate rather than to overstate his reasons.

"But, Sir John," she protested, "if every man is to be condemned for the sins of his forbears, but few could escape condemnation, and wherever shall you find me a husband deserving your approval?"

"His father...." began Sir John.

"Tell me not of his father, but of himself," she interrupted.

He frowned impatiently—they were sitting in that bower of hers above the river.

"I was coming to 't," he answered, a thought testily, for these interruptions which made him keep to the point robbed him of his best arguments. "However, suffice it that many of his father's vicious qualities he has inherited, as we see in his ways of life; that he has not inherited others only the future can assure us."

"In other words," she mocked him, yet very seriously, "I am to wait until he dies of old age to make quite sure that he has no such sins as must render him an unfitting husband?"

"No, no," he cried. "Good lack! what a perverseness is thine!"

"The perverseness is your own, Sir John. I am but the mirror of it."

He shifted in his chair and grunted. "Be it so, then," he snapped. "We will deal with the qualities that already he displays." And Sir John enumerated them.

"But this is no more than your judgment of him—no more than what you think him."

"'Tis what all the world thinks him."

"But I shall not marry a man for what others think of him, but for what I think of him myself. And in my view you cruelly malign him. I discover no such qualities in Sir Oliver."

"'Tis that you should be spared such a discovery that I am beseeching you not to wed him."

"Yet unless I wed him I shall never make such a discovery; and until I make it I shall ever continue to love him and to desire to wed him. Is all my life to be spent so?" She laughed outright, and came to stand beside him. She put an arm about his neck as she might have put it about the neck of her father, as she had been in the habit of doing any day in these past ten years—and thereby made him feel himself to have reached an unconscionable age. With her hand she rubbed his brow.

"Why, here are wicked wrinkles of ill-humour," she cried to him. "You are all undone, and by a woman's wit, and you do not like it."

"I am undone by a woman's wilfulness, by a woman's headstrong resolve not to see."

"You have naught to show me, Sir John."

"Naught? Is all that I have said naught?"

"Words are not things; judgments are not facts. You say that he is so, and so and so. But when I ask you upon what facts you judge him, your only answer is that you think him to be what you say he is. Your thoughts may be honest, Sir John, but your logic is contemptible." And she laughed again at his gaping discomfiture. "Come, now, deal like an honest upright judge, and tell me one act of his—one thing that he has ever done and of which you have sure knowledge—that will bear him out to be what you say he is. Now, Sir John!"

He looked up at her impatiently. Then, at last he smiled.

"Rogue!" he cried—and upon a distant day he was to bethink him of those words. "If ever he be brought to judgment I can desire him no better advocate than thou."

Thereupon following up her advantage swiftly, she kissed him. "Nor could I desire him a more honest judge than you."

What was the poor man to do thereafter? What he did. Live up to her pronouncement, and go forthwith to visit Sir Oliver and compose their quarrel.

The acknowledgment of his fault was handsomely made, and Sir Oliver received it in a spirit no less handsome. But when Sir John came to the matter of Mistress Rosamund he was, out of his sense of duty to her, less generous. He announced that since he could not bring himself to look upon Sir Oliver as a suitable husband for her, nothing that he had now said must mislead Sir Oliver into supposing him a consenting party to any such union.

"But that," he added, "is not to say that I oppose it. I disapprove, but I stand aside. Until she is of full age her brother will refuse his sanction. After that, the matter will concern neither him nor myself."

"I hope," said Sir Oliver, "he will take as wise a view. But whatever view he takes will be no matter. For the rest, Sir John, I thank you for your frankness, and I rejoice to know that if I may not count you for my friend, at least I need not reckon you among my enemies."

But if Sir John was thus won round to a neutral attitude, Master Peter's rancour abated nothing; rather it increased each day, and presently there came another matter to feed it, a matter of which Sir Oliver had no suspicion.

He knew that his brother Lionel rode almost daily to Malpas, and he knew the object of those daily rides. He knew of the lady who kept a sort of court there for the rustic bucks of Truro, Penryn, and Helston, and he knew something of the ill-repute that had attached to her in town—a repute, in fact, which had been the cause of her withdrawal into the country. He told his brother some frank and ugly truths, concerning her, by way of warning him, and therein, for the first time, the twain went very near to quarrelling.

After that he mentioned her no more. He knew that in his indolent way Lionel could be headstrong, and he knew human nature well enough to be convinced that interference here would but set up a breach between himself and his brother without in the least achieving its real object. So Oliver shrugged re-signedly, and held his peace.

There he left the affair, nor ever spoke again of Malpas and the siren who presided there. And meanwhile the autumn faded into winter, and with the coming of stormy weather Sir Oliver and Rosamund had fewer opportunities of meeting. To Godolphin Court he would not go since she did not desire it; and himself he deemed it best to remain away since otherwise he must risk a quarrel with its master, who had forbidden him the place. In those days he saw Peter Godolphin but little, and on the rare occasions when they did meet they passed each other with a very meagre salute.

Sir Oliver was entirely happy, and men noticed how gentler were his accents, how sunnier had become a countenance that they had known for haughty and forbidding. He waited for his coming happiness with the confidence of an immortal in the future. Patience was all the service Fate asked of him, and he gave that service blithely, depending upon the reward that soon now would be his own. Indeed, the year drew near its close; and ere another winter should come round Penarrow House would own a mistress. That to him seemed as inevitable as the season itself. And yet for all his supreme confidence, for all his patience and the happiness he culled from it, there were moments when he seemed oppressed by some elusive sense of overhanging doom, by some subconsciousness of an evil in the womb of Destiny. Did he challenge his oppression, did he seek to translate it into terms of reason, he found nothing upon which his wits could fasten—and he came ever to conclude that it was his very happiness by its excessiveness that was oppressing him, giving him at times that sense of premonitory weight about the heart as if to check its joyous soarings.

One day, a week from Christmas, he had occasion to ride to Helston on some trifling affair. For half a week a blizzard had whirled about the coast, and he had been kept chafing indoors what time layer upon layer of snow was spread upon the countryside. On the fourth day, the storm being spent, the sun came forth, the skies were swept clear of clouds and all the countryside lay robed in a sun-drenched, dazzling whiteness. Sir Oliver called for his horse and rode forth alone through the crisp snow. He turned homeward very early in the afternoon, but when a couple of miles from Helston he found that his horse had cast a shoe. He dismounted, and bridle over arm tramped on through the sunlit vale between the heights of Pendennis and Arwenack, singing as he went. He came thus to Smithick and the door of the forge. About it stood a group of fishermen and rustics, for, in the absence of any inn just there, this forge was ever a point of congregation. In addition to the rustics and an itinerant merchant with his pack-horses, there were present Sir Andrew Flack, the parson from Penryn, and Master Gregory Baine, one of the Justices from the neighbourhood of Truro. Both were well known to Sir Oliver, and he stood in friendly gossip with them what time he waited for his horse.

It was all very unfortunate, from the casting of that shoe to the meeting with those gentlemen; for as Sir Oliver stood there, down the gentle slope from Arwenack rode Master Peter Godolphin.

It was said afterwards by Sir Andrew and Master Baine that Master Peter appeared to have been carousing, so flushed was his face, so unnatural the brightness of his eye, so thick his speech and so extravagant and foolish what he said. There can be little doubt that it was so. He was addicted to Canary, and so indeed was Sir John Killigrew, and he had been dining with Sir John. He was of those who turn quarrelsome in wine—which is but another way of saying that when the wine was in and the restraint out, his natural humour came uppermost untrammelled. The sight of Sir Oliver standing there gave the lad precisely what he needed to indulge that evil humour of his, and he may have been quickened in his purpose by the presence of those other gentlemen. In his half-fuddled state of mind he may have recalled that once he had struck Sir Oliver and Sir Oliver had laughed and told him that none would believe it.

He drew rein suddenly as he came abreast of the group, so suddenly that he pulled his horse until it almost sat down like a cat; yet he retained his saddle. Then he came through the snow that was all squelched and mudded just about the forge, and leered at Sir Oliver.

"I am from Arwenack," he announced unnecessarily. "We have been talking of you."

"You could have had no better subject of discourse," said Sir Oliver, smiling, for all that his eyes were hard and something scared—though his fears did not concern himself.

"Marry, you are right; you make an engrossing topic—you and your debauched father."

"Sir," replied Sir Oliver, "once already have I deplored your mother's utter want of discretion."

The words were out of him in a flash under the spur of the gross insult flung at him, uttered in the momentary blind rage aroused by that inflamed and taunting face above him. No sooner were they sped than he repented them, the more bitterly because they were greeted by a guffaw from the rustics. He would have given half his fortune in that moment to have recalled them.

Master Godolphin's face had changed as utterly as if he had removed a mask. From flushed that it had been it was livid now and the eyes were blazing, the mouth twitching. Thus a moment he glowered upon his enemy. Then standing in his stirrups he swung aloft his whip.

"You dog!" he cried, in a snarling sob. "You dog!" And his lash came down and cut a long red wheal across Sir Oliver's dark face.

With cries of dismay and anger the others, the parson, the Justice and the rustics got between the pair, for Sir Oliver was looking very wicked, and all the world knew him for a man to be feared.

"Master Godolphin, I cry shame upon you," ex-claimed the parson. "If evil comes of this I shall testify to the grossness of your aggression. Get you gone from here!"

"Go to the devil, sir," said Master Godolphin thickly. "Is my mother's name to be upon the lips of that bastard? By God, man, the matter rests not here. He shall send his friends to me, or I will horse-whip him every time we meet. You hear, Sir Oliver?"

Sir Oliver made him no reply.

"You hear?" he roared. "There is no Sir John Killigrew this time upon whom you can shift the quarrel. Come you to me and get the punishment of which that whiplash is but an earnest." Then with a thick laugh he drove spurs into his horse's flanks, so furiously that he all but sent the parson and another sprawling.

"Stay but a little while for me," roared Sir Oliver after him. "You'll ride no more, my drunken fool!"

And in a rage he bellowed for his horse, flinging off the parson and Master Baine, who endeavoured to detain and calm him. He vaulted to the saddle when the nag was brought him, and whirled away in furious pursuit.

The parson looked at the Justice and the Justice shrugged, his lips tight-pressed.

"The young fool is drunk," said Sir Andrew, shaking his white head. "He's in no case to meet his Maker."

"Yet he seems very eager," quoth Master Justice Baine. "I doubt I shall hear more of the matter." He turned and looked into the forge where the bellows now stood idle, the smith himself grimy and aproned in leather in the doorway, listening to the rustics account of the happening. Master Baine it seems had a taste for analogies. "Faith," he said, "the place was excellently well chosen. They have forged here to-day a sword which it will need blood to temper."

CHAPTER IV. THE INTERVENER

The parson had notions of riding after Sir Oliver, and begged Master Baine to join him. But the Justice looked down his long nose and opined that no good purpose was to be served; that Tressilians were ever wild and bloody men; and that an angry Tressilian was a thing to be avoided. Sir Andrew, who was far from valorous, thought there might be wisdom in the Justice's words, and remembered that he had troubles enough of his own with a froward wife without taking up the burdens of others. Master Godolphin and Sir Oliver between them, quoth the justice, had got up this storm of theirs. A God's name let them settle it, and if in the settling they should cut each other's throats haply the countryside would be well rid of a brace of turbulent fellows. The pedlar deemed them a couple of madmen, whose ways were beyond the understanding of a sober citizen. The others—the fishermen and the rustics—had not the means to follow even had they had the will.

They dispersed to put abroad the news of that short furious quarrel and to prophesy that blood would be let in the adjusting of it. This prognostication the they based entirely upon their knowledge of the short Tressilian way. But it was a matter in which they were entirely wrong. It is true that Sir Oliver went galloping along that road that follows the Penryn river and that he pounded over the bridge in the town of Penryn in Master Godolphin's wake with murder in his heart. Men who saw him riding wildly thus with the red wheal across his white furious face said that he looked a very devil.

He crossed the bridge at Penryn a half-hour after sunset, as dusk was closing into night, and it may be that the sharp, frosty air had a hand in the cooling of his blood. For as he reached the river's eastern bank he slackened his breakneck pace, even as he slackened the angry galloping of his thoughts. The memory of that oath he had sworn three months ago to Rosamund smote him like a physical blow. It checked his purpose, and, reflecting this, his pace fell to an amble. He shivered to think how near he had gone to wrecking all the happiness that lay ahead of him. What was a boy's whiplash, that his resentment of it; should set all his future life in jeopardy? Even though men should call him a coward for submitting to it and leaving the insult unavenged, what should that matter? Moreover, upon the body of him who did so proclaim him he could brand the lie of a charge so foolish. Sir Oliver raised his eyes to the deep sapphire dome of heaven where an odd star was glittering frostily, and thanked God from a swelling heart that he had not overtaken Peter Godolphin whilst his madness was upon him.

A mile or so below Penryn, he turned up the road that ran down to the ferry there, and took his way home over the shoulder of the hill with a slack rein. It was not his usual way. He was wont ever to go round by Trefusis Point that he might take a glimpse at the walls of the house that harboured Rosamund and a glance at the window of her bower. But to-night he thought the shorter road over the hill would be the safer way. If he went by Godolphin Court he might chance to meet Peter again, and his past anger warned him against courting such a meeting, warned him to avoid it lest evil should betide. Indeed, so imperious was the warning, and such were his fears of himself after what had just passed, that he resolved to leave Penarrow on the next day. Whither he would go he did not then determine. He might repair to London, and he might even go upon another cruise—an idea which he had lately dismissed under Rosamund's earnest intercession. But it was imperative that he should quit the neighbourhood, and place a distance between Peter Godolphin and himself until such time as he might take Rosamund to wife. Eight months or so of exile; but what matter? Better so than that he should be driven into some deed that would compel him to spend his whole lifetime apart from her. He would write, and she would understand and approve when he told her what had passed that day.

The resolve was firmly implanted in him by the time he reached Penarrow, and he felt himself uplifted by it and by the promise it afforded him that thus his future happiness would be assured.

Himself he stabled his horse; for of the two grooms he kept, one had by his leave set out yesterday to spend Christmas in Devon with his parents, the other had taken a chill and had been ordered to bed that very day by Sir Oliver, who was considerate with those that served him. In the dining-room he found supper spread, and a great log fire blazed in the enormous cowled fire-place, diffusing a pleasant warmth through the vast room and flickering ruddily upon the trophies of weapons that adorned the walls, upon the tapestries and the portraits of dead Tressilians. Hearing his step, old Nicholas entered bearing a great candle-branch which he set upon the table.

"You'm late, Sir Oliver," said the servant, "and Master Lionel bain't home yet neither."

Sir Oliver grunted and scowled as he crunched a log and set it sizzling under his wet heel. He thought of Malpas and cursed Lionel's folly, as, without a word, he loosed his cloak and flung it on an oaken coffer by the wall where already he had cast his hat. Then he sat down, and Nicholas came forward to draw off his boots.

When that was done and the old servant stood up again, Sir Oliver shortly bade him to serve supper.

"Master Lionel cannot be long now," said he. "And give me to drink, Nick. 'Tis what I most require."

"I've brewed ee a posset o' canary sack," announced Nicholas; "there'm no better supping o' a frosty winter's night, Sir Oliver."

He departed to return presently with a black jack that was steaming fragrantly. He found his master still in the same attitude, staring at the fire, and frowning darkly. Sir Oliver's thoughts were still of his brother and Malpas, and so insistent were they that his own concerns were for the moment quite neglected; he was considering whether it was not his duty, after all, to attempt a word of remonstrance. At length he rose with a sigh and got to table. There he bethought him of his sick groom, and asked Nicholas for news of him. Nicholas reported the fellow to be much as he had been, whereupon Sir Oliver took up a cup and brimmed it with the steaming posset.

"Take him that," he said. "There's no better medicine for such an ailment."

Outside fell a clatter of hooves.

"Here be Master Lionel at last," said the servant.

"No doubt," agreed Sir Oliver. "No need to stay for him. Here is all he needs. Carry that to Tom ere it cools."

It was his object to procure the servant's absence when Lionel should arrive, resolved as he was to greet him with a sound rating for his folly. Reflection had brought him the assurance that this was become his duty in view of his projected absence from Penarrow; and in his brother's interest he was determined not to spare him.

He took a deep draught of the posset, and as he set it down he heard Lionel's step without. Then the door was flung open, and his brother stood on the threshold a moment at gaze.

Sir Oliver looked round with a scowl, the well-considered reproof already on his lips.

"So...." he began, and got no further. The sight that met his eyes drove the ready words from his lips and mind; instead it was with a sharp gasp of dismay that he came immediately to his feet. "Lionel!"

Lionel lurched in, closed the door, and shot home one of its bolts. Then he leaned against it, facing his brother again. He was deathly pale, with great dark stains under his eyes; his ungloved right hand was pressed to his side, and the fingers of it were all smeared with blood that was still oozing and dripping from between them. Over his yellow doublet on the right side there was a spreading dark stain whose nature did not intrigue Sir Oliver a moment.

"My God!" he cried, and ran to his brother. "What's happened, Lal? Who has done this?"

"Peter Godolphin," came the answer from lips that writhed in a curious smile.

Never a word said Sir Oliver, but he set his teeth and clenched his hands until the nails cut into his palms. Then he put an arm about this lad he loved above all save one in the whole world, and with anguish in his mind he supported him forward to the fire. There Lionel dropped to the chair that Sir Oliver had lately occupied.

"What is your hurt, lad? Has it gone deep?" he asked, in terror almost.

"'Tis naught—a flesh wound; but I have lost a mort of blood. I thought I should have been drained or ever I got me home."

With fearful speed Sir Oliver drew his dagger and ripped away doublet, vest, and shirt, laying bare the lad's white flesh. A moment's examination, and he breathed more freely.

"Art a very babe, Lal," he cried in his relief. "To ride without thought to stanch so simple a wound, and so lose all this blood—bad Tressilian blood though it be." He laughed in the immensity of his reaction from that momentary terror. "Stay thou there whilst I call Nick to help us dress this scratch."

"No, no!" There was note of sudden fear in the lad's voice, and his hand clutched at his brother's sleeve. "Nick must not know. None must know, or I am undone else."

Sir Oliver stared, bewildered. Lionel smiled again that curious twisted, rather frightened smile.

"I gave better than I took, Noll," said he. "Master Godolphin is as cold by now as the snow on which I left him."

His brother's sudden start and the fixed stare from out of his slowly paling face scared Lionel a little. He observed, almost subconsciously, the dull red wheal that came into prominence as the colour faded out of Sir Oliver's face, yet never thought to ask how it came there. His own affairs possessed him too completely.

"What's this?" quoth Oliver at last, hoarsely.

Lionel dropped his eyes, unable longer to meet a glance that was becoming terrible.

"He would have it," he growled almost sullenly, answering the reproach that was written in every line of his brother's taut body. "I had warned him not to cross my path. But to-night I think some madness had seized upon him. He affronted me, Noll; he said things which it was beyond human power to endure, and...." He shrugged to complete his sentence.

"Well, well," said Oliver in a small voice. "First let us tend this wound of yours."

"Do not call Nick," was the other's swift admonition. "Don't you see, Noll?" he explained in answer to the inquiry of his brother's stare, "don't you see that we fought there almost in the dark and without witnesses. It...." he swallowed, "it will be called murder, fair fight though it was; and should it be discovered that it was I...." He shivered and his glance grew wild; his lips twitched.

"I see," said Oliver, who understood at last, and he added bitterly: "You fool!"

"I had no choice," protested Lionel. "He came at me with his drawn sword. Indeed, I think he was half-drunk. I warned him of what must happen to the other did either of us fall, but he bade me not concern myself with the fear of any such consequences to himself. He was full of foul words of me and you and all whoever bore our name. He struck me with the flat of his blade and threatened to run me through as I stood unless I drew to defend myself. What choice had I? I did not mean to kill him—as God's my witness, I did not, Noll."

Without a word Oliver turned to a side-table, where stood a metal basin and ewer. He poured water, then came in the same silence to treat his brother's wound. The tale that Lionel told made blame impossible, at least from Oliver. He had but to recall the mood in which he himself had ridden after Peter Godolphin; he had but to remember, that only the consideration of Rosamund—only, indeed, the consideration of his future—had set a curb upon his own bloodthirsty humour.

When he had washed the wound he fetched some table linen from a press and ripped it into strips with his dagger; he threaded out one of these and made a preliminary crisscross of the threads across the lips of the wound—for the blade had gone right through the muscles of the breast, grazing the ribs; these threads would help the formation of a clot. Then with the infinite skill and cunning acquired in the course of his rovings he proceeded to the bandaging.

That done, he opened the window and flung out the blood-tinted water. The cloths with which he had mopped the wound and all other similar evidences of the treatment he cast upon the fire. He must remove all traces even from the eyes of Nicholas. He had the most implicit trust in the old servant's fidelity. But the matter was too grave to permit of the slightest risk. He realized fully the justice of Lionel's fears that however fair the fight might have been, a thing done thus in secret must be accounted murder by the law.

Bidding Lionel wrap himself in his cloak, Sir Oliver unbarred the door, and went upstairs in quest of a fresh shirt and doublet for his brother. On the landing he met Nicholas descending. He held him a moment in talk of the sick man above, and outwardly at least he was now entirely composed. He dispatched him upstairs again upon a trumped-up errand that must keep him absent for some little time, whilst himself he went to get the things he needed.

He returned below with them, and when he had assisted his brother into fresh garments with as little movement as possible so as not to disturb his dressing of the wound or set it bleeding afresh, he took the blood-stained doublet, vest, and shirt which he had ripped and flung them, too, into the great fire.

When some moments later Nicholas entered the vast room he found the brothers sitting composedly at table. Had he faced Lionel he would have observed little amiss with him beyond the deep pallor of his face. But he did not even do so much. Lionel sat with his back to the door and the servant's advance into the room was checked by Sir Oliver with the assurance that they did not require him. Nicholas withdrew again, and the brothers were once more alone.

Lionel ate very sparingly. He thirsted and would have emptied the measure of posset, but that Sir Oliver restrained him, and refused him anything but water lest he should contract a fever. Such a sparing meal as they made—for neither had much appetite—was made in silence. At last Sir Oliver rose, and with slow, heavy steps, suggestive of his humour, he crossed to the fire-place. He threw fresh logs on the blaze, and took from the tall mantelshelf his pipe and a leaden jar of tobacco. He filled the pipe pensively, then with the short iron tongs seized a fragment of glowing wood and applied it to the herb.

He returned to the table, and standing over his brother, he broke at last the silence that had now endured some time.

"What," he asked gruffly, "was the cause of your quarrel?"

Lionel started and shrank a little; between finger and thumb he kneaded a fragment of bread, his eyes upon it. "I scarce know," he replied.

"Lal, that is not the truth."

"How?"

"'Tis not the truth. I am not to be put off with such an answer. Yourself you said that you had warned him not to cross your path. What path was in your mind?"

Lionel leaned his elbows on the table and took his head in his hands. Weak from loss of blood, overwrought mentally as well, in a state of revulsion and reaction also from the pursuit which had been the cause of to-night's tragic affair, he had not strength to withhold the confidence his brother asked. On the contrary, it seemed to him that in making such a confidence, he would find a haven and refuge in Sir Oliver.

"'Twas that wanton at Malpas was the cause of all," he complained. And Sir Oliver's eye flashed at the words. "I deemed her quite other; I was a fool, a fool! I"—he choked, and a sob shook him—"I thought she loved me. I would have married her, I would so, by God."

Sir Oliver swore softly under his breath.

"I believed her pure and good, and...." He checked. "After all, who am I to say even now that she was not? 'Twas no fault of hers. 'Twas he, that foul dog Godolphin, who perverted her. Until he came all was well between us. And then...."

"I see," said Sir Oliver quietly. "I think you have something for which to thank him, if he revealed to you the truth of that strumpet's nature. I would have warned thee, lad. But... Perhaps I have been weak in that."

"It was not so; it was not she...."

"I say it was, and if I say so I am to be believed, Lionel. I'd smirch no woman's reputation without just cause. Be very sure of that."

Lionel stared up at him. "O God!" he cried presently, "I know not what to believe. I am a shuttle-cock flung this way and that way."

"Believe me," said Sir Oliver grimly. "And set all doubts to rest." Then he smiled. "So that was the virtuous Master Peter's secret pastime, eh? The hypocrisy of man! There is no plumbing the endless depths of it!"

He laughed outright, remembering all the things that Master Peter had said of Ralph Tressilian—delivering himself as though he were some chaste and self-denying anchorite. Then on that laugh he caught his breath quite suddenly. "Would she know?" he asked fearfully. "Would that harlot know, would she suspect that 'twas your hand did this?"

"Aye—would she," replied the other. "I told her to-night, when she flouted me and spoke of him, that I went straight to find him and pay the score between us. I was on my way to Godolphin Court when I came upon him in the park."

"Then you lied to me again, Lionel. For you said 'twas he attacked you."

"And so he did." Lionel countered instantly. "He never gave me time to speak, but flung down from his horse and came at me snarling like a cross-grained mongrel. Oh, he was as ready for the fight as I—as eager."

"But the woman at Malpas knows," said Sir Oliver gloomily. "And if she tells...."

"She'll not," cried Lionel. "She dare not for her reputation's sake."

"Indeed, I think you are right," agreed his brother with relief. "She dare not for other reasons, when I come to think of it. Her reputation is already such, and so well detested is she that were it known she had been the cause, however indirect, of this, the countryside would satisfy certain longings that it entertains concerning her. You are sure none saw you either going or returning?"

"None."

Sir Oliver strode the length of the room and back, pulling at his pipe. "All should be well, then, I think," said he at last. "You were best abed. I'll carry you thither."

He took up his stripling brother in his powerful arms and bore him upstairs as though he were a babe.

When he had seen him safely disposed for slumber, he returned below, shut the door in the hall, drew up the great oaken chair to the fire, and sat there far into the night smoking and thinking.

He had said to Lionel that all should be well. All should be well for Lionel. But what of himself with the burden of this secret on his soul? Were the victim another than Rosamund's brother the matter would have plagued him but little. The fact that Godolphin was slain, it must be confessed, was not in itself the source of his oppression. Godolphin had more than deserved his end, and he would have come by it months ago at Sir Oliver's own hand but for the fact that he was Rosamund's brother, as we know. There was the rub, the bitter, cruel rub. Her own brother had fallen by the hand of his. She loved her brother more than any living being next to himself, just as he loved Lionel above any other but herself. The pain that must be hers he knew; he experienced some of it in anticipation, participating it because it was hers and because all things that were hers he must account in some measure his own.

He rose up at last, cursing that wanton at Malpas who had come to fling this fresh and terrible difficulty where already he had to face so many. He stood leaning upon the overmantel, his foot upon one of the dogs of the fender, and considered what to do. He must bear his burden in silence, that was all. He must keep this secret even from Rosamund. It split his heart to think that he must practise this deceit with her. But naught else was possible short of relinquishing her, and that was far beyond his strength.

The resolve adopted, he took up a taper and went off to bed.

CHAPTER V. THE BUCKLER

It was old Nicholas who brought the news next morning to the brothers as they were breaking their fast.

Lionel should have kept his bed that day, but dared not, lest the fact should arouse suspicion. He had a little fever, the natural result both of his wound and of his loss of blood; he was inclined to welcome rather than deplore it, since it set a flush on cheeks that otherwise must have looked too pale.

So leaning upon his brother's arm he came down to a breakfast of herrings and small ale before the tardy sun of that December morning was well risen.

Nicholas burst in upon them with a white face and shaking limbs. He gasped out his tale of the event in a voice of terror, and both brothers affected to be shocked, dismayed and incredulous. But the worst part of that old man's news, the true cause of his terrible agitation, was yet to be announced.

"And they do zay," he cried with anger quivering through his fear, "they do zay that it were you that killed he, Sir Oliver."

"I?" quoth Sir Oliver, staring, and suddenly like a flood there burst upon his mind a hundred reasons overlooked until this moment, that inevitably must urge the countryside to this conclusion, and to this conclusion only. "Where heard you that foul lie?"

In the tumult of his mind he never heeded what answer was returned by Nicholas. What could it matter where the fellow had heard the thing; by now it would be the accusation on the lips of every man. There was one course to take and he must take it instantly—as he had taken it once before in like case. He must straight to Rosamund to forestall the tale that others would carry to her. God send he did not come too late already.

He stayed for no more than to get his boots and hat, then to the stables for a horse, and he was away over the short mile that divided Penarrow from Godolphin Court, going by bridle and track meadow straight to his goal. He met none until he fetched up in the courtyard at Godolphin Court. Thence a babble of excited voices had reached him as he approached. But at sight of him there fell a general silence, ominous and staring. A dozen men or more were assembled there, and their eyes considered him first with amazement and curiosity, then with sullen anger.

He leapt down from his saddle, and stood a moment waiting for one of the three Godolphin grooms he had perceived in that assembly to take his reins. Seeing that none stirred—

"How now?" he cried. "Does no one wait here? Hither, sirrah, and hold my horse."

The groom addressed hesitated a moment, then, under the stare of Sir Oliver's hard, commanding eye, he shuffled sullenly forward to do as he was bid. A murmur ran through the group. Sir Oliver flashed a glance upon it, and every tongue trembled into silence.

In that silence he strode up the steps, and entered the rush-strewn hall. As he vanished he heard the hubbub behind him break out anew, fiercer than it had been before. But he nothing heeded it.

He found himself face to face with a servant, who shrank before him, staring as those in the courtyard had stared. His heart sank. It was plain that he came a little late already; that the tale had got there ahead of him.

"Where is your mistress?" said he.

"I...I will tell her you are here, Sir Oliver," the man replied in a voice that faltered; and he passed through a doorway on the right. Sir Oliver stood a moment tapping his boots with his whip, his face pale, a deep line between his brows. Then the man reappeared, closing the door after him.

"Mistress Rosamund bids you depart, sir. She will not see you."

A moment Sir Oliver scanned the servant's face—or appeared to scan it, for it is doubtful if he saw the fellow at all. Then for only answer he strode forward towards the door from which the man had issued. The servant set his back to it, his face resolute.

"Sir Oliver, my mistress will not see you."

"Out of my way!" he muttered in his angry, contemptuous fashion, and as the man persistent in his duty stood his ground, Sir Oliver took him by the breast of his jacket, heaved him aside and went in.

She was standing in mid-apartment, dressed by an odd irony all in bridal white, that yet was not as white as was her face. Her eyes looked like two black stains, solemn and haunting as they fastened up on this intruder who would not be refused. Her lips parted, but she had no word for him. She just stared in a horror that routed all his audacity and checked the masterfulness of his advance. At last he spoke.

"I see that you have heard," said he, "the lie that runs the countryside. That is evil enough. But I see that you have lent an ear to it; and that is worse."

She continued to regard him with a cold look of loathing, this child that but two days ago had lain against his heart gazing up at him in trust and adoration.

"Rosamund!" he cried, and approached her by another step. "Rosamund! I am here to tell you that it is a lie."

"You had best go," she said, and her voice had in it a quality that made him tremble.

"Go?" he echoed stupidly. "You bid me go? You will not hear me?"

"I consented to hear you more than once; refused to hear others who knew better than I, and was heedless of their warnings. There is no more to be said between us. I pray God that they may take and hang you."

He was white to the lips, and for the first time in his life he knew fear and felt his great limbs trembling under him.

"They may hang me and welcome since you believe this thing. They could not hurt me more than you are doing, nor by hanging me could they deprive me of aught I value, since your faith in me is a thing to be blown upon by the first rumour of the countryside."

He saw the pale lips twist themselves into a dreadful smile. "There is more than rumour, I think," said she. "There is more than all your lies will ever serve to cloak."

"My lies?" he cried. "Rosamund, I swear to you by my honour that I have had no hand in the slaying of Peter. May God rot me where I stand if this be not true!"

"It seems," said a harsh voice behind him, "that you fear God as little as aught else."

He wheeled sharply to confront Sir John Killigrew, who had entered after him.

"So," he said slowly, and his eyes grew hard and bright as agates, "this is your work." And he waved a hand towards Rosamund. It was plain to what he alluded.

"My work?" quoth Sir John. He closed the door, and advanced into the room. "Sir, it seems your audacity, your shamelessness, transcends all bounds. Your...."

"Have done with that," Sir Oliver interrupted him and smote his great fist upon the table. He was suddenly swept by a gust of passion. "Leave words to fools, Sir John, and criticisms to those that can defend them better."

"Aye, you talk like a man of blood. You come hectoring it here in the very house of the dead—in the very house upon which you have cast this blight of sorrow and murder...."

"Have done, I say, or murder there will be!"

His voice was a roar, his mien terrific. And bold man though Sir John was, he recoiled. Instantly Sir Oliver had conquered himself again. He swung to Rosamund. "Ah, forgive me!" he pleaded. "I am mad—stark mad with anguish at the thing imputed. I have not loved your brother, it is true. But as I swore to you, so have I done. I have taken blows from him, and smiled; but yesterday in a public place he affronted me, lashed me across the face with his riding-whip, as I still bear the mark. The man who says I were not justified in having killed him for it is a liar and a hypocrite. Yet the thought of you, Rosamund, the thought that he was your brother sufficed to quench the rage in which he left me. And now that by some grim mischance he has met his death, my recompense for all my patience, for all my thought for you is that I am charged with slaying him, and that you believe this charge."

"She has no choice," rasped Killigrew.

"Sir John," he cried, "I pray you do not meddle with her choice. That you believe it, marks you for a fool, and a fool's counsel is a rotten staff to lean upon at any time. Why God o' mercy! assume that I desired to take satisfaction for the affront he had put upon me; do you know so little of men, and of me of all men, that you suppose I should go about my vengeance in this hole-and-corner fashion to set a hangman's noose about my neck. A fine vengeance that, as God lives! Was it so I dealt with you, Sir John, when you permitted your tongue to wag too freely, as you have yourself confessed? Heaven's light, man; take a proper view; consider was this matter likely. I take it you are a more fearsome antagonist than was ever poor Peter Godolphin, yet when I sought satisfaction of you I sought it boldly and openly, as is my way. When we measured swords in your park at Arwenack we did so before witnesses in proper form, that the survivor might not be troubled with the Justices. You know me well, and what manner of man I am with my weapons. Should I not have done the like by Peter if I had sought his life? Should I not have sought it in the same open fashion, and so killed him at my pleasure and leisure, and without risk or reproach from any?"

Sir John was stricken thoughtful. Here was logic hard and clear as ice; and the knight of Arwenack was no fool. But whilst he stood frowning and perplexed at the end of that long tirade, it was Rosamund who gave Sir Oliver his answer.

"You ran no risk of reproach from any, do you say?"

He turned, and was abashed. He knew the thought that was running in her mind.

"You mean," he said slowly, gently, his accents charged with reproachful incredulity, "that I am so base and false that I could in this fashion do what I dared not for your sake do openly? 'Tis what you mean. Rosamund! I burn with shame for you that you can think such thoughts of one whom... whom you professed to love."

Her coldness fell from her. Under the lash of his bitter, half-scornful accents, her anger mounted, whelming for a moment even her anguish in her brother's death.

"You false deceiver!" she cried. "There are those who heard you vow his death. Your very words have been reported to me. And from where he lay they found a trail of blood upon the snow that ran to your own door. Will you still lie?"

They saw the colour leave his face. They saw his arms drop limply to his sides, and his eyes dilate with obvious sudden fear.

"A... a trail of blood?" he faltered stupidly.

"Aye, answer that!" cut in Sir John, fetched suddenly from out his doubts by that reminder.

Sir Oliver turned upon Killigrew again. The knight's words restored to him the courage of which Rosamund's had bereft him. With a man he could fight; with a man there was no need to mince his words.

"I cannot answer it," he said, but very firmly, in a tone that brushed aside all implications. "If you say it was so, so it must have been. Yet when all is said, what does it prove? Does it set it beyond doubt that it was I who killed him? Does it justify the woman who loved me to believe me a murderer and something worse?" He paused, and looked at her again, a world of reproach in his glance.

She had sunk to a chair, and rocked there, her fingers locking and interlocking, her face a mask of pain unutterable.

"Can you suggest what else it proves, sir?" quoth Sir John, and there was doubt in his voice.

Sir Oliver caught the note of it, and a sob broke from him.

"O God of pity!" he cried out. "There is doubt in your voice, and there is none in hers. You were my enemy once, and have since been in a mistrustful truce with me, yet you can doubt that I did this thing. But she... she who loved me has no room for any doubt!"

"Sir Oliver," she answered him, "the thing you have done has broken quite my heart. Yet knowing all the taunts by which you were brought to such a deed I could have forgiven it, I think, even though I could no longer be your wife; I could have forgiven it, I say, but for the baseness of your present denial."

He looked at her, white-faced an instant, then turned on his heel and made for the door. There he paused.

"Your meaning is quite plain," said he. "It is your wish that I shall take my trial for this deed." He laughed. "Who will accuse me to the Justices? Will you, Sir John?"

"If Mistress Rosamund so desires me," replied the knight.

"Ha! Be it so. But do not think I am the man to suffer myself to be sent to the gallows upon such paltry evidence as satisfies that lady. If any accuser comes to bleat of a trail of blood reaching to my door, and of certain words I spoke yesterday in anger, I will take my trial—but it shall be trial by battle upon the body of my accuser. That is my right, and I will have every ounce of it. Do you doubt how God will pronounce? I call upon him solemnly to pronounce between me and such an one. If I am guilty of this thing may He wither my arm when I enter the lists."

"Myself I will accuse you," came Rosamund's dull voice. "And if you will, you may claim your rights against me and butcher me as you butchered him."

"God forgive you, Rosamund!" said Sir Oliver, and went out.

He returned home with hell in his heart. He knew not what the future might hold in store for him; but such was his resentment against Rosamund that there was no room in his bosom for despair. They should not hang him. He would fight them tooth and claw, and yet Lionel should not suffer. He would take care of that. And then the thought of Lionel changed his mood a little. How easily could he have shattered their accusation, how easily have brought her to her proud knees imploring pardon of him! By a word he could have done it, yet he feared lest that word must jeopardize his brother.

In the calm, still watches of that night, as he lay sleepless upon his bed and saw things without heat, there crept a change into his mental attitude. He reviewed all the evidence that had led her to her conclusions, and he was forced to confess that she was in some measure justified of them. If she had wronged him, he had wronged her yet more. For years she had listened to all the poisonous things that were said of him by his enemies—and his arrogance had made him not a few. She had disregarded all because she loved him; her relations with her brother had become strained on that account, yet now, all this returned to crush her; repentance played its part in her cruel belief that it was by his hand Peter Godolphin had fallen. It must almost seem to her that in a sense she had been a party to his murder by the headstrong course to which she had kept in loving the man her brother hated.

He saw it now, and was more merciful in judging her. She had been more than human if she had not felt as he now saw that she must feel, and since reactions are to be measured by the mental exaltations from which they spring, so was it but natural that now she must hate him fiercely whom she had loved wellnigh as fiercely.

It was a heavy cross to bear. Yet for Lionel's sake he must bear it with what fortitude he could. Lionel must not be sacrificed to his egoism for a deed that in Lionel he could not account other than justified. He were base indeed did he so much as contemplate such a way of escape as that.

But if he did not contemplate it, Lionel did, and went in terror during those days, a terror that kept him from sleep and so fostered the fever in him that on the second day after that grim affair he had the look of a ghost, hollow-eyed and gaunt. Sir Oliver remonstrated with him and in such terms as to put heart into him anew. Moreover, there was other news that day to allay his terrors: the Justices, at Truro had been informed of the event and the accusation that was made; but they had refused point-blank to take action in the matter. The reason of it was that one of them was that same Master Anthony Baine who had witnessed the affront offered Sir Oliver. He declared that whatever had happened to Master Godolphin as a consequence was no more than he deserved, no more than he had brought upon himself, and he gave it as his decision that his conscience as a man of honour would not permit him to issue any warrant to the constable.

Sir Oliver received this news from that other witness, the parson, who himself had suffered such rudeness at Godolphin's hands, and who, man of the Gospel and of peace though he was, entirely supported the Justice's decision—or so he declared.

Sir Oliver thanked him, protesting that it was kind in him and in Master Baine to take such a view, but for the rest avowing that he had had no hand in the affair, however much appearances might point to him.

When, however, it came to his knowledge two days later that the whole countryside was in a ferment against Master Baine as a consequence of the attitude he had taken up, Sir Oliver summoned the parson and straightway rode with him to the Justice's house at Truro, there to afford certain evidence which he had withheld from Rosamund and Sir John Killigrew.

"Master Baine," he said, when the three of them were closeted in that gentleman's library, "I have heard of the just and gallant pronouncement you have made, and I am come to thank you and to express my admiration of your courage."

Master Baine bowed gravely. He was a man whom Nature had made grave.

"But since I would not that any evil consequences might attend your action, I am come to lay proof before you that you have acted more rightly even than you think, and that I am not the slayer."

"You are not?" ejaculated Master Baine in amazement.

"Oh, I assure you I use no subterfuge with you, as you shall judge. I have proof to show you, as I say; and I am come to do so now before time might render it impossible. I do not desire it to be made public just yet, Master Baine; but I wish you to draw up some such document as would satisfy the courts at any future time should this matter be taken further, as well it may."

It was a shrewd plea. The proof that was not upon himself was upon Lionel; but time would efface it, and if anon publication were made of what he was now about to show, it would then be too late to look elsewhere.

"I assure you, Sir Oliver, that had you killed him after what happened I could not hold you guilty of having done more than punish a boorish and arrogant offender."

"I know sir. But it was not so. One of the pieces of evidence against me—indeed the chief item—is that from Godolphin's body to my door there was a trail of blood."

The other two grew tensely interested. The parson watched him with unblinking eyes.

"Now it follows logically, I think, inevitably indeed, that the murderer must have been wounded in the encounter. The blood could not possibly have been the victim's, therefore it must have been the slayer's. That the slayer was wounded indeed we know, since there was blood upon Godolphin's sword. Now, Master Baine, and you, Sir Andrew, shall be witnesses that there is upon my body not so much as a scratch of recent date. I will strip me here as naked as when first I had the mischance to stray into this world, and you shall satisfy yourselves of that. Thereafter I shall beg you, Master Baine, to indite the document I have mentioned." And he removed his doublet as he spoke. "But since I will not give these louts who accuse me so much satisfaction, lest I seem to go in fear of them, I must beg, sirs, that you will keep this matter entirely private until such time as its publication may be rendered necessary by events."

They saw the reasonableness of his proposal, and they consented, still entirely sceptical. But when they had made their examination they were utterly dumbfounded to find all their notions entirely overset. Master Baine, of course, drew up the required document, and signed and sealed it, whilst Sir Andrew added his own signature and seal as witness thereunto.

With this parchment that should be his buckler against any future need, Sir Oliver rode home, uplifted. For once it were safe to do so, that parchment should be spread before the eyes of Sir John Killigrew and Rosamund, and all might yet be well.

CHAPTER VI. JASPER LEIGH

If that Christmas was one of sorrow at Godolphin Court, it was nothing less at Penarrow.

Sir Oliver was moody and silent in those days, given to sit for long hours staring into the heart of the fire and repeating to himself again and again every word of his interview with Rosamund, now in a mood of bitter resentment against her for having so readily believed his guilt, now in a gentler sorrowing humour which made full allowance for the strength of the appearances against him.

His half-brother moved softly about the house now in a sort of self-effacement, never daring to intrude upon Sir Oliver's abstractions. He was well acquainted with their cause. He knew what had happened at Godolphin Court, knew that Rosamund had dismissed Sir Oliver for all time, and his heart smote him to think that he should leave his brother to bear this burden that rightly belonged to his own shoulders.

The thing preyed so much upon his mind that in an expansive moment one evening he gave it tongue.

"Noll," he said, standing beside his brother's chair in the firelit gloom, and resting a hand upon his brother's shoulder, "were it not best to tell the truth?"

Sir Oliver looked up quickly, frowning. "Art mad?" quoth he. "The truth would hang thee, Lal."

"It might not. And in any case you are suffering something worse than hanging. Oh, I have watched you every hour this past week, and I know the pain that abides in you. It is not just." And he insisted—"We had best tell the truth."

Sir Oliver smiled wistfully. He put out a hand and took his brother's.

"'Tis noble in you to propose it, Lal."

"Not half so noble as it is in you to bear all the suffering for a deed that was my own."

"Bah!" Sir Oliver shrugged impatiently; his glance fell away from Lionel's face and returned to the consideration of the fire. "After all, I can throw off the burden when I will. Such knowledge as that will enhearten a man through any trial."

He had spoken in a harsh, cynical tone, and Lionel had turned cold at his words. He stood a long while in silence there, turning them over in his mind and considering the riddle which they presented him. He thought of asking his brother bluntly for the key to it, for the precise meaning of his disconcerting statement, but courage failed him. He feared lest Sir Oliver should confirm his own dread interpretation of it.

He drew away after a time, and soon after went to bed. For days thereafter the phrase rankled in his mind—"I can throw off the burden when I will." Conviction grew upon him that Sir Oliver meant that he was enheartened by the knowledge that by speaking if he choose he could clear himself. That Sir Oliver would so speak he could not think. Indeed, he was entirely assured that Sir Oliver was very far from intending to throw off his burden. Yet he might come to change his mind. The burden might grow too heavy, his longings for Rosamund too clamorous, his grief at being in her eyes her brother's murderer too overwhelming.

Lionel's soul shuddered to contemplate the consequences to himself. His fears were self-revelatory. He realized how far from sincere had been his proposal that they should tell the truth; he perceived that it had been no more than the emotional outburst of the moment, a proposal which if accepted he must most bitterly have repented. And then came the reflection that if he were guilty of emotional outbursts that could so outrageously play the traitor to his real desires, were not all men subject to the same? Might not his brother, too, come to fall a prey to one of those moments of mental storm when in a climax of despair he would find his burden altogether too overwhelming and in rebellion cast it from him?

Lionel sought to assure himself that his brother was a man of stern fibres, a man who never lost control of himself. But against this he would argue that what had happened in the past was no guarantee of what might happen in the future; that a limit was set to the endurance of every man be he never so strong, and that it was far from impossible that the limit of Sir Oliver's endurance might be reached in this affair. If that happened in what case should he find himself? The answer to this was a picture beyond his fortitude to contemplate. The danger of his being sent to trial and made to suffer the extreme penalty of the law would be far greater now than if he had spoken at once. The tale he could then have told must have compelled some attention, for he was accounted a man of unsmirched honour and his word must carry some weight. But now none would believe him. They would argue from his silence and from his having suffered his brother to be unjustly accused that he was craven-hearted and dishonourable, and that if he had acted thus it was because he had no good defence to offer for his deed. Not only would he be irrevocably doomed, but he would be doomed with ignominy, he would be scorned by all upright men and become a thing of contempt over whose end not a tear would be shed.

Thus he came to the dread conclusion that in his endeavours to screen himself he had but enmeshed himself the more inextricably. If Oliver but spoke he was lost. And back he came to the question: What assurance had he that Oliver would not speak?

The fear of this from occurring to him occasionally began to haunt him day and night, and for all that the fever had left him and his wound was entirely healed, he remained pale and thin and hollow-eyed. Indeed the secret terror that was in his soul glared out of his eyes at every moment. He grew nervous and would start up at the least sound, and he went now in a perpetual mistrust of Oliver, which became manifest in a curious petulance of which there were outbursts at odd times.

Coming one afternoon into the dining-room, which was ever Sir Oliver's favourite haunt in the mansion of Penarrow, Lionel found his half-brother in that brooding attitude, elbow on knee and chin on palm, staring into the fire. This was so habitual now in Sir Oliver that it had begun to irritate Lionel's tense nerves; it had come to seem to him that in this listlessness was a studied tacit reproach aimed at himself.

"Why do you sit ever thus over the fire like some old crone?" he growled, voicing at last the irritability that so long had been growing in him.

Sir Oliver looked round with mild surprise in his glance. Then from Lionel his eyes travelled to the long windows.

"It rains," he said.

"It was not your wont to be driven to the fireside by rain. But rain or shine 'tis ever the same. You never go abroad."

"To what end?" quoth Sir Oliver, with the same mildness, but a wrinkle of bewilderment coming gradually between his dark brows. "Do you suppose I love to meet lowering glances, to see heads approach one another so that confidential curses of me may be muttered?"

"Ha!" cried Lionel, short and sharp, his sunken eyes blazing suddenly. "It has come to this, then, that having voluntarily done this thing to shield me you now reproach me with it."

"I?" cried Sir Oliver, aghast.

"Your very words are a reproach. D'ye think I do not read the meaning that lies under them?"

Sir Oliver rose slowly, staring at his brother. He shook his head and smiled.

"Lal, Lal!" he said. "Your wound has left you disordered, boy. With what have I reproached you? What was this hidden meaning of my words? If you will read aright you will see it to be that to go abroad is to involve myself in fresh quarrels, for my mood is become short, and I will not brook sour looks and mutterings. That is all."

He advanced and set his hands upon his brother's shoulders. Holding him so at arm's length he considered him, what time Lionel drooped his head and a slow flush overspread his cheeks. "Dear fool!" he said, and shook him. "What ails you? You are pale and gaunt, and not yourself at all. I have a notion. I'll furnish me a ship and you shall sail with me to my old hunting-grounds. There is life out yonder—life that will restore your vigour and your zest, and perhaps mine as well. How say you, now?"

Lionel looked up, his eye brightening. Then a thought occurred to him; a thought so mean that again the colour flooded into his cheeks, for he was shamed by it. Yet it clung. If he sailed with Oliver, men would say that he was a partner in the guilt attributed to his brother. He knew—from more than one remark addressed him here or there, and left by him uncontradicted—that the belief was abroad on the countryside that a certain hostility was springing up between himself and Sir Oliver on the score of that happening in Godolphin Park. His pale looks and hollow eyes had contributed to the opinion that his brother's sin was weighing heavily upon him. He had ever been known for a gentle, kindly lad, in all things the very opposite of the turbulent Sir Oliver, and it was assumed that Sir Oliver in his present increasing harshness used his brother ill because the lad would not condone his crime. A deal of sympathy was consequently arising for Lionel and was being testified to him on every hand. Were he to accede to such a proposal as Oliver now made him, assuredly he must jeopardize all that.

He realized to the full the contemptible quality of his thought and hated himself for conceiving it. But he could not shake off its dominion. It was stronger than his will.

His brother observing this hesitation, and misreading it drew him to the fireside and made him sit.

"Listen," he said, as he dropped into the chair opposite. "There is a fine ship standing in the road below, off Smithick. You'll have seen her. Her master is a desperate adventurer named Jasper Leigh, who is to be found any afternoon in the alehouse at Penycumwick. I know him of old, and he and his ship are to be acquired. He is ripe for any venture, from scuttling Spaniards to trading in slaves, and so that the price be high enough we may buy him body and soul. His is a stomach that refuses nothing, so there be money in the venture. So here is ship and master ready found; the rest I will provide—the crew, the munitions, the armament, and by the end of March we shall see the Lizard dropping astern. What do you say, Lal? 'Tis surely better than to sit, moping here in this place of gloom."

"I'll...I'll think of it," said Lionel, but so listlessly that all Sir Oliver's quickening enthusiasm perished again at once and no more was said of the venture.

But Lionel did not altogether reject the notion. If on the one hand he was repelled by it, on the other he was attracted almost despite himself. He went so far as to acquire the habit of riding daily over to Penycumwick, and there he made the acquaintance of that hardy and scarred adventurer of whom Sir Oliver had spoken, and listened to the marvels the fellow had to tell—many of them too marvellous to be true—of hazards upon distant seas.

But one day in early March Master Jasper Leigh had a tale of another kind for him, news that dispelled from Lionel's mind all interest in the captain's ventures on the Spanish Main. The seaman had followed the departing Lionel to the door of the little inn and stood by his stirrup after he had got to horse.

"A word in your ear, good Master Tressilian," said he. "D'ye know what is being concerted here against our brother?"

"Against my brother?"

"Ay—in the matter of the killing of Master Peter Godolphin last Christmas. Seeing that the Justices would not move of theirselves, some folk ha' petitioned the Lieutenant of Cornwall to command them to grant a warrant for Sir Oliver's arrest on a charge o' murder. But the Justices ha' refused to be driven by his lordship, answering that they hold their office direct from the Queen and that in such a matter they are answerable to none but her grace. And now I hear that a petition be gone to London to the Queen herself, begging her to command her Justices to perform their duty or quit their office."

Lionel drew a sharp breath, and with dilating eyes regarded the mariner, but made him no answer.

Jasper laid a long finger against his nose and his eyes grew cunning. "I thought I'd warn you, sir, so as you may bid Sir Oliver look to hisself. 'Tis a fine seaman and fine seamen be none so plentiful."

Lionel drew his purse from his pocket and without so much as looking into its contents dropped it into the seaman's ready hand, with a muttered word of thanks.

He rode home in terror almost. It was come. The blow was about to fall, and his brother would at last be forced to speak. At Penarrow a fresh shock awaited him. He learnt from old Nicholas that Sir Oliver was from home, that he had ridden over to Godolphin Court.

The instant conclusion prompted by Lionel's terror was that already the news had reached Sir Oliver and that he had instantly taken action; for he could not conceive that his brother should go to Godolphin Court upon any other business.

But his fears on that score were very idle. Sir Oliver, unable longer to endure the present state of things, had ridden over to lay before Rosamund that proof with which he had taken care to furnish himself. He could do so at last without any fear of hurting Lionel. His journey, however, had been entirely fruitless. She had refused point-blank to receive him, and for all that with a humility entirely foreign to him he had induced a servant to return to her with a most urgent message, yet he had been denied. He returned stricken to Penarrow, there to find his brother awaiting him in a passion of impatience.

"Well?" Lionel greeted him. "What will you do now?"

Sir Oliver looked at him from under brows that scowled darkly in reflection of his thoughts.

"Do now? Of what do you talk?" quoth he.

"Have you not heard?" And Lionel told him the news.

Sir Oliver stared long at him when he had done, then his lips tightened and he smote his brow.

"So!" he cried. "Would that be why she refused to see me? Did she conceive that I went perhaps to plead? Could she think that? Could she?"

He crossed to the fireplace and stirred the logs with his boot angrily. "Oh! 'Twere too unworthy. Yet of a certainty 'tis her doing, this."

"What shall you do?" insisted Lionel, unable to repress the question that was uppermost in his mind; and his voice shook.

"Do?" Sir Oliver looked at him over his shoulder. "Prick this bubble, by heaven! Make an end of it for them, confound them and cover them with shame."

He said it roughly, angrily, and Lionel recoiled, deeming that roughness and anger aimed at himself. He sank into a chair, his knees loosened by his sudden fear. So it seemed that he had had more than cause for his apprehensions. This brother of his who boasted such affection for him was not equal to bearing this matter through. And yet the thing was so unlike Oliver that a doubt still lingered with him.

"You... you will tell them the truth?" he said, in small, quavering voice.

Sir Oliver turned and considered him more attentively.

"A God's name, Lal, what's in thy mind now?" he asked, almost roughly. "Tell them the truth? Why, of course—but only as it concerns myself. You're not supposing that I shall tell them it was you? You'll not be accounting me capable of that?"

"What other way is there?"

Sir Oliver explained the matter. The explanation brought Lionel relief. But this relief was ephemeral. Further reflection presented a new fear to him. It came to him that if Sir Oliver cleared himself, of necessity his own implication must follow. His terrors very swiftly magnified a risk that in itself was so slender as to be entirely negligible. In his eyes it ceased to be a risk; it became a certain and inevitable danger. If Sir Oliver put forward this proof that the trail of blood had not proceeded from himself, it must, thought Lionel, inevitably be concluded that it was his own. As well might Sir Oliver tell them the whole truth, for surely they could not fail to infer it. Thus he reasoned in his terror, accounting himself lost irrevocably.

Had he but gone with those fears of his to his brother, or had he but been able to abate them sufficiently to allow reason to prevail, he must have been brought to understand how much further they carried him than was at all justified by probability. Oliver would have shown him this, would have told him that with the collapsing of the charge against himself no fresh charge could be levelled against any there, that no scrap of suspicion had ever attached to Lionel, or ever could. But Lionel dared not seek his brother in this matter. In his heart he was ashamed of his fears; in his heart he knew himself for a craven. He realized to the full the hideousness of his selfishness, and yet, as before, he was not strong enough to conquer it. In short, his love of himself was greater than his love of his brother, or of twenty brothers.

The morrow—a blustering day of late March found him again at that alehouse at Penycumwick in the company of Jasper Leigh. A course had occurred to him, as the only course now possible. Last night his brother had muttered something of going to Killigrew with his proofs since Rosamund refused to receive him. Through Killigrew he would reach her, he had said; and he would yet see her on her knees craving his pardon for the wrong she had done him, for the cruelty she had shown him.

Lionel knew that Killigrew was absent from home just then; but he was expected to return by Easter, and to Easter there was but a week. Therefore he had little time in which to act, little time in which to execute the project that had come into his mind. He cursed himself for conceiving it, but held to it with all the strength of a weak nature.

Yet when he came to sit face to face with Jasper Leigh in that little inn-parlour with the scrubbed table of plain deal between them, he lacked the courage to set his proposal forth. They drank sherry sack stiffly laced with brandy by Lionel's suggestion, instead of the more customary mulled ale. Yet not until he had consumed the best part of a pint of it did Lionel feel himself heartened to broaching his loathsome business. Through his head hummed the words his brother had said some time ago when first the name of Jasper Leigh had passed between them—"a desperate adventurer ripe for anything. So the price be high enough you may buy him body and soul." Money enough to buy Jasper Leigh was ready to Lionel's hand; but it was Sir Oliver's money—the money that was placed at Lionel's disposal by his half-brother's open-handed bounty. And this money he was to employ for Oliver's utter ruin! He cursed himself for a filthy, contemptible hound; he cursed the foul fiend that whispered such suggestions into his mind; he knew himself, despised himself and reviled himself until he came to swear to be strong and to go through with whatever might await him sooner than be guilty of such a baseness; the next moment that same resolve would set him shuddering again as he viewed the inevitable consequences that must attend it.

Suddenly the captain set him a question, very softly, that fired the train and blew all his lingering self-resistance into shreds.

"You'll ha' borne my warning to Sir Oliver?" he asked, lowering his voice so as not to be overheard by the vintner who was stirring beyond the thin wooden partition.

Master Lionel nodded, nervously fingering the jewel in his ear, his eyes shifting from their consideration of the seaman's coarse, weather-tanned and hairy countenance.

"I did," he said. "But Sir Oliver is headstrong. He will not stir."

"Will he not?" The captain stroked his bushy red beard and cursed profusely and horribly after the fashion of the sea. "Od's wounds! He's very like to swing if he bides him here."

"Ay," said Lionel, "if he bides." He felt his mouth turn dry as he spoke; his heart thudded, but its thuds were softened by a slight insensibility which the liquor had produced in him.

He uttered the words in so curious a tone that the sailor's dark eyes peered at him from under his heavy sandy eyebrows. There was alert inquiry in that glance. Master Lionel got up suddenly.

"Let us take a turn outside, captain," said he.

The captain's eyes narrowed. He scented business. There was something plaguily odd about this young gentleman's manner. He tossed off the remains of his sack, slapped down the pot and rose.

"Your servant, Master Tressilian," said he.

Outside our gentleman untethered his horse from the iron ring to which he had attached the bridle; leading his horse he turned seaward and strode down the road that wound along the estuary towards Smithick.

A sharp breeze from the north was whipping the water into white peaks of foam; the sky was of a hard brightness and the sun shone brilliantly. The tide was running out, and the rock in the very neck of the haven was thrusting its black crest above the water. A cable's length this side of it rode the black hull and naked spars of the Swallow—Captain Leigh's ship.

Lionel stepped along in silence, very gloomy and pensive, hesitating even now. And the crafty mariner reading this hesitation, and anxious to conquer it for the sake of such profit as he conceived might lie in the proposal which he scented, paved the way for him at last.

"I think that ye'll have some matter to propose to me." said he slyly. "Out with it, sir, for there never was a man more ready to serve you."

"The fact is," said Lionel, watching the other's face with a sidelong glance, "I am in a difficult position, Master Leigh."

"I've been in a many," laughed the captain, "but never yet in one through which I could not win. Strip forth your own, and haply I can do as much for you as I am wont to do for myself."

"Why, it is this wise," said the other. "My brother will assuredly hang as you have said if he bides him here. He is lost if they bring him to trial. And in that case, faith, I am lost too. It dishonours a man's family to have a member of it hanged. 'Tis a horrible thing to have happen."

"Indeed, indeed!" the sailor agreed encouragingly.

"I would abstract him from this," pursued Lionel, and at the same time cursed the foul fiend that prompted him such specious words to cloak his villainy. "I would abstract him from it, and yet 'tis against my conscience that he should go unpunished for I swear to you, Master Leigh, that I abhor the deed—a cowardly, murderous deed!"

"Ah!" said the captain. And lest that grim ejaculation should check his gentleman he made haste to add—"To be sure! To be sure!"

Master Lionel stopped and faced the other squarely, his shoulders to his horse. They were quite alone in as lonely a spot as any conspirator could desire. Behind him stretched the empty beach, ahead of him the ruddy cliffs that rise gently to the wooded heights of Arwenack.

"I'll be quite plain and open with you, Master Leigh. Peter Godolphin was my friend. Sir Oliver is no more than my half-brother. I would give a deal to the man who would abstract Sir Oliver secretly from the doom that hangs over him, and yet do the thing in such a way that Sir Oliver should not thereby escape the punishment he deserves."

It was strange, he thought, even as he said it, that he could bring his lips so glibly to utter words that his heart detested.

The captain looked grim. He laid a finger upon Master Lionel's velvet doublet in line with that false heart of his.

"I am your man," said he. "But the risk is great. Yet ye say that ye'ld give a deal...."

"Yourself shall name the price," said Lionel quickly, his eyes burning feverishly, his cheeks white.

"Oh I can contrive it, never fear," said the captain. "I know to a nicety what you require. How say you now: if I was to carry him overseas to the plantations where they lack toilers of just such thews as his?" He lowered his voice and spoke with some slight hesitation, fearing that he proposed perhaps more than his prospective employer might desire.

"He might return," was the answer that dispelled all doubts on that score.

"Ah!" said the skipper. "What o' the Barbary rovers, then! They lack slaves and are ever ready to trade, though they be niggardly payers. I never heard of none that returned once they had him safe aboard their galleys. I ha' done some trading with them, bartering human freights for spices and eastern carpets and the like."

Master Lionel breathed hard. "'Tis a horrible fate, is't not?"

The captain stroked his beard. "Yet 'tis the only really safe bestowal, and when all is said 'tis not so horrible as hanging, and certainly less dishonouring to a man's kin. Ye'ld be serving Sir Oliver and yourself."

"'Tis so, tis so," cried Master Lionel almost fiercely. "And the price?"

The seaman shifted on his short, sturdy legs, and his face grew pensive. "A hundred pound?" he suggested tentatively.

"Done with you for a hundred pounds," was the prompt answer—so prompt that Captain Leigh realized he had driven a fool's bargain which it was incumbent upon him to amend.

"That is, a hundred pound for myself," he corrected slowly. "Then there be the crew to reckon for—to keep their counsel and lend a hand; 'twill mean another hundred at the least."

Master Lionel considered a moment. "It is more than I can lay my hands on at short notice. But, look you, you shall have a hundred and fifty pounds in coin and the balance in jewels. You shall not be the loser in that, I promise you. And when you come again, and bring me word that all is done as you now undertake there shall be the like again."

Upon that the bargain was settled. And when Lionel came to talk of ways and means he found that he had allied himself to a man who understood his business thoroughly. All the assistance that the skipper asked was that Master Lionel should lure his gentleman to some concerted spot conveniently near the waterside. There Leigh would have a boat and his men in readiness, and the rest might very safely be left to him.

In a flash Lionel bethought him of the proper place for this. He swung round, and pointed across the water to Trefusis Point and the grey pile of Godolphin Court all bathed in sunshine now.

"Yonder, at Trefusis Point in the shadow of Godolphin Court at eight tomorrow night, when there will be no moon. I'll see that he is there. But on your life do not miss him."

"Trust me," said Master Leigh. "And the money?"

"When you have him safely aboard come to me at Penarrow," he replied, which showed that after all he did not trust Master Leigh any further than he was compelled.

The captain was quite satisfied. For should his gentleman fail to disburse he could always return Sir Oliver to shore.

On that they parted. Lionel mounted and rode away, whilst Master Leigh made a trumpet of his hands and hallooed to the ship.

As he stood waiting for the boat that came off to fetch him, a smile slowly overspread the adventurer's rugged face. Had Master Lionel seen it he might have asked himself how far it was safe to drive such bargains with a rogue who kept faith only in so far as it was profitable. And in this matter Master Leigh saw a way to break faith with profit. He had no conscience, but he loved as all rogues love to turn the tables upon a superior rogue. He would play Master Lionel most finely, most poetically false; and he found a deal to chuckle over in the contemplation of it.

CHAPTER VII. TREPANNED

Master Lionel was absent most of the following day from Penarrow, upon a pretext of making certain purchases in Truro. It would be half-past seven when he returned; and as he entered he met Sir Oliver in the hall.

"I have a message for you from Godolphin Court," he announced, and saw his brother stiffen and his face change colour. "A boy met me at the gates and bade me tell you that Mistress Rosamund desires a word with you forthwith."

Sir Oliver's heart almost stopped, then went off at a gallop. She asked for him! She had softened perhaps from her yesterday's relentlessness. She would consent at last to see him!

"Be thou blessed for these good tidings!" he answered on a note of high excitement. "I go at once." And on the instant he departed. Such was his eagerness, indeed, that under the hot spur of it he did not even stay to fetch that parchment which was to be his unanswerable advocate. The omission was momentous.

Master Lionel said no word as his brother swept out. He shrank back a little into the shadows. He was white to the lips and felt as he would stifle. As the door closed he moved suddenly. He sprang to follow Sir Oliver. Conscience cried out to him that he could not do this thing. But Fear was swift to answer that outcry. Unless he permitted what was planned to take its course, his life might pay the penalty.

He turned, and lurched into the dining-room upon legs that trembled.

He found the table set for supper as on that other night when he had staggered in with a wound in his side to be cared for and sheltered by Sir Oliver. He did not approach the table; he crossed to the fire, and sat down there holding out his hands to the blaze. He was very cold and could not still his trembling. His very teeth chattered.

Nicholas came in to know if he would sup. He answered unsteadily that despite the lateness of the hour he would await Sir Oliver's return.

"Is Sir Oliver abroad?" quoth the servant in surprise.

"He went out a moment since, I know not whither," replied Lionel. "But since he has not supped he is not like to be long absent."

Upon that he dismissed the servant, and sat huddled there, a prey to mental tortures which were not to be repressed. His mind would turn upon naught but the steadfast, unwavering affection of which Sir Oliver ever had been prodigal towards him. In this very matter of Peter Godolphin's death, what sacrifices had not Sir Oliver made to shield him? From so much love and self-sacrifice in the past he inclined to argue now that not even in extreme peril would his brother betray him. And then that bad streak of fear which made a villain of him reminded him that to argue thus was to argue upon supposition, that it would be perilous to trust such an assumption; that if, after all, Sir Oliver should fail him in the crucial test, then was he lost indeed.

When all is said, a man's final judgment of his fellows must be based upon his knowledge of himself; and Lionel, knowing himself incapable of any such sacrifice for Sir Oliver, could not believe Sir Oliver capable of persisting in such a sac-sacrifice as future events might impose. He reverted to those words Sir Oliver had uttered in that very room two nights ago, and more firmly than ever he concluded that they could have but one meaning.

Then came doubt, and, finally, assurance of another sort, assurance that this was not so and that he knew it; assurance that he lied to himself, seeking to condone the thing he did. He took his head in his hands and groaned loud. He was a villain, a black-hearted, soulless villain! He reviled himself again. There came a moment when he rose shuddering, resolved even in this eleventh hour to go after his brother and save him from the doom that awaited him out yonder in the night.

But again that resolve was withered by the breath of selfish fear. Limply he resumed his seat, and his thoughts took a fresh turn. They considered now those matters which had engaged them on that day when Sir Oliver had ridden to Arwenack to claim satisfaction of Sir John Killigrew. He realized again that Oliver being removed, what he now enjoyed by his brother's bounty he would enjoy henceforth in his own unquestioned right. The reflection brought him a certain consolation. If he must suffer for his villainy, at least there would be compensations.

The clock over the stables chimed the hour of eight. Master Lionel shrank back in his chair at the sound. The thing would be doing even now. In his mind he saw it all—saw his brother come running in his eagerness to the gates of Godolphin Court, and then dark forms resolve themselves from the surrounding darkness and fall silently upon him. He saw him struggling a moment on the ground, then, bound hand and foot, a gag thrust into his mouth, he beheld him in fancy borne swiftly down the slope to the beach and so to the waiting boat.

Another half-hour sat he there. The thing was done by now, and this assurance seemed to quiet him a little.

Then came Nicholas again to babble of some possible mischance having overtaken his master.

"What mischance should have overtaken him?" growled Lionel, as if in scorn of the idea.

"I pray none indeed," replied the servant. "But Sir Oliver lacks not for enemies nowadays, and 'tis scarce zafe for he to be abroad after dark."

Master Lionel dismissed the notion contemptuously. For pretence's sake he announced that he would wait no longer, whereupon Nicholas brought in his supper, and left him again to go and linger about the door, looking out into the night and listening for his master's return. He paid a visit to the stables, and knew that Sir Oliver had gone forth afoot.

Meanwhile Master Lionel must make pretence of eating though actual eating must have choked him. He smeared his platter, broke food, and avidly drank a bumper of claret. Then he, too, feigned a growing anxiety and went to join Nicholas. Thus they spent the weary night, watching for the return of one who Master Lionel knew would return no more.

At dawn they roused the servants and sent them to scour the countryside and put the news of Sir Oliver's disappearance abroad. Lionel himself rode out to Arwenack to ask Sir John Killigrew bluntly if he knew aught of this matter.

Sir John showed a startled face, but swore readily enough that he had not so much as seen Sir Oliver for days. He was gentle with Lionel, whom he liked, as everybody liked him. The lad was so mild and kindly in his ways, so vastly different from his arrogant overbearing brother, that his virtues shone the more brightly by that contrast.

"I confess it is natural you should come to me," said Sir John. "But, my word on it, I have no knowledge of him. It is not my way to beset my enemies in the dark."

"Indeed, indeed, Sir John, I had not supposed it in my heart," replied the afflicted Lionel. "Forgive me that I should have come to ask a question so unworthy. Set it down to my distracted state. I have not been the same man these months, I think, since that happening in Godolphin Park. The thing has preyed upon my mind. It is a fearsome burden to know your own brother—though I thank God he is no more than my half-brother—guilty of so foul a deed."

"How?" cried Killigrew, amazed. "You say that? You believed it yourself?"

Master Lionel looked confused, a look which Sir John entirely misunderstood and interpreted entirely in the young man's favour. And it was thus and in that moment that was sown the generous seed of the friendship that was to spring up between these two men, its roots fertilized by Sir John's pity that one so gentle-natured, so honest, and so upright should be cursed with so villainous a brother.

"I see, I see," he said. And he sighed. "You know that we are daily expecting an order from the Queen to her Justices to take the action which hitherto they have refused against your... against Sir Oliver." He frowned thoughtfully. "D'ye think Sir Oliver had news of this?"

At once Master Lionel saw the drift of what was in the other's mind.

"I know it," he replied. "Myself I bore it him. But why do you ask?"

"Does it not help us perhaps to understand and explain Sir Oliver's disappearance? God lack! Surely, knowing that, he were a fool to have tarried here, for he would hang beyond all doubt did he stay for the coming of her grace's messenger."

"My God!" said Lionel, staring. "You... you think he is fled, then?"

Sir John shrugged. "What else is to be thought?"

Lionel hung his head. "What else, indeed?" said he, and took his leave like a man overwrought, as indeed he was. He had never considered that so obvious a conclusion must follow upon his work so fully to explain the happening and to set at rest any doubt concerning it.

He returned to Penarrow, and bluntly told Nicholas what Sir John suspected and what he feared himself must be the true reason of Sir Oliver's disappearance. The servant, however, was none so easy to convince.

"But do ee believe that he done it?" cried Nicholas. "Do ee believe it, Master Lionel?" There was reproach amounting to horror in the servant's voice.

"God help me, what else can I believe now that he is fled."

Nicholas sidled up to him with tightened lips. He set two gnarled fingers on the young man's arm.

"He'm not fled, Master Lionel," he announced with grim impressiveness. "He'm never a turntail. Sir Oliver he don't fear neither man nor devil, and if so be him had killed Master Godolphin, he'd never ha' denied it. Don't ee believe Sir John Killigrew. Sir John ever hated he."

But in all that countryside the servant was the only one to hold this view. If a doubt had lingered anywhere of Sir Oliver's guilt, that doubt was now dispelled by this flight of his before the approach of the expected orders from the Queen.

Later that day came Captain Leigh to Penarrow inquiring for Sir Oliver.

Nicholas brought word of his presence and his inquiry to Master Lionel, who bade him be admitted.

The thick-set little seaman rolled in on his bowed legs, and leered at his employer when they were alone.

"He's snug and safe aboard," he announced. "The thing were done as clean as peeling an apple, and as quiet."

"Why did you ask for him?" quoth Master Lionel.

"Why?" Jasper leered again. "My business was with him. There was some talk between us of him going a voyage with me. I've heard the gossip over at Smithick. This will fit in with it." He laid that finger of his to his nose. "Trust me to help a sound tale along. 'T were a clumsy business to come here asking for you, sir. Ye'll know now how to account for my visit."

Lionel paid him the price agreed and dismissed him upon receiving the assurance that the Swallow would put to sea upon the next tide.

When it became known that Sir Oliver had been in treaty with Master Leigh for a passage overseas, and that it was but on that account that Master Leigh had tarried in that haven, even Nicholas began to doubt.

Gradually Lionel recovered his tranquillity as the days flowed on. What was done was done, and, in any case, being now beyond recall, there was no profit in repining. He never knew how fortune aided him, as fortune will sometimes aid a villain. The royal pour-suivants arrived some six days later, and Master Baine was the recipient of a curt summons to render himself to London, there to account for his breach of trust in having refused to perform his sworn duty. Had Sir Andrew Flack but survived the chill that had carried him off a month ago, Master Justice

Baine would have made short work of the accusation lodged against him. As it was, when he urged the positive knowledge he possessed, and told them how he had made the examination to which Sir Oliver had voluntarily submitted, his single word carried no slightest conviction. Not for a moment was it supposed that this was aught but the subterfuge of one who had been lax in his duty and who sought to save himself from the consequences of that laxity. And the fact that he cited as his fellow-witness a gentleman now deceased but served to confirm his judges in this opinion. He was deposed from his office and subjected to a heavy fine, and there the matter ended, for the hue-and-cry that was afoot entirely failed to discover any trace of the missing Sir Oliver.

For Master Lionel a new existence set in from that day. Looked upon as one in danger of suffering for his brother's sins, the countryside determined to help him as far as possible to bear his burden. Great stress was laid upon the fact that after all he was no more than Sir Oliver's half-brother; some there were who would have carried their kindness to the lengths of suggesting that perhaps he was not even that, and that it was but natural that Ralph Tressilian's second wife should have repaid her husband in kind for his outrageous infidelities. This movement of sympathy was led by Sir John Killigrew, and it spread in so rapid and marked a manner that very soon Master Lionel was almost persuaded that it was no more than he deserved, and he began to sun himself in the favour of a countryside that hitherto had shown little but hostility for men of the Tressilian blood.

CHAPTER VIII. THE SPANIARD

The Swallow, having passed through a gale in the Bay of Biscay—a gale which she weathered like the surprisingly steady old tub she was—rounded Cape Finisterre and so emerged from tempest into peace, from leaden skies and mountainous seas into a sunny azure calm. It was like a sudden transition from winter into spring, and she ran along now, close hauled to the soft easterly breeze, with a gentle list to port.

It had never been Master Leigh's intent to have got so far as this without coming to an understanding with his prisoner. But the wind had been stronger than his intentions, and he had been compelled to run before it and to head to southward until its fury should abate. Thus it fell out—and all marvellously to Master Lionel's advantage, as you shall see—that the skipper was forced to wait until they stood along the coast of Portugal—but well out to sea, for the coast of Portugal was none too healthy just then to English seamen—before commanding Sir Oliver to be haled into his presence.

In the cramped quarters of the cabin in the poop of the little vessel sat her captain at a greasy table, over which a lamp was swinging faintly to the gentle heave of the ship. He was smoking a foul pipe, whose fumes hung heavily upon the air of that little chamber, and there was a bottle of Nantes at his elbow.

To him, sitting thus in state, was Sir Oliver introduced—his wrists still pinioned behind him. He was haggard and hollow-eyed, and he carried a week's growth of beard on his chin. Also his garments were still in disorder from the struggle he had made when taken, and from the fact that he had been compelled to lie in them ever since.

Since his height was such that it was impossible for him to stand upright in that low-ceilinged cabin, a stool was thrust forward for him by one of the ruffians of Leigh's crew who had haled him from his confinement beneath the hatchway.

He sat down quite listlessly, and stared vacantly at the skipper. Master Leigh was somewhat discomposed by this odd calm when he had looked for angry outbursts. He dismissed the two seamen who fetched Sir Oliver, and when they had departed and closed the cabin door he addressed his captive.

"Sir Oliver," said he, stroking his red beard, "ye've been most foully abused."

The sunshine filtered through one of the horn windows and beat full upon Sir Oliver's expressionless face.

"It was not necessary, you knave, to bring me hither to tell me so much." he answered.

"Quite so," said Master Leigh. "But I have something more to add. Ye'll be thinking that I ha' done you a disservice. There ye wrong me. Through me you are brought to know true friends from secret enemies; henceforward ye'll know which to trust and which to mistrust."

Sir Oliver seemed to rouse himself a little from his passivity, stimulated despite himself by the impudence of this rogue. He stretched a leg and smiled sourly.

"You'll end by telling me that I am in your debt," said he.

"You'll end by saying so yourself," the captain assured him. "D'ye know what I was bidden do with you?"

"Faith, I neither know nor care," was the surprising answer, wearily delivered. "If it is for my entertainment that you propose to tell me, I beg you'll spare yourself the trouble."

It was not an answer that helped the captain. He pulled at his pipe a moment.

"I was bidden," said he presently, "to carry you to Barbary and sell you there into the service of the Moors. That I might serve you, I made believe to accept this task."

"God's death!" swore Sir Oliver. "You carry make-believe to an odd length."

"The weather has been against me. It were no intention o' mine to ha' come so far south with you. But we've been driven by the gale. That is overpast, and so that ye'll promise to bear no plaint against me, and to make good some of the loss I'll make by going out of my course, and missing a cargo that I wot of, I'll put about and fetch you home again within a week."

Sir Oliver looked at him and smiled grimly. "Now what a rogue are you that can keep faith with none!" he cried. "First you take money to carry me off; and then you bid me pay you to carry me back again."

"Ye wrong me, sir, I vow ye do! I can keep faith when honest men employ me, and ye should know it, Sir Oliver. But who keeps faith with rogues is a fool—and that I am not, as ye should also know. I ha' done this thing that a rogue might be revealed to you and thwarted, as well as that I might make some little profit out of this ship o' mine. I am frank with ye, Sir Oliver. I ha' had some two hundred pounds in money and trinkets from your brother. Give me the like and...."

But now of a sudden Sir Oliver's listlessness was all dispelled. It fell from him like a cloak, and he sat forward, wide awake and with some show of anger even.

"How do you say?" he cried, on a sharp, high note.

The captain stared at him, his pipe neglected. "I say that if so be as ye'll pay me the same sum which your brother paid me to carry you off...."

"My brother?" roared the knight. "Do you say my brother?"

"I said your brother."

"Master Lionel?" the other demanded still.

"What other brothers have you?" quoth Master Leigh.

There fell a pause and Sir Oliver looked straight before him, his head sunken a little between his shoulders. "Let me understand," he said at length. "Do you say that my brother Lionel paid you money to carry me off—in short, that my presence aboard this foul hulk of yours is due to him?"

"Whom else had ye suspected? Or did ye think that I did it for my own personal diversion?"

"Answer me," bellowed Sir Oliver, writhing in his bonds.

"I ha' answered you more than once already. Still, I tell you once again, since ye are slow to understand it, that I was paid a matter of two hundred pound by your brother, Master Lionel Tressilian, to carry you off to Barbary and there sell you for a slave. Is that plain to you?"

"As plain as it is false. You lie, you dog!"

"Softly, softly!" quoth Master Leigh, good-humouredly.

"I say you lie!"

Master Leigh considered him a moment. "Sets the wind so!" said he at length, and without another word he rose and went to a sea-chest ranged against the wooden wall of the cabin. He opened it and took thence a leather bag. From this he produced a handful of jewels. He thrust them under Sir Oliver's nose. "Haply," said he, "ye'll be acquainted with some of them. They was given me to make up the sum since your brother had not the whole two hundred pound in coin. Take a look at them."

Sir Oliver recognized a ring and a long pear-shaped pearl earring that had been his brother's; he recognized a medallion that he himself had given Lionel two years ago; and so, one by one, he recognized every trinket placed before him.

His head drooped to his breast, and he sat thus awhile like a man stunned. "My God!" he groaned miserably, at last. "Who, then, is left to me! Lionel too! Lionel!" A sob shook the great frame. Two tears slowly trickled down that haggard face and were lost in the stubble of beard upon his chin. "I am accursed!" he said.

Never without such evidence could he have believed this thing. From the moment that he was beset outside the gates of Godolphin Court he had conceived it to be the work of Rosamund, and his listlessness was begotten of the thought that she could have suffered conviction of his guilt and her hatred of him to urge her to such lengths as these. Never for an instant had he doubted the message delivered him by Lionel that it was Mistress Rosamund who summoned him. And just as he believed himself to be going to Godolphin Court in answer to her summons, so did he conclude that the happening there was the real matter to which she had bidden him, a thing done by her contriving, her answer to his attempt on the previous day to gain speech with her, her manner of ensuring that such an impertinence should never be repeated.

This conviction had been gall and wormwood to him; it had drugged his very senses, reducing him to a listless indifference to any fate that might be reserved him. Yet it had not been so bitter a draught as this present revelation. After all, in her case there were some grounds for the hatred that had come to take the place of her erstwhile love. But in Lionel's what grounds were possible? What motives could exist for such an action as this, other than a monstrous, a loathly egoism which desired perhaps to ensure that the blame for the death of Peter Godolphin should not be shifted from the shoulders that were unjustly bearing it, and the accursed desire to profit by the removal of the man who had been brother, father and all else to him? He shuddered in sheer horror. It was incredible, and yet beyond a doubt it was true. For all the love which he had showered upon Lionel, for all the sacrifices of self which he had made to shield him, this was Lionel's return. Were all the world against him he still must have believed Lionel true to him, and in that belief must have been enheartened a little. And now...His sense of loneliness, of utter destitution overwhelmed him. Then slowly of his sorrow resentment was begotten, and being begotten it grew rapidly until it filled his mind and whelmed in its turn all else. He threw back his great head, and his bloodshot, gleaming eyes fastened upon Captain Leigh, who seated now upon the sea-chest was quietly observing him and waiting patiently until he should recover the wits which this revelation had scattered.

"Master Leigh," said he, "what is your price to carry me home again to England?"

"Why, Sir Oliver," said he, "I think the price I was paid to carry you off would be a fair one. The one would wipe out t'other as it were."

"You shall have twice the sum when you land me on Trefusis Point again," was the instant answer.

The captain's little eyes blinked and his shaggy red eyebrows came together in a frown. Here was too speedy an acquiescence. There must be guile behind it, or he knew naught of the ways of men.

"What mischief are ye brooding?" he sneered.

"Mischief, man? To you?" Sir Oliver laughed hoarsely. "God's light, knave, d'ye think I consider you in this matter, or d'ye think I've room in my mind for such petty resentments together with that other?"

It was the truth. So absolute was the bitter sway of his anger against Lionel that he could give no thought to this rascally seaman's share in the adventure.

"Will ye give me your word for that?"

"My word? Pshaw, man! I have given it already. I swear that you shall be paid the sum I've named the moment you set me ashore again in England. Is that enough for you? Then cut me these bonds, and let us make an end of my present condition."

"Faith, I am glad to deal with so sensible a man! Ye take it in the proper spirit. Ye see that what I ha' done I ha' but done in the way of my calling, that I am but a tool, and that what blame there be belongs to them which hired me to this deed."

"Aye, ye're but a tool—a dirty tool, whetted with gold; no more. 'Tis admitted. Cut me these bonds, a God's name! I'm weary o' being trussed like a capon."

The captain drew his knife, crossed to Sir Oliver's side and slashed his bonds away without further word. Sir Oliver stood up so suddenly that he smote his head against the low ceiling of the cabin, and so sat down again at once. And in that moment from without and above there came a cry which sent the skipper to the cabin door. He flung it open, and so let out the smoke and let in the sunshine. He passed out on to the poop-deck, and Sir Oliver—conceiving himself at liberty to do so—followed him.

In the waist below a little knot of shaggy seamen were crowding to the larboard bulwarks, looking out to sea; on the forecastle there was another similar assembly, all staring intently ahead and towards the land. They were off Cape Roca at the time, and when Captain Leigh saw by how much they had lessened their distance from shore since last he had conned the ship, he swore ferociously at his mate who had charge of the wheel. Ahead of them away on their larboard bow and in line with the mouth of the Tagus from which she had issued—and where not a doubt but she had been lying in wait for such stray craft as this—came a great tall-masted ship, equipped with top-gallants, running wellnigh before the wind with every foot of canvas spread.

Close-hauled as was the Swallow and with her top-sails and mizzen reefed she was not making more than one knot to the Spaniard's five—for that she was a Spaniard was beyond all doubt judging by the haven whence she issued.

"Luff alee!" bawled the skipper, and he sprang to the wheel, thrusting the mate aside with a blow of his elbow that almost sent him sprawling.

"'Twas yourself set the course," the fellow protested.

"Thou lubberly fool," roared the skipper. "I bade thee keep the same distance from shore. If the land comes jutting out to meet us, are we to keep straight on until we pile her up?" He spun the wheel round in his hands, and turned her down the wind. Then he relinquished the helm to the mate again. "Hold her thus," he commanded, and bellowing orders as he went, he heaved himself down the companion to see them executed. Men sprang to the ratlines to obey him, and went swarming aloft to let out the reefs of the topsails; others ran astern to do the like by the mizzen and soon they had her leaping and plunging through the green water with every sheet unfurled, racing straight out to sea.

From the poop Sir Oliver watched the Spaniard. He saw her veer a point or so to starboard, heading straight to intercept them, and he observed that although this manceuvre brought her fully a point nearer to the wind than the Swallow, yet, equipped as she was with half as much canvas again as Captain Leigh's piratical craft, she was gaining steadily upon them none the less.

The skipper came back to the poop, and stood there moodily watching that other ship's approach, cursing himself for having sailed into such a trap, and cursing his mate more fervently still.

Sir Oliver meanwhile took stock of so much of the Swallow's armament as was visible and wondered what like were those on the main-deck below. He dropped a question on that score to the captain, dispassionately, as though he were no more than an indifferently interested spectator, and with never a thought to his position aboard.

"Should I be racing her afore the Wind if I as properly equipped?" growled Leigh. "Am I the man to run before a Spaniard? As it is I do no more than lure her well away from land."

Sir Oliver understood, and was silent thereafter. He observed a bo'sun and his mates staggering in the waist under loads of cutlasses and small arms which they stacked in a rack about the mainmast. Then the gunner, a swarthy, massive fellow, stark to the waist with a faded scarf tied turban-wise about his head, leapt up the companion to the brass carronade on the larboard quarter, followed by a couple of his men.

Master Leigh called up the bo'sun, bade him take the wheel, and dispatched the mate forward to the forecastle, where another gun was being prepared for ac tion.

Thereafter followed a spell of racing, the Spaniard ever lessening the distance between them, and the land dropping astern until it was no more than a hazy line above the shimmering sea. Suddenly from the Spaniard appeared a little cloud of white smoke, and the boom of a gun followed, and after it came a splash a cable's length ahead of the Swallow's bows.

Linstock in hand the brawny gunner on the poop stood ready to answer them when the word should be given. From below came the gunner's mate to report himself ready for action on the main-deck and to receive his orders.

Came another shot from the Spaniard, again across the bows of the Swallow.

"'Tis a clear invitation to heave to," said Sir Oliver.

The skipper snarled in his fiery beard. "She has a longer range than most Spaniards," said he. "But I'll not waste powder yet for all that. We've none to spare."

Scarcely had he spoken when a third shot boomed. There was a splintering crash overhead followed by a sough and a thud as the maintopmast came hurtling to the deck and in its fall stretched a couple of men in death. Battle was joined, it seemed. Yet Captain Leigh did nothing in a hurry.

"Hold there!" he roared to the gunner who swung his linstock at that moment in preparation.

She was losing way as a result of that curtailment of her mainmast, and the Spaniard came on swiftly now. At last the skipper accounted her near enough, and gave the word with an oath. The Swallow fired her first and last shot in that encounter. After the deafening thunder of it and through the cloud of suffocating smoke, Sir Oliver saw the high forecastle of the Spaniard rent open.

Master Leigh was cursing his gunner for having aimed too high. Then he signalled to the mate to fire the culverin of which he had charge. That second shot was to be the signal for the whole broadside from the main-deck below. But the Spaniard anticipated them. Even as the skipper of the Swallow signalled the whole side of the Spaniard burst into flame and smoke.

The Swallow staggered under the blow, recovered an instant, then listed ominously to larboard.

"Hell!" roared Leigh. "She's bilging!" and Sir Oliver saw the Spaniard standing off again, as if satisfied with what she had done. The mate's gun was never fired, nor was the broadside from below. Indeed that sudden list had set the muzzles pointing to the sea; within three minutes of it they were on a level with the water. The Swallow had received her death-blow, and she was settling down.

Satisfied that she could do no further harm, the Spaniard luffed and hove to, awaiting the obvious result and intent upon picking up what slaves she could to man the galleys of his Catholic Majesty on the Mediterranean.

Thus the fate intended Sir Oliver by Lionel was to be fulfilled; and it was to be shared by Master Leigh himself, which had not been at all in that venal fellow's reckoning.

PART II. SAKR-EL-BAHR

CHAPTER I. THE CAPTIVE

Sakr-el-Bahr, the hawk of the sea, the scourge of the Mediterranean and the terror of Christian Spain, lay prone on the heights of Cape Spartel.

Above him on the crest of the cliff ran the dark green line of the orange groves of Araish—the reputed Garden of the Hesperides of the ancients, where the golden apples grew. A mile or so to eastward were dotted the huts and tents of a Bedouin encampment on the fertile emerald pasture-land that spread away, as far as eye could range, towards Ceuta. Nearer, astride of a grey rock an almost naked goatherd, a lithe brown stripling with a cord of camel-hair about his shaven head, intermittently made melancholy and unmelodious sounds upon a reed pipe. From somewhere in the blue vault of heaven overhead came the joyous trilling of a lark, from below the silken rustling of the tideless sea.

Sakr-el-Bahr lay prone upon a cloak of woven camel-hair amid luxuriating fern and samphire, on the very edge of the shelf of cliff to which he had climbed. On either side of him squatted a negro from the Sus both naked of all save white loin-cloths, their muscular bodies glistening like ebony in the dazzling sunshine of mid-May. They wielded crude fans fashioned from the yellowing leaves of date palms, and their duty was to wave these gently to and fro above their lord's head, to give him air and to drive off the flies.

Sakr-el-Bahr was in the very prime of life, a man of a great length of body, with a deep Herculean torso and limbs that advertised a giant strength. His hawk-nosed face ending in a black forked beard was of a swarthiness accentuated to exaggeration by the snowy white turban wound about his brow. His eyes, by contrast, were singularly light. He wore over his white shirt a long green tunic of very light silk, woven along its edges with arabesques in gold; a pair of loose calico breeches reached to his knees; his brown muscular calves were naked, and his feet were shod in a pair of Moorish shoes of crimson leather, with up-curling and very pointed toes. He had no weapons other than the heavy-bladed knife with a jewelled hilt that was thrust into his girdle of plaited leather.

A yard or two away on his left lay another supine figure, elbows on the ground, and hands arched above his brow to shade his eyes, gazing out to sea. He, too, was a tall and powerful man, and when he moved there was a glint of armour from the chain mail in which his body was cased, and from the steel casque about which he had swathed his green turban. Beside him lay an enormous curved scimitar in a sheath of brown leather that was heavy with steel ornaments. His face was handsome, and bearded, but swarthier far than his companion's, and the backs of his long fine hands were almost black.

Sakr-el-Bahr paid little heed to him. Lying there he looked down the slope, clad with stunted cork-trees and evergreen oaks; here and there was the golden gleam of broom; yonder over a spur of whitish rock sprawled the green and living scarlet of a cactus. Below him about the caves of Hercules was a space of sea whose clear depths shifted with its slow movement from the deep green of emerald to all the colours of the opal. A little farther off behind a projecting screen of rock that formed a little haven two enormous masted galleys, each of fifty oars, and a smaller galliot of thirty rode gently on the slight heave of the water, the vast yellow oars standing out almost horizontally from the sides of each vessel like the pinions of some gigantic bird. That they lurked there either in concealment or in ambush was very plain. Above them circled a flock of seagulls noisy and insolent.

Sakr-el-Bahr looked out to sea across the straits towards Tarifa and the faint distant European coastline just visible through the limpid summer air. But his glance was not concerned with that hazy horizon; it went no further than a fine white-sailed ship that, close-hauled, was beating up the straits some four miles off. A gentle breeze was blowing from the east, and with every foot of canvas spread to catch it she stood as close to it as was possible. Nearer she came on her larboard tack, and not a doubt but her master would be scanning the hostile African littoral for a sight of those desperate rovers who haunted it and who took toll of every Christian ship that ventured over-near. Sakr-el-Bahr smiled to think how little the presence of his galleys could be suspected, how innocent must look the sun-bathed shore of Africa to the Christian skipper's diligently searching spy-glass. And there from his height, like the hawk they had dubbed him, poised in the cobalt heavens to plumb down upon his prey, he watched the great white ship and waited until she should come within striking distance.

A promontory to eastward made something of a lee that reached out almost a mile from shore. From the watcher's eyrie the line of demarcation was sharply drawn; they could see the point at which the white crests of the wind-whipped wavelets ceased and the water became smoother. Did she but venture as far southward on her present tack, she would be slow to go about again, and that should be their opportunity. And all unconscious of the lurking peril she held steadily to her course, until not half a mile remained between her and that inauspicious lee.

Excitement stirred the mail-clad corsair; he kicked his heels in the air, then swung round to the impassive and watchful Sakr-el-Bahr.

"She will come! She will come!" he cried in the Frankish jargon—the lingua franca of the African littoral.

"Insh' Allah!" was the laconic answer—"If God will."

A tense silence fell between them again as the ship drew nearer so that now with each forward heave of her they caught a glint of the white belly under her black hull. Sakr-el-Bahr shaded his eyes, and concentrated his vision upon the square ensign flying from, her mainmast. He could make out not only the red and yellow quarterings, but the devices of the castle and the lion.

"A Spanish ship, Biskaine," he growled to his companion. "It is very well. The praise to the One!"

"Will she venture in?" wondered the other.

"Be sure she will venture," was the confident answer. "She suspects no danger, and it is not often that our galleys are to be found so far westward. Aye, there she comes in all her Spanish pride."

Even as he spoke she reached that line of demarcation. She crossed it, for there was still a moderate breeze on the leeward side of it, intent no doubt upon making the utmost of that southward run.

"Now!" cried Biskaine—Biskaine-el-Borak was he called from the lightning-like impetuousness in which he was wont to strike. He quivered with impatience, like a leashed hound.

"Not yet," was the calm, restraining answer. "Every inch nearer shore she creeps the more certain is her doom. Time enough to sound the charge when she goes about. Give me to drink, Abiad," he said to one of his negroes, whom in irony he had dubbed "the White."

The slave turned aside, swept away a litter of ferns and produced an amphora of porous red clay; he removed the palm-leaves from the mouth of it and poured water into a cup. Sakr-el-Bahr drank slowly, his eyes never leaving the vessel, whose every ratline was clearly defined by now in the pellucid air. They could see men moving on her decks, and the watchman stationed in the foremast fighting-top. She was not more than half a mile away when suddenly came the manceuvre to go about.

Sakr-el-Bahr leapt instantly to his great height and waved a long green scarf. From one of the galleys behind the screen of rocks a trumpet rang out in immediate answer to that signal; it was followed by the shrill whistles of the bo'suns, and that again by the splash and creak of oars, as the two larger galleys swept out from their ambush. The long armoured poops were a-swarm with turbaned corsairs, their weapons gleaming in the sunshine; a dozen at least were astride of the crosstree of each mainmast, all armed with bows and arrows, and the ratlines on each side of the galleys were black with men who swarmed there like locusts ready to envelop and smother their prey.

The suddenness of the attack flung the Spaniard into confusion. There was a frantic stir aboard her, trumpet blasts and shootings and wild scurryings of men hither and thither to the posts to which they were ordered by their too reckless captain. In that confusion her manceuvre to go about went all awry, and precious moments were lost during which she stood floundering, with idly flapping sails. In his desperate haste the captain headed her straight to leeward, thinking that by running thus before the wind he stood the best chance of avoiding the trap. But there was not wind enough in that sheltered spot to make the attempt successful. The galleys sped straight on at an angle to the direction in which the Spaniard was moving, their yellow dripping oars flashing furiously, as the bo'suns plied their whips to urge every ounce of sinew in the slaves.

Of all this Sakr-el-Bahr gathered an impression as, followed by Biskaine and the negroes, he swiftly made his way down from that eyrie that had served him so well. He sprang from red oak to cork-tree and from cork-tree to red oak; he leapt from rock to rock, or lowered himself from ledge to ledge, gripping a handful of heath or a projecting stone, but all with the speed and nimbleness of an ape. He dropped at last to the beach, then sped across it at a run, and went bounding along a black reef until he stood alongside of the galliot which had been left behind by the other Corsair vessels. She awaited him in deep water, the length of her oars from the rock, and as he came alongside, these oars were brought to the horizontal, and held there firmly. He leapt down upon them, his companions following him, and using them as a gangway, reached the bulwarks. He threw a leg over the side, and alighted on a decked space between two oars and the two rows of six slaves that were manning each of them.

Biskaine followed him and the negroes came last. They were still astride of the bulwarks when Sakr-el-Bahr gave the word. Up the middle gangway ran a bo'sun and two of his mates cracking their long whips of bullock-hide. Down went the oars, there was a heave, and they shot out in the wake of the other two to join the fight.

Sakr-el-Bahr, scimitar in hand, stood on the prow, a little in advance of the mob of eager babbling corsairs who surrounded him, quivering in their impatience to be let loose upon the Christian foe. Above, along the yardarm and up the ratlines swarmed his bowmen. From the mast-head floated out his standard, of crimson charged with a green crescent.

The naked Christian slaves groaned, strained and sweated under the Moslem lash that drove them to the destruction of their Christian brethren.

Ahead the battle was already joined. The Spaniard had fired one single hasty shot which had gone wide, and now one of the corsair's grappling-irons had seized her on the larboard quarter, a withering hail of arrows was pouring down upon her decks from the Muslim crosstrees; up her sides crowded the eager Moors, ever most eager when it was a question of tackling the Spanish dogs who had driven them from their Andalusian Caliphate. Under her quarter sped the other galley to take her on the starboard side, and even as she went her archers and stingers hurled death aboard the galleon.

It was a short, sharp fight. The Spaniards in confusion from the beginning, having been taken utterly by surprise, had never been able to order themselves in a proper manner to receive the onslaught. Still, what could be done they did. They made a gallant stand against this pitiless assailant. But the corsairs charged home as gallantly, utterly reckless of life, eager to slay in the name of Allah and His Prophet and scarcely less eager to die if it should please the All-pitiful that their destinies should be here fulfilled. Up they went, and back fell the Castilians, outnumbered by at least ten to one.

CHAPTER I. THE CAPTIVE

When Sakr-el-Bahr's galliot came alongside, that brief encounter was at an end, and one of his corsairs was aloft, hacking from the mainmast the standard of Spain and the wooden crucifix that was nailed below it. A moment later and to a thundering roar of "Al-hamdolliah!" the green crescent floated out upon the breeze.

Sakr-el-Bahr thrust his way through the press in the galleon's waist; his corsairs fell back before him, making way, and as he advanced they roared his name deliriously and waved their scimitars to acclaim him this hawk of the sea, as he was named, this most valiant of all the servants of Islam. True he had taken no actual part in the engagement. It had been too brief and he had arrived too late for that. But his had been the daring to conceive an ambush at so remote a western point, and his the brain that had guided them to this swift sweet victory in the name of Allah the One.

The decks were slippery with blood, and strewn with wounded and dying men, whom already the Muslimeen were heaving overboard—dead and wounded alike when they were Christians, for to what end should they be troubled with maimed slaves?

About the mainmast were huddled the surviving Spaniards, weaponless and broken in courage, a herd of timid, bewildered sheep.

Sakr-el-Bahr stood forward, his light eyes considering them grimly. They must number close upon a hundred, adventurers in the main who had set out from Cadiz in high hope of finding fortune in the Indies. Their voyage had been a very brief one; their fate they knew—to toil at the oars of the Muslim galleys, or at best, to be taken to Algiers or Tunis and sold there into the slavery of some wealthy Moor.

Sakr-el-Bahr's glance scanned them appraisingly, and rested finally on the captain, who stood slightly in advance, his face livid with rage and grief. He was richly dressed in the Castilian black, and his velvet thimble-shaped hat was heavily plumed and decked by a gold cross.

Sakr-el-Bahr salaamed ceremoniously to him. "Fortuna de guerra, senor capitan," said he in fluent Spanish. "What is your name?"

"I am Don Paulo de Guzman," the man answered, drawing himself erect, and speaking with conscious pride in himself and manifest contempt of his interlocutor.

"So! A gentleman of family! And well-nourished and sturdy, I should judge. In the sôk at Algiers you might fetch two hundred philips. You shall ransom yourself for five hundred."

"Por las Entranas de Dios!" swore Don Paulo who, like all pious Spanish Catholics, favoured the oath anatomical. What else he would have added in his fury is not known, for Sakr-el-Bahr waved him contemptuously away.

"For your profanity and want of courtesy we will make the ransom a thousand philips, then," said he. And to his followers—"Away with him! Let him have courteous entertainment against the coming of his ransom."

He was borne away cursing.

Of the others Sakr-el-Bahr made short work. He offered the privilege of ransoming himself to any who might claim it, and the privilege was claimed by three. The rest he consigned to the care of Biskaine, who acted as his Kayla, or lieutenant. But before doing so he bade the ship's bo'sun stand forward, and demanded to know what slaves there might be on board. There were, he learnt, but a dozen, employed upon menial duties on the ship—three Jews, seven Muslimeen and two heretics—and they had been driven under the hatches when the peril threatened.

By Sakr-el-Bahr's orders these were dragged forth from the blackness into which they had been flung. The Muslimeen upon discovering that they had fallen into the hands of their own people and that their slavery was at an end, broke into cries of delight, and fervent praise of Allah than whom they swore there was no other God. The three Jews, lithe, stalwart young men in black tunics that fell to their knees and black skull-caps upon their curly black locks, smiled ingratiatingly, hoping for the best since they were fallen into the hands of people who were nearer akin to them than Christians and allied to them, at least, by the bond of common enmity to Spain and common suffering at the hands of Spaniards. The two heretics stood in stolid apathy, realizing that with them it was but a case of passing from Charybdis to Scylla, and that they had as little to hope for from heathen as from Christian. One of these was a sturdy bowlegged fellow, whose garments were little better than rags; his weather-beaten face was of the colour of mahogany and his eyes of a dark blue under tufted eyebrows that once had been red—like his hair and beard—but were now thickly intermingled with grey. He was spotted like a leopard on the hands by enormous dark brown freckles.

Of the entire dozen he was the only one that drew the attention of Sakr-el-Bahr. He stood despondently before the corsair, with bowed head and his eyes upon the deck, a weary, dejected, spiritless slave who would as soon die as live. Thus some few moments during which the stalwart Muslim stood regarding him; then as if drawn by that persistent scrutiny he raised his dull, weary eyes. At once they quickened, the dulness passed out of them; they were bright and keen as of old. He thrust his head forward, staring in his turn; then, in a bewildered way he looked about him at the ocean of swarthy faces under turbans of all colours, and back again at Sakr-el-Bahr.

"God's light!" he said at last, in English, to vent his infinite amazement. Then reverting to the cynical manner that he had ever affected, and effacing all surprise—

"Good day to you, Sir Oliver," said he. "I suppose ye'll give yourself the pleasure of hanging me."

"Allah is great!" said Sakr-el-Bahr impassively.

CHAPTER II. THE RENEGADE

How it came to happen that Sakr-el-Bahr, the Hawk of the Sea, the Muslim rover, the scourge of the Mediterranean, the terror of Christians, and the beloved of Asad-ed-Din, Basha of Algiers, would be one and the same as Sir Oliver Tressilian, the Cornish gentleman of Penarrow, is at long length set forth in the chronicles of Lord Henry Goade. His lordship conveys to us some notion of how utterly overwhelming he found that fact by the tedious minuteness with which he follows step by step this extraordinary metamorphosis. He devotes to it two entire volumes of those eighteen which he has left us. The whole, however, may with advantage be summarized into one short chapter.

Sir Oliver was one of a score of men who were rescued from the sea by the crew of the Spanish vessel that had sunk the Swallow; another was Jasper Leigh, the skipper. All of them were carried to Lisbon, and there handed over to the Court of the Holy Office. Since they were heretics all—or nearly all—it was fit and proper that the Brethren of St. Dominic should undertake their conversion in the first place. Sir Oliver came of a family that never had been famed for rigidity in religious matters, and he was certainly not going to burn alive if the adoption of other men's opinions upon an extremely hypothetical future state would suffice to save him from the stake. He accepted Catholic baptism with an almost contemptuous indifference. As for Jasper Leigh, it will be conceived that the elasticity of the skipper's conscience was no less than Sir Oliver's, and he was certainly not the man to be roasted for a trifle of faith.

No doubt there would be great rejoicings in the Holy House over the rescue of these two unfortunate souls from the certain perdition that had awaited them. It followed that as converts to the Faith they were warmly cherished, and tears of thanksgiving were profusely shed over them by the Hounds of God. So much for their heresy. They were completely purged of it, having done penance in proper form at an Auto held on the Rocio at Lisbon, candle in hand and sanbenito on their shoulders. The Church dismissed them with her blessing and an injunction to persevere in the ways of salvation to which with such meek kindness she had inducted them.

Now this dismissal amounted to a rejection. They were, as a consequence, thrown back upon the secular authorities, and the secular authorities had yet to punish them for their offence upon the seas. No offence could be proved, it is true. But the courts were satisfied that this lack of offence was but the natural result of a lack of opportunity. Conversely, they reasoned, it was not to be doubted that with the opportunity the offence would have been forthcoming. Their assurance of this was based upon the fact that when the Spaniard fired across the bows of the Swallow as an invitation to heave to, she had kept upon her course. Thus, with unanswerable Castilian logic was the evil conscience of her skipper proven. Captain Leigh protested on the other hand that his action had been dictated by his lack of faith in Spaniards and his firm belief that all Spaniards were pirates to be avoided by every honest seaman who was conscious of inferior strength of armaments. It was a plea that won him no favour with his narrow-minded judges.

Sir Oliver fervently urged that he was no member of the crew of the Swallow, that he was a gentleman who found himself aboard her very much against his will, being the victim of a villainous piece of trepanning executed by her venal captain. The court heard his plea with respect, and asked to know his name and rank. He was so very indiscreet as to answer truthfully. The result was extremely educative to Sir Oliver; it showed him how systematically conducted was the keeping of the Spanish archives. The court produced documents enabling his judges to recite to him most of that portion of his life that had been spent upon the seas, and many an awkward little circumstance which had slipped his memory long since, which he now recalled, and which certainly was not calculated to make his sentence lighter.

Had he not been in the Barbados in such a year, and had he not there captured the galleon Maria de las Dolores? What was that but an act of villainous piracy? Had he not scuttled a Spanish carack four years ago in the bay of Funchal? Had he not been with that pirate Hawkins in the affair at San Juan de Ulloa? And so on. Questions poured upon him and engulfed him.

He almost regretted that he had given himself the trouble to accept conversion and all that it entailed at the hands of the Brethren of St. Dominic. It began to appear to him that he had but wasted time and escaped the clerical fire to be dangled on a secular rope as an offering to the vengeful gods of outraged Spain.

So much, however, was not done. The galleys in the Mediterranean were in urgent need of men at the time, and to this circumstance Sir Oliver, Captain Leigh, and some others of the luckless crew of the Swallow owed their lives, though it is to be doubted whether any of them found the matter one for congratulation. Chained each man to a fellow, ankle to ankle, with but a short length of links between, they formed part of a considerable herd of unfortunates, who were driven across Portugal into Spain and then southward to Cadiz. The last that Sir Oliver saw of Captain Leigh was on the morning on which he set out from the reeking Lisbon gaol. Thereafter throughout that weary march each knew the other to be somewhere in that wretched regiment of galley-slaves; but they never came face to face again.

In Cadiz Sir Oliver spent a month in a vast enclosed space that was open to the sky, but nevertheless of an indescribable foulness, a place of filth, disease, and suffering beyond human conception, the details of which the curious may seek for himself in my Lord Henry's chronicles. They are too revolting by far to be retailed here.

At the end of that month he was one of those picked out by an officer who was manning a galley that was to convey the Infanta to Naples. He owed this to his vigorous constitution which had successfully withstood the infections of that mephitic place of torments, and to the fine thews which the officer pummelled and felt as though he were acquiring a beast of burden—which, indeed, is precisely what he was doing.

The galley to which our gentleman was dispatched was a vessel of fifty oars, each manned by seven men. They were seated upon a sort of staircase that followed the slope of the oar, running from the gangway in the vessel's middle down to the shallow bulwarks.

The place allotted to Sir Oliver was that next the gangway. Here, stark naked as when he was born, he was chained to the bench, and in those chains, let us say at once, he remained, without a single moment's intermission, for six whole months.

Between himself and the hard timbers of his seat there was naught but a flimsy and dirty sheepskin. From end to end the bench was not more than ten feet in length, whilst the distance separating it from the next one was a bare four feet. In that cramped space of ten feet by four, Sir Oliver and his six oar-mates had their miserable existence, waking and sleeping—for they slept in their chains at the oar without sufficient room in which to lie at stretch.

Anon Sir Oliver became hardened and inured to that unspeakable existence, that living death of the galley-slave. But that first long voyage to Naples was ever to remain the most terrible experience of his life. For spells of six or eight endless hours at a time, and on one occasion for no less than ten hours, did he pull at his oar without a single moment's pause. With one foot on the stretcher, the other on the bench in front of him, grasping his part of that appallingly heavy fifteen-foot oar, he would bend his back to thrust forward—and upwards so to clear the shoulders of the groaning, sweating slaves in front of him—then he would lift the end so as to bring the blade down to the water, and having gripped he would rise from his seat to throw his full weight into the pull, and so fall back with clank of chain upon the groaning bench to swing forward once more, and so on until his senses reeled, his sight became blurred, his mouth parched and his whole body a living, straining ache. Then would come the sharp fierce cut of the boatswain's whip to revive energies that flagged however little, and sometimes to leave a bleeding stripe upon his naked back.

Thus day in day out, now broiled and blistered by the pitiless southern sun, now chilled by the night dews whilst he took his cramped and unrefreshing rest, indescribably filthy and dishevelled, his hair and beard matted with endless sweat, unwashed save by the rains which in that season were all too rare, choked almost by the stench of his miserable comrades and infested by filthy crawling things begotten of decaying sheepskins and Heaven alone knows what other foulnesses of that floating hell. He was sparingly fed upon weevilled biscuit and vile messes of tallowy rice, and to drink he was given luke-warm water that was often stale, saving that sometimes when the spell of rowing was more than usually protracted the boatswains would thrust lumps of bread sodden in wine into the mouths of the toiling slaves to sustain them.

The scurvy broke out on that voyage, and there were other diseases among the rowers, to say nothing of the festering sores begotten of the friction of the bench which were common to all, and which each must endure as best he could. With the slave whose disease conquered him or who, reaching the limit of his endurance, permitted himself to swoon, the boat-swains had a short way. The diseased were flung overboard; the swooning were dragged out upon the gangway or bridge and flogged there to revive them; if they did not revive they were flogged on until they were a horrid bleeding pulp, which was then heaved into the sea.

Once or twice when they stood to windward the smell of the slaves being wafted abaft and reaching the fine gilded poop where the Infanta and her attendants travelled, the helmsmen were ordered to put about, and for long weary hours the slaves would hold the galley in position, backing her up gently against the wind so as not to lose way.

The number that died in the first week of that voyage amounted to close upon a quarter of the total. But there were reserves in the prow, and these were drawn upon to fill the empty places. None but the fittest could survive this terrible ordeal.

Of these was Sir Oliver, and of these too was his immediate neighbour at the oar, a stalwart, powerful, impassive, uncomplaining young Moor, who accepted his fate with a stoicism that aroused Sir Oliver's admiration. For days they exchanged no single word together, their religions marking them out, they thought, for enemies despite the fact that they were fellows in misfortune. But one evening when an aged Jew who had collapsed in merciful unconsciousness was dragged out and flogged in the usual manner, Sir Oliver, chancing to behold the scarlet prelate who accompanied the Infanta looking on from the poop-rail with hard unmerciful eyes, was filled with such a passion at all this inhumanity and at the cold pitilessness of that professed servant of the Gentle and Pitiful Saviour, that aloud he cursed all Christians in general and that scarlet Prince of the Church in particular.

He turned to the Moor beside him, and addressing him in Spanish—

"Hell," he said, "was surely made for Christians, which may be why they seek to make earth like it."

Fortunately for him the creak and dip of the oars, the clank of chains, and the lashes beating sharply upon the wretched Jew were sufficient to muffle his voice. But the Moor heard him, and his dark eyes gleamed.

"There is a furnace seven times heated awaiting them,) my brother," he replied, with a confidence which seemed to be the source of his present stoicism. "But art thou, then, not a Christian?"

He spoke in that queer language of the North African seaboard, that lingua franca, which sounded like some French dialect interspersed with Arabic words.

But Sir Oliver made out his meaning almost by intuition. He answered him in Spanish again, since although the Moor did not appear to speak it yet it was plain he understood it.

"I renounce from this hour," he answered in his passion. "I will acknowledge no religion in whose name such things are done. Look me at that scarlet fruit of hell up yonder. See how daintily he sniffs at his pomander lest his saintly nostrils be offended by the exhalations of our misery. Yet are we God's creatures made in God's image like himself. What does he know of God? Religion he knows as he knows good wine, rich food, and soft women. He preaches self-denial as the way to heaven, and by his own tenets is he damned." He growled an obscene oath as he heaved the great oar forward. "A Christian I?" he cried, and laughed for the first time since he had been chained to that bench of agony. "I am done with Christians and Christianity!"

"Verily we are God's, and to Him shall we return," said the Moor.

That was the beginning of a friendship between Sir Oliver and this man, whose name was Yusuf-ben-Moktar. The Muslim conceived that in Sir Oliver he saw one upon whom the grace of Allah had descended, one who was ripe to receive the Prophet's message. Yusuf was devout, and he applied himself to the conversion of his fellow-slave. Sir Oliver listened to him, however, with indifference. Having discarded one creed he would need a deal of satisfying on the score of another before he adopted it, and it seemed to him that all the glorious things urged by Yusuf in praise of Islam he had heard before in praise of Christianity. But he kept his counsel on that score, and meanwhile his intercourse with the Muslim had the effect of teaching him the lingua franca, so that at the end of six months he found himself speaking it like a Mauretanian with all the Muslim's imagery and with more than the ordinary seasoning of Arabic.

It was towards the end of that six months that the event took place which was to restore Sir Oliver to liberty. In the meanwhile those limbs of his which had ever been vigorous beyond the common wont had acquired an elephantine strength. It was ever thus at the oar. Either you died under the strain, or your thews and sinews grew to be equal to their relentless task. Sir Oliver in those six months was become a man of steel and iron, impervious to fatigue, superhuman almost in his endurance.

They were returning home from a trip to Genoa when one evening as they were standing off Minorca in the Balearic Isles they were surprised by a fleet of four Muslim galleys which came skimming round a promontory to surround and engage them.

Aboard the Spanish vessel there broke a terrible cry of "Asad-ed-Din"—the name of the most redoubtable Muslim corsair since the Italian renegade Ochiali—the Ali Pasha who had been killed at Lepanto. Trumpets blared and drums beat on the poop, and the Spaniards in morion and corselet, armed with calivers and pikes, stood to defend their lives and liberty. The gunners sprang to the culverins. But fire had to be kindled and linstocks ignited, and in the confusion much time was lost—so much that not a single cannon shot was fired before the grappling irons of the first galley clanked upon and gripped the Spaniard's bulwarks. The shock of the impact was terrific. The armoured prow of the Muslim galley—Asad-ed-Din's own—smote the Spaniard a slanting blow amidships that smashed fifteen of the oars as if they had been so many withered twigs.

There was a shriek from the slaves, followed by such piteous groans as the damned in hell may emit. Fully two score of them had been struck by the shafts of their oars as these were hurled back against them. Some had been killed outright, others lay limp and crushed, some with broken backs, others with shattered limbs and ribs.

Sir Oliver would assuredly have been of these but for the warning, advice, and example of Yusuf, who was well versed in galley-fighting and who foresaw clearly what must happen. He thrust the oar upward and forward as far as it would go, compelling the others at his bench to accompany his movement. Then he slipped down upon his knees, released his hold of the timber, and crouched down until his shoulders were on a level with the bench. He had shouted to Sir Oliver to follow his example, and Sir Oliver without even knowing what the manoeuvre should portend, but gathering its importance from the other's urgency of tone, promptly obeyed. The oar was struck an instant later and ere it snapped off it was flung back, braining one of the slaves at the bench and mortally injuring the others, but passing clean over the heads of Sir Oliver and Yusuf. A moment later the bodies of the oarsmen of the bench immediately in front were flung back atop of them with yells and curses.

When Sir Oliver staggered to his feet he found the battle joined. The Spaniards had fired a volley from their calivers and a dense cloud of smoke hung above the bulwarks; through this surged now the corsairs, led by a tall, lean, elderly man with a flowing white beard and a swarthy eagle face. A crescent of emeralds flashed from his snowy turban; above it rose the peak of a steel cap, and his body was cased in chain mail. He swung a great scimitar, before which Spaniards went down like wheat to the reaper's sickle. He fought like ten men, and to support him poured a never-ending stream of Muslimeen to the cry of "Din! Din! Allah, Y'Allah!" Back and yet back went the Spaniards before that irresistible onslaught.

Sir Oliver found Yusuf struggling in vain to rid himself of his chain, and went to his assistance. He stooped, seized it in both hands, set his feet against the bench, exerted all his strength, and tore the staple from the wood. Yusuf was free, save, of course, that a length of heavy chain was dangling from his steel anklet. In his turn he did the like service by Sir Oliver, though not quite as speedily, for strong man though he was, either his strength was not equal to the Cornishman's or else the latter's staple had been driven into sounder timber. In the end, however, it yielded, and Sir Oliver too was free. Then he set the foot that was hampered by the chain upon the bench, and with the staple that still hung from the end of it he prised open the link that attached it to his anklet.

That done he took his revenge. Crying "Din!" as loudly as any of the Muslimeen boarders, he flung himself upon the rear of the Spaniards brandishing his chain. In his hands it became a terrific weapon. He used it as a scourge, lashing it to right and left of him, splitting here a head and crushing there a face, until he had hacked a way clean through the Spanish press, which bewildered by this sudden rear attack made but little attempt to retaliate upon the escaped galley-slave. After him, whirling the remaining ten feet of the broken oar, came Yusuf.

Sir Oliver confessed afterwards to knowing very little of what happened in those moments. He came to a full possession of his senses to find the fight at an end, a cloud of turbaned corsairs standing guard over a huddle of Spaniards, others breaking open the cabin and dragging thence the chests that it contained, others again armed with chisels and mallets passing along the benches liberating the surviving slaves, of whom the great majority were children of Islam.

Sir Oliver found himself face to face with the white-bearded leader of the corsairs, who was leaning upon his scimitar and regarding him with eyes at once amused and amazed. Our gentleman's naked body was splashed from head to foot with blood, and in his right hand he still clutched that yard of iron links with which he had wrought such ghastly execution. Yusuf was standing at the corsair leader's elbow speaking rapidly.

"By Allah, was ever such a lusty fighter seen!" cried the latter. "The strength of the Prophet is within him thus to smite the unbelieving pigs."

Sir Oliver grinned savagely.

"I was returning them some of their whip-lashes—with interest," said he.

And those were the circumstances under which he came to meet the formidable Asad-ed-Din, Basha of Algiers, those the first words that passed between them.

Anon, when aboard Asad's own galley he was being carried to Barbary, he was washed and his head was shaved all but the forelock, by which the Prophet should lift him up to heaven when his earthly destiny should come to be fulfilled. He made no protest. They washed and fed him and gave him ease; and so that they did these things to him they might do what else they pleased. At last arrayed in flowing garments that were strange to him, and with a turban wound about his head, he was conducted to the poop, where Asad sat with Yusuf under an awning, and he came to understand that it was in compliance with the orders of Yusuf that he had been treated as if he were a True-Believer.

Yusuf-ben-Moktar was discovered as a person of great consequence, the nephew of Asad-ed-Din, and a favourite with that Exalted of Allah the Sublime Portal himself, a man whose capture by Christians had been a thing profoundly deplored. Accordingly his delivery from that thraldom was matter for rejoicing. Being delivered, he bethought him of his oar-mate, concerning whom indeed Asad-ed-Din manifested the greatest curiosity, for in all this world there was nothing the old corsair loved so much as a fighter, and in all his days, he vowed, never had he seen the equal of that stalwart galley-slave, never the like of his performance with that murderous chain. Yusuf had informed him that the man was a fruit ripe for the Prophet's plucking, that the grace of Allah was upon him, and in spirit already he must be accounted a good Muslim.

When Sir Oliver, washed, perfumed, and arrayed in white caftan and turban, which gave him the air of being even taller than he was, came into the presence of Asad-ed-Din, it was conveyed to him that if he would enter the ranks of the Faithful of the Prophet's House and devote the strength and courage with which Allah the One had endowed him to the upholding of the true Faith and to the chastening of the enemies of Islam, great honour, wealth and dignity were in store for him.

Of all that proposal, made at prodigious length and with great wealth of Eastern circumlocution, the only phrase that took root in his rather bewildered mind was that which concerned the chastening of the enemies of Islam. The enemies of Islam he conceived, were his own enemies; and he further conceived that they stood in great need of chastening, and that to take a hand in that chastening would be a singularly grateful task. So he considered the proposals made him. He considered, too, that the alternative—in the event of his refusing to make the protestations of Faith required of him—was that he must return to the oar of a galley, of a Muslim galley now. Now that was an occupation of which he had had more than his fill, and since he had been washed and restored to the normal sensations of a clean human being he found that whatever might be within the scope of his courage he could not envisage returning to the oar. We have seen the ease with which he had abandoned the religion in which he was reared for the Roman faith, and how utterly deluded he had found himself. With the same degree of ease did he now go over to Islam and with much greater profit. Moreover, he embraced the Religion of Mahomet with a measure of fierce conviction that had been entirely lacking from his earlier apostasy.

He had arrived at the conclusion whilst aboard the galley of Spain, as we have seen, that Christianity as practised in his day was a grim mockery of which the world were better rid. It is not to be supposed that his convictions that Christianity was at fault went the length of making him suppose that Islam was right, or that his conversion to the Faith of Mahomet was anything more than superficial. But forced as he was to choose between the rower's bench and the poop-deck, the oar and the scimitar, he boldly and resolutely made the only choice that in his case could lead to liberty and life.

Thus he was received into the ranks of the Faithful whose pavilions wait them in Paradise, set in an orchard of never-failing fruit, among rivers of milk, of wine, and of clarified honey. He became the Kayia or lieutenant to Yusuf on the galley of that corsair's command and seconded him in half a score of engagements with an ability and a conspicuity that made him swiftly famous throughout the ranks of the Mediterranean rovers. Some six months later in a fight off the coast of Sicily with one of the galleys of the Religion—as the vessels of the Knights of Malta were called—Yusuf was mortally wounded in the very moment of the victory. He died an hour later in the arms of Sir Oliver, naming the latter his successor in the command of the galley, and enjoining upon all implicit obedience to him until they should be returned to Algiers and the Basha should make known his further will in the matter.

CHAPTER II. THE RENEGADE

The Basha's will was to confirm his nephew's dying appointment of a successor, and Sir Oliver found himself in full command of a galley. From that hour he became Oliver-Reis, but very soon his valour and fury earned him the by-name of Sakr-el-Bahr, the Hawk of the Sea. His fame grew rapidly, and it spread across the tideless sea to the very shores of Christendom. Soon he became Asad's lieutenant, the second in command of all the Algerine galleys, which meant in fact that he was the commander-in-chief, for Asad was growing old and took the sea more and more rarely now. Sakr-el-Bahr sallied forth in his name and his stead, and such was his courage, his address, and his good fortune that never did he go forth to return empty-handed.

It was clear to all that the favour of Allah was upon him, that he had been singled out by Allah to be the very glory of Islam. Asad, who had ever esteemed him, grew to love him. An intensely devout man, could he have done less in the case of one for whom the Pitying the Pitiful showed so marked a predilection? It was freely accepted that when the destiny of Asad-ed-Din should come to be fulfilled, Sakr-el-Bahr must succeed him in the Bashalik of Algiers, and that thus Oliver-Reis would follow in the footsteps of Barbarossa, Ochiali, and other Christian renegades who had become corsair-princes of Islam.

In spite of certain hostilities which his rapid advancement begot, and of which we shall hear more presently, once only did his power stand in danger of suffering a check. Coming one morning into the reeking bagnio at Algiers, some six months after he had been raised to his captaincy, he found there a score of countrymen of his own, and he gave orders that their letters should instantly be struck off and their liberty restored them.

Called to account by the Basha for this action he took a high-handed way, since no other was possible. He swore by the beard of the Prophet that if he were to draw the sword of Mahomet and to serve Islam upon the seas, he would serve it in his own way, and one of his ways was that his own countrymen were to have immunity from the edge of that same sword. Islam, he swore, should not be the loser, since for every Englishman he restored to liberty he would bring two Spaniards, Frenchmen, Greeks, or Italians into bondage.

He prevailed, but only upon condition that since captured slaves were the property of the state, if he desired to abstract them from the state he must first purchase them for himself. Since they would then be his own property he could dispose of them at his good pleasure. Thus did the wise and just Asad resolve the difficulty which had arisen, and Oliver-Reis bowed wisely to that decision.

Thereafter what English slaves were brought to Algiers he purchased, manumitted, and found means to send home again. True, it cost him a fine price yearly, but he was fast amassing such wealth as could easily support this tax.

As you read Lord Henry Goade's chronicles you might come to the conclusion that in the whorl of that new life of his Sir Oliver had entirely forgotten the happenings in his Cornish home and the woman he had loved, who so readily had believed him guilty of the slaying of her brother. You might believe this until you come upon the relation of how he found one day among some English seamen brought captive to Algiers by Biskaine-el-Borak—who was become his own second in command—a young Cornish lad from Helston named Pitt, whose father he had known.

He took this lad home with him to the fine palace which he inhabited near the Bab-el-Oueb, treated him as an honoured guest, and sat through a whole summer night in talk with him, questioning him upon this person and that person, and thus gradually drawing from him all the little history of his native place during the two years that were sped since he had left it. In this we gather an impression of the wistful longings the fierce nostalgia that must have overcome the renegade and his endeavours to allay it by his endless questions. The Cornish lad had brought him up sharply and agonizingly with that past of his upon which he had closed the door when he became a Muslim and a corsair. The only possible inference is that in those hours of that summer's night repentance stirred in him, and a wild longing to return. Rosamund should reopen for him that door which, hard-driven by misfortune, he had slammed. That she would do so when once she knew the truth he had no faintest doubt. And there was now no reason why he should conceal the truth, why he should continue to shield that dastardly half-brother of his, whom he had come to hate as fiercely as he had erstwhile loved him.

In secret he composed a long letter giving the history of all that had happened to him since his kidnapping, and setting forth the entire truth of that and of the deed that had led to it. His chronicler opines that it was a letter that must have moved a stone to tears. And, moreover, it was not a mere matter of passionate protestations of innocence, or of unsupported accusation of his brother. It told her of the existence of proofs that must dispel all doubt. It told her of that parchment indited by Master Baine and witnessed by the parson, which document was to be delivered to her together with the letter. Further, it bade her seek confirmation of that document's genuineness, did she doubt it, at the hands of Master Baine himself. That done, it besought her to lay the whole matter before the Queen, and thus secure him faculty to return to England and immunity from any consequences of his subsequent regenade act to which his sufferings had driven him. He loaded the young Cornishman with gifts, gave him that letter to deliver in person, and added instructions that should enable him to find the document he was to deliver with it. That precious parchment had been left between the leaves of an old book on falconry in the library at Penarrow, where it would probably be found still undisturbed since his brother would not suspect its presence and was himself no scholar. Pitt was to seek out Nicholas at Penarrow and enlist his aid to obtain possession of that document, if it still existed.

Then Sakr-el-Bahr found means to conduct Pitt to Genoa, and there put him aboard an English vessel.

Three months later he received an answer—a letter from Pitt, which reached him by way of Genoa—which was at peace with the Algerines, and served then as a channel of communication with Christianity. In this letter Pitt informed him that he had done all that Sir Oliver had desired him; that he had found the document by the help of Nicholas, and that in person he had waited upon Mistress

Rosamund Godolphin, who dwelt now with Sir John Killigrew at Arwenack, delivering to her the letter and the parchment; but that upon learning on whose behalf he came she had in his presence flung both unopened upon the fire and dismissed him with his tale untold.

Sakr-el-Bahr spent the night under the skies in his fragrant orchard, and his slaves reported in terror that they had heard sobs and weeping. If indeed his heart wept, it was for the last time; thereafter he was more inscrutable, more ruthless, cruel and mocking than men had ever known him, nor from that day did he ever again concern himself to manumit a single English slave. His heart was become a stone.

Thus five years passed, counting from that spring night when he was trepanned by Jasper Leigh, and his fame spread, his name became a terror upon the seas, and fleets put forth from Malta, from Naples, and from Venice to make an end of him and his ruthless piracy. But Allah kept watch over him, and Sakr-el-Bahr never delivered battle but he wrested victory to the scimitars of Islam.

Then in the spring of that fifth year there came to him another letter from the Cornish Pitt, a letter which showed him that gratitude was not as dead in the world as he supposed it, for it was purely out of gratitude that the lad whom he had delivered from thraldom wrote to inform him of certain matters that concerned him. This letter reopened that old wound; it did more; it dealt him a fresh one. He learnt from it that the writer had been constrained by Sir John Killigrew to give such evidence of Sir Oliver's conversion to Islam as had enabled the courts to pronounce Sir Oliver as one to be presumed dead at law, granting the succession to his half-brother, Master Lionel Tressilian. Pitt professed himself deeply mortified at having been forced unwittingly to make Sir Oliver so evil a return for the benefits received from him, and added that sooner would he have suffered them to hang him than have spoken could he have foreseen the consequences of his testimony.

So far Sir Oliver read unmoved by any feeling other than cold contempt. But there was more to follow. The letter went on to tell him that Mistress Rosamund was newly returned from a two years' sojourn in France to become betrothed to his half-brother Lionel, and that they were to be wed in June. He was further informed that the marriage had been contrived by Sir John Killigrew in his desire to see Rosamund settled and under the protection of a husband, since he himself was proposing to take the seas and was fitting out a fine ship for a voyage to the Indies. The writer added that the marriage was widely approved, and it was deemed to be an excellent measure for both houses, since it would weld into one the two contiguous estates of Penarrow and Godolphin Court.

Oliver-Reis laughed when he had read thus far. The marriage was approved not for itself, it would seem, but because by means of it two stretches of earth were united into one. It was a marriage of two parks, of two estates, of two tracts of arable and forest, and that two human beings were concerned in it was apparently no more than an incidental circumstance.

Then the irony of it all entered his soul and spread it with bitterness. After dismissing him for the supposed murder of her brother, she was to take the actual murderer to her arms. And he, that cur, that false villain!—out of what depths of hell did he derive the courage to go through with this mummery?—had he no heart, no conscience, no sense of decency, no fear of God?

He tore the letter into fragments and set about effacing the matter from his thoughts. Pitt had meant kindly by him, but had dealt cruelly. In his efforts to seek distraction from the torturing images ever in his mind he took to the sea with three galleys, and thus some two weeks later came face to face with Master Jasper Leigh aboard the Spanish carack which he captured under Cape Spartel.

CHAPTER III. HOMEWARD BOUND

In the cabin of the captured Spaniard, Jasper Leigh found himself that evening face to face with Sakr-el-Bahr, haled thither by the corsair's gigantic Nubians.

Sakr-el-Bahr had not yet pronounced his intentions concerning the piratical little skipper, and Master Leigh, full conscious that he was a villain, feared the worst, and had spent some miserable hours in the fore-castle awaiting a doom which he accounted foregone.

"Our positions have changed, Master Leigh, since last we talked in a ship's cabin," was the renegade's inscrutable greeting.

"Indeed," Master Leigh agreed. "But I hope ye'll remember that on that occasion I was your friend."

"At a price," Sakr-el-Bahr reminded him. "And at a price you may find me your friend to-day."

The rascally skipper's heart leapt with hope.

"Name it, Sir Oliver," he answered eagerly. "And so that it ties within my wretched power I swear I'll never boggle at it. I've had enough of slavery," he ran on in a plaintive whine. "Five years of it, and four of them spent aboard the galleys of Spain, and no day in all of them but that I prayed for death. Did you but know what I ha' suffered."

"Never was suffering more merited, never punishment more fitting, never justice more poetic," said Sakr-el-Bahr in a voice that made the skipper's blood run cold. "You would have sold me, a man who did you no hurt, indeed a man who once befriended you—you would have sold me into slavery for a matter of two hundred pounds...."

"Nay, nay," cried the other fearfully, "as God's my witness, 'twas never part of my intent. Ye'll never ha' forgot the words I spoke to you, the offer that I made to carry you back home again."

"Ay, at a price, 'tis true," Sakr-el-Bahr repeated. "And it is fortunate for you that you are to-day in a position to pay a price that should postpone your dirty neck's acquaintance with a rope. I need a navigator," he added in explanation, "and what five years ago you would have done for two hundred pounds, you shall do to-day for your life. How say you: will you navigate this ship for me?"

"Sir," cried Jasper Leigh, who could scarce believe that this was all that was required of him, "I'll sail it to hell at your bidding."

"I am not for Spain this voyage," answered Sakr-el-Bahr. "You shall sail me precisely as you would have done five years ago, back to the mouth of the Fal, and set me ashore there. Is that agreed?"

"Ay, and gladly," replied Master Leigh without a second's pause.

"The conditions are that you shall have your life and your liberty," Sakr-el-Bahr explained. "But do not suppose that arrived in England you are to be permitted to depart. You must sail us back again, though once you have done that I shall find a way to send you home if you so desire it, and perhaps there will be some measure of reward for you if you serve me faithfully throughout. Follow the habits of a lifetime by playing me false and there's an end to you. You shall have for constant bodyguard these two lilies of the desert," and he pointed to the colossal Nubians who stood there invisible almost in the shadow but for the flash of teeth and eyeballs. "They shall watch over you, and see that no harm befalls you so long as you are honest with me, and they shall strangle you at the first sign of treachery. You may go. You have the freedom of the ship, but you are not to leave it here or elsewhere save at my express command."

Jasper Leigh stumbled out counting himself fortunate beyond his expectations or deserts, and the Nubians followed him and hung behind him ever after like some vast twin shadow.

To Sakr-el-Bahr entered now Biskaine with a report of the prize captured. Beyond the prisoners, however, and the actual vessel, which had suffered nothing in the fight, the cargo was of no account. Outward bound as she was it was not to be expected that any treasures would be discovered in her hold. They found great store of armaments and powder and a little money; but naught else that was worthy of the corsairs' attention.

Sakr-el-Bahr briefly issued his surprising orders.

"Thou'lt set the captives aboard one of the galleys, Biskaine, and thyself convey them to Algiers, there to be sold. All else thou'lt leave aboard here, and two hundred picked corsairs to go a voyage with me overseas, men that will act as mariners and fighters."

"Art thou, then, not returning to Algiers, O Sakr-el-Bahr?"

"Not yet. I am for a longer voyage. Convey my service to Asad-ed-Din, whom Allah guard and cherish, and tell him to look for me in some six weeks time."

This sudden resolve of Oliver-Reis created no little excitement aboard the galleys. The corsairs knew nothing of navigation upon the open seas, none of them had ever been beyond the Mediterranean, few of them indeed had ever voyaged as far west as Cape Spartel, and it is doubtful if they would have followed any other leader into the perils of the open Atlantic. But Sakr-el-Bahr, the child of Fortune, the protected of Allah, had never yet led them to aught but victory, and he had but to call them to heel and they would troop after him whithersoever he should think well to go. So now there was little trouble in finding the two hundred Muslimeen he desired for his fighting crew. Rather was the difficulty to keep the number of those eager for the adventure within the bounds he had indicated.

CHAPTER III. HOMEWARD BOUND

You are not to suppose that in all this Sir Oliver was acting upon any preconcerted plan. Whilst he had lain on the heights watching that fine ship beating up against the wind it had come to him that with such a vessel under him it were a fond adventure to sail to England, to descend upon that Cornish coast abruptly as a thunderbolt, and present the reckoning to his craven dastard of a brother. He had toyed with the fancy, dreamily almost as men build their castles in Spain. Then in the heat of conflict it had entirely escaped his mind, to return in the shape of a resolve when he came to find himself face to face with Jasper Leigh.

The skipper and the ship conjointly provided him with all the means to realize that dream he had dreamt. There was none to oppose his will, no reason not to indulge his cruel fancy. Perhaps, too, he might see Rosamund again, might compel her to hear the truth from him. And there was Sir John Killigrew. He had never been able to determine whether Sir John had been his friend or his foe in the past; but since it was Sir John who had been instrumental in setting up Lionel in Sir Oliver's place—by inducing the courts to presume Sir Oliver's death on the score that being a renegade he must be accounted dead at law—and since it was Sir John who was contriving this wedding between Lionel and Rosamund, why, Sir John, too, should be paid a visit and should be informed of the precise nature of the thing he did.

With the forces at his disposal in those days of his absolute lordship of life and death along the African littoral, to conceive was with Oliver-Reis no more than the prelude to execution. The habit of swift realization of his every wish had grown with him, and that habit guided now his course.

He made his preparations quickly, and on the morrow the Spanish carack—lately labelled Nuestra Senora de las Llagas, but with that label carefully effaced from her quarter—trimmed her sails and stood out for the open Atlantic, navigated by Captain Jasper Leigh. The three galleys under the command of Biskaine-el-Borak crept slowly eastward and homeward to Algiers, hugging the coast, as was the corsair habit. The wind favoured Oliver so well that within ten days of rounding Cape St. Vincent he had his first glimpse of the Lizard.

CHAPTER IV. THE RAID

In the estuary of the River Fal a splendid ship, on the building of which the most cunning engineers had been employed and no money spared, rode proudly at anchor just off Smithick under the very shadow of the heights crowned by the fine house of Arwenack. She was fitting out for a distant voyage and for days the work of bringing stores and munitions aboard had been in progress, so that there was an unwonted bustle about the little forge and the huddle of cottages that went to make up the fishing village, as if in earnest of the great traffic that in future days was to be seen about that spot. For Sir John Killigrew seemed at last to be on the eve of prevailing and of laying there the foundations of the fine port of his dreams.

To this state of things his friendship with Master Lionel Tressilian had contributed not a little. The opposition made to his project by Sir Oliver—and supported, largely at Sir Oliver's suggestion, by Truro and Helston—had been entirely withdrawn by Lionel; more, indeed Lionel had actually gone so far in the opposite direction as to support Sir John in his representations to Parliament and the Queen. It followed naturally enough that just as Sir Oliver's opposition of that cherished project had been the seed of the hostility between Arwenack and Penarrow, so Lionel's support of it became the root of the staunch friendship that sprang up between himself and Sir John.

What Lionel lacked of his brother's keen intelligence he made up for in cunning. He realized that although at some future time it was possible that Helston and Truro and the Tressilian property there might come to suffer as a consequence of the development of a port so much more advantageously situated, yet that could not be in his own lifetime; and meanwhile he must earn in return Sir John's support for his suit of Rosamund Godolphin and thus find the Godolphin estates merged with his own. This certain immediate gain was to Master Lionel well worth the other future possible loss.

It must not, however, be supposed that Lionel's courtship had thenceforward run a smooth and easy course. The mistress of Godolphin Court showed him no favour and it was mainly that she might abstract herself from the importunities of his suit that she had sought and obtained Sir John Killigrew's permission to accompany the latter's sister to France when she went there with her husband, who was appointed English ambassador to the Louvre. Sir John's authority as her guardian had come into force with the decease of her brother.

Master Lionel moped awhile in her absence; but cheered by Sir John's assurance that in the end he should prevail, he quitted Cornwall in his turn and went forth to see the world. He spent some time in London about the Court, where, however, he seems to have prospered little, and then he crossed to France to pay his devoirs to the lady of his longings.

His constancy, the humility with which he made his suit, the obvious intensity of his devotion, began at last to wear away that gentlewoman's opposition, as dripping water wears away a stone. Yet she could not bring herself to forget that he was Sir Oliver's brother—the brother of the man she had loved, and the brother of the man who had killed her own brother. Between them stood, then, two things; the ghost of that old love of hers and the blood of Peter Godolphin.

Of this she reminded Sir John on her return to Cornwall after an absence of some two years, urging these matters as reasons why an alliance between herself and Lionel Tressilian must be impossible.

Sir John did not at all agree with her.

"My dear," he said, "there is your future to be thought of. You are now of full age and mistress of your own actions. Yet it is not well for a woman and a gentlewoman to dwell alone. As long as I live, or as long as I remain in England, all will be well. You may continue indefinitely your residence here at Arwenack, and you have been wise, I think, in quitting the loneliness of Godolphin Court. Yet consider that that loneliness may be yours again when I am not here."

"I should prefer that loneliness to the company you would thrust upon me," she answered him.

"Ungracious speech!" he protested. "Is this your gratitude for that lad's burning devotion, for his patience, his gentleness, and all the rest!"

"He is Oliver Tressilian's brother," she replied.

"And has he not suffered enough for that already? Is there to be no end to the price that he must pay for his brother's sins? Besides, consider that when all is said they are not even brothers. They are but half-brothers."

"Yet too closely kin," she said. "If you must have me wed I beg you'll find me another husband."

To this he would answer that expediently considered no husband could be better than the one he had chosen her. He pointed out the contiguity of their two estates, and how fine and advantageous a thing it would be to merge these two into one.

He was persistent, and his persistence was increased when he came to conceive his notion to take the seas again. His conscience would not permit him to heave anchor until he had bestowed her safely in wedlock. Lionel too was persistent, in a quiet, almost self-effacing way that never set a strain upon her patience, and was therefore the more difficult to combat.

In the end she gave way under the pressure of these men's wills, and did so with the best grace she could summon, resolved to drive from her heart and mind the one real obstacle of which, for very shame, she had made no mention to Sir John. The fact is that in spite of all, her love for Sir Oliver was not dead. It was stricken down, it is true, until she herself failed to recognize it for what it really was. But she caught herself thinking of him frequently and wistfully; she found herself comparing him with his brother; and for all that she had bidden Sir John find her some other husband than Lionel, she knew full well that any suitor brought before her must be submitted to that same comparison to his inevitable undoing. All this she accounted evil in herself. It was in vain that she lashed her mind with the reminder that Sir Oliver was Peter's murderer. As time went on she found herself actually making excuses for her sometime lover; she would admit that Peter had driven him to the step, that for her sake Sir Oliver had suffered insult upon insult from Peter, until, being but human, the cup of his endurance had overflowed in the end, and weary of submitting to the other's blows he had risen up in his anger and smitten in his turn.

She would scorn herself for such thoughts as these, yet she could not dismiss them. In act she could be strong—as witness how she had dealt with that letter which Oliver sent her out of Barbary by the hand of Pitt—but her thoughts she could not govern, and her thoughts were full often traitors to her will. There were longings in her heart for Oliver which she could not stifle, and there was ever the hope that he would one day return, although she realized that from such a return she might look for nothing.

When Sir John finally slew the hope of that return he did a wiser thing than he conceived. Never since Oliver's disappearance had they heard any news of him until Pitt came to Arwenack with that letter and his story. They had heard, as had all the world, of the corsair Sakr-el-Bahr, but they had been far indeed from connecting him with Oliver Tressilian. Now that his identity was established by Pitt's testimony, it was an easy matter to induce the courts to account him dead and to give Lionel the coveted inheritance.

This to Rosamund was a small matter. But a great one was that Sir Oliver was dead at law, and must be so in fact, should he ever again set foot in England. It extinguished finally that curiously hopeless and almost subconscious hope of hers that one day he would return. Thus it helped her perhaps to face and accept the future which Sir John was resolved to thrust upon her.

Her betrothal was made public, and she proved if not an ardently loving, at least a docile and gentle mistress to Lionel. He was content. He could ask no more in reason at the moment, and he was buoyed up by every lover's confidence that given opportunity and time he could find the way to awaken a response. And it must be confessed that already during their betrothal he gave some proof of his reason for his confidence. She had been lonely, and he dispelled her loneliness by his complete surrender of himself to her; his restraint and his cautious, almost insidious creeping along a path which a more clumsy fellow would have taken at a dash made companionship possible between them and very sweet to her. Upon this foundation her affection began gradually to rise, and seeing them together and such excellent friends, Sir John congratulated himself upon his wisdom and went about the fitting out of that fine ship of his—the Silver Heron—for the coming voyage.

Thus they came within a week of the wedding, and Sir John all impatience now. The marriage bells were to be his signal for departure; as they fell silent the Silver Heron should spread her wings.

It was the evening of the first of June; the peal of the curfew had faded on the air and lights were being set in the great dining-room at Arwenack where the company was to sup. It was a small party. Just Sir John and Rosamund and Li onel, who had lingered on that day, and Lord Henry Goade—our chronicler—the Queen's Lieutenant of Cornwall, together with his lady. They were visiting Sir John and they were to remain yet a week his guests at Arwenack that they might grace the coming nuptials.

Above in the house there was great stir of preparation for the departure of Sir John and his ward, the latter into wedlock, the former into unknown seas. In the turret chamber a dozen sempstresses were at work upon the bridal outfit under the directions of that Sally Pentreath who had been no less assiduous in the preparation of swaddling clothes and the like on the eve of Rosamund's appearance in this world.

At the very hour at which Sir John was leading his company to table Sir Oliver Tressilian was setting foot ashore not a mile away.

He had deemed it wiser not to round Pendennis Point. So in the bay above Swanpool on the western side of that promontory he had dropped anchor as the evening shadows were deepening. He had launched the ship's two boats, and in these he had conveyed some thirty of his men ashore. Twice had the boats returned, until a hundred of his corsairs stood ranged along that foreign beach. The other hundred he left on guard aboard. He took so great a force upon an expedition for which a quarter of the men would have sufficed so as to ensure by overwhelming numbers the avoidance of all unnecessary violence.

Absolutely unobserved he led them up the slope towards Arwenack through the darkness that had now closed in. To tread his native soil once more went near to drawing tears from him. How familiar was the path he followed with such confidence in the night; how well known each bush and stone by which he went with his silent multitude hard upon his heels. Who could have foretold him such a return as this.

Who could have dreamt when he roamed amain in his youth here with dogs and fowling-piece that he would creep one night over these dunes a renegade Muslim leading a horde of infidels to storm the house of Sir John Killigrew of Arwenack?

Such thoughts begot a weakness in him; but he made a quick recovery when his mind swung to all that he had so unjustly suffered, when he considered all that he came thus to avenge.

First to Arwenack to Sir John and Rosamund to compel them to hear the truth at least, and then away to Penarrow for Master Lionel and the reckoning. Such was the project that warmed him, conquered his weakness and spurred him, relentless, onward and upward to the heights and the fortified house that dominated them.

He found the massive iron-studded gates locked, as was to have been expected at that hour. He knocked, and presently the postern gaped, and a lantern was advanced. Instantly that lantern was dashed aside and Sir Oliver had leapt over the sill into the courtyard. With a hand gripping the porter's throat to choke all utterance, Sir Oliver heaved him out to his men, who swiftly gagged him.

That done they poured silently through that black gap of the postern into the spacious gateway. On he led them, at a run almost, towards the tall mullioned windows whence a flood of golden light seemed invitingly to beckon them.

With the servants who met them in the hall they dealt in the same swift silent fashion as they had dealt with the gatekeeper, and such was the speed and caution of their movements that Sir John and his company had no suspicion of their presence until the door of the dining-room crashed open before their eyes.

The sight which they beheld was one that for some moments left them mazed and bewildered. Lord Henry tells us how at first he imagined that here was some mummery, some surprise prepared for the bridal couple by Sir John's tenants or the folk of Smithick and Penycumwick, and he adds that he was encouraged in this belief by the circumstance that not a single weapon gleamed in all that horde of outlandish intruders.

Although they came full armed against any eventualities, yet by their leader's orders not a blade was bared. What was to do was to be done with their naked hands alone and without bloodshed. Such were the orders of Sakr-el-Bahr, and Sakr-el-Bahr's were not orders to be disregarded.

Himself he stood forward at the head of that legion of brown-skinned men arrayed in all the colours of the rainbow, their heads swathed in turbans of every hue. He considered the company in grim silence, and the company in amazement considered this turbaned giant with the masterful face that was tanned to the colour of mahogany, the black forked beard, and those singularly light eyes glittering like steel under his black brows.

Thus a little while in silence, then with a sudden gasp Lionel Tressilian sank back in his tall chair as if bereft of strength.

The agate eyes flashed upon him smiling, cruelly.

"I see that you, at least, I recognize me," said Sakr-el-Bahr in his deep voice. "I was assured I could depend upon the eyes of brotherly love to pierce the change that time and stress have wrought in me."

Sir John was on his feet, his lean swarthy face flushing darkly, an oath on his lips. Rosamund sat on as if frozen with horror, considering Sir Oliver with dilating eyes, whilst her hands clawed the table before her. They too recognized him now, and realized that here was no mummery. That something sinister was intended Sir John could not for a moment doubt. But of what that something might be he could form no notion. It was the first time that Barbary rovers were seen in England. That famous raid of theirs upon Baltimore in Ireland did not take place until some thirty years after this date.

"Sir Oliver Tressilian!" Killigrew gasped, and "Sir Oliver Tressilian!" echoed Lord Henry Goade, to add "By God!"

"Not Sir Oliver Tressilian, came the answer, but Sakr-el-Bahr, the scourge of the sea, the terror of Christendom, the desperate corsair your lies, cupidity, and false-heartedness have fashioned out of a sometime Cornish gentleman." He embraced them all in his denunciatory gesture. "Behold me here with my sea-hawks to present a reckoning long overdue."

Writing now of what his own eyes beheld, Lord Henry tells us how Sir John leapt to snatch a weapon from the armoured walls; how Sakr-el-Bahr barked out a single word in Arabic, and how at that word a half-dozen of his supple blackamoors sprang upon the knight like greyhounds upon a hare and bore him writhing to the ground.

Lady Henry screamed; her husband does not appear to have done anything, or else modesty keeps him silent on the score of it. Rosamund, white to the lips, continued to look on, whilst Lionel, overcome, covered his face with his hands in sheer horror. One and all of them expected to see some ghastly deed of blood performed there, coldly and callously as the wringing of a capon's neck. But no such thing took place. The corsairs merely turned Sir John upon his face, dragged his wrists behind him to make them fast, and having performed that duty with a speedy, silent dexterity they abandoned him.

Sakr-el-Bahr watched their performance with those grimly smiling eyes of his. When it was done he spoke again and pointed to Lionel, who leapt up in sudden terror, with a cry that was entirely inarticulate. Lithe brown arms encircled him like a legion of snakes. Powerless, he was lifted in the air and borne swiftly away. For an instant he found himself held face to face with his turbaned brother. Into that pallid terror-stricken human mask the renegade's eyes stabbed like two daggers. Then deliberately and after the fashion of the Muslim he was become he spat upon it.

"Away!" he growled, and through the press of corsairs that thronged the hall behind him a lane was swiftly opened and Lionel was swallowed up, lost to the view of those within the room.

"What murderous deed do you intend?" cried Sir John indomitably. He had risen and stood grimly dignified in his bonds.

"Will you murder your own brother as you murdered mine?" demanded Rosamund, speaking now for the first time, and rising as she spoke, a faint flush coming to overspread her pallor. She saw him wince; she saw the mocking lustful anger perish in his face, leaving it vacant for a moment. Then it became grim again with a fresh resolve. Her words had altered all the current of his intentions. They fixed in him a dull, fierce rage. They silenced the explanations which he was come to offer, and which he scorned to offer here after that taunt.

"It seems you love that—whelp, that thing that was my brother," he said, sneering. "I wonder will you love him still when you come to be better acquainted with him? Though, faith, naught would surprise me in a woman and her love. Yet

I am curious to see—curious to see." He laughed. "I have a mind to gratify myself. I will not separate you—not just yet."

He advanced upon her. "Come thou with me, lady," he commanded, and held out his hand.

And now Lord Henry seems to have been stirred to futile action.

"At that," he writes, "I thrust myself between to shield her. 'Thou dog,' I cried,'thou shalt be made to suffer!'

"'Suffer?' quoth he, and mocked me with his deep laugh. 'I have suffered already. 'Tis for that reason I am here.'

"'And thou shalt suffer again, thou pirate out of hell!' I warned him. 'Thou shalt suffer for this outrage as God's my life!'

"'Shall I so?' quoth he, very calm and sinister. 'And at whose hands, I pray you?'

"'At mine, sir, I roared, being by now stirred to a great fury.

"'At thine?' he sneered. 'Thou'lt hunt the hawk of the sea? Thou? Thou plump partridge! Away! Hinder me not!'"

And he adds that again Sir Oliver spoke that short Arabic command, whereupon a dozen blackamoors whirled the Queen's Lieutenant aside and bound him to a chair.

Face to face stood now Sir Oliver with Rosamund—face to face after five long years, and he realized that in every moment of that time the certainty had never departed from him of some such future meeting.

"Come, lady," he bade her sternly.

A moment she looked at him with hate and loathing in the clear depths of her deep blue eyes. Then swiftly as lightning she snatched a knife from the board and drove it at his heart. But his hand moved as swiftly to seize her wrist, and the knife clattered to the ground, its errand unfulfilled.

A shuddering sob escaped her then to express at once her horror of her own attempt and of the man who held her. That horror mounting until it overpowered her, she sank suddenly against him in a swoon.

Instinctively his arms went round her, and a moment he held her thus, recalling the last occasion on which she had lain against his breast, on an evening five years and more ago under the grey wall of Godolphin Court above the river. What prophet could have told him that when next he so held her the conditions would be these? It was all grotesque and incredible, like the fantastic dream of some sick mind. But it was all true, and she was in his arms again.

He shifted his grip to her waist, heaved her to his mighty shoulder, as though she were a sack of grain, and swung about, his business at Arwenack accomplished—indeed, more of it accomplished than had been his intent, and also something less.

"Away, away!" he cried to his rovers, and away they sped as fleetly and silently as they had come, no man raising now so much as a voice to hinder them.

Through the hall and across the courtyard flowed that human tide; out into the open and along the crest of the hill it surged, then away down the slope towards the beach where their boats awaited them. Sakr-el-Bahr ran as lightly as though the swooning woman he bore were no more than a cloak he had flung across his shoulder. Ahead of him went a half-dozen of his fellows carrying his gagged and pinioned brother.

Once only before they dipped from the heights of Arwenack did Oliver check. He paused to look across the dark shimmering water to the woods that screened the house of Penarrow from his view. It had been part of his purpose to visit it, as we know. But the necessity had now been removed, and he was conscious of a pang of disappointment, of a hunger to look again upon his home. But to shift the current of his thoughts just then came two of his officers—Othmani and Ali, who had been muttering one with the other. As they overtook him, Othmani set now a hand upon his arm, and pointed down towards the twinkling lights of Smithick and Penycumwick.

"My lord," he cried, "there will be lads and maidens there should fetch fat prices in the sôk-el-Abeed."

"No doubt," said Sakr-el-Bahr, scarce heeding him, heeding indeed little in this world but his longings to look upon Penarrow.

"Why, then, my lord, shall I take fifty True-Believers and make a raid upon them? It were an easy task, all unsuspicious as they must be of our presence."

Sakr-el-Bahr came out of his musings. "Othmani," said he, "art a fool, the very father of fools, else wouldst thou have come to know by now that those who once were of my own race, those of the land from which I am sprung, are sacred to me. Here we take no slave but these we have. On, then, in the name of Allah!"

But Othmani was not yet silenced. "And is our perilous voyage across these unknown seas into this far heathen land to be rewarded by no more than just these two captives? Is that a raid worthy of Sakr-el-Bahr?"

"Leave Sakr-el-Bahr to judge," was the curt answer.

"But reflect, my lord: there is another who will judge. How shall our Basha, the glorious Asad-ed-Din, welcome thy return with such poor spoils as these? What questions will he set thee, and what account shalt thou render him for having imperilled the lives of all these True-Believers upon the seas for so little profit?"

"He shall ask me what he pleases, and I shall answer what I please and as Allah prompts me. On, I say!"

And on they went, Sakr-el-Bahr conscious now of little but the warmth of that body upon his shoulder, and knowing not, so tumultuous were his emotions, whether it fired him to love or hate.

They gained the beach; they reached the ship whose very presence had continued unsuspected. The breeze was fresh and they stood away at once. By sunrise there was no more sign of them than there had been at sunset, there was no more clue to the way they had taken than to the way they had come. It was as if they had dropped from the skies in the night upon that Cornish coast, and but for the mark of their swift, silent passage, but for the absence of Rosamund and Lionel

Tressilian, the thing must have been accounted no more than a dream of those few who had witnessed it.

Aboard the carack, Sakr-el-Bahr bestowed Rosamund in the cabin over the quarter, taking the precaution to lock the door that led to the stern-gallery. Lionel he ordered to be dropped into a dark hole under the hatchway, there to lie and meditate upon the retribution that had overtaken him until such time as his brother should have determined upon his fate—for this was a matter upon which the renegade was still undecided.

Himself he lay under the stars that night and thought of many things. One of these things, which plays some part in the story, though it is probable that it played but a slight one in his thoughts, was begotten of the words Othmani had used. What, indeed, would be Asad's welcome of him on his return if he sailed into Algiers with nothing more to show for that long voyage and the imperilling of the lives of two hundred True-Believers than just those two captives whom he intended, moreover, to retain for himself? What capital would not be made out of that circumstance by his enemies in Algiers and by Asad's Sicilian wife who hated him with all the bitterness of a hatred that had its roots in the fertile soil of jealousy?

This may have spurred him in the cool dawn to a very daring and desperate enterprise which Destiny sent his way in the shape of a tall-masted Dutchman homeward bound. He gave chase, for all that he was full conscious that the battle he invited was one of which his corsairs had no experience, and one upon which they must have hesitated to venture with another leader than himself. But the star of Sakr-el-Bahr was a star that never led to aught but victory, and their belief in him, the very javelin of Allah, overcame any doubts that may have been begotten of finding themselves upon an unfamiliar craft and on a rolling, unfamiliar sea.

This fight is given in great detail by my Lord Henry from the particulars afforded him by Jasper Leigh. But it differs in no great particular from other sea-fights, and it is none of my purpose to surfeit you with such recitals. Enough to say that it was stern and fierce, entailing great loss to both combatants; that cannon played little part in it, for knowing the quality of his men Sakr-el-Bahr made haste to run in and grapple. He prevailed of course as he must ever pre-vail by the very force of his personality and the might of his example. He was the first to leap aboard the Dutchman, clad in mail and whirling his great scimitar, and his men poured after him shouting his name and that of Allah in a breath.

Such was ever his fury in an engagement that it infected and inspired his followers. It did so now, and the shrewd Dutchmen came to perceive that this heathen horde was as a body to which he supplied the brain and soul. They attacked him fiercely in groups, intent at all costs upon cutting him down, convinced almost by instinct that were he felled the victory would easily be theirs. And in the end they succeeded. A Dutch pike broke some links of his mail and dealt him a flesh wound which went unheeded by him in his fury; a Dutch rapier found the breach thus made in his de-fences, and went through it to stretch him bleeding upon the deck. Yet he staggered up, knowing as full as did they that if he succumbed then all was lost. Armed now with a short axe which he had found under his hand when he went down, he hacked a way to the bulwarks, set his back against the timbers, and hoarse of voice, ghastly of face, spattered with the blood of his wound he urged on his men until the victory was theirs—and this was fortunately soon. And then, as if he had been sustained by no more than the very force of his will, he sank down in a heap among the dead and wounded huddled against the vessel's bulwarks.

Grief stricken his corsairs bore him back aboard the carack. Were he to die then was their victory a barren one indeed. They laid him on a couch prepared for him amidships on the main deck, where the vessel's pitching was least discomfiting. A Moorish surgeon came to tend him, and pronounced his hurt a grievous one, but not so grievous as to close the gates of hope.

This pronouncement gave the corsairs all the assurance they required. It could not be that the Gardener could already pluck so fragrant a fruit from Allah's garden. The Pitiful must spare Sakr-el-Bahr to continue the glory of Islam.

Yet they were come to the straits of Gibraltar before his fever abated and he recovered complete consciousness, to learn of the final issue of that hazardous fight into which he had led those children of the Prophet.

The Dutchman, Othmani informed him, was following in their wake, with Ali and some others aboard her, steering ever in the wake of the carack which continued to be navigated by the Nasrani dog, Jasper Leigh. When Sakr-el-Bahr learnt the value of the capture, when he was informed that in addition to a hundred able-bodied men under the hatches, to be sold as slaves in the sôk-el-Abeed, there was a cargo of gold and silver, pearls, amber, spices, and ivory, and such lesser matters as gorgeous silken fabrics, rich beyond anything that had ever been seen upon the seas at any one time, he felt that the blood he had shed had not been wasted.

Let him sail safely into Algiers with these two ships both captured in the name of Allah and his Prophet, one of them an argosy so richly fraught, a floating treasure-house, and he need have little fear of what his enemies and the crafty evil Sicilian woman might have wrought against him in his absence.

Then he made inquiry touching his two English captives, to be informed that Othmani had taken charge of them, and that he had continued the treatment meted out to them by Sakr-el-Bahr himself when first they were brought aboard.

He was satisfied, and fell into a gentle healing sleep, whilst, on the decks above, his followers rendered thanks to Allah the Pitying the Pitiful, the Master of the Day of Judgment, who Alone is All-Wise, All-Knowing.

CHAPTER V. THE LION OF THE FAITH

Asad-ed-Din, the Lion of the Faith, Basha of Algiers, walked in the evening cool in the orchard of the Kasbah upon the heights above the city, and at his side, stepping daintily, came Fenzileh, his wife, the first lady of his hareem, whom eighteen years ago he had carried off in his mighty arms from that little white-washed village above the Straits of Messina which his followers had raided.

She had been a lissom maid of sixteen in those far-off days, the child of humble peasant-folk, and she had gone uncomplaining to the arms of her swarthy ravisher. To-day, at thirty-four, she was still beautiful, more beautiful indeed than when first she had fired the passion of Asad-Reis—as he then was, one of the captains of the famous Ali-Basha. There were streaks of red in her heavy black tresses, her skin was of a soft pearliness that seemed translucent, her eyes were large, of a golden-brown, agleam with sombre fires, her lips were full and sensuous. She was tall and of a shape that in Europe would have been accounted perfect, which is to say that she was a thought too slender for Oriental taste; she moved along beside her lord with a sinuous, languorous grace, gently stirring her fan of ostrich plumes. She was unveiled; indeed it was her immodest habit to go naked of face more often than was seemly, which is but the least of the many undesirable infidel ways which had survived her induction into the Faith of Islam—a necessary step before Asad, who was devout to the point of bigotry, would consent to make her his wife. He had found her such a wife as it is certain he could never have procured at home; a woman who, not content to be his toy, the plaything of his idle hour, insinuated herself into affairs, demanded and obtained his confidences, and exerted over him much the same influence as the wife of a European prince might exert over her consort. In the years during which he had lain under the spell of her ripening beauty he had accepted the situation willingly enough; later, when he would have curtailed her interferences, it was too late; she had taken a firm grip of the reins, and Asad was in no better case than many a European husband—an anomalous and outrageous condition this for a Basha of the Prophet's House. It was also a dangerous one for Fenzileh; for should the burden of her at any time become too heavy for her lord there was a short and easy way by which he could be rid of it. Do not suppose her so foolish as not to have realized this—she realized it fully; but her Sicilian spirit was daring to the point of recklessness; her very dauntlessness which had enabled her to seize a control so unprecedented in a Muslim wife urged her to maintain it in the face of all risks.

Dauntless was she now, as she paced there in the cool of the orchard, under the pink and white petals of the apricots, the flaming scarlet of pomegranate blossoms, and through orange-groves where the golden fruit glowed and amid foliage of sombre green. She was at her eternal work of poisoning the mind of her lord against Sakr-el-Bahr, and in her maternal jealousy she braved the dangers of such an undertaking, fully aware of how dear to the heart of Asad ed Din was that absent renegade corsair. It was this very affection of the Basha's for his lieutenant that was the fomenter of her own hate of Sakr-el-Bahr, for it was an affection that transcended Asad's love for his own son and hers, and it led to the common rumour that for Sakr-el-Bahr was reserved the high destiny of succeeding Asad in the Bashalik.

"I tell thee thou'rt abused by him, O source of my life."

"I hear thee," answered Asad sourly. "And were thine own hearing less infirm, woman, thou wouldst have heard me answer thee that thy words weigh for naught with me against his deeds. Words may be but a mask upon our thoughts; deeds are ever the expression of them. Bear thou that in mind, O Fenzileh."

"Do I not bear in mind thine every word, O fount of wisdom?" she protested, and left him, as she often did, in doubt whether she fawned or sneered. "And it is his deeds I would have speak for him, not indeed my poor words and still less his own."

"Then, by the head of Allah, let those same deeds speak, and be thou silent."

The harsh tone of his reproof and the scowl upon his haughty face, gave her pause for a moment. He turned about.

"Come!" he said. "Soon it will be the hour of prayer." And he paced back towards the yellow huddle of walls of the Kasbah that overtopped the green of that fragrant place.

He was a tall, gaunt man, stooping slightly at the shoulders under the burden of his years; but his eagle face was masterful, and some lingering embers of his youth still glowed in his dark eyes. Thoughtfully, with a jewelled hand, he stroked his long white beard; with the other he leaned upon her soft plump arm, more from habit than for support, for he was full vigorous still.

High in the blue overhead a lark burst suddenly into song, and from the depths of the orchard came a gentle murmur of doves as if returning thanks for the lessening of the great heat now that the sun was sinking rapidly towards the world's edge and the shadows were lengthening.

Came Fenzileh's voice again, more musical than either, yet laden with words of evil, poison wrapped in honey.

"O my dear lord, thou'rt angered with me now. Woe me! that never may I counsel thee for thine own glory as my heart prompts me, but I must earn thy coldness."

"Abuse not him I love," said the Basha shortly. "I have told thee so full oft already."

She nestled closer to him, and her voice grew softer, more akin to the amorous cooing of the doves. "And do I not love thee, O master of my soul? Is there in all the world a heart more faithful to thee than mine? Is not thy life my life? Have not my days been all devoted to the perfecting of thine happiness? And wilt thou then frown upon me if I fear for thee at the hands of an intruder of yesterday?"

"Fear for me?" he echoed, and laughed jeeringly. "What shouldst thou fear for me from Sakr-el-Bahr?"

"What all believers must ever fear from one who is no true Muslim, from one who makes a mock and travesty of the True Faith that he may gain advancement."

The Basha checked in his stride, and turned upon her angrily.

"May thy tongue rot, thou mother of lies!"

"I am as the dust beneath thy feet, O my sweet lord, yet am I not what thine heedless anger calls me."

"Heedless?" quoth he. "Not heedless but righteous to hear one whom the Prophet guards, who is the very javelin of Islam against the breast of the unbeliever, who carries the scourge of Allah against the infidel Frankish pigs, so maligned by thee! No more, I say! Lest I bid thee make good thy words, and pay the liar's price if thou shouldst fail."

"And should I fear the test?" she countered, nothing daunted. "I tell thee, O father of Marzak, that I should hail it gladly. Why, hear me now. Thou settest store by deeds, not words. Tell me, then, is it the deed of a True-Believer to waste substance upon infidel slaves, to purchase them that he may set them free?"

Asad moved on in silence. That erstwhile habit of Sakr-el-Bahr's was one not easy to condone. It had occasioned him his moments of uneasiness, and more than once had he taxed his lieutenant with the practice ever to receive the same answer, the answer which he now made to Fenzileh. "For every slave that he so manumitted, he brought a dozen into bondage."

"Perforce, else would he be called to account. 'Twas so much dust he flung into the face of true Muslimeen. Those manumissions prove a lingering fondness for the infidel country whence he springs. Is there room for that in the heart of a true member of the Prophet's immortal House? Hast ever known me languish for the Sicilian shore from which in thy might thou wrested me, or have I ever besought of thee the life of a single Sicilian infidel in all these years that I have lived to serve thee? Such longings are betrayed, I say, by such a practice, and such longings could have no place in one who had uprooted infidelity from his heart. And now this voyage of his beyond the seas—risking a vessel that he captured from the arch-enemy of Islam, which is not his to risk but thine in whose name he captured it; and together with it he imperils the lives of two hundred True-Believers. To what end? To bear him overseas, perchance that he may look again upon the unhallowed land that gave him birth. So Biskaine reported. And what if he should founder on the way?"

"Thou at least wouldst be content, thou fount of malice," growled Asad.

"Call me harsh names, O sun that warms me! Am I not thine to use and abuse at thy sweet pleasure? Pour salt upon the heart thou woundest; since it is thy hand

I'll never murmur a complaint. But heed me—heed my words; or since words are of no account with thee, then heed his deeds which I am drawing to thy tardy notice. Heed them, I say, as my love bids me even though thou shouldst give me to be whipped or slain for my temerity."

"Woman, thy tongue is like the clapper of a bell with the devil swinging from the rope. What else dost thou impute?"

"Naught else, since thou dost but mock me, withdrawing thy love from thy fond slave."

"The praise to Allah, then," said he. "Come, it is the hour of prayer!"

But he praised Allah too soon. Woman-like, though she protested she had done, she had scarce begun as yet.

"There is thy son, O father of Marzak."

"There is, O mother of Marzak."

"And a man's son should be the partner of his soul. Yet is Marzak passed over for this foreign upstart; yet does this Nasrani of yesterday hold the place in thy heart and at thy side that should be Marzak's."

"Could Marzak fill that place," he asked. "Could that beardless boy lead men as Sakr-el-Bahr leads them, or wield the scimitar against the foes of Islam and increase as Sakr-el-Bahr increases the glory of the Prophet's Holy Law upon the earth?"

"If Sakr-el-Bahr does this, he does it by thy favour, O my lord. And so might Marzak, young though he be. Sakr-el-Bahr is but what thou hast made him—no more, no less."

"There art thou wrong, indeed, O mother of error. Sakr-el-Bahr is what Allah hath made him. He is what Allah wills. He shall become what Allah wills. Hast yet to learn that Allah has bound the fate of each man about his neck?"

And then a golden glory suffused the deep sapphire of the sky heralding the setting of the sun and made an end of that altercation, conducted by her with a daring as singular as the patience that had endured it. He quickened his steps in the direction of the courtyard. That golden glow paled as swiftly as it had spread, and night fell as suddenly as if a curtain had been dropped.

In the purple gloom that followed the white cloisters of the courtyard glowed with a faintly luminous pearliness. Dark forms of slaves stirred as Asad entered from the garden followed by Fenzileh, her head now veiled in a thin blue silken gauze. She flashed across the quadrangle and vanished through one of the archways, even as the distant voice of a Mueddin broke plaintively upon the brooding stillness reciting the Shehad—

"La illaha, illa Allah! Wa Muhammad er Rasool Allah!"

A slave spread a carpet, a second held a great silver bowl, into which a third poured water. The Basha, having washed, turned his face towards Mecca, and testified to the unity of Allah, the Compassionate, the Merciful, King of the Day of judgment, whilst the cry of the Mueddin went echoing over the city from minaret to minaret.

As he rose from his devotions, there came a quick sound of steps without, and a sharp summons. Turkish janissaries of the Basha's guard, invisible almost in their flowing black garments, moved to answer that summons and challenge those who came.

From the dark vaulted entrance of the courtyard leapt a gleam of lanterns containing tiny clay lamps in which burned a wick that was nourished by mutton fat. Asad, waiting to learn who came, halted at the foot of the white glistening steps, whilst from doors and lattices of the palace flooded light to suffuse the courtyard and set the marbles shimmering.

A dozen Nubian javelin-men advanced, then ranged themselves aside whilst into the light stepped the imposing, gorgeously robed figure of Asad's wazeer, Tsamanni. After him came another figure in mail that clanked faintly and glimmered as he moved.

"Peace and the Prophet's blessings upon thee, O mighty Asad!" was the wazeer's greeting.

"And peace upon thee, Tsamanni," was the answer. "Art the bearer of news?"

"Of great and glorious tidings, O exalted one! Sakr-el-Bahr is returned."

"The praise to Him!" exclaimed the Basha, with uplifted hands; and there was no mistaking the thrill of his voice.

There fell a soft step behind him and a shadow from the doorway. He turned. A graceful stripling in turban and caftan of cloth of gold salaamed to him from the topmast step. And as he came upright and the light of the lanterns fell full upon his face the astonishingly white fairness of it was revealed—a woman's face it might have been, so softly rounded was it in its beardlessness.

Asad smiled wrily in his white beard, guessing that the boy had been sent by his ever-watchful mother to learn who came and what the tidings that they bore.

"Thou hast heard, Marzak?" he said. "Sakr-el-Bahr is returned."

"Victoriously, I hope," the lad lied glibly.

"Victorious beyond aught that was ever known," replied Tsamanni. "He sailed at sunset into the harbour, his company aboard two mighty Frankish ships, which are but the lesser part of the great spoil he brings."

"Allah is great," was the Basha's glad welcome of this answer to those insidious promptings of his Sicilian wife. "Why does he not come in person with his news?"

"His duty keeps him yet awhile aboard, my lord," replied the wazeer. "But he hath sent his kayia Othmani here to tell the tale of it."

"Thrice welcome be thou, Othmani." He beat his hands together, whereat slaves placed cushions for him upon the ground. He sat, and beckoned Marzak to his side. "And now thy tale!"

And Othmani standing forth related how they had voyaged to distant England in the ship that Sakr-el-Bahr had captured, through seas that no corsair yet had ever crossed, and how on their return they had engaged a Dutchman that was their superior in strength and numbers; how none the less Sakr-el-Bahr had wrested victory by the help of Allah, his protector, how he had been dealt a wound that must have slain any but one miraculously preserved for the greater glory of Islam, and of the surpassing wealth of the booty which at dawn tomorrow should be laid at Asad's feet for his division of it.

CHAPTER VI. THE CONVERT

That tale of Othmani's being borne anon to Fenzileh by her son was gall and wormwood to her jealous soul. Evil enough to know that Sakr-el-Bahr was returned in spite of the fervent prayers for his foundering which she had addressed both to the God of her forefathers and to the God of her adoption. But that he should have returned in triumph bringing with him heavy spoils that must exalt him further in the affection of Asad and the esteem of the people was bitterness indeed. It left her mute and stricken, bereft even of the power to curse him.

Anon, when her mind recovered from the shock she turned it to the consideration of what at first had seemed a trivial detail in Othmani's tale as reported by Marzak.

"It is most singularly odd that he should have undertaken that long voyage to England to wrest thence just those two captives; that being there he should not have raided in true corsair fashion and packed his ship with slaves. Most singularly odd!"

They were alone behind the green lattices through which filtered the perfumes of the garden and the throbbing of a nightingale's voice laden with the tale of its love for the rose. Fenzileh reclined upon a divan that was spread with silken Turkey carpets, and one of her gold-embroidered slippers had dropped from her henna-stained toes. Her lovely arms were raised to support her head, and she stared up at the lamp of many colours that hung from the fretted ceiling.

Marzak paced the length of the chamber back and forth, and there was silence save for the soft swish of his slippers along the floor.

"Well?" she asked him impatiently at last. "Does it not seem odd to thee?"

"Odd, indeed, O my mother," the youth replied, coming to a halt before her.

"And canst think of naught that was the cause of it?"

"The cause of it?" quoth he, his lovely young face, so closely modelled upon her own, looking blank and vacant.

"Ay, the cause of it," she cried impatiently. "Canst do naught but stare? Am I the mother of a fool? Wilt thou simper and gape and trifle away thy days whilst that dog-descended Frank tramples thee underfoot, using thee but as a stepping-stone to the power that should be thine own? And that be so, Marzak, I would thou hadst been strangled in my womb."

He recoiled before the Italian fury of her, was dully resentful even, suspecting that in such words from a woman were she twenty times his mother, there was something dishonouring to his manhood.

"What can I do?" he cried.

"Dost ask me? Art thou not a man to think and act? I tell thee that misbegotten son of a Christian and a Jew will trample thee in the dust. He is greedy as the locust, wily as the serpent, and ferocious as the panther. By Allah! I would I had never borne a son. Rather might men point at me the finger of scorn and call me mother of the wind than that I should have brought forth a man who knows not how to be a man."

"Show me the way," he cried. "Set me a task; tell me what to do and thou shalt not find me lacking, O my mother. Until then spare me these insults, or I come no more to thee."

At this threat that strange woman heaved herself up from her soft couch. She ran to him and flung her arms about his neck, set her cheek against his own. Not eighteen years in the Basha's hareem had stifled the European mother in her, the passionate Sicilian woman, fierce as a tiger in her maternal love.

"O my child, my lovely boy," she almost sobbed. "It is my fear for thee that makes me harsh. If I am angry it is but my love that speaks, my rage for thee to see another come usurping the place beside thy father that should be thine. Ah! but we will prevail, sweet son of mine. I shall find a way to return that foreign offal to the dung-heap whence it sprang. Trust me, O Marzak! Sh! Thy father comes. Away! Leave me alone with him."

She was wise in that, for she knew that alone Asad was more easily controlled by her, since the pride was absent which must compel him to turn and rend her did she speak so before others. Marzak vanished behind the screen of fretted sandalwood that masked one doorway even as Asad loomed in the other.

He came forward smiling, his slender brown fingers combing his long beard, his white djellaba trailing behind him along the ground.

"Thou hast heard, not a doubt, O Fenzileh," said he. "Art thou answered enough?"

She sank down again upon her cushions and idly considered herself in a steel mirror set in silver.

"Answered?" she echoed lazily, with infinite scorn and a hint of rippling contemptuous laughter running through the word. "Answered indeed. Sakr-el-Bahr risks the lives of two hundred children of Islam and a ship that being taken was become the property of the State upon a voyage to England that has no object but the capturing of two slaves—two slaves, when had his purpose been sincere, it might have been two hundred."

"Ha! And is that all that thou hast heard?" he asked her mocking in his turn.

"All that signifies," she replied, still mirroring herself. "I heard as a matter of lesser import that on his return, meeting fortuitously a Frankish ship that chanced to be richly laden, he seized it in thy name."

"Fortuitously, sayest thou?"

"What else?" She lowered the mirror, and her bold, insolent eyes met his own quite fearlessly. "Thou'lt not tell me that it was any part of his design when he went forth?"

He frowned; his head sank slowly in thought. Observing the advantage gained she thrust it home. "It was a lucky wind that blew that Dutchman into his path, and luckier still her being so richly fraught that he may dazzle thine eyes with the sight of gold and gems, and so blind thee to the real purpose of his voyage."

"Its real purpose?" he asked dully. "What was its real purpose?" She smiled a smile of infinite knowledge to hide her utter ignorance, her inability to supply even a reason that should wear an air of truth.

"Dost ask me, O perspicuous Asad? Are not thine eyes as sharp, thy wits as keen at least as mine, that what is clear to me should be hidden from thee? Or hath this Sakr-el-Bahr bewitched thee with enchantments of Babyl?"

He strode to her and caught her wrist in a cruelly rough grip of his sinewy old hand.

"His purpose, thou jade! Pour out the foulness of thy mind. Speak!"

She sat up, flushed and defiant.

"I will not speak," said she.

"Thou wilt not? Now, by the Head of Allah! dost dare to stand before my face and defy me, thy Lord? I'll have thee whipped, Fenzileh. I have been too tender of thee these many years—so tender that thou hast forgot the rods that await the disobedient wife. Speak then ere thy flesh is bruised or speak thereafter, at thy pleasure."

"I will not," she repeated. "Though I be flung to the hooks, not another word will I say of Sakr-el-Bahr. Shall I unveil the truth to be spurned and scorned and dubbed a liar and the mother of lies?" Then abruptly changing she fell to weeping. "O source of my life!" she cried to him, "how cruelly unjust to me thou art!" She was grovelling now, a thing of supplest grace, her lovely arms entwining his knees. "When my love for thee drives me to utter what I see, I earn but thy anger, which is more than I can endure. I swoon beneath the weight of it."

He flung her off impatiently. "What a weariness is a woman's tongue!" he cried, and stalked out again, convinced from past experiences that did he linger he would be whelmed in a torrent of words.

But her poison was shrewdly administered, and slowly did its work. It abode in his mind to torture him with the doubts that were its very essence. No reason, however well founded, that she might have urged for Sakr-el-Bahr's strange conduct could have been half so insidious as her suggestion that there was a reason. It gave him something vague and intangible to consider. Something that he could not repel since it had no substance he could grapple with. Impatiently he awaited the morning and the coming of Sakr-el-Bahr himself, but he no longer awaited it with the ardent whole-hearted eagerness as of a father awaiting the coming of a beloved son.

Sakr-el-Bahr himself paced the poop deck of the carack and watched the lights perish one by one in the little town that straggled up the hillside before him. The moon came up and bathed it in a white hard light, throwing sharp inky shadows of rustling date palm and spearlike minaret, and flinging shafts of silver athwart the peaceful bay.

His wound was healed and he was fully himself once more. Two days ago he had come on deck for the first time since the fight with the Dutchman, and he had spent there the greater portion of the time since then. Once only had he visited his captives. He had risen from his couch to repair straight to the cabin in the poop where Rosamund was confined. He had found her pale and very wistful, but with her courage entirely unbroken. The Godolphins were a stiff-necked race, and Rosamund bore in her frail body the spirit of a man. She looked up when he entered, started a little in surprise to see him at last, for it was the first time he stood before her since he had carried her off from Arwenack some four weeks ago. Then she had averted her eyes, and sat there, elbows on the table, as if carved of wood, as if blind to his presence and deaf to his words.

To the expressions of regret—and they were sincere, for already he repented him his unpremeditated act so far as she was concerned—she returned no slightest answer, gave no sign indeed that she heard a word of it. Baffled, he stood gnawing his lip a moment, and gradually, unreasonably perhaps, anger welled up from his heart. He turned and went out again. Next he had visited his brother, to consider in silence a moment the haggard, wild-eyed, unshorn wretch who shrank and cowered before him in the consciousness of guilt. At last he returned to the deck, and there, as I have said, he spent the greater portion of the last three days of that strange voyage, reclining for the most part in the sun and gathering strength from its ardour.

To-night as he paced under the moon a stealthy shadow crept up the companion to call him gently by his English name—

"Sir Oliver!"

He started as if a ghost had suddenly leapt up to greet him. It was Jasper Leigh who hailed him thus.

"Come up," he said. And when the fellow stood before him on the poop—"I have told you already that here is no Sir Oliver. I am Oliver-Reis or Sakr-el-Bahr, as you please, one of the Faithful of the Prophet's House. And now what is your will?"

"Have I not served you faithfully and well?" quoth Captain Leigh.

"Who has denied it?"

"None. But neither has any acknowledged it. When you lay wounded below it had been an easy thing for me to ha' played the traitor. I might ha' sailed these ships into the mouth of Tagus. I might so by God!"

"You'ld have been carved in pieces on the spot," said Sakr-el-Bahr.

"I might have hugged the land and run the risk of capture and then claimed my liberation from captivity."

"And found yourself back on the galleys of his Catholic Majesty. But there! I grant that you have dealt loyally by me. You have kept your part of the bond. I shall keep mine, never doubt it."

"I do not. But your part of the bond was to send me home again."

"Well?"

"The hell of it is that I know not where to find a home, I know not where home may be after all these years. If ye send me forth, I shall become a wanderer of no account."

"What else am I to do with you?"

"Faith now I am as full weary of Christians and Christendom as you was yourself when the Muslims took the galley on which you toiled. I am a man of parts, Sir Ol-Sakr-el-Bahr. No better navigator ever sailed a ship from an English port, and I ha' seen a mort o' fighting and know the art of it upon the sea. Can ye make naught of me here?"

"You would become a renegade like me?" His tone was bitter.

"I ha' been thinking that 'renegade' is a word that depends upon which side you're on. I'd prefer to say that I've a wish to be converted to the faith of Mahound."

"Converted to the faith of piracy and plunder and robbery upon the seas is what you mean," said Sakr-el-Bahr.

"Nay, now. To that I should need no converting, for all that I were afore," Captain Leigh admitted frankly. "I ask but to sail under another flag than the Jolly Roger."

"You'll need to abjure strong drink," said Sakr-el-Bahr.

"There be compensations," said Master Leigh.

Sakr-el-Bahr considered. The rogue's appeal smote a responsive chord in his heart. It would be good to have a man of his own race beside him, even though it were but such a rascal as this.

"Be it as you will," he said at last. "You deserve to be hanged in spite of what promises I made you. But no matter for that. So that you become a Muslim I will take you to serve beside me, one of my own lieutenants to begin with, and so long as you are loyal to me, Jasper, all will be well. But at the first sign of faithlessness, a rope and the yard-arm, my friend, and an airy dance into hell for you."

The rascally skipper stooped in his emotion, caught up Sakr-el-Bahr's hand and bore it to his lips. "It is agreed," he said. "Ye have shown me mercy who have little deserved it from you. Never fear for my loyalty. My life belongs to you, and worthless thing though it may be, ye may do with it as ye please."

Despite himself Sakr-el-Bahr tightened his grip upon the rogue's hand, and Jasper shuffled off and down the companion again, touched to the heart for once in his rough villainous life by a clemency that he knew to be undeserved, but which he swore should be deserved ere all was done.

CHAPTER VII. MARZAK-BEN-ASAD

It took no less than forty camels to convey the cargo of that Dutch argosy from the mole to the Kasbah, and the procession—carefully marshalled by Sakr-el-Bahr, who knew the value of such pageants to impress the mob—was such as never yet had been seen in the narrow streets of Algiers upon the return of any corsair. It was full worthy of the greatest Muslim conqueror that sailed the seas, of one who, not content to keep to the tideless Mediterranean as had hitherto been the rule of his kind, had ventured forth upon the wider ocean.

Ahead marched a hundred of his rovers in their short caftans of every conceivable colour, their waists swathed in gaudy scarves, some of which supported a very arsenal of assorted cutlery; many wore body armour of mail and the gleaming spike of a casque thrust up above their turbans. After them, dejected and in chains, came the five score prisoners taken aboard the Dutchman, urged along by the whips of the corsairs who flanked them. Then marched another regiment of corsairs, and after these the long line of stately, sneering camels, shuffling cumbrously along and led by shouting Saharowis. After them followed yet more corsairs, and then mounted, on a white Arab jennet, his head swathed in a turban of cloth of gold, came Sakr-el-Bahr. In the narrower streets, with their white and yellow washed houses, which presented blank windowless walls broken here and there by no more than a slit to admit light and air, the spectators huddled themselves fearfully into doorways to avoid being crushed to death by the camels, whose burdens bulging on either side entirely filled those narrow ways. But the more open spaces, such as the strand on either side of the mole, the square before the sôk, and the approaches of Asad's fortress, were thronged with a motley roaring crowd. There were stately Moors in flowing robes cheek by jowl with half-naked blacks from the Sus and the Draa; lean, enduring Arabs in their spotless white djellabas rubbed shoulders with Berbers from the highlands in black camel-hair cloaks; there were Levantine Turks, and Jewish refugees from Spain ostentatiously dressed in European garments, tolerated there because bound to the Moor by ties of common suffering and common exile from that land that once had been their own.

Under the glaring African sun this amazing crowd stood assembled to welcome Sakr-el-Bahr; and welcome him it did, with such vocal thunder that an echo of it from the mole reached the very Kasbah on the hilltop to herald his approach.

By the time, however, that he reached the fortress his procession had dwindled by more than half. At the sôk his forces had divided, and his corsairs, headed by Othmani, had marched the captives away to the bagnio—or banyard, as my Lord Henry calls it—whilst the camels had continued up the hill. Under the great gateway of the Kasbah they padded into the vast courtyard to be ranged along two sides of it by their Saharowi drivers, and there brought clumsily to their knees. After them followed but some two score corsairs as a guard of honour to their leader. They took their stand upon either side of the gateway after profoundly salaaming to Asad-ed-Din. The Basha sat in the shade of an awning enthroned upon a divan, attended by his wazeer Tsamanni and by Marzak, and guarded by a half-dozen janissaries, whose sable garments made an effective background to the green and gold of his jewelled robes. In his white turban glowed an emerald crescent.

The Basha's countenance was dark and brooding as he watched the advent of that line of burdened camels. His thoughts were still labouring with the doubt of Sakr-el-Bahr which Fenzileh's crafty speech and craftier reticence had planted in them. But at sight of the corsair leader himself his countenance cleared suddenly, his eyes sparkled, and he rose to his feet to welcome him as a father might welcome a son who had been through perils on a service dear to both.

Sakr-el-Bahr entered the courtyard on foot, having dismounted at the gate. Tall and imposing, with his head high and his forked beard thrusting forward, he stalked with great dignity to the foot of the divan followed by Ali and a mahogany-faced fellow, turbaned and red-bearded, in whom it needed more than a glance to recognize the rascally Jasper Leigh, now in all the panoply of your complete renegado.

Sakr-el-Bahr went down upon his knees and prostrated himself solemnly before his prince.

"The blessing of Allah and His peace upon thee, my lord," was his greeting.

And Asad, stooping to lift that splendid figure in his arms, gave him a welcome that caused the spying Fenzileh to clench her teeth behind the fretted lattice that concealed her.

"The praise to Allah and to our Lord Mahomet that thou art returned and in health, my son. Already hath my old heart been gladdened by the news of thy victories in the service of the Faith."

Then followed the display of all those riches wrested from the Dutch, and greatly though Asad's expectations had been fed already by Othmani, the sight now spread before his eyes by far exceeded all those expectations.

In the end all was dismissed to the treasury, and Tsamanni was bidden to go cast up the account of it and mark the share that fell to the portion of those concerned—for in these ventures all were partners, from the Basha himself, who represented the State down to the meanest corsair who had manned the victorious vessels of the Faith, and each had his share of the booty, greater or less according to his rank, one twentieth of the total falling to Sakr-el-Bahr himself.

In the courtyard were left none but Asad, Marzak and the janissaries, and Sakr-el-Bahr with Ali and Jasper. It was then that Sakr-el-Bahr presented his new officer to the Bashal as one upon whom the grace of Allah had descended, a great fighter and a skilled seaman, who had offered up his talents and his life to the service of Islam, who had been accepted by Sakr-el-Bahr, and stood now before Asad to be confirmed in his office.

Marzak interposed petulantly, to exclaim that already were there too many erstwhile Nasrani dogs in the ranks of the soldiers of the Faith, and that it was unwise to increase their number and presumptuous in Sakr-el-Bahr to take so much upon himself.

Sakr-el-Bahr measured him with an eye in which scorn and surprise were nicely blended.

"Dost say that it is presumptuous to win a convert to the banner of Our Lord Mahomet?" quoth he. "Go read the Most Perspicuous Book and see what is there enjoined as a duty upon every True-Believer. And bethink thee, O son of Asad, that when thou dost in thy little wisdom cast scorn upon those whom Allah has blessed and led from the night wherein they dwelt into the bright noontide of Faith, thou dost cast scorn upon me and upon thine own mother, which is but a little matter, and thou dost blaspheme the Blessed name of Allah, which is to tread the ways that lead unto the Pit."

Angry but defeated and silenced, Marzak fell back a step and stood biting his lip and glowering upon the corsair, what time Asad nodded his head and smiled approval.

"Verily art thou full learned in the True Belief, Sakr-el-Bahr," he said. "Thou art the very father of wisdom as of valour." And thereupon he gave welcome to Master Leigh, whom he hailed to the ranks of the Faithful under the designation of Jasper-Reis.

That done, the renegade and Ali were both dismissed, as were also the janissaries, who, quitting their position behind Asad, went to take their stand on guard at the gateway. Then the Basha beat his hands together, and to the slaves who came in answer to his summons he gave orders to set food, and he bade Sakr-el-Bahr to come sit beside him on the divan.

Water was brought that they might wash. That done, the slaves placed before them a savoury stew of meat and eggs with olives, limes, and spices.

Asad broke bread with a reverently pronounced "Bismillah!" and dipped his fingers into the earthenware bowl, leading the way for Sakr-el-Bahr and Marzak, and as they ate he invited the corsair himself to recite the tale of his adventure.

When he had done so, and again Asad had praised him in high and loving terms, Marzak set him a question.

"Was it to obtain just these two English slaves that thou didst undertake this perilous voyage to that distant land?"

"That was but a part of my design," was the calm reply. "I went to rove the seas in the Prophet's service, as the result of my voyage gives proof."

"Thou didst not know that this Dutch argosy would cross thy path," said Marzak, in the very words his mother had prompted him.

"Did I not?" quoth Sakr-el-Bahr, and he smiled confidently, so confidently that Asad scarce needed to hear the words that so cunningly gave the lie to the innuendo. "Had I no trust in Allah the All-wise, the All-knowing?

"Well answered, by the Koran!" Asad approved him heartily, the more heartily since it rebutted insinuations which he desired above all to hear rebutted.

But Marzak did not yet own himself defeated. He had been soundly schooled by his guileful Sicilian mother.

"Yet there is something in all this I do not understand," he murmured, with false gentleness.

"All things are possible to Allah!" said Sakr-el-Bahr, in tones of incredulity, as if he suggested—not without a suspicion of irony—that it was incredible there should be anything in all the world that could elude the penetration of Marzak.

The youth bowed to him in acknowledgment. "Tell me, O mighty Sakr-el-Bahr," he begged, "how it came to pass that having reached those distant shores thou wert content to take thence but two poor slaves, since with thy followers and the favour of the All-seeing thou might easily have taken fifty times that number." And he looked ingenuously into the corsair's swarthy, rugged face, whilst Asad frowned thoughtfully, for the thought was one that had occurred to him already.

It became necessary that Sakr-el-Bahr should lie to clear himself. Here no high-sounding phrase of Faith would answer. And explanation was unavoidable, and he was conscious that he could not afford one that did not go a little lame.

"Why, as to that," said he, "these prisoners were wrested from the first house upon which we came, and their capture occasioned some alarm. Moreover, it was night-time when we landed, and I dared not adventure the lives of my followers by taking them further from the ship and attacking a village which might have risen to cut off our good retreat."

The frown remained stamped upon the brow of Asad, as Marzak slyly observed.

"Yet Othmani," said he, "urged thee to fall upon a slumbering village all unconscious of thy presence, and thou didst refuse."

Asad looked up sharply at that, and Sakr-el-Bahr realized with a tightening about the heart something of the undercurrents at work against him and all the pains that had been taken to glean information that might be used to his undoing.

"Is it so?" demanded Asad, looking from his son to his lieutenant with that lowering look that rendered his face evil and cruel.

Sakr-el-Bahr took a high tone. He met Asad's glance with an eye of challenge.

"And if it were so my lord?" he demanded.

"I asked thee is it so?"

"Ay, but knowing thy wisdom I disbelieved my ears," said Sakr-el-Bahr. "Shall it signify what Othmani may have said? Do I take my orders or am I to be guided by Othmani? If so, best set Othmani in my place, give him the command

and the responsibility for the lives of the Faithful who fight beside him." He ended with an indignant snort.

"Thou art over-quick to anger," Asad reproved him, scowling still

"And by the Head of Allah, who will deny my right to it? Am I to conduct such an enterprise as this from which I am returned laden with spoils that might well be the fruits of a year's raiding, to be questioned by a beardless stripling as to why I was not guided by Othmani?"

He heaved himself up and stood towering there in the intensity of a passion that was entirely simulated. He must bluster here, and crush down suspicion with whorling periods and broad, fierce gesture.

"To what should Othmani have guided me?" he demanded scornfully. "Could he have guided me to more than I have this day laid at thy feet? What I have done speaks eloquently with its own voice. What he would have had me do might well have ended in disaster. Had it so ended, would the blame of it have fallen upon Othmani? Nay, by Allah! but upon me. And upon me rests then the credit, and let none dare question it without better cause."

Now these were daring words to address to the tyrant Asad, and still more daring was the tone, the light hard eyes aflash and the sweeping gestures of contempt with which they were delivered. But of his ascendancy over the Basha there was no doubt. And here now was proof of it.

Asad almost cowered before his fury. The scowl faded from his face to be replaced by an expression of dismay.

"Nay, nay, Sakr-el-Bahr, this tone!" he cried.

Sakr-el-Bahr, having slammed the door of conciliation in the face of the Basha, now opened it again. He became instantly submissive.

"Forgive it," he said. "Blame the devotion of thy servant to thee and to the Faith he serves with little reck to life. In this very expedition was I wounded nigh unto death. The livid scar of it is a dumb witness to my zeal. Where are thy scars, Marzak?"

Marzak quailed before the sudden blaze of that question, and Sakr-el-Bahr laughed softly in contempt.

"Sit," Asad bade him. "I have been less than just."

"Thou art the very fount and spring of justice, O my lord, as this thine admission proves," protested the corsair. He sat down again, folding his legs under him. "I will confess to you that being come so near to England in that cruise of mine I determined to land and seize one who some years ago did injure me, and between whom and me there was a score to settle. I exceeded my intentions in that I carried off two prisoners instead of one. These prisoners," he ran on, judging that the moment of reaction in Asad's mind was entirely favourable to the preferment of the request he had to make, "are not in the bagnio with the others. They are still confined aboard the carack I seized."

"And why is this?" quoth Asad, but without suspicion now.

"Because, my lord, I have a boon to ask in some reward for the service I have rendered."

"Ask it, my son."

"Give me leave to keep these captives for myself."

Asad considered him, frowning again slightly. Despite himself, despite his affection for Sakr-el-Bahr, and his desire to soothe him now that rankling poison of Fenzileh's infusing was at work again in his mind.

"My leave thou hast," said he. "But not the law's, and the law runs that no corsair shall subtract so much as the value of an asper from his booty until the division has been made and his own share allotted him," was the grave answer.

"The law?" quoth Sakr-el-Bahr. "But thou art the law, exalted lord."

"Not so, my son. The law is above the Basha, who must himself conform to it so that he be just and worthy of his high office. And the law I have recited thee applies even should the corsair raider be the Basha himself. These slaves of thine must forthwith be sent to the bagnio to join the others that tomorrow all may be sold in the sôk. See it done, Sakr-el-Bahr."

The corsair would have renewed his pleadings, but that his eye caught the eager white face of Marzak and the gleaming expectant eyes, looking so hopefully for his ruin. He checked, and bowed his head with an assumption of indifference.

"Name thou their price then, and forthwith will I pay it into thy treasury."

But Asad shook his head. "It is not for me to name their price, but for the buyers," he replied. "I might set the price too high, and that were unjust to thee, or too low, and that were unjust to others who would acquire them. Deliver them over to the bagnio."

"It shall be done," said Sakr-el-Bahr, daring to insist no further and dissembling his chagrin.

Very soon thereafter he departed upon that errand, giving orders, however, that Rosamund and Lionel should be kept apart from the other prisoners until the hour of the sale on the morrow when perforce they must take their place with the rest.

Marzak lingered with his father after Oliver had taken his leave, and presently they were joined there in the courtyard by Fenzileh—this woman who had brought, said many, the Frankish ways of Shaitan into Algiers.

CHAPTER VIII. MOTHER AND SON

Early on the morrow—so early that scarce had the Shehad been recited—came Biskaine-el-Borak to the Basha. He had just landed from a galley which had come upon a Spanish fishing boat, aboard of which there was a young Morisco who was being conducted over seas to Algiers. The news of which the fellow was the bearer was of such urgency that for twenty hours without intermission the slaves had toiled at the oars of Biskaine's vessel—the capitana of his fleet—to bring her swiftly home.

The Morisco had a cousin—a New-Christian like himself, and like himself, it would appear, still a Muslim at heart—who was employed in the Spanish treasury at Malaga. This man had knowledge that a galley was fitting out for sea to convey to Naples the gold destined for the pay of the Spanish troops in garrison there. Through parsimony this treasure-galley was to be afforded no escort, but was under orders to hug the coast of Europe, where she should be safe from all piratical surprise. It was judged that she would be ready to put to sea in a week, and the Morisco had set out at once to bring word of it to his Algerine brethren that they might intercept and capture her.

Asad thanked the young Morisco for his news, bade him be housed and cared for, and promised him a handsome share of the plunder should the treasure-galley be captured. That done he sent for Sakr-el-Bahr, whilst Marzak, who had been present at the interview, went with the tale of it to his mother, and beheld her fling into a passion when he added that it was Sakr-el-Bahr had been summoned that he might be entrusted with this fresh expedition, thus proving that all her crafty innuendoes and insistent warnings had been so much wasted labour.

With Marzak following at her heels, she swept like a fury into the darkened room where Asad took his ease.

"What is this I hear, O my lord?" she cried, in tone and manner more the European shrew than the submissive Eastern slave. "Is Sakr-el-Bahr to go upon this expedition against the treasure-galley of Spain?"

Reclining on his divan he looked her up and down with a languid eye. "Dost know of any better fitted to succeed?" quoth he.

"I know of one whom it is my lord's duty to prefer to that foreign adventurer. One who is entirely faithful and entirely to be trusted. One who does not attempt to retain for himself a portion of the booty garnered in the name of Islam."

"Bah!" said Asad. "Wilt thou talk forever of those two slaves? And who may be this paragon of thine?"

"Marzak," she answered fiercely, flinging out an arm to drag forward her son. "Is he to waste his youth here in softness and idleness? But yesternight that ribald mocked him with his lack of scars. Shall he take scars in the orchard of the Kasbah here? Is he to be content with those that come from the scratch of a bramble, or is he to learn to be a fighter and leader of the Children of the Faith that himself he may follow in the path his father trod?"

"Whether he so follows," said Asad, "is as the Sultan of Istambul, the Sublime Portal, shall decree. We are but his vicegerents here."

"But shall the Grand Sultan appoint him to succeed thee if thou hast not equipped him so to do? I cry shame on thee, O father of Marzakl, for that thou art lacking in due pride in thine own son."

"May Allah give me patience with thee! Have I not said that he is still over young."

"At his age thyself thou wert upon the seas, serving with the great Ochiali."

"At his age I was, by the favour of Allah, taller and stronger than is he. I cherish him too dearly to let him go forth and perchance be lost to me before his strength is full grown."

"Look at him," she commanded. "He is a man, Asad, and such a son as another might take pride in. Is it not time he girt a scimitar about his waist and trod the poop of one of thy galleys?"

"Indeed, indeed, O my father!" begged Marzak himself.

"What?" barked the old Moor. "And is it so? And wouldst thou go forth then against the Spaniard? What knowledge hast thou that shall equip thee for such a task?"

"What can his knowledge be since his father has never been concerned to school him?" returned Fenzileh. "Dost thou sneer at shortcomings that are the natural fruits of thine own omissions?"

"I will be patient with thee," said Asad, showing every sign of losing patience. "I will ask thee only if in thy judgment he is in case to win a victory for Islam? Answer me straightly now."

"Straightly I answer thee that he is not. And, as straightly, I tell thee that it is full time he were. Thy duty is to let him go upon this expedition that he may learn the trade that lies before him."

Asad considered a moment. Then: "Be it so," he answered slowly. "Shalt set forth, then, with Sakr-el-Bahr, my son."

"With Sakr-el-Bahr?" cried Fenzilch aghast.

"I could find him no better preceptor."

"Shall thy son go forth as the servant of another?"

"As the pupil," Asad amended. "What else?"

"Were I a man, O fountain of my soul," said she, "and had I a son, none but myself should be his preceptor. I should so mould and fashion him that he should be another me. That, O my dear lord, is thy duty to Marzak. Entrust not his training to another and to one whom despite thy love for him I cannot trust. Go forth thyself upon this expedition with Marzak here for thy kayia."

Asad frowned. "I grow too old," he said. "I have not been upon the seas these two years past. Who can say that I may not have lost the art of victory. No, no." He shook his head, and his face grew overcast and softened by wistfulness. "Sakr-el-Bahr commands this time, and if Marzak goes, he goes with him."

"My lord...." she began, then checked. A Nubian had entered to announce that Sakr-el-Bahr was come and was awaiting the orders of his lord in the courtyard. Asad rose instantly and for all that Fenzileh, greatly daring as ever, would still have detained him, he shook her off impatiently, and went out.

She watched his departure with anger in those dark lovely eyes of hers, an anger that went near to filming them in tears, and after he had passed out into the glaring sunshine beyond the door, a silence dwelt in the cool darkened chamber—a silence disturbed only by distant trills of silvery laughter from the lesser women of the Basha's house. The sound jarred her taut nerves. She moved with an oath and beat her hands together. To answer her came a negress, lithe and muscular as a wrestler and naked to the waist; the slave ring in her ear was of massive gold.

"Bid them make an end of that screeching," she snapped to vent some of her fierce petulance. "Tell them I will have the rods to them if they again disturb me."

The negress went out, and silence followed, for those other lesser ladies of the Basha's hareem were more obedient to the commands of Fenzileh than to those of the Basha himself.

Then she drew her son to the fretted lattice commanding the courtyard, a screen from behind which they could see and hear all that passed out yonder. Asad was speaking, informing Sakr-el-Bahr of what he had learnt, and what there was to do.

"How soon canst thou put to sea again?" he ended

"As soon as the service of Allah and thyself require," was the prompt answer.

"It is well, my son." Asad laid a hand, affectionately upon the corsair's shoulder, entirely conquered by this readiness. "Best set out at sunrise to-morrow. Thou'lt need so long to make thee ready for the sea."

"Then by thy leave I go forthwith to give orders to prepare," replied Sakr-el-Bahr, for all that he was a little troubled in his mind by this need to depart again so soon.

"What galleys shalt thou take?"

"To capture one galley of Spain? My own galeasse, no more; she will be full equal to such an enterprise, and I shall be the better able, then, to lurk and take cover—a thing which might well prove impossible with a fleet."

"Ay—thou art wise in thy daring," Asad approved him. "May Allah prosper thee upon the voyage."

"Have I thy leave to go?"

"A moment yet. There is my son Marzak. He is approaching manhood, and it is time he entered the service of Allah and the State. It is my desire that he sail as thy lieutenant on this voyage, and that thou be his preceptor even as I was thine of old."

Now here was something that pleased Sakr-el-Bahr as little as it pleased Marzak. Knowing the bitter enmity borne him by the son of Fenzileh he had every cause to fear trouble if this project of Asad's were realized.

"As I was thine of old!" he answered with crafty wistfulness. "Wilt thou not put to sea with us to-morrow, O Asad? There is none like thee in all Islam, and what a joy were it not to stand beside thee on the prow as of old when we grapple with the Spaniard."

Asad considered him. "Dost thou, too, urge this?" quoth he.

"Have others urged it?" The man's sharp wits, rendered still sharper by his sufferings, were cutting deeply and swiftly into this matter. "They did well, but none could have urged it more fervently than I, for none knows so well as I the joy of battle against the infidel under thy command and the glory of prevailing in thy sight. Come, then, my lord, upon this enterprise, and be thyself thine own son's preceptor since 'tis the highest honour thou canst bestow upon him."

Thoughtfully Asad stroked his long white beard, his eagle eyes growing narrow. "Thou temptest me, by Allah!"

"Let me do more...."

"Nay, more thou canst not. I am old and worn, and I am needed here. Shall an old lion hunt a young gazelle? Peace, peace! The sun has set upon my fighting day. Let the brood of fighters I have raised up keep that which my arm conquered and maintain my name and the glory of the Faith upon the seas." He leaned upon Sakr-el-Bahr's shoulder and sighed, his eyes wistfully dreamy. "It were a fond adventure in good truth. But no...I am resolved. Go thou and take Marzak with thee, and bring him safely home again."

"I should not return myself else," was the answer. "But my trust is in the All-knowing."

Upon that he departed, dissembling his profound vexation both at the voyage and the company, and went to bid Othmani make ready his great galeasse, equipping it with carronades, three hundred slaves to row it, and three hundred fighting men.

Asad-el-Din returned to that darkened room in the Kasbah overlooking the courtyard, where Fenzileh and Marzak still lingered. He went to tell them that in compliance with the desires of both Marzak should go forth to prove himself upon this expedition.

But where he had left impatience he found thinly veiled wrath

"O sun that warms me," Fenzileh greeted him, and from long experience he knew that the more endearing were her epithets the more vicious was her mood, "do then my counsels weigh as naught with thee, are they but as the dust upon thy shoes?"

"Less," said Asad, provoked out of his habitual indulgence of her licences of speech.

"That is the truth, indeed!" she cried, bowing her head, whilst behind her the handsome face of her son was overcast.

"It is," Asad agreed. "At dawn, Marzak, thou settest forth upon the galeasse of Sakr-el-Bahr to take the seas under his tutelage and to emulate the skill and valour that have rendered him the stoutest bulwark of Islam, the very javelin of Allah."

But Marzak felt that in this matter his mother was to be supported, whilst his detestation of this adventurer who threatened to usurp the place that should rightly be his own spurred him to mad lengths of daring.

"When I take the seas with that dog-descended Nasrani," he answered hoarsely, "he shall be where rightly he belongs—at the rowers' bench."

"How?" It was a bellow of rage. Upon the word Asad swung to confront his son, and his face, suddenly inflamed, was so cruel and evil in its expression that it terrified that intriguing pair. "By the beard of the Prophet! what words are these to me?" He advanced upon Marzak until Fenzileh in sudden terror stepped between and faced him, like a lioness springing to defend her cub. But the Basha, enraged now by this want of submission in his son, enraged both against that son and the mother who he knew had prompted him, caught her in his sinewy old hands, and flung her furiously aside, so that she stumbled and fell in a panting heap amid the cushions of her divan.

"The curse of Allah upon thee!" he screamed, and Marzak recoiled before him. "Has this presumptuous hellcat who bore thee taught thee to stand before my face, to tell me what thou wilt and wilt not do? By the Koran! too long have I endured her evil foreign ways, and now it seems she has taught thee how to tread them after her and how to beard thy very father! To-morrow thou'lt take the sea with Sakr-el-Bahr, I have said it. Another word and thou'lt go aboard his galeasse even as thou saidst should be the case with him—at the rowers' bench, to learn submission under the slave master's whip."

Terrified, Marzak stood numb and silent, scarcely daring to draw breath. Never in all his life had he seen his father in a rage so royal. Yet it seemed to inspire no fear in Fenzileh, that congenital shrew whose tongue not even the threat of rods or hooks could silence.

"I shall pray Allah to restore sight to thy soul, O father of Marzak," she panted, "to teach thee to discriminate between those that love thee and the self-seekers that abuse thy trust."

"How!" he roared at her. "Art not yet done?"

"Nor ever shall be until I am lain dumb in death for having counselled thee out of my great love, O light of these poor eyes of mine."

"Maintain this tone," he said, with concentrated anger, "and that will soon befall."

"I care not so that the sleek mask be plucked from the face of that dog-descended Sakr-el-Bahr. May Allah break his bones! What of those slaves of his—those two from England, O Asad? I am told that one is a woman, tall and of that white beauty which is the gift of Eblis to these Northerners. What is his purpose with her—that he would not show her in the suk as the law prescribes, but comes slinking here to beg thee set aside the law for him? Ha! I talk in vain. I have shown thee graver things to prove his vile disloyalty, and yet thou'lt fawn upon him whilst thy fangs are bared to thine own son."

He advanced upon her, stooped, caught her by the wrist, and heaved her up.

His face showed grey under its deep tan. His aspect terrified her at last and made an end of her reckless forward courage.

He raised his voice to call.

"Ya anta! Ayoub!"

She gasped, livid in her turn with sudden terror. "My lord, my lord!" she whimpered. "Stream of my life, be not angry! What wilt thou do?"

He smiled evilly. "Do?" he growled. "What I should have done ten years ago and more. We'll have the rods to thee." And again he called, more insistently—"Ayoub!"

"My lord, my lord!" she gasped in shuddering horror now that at last she found him set upon the thing to which so often she had dared him. "Pity! Pity!" She grovelled and embraced his knees. "In the name of the Pitying the Pitiful be merciful upon the excesses to which my love for thee may have driven this poor tongue of mine. O my sweet lord! O father of Marzak!"

Her distress, her beauty, and perhaps, more than either, her unusual humility and submission may have moved him. For even as at that moment Ayoub—the sleek and portly eunuch, who was her wazeer and chamberlain—loomed in the inner doorway, salaaming, he vanished again upon the instant, dismissed by a peremptory wave of the Basha's hand.

Asad looked down upon her, sneering. "That attitude becomes thee best," he said. "Continue it in future." Contemptuously he shook himself free of her grasp, turned and stalked majestically out, wearing his anger like a royal mantle, and leaving behind him two terror-shaken beings, who felt as if they had looked over the very edge of death.

There was a long silence between them. Then at long length Fenzileh rose and crossed to the meshra-biyah—the latticed window-box. She opened it and took from one of its shelves an earthenware jar, placed there so as to receive the slightest breeze. From it she poured water into a little cup and drank greedily. That she could perform this menial service for herself when a mere clapping of hands would have brought slaves to minister to her need betrayed something of her disordered state of mind.

She slammed the inner lattice and turned to Marzak. "And now?" quoth she.

"Now?" said the lad.

"Ay, what now? What are we to do? Are we to lie crushed under his rage until we are ruined indeed? He is bewitched. That jackal has enchanted him, so that he must deem well done all that is done by him. Allah guide us here, Marzak, or thou'lt be trampled into dust by Sakr-el-Bahr."

Marzak hung his head; slowly he moved to the divan and flung himself down upon its pillows; there he lay prone, his hands cupping his chin, his heels in the air.

"What can I do?" he asked at last.

"That is what I most desire to know. Something must be done, and soon. May his bones rot! If he lives thou art destroyed."

"Ay," said Marzak, with sudden vigour and significance. "If he lives!" And he sat up. "Whilst we plan and plot, and our plans and plots come to naught save to provoke the anger of my father, we might be better employed in taking the shorter way."

She stood in the middle of the chamber, pondering him with gloomy eyes "I too have thought of that," said she. "I could hire me men to do the thing for a handful of gold. But the risk of it...."

"Where would be the risk once he is dead?"

"He might pull us down with him, and then what would our profit be in his death? Thy father would avenge him terribly."

"If it were craftily done we should not be discovered."

"Not be discovered?" she echoed, and laughed without mirth. "How young and blind thou art, O Marzak! We should be the first to be suspected. I have made no secret of my hate of him, and the people do not love me. They would urge thy father to do justice even were he himself averse to it, which I will not credit would be the case. This Sakr-el-Bahr—may Allah wither him!—is a god in their eyes. Bethink thee of the welcome given him! What Basha returning in triumph was ever greeted by the like? These victories that fortune has vouchsafed him have made them account him divinely favoured and protected. I tell thee, Marzak, that did thy father die to-morrow Sakr-el-Bahr would be proclaimed Basha of Algiers in his stead, and woe betide us then. And Asad-el-Din grows old. True, he does not go forth to fight. He clings to life and may last long. But if he should not, and if Sakr-el-Bahr should still walk the earth when thy father's destiny is fulfilled, I dare not think what then will be thy fate and mine."

"May his grave be defiled!" growled Matzak.

"His grave?" said she. "The difficulty is to dig it for him without hurt to ourselves. Shaitan protects the dog."

"May he make his bed in hell!" said Marzak.

"To curse him will not help us. Up, Marzak, and consider how the thing is to be done."

Marzak came to his feet, nimble and supple as a greyhound. "Listen now," he said. "Since I must go this voyage with him, perchance upon the seas on some dark night opportunity may serve me."

"Wait! Let me consider it. Allah guide me to find some way!" She beat her hands together and bade the slave girl who answered her to summon her wazeer Ayoub, and bid a litter be prepared for her. "We'll to the sôk, O Marzak, and see these slaves of his. Who knows but that something may be done by means of them! Guile will serve us better than mere strength against that misbegotten son of shame."

"May his house be destroyed!" said Marzak.

CHAPTER IX. COMPETITORS

The open space before the gates of the sôk-el-Abeed was thronged with a motley, jostling, noisy crowd that at every moment was being swelled by the human streams pouring to mingle in it from the debauching labyrinth of narrow, unpaved streets.

There were brown-skinned Berbers in black goat-hair cloaks that were made in one piece with a cowl and decorated by a lozenge of red or orange colour on the back, their shaven heads encased in skull-caps or simply bound in a cord of plaited camel-hair; there were black Saharowi who went almost naked, and stately Arabs who seemed overmuffled in their flowing robes of white with the cowls overshadowing their swarthy, finely featured faces; there were dignified and prosperous-looking Moors in brightly coloured selhams astride of sleek mules that were richly caparisoned; and there were Tagareenes, the banished Moors of Andalusia, most of whom followed the trade of slave-dealers; there were native Jews in sombre black djellabas, and Christian-Jews—so-called because bred in Christian countries, whose garments they still wore; there were Levantine Turks, splendid of dress and arrogant of demeanour, and there were humble Cololies, Kabyles and Biscaries. Here a water-seller, laden with his goatskin vessel, tinkled his little bell; there an orange-hawker, balancing a basket of the golden fruit upon his ragged turban, bawled his wares. There were men on foot and men on mules, men on donkeys and men on slim Arab horses, an ever-shifting medley of colours, all jostling, laughing, cursing in the ardent African sunshine under the blue sky where pigeons circled. In the shadow of the yellow tapia wall squatted a line of whining beggars and cripples soliciting alms; near the gates a little space had been cleared and an audience had gathered in a ring about a Meddah—a beggar-troubadour—who, to the accompaniment of gimbri and gaitah from two acolytes, chanted a doleful ballad in a thin, nasal voice.

Those of the crowd who were patrons of the market held steadily amain, and, leaving their mounts outside, passed through the gates through which there was no admittance for mere idlers and mean folk. Within the vast quadrangular space of bare, dry ground, enclosed by dust-coloured walls, there was more space. The sale of slaves had not yet begun and was not due to begin for another hour, and meanwhile a little trading was being done by those merchants who had obtained the coveted right to set up their booths against the walls; they were vendors of wool, of fruit, of spices, and one or two traded in jewels and trinkets for the adornment of the Faithful.

A well was sunk in the middle of the ground, a considerable octagon with a low parapet in three steps. Upon the nethermost of these sat an aged, bearded Jew in a black djellaba, his head swathed in a coloured kerchief. Upon his knees reposed a broad, shallow black box, divided into compartments, each filled with lesser gems and rare stones, which he was offering for sale; about him stood a little group of young Moors and one or two Turkish officers, with several of whom the old Israelite was haggling at once.

The whole of the northern wall was occupied by a long penthouse, its contents completely masked by curtains of camel-hair; from behind it proceeded a subdued murmur of human voices. These were the pens in which were confined the slaves to be offered for sale that day. Before the curtains, on guard, stood some dozen corsairs with attendant negro slaves.

Beyond and above the wall glistened the white dome of a zowia, flanked by a spear-like minaret and the tall heads of a few date palms whose long leaves hung motionless in the hot air.

Suddenly in the crowd beyond the gates there was a commotion. From one of the streets six colossal Nubians advanced with shouts of—

"Oak! Oak! Warda! Way! Make way!"

They were armed with great staves, grasped in their two hands, and with these they broke a path through that motley press, hurling men to right and left and earning a shower of curses in return.

"Balâk! Make way! Way for the Lord Asad-ed-Din, the exalted of Allah! Way!"

The crowd, pressing back, went down upon its knees and grovelled as Asad-ed-Din on a milk-white mule rode forward, escorted by Tsamanni his wazeer and a cloud of black-robed janissaries with flashing scimitars.

The curses that had greeted the violence of his negroes were suddenly silenced; instead, blessings as fervent filled the air.

"May Allah increase thy might! May Allah lengthen thy days! The blessings of our Lord Mahomet upon thee! Allah send thee more victories!" were the benedictions that showered upon him on every hand. He returned them as became a man who was supremely pious and devout.

"The peace of Allah upon the Faithful of the Prophet's House," he would murmur in response from time to time, until at last he had reached the gates. There he bade Tsamanni fling a purse to the crouching beggars—for is it not written in the Most Perspicuous Book that of alms ye shall bestow what ye can spare, for such as are saved from their own greed shall prosper, and whatever ye give in alms, as seeking the face of Allah shall be doubled unto you?

Submissive to the laws as the meanest of his subjects, Asad dismounted and passed on foot into the sôk. He came to a halt by the well, and, facing the curtained penthouse, he blessed the kneeling crowd and commanded all to rise.

He beckoned Sakr-el-Bahr's officer Ali—who was in charge of the slaves of the corsair's latest raid and announced his will to inspect the captives. At a sign from Ali, the negroes flung aside the camel-hair curtains and let the fierce sunlight beat in upon those pent-up wretches; they were not only the captives taken by Sakr-el-Bahr, but some others who were the result of one or two lesser raids by Biskaine.

Asad beheld a huddle of men and women—though the proportion of women was very small—of all ages, races, and conditions; there were pale fair-haired men from France or the North, olive-skinned Italians and swarthy Spaniards, negroes and half-castes; there were old men, young men and mere children, some handsomely dressed, some almost naked, others hung with rags. In the hopeless dejection of their countenances alone was there any uniformity. But it was not a dejection that could awaken pity in the pious heart of Asad. They were unbelievers who would never look upon the face of God's Prophet, accursed and unworthy of any tenderness from man. For a moment his glance was held by a lovely black-haired Spanish girl, who sat with her locked hands held fast between her knees, in an attitude of intense despair and suffering—the glory of her eyes increased and magnified by the dark brown stains of sleeplessness surrounding them. Leaning on Tsamanni's arm, he stood considering her for a little while; then his glance travelled on. Suddenly he tightened his grasp of Tsamanni's arm and a quick interest leapt into his sallow face.

On the uppermost tier of the pen that he was facing sat a very glory of womanhood, such a woman as he had heard tell existed but the like of which he had never yet beheld. She was tall and graceful as a cypress-tree; her skin was white as milk, her eyes two darkest sapphires, her head of a coppery golden that seemed to glow like metal as the sunlight caught it. She was dressed in a close gown of white, the bodice cut low and revealing the immaculate loveliness of her neck.

Asad-ed-Din turned to Ali. "What pearl is this that hath been cast upon this dung-heap?" he asked.

"She is the woman our lord Sakr-el-Bahr carried off from England." Slowly the Basha's eyes returned to consider her, and insensible though she had deemed herself by now, he saw her cheeks slowly reddening under the cold insult of his steady, insistent glance. The glow heightened her beauty, effacing the weariness which the face had worn.

"Bring her forth," said the Basha shortly.

She was seized by two of the negroes, and to avoid being roughly handled by them she came at once, bracing herself to bear with dignity whatever might await her. A golden-haired young man beside her, his face haggard and stubbled with a beard of some growth, looked up in alarm as she was taken from his side. Then, with a groan, he made as if to clutch her, but a rod fell upon his raised arms and beat thbm down.

Asad was thoughtful. It was Fenzileh who had bidden him come look at the infidel maid whom Sakr-el-Bahr had risked so much to snatch from England, suggesting that in her he would behold some proof of the bad faith which she was forever urging against the corsair leader. He beheld the woman, but he discovered about her no such signs as Fenzileh had suggested he must find, nor indeed did he look for any. Out of curiosity had he obeyed her prompting. But that and all else were forgotten now in the contemplation of this noble ensample of Northern womanhood, statuesque almost in her terrible restraint.

He put forth a hand to touch her arm, and she drew it back as if his fingers were of fire.

He sighed. "How inscrutable are the ways of Allah, that He should suffer so luscious a fruit to hang from the foul tree of infidelity!"

Tsamanni watching him craftily, a master-sycophant profoundly learned in the art of playing upon his master's moods, made answer:

"Even so perchance that a Faithful of the Prophet's House may pluck it. Verily all things are possible to the One!"

"Yet is it not set down in the Book to be Read that the daughters of the infidel are not for True-Believers?" And again he sighed.

But Tsamanni knowing full well how the Basha would like to be answered, trimmed his reply to that desire.

"Allah is great, and what hath befallen once may well befall again, my lord."

Asad's kindling eyes flashed a glance at his wazeer.

"Thou meanest Fenzileh. But then, by the mercy of Allah, I was rendered the instrument of her enlightenment."

"It may well be written that thou shalt be the same again, my lord," murmured the insidious Tsamanni. There was more stirring in his mind than the mere desire to play the courtier now. 'Twixt Fenzileh and himself there had long been a feud begotten of the jealousy which each inspired in the other where Asad was concerned. Were Fenzileh removed the wazeer's influence must grow and spread to his own profit. It was a thing of which he had often dreamed, but a dream he feared that was never like to be realized, for Asad was ageing, and the fires that had burned so fiercely in his earlier years seemed now to have consumed in him all thought of women. Yet here was one as by a miracle, of a beauty so amazing and so diverse from any that ever yet had feasted the Basha's sight, that plainly she had acted as a charm upon his senses.

"She is white as the snows upon the Atlas, luscious as the dates of Tafilalt," he murmured fondly, his gleaming eyes considering her what time she stood immovable before him. Suddenly he looked about him, and wheeled upon Tsamanni, his manner swiftly becoming charged with anger.

"Her face has been bared to a thousand eyes and more," he cried.

"Even that has been so before," replied Tsamanni.

And then quite suddenly at their elbow a voice that was naturally soft and musical of accent but now rendered harsh, cut in to ask:

"What woman may this be?"

Startled, both the Basha and his wazeer swung round. Fenzileh, becomingly veiled and hooded, stood before them, escorted by Marzak. A little behind them were the eunuchs and the litter in which, unperceived by Asad, she had been borne thither. Beside the litter stood her wazeer Ayoub-el-Samin.

Asad scowled down upon her, for he had not yet recovered from the resentment she and Marzak had provoked in him. Moreover, that in private she should be lacking in the respect which was his due was evil enough, though he had tolerated it. But that she should make so bold as to thrust in and question him in this peremptory fashion before all the world was more than his dignity could suffer. Never yet had she dared so much nor would she have dared it now but that her sudden anxiety had effaced all caution from her mind. She had seen the look with which Asad had been considering that lovely slave, and not only jealousy but positive fear awoke in her. Her hold upon Asad was growing tenuous. To snap it utterly no more was necessary than that he who of late years had scarce bestowed a thought or glance upon a woman should be taken with the fancy to bring some new recruit to his hareem.

Hence her desperate, reckless courage to stand thus before him now, for although her face was veiled there was hardy arrogance in every line of her figure. Of his scowl she took no slightest heed.

"If this be the slave fetched by Sakr-el-Bahr from England, then rumour has lied to me," she said. "I vow it was scarce worth so long a voyage and the endangering so many valuable Muslim lives to fetch this yellow-faced, long-shanked daughter of perdition into Barbary."

Asad's surprise beat down his anger. He was not subtle.

"Yellow-faced? Long-shanked?" quoth he. Then reading Fenzileh at last, he displayed a slow, crooked smile. "Already have I observed thee to grow hard of hearing, and now thy sight is failing too, it seems. Assuredly thou art growing old." And he looked her over with such an eye of displeasure that she recoiled.

He stepped close up to her. "Too long already hast thou queened it in my hareem with thine infidel, Frankish ways," he muttered, so that none but those immediately about overheard his angry words. "Thou art become a very scandal in the eyes of the Faithful," he added very grimly. "It were well, perhaps, that we amended that."

Abruptly then he turned away, and by a gesture he ordered Ali to return the slave to her place among the others. Leaning on the arm of Tsamanni he took some steps towards the entrance, then halted, and turned again to Fenzileh:

"To thy litter," he bade her peremptorily, rebuking her thus before all, "and get thee to the house as becomes a seemly Muslim woman. Nor ever again let thyself be seen roving the public places afoot."

She obeyed him instantly, without a murmur; and he himself lingered at the gates with Tsamanni until her litter had passed out, escorted by Ayoub and Marzak walking each on one side of it and neither daring to meet the angry eye of the Basha.

Asad looked sourly after that litter, a sneer on his heavy lips.

"As her beauty wanes so her presumption waxes," he growled. "She is growing old, Tsamanni—old and lean and shrewish, and no fit mate for a Member of the

Prophet's House. It were perhaps a pleasing thing in the sight of Allah that we replaced her." And then, referring obviously to that other one, his eye turning towards the penthouse the curtains of which were drawn again, he changed his tone.

"Didst thou mark, O Tsamanni, with what a grace she moved?—lithely and nobly as a young gazelle. Verily, so much beauty was never created by the All-Wise to be cast into the Pit."

"May it not have been sent to comfort some True-Believer?" wondered the subtle wazeer. "To Allah all things are possible."

"Why else, indeed?" said Asad. "It was written; and even as none may obtain what is not written, so none may avoid what is. I am resolved. Stay thou here, Tsamanni. Remain for the outcry and purchase her. She shall be taught the True Faith. She shall be saved from the furnace." The command had come, the thing that Tsamanni had so ardently desired.

He licked his lips. "And the price, my lord?" he asked, in a small voice.

"Price?" quoth Asad. "Have I not bid thee purchase her? Bring her to me, though her price be a thousand philips."

"A thousand philips!" echoed Tsamanni amazed. "Allah is great!"

But already Asad had left his side and passed out under the arched gateay, where the grovelling anew at the sight of him.

It was a fine thing for Asad to bid him remain for the sale. But the dalal would part with no slave until the money was forthcoming, and Tsamanni had no considerable sum upon his person. Therefore in the wake of his master he set out forthwith to the Kasbah. It wanted still an hour before the sale would be held and he had time and to spare in which to go and return.

It happened, however, that Tsamanni was malicious, and that the hatred of Fenzileh which so long he had consumed in silence and dissembled under fawning smiles and profound salaams included also her servants. There was none in all the world of whom he entertained a greater contempt than her sleek and greasy eunuch Ayoub-el-Samin of the majestic, rolling gait and fat, supercilious lips.

It was written, too, that in the courtyard of the Kasbah he should stumble upon Ayoub, who indeed had by his mistress's commands been set to watch for the wazeer. The fat fellow rolled forward, his hands supporting his paunch, his little eyes agleam.

"Allah increase thy health, Tsamanni," was his courteous greeting. "Thou bearest news?"

"News? What news?" quoth Tsamanni. "In truth none that will gladden thy mistress."

"Merciful Allah! What now? Doth it concern that Frankish slave-girl?"

Tsamanni smiled, a thing that angered Ayoub, who felt that the ground he trod was becoming insecure; it followed that if his mistress fell from influence he fell with her, and became as the dust upon Tsamanni's slippers.

"By the Koran thou tremblest, Ayoub!" Tsamanni mocked him. "Thy soft fat is all a-quivering; and well it may, for thy days are numbered, O father of nothing."

"Dost deride me, dog?" came the other's voice, shrill now with anger.

"Callest me dog? Thou?" Deliberately Tsamanni spat upon his shadow. "Go tell thy mistress that I am bidden by my lord to buy the Frankish girl. Tell her that my lord will take her to wife, even as he took Fenzileh, that he may lead her into the True Belief and cheat Shaitan of so fair a jewel. Add that I am bidden to buy her though she cost my lord a thousand philips. Bear her that message, O father of wind, and may Allah increase thy paunch!" And he was gone, lithe, active, and mocking.

"May thy sons perish and thy daughters become harlots," roared the eunuch, maddened at once by this evil news and the insult with which it was accompanied.

But Tsamanni only laughed, as he answered him over his shoulder—

"May thy sons be sultans all, Ayoub!"

Quivering still with a rage that entirely obliterated his alarm at what he had learnt, Ayoub rolled into the presence of his mistress with that evil message.

She listened to him in a dumb white fury. Then she fell to reviling her lord and the slave-girl in a breath, and called upon Allah to break their bones and blacken their faces and rot their flesh with all the fervour of one born and bred in the True Faith. When she recovered from that burst of fury it was to sit brooding awhile. At length she sprang up and bade Ayoub see that none lurked to listen about the doorways.

"We must act, Ayoub, and act swiftly, or I am destroyed and with me will be destroyed Marzak, who alone could not stand against his father's face. Sakr-el-Bahr will trample us into the dust." She checked on a sudden thought. "By Allah it may have been a part of his design to have brought hither that white-faced wench. But we must thwart him and we must thwart Asad, or thou art ruined too, Ayoub."

"Thwart him?" quoth her wazeer, gaping at the swift energy of mind and body with which this woman was endowed, the like of which he had never seen in any woman yet. "Thwart him?" he repeated.

"First, Ayoub, to place this Frankish girl beyond his reach."

"That is well thought—but how?"

"How? Can thy wit suggest no way? Hast thou wits at all in that fat head of thine? Thou shalt outbid Tsamanni, or, better still, set someone else to do it for thee, and so buy the girl for me. Then we'll contrive that she shall vanish quietly and quickly before Asad can discover a trace of her."

His face blanched, and the wattles about his jaws were shaking. "And... and the cost? Hast thou counted the cost, O Fenzileh? What will happen when Asad gains knowledge of this thing?"

"He shall gain no knowledge of it," she answered him. "Or if he does, the girl being gone beyond recall, he shall submit him to what was written. Trust me to know how to bring him to it."

"Lady, lady!" he cried, and wrung his bunches of fat fingers. "I dare not engage in this!"

"Engage in what? If I bid thee go buy this girl, and give thee the money thou'lt require, what else concerns thee, dog? What else is to be done, a man shall do.

Come now, thou shalt have the money, all I have, which is a matter of some fifteen hundred philips, and what is not laid out upon this purchase thou shalt retain for thyself."

He considered an instant, and conceived that she was right. None could blame him for executing the commands she gave him. And there would be profit in it, clearly—ay, and it would be sweet to outbid that dog Tsamanni and send him empty-handed home to face the wrath of his frustrated master. He spread his hands and salaamed in token of complete acquiescence.

CHAPTER X. THE SLAVE-MARKET

At the sôk-el-Abeed it was the hour of the outcry, announced by a blast of trumpets and the thudding of tom-toms. The traders that until then had been licensed to ply within the enclosure now put up the shutters of their little booths. The Hebrew pedlar of gems closed his box and effaced himself, leaving the steps about the well clear for the most prominent patrons of the market. These hastened to assemble there, surrounding it and facing outwards, whilst the rest of the crowd was ranged against the southern and western walls of the enclosure.

Came negro water-carriers in white turbans with aspersers made of palmetto leaves to sprinkle the ground and lay the dust against the tramp of slaves and buyers. The trumpets ceased for an instant, then wound a fresh imperious blast and fell permanently silent. The crowd about the gates fell back to right and left, and very slowly and stately three tall dalals, dressed from head to foot in white and with immaculate turbans wound about their heads, advanced into the open space. They came to a halt at the western end of the long wall, the chief dalal standing slightly in advance of the other two.

The chattering of voices sank upon their advent, it became a hissing whisper, then a faint drone like that of bees, and then utter silence. In the solemn and grave demeanour of the dalals there was something almost sacerdotal, so that when that silence fell upon the crowd the affair took on the aspect of a sacrament.

The chief dalal stood forward a moment as if in an abstraction with downcast eyes; then with hands outstretched to catch a blessing he raised his voice and began to pray in a monotonous chant:

"In the name of Allah the Pitying the Pitiful Who created man from clots of blood! All that is in the Heavens and in the Earth praiseth Allah, Who is the Mighty, the Wise! His the kingdom of the Heavens and of the Earth. He maketh alive and killeth, and He hath power over all things. He is the first and the last, the seen and the unseen, and He knoweth all things."

"Ameen," intoned the crowd.

"The praise to Him who sent us Mahomet His Prophet to give the world the True Belief, and curses upon Shaitan the stoned who wages war upon Allah and His children."

"Ameen."

"The blessings of Allah and our Lord Mahomet upon this market and upon all who may buy and sell herein, and may Allah increase their wealth and grant them length of days in which to praise Him."

"Ameen," replied the crowd, as with a stir and rustle the close ranks relaxed from the tense attitude of prayer, and each man sought elbow-room.

The dalal beat his hands together, whereupon the curtains were drawn aside and the huddled slaves displayed—some three hundred in all, occupying three several pens.

In the front rank of the middle pen—the one containing Rosamund and Lionel—stood a couple of stalwart young Nubians, sleek and muscular, who looked on with completest indifference, no whit appalled by the fate which had haled them thither. They caught the eye of the dalal, and although the usual course was for a buyer to indicate a slave he was prepared to purchase, yet to the end that good beginning should be promptly made, the dalal himself pointed out that stalwart pair to the corsairs who stood on guard. In compliance the two negroes were brought forth.

"Here is a noble twain," the dalal announced, "strong of muscle and long of limb, as all may see, whom it were a shameful thing to separate. Who needs such a pair for strong labour let him say what he will give." He set out on a slow circuit of the well, the corsairs urging the two slaves to follow him that all buyers might see and inspect them.

In the foremost ranks of the crowd near the gate stood Ali, sent thither by Othmani to purchase a score of stout fellows required to make up the contingent of the galeasse of Sakr-el-Bahr. He had been strictly enjoined to buy naught but the stoutest stuff the market could afford—with one exception. Aboard that galeasse they wanted no weaklings who would trouble the boatswain with their swoonings. Ali announced his business forthwith.

"I need such tall fellows for the oars of Sakr-el-Bahr," said he with loud importance, thus drawing upon himself the eyes of the assembly, and sunning himself in the admiring looks bestowed upon one of the officers of Oliver-Reis, one of the rovers who were the pride of Islam and a sword-edge to the infidel.

"They were born to toil nobly at the oar, O Ali-Reis," replied the dalal in all solemnity. "What wilt thou give for them?"

"Two hundred philips for the twain."

The dalal paced solemnly on, the slaves following in his wake.

"Two hundred philips am I offered for a pair of the lustiest slaves that by the favour of Allah were ever brought into this market. Who will say fifty philips more?"

A portly Moor in a flowing blue selham rose from his seat on the step of the well as the dalal came abreast of him, and the slaves scenting here a buyer, and preferring any service to that of the galleys with which they were threatened, came each in turn to kiss his hands and fawn upon him, for all the world like dogs.

Calm and dignified he ran his hands over them feeling their muscles, and then forced back their lips and examined their teeth and mouths.

"Two hundred and twenty for the twain," he said, and the dalal passed on with his wares, announcing the increased price he had been offered.

Thus he completed the circuit and came to stand once more before Ali.

"Two hundred and twenty is now the price, O Ali! By the Koran, they are worth three hundred at the least. Wilt say three hundred?"

"Two hundred and thirty," was the answer.

Back to the Moor went the dalal. "Two hundred and thirty I am now offered, O Hamet. Thou wilt give another twenty?"

"Not I, by Allah!" said Hamet, and resumed his seat. "Let him have them."

"Another ten philips?" pleaded the dalal.

"Not another asper."

"They are thine, then, O Ali, for two hundred and thirty. Give thanks to Allah for so good a bargain."

The Nubians were surrendered to Ali's followers, whilst the dalal's two assistants advanced to settle accounts with the corsair.

"Wait wait," said he, "is not the name of Sakr-el-Bahr good warranty?"

"The inviolable law is that the purchase money be paid ere a slave leaves the market, O valiant Ali."

"It shall be observed," was the impatient answer, "and I will so pay before they leave. But I want others yet, and we will make one account an it please thee. That fellow yonder now. I have orders to buy him for my captain." And he indicated Lionel, who stood at Rosamund's side, the very incarnation of woefulness and debility.

Contemptuous surprise flickered an instant in the eyes of the dalal. But this he made haste to dissemble.

"Bring forth that yellow-haired infidel," he commanded.

The corsairs laid hands on Lionel. He made a vain attempt to struggle, but it was observed that the woman leaned over to him and said something quickly, whereupon his struggles ceased and he suffered himself to be dragged limply forth into the full view of all the market.

"Dost want him for the oar, Ali?" cried Ayoub-el-Samin across the quadrangle, a jest this that evoked a general laugh.

"What else?" quoth Ali. "He should be cheap at least."

"Cheap?" quoth the dalal in an affectation of surprise. "Nay, now. 'Tis a comely fellow and a young one. What wilt thou give, now? a hundred philips?"

"A hundred philips!" cried Ali derisively. "A hundred philips for that skinful of bones! Ma'sh'-Allah! Five philips is my price, O dalal."

Again laughter crackled through the mob. But the dalal stiffened with increasing dignity. Some of that laughter seemed to touch himself, and he was not a person to be made the butt of mirth.

"'Tis a jest, my master," said he, with a forgiving yet contemptuous wave. "Behold how sound he is." He signed to one of the corsairs, and Lionel's doublet was slit from neck to girdle and wrenched away from his body, leaving him naked to the waist, and displaying better proportions than might have been expected. In a passion at that indignity Lionel writhed in the grip of his guards, until one of the corsairs struck him a light blow with a whip in earnest of what to expect if he continued to be troublesome. "Consider him now," said the dalal, pointing to that white torso. "And behold how sound he is. See how excellent are his teeth." He seized Lionel's head and forced the jaws apart.

"Ay," said Ali, "but consider me those lean shanks and that woman's arm."

"'Tis a fault the oar will mend," the dalal insisted.

"You filthy blackamoors!" burst from Lionel in a sob of rage.

"He is muttering curses in his infidel tongue," said Ali. "His temper is none too good, you see. I have said five philips. I'll say no more."

With a shrug the dalal began his circuit of the well, the corsairs thrusting Lionel after him. Here one rose to handle him, there another, but none seemed disposed to purchase.

"Five philips is the foolish price offered me for this fine young Frank," cried the dalal. "Will no True-Believer pay ten for such a slave? Wilt not thou, O Ayoub? Thou, Hamet—ten philips?"

But one after another those to whom he was offered shook their heads. The haggardness of Lionel's face was too unprepossessing. They had seen slaves with that look before, and experience told them that no good was ever to be done with such fellows. Moreover, though shapely, his muscles were too slight, his flesh looked too soft and tender. Of what use a slave who must be hardened and nourished into strength, and who might very well die in the process? Even at five philips he would be dear. So the disgusted dalal came back to Ali.

"He is thine, then, for five philips—Allah pardon thy avarice."

Ali grinned, and his men seized upon Lionel and bore him off into the background to join the two negroes previously purchased.

And then, before Ali could bid for another of the slaves he desired to acquire, a tall, elderly Jew, dressed in black doublet and hose like a Castilian gentleman, with a ruffle at his neck, a plumed bonnet on his grey locks, and a serviceable dagger hanging from his girdle of hammered gold, had claimed the attention of the dalal.

In the pen that held the captives of the lesser raids conducted by Biskaine sat an Andalusian girl of perhaps some twenty years, of a beauty entirely Spanish.

Her face was of the warm pallor of ivory, her massed hair of an ebony black, her eyebrows were finely pencilled, and her eyes of deepest and softest brown. She was dressed in the becoming garb of the Castilian peasant, the folded kerchief of red and yellow above her bodice leaving bare the glories of her neck. She was very pale, and her eyes were wild in their look, but this detracted nothing from her beauty.

She had attracted the jew's notice, and it is not impossible that there may have stirred in him a desire to avenge upon her some of the cruel wrongs, some of the rackings, burning, confiscations, and banishment suffered by the men of his race at the hands of the men of hers. He may have bethought him of invaded ghettos, of Jewish maidens ravished, and Jewish children butchered in the name of the God those Spanish Christians worshipped, for there was something almost of contemptuous fierceness in his dark eyes and in the hand he flung out to indicate her.

"Yonder is a Castilian wench for whom I will give fifty Philips, O dalal," he announced. The datal made a sign, whereupon the corsairs dragged her struggling forth.

"So much loveliness may not be bought for fifty Philips, O Ibrahim," said he. "Yusuf here will pay sixty at least." And he stood expectantly before a resplendent Moor.

The Moor, however, shook his head.

"Allah knows I have three wives who would destroy her loveliness within the hour and so leave me the loser."

The dalal moved on, the girl following him but contesting every step of the way with those who impelled her forward, and reviling them too in hot Castilian. She drove her nails into the arms of one and spat fiercely into the face of another of her corsair guards. Rosamund's weary eyes quickened to horror as she watched her—a horror prompted as much by the fate awaiting that poor child as by the undignified fury of the futile battle she waged against it. But it happened that her behaviour impressed a Levantine Turk quite differently. He rose, a short squat figure, from his seat on the steps of the well.

"Sixty Philips will I pay for the joy of taming that wild cat," said he.

But Ibrahim was not to be outbidden. He offered seventy, the Turk countered with a bid of eighty, and Ibrahim again raised the price to ninety, and there fell a pause.

The dalal spurred on the Turk. "Wilt thou be beaten then, and by an Israelite? Shall this lovely maid be given to a perverter of the Scriptures, to an inheritor of the fire, to one of a race that would not bestow on their fellow-men so much as the speck out of a date-stone? It were a shame upon a True-Believer."

Urged thus the Turk offered another five Philips, but with obvious reluctance. The Jew, however, entirely unabashed by a tirade against him, the like of which he heard a score of times a day in the course of trading, pulled forth a heavy purse from his girdle.

"Here are one hundred Philips," he announced. "'Tis overmuch. But I offer it."

Ere the dalal's pious and seductive tongue could urge him further the Turk sat down again with a gesture of finality.

"I give him joy of her," said he.

"She is thine, then, O Ibrahim, for one hundred philips."

The Israelite relinquished the purse to the dalal's white-robed assistants and advanced to receive the girl. The corsairs thrust her forward against him, still vainly battling, and his arms closed about her for a moment.

"Thou has cost me dear, thou daughter of Spain," said he. "But I am content. Come." And he made shift to lead her away. Suddenly, however, fierce as a tiger-cat she writhed her arms upwards and clawed at his face. With a scream of pain he relaxed his hold of her and in that moment, quick as lightning she plucked the dagger that hung from his girdle so temptingly within her reach.

"Valga me Dios!" she cried, and ere a hand could be raised to prevent her she had buried the blade in her lovely breast and sank in a laughing, coughing, heap at his feet. A final convulsive heave and she lay there quite still, whilst Ibrahim glared down at her with eyes of dismay, and over all the market there hung a hush of sudden awe.

Rosamund had risen in her place, and a faint colour came to warm her pallor, a faint light kindled in her eyes. God had shown her the way through this poor Spanish girl, and assuredly God would give her the means to take it when her own turn came. She felt herself suddenly uplifted and enheartened. Death was a sharp, swift severing, an easy door of escape from the horror that threatened her, and God in His mercy, she knew, would justify self-murder under such circumstances as were her own and that poor dead Andalusian maid's.

At length Ibrahim roused himself from his momentary stupor. He stepped deliberately across the body, his face inflamed, and stood to beard the impassive dalal.

"She is dead!" he bleated. "I am defrauded. Give me back my gold!"

"Are we to give back the price of every slave that dies?" the dalal questioned him.

"But she was not yet delivered to me," raved the Jew. "My hands had not touched her. Give me back my gold."

"Thou liest, son of a dog," was the answer, dispassionately delivered. "She was thine already. I had so pronounced her. Bear her hence, since she belongs to thee."

The Jew, his face empurpling, seemed to fight for breath

"How?" he choked. "Am I to lose a hundred philips?"

"What is written is written," replied the serene dalal.

Ibrahim was frothing at the lips, his eyes were blood-injected. "But it was never written that...."

"Peace," said the dalal. "Had it not been written it could not have come to pass. It is the will of Allah! Who dares rebel against it?"

The crowd began to murmur.

"I want my hundred philips," the Jew insisted, whereupon the murmur swelled into a sudden roar.

"Thou hearest?" said the dalal. "Allah pardon thee, thou art disturbing the peace of this market. Away, ere ill betide thee."

"Hence! hence!" roared the crowd, and some advanced threateningly upon the luckless Ibrahim. "Away, thou perverter of Holy Writ! thou filth! thou dog! Away!"

Such was the uproar, such the menace of angry countenances and clenched fists shaken in his very face, that Ibrahim quailed and forgot his loss in fear.

"I go, I go," he said, and turned hastily to depart.

But the dalal summoned him back. "Take hence thy property," said he, and pointed to the body. And so Ibrahim was forced to suffer the further mockery of summoning his slaves to bear away the lifeless body for which he had paid in lively potent gold.

Yet by the gates he paused again. "I will appeal me to the Basha," he threatened. "Asad-ed-Din is just, and he will have my money restored to me."

"So he will," said the dalal, "when thou canst restore the dead to life," and he turned to the portly Ayoub, who was plucking at his sleeve. He bent his head to catch the muttered words of Fenzileh's wazeer. Then, in obedience to them, he ordered Rosamund to be brought forward.

She offered no least resistance, advancing in a singularly lifeless way, like a sleep-walker or one who had been drugged. In the heat and glare of the open market she stood by the dalal's side at the head of the well, whilst he dilated upon her physical merits in that lingua franca which he used since it was current coin among all the assorted races represented there—a language which the knowledge of French that her residence in France had taught her she was to her increasing horror and shame able to understand.

The first to make an offer for her was that same portly Moor who had sought to purchase the two Nubeans. He rose to scrutinize her closely, and must have been satisfied, for the price he offered was a good one, and he offered it with contemptuous assurance that he would not be outbidden.

"One hundred philips for the milk-faced girl."

"'Tis not enough. Consider me the moon-bright loveliness of her face," said the dalal as he moved on. "Chigil yields us fair women, but no woman of Chigil was ever half so fair."

"One hundred and fifty," said the Levantine Turk with a snap.

"Not yet enough. Behold the stately height which Allah hath vouchsafed her. See the noble carriage of her head, the lustre of her eye! By Allah, she is worthy to grace the Sultan's own hareem."

He said no more than the buyers recognized to be true, and excitement stirred faintly through their usually impassive ranks. A Tagareen Moor named Yusuf offered at once two hundred.

But still the dalal continued to sing her praises. He held up one of her arms for inspection, and she submitted with lowered eyes, and no sign of resentment beyond the slow flush that spread across her face and vanished again.

"Behold me these limbs, smooth as Arabian silks and whiter than ivory. Look at those lips like pomegranate blossoms. The price is now two hundred philips. What wilt thou give, O Hamet?"

Hamet showed himself angry that his original bid should so speedily have been doubled. "By the Koran, I have purchased three sturdy girls from the Sus for less."

"Wouldst thou compare a squat-faced girl from the Sus with this narcissus-eyed glory of womanhood?" scoffed the dalal.

"Two hundred and ten, then," was Hamet's sulky grunt.

The watchful Tsamanni considered that the time had come to buy her for his lord as he had been bidden.

"Three hundred," he said curtly, to make an end of matters, and—

"Four hundred," instantly piped a shrill voice behind him.

He spun round in his amazement and met the leering face of Ayoub. A murmur ran through the ranks of the buyers, the people craned their necks to catch a glimpse of this open-handed purchaser.

Yusuf the Tagareen rose up in a passion. He announced angrily that never again should the dust of the sôk of Algiers defile his slippers, that never again would he come there to purchase slaves.

"By the Well of Zem-Zem," he swore, "all men are bewitched in this market. Four hundred philips for a Frankish girl! May Allah increase your wealth, for verily you'll need it." And in his supreme disgust he stalked to the gates, and elbowed his way through the crowd, and so vanished from the sôk.

Yet ere he was out of earshot her price had risen further. Whilst Tsamanni was recovering from his surprise at the competitor that had suddenly appeared before him, the dalal had lured an increased offer from the Turk.

"'Tis a madness," the latter deplored. "But she pleaseth me, and should it seem good to Allah the Merciful to lead her into the True Faith she may yet become the light of my hareem. Four hundred and twenty philips, then, O dalal, and Allah pardon me my prodigality."

Yet scarcely was his little speech concluded than Tsamanni with laconic eloquence rapped out: "Five hundred."

"Y'Allah!" cried the Turk, raising his hands to heaven, and "Y'Allah!" echoed the crowd.

"Five hundred and fifty," shrilled Ayoub's voice above the general din.

"Six hundred," replied Tsamanni, still unmoved.

And now such was the general hubbub provoked by these unprecedented prices that the dalal was forced to raise his voice and cry for silence.

When this was restored Ayoub at once raised the price to seven hundred.

"Eight hundred," snapped Tsamanni, showing at last a little heat.

"Nine hundred," replied Ayoub.

Tsamanni swung round upon him again, white now with fury.

"Is this a jest, O father of wind?" he cried, and excited laughter by the taunt implicit in that appellation.

"And thou'rt the jester," replied Ayoub with forced calm, "thou'lt find the jest a costly one."

With a shrug Tsamanni turned again to the dalal. "A thousand philips," said he shortly.

"Silence there!" cried the dalal again. "Silence, and praise Allah who sends good prices."

"One thousand and one hundred," said Ayoub the irrepressible

And now Tsamanni not only found himself outbidden, but he had reached the outrageous limit appointed by Asad. He lacked authority to go further, dared not do so without first consulting the Basha. Yet if he left the sôk for that purpose Ayoub would meanwhile secure the girl. He found himself between sword and wall. On the one hand did he permit himself to be outbidden his master might visit upon him his disappointment. On the other, did he continue beyond the limit so idly mentioned as being far beyond all possibility, it might fare no less ill with him.

He turned to the crowd, waving his arms in furious gesticulation. "By the beard of the Prophet, this bladder of wind and grease makes sport of us. He has no intent to buy. What man ever heard of the half of such a price for a slave girl?"

Ayoub's answer was eloquent; he produced a fat bag and flung it on the ground, where it fell with a mellow chink. "There is my sponsor," he made answer, grinning in the very best of humours, savouring to the full his enemy's rage and discomfiture, and savouring it at no cost to himself. "Shall I count out one thousand and one hundred philips, O dalal."

"If the wazeer Tsamanni is content."

"Dost thou know for whom I buy?" roared Tsamanni. "For the Basha himself, Asad-ed-Din, the exalted of Allah," He advanced upon Ayoub with hands upheld. "What shalt thou say to him, O dog, when he calls thee to account for daring to outbid him."

But Ayoub remained unruffled before all this fury. He spread his fat hands, his eyes twinkling, his great lips pursed. "How should I know, since Allah has not made me all-knowing? Thou shouldst have said so earlier. 'Tis thus I shall answer the Basha should he question me, and the Basha is just."

"I would not be thee, Ayoub—not for the throne of Istambul."

"Nor I thee, Tsamanni; for thou art jaundiced with rage."

And so they stood glaring each at the other until the dalal called them back to the business that was to do.

"The price is now one thousand and one hundred philips. Wilt thou suffer defeat, O wazeer?"

"Since Allah wills. I have no authority to go further."

"Then at one thousand and one hundred philips, Ayoub, she is...."

But the sale was not yet to be completed. From the dense and eager throng about the gates rang a crisp voice—

"One thousand and two hundred philips for the Frankish girl."

The dalal, who had conceived that the limits of madness had been already reached, stood gaping now in fresh amazement. The mob crowed and cheered and roared between enthusiasm and derision, and even Tsamanni brightened to see another champion enter the lists who perhaps would avenge him upon Ayoub. The crowd parted quickly to right and left, and through it into the open strode Sakr-el-Bahr. They recognized him instantly, and his name was shouted in acclamation by that idolizing multitude.

That Barbary name of his conveyed no information to Rosamund, and her back being turned to the entrance she did not see him. But she had recognized his voice, and she had shuddered at the sound. She could make nothing of the bidding, nor what the purpose that surely underlay it to account for the extraordinary excitement of the traders. Vaguely had she been wondering what dastardly purpose Oliver might intend to serve, but now that she heard his voice that wonder ceased and understanding took its place. He had hung there somewhere in the crowd waiting until all competitors but one should have been outbidden, and now he stepped forth to buy her for his own—his slave! She closed her eyes a moment and prayed God that he might not prevail in his intent. Any fate but that; she would rob him even of the satisfaction of driving her to sheathe a poniard in her heart as that poor Andalusian girl had done. A wave almost of unconsciousness passed over her in the intensity of her horror. For a moment the ground seemed to rock and heave under her feet.

Then the dizziness passed, and she was herself again. She heard the crowd thundering "Ma'sh'Allah!" and "Sakr-el-Bahr!" and the dalal clamouring sternly for silence. When this was at last restored she heard his exclamation—

"The glory to Allah who sends eager buyers! What sayest thou, O wazeer Ayoub?"

"Ay!" sneered Tsamanni, "what now?"

"One thousand and three hundred," said Ayoub with a quaver of uneasy defiance.

"Another hundred, O dalal," came from Sakr-el-Bahr in a quiet voice.

"One thousand and five hundred," screamed Ayoub, thus reaching not only the limit imposed by his mistress, but the very limit of the resources at her immediate disposal. Gone, too, with that bid was all hope of profit to himself.

But Sakr-el-Bahr, impassive as Fate, and without so much as deigning to bestow a look upon the quivering eunuch, said again—

"Another hundred, O dalal."

"One thousand and six hundred philips!" cried the dalal, more in amazement than to announce the figure reached. Then controlling his emotions he bowed his head in reverence and made confession of his faith. "All things are possible if Allah wills them. The praise to Him who sends wealthy buyers."

He turned to the crestfallen Ayoub, so crestfallen that in the contemplation of him Tsamanni was fast gathering consolation for his own discomfiture, vicariously tasting the sweets of vengeance. "What say you now, O perspicuous wazeer?"

"I say," choked Ayoub, "that since by the favour of Shaitan he hath so much wealth he must prevail."

But the insulting words were scarcely uttered than Sakr-el-Bahr's great hand had taken the wazeer by the nape of his fat neck, a growl of anger running through the assembly to approve him.

"By the favour of Shaitan, sayest thou, thou sex-less dog?" he growled, and tightened his grip so that the wazeer squirmed and twisted in an agony of pain. Down was his head thrust, and still down, until his fat body gave way and he lay supine and writhing in the dust of the sôk. "Shall I strangle thee, thou father of filth, or shall I fling thy soft flesh to the hooks to teach thee what is a man's due from thee?" And as he spoke he rubbed the too daring fellow's face roughly on the ground.

"Mercy!" squealed the wazeer. "Mercy, O mighty Sakr-el-Bahr, as thou lookest for mercy!"

"Unsay thy words, thou offal. Pronounce thyself a liar and a dog."

"I do unsay them. I have foully lied. Thy wealth is the reward sent thee by Allah for thy glorious victories over the unbelieving."

"Put out thine offending tongue," said Sakr-el-Bahr, "and cleanse it in the dust. Put it forth, I say."

Ayoub obeyed him in fearful alacrity, whereupon Sakr-el-Bahr released his hold and allowed the unfortunate fellow to rise at last, half-choked with dirt, livid of face, and quaking like a jelly, an object of ridicule and cruel mockery to all assembled.

"Now get thee hence, ere my sea-hawks lay their talons on thee. Go!"

Ayoub departed in all haste to the increasing jeers of the multitude and the taunts of Tsamanni, whilst Sakr-el-Bahr turned him once more to the dalal.

"At one thousand and six hundred philips this slave is thine, O Sakr-el-Bahr, thou glory of Islam. May Allah increase thy victories!"

"Pay him, Ali," said the corsair shortly, and he advanced to receive his purchase.

Face to face stood he now with Rosamund, for the first time since that day before the encounter with the Dutch argosy when he had sought her in the cabin of the carack.

One swift glance she bestowed on him, then, her senses reeling with horror at her circumstance she shrank back, her face of a deathly pallor. In his treatment of Ayoub she had just witnessed the lengths of brutality of which he was capable, and she was not to know that this brutality had been a deliberate piece of mummery calculated to strike terror into her.

Pondering her now he smiled a tight-lipped cruel smile that only served to increase her terror.

"Come," he said in English.

She cowered back against the dalal as if for protection. Sakr-el-Bahr reached forward, caught her by the wrists, and almost tossed her to his Nubians, Abiad and Zal-Zer, who were attending him.

"Cover her face," he bade them. "Bear her to my house. Away!"

CHAPTER XI. THE TRUTH

The sun was dipping swiftly to the world's rim when Sakr-el-Bahr with his Nubians and his little retinue of corsairs came to the gates of that white house of his on its little eminence outside the Bab-el-Oueb and beyond the walls of the city.

When Rosamund and Lionel, brought in the wake of the corsair, found themselves in the spacious courtyard beyond the dark and narrow entrance, the blue of the sky contained but the paling embers of the dying day, and suddenly, sharply upon the evening stillness, came a mueddin's voice calling the faithful unto prayer.

Slaves fetched water from the fountain that played in the middle of the quadrangle and tossed aloft a slender silvery spear of water to break into a myriad gems and so shower down into the broad marble basin. Sakr-el-Bahr washed, as did his followers, and then he went down upon the praying-mat that had been set for him, whilst his corsairs detached their cloaks and spread them upon the ground to serve them in like stead.

The Nubians turned the two slaves about, lest their glances should defile the orisons of the faithful, and left them so facing the wall and the green gate that led into the garden whence were wafted on the cooling air the perfumes of jessamine and lavender. Through the laths of the gate they might have caught a glimpse of the riot of colour there, and they might have seen the slaves arrested by the Persian waterwheel at which they had been toiling and chanting until the call to prayer had come to strike them into statues.

Sakr-el-Bahr rose from his devotions, uttered a sharp word of command, and entered the house. The Nubians followed him, urging their captives before them up the narrow stairs, and so brought them out upon the terrace on the roof, that space which in Eastern houses is devoted to the women, but which no woman's foot had ever trodden since this house had been tenanted by Sakr-el-Bahr the wifeless.

This terrace, which was surrounded by a parapet some four feet high, commanded a view of the city straggling up the hillside to eastward, from the harbour and of the island at the end of the mole which had been so laboriously built by the labour of Christian slaves from the stones of the ruined fortress—the Peñon, which Kheyr-ed-Din Barbarossa had wrested from the Spaniards. The deepening shroud of evening was now upon all, transmuting white and yellow walls alike to a pearly greyness. To westward stretched the fragrant gardens of the house, where the doves were murmuring fondly among the mulberries and lotus trees. Beyond it a valley wound its way between the shallow hills, and from a pool fringed with sedges and bullrushes above which a great stork was majestically sailing came the harsh croak of frogs.

An awning supported upon two gigantic spears hung out from the southern wall of the terrace which rose to twice the height of that forming the parapet on its other three sides. Under this was a divan and silken cushions, and near it a small Moorish table of ebony inlaid with mother-of-pearl and gold. Over the opposite parapet, where a lattice had been set, rioted a trailing rose-tree charged with blood-red blossoms, though now their colours were merged into the all-encompassing greyness.

Here Lionel and Rosamund looked at each other in the dim light, their faces gleaming ghostly each to each, whilst the Nubians stood like twin statues by the door that opened from the stair-head.

The man groaned, and clasped his hands before him. The doublet which had been torn from him in the sôk had since been restored and temporarily repaired by a strand of palmetto cord. But he was woefully bedraggled. Yet his thoughts, if his first words are to be taken as an indication of them were for Rosamund's condition rather than his own.

"O God, that you should be subjected to this!" he cried. "That you should have suffered what you have suffered! The humiliation of it, the barbarous cruelty! Oh!" He covered his haggard face with his hands.

She touched him gently on the arm.

"What I have suffered is but a little thing," she said, and her voice was wonderfully steady and soothing. Have I not said that these Godolphins were brave folk? Even their women were held to have something of the male spirit in their breasts; and to this none can doubt that Rosamund now bore witness. "Do not pity me, Lionel, for my sufferings are at an end or very nearly." She smiled strangely, the smile of exaltation that you may see upon the martyr's face in the hour of doom.

"How?" quoth he, in faint surprise.

"How?" she echoed. "Is there not always a way to thrust aside life's burden when it grows too heavy—heavier than God would have us bear?"

His only answer was a groan. Indeed, he had done little but groan in all the hours they had spent together since they were brought ashore from the carack; and had the season permitted her so much reflection, she might have considered that she had found him singularly wanting during those hours of stress when a man of worth would have made some effort, however desperate, to enhearten her rather than repine upon his own plight.

Slaves entered bearing four enormous flaming torches which they set in iron sconces protruding from the wall of the house. Thence they shed a lurid ruddy glow upon the terrace. The slaves departed again, and presently, in the black gap of the doorway between the Nubians, a third figure appeared unheralded. It was Sakr-el-Bahr.

He stood a moment at gaze, his attitude haughty, his face expressionless; then slowly he advanced. He was dressed in a short white caftan that descended to his knees, and was caught about his waist in a shimmering girdle of gold that quivered like fire in the glow of the torches as he moved. His arms from the elbow and his legs from the knee were bare, and his feet were shod with gold-embroidered red Turkish slippers. He wore a white turban decked by a plume of osprey attached by a jewelled clasp.

He signed to the Nubians and they vanished silently, leaving him alone with his captives.

He bowed to Rosamund. "This, mistress," he said, "is to be your domain henceforth which is to treat you more as wife than slave. For it is to Muslim wives that the housetops in Barbary are allotted. I hope you like it."

Lionel staring at him out of a white face, his conscience bidding him fear the very worst, his imagination painting a thousand horrid fates for him and turning him sick with dread, shrank back before his half-brother, who scarce appeared to notice him just then.

But Rosamund confronted him, drawn to the full of her splendid height, and if her face was pale, yet it was as composed and calm as his own; if her bosom rose and fell to betray her agitations yet her glance was contemptuous and defiant, her voice calm and steady, when she answered him with the question—"What is your intent with me?"

"My intent?" said he, with a little twisted smile. Yet for all that he believed he hated her and sought to hurt, to humble and to crush her, he could not stifle his admiration of her spirit's gallantry in such an hour as this.

From behind the hills peeped the edge of the moon—a sickle of burnished copper.

"My intent is not for you to question," he replied. "There was a time, Rosamund, when in all the world you had no slave more utter than was I. Yourself in your heartlessness, and in your lack of faith, you broke the golden fetters of that servitude. You'll find it less easy to break the shackles I now impose upon you."

She smiled her scorn and quiet confidence. He stepped close to her. "You are my slave, do you understand?—bought in the market-place as I might buy me a mule, a goat, or a camel—and belonging to me body and soul. You are my property, my thing, my chattel, to use or abuse, to cherish or break as suits my whim, without a will that is not my will, holding your very life at my good pleasure."

She recoiled a step before the dull hatred that throbbed in his words, before the evil mockery of his swarthy bearded face.

"You beast!" she gasped.

"So now you understand the bondage into which you are come in exchange for the bondage which in your own wantonness you dissolved."

"May God forgive you," she panted.

"I thank you for that prayer," said he. "May He forgive you no less."

And then from the background came an inarticulate sound, a strangled, snarling sob from Lionel.

Sakr-el-Bahr turned slowly. He eyed the fellow a moment in silence, then he laughed.

"Ha! My sometime brother. A pretty fellow, as God lives is it not? Consider him Rosamund. Behold how gallantly misfortune is borne by this pillar of manhood upon which you would have leaned, by this stalwart husband of your choice. Look at him! Look at this dear brother of mine."

Under the lash of that mocking tongue Lionel's mood was stung to anger where before it had held naught but fear.

"You are no brother of mine," he retorted fiercely. "Your mother was a wanton who betrayed my father."

Sakr-el-Bahr quivered a moment as if he had been struck. Yet he controlled himself.

"Let me hear my mother's name but once again on thy foul tongue, and I'll have it ripped out by the roots. Her memory, I thank God, is far above the insults of such a crawling thing as you. None the less, take care not to speak of the only woman whose name I reverence."

And then turning at bay, as even the rat will do, Lionel sprang upon him, with clawing hands outstretched to reach his throat. But Sakr-el-Bahr caught him in a grip that bent him howling to his knees.

"You find me strong, eh?" he gibed. "Is it matter for wonder? Consider that for six endless months I toiled at the oar of a galley, and you'll understand what it was that turned my body into iron and robbed me of a soul."

He flung him off, and sent him crashing into the rosebush and the lattice over which it rambled.

"Do you realize the horror of the rower's bench? to sit day in day out, night in night out, chained naked to the oar, amid the reek and stench of your fellows in misfortune, unkempt, unwashed save by the rain, broiled and roasted by the sun, festering with sores, lashed and cut and scarred by the boatswain's whip as you faint under the ceaseless, endless, cruel toil?"

"Do you realize it?" From a tone of suppressed fury his voice rose suddenly to a roar. "You shall. For that horror which was mine by your contriving shall now be yours until you die."

He paused; but Lionel made no attempt to avail himself of this. His courage all gone out of him again, as suddenly as it had flickered up, he cowered where he had been flung.

"Before you go there is something else," Sakr-el-Bahr resumed, "something for which I have had you brought hither to-night.

"Not content with having delivered me to all this, not content with having branded me a murderer, destroyed my good name, filched my possessions and driven me into the very path of hell, you must further set about usurping my place in the false heart of this woman I once loved."

"I hope," he went on reflectively, "that in your own poor way you love her, too, Lionel. Thus to the torment that awaits your body shall be added torment for your treacherous soul—such torture of mind as only the damned may know. To that end have I brought you hither. That you may realize something of what is in store for this woman at my hands; that you may take the thought of it with you to be to your mind worse than the boatswain's lash to your pampered body."

"You devil!" snarled Lionel. "Oh, you fiend out of hell!"

"If you will manufacture devils, little toad of a brother, do not upbraid them for being devils when next you meet them."

"Give him no heed, Lionel!" said Rosamund. "I shall prove him as much a boaster as he has proved himself a villain. Never think that he will be able to work his evil will."

"'Tis you are the boaster there," said Sakr-el-Bahr. "And for the rest, I am what you and he, between you, have made me."

"Did we make you liar and coward?—for that is what you are indeed," she answered.

"Coward?" he echoed, in genuine surprise. "'Twill be some lie that he has told you with the others. In what, pray, was I ever a coward?"

"In what? In this that you do now; in this taunting and torturing of two helpless beings in our power."

"I speak not of what I am," he replied, "for I have told you that I am what you have made me. I speak of what I was. I speak of the past."

She looked at him and she seemed to measure him with her unwavering glance.

"You speak of the past?" she echoed, her voice low. "You speak of the past and to me? You dare?"

"It is that we might speak of it together that I have fetched you all the way from England; that at last I may tell you things I was a fool to have kept from you five years ago; that we may resume a conversation which you interrupted when you dismissed me."

"I did you a monstrous injury, no doubt," she answered him, with bitter irony. "I was surely wanting in consideration. It would have become me better to have smiled and fawned upon my brother's murderer."

"I swore to you, then, that I was not his murderer," he reminded her in a voice that shook.

"And I answered you that you lied."

"Ay, and on that you dismissed me—the word of the man whom you professed to love, the word of the man to whom you had given your trust weighing for naught with you."

"When I gave you my trust," she retorted, "I did so in ignorance of your true self, in a headstrong wilful ignorance that would not be guided by what all the world said of you and your wild ways. For that blind wilfulness I have been punished, as perhaps I deserved to be."

"Lies—all lies!" he stormed. "Those ways of mine—and God knows they were none so wild, when all is said—I abandoned when I came to love you. No lover since the world began was ever so cleansed, so purified, so sanctified by love as was I."

"Spare me this at least!" she cried on a note of loathing

"Spare you?" he echoed. "What shall I spare you?"

"The shame of it all; the shame that is ever mine in the reflection that for a season I believed I loved you."

He smiled. "If you can still feel shame, it shall overwhelm you ere I have done. For you shall hear me out. Here there are none to interrupt us, none to thwart my sovereign will. Reflect then, and remember. Remember what a pride you took in the change you had wrought in me. Your vanity welcomed that flattery, that tribute to the power of your beauty. Yet, all in a moment, upon the paltriest grounds, you believed me the murderer of your brother."

"The paltriest grounds?" she cried, protesting almost despite herself

"So paltry that the justices at Truro would not move against me."

"Because," she cut in, "they accounted that you had been sufficiently provoked. Because you had not sworn to them as you swore to me that no provocation should ever drive you to raise your hand against my brother. Because they did not realize how false and how forsworn you were."

He considered her a moment. Then he took a turn on the terrace. Lionel crouching ever by the rose-tree was almost entirely forgotten by him now.

"God give me patience with you!" he said at length. "I need it. For I desire you to understand many things this night. I mean you to see how just is my resentment; how just the punishment that is to overtake you for what you have made of my life and perhaps of my hereafter. Justice Baine and another who is dead, knew me for innocent."

"They knew you for innocent?" There was scornful amazement in her tone. "Were they not witnesses of the quarrel betwixt you and Peter and of your oath that you would kill him?"

"That was an oath sworn in the heat of anger. Afterwards I bethought me that he was your brother."

"Afterwards?" said she. "After you had murdered him?"

"I say again," Oliver replied calmly, "that I did not do this thing."

"And I say again that you lie."

He considered her for a long moment; then he laughed. "Have you ever," he asked, "known a man to lie without some purpose? Men lie for the sake of profit, they lie out of cowardice or malice, or else because they are vain and vulgar boasters. I know of no other causes that will drive a man to falsehood, save that—ah, yes!—" (and he flashed a sidelong glance at Lionel)—"save that sometimes a man will lie to shield another, out of self-sacrifice. There you have all the spurs that urge a man to falsehood. Can any of these be urging me to-night? Reflect! Ask yourself what purpose I could serve by lying to you now. Consider further that I have come to loathe you for your unfaith; that I desire naught so much as to punish you for that and for all its bitter consequences to me that I have brought you hither to exact payment from you to the uttermost farthing. What end then can I serve by falsehood?"

"All this being so, what end could you serve by truth?" she countered.

"To make you realize to the full the injustice that you did. To make you understand the wrongs for which you are called to pay. To prevent you from conceiving yourself a martyr; to make you perceive in all its deadly bitterness that what now comes to you is the inevitable fruit of your own faithlessness."

"Sir Oliver, do you think me a fool?" she asked him.

"Madam, I do—and worse," he answered.

"Ay, that is clear," she agreed scornfully, "since even now you waste breath in attempting to persuade me against my reason. But words will not blot out facts. And though you talk from now till the day of judgment no word of yours can efface those bloodstains in the snow that formed a trail from that poor murdered body to your own door; no word of yours can extinguish the memory of the hatred between him and you, and of your own threat to kill him; nor can it stifle the recollection of the public voice demanding your punishment. You dare to take such a tone as you are taking with me? You dare here under Heaven to stand and lie to me that you may give false gloze to the villainy of your present deed—for that is the purpose of your falsehood, since you asked me what purpose there could be for it. What had you to set against all that, to convince me that your hands were clean, to induce me to keep the troth which—God forgive me!—I had plighted to you?"

"My word," he answered her in a ringing voice.

"Your lie," she amended.

"Do not suppose," said he, "that I could not support my word by proofs if called upon to do so."

"Proofs?" She stared at him, wide-eyed a moment. Then her lip curled. "And that no doubt was the reason of your flight when you heard that the Queen's pursuivants were coming in response to the public voice to call you to account."

He stood at gaze a moment, utterly dumbfounded. "My flight?" he said. "What fable's that?"

"You will tell me next that you did not flee. That that is another false charge against you?"

"So," he said slowly, "it was believed I fled!"

And then light burst upon him, to dazzle and stun him. It was so inevitably what must have been believed, and yet it had never crossed his mind. O the damnable simplicity of it! At another time his disappearance must have provoked comment and investigation, perhaps. But, happening when it did, the answer to it came promptly and convincingly and no man troubled to question further. Thus was Lionel's task made doubly easy, thus was his own guilt made doubly sure in the eyes of all. His head sank upon his breast. What had he done? Could he still blame Rosamund for having been convinced by so overwhelming a piece of evidence? Could he still blame her if she had burnt unopened the letter which he had sent her by the hand of Pitt? What else indeed could any suppose, but that he had fled? And that being so, clearly such a flight must brand him irrefutably for the murderer he was alleged to be. How could he blame her if she had ultimately been convinced by the only reasonable assumption possible?

A sudden sense of the wrong he had done rose now like a tide about him.

"My God!" he groaned, like a man in pain. "My God!"

He looked at her, and then averted his glance again, unable now to endure the haggard, strained yet fearless gaze of those brave eyes of hers.

"What else, indeed, could you believe?" he muttered brokenly, thus giving some utterance to what was passing through his mind.

"Naught else but the whole vile truth," she answered fiercely, and thereby stung him anew, whipped him out of his sudden weakening back to his mood of resentment and vindictiveness.

She had shown herself, he thought in that moment of reviving anger, too ready to believe what told against him.

"The truth?" he echoed, and eyed her boldly now. "Do you know the truth when you see it? We shall discover. For by God's light you shall have the truth laid stark before you now, and you shall find it hideous beyond all your hideous imaginings."

There was something so compelling now in his tone and manner that it drove her to realize that some revelation was impending. She was conscious of a faint excitement, a reflection perhaps of the wild excitement that was astir in him.

"Your brother," he began, "met his death at the hands of a false weakling whom I loved, towards whom I had a sacred duty. Straight from the deed he fled to me for shelter. A wound he had taken in the struggle left that trail of blood to mark the way he had come." He paused, and his tone became gentler, it assumed the level note of one who reasons impassively. "Was it not an odd thing, now, that none should ever have paused to seek with certainty whence that blood proceeded, and to consider that I bore no wound in those days? Master Baine knew it, for I submitted my body to his examination, and a document was drawn up and duly attested which should have sent the Queen's pursuivants back to London with drooping tails had I been at Penarrow to receive them."

Faintly through her mind stirred the memory that Master Baine had urged the existence of some such document, that in fact he had gone so far as to have made oath of this very circumstance now urged by Sir Oliver; and she remembered that the matter had been brushed aside as an invention of the justice's to answer the charge of laxity in the performance of his duty, particularly as the only co-witness he could cite was Sir Andrew Flack, the parson, since deceased. Sir Oliver's voice drew her attention from that memory.

"But let that be," he was saying. "Let us come back to the story itself. I gave the craven weakling shelter. Thereby I drew down suspicion upon myself, and since I could not clear myself save by denouncing him, I kept silent. That suspicion drew to certainty when the woman to whom I was betrothed, recking nothing of my oaths, freely believing the very worst of me, made an end of our betrothal and thereby branded me a murderer and a liar in the eyes of all. Indignation swelled against me. The Queen's pursuivants were on their way to do what the justices of Truro refused to do.

"So far I have given you facts. Now I give you surmise—my own conclusions—but surmise that strikes, as you shall judge, the very bull's-eye of truth. That dastard to whom I had given sanctuary, to whom I had served as a cloak, measured my nature by his own and feared that I must prove unequal to the fresh burden to be cast upon me. He feared lest under the strain of it I should speak out, advance my proofs, and so destroy him. There was the matter of that wound, and there was something still more unanswerable he feared I might have urged. There was a certain woman—a wanton up at Malpas—who could have been made to speak, who could have revealed a rivalry concerning her betwixt the slayer and your brother. For the affair in which Peter Godolphin met his death was a pitifully, shamefully sordid one at bottom."

For the first time she interrupted him, fiercely. "Do you malign the dead?"

"Patience, mistress," he commanded. "I malign none. I speak the truth of a dead man that the truth may be known of two living ones. Hear me out, then! I have waited long and survived a deal that I might tell you this

"That craven, then, conceived that I might become a danger to him; so he decided to remove me. He contrived to have me kidnapped one night and put aboard a vessel to be carried to Barbary and sold there as a slave. That is the truth of my disappearance. And the slayer, whom I had befriended and sheltered at my own bitter cost, profited yet further by my removal. God knows whether the prospect of such profit was a further temptation to him. In time he came to succeed me in my possessions, and at last to succeed me even in the affections of the faithless woman who once had been my affianced wife."

At last she started from the frozen patience in which she had listened hitherto. "Do you say that... that Lionel...?" she was beginning in a voice choked by indignation.

And then Lionel spoke at last, straightening himself into a stiffly upright attitude.

"He lies!" he cried. "He lies, Rosamund! Do not heed him."

"I do not," she answered, turning away.

A wave of colour suffused the swarthy face of Sakr-el-Bahr. A moment his eyes followed her as she moved away a step or two, then they turned their blazing light of anger upon Lionel. He strode silently across to him, his mien so menacing that Lionel shrank back in fresh terror.

Sakr-el-Bahr caught his brother's wrist in a grip that was as that of a steel manacle. "We'll have the truth this night if we have to tear it from you with red-hot pincers," he said between his teeth.

He dragged him forward to the middle of the terrace and held him there before Rosamund, forcing him down upon his knees into a cowering attitude by the violence of that grip upon his wrist.

"Do you know aught of the ingenuity of Moorish torture?" he asked him. "You may have heard of the rack and the wheel and the thumbscrew at home. They are instruments of voluptuous delight compared with the contrivances of Barbary to loosen stubborn tongues."

White and tense, her hands clenched, Rosamund seemed to stiffen before him.

"You coward! You cur! You craven renegade dog!" she branded him.

Oliver released his brother's wrist and beat his hands together. Without heeding Rosamund he looked down upon Lionel, who cowered shuddering at his feet.

"What do you say to a match between your fingers? Or do you think a pair of bracelets of living fire would answer better, to begin with?"

A squat, sandy-bearded, turbaned fellow, rolling slightly in his gait, came—as had been prearranged—to answer the corsair's summons.

With the toe of his slipper Sakr-el-Bahr stirred his brother.

"Look up, dog," he bade him. "Consider me that man, and see if you know him again. Look at him, I say!" And Lionel looked, yet since clearly he did so without recognition his brother explained: "His name among Christians was Jasper Leigh. He was the skipper you bribed to carry me into Barbary. He was taken in his own toils when his ship was sunk by Spaniards. Later he fell into my power, and because I forebore from hanging him he is to-day my faithful follower. I should bid him tell you what he knows," he continued, turning to Rosamund, "if I thought you would believe his tale. But since I am assured you would not, I will take other means." He swung round to Jasper again. "Bid Ali heat me a pair of steel manacles in a brazier and hold them in readiness against my need of them." And he waved his hand.

Jasper bowed and vanished.

"The bracelets shall coax confession from your own lips, my brother."

"I have naught to confess," protested Lionel. "You may force lies from me with your ruffianly tortures."

Oliver smiled. "Not a doubt but that lies will flow from you more readily than truth. But we shall have truth, too, in the end, never doubt it." He was mocking, and there was a subtle purpose underlying his mockery. "And you shall tell a full story," he continued, "in all its details, so that Mistress Rosamund's last doubt shall vanish. You shall tell her how you lay in wait for him that evening in Godolphin Park; how you took him unawares, and...."

"That is false!" cried Lionel in a passion of sincerity that brought him to his feet.

It was false, indeed, and Oliver knew it, and deliberately had recourse to falsehood, using it as a fulcrum upon which to lever out the truth. He was cunning as all the fiends, and never perhaps did he better manifest his cunning.

"False?" he cried with scorn. "Come, now, be reasonable. The truth, ere torture sucks it out of you. Reflect that I know all—exactly as you told it me. How was it, now? Lurking behind a bush you sprang upon him unawares and ran him through before he could so much as lay a hand to his sword, and so...."

"The lie of that is proven by the very facts themselves," was the furious interruption. A subtle judge of tones might have realized that here was truth indeed, angry indignant truth that compelled conviction. "His sword lay beside him when they found him."

But Oliver was loftily disdainful. "Do I not know? Yourself you drew it after you had slain him."

The taunt performed its deadly work. For just one instant Lionel was carried off his feet by the luxury of his genuine indignation, and in that one instant he was lost.

"As God's my witness, that is false!" he cried wildly. "And you know it. I fought him fair...."

He checked on a long, shuddering, indrawn breath that was horrible to hear.

Then silence followed, all three remaining motionless as statues: Rosamund white and tense, Oliver grim and sardonic, Lionel limp, and overwhelmed by the consciousness of how he had been lured into self-betrayal.

At last it was Rosamund who spoke, and her voice shook and shifted from key to key despite her strained attempt to keep it level.

"What... what did you say, Lionel?" she asked. Oliver laughed softly. "He was about to add proof of his statement, I think," he jeered. "He was about to mention the wound he took in that fight, which left those tracks in the snow, thus to prove that I lied—as indeed I did—when I said that he took Peter unawares.

"Lionel!" she cried. She advanced a step and made as if to hold out her arms to him, then let them fall again beside her. He stood stricken, answering nothing. "Lionel!" she cried again, her voice growing suddenly shrill. "Is this true?"

"Did you not hear him say it?" quoth Oliver.

She stood swaying a moment, looking at Lionel, her white face distorted into a mask of unutterable pain. Oliver stepped towards her, ready to support her, fearing that she was about to fall. But with an imperious hand she checked his advance, and by a supreme effort controlled her weakness. Yet her knees shook under her, refusing their office. She sank down upon the divan and covered her face with her hands.

"God pity me!" she moaned, and sat huddled there, shaken with sobs.

Lionel started at that heart-broken cry. Cowering, he approached her, and Oliver, grim and sardonic, stood back, a spectator of the scene he had precipitated. He knew that given rope Lionel would enmesh himself still further. There must be explanations that would damn him utterly. Oliver was well content to look on.

"Rosamund!" came Lionel's piteous cry. "Rose! Have mercy! Listen ere you judge me. Listen lest you misjudge me!"

"Ay, listen to him," Oliver flung in, with his soft hateful laugh. "Listen to him. I doubt he'll be vastly entertaining."

That sneer was a spur to the wretched Lionel. "Rosamund, all that he has told you of it is false. I...I...It was done in self-defence. It is a lie that I took him unawares." His words came wildly now. "We had quarrelled about... about... a certain matter, and as the devil would have it we met that evening in Godolphin Park, he and I. He taunted me; he struck me, and finally he drew upon me and forced me to draw that I might defend my life. That is the truth. I swear to you here on my knees in the sight of Heaven! And...."

"Enough, sir! Enough!" she broke in, controlling herself to check these protests that but heightened her disgust.

"Nay, hear me yet, I implore you; that knowing all you may be merciful in your judgment."

"Merciful?" she cried, and almost seemed to laugh

"It was an accident that I slew him," Lionel raved on. "I never meant it. I never meant to do more than ward and preserve my life. But when swords are crossed more may happen than a man intends. I take God to witness that his death was an accident resulting from his own fury."

She had checked her sobs, and she considered him now with eyes that were hard and terrible.

"Was it also an accident that you left me and all the world in the belief that the deed was your brother's?" she asked him.

He covered his face, as if unable to endure her glance. "Did you but know how I loved you—even in those days, in secret—you would perhaps pity me a little," he whimpered.

"Pity?" She leaned forward and seemed to spit the word at him. "'Sdeath, man! Do you sue for pity—you?"

"Yet you must pity me did you know the greatness of the temptation to which I succumbed."

"I know the greatness of your infamy, of your falseness, of your cowardice, of your baseness. Oh!"

He stretched out suppliant hands to her; there were tears now in his eyes. "Of your charity, Rosamund...." he was beginning, when at last Oliver intervened:

"I think you are wearying the lady," he said, and stirred him with his foot. "Relate to us instead some more of your astounding accidents. They are more diverting. Elucidate the accident, by which you had me kidnapped to be sold into slavery. Tell us of the accident by which you succeeded to my property. Expound to the full the accidental circumstances of which throughout you have been the unfortunate victim. Come, man, ply your wits. 'Twill make a pretty tale."

And then came Jasper to announce that Ali waited with the brazier and the heated manacles.

"They are no longer needed," said Oliver. "Take this slave hence with you. Bid Ali to take charge of him, and at dawn to see him chained to one of the oars of my galeasse. Away with him."

Lionel rose to his feet, his face ashen. "Wait! Ah, wait! Rosamund!" he cried.

Oliver caught him by the nape of his neck, spun him round, and flung him into the arms of Jasper. "Take him away!" he growled, and Jasper took the wretch by the shoulders and urged him out, leaving Rosamund and Oliver alone with the truth under the stars of Barbary.

CHAPTER XII. THE SUBTLETY OF FENZILEH

Oliver considered the woman for a long moment as she sat half-crouching on the divan, her hands locked, her face set and stony, her eyes lowered. He sighed gently and turned away. He paced to the parapet and looked out upon the city bathed in the white glare of the full risen moon. There arose thence a hum of sound, dominated, however, by the throbbing song of a nightingale somewhere in his garden and the croaking of the frogs by the pool in the valley.

Now that truth had been dragged from its well, and tossed, as it were, into Rosamund's lap, he felt none of the fierce exultation which he had conceived that such an hour as this must bring him. Rather, indeed, was he saddened and oppressed. To poison the unholy cup of joy which he had imagined himself draining with such thirsty zest there was that discovery of a measure of justification for her attitude towards him in her conviction that his disappearance was explained by flight.

He was weighed down by a sense that he had put himself entirely in the wrong; that in his vengeance he had overreached himself; and he found the fruits of it, which had seemed so desirably luscious, turning to ashes in his mouth.

Long he stood there, the silence between them entirely unbroken. Then at length he stirred, turned from the parapet, and paced slowly back until he came to stand beside the divan, looking down upon her from his great height.

"At last you have heard the truth," he said. And as she made no answer he continued: "I am thankful it was surprised out of him before the torture was applied, else you might have concluded that pain was wringing a false confession from him." He paused, but still she did not speak; indeed, she made no sign that she had heard him. "That," he concluded, "was the man whom you preferred to me. Faith, you did not flatter me, as perhaps you may have learnt."

At last she was moved from her silence, and her voice came dull and hard. "I have learnt how little there is to choose between you," she said. "It was to have been expected. I might have known two brothers could not have been so dissimilar in nature. Oh, I am learning a deal, and swiftly!"

It was a speech that angered him, that cast out entirely the softer mood that had been growing in him.

"You are learning?" he echoed. "What are you learning?"

"Knowledge of the ways of men."

His teeth gleamed in his wry smile. "I hope the knowledge will bring you as much bitterness as the knowledge of women—of one woman—has brought me. To have believed me what you believed me—me whom you conceived yourself to love!" He felt, perhaps the need to repeat it that he might keep the grounds of his grievance well before his mind.

"If I have a mercy to beg of you it is that you will not shame me with the reminder."

"Of your faithlessness?" he asked. "Of your disloyal readiness to believe the worst evil of me?"

"Of my ever having believed that I loved you. That is the thought that shames me, as nothing else in life could shame me, as not even the slave-market and all the insult to which you have submitted me could shame me. You taunt me with my readiness to believe evil of you...."

"I do more than taunt you with it," he broke in, his anger mounting under the pitiless lash of her scorn. "I lay to your charge the wasted years of my life, all the evil that has followed out of it, all that I have suffered, all that I have lost, all that I am become."

She looked up at him coldly, astonishingly mistress of herself. "You lay all this to my charge?" she asked him.

"I do." He was very vehement. "Had you not used me as you did, had you not lent a ready ear to lies, that whelp my brother would never have gone to such lengths, nor should I ever have afforded him the opportunity."

She shifted on the cushions of the divan and turned her shoulder to him.

"All this is very idle," she said coldly. Yet perhaps because she felt that she had need to justify herself she continued: "If, after all, I was so ready to believe evil of you, it is that my instincts must have warned me of the evil that was ever in you. You have proved to me to-night that it was not you who murdered Peter; but to attain that proof you have done a deed that is even fouler and more shameful, a deed that reveals to the full the blackness of your heart. Have you not proved yourself a monster of vengeance and impiety?" She rose and faced him again in her sudden passion. "Are you not—you that were born a Cornish Christian gentleman—become a heathen and a robber, a renegade and a pirate? Have you not sacrificed your very God to your vengeful lust?"

He met her glance fully, never quailing before her denunciation, and when she had ended on that note of question he counter-questioned her.

"And your instincts had forewarned you of all this? God's life, woman! can you invent no better tale than that?" He turned aside as two slaves entered bearing an earthenware vessel. "Here comes your supper. I hope your appetite is keener than your logic."

They set the vessel, from which a savoury smell proceeded, upon the little Moorish table by the divan. On the ground beside it they placed a broad dish of baked earth in which there were a couple of loaves and a red, short-necked amphora of water with a drinking-cup placed over the mouth of it to act as a stopper.

They salaamed profoundly and padded softly out again.

"Sup," he bade her shortly.

"I want no supper," she replied, her manner sullen.

His cold eye played over her. "Henceforth, girl, you will consider not what you want, but what I bid you do. I bid you eat; about it, therefore."

"I will not."

"Will not?" he echoed slowly. "Is that a speech from slave to master? Eat, I say."

"I cannot! I cannot!" she protested.

"A slave may not live who cannot do her master's bidding."

"Then kill me," she answered fiercely, leaping up to confront and dare him. "Kill me. You are used to killing, and for that at least I should be grateful."

"I will kill you if I please," he said in level icy tones. "But not to please you. You don't yet understand. You are my slave, my thing, my property, and I will not suffer you to be damaged save at my own good pleasure. Therefore, eat, or my Nubians shall whip you to quicken appetite."

For a moment she stood defiant before him, white and resolute. Then quite suddenly, as if her will was being bent and crumpled under the insistent pressure of his own, she drooped and sank down again to the divan. Slowly, reluctantly she drew the dish nearer. Watching her, he laughed quite silently.

She paused, appearing to seek for something. Failing to find it she looked up at him again, between scorn and intercession.

"Am I to tear the meat with my fingers?" she demanded.

His eyes gleamed with understanding, or at least with suspicion. But he answered her quite calmly—"It is against the Prophet's law to defile meat or bread by the contact of a knife. You must use the hands that God has given you."

"Do you mock me with the Prophet and his laws? What are the Prophet's laws to me? If eat I must, at least I will not eat like a heathen dog, but in Christian fashion."

To indulge her, as it seemed, he slowly drew the richly hilted dagger from his girdle. "Let that serve you, then," he said; and carelessly he tossed it down beside her.

With a quick indrawn breath she pounced upon it. "At last," she said, "you give me something for which I can be grateful to you." And on the words she laid the point of it against her breast.

Like lightning he had dropped to one knee, and his hand had closed about her wrist with such a grip that all her arm felt limp and powerless. He was smiling into her eyes, his swarthy face close to her own.

"Did you indeed suppose I trusted you? Did you really think me deceived by your sudden pretence of yielding? When will you learn that I am not a fool? I did it but to test your spirit."

"Then now you know its temper," she replied. "You know my intention."

"Forewarned, forearmed," said he.

She looked at him, with something that would have been mockery but for the contempt that coloured it too deeply. "Is it so difficult a thing," she asked, "to snap the thread of life? Are there no ways of dying save by the knife? You boast yourself my master; that I am your slave; that, having bought me in the market-place, I belong to you body and soul. How idle is that boast. My body you may bind and confine; but my soul.... Be very sure that you shall be cheated of your bargain. You boast yourself lord of life and death. A lie! Death is all that you can command."

Quick steps came pattering up the stairs, and before he could answer her, before he had thought of words in which to do so, Ali confronted him with the astounding announcement that there was a woman below asking urgently to speak with him.

"A woman?" he questioned, frowning. "A Nasrani woman, do you mean?"

"No, my lord. A Muslim," was the still more surprising information.

"A Muslim woman, here? Impossible!"

But even as he spoke a dark figure glided like a shadow across the threshold on to the terrace. She was in black from head to foot, including the veil that shrouded her, a veil of the proportions of a mantle, serving to dissemble her very shape.

Ali swung upon her in a rage. "Did I not bid thee wait below, thou daughter of shame?" he stormed. "She has followed me up, my lord, to thrust herself in here upon you. Shall I drive her forth?"

"Let her be," said Sakr-el-Bahr. And he waved Ali away. "Leave us!"

Something about that black immovable figure arrested his attention and fired his suspicions. Unaccountably almost it brought to his mind the thought of Ayoub-el-Sarnin and the bidding there had been for Rosamund in the sôk.

He stood waiting for his visitor to speak and disclose herself. She on her side continued immovable until Ali's footsteps had faded in the distance. Then, with a boldness entirely characteristic, with the recklessness that betrayed her European origin, intolerant of the Muslim restraint imposed upon her sex, she did what no True-believing woman would have done. She tossed back that long black veil and disclosed the pale countenance and languorous eyes of Fenzileh.

For all that it was no more than he had expected, yet upon beholding her—her countenance thus bared to his regard—he recoiled a step.

"Fenzileh!" he cried. "What madness is this?"

Having announced herself in that dramatic fashion she composedly readjusted her veil so that her countenance should once more be decently concealed.

"To come here, to my house, and thus!" he protested. "Should this reach the ears of thy lord, how will it fare with thee and with me? Away, woman, and at once!" he bade her.

"No need to fear his knowing of this unless, thyself, thou tell him," she answered. "To thee I need no excuse if thou'lt but remember that like thyself I was not born a Muslim."

"But Algiers is not thy native Sicily, and whatever thou wast born it were well to remember what thou art become."

He went on at length to tell her of the precise degree of her folly, but she cut in, stemming his protestation in full flow.

"These are idle words that but delay me."

"To thy purpose then, in Allah's name, that thus thou mayest depart the sooner."

She came to it straight enough on that uncompromising summons. She pointed to Rosamund. "It concerns that slave," said she. "I sent my wazeer to the sôk today with orders to purchase her for me."

"So I had supposed," he said.

"But it seems that she caught thy fancy, and the fool suffered himself to be outbidden."

"Well?"

"Thou'lt relinquish her to me at the price she cost thee?" A faint note of anxiety trembled in her voice.

"I am anguished to deny thee, O Fenzileh. She is not for sale."

"Ah, wait," she cried. "The price paid was high—many times higher than I have ever heard tell was given for a slave, however lovely. Yet I covet her. 'Tis a whim of mine, and I cannot suffer to be thwarted in my whims. To gratify this one I will pay three thousand philips."

He looked at her and wondered what devilries might be stirring in her mind, what evil purpose she desired to serve.

"Thou'lt pay three thousand philips?" he said slowly. Then bluntly asked her: "Why?"

"To gratify a whim, to please a fancy."

"What is the nature of this costly whim?" he insisted.

"The desire to possess her for my own," she answered evasively.

"And this desire to possess her, whence is it sprung?" he returned, as patient as he was relentless.

"You ask too many questions," she exclaimed with a flash of anger.

He shrugged and smiled. "You answer too few."

She set her arms akimbo and faced him squarely. Faintly through her veil he caught the gleam of her eyes, and he cursed the advantage she had in that her face was covered from his reading.

"In a word, Oliver-Reis," said she, "wilt sell her for three thousand philips?"

"In a word—no," he answered her.

"Thou'lt not? Not for three thousand philips?" Her voice was charged with surprise, and he wondered was it real or assumed.

"Not for thirty thousand," answered he. "She is mine, and I'll not relinquish her. So since I have proclaimed my mind, and since to tarry here is fraught with peril for us both, I beg thee to depart."

There fell a little pause, and neither of them noticed the alert interest stamped upon the white face of Rosamund. Neither of them suspected her knowledge of French which enabled her to follow most of what was said in the lingua franca they employed.

Fenzileh drew close to him. "Thou'lt not relinquish her, eh?" she asked, and he was sure she sneered. "Be not so confident. Thou'lt be forced to it, my friend—if not to me, why then, to Asad. He is coming for her, himself, in person."

"Asad?" he cried, startled now.

"Asad-ed-Din," she answered, and upon that resumed her pleading. "Come, then! It were surely better to make a good bargain with me than a bad one with the Basha."

He shook his head and planted his feet squarely. "I intend to make no bargain with either of you. This slave is not for sale."

"Shalt thou dare resist Asad? I tell thee he will take her whether she be for sale or not."

"I see," he said, his eyes narrowing. "And the fear of this, then, is the source of thy whim to acquire her for thyself. Thou art not subtle, O Fenzileh. The consciousness that thine own charms are fading sets thee trembling lest so much loveliness should entirely cast thee from thy lord's regard, eh?"

If he could not see her face, and study there the effect of that thrust of his, at least he observed the quiver that ran through her muffled figure, he caught the note of anger that throbbed in her reply—"And if that were so, what is't to thee?"

"It may be much or little," he replied thoughtfully.

"Indeed, it should be much," she answered quickly, breathlessly. "Have I not ever been thy friend? Have I not ever urged thy valour on my lord's notice and wrought like a true friend for thine advancement, Sakr-el-Bahr?"

He laughed outright. "Hast thou so?" quoth he.

"Laugh as thou wilt, but it is true," she insisted. "Lose me and thy most valuable ally is lost—one who has the ear and favour of her lord. For look, Sakr-el-Bahr, it is what would befall if another came to fill my place, another who might poison Asad's mind with lies against thee—for surely she cannot love thee, this Frankish girl whom thou hast torn from her home!"

"Be not concerned for that," he answered lightly, his wits striving in vain to plumb the depths and discover the nature of her purpose. "This slave of mine shall never usurp thy place beside Asad."

"O fool, Asad will take her whether she be for sale or not."

He looked down upon her, head on one side and arms akimbo. "If he can take her from me, the more easily can he take her from thee. No doubt thou hast considered that, and in some dark Sicilian way considered too how to provide against it. But the cost—hast thou counted that? What will Asad say to thee when he learns how thou hast thwarted him?"

"What do I care for that?" she cried in sudden fury, her gestures becoming a little wild. "She will be at the bottom of the harbour by then with a stone about her neck. He may have me whipped. No doubt he will. But 'twill end there. He will require me to console him for his loss, and so all will be well again."

At last he had drawn her, pumped her dry, as he imagined. Indeed, indeed, he thought, he had been right to say she was not subtle. He had been a fool to have permitted himself to be intrigued by so shallow, so obvious a purpose. He shrugged and turned away from her.

"Depart in peace, O Fenzileh," he said. "I yield her to none—be his name Asad or Shaitan."

His tone was final, and her answer seemed to accept at last his determination. Yet she was very quick with that answer; so quick that he might have suspected it to be preconceived.

"Then it is surely thine intent to wed her." No voice could have been more in nocent and guileless than was hers now. "If so," she went on, "it were best done quickly, for marriage is the only barrier Asad will not overthrow. He is devout, and out of his deep reverence for the Prophet's law he would be sure to respect such a bond as that. But be very sure that he will respect nothing short of it."

Yet notwithstanding her innocence and assumed simplicity—because of it, perhaps—he read her as if she had been an open book; it no longer mattered that her face was veiled.

"And thy purpose would be equally well served, eh?" he questioned her, sly in his turn.

"Equally," she admitted.

"Say 'better,' Fenzileh," he rejoined. "I said thou art not subtle. By the Koran, I lied. Thou art subtle as the serpent. Yet I see whither thou art gliding. Were I to be guided by thine advice a twofold purpose would be served. First, I should place her beyond Asad's reach, and second, I should be embroiled with him for having done so. What could more completely satisfy thy wishes?"

"Thou dost me wrong," she protested. "I have ever been thy friend. I would that...." She broke off suddenly to listen. The stillness of the night was broken by cries from the direction of the Bab-el-Oueb. She ran swiftly to the parapet whence the gate was to be seen and leaned far out.

"Look, look!" she cried, and there was a tremor of fear in her voice. "It is he—Asad-ed-Din."

Sakr-el-Bahr crossed to her side and in a glare of torches saw a body of men coming forth from the black archway of the gate.

"It almost seems as if, departing from thy usual custom, thou hast spoken truth, O Fenzileh."

She faced him, and he suspected the venomous glance darted at him through her veil. Yet her voice when she spoke was cold. "In a moment thou'lt have no single doubt of it. But what of me?" The question was added in a quickening tone. "He must not find me here. He would kill me, I think."

"I am sure he would," Sakr-el-Bahr agreed. "Yet muffled thus, who should recognize thee? Away, then, ere he comes. Take cover in the courtyard until he shall have passed. Didst thou come alone?"

"Should I trust anyone with the knowledge that I had visited thee?" she asked, and he admired the strong Sicilian spirit in her that not all these years in the Basha's hareem had sufficed to extinguish.

She moved quickly to the door, to pause again on the threshold.

"Thou'lt not relinquish her? Thou'lt not."

"Be at ease," he answered her, on so resolved a note that she departed satisfied.

CHAPTER XIII. IN THE SIGHT OF ALLAH

Sakr-el-Bahr stood lost in thought after she had gone. Again he weighed her every word and considered precisely how he should meet Asad, and how refuse him, if the Basha's were indeed such an errand as Fenzileh had heralded.

Thus in silence he remained waiting for Ali or another to summon him to the presence of the Basha. Instead, however, when Ali entered it was actually to announce Asad-ed-Din, who followed immediately upon his heels, having insisted in his impatience upon being conducted straight to the presence of Sakr-el-Bahr.

"The peace of the Prophet upon thee, my son, was the Basha's greeting.

"And upon thee, my lord." Sakr-el-Bahr salaamed. "My house is honoured." With a gesture he dismissed Ali.

"I come to thee a suppliant," said Asad, advancing.

"A suppliant, thou? No need, my lord. I have no will that is not the echo of thine own."

The Basha's questing eyes went beyond him and glowed as they rested upon Rosamund.

"I come in haste," he said, "like any callow lover, guided by my every instinct to the presence of her I seek—this Frankish pearl, this pen-faced captive of thy latest raid. I was away from the Kasbah when that pig Tsamanni returned thither from the sôk; but when at last I learnt that he had failed to purchase her as I commanded, I could have wept for very grief. I feared at first that some merchant from the Sus might have bought her and departed; but when I heard—blessed be Allah!—that thou wert the buyer, I was comforted again. For thou'lt yield her up to me, my son."

He spoke with such confidence that Oliver had a difficulty in choosing the words that were to disillusion him. Therefore he stood in hesitancy a moment.

"I will make good thy, loss," Asad ran on. "Thou shalt have the sixteen hundred philips paid and another five hundred to console thee. Say that will content thee; for I boil with impatience."

Sakr-el-Bahr smiled grimly. "It is an impatience well known to me, my lord, where she is concerned," he answered slowly. "I boiled with it myself for five interminable years. To make an end of it I went a distant perilous voyage to England in a captured Frankish vessel. Thou didst not know, O Asad, else thou wouldst...."

"Bah!" broke in the Basha. "Thou'rt a huckster born. There is none like thee, Sakr-el-Bahr, in any game of wits. Well, well, name thine own price, strike thine own profit out of my impatience and let us have done."

"My lord," he said quietly, "it is not the profit that is in question. She is not for sale."

Asad blinked at him, speechless, and slowly a faint colour crept into his sallow cheeks.

"Not... not for sale?" he echoed, faltering in his amazement.

"Not if thou offered me thy Bashalik as the price of her," was the solemn answer. Then more warmly, in a voice that held a note of intercession—"Ask anything else that is mine," he continued, "and gladly will I lay it at thy feet in earnest of my loyalty and love for thee."

"But I want nothing else." Asad's tone was impatient, petulant almost. "I want this slave."

"Then," replied Oliver, "I cast myself upon thy mercy and beseech thee to turn thine eyes elsewhere."

Asad scowled upon him. "Dost thou deny me?" he demanded, throwing back his head.

"Alas!" said Sakr-el-Bahr.

There fell a pause. Darker and darker grew the countenance of Asad, fiercer glowed the eyes he bent upon his lieutenant. "I see," he said at last, with a calm so oddly at variance with his looks as to be sinister. "I see. It seems that there is more truth in Fenzileh than I suspected. So!" He considered the corsair a moment with his sunken smouldering eyes.

Then he addressed him in a tone that vibrated with his suppressed anger. "Bethink thee, Sakr-el-Bahr, of what thou art, of what I have made thee. Bethink thee of all the bounty these hands have lavished on thee. Thou art my own lieutenant, and mayest one day be more. In Algiers there is none above thee save myself. Art, then, so thankless as to deny me the first thing I ask of thee? Truly is it written 'Ungrateful is Man.'"

"Didst thou know," began Sakr-el-Bahr, "all that is involved for me in this...."

"I neither know nor care," Asad cut in. "Whatever it may be, it should be as naught when set against my will." Then he discarded anger for cajolery. He set a hand upon Sakr-el-Bahr's stalwart shoulder. "Come, my son. I will deal generously with thee out of my love, and I will put thy refusal from my mind."

"Be generous, my lord, to the point of forgetting that ever thou didst ask me for her."

"Dost still refuse?" The voice, honeyed an instant ago, rang harsh again. "Take care how far thou strain my patience. Even as I have raised thee from the dirt, so at a word can I cast thee down again. Even as I broke the shackles that chained thee to the rowers' bench, so can I rivet them on thee anew."

"All this canst thou do," Sakr-el-Bahr agreed. "And since, knowing it, I still hold to what is doubly mine—by right of capture and of purchase—thou mayest conceive how mighty are my reasons. Be merciful, then, Asad...."

"Must I take her by force in spite of thee?" roared the Basha.

Sakr-el-Bahr stiffened. He threw back his head and looked the Basha squarely in the eyes.

"Whilst I live, not even that mayest thou do," he answered.

"Disloyal, mutinous dog! Wilt thou resist me—me?"

"It is my prayer that thou'lt not be so ungenerous and unjust as to compel thy servant to a course so hateful."

Asad sneered. "Is that thy last word?" he demanded.

"Save only that in all things else I am thy slave, O Asad."

A moment the Basha stood regarding him, his glance baleful. Then deliberately, as one who has taken his resolve, he strode to the door. On the threshold he paused and turned again. "Wait!" he said, and on that threatening word departed.

Sakr-el-Bahr remained a moment where he had stood during the interview, then with a shrug he turned. He met Rosamund's eyes fixed intently upon him, and invested with a look he could not read. He found himself unable to meet it, and he turned away. It was inevitable that in such a moment the earlier stab of remorse should be repeated. He had overreached himself indeed. Despair settled down upon him, a full consciousness of the horrible thing he had done, which seemed now so irrevocable. In his silent anguish he almost conceived that he had mistaken his feelings for Rosamund; that far from hating her as he had supposed, his love for her had not yet been slain, else surely he should not be tortured now by the thought of her becoming Asad's prey. If he hated her, indeed, as he had supposed, he would have surrendered her and gloated.

He wondered was his present frame of mind purely the result of his discovery that the appearances against him had been stronger far than he imagined, so strong as to justify her conviction that he was her brother's slayer.

And then her voice, crisp and steady, cut into his torture of consideration.

"Why did you deny him?"

He swung round again to face her, amazed, horror-stricken.

"You understood?" he gasped.

"I understood enough," said she. "This lingua franca is none so different from French." And again she asked—"Why did you deny him?"

He paced across to her side and stood looking down at her.

"Do you ask why?"

"Indeed," she said bitterly, "there is scarce the need perhaps. And yet can it be that your lust of vengeance is so insatiable that sooner than willingly forgo an ounce of it you will lose your head?"

His face became grim again. "Of course," he sneered, "it would be so that you'd interpret me."

"Nay. If I have asked it is because I doubt."

"Do you realize what it can mean to become the prey of Asad-ed-Din?"

She shuddered, and her glance fell from his, yet her voice was composed when she answered him—"Is it so very much worse than becoming the prey of Oliver-Reis or Sakr-el-Bahr, or whatever they may call you?"

"If you say that it is all one to you there's an end to my opposing him," he answered coldly. "You may go to him. If I resisted him—like a fool, perhaps—it was for no sake of vengeance upon you. It was because the thought of it fills me with horror."

"Then it should fill you with horror of yourself no less," said she.

His answer startled her.

"Perhaps it does," he said, scarcely above a murmur. "Perhaps it does."

She flashed him an upward glance and looked as if she would have spoken. But he went on, suddenly passionate, without giving her time to interrupt him. "O God! It needed this to show me the vileness of the thing I have done. Asad has no such motives as had I. I wanted you that I might punish you. But he...O God!" he groaned, and for a moment put his face to his hands.

She rose slowly, a strange agitation stirring in her, her bosom galloping. But in his overwrought condition he failed to observe it. And then like a ray of hope to illumine his despair came the counsel that Fenzileh had given him, the barrier which she had said that Asad, being a devout Muslim, would never dare to violate.

"There is a way," he cried. "There is the way suggested by Fenzileh at the promptings of her malice." An instant he hesitated, his eyes averted. Then he made his plunge. "You must marry me."

It was almost as if he had struck her. She recoiled. Instantly suspicion awoke in her; swiftly it drew to a conviction that he had but sought to trick her by a pretended penitence.

"Marry you!" she echoed.

"Ay," he insisted. And he set himself to explain to her how if she were his wife she must be sacred and inviolable to all good Muslimeen, that none could set a finger upon her without doing outrage to the Prophet's holy law, and that, whoever might be so disposed, Asad was not of those, since Asad was perfervidly devout. "Thus only," he ended, "can I place you beyond his reach."

But she was still scornfully reluctant.

"It is too desperate a remedy even for so desperate an ill," said she, and thus drove him into a frenzy of impatience with her.

"You must, I say," he insisted, almost angrily. "You must—or else consent to be borne this very night to Asad's hareem—and not even as his wife, but as his slave. Oh, you must trust me for your own sake! You must!"

"Trust you!" she cried, and almost laughed in the intensity of her scorn. "Trust you! How can I trust one who is a renegade and worse?"

He controlled himself that he might reason with her, that by cold logic he might conquer her consent.

"You are very unmerciful," he said. "In judging me you leave out of all account the suffering through which I have gone and what yourself contributed to it. Knowing now how falsely I was accused and what other bitter wrongs I suffered, consider that I was one to whom the man and the woman I most loved in all this world had proven false. I had lost faith in man and in God, and if I became a Muslim, a renegade, and a corsair, it was because there was no other gate by which I could escape the unutterable toil of the oar to which I had been chained." He looked at her sadly. "Can you find no excuse for me in all that?"

It moved her a little, for if she maintained a hostile attitude, at least she put aside her scorn.

"No wrongs," she told him, almost with sorrow in her voice, "could justify you in outraging chivalry, in dishonouring your manhood, in abusing your strength to persecute a woman. Whatever the causes that may have led to it, you have fallen too low, sir, to make it possible that I should trust you."

He bowed his head under the rebuke which already he had uttered in his own heart. It was just and most deserved, and since he recognized its justice he found it impossible to resent it.

"I know," he said. "But I am not asking you to trust me to my profit, but to your own. It is for your sake alone that I implore you to do this." Upon a sudden inspiration he drew the heavy dagger from his girdle and proffered it, hilt foremost. "If you need an earnest of my good faith," he said, "take this knife with which to-night you attempted to stab yourself. At the first sign that I am false to my trust, use it as you will—upon me or upon yourself."

She pondered him in some surprise. Then slowly she put out her hand to take the weapon, as he bade her.

"Are you not afraid," she asked him, "that I shall use it now, and so make an end?"

"I am trusting you," he said, "that in return you may trust me. Further, I am arming you against the worst. For if it comes to choice between death and Asad, I shall approve your choice of death. But let me add that it were foolish to choose death whilst yet there is a chance of life."

"What chance?" she asked, with a faint return of her old scorn. "The chance of life with you?"

"No," he answered firmly. "If you will trust me, I swear that I will seek to undo the evil I have done. Listen. At dawn my galeasse sets out upon a raid. I will convey you secretly aboard and find a way to land you in some Christian country—Italy or France—whence you may make your way home again."

"But meanwhile," she reminded him, "I shall have become your wife."

He smiled wistfully. "Do you still fear a trap? Can naught convince you of my sincerity? A Muslim marriage is not binding upon a Christian, and I shall account it no marriage. It will be no more than a pretence to shelter you until we are away."

"How can I trust your word in that?"

"How?" He paused, baffled; but only for a moment. "You have the dagger," he answered pregnantly.

She stood considering, her eyes upon the weapon's lividly gleaming blade. "And this marriage?" she asked. "How is it to take place?"

He explained to her then that by the Muslim law all that was required was a declaration made before a kadi, or his superior, and in the presence of witnesses.

He was still at his explanation when from below there came a sound of voices, the tramp of feet, and the flash of torches.

"Here is Asad returning in force," he cried, and his voice trembled. "Do you consent?"

"But the kadi?" she inquired, and by the question he knew that she was won to his way of saving her.

"I said the kadi or his superior. Asad himself shall be our priest, his followers our witnesses."

"And if he refuses? He will refuse!" she cried, clasping her hands before her in her excitement.

"I shall not ask him. I shall take him by surprise."

"It... it must anger him. He may avenge himself for what he must deem a trick."

"Ay," he answered, wild-eyed. "I have thought of that, too. But it is a risk we must run. If we do not prevail, then—"

"I have the dagger," she cried fearlessly.

"And for me there will be the rope or the sword," he answered. "Be calm! They come!"

But the steps that pattered up the stairs were Ali's. He flung upon the terrace in alarm.

"My lord, my lord! Asad-ed-Din is here in force. He has an armed following with him!"

"There is naught to fear," said Sakr-el-Bahr, with every show of calm. "All will be well."

Asad swept up the stairs and out upon that terrace to confront his rebellious lieutenant. After him came a dozen black-robed janissaries with scimitars along which the light of the torches rippled in little runnels as of blood.

The Basha came to a halt before Sakr-el-Bahr, his arms majestically folded, his head thrown back, so that his long white beard jutted forward.

"I am returned," he said, "to employ force where gentleness will not avail. Yet I pray that Allah may have lighted thee to a wiser frame of mind."

"He has, indeed, my lord," replied Sakr-el-Bahr.

"The praise to Him!" exclaimed Asad in a voice that rang with joy. "The girl, then!" And he held out a hand.

Sakr-el-Bahr stepped back to her and took her hand in his as if to lead her forward. Then he spoke the fateful words.

"In Allah's Holy Name and in His All-seeing eyes, before thee, Asad-ed-Din, and in the presence of these witnesses, I take this woman to be my wife by the merciful law of the Prophet of Allah the All-wise, the All-pitying."

The words were out and the thing was done before Asad had realized the corsair's intent. A gasp of dismay escaped him; then his visage grew inflamed, his eyes blazed.

But Sakr-el-Bahr, cool and undaunted before that royal anger, took the scarf that lay about Rosamund's shoulders, and raising it, flung it over her head, so that her face was covered by it.

"May Allah rot off the hand of him who in contempt of our Lord Mahomet's holy law may dare to unveil that face, and may Allah bless this union and cast into the pit of Gehenna any who shall attempt to dissolve a bond that is tied in His All-seeing eyes."

It was formidable. Too formidable for Asad ed Din. Behind him his janissaries like hounds in leash stood eagerly awaiting his command. But none came. He stood there breathing heavily, swaying a little, and turning from red to pale in the battle that was being fought within him between rage and vexation on the one hand and his profound piety on the other. And as he yet hesitated perhaps Sakr-el-Bahr assisted his piety to gain the day.

"Now you will understand why I would not yield her, O mighty Asad," he said. "Thyself hast thou oft and rightly reproached me with my celibacy, reminding me that it is not pleasing in the sight of Allah, that it is unworthy a good Muslim. At last it hath pleased the Prophet to send me such a maid as I could take to wife."

Asad bowed his head. "What is written is written," he said in the voice of one who admonished himself. Then he raised his arms aloft. "Allah is All-knowing," he declared. "His will be done!"

"Ameen," said Sakr-el-Bahr very solemnly and with a great surge of thankful prayer to his own long-forgotten God.

The Basha stayed yet a moment, as if he would have spoken. Then abruptly he turned and waved a hand to his janissaries. "Away!" was all he said to them, and stalked out in their wake.

CHAPTER XIV. THE SIGN

From behind her lattice, still breathless from the haste she had made, and with her whelp Marzak at her side, Fenzileh had witnessed that first angry return of the Basha from the house of Sakr-el-Bahr.

She had heard him bawling for Abdul Mohktar, the leader of his janissaries, and she had seen the hasty mustering of a score of these soldiers in the courtyard, where the ruddy light of torches mingled with the white light of the full moon. She had seen them go hurrying away with Asad himself at their head, and she had not known whether to weep or to laugh, whether to fear or to rejoice.

"It is done," Marzak had cried exultantly. "The dog hath withstood him and so destroyed himself. There will be an end to Sakr-el-Bahr this night." And he had added: "The praise to Allah!"

But from Fenzileh came no response to his prayer of thanksgiving. True, Sakr-el-Bahr must be destroyed, and by a sword that she herself had forged. Yet was it not inevitable that the stroke which laid him low must wound her on its repercussion? That was the question to which now she sought an answer. For all her eagerness to speed the corsair to his doom, she had paused sufficiently to weigh the consequences to herself; she had not overlooked the circumstance that an inevitable result of this must be Asad's appropriation of that Frankish slave-girl. But at the time it had seemed to her that even this price was worth paying to remove Sakr-el-Bahr definitely and finally from her son's path—which shows that, after all, Fenzileh the mother was capable of some self-sacrifice. She comforted herself now with the reflection that the influence, whose waning she feared might be occasioned by the introduction of a rival into Asad's hareem, would no longer be so vitally necessary to herself and Marzak once Sakr-el-Bahr were removed. The rest mattered none so much to her. Yet it mattered something, and the present state of things left her uneasy, her mind a cockpit of emotions. Her grasp could not encompass all her desires at once, it seemed; and whilst she could gloat over the gratification of one, she must bewail the frustration of another. Yet in the main she felt that she should account herself the gainer.

In this state of mind she had waited, scarce heeding the savagely joyous and entirely selfish babblings of her cub, who cared little what might betide his mother as the price of the removal of that hated rival from his path. For him, at least, there was nothing but profit in the business, no cause for anything but satisfaction; and that satisfaction he voiced with a fine contempt for his mother's feelings.

Anon they witnessed Asad's return. They saw the janissaries come swinging into the courtyard and range themselves there whilst the Basha made his appearance, walking slowly, with steps that dragged a little, his head sunk upon his breast, his hands behind him. They waited to see slaves following him, leading or carrying the girl he had gone to fetch. But they waited in vain, intrigued and uneasy.

They heard the harsh voice in which Asad dismissed his followers, and the clang of the closing gate; and they saw him pacing there alone in the moonlight, ever in that attitude of dejection.

What had happened? Had he killed them both? Had the girl resisted him to such an extent that he had lost all patience and in one of those rages begotten of such resistance made an end of her?

Thus did Fenzileh question herself, and since she could not doubt but that Sakr-el-Bahr was slain, she concluded that the rest must be as she conjectured. Yet, the suspense torturing her, she summoned Ayoub and sent him to glean from Abdul Mohktar the tale of what had passed. In his own hatred of Sakr-el-Bahr, Ayoub went willingly enough and hoping for the worst. He returned disappointed, with a tale that sowed dismay in Fenzileh and Marzak.

Fenzileh, however, made a swift recovery. After all, it was the best that could have happened. It should not be difficult to transmute that obvious dejection of Asad's into resentment, and to fan this into a rage that must end by consuming Sakr-el-Bahr. And so the thing could be accomplished without jeopardy to her own place at Asad's side. For it was inconceivable that he should now take Rosamund to his hareem. Already the fact that she had been paraded with naked face among the Faithful must in itself have been a difficult obstacle to his pride. But it was utterly impossible that he could so subject his self-respect to his desire as to take to himself a woman who had been the wife of his servant.

Fenzileh saw her way very clearly. It was through Asad's devoutness—as she herself had advised, though scarcely expecting such rich results as these—that he had been thwarted by Sakr-el-Bahr. That same devoutness must further be played upon now to do the rest.

Taking up a flimsy silken veil, she went out to him where he now sat on the divan under the awning, alone there in the tepid-scented summer night. She crept to his side with the soft, graceful, questing movements of a cat, and sat there a moment unheeded almost—such was his abstraction—her head resting lightly against his shoulder.

"Lord of my soul," she murmured presently, "thou art sorrowing." Her voice was in itself a soft and soothing caress.

He started, and she caught the gleam of his eyes turned suddenly upon her.

"Who told thee so?" he asked suspiciously.

"My heart," she answered, her voice melodious as a viol. "Can sorrow burden thine and mine go light?" she wooed him. "Is happiness possible to me when thou art downcast? In there I felt thy melancholy, and thy need of me, and I am come to share thy burden, or to bear it all for thee." Her arms were raised, and her fingers interlocked themselves upon his shoulder.

He looked down at her, and his expression softened. He needed comfort, and never was she more welcome to him.

Gradually and with infinite skill she drew from him the story of what had happened. When she had gathered it, she loosed her indignation.

"The dog!" she cried. "The faithless, ungrateful hound! Yet have I warned thee against him, O light of my poor eyes, and thou hast scorned me for the warnings uttered by my love. Now at last thou knowest him, and he shall trouble thee no longer. Thou'lt cast him off, reduce him again to the dust from which thy bounty raised him."

But Asad did not respond. He sat there in a gloomy abstraction, staring straight before him. At last he sighed wearily. He was just, and he had a conscience, as odd a thing as it was awkward in a corsair Basha.

"In what hath befallen," he answered moodily, "there is naught to justify me in casting aside the stoutest soldier of Islam. My duty to Allah will not suffer it."

"Yet his duty to thee suffered him to thwart thee, O my lord," she reminded him very softly.

"In my desires—ay!" he answered, and for a moment his voice quivered with passion. Then he repressed it, and continued more calmly—"Shall my self-seeking overwhelm my duty to the Faith? Shall the matter of a slave-girl urge me to sacrifice the bravest soldier of Islam, the stoutest champion of the Prophet's law? Shall I bring down upon my head the vengeance of the One by destroying a man who is a scourge of scorpions unto the infidel—and all this that I may gratify my personal anger against him, that I may avenge the thwarting of a petty desire?"

"Dost thou still say, O my life, that Sakr-el-Bahr is the stoutest champion of the Prophet's law?" she asked him softly, yet on a note of amazement.

"It is not I that say it, but his deeds," he answered sullenly.

"I know of one deed no True-Believer could have wrought. If proof were needed of his infidelity he hath now afforded it in taking to himself a Nasrani wife. Is it not written in the Book to be Read: 'Marry not idolatresses'? Is not that the Prophet's law, and hath he not broken it, offending at once against Allah and against thee, O fountain of my soul?"

Asad frowned. Here was truth indeed, something that he had entirely overlooked. Yet justice compelled him still to defend Sakr-el-Bahr, or else perhaps he but reasoned to prove to himself that the case against the corsair was indeed complete.

"He may have sinned in thoughtlessness," he suggested.

At that she cried out in admiration of him. "What a fount of mercy and forbearance art thou, O father of Marzak! Thou'rt right as in all things. It was no doubt in thoughtlessness that he offended, but would such thoughtlessness be possible in a True-Believer—in one worthy to be dubbed by thee the champion of the Prophet's Holy Law?"

It was a shrewd thrust, that pierced the armour of conscience in which he sought to empanoply himself. He sat very thoughtful, scowling darkly at the inky shadow of the wall which the moon was casting. Suddenly he rose.

"By Allah, thou art right!" he cried. "So that he thwarted me and kept that Frankish woman for himself, he cared not how he sinned against the law."

She glided to her knees and coiled her arms about his waist, looking up at him. "Still art thou ever merciful, ever sparing in adverse judgment. Is that all his fault, O Asad?"

"All?" he questioned, looking down at her. "What more is there?"

"I would there were no more. Yet more there is, to which thy angelic mercy blinds thee. He did worse. Not merely was he reckless of how he sinned against the law, he turned the law to his own base uses and so defiled it."

"How?" he asked quickly, eagerly almost.

"He employed it as a bulwark behind which to shelter himself and her. Knowing that thou who art the Lion and defender of the Faith wouldst bend obediently to what is written in the Book, he married her to place her beyond thy reach."

"The praise to Him who is All-wise and lent me strength to do naught unworthy!" he cried in a great voice, glorifying himself. "I might have slain him to dissolve the impious bond, yet I obeyed what is written."

"Thy forbearance hath given joy to the angels," she answered him, "and yet a man was found so base as to trade upon it and upon thy piety, O Asad!"

He shook off her clasp, and strode away from her a prey to agitation. He paced to and fro in the moonlight there, and she, well-content, reclined upon the cushions of the divan, a thing of infinite grace, her gleaming eyes discreetly veiled from him—waiting until her poison should have done its work.

She saw him halt, and fling up his arms, as if apostrophizing Heaven, as if asking a question of the stars that twinkled in the wide-flung nimbus of the moon.

Then at last he paced slowly back to her. He was still undecided. There was truth in what she had said; yet he knew and weighed her hatred of Sakr-el-Bahr, knew how it must urge her to put the worst construction upon any act of his, knew her jealousy for Marzak, and so he mistrusted her arguments and mistrusted himself. Also there was his own love of Sakr-el-Bahr that would insist upon a place in the balance of his judgment. His mind was in turmoil.

"Enough," he said almost roughly. "I pray that Allah may send me counsel in the night." And upon that he stalked past her, up the steps, and so into the house.

She followed him. All night she lay at his feet to be ready at the first peep of dawn to buttress a purpose that she feared was still weak, and whilst he slept fitfully, she slept not at all, but lay wide-eyed and watchful.

At the first note of the mueddin's voice, he leapt from his couch obedient to its summons, and scarce had the last note of it died upon the winds of dawn than he was afoot, beating his hands together to summon slaves and issuing his orders, from which she gathered that he was for the harbour there and then.

"May Allah have inspired thee, O my lord!" she cried. And asked him: "What is thy resolve?"

"I go to seek a sign," he answered her, and upon that departed, leaving her in a frame of mind that was far from easy.

She summoned Marzak, and bade him accompany his father, breathed swift instructions of what he should do and how do it.

"Thy fate has been placed in thine own hands," she admonished him. "See that thou grip it firmly now."

In the courtyard Marzak found his father in the act of mounting a white mule that had been brought him.

He was attended by his wazeer Tsamanni, Biskaine, and some other of his captains. Marzak begged leave to go with him. It was carelessly granted, and they set out, Marzak walking by his father's stirrup, a little in advance of the others. For a while there was silence between father and son, then the latter spoke.

"It is my prayer, O my father, that thou art resolved to depose the faithless Sakr-el-Bahr from the command of this expedition."

Asad considered his son with a sombre eye. "Even now the galeasse should be setting out if the argosy is to be intercepted," he said. "If Sakr-el-Bahr does not command, who shall, in Heaven's name?"

"Try me, O my father," cried Marzak.

Asad smiled with grim wistfulness. "Art weary of life, O my son, that thou wouldst go to thy death and take the galeasse to destruction?"

"Thou art less than just, O my father," Marzak protested.

"Yet more than kind, O my son," replied Asad, and they went on in silence thereafter, until they came to the mole.

The splendid galeasse was moored alongside, and all about her there was great bustle of preparation for departure. Porters moved up and down the gangway that connected her with the shore, carrying bales of provisions, barrels of water, kegs of gunpowder, and other necessaries for the voyage, and even as Asad and his followers reached the head of that gangway, four negroes were staggering down it under the load of a huge palmetto bale that was slung from staves yoked to their shoulders.

On the poop stood Sakr-el-Bahr with Othmani, Ali, Jasper-Reis, and some other officers. Up and down the gangway paced Larocque and Vigitello, two renegade boatswains, one French and the other Italian, who had sailed with him on every voyage for the past two years. Larocque was superintending the loading of the vessel, bawling his orders for the bestowal of provisions here, of water yonder, and of powder about the mainmast. Vigitello was making a final inspection of the slaves at the oars.

As the palmetto pannier was brought aboard, Larocque shouted to the negroes to set it down by the mainmast. But here Sakr-el-Bahr interfered, bidding them, instead, to bring it up to the stern and place it in the poop-house.

Asad had dismounted, and stood with Marzak at his side at the head of the gangway when the youth finally begged his father himself to take command of this expedition, allowing him to come as his lieutenant and so learn the ways of the sea.

Asad looked at him curiously, but answered nothing. He went aboard, Marzak and the others following him. It was at this moment that Sakr-el-Bahr first became aware of the Basha's presence, and he came instantly forward to do the honhonours of his galley. If there was a sudden uneasiness in his heart his face was calm and his glance as arrogant and steady as ever.

"May the peace of Allah overshadow thee and thy house, O mighty Asad," was his greeting. "We are on the point of casting off, and I shall sail the more securely for thy blessing."

Asad considered him with eyes of wonder. So much effrontery, so much ease after their last scene together seemed to the Basha a thing incredible, unless, indeed, it were accompanied by a conscience entirely at peace.

"It has been proposed to me that I shall do more than bless this expedition—that I shall command it," he answered, watching Sakr-el-Bahr closely. He observed the sudden flicker of the corsair's eyes, the only outward sign of his inward dismay.

"Command it?" echoed Sakr-el-Bahr. "'Twas proposed to thee?" And he laughed lightly as if to dismiss that suggestion.

That laugh was a tactical error. It spurred Asad. He advanced slowly along the vessel's waist-deck to the mainmast—for she was rigged with main and foremasts. There he halted again to look into the face of Sakr-el-Bahr who stepped along beside him.

"Why didst thou laugh?" he questioned shortly.

"Why? At the folly of such a proposal," said Sakr-el-Bahr in haste, too much in haste to seek a diplomatic answer.

Darker grew the Basha's frown. "Folly?" quoth he. "Wherein lies the folly?"

Sakr-el-Bahr made haste to cover his mistake. "In the suggestion that such poor quarry as waits us should be worthy thine endeavour, should warrant the Lion of the Faith to unsheathe his mighty claws. Thou," he continued with ringing scorn, "thou the inspirer of a hundred glorious fights in which whole fleets have been engaged, to take the seas upon so trivial an errand—one galeasse to swoop upon a single galley of Spain! It were unworthy thy great name, beneath the dignity of thy valour!" and by a gesture he contemptuously dismissed the subject.

But Asad continued to ponder him with cold eyes, his face inscrutable. "Why, here's a change since yesterday!" he said.

"A change, my lord?"

"But yesterday in the market-place thyself didst urge me to join this expedition and to command it," Asad reminded him, speaking with deliberate emphasis. "Thyself invoked the memory of the days that are gone, when, scimitar in hand, we charged side by side aboard the infidel, and thou didst beseech me to engage again beside thee. And now...." He spread his hands, anger gathered in his eyes. "Whence this change?" he demanded sternly.

Sakr-el-Bahr hesitated, caught in his own toils. He looked away from Asad a moment; he had a glimpse of the handsome flushed face of Marzak at his father's elbow, of Biskaine, Tsamanni, and the others all staring at him in amazement, and even of some grimy sunburned faces from the rowers' bench on his left that were looking on with dull curiosity.

He smiled, seeming outwardly to remain entirely unruffled. "Why... it is that I have come to perceive thy reasons for refusing. For the rest, it is as I say, the quarry is not worthy of the hunter."

Marzak uttered a soft sneering laugh, as if the true reason of the corsair's attitude were quite clear to him. He fancied too, and he was right in this, that Sakr-el-Bahr's odd attitude had accomplished what persuasions addressed to Asad-ed-Din might to the end have failed to accomplish—had afforded him the sign he was come to seek. For it was in that moment that Asad determined to take command himself.

"It almost seems," he said slowly, smiling, "as if thou didst not want me. If so, it is unfortunate; for I have long neglected my duty to my son, and I am resolved at last to repair that error. We accompany thee upon this expedition, Sakr-el-Bahr. Myself I will command it, and Marzak shall be my apprentice in the ways of the sea."

Sakr-el-Bahr said not another word in protest against that proclaimed resolve. He salaamed, and when he spoke there was almost a note of gladness in his voice.

"The praise to Allah, then, since thou'rt determined. It is not for me to urge further the unworthiness of the quarry since I am the gainer by thy resolve."

CHAPTER XV. THE VOYAGE

His resolve being taken, Asad drew Tsamanni aside and spent some moments in talk with him, giving him certain instructions for the conduct of affairs ashore during his absence. That done, and the wazeer dismissed, the Basha himself gave the order to cast off, an order which there was no reason to delay, since all was now in readiness.

The gangway was drawn ashore, the boatswains whistle sounded, and the steersmen leapt to their niches in the stern, grasping the shafts of the great steering-oars. A second blast rang out, and down the gangway-deck came Vigitello and two of his mates, all three armed with long whips of bullock-hide, shouting to the slaves to make ready. And then, on the note of a third blast of Larocque's whistle, the fifty-four poised oars dipped to the water, two hundred and fifty bodies bent as one, and when they heaved themselves upright again the great galeasse shot forward and so set out upon her adventurous voyage. From her mainmast the red flag with its green crescent was unfurled to the breeze, and from the crowded mole, and the beach where a long line of spectators had gathered, there burst a great cry of valediction.

That breeze blowing stiffly from the desert was Lionel's friend that day. Without it his career at the oar might have been short indeed. He was chained, like the rest, stark naked, save for a loincloth, in the place nearest the gangway on the first starboard bench abaft the narrow waist-deck, and ere the galeasse had made the short distance between the mole and the island at the end of it, the boatswain's whip had coiled itself about his white shoulders to urge him to better exertion than he was putting forth. He had screamed under the cruel cut, but none had heeded him. Lest the punishment should be repeated, he had thrown all his weight into the next strokes of the oar, until by the time the Peñon was reached the sweat was running down his body and his heart was thudding against his ribs. It was not possible that it could have lasted, and his main agony lay in that he realized it, and saw himself face to face with horrors inconceivable that must await the exhaustion of his strength. He was not naturally robust, and he had led a soft and pampered life that was very far from equipping him for such a test as this.

But as they reached the Peñon and felt the full vigour of that warm breeze, Sakr-el-Bahr, who by Asad's command remained in charge of the navigation, ordered the unfurling of the enormous lateen sails on main and foremasts. They ballooned out, swelling to the wind, and the galeasse surged forward at a speed that was more than doubled. The order to cease rowing followed, and the slaves were left to return thanks to Heaven for their respite, and to rest in their chains until such time as their sinews should be required again.

The vessel's vast prow, which ended in a steel ram and was armed with a culverin on either quarter, was crowded with lounging corsairs, who took their ease there until the time to engage should be upon them. They leaned on the high bulwarks or squatted in groups, talking, laughing, some of them tailoring and repairing garments, others burnishing their weapons or their armour, and one swarthy youth there was who thrummed a gimri and sang a melancholy Shilha love-song to the delight of a score or so of bloodthirsty ruffians squatting about him in a ring of variegated colour.

The gorgeous poop was fitted with a spacious cabin, to which admission was gained by two archways curtained with stout silken tapestries upon whose deep red ground the crescent was wrought in brilliant green. Above the cabin stood the three cressets or stern-lamps, great structures of gilded iron surmounted each by the orb and crescent. As if to continue the cabin forward and increase its size, a green awning was erected from it to shade almost half the poop-deck. Here cushions were thrown, and upon these squatted now Asad-ed-Din with Marzak, whilst Biskaine and some three or four other officers who had escorted him aboard and whom he had retained beside him for that voyage, were lounging upon the gilded balustrade at the poop's forward end, immediately above the rowers' benches.

Sakr-el-Bahr alone, a solitary figure, resplendent in caftan and turban that were of cloth of silver, leaned upon the bulwarks of the larboard quarter of the poop-deck, and looked moodily back upon the receding city of Algiers which by now was no more than an agglomeration of white cubes piled up the hillside in the morning sunshine.

Asad watched him silently awhile from under his beetling brows, then summoned him. He came at once, and stood respectfully before his prince.

Asad considered him a moment solemnly, whilst a furtive malicious smile played over the beautiful countenance of his son.

"Think not, Sakr-el-Bahr," he said at length, "that I bear thee resentment for what befell last night or that that happening is the sole cause of my present determination. I had a duty—a long-neglected duty—to Marzak, which at last I have undertaken to perform." He seemed to excuse himself almost, and Marzak misliked both words and tone. Why, he wondered, must this fierce old man, who had made his name a terror throughout Christendom, be ever so soft and yielding where that stalwart and arrogant infidel was concerned?

Sakr-el-Bahr bowed solemnly. "My lord," he said, "it is not for me to question thy resolves or the thoughts that may have led to them. It suffices me to know thy wishes; they are my law."

"Are they so?" said Asad tartly. "Thy deeds will scarce bear out thy protestations." He sighed. "Sorely was I wounded yesternight when thy marriage thwarted me and placed that Frankish maid beyond my reach. Yet I respect this marriage of thine, as all Muslims must—for all that in itself it was unlawful. But there!" he ended with a shrug. "We sail together once again to crush the Spaniard. Let no ill-will on either side o'er-cloud the splendour of our task."

"Ameen to that, my lord," said Sakr-el-Bahr devoutly. "I almost feared...."

"No more!" the Basha interrupted him. "Thou wert never a man to fear anything, which is why I have loved thee as a son."

But it suited Marzak not at all that the matter should be thus dismissed, that it should conclude upon a note of weakening from his father, upon what indeed amounted to a speech of reconciliation. Before Sakr-el-Bahr could make answer he had cut in to set him a question laden with wicked intent.

"How will thy bride beguile the season of thine absence, O Sakr-el-Bahr?"

"I have lived too little with women to be able to give thee an answer," said the corsair.

Marzak winced before a reply that seemed to reflect upon himself. But he returned to the attack.

"I compassionate thee that art the slave of duty, driven so soon to abandon the delight of her soft arms. Where hast thou bestowed her, O captain?"

"Where should a Muslim bestow his wife but according to the biddings of the Prophet—in the house?"

Marzak sneered. "Verily, I marvel at thy fortitude in quitting her so soon!"

But Asad caught the sneer, and stared at his son. "What cause is there to marvel in that a true Muslim should sacrifice his inclinations to the service of the Faith?" His tone was a rebuke; but it left Marzak undismayed. The youth sprawled gracefully upon his cushions, one leg tucked under him.

"Place no excess of faith in appearances, O my father!" he said.

"No more!" growled the Basha. "Peace to thy tongue, Marzak, and may Allah the All-knowing smile upon our expedition, lending strength to our arms to smite the infidel to whom the fragrance of the garden is forbidden."

To this again Sakr-el-Bahr replied "Ameen," but an uneasiness abode in his heart summoned thither by the questions Marzak had set him. Were they idle words calculated to do no more than plague him, and to keep fresh in Asad's mind the memory of Rosamund, or were they based upon some actual knowledge?

His fears were to be quickened soon on that same score. He was leaning that afternoon upon the rail, idly observing the doling out of the rations to the slaves, when Marzak came to join him.

For some moments he stood silently beside Sakr-el-Bahr watching Vigitello and his men as they passed from bench to bench serving out biscuits and dried dates to the rowers—but sparingly, for oars move sluggishly when stomachs are too well nourished—and giving each to drink a cup of vinegar and water in which floated a few drops of added oil.

Then he pointed to a large palmetto bale that stood on the waist-deck near the mainmast about which the powder barrels were stacked.

"That pannier," he said, "seems to me oddly in the way yonder. Were it not better to bestow it in the hold, where it will cease to be an encumbrance in case of action?"

Sakr-el-Bahr experienced a slight tightening at the heart. He knew that Marzak had heard him command that bale to be borne into the poop-cabin, and that anon he had ordered it to be fetched thence when Asad had announced his intention of sailing with him. He realized that this in itself might be a suspicious circumstance; or, rather, knowing what the bale contained, he was too ready to fear suspicion. Nevertheless he turned to Marzak with a smile of some disdain.

"I understood, Marzak, that thou art sailing with us as apprentice."

"What then?" quoth Marzak.

"Why merely that it might become thee better to be content to observe and learn. Thou'lt soon be telling me how grapnels should be slung, and how an action should be fought." Then he pointed ahead to what seemed to be no more than a low cloud-bank towards which they were rapidly skimming before that friendly wind. "Yonder," he said, "are the Balearics. We are making good speed."

Although he said it without any object other than that of turning the conversation, yet the fact itself was sufficiently remarkable to be worth a comment. Whether rowed by her two hundred and fifty slaves, or sailed under her enormous spread of canvas, there was no swifter vessel upon the Mediterranean than the galeasse of Sakr-el-Bahr. Onward she leapt now with bellying tateens, her well-greased keel slipping through the wind-whipped water at a rate which perhaps could not have been bettered by any ship that sailed.

"If this wind holds we shall be under the Point of Aguila before sunset, which will be something to boast of hereafter," he promised.

Marzak, however, seemed but indifferently interested; his eyes continued awhile to stray towards that palmetto bale by the mainmast. At length, without another word to Sakr-el-Bahr, he made his way abaft, and flung himself down under the awning, beside his father. Asad sat there in a moody abstraction, already regretting that he should have lent an ear to Fenzileh to the extent of coming upon this voyage, and assured by now that at least there was no cause to mistrust Sakr-el-Bahr. Marsak came to revive that drooping mistrust. But the moment was ill-chosen, and at the first words he uttered on the subject, he was growled into silence by his sire.

"Thou dost but voice thine own malice," Asad rebuked him. "And I am proven a fool in that I have permitted the malice of others to urge me in this matter. No more, I say."

Thereupon Marzak fell silent and sulking, his eyes ever following Sakr-el-Bahr, who had descended the three steps from the poop to the gangway and was pacing slowly down between the rowers' benches.

The corsair was supremely ill at ease, as a man must be who has something to conceal, and who begins to fear that he may have been betrayed. Yet who was there could have betrayed him? But three men aboard that vessel knew his secret—Ali, his lieutenant, Jasper, and the Italian Vigitello. And Sakr-el-Bahr would have staked all his possessions that neither Ali nor Vigitello would have betrayed him, whilst he was fairly confident that in his own interests Jasper also must have kept faith. Yet Marzak's allusion to that palmetto bale had filled him with an uneasiness that sent him now in quest of his Italian boatswain whom he trusted above all others.

"Vigitello," said he, "is it possible that I have been betrayed to the Basha?"

Vigitello looked up sharply at the question, then smiled with confidence. They were standing alone by the bulwarks on the waist deck.

"Touching what we carry yonder?" quoth he, his glance shifting to the bale. "Impossible. If Asad had knowledge he would have betrayed it before we left Algiers, or else he would never have sailed without a stouter bodyguard of his own.

"What need of bodyguard for him?" returned Sakr-el-Bahr. "If it should come to grips between us—as well it may if what I suspect be true—there is no doubt as to the side upon which the corsairs would range themselves."

"Is there not?" quoth Vigitello, a smile upon his swarthy face. "Be not so sure. These men have most of them followed thee into a score of fights. To them thou art the Basha, their natural leader."

"Maybe. But their allegiance belongs to Asad-ed-Din, the exalted of Allah. Did it come to a choice between us, their faith would urge them to stand beside him in spite of any past bonds that may have existed between them and me."

"Yet there were some who murmured when thou wert superseded in the command of this expedition," Vigitello informed him. "I doubt not that many would be influenced by their faith, but many would stand by thee against the Grand Sultan himself. And do not forget," he added, instinctively lowering his voice, "that many of us are renegadoes like myself and thee, who would never know a moment's doubt if it came to a choice of sides. But I hope," he ended in another tone, "there is no such danger here."

"And so do I, in all faith," replied Sakr-el-Bahr, with fervour. "Yet I am uneasy, and I must know where I stand if the worst takes place. Go thou amongst the men, Vigitello, and probe their real feelings, gauge their humour and endeavour to ascertain upon what numbers I may count if I have to declare war upon Asad or if he declares it upon me. Be cautious."

Vigitello closed one of his black eyes portentously. "Depend upon it," he said, "I'll bring you word anon."

On that they parted, Vigitello to make his way to the prow and there engage in his investigations, Sakr-el-Bahr slowly to retrace his steps to the poop. But at the first bench abaft the gangway he paused, and looked down at the dejected, white-fleshed slave who sat shackled there. He smiled cruelly, his own anxieties forgotten in the savour of vengeance.

"So you have tasted the whip already," he said in English. "But that is nothing to what is yet to come. You are in luck that there is a wind to-day. It will not always be so. Soon shall you learn what it was that I endured by your contriving."

Lionel looked up at him with haggard, blood-injected eyes. He wanted to curse his brother, yet was he too overwhelmed by the sense of the fitness of this punishment.

"For myself I care nothing," he replied.

"But you will, sweet brother," was the answer. "You will care for yourself most damnably and pity yourself most poignantly. I speak from experience. 'Tis odds you will not live, and that is my chief regret. I would you had my thews to keep you alive in this floating hell."

"I tell you I care nothing for myself," Lionel insisted. "What have you done with Rosamund?"

"Will it surprise you to learn that I have played the gentleman and married her?" Oliver mocked him.

"Married her?" his brother gasped, blenching at the very thought. "You hound!"

"Why abuse me? Could I have done more?" And with a laugh he sauntered on, leaving Lionel to writhe there with the torment of his half-knowledge.

An hour later, when the cloudy outline of the Balearic Isles had acquired density and colour, Sakr-el-Bahr and Vigitello met again on the waist-deck, and they exchanged some few words in passing.

"It is difficult to say exactly," the boatswain murmured, "but from what I gather I think the odds would be very evenly balanced, and it were rash in thee to precipitate a quarrel."

"I am not like to do so," replied Sakr-el-Bahr. "I should not be like to do so in any case. I but desired to know how I stand in case a quarrel should be forced upon me." And he passed on.

Yet his uneasiness was no whit allayed; his difficulties were very far from solved. He had undertaken to carry Rosamund to France or Italy; he had pledged her his word to land her upon one or the other shore, and should he fail, she might even come to conclude that such had never been his real intention. Yet how was he to succeed, now, since Asad was aboard the galeasse? Must he be constrained to carry her back to Algiers as secretly as he had brought her thence, and to keep her there until another opportunity of setting her ashore upon a Christian country should present itself? That was clearly impracticable and fraught with too much risk of detection. Indeed, the risk of detection was very imminent now. At any moment her presence in that pannier might be betrayed. He could think of no way in which to redeem his pledged word. He could but wait and hope, trusting to his luck and to some opportunity which it was impossible to foresee.

And so for a long hour and more he paced there moodily to and fro, his hands clasped behind him, his turbaned head bowed in thought, his heart very heavy within him. He was taken in the toils of the evil web which he had spun; and it seemed very clear to him now that nothing short of his life itself would be demanded as the price of it. That, however, was the least part of his concern. All things had miscarried with him and his life was wrecked. If at the price of it he could ensure safety to Rosamund, that price he would gladly pay. But his dismay and uneasiness all sprang from his inability to discover a way of achieving that most desired of objects even at such a sacrifice. And so he paced on alone and very lonely, waiting and praying for a miracle.

CHAPTER XVI. THE PANNIER

He was still pacing there when an hour or so before sunset—some fifteen hours after setting out—they stood before the entrance of a long bottle-necked cove under the shadow of the cliffs of Aquila Point on the southern coast of the Island of Formentera. He was rendered aware of this and roused from his abstraction by the voice of Asad calling to him from the poop and commanding him to make the cove.

Already the wind was failing them, and it became necessary to take to the oars, as must in any case have happened once they were through the coves narrow neck in the becalmed lagoon beyond. So Sakr-el-Bahr, in his turn, lifted up his voice, and in answer to his shout came Vigitello and Larocque.

A blast of Vigitello's whistle brought his own men to heel, and they passed rapidly along the benches ordering the rowers to make ready, whilst Jasper and a half-dozen Muslim sailors set about furling the sails that already were beginning to flap in the shifting and intermittent gusts of the expiring wind. Sakr-el-Bahr gave the word to row, and Vigitello blew a second and longer blast. The oars dipped, the slaves strained and the galeasse ploughed forward, time being kept by a boatswain's mate who squatted on the waist-deck and beat a tomtom rhythmically. Sakr-el-Bahr, standing on the poop-deck, shouted his orders to the steersmen in their niches on either side of the stern, and skilfully the vessel was manoeuvred through the narrow passage into the calm lagoon whose depths were crystal clear. Here before coming to rest, Sakr-el-Bahr followed the invariable corsair practice of going about, so as to be ready to leave his moorings and make for the open again at a moment's notice.

She came at last alongside the rocky buttresses of a gentle slope that was utterly deserted by all save a few wild goats browsing near the summit. There were clumps of broom, thick with golden flower, about the base of the hill. Higher, a few gnarled and aged olive trees reared their grey heads from which the rays of the westering sun struck a glint as of silver.

Larocque and a couple of sailors went over the bulwarks on the larboard quarter, dropped lightly to the horizontal shafts of the oars, which were rigidly poised, and walking out upon them gained the rocks and proceeded to make fast the vessel by ropes fore and aft.

Sakr-el-Bahr's next task was to set a watch, and he appointed Larocque, sending him to take his station on the summit of the head whence a wide range of view was to be commanded.

Pacing the poop with Marzak the Basha grew reminiscent of former days when roving the seas as a simple corsair he had used this cove both for purposes of ambush and concealment. There were, he said, few harbours in all the Mediterranean so admirably suited to the corsairs' purpose as this; it was a haven of refuge in case of peril, and an unrivalled lurking-place in which to lie in wait for the prey. He remembered once having lain there with the formidable Dragut-Reis, a fleet of six galleys, their presence entirely unsuspected by the Genoese admiral, Doria, who had passed majestically along with three caravels and seven galleys.

Marzak, pacing beside his father, listened but half-heartedly to these reminiscences. His mind was all upon Sakr-el-Bahr, and his suspicions of that palmetto bale were quickened by the manner in which for the last two hours he had seen the corsair hovering thoughtfully in its neighbourhood.

He broke in suddenly upon his father's memories with an expression of what was in his mind.

"The thanks to Allah," he said, "that it is thou who command this expedition, else might this coves advantages have been neglected."

"Not so," said Asad. "Sakr-el-Bahr knows them as well as I do. He has used this vantage point afore-time. It was himself who suggested that this would be the very place in which to await this Spanish craft."

"Yet had he sailed alone I doubt if the Spanish argosy had concerned him greatly. There are other matters on his mind, O my father. Observe him yonder, all lost in thought. How many hours of this voyage has he spent thus. He is as a man trapped and desperate. There is some fear rankling in him. Observe him, I say."

"Allah pardon thee," said his father, shaking his old head and sighing over so much impetuosity of judgment. "Must thy imagination be for ever feeding on thy malice? Yet I blame not thee, but thy Sicilian mother, who has fostered this hostility in thee. Did she not hoodwink me into making this unnecessary voyage?"

"I see thou hast forgot last night and the Frankish slave-girl," said his son.

"Nay, then thou seest wrong. I have not forgot it. But neither have I forgot that since Allah hath exalted me to be Basha of Algiers, He looks to me to deal in justice. Come, Marzak, set an end to all this. Perhaps to-morrow thou shalt see him in battle, and after such a sight as that never again wilt thou dare say evil of him. Come, make thy peace with him, and let me see better relations betwixt you hereafter."

And raising his voice he called Sakr-el-Bahr, who immediately turned and came up the gangway. Marzak stood by in a sulky mood, with no notion of doing his father's will by holding out an olive branch to the man who was like to cheat him of his birthright ere all was done. Yet was it he who greeted Sakr-el-Bahr when the corsair set foot upon the poop.

"Does the thought of the coming fight perturb thee, dog of war?" he asked.

"Am I perturbed, pup of peace?" was the crisp answer.

"It seems so. Thine aloofness, thine abstractions...."

"Are signs of perturbation, dost suppose?"

"Of what else?"

Sakr-el-Bahr laughed. "Thou'lt tell me next that I am afraid. Yet I should counsel thee to wait until thou hast smelt blood and powder, and learnt precisely what fear is."

The slight altercation drew the attention of Asad's officers who were idling there. Biskaine and some three others lounged forward to stand behind the Basha, looking, on in some amusement, which was shared by him.

"Indeed, indeed," said Asad, laying a hand upon Marzak's shoulder, "his counsel is sound enough. Wait, boy, until thou hast gone beside him aboard the infidel, ere thou judge him easily perturbed."

Petulantly Marzak shook off that gnarled old hand. "Dost thou, O my father, join with him in taunting me upon my lack of knowledge. My youth is a sufficient answer. But at least," he added, prompted by a wicked notion suddenly conceived, "at least you cannot taunt me with lack of address with weapons."

"Give him room," said Sakr-el-Bahr, with ironical good-humour, "and he will show us prodigies."

Marzak looked at him with narrowing, gleaming eyes. "Give me a cross-bow," he retorted, "and I'll show thee how to shoot," was his amazing boast.

"Thou'lt show him?" roared Asad. "Thou'lt show him!" And his laugh rang loud and hearty. "Go smear the sun's face with clay, boy."

"Reserve thy judgment, O my father," begged Marzak, with frosty dignity.

"Boy, thou'rt mad! Why, Sakr-el-Bahr's quarrel will check a swallow in its flight."

"That is his boast, belike," replied Marzak.

"And what may thine be?" quoth Sakr-el-Bahr. "To hit the Island of Formentera at this distance?"

"Dost dare to sneer at me?" cried Marzak, ruffling.

"What daring would that ask?" wondered Sakr-el-Bahr.

"By Allah, thou shalt learn."

"In all humility I await the lesson."

"And thou shalt have it," was the answer viciously delivered. Marzak strode to the rail. "Ho there! Vigitello! A cross-bow for me, and another for Sakr-el-Bahr."

Vigitello sprang to obey him, whilst Asad shook his head and laughed again.

"An it were not against the Prophet's law to make a wager...." he was beginning, when Marzak interrupted him.

"Already should I have proposed one."

"So that," said Sakr-el-Bahr, "thy purse would come to match thine head for emptiness."

Marzak looked at him and sneered. Then he snatched from Vigitello's hands one of the cross-bows that he bore and set a shaft to it. And then at last Sakr-el-Bahr was to learn the malice that was at the root of all this odd pretence.

"Look now," said the youth, "there is on that palmetto bale a speck of pitch scarce larger than the pupil of my eye. Thou'lt need to strain thy sight to see it. Observe how my shaft will find it. Canst thou better such a shot?"

His eyes, upon Sakr-el-Bahr's face, watching it closely, observed the pallor by which it was suddenly overspread. But the corsair's recovery was almost as swift. He laughed, seeming so entirely careless that Marzak began to doubt whether he had paled indeed or whether his own imagination had led him to suppose it.

"Ay, thou'lt choose invisible marks, and wherever the arrow enters thou'lt say 'twas there! An old trick, O Marzak. Go cozen women with it."

"Then," said Marzak, "we will take instead the slender cord that binds the bale." And he levelled his bow. But Sakr-el-Bahr's hand closed upon his arm in an easy yet paralyzing grip.

"Wait," he said. "Thou'lt choose another mark for several reasons. For one, I'll not have thy shaft blundering through my oarsmen and haply killing one of them. Most of them are slaves specially chosen for their brawn, and I cannot spare any. Another reason is that the mark is a foolish one. The distance is not more than ten paces. A childish test, which, maybe, is the reason why thou hast chosen it."

Marzak lowered his bow and Sakr-el-Bahr released his arm. They looked at each other, the corsair supremely master of himself and smiling easily, no faintest trace of the terror that was in his soul showing upon his swarthy bearded countenance or in his hard pale eyes.

He pointed up the hillside to the nearest olive tree, a hundred paces distant. "Yonder," he said, "is a man's mark. Put me a shaft through the long branch of that first olive."

Asad and his officers voiced approval.

"A man's mark, indeed," said the Basha, "so that he be a marksman."

But Marzak shrugged his shoulders with make-believe contempt. "I knew he would refuse the mark I set," said he. "As for the olive-branch, it is so large a butt that a child could not miss it at this distance."

"If a child could not, then thou shouldst not," said Sakr-el-Bahr, who had so placed himself that his body was now between Marzak and the palmetto bale. "Let us see thee hit it, O Marzak." And as he spoke he raised his cross-bow, and scarcely seeming to take aim, he loosed his shaft. It flashed away to be checked, quivering, in the branch he had indicated.

A chorus of applause and admiration greeted the shot, and drew the attention of all the crew to what was toward.

Marzak tightened his lips, realizing how completely he had been outwitted. Willy-nilly he must now shoot at that mark. The choice had been taken out of his hands by Sakr-el-Bahr. He never doubted that he must cover himself with ridicule in the performance, and that there he would be constrained to abandon this pretended match.

"By the Koran," said Biskaine, "thou'lt need all thy skill to equal such a shot, Marzak."

"'Twas not the mark I chose," replied Marzak sullenly.

"Thou wert the challenger, O Marzak," his father reminded him. "Therefore the choice of mark was his. He chose a man's mark, and by the beard of Mohammed, he showed us a man's shot."

Marzak would have flung the bow from him in that moment, abandoning the method he had chosen to investigate the contents of that suspicious palmetto bale; but he realized that such a course must now cover him with scorn. Slowly he levelled his bow at that distant mark.

"Have a care of the sentinel on the hill-top," Sakr-el-Bahr admonished him, provoking a titter.

Angrily the youth drew the bow. The cord hummed, and the shaft sped to bury itself in the hill's flank a dozen yards from the mark.

Since he was the son of the Basha none dared to laugh outright save his father and Sakr-el-Bahr. But there was no suppressing a titter to express the mockery to which the proven braggart must ever be exposed.

Asad looked at him, smiling almost sadly. "See now," he said, "what comes of boasting thyself against Sakr-el-Bahr."

"My will was crossed in the matter of a mark," was the bitter answer. "You angered me and made my aim untrue."

Sakr-el-Bahr strode away to the starboard bulwarks, deeming the matter at an end. Marzak observed him.

"Yet at that small mark," he said, "I challenge him again." As he spoke he fitted a second shaft to his bow. "Behold!" he cried, and took aim.

But swift as thought, Sakr-el-Bahr—heedless now of all consequences—levelled at Marzak the bow which he still held.

"Hold!" he roared. "Loose thy shaft at that bale, and I loose this at thy throat. I never miss!" he added grimly.

There was a startled movement in the ranks of those who stood behind Marzak. In speechless amazement they stared at Sakr-el-Bahr, as he stood there, white-faced, his eyes aflash, his bow drawn taut and ready to launch that death-laden quarrel as he threatened.

Slowly then, smiling with unutterable malice, Marzak lowered his bow. He was satisfied. His true aim was reached. He had drawn his enemy into self-betrayal.

Asad's was the voice that shattered that hush of consternation.

"Kellamullah!" he bellowed. "What is this? Art thou mad, too, O Sakr-el-Bahr?"

"Ay, mad indeed," said Marzak; "mad with fear." And he stepped quickly aside so that the body of Biskaine should shield him from any sudden consequences of his next words. "Ask him what he keeps in that pannier, O my father."

"Ay, what, in Allah's name?" demanded the Basha, advancing towards his captain.

Sakr-el-Bahr lowered his bow, master of himself again. His composure was beyond all belief.

"I carry in it goods of price, which I'll not see riddled to please a pert boy," he said.

"Goods of price?" echoed Asad, with a snort. "They'll need to be of price indeed that are valued above the life of my son. Let us see these goods of price." And to the men upon the waist-deck he shouted, "Open me that pannier."

Sakr-el-Bahr sprang forward, and laid a hand upon the Basha's arm.

"Stay, my lord!" he entreated almost fiercely. "Consider that this pannier is my own. That its contents are my property; that none has a right to...."

"Wouldst babble of rights to me, who am thy lord?" blazed the Basha, now in a towering passion. "Open me that pannier, I say."

They were quick to his bidding. The ropes were slashed away, and the front of the pannier fell open on its palmetto hinges. There was a half-repressed chorus of amazement from the men. Sakr-el-Bahr stood frozen in horror of what must follow.

"What is it? What have you found?" demanded Asad.

In silence the men swung the bale about, and disclosed to the eyes of those upon the poop-deck the face and form of Rosamund Godolphin. Then Sakr-el-Bahr, rousing himself from his trance of horror, reckless of all but her, flung down the gangway to assist her from the pannier, and thrusting aside those who stood about her, took his stand at her side.

CHAPTER XVII. THE DUPE

For a little while Asad stood at gaze, speechless in his incredulity. Then to revive the anger that for a moment had been whelmed in astonishment came the reflection that he had been duped by Sakr-el-Bahr, duped by the man he trusted most. He had snarled at Fenzileh and scorned Marzak when they had jointly warned him against his lieutenant; if at times he had been in danger of heeding them, yet sooner or later he had concluded that they but spoke to vent their malice. And yet it was proven now that they had been right in their estimate of this traitor, whilst he himself had been a poor, blind dupe, needing Marzak's wit to tear the bandage from his eyes.

Slowly he went down the gangway, followed by Marzak, Biskaine, and the others. At the point where it joined the waist-deck he paused, and his dark old eyes smouldered under his beetling brows.

"So," he snarled. "These are thy goods of price. Thou lying dog, what was thine aim in this?"

Defiantly Sakr-el-Bahr answered him: "She is my wife. It is my right to take her with me where I go." He turned to her, and bade her veil her face, and she immediately obeyed him with fingers that shook a little in her agitation.

"None questions thy right to that," said Asad. "But being resolved to take her with thee, why not take her openly? Why was she not housed in the poop-house, as becomes the wife of Sakr-el-Bahr? Why smuggle her aboard in a pannier, and keep her there in secret?"

"And why," added Marzak, "didst thou lie to me when I questioned thee upon her whereabouts?—telling me she was left behind in thy house in Algiers?"

"All this I did," replied Sakr-el-Bahr, with a lofty—almost a disdainful—dignity, "because I feared lest I should be prevented from bearing her away with me," and his bold glance, beating full upon Asad, drew a wave of colour into the gaunt old cheeks.

"What could have caused that fear?" he asked. "Shall I tell thee? Because no man sailing upon such a voyage as this would have desired the company of his new-wedded wife. Because no man would take a wife with him upon a raid in which there is peril of life and peril of capture."

"Allah has watched over me his servant in the past," said Sakr-el-Bahr, "and I put my trust in Him."

It was a specious answer. Such words—laying stress upon the victories Allah sent him—had afore-time served to disarm his enemies. But they served not now. Instead, they did but fan the flames of Asad's wrath.

"Blaspheme not," he croaked, and his tall form quivered with rage, his sallow old face grew vulturine. "She was brought thus aboard in secret out of fear that were her presence known thy true purpose too must stand revealed."

"And whatever that true purpose may have been," put in Marzak, "it was not the task entrusted thee of raiding the Spanish treasure galley."

"'Tis what I mean, my son," Asad agreed. Then with a commanding gesture: "Wilt thou tell me without further lies what thy purpose was?" he asked.

"How?" said Sakr-el-Bahr, and he smiled never so faintly. "Hast thou not said that this purpose was revealed by what I did? Rather, then, I think is it for me to ask thee for some such information. I do assure thee, my lord, that it was no part of my intention to neglect the task entrusted me. But just because I feared lest knowledge of her presence might lead my enemies to suppose what thou art now supposing, and perhaps persuade thee to forget all that I have done for the glory of Islam, I determined to bring her secretly aboard.

"My real aim, since you must know it, was to land her somewhere on the coast of France, whence she might return to her own land, and her own people. That done, I should have set about intercepting the Spanish galley, and never fear but that by Allah's favour I should have succeeded."

"By the horns of Shaitan," swore Marzak, thrusting himself forward, "he is the very father and mother of lies. Wilt thou explain this desire to be rid of a wife thou hadst but wed?" he demanded.

"Ay," growled Asad. "Canst answer that?"

"Thou shalt hear the truth," said Sakr-el-Bahr.

"The praise to Allah!" mocked Marzak.

"But I warn you," the corsair continued, "that to you it will seem less easy to believe by much than any falsehood I could invent. Years ago in England where I was born I loved this woman and should have taken her to wife. But there were men and circumstances that defamed me to her so that she would not wed me, and I went forth with hatred of her in my heart. Last night the love of her which I believed to be dead and turned to loathing, proved to be still a living force. Loving her, I came to see that I had used her unworthily, and I was urged by a desire above all others to undo the evil I had done."

On that he paused, and after an instant's silence Asad laughed angrily and contemptuously. "Since when has man expressed his love for a woman by putting her from him?" he asked in a voice of scorn that showed the precise value he set upon such a statement.

"I warned thee it would seem incredible," said Sakr-el-Bahr.

"Is it not plain, O my father, that this marriage of his was no more than a pretence?" cried Marzak.

"As plain as the light of day," replied Asad. "Thy marriage with that woman made an impious mock of the True Faith. It was no marriage. It was a blasphemous pretence, thine only aim to thwart me, abusing my regard for the Prophet's Holy Law, and to set her beyond my reach." He turned to Vigitello, who stood a little behind Sakr-el-Bahr. "Bid thy men put me this traitor into irons," he said.

"Heaven hath guided thee to a wise decision, O my father!" cried Marzak, his voice jubilant. But his was the only jubilant note that was sounded, his the only voice that was raised.

"The decision is more like to guide you both to Heaven," replied Sakr-el-Bahr, undaunted. On the instant he had resolved upon his course. "Stay!" he said, raising his hand to Vigitello, who, indeed had shown no sign of stirring. He stepped close up to Asad, and what he said did not go beyond those who stood immediately about the Basha and Rosamund, who strained her ears that she might lose no word of it.

"Do not think, Asad," he said, "that I will submit me like a camel to its burden. Consider thy position well. If I but raise my voice to call my sea-hawks to me, only Allah can tell how many will be left to obey thee. Darest thou put this matter to the test?" he asked, his countenance grave and solemn, but entirely fearless, as of a man in whom there is no doubt of the issue as it concerns himself.

Asad's eyes glittered dully, his colour faded to a deathly ashen hue. "Thou infamous traitor...." he began in a thick voice, his body quivering with anger.

"Ah no," Sakr-el-Bahr interrupted him. "Were I a traitor it is what I should have done already, knowing as I do that in any division of our forces, numbers will be heavily on my side. Let then my silence prove my unswerving loyalty, Asad. Let it weigh with thee in considering my conduct, nor permit thyself to be swayed by Marzak there, who recks nothing so that he vents his petty hatred of me."

"Do not heed him, O my father!" cried Marzak. "It cannot be that...."

"Peace!" growled Asad, somewhat stricken on a sudden.

And there was peace whilst the Basha stood moodily combing his white beard, his glittering eyes sweeping from Oliver to Rosamund and back again. He was weighing what Sakr-el-Bahr had said. He more than feared that it might be no more than true, and he realized that if he were to provoke a mutiny here he would be putting all to the test, setting all upon a throw in which the dice might well be cogged against him.

If Sakr-el-Bahr prevailed, he would prevail not merely aboard this galley, but throughout Algiers, and Asad would be cast down never to rise again. On the other hand, if he bared his scimitar and called upon the faithful to support him, it might chance that recognizing in him the exalted of Allah to whom their loyalty was due, they would rally to him. He even thought it might be probable. Yet the stake he put upon the board was too vast. The game appalled him, whom nothing yet had appalled, and it scarce needed a muttered caution from Biskaine to determine him to hold his hand.

He looked at Sakr-el-Bahr again, his glance now sullen. "I will consider thy words," he announced in a voice that was unsteady. "I would not be unjust, nor steer my course by appearances alone. Allah forbid!"

CHAPTER XVIII. SHEIK MAT

Under the inquisitive gaping stare of all about them stood Rosamund and Sakr-el-Bahr regarding each other in silence for a little spell after the Basha's departure. The very galley-slaves, stirred from their habitual lethargy by happenings so curious and unusual, craned their sinewy necks to peer at them with a flicker of interest in their dull, weary eyes.

Sakr-el-Bahr's feelings as he considered Rosamunds's white face in the fading light were most oddly conflicting. Dismay at what had befallen and some anxious dread of what must follow were leavened by a certain measure of relief.

He realized that in no case could her concealment have continued long. Eleven mortal hours had she spent in the cramped and almost suffocating space of that pannier, in which he had intended to do no more than carry her aboard. The uneasiness which had been occasioned him by the impossibility to deliver her from that close confinement when Asad had announced his resolve to accompany them upon that voyage, had steadily been increasing as hour succeeded hour, and still he found no way to release her from a situation in which sooner or later, when the limits of her endurance were reached, her presence must be betrayed. This release which he could not have contrived had been contrived for him by the suspicions and malice of Marzak. That was the one grain of consolation in the present peril—to himself who mattered nothing and to her, who mattered all. Adversity had taught him to prize benefits however slight and to confront perils however overwhelming. So he hugged the present slender benefit, and resolutely braced himself to deal with the situation as he found it, taking the fullest advantage of the hesitancy which his words had sown in the heart of the Basha. He hugged, too, the thought that as things had fallen out, from being oppressor and oppressed, Rosamund and he were become fellows in misfortune, sharing now a common peril. He found it a sweet thought to dwell on. Therefore was it that he faintly smiled as he looked into Rosamund's white, strained face.

That smile evoked from her the question that had been burdening her mind.

"What now? What now?" she asked huskily, and held out appealing hands to him.

"Now," said he coolly, "let us be thankful that you are delivered from quarters destructive both to comfort and to dignity. Let me lead you to those I had prepared for you, which you would have occupied long since but for the ill-timed coming of Asad. Come." And he waved an inviting hand towards the gangway leading to the poop.

She shrank back at that, for there on the poop sat Asad under his awning with Marzak, Biskaine, and his other officers in attendance.

"Come," he repeated, "there is naught to fear so that you keep a bold countenance. For the moment it is Sheik Mat—check to the king."

"Naught to fear?" she echoed, staring.

"For the moment, naught," he answered firmly. "Against what the future may hold, we must determine. Be sure that fear will not assist our judgment."

She stiffened as if he had charged her unjustly.

"I do not fear," she assured him, and if her face continued white, her eyes grew steady, her voice was resolute.

"Then come," he repeated, and she obeyed him instantly now as if to prove the absence of all fear.

Side by side they passed up the gangway and mounted the steps of the companion to the poop, their approach watched by the group that was in possession of it with glances at once of astonishment and resentment.

Asad's dark, smouldering eyes were all for the girl. They followed her every movement as she approached and never for a moment left her to turn upon her companion.

Outwardly she bore herself with a proud dignity and an unfaltering composure under that greedy scrutiny; but inwardly she shrank and writhed in a shame and humiliation that she could hardly define. In some measure Oliver shared her feelings, but blent with anger; and urged by them he so placed himself at last that he stood between her and the Basha's regard to screen her from it as he would have screened her from a lethal weapon. Upon the poop he paused, and salaamed to Asad.

"Permit, exalted lord," said he, "that my wife may occupy the quarters I had prepared for her before I knew that thou wouldst honour this enterprise with thy presence."

Curtly, contemptuously, Asad waved a consenting hand without vouchsafing to reply in words. Sakr-el-Bahr bowed again, stepped forward, and put aside the heavy red curtain upon which the crescent was wrought in green. From within the cabin the golden light of a lamp came out to merge into the blue-gray twilight, and to set a shimmering radiance about the white-robed figure of Rosamund.

Thus for a moment Asad's fierce, devouring eyes observed her, then she passed within. Sakr-el-Bahr followed, and the screening curtain swung back into its place.

The small interior was furnished by a divan spread with silken carpets, a low Moorish table in coloured wood mosaics bearing the newly lighted lamp, and a tiny brazier in which aromatic gums were burning and spreading a sweetly pungent perfume for the fumigation of all True-Believers.

Out of the shadows in the farther corners rose silently Sakr-el-Bahr's two Nubian slaves, Abiad and Zal-Zer, to salaam low before him. But for their turbans and loincloths in spotless white their dusky bodies must have remained invisible, shadowy among the shadows.

The captain issued an order briefly, and from a hanging cupboard the slaves took meat and drink and set it upon the low table—a bowl of chicken cooked in rice and olives and prunes, a dish of bread, a melon, and a clay amphora of water. Then at another word from him, each took a naked scimitar and they passed out to place themselves on guard beyond the curtain. This was not an act in which there was menace or defiance, nor could Asad so interpret it. The acknowledged presence of Sakr-el-Balir's wife in that poop-house, rendered the place the equivalent of his hareem, and a man defends his hareem as he defends his honour; it is a spot sacred to himself which none may violate, and it is fitting that he take proper precaution against any impious attempt to do so.

Rosamund sank down upon the divan, and sat there with bowed head, her hands folded in her lap. Sakr-el-Bahr stood by in silence for a long moment contemplating her.

"Eat," he bade her at last. "You will need strength and courage, and neither is possible to a fasting body."

She shook her head. Despite her long fast, food was repellent. Anxiety was thrusting her heart up into her throat to choke her.

"I cannot eat," she answered him. "To what end? Strength and courage cannot avail me now."

"Never believe that," he said. "I have undertaken to deliver you alive from the perils into which I have brought you, and I shall keep my word."

So resolute was his tone that she looked up at him, and found his bearing equally resolute and confident.

"Surely," she cried, "all chance of escape is lost to me."

"Never count it lost whilst I am living," he replied. She considered him a moment, and there was the faintest smile on her lips.

"Do you think that you will live long now?" she asked him.

"Just as long as God pleases," he replied quite coolly. "What is written is written. So that I live long enough to deliver you, then... why, then, faith I shall have lived long enough."

Her head sank. She clasped and unclasped the hands in her lap. She shivered slightly.

"I think we are both doomed," she said in a dull voice. "For if you die, I have your dagger still, remember. I shall not survive you."

He took a sudden step forward, his eyes gleaming, a faint flush glowing through the tan of his cheeks. Then he checked. Fool! How could he so have misread her meaning even for a moment? Were not its exact limits abundantly plain, even without the words which she added a moment later?

"God will forgive me if I am driven to it—if I choose the easier way of honour; for honour, sir," she added, clearly for his benefit, "is ever the easier way, believe me."

"I know," he replied contritely. "I would to God I had followed it."

He paused there, as if hoping that his expression of penitence might evoke some answer from her, might spur her to vouchsafe him some word of forgiveness. Seeing that she continued, mute and absorbed, he sighed heavily, and turned to other matters.

"Here you will find all that you can require," he said. "Should you lack aught you have but to beat your hands together, one or the other of my slaves will come to you. If you address them in French they will understand you. I would I could have brought a woman to minister to you, but that was impossible, as you'll perceive." He stepped to the entrance.

"You are leaving me?" she questioned him in sudden alarm.

"Naturally. But be sure that I shall be very near at hand. And meanwhile be no less sure that you have no cause for immediate fear. At least, matters are no worse than when you were in the pannier. Indeed, much better, for some measure of ease and comfort is now possible to you. So be of good heart; eat and rest. God guard you! I shall return soon after sunrise."

Outside on the poop-deck he found Asad alone now with Marzak under the awning. Night had fallen, the great crescent lanterns on the stern rail were alight and cast a lurid glow along the vessel's length, picking out the shadowy forms and gleaming faintly on the naked backs of the slaves in their serried ranks along the benches, many of them bowed already in attitudes of uneasy slumber. Another lantern swung from the mainmast, and yet another from the poop-rail for the Basha's convenience. Overhead the clustering stars glittered in a cloudless sky of deepest purple. The wind had fallen entirely, and the world was wrapped in stillness broken only by the faint rustling break of waves upon the beach at the cove's end.

Sakr-el-Bahr crossed to Asad's side, and begged for a word alone with him.

"I am alone," said the Basha curtly.

"Marzak is nothing, then," said Sakr-el-Bahr. "I have long suspected it."

Marzak showed his teeth and growled inarticulately, whilst the Basha, taken aback by the ease reflected in the captain's careless, mocking words, could but quote a line of the Koran with which Fenzileh of late had often nauseated him.

"A man's son is the partner of his soul. I have no secrets from Marzak. Speak, then, before him, or else be silent and depart."

"He may be the partner of thy soul, Asad," replied the corsair with his bold mockery, "but I give thanks to Allah he is not the partner of mine. And what I have to say in some sense concerns my soul."

"I thank thee," cut in Marzak, "for the justice of thy words. To be the partner of thy soul were to be an infidel unbelieving dog."

"Thy tongue, O Marzak, is like thine archery," said Sakr-el-Bahr.

"Ay—in that it pierces treachery," was the swift retort.

"Nay—in that it aims at what it cannot hit. Now, Allah, pardon me! Shall I grow angry at such words as thine? Hath not the One proven full oft that he who calls me infidel dog is a liar predestined to the Pit? Are such victories as mine over the fleets of the unbelievers vouchsafed by Allah to an infidel? Foolish blasphemer, teach thy tongue better ways lest the All-wise strike thee dumb."

"Peace!" growled Asad. "Thine arrogance is out of season."

"Haply so," said Sakr-el-Bahr, with a laugh. "And my good sense, too, it seems. Since thou wilt retain beside thee this partner of thy soul, I must speak before him. Have I thy leave to sit?"

Lest such leave should be denied him he dropped forthwith to the vacant place beside Asad and tucked his legs under him.

"Lord," he said, "there is a rift dividing us who should be united for the glory of Islam."

"It is of thy making, Sakr-el-Bahr," was the sullen answer, "and it is for thee to mend it."

"To that end do I desire thine ear. The cause of this rift is yonder." And he jerked his thumb backward over his shoulder towards the poop-house. "If we remove that cause, of a surety the rift itself will vanish, and all will be well again between us."

He knew that never could all be well again between him and Asad. He knew that by virtue of his act of defiance he was irrevocably doomed, that Asad having feared him once, having dreaded his power to stand successfully against his face and overbear his will, would see to it that he never dreaded it again. He knew that if he returned to Algiers there would be a speedy end to him. His only chance of safety lay, indeed, in stirring up mutiny upon the spot and striking swiftly, venturing all upon that desperate throw. And he knew that this was precisely what Asad had cause to fear. Out of this assurance had he conceived his present plan, deeming that if he offered to heal the breach, Asad might pretend to consent so as to weather his present danger, making doubly sure of his vengeance by waiting until they should be home again.

Asad's gleaming eyes considered him in silence for a moment.

"How remove that cause?" he asked. "Wilt thou atone for the mockery of thy marriage, pronounce her divorced and relinquish her?"

"That were not to remove her," replied Sakr-el-Bahr. "Consider well, Asad, what is thy duty to the Faith. Consider that upon our unity depends the glory of Islam. Were it not sinful, then, to suffer the intrusion of aught that may mar such unity? Nay, nay, what I propose is that I should be permitted—assisted even—to bear out the project I had formed, as already I have frankly made confession. Let us put to sea again at dawn—or this very night if thou wilt—make for the coast of France, and there set her ashore that she may go back to her own people and we be rid of her disturbing presence. Then we will return—there is time and to spare—and here or elsewhere lurk in wait for this Spanish argosy, seize the booty and sail home in amity to Algiers, this incident, this little cloud in the splendour of our comradeship, behind us and forgotten as though it had never been. Wilt thou, Asad—for the glory of the Prophet's Law?"

The bait was cunningly presented, so cunningly that not for a moment did Asad or even the malicious Marzak suspect it to be just a bait and no more. It was his own life, become a menace to Asad, that Sakr-el-Bahr was offering him in exchange for the life and liberty of that Frankish slave-girl, but offering it as if unconscious that he did so.

Asad considered, temptation gripping, him. Prudence urged him to accept, so that affecting to heal the dangerous breach that now existed he might carry Sakr-el-Bahr back to Algiers, there, beyond the aid of any friendly mutineers, to have him strangled. It was the course to adopt in such a situation, the wise and sober course by which to ensure the overthrow of one who from an obedient and submissive lieutenant had suddenly shown that it was possible for him to become a serious and dangerous rival.

Sakr-el-Bahr watched the Basha's averted, gleaming eyes under their furrowed, thoughtful brows, he saw Marzak's face white, tense and eager in his anxiety that his father should consent. And since his father continued silent, Marzak, unable longer to contain himself, broke into speech.

"He is wise, O my father!" was his crafty appeal. "The glory of Islam above all else! Let him have his way in this, and let the infidel woman go. Thus shall all be well between us and Sakr-el-Bahr!" He laid such a stress upon these words that it was obvious he desired them to convey a second meaning.

Asad heard and understood that Marzak, too, perceived what was here to do; tighter upon him became temptation's grip; but tighter, too, became the grip of a temptation of another sort. Before his fierce eyes there arose a vision of a tall stately maiden with softly rounded bosom, a vision so white and lovely that it enslaved him. And so he found himself torn two ways at once. On the one hand, if he relinquished the woman, he could make sure of his vengeance upon Sakr-el-Bahr, could make sure of removing that rebel from his path. On the other hand, if he determined to hold fast to his desires and to be ruled by them, he must be prepared to risk a mutiny aboard the galeasse, prepared for battle and perhaps for defeat. It was a stake such as no sane Basha would have consented to set upon the board. But since his eyes had again rested upon Rosamund, Asad was no longer sane. His thwarted desires of yesterday were the despots of his wits.

He leaned forward now, looking deep into the eyes of Sakr-el-Bahr.

"Since for thyself thou dost not want her, why dost thou thwart me?" he asked, and his voice trembled with suppressed passion. "So long as I deemed thee honest in taking her to wife I respected that bond as became a good Muslim; but since 'tis manifest that it was no more than a pretence, a mockery to serve some purpose hostile to myself, a desecration of the Prophet's Holy Law, I, before whom this blasphemous marriage was performed, do pronounce it to be no marriage. There is no need for thee to divorce her. She is no longer thine. She is for any Muslim who can take her."

Sakr-el-Bahr laughed unpleasantly. "Such a Muslim," he announced, "will be nearer my sword than the Paradise of Mahomet." And on the words he stood up, as if in token of his readiness.

Asad rose with him in a bound of a vigour such as might scarce have been looked for in a man of his years.

"Dost threaten?" he cried, his eyes aflash.

"Threaten?" sneered Sakr-el-Bahr. "I prophesy." And on that he turned, and stalked away down the gangway to the vessel's waist. There was no purpose in his going other than his perceiving that here argument were worse than useless, and that the wiser course were to withdraw at once, avoiding it and allowing his veiled threat to work upon the Basha's mind.

Quivering with rage Asad watched his departure. On the point of commanding him to return, he checked, fearing lest in his present mood Sakr-el-Bahr should flout his authority and under the eyes of all refuse him the obedience due. He knew that it is not good to command where we are not sure of being obeyed or of being able to enforce obedience, that an authority once successfully flouted is in itself half-shattered.

Whilst still he hesitated, Marzak, who had also risen, caught him by the arm and poured into his ear hot, urgent arguments enjoining him to yield to Sakr-el-Bahr's demand.

"It is the sure way," he cried insistently. "Shall all be jeopardized for the sake of that whey-faced daughter of perdition? In the name of Shaitan, let us be rid of her; set her ashore as he demands, as the price of peace between us and him, and in the security of that peace let him be strangled when we come again to our moorings in Algiers. It is the sure way—the sure way!"

Asad turned at last to look into that handsome eager face. For a moment he was at a loss; then he had recourse to sophistry. "Am I a coward that I should refuse all ways but sure ones?" he demanded in a withering tone. "Or art thou a coward who can counsel none other?"

"My anxiety is all for thee, O my father," Marzak defended himself indignantly. "I doubt if it be safe to sleep, lest he should stir up mutiny in the night."

"Have no fear," replied Asad. "Myself I have set the watch, and the officers are all trustworthy. Biskaine is even now in the forecastle taking the feeling of the men. Soon we shall know precisely where we stand."

"In thy place I would make sure. I would set a term to this danger of mutiny. I would accede to his demands concerning the woman, and settle after-wards with himself."

"Abandon that Frankish pearl?" quoth Asad. Slowly he shook his head. "Nay, nay! She is a garden that shall yield me roses. Together we shall yet taste the sweet sherbet of Kansar, and she shall thank me for having led her into Paradise. Abandon that rosy-limbed loveliness!" He laughed softly on a note of exaltation, whilst in the gloom Marzak frowned, thinking of Fenzileh.

"She is an infidel," his son sternly reminded him, "so forbidden thee by the Prophet. Wilt thou be as blind to that as to thine own peril?" Then his voice gathering vehemence and scorn as he proceeded: "She has gone naked of face through the streets of Algiers; she has been gaped at by the rabble in the sôk; this loveliness of hers has been deflowered by the greedy gaze of Jew and Moor and Turk; galley-slaves and negroes have feasted their eyes upon her unveiled beauty; one of thy captains hath owned her his wife." He laughed. "By Allah, I do not know thee, O my father! Is this the woman thou wouldst take for thine own? This the woman for whose possession thou wouldst jeopardize thy life and perhaps the very Bashalik itself!"

Asad clenched his hands until the nails bit into his flesh. Every word his son had uttered had been as a lash to his soul. The truth of it was not to be contested. He was humiliated and shamed. Yet was he not conquered of his madness, nor diverted from his course. Before he could make answer, the tall martial figure of Biskaine came up the companion.

"Well?" the Basha greeted him eagerly, thankful for this chance to turn the subject.

Biskaine was downcast. His news was to be read in his countenance. "The task appointed me was difficult," said he. "I have done my best. Yet I could scarce go about it in such a fashion as to draw definite conclusions. But this I know, my lord, that he will be reckless indeed if he dares to take up arms against thee and challenge thine authority. So much at least I am permitted to conclude."

"No more than that?" asked Asad. "And if I were to take up arms against him, and to seek to settle this matter out of hand?"

Biskaine paused a moment ere replying. "I cannot think but that Allah would vouchsafe thee victory," he said. But his words did not delude the Basha. He recognized them to be no more than those which respect for him dictated to his officer. "Yet," continued Biskaine, "I should judge thee reckless too, my lord, as reckless as I should judge him in the like circumstances."

"I see," said Asad. "The matter stands so balanced that neither of us dare put it to the test."

"Thou hast said it."

"Then is thy course plain to thee!" cried Marzak, eager to renew his arguments. "Accept his terms, and...."

But Asad broke in impatiently. "Every thing in its own hour and each hour is written. I will consider what to do."

Below on the waist-deck Sakr-el-Bahr was pacing with Vigitello, and Vigitello's words to him were of a tenor identical almost with those of Biskaine to the Basha.

"I scarce can judge," said the Italian renegade. "But I do think that it were not wise for either thou or Asad to take the first step against the other."

"Are matters, then, so equal between us?"

"Numbers, I fear," replied Vigitello, "would be in favour of Asad. No truly devout Muslim will stand against the Basha, the representative of the Sublime Portal, to whom loyalty is a question of religion. Yet they are accustomed to obey thee, to leap at thy command, and so Asad himself were rash to put it to the test."

"Ay—a sound argument," said Sakr-el-Bahr. "It is as I had thought."

Upon that he quitted Vigitello, and slowly, thoughtfully, returned to the poop-deck. It was his hope—his only hope now—that Asad might accept the proposal he had made him. As the price of it he was fully prepared for the sacrifice of his own life, which it must entail. But, it was not for him to approach Asad again; to do so would be to argue doubt and anxiety and so to court refusal. He must possess his soul in what patience he could. If Asad persisted in his refusal undeterred by any fear of mutiny, then Sakr-el-Bahr knew not what course remained him to accomplish Rosamund's deliverance. Proceed to stir up mutiny he dared not. It was too desperate a throw. In his own view it offered him no slightest chance of success, and did it fail, then indeed all would be lost, himself destroyed, and Rosamund at the mercy of Asad. He was as one walking along a sword-edge. His only chance of present immunity for himself and Rosamund lay in the confidence that Asad would dare no more than himself to take the initiative in aggression. But that was only for the present, and at any moment Asad might give the word to put about and steer for Barbary again; in no case could that be delayed beyond the plundering of the Spanish argosy. He nourished the faint hope that in that coming fight—if indeed the Spaniards did show fight—some chance might perhaps present itself, some unexpected way out of the present situation.

He spent the night under the stars, stretched across the threshold of the curtained entrance to the poop-house, making thus a barrier of his body whilst he slept, and himself watched over in his turn by his faithful Nubians who remained on guard. He awakened when the first violet tints of dawn were in the east, and quietly dismissing the weary slaves to their rest, he kept watch alone thereafter. Under the awning on the starboard quarter slept the Basha and his son, and near them Biskaine was snoring.

CHAPTER XIX. THE MUTINEERS

Later that morning, some time after the galeasse had awakened to life and such languid movement as might be looked for in a waiting crew, Sakr-el-Bahr went to visit Rosamund.

He found her brightened and refreshed by sleep, and he brought her reassuring messages that all was well, encouraging her with hopes which himself he was very far from entertaining. If her reception of him was not expressedly friendly, neither was it unfriendly. She listened to the hopes he expressed of yet effecting her safe deliverance, and whilst she had no thanks to offer him for the efforts he was to exert on her behalf—accepting them as her absolute due, as the inadequate liquidation of the debt that lay between them—yet there was now none of that aloofness amounting almost to scorn which hitherto had marked her bearing towards him.

He came again some hours later, in the afternoon, by when his Nubians were once more at their post. He had no news to bring her beyond the fact that their sentinel on the heights reported a sail to westward, beating up towards the island before the very gentle breeze that was blowing. But the argosy they awaited was not yet in sight, and he confessed that certain proposals which he had made to Asad for landing her in France had been rejected. Still she need have no fear, he added promptly, seeing the sudden alarm that quickened in her eyes. A way would present itself. He was watching, and would miss no chance.

"And if no chance should offer?" she asked him.

"Why then I will make one," he answered, lightly almost. "I have been making them all my life, and it would be odd if I should have lost the trick of it on my life's most important occasion."

This mention of his life led to a question from her.

"How did you contrive the chance that has made you what you are? I mean," she added quickly, as if fearing that the purport of that question might be misunderstood, "that has enabled you to become a corsair captain."

"'Tis a long story that," he said. "I should weary you in the telling of it."

"No," she replied, and shook her head, her clear eyes solemnly meeting his clouded glance. "You would not weary me. Chances may be few in which to learn it."

"And you would learn it?" quoth he, and added, "That you may judge me?"

"Perhaps," she said, and her eyes fell.

With bowed head he paced the length of the small chamber, and back again. His desire was to do her will in this, which is natural enough—for if it is true that who knows all must perforce forgive all, never could it have been truer than in the case of Sir Oliver Tressilian.

So he told his tale. Pacing there he related it at length, from the days when he had toiled at an oar on one of the galleys of Spain down to that hour in which aboard the Spanish vessel taken under Cape Spartel he had determined upon that voyage to England to present his reckoning to his brother. He told his story simply and without too great a wealth of detail, yet he omitted nothing of all that had gone to place him where he stood. And she, listening, was so profoundly moved that at one moment her eyes glistened with tears which she sought vainly to repress. Yet he, pacing there, absorbed, with head bowed and eyes that never once strayed in her direction, saw none of this.

"And so," he said, when at last that odd narrative had reached its end, "you know what the forces were that drove me. Another stronger than myself might have resisted and preferred to suffer death. But I was not strong enough. Or perhaps it is that stronger than myself was my desire to punish, to vent the bitter hatred into which my erstwhile love for Lionel was turned."

"And for me, too—as you have told me," she added.

"Not so," he corrected her. "I hated you for your unfaith, and most of all for your having burnt unread the letter that I sent you by the hand of Pitt. In doing that you contributed to the wrongs I was enduring, you destroyed my one chance of establishing my innocence and seeking rehabilitation, you doomed me for life to the ways which I was treading. But I did not then know what ample cause you had to believe me what I seemed. I did not know that it was believed I had fled. Therefore I forgive you freely a deed for which at one time I confess that I hated you, and which spurred me to bear you off when I found you under my hand that night at Arwenack when I went for Lionel."

"You mean that it was no part of your intent to have done so?" she asked him.

"To carry you off together with him?" he asked. "I swear to God I had not premeditated that. Indeed, it was done because not premeditated, for had I considered it, I do think I should have been proof against any such temptation. It assailed me suddenly when I beheld you there with Lionel, and I succumbed to it. Knowing what I now know I am punished enough, I think."

"I think I can understand," she murmured gently, as if to comfort him, for quick pain had trembled in his voice.

He tossed back his turbaned head. "To understand is something," said he. "It is half-way at least to forgiveness. But ere forgiveness can be accepted the evil done must be atoned for to the full."

"If possible," said she.

"It must be made possible," he answered her with heat, and on that he checked abruptly, arrested by a sound of shouting from without.

He recognized the voice of Larocque, who at dawn had returned to his sentinel's post on the summit of the headland, relieving the man who had replaced him there during the night.

"My lord! My lord!" was the cry, in a voice shaken by excitement, and succeeded by a shouting chorus from the crew.

Sakr-el-Bahr turned swiftly to the entrance, whisked aside the curtain, and stepped out upon the poop. Larocque was in the very act of clambering over the bulwarks amidships, towards the waist-deck where Asad awaited him in company with Marzak and the trusty Biskaine. The prow, on which the corsairs had lounged at ease since yesterday, was now a seething mob of inquisitive babbling men, crowding to the rail and even down the gangway in their eagerness to learn what news it was that brought the sentinel aboard in such excited haste.

From where he stood Sakr-el-Bahr heard Larocque's loud announcement.

"The ship I sighted at dawn, my lord!"

"Well?" barked Asad.

"She is here—in the bay beneath that headland. She has just dropped anchor."

"No need for alarm in that," replied the Basha at once. "Since she has anchored there it is plain that she has no suspicion of our presence. What manner of ship is she?"

"A tall galleon of twenty guns, flying the flag of England.

"Of England!" cried Asad in surprise. "She'll need be a stout vessel to hazard herself in Spanish waters."

Sakr-el-Bahr advanced to the rail.

"Does she display no further device?" he asked.

Larocque turned at the question. "Ay," he answered, "a narrow blue pennant on her mizzen is charged with a white bird—a stork, I think."

"A stork?" echoed Sakr-el-Bahr thoughtfully. He could call to mind no such English blazon, nor did it seem to him that it could possibly be English. He caught the sound of a quickly indrawn breath behind him. He turned to find Rosamund standing in the entrance, not more than half concealed by the curtain. Her face showed white and eager, her eyes were wide.

"What is't?" he asked her shortly.

"A stork, he thinks," she said, as though that were answer enough.

"I' faith an unlikely bird," he commented. "The fellow is mistook."

"Yet not by much, Sir Oliver."

"How? Not by much?" Intrigued by something in her tone and glance, he stepped quickly up to her, whilst below the chatter of voices increased.

"That which he takes to be a stork is a heron—a white heron, and white is argent in heraldry, is't not?"

"It is. What then?"

"D'ye not see? That ship will be the Silver Heron."

He looked at her. "'S life!" said he, "I reck little whether it be the silver heron or the golden grasshopper. What odds?"

"It is Sir John's ship—Sir John Killigrew's," she explained. "She was all but ready to sail when... when you came to Arwenack. He was for the Indies. Instead—don't you see?—out of love for me he will have come after me upon a forlorn hope of overtaking you ere you could make Barbary."

"God's light!" said Sakr-el-Bahr, and fell to musing. Then he raised his head and laughed. "Faith, he's some days late for that!"

But the jest evoked no response from her. She continued to stare at him with those eager yet timid eyes.

"And yet," he continued, "he comes opportunely enough. If the breeze that has fetched him is faint, yet surely it blows from Heaven."

"Were it...?" she paused, faltering a moment.

Then, "Were it possible to communicate with him?" she asked, yet with hesitation.

"Possible—ay," he answered. "Though we must needs devise the means, and that will prove none so easy."

"And you would do it?" she inquired, an undercurrent of wonder in her question, some recollection of it in her face.

"Why, readily," he answered, "since no other way presents itself. No doubt 'twill cost some lives," he added, "but then...." And he shrugged to complete the sentence.

"Ah, no, no! Not at that price!" she protested. And how was he to know that all the price she was thinking of was his own life, which she conceived would be forfeited if the assistance of the Silver Heron were invoked?

Before he could return her any answer his attention was diverted. A sullen threatening note had crept into the babble of the crew, and suddenly one or two voices were raised to demand insistently that Asad should put to sea at once and remove his vessel from a neighbourhood become so dangerous. Now, the fault of this was Marzak's. His was the voice that first had uttered that timid suggestion, and the infection of his panic had spread instantly through the corsair ranks.

Asad, drawn to the full of his gaunt height, turned upon them the eyes that had quelled greater clamours, and raised the voice which in its day had hurled a hundred men straight into the jaws of death without a protest.

"Silence!" he commanded. "I am your lord and need no counsellors save Allah. When I consider the time come, I will give the word to row, but not before. Back to your quarters, then, and peace!"

He disdained to argue with them, to show them what sound reasons there were for remaining in this secret cove and against putting forth into the open. Enough for them that such should be his will. Not for them to question his wisdom and his decisions.

But Asad-ed-Din had lain overlong in Algiers whilst his fleets under Sakr-el-Bahr and Biskaine had scoured the inland sea. The men were no longer accustomed to the goad of his voice, their confidence in his judgment was not built upon the sound basis of past experience. Never yet had he led into battle the men of this crew and brought them forth again in triumph and enriched by spoil.

So now they set their own judgment against his. To them it seemed a recklessness—as, indeed, Marzak had suggested—to linger here, and his mere announcement of his purpose was far from sufficient to dispel their doubts.

The murmurs swelled, not to be overborne by his fierce presence and scowling brow, and suddenly one of the renegades—secretly prompted by the wily Vigitello—raised a shout for the captain whom they knew and trusted.

"Sakr-el-Bahr! Sakr-el-Bahr! Thou'lt not leave us penned in this cove to perish like rats!"

It was as a spark to a train of powder. A score of voices instantly took up the cry; hands were flung out towards Sakr-el-Bahr, where he stood above them and in full view of all, leaning impassive and stern upon the poop-rail, whilst his agile mind weighed the opportunity thus thrust upon him, and considered what profit was to be extracted from it.

Asad fell back a pace in his profound mortification. His face was livid, his eyes blared furiously, his hand flew to the jewelled hilt of his scimitar, yet forbore from drawing the blade. Instead he let loose upon Marzak the venom kindled in his soul by this evidence of how shrunken was his authority.

"Thou fool!" he snarled. "Look on thy craven's work. See what a devil thou hast raised with thy woman's counsels. Thou to command a galley! Thou to become a fighter upon the seas! I would that Allah had stricken me dead ere I begat me such a son as thou!"

Marzak recoiled before the fury of words that he feared might be followed by yet worse. He dared make no answer, offer no excuse; in that moment he scarcely dared breathe.

Meanwhile Rosamund in her eagerness had advanced until she stood at Sakr-el-Bahr's elbow.

"God is helping us!" she said in a voice of fervent gratitude. "This is your opportunity. The men will obey you."

He looked at her, and smiled faintly upon her eagerness. "Ay, mistress, they will obey me," he said. But in the few moments that were sped he had taken his resolve. Whilst undoubtedly Asad was right, and the wise course was to lie close in this sheltering cove where the odds of their going unperceived were very heavily in their favour, yet the men's judgment was not altogether at fault. If they were to put to sea, they might by steering an easterly course pass similarly unperceived, and even should the splash of their oars reach the galleon beyond the headland, yet by the time she had weighed anchor and started in pursuit they would be well away straining every ounce of muscle at the oars, whilst the breeze—a heavy factor in his considerations—was become so feeble that they could laugh at pursuit by a vessel that depended upon wind alone. The only danger, then, was the danger of the galleon's cannon, and that danger was none so great as from experience Sakr-el-Bahr well knew.

Thus was he reluctantly forced to the conclusion that in the main the wiser policy was to support Asad, and since he was full confident of the obedience of the men he consoled himself with the reflection that a moral victory might be in store for him out of which some surer profit might presently be made.

In answer, then, to those who still called upon him, he leapt down the companion and strode along the gangway to the waist-deck to take his stand at the Basha's side. Asad watched his approach with angry misgivings; it was with him a foregone conclusion that things being as they were Sakr-el-Bahr would be ranged against him to obtain complete control of these mutineers and to cull the fullest advantage from the situation. Softly and slowly he unsheathed his scimitar, and Sakr-el-Bahr seeing this out of the corner of his eye, yet affected not to see, but stood forward to address the men.

"How now?" he thundered wrathfully. "What shall this mean? Are ye all deaf that ye have not heard the commands of your Basha, the exalted of Allah, that ye dare raise your mutinous voices and say what is your will?"

Sudden and utter silence followed that exhortation. Asad listened in relieved amazement; Rosamund caught her breath in sheer dismay.

What could he mean, then? Had he but fooled and duped her? Were his intentions towards her the very opposite to his protestations? She leant upon the poop-rail straining to catch every syllable of that speech of his in the lingua franca, hoping almost that her indifferent knowledge of it had led her into error on the score of what he had said.

She saw him turn with a gesture of angry command upon Larocque, who stood there by the bulwarks, waiting.

"Back to thy post up yonder, and keep watch upon that vessel's movements, reporting them to us. We stir not hence until such be our lord Asad's good pleasure. Away with thee!"

Larocque without a murmur threw a leg over the bulwarks and dropped to the oars, whence he clambered ashore as he had been bidden. And not a single voice was raised in protest.

Sakr-el-Bahr's dark glance swept the ranks of the corsairs crowding the forecastle.

"Because this pet of the hareem," he said, immensely daring, indicating Marzak by a contemptuous gesture, "bleats of danger into the ears of men, are ye all to grow timid and foolish as a herd of sheep? By Allah! What are ye? Are ye the fearless sea-hawks that have flown with me, and struck where the talons of my grappling-hooks were flung, or are ye but scavenging crows?"

He was answered by an old rover whom fear had rendered greatly daring.

"We are trapped here as Dragut was trapped at Jerba."

"Thou liest," he answered. "Dragut was not trapped, for Dragut found a way out. And against Dragut there was the whole navy of Genoa, whilst against us there is but one single galleon. By the Koran, if she shows fight, have we no teeth? Will it be the first galleon whose decks we have overrun? But if ye prefer a coward's counsel, ye sons of shame, consider that once we take the open sea our discovery will be assured, and Larocque hath told you that she carries twenty guns. I tell you that if we are to be attacked by her, best be attacked at close quarters, and I tell you that if we lie close and snug in here it is long odds that we shall never be attacked at all. That she has no inkling of our presence is proven, since she has cast anchor round the headland. And consider that if we fly from a danger that doth not exist, and in our flight are so fortunate as not to render real that danger and to court it, we abandon a rich argosy that shall bring profit to us all."

"But I waste my breath in argument," he ended abruptly. "You have heard the commands of your lord, Asad-ed-Din, and that should be argument enough. No more of this, then."

Without so much as waiting to see them disperse from the rail and return to their lounging attitudes about the forecastle, he turned to Asad.

"It might have been well to hang the dog who spoke of Dragut and Jerba," he said. "But it was never in my nature to be harsh with those who follow me." And that was all.

Asad from amazement had passed quickly to admiration and a sort of contrition, into which presently there crept a poisonous tinge of jealousy to see Sakr-el-Bahr prevail where he himself alone must utterly have failed. This jealousy spread all-pervadingly, like an oil stain. If he had come to bear ill-will to Sakr-el-Bahr before, that ill-will was turned of a sudden into positive hatred for one in whom he now beheld a usurper of the power and control that should reside in the Basha alone. Assuredly there was no room for both of them in the Bashalik of Algiers.

Therefore the words of commendation which had been rising to his lips froze there now that Sakr-el-Bahr and he stood face to face. In silence he considered his lieutenant through narrowing evil eyes, whose message none but a fool could have misunderstood.

Sakr-el-Bahr was not a fool, and he did not misunderstand it for a moment. He felt a tightening at the heart, and ill-will sprang to life within him responding to the call of that ill-will. Almost he repented him that he had not availed himself of that moment of weakness and mutiny on the part of the crew to attempt the entire superseding of the Basha.

The conciliatory words he had in mind to speak he now suppressed. To that venomous glance he opposed his ever ready mockery. He turned to Biskaine.

"Withdraw," he curtly bade him, "and take that stout sea-warrior with thee." And he indicated Marzak.

Biskaine turned to the Basha. "Is it thy wish, my lord?" he asked.

Asad nodded in silence, and motioned him away together with the cowed Marzak.

"My lord," said Sakr-el-Bahr, when they were alone, "yesterday I made thee a proposal for the healing of this breach between us, and it was refused. But now had I been the traitor and mutineer thou hast dubbed me I could have taken full advantage of the humour of my corsairs. Had I done that it need no longer have been mine to propose or to sue. Instead it would have been mine to dictate. Since I have given thee such crowning proof of my loyalty, it is my hope and trust that I may be restored to the place I had lost in thy confidence, and that this being so thou wilt accede now to that proposal of mine concerning the Frankish woman yonder."

It was unfortunate perhaps that she should have been standing there unveiled upon the poop within the range of Asad's glance; for the sight of her it may have been that overcame his momentary hesitation and stifled the caution which prompted him to accede. He considered her a moment, and a faint colour kindled in his cheeks which anger had made livid.

"It is not for thee, Sakr-el-Bahr," he answered at length, "to make me proposals. To dare it, proves thee far removed indeed from the loyalty thy lips profess. Thou knowest my will concerning her. Once hast thou thwarted and defied me, misusing to that end the Prophet's Holy Law. Continue a barrier in my path and it shall be at thy peril." His voice was raised and it shook with anger.

"Not so loud," said Sakr-el-Bahr, his eyes gleaming with a response of anger. "For should my men overhear these threats of thine I will not answer for what may follow. I oppose thee at my peril sayest thou. Be it so, then." He smiled grimly. "It is war between us, Asad, since thou hast chosen it. Remember hereafter when the consequences come to overwhelm thee that the choice was thine."

"Thou mutinous, treacherous son of a dog!" blazed Asad.

Sakr-el-Bahr turned on his heel. "Pursue the path of an old man's folly," he said over his shoulder, "and see whither it will lead thee."

Upon that he strode away up the gangway to the poop, leaving the Basha alone with his anger and some slight fear evoked by that last bold menace. But notwithstanding that he menaced boldly the heart of Sakr-el-Bahr was surcharged with anxiety. He had conceived a plan; but between the conception and its execution he realized that much ill might lie.

"Mistress," he addressed Rosamund as he stepped upon the poop. "You are not wise to show yourself so openly."

To his amazement she met him with a hostile glance.

"Not wise?" said she, her countenance scornful. "You mean that I may see more than was intended for me. What game do you play here, sir, that you tell me one thing and show me by your actions that you desire another?"

He did not need to ask her what she meant. At once he perceived how she had misread the scene she had witnessed.

"I'll but remind you," he said very gravely, "that once before you did me a wrong by over-hasty judgment, as has been proven to you."

It overthrew some of her confidence. "But then...." she began.

"I do but ask you to save your judgment for the end. If I live I shall deliver you. Meanwhile I beg that you will keep your cabin. It does not help me that you be seen."

She looked at him, a prayer for explanation trembling on her lips. But before the calm command of his tone and glance she slowly lowered her head and withdrew beyond the curtain.

CHAPTER XX. THE MESSENGER

For the rest of the day she kept the cabin, chafing with anxiety to know what was toward and the more racked by it because Sakr-el-Bahr refrained through all those hours from coming to her. At last towards evening, unable longer to contain herself, she went forth again, and as it chanced she did so at an untimely moment.

The sun had set, and the evening prayer was being recited aboard the galeasse, her crew all prostrate. Perceiving this, she drew back again instinctively, and remained screened by the curtain until the prayer was ended. Then putting it aside, but without stepping past the Nubians who were on guard, she saw that on her left Asad-ed-Din, with Marzak, Biskaine, and one or two other officers, was again occupying the divan under the awning. Her eyes sought Sakr-el-Bahr, and presently they beheld him coming up the gangway with his long, swinging stride, in the wake of the boat-swain's mates who were doling out the meagre evening meal to the slaves.

Suddenly he halted by Lionel, who occupied a seat at the head of his oar immediately next to the gangway. He addressed him harshly in the lingua franca, which Lionel did not understand, and his words rang clearly and were heard—as he intended that they should be—by all upon the poop.

"Well, dog? How does galley-slave fare suit thy tender stomach?"

Lionel looked up at him.

"What are you saying?" he asked in English.

Sakr-el-Bahr bent over him, and his face as all could see was evil and mocking. No doubt he spoke to him in English also, but no more than a murmur reached the straining ears of Rosamund, though from his countenance she had no doubt of the purport of his words. And yet she was far indeed from a correct surmise. The mockery in his countenance was but a mask.

"Take no heed of my looks," he was saying. "I desire them up yonder to think that I abuse you. Look as a man would who were being abused. Cringe or snarl, but listen. Do you remember once when as lads we swam together from Penarrow to Trefusis Point?"

"What do you mean?" quoth Lionel, and the natural sullenness of his mien was all that Sakr-el-Bahr could have desired.

"I am wondering whether you could still swim as far. If so you might find a more appetizing supper awaiting you at the end—aboard Sir John Killigrew's ship. You had not heard? The Silver Heron is at anchor in the bay beyond that headland. If I afford you the means, could you swim to her do you think?"

Lionel stared at him in profoundest amazement. "Do you mock me?" he asked at length.

"Why should I mock you on such a matter?"

"Is it not to mock me to suggest a way for my deliverance?"

Sakr-el-Bahr laughed, and he mocked now in earnest. He set his left foot upon the rowers' stretcher, and leaned forward and down his elbow upon his raised knee so that his face was close to Lionel's.

"For your deliverance?" said he. "God's life! Lionel, your mind was ever one that could take in naught but your own self. 'Tis that has made a villain of you. Your deliverance! God's wounds! Is there none but yourself whose deliverance I might desire? Look you, now I want you to swim to Sir John's ship and bear him word of the presence here of this galeasse and that Rosamund is aboard it. 'Tis for her that I am concerned, and so little for you that should you chance to be drowned in the attempt my only regret will be that the message was not delivered. Will you undertake that swim? It is your one sole chance short of death itself of escaping from the rower's bench. Will you go?"

"But how?" demanded Lionel, still mistrusting him.

"Will you go?" his brother insisted.

"Afford me the means and I will," was the answer.

"Very well." Sakr-el-Bahr leaned nearer still. "Naturally it will be supposed by all who are watching us that I am goading you to desperation. Act, then, your part. Up, and attempt to strike me. Then when I return the blow—and I shall strike heavily that no make-believe may be suspected—collapse on your oar pretending to swoon. Leave the rest to me. Now," he added sharply, and on the word rose with a final laugh of derision as if to take his departure.

But Lionel was quick to follow the instructions. He leapt up in his bonds, and reaching out as far as they would permit him, he struck Sakr-el-Bahr heavily upon the face. On his side, too, there was to be no make-believe apparent. That done he sank down with a clank of shackles to the bench again, whilst every one of his fellow-slaves that faced his way looked on with fearful eyes.

Sakr-el-Bahr was seen to reel under the blow, and instantly there was a commotion on board. Biskaine leapt to his feet with a half-cry of astonishment; even Asad's eyes kindled with interest at so unusual a sight as that of a galley-slave attacking a corsair. Then with a snarl of anger, the snarl of an enraged beast almost, Sakr-el-Bahr's great arm was swung aloft and his fist descended like a hammer upon Lionel's head.

Lionel sank forward under the blow, his senses swimming. Sakr-el-Bahr's arm swung up a second time.

"Thou dog!" he roared, and then checked, perceiving that Lionel appeared to have swooned.

He turned and bellowed for Vigitello and his mates in a voice that was hoarse with passion. Vigitello came at a run, a couple of his men at his heels.

"Unshackle me this carrion, and heave it overboard," was the harsh order. "Let that serve as an example to the others. Let them learn thus the price of mutiny in their lousy ranks. To it, I say."

Away sped a man for hammer and chisel. He returned with them at once. Four sharp metallic blows rang out, and Lionel was dragged forth from his place to the gangway-deck. Here he revived, and screamed for mercy as though he were to be drowned in earnest.

Biskaine chuckled under the awning, Asad looked on approvingly, Rosamund drew back, shuddering, choking, and near to fainting from sheer horror.

She saw Lionel borne struggling in the arms of the boatswain's men to the starboard quarter, and flung over the side with no more compunction or care than had he been so much rubbish. She heard the final scream of terror with which he vanished, the splash of his fall, and then in the ensuing silence the laugh of Sakr-el-Bahr.

For a spell she stood there with horror and loathing of that renegade corsair in her soul. Her mind was bewildered and confused. She sought to restore order in it, that she might consider this fresh deed of his, this act of wanton brutality and fratricide. And all that she could gather was the firm conviction that hitherto he had cheated her; he had lied when he swore that his aim was to effect her deliverance. It was not in such a nature to know a gentle mood of penitence for a wrong done. What might be his purpose she could not yet perceive, but that it was an evil one she never doubted, for no purpose of his could be aught but evil. So overwrought was she now that she forgot all Lionel's sins, and found her heart filled with compassion for him hurled in that brutal fashion to his death.

And then, quite suddenly a shout rang out from the forecastle.

"He is swimming!"

Sakr-el-Bahr had been prepared for the chance of this.

"Where? Where?" he cried, and sprang to the bulwarks.

"Yonder!" A man was pointing. Others had joined him and were peering through the gathering gloom at the moving object that was Lionel's head and the faintly visible swirl of water about it which indicated that he swam.

"Out to sea!" cried Sakr-el-Bahr. "He'll not swim far in any case. But we will shorten his road for him." He snatched a cross-bow from the rack about the mainmast, fitted a shaft to it and took aim.

On the point of loosing the bolt he paused.

"Marzak!" he called. "Here, thou prince of marksmen, is a butt for thee!"

From the poop-deck whence with his father he too was watching the swimmer's head, which at every moment became more faint in the failing light, Marzak looked with cold disdain upon his challenger, making no reply. A titter ran through the crew.

"Come now," cried Sakr-el-Bahr. "Take up thy bow!"

"If thou delay much longer," put in Asad, "he will be beyond thine aim. Already he is scarcely visible."

"The more difficult a butt, then," answered Sakr-el-B ahr, who was but delaying to gain time. "The keener test. A hundred philips, Marzak, that thou'lt not hit me that head in three shots, and that I'll sink him at the first! Wilt take the wager?"

"The unbeliever is for ever peeping forth from thee," was Marzak's dignified reply. "Games of chance are forbidden by the Prophet."

"Make haste, man!" cried Asad. "Already I can scarce discern him. Loose thy quarrel."

"Pooh," was the disdainful answer. "A fair mark still for such an eye as mine. I never miss—not even in the dark."

"Vain boaster," said Marzak.

"Am I so?" Sakr-el-Bahr loosed his shaft at last into the gloom, and peered after it following its flight, which was wide of the direction of the swimmer's head. "A hit!" he cried brazenly. "He's gone!"

"I think I see him still," said one.

"Thine eyes deceive thee in this light. No man was ever known to swim with an arrow through his brain."

"Ay," put in Jasper, who stood behind Sakr-el-Bahr. "He has vanished."

"'Tis too dark to see," said Vigitello.

And then Asad turned from the vessel's side. "Well, well—shot or drowned, he's gone," he said, and there the matter ended.

Sakr-el-Bahr replaced the cross-bow in the rack, and came slowly up to the poop.

In the gloom he found himself confronted by Rosamund's white face between the two dusky countenances of his Nubians. She drew back before him as he approached, and he, intent upon imparting his news to her, followed her within the poop-house, and bade Abiad bring lights.

When these had been kindled they faced each other, and he perceived her profound agitation and guessed the cause of it. Suddenly she broke into speech.

"You beast! You devil!" she panted. "God will punish you! I shall spend my every breath in praying Him to punish you as you deserve. You murderer! You hound! And I like a poor simpleton was heeding your false words. I was believing you sincere in your repentance of the wrong you have done me. But now you have shown me...."

"How have I hurt you in what I have done to Lionel?" he cut in, a little amazed by so much vehemence.

"Hurt me!" she cried, and on the words grew cold and calm again with very scorn. "I thank God it is beyond your power to hurt me. And I thank you for correcting my foolish misconception of you, my belief in your pitiful pretence that it was your aim to save me. I would not accept salvation at your murderer's hands. Though, indeed, I shall not be put to it. Rather," she pursued, a little wildly now in her deep mortification, "are you like to sacrifice me to your own vile ends, whatever they may be. But I shall thwart you, Heaven helping me. Be sure I shall not want courage for that." And with a shuddering moan she covered her face, and stood swaying there before him.

He looked on with a faint, bitter smile, understanding her mood just as he understood her dark threat of thwarting him.

"I came," he said quietly, "to bring you the assurance that he has got safely away, and to tell you upon what manner of errand I have sent him."

Something compelling in his voice, the easy assurance with which he spoke, drew her to stare at him again.

"I mean Lionel, of course," he said, in answer to her questioning glance. "That scene between us—the blow and the swoon and the rest of it—was all make-believe. So afterwards the shooting. My challenge to Marzak was a ruse to gain time—to avoid shooting until Lionel's head should have become so dimly visible in the dusk that none could say whether it was still there or not. My shaft went wide of him, as I intended. He is swimming round the head with my message to Sir John Killigrew. He was a strong swimmer in the old days, and should easily reach his goal. That is what I came to tell you."

For a long spell she continued to stare at him in silence.

"You are speaking the truth?" she asked at last, in a small voice.

He shrugged. "You will have a difficulty in perceiving the object I might serve by falsehood."

She sat down suddenly upon the divan; it was almost as if she collapsed bereft of strength; and as suddenly she fell to weeping softly.

"And... and I believed that you... that you...."

"Just so," he grimly interrupted. "You always did believe the best of me."

And on that he turned and went out abruptly.

CHAPTER XXI. MORITURUS

He departed from her presence with bitterness in his heart, leaving a profound contrition in her own. The sense of this her last injustice to him so overwhelmed her that it became the gauge by which she measured that other earlier wrong he had suffered at her hands. Perhaps her overwrought mind falsified the perspective, exaggerating it until it seemed to her that all the suffering and evil with which this chronicle has been concerned were the direct fruits of her own sin of unfaith.

Since all sincere contrition must of necessity bring forth an ardent desire to atone, so was it now with her. Had he but refrained from departing so abruptly he might have had her on her knees to him suing for pardon for all the wrongs which her thoughts had done him, proclaiming her own utter unworthiness and baseness. But since his righteous resentment had driven him from her presence she could but sit and brood upon it all, considering the words in which to frame her plea for forgiveness when next he should return.

But the hours sped, and there was no sign of him. And then, almost with a shock of dread came the thought that ere long perhaps Sir John Killigrew's ship would be upon them. In her distraught state of mind she had scarcely pondered that contingency. Now that it occurred to her all her concern was for the result of it to Sir Oliver. Would there be fighting, and would he perhaps perish in that conflict at the hands either of the English or of the corsairs whom for her sake he had betrayed, perhaps without ever hearing her confession of penitence, without speaking those words of forgiveness of which her soul stood in such thirsty need?

It would be towards midnight when unable longer to bear the suspense of it, she rose and softly made her way to the entrance. Very quietly she lifted the curtain, and in the act of stepping forth almost stumbled over a body that lay across the threshold. She drew back with a startled gasp; then stooped to look, and by the faint rays of the lanterns on mainmast and poop-rail she recognized Sir Oliver, and saw that he slept. She never heeded the two Nubians immovable as statues who kept guard. She continued to bend over him, and then gradually and very softly sank down on her knees beside him. There were tears in her eyes—tears wrung from her by a tender emotion of wonder and gratitude at so much fidelity. She did not know that he had slept thus last night. But it was enough for her to find him here now. It moved her oddly, profoundly, that this man whom she had ever mistrusted and misjudged should even when he slept make of his body a barrier for her greater security and protection.

A sob escaped her, and at the sound, so lightly and vigilantly did he take his rest, he came instantly if silently to a sitting attitude; and so they looked into each other's eyes, his swarthy, bearded hawk face on a level with her white gleaming countenance.

"What is it?" he whispered.

She drew back instantly, taken with sudden panic at that question. Then recovering, and seeking womanlike to evade and dissemble the thing she was come to do, now that the chance of doing it was afforded her—"Do you think," she faltered, "that Lionel will have reached Sir John's ship?"

He flashed a glance in the direction of the divan under the awning where the Basha slept. There all was still. Besides, the question had been asked in English. He rose and held out a hand to help her to her feet. Then he signed to her to reenter the poop-house, and followed her within.

"Anxiety keeps you wakeful?" he said, half-question, half-assertion.

"Indeed," she replied.

"There is scarce the need," he assured her. "Sir John will not be like to stir until dead of night, that he may make sure of taking us unawares. I have little doubt that Lionel would reach him. It is none so long a swim. Indeed, once outside the cove he could take to the land until he was abreast of the ship. Never doubt he will have done his errand."

She sat down, her glance avoiding his; but the light falling on her face showed him the traces there of recent tears.

"There will be fighting when Sir John arrives?" she asked him presently.

"Like enough. But what can it avail? We shall be caught—as was said today—in just such a trap as that in which Andrea Doria caught Dragut at Jerba, saving that whilst the wily Dragut found a way out for his galleys, here none is possible. Courage, then, for the hour of your deliverance is surely at hand."

He paused, and then in a softer voice, humbly almost, "It is my prayer," he added, "that hereafter in a happy future these last few weeks shall come to seem no more than an evil dream to you."

To that prayer she offered no response. She sat bemused, her brow wrinkled.

"I would it might be done without fighting," she said presently, and sighed wearily.

"You need have no fear," he assured her. "I shall take all precautions for you. You shall remain here until all is over and the entrance will be guarded by a few whom I can trust."

"You mistake me," she replied, and looked up at him suddenly. "Do you suppose my fears are for myself?" She paused again, and then abruptly asked him, "What will befall you?"

"I thank you for the thought," he replied gravely. "No doubt I shall meet with my deserts. Let it but come swiftly when it comes."

"Ah, no, no!" she cried. "Not that!" And rose in her sudden agitation.

"What else remains?" he asked, and smiled. "What better fate could anyone desire me?"

"You shall live to return to England," she surprised him by exclaiming. "The truth must prevail, and justice be done you."

He looked at her with so fierce and searching a gaze that she averted her eyes. Then he laughed shortly.

"There's but one form of justice I can look for in England," said he. "It is a justice administered in hemp. Believe me, mistress, I am grown too notorious for mercy. Best end it here to-night. Besides," he added, and his mockery fell from him, his tone became gloomy, "bethink you of my present act of treachery to these men of mine, who, whatever they may be, have followed me into a score of perils and but to-day have shown their love and loyalty to me to be greater than their devotion to the Basha himself. I shall have delivered them to the sword. Could I survive with honour? They may be but poor heathens to you and yours, but to me they are my sea-hawks, my warriors, my faithful gallant followers, and I were a dog indeed did I survive the death to which I have doomed them."

As she listened and gathered from his words the apprehension of a thing that had hitherto escaped her, her eyes grew wide in sudden horror.

"Is that to be the cost of my deliverance?" she asked him fearfully.

"I trust not," he replied. "I have something in mind that will perhaps avoid it."

"And save your own life as well?" she asked him quickly.

"Why waste a thought upon so poor a thing? My life was forfeit already. If I go back to Algiers they will assuredly hang me. Asad will see to it, and not all my sea-hawks could save me from my fate."

She sank down again upon the divan, and sat there rocking her arms in a gesture of hopeless distress.

"I see," she said. "I see. I am bringing this fate upon you. When you sent Lionel upon that errand you voluntarily offered up your life to restore me to my own people. You had no right to do this without first consulting me. You had no right to suppose I would be a party to such a thing. I will not accept the sacrifice. I will not, Sir Oliver."

"Indeed, you have no choice, thank God!" he answered her. "But you are astray in your conclusions. It is I alone who have brought this fate upon myself. It is the very proper fruit of my insensate deed. It recoils upon me as all evil must upon him that does it." He shrugged his shoulders as if to dismiss the matter. Then in a changed voice, a voice singularly timid, soft, and gentle, "it were perhaps too much to ask," said he, "that you should forgive me all the suffering I have brought you?"

"I think," she answered him, "that it is for me to beg forgiveness of you."

"Of me?"

"For my unfaith, which has been the source of all. For my readiness to believe evil of you five years ago, for having burnt unread your letter and the proof of your innocence that accompanied it."

He smiled upon her very kindly. "I think you said your instinct guided you. Even though I had not done the thing imputed to me, your instinct knew me for evil; and your instinct was right, for evil I am—I must be. These are your own words. But do not think that I mock you with them. I have come to recognize their truth."

She stretched out her hands to him. "If... if I were to say that I have come to realize the falsehood of all that?"

"I should understand it to be the charity which your pitiful heart extends to one in my extremity. Your instinct was not at fault."

"It was! It was!"

But he was not to be driven out of his conviction. He shook his head, his countenance gloomy. "No man who was not evil could have done by you what I have done, however deep the provocation. I perceive it clearly now—as men in their last hour perceive hidden things."

"Oh, why are you so set on death?" she cried upon a despairing note.

"I am not," he answered with a swift resumption of his more habitual manner. "'Tis death that is so set on me. But at least I meet it without fear or regret. I face it as we must all face the inevitable—the gifts from the hands of destiny. And I am heart-ened—gladdened almost—by your sweet forgive-ness."

She rose suddenly, and came to him. She caught his arm, and standing very close to him, looked up now into his face.

"We have need to forgive each other, you and I, Oliver," she said. "And since forgiveness effaces all, let... let all that has stood between us these last five years be now effaced."

He caught his breath as he looked down into her white, straining face

"Is it impossible for us to go back five years? Is it impossible for us to go back to where we stood in those old days at Godolphin Court?"

The light that had suddenly been kindled in his face faded slowly, leaving it grey and drawn. His eyes grew clouded with sorrow and despair.

"Who has erred must abide by his error—and so must the generations that come after him. There is no going back ever. The gates of the past are tight-barred against us."

"Then let us leave them so. Let us turn our backs upon that past, you and I, and let us set out afresh together, and so make amends to each other for what our folly has lost to us in those years."

He set his hands upon her shoulders, and held her so at arm's length from him considering her with very tender eyes.

"Sweet lady!" he murmured, and sighed heavily. "God! How happy might we not have been but for that evil chance...." He checked abruptly. His hands fell from her shoulders to his sides, he half-turned away, brusque now in tone and manner. "I grow maudlin. Your sweet pity has so softened me that I had almost spoke of love; and what have I to do with that? Love belongs to life; love is life; whilst I... Moriturus te salutat!"

"Ah, no, no!" She was clinging to him again with shaking hands, her eyes wild.

"It is too late," he answered her. "There is no bridge can span the pit I have dug myself. I must go down into it as cheerfully as God will let me."

"Then," she cried in sudden exaltation, "I will go down with you. At the last, at least, we shall be together."

"Now here is midsummer frenzy!" he protested, yet there was a tenderness in the very impatience of his accents. He stroked the golden head that lay against his shoulder. "How shall that help me?" he asked her. "Would you embitter my last hour—rob death of all its glory? Nay, Rosamund, you can serve me better far by living. Return to England, and publish there the truth of what you have learnt. Be yours the task of clearing my honour of this stain upon it, proclaiming the truth of what drove me to the infamy of becoming a renegade and a corsair." He started from her. "Hark! What's that?"

From without had come a sudden cry, "Afoot! To arms! To arms! Holâ! Balâk! Balâk!"

"It is the hour," he said, and turning from her suddenly sprang to the entrance and plucked aside the curtain.

CHAPTER XXII. THE SURRENDER

Up the gangway between the lines of slumbering slaves came a quick patter of feet. Ali, who since sunset had been replacing Larocque on the heights, sprang suddenly upon the poop still shouting.

"Captain! Captain! My lord! Afoot! Up! or we are taken!"

Throughout the vessel's length came the rustle and stir of waking men. A voice clamoured somewhere on the forecastle. Then the flap of the awning was suddenly whisked aside and Asad himself appeared with Marzak at his elbow.

From the starboard side as suddenly came Biskaine and Othmani, and from the waist Vigitello, Jasper—that latest renegade—and a group of alarmed corsairs.

"What now?" quoth the Basha.

Ali delivered his message breathlessly. "The galleon has weighed anchor. She is moving out of the bay."

Asad clutched his beard, and scowled. "Now what may that portend? Can knowledge of our presence have reached them?"

"Why else should she move from her anchorage thus in the dead of night?" said Biskaine.

"Why else, indeed?" returned Asad, and then he swung upon Oliver standing there in the entrance of the poop-house. "What sayest thou, Sakr-el-Bahr?" he appealed to him.

Sakr-el-Bahr stepped forward, shrugging. "What is there to say? What is there to do?" he asked. "We can but wait. If our presence is known to them we are finely trapped, and there's an end to all of us this night."

His voice was cool as ice, contemptuous almost, and whilst it struck anxiety into more than one it awoke terror in Marzak.

"May thy bones rot, thou ill-omened prophet!" he screamed, and would have added more but that Sakr-el-Bahr silenced him.

"What is written is written!" said he in a voice of thunder and reproof.

"Indeed, indeed," Asad agreed, grasping at the fatalist's consolation. "If we are ripe for the gardeners hand, the gardener will pluck us."

Less fatalistic and more practical was the counsel of Biskaine.

"It were well to act upon the assumption that we are indeed discovered, and make for the open sea while yet there may be time."

"But that were to make certain what is still doubtful," broke in Marzak, fearful ever. "It were to run to meet the danger."

"Not so!" cried Asad in a loud, confident voice. "The praise to Allah who sent us this calm night. There is scarce a breath of wind. We can row ten leagues while they are sailing one."

A murmur of quick approval sped through the ranks of officers and men.

"Let us but win safely from this cove and they will never overtake us," announced Biskaine.

"But their guns may," Sakr-el-Bahr quietly reminded them to damp their confidence. His own alert mind had already foreseen this one chance of escaping from the trap, but he had hoped that it would not be quite so obvious to the others.

"That risk we must take," replied Asad. "We must trust to the night. To linger here is to await certain destruction." He swung briskly about to issue his orders. "Ali, summon the steersmen. Hasten! Vigitello, set your whips about the slaves, and rouse them." Then as the shrill whistle of the boatswain rang out and the whips of his mates went hissing and cracking about the shoulders of the already half-awakened slaves, to mingle with all the rest of the stir and bustle aboard the galeasse, the Basha turned once more to Biskaine. "Up thou to the prow," he commanded, "and marshal the men. Bid them stand to their arms lest it should come to boarding. Go!" Biskaine salaamed and sprang down the companion. Above the rumbling din and scurrying toil of preparation rang Asad's voice.

"Crossbowmen, aloft! Gunners to the carronades! Kindle your linstocks! Put out all lights!"

An instant later the cressets on the poop-rail were extinguished, as was the lantern swinging from the rail, and even the lamp in the poop-house which was invaded by one of the Basha's officers for that purpose. The lantern hanging from the mast alone was spared against emergencies; but it was taken down, placed upon the deck, and muffled.

Thus was the galeasse plunged into a darkness that for some moments was black and impenetrable as velvet. Then slowly, as the eyes became accustomed to it, this gloom was gradually relieved. Once more men and objects began to take shape in the faint, steely radiance of the summer night.

After the excitement of that first stir the corsairs went about their tasks with amazing calm and silence. None thought now of reproaching the Basha or Sakr-el-Bahr with having delayed until the moment of peril to take the course which all of them had demanded should be taken when first they had heard of the neighbourhood of that hostile ship. In lines three deep they stood ranged along the ample fighting platform of the prow; in the foremost line were the archers, behind them stood the swordsmen, their weapons gleaming lividly in the darkness. They crowded to the bulwarks of the waist-deck and swarmed upon the rat-lines of the mainmast. On the poop three gunners stood to each of the two small cannon, their faces showing faintly ruddy in the glow of the ignited match.

Asad stood at the head of the companion, issuing his sharp brief commands, and Sakr-el-Bahr, behind him, leaning against the timbers of the poop-house with

Rosamund at his side, observed that the Basha had studiously avoided entrusting any of this work of preparation to himself.

The steersmen climbed to their niches, and the huge steering oars creaked as they were swung out. Came a short word of command from Asad and a stir ran through the ranks of the slaves, as they threw forward their weight to bring the oars to the level. Thus a moment, then a second word, the premonitory crack of a whip in the darkness of the gangway, and the tomtom began to beat the time. The slaves heaved, and with a creak and splash of oars the great galeasse skimmed forward towards the mouth of the cove.

Up and down the gangway ran the boatswain's mates, cutting fiercely with their whips to urge the slaves to the very utmost effort. The vessel gathered speed. The looming headland slipped by. The mouth of the cove appeared to widen as they approached it. Beyond spread the dark steely mirror of the dead-calm sea.

Rosamund could scarcely breathe in the intensity of her suspense. She set a hand upon the arm of Sakr-el-Bahr.

"Shall we elude them, after all?" she asked in a trembling whisper.

"I pray that we may not," he answered, muttering. "But this is the handiwork I feared. Look!" he added sharply, and pointed.

They had shot clear to the headland. They were out of the cove, and suddenly they had a view of the dark bulk of the galleon, studded with a score of points of light, riding a cable's length away on their larboard quarter.

"Faster!" cried the voice of Asad. "Row for your lives, you infidel swine! Lay me your whips upon these hides of theirs! Bend me these dogs to their oars, and they'll never overtake us now."

Whips sang and thudded below them in the waist, to be answered by more than one groan from the tormented panting slaves, who already were spending every ounce of strength in this cruel effort to elude their own chance of salvation and release. Faster beat the tomtom marking the desperate time, and faster in response to it came the creak and dip of oars and the panting, stertorous breathing of the rowers.

"Lay on! Lay on!" cried Asad, inexorable. Let them burst their lungs—they were but infidel lungs!—so that for an hour they but maintained the present pace.

"We are drawing away!" cried Marzak in jubilation. "The praise to Allah!"

And so indeed they were. Visibly the lights of the galleon were receding. With every inch of canvas spread yet she appeared to be standing still, so faint was the breeze that stirred. And whilst she crawled, the galeasse raced as never yet she had raced since Sakr-el-Bahr had commanded her, for Sakr-el-Bahr had never yet turned tail upon the foe in whatever strength he found him.

Suddenly over the water from the galleon came a loud hail. Asad laughed, and in the darkness shook his fist at them, cursing them in the name of Allah and his Prophet. And then, in answer to that curse of his, the galleon's side belched fire; the calm of the night was broken by a roar of thunder, and something smote the water ahead of the Muslim vessel with a resounding thudding splash.

In fear Rosamund drew closer to Sakr-el-Bahr. But Asad laughed again.

"No need to fear their marksmanship," he cried. "They cannot see us. Their own lights dazzle them. On! On!"

"He is right," said Sakr-el-Bahr. "But the truth is that they will not fire to sink us because they know you to be aboard."

She looked out to sea again, and beheld those friendly lights falling farther and farther astern.

"We are drawing steadily away," she groaned. "They will never overtake us now."

So feared Sakr-el-Bahr. He more than feared it. He knew that save for some miraculous rising of the wind it must be as she said. And then out of his despair leapt inspiration—a desperate inspiration, true child of that despair of which it was begotten.

"There is a chance," he said to her. "But it is as a throw of the dice with life and death for stakes."

"Then seize it," she bade him instantly. "For though it should go against us we shall not be losers."

"You are prepared for anything?" he asked her.

"Have I not said that I will go down with you this night? Ah, don't waste time in words!"

"Be it so, then," he replied gravely, and moved away a step, then checked. "You had best come with me," he said.

Obediently she complied and followed him, and some there were who stared as these two passed down the gangway, yet none attempted to hinder her movements. Enough and to spare was there already to engage the thoughts of all aboard that vessel.

He thrust a way for her, past the boatswain's mates who stood over the slaves ferociously plying tongues and whips, and so brought her to the waist. Here he took up the lantern which had been muffled, and as its light once more streamed forth, Asad shouted an order for its extinction. But Sakr-el-Bahr took no least heed of that command. He stepped to the mainmast, about which the powder kegs had been stacked. One of these had been broached against its being needed by the gunners on the poop. The unfastened lid rested loosely atop of it. That lid Sakr-el-Bahr knocked over; then he pulled one of the horn sides out of the lantern, and held the now half-naked flame immediately above the powder.

A cry of alarm went up from some who had watched him. But above that cry rang his sharp command:

"Cease rowing!"

The tomtom fell instantly silent, but the slaves took yet another stroke.

"Cease rowing!" he commanded again. "Asad!" he called. "Bid them pause, or I'll blow you all straight into the arms of Shaitan." And he lowered the lantern until it rested on the very rim of the powder keg.

At once the rowing ceased. Slaves, corsairs, officers, and Asad himself stood paralyzed, all at gaze upon that grim figure illumined by the lantern, threatening them with doom. It may have crossed the minds of some to throw themselves forthwith upon him; but to arrest them was the dread lest any movement towards him should precipitate the explosion that must blow them all into the next world.

At last Asad addressed him, his voice half-choked with rage.

"May Allah strike thee dead! Art thou djinn-possessed?"

Marzak, standing at his father's side, set a quarrel to the bow which he had snatched up. "Why do you all stand and stare?" he cried. "Cut him down, one of you!" And even as he spoke he raised his bow. But his father checked him, perceiving what must be the inevitable result.

"If any man takes a step towards me, the lantern goes straight into the gunpowder," said Sakr-el-Bahr serenely. "And if you shoot me as you intend, Marzak, or if any other shoots, the same will happen of itself. Be warned unless you thirst for the Paradise of the Prophet."

"Sakr-el-Bahr!" cried Asad, and from its erstwhile anger his voice had now changed to a note of intercession. He stretched out his arms appealingly to the captain whose doom he had already pronounced in his heart and mind. "Sakr-el-Bahr, I conjure thee by the bread and salt we have eaten together, return to thy senses, my son."

"I am in my sense," was the answer, "and being so I have no mind for the fate reserved me in Algiers—by the memory of that same bread and salt. I have no mind to go back with thee to be hanged or sent to toil at an oar again."

"And if I swear to thee that naught of this shall come to pass?"

"Thou'lt be forsworn. I would not trust thee now, Asad. For thou art proven a fool, and in all my life I never found good in a fool and never trusted one—save once, and he betrayed me. Yesterday I pleaded with thee, showing thee the wise course, and affording thee thine opportunity. At a slight sacrifice thou mightest have had me and hanged me at thy leisure. 'Twas my own life I offered thee, and for all that thou knewest it, yet thou knewest not that I knew." He laughed. "See now what manner of fool art thou? Thy greed hath wrought thy ruin. Thy hands were opened to grasp more than they could hold. See now the consequence. It comes yonder in that slowly but surely approaching galleon."

Every word of it sank into the brain of Asad thus tardily to enlighten him. He wrung his hands in his blended fury and despair. The crew stood in appalled silence, daring to make no movement that might precipitate their end.

"Name thine own price," cried the Basha at length, "and I swear to thee by the beard of the Prophet it shall be paid thee."

"I named it yesterday, but it was refused. I offered thee my liberty and my life if that were needed to gain the liberty of another."

Had he looked behind him he might have seen the sudden lighting of Rosamund's eyes, the sudden clutch at her bosom, which would have announced to him that his utterances were none so cryptic but that she had understood them.

"I will make thee rich and honoured, Sakr-el-Bahr," Asad continued urgently. "Thou shalt be as mine own son. The Bashalik itself shall be thine when I lay it down, and all men shall do thee honour in the meanwhile as to myself."

"I am not to be bought, O mighty Asad. I never was. Already wert thou set upon my death. Thou canst command it now, but only upon the condition that thou share the cup with me. What is written is written. We have sunk some tall ships together in our day, Asad. We'll sink together in our turn to-night if that be thy desire."

"May thou burn for evermore in hell, thou black-hearted traitor!" Asad cursed him, his anger bursting all the bonds he had imposed upon it.

And then, of a sudden, upon that admission of defeat from their Basha, there arose a great clamour from the crew. Sakr-el-Bahr's sea-hawks called upon him, reminding him of their fidelity and love, and asking could he repay it now by dooming them all thus to destruction.

"Have faith in me!" he answered them. "I have never led you into aught but victory. Be sure that I shall not lead you now into defeat—on this the last occasion that we stand together."

"But the galleon is upon us!" cried Vigitello. And so, indeed, it was, creeping up slowly under that faint breeze, her tall bulk loomed now above them, her prow ploughing slowly forward at an acute angle to the prow of the galeasse. Another moment and she was alongside, and with a swing and clank and a yell of victory from the English seamen lining her bulwarks her grappling irons swung down to seize the corsair ship at prow and stern and waist. Scarce had they fastened, than a torrent of men in breast-plates and morions poured over her side, to alight upon the prow of the galeasse, and not even the fear of the lantern held above the powder barrel could now restrain the corsairs from giving these hardy boarders the reception they reserved for all infidels. In an instant the fighting platform on the prow was become a raging, seething hell of battle luridly illumined by the ruddy glow from the lights aboard the Silver Heron. Foremost among those who had leapt down had been Lionel and Sir John Killigrew. Foremost among those to receive them had been Jasper Leigh, who had passed his sword through Lionel's body even as Lionel's feet came to rest upon the deck, and before the battle was joined.

A dozen others went down on either side before Sakr-el-Bahr's ringing voice could quell the fighting, before his command to them to hear him was obeyed.

"Hold there!" he had bellowed to his sea-hawks, using the lingua franca. "Back, and leave this to me. I will rid you of these foes." Then in English he had summoned his countrymen also to desist. "Sir John Killigrew!" he called in a loud voice. "Hold your hand until you have heard me! Call your men back and let none others come aboard! Hold until you have heard me, I say, then wreak your will."

Sir John, perceiving him by the mainmast with Rosamund at his side, and leaping at the most inevitable conclusion that he meant to threaten her life, perhaps to destroy her if they continued their advance, flung himself before his men, to check them.

Thus almost as suddenly as it had been joined the combat paused

"What have you to say, you renegade dog?" Sir John demanded.

"This, Sir John, that unless you order your men back aboard your ship, and make oath to desist from this encounter, I'll take you straight down to hell with us at once. I'll heave this lantern into the powder here, and we sink and you come down with us held by your own grappling hooks. Obey me and you shall have all that you have come to seek aboard this vessel. Mistress Rosamund shall be delivered up to you."

Sir John glowered upon him a moment from the poop, considering. Then—

"Though not prepared to make terms with you," he announced, "yet I will accept the conditions you impose, but only provided that I have all indeed that I am come to seek. There is aboard this galley an infamous renegade hound whom I am bound by my knightly oath to take and hang. He, too, must be delivered up to me. His name was Oliver Tressilian."

Instantly, unhesitatingly, came the answer—"Him, too, will I surrender to you upon your sworn oath that you will then depart and do here no further hurt."

Rosamund caught her breath, and clutched Sakr-el-Bahr's arm, the arm that held the lantern.

"Have a care, mistress," he bade her sharply, "or you will destroy us all."

"Better that!" she answered him.

And then Sir John pledged him his word that upon his own surrender and that of Rosamund he would withdraw nor offer hurt to any there.

Sakr-el-Bahr turned to his waiting corsairs, and briefly told them what the terms he had made.

He called upon Asad to pledge his word that these terms would be respected, and no blood shed on his behalf, and Asad answered him, voicing the anger of all against him for his betrayal.

"Since he wants thee that he may hang thee, he may have thee and so spare us the trouble, for 'tis no less than thy treachery deserves from us."

"Thus, then, I surrender," he announced to Sir John, and flung the lantern overboard.

One voice only was raised in his defence, and that voice was Rosamund's. But even that voice failed, conquered by weary nature. This last blow following upon all that lately she had endured bereft her of all strength. Half swooning she collapsed against Sakr-el-Bahr even as Sir John and a handful of his followers leapt down to deliver her and make fast their prisoner.

The corsairs stood looking on in silence; the loyalty to their great captain, which would have made them spend their last drop of blood in his defence, was quenched by his own act of treachery which had brought the English ship upon them. Yet when they saw him pinioned and hoisted to the deck of the Silver Heron, there was a sudden momentary reaction in their ranks. Scimitars were waved aloft, and cries of menace burst forth. If he had betrayed them, yet he had so contrived that they should not suffer by that betrayal. And that was worthy of the Sakr-el-Bahr they knew and loved; so worthy that their love and loyalty leapt full-armed again upon the instant.

But the voice of Asad called upon them to bear in mind what in their name he had promised, and since the voice of Asad alone might not have sufficed to quell that sudden spark of revolt, there came down to them the voice of Sakr-el-Bahr himself issuing his last command.

"Remember and respect the terms I have made for you! Mektub! May Allah guard and prosper you!"

A wail was his reply, and with that wail ringing in his ears to assure him that he did not pass unloved, he was hurried below to prepare him for his end.

The ropes of the grapnels were cut, and slowly the galleon passed away into the night, leaving the galley to replace what slaves had been maimed in the encounter and to head back for Algiers, abandoning the expedition against the argosy of Spain.

Under the awning upon the poop Asad now sat like a man who has awakened from an evil dream. He covered his head and wept for one who had been as a son to him, and whom through his madness he had lost. He cursed all women, and he cursed destiny; but the bitterest curse of all was for himself.

In the pale dawn they flung the dead overboard and washed the decks, nor did they notice that a man was missing in token that the English captain, or else his followers, had not kept strictly to the letter of the bond.

They returned in mourning to Algiers—mourning not for the Spanish argosy which had been allowed to go her ways unmolested, but for the stoutest captain that ever bared his scimitar in the service of Islam. The story of how he came to be delivered up was never clearly told; none dared clearly tell it, for none who had participated in the deed but took shame in it thereafter, however clear it might be that Sakr-el-Bahr had brought it all upon himself. But, at least, it was understood that he had not fallen in battle, and hence it was assumed that he was still alive. Upon that presumption there was built up a sort of legend that he would one day come back; and redeemed captives returning a half-century later related how in Algiers to that day the coming of Sakr-el-Bahr was still confidently expected and looked for by all true Muslimeen.

CHAPTER XXIII. THE HEATHEN CREED

Sakr-el-Bahr was shut up in a black hole in the forecastle of the Silver Heron to await the dawn and to spend the time in making his soul. No words had passed between him and Sir John since his surrender. With wrists pinioned behind him, he had been hoisted aboard the English ship, and in the waist of her he had stood for a moment face to face with an old acquaintance—our chronicler, Lord Henry Goade. I imagine the florid countenance of the Queen's Lieutenant wearing a preternaturally grave expression, his eyes forbidding as they rested upon the renegade. I know—from Lord Henry's own pen—that no word had passed between them during those brief moments before Sakr-el-Bahr was hurried away by his guards to be flung into those dark, cramped quarters reeking of tar and bilge.

For a long hour he lay where he had fallen, believing himself alone; and time and place would no doubt conduce to philosophical reflection upon his condition. I like to think that he found that when all was considered, he had little with which to reproach himself. If he had done evil he had made ample amends. It can scarcely be pretended that he had betrayed those loyal Muslimeen followers of his, or, if it is, at least it must be added that he himself had paid the price of that betrayal. Rosamund was safe, Lionel would meet the justice due to him, and as for himself, being as good as dead already, he was worth little thought. He must have derived some measure of content from the reflection that he was spending his life to the very best advantage. Ruined it had been long since. True, but for his ill-starred expedition of vengeance he might long have continued to wage war as a corsair, might even have risen to the proud Muslim eminence of the Bashalik of Algiers and become a feudatory prince of the Grand Turk. But for one who was born a Christian gentleman that would have been an unworthy way to have ended his days. The present was the better course.

A faint rustle in the impenetrable blackness of his prison turned the current of his thoughts. A rat, he thought, and drew himself to a sitting attitude, and beat his slippered heels upon the ground to drive away the loathly creature. Instead, a voice challenged him out of the gloom.

"Who's there?"

It startled him for a moment, in his complete assurance that he had been alone.

"Who's there?" the voice repeated, querulously to add: "What black hell be this? Where am I?"

And now he recognized the voice for Jasper Leigh's, and marvelled how that latest of his recruits to the ranks of Mohammed should be sharing this prison with him.

"Faith," said he, "you're in the forecastle of the Silver Heron; though how you come here is more than I can answer."

"Who are ye?" the voice asked.

"I have been known in Barbary as Sakr-el-Bahr."

"Sir Oliver!"

"I suppose that is what they will call me now. It is as well perhaps that I am to be buried at sea, else it might plague these Christian gentlemen what legend to inscribe upon my headstone. But you—how come you hither? My bargain with Sir John was that none should be molested, and I cannot think Sir John would be forsworn."

"As to that I know nothing, since I did not even know where I was bestowed until ye informed me. I was knocked senseless in the fight, after I had put my bilbo through your comely brother. That is the sum of my knowledge."

Sir Oliver caught his breath. "What do you say? You killed Lionel?"

"I believe so," was the cool answer. "At least I sent a couple of feet of steel through him—'twas in the press of the fight when first the English dropped aboard the galley; Master Lionel was in the van—the last place in which I should have looked to see him."

There fell a long silence. At length Sir Oliver spoke in a small voice.

"Not a doubt but you gave him no more than he was seeking. You are right, Master Leigh; the van was the last place in which to look for him, unless he came deliberately to seek steel that he might escape a rope. Best so, no doubt. Best so! God rest him!"

"Do you believe in God?" asked the sinful skipper on an anxious note.

"No doubt they took you because of that," Sir Oliver pursued, as if communing with himself. "Being in ignorance perhaps of his deserts, deeming him a saint and martyr, they resolved to avenge him upon you, and dragged you hither for that purpose." He sighed. "Well, well, Master Leigh, I make no doubt that knowing yourself for a rascal you have all your life been preparing your neck for a noose; so this will come as no surprise to you."

The skipper stirred uneasily, and groaned. "Lord, how my head aches!" he complained.

"They've a sure remedy for that," Sir Oliver comforted him. "And you'll swing in better company than you deserve, for I am to be hanged in the morn-ing too. You've earned it as fully as have I, Master Leigh. Yet I am sorry for you—sorry you should suffer where I had not so intended."

Master Leigh sucked in a shuddering breath, and was silent for a while.

Then he repeated an earlier question.

"Do you believe in God, Sir Oliver?"

"There is no God but God, and Mohammed is his Prophet," was the answer, and from his tone Master Leigh could not be sure that he did not mock.

"That's a heathen creed," said he in fear and loathing.

"Nay, now; it's a creed by which men live. They perform as they preach, which is more than can be said of any Christians I have ever met."

"How can you talk so upon the eve of death?" cried Leigh in protest.

"Faith," said Sir Oliver, "it's considered the season of truth above all others."

"Then ye don't believe in God?"

"On the contrary, I do."

"But not in the real God?" the skipper insisted.

"There can be no God but the real God—it matters little what men call Him."

"Then if ye believe, are ye not afraid?"

"Of what?"

"Of hell, damnation, and eternal fire," roared the skipper, voicing his own belated terrors.

"I have but fulfilled the destiny which in His Omniscience He marked out for me," replied Sir Oliver. "My life hath been as He designed it, since naught may exist or happen save by His Will. Shall I then fear damnation for having been as God fashioned me?"

"'Tis the heathen Muslim creed!" Master Leigh protested.

"'Tis a comforting one," said Sir Oliver, "and it should comfort such a sinner as thou."

But Master Leigh refused to be comforted. "Oh!" he groaned miserably. "I would that I did not believe in God!"

"Your disbelief could no more abolish Him than can your fear create Him," replied Sir Oliver. "But your mood being what it is, were it not best you prayed?"

"Will not you pray with me?" quoth that rascal in his sudden fear of the hereafter.

"I shall do better," said Sir Oliver at last. "I shall pray for you—to Sir John Killigrew, that your life be spared."

"Sure he'll never heed you!" said Master Leigh with a catch in his breath.

"He shall. His honour is concerned in it. The terms of my surrender were that none else aboard the galley should suffer any hurt."

"But I killed Master Lionel."

"True—but that was in the scrimmage that preceded my making terms. Sir John pledged me his word, and Sir John will keep to it when I have made it clear to him that honour demands it."

A great burden was lifted from the skipper's mind—that great shadow of the fear of death that had overhung him. With it, it is greatly to be feared that his desperate penitence also departed. At least he talked no more of damnation, nor took any further thought for Sir Oliver's opinions and beliefs concerning the hereafter. He may rightly have supposed that Sir Oliver's creed was Sir Oliver's affair, and that should it happen to be wrong he was scarcely himself a qualified person to correct it. As for himself, the making of his soul could wait until another day, when the necessity for it should be more imminent.

Upon that he lay down and attempted to compose himself to sleep, though the pain in his head proved a difficulty. Finding slumber impossible after a while he would have talked again; but by that time his companion's regular breathing warned him that Sir Oliver had fallen asleep during the silence.

Now this surprised and shocked the skipper. He was utterly at a loss to understand how one who had lived Sir Oliver's life, been a renegade and a heathen, should be able to sleep tranquilly in the knowledge that at dawn he was to hang. His belated Christian zeal prompted him to rouse the sleeper and to urge him to spend the little time that yet remained him in making his peace with God. Humane compassion on the other hand suggested to him that he had best leave him in the peace of that oblivion. Considering matters he was profoundly touched to reflect that in such a season Sir Oliver could have found room in his mind to think of him and his fate and to undertake to contrive that he should be saved from the rope. He was the more touched when he bethought him of the extent to which he had himself been responsible for all that happened to Sir Oliver. Out of the consideration of heroism, a certain heroism came to be begotten in him, and he fell to pondering how in his turn he might perhaps serve Sir Oliver by a frank confession of all that he knew of the influences that had gone to make Sir Oliver what he was. This resolve uplifted him, and oddly enough it uplifted him all the more when he reflected that perhaps he would be jeopardizing his own neck by the confession upon which he had determined.

So through that endless night he sat, nursing his aching head, and enheartened by the first purpose he had ever conceived of a truly good and altruistic deed. Yet fate it seemed was bent upon frustrating that purpose of his. For when at dawn they came to hale Sir Oliver to his doom, they paid no heed to Jasper Leigh's demands that he, too, should be taken before Sir John.

"Thee bean't included in our orders," said a seaman shortly.

"Maybe not," retorted Master Leigh, "because Sir John little knows what it is in my power to tell him. Take me before him, I say, that he may hear from me the truth of certain matters ere it be too late."

"Be still," the seaman bade him, and struck him heavily across the face, so that he reeled and collapsed into a corner. "Thee turn will come soon. Just now our business be with this other heathen."

"Naught that you can say would avail," Sir Oliver assured him quietly. "But I thank you for the thought that marks you for my friend. My hands are bound, Jasper. Were it otherwise I would beg leave to clasp your own. Fare you well!"

Sir Oliver was led out into the golden sunlight which almost blinded him after his long confinement in that dark hole. They were, he gathered, to conduct him to the cabin where a short mockery of a trial was to be held. But in the waist their progress was arrested by an officer, who bade them wait.

Sir Oliver sat down upon a coil of rope, his guard about him, an object of curious inspection to the rude seamen. They thronged the forecastle and the hatchways to stare at this formidable corsair who once had been a Cornish gentleman and who had become a renegade Muslim and a terror to Christianity.

Truth to tell, the sometime Cornish gentleman was difficult to discern in him as he sat there still wearing the caftan of cloth of silver over his white tunic and a turban of the same material swathed about his steel headpiece that ended in a spike. Idly he swung his brown sinewy legs, naked from knee to ankle, with the inscrutable calm of the fatalist upon his swarthy hawk face with its light agate eyes and black forked beard; and those callous seamen who had assembled there to jeer and mock him were stricken silent by the intrepidity and stoicism of his bearing in the face of death.

If the delay chafed him, he gave no outward sign of it. If his hard, light eyes glanced hither and thither it was upon no idle quest. He was seeking Rosamund, hoping for a last sight of her before they launched him upon his last dread voyage.

But Rosamund was not to be seen. She was in the cabin at the time. She had been there for this hour past, and it was to her that the present delay was due.

CHAPTER XXIV. THE JUDGES

In the absence of any woman into whose care they might entrust her, Lord Henry, Sir John, and Master Tobias, the ship's surgeon, had amongst them tended Rosamund as best they could when numbed and half-dazed she was brought aboard the Silver Heron.

Master Tobias had applied such rude restoratives as he commanded, and having made her as comfortable as possible upon a couch in the spacious cabin astern, he had suggested that she should be allowed the rest of which she appeared so sorely to stand in need. He had ushered out the commander and the Queen's Lieutenant, and himself had gone below to a still more urgent case that was demanding his attention—that of Lionel Tressilian, who had been brought limp and unconscious from the galeasse together with some four other wounded members of the Silver Heron's crew.

At dawn Sir John had come below, seeking news of his wounded friend. He found the surgeon kneeling over Lionel.

As he entered, Master Tobias turned aside, rinsed his hands in a metal basin placed upon the floor, and rose wiping them on a napkin.

"I can do no more, Sir John," he muttered in a desponding voice. "He is sped."

"Dead, d'ye mean?" cried Sir John, a catch in his voice.

The surgeon tossed aside the napkin, and slowly drew down the upturned sleeves of his black doublet. "All but dead," he answered. "The wonder is that any spark of life should still linger in a body with that hole in it. He is bleeding inwardly, and his pulse is steadily weakening. It must continue so until imperceptibly he passes away. You may count him dead already, Sir John." He paused. "A merciful, painless end," he added, and sighed perfunctorily, his pale shaven face decently grave, for all that such scenes as these were commonplaces in his life. "Of the other four," he continued, "Blair is dead; the other three should all recover."

But Sir John gave little heed to the matter of those others. His grief and dismay at this quenching of all hope for his friend precluded any other consideration at the moment.

"And he will not even recover consciousness?" he asked insisting, although already he had been answered.

"As I have said, you may count him dead already, Sir John. My skill can do nothing for him."

Sir John's head drooped, his countenance drawn and grave. "Nor can my justice," he added gloomily. "Though it avenge him, it cannot give me back my friend." He looked at the surgeon. "Vengeance, sir, is the hollowest of all the mockeries that go to make up life."

"Your task, Sir John," replied the surgeon, "is one of justice, not vengeance."

"A quibble, when all is said." He stepped to Lionel's side, and looked down at the pale handsome face over which the dark shadows of death were already creeping. "If he would but speak in the interests of this justice that is to do! If we might but have the evidence of his own words, lest I should ever be asked to justify the hanging of Oliver Tressilian."

"Surely, sir," the surgeon ventured, "there can be no such question ever. Mistress Rosamund's word alone should suffice, if indeed so much as that even were required."

"Ay! His offenses against God and man are too notorious to leave grounds upon which any should ever question my right to deal with him out of hand."

There was a tap at the door and Sir John's own body servant entered with the announcement that Mistress Rosamund was asking urgently to see him.

"She will be impatient for news of him," Sir John concluded, and he groaned. "My God! How am I to tell her? To crush her in the very hour of her deliverance with such news as this! Was ever irony so cruel?" He turned, and stepped heavily to the door. There he paused. "You will remain by him to the end?" he bade the surgeon interrogatively.

Master Tobias bowed. "Of course, Sir John." And he added, "'Twill not be long."

Sir John looked across at Lionel again—a glance of valediction. "God rest him!" he said hoarsely, and passed out.

In the waist he paused a moment, turned to a knot of lounging seamen, and bade them throw a halter over the yard-arm, and hale the renegade Oliver Tressilian from his prison. Then with slow heavy step and heavier heart he went up the companion to the vessel's castellated poop.

The sun, new risen in a faint golden haze, shone over a sea faintly rippled by the fresh clean winds of dawn to which their every stitch of canvas was now spread. Away on the larboard quarter, a faint cloudy outline, was the coast of Spain.

Sir John's long sallow face was preternaturally grave when he entered the cabin, where Rosamund awaited him. He bowed to her with a grave courtesy, doffing his hat and casting it upon a chair. The last five years had brought some strands of white into his thick black hair, and at the temples in particular it showed very grey, giving him an appearance of age to which the deep lines in his brow contributed.

He advanced towards her, as she rose to receive him. "Rosamund, my dear!" he said gently, and took both her hands. He looked with eyes of sorrow and concern into her white, agitated face.

"Are you sufficiently rested, child?"

"Rested?" she echoed on a note of wonder that he should suppose it.

"Poor lamb, poor lamb!" he murmured, as a mother might have done, and drew her towards him, stroking that gleaming auburn head. "We'll speed us back to England with every stitch of canvas spread. Take heart then, and...."

But she broke in impetuously, drawing away from him as she spoke, and his heart sank with foreboding of the thing she was about to inquire.

"I overheard a sailor just now saying to another that it is your intent to hang Sir Oliver Tressilian out of hand—this morning."

He misunderstood her utterly. "Be comforted," he said. "My justice shall be swift; my vengeance sure. The yard-arm is charged already with the rope on which he shall leap to his eternal punishment."

She caught her breath, and set a hand upon her bosom as if to repress its sudden tumult.

"And upon what grounds," she asked him with an air of challenge, squarely facing him, "do you intend to do this thing?"

"Upon what grounds?" he faltered. He stared and frowned, bewildered by her question and its tone. "Upon what grounds?" he repeated, foolishly almost in the intensity of his amazement. Then he considered her more closely, and the wildness of her eyes bore to him slowly an explanation of words that at first had seemed beyond explaining.

"I see!" he said in a voice of infinite pity; for the conviction to which he had leapt was that her poor wits were all astray after the horrors through which she had lately travelled. "You must rest," he said gently, "and give no thought to such matters as these. Leave them to me, and be very sure that I shall avenge you as is due."

"Sir John, you mistake me, I think. I do not desire that you avenge me. I have asked you upon what grounds you intend to do this thing, and you have not answered me."

In increasing amazement he continued to stare. He had been wrong, then. She was quite sane and mistress of her wits. And yet instead of the fond inquiries concerning Lionel which he had been dreading came this amazing questioning of his grounds to hang his prisoner.

"Need I state to you—of all living folk—the offences which that dastard has committed?" he asked, expressing thus the very question that he was setting himself.

"You need to tell me," she answered, "by what right you constitute yourself his judge and executioner; by what right you send him to his death in this peremptory fashion, without trial." Her manner was as stern as if she were invested with all the authority of a judge.

"But you," he faltered in his ever-growing bewilderment, "you, Rosamund, against whom he has offended so grievously, surely you should be the last to ask me such a question! Why, it is my intention to proceed with him as is the manner of the sea with all knaves taken as Oliver Tressilian was taken. If your mood be merciful towards him—which as God lives, I can scarce conceive—consider that this is the greatest mercy he can look for."

"You speak of mercy and vengeance in a breath, Sir John." She was growing calm, her agitation was quieting and a grim sternness was replacing it.

He made a gesture of impatience. "What good purpose could it serve to take him to England?" he demanded. "There he must stand his trial, and the issue is foregone. It were unnecessarily to torture him."

"The issue may be none so foregone as you suppose," she replied. "And that trial is his right."

Sir John took a turn in the cabin, his wits all confused. It was preposterous that he should stand and argue upon such a matter with Rosamund of all people, and yet she was compelling him to it against his every inclination, against common sense itself.

"If he so urges it, we'll not deny him," he said at last, deeming it best to humour her. "We'll take him back to England if he demands it, and let him stand his trial there. But Oliver Tressilian must realize too well what is in store for him to make any such demand." He passed before her, and held out his hands in entreaty. "Come, Rosamund, my dear! You are distraught, you...."

"I am indeed distraught, Sir John," she answered, and took the hands that he extended. "Oh, have pity!" she cried with a sudden change to utter intercession. "I implore you to have pity!"

"What pity can I show you, child? You have but to name...."

"'Tis not pity for me, but pity for him that I am beseeching of you."

"For him?" he cried, frowning again.

"For Oliver Tressilian."

He dropped her hands and stood away. "God's light!" he swore. "You sue for pity for Oliver Tressilian, for that renegade, that incarnate devil? Oh, you are mad!" he stormed. "Mad!" and he flung away from her, whirling his arms.

"I love him," she said simply.

That answer smote him instantly still. Under the shock of it he just stood and stared at her again, his jaw fallen.

"You love him!" he said at last below his breath. "You love him! You love a man who is a pirate, a renegade, the abductor of yourself and of Lionel, the man who murdered your brother!"

"He did not." She was fierce in her denial of it. "I have learnt the truth of that matter."

"From his lips, I suppose?" said Sir John, and he was unable to repress a sneer. "And you believed him?"

"Had I not believed him I should not have married him."

"Married him?" Sudden horror came now to temper his bewilderment. Was there to be no end to these astounding revelations? Had they reached the climax yet, he wondered, or was there still more to come? "You married that infamous villain?" he asked, and his voice was expressionless.

"I did—in Algiers on the night we landed there." He stood gaping at her whilst a man might count to a dozen, and then abruptly he exploded. "It is enough!" he roared, shaking a clenched fist at the low ceiling of the cabin. "It is enough, as God's my Witness. If there were no other reason to hang him, that would be reason and to spare. You may look to me to make an end of this infamous marriage within the hour."

"Ah, if you will but listen to me!" she pleaded.

"Listen to you?" He paused by the door to which he had stepped in his fury, intent upon giving the word that there and then should make an end, and summoning Oliver Tressilian before him, announce his fate to him and see it executed on the spot. "Listen to you?" he repeated, scorn and anger blending in his voice. "I have heard more than enough already!"

It was the Killigrew way, Lord Henry Goade assures us, pausing here at long length for one of those digressions into the history of families whose members chance to impinge upon his chronicle. "They were," he says, "ever an impetuous, short-reasoning folk, honest and upright enough so far as their judgment carried them, but hampered by a lack of penetration in that judgment."

Sir John, as much in his earlier commerce with the Tressilians as in this pregnant hour, certainly appears to justify his lordship of that criticism. There were a score of questions a man of perspicuity would not have asked, not one of which appears to have occurred to the knight of Arwenack. If anything arrested him upon the cabin's threshold, delayed him in the execution of the thing he had resolved upon, no doubt it was sheer curiosity as to what further extravagances Rosamund might yet have it in her mind to utter.

"This man has suffered," she told him, and was not put off by the hard laugh with which he mocked that statement. "God alone knows what he has suffered in body and in soul for sins which he never committed. Much of that suffering came to him through me. I know to-day that he did not murder Peter. I know that but for a disloyal act of mine he would be in a position incontestably to prove it without the aid of any man. I know that he was carried off, kidnapped before ever he could clear himself of the accusation, and that as a consequence no life remained him but the life of a renegade which he chose. Mine was the chief fault. And I must make amends. Spare him to me! If you love me...."

But he had heard enough. His sallow face was flushed to a flaming purple.

"Not another word!" he blazed at her. "It is because I do love you—love and pity you from my heart—that I will not listen. It seems I must save you not only from that knave, but from yourself. I were false to my duty by you, false to your dead father and murdered brother else. Anon, you shall thank me, Rosamund." And again he turned to depart.

"Thank you?" she cried in a ringing voice. "I shall curse you. All my life I shall loathe and hate you, holding you in horror for a murderer if you do this thing. You fool! Can you not see? You fool!"

He recoiled. Being a man of position and importance, quick, fearless, and vindictive of temperament—and also, it would seem, extremely fortunate—it had never happened to him in all his life to be so uncompromisingly and frankly judged. She was by no means the first to account him a fool, but she was certainly the first to call him one to his face; and whilst to the general it might have proved her extreme sanity, to him it was no more than the culminating proof of her mental distemper.

"Pish!" he said, between anger and pity, "you are mad, stark mad! Your mind's unhinged, your vision's all distorted. This fiend incarnate is become a poor victim of the evil of others; and I am become a murderer in your sight—a murderer and a fool. God's Life! Bah! Anon when you are rested, when you are restored, I pray that things may once again assume their proper aspect."

He turned, all aquiver still with indignation, and was barely in time to avoid being struck by the door which opened suddenly from without.

Lord Henry Goade, dressed—as he tells us—entirely in black, and with his gold chain of office—an ominous sign could they have read it—upon his broad chest, stood in the doorway, silhouetted sharply against the flood of morning sunlight at his back. His benign face would, no doubt, be extremely grave to match the suit he had put on, but its expression will have lightened somewhat when his glance fell upon Rosamund standing there by the table's edge.

"I was overjoyed," he writes, "to find her so far recovered, and seeming so much herself again, and I expressed my satisfaction."

"She were better abed," snapped Sir John, two hectic spots burning still in his sallow cheeks. "She is distempered, quite."

"Sir John is mistaken, my lord," was her calm assurance, "I am very far from suffering as he conceives."

"I rejoice therein, my dear," said his lordship, and I imagine his questing eyes speeding from one to the other of them, and marking the evidences of Sir John's temper, wondering what could have passed. "It happens," he added sombrely, "that we may require your testimony in this grave matter that is toward." He turned to Sir John. "I have bidden them bring up the prisoner for sentence. Is the ordeal too much for you, Rosamund?"

"Indeed, no, my lord," she replied readily. "I welcome it." And threw back her head as one who braces herself for a trial of endurance.

"No, no," cut in Sir John, protesting fiercely. "Do not heed her, Harry. She...."

"Considering," she interrupted, "that the chief count against the prisoner must concern his... his dealings with myself, surely the matter is one upon which I should be heard."

"Surely, indeed," Lord Henry agreed, a little bewildered, he confesses, "always provided you are certain it will not overtax your endurance and distress you overmuch. We could perhaps dispense with your testimony."

"In that, my lord, I assure you that you are mistaken," she answered. "You cannot dispense with it."

"Be it so, then," said Sir John grimly, and he strode back to the table, prepared to take his place there.

Lord Henry's twinkling blue eyes were still considering Rosamund somewhat searchingly, his fingers tugging thoughtfully at his short tuft of ashen-coloured beard. Then he turned to the door. "Come in, gentlemen," he said, "and bid them bring up the prisoner."

Steps clanked upon the deck, and three of Sir John's officers made their appearance to complete the court that was to sit in judgment upon the renegade corsair, a judgment whose issue was foregone.

CHAPTER XXV. THE ADVOCATE

Chairs were set at the long brown table of massive oak, and the officers sat down, facing the open door and the blaze of sunshine on the poop-deck, their backs to the other door and the horn windows which opened upon the stern-gallery. The middle place was assumed by Lord Henry Goade by virtue of his office of Queen's Lieutenant, and the reason for his chain of office became now apparent. He was to preside over this summary court. On his right sat Sir John Killigrew, and beyond him an officer named Youldon. The other two, whose names have not survived, occupied his lordship's left.

A chair had been set for Rosamund at the table's extreme right and across the head of it, so as to detach her from the judicial bench. She sat there now, her elbows on the polished board, her face resting in her half-clenched hands, her eyes scrutinizing the five gentlemen who formed this court.

Steps rang on the companion, and a shadow fell athwart the sunlight beyond the open door. From the vessel's waist came a murmur of voices and a laugh. Then Sir Oliver appeared in the doorway guarded by two fighting seamen in corselet and morion with drawn swords.

He paused an instant in the doorway, and his eyelids flickered as if he had received a shock when his glance alighted upon Rosamund. Then under the suasion of his guards he entered, and stood forward, his wrists still pinioned behind him, slightly in advance of the two soldiers.

He nodded perfunctorily to the court, his face entirely calm.

"A fine morning, sirs," said he.

The five considered him in silence, but Lord Henry's glance, as it rested upon the corsair's Muslim garb, was eloquent of the scorn which he tells us filled his heart.

"You are no doubt aware, sir," said Sir John after a long pause, "of the purpose for which you have been brought hither."

"Scarcely," said the prisoner. "But I have no doubt whatever of the purpose for which I shall presently be taken hence. However," he continued, cool and critical, "I can guess from your judicial attitudes the superfluous mockery that you intend. If it will afford you entertainment, faith, I do not grudge indulging you. I would observe only that it might be considerate in you to spare Mistress Rosamund the pain and weariness of the business that is before you."

"Mistress Rosamund herself desired to be present," said Sir John, scowling.

"Perhaps," said Sir Oliver, "she does not realize...."

"I have made it abundantly plain to her," Sir John interrupted, almost vindictively.

The prisoner looked at her as if in surprise, his brows knit. Then with a shrug he turned to his judges again.

"In that case," said he, "there's no more to be said. But before you proceed, there is another matter upon which I desire an understanding.

"The terms of my surrender were that all others should be permitted to go free. You will remember, Sir John, that you pledged me your knightly word for that. Yet I find aboard here one who was lately with me upon my galeasse—a sometime English seaman, named Jasper Leigh, whom you hold a prisoner."

"He killed Master Lionel Tressilian," said Sir John coldly

"That may be, Sir John. But the blow was delivered before I made my terms with you, and you cannot violate these terms without hurt to your honour."

"D'ye talk of honour, sir?" said Lord Henry.

"Of Sir John's honour, my lord," said the prisoner, with mock humility.

"You are here, sir, to take your trial," Sir John reminded him.

"So I had supposed. It is a privilege for which you agreed to pay a certain price, and now it seems you have been guilty of filching something back. It seems so, I say. For I cannot think but that the arrest was inadvertently effected, and that it will suffice that I draw your attention to the matter of Master Leigh's detention."

Sir John considered the table. It was beyond question that he was in honour bound to enlarge Master Leigh, whatever the fellow might have done; and, indeed, his arrest had been made without Sir John's knowledge until after the event.

"What am I do with him?" he growled sullenly.

"That is for yourself to decide, Sir John. But I can tell you what you may not do with him. You may not keep him a prisoner, or carry him to England or injure him in any way. Since his arrest was a pure error, as I gather, you must repair that error as best you can. I am satisfied that you will do so, and need say no more. Your servant, sirs," he added to intimate that he was now entirely at their disposal, and he stood waiting.

There was a slight pause, and then Lord Henry, his face inscrutable, his glance hostile and cold, addressed the prisoner.

"We have had you brought hither to afford you an opportunity of urging any reasons why we should not hang you out of hand, as is our right."

Sir Oliver looked at him in almost amused surprise. "Faith!" he said at length. "It was never my habit to waste breath."

"I doubt you do not rightly apprehend me, sir," returned his lordship, and his voice was soft and silken as became his judicial position. "Should you demand a formal trial, we will convey you to England that you may have it."

"But lest you should build unduly upon that," cut in Sir John fiercely, "let me warn you that as the offences for which you are to suffer were chiefly committed within Lord Henry Goade's own jurisdiction, your trial will take place in Cornwall, where Lord Henry has the honour to be Her Majesty's Lieutenant and dispenser of justice."

"Her Majesty is to be congratulated," said Sir Oliver elaborately.

"It is for you to choose, sir," Sir John ran on, "whether you will be hanged on sea or land."

"My only possible objection would be to being hanged in the air. But you're not likely to heed that," was the flippant answer.

Lord Henry leaned forward again. "Let me beg you, sir, in your own interests to be serious," he admonished the prisoner.

"I confess the occasion, my lord. For if you are to sit in judgment upon my piracy, I could not desire a more experienced judge of the matter on sea or land than Sir John Killigrew."

"I am glad to deserve your approval," Sir John replied tartly. "Piracy," he added, "is but the least of the counts against you."

Sir Oliver's brows went up, and he stared at the row of solemn faces.

"As God's my life, then, your other counts must needs be sound—or else, if there be any justice in your methods, you are like to be disappointed of your hopes of seeing me swing. Proceed, sirs, to the other counts. I vow you become more interesting than I could have hoped."

"Can you deny the piracy?" quoth Lord Henry.

"Deny it? No. But I deny your jurisdiction in the matter, or that of any English court, since I have committed no piracy in English waters."

Lord Henry admits that the answer silenced and bewildered him, being utterly unexpected. Yet what the prisoner urged was a truth so obvious that it was difficult to apprehend how his lordship had come to overlook it. I rather fear that despite his judicial office, jurisprudence was not a strong point with his lordship. But Sir John, less perspicuous or less scrupulous in the matter, had his retort ready.

"Did you not come to Arwenack and forcibly carry off thence...."

"Nay, now, nay, now," the corsair interrupted, good-humouredly. "Go back to school, Sir John, to learn that abduction is not piracy."

"Call it abduction, if you will," Sir John admitted.

"Not if I will, Sir John. We'll call it what it is, if you please."

"You are trifling, sir. But we shall mend that presently," and Sir John banged the table with his fist, his face flushing slightly in anger. (Lord Henry very properly deplores this show of heat at such a time.) "You cannot pretend to be ignorant," Sir John continued, "that abduction is punishable by death under the law of England." He turned to his fellow-judges. "We will then, sirs, with your concurrence, say no more of the piracy."

"Faith," said Lord Henry in his gentle tones, "in justice we cannot." And he shrugged the matter aside. "The prisoner is right in what he claims. We have no jurisdiction in that matter, seeing that he committed no piracy in English waters, nor—so far as our knowledge goes—against any vessel sailing under the English flag."

Rosamund stirred. Slowly she took her elbows from the table, and folded her arms resting them upon the edge of it. Thus leaning forward she listened now with an odd brightness in her eye, a slight flush in her cheeks reflecting some odd excitement called into life by Lord Henry's admission—an admission which sensibly whittled down the charges against the prisoner.

Sir Oliver, watching her almost furtively, noted this and marvelled, even as he marvelled at her general composure. It was in vain that he sought to guess what might be her attitude of mind towards himself now that she was safe again among friends and protectors.

But Sir John, intent only upon the business ahead, plunged angrily on.

"Be it so," he admitted impatiently. "We will deal with him upon the counts of abduction and murder. Have you anything to say?"

"Nothing that would be like to weigh with you," replied Sir Oliver. And then with a sudden change from his slightly derisive manner to one that was charged with passion: "Let us make an end of this comedy," he cried, "of this pretence of judicial proceedings. Hang me, and have done, or set me to walk the plank. Play the pirate, for that is a trade you understand. But a' God's name don't disgrace the Queen's commission by playing the judge."

Sir John leapt to his feet, his face aflame. "Now, by Heaven, you insolent knave...."

But Lord Henry checked him, placing a restraining hand upon his sleeve, and forcing him gently back into his seat. Himself he now addressed the prisoner.

"Sir, your words are unworthy one who, whatever his crimes, has earned the repute of being a sturdy, valiant fighter. Your deeds are so notorious—particularly that which caused you to flee from England and take to roving, and that of your reappearance at Arwenack and the abduction of which you were then guilty—that your sentence in an English court is a matter foregone beyond all possible doubt. Nevertheless, it shall be yours, as I have said, for the asking.

"Yet," he added, and his voice was lowered and very earnest, "were I your friend, Sir Oliver, I would advise you that you rather choose to be dealt with in the summary fashion of the sea."

"Sirs," replied Sir Oliver, "your right to hang me I have not disputed, nor do I. I have no more to say."

"But I have."

Thus Rosamund at last, startling the court with her crisp, sharp utterance. All turned to look at her as she rose, and stood tall and compelling at the table's end.

"Rosamund!" cried Sir John, and rose in his turn. "Let me implore you...."

She waved him peremptorily, almost contemptuously, into silence.

"Since in this matter of the abduction with which Sir Oliver is charged," she said, "I am the person said to have been abducted, it were perhaps well that before going further in this matter you should hear what I may hereafter have to say in an English court."

Sir John shrugged, and sat down again. She would have her way, he realized; just as he knew that its only result could be to waste their time and protract the agony of the doomed man.

Lord Henry turned to her, his manner full of deference. "Since the prisoner has not denied the charge, and since wisely he refrains from demanding to be taken to trial, we need not harass you, Mistress Rosamund. Nor will you be called upon to say anything in an English court."

"There you are at fault, my lord," she answered, her voice very level. "I shall be called upon to say something when I impeach you all for murder upon the high seas, as impeach you I shall if you persist in your intent."

"Rosamund!" cried Oliver in his sudden amazement—and it was a cry of joy and exultation.

She looked at him, and smiled—a smile full of courage and friendliness and something more, a smile for which he considered that his impending hanging was but a little price to pay. Then she turned again to that court, into which her words had flung a sudden consternation.

"Since he disdains to deny the accusation, I must deny it for him," she informed them. "He did not abduct me, sirs, as is alleged. I love Oliver Tressilian. I am of full age and mistress of my actions, and I went willingly with him to Algiers where I became his wife."

Had she flung a bomb amongst them she could hardly have made a greater disorder of their wits. They sat back, and stared at her with blank faces, muttering incoherencies.

"His... his wife?" babbled Lord Henry. "You became his...."

And then Sir John cut in fiercely. "A lie! A lie to save that foul villain's neck!"

Rosamund leaned towards him, and her smile was almost a sneer. "Your wits were ever sluggish, Sir John," she said. "Else you would not need reminding that I could have no object in lying to save him if he had done me the wrong that is imputed to him." Then she looked at the others. "I think, sirs, that in this matter my word will outweigh Sir John's or any man's in any court of justice."

"Faith, that's true enough!" ejaculated the bewildered Lord Henry. "A moment, Killigrew!" And again he stilled the impetuous Sir John. He looked at Sir Oliver, who in truth was very far from being the least bewildered in that company. "What do you say to that, sir?" he asked.

"To that?" echoed the almost speechless corsair. "What is there left to say?" he evaded.

"'Tis all false," cried Sir John again. "We were witnesses of the event—you and I, Harry—and we saw...."

"You saw," Rosamund interrupted. "But you did not know what had been concerted."

For a moment that silenced them again. They were as men who stand upon crumbling ground, whose every effort to win to a safer footing but occasioned a fresh slide of soil. Then Sir John sneered, and made his riposte.

"No doubt she will be prepared to swear that her betrothed, Master Lionel Tressilian, accompanied her willingly upon that elopement."

"No," she answered. "As for Lionel Tressilian he was carried off that he might expiate his sins—sins which he had fathered upon his brother there, sins which are the subject of your other count against him."

"Now what can you mean by that?" asked his lordship.

"That the story that Sir Oliver killed my brother is a calumny; that the murderer was Lionel Tressilian, who, to avoid detection and to complete his work, caused Sir Oliver to be kidnapped that he might be sold into slavery."

"This is too much!" roared Sir John. "She is trifling with us, she makes white black and black white. She has been bewitched by that crafty rogue, by Moorish arts that...."

"Wait!" said Lord Henry, raising his hand. "Give me leave." He confronted her very seriously. "This... this is a grave statement, mistress. Have you any proof—anything that you conceive to be a proof—of what you are saying?"

But Sir John was not to be repressed. "'Tis but the lying tale this villain told her. He has bewitched her, I say. 'Tis plain as the sunlight yonder."

Sir Oliver laughed outright at that. His mood was growing exultant, buoyant, and joyous, and this was the first expression of it. "Bewitched her? You're determined never to lack for a charge. First 'twas piracy, then abduction and murder, and now 'tis witchcraft!"

"Oh, a moment, pray!" cried Lord Henry, and he confesses to some heat at this point. "Do you seriously tell us, Mistress Rosamund, that it was Lionel Tressilian who murdered Peter Godolphin?"

"Seriously?" she echoed, and her lips were twisted in a little smile of scorn. "I not merely tell it you, I swear it here in the sight of God. It was Lionel who murdered my brother and it was Lionel who put it about that the deed was Sir Oliver's. It was said that Sir Oliver had run away from the consequences of something discovered against him, and I to my shame believed the public voice. But I have since discovered the truth...."

"The truth, do you say, mistress?" cried the impetuous Sir John in a voice of passionate contempt. "The truth...."

Again his Lordship was forced to intervene.

"Have patience, man," he admonished the knight. "The truth will prevail in the end, never fear, Killigrew."

"Meanwhile we are wasting time," grumbled Sir John, and on that fell moodily silent.

"Are we further to understand you to say, mistress," Lord Henry resumed, "that the prisoner's disappearance from Penarrow was due not to flight, as was supposed, but to his having been trepanned by order of his brother?"

"That is the truth as I stand here in the sight of Heaven," she replied in a voice that rang with sincerity and carried conviction to more than one of the officers seated at that table. "By that act the murderer sought not only to save himself from exposure, but to complete his work by succeeding to the Tressilian estates.

Sir Oliver was to have been sold into slavery to the Moors of Barbary. Instead the vessel upon which he sailed was captured by Spaniards, and he was sent to the galleys by the Inquisition. When his galley was captured by Muslim corsairs he took the only way of escape that offered. He became a corsair and a leader of corsairs, and then...."

"What else he did we know," Lord Henry interrupted. "And I assure you it would all weigh very lightly with us or with any court if what else you say is true."

"It is true. I swear it, my lord," she repeated.

"Ay," he answered, nodding gravely. "But can you prove it?"

"What better proof can I offer you than that I love him, and have married him?"

"Bah!" said Sir John.

"That, mistress," said Lord Henry, his manner extremely gentle, "is proof that yourself you believe this amazing story. But it is not proof that the story itself is true. You had it, I suppose," he continued smoothly, "from Oliver Tressilian himself?"

"That is so; but in Lionel's own presence, and Lionel himself confirmed it—admitting its truth."

"You dare say that?" cried Sir John, and stared at her in incredulous anger. "My God! You dare say that?"

"I dare and do," she answered him, giving him back look for look.

Lord Henry sat back in his chair, and tugged gently at his ashen tuft of beard, his florid face overcast and thoughtful. There was something here he did not understand at all. "Mistress Rosamund," he said quietly, "let me exhort you to consider the gravity of your words. You are virtually accusing one who is no longer able to defend himself; if your story is established, infamy will rest for ever upon the memory of Lionel Tressilian. Let me ask you again, and let me entreat you to answer scrupulously. Did Lionel Tressilian admit the truth of this thing with which you say that the prisoner charged him?"

"Once more I solemnly swear that what I have spoken is true; that Lionel Tressilian did in my presence, when charged by Sir Oliver with the murder of my brother and the kidnapping of himself, admit those charges. Can I make it any plainer, sirs?"

Lord Henry spread his hands. "After that, Killigrew, I do not think we can go further in this matter. Sir Oliver must go with us to England, and there take his trial."

But there was one present—that officer named Youldon—whose wits, it seems, were of keener temper.

"By your leave, my lord," he now interposed, and he turned to question the witness. "What was the occasion on which Sir Oliver forced this admission from his brother?"

Truthfully she answered. "At his house in Algiers on the night he...." She checked suddenly, perceiving then the trap that had been set for her. And the others perceived it also. Sir John leapt into the breach which Youldon had so shrewdly made in her defences.

"Continue, pray," he bade her. "On the night he...."

"On the night we arrived there," she answered desperately, the colour now receding slowly from her face.

"And that, of course," said Sir John slowly, mockingly almost, "was the first occasion on which you heard this explanation of Sir Oliver's conduct?"

"It was," she faltered—perforce.

"So that," insisted Sir John, determined to leave her no loophole whatsoever, "so that until that night you had naturally continued to believe Sir Oliver to be the murderer of your brother?"

She hung her head in silence, realizing that the truth could not prevail here since she had hampered it with a falsehood, which was now being dragged into the light.

"Answer me!" Sir John commanded.

"There is no need to answer," said Lord Henry slowly, in a voice of pain, his eyes lowered to the table. "There can, of course, be but one answer. Mistress Rosamund has told us that he did not abduct her forcibly; that she went with him of her own free will and married him; and she has urged that circumstance as a proof of her conviction of his innocence. Yet now it becomes plain that at the time she left England with him she still believed him to be her brother's slayer. Yet she asks us to believe that he did not abduct her." He spread his hands again and pursed his lips in a sort of grieved contempt.

"Let us make an end, a' God's name!" said Sir John, rising.

"Ah, wait!" she cried. "I swear that all that I have told you is true—all but the matter of the abduction. I admit that, but I condoned it in view of what I have since learnt."

"She admits it!" mocked Sir John.

But she went on without heeding him. "Knowing what he has suffered through the evil of others, I gladly own him my husband, hoping to make some amends to him for the part I had in his wrongs. You must believe me, sirs. But if you will not, I ask you is his action of yesterday to count for naught? Are you not to remember that but for him you would have had no knowledge of my whereabouts?"

They stared at her in fresh surprise.

"To what do you refer now, mistress? What action of his is responsible for this?"

"Do you need to ask? Are you so set on murdering him that you affect ignorance? Surely you know that it was he dispatched Lionel to inform you of my whereabouts?"

Lord Henry tells us that at this he smote the table with his open palm, displaying an anger he could no longer curb. "This is too much!" he cried. "Hitherto I have believed you sincere but misguided and mistaken. But so deliberate a falsehood transcends all bounds. What has come to you, girl? Why, Lionel himself told us the circumstances of his escape from the galeasse. Himself he told us how that villain had him flogged and then flung him into the sea for dead."

"Ah!" said Sir Oliver between his teeth. "I recognize Lionel there! He would be false to the end, of course. I should have thought of that."

Rosamund at bay, in a burst of regal anger leaned forward to face Lord Henry and the others. "He lied, the base, treacherous dog!" she cried.

"Madam," Sir John rebuked her, "you are speaking of one who is all but dead."

"And more than damned," added Sir Oliver. "Sirs," he cried, "you prove naught but your own stupidity when you accuse this gentle lady of falsehood."

"We have heard enough, sir," Lord Henry interrupted.

"Have you so, by God!" he roared, stung suddenly to anger. "You shall hear yet a little more. The truth will prevail, you have said yourself; and prevail the truth shall since this sweet lady so desires it."

He was flushed, and his light eyes played over them like points of steel, and like points of steel they carried a certain measure of compulsion. He had stood before them half-mocking and indifferent, resigned to hang and desiring the thing might be over and ended as speedily as possible. But all that was before he suspected that life could still have anything to offer him, whilst he conceived that Rosamund was definitely lost to him. True, he had the memory of a certain tenderness she had shown him yesternight aboard the galley, but he had deemed that tenderness to be no more than such as the situation itself begot. Almost he had deemed the same to be here the case until he had witnessed her fierceness and despair in fighting for his life, until he had heard and gauged the sincerity of her avowal that she loved him and desired to make some amends to him for all that he had suffered in the past. That had spurred him, and had a further spur been needed, it was afforded him when they branded her words with falsehood, mocked her to her face with what they supposed to be her lies. Anger had taken him at that to stiffen his resolve to make a stand against them and use the one weapon that remained him—that a merciful chance, a just God had placed within his power almost despite himself.

"I little knew, sirs," he said, "that Sir John was guided by the hand of destiny itself when last night, in violation of the terms of my surrender, he took a prisoner from my galeasse. That man is, as I have said, a sometime English seaman, named Jasper Leigh. He fell into my hands some months ago, and took the same road to escape from thraldom that I took myself under the like circumstances. I was merciful in that I permitted him to do so, for he is the very skipper who was suborned by Lionel to kidnap me and carry me into Barbary. With me he fell into the hands of the Spaniards. Have him brought hither, and question him."

In silence they all looked at him, but on more than one face he saw the reflection of amazement at his impudence, as they conceived it.

It was Lord Henry who spoke at last. "Surely, sir, this is most oddly, most suspiciously apt," he said, and there could be no doubt that he was faintly sneering. "The very man to be here aboard, and taken prisoner thus, almost by chance...."

"Not quite by chance, though very nearly. He conceives that he has a grudge against Lionel, for it was through Lionel that misfortune overtook him. Last night when Lionel so rashly leapt aboard the galley, Jasper Leigh saw his opportunity to settle an old score and took it. It was as a consequence of that that he was arrested."

"Even so, the chance is still miraculous."

"Miracles, my lord, must happen sometimes if the truth is to prevail," Sir Oliver replied with a tinge of his earlier mockery. "Fetch him hither, and question him. He knows naught of what has passed here. It were a madness to suppose him primed for a situation which none could have foreseen. Fetch him hither, then."

Steps sounded outside but went unheeded at the moment.

"Surely," said Sir John, "we have been trifled with by liars long enough!"

The door was flung open, and the lean black figure of the surgeon made its appearance.

"Sir John!" he called urgently, breaking without ceremony into the proceedings, and never heeding Lord Henry's scowl. "Master Tressilian has recovered consciousness. He is asking for you and for his brother. Quick, sirs! He is sinking fast."

CHAPTER XXVI. THE JUDGMENT

To that cabin below the whole company repaired in all speed in the surgeon's wake, Sir Oliver coming last between his guards. They assembled about the couch where Lionel lay, leaden-hued of face, his breathing laboured, his eyes dull and glazing.

Sir John ran to him, went down upon one knee to put loving arms about that chilling clay, and very gently raised him in them, and held him so resting against his breast.

"Lionel!" he cried in stricken accents. And then as if thoughts of vengeance were to soothe and comfort his sinking friend's last moments, he added: "We have the villain fast."

Very slowly and with obvious effort Lionel turned his head to the right, and his dull eyes went beyond Sir John and made quest in the ranks of those that stood about him.

"Oliver?" he said in a hoarse whisper. "Where is Oliver?"

"There is not the need to distress you...." Sir John was beginning, when Lionel interrupted him.

"Wait!" he commanded in a louder tone. "Is Oliver safe?"

"I am here," said Sir Oliver's deep voice, and those who stood between him and his brother drew aside that they might cease from screening him.

Lionel looked at him for a long moment in silence, sitting up a little. Then he sank back again slowly against Sir John's breast.

"God has been merciful to me a sinner," he said, "since He accords me the means to make amends, tardily though it be."

Then he struggled up again, and held out his arms to Sir Oliver, and his voice came in a great pleading cry. "Noll! My brother! Forgive!"

Oliver advanced, none hindering until, with his hands still pinioned behind him he stood towering there above his brother, so tall that his turban brushed the low ceiling of the cabin. His countenance was stern and grim.

"What is it that you ask me to forgive?" he asked. Lionel struggled to answer, and sank back again into Sir John's arms, fighting for breath; there was a trace of blood-stained foam about his lips.

"Speak! Oh, speak, in God's name!" Rosamund exhorted him from the other side, and her voice was wrung with agony.

He looked at her, and smiled faintly. "Never fear," he whispered, "I shall speak. God has spared me to that end. Take your arms from me, Killigrew. I am the... the vilest of men. It... it was I who killed Peter Godolphin."

"My God!" groaned Sir John, whilst Lord Henry drew a sharp breath of dismay and realization.

"Ah, but that is not my sin," Lionel continued. "There was no sin in that. We fought, and in self-defence I slew him—fighting fair. My sin came afterwards. When suspicion fell on Oliver, I nourished it...Oliver knew the deed was mine, and kept silent that he might screen me. I feared the truth might become known for all that... and... and I was jealous of him, and... and I had him kidnapped to be sold...."

His fading voice trailed away into silence. A cough shook him, and the faint crimson foam on his lips was increased. But he rallied again, and lay there panting, his fingers plucking at the coverlet.

"Tell them," said Rosamund, who in her desperate fight for Sir Oliver's life kept her mind cool and steady and directed towards essentials, "tell them the name of the man you hired to kidnap him."

"Jasper Leigh, the skipper of the Swallow," he answered, whereupon she flashed upon Lord Henry a look that contained a gleam of triumph for all that her face was ashen and her lips trembled.

Then she turned again to the dying man, relentlessly almost in her determination to extract all vital truth from him ere he fell silent.

"Tell them," she bade him, "under what circumstances Sir Oliver sent you last night to the Silver Heron."

"Nay, there is no need to harass him," Lord Henry interposed. "He has said enough already. May God forgive us our blindness, Killigrew!"

Sir John bowed his head in silence over Lionel.

"Is it you, Sir John?" whispered the dying man. "What? Still there? Ha!" he seemed to laugh faintly, then checked. "I am going...." he muttered, and again his voice grew stronger, obeying the last flicker of his shrinking will. "Noll! I am going! I...I have made reparation... all that I could. Give me... give me thy hand!" Gropingly he put forth his right.

"I should have given it you ere this but that my wrists are bound," cried Oliver in a sudden frenzy. And then exerting that colossal strength of his, he suddenly snapped the cords that pinioned him as if they had been thread. He caught his brother's extended hand, and dropped upon his knees beside him. "Lionel...Boy!" he cried. It was as if all that had befallen in the last five years had been wiped out of existence. His fierce relentless hatred of his half-brother, his burning sense of wrong, his parching thirst for vengeance, became on the instant all dead, buried, and forgotten. More, it was as if they had never been. Lionel in that moment was again the weak, comely, beloved brother whom he had cherished and screened and guarded, and for whom when the hour arrived he had sacrificed his good name, and the woman he loved, and placed his life itself in jeopardy.

"Lionel, boy!" was all that for a moment he could say. Then: "Poor lad! Poor lad!" he added. "Temptation was too strong for thee." And reaching forth he took the other white hand that lay beyond the couch, and so held both tight-clasped within his own.

From one of the ports a ray of sunshine was creeping upwards towards the dying man's face. But the radiance that now overspread it was from an inward source. Feebly he returned the clasp of his brother's hands.

"Oliver, Oliver!" he whispered. "There is none like thee! I ever knew thee as noble as I was base. Have I said enough to make you safe? Say that he will be safe now," he appealed to the others, "that no...."

"He will be safe," said Lord Henry stoutly. "My word on't."

"It is well. The past is past. The future is in your hands, Oliver. God's blessing on't." He seemed to collapse, to rally yet again. He smiled pensively, his mind already wandering. "That was a long swim last night—the longest I ever swam. From Penarrow to Trefusis—a fine long swim. But you were with me, Noll. Had my strength given out...I could have depended on you. I am still chill from it, for it was cold... cold... ugh!" He shuddered, and lay still.

Gently Sir John lowered him to his couch. Beyond it Rosamund fell upon her knees and covered her face, whilst by Sir John's side Oliver continued to kneel, clasping in his own his brother's chilling hands.

There ensued a long spell of silence. Then with a heavy sigh Sir Oliver folded Lionel's hands across his breast, and slowly, heavily rose to his feet.

The others seemed to take this for a signal. It was as if they had but waited mute and still out of deference to Oliver. Lord Henry moved softly round to Rosamund and touched her lightly upon the shoulder. She rose and went out in the wake of the others, Lord Henry following her, and none remaining but the surgeon.

Outside in the sunshine they checked. Sir John stood with bent head and hunched shoulders, his eyes upon the white deck. Timidly almost—a thing never seen before in this bold man—he looked at Sir Oliver.

"He was my friend," he said sorrowfully, and as if to excuse and explain himself, "and... and I was misled through love of him."

"He was my brother," replied Sir Oliver solemnly. "God rest him!"

Sir John, resolved, drew himself up into an attitude preparatory to receiving with dignity a rebuff should it be administered him.

"Can you find it in your generosity, sir, to forgive me?" he asked, and his air was almost one of challenge.

Silently Sir Oliver held out his hand. Sir John fell upon it almost in eagerness.

"We are like to be neighbours again," he said, "and I give you my word I shall strive to be a more neighbourly one than in the past."

"Then, sirs," said Sir Oliver, looking from Sir John to Lord Henry, "I am to understand that I am no longer a prisoner."

"You need not hesitate to return with us to England, Sir Oliver," replied his lordship. "The Queen shall hear your story, and we have Jasper Leigh to confirm it if need be, and I will go warranty for your complete reinstatement. Count me your friend, Sir Oliver, I beg." And he, too, held out his hand. Then turning to the others: "Come, sirs," he said, "we have duties elsewhere, I think."

They tramped away, leaving Oliver and Rosamund alone. The twain looked long each at the other. There was so much to say, so much to ask, so much to explain, that neither knew with what words to begin. Then Rosamund suddenly came up to him, holding out her hands. "Oh, my dear!" she said, and that, after all, summed up a deal.

One or two over-inquisitive seamen, lounging on the forecastle and peeping through the shrouds, were disgusted to see the lady of Godolphin Court in the arms of a beturbaned bare-legged follower of Mahound.

The Complete Richard Hannay - 39 Steps, Greenmantle, Mr Steadfast, Three Hostages, Island of Sheep.
John Buchan
Benediction Classics, 2012
908 pages
ISBN: 978-1-78139-203-4

Available from www.amazon.com, www.amazon.co.uk

The Complete Richard Hannay includes the five John Buchan novels that feature the hero: 39 Steps, Greenmantle, Mr Steadfast, Three Hostages, Island of Sheep. Richard Hannay was one of the first modern spy thriller heroes and has shaped the genre. Hannay is strong and silent, combining the Scottish dourness with the English "stiff upper lip". He is tough and shrewd, courageous and resourceful. However, unlike later spy thrillers he has a greater breadth of emotion. He is philosophical and refuses to demonise his enemies, he falls in love, he is dependent upon his friends and he is religious. These books are exciting, with Richard Hannay being chased over moor and glen, they are page turning thrillers.

John Macnab
John Buchan
Benediction Classics, 2011
208 pages
ISBN: 978-1-84902-423-5

Available from www.amazon.com,
www.amazon.co.uk

John Macnab is the second most famous novel by John Buchan, published in 1925. It is a story of three successful men - a barrister, cabinet minister and banker who are bored. They decide to alleviate the boredom by anonymously informing three Scottish estates that they intend to poach a stag or a salmon and returning it to them undetected. It is about daring thinking and high living set in the beautiful Highlands of Scotland and evoking images of the hunting, shooting and fishing lifestyle.

The Scarlet Pimpernel Omnibus - Unabridged - The Scarlet Pimpernel, I Will Repay, Eldorado, Sir Percy Hits Back
Baroness Orczy
Oxford City Press, 2012
824 pages
ISBN: 978-1-78139-228-7

Available from www.amazon.com, www.amazon.co.uk

The Scarlet Pimpernel appears in a play and a series of novels and short stories by Baroness Emmuska Orczy. They are set at the start of the French Revolution, Pimpernel being a master of disguise and a precursor to other heroes such as Zorro and Batman. The play and the tales brought Orczy international acclaim, being translated into sixteen languages. This omnibus edition includes the following unabridged stories: The Scarlet Pimpernel, I Will Repay, Eldorado, and Sir Percy Hits Back

The Gallant Pimpernel - Unabridged - Lord Tony's Wife, The Way of the Scarlet Pimpernel, Sir Percy Leads the Band, The Triumph of the Scarlet Pimpernel
Baroness Orczy
Oxford City Press, 2012
804 pages
ISBN: 978-1-78139-227-0

Available from www.amazon.com, www.amazon.co.uk

The Scarlet Pimpernel appears in a play and a series of novels and short stories by Baroness Emmuska Orczy. They are set at the start of the French Revolution, Pimpernel being a master of disguise and a precursor to other heroes such as Zorro and Batman. The play and the tales brought Orczy international acclaim, being translated into sixteen languages. This omnibus edition includes the following unabridged stories: Lord Tony's Wife, The Way of the Scarlet Pimpernel, Sir Percy Leads the Band, and The Triumph of the Scarlet Pimpernel.

Also from Benediction Books ...

Wandering Between Two Worlds: Essays on Faith and Art
Anita Mathias
Benediction Books, 2007
152 pages
ISBN: 0955373700

Available from www.amazon.com, www.amazon.co.uk

In these wide-ranging lyrical essays, Anita Mathias writes, in lush, lovely prose, of her naughty Catholic childhood in Jamshedpur, India; her large, eccentric family in Mangalore, a sea-coast town converted by the Portuguese in the sixteenth century; her rebellion and atheism as a teenager in her Himalayan boarding school, run by German missionary nuns, St. Mary's Convent, Nainital; and her abrupt religious conversion after which she entered Mother Teresa's convent in Calcutta as a novice. Later rich, elegant essays explore the dualities of her life as a writer, mother, and Christian in the United States-- Domesticity and Art, Writing and Prayer, and the experience of being "an alien and stranger" as an immigrant in America, sensing the need for roots.

About the Author

Anita Mathias is the author of *Wandering Between Two Worlds: Essays on Faith and Art*. She has a B.A. and M.A. in English from Somerville College, Oxford University, and an M.A. in Creative Writing from the Ohio State University, USA. Anita won a National Endowment of the Arts fellowship in Creative Non-fiction in 1997. She lives in Oxford, England with her husband, Roy, and her daughters, Zoe and Irene.

Anita's website:
http://www.anitamathias.com, and
Anita's blog Dreaming Beneath the Spires:
http://dreamingbeneaththespires.blogspot.com

The Church That Had Too Much
Anita Mathias
Benediction Books, 2010
52 pages
ISBN: 9781849026567

Available from www.amazon.com, www.amazon.co.uk

The Church That Had Too Much was very well-intentioned. She wanted to love God, she wanted to love people, but she was both hampered by her muchness and the abundance of her possessions, and beset by ambition, power struggles and snobbery. Read about the surprising way The Church That Had Too Much began to resolve her problems in this deceptively simple and enchanting fable.

About the Author

Anita Mathias is the author of *Wandering Between Two Worlds: Essays on Faith and Art*. She has a B.A. and M.A. in English from Somerville College, Oxford University, and an M.A. in Creative Writing from the Ohio State University, USA. Anita won a National Endowment of the Arts fellowship in Creative Non-fiction in 1997. She lives in Oxford, England with her husband, Roy, and her daughters, Zoe and Irene.

Anita's website:
    http://www.anitamathias.com, and
Anita's blog Dreaming Beneath the Spires:
    http://dreamingbeneaththespires.blogspot.com

www.ingramcontent.com/pod-product-compliance
Lightning Source LLC
Chambersburg PA
CBHW080811020826
48982CB00017B/900
* 9 7 8 1 7 8 1 3 9 2 5 1 5 *